STANFIELD HALL.

A ROMANCE.

BY J. F. SMITH, ESQ.

IN TWO CHRONICLES

———

LONDON:

PUBLISHED BY E. LLOYD, SALISBURY-SQUARE, FLEET-STREET.

THE CHRONICLES OF STANFIELD HALL.

BY F. SMITH, Esq.

AUTHOR OF "AMY LAWRENCE," "THE YOUNG CHEVALIER," &c., &c.

THE PRELATE DETERMINES TO PROTECT ULRIC FROM HERMAN'S VENGEANCE.

CHAPTER I.

A tale of love and war, of olden times,
When heathen gods in this scarce Christian land
Were worshipped in secret and in terror.

STANFIELD HALL, the scene of so many remarkable events and fearful crimes, is one of the oldest manors in England. It is called in the Norman register, known by the name of the "Doomsday Book," Stainsfields, and sometimes Stanfells. It seems to have been erected into a lordship as early as the Heptarchy, having probably been held at that remote period by one of the powerful franklins of the East Angles. In the reign of Edward the Confessor, it was possessed by the rich and ancient family of Hale, or Held, as they are denominated in the chronicles of Walter of Cotessy, a monkish writer of the twelfth century, whose quaint histories and obscure Latin will well repay the labour of those who have either time or patience to pore over his musty manuscripts.

At the period at which our tale commences—the year preceding the fatal battle of Hastings—it was the chief residence of Herwald de Hale, so called by the Norman writers—the distinctive particle *de* marking their acknowledgment of the nobility of the powerful Saxon, who was more familiarly known to those of his own race as Herwald of Stanfells, or Herwald of the Tower. Stanfield, in the age of which we write, presented a far different appearance from the present comparatively modern pile, which offers a fair specimen of the mixed domestic architecture which characterised the reign of Elizabeth. A low range of buildings, built of sun-burnt bricks and rough stones, enclosed a large quadrangular court, capable, in case of need, of containing the herds of cattle, which formed no inconsiderable portion of the wealth of the Saxon proprietor; the windows—if the unglazed apertures might be so designated—were all to the exterior, a few narrow loopholes only being left in the outward walls for the purpose of reconnoitring or defence. The place, or holm, as the buildings were called, was still further strengthened by irregular turrets at its respective angles.

The principal tower, from which the Saxons gave to the lord of Stanfells his distinctive appellation, was a lofty building, with more pretension to architectural ornament than the rest. Over the low, circular arched door was a rudely sculptured shield, displaying a bittern in the centre of a cross engrailed—the arms, doubtless, of its founder; but how obtained, or by whom bestowed, it might puzzle the Heralds' College to decide. A corresponding door on the opposite side gave admittance into the interior of the quadrangle, of which it formed the principal object and defence. The lands surrounding the edifice were rich pasture, well drained by irregular channels, cut to convey the water to the extensive moat, which said moat was crossed by a rude drawbridge of wood, extending partially over the stream, and resting on an irregular bridge of stone, whose arches reached to the middle only of the moat. The drawbridge was capable of being either moved or destroyed upon the first approach of danger. Low thick woods extended from the clear pasture lands, even to the limits of the town of Wymondham, or Wyndham, as the inhabitants now call it, then celebrated as the residence of a sainted anchorite, upon the ruins of whose cell the present church is built. These woods served as the retreat for vast herds of swine, which lived in a half-savage state within its almost impervious recesses, which served as shelter to the deer and game for which that part of England has so long been celebrated.

Herwald of the Tower, the owner of the edifice we have endeavoured to describe, was a true Saxon, generous, fierce, and impetuous —a mixture of the good and evil qualities of his unhappy race. Passionately addicted to war, and its mimic pastime, the chase, his character naturally bore the impress of his pursuits. He was proud of his wealth and lineage, but still prouder of the object in which they were both to centre—his only child, Edith, the heiress of Stanfield, and many a broad land beside. Resolute as the franklin was, he had seldom been known to resist the slightest wish of his daughter, who might, without impropriety, have been called Our Lady of *Bon Secours* by all who stood in fear of her impetuous father's resentment. As good as she was beautiful, even the extravagant indulgence of her sire had failed to spoil her—an indulgence more frequently forced upon her than sought. Edith possessed neither the blue eyes nor fair hair so characteristic of her race; on the contrary, her tresses might have vied with the raven's wing in blackness; her eyes, of the same colour, were chastened in their brilliancy by a melancholy expression, which seemed to foreshadow some impending doom; but the maiden's complexion was fair as e'en the fairest of her race—so pure, so transparent, and so clear, that her rising thoughts might be read in its roseate changes, as clouds are seen reflected on the bosom of some tranquil lake. To the advantage of personal beauty, Edith added that of simple as well as rich attire. It is true the arms and neck of the noble Saxon maiden were circled with jewelled bracelets and a collar of gold—ornaments indispensable to her birth and station; but her robes were made in the simplest form, and generally of white; the girdle which bound them to her slender waist being of needlework, and matching with the embroidered hem of the ample veil which floated round her.

It was in a costume much like the one we have attempted to describe, that Edith, surrounded by her handmaidens, and two or three officers of her father's household, stood, at the close of a cold autumnal day, within the narrow entrance of the principal tower of Stanfield, to await the franklin's return. Darkness already obscured the horizon, and a shower of sleet began to fall.

"I wish," exclaimed Judith, Edith's

favourite attendant and foster-sister, shivering, and drawing her wimple closer round her shoulders, "our master would return, or that you, noble lady, would retire to your chamber. The sleet reaches you even here; and it is not so long," she added, in a lower tone, "since your illness, that you should unnecessarily brave it. Be persuaded, dear lady, and let us in."

"Not so," mildly replied Edith, whom the whispered allusion to her illness had evidently disconcerted, but not angered. "Thou knowest, Judith, that my father is displeased if his daughter's step fail to meet him at the threshold on his return; and I must not anger him—disobedience in a child is a sin: in me it would, I fear, be a fearful one," she added, tears suffusing her eyes as she spoke, "having so kind a parent."

"The kindest are sometimes unreasonable," thought Judith, who, however, was far too prudent to give utterance to her opinion, certain that it would be disapproved by her young mistress. Perhaps her knowledge of her lady's secret cause of uneasiness was present to her thoughts, for she knew that Edith loved, and that her love was not blessed with her father's smile.

"Our master will soon be here," exclaimed old Hubert, the nominal seneschal of the holm—we say nominal, for, on account of his great age and blindness, the duties of his office were performed by his nephew, Huon, a sturdy man-at-arms, whose tender assiduities had, it was supposed by the gossips of the household, at length found favour with the pretty Judith.

"Soon be here, indeed!" repeated Huon; "why, uncle, do you pretend to the gift of second-sight? Our eyes are young and keen enough, yet we can discover no traces of our lord's approach."

"If my eyes are dim, boy," answered the old man, "praise to St. Cuthbert, my ears are as true as ever. Hark!" he added, forming a hollow with his hand to his ear, to aid the sense as he spoke, "black Hubert is giving tongue right merrily. There are other dogs than our lord's," he added, after a pause, during which the rest of the attendants, who had more faith in his perception than his ungracious nephew, had vainly listened for the distant sounds; "some stranger of note is with our master. In, knaves, in, and prepare for the reception of an honoured guest."

"By Hengist, lady, but old Hubert is right!" said Judith, who at last caught the distant baying of the deep-mouthed hounds; "your honoured father approaches, but whether accompanied by guests or no is more than I can guess or tell, though any guest

were welcome, provided he were young and handsome, to these old towers."

"Peace, Judith," answered her mistress, with a smile; "thy tongue outruns discretion. See!" she added, as the hunting party appeared in sight, emerging from the thick, umbrageous wood, "my father comes: let us forth to meet him."

Scarcely had the expecting party, who followed their young mistress, gained the drawbridge, than the hunters reached it. The franklin, a hale, powerful man of fifty, was the first to cross it. Leaping from his horse, which he left to his numerous attendants to catch, he hastily approached his lovely child.

"Why, how now, Edith, bird!" he exclaimed—"why have you quitted your tapestried nook to expose your cheek to the keen blast? This is no night for maidens to be abroad in. Come," he added, throwing his mantle around her shoulders, after first kissing her on the forehead, "let us in. I must see you with your brightest eyes and sweetest smiles to-night—we have a guest at Stanfield." Her father indicated, with a glance, at the conclusion of his speech, a man of about five-and-twenty, who was in the act of dismounting, that he might in a more seemly manner pay his homage to the Lady Edith.

"My uncle said we should have guests," muttered Huon, aside; "but little did I dream that it would be our lord's nephew. What brings him here?—the old scent, I suppose."

"Whatever brings him," whispered Judith, who had heard the remark, "it bodes our lady no good. The two years accorded by her father are not yet expired."

"Perhaps," answered Huon, "he comes to renounce his claim to the Lady Edith's hand, seeing that she hath scant love for him."

"He renounce his claim to her hand!" answered Judith, her lip curling with scorn. "No, no; you know him too well to think or hope it—he will never renounce it while she is the heiress of broad lands, or his craven heart thirsts for gold. He resign it! As well ask thy hawk, Master Huon, to forego its prey, when poised to make the deadly swoop, or lure the bloodhound from the track it hath followed for days, as expect Herman of the Burg to forego the prize which he believes to be within his reach."

"Believes within his reach! If our lord's will does not alter, he is sure it is within his reach."

"Perhaps," replied the damsel, with a smile of intelligence; "but wills as stern as the franklin's have ere now been thwarted, and by as weak a thing as woman's resolution."

The effect produced by the appearance of

Herman of the Burg upon the lovely Edith was most distressing; the blood forsook her lips and cheeks, and her mild eyes were cast hopelessly round, as if to seek a refuge from some impending evil. Her wily suitor either did not see or would not notice her distress; with a high-bred courtesy, whose refinement was a mockery, he half bent the knee as he saluted his cousin's hand. His triumphant glance gave the lie to the humility of the action—the latter was for his uncle, the former for his intended victim.

"Come, my children," uttered Herwald, who at last perceived his daughter's agitation, "this is no place for greeting. You, Herman, go and change your rough riding gear—women love not to look upon soiled garments and stained plumes; and you, Edith," he added, "to your tire-women. Remember," he whispered, in reply to her glance of supplication, "your brightest smiles and gayest robes to-night."

The passionate fondness of the Saxon franklin for his daughter will at first, perhaps, appear to our readers incompatible with the violence which he evidently placed upon her inclinations. A few words will explain the seeming incongruity. Herman of the Burg was the heir of his name, and consequently preferred by him as a suitor for his daughter's hand. In Herwald the love of his child, deep and indulgent as was the sentiment, was second only to his pride of ancestry. No other Saxon, no matter how noble his lineage, how valiant his achievements, could perpetuate to his race the name which he himself so proudly bore; and to this vain pride the happiness of his child was to be coldly sacrificed. Indulgent to excess in every other matter, he would listen to no remonstrance in this. Two years previous to the commencement of our history he had quarrelled violently with his oldest friend and brother in arms, Edda the Saxon, because his son Edward had presumed to love his daughter. In birth, disposition, and fortune, they were equal; as children, they were reared together. The gentle disposition of the gallant boy had won the maiden's heart, and they mutually loved, in the confiding innocence of their natures, before they were aware that the fatal passion had found an entrance to their souls. Time at last revealed to Edward the nature of his hopes and wishes. His high sense of honour told him how to act: he sought his father, confessed his passion, and besought him to demand the hand of Edith of the franklin. The result of their interview has been already stated. The two fathers, who had so long been sworn friends, parted declared enemies; each commanding their offspring never to think of such a marriage more.

How easy it is for parents to utter commands which the heart finds it impossible to obey! Edith, who, until that moment, had found her chief happiness in fulfilling her father's wishes, for the first time in her life found them harsh and difficult. Edward, till then all submission to his venerable parent, declared obedience impossible. Vainly they strove to forget each other—memory had too fondly treasured each loved image in its shrine for mere commands to part them. In short, aided by the faithful Judith, whose indignation at her master's cruelty was often loudly and vehemently expressed, the lovers contrived to meet. Eloquence is doubly persuasive when uttered by those we love. Edward succeeded in persuading the object of his passion to consent to a clandestine union; and the unhappy Edith was, at the period of which we write, both a wife and mother.

"Now may the Mother of Heaven aid me!" exclaimed the unhappy Edith, as soon as she had reached her chamber, throwing herself at the same time on the neck of her faithful Judith. "The hour I have so long dreaded has arrived—the hour when I must have a father's curse. Oh! the sin," she added, wringing her hands as she spoke, "the bitter sin of disobedience!"

"Be comforted, dear lady," soothingly uttered her attendant, alarmed at the despair of her mistress; "your noble father loves you dearer than aught on earth; he will never resist your prayers and tears; besides, you have an advocate in your fair boy. Think you that when he sees the heir of his proud name, the son of his loved Edith, his iron nature will not at last give way? And," she added, with a half smile, "at the worst it is but running away: your lord hath a fair castle to receive, and brave friends to protect you. Things are never so bad but they may be mended, or but they might be worse."

"This visit, this ill-omenened visit!" murmured Edith, scarcely conscious of the utterance of her thoughts; "this very night, too, I was to have seen my Edward——"

"And your boy—your fair, sweet boy!" interrupted Judith, willing to change the current of her thoughts; "you must think of him—act for him. I would that black Herman had met the foul fiend in his path ere he had crossed yours; but since it is so, let's meet him bravely. At ten to-night your lord and infant will arrive at my mother's cottage. The little rogue, how I do long to kiss him! You must contrive to see him, and consult what is to be done."

"Impossible! I must remain within the banquet hall—you heard my father's words? And even supposing I could contrive to escape the feast how quit the manor?"

"Leave that to me," answered Judith. "Huon keeps the keys, and never more shall he have smile or fair word of me unless he do my bidding. And now," she continued, "dear lady, let me arrange your hair: your veil is damp with the night dew and the sleet. The bell will soon sound, and your noble father is impatient of being kept waiting."

Edith, seating herself upon a faldstool, resigned herself into the busy hands of her attendant, who, removing the veil and fastening from her mistress's head, suffered her long tresses to flow for a few seconds over her shoulders, while she sought, in a small quaintly-carved ivory cabinet, a rich circlet of gems, to replace the simple bandeau which she had removed. While so occupied, Edith sat like a statue of Grief, fair in its pensive loveliness; her long hair, like a sable veil, shading her pallid features; her pure heart torn by the agony of conflicting emotions; her mind absorbed, calmed by the intenseness of its agonies.

CHAPTER II.

The bannered hall hung with the trophies
Of the manly chase—the seat of old
Of council, hospitality, and mirth.

HE great hall of Stanfield was illuminated with huge candles of coarse yellow wax, placed in iron sconces, at irregular distances, on the wall. The logs of wood burnt briskly in the wide chimney: their dancing flames and crackling embers sent forth a genial heat, and gave a comparatively comfortable appearance to the desolate apartment. The broad-chested staghounds were lying at their ease before the fire, fatigued with the day's protracted chase. A careless observer would, from their half-closed eyes, have pronounced them to be sleeping; but whenever a fresh footstep fell on the rough stone pavement, the open eye and pricked ear showed that they were wakefully attentive to all that passed. The numerous domestics had already placed the manchet bread and spiced cover, when Herwald entered the hall, accompanied by Herman, and others of his guests: his pet hound rose lazily to meet him, and with the familiarity of an admitted favourite, thrust his long nose into the franklin's hand, in order to attract his attention, and obtain the customary caress.

"Down, Odin, down!" cried his master, peevishly, his displeasure excited at the absence of his daughter, Edith, who had not yet made her appearance. "What do the hounds do here?—is there no chenery at Stanfield, that we meet them in our very chambers? See to it, knaves, for the future, and force not me to look to it!"

The faithful animal was not to be repulsed with words, but continued to press his claim to notice; the canine courtier not knowing, like his human brother, that there are moments of ennui in the lives of despots when even flattery offends and homage fatigues—a truth of which poor Odin soon received a practical illustration: an impatient kick sent him howling to a distant corner of the apartment.

"Come," continued Herwald, "let us to the feast; and you, Huon, must serve my cup to-night—it seems my child hath forgot it is her father's hour of service."

"Not for lack of being reminded," said Herman, "for 'tis not so long since you bade her to the feast."

"Humph!" muttered the franklin, "that speech were better from her father's lips. Thou hast scant courtesy, Herman, in that rugged heart of thine; and I sometimes wish that thou wert other than my brother's son. What right hast thou to blame her?"

The wily nephew perceived that he had gone too far. Herwald's parental love and pride took the alarm that another should presume to blame his child. Herman knew that his uncle loved him not for himself, but as the heritor of his name, and that, if provoked, he was capable of sacrificing even the fixed purpose of his life to Edith's tears and his own resentment.

"You deal not fairly with me, noble franklin," he replied: "you first cut short my speech, then blame me for its harshness. I was about to express my fear that the keen blast and sleet which blanched my cousin's cheek had chilled her blood—that illness might——"

"Illness!" interrupted Herwald, his love for Edith changing the current of his thoughts. "What a churl am I to blame her! It must be so. I marked her pallid cheek and clouded eye, and thought they both proceeded from a different cause. . Now, knaves, can ye not stir? Haste to your lady's chamber; tell her——"

His further words were cut short by the entrance of Edith, who at last had mustered sufficient courage to meet her father's glance—to endure her cousin's detested assiduities.

"Why, this is well!" cried the franklin, kindly taking her by the hand, to lead her to a seat, his eye glancing in approbation on her improved attire: "our feast were dull, Edith, without thy presence. To your places," he added, turning to his guests; "our worthy chaplain will ask the blessing, and my daughter speak her father's welcome."

The portly ecclesiastic spoke the hurried benediction, and the flowing wine-cup soon began to circle in the hall of Stanfield.

In a distant chamber of the holm a different scene was passing. Hubert, the aged seneschal, was sleeping in a rough settle, lined with deer-skin, beside a smouldering fire, whose red, flickering blaze, as it alternately rose and fell, gave a Rembrandt-like expression to his features; his bunch of ponderous keys hung on a hook within reach of his shrivelled hand; the doors had all been fastened for the night, and the faithful servitor, conscious that he had fulfilled his duty, was indulging in repose. A flagon of mead, half-emptied, and the remains of a pasty, showed that he had already supped. So deep was his sleep, that the sound of music and revelry in the hall failed to wake him—perhaps because, although loud, it was distant: a nearer sound, far less distinct, might, as it soon after proved, have roused him.

The sounds of revelry came louder and louder, when Huon, followed by Judith, appeared cautiously at the door of the chamber in which his uncle sat, and, after reconnoitring awhile, slowly, and with the stealthy pace of a cat, approached the old man's chair. His manner would have seemed suspicious, had not the open, manly expression of his rough, handsome face, and the half-laughing, half-anxious countenance of the damsel, who was watching him, precluded all idea of any sinister design. Comparatively noiseless as were the steps of Huon, they fell upon the sleeper's ear, or perchance his breath fell upon his aged face, as he leant over him to reach the keys; for at the very moment he grasped them Hubert awoke, and caught the culprit's receding arm.

"Eh! what?" exclaimed the seneschal—"have we thieves in Stanfield? What, ho! Help, knaves!—help, I say!"

Fortunately, at that moment, a fresh burst from the banquet-chamber covered the speaker's voice.

"Silence, uncle, silence!" whispered Huon. "'Tis I, your nephew. Have you been dreaming, or do you suppose that I am come to rob you?"

"I don't know," replied the old man, suspiciously; "the world is grown so changed and wicked. What want you with the keys? The gates are all made fast; and, without the franklin's order, none may enter or have egress to-night."

"Pshaw! uncle—our master carouses: would you have me disturb him for a trifle like this? It is only for Judith, who is anxious to visit her mother's cottage to-night. Her young lady hath given her permission to be absent, and——here, Judith," he added, "come and speak for yourself."

The maiden advanced, and laid her hand upon the arm of the vigilant guardian, half-smiling and half-pouting as she did so.

"Come, Hubert, you surely won't refuse me?" she said: "my poor mother is ill, and tards to see her child."

"Well, well," replied the old man, gradually relaxing his grasp upon the keys, for Judith was a favourite with him, "I am glad it is no worse. Thou art a duteous child," he added, "unlike my roystering scapegrace: thou canst honour gray hairs. There, take the key; but who is to go with thee? True, the land is quiet, and there is little fear of robbers; but still it is not seemly that my old cummer's daughter should cross the wold like a wayfarer or runaway serf."

"I shall accompany her, uncle: under my care, it must be a bold arm that would do her wrong." Huon's glance of affection as he spake was answered by Judith with a corresponding one of innocent confidence.

"Ho! ho!" laughingly exclaimed the old man. "What! is my dainty springer caught at last? Huon," he added, checking his tone, and speaking in a more serious voice, "this must be no light love."

"Uncle!"

"Well, well—there, now, I'll trust thee—I'll trust thee;" and the aged man sank chuckling in his warm seat by the fire, his thoughts gradually becoming confused, wandering from Huon and Judith to the recollection of his own all but forgotten boyish passion.

"In an hour meet me at the gate," whispered Judith to her lover; "by that time the household will have retired to rest, and I may pass forth unperceived."

"But my guerdon?" replied the esquire, not willing to be baulked of his promised reward.

"Out on thee for an unreasonable creditor!" said his mistress. "Wouldst have me pay thy service before it is performed? It were poor wisdom, that."

Huon, expecting that he would have a fair opportunity of urging his suit during their walk to the cottage, grumblingly submitted to the postponement of the kiss—the bribe for which he had been tempted to steal the keys from his uncle, to whose charge, after the fastening of the doors, they were invariably given.

On reaching her chamber, Judith found her young mistress—who, under the plea of indisposition, had contrived to withdraw from the banquet—awaiting her return. The triumphant confidence of Herman terrified her; her father's open allusions, when warmed with wine, to her approaching union, too plainly told her how fixed was his resolution—how hopeless was the chance of moving him from his long-settled purpose; and the timid girl, with a firmness springing from desperation, almost rejoiced at the insuperable bar which her secret marriage placed to the intended union. A few moments under the hands of her nimble confidant served to remove the jewels and gay attire which, in obedience to the franklin, she had assumed. A dark dress and linen wimple supplied their place; and as they passed forth together, the heiress of Stanfield might have been taken by any straggling domestic for a fellow-servant passing to perform some household duty.

"How now!" whispered Huon, as they reached the gate, where, by appointment, he waited the arrival of Judith: "a companion! This is more than I bargained for. Surely," he added, in a tone of reproach, "you cannot mistrust me?"

"And surely," said his mistress, in a corresponding voice, "you cannot judge so lightly of me as to suppose that I would quit the holm at such an hour alone with any man? No, Huon, no: evil tongues are too often busy with a maiden's fame. They may say that I have a careless laugh and a light word, but none shall say that my acts were not of honesty and virtue."

There was a quiet impressiveness which gave weight to her words, and told her lover that reply would be as useless as imprudent. Perhaps, in his heart, he secretly loved her better for her resolution.

"Tell me, at least, who is to be our companion," he replied, at the same time opening the great door.

Edith, who overheard the words, passed hastily through the portal.

"Humph! it can't be old Alice," he continued; "her step is too nimble for her."

"Perhaps," said Judith, "it is deaf Ann; but no matter who it is. Give us your arm: make fast the tower, and Heaven and St. Cuthbert guide us on our way!"

The astonishment of Huon on his arrival at the cottage may be imagined, when he found that he had been instrumental in the absence of his young lady; but his fair tempter's smile reassured him, and the visions of punishment and terror of his master, which the discovery at first conjured up, gradually gave way to the smile of Judith and the iterated thanks of Edward and his lady.

* * * * *

The jest and song had long ceased in the hall of Stanfield, and its inmates retired to rest, when a phantom-like figure might be seen approaching the walls. With the utmost deliberation he counted the loopholes, commencing from the left of the principal tower, and paused at the twelfth. Looking carefully around, he threw himself into a crouching position beneath the shade of an ancient pollard, and placing his fingers to his lips, imitated the peculiar cry of the bittern, paused for a few moments twice, and at each pause renewed it. At the end of the third signal, Herman and his confidant, Unolff, appeared upon the walls, their usual costume hid by the close leathern shirt usually worn by the superior vassals and ecclesiastical serfs. A cord, which the squire fixed to one of the rough projecting stones of the tower, enabled them to descend, and in a few moments from their first appearance on the walls they stood before the holm. At a signal from Herman the crouching man approached.

"Speak!" whispered the Saxon, repressed passion causing the words to whistle through his close-set teeth, "have you dogged him to the lair?"

"I have, noble franklin," replied the man. "I followed him for many a weary mile, often burying myself in the bog to the shoulders, to avoid recognition; sometimes trailing my limbs like a serpent through the woods; but I housed him safely at last in the cottage."

"Thou art the best of bloodhounds!" exclaimed his master, a gleam of ferocious joy lighting up his pale and agitated features. "Are your fellows posted? 'Tis well," he continued, in answer to a sign of assent. "Now, then, follow me. Let your hearts be firm, and your hands sure; you know the recompense."

His two companions inclined their heads in token of obedience, and the doomed murderer sullenly pursued his path, bent on his cruel purpose, reckless alike of human or divine retribution, which sooner or later, with its iron hand, crushes the mail of guilt, lays bare the sinner's breast, and vindicates the eternal laws of justice unto man.

How sweet, how ennobling are the sentiments of maternity! how vast the courage inspired by a pure and virtuous love! In the caresses of her child and husband, the sorrows, the wild despair of Edith became calm, and she viewed the inevitable *éclaircissement* no longer with the sullen stupor of a hopeless heart, but with the calmness of reason and the trustfulness of religion. Perhaps she drew fortitude from the crisis. We have frequently observed and wondered at that peculiar elasticity in the soul of woman. Trifles oppress them, misfortunes elevate them. When skies are bright, and all around is fair, woman is then timidity and love; let the storm rage, and man, superior man, hath not the courage and fortitude of soul that can sustain a woman in that hour.

It was finally arranged that Edith should disclose her marriage to her father, trusting to his extreme affection, and the impression likely to be produced by the sight of his infant grandson, who was consigned to the faithful Judith's care, to effect a reconciliation.

"Trust me, dearest Edith," said her husband, as the parting moment arrived, "that all will yet be well. Stern as is the franklin's heart, it hath a stream of tendernes for thee too deep for anger to freeze—too pure to be sullied by unreasonable resentment. At first, I doubt not but his rage will be fearful; fortunately, violent emotions soon exhaust themselves. Would," he added, "that I could be the first to bear the brunt of his indignation —to turn his wrath from thy dear head! Remember, it is for our boy you plead; a mother's eloquence is ever irresistible. Take courage, Edith; and many a joyous hour in Stanfield's halls will repay thee for each sorrow past."

With this and similar arguments did Edward sustain the courage of his trembling wife, whose resolution rose and fell as hope and fear alternately prevailed. The hour of parting at last arrived; the iron tongue of night had long told the birth of morning, when Edith and her attendants set forward to return to the hall.

"I must to my father," said Edward; " I can trust his generous nature for forgiveness; his anger, like a summer's storm, is fierce, but quickly dies away. With the morning, I am sure, he will be at Stanfield, to calm your father's wrath, or, at the worst, protect his child."

The parting kiss was given—the last that cruel destiny permitted them on earth: a serpent, envious of their happiness, was in their path; and Edward's guardian angel slept. Agreeable to his intention of seeking his parent, he directed his steps towards the distant village where his horses and attendants waited him; chewing, as he walked along, the cud of many a sweet and bitter fancy, hope and confidence alternately giving way to the gloomy forebodings of despair. Just as the first streak of ruddy day, piercing the veil of night, appeared above the horizon, he reached a rising knoll, where rustic piety had erected a rude cross and seat, to invite the traveller to prayer or repose. Just as he gained the spot, the distant matin bell fell upon his ear. Kneeling on the turf-raised altar, he commended his wife and child to the protection of that Being whose arm can sustain the weak, whose wisdom guide them through the storms of life. While absorbed in prayer, he might be seen suddenly to spring from the earth: one convulsive bound, and all was over. The being lately life, intelligence, and animation, lay a senseless corse—a bolt winged from an arbalet had pierced his manly heart; sent him in the moment of prayer, his pure soul raised to God, strong in the hopefulness of youth, in the confidence of a happy future, to meet the Judge whose ear was even then mercifully inclined to his supplication. A few moments afterwards, and Herman, together with his companions, stood by the dead man's side.

As the hour drew nigh in which Edith was to meet her father, and confess the secret of her marriage, her high-wrought courage began to fail her. It needed all the encouragement of her faithful Judith, and the contemplation of her slumbering child, to nerve her for the task. She was in the act of rising from her knees, which had been bent in prayer, when the franklin entered the room. Despite her resolution, she trembled at the sight of him.

"Edith, my child," he said, kindly taking her hand, "why start? A daughter's prayer should ever be fitted for a parent's ear; and thine, I doubt not, has been to bend thy unreasonable objections to my will. Is it not so, my child?"

Edith remained silent.

"Listen to me," resumed her father. "When thy mother died there was left a tender, gentle flower, so fragile, that the slightest breath of coldness or unkindness would have cut the slender thread of its existence. Edith, thou hast known me only as the rough hunter, the successful soldier, or stern franklin."

"More," interrupted his hearer, weeping, and passionately kissing his hand, "as the father, the kind, the generous, too indulgent father."

"Somewhat, perhaps, too much so," he resumed. "It was my nature, and I cannot change it. But I have been thy nurse, Edith: watched night after night the little cot where slept my motherless treasure; schooled my rough voice to woman's softness, not to disturb thy slumbers; tended thee with more than a father's fondness—with almost the yearning tenderness of a mother's love. Say, have I not the right to demand some recompense?"

His daughter clasped her hands in silence.

"For thy sake I have sought to rear no other heritor to my proud name. Must, then, that name, which is dear to me as my own existence, be transmitted through another? Must the long-cherished hopes of years be disappointed? Will the child whom I have so blindly loved blight the only hope of my existence, or by an effort worthy of herself assure her father's happiness? Think what will be your feelings, when, standing by my grave, you will be enabled to say, 'I have done my duty—I have closed my father's eyes in peace!'"

During the franklin's last address the agitation of Edith had visibly increased. The tone of affectionate entreaty pierced her very soul; and had the sacrifice been possible, at that moment of excitement gladly would his child have submitted to become its victim.

"Would—would that it were possible!" she replied; "in this bitter hour I feel the sin, the curse of disobedience."

"What mean you?" uttered the franklin; "what fearful mystery is this? Speak!—have I still a child?"

"You have—you have!" frantically exclaimed his daughter; "but know that child is——"

"What?"

"A wife and mother!"

Edith, exhausted by the effort, remained gazing in speechless agony upon her father's face: life, hope, happiness, all seemed to hang upon his lips.

Had a thunderbolt fallen at the feet of Herwald he could not have been more astonished.

"Married!" he exclaimed, "and a mother! Well, well—I have no child now!"

"Do not say that!" sobbed Edith—"do not say that! Speak to me—look upon me —call me daughter—for Heaven's sake call me daughter!"

"No!" sternly answered the franklin, shaking himself from her grasp. "My curse pursue thee! Hear it in the arms of thy husband—tremble at it when the tempest rages; and when the sun shines upon thy father's grave, remember whose disobedience laid him there! When the thunder roars mayst thou fancy thou hear'st thy father's curse! If thou hast children——"

At this moment Judith, who had been a trembling spectator of the interview, with one of those sudden acts of inspiration which only woman's heart can inspire, and which no philosophy can teach, placed his infant grandson at his enraged grandfather's feet. The shock was electrical: vainly he struggled to continue his malediction: nature was too powerful for passion—pity too strong for anger. The kneeling mother and her helpless infant formed an appeal he could not resist.

"No, no," he murmured, in a broken voice; "I cannot, dare not curse thy child— Edith's child!" he added, gazing almost with love upon the little stranger who lay smiling at his feet. "Edith," he added, after a short struggle with his better nature, "'tis past;

this boy hath made thy peace; come to thy father's arms—once more his child!"

With a cry of joy, which burst from the deepest recesses of her heart, a smile as pure, as glad as the redeemed spirit when first winged from Heaven, Edith threw herself into the arms of her forgiving father.

The words of parental forgiveness, the caress of parental love, were the last rays of happiness the unfortunate Edith was destined to taste on earth. Scarcely had the reconciled Saxon and his child recovered from the agitation of the scene which we have so faintly endeavoured to describe, than the recluse of Wymondham entered the apartment unannounced, the universal reverence in which he was held rendering his visits everywhere a welcome honour.

"Franklin!" he exclaimed, "to horse! Blood hath been shed upon thy land—the blood of the noble and the good! Edward, the son of thy oldest friend, Edda, the Saxon, lies murdered at the foot of the cross!"

A piercing shriek burst from the lips of Edith—a shriek fearful as the despairing agony of a departing soul, and the heiress of Stanfield lay a senseless maniac at the feet of her agonised father!

CHAPTER III.

Vers'd in the Druids' lore of old,
A priest of whom strange deeds were told,
Of wondrous power; but none may tell
If won from Heaven or wrung from hell.

IT would be impossible to describe the rage and confusion of Herman when his uncle informed him not only of Edith's marriage, but of the birth of an heir to Stanfield. The prize for which he had imbrued his hands in blood, and yielded his soul to the dark fiend, seemed for ever to have escaped him. 'Tis true, the melancholy state of Edith gave but little hope of recovery; but the boy lived—Edward's boy—to become the inheritor of the broad lands for which his cupidity panted, and perhaps the avenger of his father's assassination. This last consideration, or both combined, determined him on attempting to remove the infant heir. Open force, guarded as was the holm, he knew to be hopeless; he determined, therefore, to seek by other means the accomplishment of his detestable purpose. As prompt in execution as in thought, he mounted his horse, and attended only by the easy confidant of his crimes and pleasures, directed its head towards

the thick wood of Wymondham, where he trusted to find a fit agent for the crime he meditated.

In the deepest recesses of the wood in question stood a rude hut, partially formed of unhewn stones and logs of wood; strength, more than convenience, seemed to have been the builder's object, not less in choice of material than situation. A thick stagnant pool cut off all access to the back part of the building, where the only apertures for admitting light were situated. The stout oaken door was thickly studded with nails, and, from its solidity and strength, seemed to defy intrusion, the danger of which was still further lessened by the absence of all regular road, and the thick, stunted pollards, which prevented the traveller or hunter from seeing the edifice till close upon it. When by accident any such approached, they hastily crossed themselves and fled, casting glances in their flight, to assure themselves that they were not followed by its mysterious inmate, Haga, or the Dark Man of the Wold, as the occupant was called. He bore a most equivocal character for miles around: none knew his place of birth, or the history of his past life. Deeply skilled in medicine, and in the knowledge of all healing plants, his wisdom was seldom taxed by the superstitious boors or neighbouring franklins, and then only in extreme cases, when all other remedies had failed. In his intercourse with such rare visitors his words were few, but to the purpose; his manners cold, stern, and dignified, added to which he invariably rejected all gifts or proffers of remuneration. In person, Haga was tall, though bent with age; a long beard fell over his ample dark tunic, reaching the silver girdle which bound it to his waist; on it were engraved certain runic characters, the meaning of which was known only to the Druids and bards of the Saxon nation. Indeed, by some he was considered as belonging to the all but extinct order of the former sacerdotal race—a supposition in some measure confirmed by his never having been seen, within the memory of man, in any building dedicated to Christian worship. From whatever source he obtained his means, they were ample; indeed, he had been frequently known to bestow on the wayfarer or the unfortunate an alms which many a noble and wealthy franklin would have grudged. Still he was not beloved; but fear served him as a more efficient protection, for the wretch who would have plundered and fired the roof which sheltered him trembled as he passed the rude hut of Haga of the Wold. The fact of several children having been missed from the neighbouring villages still further tended to increase the superstitious dread in which he was universally held; for, although few tongues ventured to accuse, there were many who doubted not but that Haga was in some way connected with their disappearance; some, more charitably inclined, suggested that they had probably wandered too far into the woods, and either perished of hunger or from the attacks of the wolves, at that period so plentiful in England.

When Herman had approached within bow-shot of the hut, he reined his steed, and dismounting, took from his attendant a dark hunting cloak, in which he enveloped his person so as effectually to prevent recognition, and directed his steps towards the unhallowed spot, leaving his reckless squire lost in admiration at his master's hardy courage.

"Enter!" exclaimed the deep voice of the inmate, as the third blow of Herman's dagger fell on the iron-studded door of the hut: "be thou poor or wretched, rich or noble, weak or strong, craven or brave, enter the hut of the recluse."

The visitor did as he was commanded, and found himself, for the first time in his life, face to face with the being whose name was seldom pronounced without awe, and even whose benefits were received with a secret malediction.

The interior of the cottage presented a far more comfortable appearance than its exterior seemed to promise. A long carved oaken settle extended on one side of the wall; over it were hung several antique bronze instruments, such as are still occasionally found in cairns and Druid mounds, and which modern antiquaries have alternately decided to be instruments of sacrifice or divination; a withered wreath of ivy lay upon the huge block of wood which served as a table, and whose roots, still deeply imbedded in the earth, showed that it retained its primeval position.

Haga was occupied in sorting a collection of herbs, gathered in the neighbouring woods, when Herman entered, and seated himself opposite to him. For a few moments they gazed on each other without speaking. The recluse was the first to break silence.

"What brings the franklin to my secluded dwelling?" he demanded. "His cheek seems flushed with health. Why comes he disguised?" he added, a shade of displeasure passing over his haughty brow: "it was not thus his fathers of yore sought the wise men of their race."

"The wisdom of the sage," replied his guest, "is medicine alike unto the body and the mind; if my cheek is flushed with health, and my limbs are strong, my heart is sick—"

"For vengeance!" interrupted the old man—"for vengeance! I read it in thy knitted brow—the paleness of thy lip, which shames thy cheek's deep red. Thou wouldst remove a rival from thy path of love or of ambition. Begone! I cannot aid thee."

"Will not, rather," answered his guest. "Come, let us understand each other. Although I give not credence to the idle tongues of superstitious fools, I have not now to learn that thou art skilled in herbs—that nature, like one vast book, is open to thy gaze, and that thy wisdom may be turned to good or evil. Come, sell me a draught the slightest drop of which shall stop life's current at its very spring, yet leave no tell-tale evidence behind. I'll pay thy price in gold!"

"Gold!" replied Haga, with a scornful laugh: "were a mine of the pale yellow dross beneath my feet, I would not raise the soil which covers it. Gold! I loathe it more than I loathe humanity, for 'tis its worst weapon. Go, man, go: the outcast of the world—the condemned of men's opinion—will not justify their judgment by participating in a crime like this."

"This is cant!" exclaimed Herman, starting to his feet with ill-suppressed rage—"mere cant, to enhance the value of the service I demand. Fear not to tax my purse: it shall pay thee both for thy conscience and thy nostrum. Why, man," he added, "if what men say of thee be true, thou art already damned beyond the reach of mercy: earth hath no absolution, holy church no prayer for crimes so black as thine."

"Such is thy Christian creed," retorted Haga. "I trust it not—it binds not me; I worship not in temples made with hands. The umbrageous forest is my tabernacle—primeval rocks my altar—my matin hymn the feathered minstrel's song—my oracles the running stream or brook."

"Thou art a Druid," observed Herman—"one of a race proscribed."

"The last of a race proscribed, thou mightest have said," proudly answered the old man. "Cruel hath been our persecutions, and cruel vengeance follows it; the Norman is at hand, the avenger of our sacred race; Odin and Thor no longer guard a land where their altars are deserted and their priests unhonoured—soon, soon will their judgments be accomplished."

"Pagan," said the Saxon franklin, at the same time devoutly crossing himself—for, like most of the nobles of his age, his character formed a strange mixture of cruelty and superstition—"darest thou avow such heresies to me? Although the sainted Edward no longer wears a mortal crown, the church is powerful still."

"And who will be my denouncer?" demanded the Druid, with a sneer. "The noble franklin who came to solicit a poison at my hands to remove from his path a rival whom he fears, perchance, to meet in open fight? I have no fear of such an accuser."

"No man have I ever feared to meet on equal terms, or against such sought the aid of ministry like thine," said Herman. "It is an opening flower I would close, not uproot an oak. I would efface the stain upon an ancient house, without, if possible, steeping my hand in an infant's blood."

"An infant?" eagerly demanded Haga: "hath it been baptised?" He fixed his eyes keenly on Herman, as if he would read his very soul. There was a pause, during which the latter weighed in his mind the import of the question.

"It hath," he slowly answered.

The old man rose, and paced the narrow limits of the chamber, as if communing with himself. His mind seemed at last made up. Laying his hand upon the arm of the franklin, which trembled beneath his touch, he whispered—

"I'll make a compact with thee. I'll give thee means to steep the child in sleep, but not in death—in sleep so deep and calm, that not one pulse shall indicate that life remains within its secret sanctuary: the mother's kiss shall not detect the lingering breath upon its lips—the eye of hate discover the latent bloom upon its cheek. I will do this upon one condition."

"Condition!" faltered Herman, whose superstition recoiled from the Druid's words, "what condition?"

"That when he sleeps this sleep of seeming death," replied the old man, "you shall convey him here to me; that I shall remain sole master of his fate—no question asked—no future count demanded."

"Horror!" exclaimed the Saxon: "wouldst have me barter the infant to the fiend? Never, never: though criminal, I am a Christian."

"Begone, then, at once!" said the tempter. "Thou knowest the only terms on which my services are to be bought. The child here, living at my absolute disposal, what is't to thee whether his blood bedew the shrine of Odin, or that I rear him to serve his neglected altars? Thy conscience," he added, with a sneer, "will be free."

"True," muttered Herman; "and holy church may yet absolve me."

"It may," sarcastically resumed the Druid. "Gold will buy pardon for a heavier sin. Is it a compact?"

"It is!" after a struggle answered

the wretched man. "There is no other way."

The Druid, without further word, went to a dark recess, and after searching for some time amongst its contents, drew a small crystal phial from it, and placed it in the hands of the trembling homicide.

"There is the drug you seek," he exclaimed. "One drop, and the drinker will for hours appear as dead. Once in its death-like trance, it will be easy to remove the body here. In five days I shall expect you. Beware," he added, "how you break faith with me. None ever did so with impunity, and Herman of the Burg shall not be the first."

His hearer started at the ominous manner in which the speaker pronounced his name.

"You know me, then?" he murmured, his countenance changing with fear and passion.

"Well," resumed the old man; "know thee as the murderer of Edward, heir to the Saxon Edda; know thee as the betrothed of a bride thou never shalt possess—as the heir of a name which, if thou keep not faith with me, never shall be thine! Farewell! Pass on thy way, and till the deed is accomplished, darken my door no more."

That very night Herman, under pretence of leaving the franklin to indulge in his natural grief, and watch over his unhappy child, started from Stanfield on his way to Burg, a strong fortress which he possessed, built on the ruins of the Garionorum of Cæsar, the Roman remains of which have survived the more modern structure, and still attract the attention of the antiquary and traveller as he passes over the shallow waters of Braidon, which wash their base. But although he left the home of his destined victim, instruments worthy of their master remained behind to work his will. Before the five days were elapsed a fire broke out in that part of the holm where the infant heir reposed. His attendants had been drugged with the Druid's fatal gift, and slept when they should have watched. The unfortunate wretches perished in the flames, in which the infant was also supposed to have found an untimely grave. It was long ere Edith and her repentant father recovered this second blow.

CHAPTER IV.

Time calms the rooted grief, but seldom cures it;
A look, a word, will jar 'gainst memory's chords,
And bid the old thoughts return.

EIGHTEEN years had elapsed since the fire at Stanfield, in which so many persons perished. The base contriver of the deed remained unsuspected; but the vast political changes which had placed the Norman on the throne prevented his profiting, as he anticipated, by the deed. It was the policy both of William and his successors to amalgamate as far as possible the still hostile races. In many instances confiscation was avoided by the Saxon heiress marrying some Norman knight, who thus became an inheritor of the soil. The wealthy franklin purchased the peaceable possession of his ancestral domains by allying himself with some powerful noble of the invader's blood, whose dowerless daughter bestowed at least security with the possession of her hand.

Stanfield, as may be supposed, was too rich a prize to escape the Conqueror's cupidity. Had her own safety only been at stake, Edith would have defied the utmost malice of her fate; but when she reflected that her father— her indulgent father—even if his life were spared, must wander forth unhonoured and defenceless, exposed not only to the reverse of fortune, but to the conquerors' unpitying scoffs, her last resolve gave way, and she bestowed her hand on Hugh de Bigod, created, for his services at the battle of Hastings, Earl of Norwich, and marshal of the king in that portion of his dominions formerly comprised under the name of the East Angles. Fortunately for Edith, she met with no ungenerous wooer or stern lord. Love it was not in her power to bestow; but as the manly qualities of the earl's nature developed themselves, her friendship became his. Like herself, he had mourned the loss of the object of his first affections, two infant pledges of which, a boy and a girl, remained to him. The spirited Norman and his sister Matilda gazed at first with fear upon the pale cheek and gloomy brow of their new mother, whose gentleness, however, gradually won their hearts, and on whom she soon bestowed some portion of that love which her heart still treasured for the memory of her own lost boy. The franklin, full of years, had long since slumbered at peace. Even the deeply guilty Herman shared in the protection which the union of Edith with the powerful favourite of the Conqueror extended to her race. He was a frequent visitor at the castle of Norwich, where the earl and countess generally resided, and if not a welcome, was at least a tolerated guest. Age had not taught him penitence, or cured him of his ambitious dreams: the murderer plotted still.

The sun was shining cheerfully on a fine morning in September, gilding the lofty tower of the cathedral, which still remains the pride and admiration of the ancient city of Norwich; its rays, after striking the lofty pinnacle and fretted nooks, rich in many a quaint device and sculptured saint, fell in quiet repose upon the emerald turf enclosed by the cloisters of the sacred edifice, causing the shadows from the western windows to fall upon the pavement. The last chant of the matin hymn was fading through the aisles, when an ecclesiastic, whose chain and cross indicated his episcopal rank, entered from one of the side doors of the church, and began to pace the cloister: his rich purple soutan fell in graceful folds around his stately form, which seemed bent less by age than sorrow. The arched brow, piercing eye, and aquiline nose of the individual, sufficiently indicated his Norman blood. To a casual observer, the general expression of his countenance would have been taken for pride: to those who examined closer, a decided character of benevolence redeemed it. Such as we have endeavoured to describe him was Herbert de Lozinga, Bishop of Norwich, and chancellor to William the Conqueror—a man of whom even his enemies said much good, and whose friends were enthusiastic in his praise. Born of high rank, and elevated to ecclesiastical dignities, he possessed some of the prejudices of his birth, and many of the virtues of his state. Those who saw in him only the noble and the prelate, envied him: the few who knew the man wondered that he was unhappy: a subdued melancholy seemed to be the prevailing feature of his disposition. Perhaps in the priest he had not learnt to subdue all the recollections of the man. The general companion of his solitary morning walk within the cloisters was a young orphan named Ulrick, whom he had reared from infancy, and to whom scandal assigned a nearer claim upon his bounty than mere charity.

"How keen and fresh blows the mountain breeze!" muttered the prelate to himself, as he paced the cloister, his eye glancing alternately from the fretted roof to the enclosed space before him. "Where can Ulrick linger? The matin song fell harshly on my ear, want-

ing his voice to give it melody. 'Tis strange," he added, "how the boy hath twined himself around my heart. I should remember that the hour will arrive when we must part—when he must mingle in the world, and seek to win by gallant deeds the name which cruel fate denies him."

The speaker continued his walk with the same languid step—sometimes lingering to catch some new point of view, as the tower and spires of the cathedral were seen through the deep fret-work of the cloister window—sometimes to listen to the echo of some distant step, as it either receded or drew near the spot where he was meditating. At last the sound of a footfall lighter than the sound of the sandalled monk's drew near, and in a few seconds the object of his thoughts presented himself.

Ulrick the Orphan, as he was generally called, was formed in a mould where symmetry and manly strength were blended. Although generally supposed to be, if not the son, at least in some way connected by blood with his patron, his features bore the impress of the Saxon rather than the Norman race—blue eyes, a fair complexion, and light chestnut curls: the first down of manhood shaded his lip and chin, redeeming the almost womanish character of his beauty. Although mildness seemed to be the general expression of his countenance, there was great determination in the mouth and nostrils, the chiselled lines of which generally indicate courage, firmness, and perseverance. His step, though light, was stately, like the young fawn's, when, sauntering from its evening lair, it snuffs the breath of morning with an air in which affection and reverence are mingled. The youth approached the spot where Herbert de Lozinga awaited him, and, silently bending the knee, he asked the usual benediction, which the prelate bestowed upon him by making the sign of the cross above his head.

"Forgive me, reverend father," said Ulrick, as he rose from his knee, "but I have been detained beyond my usual hour. I encountered the noble Mirvan in my walks, and——" Here the speaker hesitated.

"With him one," interrupted the prelate, with a melancholy smile, "whose charms, I fear, endanger Ulrick's peace."

The youth blushed at the accusation, and was silent.

"Hear me boy!" resumed Herbert. "I have long wished to speak with you on the subject, but weakly hesitated, knowing how sad it is to be sternly awakened from those blissful dreams in which youthful confidence too often plunges us. You love!"

His hearer started as the gentle voice of

his patron pronounced the fatal words which tore from his soul its sweet delusion. Still, as drowning wretches cling to the last plank, he struggled to avoid confessing, even to himself, the folly of his passion, the madness of his hopes. Matilda, the daughter of one of the most powerful nobles of the Norman race—and he, an orphan, a being without a name—the stain of doubt, perchance of infamy, upon his birth—and he to dare to raise his eyes so high! No, no; he had mistaken friendship for love; it could be nothing else.

"Think not, my lord," he replied, as soon as he recovered from the confusion into which the unexpected accusation had thrown him, "that such arrogance and pride e'er harboured here: the Lady Matilda can ne'er be viewed by me but with such awe and reverence as the shrine of some bright saint enthroned in bliss might claim. Chance, you are aware, led me to preserve her brother's life: the grateful maid hath deigned to call me friend: think, father—friend. That," he added, fixing his eyes almost imploringly upon his interrogator, "is a name distinct from love."

An expression of sadness clouded the usually calm, clear brow of the priest. For years the page of human life had been his study. Perhaps some recollection of his own youthful dreams came over him, when he, too, had struggled to blind his reason to the true nature of his heart—its weakness, passions. Perhaps his natural sympathy with humanity interested him in the struggle between truth and delusion which was evidently taking place in Ulrick's soul—a struggle which, for its victim's happiness, he was resolved at any risk to end.

"Your sentiments towards Matilda are, then, merely those of friendship—nothing more?"

Ulrick remained silent: the precipice was becoming gradually defined before him.

"Could you," continued Herbert, "with joy be present, see her wed, and her rich beauties grace another's arms? You tremble, Ulrick, at the thought. Why is this?"

"Yet 'tis not love!" passionately iterated Ulrick; "for I should be content could I but live for ever in her sight, nor frame one wish beyond. But never more to hear the music of her voice, or catch the expression of her dark blue eye when mirth illumes it, or when sorrow's tale hath gemmed its fringes with a pitying tear, would give my heart a pang."

The vehemence of the speaker betrayed too clearly, even to himself, the state of his affections. Like a child attracted by the pleasing colours of the snake, he had played with the reptile till its venom had infused itself into his soul.

"We have been both to blame!" exclaimed the prelate, rising from the rough stone on which he had been seated, and pacing the cloister with a firmer step than usual; "we have been dreamers both. You must to the world, boy: my selfish love hath too long detained thee here. Action is the best cure for sorrow and for ill. Our monarch prosecutes the war in France: honours and lordships may be won by gallant deeds. If fate denies thee a name, thy sword must win one."

"Honours and lands the sword may win, but what deed can efface the stain of infamy upon my birth?"

Ulrick's voice trembled with emotion as he spoke. The general opinion of his being the son of the bishop had at times struck him with a sad foreboding: he feared to find in the author of his being the man whom he most loved and reverenced on earth—the term, "son of a priest," being at that time the most bitter reproach an insulting enemy could bestow.

"Infamy!" repeated Herbert; "and who shall dare pronounce it so, when I, who have reared thee from thy tenderest years—I, who received thee a smiling infant in these arms, believe thee noble?"

Never before had Herbert de Lozinga been so explicit with his orphan *protegé*, whom respect, and perhaps a nameless dread, had hitherto prevented from demanding an explanation of the tie between them. The words of his protector fell like a precious balm upon his soul—they conveyed to him the assurance that he was not the wretched being he suspected.

"You, then," he exclaimed, "are not—"

The blush upon the brow of his guardian arrested Ulrick's words: he paused, and bent his eyes to the earth in silence.

"No, Ulrick," replied the prelate to the half-uttered interrogation, "I am not thy father. No offspring's tear," he added, in a voice of deep emotion, "will fall upon my grave. Thinkest thou, had I so far forgot the laws of God—my priestly vow—I could have ever gazed without a blush upon thee?"

"Pardon, pardon!" sobbed Ulrick, prostrating himself at his feet, half choked with emotion. "I am, indeed, a wretch, to have formed one doubt of purity like thine. Tell me, I entreat thee, all that thou knowest touching my wretched state."

The bishop, in his turn, seemed confused at the request, for the required explanation recalled the most painful moments of his existence—the struggles of passions which had left their scars upon his very soul. Feeling, however, how necessary it was to make the effort, he resolved to subdue the natural hesitation which he felt, and add another page to the long list of pangs he had endured.

"Be it so, Ulrick," he replied; "but not now—not now. I lack courage for the task —firmness to bring my mind to part with thee. I must seek them both in prayer. In three days thy letters shall be prepared for William's camp—all things arranged for thy departure; but ere thou leavest the solitary man whose heart has been thy home, thou shalt learn the sorrows of his life, and how thou first wert cast a helpless infant on his care. Go," he added; "take leave of thy friends at the castle—of the noble Mirvan and his gentle sister; but remember, Ulrick, not one word of love: plant not a thorn where thou wouldst place a rose. Since 'tis the lot of man to suffer—to feel his heart consume beneath the serpent-tooth of deathless passions—suffer alone, and, like the wounded eagle on the rock, pine in solitude away."

On the evening of the same day, Ulrick directed his steps towards the castle, to announce to his two friends his intended departure for the camp. With the peculiar sensitiveness of his nature, he had refused on several occasions to partake of the almost regal hospitality of the earl, whose residence emulated the splendours of the court, and who had frequently expressed a wish to meet the preserver of his son. As he crossed the open space which divided the cathedral precincts from the city, now known by the name of Tombland, his heart beat with contending emotions: he was going, for the last time, perhaps, to listen to the voice whose tone found so deep an echo in his soul—to gaze upon the eyes whose light to him was as twin stars to guide him to his destiny; was going to part—the words of love which glowed upon his tongue unspoken—the wishes, passions, and regrets which burnt within him as closely sealed as in a sepulchre. Still, despite the barriers which reason presented to his passion, his step was buoyant; hope held possession of a corner of his heart, even as she lay hidden at the bottom of Pandora's box: and that which was only not impossible seemed half achieved.

"Yes," he exclaimed, apostrophising the object of his adoration, "her name shall be my beacon in the path of honour. If I fall, she shall feel I was not altogether unworthy of her love; if I return with fame, that love may crown me."

Ulrick had crossed about half the distance which separated the city gate from the castle, when he was surrounded by a gay and laughing band of youthful nobles, who, headed by Mirvan and Herman of the Burg, had been indulging in the pleasures of the chase; his sister, and his fair cousin, Isabel of Bayeux, had accompanied them.

"So ho!" exclaimed Mirvan, dismounting from his horse, and placing his arm in Ulrick's, "I have caught the sage at last. No refusal now; not e'en my sister's word shall set you free; for once we'll have philosophy at our gay banquet, that when beauty's smiles lead our hearts astray, wisdom, in time, may pull the reins of our understanding to check us. Wouldst believe it, my fair coz," he added, turning to Isabel, "although Matilda and myself, time out of mind, have tried to tempt him, this is the first time we have lured the hermit from his cell?"

"And not soon again to return to it," said Ulrick, bowing lowly to the two lovely girls, who had reined in their stately palfreys on first perceiving him. "I am bound to the country of the Lady Isabel, to try my humble fortunes in the wars."

At the concluding words, a close observer might have seen the cheek of Matilda turn pale. Herman observed it, and his heart overflowed with bitterness and gall.

"You are right, young man," he haughtily and loudly answered. "Normandy is the land of those who have neither country nor nation, birth nor name: it is a land for adventurers. You will do well to cast your fortunes there."

To most of the young men, the bitter, sarcastic humour of the speaker was well known: they passed his observations, therefore, with a laugh. Not so Isabel, who, with the penetration of a woman's wit, had detected the desire of the franklin to humiliate Ulrick in the presence of Matilda, whose love, despite the disparity of years between them, he ridiculously aspired to.

"Sir Saxon," she exclaimed, "it is the land, at least, of courtesy, since it permits those whom it has conquered to rail unpunished against their masters. It is the land of the brave," she added, proudly, "and worthy to become the home of those who have true hearts and loyal weapons."

"By my faith! fair cousin," interrupted Mirvan, secretly annoyed at the turn the conversation had taken, "if their swords are but half as keen as thy tongue, I had rather be friends than quarrel with thy countrymen. Our kinsman meant not to offend thee: do not quarrel with him."

"Quarrel with Herman!" iterated the haughty beauty, perfectly aware of her power over Mirvan's heart—"quarrel with the spleen? No, no: he is to be endured, not quarrelled with."

"Kinsman," exclaimed the young noble, who read in the glowing cheek and flashing eye of his young friend a coming storm, "pleasure me by riding with our friends on to the castle. The ladies will accept of mine and Ulrick's escort."

The grave tone in which the request was made implied a command to the haughty Saxon. But Mirvan was too important a person for him to offend: besides, he felt that he had already lost ground in his favour by his churlish speech to one to whom he was not only sincerely attached, but deeply indebted.

"Willingly, cousin," he brought himself to answer. "My absence shall be my punishment: the fair Isabel, I doubt not, will feel it more than sufficient for the crime. At least, we part as friends," he added, raising his plumed cap as he spoke, and bowing to the very saddle-bow of his fair enemy.

"Friends!" carelessly repeated Isabel: "oh, yes—friends as much as ever."

The franklin either would not or did not see the irony of the last words of the speaker, but turned his horse's head towards the castle, attended by all but Mirvan, Ulrick, and the two ladies.

"You are too hard, Isabel," said the former, "on our kinsman: he hath a heart."

"Heart!" interrupted the maiden; "so hath the tomb its tenant. Heart! 'Tis a cold and frozen sceptre. Love, friendship, confidence, the ties which bind us to our fellow-creatures, the gushing sympathies of love, all that ennobles man, and lights this dull earth with gleams of Eden's sunshine, are his scoffs."

"I cannot argue with you," said Mirvan. Then turning to Ulrick, he continued, "And so you leave us for the wars? The cloister, then, it seems, has lost its charms. Is Mars or Venus now in the ascendant?"

"Neither, I trust," replied the conscience-stricken youth. "But I am sick of dreaming out my life in cloistered ease. 'Tis time I see the world, and mate myself with men. My guardian's influence hath oped the path of honour—I were a sluggard did I not pursue it. If I have neither name nor birth, country nor station, who shall blame me that I strive to win one?"

"Blame!" said Isabel. "Thou shalt have one Christian maiden's prayers at least for thy success; nay, I think I may venture to promise thee my pensive cousin's, too."

"You may, indeed," softly uttered Matilda, thus directly appealed to; "they are due not less to his own merits than to the preserver of my brother's life."

The quiet tone of the speaker's voice told to her cousin that her calmness was assumed; indeed, she had long suspected a mutual passion, not the less ardent for being uncon-fessed, between Matilda and the unknown orphan.

"Happy Ulrick!" exclaimed Mirvan, who, in the blindness of his own passion for the volatile Isabel, did not suspect his sister's; "did not a dearer tie withhold me, gladly would I share thy perils and behold thy triumphs. As it is, although I may not witness, perchance I can assist them. My father, as thou well knowest, stands in high favour with our valiant monarch, and, I am sure, will gladly stretch his utmost influence to serve thee: he will, doubtless, furnish thee with letters to those who can place thee foremost in the path of danger and of honour."

"I ask no more," replied Ulrick. "If I fall, it matters little: few will mourn me, and none know the wild ambitious aspirations which perish with me. Should I survive, those who interest themselves in my wretched fate shall not blush for the favour they have shown me."

On his arrival at the castle, Ulrick was presented to the earl and countess, the former of whom thanked him with stately kindness for the service he had rendered Mirvan, whose life our hero had preserved from the attack of a ferocious wolf, when, wounded and unhorsed, he lay exposed to the savage monster's fury. Edith, whose remarkable beauty time and sorrow had mellowed, but not destroyed, sighed as she gazed on the gallant youth, who modestly knelt to kiss her extended hand. Perhaps some feature jarred the chords of memory, or some mysterious sympathy formed a link between them. The pressure of his lips upon her hand had thrilled to her matron heart.

"Such," she mentally uttered, with a sigh, "such might have been my gallant Edward's boy, had cruel fortune spared him to my widowed heart!"

The modesty with which Ulrick listened to the counsel of the earl, the extreme grace of his person and purity of mind, made a favourable impression upon that powerful nobleman. His guests and officers perceived the entrainment of their host and chief, and vied with each other in courtesies. All who listened to the eager hopes and noble aspirations of the gallant youth wished him success in his career of arms, all but one—the jealous, disappointed Herman, who sat listening to his rival's praise in gloomy silence, for rivals he already felt they were. At length, unable longer to endure the gnawings of his envious heart, he quietly withdrew from the hall, to indulge in gloomy meditation.

"Bring Ulrick to the chapel," whispered Isabel to her cousin Mirvan, as, leaning on the arm of Matilda, they followed the countess from the banquet. "If we cannot dub him knight, at least we may arm him for the battle in which he is to win his spurs. I owe him," she added, "no less a debt of gratitude than Matilda, and am impatient till the debt be paid."

The last part of the maiden's speech was too flattering to Mirvan to make him wonder at the unusual request. As soon, therefore, as the feast was ended, and the principal guests retired from the hall, he took the arm of Ulrick, and led his wondering friend towards the chapel.

CHAPTER V.

Words from the lips we love will often wake
The slumbering resolution of the heart—
Urge it to high emprise and deeds of fame.

HE two fair cousins were standing near the altar when the young men entered the sacred edifice. The light from the everburning silver lamp before the shrine gave a religious, mellow tone to the scene, the segment-formed arches dimly receding till they were lost in darkness. Four purer hearts, or more devoted to each other, were seldom met than those assembled there. It is true that between Matilda and Ulrick no vow had e'er been spoken; each seemed instinctively to feel it would be wrong that it should be so. The youth felt that the idol of his worship could receive no clandestine homage; the maiden, that the favoured of her choice would fall from the high place he held within her breast by any rash avowal. And yet they loved—loved with all the pure confiding innocence of youth—the confidence of humanity ere sin or the world's treachery had blighted them. Confident in the sinlessness of her passion, Matilda advanced to meet them; her voice was firm, as her heart was pure and holy.

"Ulrick," she said, "the sister cannot permit the preserver of her brother's life to go unarmed into the battle. The sword is a strange gift from woman's hand; but when grasped by honour, 'tis the best—in thine 'twill ne'er be drawn but in the cause of virtue and of truth."

"To virtue and justice I devote it!" exclaimed Ulrick, sinking on one knee as he received the weapon from her hand. "Lady, this moment shall be graven in the cell where memory treasures up its deepest joys. Round it entwines the thread of my existence. If fortune smiles upon the soldier's arm, thy virtues will have been the inspiring cause; if death should call me on the field of honour, thy image shall console me."

For a few moments the lovers gazed on each other in silence, drinking, in that brief space, a draught for years—a happiness for ages.

"Though far less prized," exclaimed Isabel, willing to end the scene, the excitement of which she feared, "do not refuse my gift." She passed a silken scarf, embroidered by her own fair hands, over the shoulders of Ulrick as she spoke. "It was intended for another, but not more worthy object."

"Less worthy far to wear it," said Mirvan, who understood that it was for himself that the prize had originally been destined.

"Beggar that I am, in all but thanks," sighed Ulrick, as he kissed the embroidered hem of the maiden's gift, "how have I merited such goodness?"

"By prudence," replied Isabel, in a marked tone; "by courage, not in its brute contests with man to man, but in its loftier struggles. We have performed our task—farewell!"

"Farewell!" exclaimed Ulrick, kneeling, and passionately kissing the extended hands of the fair girls. "You have lit my soul with energies—armed me to brave all that the wildest fortune can wreak on me. I will return worthy of such angelic goodness, or return no more."

The excited youth rushed from the chapel as he spoke. Isabel and Matilda retired in silence to their chambers.

That night Mirvan had much for study and reflection.

How delicious is the moment when the youthful heart first feels that it is loved! The soul expands, merges into a new existence, and all around partakes of Eden's bliss.

"Yes," exclaimed Ulrick, as he left the bridge which crossed the castle-moat, "I now am armed to meet adversity—armed against all the terrors of impending fate. Matilda wills that I should gain a name; others, alone by vile ambition led, have for high deeds been raised to greatness and to honour, and can I fail when her voice bids me on? No; her name shall prove a beacon-light to guide me o'er life's waves."

"Say, rather, an *ignis fatuus,* to lure thee

to thy ruin," interrupted Herman, whose unsocial temper had driven him from the banquet, and who, unfortunately, overheard our hero's meditation.

The moon was shining brightly, and Ulrick recognised the person as well as the voice of the speaker. The recollection of their previous meeting galled him, and he answered, in a tone as haughty as his own—

"When I require counsel, it is not of Herman of the Burg that I shall seek it. When I require a confidant, it is not Herman of the Burg that I shall choose. Pass on, Sir Saxon; meddle in that which concerns you, and our Lady speed you on your way."

"It doth concern me, boy," retorted Herman, "that my kinswoman's name should not be sullied by every peasant's breath."

"Peasant!" iterated Ulrick, his eye flashing fire, and his hand instinctively grasping the sword, Matilda's gift.

Herman beheld the action, but, confident in his strength and presumed superior skill, determined to provoke him. His heart was overflowing with pent-up bitterness and gall. Ulrick appeared to be a subject on whom he might vent them safely.

"Ay, peasant!" he repeated; "or, if thou likest it better, bastard of a Norman priest!"

"Liar!" thundered Ulrick, "I thank thee for that word; it nerves my arm and justifies my hate. Draw, and defend thy life; be you, bright moon, the witness of our quarrel. Strike at the breast that never did thee wrong—aim at the heart whose manhood thou wouldst trample—strike at the life whose current thou wouldst taint; but, Saxon, guard thine own!"

So impetuous was the attack of Ulrick, that his opponent must have succumbed, despite his cunning fence and giant strength, had not the combat been interrupted by a voice all were accustomed to obey—by the earl, whose attention, in the course of his evening walk round the ramparts, had been attracted by the clashing of their weapons, and who, in his haste to separate them, had sought the spot unattended and unarmed.

"How is this?" he cried. "My kinsman and my guest at mortal strife! Put up your swords, tell me your cause of quarrel, and let me judge between you."

Ulrick dropped the upraised weapon from his hand. How explain, without compromising Matilda's name, the cause of their dispute? He bowed his head in silence.

"Well may he be silent," exclaimed Herman, with a coarse sneer of triumph. "Wouldst thou believe it, noble earl, this peasant knave, this serf in blood as well as nature, dares raise his eyes where mine have feared to gaze—e'en to your daughter's love?"

"Young man," demanded the earl sternly, his brow so deeply flushed with indignation that it was perceptible even in the pale moonlight, "can this be true?"

"An hour since, my lord, I had answered no," replied Ulrick, "for I knew not then the nature of the fire which threatens to consume me. Hear me, sir earl," he added. "If to have loved your daughter as mortals love some distant star—as pilgrims worship the virgin saint before whose shrine they bow—be criminal, I am most guilty; but never have these lips breathed one word of passion, uttered one thought of earth. I have adored as spirits worship—in the heart, in silence. Farewell, my lord! When men shall speak of the poor orphan boy who dared to love your peerless child, their tongues shall say, 'Proud was his sin, as proud was his atonement.' For you," he continued, with a contemptuous glance at Herman, "this time you have escaped me—beware the next!"

Bowing with deep reverence to the earl, the excited youth turned his hasty steps towards the episcopal palace.

"Poor boy!" said the earl, touched by the noble frankness of his manner, and perhaps viewing his passion more in the light of that chivalrous devotion which the manners of the age permitted than positive love, "were thy birth but noble as thy heart, I would not turn thee hopeless from my door."

"Perhaps, my lord," said Herman, "this moment may be suited to the words I have to offer; at least I'll seek no other. Thou knowest the wars in which our Norman sovereign is engaged have given courage to the Saxon chiefs to attempt one blow for freedom, to cast off the yoke which for many years have galled them. It is the time to knit still closer the bond of unity between us, or weaken it for ever."

"What meanest thou?" demanded the earl, his attention deeply interested by the words which the excited Herman, contrary to his usual caution, had let drop.

"It means," answered Herman, "that I love your daughter; her hand once mine, your interests are mine, your nation mine. The moment which bestows it sees the conspiracy unveiled, the traitors at your feet."

The earl, although deeply attached to the interests of his sovereign, was too generous a father to sacrifice his child to a being so base, so utterly void of honour. The hint at a conspiracy alarmed him, for well he knew the uncertain tenure by which the Normans held the land. He determined, therefore, to keep an eye upon his dangerous kinsman. With respect to the proposed alliance, he refused to entertain it for a moment.

"Franklin," he replied, "my life hath been

one of honour; so shall be my speech. The difference of your years renders your union with my child impossible. Besides, while I am resolved never to yield her but to one of equal birth, her heart must be consulted. Well I know it never can be yours, so speak of it no more. With respect to the complots of your Saxon friends, we will speak more before the council; there may be other means of recompense. Come, let us to the castle."

"No," sternly answered the Saxon; "my path is taken; to the castle I return no more. I have had enough of Norman justice, of Norman hospitality. Farewell!"

"Not so," said the earl; "you must return with me. You have said too much or too little to be further trusted."

"Must go with you!" repeated Herman, who saw too late that he had betrayed himself. "And why must?"

"Because it is my will," replied the earl; "and I have power to enforce it. What, ho! warder!" he exclaimed, elevating his voice so as to be heard by the officer who kept watch upon the distant keep, "a guard! De Bigod, to the rescue!"

Scarcely had the words passed the noble's lips than Herman sprang upon him, and a short struggle ensued. The earl, though unarmed, was strong, and succeeded in dragging his assailant towards the moat, when the sword which Ulrick had lately dropped, and left behind him in his excitement, struck against the Saxon's foot. In an instant he raised it, and plunged it into the body of the earl, who, uttering a deep groan, expired at his feet.

The alarm had been given, and Mirvan, with the knights and guests, followed by the castle guard, were seen hastily approaching over the bridge. The alarm bell pealed forth its deep, loud notes. Flight was impossible; but the assassin's presence of mind did not forsake him. He first threw from his grasp the blood-stained sword, then raising the dead body, he placed it across his knee, and called loudly for help. In a few moments he was surrounded by Mirvan and the soldiery.

"Heavens!" exclaimed Mirvan, "my noble father murdered! Who hath done this?"

"Alas! I know not," replied the hypocrite. "I came too late to save him. On my approach the assassin fled. Somewhere he dropped his sword."

A hundred torches were in an instant bent to earth. The fatal weapon was found—blood was upon it. The knight who raised it held it to the light—it bore the name of Ulrick.

"Ulrick!" exclaimed the horror-stricken Mirvan.

"Ay, Ulrick," repeated Herman, "the new friend for whom your old ones were neglected; by whom you swore. The model," he added, with a sneer, "of chivalry and virtue."

Unable to restrain his emotion, the noble youth, deeply wounded in friendship and filial love, let fall his head upon his manly bosom, to conceal the grief which honoured him.

"Approach, noble knights and valiant men-at-arms," continued the assassin, snatching the sword from the hands of the knight who first raised it. "Convince yourselves, Ulrick is the murderer!"

CHAPTER VI.

An' he be guilty, I will ne'er again
Trust looks or words. Virtue is but a mask—
A painted mockery without a meaning.

IGHT had spread her mantle o'er the twilight world, and found Herbert de Lozinga seated in an apartment of his episcopal palace. On a table near him were two antique mitres, one pertaining to him as Bishop of Norwich, the other as Abbot of Hulm, by which latter dignity his successors in the bishopric still sit in the House of Peers; before him lay a steel-clasped casket, containing various papers and memoranda, together with a ruby ring and richly mounted dagger, upon whose hilt some Saxon artist had sculptured a rude crest. The prelate had evidently prepared himself for his promised interview with Ulrick by prayer and stern control. All trace of the agitation of the morning had disappeared; his brow was calm as though passion's tempests had never ruffled it, or human sorrows ploughed one furrow on its polished surface.

The prelate wondered at his self-possession, and regretted that he had so long delayed an explanation which would have prevented many a painful impression to the disadvantage of his youthful *protégé*.

"How strange," he murmured to himself, "is the human heart!—how inexplicable in its strength and in its weakness! Philosophy cannot sound its depths—the angels who stand before the throne of God cannot pierce its mysteries! He who framed alone can read it!"

His reflections were interrupted by the entrance of Ulrick, whose flushed brow and hurried step were but the outward signs of the agitation of his soul. For a few moments his benefactor gazed on him in silence, at a loss to account for his unusual manner. The idea that he had been indulging in the wine-cup at the castle naturally presented itself, and created a painful impression in his mind.

"Ulrick!" he exclaimed, for the first time, perhaps, in his life, using the accent of reproof, "whence this flushed brow and flashing eye? A step like that might suit the battle-field, but not my peaceful halls. Is this a mood to seek my presence in?"

In an instant the words recalled the young man to himself. The fear of giving pain to one whom he so deeply venerated enabled him to check the passionate impulse of his heart, and control the bitterness of its emotions. Never before had he been exposed to scorn and contumely: the iron had entered his soul, and he felt it deeply.

"Forgive me, father," replied Ulrick, bending the knee—"forgive the boy your charity has reared, if he forgets the lowness of his state, and dares to act and feel himself a man. Scorn have I met from one I never wronged—foul-mouthed reproach, and biting, bitter taunts. Why—why," he added, passionately, "did I ever for a moment quit this calm retreat, to mingle with a world which mocks my wretchedness?"

The cold reproving manner of the prelate immediately changed. He saw that Ulrick had been wounded where youth is most sensitive. In his mind he rejoiced that his first suspicions were unfounded, and sought, by even more than his usual kindness of manner, to atone for the involuntary wrong.

"The world, 'tis true," he said, "is thickly spread with briars and foul weeds; but, trust my word, sweet flowers may still be found. What, Ulrick, foiled in thy first encounter with the world! Be more thyself; answer its injustice with high deeds; pursue life's path wherever honour leads; and even if happiness escape thy search, believe me, boy, thou'lt stumble on content."

"I feel that I have a heart to bear its dangers manfully," answered the young man, "but not to endure its sneers, its heartless falsehood, and its slanderous tongues. If the world, indeed, be such as schoolmen paint it, and as priests believe, I could, with scarce

one sigh, renounce its charms, and seek a refuge here."

The despondent tone of Ulrick alarmed his benefactor, who well knew the impressionable nature of his character, and the advantage which might be taken from it.

"Seek not within the cloister's shade for happiness," he exclaimed, "or shelter from the world: its jealousies, its slanders, and deceits, may reach thee even here. The man who wastes his spring of life, unloving and unloved, leaving unfilled the ends of his creation, casting aside the tender ties of parent, lover, friend, may reach indifference, but rarely happiness. I will relate to thee some passages of the history of my life," he added —"a life chequered by passions such as sear the heart—by hopes as bright as those which angels dream."

The prelate motioned Ulrick to seat himself beside him, and was about to commence his tale, when he was interrupted by the entrance of Father Oswald, a Saxon monk, whose frightened mien indicated that some unusual occurrence had taken place.

"Now, son," mildly demanded the bishop, "what means this untimely visit?"

"Our sanctuary is invaded," answered the intruder: "armed men are in the cloisters, and the tramp of war disturbs the voice of prayer. A pursuivant and a party of men-at-arms, in the name of the Earl of Norwich, demand an audience, venerable father."

"A pursuivant and men-at-arms!" exclaimed Herbert de Lozinga, hastily quitting the seat he had assumed; "and at an hour like this! Surely you dream. Follow me, Ulrick," he added; "but remember, boy, whatever may ensue, mine is the only voice to find an echo here."

When Herbert and his *protegé* entered the cloisters, they found a number of the brothers, like frightened sheep, gathered together, gazing on a compact body of men-at-arms, headed by Ernulf, the reckless squire of Herman of the Burg, who wore over his steel hauberk a tabard blazoned with the arms of the house of Bigod. Insolent as he generally was, his eye quailed before the firm step and indignant glance of the Norman prelate, who, casting a look of reproof upon his alarmed brethren, boldly fronted him. Ulrick and Father Oswald closely followed him.

"Now, Sir Squire," exclaimed Herbert, "what means your presence here? Why are these aisles, the house of prayer and peace, invaded in the hour of night by armed men in such discourteous guise? Was he drunk or mad who sent you here upon this valiant expedition?"

"Neither, my lord," replied Ernulf;

"but sorrowful at the stern duty others' crimes impose."

"Sorrow and duty—others' crimes! Speak not in riddles, man. Art really sent by Hugh de Bigod, or is this some jest, ill-placed, to try our patience?"

"Noble prelate, the Earl of Norwich, Hugh de Bigod, is dead."

"Dead!" interrupted Ulrick: "impossible! Not two hours since I left him full of health and vigour, giving the promise of long years of life."

"The noble earl," continued the squire, addressing himself to Herbert, "has been murdered; and I am here, in the fulfilment of mine office, to arrest his murderer. Behold him there!"

The speaker slowly raised the silver staff of his office; all eyes followed its direction till it pointed full at Ulrick. For an instant the proud glance of the prelate failed. His recollection of the agitation of his *protegé*—his flushed cheek and quivering lip, drove the blood fearfully to his heart.

"Murderer!" he slowly repeated, fixing his eyes at the same time on Ulrick—"murderer!"

The calm confidence with which the youth met his gaze restored in an instant his benefactor's confidence. Guilt ne'er wore a look so pure, so clear as that. A fearful weight fell from the good man's heart.

"And who," he demanded, with cold dignity, "is his accuser?"

"My noble master, Herman of the Burg," answered Ernulf, beginning, he knew not why, to feel uneasy at the tone of the priest, and the cold, statue-like self-possession of the accused.

"Anathema — maranathema!" shrieked Father Oswald; "be his name accursed! Herman of the Burg hath guilt upon his soul would damn his race: his path hath been of blood and human tears. He his accuser! The wolf accuse the lamb—the kite arraign the innocent dove—crime assume the judgment-seat on virtue! No," he added; "there is yet a bolt in Heaven, and a red arm to wing it!"

All were appalled at the vehemence of the speaker, whose vast age, majestic appearance, and fearful penitence, had procured him a high character for sanctity. Seldom he spoke but to demand the prayers of his confreres; his days were passed in the most rigid abstinence—his nights in fearful vigils. There was a silence of some minutes after his denunciation; the bishop was the first to break it.

"Say to your master that Sir Ulrick is prepared to meet all accusation. He will remain within these walls until the hour of trial: I grant him sanctuary, and will answer for his appearance."

"It may not be," insolently interrupted Ernulf, whose orders were at all risks to secure possession of Ulrick's person; "the murderer may escape. Advance!—secure him!"

The men-at-arms, in obedience to the order of their chief, made one step to advance towards arresting the accused, when Herbert de Lozinga interposed between them. His manner was as unruffled and dignified as when seated upon his episcopal throne in the exercise of his spiritual office—his voice as firm and calm.

"None may arrest within these sacred walls," he exclaimed. "Have you not heard I grant him sanctuary? Advance one step, and on each one I breathe the curse which in its wrath hath shattered crowns, broken the sceptres of earth's mightiest kings—the awful curse of Rome!"

The soldiers shrank at the prelate's voice as at the presence of a destroying angel, so profound was their dread of excommunication, the most tremendous engine ever yet wielded by priestly power. Even Ernulf, their bold and reckless leader, was prepared to resign a contest in which he saw defeat was certain; for not one man-at-arms, it was clear, would second him after that fearful threat.

Ulrick for the first time broke silence.

"No, father, not for me this contest. I were, indeed, unworthy of thy love could I consent to shield my honour 'neath thy sacred mantle. Let craven guilt crouch 'neath the voice of accusation: innocence fears not the lightning, but defies the storm. If Hugh de Bigod hath, indeed, been murdered, I owe it to his son," he added—"to Mirvan's friendship, as well as my own truth, to lay my heart before him. Sir Squire, I am your prisoner."

In vain did his more cautious protector struggle against the resolution of the noble youth; he well knew that innocence is not always a protection, and would have preferred to guard him within the peaceful walls of his own palace. But even his entreaties were useless. The thought that Matilda had heard the fearful calumny stung Ulrick to desperation. He imagined that to prove his innocence it was but necessary to assert it, nor dreamt that there were beings in the world so practised in the wiles of crime, that e'en from virtue's self could weave the net that should entangle it.

"Be it so," exclaimed the prelate, won, but not convinced, by his arguments; "give thyself, in the generous confidence of thy nature, blindly to those now plotting thy destruction. Despite thyself, I'll save thee.

Our royal master's confidence gives me a voice in every tribunal in the realm : at the hour of judgment thy enemies shall hear it."

Ulrick, unwilling to prolong a scene as painful to his own heart as to the prelate's, tore himself from his embrace, and surrendered his person to the men-at-arms, who, overjoyed at the unexpected turn the affair had taken, immediately surrounded him and bore him from the cloisters. The monks watched his departure with regret, for he had been reared from infancy among them, and, like some graceful tendril, had twined himself around their rugged natures. With pensive steps they retired to their cells, leaving their superior and Father Oswald alone.

"He is innocent," exclaimed Herbert to himself; "I feel he is innocent; guilt never wore a brow so clear as that. Murder scowls; in its restless eye you read the page of guilt. Yet, how to prove it? This Saxon, Herman, bears an evil name—could he? I know not what to think. I'll seek the earl; the cause of quarrel, all must be explained, the accursed author of the deed made plain, or Ulrick's life is lost."

"It will be," solemnly answered the monk, "unless we help to save him."

Herbert started at the deep tone of the speaker's voice; so absorbed had been his feelings by Ulrick's danger, that he had been unconscious of the old man's presence.

"What meanest thou, brother Oswald?" he demanded, a ray of hope, from certain recollections of the past, dawning on his mind.

"To the confessional, father," answered the speaker; "there, and there only, dare I breathe the fearful tale of guilt within thy ears—a tale," he added, clasping his brow in agony, "which fiends might laugh to hear— a tale which, uttered but in penitence, would rend this massive pile above my head, and make the very saints themselves turn pale!"

"Follow me, son," exclaimed Herbert de Lozinga, in a tone of mild authority; "and remember that there is no sin so dark, beyond the church's power to pardon—no stain so deep that tears of penitence cannot efface it."

Long and fearful was the conference which ensued; the midnight hour found the horror-stricken prelate still seated, pale as some monumental statue, in his confessional, and the guilty penitent prostrate at his feet.

Morning had just begun to dawn as Ulrick was led by his guards to the great hall of the castle, where the nobles and petty vavasours— a species of landed gentry, dependants on the late earl—were assembled. Unfortunately for the accused, Mirvan was not present; he had even a more sacred duty to perform than to avenge his father's death—to dry the despairing tears of his sister and doubly widowed mother, for such the gentle Edith had ever proved to him. Besides, gratitude to the preserver of his life, to say nothing of his natural sense of justice, prevented his assuming the judgment-seat where his feelings were so deeply interested. He had, therefore, despite the remonstrance of Isabel, and the silent tears of Matilda, delegated to Herman the authority so fatally become his, equally determined, neither by his influence to strain the course of justice, nor to suffer his friendship for the accused to impede it.

The hall, so late the scene of mirth and generous hospitality, still retained some traces of the banquet which had lately graced it. Side-tables, covered with huge flagons and silver cups, had been removed into the arched recesses on either side. The gallery, where lately rung the sound of minstrel's harp, was crowded with the sunburnt visages of men-at-arms, old Norman followers of the house of Bigod, men who had served in many a gallant field with the murdered noble, and whose stern visages bespoke a sombre resolution to avenge him. On the dais at the upper end of the hall was seated Herman de Burg. No outward indication marked his internal struggles for composure; his eye was clouded as from grief, not restless as through fear. Indeed, so completely had his sense of danger schooled him, that even his squire Ernulf, the minister of his many crimes—the instrument of his will—the companion of his thoughts—suspected him not in this. The other nobles were either seated or standing round him, conversing in low whispers; that involuntary respect which death inspires restraining even the tongues of the more youthful. The body of the deceased earl, covered with his marshal's mantle, lay extended on a bier in the centre of the apartment; two kneeling priests beside it, repeating the litanies of the dead.

"They are long upon their errand," observed an aged knight, alluding to the expedition sent to secure the person of the accused. "Surely the monks would never dream of offering resistance."

"Their superior may," replied Herman, not altogether easy at the idea the words suggested; "he hath ever shown great love for this same Ulrick. Evil tongues are busy with his name: men say the orphan is his son."

No one offered a reply; the name of Herbert de Lozinga was too much reverenced by every Norman to be lightly spoken; to be even discourteously glanced at by a Saxon's lips was offensive in the extreme.

Herman perceived the ill effect his words had produced, and endeavoured to dissipate it.

"Doubtless," he resumed, "the noble prelate deemed such idle rumours unworthy of his notice. Slander's weapons strike alike," he added, "the noble and the clown, nor stay to ask the difference of degree."

At this moment the confusion and bustle at the lower end of the hall announced the arrival of the prisoner; all eyes were fixed upon him as he advanced with a firm step towards the dais where his judges and accuser both were seated. As he passed the bier he bent his head in reverence to the dead; the only passages in life between them had been of kindness, and deeply he regretted his untimely end. As he glanced towards the table, his eye fell upon a sword stained with blood; for an instant he started, and his cheek became flushed; it was Matilda's gift to him. His judges noticed his confusion, but were silent. Ulrick was the first to speak.

"Of what am I accused?" he demanded, "and by what authority dragged from my peaceful home before this secret, strange tribunal?"

"Of murder!" solemnly answered the aged seneschal of the late earl. The slumbering echoes of the old hall were awakened at the sound, and the word "murder" was repeated as if whispered by invisible voices. A chill ran through the assembly, whose silence was again broken by the firm, manly voice of the prisoner.

"By whom am I accused?"

"By the noble Saxon Franklin, Herman of the Burg, kinsman to your victim," again answered the same officer.

For a moment the accuser and accused gazed upon each other. In the glance of the former might be read the dastard triumph of vindictive passion; in the calm, steady gaze of the latter, scorn of its baseness—bitter, proud contempt.

"I do refuse him for my judge. Hear me, noble Normans," exclaimed Ulrick: "'tis but a few hours since I sat beside you in this festive hall, the guest of him whose murderer I am called. Returning home, I was assailed by Herman; not as man should meet his foe, with unsheathed sword, but with woman's weapons—base taunts, vile slanders, poisonous words, which drink the life-blood of the noble heart by poisoning its existence, the coward's courage and the base mind's vengeance. I had chastised him then but for the interference of the man of whose blood he would accuse me."

"'Tis false!" retorted Herman, stung by the keen tone of contempt which his victim evinced.

"'Tis true as thou art false," said Ulrick. "Noble knights, did you not hear him, when first we met, this very day, breathe forth the natural venom of his leprous nature?—sneer at my unknown birth my orphan state, and mock the heart which never did him wrong?"

"We did!" exclaimed several of the younger nobles, who began to feel interested by the high courage of the prisoner, and to suspect his accuser's disinterestedness in the affair.

"I claim the trial by battle," resumed Ulrick. "Noble knights, you will not refuse me this? Give me the chance to meet yon craven dastard in the list. Heaven will uphold the righteous weapon, and decide between us."

The nobles and knights at the upper end of the hall consulted amongst themselves: several of the younger were for granting the prisoner's demand, the elder and more influential were against it. Their advice prevailed over the more generous sentiments of their confreres. Odo of Caen announced their decision.

"It may not be," he said; "the right you invoke unfortunately belongs only to the noble and the free-born."

Ulrick bowed his head in shame and silence. The unfortunate mystery of his birth precluded him from meeting his enemy in the list of honour—from appealing from the judgment of his foe to battle.

"Ulrick is noble and free-born!" exclaimed a stern voice at the end of the hall; "the mate of any here."

"Who dare utter that monstrous lie?" demanded Herman.

A stately figure, dressed in the habit of a monk, advanced from the crowd to the higher end of the dais, and steadily confronted him: slowly he raised the cowl from his still pale features, and discovered the person of Father Oswald. Ulrick's heart beat high within him.

"I dare!" he said.

There was nothing in the features of the monk which spoke to Herman's recollection. He deemed him a mere emissary of the bishop sent to watch the proceedings, and whose zeal in the behalf of the prisoner had outrun discretion; still the boldness of the assertion slightly staggered him.

"And on what proof are we to believe thee?" inquired Odo.

"On the word of a noble Saxon," firmly answered the old man. Then, as if regretting the momentary pride of human life, he added, in deep humility—"On the faith of an unworthy priest of the Most High."

The firmness of Father Oswald's manner carried weight with it, and a fresh consultation ensued, in which Herman, who now began to be seriously alarmed at the idea of being compelled to meet his victim in the list, actively joined, and decided the matter by his influence. Odo of Caen announced it.

"We neither question, father," he said, "the nobility of thy birth or sincerity of thy heart; but this is a matter of knightly judgment, and requires a knightly guarantee. We do again refuse the combat, unless some noble, or some knight, confirms by his testimony the nobility of Ulrick's birth."

The prisoner, agitated by hope and fear, turned from the haughty speaker to the extraordinary witness who had so strangely testified in his favour. The old man met his glance with a smile of encouragement and benevolence, but was silent.

"You hear?" said Herman, with a sneer; "a noble and a knight."

"He must be noble?" demanded the monk, with hesitation, but under which a closer observer than Herman might have perceived a cold smile of conscious triumph.

"He must," impatiently iterated Herman: "as noble as myself."

"And a knight?" coolly continued Oswald.

"Like myself, he must wear upon his heels the golden spurs of chivalry," haughtily replied the Saxon, "if thou canst find such a witness."

"He is found already," interrupted the monk; "thou art that witness."

All started at the firmness with which the aged man pronounced the words, and Herman himself turned pale. Ulrick, as our readers may naturally suppose, was not the least excited at the scene. The clouds, the dark clouds of mystery which had so long obscured his birth, seemed for the first time about to clear. To him, who knew the sombre character of the speaker—the holiness of his life, his rigid love of truth, his fasts and fearful penance—the words of the monk were as oracles. He feared to speak, lest his voice should break the spell—lest he should find his glimpse of happiness was but a dream.

"What should I know of the craven bastard's birth?" faintly muttered Herman, in a hoarse voice. "What jugglery is this?"

Father Oswald advanced to the wretched man, and slowly raised to his view a ruby ring, the same which Ulrick had previously noticed lying on the table of the bishop at the interview which had been interrupted by his arrest. The effect on Herman was electrical. Had an accusing angel risen before him, and displayed the record of his secret crimes, he could not have been more appalled; indeed, his agitation was so visible, that all remarked and commented on it. Could the agony of mind which he endured have effaced a life of crime, in that bitter moment Herman had atoned for all.

"Dost recognise the token?" demanded the monk, still holding the ring before his eyes.

"I do," faintly answered the conscience-stricken man.

"And Ulrick's birth is noble?" he continued.

There was a pause: involuntarily the astounded criminal's hand rested on the hilt of his dagger, and then fell motionless beside him. The cold, stony glance of his pitiless questioner seemed to have deprived him of all power of resistance, as birds are supposed to be fascinated by the eye of the rattlesnake: the struggle between hate and terror was immense, but terror conquered.

"It is," he faintly murmured.

"As noble as thine own?" added the monk.

"As noble as my own!" frantically exclaimed Herman. Unable longer to endure the recollections and terrors which the sight of the mysterious token conjured up, he rushed from the hall, leaving his brother nobles to make their comments on his conduct, and arrange for the combat, which he now felt to be inevitable.

CHAPTER VII.

Fence round the crime with all that fraud can teach,
Falsehood imagine—justice at last shall reach it.

 OR a short time after the departure of Herman, silence reigned in the assembly; surprise and consternation were upon the countenances of all; men felt that they had assisted at a scene whose mystery was yet to be unravelled. The unexpected testimony borne to the nobility of Ulrick's birth by his bitterest enemy, and through the agency of the monk, excited the imagination, and caused a more favourable sentiment towards the prisoner. Many a half-forgotten tale to the prejudice of his accuser was revived; most began to doubt the truth of the accuser; and it was finally settled that the trial by battle should take place in three days, Ulrick

in the interim remaining in close ward under the custody of Herman.

Vainly both the prisoner and the monk protested against a decision which placed the former in the power of his deadliest enemy : their resolution was not to be revoked. In vain Ulrick intreated to be allowed to converse in private with the mysterious being who seemed to possess the clue to his wretched destiny. His judges were inexorable. The youth was conducted to his dungeon, and Father Oswald slowly pursued his pathway to the monastery.

Thrice was Ernulf summoned by his impatient master, who rushed from the hall, where he had been so singularly confronted, more with the air of a raving maniac than a Christian knight. After long years of fancied security and peace, a clue seemed found to his disgrace; the baseless fabric of his honour already tottered; and conscience presented to his tortured imagination the rabble's curse, his brother nobles' scorn. He was pacing his chamber, a prey to these and similar reflections, when the ready instrument of so many of his crimes appeared before him.

"Hast thou beheld yon cursed monk?" he exclaimed. "Didst recognise the token by which he mastered me? Can this Ulrick be, indeed, the being whom I most fear to name, whose image haunts me in my dreams, the certainty of whose existence would poison all my joys, e'en were they those of paradise?"

"Impossible, my lord," replied Ernulf. "This stripling is of Norman, not of Saxon blood. The pampered prelate brought him a child to England. Why, I remember him ere he could lisp a word of Saxon tongue. Your fears betray you."

"But the ring—the ring—my father's ancient crest!" interrupted Herman, "lost on that night when my arm failed me. Cursed be the tempest's terrors which unmanned me, and doubly cursed the meddling fiend who foiled me in my purpose!"

"My lord," exclaimed Ernulf, after a few moments' reflection, "I think I can explain this seeming mystery. Some dying penitent gave the ring to yonder monk—perhaps made him the depositor of his suspicions, for proofs he had none, and the cunning churchman hath used the knowledge to his purposes—it can be nothing more."

"Perchance," muttered Herman, but half satisfied at the suggestion, yet still grasping at it, like some drowning man; "yet I would make assurance more than sure. This monk —this being who, like providence enveloped in a thunder-cloud, unseen can strike me—he must die!"

"Die!" repeated the squire, recoiling with superstitious horror at the idea of steeping his hands in a churchman's blood. "Not by my hands, my lord. 'Tis true they are stained enough already, but not with priestly blood. Oh, never—never!"

"Churl! is it redder than a noble's?" said his master, with a sneer; "beside, thy life is in the noose. Should this mad priest possess the key to my past crimes, thinkest thou they would hesitate to place thee on the rack to wring confession of them? As a noble, I might perish by the sword; but think, Ernulf, how fearful a destiny would then be thine."

The argument was artfully used, and not without its due effect upon his hearer, who well knew how little their Norman rulers hesitated to employ the torture upon men of far higher lineage than his own. Herman watched his hesitation.

"Besides," he added, "in a distant land I will enable thee to live in safety and in honour. Thou knowest I am no churlish master. Restore to me my signet-ring, no matter by what means, and let me hear the only being whom I dread on earth is dead, I'll count thee down a thousand silver marks."

"Faith! 'tis a tempting sum!" exclaimed the ruffian, his eyes sparkling with cupidity. "And for what?" continued the tempter; "for cutting the exhausted thread of an old man's life—extinguishing a dying lamp. Decide thee, man: the tithe part of the sum I offer thee would buy thee pardon for a dozen murders."

"It will be difficult," said Ernulf, musingly. "Father Oswald seldom leaves the cloister's shelter. 'Tis true he sometimes sits in the confessional, shriving such penitents as speak no Norman tongue; but then it would be sacrilege, and that——"

"Too, shall be paid for," interrupted his master. "'Tis just that every crime should have its price: are we agreed?"

"We are," replied the squire, chuckling at the anticipation of the promised gold. "Be he priest or fiend, I'll drive my weapon to his heart. Within two days you shall have news of me."

Thus did Herman and his too-willing minister continue to plot fresh crime. The forbearance of Heaven they regarded as impunity, and in the fancied security of their cunning defied its vengeance. They knew not that if the steps of Divine justice are sometimes slow, they are sure—that her hand is iron, and her blow is death.

"What was the decision in the hall below," demanded the franklin, "after the monk—curses on my weakness!—drove me from the hall?"

"The combat was decided on."

"I know—I know," muttered Herman—

"they could not well refuse it. Where is the Norman bastard?"

"Safe in a dungeon of the castle, in your custody."

"In my custody!" repeated his master. "Humph! that was kind, at least; and in how many days the combat?"

"Three days, my lord," said the squire, and a look of peculiar intelligence passed between them.

"Three days," muttered Herman, as he quitted the apartment. "The time is short; but, well employed, much may be done by then."

At a later period of the day a cavalcade might be seen approaching the castle from the episcopal palace. Heralds, with their tabards blazoned with the arms of the church, led the way: then followed a party of priests and men-at-arms, who preceded the litter in which rode Herbert de Lozinga, the ensigns of his office as Chancellor of England being borne before him. Several of the nobles beheld his arrival with dissatisfaction: they felt indignant at the idea of his lending the sanction of his name and influence to shield the assassin of one of his own order. The greeting between them was, therefore, more of sullen respect than cordial welcome. The prelate marked their manner, but disregarded it: his courage was too high, his purpose too holy, to be influenced by the opinion of his fellow-men. Just as he passed the bridge Herman appeared, and in the name of the young earl bade him welcome, at the same time bending his knee to receive the apostolic benediction; but no upraised hand, no air-drawn cross followed the act; the piety of the bishop was too sincere to permit his lips to speak the blessing his heart could not bestow. The disappointed man rose from his knee in bitter mortification, and leading the way, preceded his unwelcome guest to the late earl's private apartment, where their conversation could be carried on without interruption. Each were on their guard: the guilty one felt that a searching eye was upon him, the priest that he had to do with one a master in the art of crime, an adept in dissimulation. Herman was the first to break the silence.

"Forgive me, reverend father," he exclaimed, "if in the reception you have met with here aught has been lacking to your honour. The hand of grief is upon my kinsman's house; he mourns his father lost, his friendship stained, his confidence abused, else he had shown the reverences it is my lot to offer."

"'Tis well," replied the prelate. "The cloister's shade I quitted not for the sake of man's observance or the world's vain honours, but at the call of justice and truth. By what right have you profaned with ruffian violence our holy church, and torn the youth I cherish as a son from me, his guardian and protector? Speak!"

There was a firmness, a conscious power in the speaker's voice which grated on the listener's ear. Still he determined to yield no inch of vantage ground—the guardianship of Ulrick's person. The ring which the monk had presented to his view opened to his mind a fearful doubt, and he determined at any sacrifice to rid himself of one whom conscience clothed in the character of an avenger.

"Is it possible, my lord!" he answered, with well-feigned astonishment; "would you lend the sanction of your high name to shield a murderer? The indignant earth which drank the victim's blood groans 'neath the homicide's polluted tread, and calls for Ulrick's life."

"I deem him innocent. Men do not fall at once from virtue into the extreme of vice. I demand that he be committed to my care: my palace walls will better answer for his safety than will a dungeon here."

"You deem him innocent!" iterated the franklin. "Surely, my lord, you have not heard the proofs: his quarrel with the earl—his sword found near the spot."

"Something I heard of taunts, bitter jests, and unmanly sneers, which sting the generous soul," gravely answered Herbert, "but nothing of a quarrel with the earl. The hour of combat is appointed. You, yourself," he added, with peculiar emphasis, "are witness of the nobility of Ulrick's birth. I again demand that, till that hour he be committed to my care."

"Impossible!" said Herman: "the proposition wounds my honour."

"And would defeat your purpose."

"Can you suspect, my lord?"

"Everything," replied the bishop, drawing himself proudly up. "Herman of the Burg, I am not one whom thou may'st trifle with: Ulrick, or thou, must with me."

"I!" faltered the astonished franklin.

"Thou! If I cannot release your victim, I can at least enchain his captor."

"This is madness," said Herman, rising with a pride equal to the prelate's, and throwing open the doors of the apartment. "Enter, my lords," he cried, "and judge between us. Our reverend father hath declared that Ulrick must be released or I become his prisoner."

"Prisoner!" exclaimed the several nobles as they entered; "and on what pretence?"

"Sorcery and murder!" exclaimed the deep voice of Father Oswald, who had entered with the crowd, and commenced reading from a parchment:—"I cite, in the name of the most reverend Father Herbert de Lozinga, Bishop of Norwich and Abbot of Hulm, Herman of the Burg, to appear before the above reverend prelate to answer the charge of having sold a Christian child to the Arch-druid Haga for human sacrifice!"

All who heard it shrunk with horror at the charge. Overwhelmed as Herman was by it, his courage did not quite forsake him.

"Who," he demanded, "is my accuser?"

"I am!" thundered the priest—"I, Haga the Arch-druid!" Then sinking on his knees at the feet of the bishop, he added, in a voice of deep humility, "I, Oswald the Christian!"

CHAPTER VIII.

Foul deeds will rise,
Though all the earth o'erwhelm them to men's eyes.

SHAKESPEARE.

HE consternation of Herman at the unexpected accusation of Father Oswald—or, as he was formerly called, Haga the Arch-druid—may be more easily imagined than pourtrayed. The crime of sorcery was, in the eleventh century, the most fearful that could be imagined. Society rejected the supposed criminal with horror; the church cast him from her bosom; his children deserted him; even the sacred tie of marriage, the bond which mystically united him, body and soul, with the companion of his life, the mother of his offspring, became dissolved, and the wretched man stood like the genius of desolation in the world—alone. The Norman nobles who had hitherto supported Herman drew from his side. As superstitious as they were brave, they shrank from an encounter with one whose arms were the spiritual weapons of their mutual faith, and Herbert would have met no difficulty in securing his prisoner, had not succour arrived from a quarter where he least expected it. The franklins stepped forward to a man, and guaranteed the appearance of the accused before the ecclesiastical tribunal—a caution which, by the laws of Edward the Confessor, the bishop could not refuse to accept; but this unexpected unanimity on the part of the Saxons gave rise, in the prelate's mind, to a strange doubt. Uncertain rumours of an intended revolt of the conquered race had, indeed, reached him; but nothing tangible—nothing certain. He was, however, too cautious a statesman to betray his suspicions—too experienced a huntsman to let the ban wolf know that the hounds were on his track. Had the deceased earl been equally prudent he might have been living still.

"'Tis well, sir franklins," he said. "I accept your surety for the appearance of Herman of the Burg; but it is on one condition, and one condition only."

"Name it—name it!" cried several voices, impatiently.

"A man accused of sorcery may not be the guardian of a Christian noble; for noble Ulrick is, even by the testimony of his accuser. Resign him to my care."

"No!" exclaimed the Normans, unanimously, who, however submissive in things spiritual, bitterly resented the bishop's interference in their feudal justice. "He is a murderer."

"Grant him such; still he is a Christian, and may not be the captive of a man o'er whom the church suspends her awful malediction. Provoke me, and it falls on him and all who aid him in his crimes."

"Ulrick shall be our captive," replied Odo of Caen. "I will be answerable for his safe appearance on the day of battle; will that content you?"

"It must," murmured the crowd of nobles. "We will all answer with our lives and honours for his favourite's safety; we will keep faithful ward——"

"And honourable treatment?" demanded Herbert de Lozinga, who, finding he could obtain no better terms, was fain to accede.

"My word," answered Odo, "is the pledge of that. Till the day of battle, Sir Ulrick shall be honourably guarded and well tended, nor friends nor foes shall have access to him. I'll hold his life as sacred as I would the blazon of my shield—the honour of my house; but his safe keeping touches our feudal privileges; my lord, we will maintain them."

The decided tone of the speaker told Herbert that all farther discussion would be useless; and having, as he hoped, secured the life of his protegé against any possible machinations of his enemy, he resolved to appear satisfied with the concessions he had already obtained; but three days were to elapse before the day of battle, and in that brief space he had much to do to work for Ulrick's safety.

"Farewell, my lords," he said. "Let us not part in anger. We have each our duties to perform; judge, then, each other kindly. I leave you with every confidence in your knightly faith: Heaven will decide between us if you break it."

Every knee was bent to the earth to receive the parting benediction of the man whose arrival they had so coldly welcomed, whose reasonable demand they had so unjustly opposed. Submissive as were the Norman nobles to the church in all things spiritual, they were jealously susceptible when it trenched upon their feudal rights, and Ulrick's cause was even slightly prejudiced in their minds by a churchman's advocacy. A faint smile of mingled satisfaction and triumph passed Herman's lips as the train of the bishop crossed the castle bridge; but a deeply observant eye was upon him, for Father Oswald, who had lingered behind his superior, read that smile, interpreted its purpose, and determined to prevent it. Instead of crossing the moat with the rest of his brethren, the monk hastily drew his cowl over his features, passed quickly to the western side of the massive keep, nor paused till he reached the angle which it formed with the chapel, the entrance to which was by a low-arched door, rich in sculptured imagery. Satisfied that none observed him, he drew a key from his bosom, applied it to the door, and disappeared within its gloomy shade.

"The meddling churchman," exclaimed Herman, who, surrounded by his brother franklins, stood at the foot of Bigod's tower, watching the departure of the prelate, "to accuse one of my blood of sorcery! The hour is not far distant when dearly he may abide it. Noble Odo," he added, addressing the Norman who was standing near him, "what thinkest thou of yon shaveling's scheme to shield his pampered minion?"

"Each power claims its subjects," coolly answered the knight. "The sorcerer to the stake—the assassin to the block. Although I will not suffer mother church to interfere with my justice, I am too dutiful a son not to respect hers; ay, by my crest, and execute it too, let me but see good reason on her side!"

There was something in the tone of the speaker's voice which vibrated to the very heart of Herman, and blanched his cheek with fear. He saw that the Normans, while resolute to obtain justice on the presumed murderer of their chief and brother noble, were perfectly indifferent as to his fate; nay, that they would assist, if called on to execute,

any judgment which the ecclesiastical tribunal might pronounce upon him, even though its sentence were the stake. He felt that his only chance of safety lay in the success of the insurrection to which he was so deeply pledged.

"It would require a keener sword than even Odo of Caen's," retorted Herman, "to execute a sentence that touched either my honour or my life."

The brow of the Norman became flushed, and his hand instinctively grasped the hilt of his weapon; but with a violent effort he restrained himself.

"Sir Saxon," he replied, "I will not be tempted. Thou art the champion of a sacred cause: would 'twere in better hands! But thou art its champion, and therefore inviolate."

The speaker turned upon his heel, and entered the tower as he spoke, without deigning to cast a second glance on the unworthy franklin.

The first act of Odo on entering the castle was to give orders to his esquire, in whom he placed unlimited confidence, to conduct a party of his immediate followers to the tower where Ulrick was confined, and to keep joint watch with his gaolers; to accompany all who entered the prison, and to guard the life of the prisoner as carefully as he would his master's honour—a precaution, as the sequel will show, not unwisely taken, but which would have been defeated had not an eye more vigilant, a heart more devoted than his, watched over Ulrick's safety.

Edith, the unhappy Edith, doubly widowed by the death of Hugh de Bigod, had retired to Stanfield on her husband's death. 'Tis true he was not the object of her early choice; the passionate enthusiasm of her young heart, the dreams which, broken once, we ne'er can dream again, were long since buried in the grave of Edward; but respect, esteem, friendship—all that her blighted feelings could bestow, the earl had long since won, and she mourned his loss, if not as women mourn the being whom they love, at least with honour and respect. It was on the evening which closed the first day of her widowhood that she was pensively seated in the long unvisited cabinet we formerly described: Judith, her still faithful attendant and the confidant of her sorrows, was at her side. Many and sad were the thoughts which occupied her mind. In that apartment she had listened to the first vow of love breathed into her virgin ear; 'twas there she had so oft received her father's blessing—tasted the thrilling pleasure of her child's caress—and there she had mourned them both. Her faithful companion's words of consolation fell on a listless ear when she whispered hopes of future happiness and peace.

"Happiness!" she exclaimed; "no, Judith, no; the world knows not the word for me. All who ever loved the wretched Edith have been blighted by her fatal destiny: the gentle Edward—my kind old father and my noble boy—all, all have perished, because they were dear to me. I am a thing accursed—a withered tree without one verdant leaf; and when I fall, a stranger's hand will lay me in the grave—a stranger's foot pace through my father's halls!"

The hopeless tone in which the words were spoken silenced even the well-meaning Judith, who, with the tact which affection gives, comprehended that her attempts at consolation were ill-timed. Sinking on her knees beside her unhappy mistress, she timidly kissed her hand, and as she did so, bedewed it with her tears—a sympathy more eloquent and grateful to affliction than words, which wake no echo in the heart.

"Now thou art kind, Judith," she continued; "thou hast given me tears, not hopes. I have hoped and trusted, but now I'll trust no more: the grave is our only refuge from despair, and death the only hope which ne'er deceives us."

"Religion is a better hope, my child," exclaimed the deep-toned voice of Herbert de Lozinga, who entered the apartment. "Remember, there is no state so wretched, no fate so dark, but one kind ray of mercy yet may cheer it."

At the sight of the prelate, whom a holy and important purpose had brought to Stanfield, the widowed countess cast herself upon her knees to implore his benediction, exclaiming as she did so—

"Your blessing, father—your blessing! Pour words of peace into my bleeding heart; teach rebel nature to submit its tears, its vain regrets, and impious struggles, unto His will, who chasteneth where he loveth!"

"'Tis thine, most noble lady, it is thine!" replied Herbert. "May Heaven endue thy soul with strength to bear the trials in its wisdom laid on it! 'Tis natural," he added, raising her as he spoke, "to mourn for those we love; life, from its cradle to the grave, teaches no other lesson; but sorrow never should destroy our usefulness—never should prevent the gentle exercise of charity and mercy."

The slight tone of reproof, mingled with the earnest benevolence of the speaker, excited the attention of Edith, who misconceived, however, its tendency.

"My gold I'll freely give unto the poor. The church hath not found me, I trust, a niggard, father."

"'Tis not the altar's steaming incense, lady—the costly offering of superfluous wealth, which forms the only sacrifice that Heaven demands; 'tis the more active exercise of virtue—shielding the innocent, and aiding the oppressed."

"I do not understand you," replied the countess. "Point out the way my services can be of use to any: fear not my zeal, but tax it to the uttermost."

"Ulrick," said the priest, "is innocent; designing men conspire against the noble boy—in secret work his ruin; your voice, lady, must be heard in his defence."

"'Tis powerless, father, here. Herman wields his kinsman's delegated rights: go plead to him."

"To Herman!" iterated the bishop; "no, lady, no. He hates the gallant youth, and with untiring vengeance still pursues him. It burns as fiercely in the villain's breast as when I snatched him first an infant from his dagger's murderous aim."

"An infant!" exclaimed both Judith and the countess, the latter of whom became pale as death at the faint ray of hope which the speaker's words let dawn upon her mind.

"Though now," resumed Herbert, "I wear the mitre on my brow, and rank, and empty pomp and state are mine, when first I left the world my state was humble—a hermit's cave was my abode; to thee 'twere useless to repeat the wrongs which drove me from my native land. I was a moody, melancholy man, unloving and unloved; my ties of kindred, my ancestral rank, I cast aside, and in this distant isle sought refuge for myself; perhaps the recluse in Windham's lonely cell was happier than the prelate in his halls."

"Is't possible!" interrupted Edith, with unfeigned surprise: "art thou the hermit of St. Mary's cave?"

"E'en so," said Herbert, with a melancholy smile. "He whose first errand was of grief and death—he who announced the murder of thy lord—perchance his second is of peace and hope."

"Hope!" murmured his listener; "what have I on earth to hope or fear?" A glance from the prelate thrilled her very soul. "Speak, father!" she exclaimed; "you have raised thoughts that will restore or crush me."

"One stormy night," he continued, resuming his narrative, "a traveller, driven by the unpitying tempest, sought shelter at my cave; nestled at his breast an infant lay, whose innocent smile had won e'en fiends to mercy. Refreshed, I left him to repose; returning to perform a midnight penance, I beheld the ruffian aim his dagger at the infant's throat. Heaven lent me courage; I wrenched the weapon from the murderer's grasp; he fled the spot, and never more returned."

"When was this?" gasped Edith.

"Twenty years ago, St. Hubert's eve," replied the bishop. "This ring," he continued, at the same time producing the ruby (whose effect upon her unworthy kinsman we have already described) dropped in the struggle, "bears the well-known crest of Herman's ancient house: confounded at the sight of it, he hath already owned that Ulrick's birth is noble."

"It is—it is!" shrieked Edith. "Father, it was my child thy guardian hand preserved! Oh, wretched mother! to have seen my boy, yet felt no token of his presence! Had not my heart been cold—seared as the inmates of a charnel-house—it sure had leaped to meet him. Norman," she continued, casting herself at his feet, "swear thou dost not deceive me—by thine order's oath, thy mother's blessing, swear that he is mine!"

"I do believe it," answered the bishop. "Haga, the Arch-druid, whom Heaven, through its unworthy servant, hath redeemed from the dark errors of his Pagan creed, hath confessed he gave into Herman's hand a drug, of power to steep his senses in oblivious sleep, on condition that the child should be consigned to him."

"To him?—to Odin's priest?" exclaimed the excited mother. "No, no! Better that he had perished in the flames in which I deemed him lost. It is too horrible—he could not have made a compact for my boy! Father, what have I done—what deadly crime committed, that Heaven should wreak such cruel vengeance upon my sinless child?"

Edith pressed her hands to her flushed brow, as if to repress the wild pulsations of its agony. Fortunately a flood of tears relieved her o'erfraught heart, which else had yielded to its wild emotions. A pause ensued, which Herbert wisely forbore to break. He beheld the mother's tears flow on with pleasure, for he knew that nature had unsealed their fountain to afford relief.

"My boy—my poor, lost, persecuted boy!" at last sobbed Edith, her memory slightly wandering, "could no blood but thine bedew the Druid's stone?—was there no pitying angel to protect thee?"

"Heaven hath protected him," said the prelate, in a mild, reproving tone: "its justice smote the minister of blood. The night before the fearful compact was to be fulfilled, Haga was stretched upon affliction's couch: chance led me to his wild retreat, where human footsteps feared to tread. I watched, I tended—saved him. Heaven gave

eloquence to my unworthy tongue, and truth prevailed. Ere many days elapsed, I poured the regenerating waters of baptism upon his repentant head."

"But my boy—my Edward's boy?" demanded Edith.

"Herman, no doubt, would have fulfilled his pledge to Haga, but found him raging on a bed of sickness. Wandering with his burthen in the storm, he sought my cell for shelter. You know the rest."

"I do—I do! Heaven hath heard the widowed mother's prayers!"

"And doubtless will preserve him," added the prelate. "But this is the time for action, not for words. Ulrick is accused of Hugh de Bigod's death, and hath appealed unto the battle's test. Herman, his accuser, is of giant strength, and skilled in cunning fence. Should his sword prevail, the block and axe will be his victim's doom."

"The block!" exclaimed Edith, starting like a roused lioness at the appalling image. "The headsman's office for my Edward's boy! I will call up the vassals of my house. I still have kindred—friends. Enslaved, enthralled, and humbled as we are, the Saxon courage is not yet so low that Norman axe should fall on a son of mine."

"Be cautious, lady; one false step may ruin all. Edda, the father of your Edward, lives, honoured and loved, the most powerful noble of the Saxon race. Seek his presence; fly to him for aid; tell him the heir of his long line yet lives. His strength will aid thy weakness—his wisdom find a clue to this disastrous maze."

It was arranged that Edith, that very night, should, under the escort of the benevolent prelate, seek the protection of the aged franklin, whose stronghold was but a few hours' ride from Stanfield. Judith was accordingly sent to give orders for the departure of her excited mistress. The faithful attendant soon returned, with consternation marked in every feature. It seems that, during the interview, Herman, accompanied by a numerous body of vassals, had arrived at the holm, and, learning that the prelate had preceded him, had taken possession of the hall, giving strict orders that no one should be permitted to quit the building without his permission. His conscience told him that all had been discovered; he determined, therefore, to throw off the mask, and by one bold step secure himself, if possible, against the punishment of his many crimes. His followers, as deeply implicated as himself in the conspiracy against the Norman race, applauded, and were the willing instruments of his design. He persuaded them that their schemes were all betrayed, and that if

Herbert de Lozinga left the place alive, the cord and axe would be their general doom. "Let them perish!" he exclaimed. "The hunter hath fallen into the lion's lair, and prudence commands that he should die!" It was secretly resolved that that part of the holm in which the apartments of Edith were situated should be fired, care being taken that none of its inmates escaped.

"Lost—lost!" said Edith, when Judith had concluded her report. "Fortune hath cheated me with a gleam of happiness, to make me feel my misery the stronger!"

"Courage, dear lady," replied her faithful friend; "hope hath not yet abandoned us. I have heard that from this very chamber one of your ancestors, pressed by the enemy, once fled through a secret passage."

"Known but to one ancient follower of our house," replied the countess, "who, even if he live, must be so aged that memory's seat is shaken."

"Shaken," said Judith, "but not destroyed. At times flashes will fall from memory's torch, and shed a vivid light on scenes long past."

"Seek him," said the bishop. "I know the man with whom we have to cope. 'Tis our last hope; and should it fail, and death becomes inevitable, remember that the priest is present for his office, and that Heaven is near!"

CHAPTER IX.

Time was men worked for love as well
As the mere hireling's wages. Times are changed:
The faithful service of the antique world
Is but tradition now.

UDITH required no second command, but hastened to the remote apartment of the venerable servitor, whose vast age had long disqualified him for all active service, but who had been retained to dream away the winter of his life beneath the roof of those whom he had so long and faithfully obeyed. The period of her absence, though short, appeared to the prelate and unhappy mother an age. Slight as was the chance of escape, the return of the faithful attendant, leading the seneschal, long since blind with age, was a relief that seemed to say all hope was not extinct.

"Where—where do you lead me?" fretfully exclaimed the old man, displeased at being taken from his favourite nook. "Why have you dragged me here? I passed the court—where am I? There used to be a step. Yes, yes—there used to be a step."

It was evident that he was endeavouring to recollect the spot to which Judith had conducted him, but that memory was struggling with the infirmities of age.

"Knowest thou where thou art?" demanded Herbert de Lozinga, in a soothing tone.

"No—no!" petulantly replied Hubert. "Who is it that questions me? Thine is no Saxon tongue. Lead me back, I pray. The air blows damp and chill, and my limbs tremble."

"Hopeless—hopeless!" said Edith, sinking on her chair. "His mind is gone—quite gone!"

It was curious to mark the effect of Edith's voice. The old man trembled like an aspen leaf: its tone had awoke some long-forgotten echo in his heart. He had half turned, as if to find his way back from whence he came, when its sound arrested him.

"Whose voice is that?" he cried. "Speak again: its sound awakens thoughts long past."

"Speak to him, lady," whispered the prelate: "he knows your voice best."

"Hubert," said the countess, advancing and taking his hand, "hast thou forgotten me?"

"I know—I know thee!" he exclaimed: "thou art my master's child. Lady, the oldest vassal of thy house would bend the knee before thee, but 'tis stiff with age."

"Hubert," said his agitated mistress, "danger besets my steps, and I must fly—fly from my father's roof."

The word "danger" seemed to restore the old man's faculties. Twice he endeavoured to erect his curbed limbs, like some worn war-steed, who heard the distant trumpet's clang, and thirsted for the fray.

"Danger!" he repeated. "What danger can assail our lady here? Shall I raise the banner of your house?"

There was something affecting in the spirit of the old servitor, whose devotion had so long outlived his strength.

"No, Hubert, no," replied Edith. "Mine is a peril that must be met by flight. The times are changed, old man, and we must meet them. This was my grandsire's chamber," she added, "from whence I have heard there is a secret passage which leads beyond the moat—know'st thou of such?"

"Hush!" whispered the aged servitor; "there is such a passage. It—it—oh, memory, memory, do not desert me now!"

The speaker passed his thin, attenuated hand over his withered brow, to assist his broken recollections, his hearers gazing on him in anxious expectation.

"Where is it?" demanded Herbert de Lozinga, no longer able to keep silence.

The seneschal started at the sound of the prelate's voice; 'twas not the one he recognised; and, with the suspicion natural to the aged, he doggedly refused to answer him. It was some time before even Edith's voice could lead him to the subject.

"No, lady," he repeated; "there is no passage. I am old, but faithful. A stranger must not learn the secrets of your house; I have sworn to keep them—Hubert will guard his oath."

"Hubert!" exclaimed the countess, excited to desperation by the disappointment of her hopes, "I tell thee that I am beset with dangers—my life is in peril. Thou knowest the secret passage from this chamber; make one effort—recall one ray of memory to thine aid—do it, and save thy mistress from despair!"

The speaker's tears fell fast upon his hands, which in her agony she had taken.

"Despair!" he repeated, almost childishly, "and tears—my lady's tears! then I must—I must. Give me a moment: where am I?"

"In my grandsire's chamber—the one in which he died."

"The panelled one?"

"The same," said Edith, making a signal that neither of her companions should speak, as it was evident that every voice but hers disturbed his recollection and excited his suspicion.

"Tell me, lady," he resumed, "what is the hour of day?"

"'Tis night, Hubert—alas! 'tis night!" exclaimed his mistress, deeming from his question that his mind was becoming again a blank, and that the clue was for ever lost—"night, dark as my destiny!"

"Night! ah—true, true! Does the moon shine upon the oriel window?"

"It does—it does!" she replied, hope once more dawning at his question.

"When," resumed the old man, "the shadow of the cross within your ancient shield falls on the oak-carved panels, then—then—your father, lady—but we are Normans, now." And so again the old man's memory failed him, and he wandered on in a disjointed strain: an expression of childish apathy succeeded to the intelligence he had so lately displayed, and the last ray of recollection quitted him for ever. Fortunately, Herbert de Lozinga had caught every word he uttered. In the centre of the window to which he had alluded was a coat-of-arms of stained glass, the red cross in which, when struck by the rays of either the sun or moon, cast a broad shadow upon one of the rudely-carved panels in the wall. On a patient examination the prelate at length succeeded in discovering the spring, which was an iron leaf curiously concealed amidst the oaken foliage. It quickly yielded to the strong pressure of his eager hand, and the path of safety lay open to their view.

"The path is open!" he exclaimed—"not a moment must be lost!"

Judith hastily enveloped the agitated countess in a dark mantle, and prepared to follow her, when the heat, which had increased to a fearful extent in the apartment, and which, from the anxiety caused by their position, they had scarcely observed, burst into a flame: perhaps the current of fresh air which the opening of the secret passage admitted hastened the calamity.

"Heavens—the holm is in flames!" said Edith. "We cannot leave the old man to perish here; that were poor gratitude for faithful service; aid me to save him, father."

By their united efforts Hubert was led safe into the recesses of the passage, whose existence he had so miraculously disclosed, and there left till aid was sent to remove him. The three fugitives, after traversing the long, damp passage, emerged into a ruined hut, situated in the deepest recesses of the forest. The prelate cast his eyes around, and recognised the abode of Haga the Arch-druid. Fortunately, he knew the country well, and a few hours' walk brought them to one of the numerous convents which owned his spiritual sway, shelter was instantly obtained, and a strict injunction for secrecy imposed on all its inmates.

"I can brave the world securely now," thought Herman, as the flames of Stanfield reddened in the night. "Edith, who scorned my love, hath proved at last my hate. The Norman priestling, too, who thought to crush me—I trample on his ashes. World," he added, with a scornful laugh, "we shall soon be quits. My debt is lessening!"

The next day the rumour of the accidental destruction of Stanfield, and the deaths of Edith and Bishop Herbert, spread far and near. The good mourned their loss, and the evil triumphed in their fall.

The next morning Ernulf, the worthy squire of such a master as Herman, doffed

THE ABDUCTION OF THE KEYS OF THE POSTERN FROM THT OLD WARDER.

his hauberk and helmet for the sober, peaceful dress of one of the lower order of franklins, and directed his steps towards the cathedral, where he was sure at all times to find the monks ready to receive their penitents, or to perform the varied ministry of their office. Disguising his perfect knowledge of the Norman tongue, he demanded of one of the brotherhood to point out to him a confessional filled by some Saxon priest, and was, as he expected, directed to the one usually occupied by Father Oswald. It was situated in one of those quiet, gloomy chapels at the back of the high altar, which the vandalism of the modern clergy has long since consigned to neglect; the light faintly penetrated through the richly-stained glass, softening, with its mellow tone, the harsh outlines of the sculptured saint to whom its shrine was dedicated; the aged priest was in the act of shriving a penitent when the disguised murderer approached. Despite his attire, and the hypocritical meekness of his look, Oswald recognised him, and instantly comprehended his purpose; but his courage did not fail him, or the danger which he ran cause his heart to beat with increased emotion. Sternly seated on his chair, he seemed like the impersonation of one of those fabled deities which he served of old, his conscious power marked by his impassibility. Before he dismissed his kneeling penitent, he took from an ebony and silver box which hung beside him a small phial, which he placed beneath his sandalled foot, so that he could crush it by the slightest pressure, and placed a morsel of some highly-perfumed drug within his mouth.

As soon as they were left alone within the chapel—Ernulf and the priest—the former advanced towards the confessional, his eyes bent in seeming humility to the ground, but in reality to hide the ferocious joy which the anticipation of blood gave to their expression. His knee was sacrilegiously bent to the earth even at the moment his hand secretly grasped the weapon concealed beneath his flowing cloak.

"What brings the parricide and sacrilegious robber to the tribunal of penitence?" demanded Oswald, his aged eyes flashing with holy indignation on the prostrate man. "Is it to commit some new crime? Is not his soul stained with blood enough already?"

Had a thunderbolt fallen at the feet of the detected Ernulf he could not have been more surprised. The being whom he came to strike seemed armed with omniscience to confound him. The secret terror of his life—the sin which haunted him—his nightly dream—his daily curse—rose, as it were, in evidence against him. His craven heart beat wildly at the words.

"Parricide!" he murmured faintly.

"Ay; how else," demanded Oswald, "name ye those who shed a parent's blood? Have so many years elapsed that thou hast forgot the deed—so many tears of penitence been shed it has effaced the stain? Fool!" he added, "should thy life be long and wearisome as mine, and every minute of it be a prayer or tear, it would not cleanse thy hand. A father's blood is on it—his dying malediction on thy soul!"

Ernulf, overwhelmed with confusion, could only faintly exclaim—

"Mercy—mercy!"

"Mercy!" iterated the priest. "Where was thy mercy when he clung to thee, with his white hair dyed in gore, and his dying eyes, in mingled love and horror, fixed upon thee? Mercy!—ask it of the fiends," he continued, "who registered thy crime; ask it of thy father's bones, which, at the archangel's trumpet's sound, shall rise in judgment against thee; ask it of the innocent blood which thou hast shed, the purity which thou hast violated, the homes which thou hast rendered desolate, but ask it not of me. Minister of justice, as well as mercy, I close the book of life against thee, and pronounce anathema to thy despairing soul."

The voice of the old man was firm as the denunciating angel's curse when it swept over the cities of the plain. The appalled Ernulf, confronted with his crime, knew not which way to flee; terror took possession of his heart; hell seemed yawning beneath him; and the strong ruffian rolled in agony at his accuser's feet.

"And now," continued Oswald, "thou wouldst add sacrilege to murder; for base, filthy hire, profane the holy sacrament of penance, insult the indignant saints before their altars, and strike their minister before their shrine!"

"Art thou a devil, thus to read men's hearts?" demanded Ernulf, rage and shame gradually mastering his terror.

"Enough, I can read thine," said Oswald. "Ay, grasp thy weapon," he continued, as he witnessed the movement of the squire's hand beneath his cloak; "I fear it not; thou art delivered to me; the worm beneath my foot is not more hurtless than thy toothless malice."

"Indeed!" exclaimed Ernulf, casting a furtive glance around, to see if he was observed, and springing to his feet; "if thou art mortal, this will reach thee!"

He drew the concealed weapon from his cloak, and raised his impious hand to strike; but ere it could descend the sandalled foot of the monk had crushed the phial beneath it, and the confessional was instantaneously filled by a thin, subtle vapour, whose effects were electrical. The weapon of the assassin fell, as if struck by lightning to the ground, while he himself stood nerveless as a new-born infant before his judge and his accuser.

"This is the completion of thy crimes," said Oswald, after a pause: "thy dark career is run."

A party of monks, summoned by his voice, soon filled the chapel. To them he recounted the attempt upon his life, and pointed to the criminal, whose person was instantly secured, for he made no resistance: his mind, like his body, seemed to have been stricken by palsy, so extraordinary was the effect produced upon him by the means through which the priest had disarmed him—means perfectly comprehended by the scientific of the present day, but which, to Ernulf's superstitious mind, seemed like the direct interposition of providence.

CHAPTER X.

Blessings, like dew, follow the good man's prayers—
Prayers which, like incense, rise from the green altar
Of the suppliant earth.

N consideration of the nobility of Ulrick's birth, the confession of which was so strangely wrung from his accuser, he was not retained in the common dungeons of the castle—a series of subterranean cells, which extended far below the level of the moat—but in the loftiest apartment of Bigod's tower, the extreme height of which rendered all escape by external means impossible. The interior was equally well guarded, for the only staircase which conducted to it was situated in the guard-chamber, through which all who either ascended or descended were obliged to pass, and where a faithful troop of men-at-arms, who had grown gray in the service of the murdered earl, kept constant watch.

The high courage and sense of innocence which had sustained our hero in the presence of Herman and the assembled nobles gave way as the last ponderous bolt was drawn upon him by his retiring gaolers. The sound fell upon his ear like earth cast upon a coffin, and mentally he saw written over his prison-door the tremendous inscription which Dante read upon the gates of hell :—

"Lasciate Esperanza."

"Where," he exclaimed, "are now the joyous visions of my youth, my thirst of honour—of a life of usefulness, of trustful confidence, and hopeful love? Fled for ever. I have dreamt the dream which idiots dream, but, waking, found my reason. Fool," he added, bitterly, "even for one moment to suppose this world contained aught of love or happiness for thee!"

In this gloomy mood he continued to pace the floor of his prison, his heart at times cheered by the knowledge of his innocence, and the assurance that his birth was noble. Father Oswald, it was plain, possessed some key to the mystery of his fate; and, like a chained lion, Ulrick fretted his soul against the bars of his dungeon. How often did he pray but for one hour of freedom to rend the veil which obscured his destiny, and which he never felt so palpably before! At times fancy would represent him as the victor in the coming fight—his honour cleared, his innocence established; or seated in some old ancestral hall, Matilda by his side, and

offsprings who resembled her around him; then for a moment he forgot his fate, the fearful accusation which hung over him, and felt a taste of joy.

The walls of Ulrick's prison were formed of huge blocks of stone, which rose to the height of about twelve feet, where they joined the rude groining of the arch, the key-stone of which was the quaintly-sculptured head of some Saxon king, whose staring eyes, like those of the evil genius of the place, seemed to mock the prisoner; the window, narrow and strongly barred, was situated in a deep recess cut in the wall, the massive thickness of which might have withstood even the artillery of the present day. In a corresponding recess in the opposite side of the room was a singular piece of sculpture representing a crucifixion, in which the victim was a boy about twelve years of age. According to a tradition well known in Norwich, a Christian youth had been crucified by the Jews on Good Friday in mockery of the Saviour. On the miraculous discovery of his body he was canonised, and his name still appears in the Roman calendar under the name of St. William in the Wood. Similar memorials of the legend were once extremely common in the neighbourhood, and may still be found in some of the old churches and conventual remains, not only in Norfolk, but its adjoining counties.

The prisoner's reflections were interrupted by the entrance of Odo's squire, who, followed by the ordinary keepers of the tower, brought Ulrick his repast, the first he had tasted for four-and-twenty hours. To all his eager questions and entreaties they maintained a dogged silence; each one felt that he was a spy on the other, and prudence, if not fidelity, fettered their tongues.

Exhausted as the captive was, he merely broke a morsel of bread, and took a draught of the flask of wine which they had left him, and then resumed his walk, again to indulge in the reveries of his excited imagination; in dreams of hope, perhaps never to be realised; or in visions of despair, yet more gloomy than his destiny. For more than an hour he had continued to pace his prison floor, his brow gradually becoming more and more flushed, and the fire of fever burning in his cheek and haggard eye. He could no longer conceal from himself that he was ill, perhaps dying; the recollection of the wine which he had drunk flashed upon him, and fearfully explained the mystery.

"I am poisoned!" he exclaimed. "Oh, cruel treachery! My name will descend polluted to the grave. Matilda's curse, perchance, will rest upon it. I'll not die like the wolf, inglorious in his lair, without one effort. Help!" he shrieked, at the same time beating with his hands and feet frantically against the door. "Treachery—murder!"

Long did the wretched Ulrick continue to awake the echoes of his prison-tower. It was evident that he was doomed to die alone, poisoned—treacherously and cowardly poisoned—by the man who feared to meet his victim in honourable fight.

"I'll strive no more," sighed the exhausted youth, "with a destiny so wretched—lost as mine; but, since my hour is come, will meet it as a Christian and a man, and with a sigh to my love, but without one regret for earth, resign my soul to the keeping of the saints!"

Unable longer to retain his feet, Ulrick threw himself upon his rude couch; and although his mind would wander in his prayer, yet still he prayed, until his senses were absorbed in sleep—a sleep his enemy had doomed to be eternal.

The prisoner had not long been lost to consciousness when the rude stone representing the martyrdom of St. William slowly rolled aside, discovering a niche, through which Father Oswald entered the dungeon. Cautiously he approached the couch, and placed his hand upon the bosom of the expiring youth.

"As I suspected!" he murmured.— "Poisoned—poisoned! Fiend, I will defeat thee yet!"

He took from his bosom a flask, which contained some highly balsamic liquid, the exquisite perfume of which filled the prison, and applied it to the sleeper's lips, and, as the contents slowly disappeared, breathed many a prayer, made many a holy sign for Ulrick's safety. Its effects were gradual, but most satisfactory. The burning fever of the prisoner gradually yielded to a soft genial perspiration: his close-set teeth unclenched themselves, and he breathed freely.

"Saved!" exclaimed the priest, who had stood watching him with breathless anxiety. "Two trials more and thou art safe. In thine hour of need, boy, I will not fail thee."

Before he left the prison, the venerable priest emptied the rest of the poisoned wine, and refilled it from a basket which he had brought, and kneeling by the rude couch, offered up to Him who guards the fatherless a heartfelt prayer for Ulrick's safety.

The great bell of the cathedral tolled the midnight hour as the body of the murdered earl, the second evening after his death, was borne by the officers of his household towards its final resting-place within the hallowed precincts. A party of men-at-arms, every fourth bearing a lighted torch, lined the centre aisle from the west entrance to the high altar, where the black-robed priests were ready to commence the mass of the dead. The choir of the magnificent church was hung with solemn draperies, and the highly-emblazoned escutcheons of the deceased noble, whose military achievements had endeared him to his soldiers as much as his statesman-like qualities, princely hospitality, and unblemished honour, had rendered him popular with his brother nobles. The richly-carved stalls were filled by the monks; every dignitary of the order was in his place except the illustrious bishop, over whose episcopal throne a purple veil was thrown, typical of the widowhood of the church, from which many believed him violently removed.

As soon as the coffin was placed upon the dais in the centre of the choir, the low, solemn chanting of the priests began, and many a prayer was breathed by his brother knights, who, clad in steel, were standing round, for the repose of Hugh de Bigod's soul. Mirvan, as the representative of his hause, was seated at the head of the bier, his brain almost stunned at the double blow it had received by the murder of his father and the treachery of his friend. Matilda and Isabel watched and prayed in one of the dimly-lighted galleries above.

Herman, the murderer and the accuser, was there, as calm as though his life had been of innocence, his hand been pure from blood. Once or twice he looked anxiously amongst the monks, to see if he could recognise the cowled visage of Father Oswald. It was a relief to his heart that he beheld it not. Doubtless he thought that Ernulf had succeeded in his sacrilegious attempt, and smiled at the triumph of his villany.

Herbert de Lozinga and the old priest removed, the accusation of sorcery, the only danger which had given him any real uneasiness, fell to the ground, and he stood, as he thought, impenetrable in his crime. His approaching battle with Ulrick he looked forward to with pleasure rather than distrust as the consummation of his triumph; indeed, he could not doubt the result, for he had secretly contrived that a poison should be administered in his victim's food—poison of so subtle a nature, that while it spared the life of the receiver, it deprived him of all strength and energy by the slow, undermining fever which it engendered, and which must have ensured his success in the contest but for the watchful energy of Father Oswald.

The conspiracy of the Saxon nobles, of which he was the life and energy, was undertaken under circumstances so peculiarly favourable, that its failure seemed impossible. William the Conqueror had withdrawn the flower of his army to France, to continue the war which he had undertaken against its monarch, and during which he eventually terminated his career. The Normans who remained in England were in many instances divided amongst themselves. The death of Hugh de Bigod, the most energetic of their leaders, and William's marshal in England during his absence, still further augmented the Saxons' chance of success. The day of battle was the one fixed for the explosion, and Herman, in the anticipated triumph of his views, tasted as much of happiness as guilt like his could know.

The solemn chant of the monks had ceased, and the priests at the altar were about to commence the mass, when the prior, who presided in the absence of the bishop, arose in his stall, and, in a cold, stern voice, commanded Herman of the Burg to quit the church, adding, that the sacred mysteries could not be celebrated in the presence of a man accused of sorcery.

"Sorcery!" exclaimed Herman, red with passion; "and where are my accusers? where the guilty prelate, who, to shield his unworthy favourite, contrived the accusation? where the mad monk who witnessed to it? A fearful death," he added, "has removed the former; the judgment of Heaven has fallen on the false judge and the accuser."

The prior was a man cold and passionless as the altar which he served, yet even his quiet nature was indignant at the aspersion cast upon the memory of Herbert de Lozinga, whose supposed death he had many reasons for knowing had been contrived by his unblushing accuser. The impious blasphemy of attributing his own crimes to the judgment of Heaven shocked him, and increased the ill opinion he already entertained against the Saxon.

"Norman nobles," replied the prior, "through you alone I answer the slanders of that bold, bad man. Whether the venerable bishop be living or dead, Herman is accused of sorcery. The accuser and the accused may die—the accusation never. Either Herman of the Burg must quit the church, or I suspend the rites: decide between ye."

At the close of the speaker's voice, the officiating priests descended the steps of the altar, and began to remove the vestments peculiar to the service, and the monks stood up in their stalls, ready at the first signal to depart.

The frowns which he saw gathering on the brows of the Norman nobles told Herman that it would be dangerous to remain; he made a virtue, therefore, of necessity; and, after bending his knee to the high altar, left the church with an air as much like that of indignant virtue as he could assume. Seeing that their enemy had fled, the priests recommenced their interrupted rites.

For a long time Herman paced the cloister, indulging in dreams of promised vengeance. Let but the insurrection triumph, and he would waste their church and convent both with fire and sword—drive every Norman priest from out the realm. "Better," he exclaimed, "our fathers' ancient faith, than this enslaving—this aspiring priesthood!" The Norman nobles, whose haughty coldness stung his pride—they, too, must feel his wrath; in his mad thirst for vengeance he contemplated taking even the lives of those with whom he lived in terms of intimacy and friendship—whose cup he often drained—whose pleasures shared; contemplated it not with the regret of a man who offers a necessary sacrifice on the altar of freedom, but with the delight of a being whose instinct was of blood.

During his walk, his attention was attracted by the rays of a strong light which pierced through the crevices of the chapter-house doors. Finding them not to be locked, he entered, and saw preparations for a scene which gave him food for reflection. The richly-ornamented building was evidently arranged not merely for an assembly of the chapter, but the trial of a prisoner. The bishop's throne was hung with black, as if he were in person about to preside. Upon the table, in the centre of the room, upon a cushion, lay an enormous crucifix, and writing materials were placed at either side for the examiners. But what most attracted his attention were the various instruments of torture scattered on the floor—instruments, in that barbarous age, too often used to extort confession from innocence as well as guilt.

"Whose trial," he murmured, "can the monks be about to proceed with? Can Ernulf have failed in his design? hath the fool been caught in his own snare? The confident tone of yon shaveling in the church has staggered me. The accuser and the accused," he added, slowly repeating the words of the prior to himself, "may die—the accusation never."

"Never!" repeated a deep, solemn voice, so near to him that the word seemed to have been whispered in his very ear. He started and looked around, but saw no one; it was evident that he was alone. Although he attributed the sound to natural causes, it made an impression on him.

"This is childish!" he exclaimed. "I grow, indeed, infirm of heart, if a mere echo can unman it. No matter," he added, drawing a long breath to relieve himself as he spoke; "let but the next two days securely pass, and, fortune, I defy thee!"

Still, however, the preparation for the midnight trial alarmed him, and as Herman was one who left nothing to chance, he advanced to the door by which he entered, intending to quit the chapter-house, and summon an esquire in whom he could confide, to conceal himself behind one of the colossal statues of the four evangelists placed in the arched recesses of the walls; to his confusion, however, the door was locked, whether by accident or design he could not tell, but conscience made him fear the former, and he was a prisoner. In vain he thundered at the massive doors: the sound of his blows echoed through the massive cloisters, and gradually faded away, leaving him in fearful silence to commune with himself.

"It must be accident," he thought. "They would not dare to plot an outrage upon my person."

This opinion was the more confirmed as he had not heard the slightest sound of a footstep near the door; indeed, it was not impossible that the wind had done it, for the portal fastened with a spring; and he resolved, since accident had made him a prisoner, to avail himself of his position to ascertain the tactics of his enemies. With this view he concealed himself behind the statue of St. John, patiently to await the commencement of the trial.

Meanwhile, a far different scene was passing in the church. As soon as the mass was ended, Mirvan advanced to the bier, and after kneeling reverentially to the dead, respectfully removed from it his father's sword, and pressed it to his lips. Every eye in the vast choir was upon him.

"Bear witness for me, my noble countrymen," he cried, "that I receive it unstained by injustice or by treason; and that he, who so late was of the first among you, has descended to the grave with honour as bright as his own shield."

"He has!" replied the Normans with one voice, so universal was their respect for the late earl's memory.

"Amen!" ejaculated the prior from his distant stall: "peace to Hugh de Bigod's soul!"

"As the heir of his name," continued Mirvan, "I am the natural avenger of his blood. I am told the assassin claims the right of battle—is it so?"

"It is!" again answered the nobles.

"Then," resumed the speaker, "I claim the right to meet him. I might resign to another the judgment-seat, but not the danger of the listed field. I demand it," he added, laying his hand upon the coffin, "in the name of the dead, by my right of birth, by our brotherhood in knighthood, and the justice of my cause. Speak—is my claim allowed?"

A low murmur of satisfaction rose amongst the nobles, who had beheld, with secret dissatisfaction, Herman of the Burg, a man whom they despised, elevated to the position of Hugh de Bigod's avenger. It shocked their prejudice and pride that a Saxon lance should vindicate a Norman cause. The young earl's demand, therefore, was most favourably received; still they decided with that gravity of deliberation with which the nobles of the epoch treated all questions of chivalry, and after a lengthened consultation between themselves, Odo of Caen announced the decision of his brother peers.

"Your claim, brave earl, is allowed. Here, in the presence of the noble dead, whom all so truly mourn—here, on our faith as true knights, we declare that Herman of the Burg may, without dishonour, forego the fight on your claiming to be the champion in your house's cause. The seneschal," he added, "shall make known to the prisoner our decree, and God defend the right!"

"Amen!" again responded the prior, in which this time all the ecclesiastics joined.

A faint scream was heard in the gallery above, and Matilda was seen borne insensible in the arms of her attendants from the church, followed by the grieving and compassionate Isabel. Mirvan beheld their departure with a deep-drawn sigh, for already he read the secret of his sister's heart, and loved her too well not to compassionate its weakness and its sorrows.

The holy water was sprinkled on the descending corse, the priestly blessing given, and the herald's pompous duty done. As the remains of the once powerful earl, Hugh de Bigod, descended to their final resting-place, one by one the priests and nobles slowly retired, leaving Mirvan alone within the church, praying by the side of the dead.

As the vassals of the different chiefs drew up under their respective leaders, and were preparing to return in procession to the castle, their departure was delayed by the arrival of George of Erpingham, the bishop's seneschal, who, at the head of a body of troops, entered the enclosed precincts of the cathedral, and placed a guard at the only gate by which egress was possible. Whatever were the good knight's intentions, resistance was in vain, the force he commanded being sufficient to crush the slightest attempts at opposition.

"What means this, George of Erpingham?"

demanded Odo, who from his rank and influence was generally the interpreter of the sentiments of his peers. "Do we meet as enemies?"

"Heaven forbid!" exclaimed the jovial knight. "I am here to do the church's errand, not to break lance with such worthy sons as you. If the wolf hides itself amidst the flock, the flock must not murmur at being detained until the wolf be found."

As he spoke, an officer of the church approached, and whispered something in his ear.

"Pardon me, gentle knights," he resumed, "but the wolf is found, and further precautions are unnecessary."

With a wave of his hand he motioned to the guard at the gate to fall back, and give egress to the nobles and their followers, who resumed their march, wondering what circumstance could have caused so unusual a proceeding.

As the elder nobles passed the gate, the same officer who had whispered to George of Erpingham placed in their hands a paper, on reading which they resigned the conduct of their men to their esquires, and retired, with thoughtful steps, into the cathedral. It was evident that some strange event either had occurred or was about to take place, and the curiosity of those who were unsummoned was unbounded. But their patience was doomed to be exercised, as well as that of our readers, while we return to the fair cousins who so lately quitted the church.

"Speak not of consolation," replied Matilda to the tender soothings of Isabel, as soon as they reached the castle, and were retired to the privacy of their own apartment. "Grief succeeds to grief, and each fresh hour brings but fresh sorrow with it. I feel so assured of Ulrick's innocence, that I could pin my life upon his faith. But how to prove it? To-morrow he meets my brother in the listed field, and either I must mourn that brother lost, or weep the truest heart that envy and calumny e'er sacrificed at the base shrine of jealous, mean revenge!"

"Don't weep—don't weep!" sobbed the affectionate hearer, the tears at the same time coursing down her own pale cheeks. "Heaven and our Lady to our aid! We are not hopeless: the fight may be prevented yet. Had Herman been the champion, I would not have given one little sigh to have prevented the meeting in the lists. You are convinced, you say, of Ulrick's innocence?"

A reproachful glance at the doubt which the question seemed to imply was Matilda's only response.

"Be not angry, pretty coz," continued the fair girl; "remember, I am not in love with him; and I know that when the heart pleads the judgment is sometimes silent. Besides, this is not the moment for a shadow of coldness or unkindness to pass between us. Could we but see Ulrick, perhaps we might obtain some clue to this most fearful mystery; for, like you, I would fain believe him guiltless, though, unlike you, I sometimes mistrust my heart—it leads my head astray."

"Obtain but that, and fear not that he is saved!" exclaimed Matilda. "Trust me, Isabel," she added, blushing at the warmth she had betrayed; "'tis not the raving of a senseless love that speaks, but the conviction of my better reason. Men do not fall as the archangel fell: from purity to the extreme of sin a gradual change succeeds. Ulrick's mind was honour's self: a mirror, so highly polished, that Truth might view her image. I have watched its every phase, and found each thought was pure. And he, the good, the gentle, murder an aged—a defenceless man! Murder my father! Impossible! If an angel, trumpet-tongued, pronounced him guilty, Matilda never could believe it!"

Could Ulrick, from the depth of his prison, have heard the maiden's eloquent defence, he would have deemed his sorrows overpaid. Firmly she met the searching look of Isabel, as every page of feeling was displayed to invite the reader's gaze. The warm-hearted girl threw her arms around her cousin, and exclaimed—

"I do believe thee. I read it in thy dark eyes' deep intelligence—those portals of thy soul—when thy pure spirit looks upon the world, and scorns its worthlessness. You love him, coz?" she added.

"Truth needs no subterfuge—I do," simply answered Matilda.

"Then he must be saved. Rouse thee, coz—we have a game to play will need our woman's wits. Odo of Caen, you know, is plighted to my sister Jane; I have some interest with him; we both must try him—use all the artillery of sighs and tears—the weapons with which mother Nature arms our sex when we contend 'gainst proud, imperious man. Doubt not but we will bend him to our will. Kneel," added Isabel, "and ask His blessing on our enterprise who reads our purpose and who knows 'tis good."

The two fair and innocent creatures, like twin seraphs, bent the knee, and offered up a prayer as pure as ever fell from angel lips for suffering innocence. The act poured the balm of both courage and consolation into their souls. Silently enveloping themselves in their dark mourning mantles and veils, they left their chamber to seek the knight whose word alone could gain them admittance to Ulrick's presence.

CHAPTER XI.

The hand of justice, tho' unseen, is sure.
Vainly men fly the slow but steady step:
Her hand is iron, and her blow is death.—MASSINGER.

ONG and anxiously did Herman remain concealed behind the statue of the saint in the chapter-house of the cathedral. At times he thought of renewing his frantic efforts for freedom, but prudence, and the desire of witnessing proceedings in which, in all probability, he would find himself deeply interested, restrained him. At last the distant steps of the approaching brethren fell upon his ear, and, despite his long habitude in crime, and the confidence which success bestows, his heart beat wildly as they drew near.

"They come," he whispered to himself. "Courage, patience, and I triumph!"

From the position in which he was placed he could see all that passed, but ran little risk himself of being seen, as nothing could be more unlikely than that any one would take the trouble to mount the niche in which he was concealed.

First in the procession were two priests, bearing the abatial and episcopal cross; then the members of the chapter, two-and-two—the latter, as they entered, bowed to the crucifix, and took their seats in their respective stalls; the prior followed, bearing his staff of office, and assumed his seat at the head of the table.

"I see no prisoner yet," thought Herman. "Perhaps, after all, it is but some brother of their order whom they have met to judge for breach of discipline. No matter—I will see this mummery out."

His doubts, however, were soon ended by the entrance of several of the Norman nobles in deep conference with Herbert de Lozinga, who, in his episcopal robes, the mitre blazing on his brow, and the crosier in his hand, appeared living before him. From that moment Herman felt that he was lost.

"Living!" he exclaimed, almost loud enough to be heard. "Have, then, the mouldering ashes of Stanfield given up their dead, or have the fiends, who so long have served, at last deserted me?"

"Brothers and nobles," said the bishop, as soon as he was seated upon his chair of state, "believe me, that no matter of slight interest has induced me to summon you to this our sacred chapter. Danger threatens not only to your lives, but to the Norman rule throughout the realm. A vast conspiracy is organised to root us from the land. Scarce two days, and the Saxons rise upon us. The day of battle is the day appointed for the massacre of all our race. Prudence and firmness may avert the blow which want of unity must render fatal. This is no childish menace—no partial outbreak," he added, "but the organised effort of a people's strength."

There was a pause as the prelate ceased speaking; men looked upon each other as men look who have received strange news; and Herman, in the gall and bitterness of his heart, cursed the lips which uttered it. Odo of Caen was the first to speak among his fellow-nobles.

"Father, this is intelligence to stir the blood within us, and worth even the risk your sacred person ran. Deign to explain the proofs on which it rests, that, knowing whence the danger comes, we may prepare to meet it. Who is the leader of this enterprise?"

"Herman of the Burg!" solemnly answered the bishop, at the same moment striking the ground with his crosier.

"Curse him!" muttered the concealed listener. "Ernulf has betrayed me!"

At the signal which the bishop gave, the doors of the chapter-house again opened, and the guilty squire, Ernulf, was led into the assembly by a party of the bishop's guard. Father Oswald followed him. The prisoner's face was flushed, although his limbs seemed feeble. Even the presence of the Norman nobles was a relief to him: he knew that they were the inmates of the castle—friends of his master's kinsman—and trusted they might befriend him. The hope, however, was but a brief one; his eye glanced from their stern visages, and fell upon the instruments of torture lying on the ground; a cold perspiration bedewed his frame, and the strong man trembled.

"Ernulf," began the bishop.—Struck by the voice, the wretched man looked up, and recognised in his judge the being whom, four-and-twenty hours before, he had, as he imagined, consigned to inevitable death. Father Oswald's mysterious knowledge of his crimes, and, to him, miraculous means of subduing him, had excited the latent superstition in his nature. He looked upon Herbert as one arisen from the dead, and armed with supernatural terrors to confound him.

"Well may'st thou tremble, guilty man, to find me living," resumed the prelate, who marked the effect his appearance had produced, and trusted that it would enable him to bend the stubborn nature of the criminal to confession, without having recourse to those means which the rude justice of the age not only tolerated, but approved. "Hast thou not heard that it is written, 'The triumph of the wicked shall be short?' Con-

EDITH'S INTERVIEW WITH EDDA IN THE DRUIDS' CAVE.

fess thy vile conspiracy, thy master's treason, and enable me and these noble knights to unravel the dark clue of guilt, and mercy, perchance, may be extended to thy forfeited life."

A dead silence followed the speaker's words.

All waited to see their effect upon the hardy criminal, who, on discovering that the bishop was really in flesh and life before him, recovered the usual audacity of his nature, and determined in the recesses of his iron mind to endure the extreme of torture rather than

No. 6.

betray the scheme on which not only his hopes of aggrandisement, but ultimate safety, depended. He remained, therefore, sullenly silent.

"Saxon dog!" exclaimed Odo, "dost thou not answer to thy judges?"

"What should I answer, noble Odo?" replied Ernulf. "Will the word of a simple esquire weigh against the assertion of a mitred prelate? What should I know of conspiracies, which I believe exist but in the imagination of my accuser, to save his favourite's life? He hath already charged my noble master with the crime of sorcery; finding that insufficient, he now adds the charge of treason to complete his ruin."

The firm tone of the speaker shook the faith of several of his listeners, who were not disinclined to believe that Herbert would have recourse to any measures to assure Ulrick's safety. Herman silently congratulated himself upon the dogged fidelity of his accomplice.

"Have you no other proof than mere assertion, my lord?" demanded Robert of Artois, whose influence Herbert de Lozinga had frequently opposed in the council, and consequently excited his hate. "If not, I, for one, would not hang a dog on such a charge."

"Nor I," exclaimed another, "provided it were Norman. But this is a Saxon cur, and we cannot refuse to put the question, should my lord bishop, in his Christian charity, demand it."

The sneer with which this was uttered did not deter the prelate from his purpose. 'Tis true, he had obtained other and ample information, but from a source he wished at present to conceal. Though mild and gentle in his character, he could assume the tone of stern reproof, and meet the boldest with a front as lofty, a speech as cutting as their own.

"'Tis well, sir knight," he answered, "you have a churchman to contend with: but remember, if I draw no sword, that thousands are ready to achieve my bidding. That if as a priest I pronounce no sentence by which man's blood is shed, that many a belted earl and landed knight are bound by feudal tenure to pronounce it for me. Robert of Artois," he added, "and you, noble peers, no more I sue for your support—I now command it. Apply the question to yon wretched man, unless by confession he avoids the ordeal."

Slowly the nobles present proceeded to give the necessary directions, the catholic church not permitting any member of its order in any case to pronounce sentence of death, or to shed human blood. Even in the inquisition, this rule to the last was invariably observed. Its familiars were all laymen, and those who were condemned were given over to the secular power, by whom alone they could be sentenced.

As the executioners now approached the unhappy criminal, Father Oswald drew his cowl still further over his features. Devoutly did Herman, who, from his place of concealment, watched the proceedings, pray that his squire might expire under the tortures to which he was about to be submitted. Dead men, he knew, could tell no tales, and willingly would he have cut the thread of life of a being, one of whose greatest crimes was, perhaps, fidelity to himself; as it was, he awaited the result with nervous impatience.

Ernulf, having been stripped to his jerkin, was first placed by his tormentors upon a frame of iron, and bound by leather thongs; by a peculiar mechanism the machine was gradually distended till every joint cracked in its socket, and the strained sinews throbbed with agony; still the culprit spoke not, but with scowling brow and firm-clenched teeth, gazed, like a maimed wolf, upon the circle round him. Suddenly the resorts were let go, the frame returned to its natural size, and the distended joints shot in their sockets: then the first groan issued from Ernulf's breast. Father Oswald trembled, and slowly pronounced the word "Confess!"

"What should I confess?" replied the hardened man. "I know nothing, and can reveal nothing."

Again the tormentors approached their victim. Placing him upon his knees, they gathered up his long hair, and plaited into it the end of a cord which hung suspended from one of the beams. As soon as all was prepared, on a signal from Odo they elevated him so that he hung suspended by the hair of his head. For two minutes did he endure the fearful torture, his temples throbbing in agony, his eye-balls bursting from his head. Still he made no sign, uttered no word of confession. The prelate, unable longer to witness his sufferings, made sign they should release him.

By the laws of the question, three distinct species of torture were to be employed. If at the end of the third the prisoner's courage held out, he was deemed innocent, and consequently acquitted. As may be supposed, the last ordeal was the most fearful, and Herbert would willingly have spared it; but Odo, who trusted that the squire's courage would hold out, or who believed that he had nothing to confess, opposed himself strongly to it.

"We are not children, my good lord," he said: "our justice cannot be trifled with. If the prisoner pass the third question, I shall believe he hath been most foully wronged, and disbelieve this strange conspiracy; so, please you, let the executioners proceed."

"Be it so," replied Herbert, "since there is no other way; and be the crime on him whose obstinacy has left no other course."

Silently did Herman pray that Ernulf's courage might hold out, or nature yield beneath the effort. Again the fearful ministers of justice secured the wretched man, and enclosed his legs in a species of iron case, compressible by screws. Ernulf groaned with agony; still no word of confession passed his lips. The screws were about to be turned to their last extent, when Father Oswald, who stood before the prisoner, suddenly dashed back his cowl, fixed his eyes upon him, and at the same time drew back his long white hair, which hid a crimson scar upon his forehead.

"Parricide!" he exclaimed, "can nothing move thee? Confess, or perish in thy impious pride!"

The sudden change which took place in Ernulf's features was terrific. The blood which forsook his cheeks rushed into his eyes, his jaw dropped, and he seemed stricken with a paralysis of horror.

"Spare me!" he exclaimed—"spare me, avenging spirit, and I will confess—all—all! Search in the lining of my breast-piece! The letters—pardon! Mercy—mercy!"

Exhausted with his sufferings, both of mind and body, he found temporary relief in insensibility.

"Bear him to prison," exclaimed the bishop, "and let his breast-piece be placed upon the table here before us."

The mangled wretch was instantly conveyed from the chapter-house, and the assembly relieved of the presence of the executioners.

As Herbert de Lozinga demanded, the breast-plate was placed upon the table, and examined by the nobles present. Between the lining and the fold they found two papers: the first contained a detailed account of the plot, the names of the franklins and Saxon leaders most compromised, their places of meeting, and number of men-at-arms. As the bishop asserted, the day of battle was fixed for the outbreak, when, under pretence of witnessing the combat, they could assemble unsuspected. In the list of Norman nobles whose lives were to be sacrificed were the names of most present: the paper was in the hand-writing of Herman of the Burg, and attested by his seal.

"Traitor!" exclaimed Odo. "Much as I despised him, I little expected this."

"Nor I," added Robert of Artois, whom a sense of their common danger for once rendered just.

"But what are we to do?" demanded the nobles with one voice.

"Leave that to me," replied the bishop. "Do you, as peers and knights, pronounce the traitor's doom—I'll find the means to see it executed. Think you," he added, with something like an expression of contempt, "that if, like yours, my hand might grasp the sword, that long ere this I had not reached him?"

Herman, secure, as he thought, in his concealment, smiled at the churchman's threats. "Fool!" he murmured, "long ere the signal you expect shall strike, England shall be in flames. As we rush on in triumph through your halls, we will remember well each mocking gibe, and strike the oppressor dead!" and the concealed culprit smiled in the anticipation of his triumph.

While the nobles and knights were deliberating upon their sentence, Herbert de Lozinga perused the other paper found in the breast-piece of the squire. With a smile of benevolent satisfaction he whispered something to one of his attendants, who immediately left the chapter-house.

"'Tis well, my lords," he exclaimed, as Odo of Caen announced that the nobles present found Herman guilty of high treason, and sentenced him to death; "our reverend prior will draw out the sentence ready for your signing; but while he does so, pleasure me in one thing. Here is a paper, found, as you saw, in the breast-piece of yon wretched man."

"We did," they responded, one and all.

"The time for declaring its contents hath not yet arrived," continued the bishop: "please to affix your seal upon the back, that, when produced, none may question its authenticity."

Odo, and even Robert of Artois, hastened to comply with his request, so great was the ascendancy the prelate had obtained by the discovery of their common danger.

"And now, my lord," said Odo, when the last signature was affixed to the deed which proclaimed Herman as a traitor and condemned him to the block, "what steps must be taken for the arrest of this most dangerous man?"

"They are already taken," solemnly answered the bishop.

"And when the trial?"

"It is past," continued the prelate, in the same cold, unimpassioned tone.

"And the execution?"

"Behold!" exclaimed Herbert de Lozinga, striking with his crosier as he spoke. The doors of the chapter-house flew open, and a guard, commanded by George of Erpingham, formed a semicircle in the space before them.

In the centre was a kneeling man; Father Oswald, holding a crucifix; and the executioner, with an uplifted axe. Ere a word, even of astonishment, could escape their lips, it fell, and the head of Herman of the Burg rolled on the blood-stained pavement.

CHAPTER XII.

Take back thy curse—there is no terror in it:
The wrong thou speak'st of hath been all thine own;
The serpent's egg was hatched in thy own nest:
Thine is the crime, and mine the punishment.—OLD PLAY.

A COMPLETE recognition between Father Oswald and his wretched son took place: the living and the long-thought dead met in the fearful judgment-hall, where the monk, despite the sternness of his heart, his high resolve, and strong sense of justice, yielded to the throes of nature, and declared himself as the only means of inducing the wretched culprit to confess, and thereby save himself from the last fearful ordeal of the question. It was not without a severe struggle that he brought himself to make the revelation; for, although now a Christian priest, he still retained much of the pride which had distinguished Haga the Archdruid. His very errors had been those of honour, love to his nation, and devotion to the proscribed order of which he was the chief. The mere thought that a son of his should have descended to aught like servitude was a bitter humiliation to his haughty soul; but that he should have proved mean, base, and stained with crime, stung it into madness.

Immediately after the execution of Herman, the priest retired to the solitude of his cell, and fortified his soul with prayer, invoking many a saint, and many a holy name, to touch with penitence the hard, bad heart of him he blushed to call his son. Gradually the suppliant's cheek resumed its paleness, and the unnatural excitement of his eye became subdued and calm; Religion poured her soothing waters in his heart, and the fierce volcano, if not extinct, at least for awhile slumbered in repose.

Rising from his knees, the aged man slowly crossed the cloisters, and directed his steps towards the prison of Ernulf—a low stone building which formerly existed on the site of the modern deanery.

The prison in which the captive was confined was a large square chamber, the only entrance to which was by a narrow door, thickly studded with nails and plates of iron, situated under a quaintly-ornamented Saxon archway; his couch was nothing more than a stone bench, projecting from the wall; over it hung a crucifix, rudely sculptured by some former inmate, to beguile the weary hours of his captivity. So strong was the dungeon, that air and light were admitted only by a massive grating, cemented in the ceiling, too high for the prisoner to reach, too deeply imbedded in the solid masonry for any external force to remove. The bruised and maimed criminal still lay groaning on his pallet, where he had been cast by his executioners, after the torture, when Father Oswald entered the cell. Despite his resolution, he felt the kindlier sentiments of his nature struggling with his justice, as he gazed upon the being who, half-stripped of his armour, the dew of agony upon his brow, his eyes blood-shot and wandering, lay stretched on the hard couch before him. Nature whispered to him that it was his son—the being whose existence had been moulded from his own, and towards whom, despite his crimes and degenerate baseness, a secret yearning inclined his soul to pity. Perhaps conscience whispered him with some neglected duty to his offspring, or demanded whether, by precept or example, he had inculcated that high sense of honour and love of virtue whose absence he so harshly blamed. It was no longer, therefore, in the tone of an accusing spirit that he addressed him, but almost in the accents of forgiveness.

"Ernulf," he demanded, "dost thou recognise me?"

The wounded man slowly turned upon his couch of pain, and gazed upon the speaker: all excitement had passed from his pale features. In recognising in Father Oswald his living parent, the spell of his authority over him was broken; he knew that he was no parricide; and even his obdurate heart felt lighter from the load removed.

"I do," he coldly answered.

His interrogator started at the cool determination, the almost indifference, evinced by the reply, and for a few moments they regarded each other in silence, severally preparing for the mental combat about to ensue —a silence as sullen as the pause which precedes the burst of the tempest, or intervenes between the thunder and the lightning's flash. The monk was the first to break it, the pity excited by the sufferings of the prisoner gradually yielding to indignation at his obduracy.

"Hast thou no word," he demanded, "for repentance?—to implore forgiveness for the crime at which the angels shudder and e'en demons tremble?—no prayer to appease offended Heaven and thy father's wrath?"

"None."

"None!" iterated the priest—"none! Is, then, thy heart so seared by crime that nothing less than the avenging bolt can penetrate it? Knowest thou the punishment announced for parricides?—The eternal fires, the endless gnawing of the serpent tooth of an undying conscience, the sting of memory, and the hell of fear!"

"I am no parricide," doggedly retorted Ernulf, his voice slightly showing that the denunciation of the priest had moved him.

"In thought and purpose," continued the speaker, "if not in act. Thinkest thou thy crime is less because the blow inflicted on thy father as he slept reached short of life? But it is just," he added, mournfully; "thy childhood was impetuous, wayward, cruel; thy manhood stained by violence and crime; 'tis just thy age should prove a fitting sequel to thy youth."

"And whose the fault?" demanded Ernulf, starting from the couch, regardless in his excitement of his bruised limbs and aching brow; "demand it of the man who called himself my father, whose pride revolted at a child's caress, whose want of confidence repressed each rising impulse of my heart towards him; whose harsh, cold, stony, selfish nature withered my childhood, turned it on itself, to feed on its own diseased, corrupted heart. Wonder at my crimes—wonder they are not a thousand times more strange than those which madness, in her fever, paints! Taught by no faith, accustomed from thy lips to hear blasphemed the truths which now it seems the Christian priest believes, but which the Druid Haga once abhorred, where was my stay, when passion's breath assailed me?—where the arms to fight temptation in her Protean forms, resist her luring spells? No!" he added; "if I have fallen, thou art not my reprover; if I have sinned, thou canst not be my judge. Man reads the crime, but Heaven the temptation."

Each word of Ernulf fell like a drop of molten lead upon the heart of Father Oswald. As he spoke, scale after scale fell from his eyes; he saw and felt that the monster before him was of his own creation; that the plastic clay of humanity had been trusted to his hand, and that, in his presumption, ignorance, or selfishness, he had moulded it into a demon's form. He found himself weak where he had thought himself most strong; and the conviction brought bitterness and sorrow to his soul, silenced the fiery eloquence of his tongue, and humiliated his vaunted reason.

"'Tis true," resumed the prisoner, "my hand has been raised against thy life; but thou hadst first destroyed my soul. Pure it was committed to thy hands. Ask of thy conscience how thou didst execute the sacred trust. Unnatural father, I do reject thee for my judge. Priest of a faith thou never taughtest thy child, thus I breathe back thy curse!"

The gaunt form of the speaker was raised to its full height, and, despite his haggard appearance, there was something even majestic in his look, as, with his arm raised, he was about to hurl back the paternal malediction with tenfold force upon the head that uttered it.

"Hold, wretched man!" exclaimed Oswald, throwing himself at his feet, his heart crushed by the convictions his words awoke within it. "I have sinned, and my sin hath become my punishment. I here retract my curse. Spare my gray hairs—let me not hear the voice of my own son condemn me!"

It was a strange sight to see the gifted Oswald prostrate at the feet of his rude offspring. Humiliated by the voice of conscience, subjected by the power of truth, he was no longer the same being. His spiritual pride, the defect of his character, was completely subdued; for his heart had been exposed to his own view, and he felt sick within him. Even Ernulf was affected at the sight, for he knew well the nature he had humbled: he had trembled at it in its strength, and he respected it in its weakness.

"Not to me, father—not to me should the knee be bent," he answered, raising the old man as he spoke; "at least, let us part friends, exchanging mutual forgiveness. I suppose," he added, "I have not long to live, for holy church seldom relinquishes her grasp except with life, and mine is a deed that admits no chance of mercy. What is the usual punishment of sacrilege?—But I know: death—death at the least."

"The stake!" faintly uttered the old man, scarcely conscious that the words had passed his lips.

"The stake!" almost shrieked the prisoner; "and you tell me so! The stake! Is there no sentiment of nature, no tie of blood, to freeze the fearful word upon your lips? The cord, the axe—any fate rather than to perish at the burning stake!"

"Think rather of thy soul," interrupted his father: "respect the church's judgments, as thou art a Christian."

"Well thou knowest I am no Christian," replied Ernulf: "the waters of baptism have never been poured on my obdurate head. 'Tis true, that since I left my home, and mingled in the world, I passed as such—perhaps, in creed, am one—but never yet hath priestly hand sprinkled the regenerating drops upon my brow."

"Now Heaven be praised!" exclaimed his father, a beam of satisfaction illuminating his aged countenance, "and thanks to every saint! The sin of my neglect may be atoned—the soul I trifled with may be redeemed!"

"What meanest thou?"

"That were thy sins as scarlet as the crimes of all the earth, that baptism would wash their stain away. Let us kneel," continued the priest, "and let us both return thanks to Heaven for mercy—thou for a soul redeemed, e'en at destruction's brink, and I for undying anguish and remorse removed. Prepare thy soul by penitence and prayer," he added, "to receive the wondrous boon which Heaven in its wisdom hath reserved. Mine shall be the hand to perform the sacred rite which numbers thee with the redeemed on earth. May thy after-life inscribe thy name with the redeemed in Heaven!"

"But the stake?" interrupted Ernulf, listening only to his fears. "Will it secure my body from the flames—must I quit the world amid the execration of the yelling crowd—feel the fierce fire melting the very marrow of my bones—my brain to boil amid the raging heat? Is there no hope—no mercy? Speak, father, speak!"

"None!" said the old man, visibly affected by his son's despair, whose countenance, distorted by the fearful terrors his imagination conjured up, was but a feeble index of his mind. "Thou hast no hope on earth."

"Perchance nor Heaven!" added Ernulf, rolling again upon his couch in an agony of fear and horror. "'Tis but a dream, perhaps—'tis but a dream: there is no Heaven, no mercy, or I should find it. Fool! to think that priests should e'er know mercy!"

The priest began to pace the cell, as if meditating some important purpose, while Ernulf continued to exhaust himself by his ravings. At times Oswald's eye would fall upon his son with a mingled expression of scorn and interest—scorn at his unmanly terrors, pity for the danger which excited them. At last, it seemed as if his mind was resolved on some important step, for he approached the couch, and arrested the pri-

soner's wanderings with a look such as that at which, 'tis said, the maniac trembles.

"And could thy life be spared, how wouldst thou use it, boy?" solemnly demanded his father. "Speak, and let thy words be truthful as thy danger's pressing; for let me trace even the shade of falsehood in thy mind, the hope but to equivocate with truth, and the chance, the little chance that's left thee, is destroyed."

"Chance!" eagerly repeated Ernulf, catching like a drowning wretch at the word—"there is, then, a chance?"

"Answer my question," coldly replied his father, who had little sympathy with earthly fears, and who could, in his own person, have regarded the stake with indifference, and even with triumph, had he been condemned to suffer in a cause his conscience told him to be holy—"how wouldst thou pass thy life?"

"In prayer—in fasting in some hermit's cell," he answered; "or, pilgrim, staff in hand, I'd seek the burning plains of Palestine, and wet with my tears the blessed Redeemer's tomb. Let me but live," he added, "and the mortal terrors of the present hour will keep my soul from every future sin. Or do you prescribe a life of penance: well will I keep it, father."

The priest gazed upon him as if he would read his inmost soul—sift every working of his subtle mind. Perhaps the impression was satisfactory, for there was again something almost of kindliness in his parting tones.

"'Tis well, my son; dispose thyself for that which Heaven thinks best; for the rest, we are but potsherds in its hands. If, in the solitude of thy dark cell, thy many crimes should preach unto thy soul despair, let the remembrance of Heaven's unnumbered mercies whisper hope."

The speaker quitted the cell as the last words fell from his lips, and Ernulf sank once more upon his couch of pain, a saddened if not a better man.

"My sin at last has found me," exclaimed the monk, as he paced the cloister on his way to the chapter-room, where he expected to hear the sentence pronounced upon his son. "Yon wretched being answered truly. 'Tis I, unnatural father, who have destroyed him; reared him in scorn of Christian faith and every Christian tie; sought to impress him with my own dark creed; or, worse, left him in ignorance to choose one. Shall Heaven, in its mercy, have left wide the path to save his soul, and I do nothing for his mortal state? No, Ernulf!" he added, sternly; "fallen as thou art, thou art still my son; stained though thou art, thy father is not pure; degraded as thy nature hath become, one trace of Eden lingers round it yet.

Thou shalt not perish if my life can save thee!"

Full of this high resolve, he entered the chapter-house, where many of the brotherhood were assembled. By all present, even by those who loved him not for his cold, unsocial nature, he was received with respect and sympathy; for all knew his connection with the prisoner, and marvelled at his firmness under a trial beneath which even manly fortitude might well succumb, and the calm endurance of which was almost miraculous in one of his advanced age and weakness. The sentence which declared Ernulf guilty of sacrilege lay signed upon the table, together with the rescript which gave him over to the secular arm, to be dealt with as mercifully as the nature of his offence permitted—a recommendation of idle form, which was never permitted to interfere with the strict execution of the law—a law which pertained more to the spirit of the dark age in which it was framed than to the character of either the church or priesthood. With a firm hand, Father Oswald read the parchment, amid the silence of the brotherhood. To his ardent piety it seemed both natural and just that the crime of sacrilege should be expiated by blood; and he affixed his signature to the document without the least apparent emotion, thereby rendering the decision of the chapter both unanimous and valid. How he reconciled the conviction that the life of the guilty party was necessary to atone for his offence, with the desire to save that life, time will show.

"When is the execution appointed to take place?" he demanded of the assembled monks, who stood gazing on him with admiration at his firmness and his self-control, a species of virtue as highly appreciated in the cloister as in the world.

"This very day," was the reply, given with an expression of surprise. "Surely," they thought, "he will never be there!"

"And the hour?"

"Sunset."

"So soon?" thought their interrogator. "Then I must be brief, for I have still much to perform."

In his own sorrow, he resolved not to be unmindful of Ulrick's safety. He had heard of the intention expressed by Mirvan in the church to be himself the champion in the lists; and well he knew that the generous nature of the accused would submit to any alternative—even to death itself—rather than draw his sword against Matilda's brother and his bosom friend. He proposed, therefore, to withdraw him from his prison through the same passage by which he himself gained entrance to it.

On the same night on which the execution of Herman of the Burg took place, a female figure, closely veiled, attended by four men-at-arms, left the episcopal palace on foot, and directed her steps towards the ferry. Her disguised person and hurried step gave her more the air of a fugitive escaped from justice than the widow of the powerful earl whose last obsequies were then being celebrated in the cathedral. Edith, for it was no other, was bound upon an expedition of no little moment, as well as danger, and her courage rose with the occasion; the long-suppressed emotions of maternal love, now throbbing at her heart with hopeful energy, gave to her mind a strength and elasticity to which it had been long a stranger, and her decision had been prompt and clear. The men-at-arms who attended her were four of the Norman followers of Herbert de Lozinga—men who had not long arrived from his ancestral lands—men who spoke not a single word of Saxon tongue, and who had never seen the countess. Their orders were to obey her will in everything, and to protect her person with their lives. Fearful of detection—for it was necessary that the world should still believe her dead—she hurried her steps towards the tower, where resided the ferryman, and where the faithful Judith was expecting her. As she hastened on, the broken chant of the monks fell occasionally upon her ear; still she paused not—her energies were but to save the living; she had no time to mourn the dead. The ferryman, to whom on her arrival she presented a ring, bowed reverentially; for he recognised the signet of the bishop, and handed her into the boat, which already was in waiting, and took his place at the helm. The four Normans seized the oars—which, to their surprise, they found muffled—and directed their course towards Whitlingham.

"And whither go you, my dear lady?" demanded Judith, in a whisper, as soon as her mistress was seated by her side.

"To Whitlingham—to the Druid caves," calmly answered Edith.

The reply struck terror to the faithful heart of her attendant. The caves of Whitlingham bore an evil name, for superstition had clothed them in her shadowy terrors. Even in the day they were avoided; but after nightfall few men would venture to approach them. Strange lights had oft been seen streaming through their rugged openings—unholy songs and yells of triumph heard; and the idea of approaching, much more of entering them, seemed to Judith little short of madness and presumption. Nothing but this conviction could have induced her to offer even the approach to a remonstrance.

"To Whitlingham! Gracious lady, did I hear you aright? Unholy sounds have oft been heard there, and strange visions seen: 'tis said the spirits of our pagan fathers nightly assemble there, to celebrate the accursed rights of Odin and of Thor. No Christian should approach them; the church rejects them; let us not tempt their wrath."

"I fear them not," replied the countess. "Good spirits cannot harm us, and Heaven will protect us against bad. But if thy courage fails thee, Judith, tell the men to pull to land—thou canst regain the palace. I have no right to tax thee, girl, beyond thy strength—it has been tried enough already."

The idea of leaving her mistress in danger was, to the faithful creature, more terrible than even her fears of Whitlingham.

"No, no," she said; "I have not lived so long to eat your bread that I should desert you now. Be they pagans or fiends, where you go, mistress, my steps shall follow. The unholy sight may, perchance, appal; but it shall not drive me from you."

"The sight of human passions is, indeed, unholy; but beyond that," said Edith, "thou hast naught to fear. The beings who assemble in the caves are men—some of them noble, though misguided ones. There may be danger to the body, but none unto the soul."

This explanation, imperfect as it was, afforded great consolation to Judith, who, however fearful where spiritual terrors were concerned, possessed more, perhaps, than a man's contempt for earthly danger. Born a vassal on the lands of Stanfield, in early life she had been accustomed to traverse the woods, and more than once had battled with the wolf. Drawing the long Saxon knife which, since the escape from the holm, she carried concealed upon her person, she whispered—

"They must be many that would harm you, lady, while I am by. If danger press, I am prepared to strike."

"Thanks; but be cautious," replied her mistress. "If discovered, resistance would be worse than useless; but I will hope the best," she added, "for Providence favours my design. The moon is now completely veiled, and not one single star, the gems upon night's mantle, is twinkling in the heavens. If once, aided by Father Oswald's instructions, we reach the cave, we are safe; but whatever you may see, speak not, breathe not, even though it be a prayer for safety."

There was a solemn earnestness in Edith's manner which precluded further conversation, and Judith sat for the rest of the journey brooding over the mystery. A thousand times she was tempted to demand an expla-nation, but as often repressed her curiosity through affection and respect.

An hour's rowing brought them to Thorp, not, as now, a lovely village, adorned by all that wealth and culture can bestow, but a low, marshy swamp, dotted here and there with the rude wattle cabins of the Saxon herds, who tended the cattle of their Norman masters. From this point of their journey increased caution seemed necessary, and they crept slowly along the left side of the river, their noiseless course shadowed by the thick foliage of the trees and shrubs which over-hung its banks. Twice in their progress they were alarmed by the sound of a distant oar, and compelled to lie flat within their boat until the danger passed them. At last they contrived, unobserved, to reach the low shelving bank which conducted to the hills. Silently the rowers, who had evidently re-ceived their instructions, drew their boat from out the stream, and concealed it in the sedges, which grew in rank abundance on the banks. As soon as this was done, the old ferryman struck into a narrow pathway, half hid by underwood and long dank grass. The countess and Judith followed him, the rear being protected by the men-at-arms; and thus, without a word being spoken, the little party, in silence and in darkness, pursued their way till they came to a rude pile of unhewn stones, evidently the remains of some Druid temple. Here a light was struck, the men-at-arms searching the bushes round, to see if any curious eye had dogged their steps, their hands upon their long, straight swords, ready for immediate action.

The countess took an illuminated parch-ment from her bosom—it was a plan with which Father Oswald had supplied her for her enterprise—and compared the characters traced upon it with those graven upon a large upright stone, which, from its enormous weight, had resisted the zeal of the converted Saxons to overturn it. Apparently they were the same. A sigh escaped her breast, as if the discovery had relieved it from some oppressive weight; and for the first time she spoke, but in a voice so low it scarcely scared the genius of silence from the place.

"Thank Heaven!—they are the same! Quick—apply the instrument!"

Judith, whom the transactions of the last two hours had completely bewildered, beheld with increased astonishment the old ferryman draw from his breast a kind of key, of curious form and antique workmanship, and apply it to one of the interstices of the stone, which, slowly turning on a concealed axle, disclosed a narrow passage descending into the very bowels of the earth. Two of the men-at-arms advanced, lit their torches, and disappeared

A BANQUET-ROOM IN STANFIELD HALL.

through the aperture. The countess, without the least hesitation, was about to follow, when, unable longer to contain her apprehensions, Judith caught her by the robe.

"What wouldst thou?" demanded the courageous Edith.

"Kill me, dear lady," replied her attendant, "but do not ask me to descend with you through yon dark, fearful passage: it leads to death or to some charnel-house."

"To neither," interrupted her mistress:

No. 7.

"it leads to a recess within the Druid's cave, where, unseen, we may observe what passes. Patience, girl—do not lose courage now: that stone once closed, and we are safe."

"But should our enemies pursue us thither?"

"Impossible," continued the countess: "one only being knows of its existence, Haga the Archdruid, who revealed it to me. Come," she added, "one moment's hesitation may defeat my plans, peril my Ulrick's safety, and destroy my hopes. What!" she exclaimed, with increased vehemence, seeing that Judith still hesitated, "wouldst thou belie a life of proved fidelity, and desert thy mistress in an hour like this?"

The implied reproach, the mere suspicion of treason to Edith, stung the breast of her hearer with a far keener pang than her not unnatural terrors, or even her fear of death, and restored both her courage and self-possession—qualities which, under ordinary circumstances, she eminently possessed.

"Lead on, gracious lady," she replied; "you are right, quite right; why should I hesitate to follow where you lead, e'en to the grave? Should I expire at your feet, I should but end my days where I have passed the service of my life."

A quiet grasp of the hand was Edith's sole reply. She immediately descended the steps, Judith resolutely following. The concealed mechanism was again set in motion, and the Druid's stone resumed its accustomed place. For a long time they followed their guide in darkness through the many windings of the secret passage, for, unfortunately, the air was confined and too impure to admit of their burning torches. Their progress was rendered still more disagreeable by the unevenness of the road, and the flight of numerous owls and bats, whom their visit had disturbed. Their rugged pathway at last terminated in a species of hall or cave, where they could breathe more freely. The chalky and flinty walls and roof had been shaped into something like form; nay, even architectural ornament, such as it was, had been added. Here they again were enabled to light their torches; for the air, from either natural or artificial fissures, entered with reviving freshness. A flight of rude steps, at the extreme end of the hall—if we may so call the cave in which the party were assembled—seemed the only means of further progress. Edith and her now courageous attendant mounted them, and discovered that they led to a sort of parapet, too high for them to pass, but which they were sufficiently tall to look over; in fact, it was a species of wall separating the secret passage from Whitlingham cave, and contrived by the Druids for some now long-forgotten purpose.

The scene which presented itself to their astonished sight was one which Salvator Rosa's magic pencil might have well described. A huge fire blazed in the centre of the cave, which was far more lofty than at the present day, the gradual accumulation of sand and earth having considerably lessened its elevation. Torches of blazing pine were fixed at regular intervals in iron niches in the walls, their red glare falling on piles of arms, so arranged as to be ready for immediate use. Polished shields and shining helmets reflected back the blaze, and rendered all that passed distinctly visible. A considerable body of men were assembled within the cave; some were dozing off to sleep, others preparing food, or listening with excited attention to the tales of old, which one or two bards, in under tones, recited. But the chief personages of the scene were standing together near the spot where Edith and her companion were concealed. The principal personage was a tall old man, whose muscular form and stately limbs, well squared shoulders, and firm step, told he was still possessed of giant strength. A chain of massive gold was twisted round his neck, and bracelets of the same precious material adorned his arms and wrists; his tunic of green cloth fell to the middle of his legs, and was richly trimmed with sables; his countenance was strongly marked, but more, perhaps, by grief than age; a lofty brow which so overhung the eye, that it would have given a heaviness of expression to the face, had not the eyes redeemed it; they were of that piercing blue so peculiar to the Saxon race, and so expressive alike of love or hatred, scorn, passion, or revenge.

The heart of the concealed countess beat wildly as she gazed upon him; for Edda, the friend of her father, the father of her murdered Edward, stood before her—not, indeed, as when last she saw him in the brown pride of autumn's age, but changed by winter's snows; still they sat gracefully upon him. His voice was round and rich of tone as ever. Involuntarily the tears coursed each other down her cheek as its first accents fell upon her ear; for the sweet memory of olden times came over her.

"'Tis well, we are resolved at last," said Edda, addressing his brother franklins, who were standing round him. "The Saxon sword hath remained so long inactive, I thought 'twas glued for ever in its scabbard. Thank Heaven! 'tis drawn again. We have too long been dreamers: my blood has grown thick, dull, and heavy: a stirring bout," he added, "will once more send it, with youthful vigour, dancing through my veins, or end my dreams at once."

Long and patiently did Edith listen to their various arrangements. Each Saxon leader was assigned his post, whilst Edda, the head of the far most numerous sept, taking advantage of the weakness of the garrison, who were nearly all expected to assist at the trial by battle, was to storm the castle. Coolly she heard discussed before her whether the signal should be given for the attack before or after the death of Ulrick, the end of whose contest with so renowned a knight as Herman seemed anything but doubtful. The last points in their proceedings being settled, one by one the numerous franklins took their leave, and Edda, with his followers, remained alone within the cave. For awhile he occupied himself in giving orders to his men, who received them with that respectful alacrity which showed their veneration for their chief, whose countenance, since the departure of his brother nobles, had gradually lost its energetic expression, and resumed its habitual melancholy. Drawing his ample cloak around him, he began soliloquising, as he paced to and fro by the watch-fire's light within the cave.

"So," he murmured, "the Saxon wolf-dog is again unslipt to hunt its Norman master. 'Tis a desperate chance to rouse the slumbering courage of a vanquished people—raise them from slavery to freedom. Should we fail, how many widowed dames and sireless sons will curse the day we drew the powerless sword!"

"Many!" exclaimed Edith, who had left the place of her concealment, and stood before him.

He started, and gazed on her with an expression of awe and fear. He was ignorant of the secret means by which she entered. He knew that the approaches to the cave were guarded by those upon whose fidelity he could depend. It seemed as if a warning spirit had risen from the earth to turn him from his purpose.

"Who and what art thou?" he demanded.

Edith slowly raised her veil, and exposed her pale but still lovely features to his view. Though many a year had passed since they had met, he knew her at a glance.

"And what," he courteously asked, "brings Hugh de Bigod's widowed countess to this lonely cave the very night of her lord's obsequies? Has the Norman heir driven his Saxon widow from her home? If so, lady, thou art welcome—welcome for the memory of one most dear—of one whose love was the first spring-flower of thy virgin heart, though forgotten now."

"Never forgotten, father," answered Edith; "for there are lines so deeply traced upon the heart, death's icy fingers only can efface them. 'Tis true, to save my wretched race from death, my father's honoured age from beggary and shame, I gave my hand to Hugh de Bigod, whose generous nature ne'er wronged the sacrifice; but my love was buried deep in Edward's lonely grave."

The name of his son, pronounced by the lips of the woman he had so fondly loved, agitated the old man; the tone of her voice awakened many a long-forgotten thought, jarred many a broken chord; a tear dimmed his deep blue eye, but with a hasty movement of his hand he dashed it from it.

"Speak not of Edward!" he exclaimed: "I am old, and age is weak. Make not a woman of me!"

"I must speak of him, and you must listen to me."

"How?"

"His widow asks," said Edith, throwing herself upon her knees, and clasping the old man's hand—"the mother of his son!"

"Woman!" cried, or rather shrieked, the aged franklin, "what have I heard? My Edward's widow—the mother of his son! I am a lonely man, crushed by my sorrows. Do not trifle with me. The storm," he added, "which once raged here is now at peace; but words like these break the icy barriers of my heart, to spread, like Etna's lava, desolation round."

The fearful energy of the old man's words alarmed the countess, but failed to check her resolution. In his passion he had grasped her wrist so intently, that the flesh quivered beneath his pressure: still she felt it not. With her disengaged hand she took a paper from her bosom, stained by time, but still more by her tears: it was the proof of her secret marriage with his son. Eagerly the old man perused its contents. Twice he tried to speak, but his emotions choked him.

"True, true," he sobbed; "none but a heart seared by treachery could doubt a voice like thine. Child of my friend—bride of my murdered boy—come to his father's heart, which throbs to pillow thee amid life's storms!" In an instant Edith's arms were twined around the old man's neck, her head reposing on his manly breast, the warm tears trickling down his venerable cheeks mingled with hers. "But your son," he added—"Edward's boy—my boy—is he living yet? A look—a sign—and I am happy!" The anxious tone of the speaker showed how deeply every feeling was interested in the reply. He watched his helpless burthen—fate seemed to hang upon her lips.

"He lives!" murmured Edith.

"Thank Heaven! Oh, many a goodly rood of land, for this, shall grace our Lady's shrine! Where is my boy?"

"A prisoner in the castle."

"A prisoner!" echoed Edda. "I'll tear him thence, though a Norman's blood cemented every stone. A prisoner! Tyrants! are they not drunk with blood enough already? A prisoner! But enough: he lives, and Edward's boy shall not long linger in the Norman's hold. Life's purple tide rekindles at my heart; my nerves swell with the energies of former years; revenge and rage are struggling in my breast for dreadful mastery. Spirits of my fathers," he continued, casting himself upon his knees, " in whose veins the mingled blood of kings and heroes ran—Odin and Hengist, from your thrones look down, and let your power protect your wretched race—rally, immortal spirits, round my sword, and guide it to each Norman tyrant's heart !"

"Not to the Norman's, but the Saxon's, father. From our own race the serpent sprang whose venom hath undone us—Saxon the sword which made thee childless and me a widow— Saxon the tongue which would complete our ruin, and dares accuse our murdered Edward's boy !"

At the words of the countess a ray of light penetrated the mind of Edda, and he exclaimed, as the truth flashed upon him—

"Ulrick is thy son !"

"He is," continued Edith—"the noble, generous, the heroic boy ! Father, thou needst not blush to own him. Not in the history of thy honoured line, princes, or fabled heroes of thy race, will a nobler heart or mind be found than Ulrick's."

Rapidly did the excited mother relate to the powerful franklin the history of her early marriage—Ulrick's birth, supposed death, and miraculous preservation by Herbert de Lozinga, by whose direction she had been sent to warn him that the plans of the Saxon insurrection were betrayed, and measures taken to defeat them. As she proceeded in her tale, to support the truth of her assertions, she showed the signet ring, upon the production of which by Father Oswald Herman had so unexpectedly declared the nobility of Ulrick's birth; and, in conclusion, she placed in his hands a packet, bearing the seal of the prelate, the contents of which she was herself unacquainted with. Hastily Edda broke the seal, and found it to contain an agreement, signed by most of the Saxon chiefs engaged in the conspiracy, in the event of their success, to deprive him of the government of his vast possessions, and allow him during his life the enjoyment merely of a portion of his revenues, unless, to avoid the humiliation, he chose to adopt Herman as his heir. The parchment had fallen into the hands of the bishop through the agency of Father Oswald.

" What !" exclaimed Edda, as he recognised each well-known signature and seal, "would they divide the lion's spoil ere he had fallen into the snare ? Fools, they have sealed their own most righteous doom ! The pitfall they have dug shall prove their ruin !"

Long and anxiously did the countess remain in consultation with the chief, and morning had already dawned ere the lonely bark, with its silent rowers, was again launched upon the stream.

CHAPTER XIII.

Souls gush in prayer, and hearts beat,
To the lip's warm orisons.

ATE on the morning after the obsequies of Hugh de Bigod, the seneschal entered the prison of Ulrick, to announce to him the decision of the Normans, that Mirvan should be permitted to appear in the lists as the champion of the deceased earl, a ceremony which he fulfilled with all the chivalrous courtesy of the age. The impression which the announcement made upon the generous heart of the prisoner may more easily be imagined than described—love, honour, all opposed it. The haughty Saxon who had taunted him with the mystery of his birth, who had outraged his pride, infamously and falsely accused him of a crime at which his soul revolted, he could have met in the deadly strife of arms—nay, thirsted for the encounter which, in the opinions of the age, would have decided the question of innocence or guilt between them; but Mirvan was a different enemy; he was the first friend of his youth—the brother of Matilda—the son called on, as he believed, to avenge his parent's blood. Friendship, as well as principle, forbade him to draw the sword in such a contest. The struggle was short, but bitter, and he determined, whatever might be the consequence, to refuse the combat, where victory would be worse than defeat—where every blow he struck would wound a heart dearer than his own. Firmly, therefore, he declared his refusal to meet any but Herman in the lists; nor could the friendly remonstrance of the seneschal induce him even for a moment to reconsider his determination.

"You are aware," urged his visitor, "that the trial by battle once appealed to, and then declined, leaves you no other judgment : by the law of arms you will be deemed guilty, and suffer not only death, but dishonour."

"Be it so," replied Ulrick. "Better to die with an unmerited stain upon my name, than to live to bear within my heart the fires of remorse. I will not lift my arm against my earliest, though misguided friend."

"Not even to prove your innocence?" demanded the officer.

"No," answered the youth, after a moment's pause: "enough that my own heart knows it."

"Who else will know it when thou art dead, branded with a fellon's name?"

"Heaven!" exclaimed Ulrick, with a look of resignation, "and the good angels, who watch the grave of peace."

The seneschal, whom the prisoner's firmness touched, bowed respectfully and withdrew. Although unable to appreciate his motives, he respected them; his rough soldier nature admired the martyr courage which could so calmly contemplate the approach of death, rejecting the last chance of safety.

"So ends my dream of life," exclaimed Ulrick, as he neard the heavy iron bar drawn on the exterior of his prison-door. "Honour has been its dream of youth—my manhood shall not shame it at its close. Erect is my integrity; I can meet my doom, and march to the scaffold as to the victor's car."

"Such," said a deep voice behind him, "is the Christian's courage and the martyr's faith."

The prisoner started at the sound; and, turning, beheld Father Oswald, who had entered his dungeon by the secret passage. His astonishment was extreme; for, from the state of insensibility in which the poisoned wine had plunged him, he was ignorant of the monk's previous visit.

"Father Oswald! how, in the name of every saint, gained you admittance here?"

"By natural means," replied the old man, pointing to the secret passage, which he had left open; "by the same means thou mayest avoid thy fate. Follow me."

"Whither?"

"To liberty."

An expression of scorn curled the prisoner's lips: for, in his mind, flight was connected with dishonour.

"What!" he exclaimed, "fly! and live to bear a branded name! give truth the lie! and turn approver to my proper shame! Oh, never, never!"

"Then meet the Norman champion in the fight," replied the monk.

"Impossible!" said the youth, mournfully; "he is my friend! unkind, I grant you, still he is my friend!"

"Friend!" repeated Oswald, in a tone of pity; "do such dreams linger in thee yet? Natures like thine are born to be deceived; cold as this heart is it can feel for thee."

"Hast thou no faith in friendship?"

"As much as in the sea's delusive calm before the tempest breaks," bitterly answered the old man; "as much as in the serpent's innocence because it sleeps. Friendship! I tell thee, boy, it is the coin with which man cheats his fellows—a wretch plotting against his neighbour's peace and life can find no mask so sure to hide his purpose as friendship's sullied name. The bird, whose wings fan it own funereal pile, is not more purely fable than a friend. Wouldst thou be happy," he added, "dream not of friendship more."

"Mirvan is my friend," interrupted Ulrick.

"Yet he—unheard—condemned thee," coolly observed the priest.

The reply shot a pang to Ulrick's breast; for in the confidence of his nature, the generosity of his heart, he felt that he could not have judged unheard as Mirvan judged; still he endeavoured to defend him.

"His father's death," he faltered, "and the false words of an artful fiend, have blinded his better reason; so confidence has given place to doubt."

"And what is friendship, if a doubt can shake it? But come," added the priest, "for I have still a solemn ministry to be performed; and I could wish that mercy should precede justice. The path to freedom lies before thee. Fly from the enemies who seek thy blood, to those who long to welcome thee."

"Never!" resolutely answered the young man, "will I consent to stain my name by ignominious flight."

"Not though it led thee to thy mother's arms," demanded the priest—"to her maternal blessing—to a name proud as the proudest of thy Norman foes—a name which renders thee the mate of any line their pirate race e'er boasted?"

"What meanest thou, father, by those words?" demanded the youth, deeply excited. "Thou art a holy man; thy words should be of truth. Are these things so?"

The priest silently bowed his head in confirmation of his words—words which the prisoner had drunk into his very soul—words which assured him that his boyhood's hopes were no longer dreams.

"And yet," said Ulrick, despairingly, after a pause, "I cannot fly."

"Not," interrupted the monk, "if, the moment thou wert free, the evidence of thine innocence, attested by the hand of thine accuser, witnessed by those who now would judge thee, were produced, to clear thy fame beyond suspicious breath?"

"Is it possible?"

"Can't thou doubt me?" he added, seeing that Ulrick's last objection was shaken. "Men so near the grave as I am seldom lie. Here is a dress in which thou mayest pass unsuspected by the soldiery, should we encounter such, when once beyond the castle wall. Array thyself, for time is precious with me."

Ulrick hesitated no longer; the assurance that the proofs of his innocence should be placed within his hands when once beyond the castle decided him, and he hastened to assume the disguise of a lay brother, which his kind protector had brought him. Just as he had drawn the cowl over his face, the door of his prison opened, and the seneschal, who had been directed to conduct the prisoner before the nobles, to explain his extraordinary resolution of not appearing in the lists against Mirvan, entered the cell. His astonishment at the sight of the two monks was extreme,

"Where is the prisoner?" he exclaimed, after having cast a hasty glance around the cell.

"Beyond your reach," coolly replied Father Osward.

"Treachery is here!" exclaimed the seneschal, raising his voice. "What ho! guards! the prisoner hath escaped! Warders, to your posts! Treason, ho!"

The effect of the alarm was to set every man within the walls on the alert. The word was passed from post to post, and the heavy tramp of the armed soldiery was heard upon the stairs ascending to the tower.

"Too late, too late," whispered the prisoner to Father Oswald; "the guards are here."

A dozen men-at-arms rushed into the prison as he spoke. Firmly the monk gasped Ulrick's arm as he replied:—

"Were their chains upon thy limbs, boy, they should melt like wax; were the sword above thy head, I would shiver it ere it fell. Brute force is theirs—science and wisdom mine."

"Seize them!" exclaimed the seneschal; "cut them down if they attempt to pass."

The men were about to obey their chief, when Father Oswald scattered a powder upon the floor, which instantly ignited on coming in contact with the air, and filled the prison with a thick vapour, from which lurid flames occasionally flashed, and peals of thunder rolled. The affrighted Normans fell prostrate through fear and superstition, the belief of magic being universal at the time, and sanctioned by law, both civil and ecclesiastic, against it.

"The fiend! the fiend!" they shouted, and in their terror called upon every saint to save them. Gradually the flames subsided, and the dense vapour became dispersed, when they recovered sufficient courage to look around them. The two monks had disappeared: they found themselves within the prison, trembling and alone. A long winding staircase, concealed in the thickness of the wall, brought the fugitives to the very foundations of the castle, where the air felt cold and damp. Here they paused for breath, and Father Oswald lit a torch which he had brought beneath his vest. Ulrick found himself, on looking round, in a cell something similar to the one he had just quitted; the same rough sculptured crucifixion adorned the wall, representing St. William in the wood. From another concealed passage opening from its back, they proceeded in the direction of the chapel, to which they mounted by similar winding stairs to the ones they had descended.

"Caution!" exclaimed the priest, as they reached the last step, which brought them to a panel of carved oak, which evidently answered the purpose of a concealed door, the complicated mechanism by which it was opened being on their side of it. His companion arrested his step at the word, for he heard voices in the chapel. By removing a small slide, Ulrick was enabled to peep through a portion of the fretwork and see what was passing in the sacred edifice, without himself being seen by those he watched.

Isabel and Matilda were standing near the altar in earnest conversation with Odo of Caen, who seemed to defend himself but weakly against some joint request. It was the voice of the former that first met his ear.

"Impossible!" she exclaimed, pettishly, as if repeating the words of the knight; "there is nothing impossible to a willing min , or to a lady's prayer. What harm can possibly arise from my cousin and myself visiting the prisoner in his dungeon? Think you that we shall smuggle him away beneath our wimples? or all three escape on a fiery dragon?"

"Not that," replied Odo, smiling at her earnestness; "but he is under ward, and I am pledged in honour to admit neither friend nor enemy to converse with him. Be reasonable, pretty coz, and press me, therefore, no more upon this theme."

"Indeed, but I will press thee, and earnestly too," answered Isabel; "for thy objections, despite thy protestations, are as slight as thy wish to favour us. By thy vow of knighthood, thou art bound to succour innocence; and Ulrick, I tell thee, again and again, is innocent. Had Herman been the champion, tongue of mine had never wagged to prevent the fight. Heaven, I doubt not, would have protected the righteous cause, and decided well between them, for I feel assured that Herman is——"

"Herman will never more appear as champion in any cause," gravely interrupted the knight, who shuddered as he remembered his midnight execution in the cloisters of the cathedral, and his own share in it.

"The better for the cause, if it be a good one. But come," she added, "brother Odo—for I suppose I must one day call thee so—pleasure us in this. Why, thou makest more mouths to perform an act of justice, than others would to attain a point of honour. Matilda and myself both vouch for Ulrick's innocence; and surely the word of two noble Norman maidens may outweigh a Saxon's slander. Would that my sister Jane were here! thou wouldst not dare say nay to her."

Though not convinced, the knight was shaken in his resolution: the appeal to her sister's name had touched a secret chord in his stern nature; yet he yielded not at once, but continued to resist, more for honour than the hope of victory.

"Could I but see the use of such an interview—what chance!" he muttered.

"Every hope," interrupted Matilda, speaking for the first time. "There is some fearful mystery concealed in Ulrick's accusation. Woman's wit will often find the key where man's boasted wisdom fails. We judge from sympathies; cold man from reason. Did he not risk his own to save my brother's life? Was not the sword with which 'tis said the felon blow was struck my parting gift? A gift," she added, slightly blushing as the eye of the knight encountered hers, "sanctioned by my brother's presence and my cousin's smile! Odo, should either Ulrick or my brother fall in this unholy fight, eternal must be their remorse who might have stayed the contest."

"'Tis stayed already," answered Odo. "Know you not the prisoner hath refused to measure swords with Mirvan?"

"Noble Ulrick!" exclaimed Matilda, "yet not more noble than my judgment painted him; and what is the result?"

"By the law of arms," he reluctantly answered, "he is condemned to die."

"To die!" exclaimed Matilda, violently excited. "Oh, no! you cannot be so lost to every precept of humanity—to every voice of justice. Unheard to die! to quit the gorgeous scenes of this fair earth—exchange life's hopes and gushing sympathies for the vile headsman's steel, with honour's impulse throbbing at the heart—to sink to a dishonourable grave, is e'en too horrible for

thought. If it be so," she added firmly, "e'en at the place of execution one voice shall still proclaim his innocence, and vindicate his name."

Our readers may well imagine with what transport the eloquent words of the speaker fell upon the listener's ear. The sinner who heard the angel of mercy pleading for him at the judgment seat could not have felt a deeper transport. In the excitement of the moment he would have quitted his concealment, and, regardless of the danger, have cast himself at Matilda's feet, to pour out his heart in grateful prayer, had not the hand of Father Oswald wisely restrained him.

"Patience," whispered the old man; "that which is deferred is far from lost; thou yet shall thank her like thyself, my son."

Even Odo was struck by the fair speaker's confidence and despair; they naturally turned his thoughts into a fresh channel.

"Lady," he said, "thou lovest this unknown youth; and love, too often, blinds our better reason."

"Odo of Caen," replied the maiden with dignity, "this is ungenerously urged; but since it hath been so, be this my answer, that never word of love from Ulrick's lips have fallen on my ear; and I spring not from a race that could, unsought, be won. Ulrick, the unknown youth, can never be to me more than my brother's life. De Bigod's daughter weds but with a line as pure and as illustrious as her own."

The deep blush which had suffused the speaker's countenance gave way to the mortal paleness which, since her father's death, overshadowed it. The rough soldier was awed by the dignity of her manner, and the hopeless tone in which her words were uttered; if not convinced, he seemed to be convinced; though skilled to read the human heart, he generously closed the page, and strove to read no further.

For a few moments there was a pause, which Odo was the first to break.

"Lady," he said, bending the knee with courtly gallantry, "that I believe my thoughts have wronged thee, be this the proof. I yield to thy demand; I will myself conduct thee and the Lady Isabel to the prison door, and leave you to converse with the accused, of whom I'll think the better that his innocence is vouched by thee. Speak," he added, with a smile, "am I forgiven?"

"Forgiven?" said Isabel, who saw that Matilda was unable to reply; "ay, and shalt be rewarded, too. I'll plead thy cause with Jane, and on her wedding-day my cousin and myself will braid her hair, and every

STANFIELD HALL.

58

pearl we have shall go to deck it. But when," she added, "shall we to the prison? —to-morrow is the day appointed for the fight."

Odo was about to reply, when the alarm bell of the castle caught his ear, as it sent forth its iron summons. He started at the sound; his first thought was of the intended Saxon insurrection. The possibility of the prisoner's escape never struck him. Before he had even time to draw his sword, Robert of Artois rushed into the chapel.

"Speak!" cried Odo; "what means the alarm?—are the Saxon hounds upon us?"

"The prisoner hath escaped!"

Matilda and Isabel were in an instant upon their knees before the shrine in mute thanksgiving; a weight seemed to have been removed from both their hearts—Matilda for Ulrick's, and Isabel for Mirvan's safety.

"Escaped!" repeated Odo, "impossible! the tower was guarded by my own and Bigod's followers. I'll stake my life on their fidelity. There must be some witchcraft or devilry in this. But follow me," he added. "Whate'er the mystery may be, we'll see the bottom of it."

Odo, followed by Robert of Artois, left the building as he spoke.

"Now, then, follow!" whispered Father Oswald; "we must cross the chapel. On the opposite side is the entrance to another passage, which leads us beneath the castle moat, e'en to the cloisters. It were dangerous now to traverse the guarded plain between them; follow me, then, in silence."

He opened the concealed spring as he spoke, and in an instant he found himself with his companion in the chapel. So absorbed were both Isabel and Matilda in their prayer, that they heeded not the echo of the priest's sandalled foot, or the yet heavier tread of Ulrick. The latter could not, however, in his love and gratitude, forget the generous defence of his honour made by the lips most dear to him. Led by the passionate impulse of his heart, he cast himself at the maiden's feet, and printed a burning kiss upon her hand.

Matildia started with surprise at such an action from a monk, and was about to rebuke his insolence, when the voice, whose tones had so often wakened an echo in her heart, reassured her.

"Angel of mercy," he exclaimed, "farewell! thy judgment hath not wronged thy goodness; the spotless virgin in her cloistered cell—the infant smiling at its mother's breast—are not more free from blood than I am. At the hour of battle, fear not but that I shall be there, to prove my innocence or brave my doom."

Before Matilda or Isabel could reply, Ulrick had again drawn the cowl over his face, and disappeared after his mysterious conductor.

Herbert de Lozinga, Edda, and the countess, were seated in an apartment of the episcopal palace when Father Oswald, after conducting Ulrick through the subterranean passages which connected the castle with the cathedral, emerged with him into the cloisters.

"Thank Heaven!" exclaimed the priest, "we are secure at last, boy; the danger is over, and I have kept my promise to thee."

He was about to leave him as he spoke.

"Stay, father," cried the youth; "safety, indeed, thou hast secured me; but, remember, it must not be safety without honour; either the proofs you promised of my innocence, or I surrender myself once more a prisoner."

"What!" exclaimed Oswald, with a melancholy smile, "doubtful still?" He advanced and took his companion by the hand, and continued in a kinder voice: "Ulrick, I have been a man of sin and sorrow; my pride has been humbled with the dust, my wisdom confounded by a child. Yet not to redeem the past—to avoid the last fearful ordeal which awaits me—would I pollute these lips with falsehood. The proofs I promised you exist; another hand than mine will yield them to thee. Give thy present hour to nature's claims—another will be found for honour's. Remember that thou hast a mother, whose heart throbs as if it would burst its bosom to enfold thee. Follow me—I will conduct thee to her."

There was a tone in the monk's voice which at once convinced Ulrick, and forbad reply. Its sadness touched him—its truthfulness confirmed him in his confidence. With the obedience, if not the simplicity, of a child, he followed his conductor to the room where his earliest benefactor and newfound parent waited him. Eagerly did the prelate, on his appearance, advance to meet him, for he loved him like a son. Ulrick's heart was the first which in his sorrows taught him his own was human—recalled him to himself—restored him to the world; and he was now returned to him, like the shipwrecked mariner whom all thought lost, through danger and through storm, doubly welcome to his lonely heart. Fervently, therefore, was the good man's benediction given, and grateful tears accompanied it.

"Ulrick," he said, as the youth rose from his knees, "there is a blessing as sacred even as the priest's—as grateful to the heart as the anointed prelate's holy words. Does not nature whisper thee it is thy mother's? Go, ask it" he added, "of the heart which

ROBERT OF NORMANDY IN DISGUISE.

yearns to give it thee; tell her she need not blush to call thee by the endearing name of son."

"I do believe thee," exclaimed the happy Edith, as she threw her arms around the neck of Ulrick, and imprinted a mother's holy kiss upon his cheek; "come to the widowed heart which through long years hath mourned thee as the dead, yet feels its sorrows overpaid in finding thee at last. Ulrick, my boy, my good and brave! my Edward's image! my life's only flower! the thrill which struck me when I first beheld thee was Nature struggling to proclaim thee

mine; and, dullard as I am, my heart was deaf to her mute eloquence, or I had known my son."

A flood of tears relieved the o'erfraught heart, which else had burst with too much happiness. The prelate felt that there were scenes too sacred even for his ministry to witness. Silently he withdrew from the apartment, followed by Father Oswald, into the cloisters, which for awhile he paced in silence, the aged monk watching his steps.

"Brother," he at last exclaimed, turning to Oswald, "thy penance upon earth hath indeed been sore, and the last blow surpasses human justice. Fearful as have been the crimes of thy son, I feel both for him and thee."

"I can bear it," replied the old man, with a firm voice. "His will who ruleth all things be accomplished!"

"If Heaven can pardon," resumed the bishop, "should man prove relentless? May not the life of thy unhappy and misguided boy be spared—spared for repentance and for future hope?"

"My lord, he is repentant. But the crime of sacrilege must be atoned; the insulted altar calls for expiation. Our duties both are painful; yours to yield him to the arm which condemns him to the flames; mine to reconcile the victim for the sacrifice. Shrink not from yours; I am prepared for mine."

The speaker hesitated for a moment, as if struggling with some internal weakness, and then threw himself upon his knees before the bishop, who instantly endeavoured to raise him; which the old man resisted.

"No!" he exclaimed, "this posture suits me best; it is a suppliant's. Grant me the only favour I ever asked of man."

"Name it, my son," replied his superior, anxious to pleasure him.

"Let not my son, the last of a line whose royal priesthood is lost in the midst of ages, be dragged like a peasant to the stake. Clad in his knightly armour, unshamed by degradation, let him die."

"Willingly, my son."

"The heart is willing, but the flesh is weak," continued Oswald. "I cannot see him die; but I will so prepare him for his fate, that you shall find an unresisting sacrifice. Till the last hour arrives, leave him with me and Heaven."

"Be it as you wish. Orders shall be given even in justice to remember mercy. His sufferings shall be brief."

"Not so," interrupted the monk. "I would not abridge one mortal pang; for oh!" he added, "they are all too litte to atone for sacrilege, neglected duty, and a soul perverted. Your blessing, holy father," he continued—"your blessing! Pray for me at the hour of daily sacrifice, when from thy sacred lips the supplication for offending man rises to Heaven!—remember him whose youth was darkness, and whose age was sorrow!"

The clanging of an iron heel upon the pavement caused them both to start. Meekly bowing, Father Oswald rose from his kness, after receiving the episcopal benediction, and directed his steps towards the prison, for his last interview with his unhappy son.

Even the approach of an armed knight— for such the stranger proved to be—would not have diverted the prelate's mind from the chain of thought in which his interview with the monk had thrown it, had he not recognised in the red-haired and coarse-visaged stranger the son of his sovereign—the same who, shortly after, under the title of William Rufus, succeeded to the crown, and lost both his crown and life by his vexatious tyranny. On recognising him, Herbert de Lozinga immediately recovered his courtly self-possession, and advanced to meet him.

"Thanks, my lord bishop, thanks," he exclaimed, with the bluntness which characterised his manners; "we doubt not of your sincerity, but something to restore the inner man were more welcome now than compliments. We have ridden hard, my lord."

No expression on the features of his hearer showed the prelate's high-bred scorn of his unpolished guest. By a silver call, which, after the manner of the age, he wore suspended by his side, he summoned a lay brother to his presence, to whom he communicated the necessary orders for an ample refection to be instantly served in his own private apartment.

"And so the Saxon clods would rise against us!" continued William. "By the hand of Rollo, but I will break their stubborn necks, or bend them to the yoke! I will not leave a Saxon franklin in his hall, fire and sword shall purge the land of all who bear the hated name. I will make England one vast hunting-ground, and chase them at my pleasure. Our father's health, my lord, we are told, breaks fast; let me but once be king!"

"Never with such views," said Herbert, "canst thou maintain thy seat; thy very nobles, William, would forsake thee. Think by how many ties the Saxon and the Norman bloods are linked, how many holy sympathies unite the conquerors and the conquered. By conciliation only canst thou hope to reign, or hold in peace thy crown."

"I'd rather hold it by my sword," impetuously answered the fiery prince.

"Crowns have often by the sword been won, but seldom held by it. Thou saidst but now thy father's days were numbered. Ask thyself, hast thou no rival near the throne whose claims may clash with thine, despite thy father's favour?"

William started, and remembered his elder brother, the unfortunate Robert, whom he eventually supplanted both in England and Normandy, and whose eyes were barbarously put out, to render him incapable of reigning, while he was a prisoner in Cardiff Castle— put out by order of his cruel and unnatural brother.

"My father, by his sword, won this fair isle, and may will it as he pleases," proudly answered the prince. "I am not to be checked by fears like these. By Heaven, prelate, did I deem thee false, I'd place thee where thy treason should be hurtless."

A transient flush for a moment clouded the usually pale features of the bishop, and his eye was lit by a fire which showed he had once been dangerous. Still, ever master of himself, he paused till the sentiment of anger had passed away, and then answered, in his usual cold and unimpassioned tone :

"I am not of those whom princes judge. Reserve, young man, your threats for those who fear them. Were it my will, prince as thou art, to send thee bound in chains unto thy elder brother, or place thy head upon the Tower of London, I'd find the means to do it. Treason to me! forget not, prince, I am of a line as noble as thine own."

The young prince, who well knew the influence which Herbert de Lozinga possessed amongst his countrymen, felt that he had gone too far. The right of his father to leave him the crown he had acquired, to the prejudice of his elder brother Robert, might be disputed; in such a case the bishop's voice would be most important. He smothered, therefore, his secret wrath, and had recourse to that hypocrisy for which he was distinguished.

"Forgive me, my good lord," he exclaimed, with an expression of frankness too transparent not to be seen through; "but children will sometimes quarrel with their tutors—you know your pleasure ever is our will."

At this moment the lay brother returned to inform his superior that the refection waited them.

"'Tis well," said the bishop. "Prince, I attend you."

His guest for a few moment's hesitated ; in his own treacherous, cruel nature, he doubted the sincerity of all men ; he was alone, in the power of a man whom he had indiscreetly threatened, and he judged his, from what his own conduct would have been an such an occasion.

"We are friends, my lord, I trust," he said. "Remember that I came hither on your summons, slightly attended, with full confidence in your well-known loyalty and faith. You will not wrong it ?"

"The man who came on Herbert de Lozinga's summons," replied his host, "were safe, even though my brother's blood crimsoned his hand. Eat of my bread, drink of my cup, and sleep beneath my roof in peace as well as safety."

But half satisfied, the young prince followed the prelate from the cloisters. The collation once dispatched, they remained for several hours in council, where the strong mind of the ecclesiastic completely subjugated the weak one of his guest, who determined at least, on the present occasion, to be guided by his experience, and conform himself to his wishes.

CHAPTER XIV.

Strange is the human heart—uncertain, wild,
Reason its slave—philosophy a child,
That vainly flutters on the rainbow wings
Of feeble reasons, weak imaginings.

LONG after the preceding interview, Father Oswald was still occupied in prayer with his son, whose repentance, at least, appeared sincere; humbly and devoutly he had received from his parent's hand the baptismal rite, whose regenerating waters wash all guilt away; a holy calm had succeeded the frantic ravings of despair, and Ernulf felt almost resigned to die. His armour, which he had taken off for the ceremony, was piled in one corner of the room; the font and tapers occupied the centre. As the penitent rose from his knees, his father removed the stole from his neck and placed it on the couch; as he did so the great bell of the church began its solemn peal—a signal to the citizens and inmates of the abbey that the execution was about to take place. Ernulf started at the sound; despite his resignation, he turned pale.

"Fear not, boy," said the old man; "in reconciling thee to heaven, I have saved thee from the penalties of earth. It were not just that thou shouldst suffer for thy crimes, while he, whose neglect perilled thy soul, escaped."

"What meanest thou, father?" demanded

the prisoner, a faint ray of hope once more returning to his heart.

"That I have provided for thee the means of safety," answered the old man. "Thinkest thou," he added, "I would see thee perish in the flames, and feel my sins had lit thy funeral pyre? Take this packet—it contains that which in a far distant land will guard thee against want; take it, together with my robe, and fly."

"And leave you here a prisoner in my place? Never, father—never; I am not so base as that."

"Even so," impassibly answered the monk; "what should I fear?"

"The vengeance of the church," replied his son.

"Ernulf, dismiss the thought; I swear to thee no human judgment will ever reach me for the act. Besides, if my own heart approves, I value not the censure of men's tongues. My robe will pass thee safe and unquestioned through the cloisters and the city. Once beyond the walls, thou knowest too well the country to be retaken. Hark!" he continued, as the bell again struck upon his ear, "time grows short. By the obedience which a son should pay his father, I command thee assume my robe and fly!"

The love of life is perhaps the last sentiment which abandons us, and Ernulf felt it with renewed force at every sound of the signal bell. The natural horror of death—and of such a death—decided him, and he hastily assumed the robe and cowl which Father Oswald had already laid aside. Calmly, and with an untrembling hand, the old man assisted him to arrange the disguise, and placed the packet in his hand.

"Farewell, my son!" he exclaimed, in a firm voice; "on earth me meet no more. Thy safety for ever banishes thee from England, and my career on earth is short: pray that its end be happy. Forgive the harshness that oppressed thy youth, the cold neglect which closed thy opening heart, as I forgive thy disobedience and thy crime. Farewell! A priest's and father's blessing rest upon thee!"

The speaker extended his arms over the disguised criminal as he spoke, and remained for a few moments absorbed in mental prayer. Gradually recovering himself, he led him to the door of the dungeon, opened it, pressed his hand for the last time as he passed through, then closed it between them for ever.

For some moments he listened to the receding footsteps of his son, and breathed more freely as they fell fainter and fainter upon his ear.

"He is safe!" exclaimed Oswald, with a smile of triumph. "I thank thee, Father, that the soul thou gavest has not through my most grievous sin been lost. Father and son may meet again with Thee."

The old man advanced to the corner of the room where the armour of Enulf was carefully piled together, and began to pray. Louder and louder the bell of the cathedral tolled as the crowds of citizens, soldiers, and knights, entered the precincts of the cathedral to witness the execution. The fat greasy burghers of Norwich squeezed and hustled each other for the best places, with as much vulgar brutality as attends a modern execution. A compact crowd filled the space between the west front and the old tower, since replaced by the Erpingham gate, leaving little more than sufficient space for the procession and the execution of the criminal. A large body of the bishop's retainers kept the ground, headed by their commander; and the abatial and episcopal banner floated from the turret of the church. The bishop's throne was erected on the right of the square formed by the soldiers, and the seats for the secular judges faced it. The latter had long been seated before the procession issued from the gates of the cathedral. The chant of the priesthood fell upon the ear, raising the solemn hymn of the church, the "Dies iræ."

> "The day of wrath, the dreadful day,
>   When all that lives must pass away;
>   When Time shall feel that he is old,
>   The sun his glorious race is told;
>   When every blazing star shall fall,
>   And nature wear one funeral pall;
>   When death and sin shall cease to reign,
>   Thy justice shall unchanged remain.
>   Dies iræ, dies illa,
>   Solvet seclum in favillâ.
>   The day of wrath—the trumpet's sound,
>   Shall call earth's varied nations round,
>   As, to meet the eternal doom,
>   They rise in myriads from the tomb.
>   'To judgment come!' the angel cries,
>   The groaning earth, the bursting skies,
>   Piercing creation's utmost bounds,
>   Shall echo back the appalling sounds.
>   Dies iræ, dies ill,
>   Solvet seclum in favillâ."

"They come at last," exclaimed one of the Saxon franklins, at the end of the hymn; "and see, the proud prelate heads them. His own turn," he muttered, "may not be long."

"What's that, friend, you murmured?" demanded George of Erpingham, who had overheard the words.

The indiscreet Saxon quailed beneath the glance of the fierce knight, like a whipped hound. Much as he feared the Normans, he feared the church still more—a sentiment which the scene he had come to witness was not likely to decrease.

"Nothing, sir knight," he stammered,

and looking confused; "mere idle thoughts —no more."

"Such thoughts are dangerous here. Keep them to thyself, Sir Franklin, and it shall go well with thee."

The arrival of the procession cut short all further reply.

First came a noble, bareheaded, bearing the banner of the clergy, followed by the monks two and two, chanting the litany of the saints; after them marched the dignitaries of the cathedral, followed by the bishop, clothed not in the pomp of purple, but in black cope and stole, in sign of penitence. On the appearance of the prelate a suppressed murmur arose among the people —on any other occasion they would have shouted—for they loved him for his charities, had mourned him dead, and rejoiced to find him living. The prisoner followed in complete armour, surrounded by the guards.

The bishop and the clergy were no sooner seated, than the criminal walked deliberately up to the stake, to which the executioner immediately attached him, while the civil judges pronounced his sentence. "How dost thou die?" demanded the marshal of the city, whose duty it was to record the answers of the prisoner.

"A penitent," replied a deep voice, which issued from the helmet of the victim, like an echo from the grave; "a Catholic and a Christian."

A shriek of mortal agony was heard at a distance in the crowd; and a monk, whom all took for Father Oswald, was seen trying to force his way through the dense mass of people.

"Apply the flames," firmly exclaimed the prisoner, upon whose ear the scream had fallen. "At once perform your office;—my soul to God, my ashes to the winds."

The fire was applied, and, in an instant, the flames blazed with fury; for Herbert de Lozinga had humanely ordered the wood which composed the pile to be saturated with spirits and resinous gums. Again the monks raised the requiem which implored mercy for the departing sinner's soul. But a voice was heard, louder than all their music, crying, "Forbear!" and the form of a frantic monk was seen, with superhuman strength, rending the yielding crowd, which gave way like a cleft stream before him. With a last effort he broke through the inner circle, sprang into the blazing pile, and endeavoured to release the victim from the stake; his cowl fell back as he did so, and all recognised Ernulf the squire, at whose execution they imagined themselves assisting.

"Save them!" exclaimed the bishop, starting from his seat, as a fearful suspicion crossed his mind—a suspicion, alas, but too true; for at the same instant the straps which fastened the helmet of the supposed criminal gave way, and fell into the flames, exposing to the horror-stricken gaze of all the well-known features of Father Oswald, who, to save his son, had thus contrived to take his place.

The very precautions taken to shorten the sufferings of the criminal rendered it impossible to save him: but he did not die alone: for his repentant son shared his death, and mingled his ashes with his. Sadly and silently the crowd dispersed, like men stricken with a mental palsy; the scene they had witnessed having displayed another page in that mysterious book, the human heart.

CHAPTER XV.

Off with his head! So much
For Buckingham.—SHAKSPERE.

 N the plain extending from the moat which surrounded the hill upon which Norwich Castle stands the lists were erected. The simplicity of the preparations showed that they were intended for no courtly tournament, but for an encounter where life and death were set upon the issue. Close to the exterior palisades a large lodge was built, adorned with purple hangings; over it floated the banners of Odo of Caen and his brother nobles, who were to act as judges of the fight. But the rest of the buildings were plain in the extreme. In the midst of the enclosed arena was a block and post, on the former of which the accused, if defeated, was to suffer death; while to the latter his name was to be affixed by the hands of the executioner in the event of his non-appearance, a mark of infamy more

degrading than even the pillory or modern outlawry.

The sun shone brightly on the scene; and, at an early hour, the troops of the confederated franklins marched to the spot, most of them wearing the long white frock peculiar to their nation, and which the carter's smock of the present day nearly resembles. Beneath it they could conveniently hide their arms, and appear to a casual observer a peaceful body of serfs and peasants, drawn together by curiosity to witness the approaching fight. Soon after the parties began to arrange themselves, the leaders of the enterprise observed, with secret dissatisfaction, that immediately a party of Saxons arrived, and took up their position on the ground, an equal number of Normans, all of whom were well armed, placed themselves beside them, and, without seeming to do so intentionally, so intersected them, that all possibility of the conspirators acting in concert was destroyed. Several times they manœuvred to change positions, but were as often outmanœuvred by the Normans, who, whether by accident or design, thwarted by their evolutions every attempt which the Saxons made to unite themselves in one or more compact bodies. The only party which presented anything like an appearance of having unity were the followers of Edda, a numerous body of men, well armed, and commanded by a youthful knight, whose face was hid by his visor, but whose firm step and active movements showed him to be in the full pride of strength and manhood.

The Norman nobles were the last who made their appearance upon the ground; most of them, as they did so, resigned the command of their vassals to their esquires, and proceeded to the castle, where a council had been summoned by the bishop, to be held previous to the proceedings in the lists. One by one the Saxon franklins were sent for on different pretexts; so that, by the time Herbert de Lozinga arrived, escorted by a large body of his followers, under the conduct of George of Erpingham, most of the leaders, whether Norman or Saxon, were assembled in the great hall. Edda, the most powerful chief of the conquered race, walked by the side of the prelate, who divided his conversation with him and the red-haired stranger, whose real rank was known only to himself. Many a knight and vavassour followed in his train, bound by the tenure of their lands to do him feudal homage. As a Norman baron, he ranked with the most powerful; and in his double capacity of Bishop of Norwich and Abbot of Hulm, with the richest ecclesiastics in the kingdom; added to which, his known favour with the

Conqueror, and office of chancellor, made him one of the most important personages in the realm, and his influence was courted and respected by all.

A tall gaunt man appeared amongst the stragglers in the bishop's train, the mere sight of whom seemed to excite the indignation of the crowd; even the men-at-arms, who escorted him to protect him from the insults of the mob, kept at a respectful distance from him, and laughed whenever a gibe more bitter, or a curse more fierce, saluted his appearance. It was the city executioner. Whether indifference or philosophy rendered him insensible to the degradation of his position, it might have been difficult to decide; but he walked on, amidst the jests, curses, and hootings of the people, with an impassibility of feature which a Stoic might have envied. He was clothed in red—the colour of his office—and wore a large black barret, which rendered the ghastly hue of his features more apparent; in his hand he carried a leathern bag, sufficiently capacious to contain either the head of a victim or the implements of his fearful and disgusting office.

"Is Saint Peter taking tithe of heads today," whispered Brenner, one of the few Saxon leaders who remained upon the ground, "that he walks with such a collector in his train? The headsman is a bird of evil omen; ill befalls the purpose or the man whose path he crosses. Would I had met his sight on any day than this!"

"Amen!" replied his companion. "The only consolation is, he is without his axe. Have you observed," he added, looking cautiously around to assure himself that no one could overhear him, "how the Normans flank our men? I trow there is more of purpose than of chance in it. I fear we are betrayed, or at least suspected."

Brenner had previously, in his own mind, made the same observation, but remained silent, not wishing to alarm his companion by acknowledging his suspicions. At this moment they were joined by a third party— Armand of the Wold, one of the petty franklins, compelled by his position to follow blindly in the wake of his more powerful chief; a shrewd, keen, calculating man, always ready to turn with the tide he was too weak to stem. The gloomy restlessness of his features showed that he was ill at ease.

"Who has seen Herman of the Burg?" he demanded; "why is he absent at such a moment? For two days he has not appeared amongst us. I like not this."

The two first speakers confessed that they had neither seen nor could explain his absence—an avowal followed by immediate silence, each calculating how far his neighbour might be a partner in the treason, if any such existed. Brenner was the first to break it.

"Most of our party, on one pretext or another, have been summoned to the castle," whispered the first speaker. "There are invitations a prudent man always should decline."

"Especially his enemy's," observed Armand.

"And, above all, a Norman's. Ill befall the day they first set foot on England's happy soil. But look," continued Brenner, "how the bishop lures the noble Edda to the council. I thought his white hairs covered more wisdom."

"Or less treason," muttered Armand.

At this moment the seneschal, wearing his chain and carrying his wand of office, approached the speakers, and commanded them to attend the council about to sit in the castle. The summons was given in the name of the bishop chancellor. As the officer was attended by a party of men-at-arms, resistance would have been equally foolish as useless. After a mutual glance, which seemed to say, "We are fairly caught," they bowed in acquiescence, and followed their conductor to the council.

The great hall of Norwich Castle was lined with men-at-arms, and a strong body guarded the different doors. All whose rank entitled them to the *entrée* were freely admitted; but once there, none but the Normans were allowed egress. Whenever a Saxon approached the entrance, he was respectfully informed that the council was about to commence, and invited to remain in his place—the tone of the invitation rendering it equivalent to a command. Thus suspicion and mistrust were at their height. The absence of Herman was the subject of many a comment; nor did the appearance of Odo of Caen and his brother nobles in complete armour tend to tranquillise the doubts of the conspirators, which at last became so painful that the clash of arms which announced the arrival of the bishop sounded as a relief to them; at least they would learn the worst, for the doubt of ill is sometimes more difficult to bear than even ill confirmed.

As if with an instinctive feeling of hostility, or of an approaching contest, the two parties had formed into separate groups, engaged in hurried whispered conversation, when Herbert de Lozinga, with his train, entered the hall. There was an expression of care upon his brow, although both step and air were firm as ever. Mirvan raised his visor as he advanced to meet him.

"Welcome, my lord and father," he ex-claimed; "we attend your summons. Please you, we have business which the sword must judge, if the accused appear; if not, the executioner. Let us to the council, and at once."

The cold, though respectful, tone of the speaker showed that he looked upon the prelate as his enemy. Indeed, he doubted not but that it was by his secret contrivance Ulrick, whom he still continued to regard as his father's murderer, had been so singularly removed from prison.

"Patience, young man!" replied Herbert. "Is the thirst of blood so strong within thee, thou canst not wait one hour? Fear not but the accused will appear; my word shall be your gage that he will meet you."

The young earl bowed respectfully, and pointed to the chair at the end of the dais for the bishop to take his seat.

"Not so," he said, in answer to the mute invitation. "There is one amongst us to whom all claims must yield. Prince," he added, turning to the stranger, "assume your seat, and let us to the affairs of moment which detain us."

The appearance of the Conqueror's favourite son produced a varied feeling in the minds of the assembly. By the Normans he was greeted with a shout of triumph; by the Saxons he was received in sullen silence. They felt that they were betrayed—that the last hope of shaking off the Conqueror's yoke was lost.

"Venerable prelate, and you, noble peers," said the prince, as soon as he was seated, "our first duty is to inquire into the cause of the death of our faithful friend, Hugh de Bigod, to avenge his memory, to track the murderer's steps, if living; if dead, to consign his name to infamy and execration. Who are the accusers?"

"I am," exclaimed Mirvan, eagerly advancing.

"And I," calmly repeated the bishop.

"But whom do you accuse?" demanded the prince, first addressing himself to Mirvan.

"The man whom I once called my dearest friend; the man I would have trusted with more than my life—with honour; the man whose soul I once held so pure—I almost blush at my unworthiness to call him friend—Ulrick, of what race I know not, but proved by the word of a noble knight, now absent, to be of gentle blood—Ulrick, the ward of my lord bishop there," he added, pointing half scornfully to the prelate, "whose word e'en now, I pray you all remember, was given for his appearance in the lists to meet the charge against him."

"Fear not, sir earl," interrupted Edda, proudly, "but he will keep his word."

"And you, my lord, whom do you accuse?" demanded William, addressing Herbert de Lozinga, whose countenance had never varied during Mirvan's speech.

"Herman of the Burg," he calmly replied.

Several of the Saxons started, for they knew by whose hand the deceased earl had fallen; the murderer had avowed it to more than one or two; but on Mirvan the accusation fell like a thunder-clap. 'Tis true that from his rough, unamiable manner, he had never liked his kinsman, but he had ever looked upon him as a man of unblemished honour, and as such would have defended his reputation with his life. His indignation, therefore, at the accusation was as unbounded as his astonishment, in which latter sentiment even the Norman nobles, great as was their dislike to Herman, shared.

"Prince," he exclaimed, "this is a mere mockery of justice; the accused retorts on his accuser. I dare not further trust myself to speak, lest I forget the reverence that's due to age, to sacred function, and this royal presence; but ask him, pray ask him upon what grounds he dares accuse my absent kinsman."

"You hear," interrogatively observed the Prince; "on what proofs do you accuse him?"

"On his own confession," solemnly answered the bishop, "witnessed by these noble peers."

"His own confession!" mechanically repeated the young earl, as doubting the evidence of his senses.

"Thyself shalt be the judge," continued the prelate, drawing from his breast the parchment which had been found in the breastplate of the unhappy Ernulf, and which our readers will doubtless remember had been attested by the signatures and seals of Odo of Caen and the Norman nobles on the night of Herman's execution. The document, which detailed every circumstance, had been written by the murderer, and given to his esquire to convey to the assembled franklins in the caves of Whitlingham, as a still further proof of his devotion to the cause of Saxon independence. Every word was in his own handwriting, which Mirvan was well acquainted with, and witnessed by his arms.

"What have I read!" exclaimed the astonished and horror-stricken youth, as he let fall the scroll. "If this be true, as I confess it is, I am indeed doubly unhappy. I have lost my father, and have wronged my friend."

"That word regains him," exclaimed Ulrick, who, on a signal given by Herbert de Lozinga, entered the hall, and advanced gracefully to his accuser. "Mirvan," he added, "my heart hath never done thee wrong; e'en in my dungeon I accused not thee; e'en at the scaffold had not cursed thy name."

A tear dimmed the eyes of the two friends as they embraced. Let not the worldling sneer at the confession of their weakness. Such weakness is more beautiful than strength. Earth hath many a gem more prized, but none more pure than manly friendship's honest, priceless tear.

"But where," exclaimed Mirvan, "is the fiend who hath deceived me—whose hand is stained with my dead father's blood? —Prince and nobles," he added, turning towards the dias, "I demand on Herman of the Burg the judgment of his peers. The felon hath confessed. The doom! the doom! I claim the murderer's doom!"

"Herman," solemnly answered the bishop, at the same time taking the speaker by the hand, and leading him to the window, "can fear no human judgment more; he hath already passed a tribunal more awful far than man's. Behold!" One of the men-at-arms threw open the window as the prelate spoke, and Mirvan beheld, with surprise, the executioner in the act of affixing the head of the assassin on the post in the centre of the lists. For a moment he gazed upon it with a feeling of fierce satisfaction, which gradually yielded to a nobler sentiment; he felt that human justice was accomplished, and shudderingly withdrew from the hideous spectacle as the soldier closed the casement. The effect upon the assembled Saxons was to produce consternation and dismay. Ignorant of the real cause of the culprit's death, they felt convinced they were betrayed, and slowly began to disperse, too happy in being permitted to escape. The Normans suffered their departure unopposed—such were the instructions they had received: but the leaders of the contemplated insurrection were not so fortunate; they still remained virtually prisoners in the castle. Shortly afterwards the countess, Matilda, and Isabel, entered the hall; and as the subject of Ulrick's birth was gone into, it is unnecessary to repeat the proofs by which his rank and claims to Stanfield and the vast inheritance of Edda were established; even the Normans confessed themselves satisfied, and frankly admitted him as their peer amongst them. If the heart of the acknowledged youth beat high, it was when his eyes encountered the blushing cheek of Matilda; if he felt the sentiment of pride, it was when he grasped

THE FATHER AND SON IN THE CONDEMNED CELL.

the hand of his recovered friend, and felt that he could claim his friendship upon equal terms.

Herbert de Lozinga approached the seat of the young prince, and whispered to him. "Your promise, prince! your promise!"

William turned uneasily upon his chair, like a man who sought to escape from something distasteful to him, but in vain; the calm and cold eye of the bishop followed his every glance; he felt that there was no escape from his plighted word.

"Herald," he said, "perform your duty."

The officer advanced into the midst of the hall, and thrice proclaimed Ulrick Earl of Stanfield, and heir of Saxon Edda; calling upon all who felt disposed to dispute his claims to stand forth and speak, or remain for ever dumb! No voice replied to him. At each pause in the ceremony the prince cast a scrutinising glance on the young earl, whom the decision stripped of a fair portion of his large inheritance; but the heart of Mirvan was too generous to entertain any selfish feeling. William, therefore, had no choice left but to proceed.

The prelate and Edda led the newly-acknowledged noble to the prince's chair; who, taking his hands between his own, received his oath of allegiance; and solemnly confirmed, as regent of the kingdom, and his father's representative, the act of investiture; the prelate, as he did so, pronouncing a loud "Amen!"

"And now, Saxons and Normans," exclaimed William, "a few words to each.—To you," he said, turning to the discouraged franklins, "your plots are known; your treasons all unveiled; you are here within our judgment-hall, surrounded by our faithful barons and our loyal troops; the block within the lists; the headsman ready at our call. What ransom can ye offer for your lives?"

There was a silence; the Normans gazed sternly upon their rivals, who felt that they were powerless within their hands, and each internally cursed bitterly the memory of him by whom they had been deluded to their ruin.

The prince enjoyed their confusion, for he was no generous enemy, and again demanded, in a tone of taunting mockery, which displayed the natural cruelty of his disposition, and augured ill for the future, "What ransom, Saxons, for your lives?"

"Thy princely word," exclaimed the bishop, anxious to end the scene.

"And your intercession, my good lord," continued William, recalled by the grave tone of the speaker's voice to the prudence of conciliating the conquered race, as a means to his own accession to the throne. "Franklins," he added, "you are pardoned; your forfeit lands and lives are spared upon the payment of such fines as we hereafter shall impose. But remember, 'tis the last time that Mercy speaks; be wiser for the future, and tempt the lion's wrath no more, lest he should turn and rend ye."

"And for the future," said Herbert de Lozinga, advancing to the centre of the hall, "let discord end between the Norman and Saxon race; let hostile blood unite to heal the wounds which long have drained this war-divided land. Lady," he added, advancing and taking Matilda by the hand, "this is a bond would prove a pledge of unity more strong than Saxon force or Norman steel could break—a bond of peace and love. Read I aright that blush?"

Matilda turned from the impassioned gaze of her lover, who looked as if life and death hung upon her reply, to read her brother's will, whose consent alone could ratify her union.

The generous Mirvan knew too well his sister's heart not to interpret its unspoken wishes. First embracing Ulrick, he led him to the prelate, saying as he did so:—

"Father, thy wisdom interprets our unspoken wishes; complete thy holy purpose."

"Thus, then," resumed the prelate, "I do betroth ye. May Heaven bless the union of two hearts formed by their virtues for each other!"

Devoutedly did the countess and the venerable Edda join in the benediction upon the last descendant of their ancient race; and every voice within the hall, *save one*, joined in the shout, "Hail to the Lord of Stanfield! hail to his promised bride!"

On the evening of the important day on which the scenes we have endeavoured to describe took place, William had retired to his chamber in the castle; for he had become the guest of the unsuspicious earl, and was arranging himself for the approaching banquet. Robert of Artois, who had long been in his confidence, was standing near a table, covered with open caskets full of jewel-work, and which supported the rude mirror in which the prince was complacently contemplating his person—for, like most plain men, he was excessively vain. His hasty, snatchy manner showed that he was either discontented or ill at ease—his companion could not tell which, but waited patiently for the enigma he had undoubtedly been summoned to hear.

"Normans!" muttered the prince— "Normans! we are no longer worthy of the name. The hound hath changed places with the deer! We raise the head we ought to tread upon! Ah! Robert," he added, pretending to see his companion for the first time, "what thinkest thou of this goodly marriage this coupling of the carrion raven with the generous falcon's brood? We had better all turn Capuchin, and preach on Christian charity. Our swords are useless now, unless we turn them into hooks to reap with. We shall soon, good Robert, be no longer masters in the land we won."

"Not if your highness wishes to prevent the knot the holy bishop fancies he has tied. Norman hearts and hands may still be found asking no better warrant for the deed than the expression of your royal will. Speak but the word, and it is done."

"Sayest thou?" said William, turning suddenly round, and fixing a scrutinising glance upon him, as if to read his very soul; for long habit of dissimulation in himself had taught him to suspect the sincerity of others. The ambitious noble met his gaze, and in an instant they understood each other, so prompt is the intelligence of guilt. "But how to be accomplished?" demanded the prince, leaving him to propose the crime he feared to ask him.

"Remove the bridegroom," coolly answered his companion; "that were the easiest way to solve the riddle."

"No; that were dangerous. Let the clown mate him with some Saxon wench, and hold his lands in peace—at least," he added, "for the present. Lozinga loves him like a son, and I have no wish to play my future sceptre against his pastoral staff. His is a temper not to be trifled with. Wouldst thou believe it, Robert? The proud priest threatened that he would send me to my half-witted brother if I presumed to cross his path again; nay, dared to vaunt his vassal line as equal to my own."

"The ambitious traitor!" exclaimed Robert of Artois, "he must be silenced. Such men are dangerous."

"Let him rest; he is as much beyond our reach as Ulrick is beneath it. The prelate and myself, we understand each other. Whilst I act with what he is pleased to call justice and conciliation, he will not oppose our father's disposition in our favour. Let me but once securely feel the crown upon my brow, fear not but I will reckon with him fully for this day. The dotard dreamt not that with every threat he aimed an arrow at my brother's life—curse on the chance which made him born before me!"

"Why not, then, secure the bride?" demanded the ready panderer, who more than suspected the cause of the speaker's humour, well knowing how susceptible he was to the thrall of beauty, and how reckless by what means he gratified his licentious passions.

"Thou hast hit my very thought," said the prince with a smile of approbation; "but how may this be done?"

"Nothing more easy."

"Explain thyself."

"This very night the noble maidens propose to attend our lady's shrine, where prayers are nightly offered up for the repose of Earl de Bigod's soul. They are too coy to grace your highness's banquet with their presence. What if some able fowler spread the net, and cage the birds on their return?"

"Where to find such a friend?"

"I'll be' that friend," replied Robert. "Your highness knows that I would peril body as well as soul to serve your pleasures. My castle of Filby is but three hours ride; it hath ere now contained as fair a prize as these sweet piping dames. Besides," he added, "the distance is so short you might yourself visit my stronghold, whenever charity inclind your heart to solace the lone captive."

A smile of mutual understanding followed, and the prince and his unworthy favourite separated; the former to lavish hollow courtesies where he meditated the foulest wrong; the latter to arrange the treacherous snare in which he hoped to entangle the unguarded steps of trusting innocence.

CHAPTER XVI.

A land of slaves shall ne'er be mine:
Dash down yon bowl of Samian wine !--BYRON.

 HE banquet, after the fashion of the times, waxed rough and boisterous in the hall of the old castle. Never had the fickle William seemed in a more gracious mood; twice had he pledged to the union of Ulrick and Matilda in the circling cup, calling on Saxon and Norman hearts to join him in the toast. All were fascinated with his open manner and seeming sincerity; and all, save one, deceived by them. Herbert de Lozinga had watched his impassioned glances when he beheld Matilda in the hall—the look which followed her retiring footsteps; and, although he anticipated no attempt at outrage, he determined to have an eye upon him. As the banquet proceeded, his suspicions were still further strengthened by the looks of triumph which flashed from his fierce eye whenever the maiden's name became the theme of conversation.

Amongst the minstrels who occupied the gallery opposite the dais was Hella, the Saxon—admitted by all who loved the joyous science to be the chief of the all but extinct bardic tribe. Many doubted, indeed, if he were even Christian, so devoted did he appear to the old superstitions and traditions of his race, so intense was his hatred of the conquerors. It had needed all the eloquence of Edda, whom he venerated as one of the last who shared in the blood of Hengist, to induce him to be present at the banquet; nor was it till after he had been repeatedly called for that he descended into the hall with his magic harp to sing before the assembly. So great was his renown, so intense the expectation of the Normans, few of whom had ever heard his song, that even the voices of the noisiest were hushed ere the gifted strain broke forth :—

" What spell can consecrate the word?
Not priestly prayer, or kingly word;
Nor e'en the deeper spell which lies
In woman's wondrous, sunlit eyes;
No! nor the minstrel's verse of flame,
A nation's shout, the breath of fame,
Can yet the holy spell afford
To consecrate the warrior's sword.

But when drawn for broken laws,
In nature's right he sternly draws,
When liberty expiring cries,
And wrongs from hill and valley rise;
The blood by tyrants rudely shed,
A nation's tears for freedom fled,
These, these the holy spell afford
To consecrate the warrior's sword."

The few Saxons who were present hung their heads in shame; to them it was like the song of their captivity. The Normans heard the strain in gloomy silence; it sounded like a reproach upon their tyranny and misrule.

"Thou hast chosen a strange theme for our banquet, friend," exclaimed the prince; "but though our ears are nice, thy skill must not go unrewarded."

He took from his neck a chain of gold, of no great value, and sent it by his page to the aged bard, who received it with a courtly reverence, although he answered with a mocking tongue:

"The praise of princes is our noblest guerdon. Gentle page, it must not be said that Hella was ungrateful to the bearer of so precious a gift; wear this," he added, taking from his own neck a chain whose value more than doubled the Norman's, and which he hung carelessly round the neck of the youth; "and sometimes think upon the poor bard's gift." So saying, he directed his harp-bearer to take up the instrument, and with a stately step left the hall.

At a signal from the bishop, the Norman minstrels sang the praise of Rollo, and the glories of his race; the nobles listened to the exciting strain, and, in their enthusiasm, forgot the aged Saxon and his song.

For the third time, with a flushed brow, William arose from his elevated seat to give forth the hollow pledge of amity and peace; when an alarm was heard without, and the seneschal, bleeding and unhelmed, rushed into the midst of the assembly. All started at the sight, and the hand of many a knight was laid upon his sword.

"Speak," demanded the bishop; "what hath befallen?"

"To arms, nobles and knights," exclaimed the faithful officer. "Returning from the cathedral, the noble ladies Isabel and Matilda have been carried off; their escort was too feeble to protect them."

The eyes of Mirvan and Ulrick remained riveted upon the speaker, as if they scarcely comprehended the intelligence, so completely were they stunned by the blow. The prelate's searching glance was fixed upon the prince, who quailed beneath it. "Doubtless by Saxons," he stammered.

"By Normans, noble prince—by Normans! I knew too well the taste of Norman steel to be deceived, despite their Saxon dress. I'll swear their brands were Norman."

William scowled upon the officer with a look of hate. The sturdy soldier, conscious of his integrity, met his gaze unmoved. While the nobles were busy in consultation, Herbert de Lozinga drew the commander of his troops, George of Erpingham, aside, and whispered something in his ear. Whatever was the nature of the communication, it evidently surprised the stalwart knight; for, for the first time in his life, he hesitated to obey. The rapid conversation which followed removed, however, his objections; for, touching his sword in sign of fidelity, he withdrew. The bishop, instead of following his example, concealed himself behind the floating arras with which the walls of the banquet-hall were hung. At the same moment Hella, the bard, entered the assembly, and approaching Ulrick with a stately step, exclaimed :

"Thy sword! thy sword! the wolf is in thy fold! the vulture bears the trembling dove to its dark nest! Last of a race I love! why standst thou idle here?—to horse! let manly deeds answer unmanly outrage! strike for thy country's wrongs, thy outraged love, or see thy bride become the Norman's scorn!"

All the nobles present, Saxons as well as Normans, deeply felt the outrage, and rushed from the chamber, calling to arms as they did so; the alarm bell sent forth its deep loud note, and added to the horror of the scene. The treacherous prince, the contriver of the cruel scheme, paced the rush-strewn floor, triumphant in his villany; and, as he thought alone, his meditations were soon interrupted by Robert of Artois; who, having succeeded in his expedition, had thrown off his disguise, and returned to the castle, lest his absence should be remarked; leaving his followers, long accustomed to such deeds of violence, to conduct the prisoners to his stronghold of Filby.

"Thou art a bold falconer," whispered the prince, "thou hast struck the quarry fairly. Hadst thou silenced yon prating seneschal, all had been unsuspected. Despite your followers' disguise, he swears that they are Normans."

"Let him swear; oaths cannot harm us, prince. I must away to join the pursuit, lest I should be suspected. In the morning take your departure as if for London. Once beyond the city, dismiss your train, and turn your horse's head to Filby, where thou wilt find the sweetest bird that ever pined within its iron cage. Thou knowest the way to tame her."

With these words the ready panderer bowed and withdrew. William was about to follow his example, when the prelate, quitting his concealment, boldly confronted him. The tyrant saw in an instant that he was discovered. For a few moments they stood gazing on each other—the countenance of the prince pale with fear and confusion, that of the bishop full of contempt.

"So," exclaimed the latter, "this is the way thy royal word is kept! Thou hast broken thine oath, outraged the roof which shelters thee, risked plunging the land in civil war, to gratify thy passions. What prevents that I proclaim thy treason, and yield thee to the Saxons?"

"Thine own ambition, priest," doggedly answered William.

"My ambition!"

"Once king, thou knowest this hand can raise thee to a height but second to my own —the primate's envied throne!"

"Vain man!" replied Herbert, "the hermit's cell would please me better than the mitred stall. Power is worthless when the heart is ashes. I come not to implore, but to command thee. Resign thy victims, and I may consent once more to spare thee the brand of public scorn—to shield thee from the avenging swords of those whose honour thou wouldst stain. Decide!"

"Never!" exclaimed the prince, foaming with rage. "I love the fair Matilda, and rather would forego the crown itself than yield her beauties to thy favoured minion. Thou hast heard my answer."

"But mine is yet unspoken," as proudly replied the bishop. "For thy brave father's sake I would have spared thee, but now the will of Heaven and justice must be done."

He advanced towards the door which opened from the banquet hall, as if to quit the apartment or to summon aid.

The baffled tyrant, perceiving his design, threw himself between, and drawing his sword, held it levelled at the prelate's breast, to impede his departure. For a moment they stood like the stag and hound at bay, gazing on each other in silence—the churchman calm and stern, the prince trembling with passion and excitement. "You pass not on your life!" he cried.

"Advance one step," said Herbert, drawing up his person to its stately height, "lay but a finger on my sacred robe, and I will bind thee in a spell shall paralyse thy soul! Not to thy honour or thy sense of justice do I now appeal. Though lost to every tie of honour and humanity, thy terrors are my safety. The brand of Europe, and the church's curse, thou darest not meet. Fool —coward—villain!" he added, as the sword of William gradually inclined towards the ground, "I scorn, deride thy vain attempt! Back, ruffian, back—I pass thee or I perish!"

With his eye sternly fixed upon the prince, the prelate moved towards the door. Thrice the weapon was raised, but its point was as often turned aside when the glance of Herbert de Lozinga encountered his. With frantic rage he dashed it to the ground, muttering as he did so:

"'Tis true; I dare not take thy life."

William had already determined in his own mind the line of conduct to pursue. Once freed from his accuser's presence, he would mount his horse and ride to Filby. There he doubted not but he might defy the outraged lovers and their friends; for what Norman chief would march against him when once the royal banner was displayed? Herbert knew too well the risk of Matilda's honour to leave him even for a moment alone. Advancing to the door, he merely waved his hand, when George of Erpingham and a body of about sixty men, all completely armed, and wearing their visors down, entered the banquet hall. William trembled at the sight, and involuntarily looked around to find his sword.

"Wouldst murder me?" he cried, glaring on the prelate.

The bishop deigned not to reply, but addressing himself to George of Erpingham, who awaited his orders, said:

"Danger and treason are abroad. His highness goes to my poor palace; escort him thither with all due honour; let none approach him, or exchance a single word. I rely on thy fidelity and knightly faith in this."

"Traitors!" exclaimed William, "know ye not who I am? Dearly shall ye rue this outrage on your prince! Rather arrest yon plotting priest! Obey my orders, and I swear, e'en by my honour, that riches, favours beyond ambitious dreams, shall recompense the deed!"

"Honour!" interrupted Herbert, contemptuously; "does not the word blister thy tongue, palsy thy craven heart? The violator of innocence, the perjurer, and the robber dares talk of honour! Prince, spare thy eloquence; thou canst not corrupt thy guard; they speak no Norman tongue. Away with him!"

"Should he resist?" demanded Epingham, through his visor.

"Force must be employed."

"Should he escape?"

The bishop fixed his glance upon the prisoner, and paused ere he replied, wishing the import of his speech to be truly understood.

"Level thine arquebus, and strike him dead."

With these last words he quitted the apartment; and William, seeing that resistance was in vain, resigned himsef to his fate. His guards closed around him, and conducted him to the bottom of the staircase, where a close litter was in waiting. For an instant he hesitated, and looked around, as if to summon assistance. None appeared; and the few torches held by the soldiers showed him the arquebus in the hands of the mysterious knight. Inwardly cursing his fate, and the being who had crossed it, he entered the litter, and in less than an hour found himself a close prisoner in the loftiest tower of the bishop's palace.

CHAPTER XVII.

There is no pain like love to hatred turned:
Hell hath no fury like a woman scorned.—OLD PLAY.

N their arrival at Filby the fair captives were conducted to a strongly barred chamber, in the centre of the keep, and left by their ruffian captors to themselves. For awhile they sat on the rude couch—the only attempt at comfort in their prison—in speechless dismay. So sudden was the transition from happiness to despair, that both were equally stunned by the blow. To all their entreaties for an explanation, and tempting offers for freedom, their conductors had maintained a sullen silence, and imagination conjured up a thousand terrors more fearful than even the dark reality of their fate.

Isabel, from the natural buoyancy of her disposition, was the first to recover something like composure. "Do not weep, coz—do not weep," she exclaimed, endeavouring to soothe the wretched Matilda, who sat beside her, clasping her hand in hers. "Perhaps we are only captured for the sake of extorting ransom; we are no village maidens, to be spirited from our homes without an effort being made to succour us. Many a lance ere this is laid in rest, and many a pennon given to the winds. Ulrick and Mirvan will search the world but they will find us; nor will Odo of Caen tamely bear this insult to the sister of his affianced bride. Trust me, that many an hour of future joy will repay us

for the present hour. Dearly the Saxon ruffians shall repent this insult!"

"These are no Saxon outlaws," replied Matilda, struggling for firmness as she spoke; "but Normans, girl. This blow is struck by those of our own race. Didst thou not mark the armour of the knight who headed the foul enterpise?"

"Normans! sayst thou, coz? Impossible! they must be Saxons; who else would dare assail De Bigod's daughter?"

Matilda mournfully shook her head in token of denial. Accustomed from infancy to the military peculiarities which distinguished the two races, her practised eye was not to be deceived; she had recognised the Norman chief in Robert of Artois, despite his simple visor and disguise, and it was impossible to root the strong conviction from her soul.

"Normans!" again iterated Isabel; "what can be their motive—plunder or revenge?"

"Whom have we ever wronged, to provoke the latter?" said Matilda. "And who would dare avow the baseness of an act like this, by demanding of Ulrick or my brother ransom for their brides! No," she added bitterly; "I fear worse outrage yet."

Isabel bounded from her seat like the fawn startled by the hunter's step. Her cousin's words revealed a danger more fearful than her terrors had yet painted; but her courage rose with the peril: indignation filled her heart; and although her cheek was pale, insulted virtue flashed from her speaking eyes.

"Let not the ruffian leader of this enterprise hope to find in a daugher of my race," she cried, "a reed, whom the storm of violence can bend or captivity appal; there is a refuge which even insult must respect, and vice cannot approach."

"True," replied Matilda; "death—honour's last shield, and virtue's sure defence."

The word sounded dismally in the vast and dimly lighted chamber where they sat. It was evident, from the preparations made to receive them, that they were expected, for a coarse repast had been prepared, mingled, however, with some degree of luxury; for although the viands were of the plainest description, the flagons and drinking-cups were of silver, then only used in the monasteries and castles of the nobles.

"Stay," said Isabel, whose eyes had been mechanically resting on the ill-assorted banquet, and who, struck by a sullen idea, advanced towards the table, "this may, perchance, afford some clue to our vile gaoler's name." She caught up the massive flagon as she spoke, and advanced with it to one of the torches stuck in an iron sconce upon the wall. The light fell upon a shield rudely graved upon the precious metal; its blazon was a bend ingrailed, surmounted by a lion's head. Both started as they gazed upon it, for they recognised at once the well-known arms of Robert of Artois. To Isabel of Bayeux this was an additional cause of fear, for she well knew the desperate character of the bad man who bore it. Twice had she rejected his unwelcome suit, the last time with a contempt which she well knew had stung his pride. Rather would she have found herself the captive of the vilest chief who lived by petty plunder, than in the power of that bold, revengeful man.

"Isabel," she cried, clinging to her cousin, and giving way to her not unnatural terrors, "thou hast read the fearful mystery aright: these are no Saxon plunderers; ransom is not their object, for twice hath Robert of Artois dared to pollute my ear with his false tale of love. But I am rightly served," she added, bitterly. "Why did I not unfold his insolence to those who would have crushed the hateful serpent ere it had twined its venomed fold around me?"

It was now Matilda's turn to soothe her affrighted cousin, whom the discovery of her captor's name had quite unnerved; like most persons of a quiet and retiring nature, she possessed that latent courage which rises with the danger of occasion, and in the deep recesses of her innocent heart she found a strength where late was nought but timidity and weakness.

"Courage, courage," she cried, repressing her own tears to assuage her companion's, "all hope hath not yet abandoned us; though human eyes may fail to penetrate our prison, the eye of Heaven is on us, and doubt not, coz, but our guardian angels watch us even here. Soon may my brother's banner circle round these walls, and lay their towers in the dust. Mirvan will come and find thee."

"Dead!" said Isebel, interrupting her; "for if he come not soon, terror too sure will kill me. Matilda!" she added, throwing her arms suddenly round her cousin's neck, "by our girlish friendship, our sister love, the tie of blood between us, promise me one thing, or my brain will turn, and reason totter on her seated throne."

"Name it, dearest girl!"

"Let not the ruffian tear us from each other; while with thee, I can endure his threats; alone, I should go mad. Thou," she added, passionately, "canst have nought to fear; I am alone the victim. Had not thy ill-starred fortune held thee to my side, thou hadst escaped this last extreme of fate. 'Tis I who have undone thee. Wilt thou not promise me?"

"I will!" replied Matilda, willing to soothe her; "nothing but violence shall tear thee from me. Should force be used?"

"Kill me!" exclaimed Isabel; "arm thine hand with Roman courage, and strike me dead before thee. By thy brother's love, thine own unsullied purity of soul, thy house's honour, and thy virgin truth, pledge me to this!"

There was a mutual pause; Matilda eyed the no longer trembling girl, who stood erect before her, and read the sincerity of her request in her firm glance and look of almost prayer. The request was terrible to one of her gentle nature—terrible from the love she bore the tender victim—terrible from the danger which surrounded them. Calmly she advanced from the couch on which they both had been seated towards the table, and taking up a small sharp knife, concealed it in her bosom. Isabel saw the action and understood it. A slight flush suffused her pallid cheek, but passed as quickly as it came; her only comment was a kiss upon the brow of the heroic girl. Matilda understood it.

"It is, indeed, a terrible and last resort," she said: "but should all else fail, I will be near thee; fear not, Isabel, by our mutual love, living the villain's arms shall never clasp thee."

The exhausted girl, overpowered by the violence of her emotions, sank into the arms of her courageous cousin in whose promise she beheld her last resource against dishonour or a life of misery.

That same night Herbert de Lozinga was seated in his oratory. He had much to reflect upon, for his own position was not without considerable danger. In arresting the person of his monarch's favourite son, and probably future sovereign, he had irretrievably committed himself with that bold, bad man, whose cruel nature never forgave any injury or a slight. But still he quailed not; personal consideration had never yet influenced him in the path of duty, and he was determined to pursue it, regardless of all consequence to himself. Ulrick's happiness was dearer to him than his life, and he resolved at all hazards to secure it.

It was necessary, therefore, that his dangerous prisoner should be securely watched; and he determined to trust his guardianship to Walter Tyrrel, a young knight who had long been attached to his service, and over whose birth, like Ulrick's a cloud of mystery hung.

In the age of which we write, it was by no means uncommon to the great nobles and prelates to attach to their households esquires and knights of gentle birth, who were trained to arms or letters, as their respective tastes or inclinations might incline them. Raising his silver call, he summoned a lay brother to his presence, and directed him to find the youthful knight in question.

"Yes!" he exclaimed, "Tyrrel will be his surest guard. The youth whom he would deprive of his inheritance, whose life long ere this he would have taken had he but dreamt of his existence. Poor boy!" he added; "cruelly he crossed thy sainted mother's path. May he prove less dangerous to her son."

The young knight entered the oratory as he concluded, flattered by the unusual confidence, for he was not only ambitious in his nature, but reckless in the means by which he advanced his fortunes. From his cold and selfish nature, the prelate had never loved him; still he was far from suspecting the deep treachery and heartless vices which his calculation hid from even his observance. Perhaps the kind man's heart was too full of its love for his first *protegé* to interest him deeply in the second; for Ulrick was to him even as a son.

"Tyrrel," said the bishop, "I am about to bestow on thee a mark of confidence—the precursor, chance, to future favour. Thou art not ignorant that I have an inmate here—something between a guest and prisoner."

"I am aware," answered Sir Walter; "my leader, Sir George of Erpingham, told me as much when he arrived."

"Know you his rank?"

"I guess it, my good lord."

"Then you must know how necessary 'tis that unusual ward be kept. To you I confide the custody of his person; guard him with all honour, but as strictly as you would watch your mother's fame and own inheritance. Perhaps," he added, with a smile, "you may one day thank me for his capture, and the trust I now repose in you. You know where he is lodged?"

"In the eastern tower, beyond the cloisters. He must be skilled indeed who could break prison there."

"Go," continued the prelate, at the same time giving him a ring; "George of Erpingham, on the sight of this, will resign his post; send him to me, for I have further employment for his zeal. Remember, young man, those who would gain my confidence must win it by fidelity and honour. Farewell."

Walter Tyrrel quitted the oratory with a gratified air, which resulted less from pride in the confidence reposed in him, than the conviction that it was something which might be turned to his own advantage and aggrandisement, before which honour and breach of trust were idle names. Besides, he never loved the prelate. He had long been jealous of his partiality for Ulrick, whose elevation galled him, and whose agony, on the abduction of his bride, he had seen with secret pleasure. The opportunity of thwarting them was too tempting to be thrown away.

"My lord bishop plays a daring game," he muttered, as he directed his steps towards the tower where Prince William was confined; "others, perchance, may play as bold a one. 'Tis not the first time both gaoler and captive have been missing. If the Red Norman bid but high enough, the path to liberty lies straight before him. I will not baulk my fortune."

So saying, the newly appointed guard entered the chamber in the lower basement of the tower, where George of Erpingham and a company of his men were keeping watch. At the sight of the prelate's signet the brave old soldier resigned the command to the treacherous knight, and withdrew to his own quarters to remove his armour ere he sought the bishop. Herbert de Lozinga had not been long alone when the lay brother, whom he had dispatched in search of Tyrrel, returned to inform him that a pilgrim from Normandy was at the gate of the convent, and demanded to speak with him.

"Not now," replied the superior; "not now; my mind is occupied by thought of too much moment. Give him hospitality

ISABEL AND MATILDA CAPTIVES IN FILBY HOLD.

for the night; in the morning I will see him. Tell him this, and speak him welcome in my name."

"I told him so," replied the old monk. "I told him so; but he was obstinate, called me a prating dotard, and swore by Rolla that he would see you, holy father, ere he slept; then called for wine, and ordered Father Felix to bring him a manchet, as if he were in an hotel, instead of a community of Christian priests."

"Quick," exclaimed Herbert, starting from his seat, "conduct him to our presence instantly. If it be as I suspect," he mur-mured, after the old man quitted the oratory, astonished at the vehemence of his superior's manner, "the game is in my hands, and Ulrick, wronged boy, the tyrant shall himself restore to thee thy bride, or pay his crimes with forfeit of his crown."

The moment the lay brother ushered in the stranger, Herbert de Lozinga recognised, despite his disguise, the eldest son of the Conqueror, whose fate has been the theme of many a minstrel's song; who, born to inherit a crown, passed the greater portion of his life within a prison; whose courage was always rendered useless by his recklessness, and who consoled himself for the loss of liberty and power by the wine-cup and the song.

"Prince, in the name of every saint, what brings you to this land," said the ecclesiastic, "where your path is beset with perils? Know you not that your father hath decided to bestow England on your brother William, leaving you, as eldest born, the ancient fief of Normandy, and that many of the nobles approve this disposition of the crown?"

"Hang the crown," replied the impetuous Robert; "if England boasts no better wine than the lean draught your cellarer set before me, William may govern it for me; but, perhaps," he added, bursting into a jocose laugh, "where the charity is large, the wine is weak. I'll wager a hundred pieces, my good lord, none of the same vintage ever graced your table: were the fat and pious brother, who served me, to drink no other until Easter, he would require a few yards less of broad cloth in his frock."

"The draught shall be amended, prince," said Herbert; "but answer me my question: what brings you here?"

"Caprice! caprice! the whim of an heir, who rides over his estate incog., while its possessor recites his last confiteor. Our father keeps his court at Rouen; but we know, from a sure hand, his health breaks fast. Like the dying bear, 'tis dangerous to approach him; he hath already hanged two physicians, and engaged a third, an unbelieving Jew."

"What is his malady?" demanded Herbert de Lozinga, anxiously, for he foresaw the conflict which would probably follow the Conqueror's death.

"The same which ails your wine," replied the prince, with a heartless laugh; "he hath too much water in the barrel. The French king asked when his vassal brother would be brought to bed: 'twas a good jest, but must be dearly paid."

"How so?"

"Our choleric father swore to be churched in Notre Dame, with twenty thousand lances in his train. He is the man at least to keep his word; he hath already wasted the Seine with fire and sword, as first fruits of his oath."

"And for a jest," exclaimed the bishop, "an idle jest, spoken in an hour of mirth, when wine had tempted reason, and the unguarded lips utter the wayward fancies of the brain, blood must be shed, houses desolated, cities destroyed, and kind hearts broken! Earth! earth!" he added, mournfully, "such are thy rulers!"

"Earth soon will count one more and less," interrupted Robert, who contemplated his father's approaching death with any thing but dissatisfaction; indeed, the conduct of the former had been sufficiently harsh towards him to break all tie of blood between them. He had thwarted him in his dearest wishes; and urged by his partiality for the unworthy William, would have stripped his elder son even of his inheritance of Normandy, had not the consent of the king of France, as souzeran, been necessary—a consent, he well knew, it would be hopeless to solicit, the policy of the French court being to disunite the crowns of England and Normandy: their descending on one head rendered the ducal vassal more powerful than his master.

"Prince," said Herbert, gravely, "Heaven only knows whether thou art come for good or ill; but thou art come in an eventful hour—thy brother is an inmate of my palace."

Robert heard the information with evident surprise, and for a moment eyed the speaker keenly, as if to read his very heart. The examination was apparently satisfactory; for he almost instantly resumed his former expression of careless confidence, and demanded, as if it were the most unimportant circumstance in the world to him:

"A guest?"

"No," gravely answered his host.

"A prisoner?"

"Yes."

The prince's reply was a loud careless laugh; the jest seemed to strike him more than the advantage to be drawn from it, so contradictory was his character: at one moment all energy, at the next indifference to everything; capable of conceiving a bold design, but wanting the perseverance to ensure success. Well had his mother, the Queen Matilda, designated him as the weathercock of impulse and of folly—she might have added, and of fortune also.

"And so you have caged the wolf," he cried—"or rather the fox, I should say, designating our royal brother from the colour of his hair. Leave a priest alone to bait a snare! How fell he into it?"

"Prince," answered Herbert, with offended dignity, "I am not one of those who traffic in pitfalls or snares. Your brother is my prisoner, to answer for a cruel outrage on a maiden's liberty; openly I arrested him, openly I'll guard him, till the outrage is atoned and the lady free. But come," he added, "the time is dark with import, and I have matter which concerns you deeply. Lay for awhile that reckless levity of heart aside, and let us speak like men who watch the game of life."

"Willingly, my lord," replied the prince, brought to something like seriousness by the prelate's tone; "but answer me one question —the boy, whom I confided to your care— speak—lives he yet?—and may I not behold him?"

"He does. His training hath not shamed his birth. Fifteen months are past since the sword of my good lord of Kent hath dubbed him knight; he hath remained ever since attached to our court; e'en now he guards my prisoner in his tower."

A singular smile, half of mischief and half fun, passed over the still handsome features of the Norman prince at the intelligence, but it soon passed away; and motioning to the prelate to precede him, he followed to a small recess at the back of the oratory, where we shall leave them to converse on business of deep import, the result of which may soon become apparent to our readers.

The first beams of the rising sun had already tinged the east with gold, and gilded the graceful spire and turrets of the cathedral, as Ulrick had Mirvan, attended by most of the nobles who had been present at the banquet, returned from their unsuccessful pursuit. The men looked jaded, and their horses worn: still not a single complaint was heard; for rough and careless as the soldiers were, they sympathised with the despair of their two leaders, who, pale as marble, and with bloodshot eyes, gazed hopelessly upon each other. Robert of Artois, the unsuspected author of the deed, had been one of the foremost in the pursuit, carefully directing the pursuers, by his well feigned zeal, far from the path they should have taken. As the various stragglers came slowly up before the castle, he reined his tired steed, and said, "Farewell, my friends. Should chance discover the author of this outrage, which fills each heart with rage, and every honest tongue with scorn, send but a glove to Filby in token of your need, and in an hour my banner shall be spread to meet you. This present hour business of import calls me home. That once dispatched, I am again your servant."

"Thanks!" exclaimed the broken-hearted Ulrick; "he is a friend indeed who shares a sorrow as if it were his own. On your return send out your men to scour the country round. I'll fill his gauntlet with gold who brings intelligence of my lost bride, or names the villain who hath wrought this mischief; dearly the heartless ruffian should abide it."

Courageous as Robert of Artois naturally was, he quailed beneath the expression of Ulrick's eye as he pronounced the threat. A desire to find himself within his stronghold of Filby seized upon him. Raising his helmet, therefore, in sign of adieu, he cried, "Doubt not, noble youths, all that friendship can achieve shall be attempted; my men shall

spare no spur nor rein till your lost treasure's found."

Hella the bard, who had, despite his vast age, been one of the first to mingle in the pursuit, cast a suspicious glance on Robert of Artois as he rode off. Odo of Caen observed it: he had not forgiven the bard his song, which seemed indirectly to call upon the Saxons to throw off the conquerors' yoke, and to censure the misrule of the Norman race. He gladly seized, therefore, the opportunity of venting his spleen, which the unsuccessful result of the pursuit had still further tended to increase.

"Sir Saxon," he cried, "thou lovest not our brother of Artois. Heaven defend me from as dark a greeting as thy looks conveys. In what hath he displeased thee?"

"His deeds," coolly answered the aged Saxon.

"Humph!" replied his questioner; "'tis difficult for Norman deeds to please a Saxon's judgment; but what particular deed of Robert of Artois hath merited the harshness of such judgment? Sir bard, explain me that."

"His share in this night's outrage."

All started, and even Odo of Caen was staggered by the coolness and firmness of the reply. Ulrick and Mirvan gathered with the rest of the nobles round the old man, and eagerly demanded upon what proofs he grounded his assertion. Some, who saw in it only a splenetic attempt to sow dissension between the Saxon and Norman chiefs, cried shame; and had not the bereaved lovers, and several of their friends, drawn their swords, the old bard would have rued his temerity in daring to accuse one of the most powerful of the Norman chiefs. After much quarrelling and confusion, Mirvan, whose office of Marshal of the Angles gave him most authority amongst them, at last obtained something like silence.

"The wisdom of age," he cried, "is not slightly to be contemned; let Hella be heard! First I demand upon what proof he founds his accusation—an accusation monstrous if false, and terrible if true."

"Upon no proof," replied Hella; "but upon——"

The rest of his speech was lost in the clamour which the friends of Robert of Artois contrived to raise; crowding, they thronged around the old man, who gazed unmoved upon them; their looks and words were menacing, when Ulrick thrust himself between; like the young lion who first sees his prey, his blood was roused, despair had made him reckless.

"Back!" he exclaimed, tracing a circle with his sword; "let him who is most tired of life first cross it. Were ye the friends of the Norman devil, whose name Robert of Artois bears, I'd brave ye all in such a cause as this. Is this the amity ye lately swore? Is this the justice Saxons must expect at Norman hands? against an old man too! Shame on your courage, sirs."

The vast body of Edda's troops, hearing the voice of their lord, thronged instantly around him. Odo, and the more reasonable of the Normans, felt that he was right; and the assailants, seeing that they were outnumbered, sheathed their weapons.

"Let him explain his words, and justify them, if he can," they cried. "Public has been the accusation; as public be the proofs."

"Who saw Robert of Artois at the banquet?" demand the old bard. There was a pause—none remembered to have seen him. "Who can tell when and where he first joined in the pursuit?" he added.

"I—I," exclaimed several of the younger nobles; "he joined us in the market-place, and all have seen how eagerly he conducted the pursuit."

"Ay," exclaimed a third, "and well he hath been recompensed."

"Conducted the pursuit!" echoed Hella. "True, he did conduct it every where, but to the road which led to his own felon den. Who twice misled us by false intelligence? Robert of Artois. Who of all the nobles was absent at the banquet when the outrage was committed? Robert of Artois. Who alone, of all those who swore to avenge the crime, hath withdrawn from the pursuit? Robert of Artois. And who," he added, with increased energy, "is the vile ravisher of innocence? Robert of Artois."

Conviction flashed in an instant upon both Mirvan and his friend, the former of whom had frequently remarked his passionate glances directed towards Isabel. So profound was the impression Hella's words produced, that even the culprit's nearest friends were dumb. Odo of Caen was the first to break the silence.

"It must be seen to," he exclaimed. "Let the esquires give orders to refresh our men; and then towards Filby."

The words had scarcely passed the speaker's lips, when a servitor, bearing the badge of Herbert de Lozinga on his vest, galloped to the ground, and, without waiting to dismount, placed in the hands of Ulrick, who hastily tore the seal, a missive from the prelate, which detailed the treachery of Robert of Artois, but without alluding to his prisoner's share in it—a circumstance which, for many prudential reasons, he wished for awhile to remain concealed.

"It is confirmed," he cried, glancing over the letter. "Robert of Artois is the vile ravisher—the traitor who hath broken the bond of peace—stolen like some midnight thief upon my path, and robbed me of my happiness. Who will dispute his guilt when it is known that the venerable bishop is his accuser? But I will have revenge!" he added, drawing his sword—an example which was followed by the aged Edda and his Saxon followers.

"By him whose name yon stars pronounce," continued Ulrick, "whose might the roaring sea and tempest's breath alike make manifest, I here devote my soul to its fulfilment—a wild, exterminating, deep revenge!"

A shout of execration from the Normans and Saxons followed the words of Ulrick, for the insult to both was equal in the outrage offered to the brides of their leaders; eagerly they demanded to be led against the stronghold of the knightly robber, vowing not to leave one stone upon another till they had rescued his prisoners. The preparations were quickly made, and ere the sun was an hour higher in the heavens, the united hosts, under the conduct of Mirvan and Ulrick, were on their way to Filby.

Matilda had beheld with joy the excitement of her cousin at last relieved by tears, as she sank exhausted with her griefs upon the couch beside her. By a benevolent provision of nature, sorrow or pain, beyond a certain limit, stupify the brain, or life would succumb beneath them. Isabel had gradually sobbed herself into a feverish slumber, disturbed by unholy dreams and voluntary terrors, from which she would occasionally start, but recompose herself on hearing the calm, sweet voice of Matilda, or feeling the affectionate pressure of her hand. The latter slept not, but had passed the night in prayer, tempering her soul with courage. On considering her position, she felt convinced that her imprisonment was but the consequence of her companionship with Isabel. The purity of her nature did not allow her to suppose that her beauty had excited the lawless desire of any one; for, like the flowers of the field, she was unconscious of her loveliness. Partially reassured, therefore, on her own account, she resolved to devote herself to the protection of her cousin, whom she loved as a sister, and the affianced bride of her brother. The rays of morning began to penetrate through the strongly barred windows, when the watcher, seeing that her charge still slept, advanced to the casement to see if she could recognise from the surrounding country the place of their imprisonment. The view fully confirmed her suspicions that they were the captives of Robert of Artois; for Filby mere, with its sedgy islands and woody banks, lay stretched like a clouded mirror in the morning mists before her. As the sun advanced in power, the lake became more and more distinct, till she could trace the wild duck leading her brood in matron pride on its placid bosom, or the stately heron patiently watching for its finny prey from some projecting stone close by the shore, where the waters were not too deep for its long legs to wade, or neck to plunge. Sometimes she would watch the solitary drake, as, with its sharp cry, it rose from the water, and directed its arrowy flight over the distant woods of Ormsby, or the low marshy grounds which lie between them—envy its rapid flight, and sigh for freedom.

Her reveries were broken by the gentle closing of a door. In an instant the terrible reality of her position pressed upon her; and, turning to confront the intruder, she beheld, to her great relief, that it was a woman. So completely was she shielded from observation by the recess in which she stood, and so quiet had been the movement, that the stranger failed to perceive her; and there was something so peculiar in her manner, that Matilda determined to observe her. Her apparel, which was extremely rich, partook more of the Eastern than European character; a saffron-coloured short vest fell over a white cymar, which descended to the wearer's ankles; both were embroidered at the hems with gold. Her figure was tall and commanding, and her features, which were still beautiful, although marked by the strife of passions, bore the peculiar characteristics of the Jewis race. It was evident, from her costume, that she could not be a menial; for, independent of the richness of her dress, gems of considerable value glittered upon her arms and neck, or were braided in her long dark hair. Cautiously she approached the couch, and gazed upon the sleeper; her features became dreadfully agitated as she did so.

"She is beautiful," she murmured, or rather hissed through her clenched teeth; "young, too; perhaps nobly born—innocent and fair; what chance have I, withered as I am in form and mind, to retain his heart against such a rival? He will soon arrive to clasp her in his eager arms, to breathe his serpent vows into her ear, to press his poisonous kisses on her lips, and laugh to scorn the lost, degraded Rachel. Let him come," she added firmly; "he shall find the kiss of death upon her lips before him; the worm shall first supplant him in her love." As the last words fell upon the astonished listener's ear, the Jewess drew a sharp, glittering blade from beneath her vest, and advanced towards the couch. Matilda had

gradually become spell-bound with terror at the evident purpose of the stranger. Her limbs were rooted to the spot, and the powers of speech and motion seemed alike denied her; her agony became intense; vainly she struggled with the torpor which oppressed her. Nor was it till the arm of the woman was actually raised over the unconscious Isabel, that, with a piercing shriek, she burst the horrible species of fascination which bound her, exclaiming as she did so:

"Think on thy soul; shed not the blood of innocence."

So thrilling was the cry, that the affrighted Isabel started from her slumber, waking from fearful visions to a more fearful reality before her. The murderess was equally startled; it seemed as if the appealing voice of conscience had thundered in her ear, "Thou shalt do no murder." She gazed in surprise upon the fair girl who had so suddenly interposed between her and her intended victim, and who, with arm encircling the agitated Isabel, boldly confronted her.

"Who art thou?" she falteringly demanded.

"Victims, like yourself, to the foulest treachery," replied Matilda; "though, perhaps, unlike you, unwilling ones. How can this poor girl excite your hatred, that you should seek to stain your hands in blood? Rather assist us to escape our tyrant's power, for the honour of your sex and the memory of your mother's love."

The word mother seemed to touch a chord whose every tone vibrated in agony. Dropping the still upraised weapon, she clasped her hands upon her brow, as if stricken by a sudden pain. The flush of passion on her features was replaced by the purer blush of shame, and in an instant the tears gushed from her burning eyes, and relieved her overfraught heart; for, fallen as Rachel was, one trace of Eden lingered in her yet. In a voice broken by sighs, she murmured:

"Speak not of my mother, lest from the grave she rise to curse her child."

"She is mad," whispered Isabel—"mad. If friends come not soon to rescue us, reason will leave me too."

"No!" said Rachel, dashing the tears from her dark eyes, as if ashamed of her momentary weakness; "I am not mad! would to our Father Abraham I were! for madness cannot equal the pangs of a despised and unrequited love."

"You love our captor, Robert of Artois, then?" exclaimed Matilda, a ray of hope dawning on her soul.

"Ay, maiden, love him as the lost daughters of our race alone can love—beyond home, parents, honour, life—more," she added, with still increasing excitement—"more e'en than heaven itself: all but life I have already sacrificed for him, and would again, though but for one kind smile; alas! 'tis long since I received one."

"And he requites your sacrifice?"

"With scorn!" interrupted Rachel; "with scorn! whose serpent tooth gnaws deeper into a woman's heart than aught on earth beside. I once was good," she added, "gentle as yourselves, not meanly nurtured or ignobly bred. What hath it made me? a raging tigress; changed my woman's heart into a fiend's; destroyed the kindlier impulse of my nature; made me in heart, if not in deed, a murderess."

"Alas!" said Isabel; "what have I done to cause such fearful hate?"

"Loved him I love," replied Rachel, whose jealousy returned as she gazed on the lovely girl before her, and mentally compared her opening loveliness with her own faded beauty; "is't not enough to give me cause to hate thee?"

"Woman," exclaimed Isabel with dignity, "be the words thy happiness or bane, be they for good or ill, know that, if Robert of Artois were king, Isabel of Bayeux would never share his throne; but would prefer the convent's gloom, the meanest hut, the shelter of the grave itself, to his polluted couch. I loathe and scorn him."

There was a tone of sincerity in the speaker's words which carried conviction to the heart. The Jewess gazed attentively upon her for a few moments—at first suspiciously, but at last with confidence, for the candid brow of the fair girl was not one where falsehood had ever traced its crooked characters. Despite herself, she could not but believe her.

"Deceived!" she muttered to herself, "again deceived! Thank Heaven, this crime at least is spared me. Forgive me, maiden," she added, "my evil purpose; but I was stung—deceived—wrought on by jealous pangs; they told me thou wert come to be his bride—and I, who loved, too easily believed them. But if thou lovest him not," she added, "why art thou here?"

"Ask of the vulture," said Matilda, "why the wounded dove is found within its nest; ask of the tiger why the bleeding fawn is trembling in his den. Art thou answered?"

"I see—I see," exclaimed the Jewess, struggling with her evil passions, which were again excited by the idea of Robert's love for another; "but I will save thee. The fool who poured this tale of poison in my ear did it to gain my love—fool! not to know that hearts like mine can feel but once its spell, and break when it is broken. Wouldst thou be free?"

"Gladly," exclaimed both Matilda and Isabel.

"But you must swear," she added, "that if by my means the path lies open to you, no injury shall fall upon your captor. False as he is, I would not, e'en to save my perilled soul, harm one hair of his ungrateful head. Promise me this."

"Easily answered: Matilda, my cousin, and myself solemnly swear never to breathe, save in confession, our captor's fearful name."

"Away then," said Rachel, hurriedly; "morning advances, and he may soon be here—here to mar our plans, and to prevent your flight."

"It is prevented," exclaimed a stern voice behind them. They started, and Isabel beheld the object of her hate and terror, Robert of Artois, who, after leaving Ulrick and Mirvau, had returned to Filby to await the arrival of his royal accomplice in the act of villany. The effect of his appearance upon the Jewess was even greater than upon his trembling victim; in an instant her fit of jealousy returned, and springing towards Isabel, she would have completed her original purpose, had not the swift arm of her seducer arrested her.

"Release my hand," she cried, or rather shrieked; "I'll not be held! Her life or thine, Norman! ravisher! villain! coward! Christian, I spit upon and curse thee!"

It is difficult to say how the contest with the frantic woman might have terminated, had not several men-at-arms rushed into the room, on hearing the voice of their master. They were accompanied by a young esquire, whose agitated countenance, when he beheld Rachel struggling with his lord, told a deeper interest than mere pity; his hand involuntarily grasped the hilt of his poignard, but reflection held it.

"Convey this wanton to a secure cell within the keep," cried Robert, spurning the unhappy woman brutally from him. "Guard her well, Aymer, and see that I am pestered with these frantic scenes no more."

"Dog," said the Jewess, still resisting the men-at-arms, who were dragging her from the apartment, "thou hast spurned me like a hound; beware my fangs! Thou hast broken the last tie between us: beware when next we meet!"

"Believe me, I regret, fair ladies, you should have been exposed to a scene like this," said Robert of Artois, as soon as the unhappy woman was removed; "but jealousy of your superior charms has driven her mad. I will give orders she shall not mar our happiness again."

This was said with an affectation of courtesy which rendered its insolent familiarity more bitter. Isabel, on whom his eyes were licentiously fixed, shrank trembling to the side of her cousin, whose hand alone prevented her from falling, so excessive was her terror at his presence.

"Robert of Artois," said Matilda, with dignity, "I appeal not to thy honour—for this deed of thine proves that my words would wake no echo there—but to thy fears. Canst hope our presence can be long concealed within these walls? Normans and Saxons will alike unite to punish thy aggression. Release us, then; and here I solemnly renew the oath never to yield thy name to those whose swords would punish thy unmanly crime."

"Filby," replied the knight, carelessly, "hath held birds of a nest as lofty, maiden, as thine own; and I have kept the fledglings. But few hours since I left thy brother and his new found friend; we parted in honest fellowship. Suspicion's self can never glance at me, and if it does," he added, "Isabel will by that time be my bride, and thou be caged by one who knows how to put a gag upon that scornful tongue, and tame thy haughty nature."

"Thy bride!" exclaimed Isabel, gazing on him with loathing. "Never!"

"These walls have echoed often to that word," sneeringly observed the knight; "spoken as oft in vain. I know a trick to make thee sue to be the bride of him you so long have scorned. I have humbled hearts, ere now, as proud, and firmer far than thine. But why are you in this chamber? My orders were you should be separated. Solitude may tend to tame your spirits. Come," he added, approaching Isabel as he spoke, "I have a dove-cot prettier far than this; let me conduct thee thither; there I will woo thee as thou shouldst be wooed, and teach thee, maid, how Robert of Artois loves."

The flashing eyes of the speaker declared but too plainly his guilty purpose. So completely did he deem the unprotected girls within his power, that he would not even give himself the trouble to dissemble, but felt a savage joy in humbling, by brutal outrage, the high spirited being who had scorned his proffered love. Isabel read his purpose, and exclaimed, as she sank fainting in the arms of her cousin:

"Thy promise, coz, thy promise!"

The appeal was not made in vain. In the purity of her nature Matilda would rather have seen her cousin dead, nay, with her own hand have offered up the spotless victim on the shrine of honour, than polluted by the touch of the base ravisher. Drawing the knife which, from the hour of her arrival at Filby, she carried concealed in her bosom, she held it, with a determined air, over the insensible form of Isabel.

"Advance one step nearer," she cried, "and I consign her soul to God and his good angels. Robert of Artois, doubt not my purpose. Mark if my hand trembles or an eyelid quivers. I have sworn, living, thy arms should never clasp her. Lessen the distance between us but one step, a line, a breadth, a hair, and her pure blood shall rise to heaven against thee."

So firm was the voice of the speaker, so resolute her eye, that even Robert of Artois, accustomed though he was to scenes like this, could not for one moment doubt her purpose. The sharp, glittering blade was within an inch of her fair cousin's breast, her eye unflinchingly fixed upon his. Involuntarily he started back, saying as he did so, "What wouldst do?"

"Preserve her honour at the expense of life."

"Murderess!"

"Thou art the murderer," replied Matilda—"I, the priestess. Thine is the victim—mine the sacrifice; approach, and it is offered. If Heaven will not prevent, its mercy will accept it."

"Foolish girl!" exclaimed Robert; "it can neither prevent nor interfere to save thee."

Scarcely had the words passed his lips than the blast of a trumpet rang loud and deep before the drawbridge. Matilda started, for she knew the challenge of her house. 'Twas Mirvan's trumpet.

"It has interposed," she cried. "Robber, thy ruffian hold is close beset; our friends are round thy walls. Well may thy cheeks turn pale. In Heaven has been our trust, and Heaven hath answered us. Living, thou canst not guard us; dead, our friends will pile these towers in ashes o'er our grave."

"Confusion!" muttered Robert, and rushed from the apartment.

Matilda laid her insensible burthen on the couch, and sank in grateful prayer upon her knees beside her.

CHAPTER XVIII.

How calm is the rest of the dead,
How sweet is the slumber they sleep,
When the eye hath no tear drop to shed,
The heart not one sorrow to weep.
What is honour, what fortune, or fame's fleeting breath,
Compared to thy slumber, oh, beautiful death !

OBERT OF ARTOIS rushed from the chamber of the two captives, and with hasty strides gained the battlements of his stronghold, from whence the sight which met his gaze might have quailed a stronger heart than his, for the united Saxon and Norman hosts were marshalled on the plain before him. So universal was the indignation at the unmanly outrage he had committed, that even amongst those whom he called his friends not a single banner was absent. Men who would have supported him in almost any other cause, who had shared with him in the plunder of the oppressed Saxons, were now in arms against him. Had his victims been of the vanquished race, it would have been long ere a single pennon had been given to the wind, but the insult to the daughter and niece of so popular a man as the late Hugh de Bigod could not be passed over ; it was a crime which might come home to every noble's hearth : and they determined, however they might violate the rights of others, that none should tamper with their own.

About twenty paces behind the herald, whose trumpet had called the lord of Filby to the walls, stood the chief leaders of the expedition—Ulrick and Mirvan, to whose anxious hearts it seemed an age until their enemy appeared. Edda, and Odo of Caen, left the parley to the two lovers, and were busily occupied in directing the franklins and nobles where to place their men. Under the direction of such experienced commanders, every point of vantage was taken possession of, and the castle was completely invested before the inmates knew of their approach.

"Unless the fox's den be well supplied," said Odo, casting a satisfied glance on the military dispositions, "we shall starve him to a surrender ; for I defy horse or man to pass by lake or plain without being exposed to the arrows of our soldiers. But see," he added, "the ravisher appears upon the was.

May the caitiff's shrift be short and speedy, for it will be his last !"

"'Tis a strange greeting you have called me to !" exclaimed Robert, after casting a hurried survey over the scene. "Is Filby held a robber's den, nobles and knights, that you appear before it, banner displayed and lance in rest ? 'Tis well our walls are strong enough to bid defiance unto all who come. Come ye in hostile guise, or is't some riddle beyond a plain man's guessing ?"

"Robert of Artois," said Ulrick, with a strong effort to master his indignation, " though this deed of thine is of so black a treachery, it merits more the hangman's officer than knightly chastisement. Descend, and let the sword decide between us. If vanquished, thou shalt release thy captives ; if conqueror, Heaven will raise them up another champion."

"Captives ! what captives ?" demanded the villain in well-dissembled surprise ; "my castle is not a prison."

"Lying will not serve thee now," cried Mirvan ; "despite thy arts, thy treachery is known. Where is my sister ? where my cousin Isabel ? Release them, or I swear not to leave one stone upon another of this den of treachery and blood—one living soul within its ruined walls : thy knightly spurs shall be hacked off—thy escutcheon reversed, in sign of infamy, upon thy grave."

"Boys," replied Robert, " I hear and scorn you both. First, for the base-born Ulrick,—for such, despite the bishop's juggling tale, I do believe he is,—I cross no sword with men of doubtful birth. As for my captives, if I have such, I have good warrant for detaining them. For the rest, exert your strength on Filby—bend bow and mangonel : our walls can boast of brave hearts and hands which know how to defend them."

"Coward !" exclaimed Ulrick, maddened by the sneering tone of the speaker ; " cold, calculating, spiritless coward, bold only when women are to be assailed, hath thy cheek no

THE QUARREL BETWEEN ABRAM AND BRANTONE.

blush of shame? thy heart no drop of knightly blood?"

"If not with Ulrick, measure swords with me; my birth, at least, is equal to thine own," said Mirvan; "felon as thou art, I offer thee the chance of equal combat, a noble's sword for the vile headman's axe. Descend, and Heaven decide between us."

Mirvan's challenge, and the epithet of coward which Ulrick had previously applied to him, stung their enemy to the quick; for, like most cruel and licentious men, he was excessively vain, and consequently suscepti-

ble of shame. It was not, therefore, without an effort that he determined to decline the contest; for he well knew how such an act must lessen him in the estimation of his chivalrous countrymen, with whom courage was held the highest virtue. Perhaps he was influenced in his decision by the belief that the arrival of the royal partner of his crime would relieve him from his embarrassing position by causing the Normans to desert their new allies, or turn their swords against them. Perhaps, too, he lacked moral courage to face the glance and swords of those whom

No. 11.

he had so cruelly injured. Whichever was the motive, his face was livid with contending passions as he replied:

"If, for the present, I decline the contest, think not it is I fear it; the bridegroom never longed more for his bride's first kiss, than I to vindicate my honour and chastise thy boyish insolence; that which I have done I dare defend. Normans and Saxons, I defy ye both. What ho!" he added, calling to the warder, "fling out our banner; man the walls; let our keen arrows count every rivet of their armour. A hide of land and twenty silver marks to him whose arm strikes down a leader of yon vaunting host."

Scarcely had the words passed his lips, than a body of his men, who had been crouching behind the battlements suddenly started up and discharged a flight of arrows at the group of nobles near the herald. Thanks to the goodness of their armour, Ulrick and Mirvan both escaped. Odo of Caen was slightly wounded in the cheek, but the unfortunate herald was slain. The assailants raised a shout of execration as they beheld him fall; and even the cheek of Robert of Artois blanched—for his office, like his person, was sacred; and the wounding or injuring one of them was ever considered a most unknightly deed.

"Villain!" exclaimed Odo of Caen, shaking his sword, "the blood thou hast shed has to be atoned. I swear never to quit this spot alive, till I have levelled thy castle with the dust, and fixed thy head upon the ruined pile. So help me Heaven, our Lady, and St. George!"

The speaker, his face streaming with blood from the treacherous arrow, drew his sword, and kissed the golden cross upon its hilt. It was no unusual circumstance at the period of the conquest, and the ages of chivalry which succeeded it, for one or more nobles to bind themselves, like Odo of Caen, to some particular undertaking; such oaths were always most scrupulously kept by all who valued their knightly reputation; to break them was considered such dishonour, that it released the affianced bride from her contract, should her lover be proved guilty of it.

"A vow! a vow!" cried Mirvan, as Odo ceased speaking, "to which I join myself heart and soul."

"And I," "And I," exclaimed Ulrick and most of the younger nobles; at the same time touching the sword of Odo, in token of their companionship in his oath, and pronouncing the formula, "So help us Heaven, our Lady, and St. George."

The followers of Robert were preparing to send a second flight of arrows, when Edda, who marked the action, gave the signal to his

men, and in an instant a cloud of missiles swept the wall; several of the besieged fell, struck by the heavy stones which the Saxons sent from their slings with remarkable precision. Their leader received one upon his breast, which reminded him that he was without his armour by the pain it occasioned; he retired, therefore, behind a bastion, calling to his esquires to bring him his coat of mail and casque as he did so.

Filby Castle was a regularly fortified hold, built with more reference to strength than either beauty or convenience. Like most of the fortresses of the age, it consisted of a lofty keep or donjon, surrounded by offices, forming a kind of courtyard, the only entrance to which was by a strong tower; the latter generally served as storehouses for the corn and provisions of the inmates, as well as the dormitories of the guards, its flat roofs serving, in case of attack, as a battery, from whence the besieged could pour down showers of arrows and hurl masses of stone upon the assailants. The keep and tower were the only buildings of stone; the rest were made of sun-burnt brick and timber, could be fired by fire, and whose loss would not affect the carrying of the rest of the place. From the determined manner of Robert of Artois, it was evident that all hope of capitulation was in vain; he was prepared to defend himself to the last; and after a brief consultation between the Saxon and Norman leaders, it was resolved to continue the siege in due form.

"Nobles," said Edda, as soon as the resolution was concluded, "if the peace between our races is to be a lasting one, it must be cemented by an act of stern but necessary justice. The wrong which brings us here hath been offered by Robert of Artois, alike to both, and both are joined to punish him. Let the gallows be erected in sight of his vile den, his name attached to it, like that of the meanest criminal, together with a parchment, signed by us all, declaring him degraded from the dignity of knighthood, and doomed for the murder of our unoffending herald to die a felon's death. Are we agreed?" continued Edda, gazing around him.

"We are," exclaimed Ulrick and Mirvan in the same breath.

Odo of Caen and his brother nobles approved the proposition; the gibbet was accordingly erected, and the act of degradation solemnly affixed by sound of trumpet. Robert, pale with rage, witnessed the ceremony from the walls of his stronghold, and his cheek changed with rage and fear, as he marked the effect it produced upon his followers, men who, under ordinary circumstances, would have abetted him in any act of villany. Quickly, however, recovering himself from the confusion, he observed, with a loud forced laugh:

"A slip of parchment will not win Filby hold. Courage, friends! we shall soon behold a royal banner in the boasters' rear. William of Normandy, our future monarch, by whose orders I am acting, will soon be here to punish these presuming traitors, who would usurp the prerogative of justice and dispute his will."

The words had scarcely passed his lips when the sentinel who was placed upon the highest tower called out that he beheld an approaching force, headed by several knights in armour, who were directing their march towards Filby; and that, from the movement amongst the besiegers, he doubted not but that they perceived it too. The intelligence gave fresh courage to their audacious leader, who doubted not but that it was his patron marching to his succour.

"See you no banner?" he demanded.

The soldier paused a moment ere he replied, for the new actors were still at a considerable distance from the scene.

"I do," at last he answered. "There are three; one borne in advance of the others—a herald precedes it."

"By whom is it borne?"

"A knight in full armour," shouted the man. "Three leaders follow it—one is a priest."

"Can you discern its blazon?" replied Robert of Artois, at the same time straining his sight to catch it, his fears reverting to Herbert de Lozinga at the intelligence that one of the leaders was a priest.

"A lion rampant in an azure field, surmounted by a ducal crown. It is a royal banner," added the man.

"Thanks to our Lady," shouted the degraded man; "it is the prince. Now then we shall see yon scum dispersed like chaff before the wind. Shout, men, and wave our banners from the walls to welcome them! Shout, in sign of recognition for their aid! See, the enemy marshal their ranks to meet them. Would they resist their prince? Aymer," he added, turning to the young esquire who attended him, "lead a party of your men into the courtyard below. Be ready for a sally. This is the day to win thy spurs; and tell the warder at the first signal to be ready at the drawbridge; we must attack them in the rear."

Robert of Artois watched with eager eyes the expected encounter of the two hosts. What was his consternation when he beheld their leaders mutually advance in sign of amity, and their troops mingle together till they formed but one body, which, after a few moments' evolution, directed its march towards Filby! From that instant he felt the

first misgiving for the success of his villanous scheme, and half repented that he had undertaken it.

"Can the fickle-minded tyrant," he muttered, "have betrayed me? or have both Normans and Saxons yielded to the *prestige* of his birth? No, no," he added, bitterly, as the banner of the leader distinctly met his view—"by my evil star, it is the blazon of my namesake, Robert Curthose, the Conqueror's eldest son. What devil brings him to this country to mar our plans? Where can his brother be? The wily bishop, too!" he added, as George of Erpingham advanced with the pennon of his master; "the game hath fearful odds against me. No matter; I will fight it to the last. Victory or revenge shall at least be mine. I will not fall alone."

Lowering their visors to guard against any fresh act of treachery on the part of the besieged, the leaders of the now united army, preceded by a herald in the royal tabard, and a knight bearing the prince's banner, advanced close to the walls of the castle; its commander was waiting to receive them. Thrice did the herald summon him to open the gates to his highness Robert of Normandy, on pain of treason and forfeiture in case of a refusal. There was a pause, during which the traitor whispered something to one of his arquebussiers, a man equally noted for skill and determination; a nod of intelligence was the fellow's only reply, and immediately he concealed himself behind one of the projecting bastions, taking his weapon with him.

"And how am I to know," answered Robert of Artois, "that the prince is really with you? Report speaks him in Normandy. Men ere now have fallen into a snare as plain as this; the royal banner may be assumed——"

"But not the royal person," interrupted the unsuspicious prince, spurring his horse, and advancing from the group of nobles by whom he was surrounded still nearer to the walls. "Behold."

He raised his visor as he spoke, exposing to the full gaze of the besieged his frank and manly countenance. Scarcely had he done so, than the concealed ruffian, obedient to the order he had received, discharged his arquebus; but fortunately, from the crouching position he had been compelled to assume in order to conceal himself, he had not taken aim with his usual precision. The arrow missed the prince's face, but struck the golden crown upon his helmet—an emblem of the prince's future destiny; and the royal insignia fell to the ground shivered by the shock. Its incautious wearer instantly closed his visor, and raising his hand in defiance, exclaimed:

"Robert of Artois, thou art a doomed man! By the oath of my race, I swear to show no mercy to thee or any of thy fellows. The axe and cord shall be the doom of all. No further parley now. The lion's on thy track; his thirst of blood is roused; fear not but he will quench it to the full."

At the end of this imprudent speech the prince returned to his followers and friends, who, however they regretted his incaution, were silent through respect; for the resolution he had sworn to left no room for hope of an accommodation with the besieged; many of whom would perhaps have hesitated to defend their master against their monarch's son, but that he had sworn their death by an oath which none of his family were ever known to break; no other resource, therefore, was left to them but desperate resistance; they knew that the attack would be fearful, and they prepared with alacrity for their defence, their wily leader rejoicing in the indiscretion of his reckless enemy.

"We have had words enough," exclaimed Ulrick; "and nothing now remains but to draw the sword and throw away the scabbard. Beloved Matilda!" he added, "if too late to save, at least I'll honour thy loss with Filby for thy funeral pile."

Under the direction of their leaders some of the men commenced cutting down the reeds and sedges which grew upon the banks of the lake; others were sent into the wood to fell trees and brushwood; the whole of which, despite the efforts of the besieged, they succeeded in piling against the offices which, as before stated, formed the court-yard of the castle, by connecting the keep with the tower. During this operation the Saxons under Edda rendered good service; for no sooner did the Normans apper upon the walls than they were swept down by their arrows, and the heavy stones flung with astonishing deterity from their slings, Many a cauldron of seething pitch fell from the hand prepared to turn it on the besiegers' heads; on more than one cccasion, however, it fell on the unprotected limbs of the Saxons, burning them to the very bone. The Normans saw this, and knowing they were better protected by their armour, called upon them to retire whilst they took their place—an offer which the former accepted in the same generous spirit in which it was meant. Nothing, however, could induce either Ulrick or Mirvan to withdraw; reckless of the danger they ran of the missiles which were showered upon them, they continued to share in the labours of their men. In the course of a few hours the pile had reached a formidable height; the boiling matter which the enemy had poured from the walls only rendered it

the more inflammable; and as soon as the torches were applied the flames rose quickly and strong. Robert of Artois, seeing that all attempts to stop the conflagration would be vain, retired with his men to the shelter of the keep, which, from its strength, seemed to bid defiance to the besiegers' efforts.

While these proceedings are being carried on it is a fit opportunity for us to return to the Jewess, and the young squire to whose charge her seducer had consigned her. On entering her dungeon, Rachel paced its cold damp floor with the angry mien of an excited lioness; her feelings had been hurt where they were most susceptible—in her love. Pride, womanhood, and affection, had alike been outraged; the man for whom she had sacrificed her own esteem, the respect of her people, the prejudice of her faith, and her mother's love, had spurned her from him like the vilest thing. The blow had so crushed her heart that even its passion for the idol once enshrined there became extinct; it throbbed with but one sentiment—revenge.

"'Tis just!" she cried, "'tis just I should be used so; gathered like a toy in a moment of caprice—cast aside like a faded flower the moment satiety had palled. What will be my fate? I have now no refuge but the grave."

"Yes, one other!" exclaimed Aymer, throwing himself at her feet. "I have long loved you—lived but in your presence—have borne the burning pang of seeing you another's, but in the hope that you would one day smile upon my persevering suit. Speak but the word—I will contrive the means to bear you from these hated walls to a home of happiness and peace."

"Happiness!" iterated the Jewess, scornfully—"happiness with one of thy cruel race? No—I have had enough of Christian faith, of Christian love—I'll trust to them no more."

"Hear me swear—by every saint, by every knightly oath," said the esquire, casting an impassioned glance upon her.

"He, too, hath sworn," interrupted the captive, "and every vow is broken. It needs but a Christian oath to make me doubt thee more than I do already. False as he is, this withered heart will never know another love, or dream again the dream its girlhood dreamt. Stir not its slumbering ashes, Aymer, lest thou wake a flame which may consume, but never burn for thee."

"Be calm, this storm of passion else must soon destory thee."

"Yes, I will be calm," said Rachel, sternly, "as seas opposing winds, as the torn earth convulsed by fires. God of my fathers," she added, with an increased burst of passion, "was it, for this I left my peaceful home—lived the companion of his guilt and shame? Yet let the desperate libertine beware. Not the fierce tigress raging for her young—not the red lightning from Jehovah's hand, strike with more fury than a woman scorned."

The still beautiful creature stood, as she uttered her fearful denunciations, more with the aspect of an enraged pythoness than a human being; her dark black eyes flashed with intensity of hate. Aymer regarded her with pity as well as love, for he guessed but too well the fate to which Robert of Artois, to secure his own safety, would find it necessary to doom her, and from that he resolved at any rate to save her, wished her to live, though not for him.

"Rachel," he cried, at the same time taking her by the hand, "listen to me. It is not now the voice of passion, but of pity, speaks; thou hast said truly that all ties between thee and thy seducer are for ever broken; thou canst no longer hope to retain his heart; hast thou no danger to encounter from his hate?"

"His hate!" answered the wretched woman scornfully; "can it do more than his destroying love?"

"It can," replied the young man, "it can kill."

"And callest thou mercy hate?—the best boon Robert of Artois can bestow is death; for in the grave is peace."

The deep tone of sadness in the wretched woman's voice, as she answered the esquire, told him how vain were all his hopes of love: still he resolved, if possible, to save her, for like most ardent natures, there was a sentiment of generosity mingled with his wildest passions; every manly feeling was interested in a creature so outraged and so helpless; his emotion increased, therefore, as he resumed:

"There are outrages worse to a noble mind than death. Should he first resign thee to his brutal followers to be their prey—their scoff—their victim——"

"Hold!" shrieked the Jewess; "naught which wears a human form could consign the being it had loved to such a fate! Fiend, devil as he is, Robert of Artois would never contemplate so foul a deed; thou sayest this but to terrify me—to win me to thy purpose."

"No!" exclaimed Aymer; "deeply as I prize thy love, wondrous as is the enchantment of thy beauty, on my soul I would not win thee by an act of baseness. Hear me: I will provide thee with the means of flight. The lower postern by the water's edge is under my especial care, the key in my possession; soon as night draws on, I will unbar thy prison door, and thou mayst fly far from this den of infamy for ever."

"Alone?" demanded the Jewess, fixing a searching glance upon him.

"Alone," firmly replied Aymer. "If I live not for thy love, I may as well die here. Men may call me traitor; but none shall ever live to brand me with a coward's name. I could have borne that men should say, 'He fled his post in danger's hour for love;' but none shall have the right to think I quitted it through fear."

"The God of Abraham bless thee, Aymer, for thy generous heart!" exclaimed the Jewess, kissing his hand with deep emotion; "and he will bless thee, boy, with a purer, better love than mine—a love whose innocence shall cast its flowers around thy path, reminding thee of Eden's lost inheritance. I do accept thy offer; and for the remnant of my wretched days, deeply as I have suffered from Christian treachery, I will think better of its faith for thee. But why remain behind?"

"I have told thee," said the young man, calmly; "love only could, even to myself, excuse my flight in danger's hour."

Rachel gazed upon him long and sadly, and seemed, while doing so, to commune with herself. Once or twice she murmured, "So young!—so brave!" Her resolution, whatever it was, at last was taken. Her voice was calm as an infant's while she uttered it:

"Aymer," she said, "thou hast prevailed. To save thy life, I give thee the little that remains of heart within this blighted bosom. If the wreck be worth thy acceptance, take it; for it is thine. Would it were better worth thy noble nature."

"I understand thee, Rachel," answered the esquire; "I read thy generous purpose. Thou wouldst save me, despite myself, from the dangers which now threaten Filby, and then leave me to my fate alone."

"Not so," she answered. "Thou hast no right to doubt my words, for they have ever been to thee a voice of truth. I do repeat it," she added, with a slight blush—"once beyond these walls, all thou canst ask is thine."

Aymer could no longer doubt; he was like a man who in the moment of despair found the path of happiness suddenly opened to his view. Taking her hand, he covered it with passionate kisses, thanking her a thousand times, as he did so, for the generous sacrifice, and vowing that his life should be devoted to the task of effacing from her mind the recollection of past sorrows, and guarding her future happiness. There was a smile of incredulity upon the face of the Jewess as she listened to him with something like pity at the extravagant joy he manifested, a joy which she well knew was doomed to be changed to bitter disappointment.

"Leave me," she cried, gently releasing her hand. "I require to be alone. I must commune with my heart, and draw courage and resignation from myself. At the hour of escape you will find me ready. Hark!" she added, as the trumpet of the besiegers a second time echoed through the castle, "the enemy are already at the gates; hasten to thy post to avoid suspicion; but first leave me thy cloak, for my blood runs coldly, and my heart is chilled in these damp walls."

Aymer carefully enveloped the speaker's form in his ample mantle, whispered the word "adieu," and would have pressed a kiss upon her lips had not the sudden paleness which came over her warned him to desist.

"Not now—not now," she murmured "but a little, and I am wholly thine. At the appointed hour of flight thou wilt find me in my dungeon, and must lead me from these cursed walls in silence. Mark me, in silence; for my heart will be too full of the bitter memories of the past to bear the sound of human voice in sympathy."

"All, dearest Rachel," whispered Aymer, soothingly, "shall be as thou hast willed it. Till the hour arrives, farewell."

The young squire contented himself with once more pressing his lips upon her hand, and hurried from the cell.

"Poor boy!" sighed the Jewess, as the echo of his footsteps fell fainter upon her ear, "had I met a heart like thine, how different might have been my fate! Mayst thou live to find a destiny more pure and happy than I could make thee. 'Tis past," she added, brushing the tears from her dark lashes; "one sigh to the recollections of my abandoned home, my blighted youth, my broken heart; and then, like the daughter of my race of old, who smote Holofernes on his silken couch, to right my injuries in the vile Norman's blood."

For awhile Rachel continued to brood over her resolve, and arrange the means of its success. A proud smile lit her beautiful features as she contemplated, in the mirror of her mind, its concluding triumph. There was nothing of fear or doubt in its expression. For herself, she was equally insensible to danger as her heart was dead to hope. Drawing her tablets from beneath her vest, she seated herself upon a stone, and hastily traced a few lines, read them twice over, seemed satisfied with their contents, and

drawing Aymer's cloak around her, left the dungeon, which he had left unfastened.

It was evident, from the ease with which the Jewess threaded her way through the winding passages, that she was well acquainted with the locality of her prison. As she approached the battlements, however, her step became more cautious, and she drew the capuchin of the esquire's mantle over her head, so as completely to disguise her features. Of those whom she encountered, some took her for a young knight who was but just recovering from his wounds, and who for some time had inhabited the castle; others passed her without troubling themselves with a conjecture, so occupied were they with their individual danger, and calculating on their respective chances of safety in the coming contest.

Like a spectre the unhappy woman glided along the ramparts, still carefully veiling her face, and reached a solitary tower, where an old soldier kept watch; he was leaning on his bow as she approached, and seemed to contemplate the approaches of the enemy with an air of sullen indifference; so absorbed was he in his thoughts, that the light step of the intruder failed to disturb him; nor was it till he felt the pressure of her hand upon his shoulder that he started from his revery.

"Harro," she whispered, "hast thou forgotten me?" She threw back the hood which concealed her features as she spoke.

"No, lady," replied the old man, bowing reverentially; "this heart must indeed be cold when I forget the ministering angel who watched over the sick couch of my departed child; my heart may be a hard and rough one, but it retains the characters graved by the hand of gratitude the more indelibly. What brings thee to a scene like this?"

"Revenge," replied Rachel, calmly. "I have been spurned like a hound by him for whom I sacrificed all that woman can—honour, respect, and heaven. Thy master and my destroyer has doomed the victim he has made to death."

"To death!" echoed the soldier, with a look of astonishment; "surely you dream?"

"Not so," she answered; "my dream at last is ended. Wilt thou serve me in this my hour of peril? or are thy professions like those of the world, hollow and unstable as the breath which made them?"

"Speak," said the old man, "and prove them. Though it cost me my life, I will not belie my words. What am I to do?"

"Give me an arrow from thy quiver," answered the Jewess.

Harro did as he was requested, and Rachel, receiving the weapon, seated herself upon the ground, and endeavoured to affix the t blets, on which she had written in her dungeon, to the point. After searching her person for a ribbon or cord to tie them with, she quickly demanded of her companion if he had a knife. He took one from his girdle and gave it to her. Without a moment's hesitation she drew one of the long glossy tresses, which it had once been her pride to ornament, through her fingers, and severed it. In a few moments the tablets were securely fastened to the steel head of the instrument. Rising, she cast her glance around the scene before her till they rested on a distant banner, around which several knights and a man in the dark flowing robes of an ecclesiastic were assembled.

"Dost see those men," she demanded, pointing to the group, "those close by the prince's banner?"

The archer nodded his head in token of assent.

"Send me this shaft amongst them," she resumed, "and I will deem my kindness to thy child o'erpaid—thy every promise kept. Draw well thy bow," she added, as the man took the arrow and fitted it to his weapon, "for life or death hang on thy strength. Let thy arm be nerved by gratitude, as mine has been by vengeance—shoot as thou wouldst for freedom or for hate."

Harro did as she requested. Using his still great strength, he drew the missile to the very head; and so sure was his aim, that, despite the vast distance between him and his mark, he hit the very flag.

Rachel watched with eager eyes its flight, and saw with satisfaction that her design was answered; for an esquire raised the arrow, and bore it with its burthen to Herbert de Lozinga, the ecclesiastic who was conversing with the knights. The prelate read the writing to those around him; and Ulrick and Mirvan waved their scarfs in token that, whatever the request or information it conveyed, it was joyfully accepted.

"Thanks, old man!" exclaimed the Jewess; "thou hast done me the last service I shall ever ask of man; thy promise has been kept; a wretch's blessing rest upon thee! Shouldst thou escape the siege," she added, taking a collar of jewels from her neck, "these will provide thee comforts for thine age. Mayest thou live long and happy!"

She placed her gift in the archer's hand, and drawing the capuchin once more over her features, retraced her way cautiously towards the keep; her step was lighter as she did so, for she felt sure of vengeance.

"Let me but triumph in life's parting 'our," she murmured to herself, "and I will deem my sufferings o'erpaid; let the fatal ••" which didst preside over my mortal

destiny shine but propitious now, and I no more will curse its influence. Robert of Artois, I have kept my oath; I feel that we shall meet again."

Instead of returning to her dungeon, she passed along the now deserted armory, nor paused till she reached the door of the apartment where Matilda and her cousin were confined; a sentry had been placed there, who raised his partisan at her approach: his orders were that none should enter. Fortunately for Rachel's enterprise, she still retained the signet-ring of her betrayer, given to her charge in an hour of confidence, which her self-sacrifice had but too well merited. Extending her hand, she showed the glittering gem; exclaiming, as she did so:

"This signal all within the walls obey. I am charged by thy master to hold converse with his prisoners. Give me way."

The man not doubting the truth of her assertion, unhesitatingly lowered his weapon, and gave her egress to the chamber, where we must leave her for awhile, and return to the operations of the besiegers.

The flames had destroyed the buildings which connected the keep of Filby Castle with the lofty tower which served as principal entrance to the edifice. The two latter, however, still held good; the threat of Robert of Normandy binding their garrison and their chief by a sense of mutual safety. The principal efforts of the enemy were, however, directed against the keep, where they knew the captives were confined, and to which Robert of Artois and the greater number of his followers had retired. Herbert de Lozinga's men had brought several battering-rams with them, which, under the direction of George of Erpingham, they were suspending from their massive swings before the iron-plated gates of the stronghold. It was an object with the besieged to impede the progress of their labour, and it was the spot where the contest raged most fiercely. The northern side of the donjon, next the water, was unassailed, and comparatively unguarded. It was from an angle of this position that Harro had winged the shaft at the request of Rachel.

"Listen!" cried the prelate, as he reperused the billet. "We have friends within the walls. Heaven will bless our cause. Perhaps ere morning's dawn the lost brides may be restored to us."

"Read, father, read!" impatiently exclaimed both Ulrick and Mirvan.

The bishop did so:—"When the first hour of twilight falls, the little postern 'neath the northern bastion will be opened. Place your men in ambush. An esquire and a female will issue from the keep. As you would avoid the sin of deep ingratitude, harm not a hair of that man's head. His companion will explain the means by which the keep may be secured. Keep up the assault upon the western side, draw the attention of the besieged to that spot, and that alone. Once within the walls, courage and your own good swords must do the rest."

"Perhaps some snare," said Odo of Caen; "can you guess the writing?"

"Evidently a woman's hand," replied the reader, handing it at the same time to the two bereaved lovers.

Ulrick and Mirvan each in turn eagerly perused the scroll, and returned it to the prelate with a feeling of disappointment, for it was not the handwriting of either Isabel or Matilda.

"Be it from friend or foe, its counsel shall be tried," exclaimed Ulrick; "I will not lose one chance of vengeance."

"Right, boy!" cried his grandfather, the venerable Edda, who, despite his years, had been one of the foremost in the attack. "See! George of Erpingham waves his sword in signal that the battering rams are placed. Odo and I will conduct the assault, whilst you and your all but brother lead a party of your men by the wood, to avoid suspicion. Once within its friendly shade, let them steal one by one to the northern postern, if, as the writer promises, the door should open."

"Leave us to answer for the rest," interrupted the two young men, as they hastened to follow his advice, and drew off their men; "perhaps, when next we meet, we meet as victors. Farewell."

Ere the aged Saxon could reply, they were on their way.

"Allow me to join you," said Robert of Normandy, as Odo and the veteran marched to the scene of action. "My honour is engaged in this as deeply, knights, as yours. 'Tis long since I have joined in the noble game of war. My blood is warmed, and I feel eager for the sport."

The besieged, who well knew that the destruction of the portal must entail the surrender of the keep, used every means to defeat the efforts of their enemy. Huge benches were brought from the banquet hall, and hurled upon them, crushing numbers beneath their massive weight. Robert of Artois, with the courage which despair will often give, displayed a perseverance worthy of a better cause; armed with a large iron bar, he laboured to loosen one of the enormous stones which formed the battlements of his stronghold, the fall of any of which must have been fatal to his enemies and rendered their battering rams useless. He would doubtless have proved successful had his men seconded his efforts with

equal ardour to his own; but the slings of the Saxons, who were posted at a distance, so annoyed them, that they shrank behind the buttresses, and their leader only owed his safety to the strength of his armour, which was, however, bruised by the heavy blows it had received. As the battering of the huge beams fell upon the portal, he redoubled his frantic efforts, till the vast mass of stone trembled beneath his repeated shocks. So desperate did the besieged at last become, that they used the bodies of the dead and dying of their own party as missiles, and hurled them on the persevering foe.

The attention of all within the walls was directed to the western side so entirely that, as Edda had suggested, the body of men under the conduct of his grandson and Mirvan reached the postern of the lake, as their unknown correspondent had directed. The last rays of the setting sun had already kissed the bosom of the lake in token of adieu as they arrived there. With breathless impatience they waited for the promised opening of the gate; every moment seemed an age of suspense—an agony of expectation—whose endurance was torture to the mind. The massive doors at last turned slowly upon their rusty hinges, and the esquire Aymer appeared, leading a female closely veiled; in an instant he was secured and disarmed, and the portal closely guarded.

"What treachery is this?" cried Aymer, in astonishment at the unexpected attack; "am I betrayed?"

The youth was destined to a still greater surprise; for his supposed mistress, who was clad in the garments of Rachel, threw herself into the equally astonished Mirvan's arms; and raising her veil as she did, discovered the features of Isabel of Bayeux, whom the Jewess, in atonement for her former attempt upon her life, had thus contrived to save.

"Where," demanded Ulrick "is Matilda?"

"Still in the tyrant's power," sobbed the excited girl; "haste, if ye are men, to save her."

The words had scarcely passed her lips than Ulrick disappeared, followed by his men; he needed no clue—instinct seemed to guide his steps to the rescue of his betrothed. And Mirvan, after consigning his rescued cousin and her companion to a party of his archers to conduct them from the scene of danger, followed his example; for his heart was too generous to taste of happiness, while his sister's safety or his friend's peace of mind were still in peril.

The shrieks of dispair and the groans of the dying within the walls soon told to Robert of Artois that his den was in the hunter's power. Casting aside the bar which he still continued

THE SAXON LEADERS UNDER THE WALLS OF FILBY HOLD.

to wield, he rushed to the apartment where he had consigned his captives, and seizing on a female whom, from her dress, he recognised as Isabel of Bayeux, he dragged her with him to an isolated turret which rose by the side of the keep, the only communication between them being a wooden platform, which with a few blows of his sword was easily destroyed.

In a few moments Mirvan and Ulrick were masters of the keep, the enemy being entirely subdued.

"Yield thee, traitor!" cried the latter, gazing with agony on the veiled woman whom Robert of Artois still held firmly by the hand,

and whom he believed to be Matilda; "yield, and I spare thy life. But as thou art a man, harm not that trembling dove beside thee."

"Here me, vile Saxon," replied the baffled villain. "I have sworn that Isabel of Bayeux shall be mine; and here, amid the ruin of my house, the destruction of my friends, I keep my oath and triumph still."

"And I," exclaimed the Jewess, dashing aside her veil, and gazing sternly upon the destroyer of her peace, "keep mine. In life or death, I swore to be beside thee. Where is now the blooming bride thou didst prefer to Rachel's fervent love?—safe in her kindred's arms. Where is now thy hold of tyranny and blood?—the despised Rachel gave it to the triumphant foe. In death— in death we are united! This is a fitting scene for nuptials such as ours. Receive my bridal kiss."

Before the astonished Norman could recover from his disappointment and surprise, Rachel drew the knife which Harro had lent her on the bastion, and plunged it into her seducer's throat. Although her heart beat wildly as she did so, her hand was firm.

"My oath, my oath is kept!" shrieked the wretched woman, as she beheld her victim fall. "God of my fathers, have pity on the guilty child!"

Still holding the weapon with which she had struck the blow firmly in her hand, she sprang from the lofty battlements; one shriek, like some despairing angel's cry, rose on the air, and all was still.

"Such is the end of crime," exclaimed Herbert de Losinga, who with Edda and Odo of Caen had _____ _____ of Matilda, and conducted _____ _____ Filby hold be lev_____ _____ men in future may _____ _____ master's crimes."

CHAPTER XIX.

For he is one of the sacred three,
To whom the word and sign were given,
Whose might unfolds that mystery,
Which the angel read as he fell from heaven.
                                    BABYLONIA TARGUM.

ILBY HOLD having been completely destroyed, the victorious party returned to Norwich, where, in a few days, by the bishop's advice, the double marriages of Ulrick and Mirvan were in a few days celebrated, amidst the rejoicings of the _____ _____, and the vassals both of _____ _____ the young earl's _____ _____ and _____ equally rejoiced in the double tie which cemented the union of the two most powerful leaders of the rival races within the Angles, promised to that portion of the distracted kingdom at least a temporary peace. Herbert de Lozinga had urged the immediate completion of the ceremony, despite the recent death of Matilda's father; for the experienced, wary statesman saw the contest likely to ensue on the death of William the Conqueror—an event which he daily expected to hear; and he determined to place the happiness of his favourite beyond the chance of war, by a tie which, even in that rude age of despotism and cruelty, was too powerful to be broken—the sanction of the church.

"Bless you, my children!" he exclaimed, as the two noble youths and their trembling brides knelt to receive his benediction; "may your lives flow on pure as the current of your thoughts, calm as the exercise of your virtues; may children who resemble you spring like fragrant flowers around you, adorn your path of life, and cheer its _____ close; may the future crown you with its hopes, and past sorrows be repaid you in the present."

Tears—but they were now tears of joy—bedewed the cheeks of Edith as her maternal heart echoed the prelate's benediction; and she breathed a silent prayer that Ulrick's life might prove happier—far happier than her own. Edda too, the venerable Edda, beheld in his grandson's marriage the promise of his race renewed; and added a blessing equally sincere, but equally destined to be vain.

The day was passed in rejoicing, usual at the period the poor were plentifully regaled, the vassals contend led in trials of manly skill and strength, whilst their lords jousted in the lists, where Matilda and Isabel, as queens of beauty, sat to reward and encourage by their smiles the victors and the combatants. The day was a glorious one, and the shields of the nobles and knights, which were affixed to lances round the lists, showed their rich blazonry in the rays of the sun. The two bridegrooms had proved successful in almost every encounter, and thrice laid their trophies at the fair umpires' feet. Even Odo of Caen had been unhelmed by Ulrick, and laughingly observed that if marriage gave such strength of arm, he too must become a Benedict. Robert of Normandy, although passionately addicted to the knightly sport, gallantly declined to joust, declaring that the champions of two such dames must be invincible. It was the law of the tournament that any knight who wished to try the prowess of another should challenge him by touching the shield affixed for that purpose beneath his pennon with his lance—its owner, armed *cap-à-pie*, generally remaining on horseback by its side, unless when engaged in the *mêlée*, or in some separate contest. The sports were nearly ended, when an arrow, sent by some unknown hand amongst the crowd, transfixed the shield of Ulrick. The method of conveying a challenge was so unusual, that most men thought it accident, till Edda, as marshal of the lists, drawing it out, discovered a label of parchment affixed to it, with these ominous words: "Foiled, but not subdued!" The old man mournfully shook his head as he read the inscription, which he crushed quickly in his hand to conceal it from his grandson, unwilling that a cloud of doubt should mar the sunshine of his present hour.

"This is no common arrow," said Odo of Caen, regarding it attentively. "Its feather has been plucked from the ill-omend raven's wing; the spirit of Artois hovers round us still. I fear more evil yet,"

"I fear so too," observed Hella, the bard, who was standing near his patron, and to whose excitable imagination the circumstance seemed fraught with evil fortune. Had he seen the writing, the impression would have been even more gloomy and profound, for he was one of those who drew omens from birds, and mysteries from every thing. "Who saw the traitor's body?" he demanded.

Neither Edda, Odo of Caen, nor any of the nobles who were standing round, remembered to have seen it.

"Perhaps," resumed the speaker, "the wolf is only wounded, not destroyed. Ulrick may live to feel its fangs again."

"Psha!" interrupted the bridegroom, who had seen the flight of the arrow, and who arrived on the spot time enough to hear the last observation; "the Jewess struck home; and there is no blow so sure as that which is nerved by hate. Besides, tower and keep are both levelled with the dust, and our enemy's bones, doubtless, lie crushed beneath them. But be he living or dead, in body or in spirit, with my good sword, and friends like these around me, I can defy him."

Many a friendly glance answered the appeal; and Ulrick, in the sincerity of his own heart, believed them.

At this instant the prince gave the signal to end the jousts by throwing down his truncheon, and the brides were conducted to the castle, amid the shouting of the multitude and the benedictions of the poor, to keep their marriage feasts. This time the gifted Saxon bard poured out no unwelcome song as his harp sent forth its strain in honour of the bridegrooms and their brides:

"Lady, although thy cheek be pale,
  Thy grief is but the bride's sweet sorrow;
Fling over her the silver veil,
  Her eyes will sparkle bright to-morrow.
The jewels in her bridal wreath,
  Like rays of light and dewdrops clashing,
Are rivalled by the gems beneath—
  The eyes, through beauty's glad tears flashing.
Fill to the bride a ruby cup,
  And twine it with the choicest flowers;
With wine and nectar fill it up,
  As emblem of her future hours.
Hail to the bridegroom and the bride!
  Warm hearts are now around them pressing,
Hands that would aid whate'er betide,
  And kindred lips pronounce their blessing.
Then, lady, though thy cheek be pale,
  Thy tears are but the bride's sweet sorrow;
Fling over her the silver veil,
  Her eyes will sparkle bright to-morrow."

The revel was continued to a late hour; and long after the wine-cup had been pledged to the new-made brides, the song and merry laugh echoed through the old walls of Norwich Castle.

In a remote corner of the city, near the old church of St. Julian, stood a lone house, whose neglected and time-stricken exterior would have conveyed the idea that it was uninhabited, had not the well-cultivated garden, which extended from the back even to the cemetery, proved that careful hands attended it. Plants of foliage and blossom unknown to Europe were to be found within its low-walled enclosure. This garden was an object of considerable interest and curiosity to the thinly scattered inhabitants who dwelt between it and the water's edge. No human eye had ever seen the mysterious gardener at his work; still his labours were evident in the weeded walks, and careful training of its flowers and fruits. The house, unlike the ordinary buildings of the period, was entirely of stone. The only apertures for the admission of light were to the back, and so narrow and guarded by coarse wooden slides, that it more resembled a fortress than an ordinary dwelling. Its doors—for it had but two, one to the back and front—were studded with thick iron nails. Few persons, however, had ever seen them open; and such casual passengers or watchers who had, shrunk with terror from its inmates, for they were of the despised race of Israel—a people looked upon with abhorrence by the lower orders, and cruelly persecuted on account of their wealth by the nobles and petty vavasours of the lands in which they dwelt. Sometimes, however, they secured toleration from their skill in medicine; and many a feudal lord, who would have wrung the last mark from the Hebrew, protected his physician. In their latter character even the church respected them; and mitred abbots and dignified prelates, when suffering from the surfeit or the spleen, condescended to invoke their aid.

It was to the reputation which the master of the lone house in question had acquired in the capacity of leech that he owed the degree of safety he enjoyed. Abram, for such was his name, was from [the East—the land of gold and gems, of mystery and beauty—alike the cradle of the faith and superstitions of mankind. 'Tis strange when we reflect how little Europe has really given to the world; it has perfected science more than created it; it has accepted religion—split and divided it into sects, but founded none. The East seems to have been like the first-born child, endowed with the Creator's peculiar blessing.

On the night of Ulrick's nuptials, a boat carefully rowed glided down the river which half encircles the city, past the abbey of Carrow, and stopped only when it reached the shore facing the mansion of the Jew. The rowers carefully drew the boat from out the stream, and having formed a sort of litter with their oars, placed something like a human form upon it; it was difficult to distinguish what, so carefully was it enveloped in the boatmen's cloaks. Gently they raised their burthen on their shoulders, and, preceded by a man in armour who had conducted the operation, slowly directed their steps towards the house we have described. Whatever might be the purport of their visit, it was evident that they were expected; for, on the first signal, the door was opened to them, and closed the instant they had passed the threshold with their burthen.

They were received by a tall, aged man, bearing a brazen lamp, whose strange costume and venerable appearance impressed even the leader of the little band with awe and respect. His beard of silvery whiteness, worn long, after the fashion of the East, flowed loosely over his dark gaberdine, which, although made in the prescribed form, differed in richness of materials from those generally worn by his persecuted race; a girdle of silver confined it to his waist; the plates which composed it were graved with Hebrew characters, as was the case of writing materials, and the clasp of a pocket curiously ornamented with needle-work, which, from chains of the same metal, depended from it. The wearer's features were sharp and intellectual; the forehead was magnificently high; the eyes, despite his age, quick and penetrating, but characterised by that restlessness of expression which long habits of watchfulness in scenes of continued danger give; the aquiline nose

and peculiar lip marked his descent from the despised nation of the Jews.

"Place your burden there," said the old man, pointing to a low couch covered with deer-skins and soft matting. "Holy Abraham! but 'tis a fearful risk to run. The prince and nobles have doomed him to the gibbet, and should it be discovered that I have aided him, little would they reck in their fury of the poor leech's life. 'Tis a fearful risk; but it must be run—it must be run. Persecuted as we are ourselves, we owe something to humanity."

"And something to thine interest, Jew," replied the esquire. "The day will come when he who sheltered Robert of Artois may lift his head with the proudest. My master hath friends more powerful than thou wotst of. This unnatural league between the Norman and the Saxon race cannot last long. The Conqueror draws near to his last breath; his successor will dearly avenge his favourite's wrongs on those who have assailed him; and my master's blazon will once more shine with the proudest. His future sovereign's favour awaits him, should be live; if not, it will avenge him."

"I am no stranger to the value of a prince's gratitude," replied Abram, with a quiet smile; "but say, how didst thou save him from the ruins of his strong castle? The world reports him dead; and those who trembled at his name, whilst living, now fearlessly curse his memory."

"I alone," replied the esquire, "was with him in the tower, except the daughter of thy accursed race, whose jealous hand struck the fatal wound. I saw him fall, and would have avenged, had not the traitress done justice on herself by plunging from the dizzy height, ending her vile career by death. I drew him from the battlements to a secret vault beneath, where for days he hath remained concealed alike from friend or foe; the fools who levelled both keep and tower in dust little thought that every stone which fell but added to my master's safety by hiding the entrance of his concealment. Thou knowest the rest."

"A Jewess!" exclaimed the old man, vainly endeavouring to suppress his agitation; "how came one of our nation to rise her rebellious hand against a Christian's life? But thou hast answered me; thou speakest of jealousy —knowest thou the maiden's name?"

"Rachel," replied the Norman; "she was the daughter of the chief rabi of Rouen; my lord took her at the sacking of the city, when Duke Robert seized it from the French. For awhile she was all in all, but at last became so jealous that his love soon tired: too much fondness fatigues us in a woman; it is the chasing of the deer gives pleasure to the hunter; few prize the game which is so easily won."

A half-suppressd groan broke from the bosom of the old man when he heard the name of the unfortunate being who had been alike the victim of her own passions and Robert ot Artois' cruelty. With a violent effort of self-control he mastered his emotion, and pointed to the men who had borne the wounded noble to his house, to remove the cloaks in which he had been wrapped. Brantone—for such was the name of the esquire—would have started, had he seen the fierce glance of hate which flashed from the eyes of the leech when the pale features of the wounded man first met his view—the basilisk's alone could have been less fearful. Drawing a small silver probe from the case of instruments which he wore suspended by his side, he proceeded to examine the wound, which was situated in the lower part of the throat, just between the juncture of the neck-piece and the coat of mail.

"Has thy master no friends or kinsmen near," demanded the Jew, "in whom he can confide?"

"I know but one," replied Brantone; "the prior of the Dominicans—his uncle, by the mother's side; all else have failed him."

"Send for him quickly, then." resumed the old man; "for in twenty-four hours he must answer for his sins. All human aid is in vain. The blow hath been too deeply struck for human skill to save him; and I would not, for the world, a Christian noble should expire beneath my roof."

"Dog!" said the soldier, raising his hand to strike him, "were it a palace, he would honour it."

Abram started back, and drew a long sharp-pointed weapon from his bosom, and calmly awaited the attack of the infuriated esquire, who paused, half ashamed of his own violence, and half awed by the calm attitude of the aged man before him, who seemed so bowed by years, that he felt that he could crush him with a breath.

"Back!" exclaimed the Jew; "for did the blood of thousands circle in thy veins, thy death were instant. Willingly I would not take thy life; for the fierce storm which once raged here is now at peace. A blow would thaw the frozen barriers of my blood, and spread, like Etna's lava, desolation around."

"Patience, old man!" cried the superstitious Norman; "I did not mean to harm thee. Let there be peace between us."

"Fear not," resumed Abram; "I am cool—quite cool. Reptiles only sting without discernment. Approach, young man," he added, willing to increase the impression he had already made upon the terrors of the strong soldier; "nay, fear me not. Observe

how wisdom may contend with stre how palsied age may bid defiance to th of youth. Look on this tiny instrum observe it well; 'tis formed of that p steel which in the East men prize fa than gold. Tempered in fires lit fi nature's hand, then quenched in snows with the world, the slender point infl gaping wound, but a slight puncture —a sempstress's needle would give as scratch; but the point is venomed—an with —— Enough! this land breeds r reptile from whose sting 'twas ta'en."

"It might serve thee against one, gedly answered Brantone, struggling ceal his terrors, "but would be useless our numbers, were we inclined to outr

"Thou wouldst not be that one," s leech, with an accent of cold contempt I am armed, were it against thousands. ing not death, I have surrounded n hearth with them. Norman, there's no within these walls but hides a grav blow," he added, catching up an ebon and pointing to a globe of coarse gla pended from the ceiling, "and a storn fearful than the simoom's breath would these strong-built walls, and tear their i limb from quivering limb. Away!" he "thou knowest my power—knowest ho that the old leech fears thee. Away, my bidding to the prior. Tell him, four-and-twenty hours shall pass, his n sleep will be eternal. I have staunche a wound—recalled the fleeting life t a lance-pierced breast; but here e'en A skill must fail."

Whether the physician spoke from conscious power, or from his knowledg human heart, so prone to superstition, i perhaps be difficult to decide. Certa that he possessed vast knowledge, wit charlatanism mixed with it. His however, produced the desired effect u hearers—ruffians who, under ordinary stances, would have desired no bette than to ill-treat and persecute a Jew. out a single word they retired from the nor breathed freely till they found the beneath the shadow of the church, wher according to the superstition of the evil power could approach them.

"Praise be to our Lady!" exclaimed the men, devoutly crossing himself, " safe from yon den of sin. I would have another such a siege as Filby the an hour in it. Think you, sir squire, Christian's part to leave our master keeping? 'Tis true his body is past for, but then his soul!"

"Pooh!" answered Brantone; "his the worthy prior, will care for that;

sinner will be too well paid to play him false; the church would know how to deal with him should the Jew attempt aught against his salvation."

"Ay, ay," interrupted a third; "leave the church alone to deal with infidels and sorcerers; a sprinkling of holy water would take the devil from out the best of them. I saw the Archbishop of Rouen lately burn three of them: they were fine robust fellows when they went into the prison, and fought with their guards like troopers, but the church soon tamed them; they walked on the morning of their execution as meekly to the stake as a lamb does to the slaughterhouse, and sang their own funeral service as piously as any monk of them all."

"Our master, I tell you again, is safe," interrupted the esquire, who well knew his companion's tediousness when once mounted upon his favourite hobby—sorcerers and infidels. "'Tis time that we should separate; I must to the holy prior, who will doubtless repay our fidelity to his nephew with something more solid than benedictions, and you to your hiding-place in Filby woods. When all is over, we can pass to Normandy, where a good lance never lacks employment, or a good sword need hang rusty in its scabbard."

With these words the group separated; the men to regain their boats, and the esquire to the distant monastery of the Dominicans, where dwelt the uncle of the unworthy Robert of Artois.

As the party left the house of the Jew, the old man carefully closed the iron-bound door, and secured it by a massive chain and many a well-forged bolt; then raising his lamp from the stone floor, where he had placed it, he slowly directed his steps to the chamber where he had left the wounded man. Going to a small cabinet, he carefully drew from it various balsams and dressings, and spread them on the table in the middle of the room. To have gazed upon him, few would have suspected the storm of passions raging in his breast, his manner was so calm, his actions so deliberate. A slight impatient quivering only in the fingers, something like the half clutch of the impatient vulture's claw, might have indicated to a very close observer that his office was not one of love, but a ministry of hate. Cautiously he cleansed the wound, and poured in the healing styptic, bound the throat, and then prepared a draught for his exhausted patient.

"Precious elixir!" he murmured, "few in this island have ever tasted of thy healing virtues. I shall never more behold the flowers from which thy subtle essence was distilled. Little did I dream, when first in Syria's land of wisdom I prepared it, that I should ever waste it on my bitterest foe. But he must live," he added fiercely between his teeth; "live for a vengeance unheard of until now; for a vengeance which alone can expiate a wrong like mine."

The sweet perfume of the balsam filled the chamber as it flowed into the cup. Highly as the Jew prized it, he poured it with no niggard hand; so true is it that hate can sometimes be as liberal as love. With almost a mother's care he raised the head of the wounded man, and poured the rich draught down his throat, then gently replaced him on his pillow, and, with his finger fixed upon his pulse, watched by him till he slept.

As soon as the deep breathing of Robert of Artois convinced the old man that the medicine had taken effect, he rose from his seat beside him, and walking to the foot of the couch, gazed upon him for a few moments in fearful silence.

"Yes," he exclaimed, "the God of Israel, though slow, is just; the destroyer of my fair and innocent child, like a helpless infant, is prostrate at my mercy. Rachel," he added, passionately, "why did I not sooner know thy destiny? For years so near thee, yet ignorant of the casket which contained my treasure. I would have ransomed all thy tears with pearls: as it is, they shall be repaid thee by his groans. He scorned thee too, poor girl! He shall have scorn for scorn, become his brother nobles' jest, be scourged from the hall of his fathers, like some vile impostor, and die despairing and accursed. If I could not save my offspring, I can at least avenge her. But stay," he added, "something the Nazarene spoke of thy heroic death. Thy bones must not bleach amidst the ruins of thy tyrant's hold! No Christian foot shall ere profane them. I will myself go forth while thy destroyer sleeps, and, as the patriarch of old sought for the body of his son, so will I seek Rachel, lost child, for thine."

The bereaved parent struck a gong suspended by the side of his cabinet; its low musical sound was echoed through the house, and answered by a being who was half giant and half dwarf, so disproportionate was the contrast between his height and the vast breadth of his shoulders, the length of his arms, and the shortness of his legs, the muscles of both of which indicated agility and strength. Although somewhat advanced in years, he was far less aged than his master, whom he looked upon with a love and veneration amounting to idolatry, not only as a high priest of his nation, but as one of the wisest and best of created beings. To him his will was law; and he would as soon have thought of questioning the slightest expression of it, as of disputing the law of Moses, or the authenticity of the Pentateuch. Unlike most persons of his peculiar formation, there was nothing repulsive in his features ; on the contrary, they were indicative not only of benevolence and intellect, but were distinguished by manly beauty. From his earliest childhood he had lived in the family of Abram, had partaken with him persecution and sorrow, as well as shared the few brief moments of sunshine in the old man's chequered wandering life.

" Erza," said his master, " hast thou heard of the destruction of Filby hold, the castle of the bold bad man who now lies sleeping here?"

" I have, father of the faithful race of Israel," answered the dwarf. " Eli, who purchased many vessels and much goodly plate of the spoilers, told me a strange tale concerning it; it seems the castle was betrayed into the hands of his enemies by some wanton daughter of our race, the discarded paramour of his fierce lusts."

" Speak not thus harshly of her," interrupted his master; " for, oh! she was my child; flesh of my flesh, blood of my blood; my long-lost, only child. When," he added bitterly, " shall Israel efface the stains of her captivity amongst the heathen?"

The dwarf was struck to the heart by the tone of anguish in the old man's voice; he too had known and loved the erring Rachel, had watched her little footsteps when a child, heard her repeat her infant prayers, and when her ripening beauties opened to womanhood, guarded her with a parent's love, with almost a lover's jealous care. Her loss, which occurred during the siege of Rouen, was scarcely more felt by her father than himself. Madly he rushed from street to street, calling frantically upon the name of Rachel, and proffering sums so fabulous for her recovery that all who heard him deemed him mad. The sight of the being who had caused so much misery to himself and master excited his fury, and with a spring he bounded towards the couch, and doubtless would have strangled him, had not the voice of Abram restrained him from his purpose.

" Hold, Erza!" he cried; " would that be vengeance?"

" No!" answered the dwarf, turning his eyes from the sleeper, as if fearful to trust them further.

" Leave him to me," resumed the old man; " at present we must go forth, whilst night favours our design. My Rachel's bones shall not be left to be trampled on by Christian feet. Bring our cloaks, and let the boat be ready."

Carefully securing the house, the disguised Israelites made their way to the water-side,

from whence a boat, rowed by the strong arms of Erza, took them to Acle, where horses were easily procured, to Filby. Abram found, by inquiries from one of his people, whom the thirst of gain led to remain all night about the ruins, that his daughter's remains had been interred, by order of Ulrick, under an oak, at a bow-shot from the spot where she had fallen. By the aid of his companions, it was quickly removed; and the dwarf, taking it in his arms, mounted with it on horseback, the living and the dead both being covered by a cloak. Day light had dawned when they reached the house.

The lordly prior of the Dominicans was seated at his morning repast when a servitor announced the arrival of the esquire of his nephew, whose supposed loss he bore with wonderful equanimity, although the world had previously given him credit for entertaining a sincere affection for him. The order to admit him was immediately given, for he hoped to find him the bearer of certain letters which had passed between himself and his relative, the discovery of which would seriously compromise with Herbert de Lozinga, his spiritual superior Hastily draining the remainder of the spiced hypocras in the flagon before him, he wiped his full lips with his linen kerchief, and prepared to receive him. Brantone, as was usual when approaching churchmen of his rank, bent the knee as he entered the apartment, exclaiming as he did so :

" Your benediction, reverend father! your benediction!"

" *Pax Dei sit semper vobiscum !*" muttered the priest, at the same time swallowing the remaining morsel of the manchet-bread. " Hast brought me any letters from my nephew?"

" Alas! reverend father, you must be aware that he is unable to write."

" I should think so," drily answered the prior, who imagined that the esquire was trying the depth of his feelings, and the soldier on his part supposing that the uncle had been informed of his nephew's almost miraculous escape.

" It will be some time before you will hear from him again."

" I should hope so," answered the priest, not altogether pleased with what he considered Brantone's familiarity.

" Besides, even if he could find strength to write, it would be difficult to find a messenger in his present abode."

" I should think so, friend," replied the ecclesiastic, crossing himself; " but answer me, did your master, previous to his death, confide any papers to your charge? If so,

kly let me have them. Poor fellow," he
d, "his fate should be a warning to us
ow we indulge in our sinful passions, or
ge in dangerous enterprise."

How, reverend father!" exclaimed the
er. "You are not yet aware that your
ew, Robert of Artois, still lives?"

Lives!" echoed the uncle, with an ex-
ion of anything like agreeable surprise;
d what does he want with me? Doubt-
gold—more gold. I had need hold the
acy and my poor priory to boot to
ly half his extravagance; it hath nearly
d me already."

My noble master will never need gold
; he is wounded unto death."

And where is he concealed?"

In the house of the Jew-leech Abram,
e skill none can question, whatever they
his honesty. He will not answer for
fe more than for four-and-twenty hours.
nust not die," added the man, "with-
he church's aid."

Doubtless! doubtless!" muttered the
t. "I will dispatch brother Felix—he
alous and discreet; besides, I will order
es to be said for his repose. The church,
gh poor in worldly wealth, is rich in
ual grace."

Had you not better shrive him your-
? demanded the esquire, bluntly. "Me-
s it were but kind to do him that last
office, considering he is your sister's

. . . enter the house of an unbelieving Jew?
aema! Think on the scandal, my dear
Should the prior of the Dominicans be
to enter such a den of wickedness, it
l be a blister on my name."

Better that, than other ears should
to the confession of your nephew,"
d Brantone, who began to see through
lespise the selfish nature of the church-
s fears. "You know best what has
d between your kinsman and yourself;
es, none but you can prevail on the
e of St. Julian to receive his body into
crated ground. Sir prior," he added
, "you must come."

Well, I suppose I must. Blessed St.
inic! shield thy unworthy servant—
him from this labyrinth; and if ever
——But how," he added, interrupting
elf in his invocation when he observed
soldier regarding him—"how, without
al, am I to get there?"

Of course, reverend father, you are free
ave the convent at your pleasure."

Certes I am," answered the prior.

Nothing more easy," continued Bran-
. "As soon as nightfall, conceal your
in my horseman's cloak; I will be

your escort to the Jew's, where you may
give my master a cast of your holy office, and
none the wiser; long ere the matin bell, you
can return in safety to your nest."

"Thou sayst he has not many hours to
live?" said the priest, regarding him with a
keen glance.

"Thou mayst take the Jew's word for it,
father, if not mine."

"Then I will go," said the prior, firmly,
"and trust my person to thy escort; return
at evening's close. And here," he added,
drawing a piece of gold from his pouch, "is
something for thine entertainment; but first
go to the curate of St. Julian's, and tell him
in my name to meet me at the house of the
accursed Jew. Fortunately his cure is a
dependancy upon our priory, and he may
look for advancement at our hands. Heaven speed thee, my son; be fortunate, and
above all discreet."

The esquire bowed reverentially to the
dignitary, pocketed the coin, and quitted the
apartment.

At the curfew, or the following hour, the
reverend uncle was seated by the side of his
wounded nephew in the lone house of Abram.
Contrary to his expectation, he found the
wounded man apparently recovering from
his hurt; his voice, though low, was clear,
and his eye bright as ever, although his
cheek was pale.

"Dog of an unbelieving race," said the
ecclesiastic, who stood calmly beside the
couch of his patient, "didst thou not send
me word the days of my nephew were numbered: nay, his very hours? and yet I find
him strong."

"My words are of truth," replied the
leech; "the strength thou seest is but the
last rallying of life, a flash before the lamp
expires. The sun which gilds the coming
day will shine upon his corse."

"Liar!" shouted Robert of Artois; "I
have been wounded nearer to death than
this! I shall live—I will live for vengeance! I will be a brand to thy accursed
race! My enemies shall bite the dust before
me! Exert thy skill—thou hast not expended
all thy nostrums. Stretch the utmost efforts
of thine art; mine uncle here will glut thine
avarice with gold, pour it like water on thy
thirsty palm; he hath my hoarded treasure in
his keeping; all shall be thine, save but my
fleeting life!"

The dignitary winced uneasily upon his
seat, and muttered something about his nephew
raving.

"It shall be tried," murmured the old man,
"not so much for the gold as for the pleasuring your reverend kinsman."

Abram left the room for a few minutes;

ULRICK, DISGUISED, AT THE BARRIER OF LUDGATE.

when he returned he bore a small silver cup in his hand, which contained a highly balsamic liquid, and offered it to the lips of the impatient knight.

"Drink!" he exclaimed; "'tis thy last chance of life—a frail one, it is true. Should it fail, all human aid is hopeless; a few, a very few short moments will decide."

Robert of Artois eagerly drained the draught, and sank exhausted upon his pillow. The old man quietly took his seat beside him. Something like a smile of satisfaction was visible on his features as his long, sharp, bony hand encircled the wrist of the drinker. For more than a quarter of an hour he watched his patient in silence, accustomed to veil every emotion of his heart under a mask of cold impassibility. He hid, even from the keen churchman, the fierce joy he felt as the pulse beat fainter and fainter beneath the pressure of his finger. Seeing that the draught had operated, he rose from his seat and whispered to the prior:

"All that human skill can accomplish hath been done; what now remains rests between the priest, his conscience, and his God. In an hour Robert of Artois will slumber with the dead."

No. 13.

"I'll have no priest!" shrieked Robert, as Abram left the chamber. "I call upon the fiends to save me. Can I not make a compact but for one year of life? I'll give my wealth, possessions — my soul," he added, "but to live! Will not the tempter hear, or is it but a fable? Is there no heaven or hell, angel or demon to assist me?"

The Jew smiled as he withdrew yet further from the chamber. The despairing curses of the destroyer of his child fell like music on his ear. They were the promise of the completion of his deeply-meditated vengeance.

The hour, as the leech had predicted, had scarcely passed when the prior summoned the curate of St. Julian's to his presence; he was followed both by Brantone and Abram. It was clear from the livid cheek of the churchman that his nephew's confession had been a fearful one, for the blood had entirely forsaken his features, and the perspiration hung in thick drops upon his clouded brow. The appearance of the couch was yet more terrible: the teeth were firmly set, the eyes distended as if they would leap from the head, and its fingers entangled in the fragments of the coverlid which had been torn in its last fearful agony. So terrible was the appearance of the body, that all but the Jew turned from it in disgust.

"Brother," said the dignitary, addressing his subordinate with that tone of blandness with which a superior intimates a command, which the conscience of the hearer should reject; "thou knowest of the misfortune which hath fallen on my house; my nephew is no more; praise to our Lady, he died penitent. See the body secretly interred this very night within the vaults of the chapelry, and in the

morning visit me at my priory. We have long watched thy zeal and diligence in the fold of which we are but an unworthy shepherd, and it is our intention to remove thee to a more extended field of usefulness. For thee, Jew," he added, "the worthy curate on his return will pay thee for thy skill and kindness shown towards the deceased; although the former was but valueless, I need not tell thee to be silent on the events of which thou hast been a witness. Remember this, I caution not twice. Brantone will escort me on my return. Farewell, and benedicite!"

Abram and the priest both bowed low as the prior, without casting a glance upon the couch where lay the body of his nephew, quitted the apartment, and issued from the house. That very night Robert of Artois, the noble Norman, whose sword had been the terror of the country, whose exactions desolated the hearts of many a peasant and petty franklin, was consigned to what the world deemed his last resting-place, by the hands of two Jews; no knightly banner waved over his remains, no sculptured scutcheon marked his resting-place.

"He will rest securely there," said the curate, as he turned the key in the massive lock of the vault. "The funeral rites must be celebrated at some fitting time. Farewell, friends! I will convey the prior's benefaction to you in the morning; that once done, forget that we have met."

And the pious man pursued his way towards his quiet cell, wondering as he went at his good fortune. The Israelite and his attendant dogged his foot-steps till they saw him housed, and then retraced their pathway to the church.

CHAPTER XX.

Hail, king! for so thou art the time is free
I see thee compass'd with thy kingdom's pearl,
Who speak my salutations in their minds;
Whose voices I desire aloud with mine,—
Hail, king of Scotland!—SHAKSPERE.

AUTIOUSLY the two Isrealites entered the church, and groped their way to the steps which conducted to the vaults where rested the body of Robert of Artois. It was not till they had descended that they ventured to light the torch which the dwarf had brought with him for that purpose; for the expedition they were engaged in was one of danger, should any curious eye discover their proceedings. The superstitious as well as religious feelings of the age being opposed to the mere entrance of any of their hated nation within the consecrated precincts even in open

day, much more so at the lone hour of night, when, according to popular belief, pale witchcraft celebrated its fearful rites—their mere presence under such circumstances was sufficient to condemn them to the stake. The body of the knight had been deposited in an old stone coffin, which had previously served some former inmate, but which in the revolution of time had been despoiled of its original tenant; the rudely-sculptured cross upon its lid indicated that it had been intended as the final resting-place of an ecclesiastic:

" Some lordly abbot or some mitred priest,
  Whose hand had grasped the crosier's holy staff,
  Or scattered benedictions on the crowd."

"Help me to raise the lid," whispered Abram; "the carrion may be stifled else within its narrow cell. Holy Jacob! how these Nazarene dogs guard their vile ashes from their heir, the worm! Their pride revolts lest their polluted dust should mingle with its purer kindred earth. So much for Christian vanity in death!"

By the aid of Erza's powerful arm the lid of the sarcophagus was soon removed, and the features of the supposed corpse once more exposed to the sweet air of heaven. The elder Israelite gazed upon his destined victim, with an air of ferocious joy, as he placed his hand upon his pallid brow, and felt the gentle moisture which already began to ooze from the sleeper's skin; for our readers, doubtless, have already suspected that the draught which the leech had administered to Robert of Artois in the presence of the prior was nothing more than a powerful soporific, the wound he had received being anything but likely to cause his death, although from neglect and loss of blood it had occasioned considerable exhaustion.

"We must be brief," said Erza, disturbing the old man's reverie of vengeance; "day soon will dawn; and it is not good men's eyes should gaze upon us, bearing the body to the house—shall I raise him?"

Abram made a sign of assent, and his companion soon removed the sleeper from his recumbent position; and, with the assistance of the old man, was proceeding to envelop him in a cloak brought with them for the purpose, when a deep voice startled them. The curate had recollected that the body had been interred with several articles of value, which the prior, in the agitation of the moment, had either forgotten or not thought it worth while to remove; amongst them a chain of gold and precious signet ring had attracted his avarice, and he was returning to the vault to secure them, when he was startled by the sight of the two Jews, whom he doubted not were there with the same intention. So servile was the respect and deference which all

of their race paid to the humblest member of his sacred profession, so accustomed was he, in trampling upon them, to find an unresisting neck, that the idea of any possible danger to himself never once crossed his imagination.

"Dogs!" he exclaimed; "is it thus ye abuse the mercy of our holy church, which suffers ye to draw your polluted breath in Christian lands in peace?—violate the dead! break open the sepulchre of a noble knight for the sake of the treasures he can no longer defend! Alas! alas! what will not the thirst of gold lead men to?"

"Especially priests," interrupted Erza, in a cold sneering tone; "the reverend father measures the strength of others' conscience by the weakness of his own. It were a curious speculation to decide what brings him here."

The curate coloured with mingled shame and anger at the implied accusation, which a secret monitor whispered him was just; still, as no proof existed of his intentions, he answered boldly with the assumed confidence of insulted innocence.

"My motives are known to Heaven; I parley not with unbelievers of the duties of mine office, which alone have brought me here. You will answer to the church for this outrage on its laws—this robbery of the dead. Infidels, I arrest ye both."

A low laugh, like the hiss of a serpent, rang through the vault as Erza sprang upon the speaker, caught him in his giant arms, and forced him upon his knees beside the empty coffin; then twining his long bony fingers in the hair of the priest, he kept him like an infant immovable in the position he had placed him in. For the first time the intruder's heart beat wildly, and he lost his haughty tone.

"What would you, masters?" he cried, his cheek becoming paler as he spoke. "The crime may be atoned without the price of blood. Holy church is not relentless, and a slight fine, perchance—"

"Ha, ha, ha! a fine!" exclaimed his captor. "The Christian dog prates as if he were in his presbytery, and we captives and bound before him. A fine! how holy church loves gold!—ha, ha! a fine!—how much, how much?"

"Mercy!" exclaimed the curate, now seriously alarmed for his life, which, after such outrage upon his person, he could no longer deem secure. "I'll be silent!—bind me by what oath you will—upon the evangile, nay, on the consecrated host itself; only spare my life!—I'll show you," he added, "where the sacred vessels of the church are all concealed; they are of gold. Dogs! you will not dare to shed a Christian's blood?"

"Is it redder than a Jew's?" demanded Erza, still keeping him, despite his frantic struggles, on his knees. "Father," he added, addressing his companion in a tone of deep respect, "decide; day will soon break. What shall be his fate?"

"Death!" said Abram, who had listened to the curate's offers of betraying the vessels of the church with contempt. "In the oath of a false priest there is no reliance; in the heart of a coward mercy hath no dwelling. Once free, he would break his vow of secrecy, and laugh at the credulous Jews as he consigned them to the flames."

"As thou art a man—as thou art human," shrieked the now thoroughly terrified priest, "have pity!"

"Am I a man?" replied the Hebrew, in a low stern voice. "Why am I hunted, then, like a vile beast of prey, by those who call themselves my fellow men? E'en from his mother's womb the Jew is made the scoff of a superstitious rabble, less brutal than their teachers; his blood is thirsted for e'en as the traveller lost in the desert thirsteth for the well. Ye have made earth no more a heritage for its once chosen people. Ye reckon us like herds, yet hold us in far less estimation; ye rend the flesh from off our aching bones, doom, despoil us, beat us, rob us of our children and our wealth. In your Christian pride, ye trample us like potsherds 'neath your feet, yet, in the hour of vengeance, prate to us of humanity and mercy."

"Pity!" murmured the fainting man, already half dead with terror.

"Pity!" iterated the Israelite, in a tone of scorn; "were we in open day, and I grovelling like a worm beneath thy feet, what pity wouldst thou render me? What would be thy answer to my prayers and tears? Scoffs and bitter mockeries. And why?—because chance made thee a Christian and me a Jew. Still it shall not be said that Abram, without necessity, was cruel. As gently as the shadow of the destroying angel's wing fell on the sleeping heathen's host, so death shall fall on thee. I sacrifice thy life not to my vengeance, but to my safety, priest."

The speaker drew from his vest the envenomed instrument with which, on a previous occasion, he had menaced the esquire of Robert of Artois, and with a firm hand inflicted a slight puncture upon the neck of the kneeling man, immediately below the left ear; so small was the orifice, that but a single drop of blood trickled from the wound, although the effect was mortal. The head of the priest fell gently upon his breast, as the hand of Erza was withdrawn; and, with

a gentle sigh, the spirit fled from its earthly tabernacle for ever.

"How shall we dispose of the Nazarene's body?" demanded the dwarf.

"I have bethought me," said his master. "Clothe him in the garments of the sleeper, and place him in the empty sepulchre. Should suspicion lead men to search the tomb, they will find, at least, a mouldering corse, and the ring and chain of Robert of Artois—his gown and cowl we must reduce to ashes."

"'Tis well," exclaimed Erza; "but if the seekers come soon they will never take the features of the fat priest for the stately face of the Norman knight, although the colour of their hair and beards are not unlike. How the craven proffered oaths and gold to save his life! I question if he would have hesitated to have thrown his soul into the bargain."

"Silence!" said Abram in a tone of calm authority. "Sport not with the dead; we are no more its judges. As for the discovery thou pratest of, let but twelve hours elapse, and the eye even of the mother who bore him would fail to recognise the inmate of yon coffin. To thy work, Erza, and perform it diligently," he added; "for it is a task in which I cannot aid thee; the corse of an unbeliever would pollute the hand of a sacred Levite."

The bodies of the living and the dead were quickly stripped by the dwarf, and arrayed each in the other's clothes. The latter was then lifted into the coffin from which the former had been so recently removed. Although so lately deceased, traces of decomposition already began to be visible upon the features of the priest, and it was with a feeling of perfect security that Erza closed the ponderous lid.

"Now raise the knight upon thy shoulders, and follow me," exclaimed the elder Israelite. "Once in the church, I will extinguish the torch; darkness will best protect us."

Daylight had already begun to dawn, when the two Hebrews, unseen by mortal eyes, left the profaned sanctuary of St. Julian, and regained the secure shelter of their lonely habitation.

Three days after the marriage of Ulrick and Mirvan, the two bridegrooms were summoned, together with most of the Norman and Saxon nobles, to attend a council to be held by Herbert de Lozinga, at the episcopal palace, where matters of grave import were to be discussed, affecting nothing less than the succession to the crown. By some means, the share which William of Normandy had taken in the abduction of the two brides had got whispered about—probably from some of the garrison of Filby; and men's minds were violently disposed against him. As soon as the principal personages who had been summoned were assembled, the prelate who presided exposed to them the villany of the prince; his father's well known disposition in his favour, contrary to the rights of his elder brother Robert; and concluded by demanding if they were willing to assist in placing a tyrant on the throne who had proved so reckless of their rights and honour, whose deceit and cruelty were known to all, and whose reign could hardly fail of proving destructive alike to Norman as to Saxon independence.

"Never, by Heaven!" exclaimed Ulrick; "let others bow a vassal knee to this unknightly robber; mine ne'er shall bend before him. If England must own a foreign king, let him at least be one whom primogeniture hath pointed out the Conqueror's natural successor. This isle," he added, "is not a petty fief, to be transferred at his caprice or pleasure. Robert of Normandy shall be my sovereign, let who will else acknowledge William's title to the crown. Nobles, it is for you to say if I have spoken well."

"You have," answered Mirvan and Odo of Caen, with one voice, both equally excited as himself by the unmanly outrage which had been offered to Matilda and Isabel. "Long live our valiant brother in arms, and future king, Prince Robert of Normandy!"

Edda and the rest of the nobles, entranced—the former by his love for his grandson, and the latter by the example of two such powerful leaders as Mirvan and Odo—joined in the shout; and all but Eborard, the wily prior of the Dominicans, added their voices to a cry, which was enthusiastically repeated amid the clash of swords, which the assembly waved above their heads in token of adherence and fidelity to the cause of their future sovereign.

Robert, who was present, gracefully bowed his thanks. He could, despite the natural familiarity of his manners, assume, when occasion required it, both the language and bearing of a prince. His words were brief, but to the purpose. He pledged himself—should he by their aid defeat the unnatural disposition of his father in his brother's favour—to govern justly, confirm the existing rights of the nobility, and look upon his Norman and Saxon subjects but as children of the same great family. When he had finished speaking, the shout again echoed through the hall—"Long live Robert of Normandy!"

"Words," said Herbert de Lozinga, rising as soon as the tumult had subsided, "are but air, and leave no impress of their purport. Let all here prove that they are men who dare maintain by acts the resolution they have spoken. Here is a deed," he added, throwing at the same time a parchment which he drew from his breast upon the table, "by which we bind ourselves to venture our lives and fortunes, lands and honours, in the cause. I'll be the first to sign it; and may Heaven reward me for the act, as I believe it to be just and holy!"

No sooner had the prelate affixed his signature than the nobles crowded round the table, impatient which should be the first to follow his example; even the prior, who saw no hope of escape, and who began to look on William's cause as hopeless, did as the rest; George of Erpingham and Walter Tyrrel were the last to sign. As leaders of the forces of the bishop, they had both been summoned to the meeting. As soon as the ceremony was completed, Herbert de Lozinga folded the parchment, and placed it in his bosom.

"Thanks, nobles, vavasours, and knights," exclaimed Robert, his eyes flashing with the anticipation of a crown. "It is to you that I shall owe my throne; and, trust me, your future sovereign——"

"Our actual king!" interrupted the prelate, sinking on his knee and kissing the speaker's hand. "Your royal father sleeps his last sleep. William the Conqueror, of all his vast possessions, retains but six feet of earth; he expired ten days since at the monastery of St. Gervas. May God assoil his soul in peace."

So unexpected was the intelligence, that for a few moments those who heard it were mute with surprise. News did not then fly with the celerity of the present day; none but the speaker and Robert suspected even the monarch's illness. As soon as they recovered themselves, every knee was bent to the earth; and one simultaneous cry rose of "God save the king."

"Sire," exclaimed Mirvan, "the present is the time for action, not for words. Might I presume to counsel you, with the dawn, surrounded by your faithful nobles, you must commence your march towards London. Your brother has many friends, active as he is ambitious. A single day's delay might prejudice your cause; therefore, again I say, on to London."

A smile passed between Herbert de Lozinga and the prince; for no others, except his gaoler, were aware of the captivity of William, so faithfully had the secret of his arrest been kept by those who had undertaken its execution.

"Small danger from our brother," replied Robert, "since our good friend and faithful counsellor (bowing to the bishop) holds him in safe ward. We can arrange our differences without an appeal to arms. Where the lion's skin will not avail him," he added, "William can assume the fox's; doubt not but he will listen to such reasons as we offer."

"And may I ask your highness," demanded Odo of Caen,—for the kings of England did not, till a much latter date, assume the title of majesty,—"what terms you intend proposing to the prince?"

"The plain fulfilment of our father's will," replied Robert, "simply substituting my name for his. England for the elder born, Normandy for the younger; they are not too hard, methinks, since both by right of primogeniture are mine."

"And what security will your highness exact," said Edda, "that he keep faith with you?"

"His knightly oath," said the prince, "and my own good sword, will prove sufficient pledges for his faith."

There was a pause, for not one present but was struck with the worthlessness of the first, and the little reliance which was to be placed upon the second part of the security. Thoughts dangerous to the captive's safety were passing in the minds of many, yet no one was found hardy enough to give utterance to the suggestions of his mind. Odo of Caen was the first to break the silence which oppressed them; and make himself the interpreter of the thoughts of all.

"Prince," he began, "there are men to whom oaths are as water or the changing wind—men whom no ties, however sacred, can hold—men whom the slightest breath of passion can induce to break their deep-sworn faith. William is one of these. A nation's peace, the safety of your friends, and the stability of the throne, demand a surer pledge than these."

"I understand," replied Robert, his cheek blanching as he spoke; "you mean the tomb. But no, rather would I forego the crown itself, wander, a simple knight, the wide world through, seek fortune in the desert, than stain my hand in my unnatural brother's blood. True, he has wronged me, but the same womb bore us. True he would rob me of my birthright, yet I have never read that Esau slew his brother. My hand would lack the strength to grasp the sceptre were it stained in William's blood. Think not of it more."

"It needs not, prince," said Walter Tyrrel, who already looked upon his captive's

fortunes as for ever set, and who was anxious to render himself acceptable to the new monarch. "William is under my guard; leave it to me, and he shall never cross your path again."

"Boy!" exclaimed the prince, "greatness is ever cursed by ready tools like thee! Thou dost belie thy blood by such degrading service; we had thoughts to have held thee near our person, and fostered thy career. This proffered baseness changes our intent. Retire from the council, sir; nor presume to approach our presence until summoned, Father," he added, in a whisper to the bishop, "there is a curse upon our race; the tiger's whelp, reared in the peaceful fold, betrays its lineage by its instinctive thirst for blood. Can the wild legend of our land be true? Are we indeed Robert the Devil's brood?"

Bowing lowly to conceal the rage and mortification but too visible upon his features, Walter Tyrrel left the apartment. A quiet smile of satisfaction played on the features of the prior of the Dominicans, as he did so, for he saw that the prince had made an implacable enemy, and that he himself had found a tool fitted for his purpose.

"Wisely hast thou spoken, prince," said Herbert de Lozinga; "for what blessing could attend a crown bought with a brother's blood? But there are other means than oaths to bind this man,—a means to draw the venom from his fangs, yet leave him still with life. Let him, in an assembly of the nobles, from my hands accept the priestly vows. No bishop then could consecrate him, no sword be drawn for his pretended rights. Once devoted to the altar, the church would know well how to guard her own."

"By Rollo, priest, but thou hast hit the mark," exclaimed Robert, whose heart began to beat freely for the first time since the disposal of his brother's person had been debated. "William will make a jovial monk, and many an abbey and fat benefice shall mark our loving favour."

A murmur of approbation arose amidst the nobles, who saw in the proposal of the prelate a bloodless solution of their difficulty. It was finally resolved that on the following day the prisoner should be brought before them, and compelled to conform himself to their decision, which the bishop undertook previously to make him acquainted with; and with this understanding the council separated.

As Eborard crossed the cloisters on his way to his litter, he encountered Walter Tyrrel, who, still smarting under the reproof he had received, paced their deep shades, meditating schemes of vengeance. The wily churchman read his purpose in his knit brow and quick, impatient step, and foresaw that his advances would be gladly met.

"Methinks, sir knight," he whispered, "devotion like thine demands at least some courtesy; even in its refusal, William had received its proffer better. Our new-made monarch must feel the crown securely on his brow ere he ventured to spurn the hand that might have rent it from him."

"That might have rent it from him!" iterated the excited man; "that will I Father, I know thou lovest not this same Robert; I marked thy hesitation when the bishop proposed the signing of the traitorous act. Set but thy foot to mine, and the withered leaf the wind makes sport of shall not prove more worthless."

"What meanest thou, son?" demanded the prior, with an air of well-affected simplicity.

"Thou lovest not this would-be king—this Robert of Normandy?"

"Certes, he hath proved himself scant friend to me or to my order," replied the priest, with a shrug.

"That is as plain as words can say," resumed Tyrrel, "thou hatest him—so I do; the lightning is not less dangerous because it slumbers in the thunder cloud, nor thy hatred less to be feared because veiled in outward calm and priestly unction. Wilt thou join hands with me in this?"

"I will," replied Eborard, in a voice so low that the impetuous questioner caught the sense of his reply more from the look which accompanied it than the sound of the words. "Tell me," he added, "how can I aid thee in the enterprise? Speak in all confidence; let there be faith, my son, between us."

"I am William's gaoler," answered the traitor, in the same subdued tone. "Hast thou two fleet steeds within thy stables?"

"I have," said the priest, with a smile of intelligence, for he began clearly to see Tyrrel's purpose; "and they are both at thy disposal; better ne'er bore a knight unto the field; kings might mount them to do battle for their crowns."

"'Tis well, father! 'tis well! let them be waiting saddled at the city gates. I will find horsemen for them both."

"When?" demanded the churchman.

"At midnight; we have scant time to lose."

The prior bowed his head in token of acquiescence, and requested to know if the fugitives would require gold for their journey, which he offered to supply them with, so anxious was he to secure the success of a project on which his future fortunes hung. His contentment increased when Tyrrel informed him that he had coin enough.

"But, how—how," he demanded, "will you provide for his escape? All else seems easy after that."

"Leave it to me," replied the knight; "long ere the dawn the prince shall be upon the road for London. Lanfranc, the primate, is his friend. The citizens will eagerly receive him. Once securely king, doubt not but William's gratitude will find within the church a position more suited to thy services and zeal."

"Heaven knows best, my son," said his hearer, trying hard to look humble and indifferent; "we court not worldly honours, but are content to be an humble watch-dog in the fold. Let us not waste the time in vain discourse," he added, casting at the same time a hasty glance to see if their conversation was observed, "lest evil eyes behold us. Keep but thy purpose, and the horses shall not fail thee. Farewell! our Lady prosper thy intent."

With these words the two conspirator separated—the prior to find his litter, and Walter Tyrrel to the tower, where William of Normandy, like a caged lion, fretted away the hours of his captivity. He had not long regained his post, when Herbert de Lozinga arrived to communicate to his prisoner the decision of his brother and the nobles. His faithful marshal, George of Erpingham, attended him.

"'Tis well, sir knight," said the bishop, as Tyrrel rose and saluted him; "you keep good ward. Continue thy services, and the present cloud upon thy fortunes will pass away. How fares our prisoner? impatient, doubtless, of his durance?"

"As a wolf caught in a springe, my lord; but I exchange few words with him. Curses and threats are sweetest words with him. My own temper is none of the most patient, and I avoid him, lest I should forget the respect due to his birth, as well as to his defenceless state; an' he escape, let our new monarch look to it."

"Small fear of that," replied the prelate; "our towers are high, and you keep faithful guard. After to-morrow's evening, come to me in my oratory. I have much to speak with you upon, as well as reconcile you to your offended prince, in whose good favour, after all, you have a pleader whom you wot not of."

The knight merely bowed his acquiescence, and the speaker, with his companion, entered the prison.

"'Tis the last time," murmured Tyrrel to himself, "I shall be forced to wear the mask before him. When next we meet, my deeds shall make me known; but till that hour arrives, patience—patience." And once more he resumed his watch before the tower.

William was pacing his chamber with impatient strides when the churchman and his attendant entered: it was the first time of their meeting since the moment of his arrest. To one of his restless character, captivity was galling enough, but uncertainty was even worse than actual restraint. In the hours of his solitude he had pondered on its probable result, and formed a thousand schemes of vengeance on the man whose energy had baffled him; he longed, yet feared the encounter, for experience had taught him he had to deal with one with whom to resolve was to execute. He felt that he was too dangerous a captive to be lightly loosed. The prelate felt on his part that he had a difficult mission to fulfil; to bend an ambitious, proud, and stubborn mind, to the resignation of its long cherished hopes of rule and ambition. For a moment, therefore, they regarded each other in silence, measuring, like skilful wrestlers, each the other's strength. The passionate prisoner was the first to speak.

"So, my lord, you are come at last. I trust it is to implore our pardon for this strange outrage on your monarch's son. You have taken a strange way, methinks, to repay our royal father's favour, by holding his son a captive. Tremble at his wrath when he shall hear of it; his indignant hand will rend the mitre from thy brow, e'en though the pontiff's self had placed it there."

"The vilest slave, the poorest serf," replied Herbert de Lozinga, unmoved by the prince's threats, "will never more start at the Conqueror's wrath, or fear his frown: thy father sleeps his last sleep; the archangel's trump alone can awaken him."

"Dead!" exclaimed William, to whom the intelligence, in his present position, brought tenfold danger. "Dead! Where is thy knee, sir priest? forgettest thou that thou speakest to England's king, or do I see a traitor?"

"Traitor I am none. My knee hath already offered earthly homage to its lawful sovereign, thy elder brother Robert. The assembled nobles," added the churchman, "have confirmed my voice; in two days he marches on to London."

"To be crowned!" shrieked Robert. "Priest of Belial! 'tis thou hast plotted this —my witless brother hath not brains to springe a woodcock with. Tell me," he added fiercely, "what is the bribe for which he bought thy soul? Try if I cannot outbid him. Was't gold—was't power? for priests, I know, love both. Tell me thy price, my ransacked kingdom shall be ground to pay it; thy voice in England shall be but second to mine own."

"Prince," interrupted his visitor, "it is already greater far than thine, since by my mouth the king thy brother speaks."

"I say the traitor Robert Duke of Normandy!" exclaimed the prisoner, foaming with impotent passion, and striking his clenched fist upon the table till the blood trickled from his knuckles; then controlling himself with a violent effort, he added, "and what would our loving brother with the fool his knavish tool hath snared? But I guess: imprisoned monarchs seldom have long to live!"

"Unhappy man! thy words are but the echoes of thine own evil heart. Robert's voice was the first to spare thy life; he would not wear a crown bought with thy blood. Learn," he added, presenting him with a paper, "upon what terms thou still mayst live, if not a monarch, at least in honourable state."

William eagerly perused the paper, and his cheek became alternately red and pale, as rage or fear predominated while he did so. As he concluded, his passion broke all bounds; he tore the document in a thousand pieces, exclaiming as he did so:

"Accursed priest! this is thy work. In every line I read thy subtle malice. But thou shalt tear the quivering flesh from off these bones with pincers—pour molten lead into my throbbing veins—rend out my heart, ere I consent to pronounce the damning vow. A priest! Moloch shall be my god, and blood my consecration; thy life shall be the first I offer at his shrine."

The infuriated man sprang upon the prelate, and, unarmed as he was, would have strangled him or dashed his brains out against his prison wall, had not George of Erpingham interposed his giant strength between them. With his mailed hand he thrust him back, and William, exhausted by his passions, sank upon a seat—his hair erect, his eyes glaring upon the churchman like a foiled tiger, disappointed in its spring.

Herbert de Lozinga gazed on him with a mingled sentiment of pity and contempt.

"Prince," he said, in a tone unmoved by anger, "thou hast heard thy doom. Twenty-four hours are given thee for reflection. That space elapsed, I resign thee to the charge of those who well know how to deal with natures such as thine. For thy attempt to lay hands upon the priest of the Most High, we scorn and pardon thee. Farewell!"

Without waiting a reply, the bishop, attended by his faithful marshal, quitted the tower.

"A priest!" iterated William, as soon as he was alone; "rather the dungeon or the grave. Fool! to be thus caught. For every moment of my thraldom, a life should answer it, were I but once more free. The hoary villain is not to be bribed. Robert hath

PRINCE HENRY FORCES HIS COMPANY UPON ULRICK.

bought him; body and soul he is his. Since my good angel hath deserted me, I call upon the fiends to aid me. Wretch that I am," he added, after a pause, "I am so lost that Lucifer himself would scorn to tempt me. No hope of freedom!—no loophole for escape! —here and hereafter cursed!—undone for ever!"

The captive sullenly dashed himself upon his couch, and gave himself up to the bitterness of despair. His reverie was not of long duration, for his solitude was broken by the entrance of Walter Tyrrel in his cell. At first he scarcely deigned to notice him; suddenly the idea of tempting him flashed upon his mind, and starting from his recumbent position he abruptly demanded:

"Knight, art thou ambitious?"

"Like most men," answered Tyrrel, coolly, "I seek to mend my fortune; for, like your highness's, it has proved a scurvy one at present. Patience or time, I suppose, will better it; if not, I must endure it."

"I'll better it," exclaimed William; "satiate thy thirst with gold, thy pride with honour."

"It must be in the church, then," answered the young man carelessly, for it was no part of his plan to be too easily persuaded; "if rumour speaks rightly, prince, you are likely to possess st... of the patronage, and I have little d... cowl."

"With ti... sinking his v... broadest... with weal... Knowest...

"I... elder brother, Rober... morning, at the coun... him so."

W... reply, and even then... should... succeed in... to... purpose, to repa... of expectation and dis... the pang it gave him. Wh... oath more or less o... the... those already...

"... monarch from the... traitor... have woven... the fetters which my vows... to c... thy na... honour—to place my foot upon the throne where thou shalt stand the nearest... urged William, "an earldom w... no mean price e'en for so vast a favour: what from my brother canst thou hope for more?"

"I... not half so much," replied Tyrrel... then I risk not life and honour. Besides, a prince's promise is so soon forgot."

"Shall I... ?" exclaimed the captive, beginning... to compliment the man with whom... deal; ... promise...

The... did so... and the prince eagerly... binding himself by every saint to... the promised recompense as soon as the crown should be securely his, and imprecating the most fearful vengeance upon himself if he broke his oath to him.

"If I fail my... "may the arrow... blood of my heart! may my days be but one long agony of doubt! may all good men execrate my name, and history hold me to the scorn of future ages!"

The triumphant Tyrrel sank upon his knee, and kissed the hand the speaker held to him.

"Pardon me, sire, my doubts," he cried; "but my future devotion shall atone them. This very night I'll break your chains; true friends are watching eagerly to aid us."

"Name them," said the now joyous captive, who felt confident that his escape was certain.

"The prior of the Dominicans."

"Good! he may be trusted; all church-not men are traitors."

"By his orders horses at midnight will be waiting for us at the city gates. Long ere the day which was to seal your degradation dawns, leagues shall divide you from your enemies. In three days, at most, your high-... sleep in London, where the vener-... prelate and your father's friends impa-...ly await you. Once there——"

"My enemies shall... thou... wrath," interrupted William; "... make their homes a desert—their name a scorn, and thou shalt be my instrument of v...; like the faithful jackal, thou sh... hunt down the quarry, and we'll d... the victim's spoil between us. Fear not, good Tyrrel," he added... placing his hand upon the sh... of the... in his... "there will be enow... before us. The heads-

It was... that the knight would... disguise to the palace... however, to assume it... when all danger... of... would... would have no...

"... mask am I to wear... when all was... about to leave the...

"... he continued... "'tis like the... which wounds it... coming... with a... of its own... I'll... my cowl sooner than my loving brother thinks, though not so long perhaps. Farewell, I have my instructions and will follow them."

"Farewell, my liege," answered the traitor, who little thought that in aiding the... of William he was marring his own prospect... "when next we meet thou... as well as great, a monarch."

"And thou a belted earl," said the tempter graciously; "the first and nearest to our throne."

With these words they separated—the youth to indulge in dreams of future greatness, the tyrant to meditate of schemes of future vengeance.

As the clock of the cathedral struck the hour of twelve the same night, a group of four men might be seen leading two well-appointed steeds towards the gate of St. Stephen's—then, as now, the direct road to London; three were in the dress usually worn by the men-at-arms of the period; the fourth, enveloped in an ample cloak and barret, might have been taken either for a noble in travelling costume or a priest. From the number of franklins and personages of note whom late events had assembled in the city, the departure of such a pary even at so late an hour created no surprise to the warders—men selected from the burgher-guard—sleepy, fat-headed fellows, more inclined to drink their ale in peace than challenge for the pass-word three determined men who seemed both able and willing to dispute it.

"Thank Heaven!" exclaimed the prior —for it was no other—as soon as they were about a bow-shot from the gate, "we are here at last. I trust our friends may arrive as safely. Bring the horses under the shadow of this tree," he added, pointing to an old oak, whose wide-spreading branches would have afforded obscurity to a much larger party; "here we will wait the arrival of the fugitives. Holy mother! but this night's work has fatigued me."

The churchman seated himself upon the grass as he spoke, while the men secured the horses, and all awaited in silence the arrival of the prince and his companion. They had not long been thus occupied, when they were startled by a rustling in the branches above them. In an instant every one was on the alert; the men-at-arms, with their arrows drawn to the head, ready to fire into the tree. There was a pause, for the noise was not repeated.

"Waste not your shafts," said the prior; "'tis but an owl, or some bird whose rest we have disturbed. Hark!"

"Whoo! whoo!" was heard distinctly from the foliage, followed by the shrill sharp cry peculiar to the obscene bird.

"I told you so," he continued; "three men-at-arms, and frightened by an owl! ha! ha! ha!"

The speaker's raillery was cut short by the arrival of the two fugitives, who, dressed in the habits of monks, had contrived, through the treachery of Tyrrel, to pass unsuspected by the guard.

"Benedicite!" said the priest, as soon as he beheld them; "thank Heaven! they are arrived at last."

William and his companion threw of their disguise in silence, and appeared well armed in riding dresses underneath. The prince was first to speak.

"Sir prior, we are your debtor; deeds, not words, must speak our thanks. Are these men to be relied on?"

"Body and soul, they are your highness's servants."

"'Tis well," replied the prince, as he mounted his horse; "let them attend us till we pass the outward post, when all danger for the moment ceases; and you, reverend father, accept our signet-ring—it might betray its wearer, for not an officer in our realm but knows its impress; we will redeem it with a monarch's ransom. And now, my men," he added, "forward! If we pass unchallenged at the outward post, return to the good prior; if not, prove to the traitors you can use your swords. Adieu."

The two fugitives, preceded by the men-at-arms, advanced upon their way, leaving the churchman beneath the shadow of the oak, watching their progress with interest.

"He must succeed," murmured Eborard; "with less valour than his brother, he has ten times his cunning and perseverance; besides, the primate loves him, and will respect the Conqueror's will. Once king, our haughty bishop may rue his traitorous zeal in Robert's cause. I'd give my life," he added, "but once to feel my foot upon his neck; he hath thwarted me at every turn. Life!" he added, "I'd almost give my hope of heaven."

"Agreed!" cried a voice from the centre of the oak—"agreed!"

Unnerved with terror, the blasphemer sank upon his knees, trying to mutter a prayer.

"*In nomine confiteor Dei.* Heaven have mercy upon me. Blessed St. Dominic, *ora pro me.*"

The invocation was interrupted by a scream of horror, as a figure, scarcely human in its proportion, dropped from the branches beside him, and seized him by the neck with a giant's grasp.

"Priest of Belial," whispered the dwarf —for it was no other than Erza, who had been out to collect simples for his master, and had concealed himself in the tree on the approach of the party—"it is a compact. Thou art mine."

At this moment, overcome with fear, the prior fainted.

In this state he was discovered by the men-at-arms, on their return. With some difficulty they recovered him from his swoon. But the ring—the prince's signet-ring—was gone!

CHAPTER XXI.

The very menial whom I fed
Hath, like a beggar, spurned me
From my door.—AFFRAIN.

GREAT was the surprise and indignation of the nobles on the following morning, when at the hour of their assembling the flight of their captive and the treacherous Tyrrel was made known to them. Success, which before seemed certain, was once more reduced to the chance of cival war—a risk which many were anxious to avoid, whilst others secretly rejoiced at it as a means of increasing their fortunes by the plunder and confiscation of their enemy's domains. Few, however, ventured to express either content or dissatisfaction at the probable result, for the principal leaders remained as firmly as ever united in the cause of the monarch whom they had unanimously acknowledged. But to Robert the intelligence was a death-blow to his hopes; the crown which he had grasped, already seemed to elude him, and the share which Tyrrel had taken in his brother's escape deeply wounded him. The curse of his race, the hand of fatality, seemed to be upon him. Of the other members of the league, Herbert de Lozinga alone perhaps foresaw the probable downfall of their enterprise; for he knew how popular, by his largess and courage, the fugitive had contrived to make himself with the army, to whom his competitor was comparatively unknown. The implicit obedience which the primate Lanfranc would be sure to pay to the last will of the Conqueror, by whom he had been raised to his elevated position, as well as his love for William, whom he had educated, and who had received the honour of knighthood at his hands, was another obstacle in their path; and the mere fact of that prince being acknowledged and crowned by a prelate possessed of such influence in the kingdom, both from his high rank and virtue, together with the possession of the late king's treasures, would give him an immense advantage over his generous and less prudent rival. Still the prelate did not despair of retiring with his brother peers from the league with honour as well as safety; for the most of the nobles possessed estates in England as well as Normandy, and would naturally favour any arrangement which promised them security for their pos-

sessions in both countries; their party was sufficiently powerful to be feared, and by remaining in arms, or by advancing towards London, they might probably secure by treaty a sufficient guarantee for their lives and liberties, as well as the confirmed investiture of their lands. With this clear view of their position, his object was to urge them to immediate action; and his voice was the first which predominated above the confusion which the unexpected intelligence had caused.

"Hear me, most noble prince and lords," he cried: "this is the hour for action, not for words; firmness and promptitude will oft assure the triumph despair would resign as hopeless. Are we less unanimous or less determined than before?—is our cause less just?—or Robert's right to possess the crown less sacred?"

"No!" shouted the assembly, with one voice; "Robert is our lawful king, and we swear never to own another whilst he lives."

"'Tis well!" resumed the speaker; "leave words for women, then—deeds are for men; and ours must answer for us. The *élite* of the army of the late king is still in France; discontent is rife within the land; the men of Kent bitterly resent the captivity of their earl, Odo, Bishop of Bayeux, the Conqueror's uterine brother. I have already sent trusty emissaries to inform them of our purpose, and doubt not but that they will rise to second us. London, between two armies, must surrender. Hold we, then, our first resolve, and advance towards it?"

"We do!" was the cheerful cry of all; and it was finally agreed that on the following morning they should commence their march—the young men eager to win fame and honour, the old ones to take advantage of events as they might rise. Just as the assembly was about to disperse, the door of the council chamber was thrown hastily open, and a stranger, clothed in complete armour, entered the hall, without saluting any of the astonished nobles; he made his way to the spot where Robert was standing, and embraced him with a familiarity which nothing but equality of rank or the tie of blood could warrant. The prince's first words explained the mystery of the stranger's want of ceremony.

"Welcome, my reverend uncle!" he exclaimed, at the same time, according to the age, saluting him on the cheek. "By what good providence do we see you at liberty? It is not often that our father's captives break their cage."

"By our faith, nephew," replied Odo of Bayeux,—for it was no other than that warlike prelate, whom the Conqueror had with great difficulty been prevailed upon, when dying, to release,—"but our brother's cage has proved a strong one. For the past, let us forget it. William, I trust, sleeps in peace, and all my enmity is buried with him; but first," he added, "let me offer the homage of a subject to his sovereign, and then to affairs touching our mutual interests."

The speaker would have bent his knee in token of fealty, had not his nephew, whose hopes his presence had revived, gracefully prevented him, saying as he did so:

"The nephew can receive no homage from his uncle; the king demands no pledge from one whose loyalty is so well assured. Besides, my lord," he added, "as a spiritual peer, it is not thus that you should do me service."

"True," replied the warlike churchman, with a smile; "but 'tis always thus; whenever I have harness on my back I forget my priesthood and assume the baron. See how gravely our brother of Norwich looks, as if to remind us of it. But come," he continued, "present me to your friends."

The shout of "Long live the valiant Odo!" "Long live the valiant bishop!" echoed through the council-chamber.

"Now then, to work," continued the prelate, as soon as the cries subsided; "let's see the muster-roll,—what nobles adhere to your standard; what friends you have to count upon; what enemies to crush or to win over to your cause."

A few words made the speaker acquainted with the position of affairs, and the declaration by which the Norman and Saxon barons acknowledged Robert as their king, and pledged their lives and fortunes to support his claims, was submitted to his inspection by Herbert de Lozinga. He perused it eagerly, and with evident satisfaction.

"Ay!" he exclaimed, "this is something tangible. No vague promises, signifying nothing; no equivocation here. Lives and lands are engaged; and my unworthy name will be honoured by appearing in such goodly company."

Snatching a pen from the table, the speaker added his signature to the list, which he handed over to his brother bishop.

"When do we march for London?" he demanded; "'tis there the battle must be fought and won."

"With the rising sun," replied the now hopeful Robert.

"Good! I will prepare for our reception there; I have friends amongst the greasy citizens. Find me, my lords, a trusty messenger: one with a soldier's eye and statesman's head; the less likely to be recognised the better; he must be noble, for he will have to treat with nobles; brave, for the service is of danger; speaking Saxon as well as Norman tongue; for, in his mission, he must have speech with both."

Eborard, the prior of the Dominicans, although scarcely recovered from the fright he had received the previous evening, had, to avoid suspicion falling upon him for his share in the escape of William, contrived to be present; he saw that an excellent opportunity was at hand for serving the cause to which he was so deeply committed, could he obtain possession of the papers. Blandly, therefore, he proffered the services of his esquire, a creature devoted to his interest, to be the bearer of the important letters; vouching, at the same time, for his nobility, which was even more questionable than his fidelity. Perhaps there was something too eager in his manner of making the offer, or Odo of Bayeux knew too much of his character, for he refused it so drily, that even the effrontery of Eborard did not allow him again to renew it. The concluding words of his refusal were even more significant.

"Churchmen, in the simplicity of their unworldly natures, are but poor judges of character, reverend prior; therefore we will choose another messenger. Robert," he added, "let orders be given that no travellers be permitted to pass the city gates without a permission signed by some military chief on which we can rely. We must guard against treachery from within as from without: not that I suspect aught like treachery from any here."

The prior bit his lips, and resumed his seat in silence.

"I am less likely to be recognised," said Ulrick, "and, should the council deem me worthy of such trust, willing—nay, eager to undertake the expedition, for I would fain do something to prove myself worthy of my place amongst you."

The warlike bishop eyed him for a few minutes as he would read his very soul. Experience had taught him that bitter lesson, learnt sooner or later in the world—suspicion; but there was something so open in the offer, so modest in the way in which it was made, that he resolved at once to trust him. Some natures require no guarantee for their honour and fidelity, for God has endorsed truth upon their brow, and art can never imitate the signature. Ulrick was one of these.

"Be it so, young man," replied Odo. "I neither ask thy name nor birth, for something tells me that thy heart is nobler far than either. Short time for preparation waits thee: within an hour thou must depart. Take such precautions as seem best to thee to travel unsuspected; but remember it is an enterprise where prudence will avail thee more than courage, and wit protect thee better than thy sword."

Most present approved of the churchman's choice, for during the attack on Filby Castle they had witnessed the courage and cool presence of mind of the young Lord of Stanfield.

"Farewell, my lords," said the young man, as he quitted the assembly to bid adieu to Matilda and his mother; "within the hour, I shall be ready for my departure."

"Had the guard of your prisoner, nephew," said Odo of Bayeux, "been confided to that young knight, instead of the worthless traitor who deceived you, our task might have been easier."

Robert heard the observation in silence, for there were circumstances which made the comparison between Ulrick and Tyrrel deeply painful to his nature.

The number of vassals which each noble could bring into the field was next gone into; and the line of march drawn out. Here Edda's knowledge of the country was of inestimable value, for he enabled them so to trace their route that all doubtful places or towns likely to be in possession of the enemy were avoided, the great object being to arrive before the walls of London with as little delay as possible. Their army was to be preceded by proclamation, in which Robert's claim to the crown as eldest son of the Conqueror would be duly set forth, and such promises of equal government held out, as would induce the oppressed Saxon population to hasten to his standard.

The council soon afterwards dispersed, the nobles to give orders for the departure of their troops, and arrange the order of march. As Eborard mounted his litter at the palace gate, he whispered something to one of his attendants, who set off immediately towards the house of Abram the Jew.

"So," exclaimed the prior, as soon as he was seated in his comfortable cell in the Dominican convent of the city, "my lord of Bayeux already doubts me—let him; doubts are not proofs. The time will soon arrive when I may avow the step I have taken proudly to the world, and trample on my enemies. Robert, thy star is on the wane. William's is rising, and my fortune with it. Why loiters this cursed Jew?" he added, starting from his seat, and pacing the floor impatiently. "I must employ him as my messenger to London. Ulrick shall find friends, whom he wots not of, to meet him there. Robert of Artois' death shall yet be paid me at his hands."

At this moment Abram was ushered into the apartment, and stood bowing reverentially before him. "So, infidel, thou art come," said the churchman. "I have employment for thee, in which thou mayest win not only gold, but friends, so that thou executest faithfully the trust I shall confide in thee."

"Abram," said the old man meekly, "is the servant of his lord. Let the master speak, the slave hears but to obey. Is the reverend prior ill? the leech is ready with his drugs to cure him."

"Satan confound thee, unbeliever, with thy drugs and charms! I am for none of these; thou must gird up thy loins, and journey for me even unto London."

"To London!" ejaculated the old man with unfeigned astonishment. "What should the leech do there?"

"That I will tell thee. Seek out the king, and deliver to him word for word my message. Tell him that his uncle, Odo of Bayeux, hath arrived, and that the rebellious nobles plot against his crown; that the men of Kent are expected to rise in Robert's favour. Bid him look to Pevensy and Rochester—both."

"Alas! my lord, but these are fearful words to fall from lips like mine; had not your reverend priorship better write?"

"No, heathen!" thundered the priest. "I place my life in no man's hands. If thou art caught, stoned, burnt, or hanged, 'tis but a Jew the less; for who would listen to his word against a Christian and a noble?"

"True," said the leech, bitterly; "the reverend priest speaks truly. The Hebrew's life is but as the twice pressed grape, a thing fit to be trodden under foot by every brutal clown or steel-clad noble. But how, please you, without a letter, am I to obtain an audience of the king? they would spurn thy servant from his palace gate, e'en as an unclean beast from out the city walls."

"I will provide thee with a token that shall procure thee access; but remember Ulrick, this new-found Earl of Stanfield, as he calls himself, is the bearer of letters to those of their friends about the court. It is of the utmost consequence he should be secured. Use every diligence to arrive before him. It is well known that thy people possess facilities for travel organised in the interests of their vile commerce. Say, dost thou understand me, Jew? and art thou willing to pleasure me in this?"

"My lord hath spoken," said Abram, bowing low, "and his servant hears but to obey his will."

"'Tis well," answered the churchman; "so, on thy return, shalt thou find protection at our hand."

"Not for shekels of gold," replied the Hebrew, "or shekels of silver, will I consent to do this thing, but for thy favour."

"How can it serve thee?" demanded the prior, rejoiced to hear that his purse-strings were to remain undrawn.

"There is a bark lying in the harbour near," replied Abram, "which brought thee goodly wine from Rouen. Two of my kindred, who are tarrying with me, would fain return unto their native city sundry bales of merchandise;—an order from thy hand, under thy seal, would secure their passage, and good treatment from the rude captain: this is the only guerdon I would ask in requital for my pains.

"Holy mother!" exclaimed the prior, "but thou seemest well acquainted with our affairs. It seems our convent cannot import wine for the poor and sick, but a Jew's nose must scent it; besides," he added, willing to make the obligation greater that it really was, "it were an ill example for a Christian prelate to connive at a Jew's escape."

"Then seek some other messenger," replied the old man, firmly, "for thou hast heard the only conditions on which Abram will do thy bidding."

"Dog! this insolence to me! Dost thou not know that I can crush thee like a vile worm beneath my foot? The church's arm, though slow to strike, is terrible when roused. Thou art too much honoured in our condescension; our confidence hath made thee bold. Let me but raise my voice against thee, and thou art lost."

"But thou never wilt raise it," coolly answered the Jew.

The calm tone of his voice, so different from the usual tone of supplication with which those of his race addressed all who belonged to the church, astonished the crafty prior, whose first impulse was to summon the assistance of his lay brothers, and consign him to one of the numerous prisons of the convent; but an instant's reflection taught him that the Jew must possess a surer guarantee for his personal safety than the mere confidence which had passed between them ere he ventured to brave his wrath. It was, therefore, in an accent as free from anger as he could command, that he demanded why he should not raise it.

"Because, priest of Belial," said Abram, firmly, "it would be the signal of thy destruction. Hast thou forgot thy correspondence with thy vile nephew, Robert of Artois? The letters are in my possession."

"Go on," said the priest, clenching his teeth with suppressed rage; his eye glancing menacingly on the speaker.

"Remember, too, thy treachery last night; were it but known that the prior of the Dominicans aided the flight of William of Normandy, and, churchman though he be, his life would be of as little purchase as the despised Jew's."

"And who would believe the Hebrew's word?" demanded his hearer with a sneer.

"None," replied Abram; "but all would listen to his proofs,—the nephew's letters, and the prince's ring."

"Sorcerer!" shouted Eborard, starting from his seat; "dost deal with fiends? I'll have thee racked for this; rend the flesh from off thy unbelieving bones; bathe thee in molten fire; tear out thy accursed tongue! Fool! idiot!" he added, "with such a secret, to enter in these walls!"

The firm glance and self-possession of the Hebrew, during these fearful threats, were not lost upon the speaker, who, in the very torrent of his wrath, calculated every chance affecting his own safety, which some secret presentiment seemed to assure him would be compromised by proceeding to extremities with the being who had ventured to defy him; he hesitated, therefore, to give the signal which might lead to their mutual destruction; they remained gazing on each other for awhile in silence.

"Hear me," at last replied Abram. "Thy crimes and my knowledge of them enable the despised Israelite and the haughty priest to treat as equals. I did not venture within these walls without good precaution for my safety; if I return not within the hour in safety to my dwelling, the letters which thou wotest of, and the prince's signet-ring, will be placed in the hands of Odo of Bayeux. Now, then, decide; I speak no more."

In an instant the manner of Eborard changed. He felt that he was check-mated by the wily Jew, and he inwardly consoled himself for his present humiliation by anticipations of future vengeance when the success of William should render further temporising unnecessary.

"'Tis well, Jew; at length I know the terms on which we treat as equals. Be it so; but remember, that the least treachery on thy part will cost thee dear, for even should I fall I leave behind many who would avenge me. There," added the speaker, hastily writing the order to the captain, and sealing it with his seal, "there is the paper thou demandest for thy friends. See that the price be thy fidelity; thy mission faithfully accomplished, and we are quits."

"Thanks, most reverend prior," said Abram, bowing with his usual humility; "hast thou further orders for thy servant?"

"None; thou knowest my message—see that it be delivered, or woe upon thy head."

The aged Israelite carefully folded the important paper, and placed it in a pouch in the inner lining of his garment. His dress was far less costly than the one we have described him as wearing in his house; instead of goodly cloth, his gaberdine was made of a threadbare stuff, patched in several places, and a plain cord, instead of the engraved silver girdle, bound it to his waist; yet, wretched as it was, probably an earl's fee would scarcely have purchased that miserable vestment, for gems of price were quilted for security within its folds, and the bond of many a noble for moneys lent sown between the linings.

In Abram's way from the priory, the only remains of which at the present day is St. Andrew's Hall, where the greasy citizens of Norwich, in the days of its corporate corruption, fed upon the flesh-pots of Egypt, he had to pass that part of the city known as the Castle Ditches, being the space comprised between the inner and outer moats, and where the retainers of the nobles and the men-at-arms were in the habit of amusing themselves by wrestling, playing the game of quoits, or contending in feats of strength. For some time the old man made his way comparatively unmolested, except by an occasional gibe or rude curse—insults with which he was too much accustomed to notice. At last he approached a party of soldiers, who had been playing for a wager at some game of agility, and who were clamorously urging upon the loser, a square-built, beetle-browed, ill-looking ruffian, to pay his loss.

"By St. Martin, masters!" he exclaimed, "but you are hard upon me; you cannot have more of a fox than his skin. St. Martin," he added, as he beheld the Jew approach, "never leaves his votaries in the lurch. Here comes my treasurer; now, then, ye cormorants, ye shall be paid in full."

To seize on the person of Abram and drag him into the midst of the circle was the work of a moment: the feat was so dexterously accomplished, that his companions hailed it with a laughing shout of approbation.

"What would ye, gentle masters?" demanded the old man, in his usual quiet and submissive tone.

"Money," replied the ruffian; "I have played on credit, and the saints have sent thee to pay my score."

"Money!" iterated the Jew; "and where

should I obtain it? I have been despoiled of every thing but the garments which I wear. The air I breathe is taxed, the light of heaven is taxed, my very prayers are taxed. Were you to rend the flesh from off my bones you could not wring a silver penny from me. I am poor."

The declaration was received with a shout of derision, as one of the pleasantest jests imaginable; the idea of the Jew being poor seemed to them so ludicrous, so accustomed were the brutal soldiery to such asseverations, when they practised their unlicensed extortion upon them.

"We shall see," said the fellow, tightening his grasp upon his prisoner. "Were thy gold secreted in thy very heart, I know a trick to squeeze it forth. Be reasonable; twelve silver pennies, and thou art free. Thou canst not object to that, in honour of the saint who hath sent thee to pay my debt."

"I have already told thee that I have no money. I am old, and in thy hands, weak, and cannot resist thee; dispose of me as thou wilt, for when did Christian ever spare one of our persecuted race?"

"He blasphemes!" cried the fellows, who had gathered round, delighted at the sport of tormenting a Jew.

"Try the cord upon his thumbs," shouted one.

"Strip the unbeliever," said another, "and burn his greasy rags—the ashes will be worth sifting."

The latter proposal seemed to hit their humour best, and, despite his feeble resistance, the gaberdine was nearly torn from off their victim's back, when they were arrested by the voice of Ulrick, who, in his way to the palace to receive his letters of Odo of Bayeux, came suddenly upon him. As the party who attended him were numerously armed, the plunderers paused at his command.

"What would ye do, my masters?" he exclaimed. "Is it thus you show your courage, in despoiling an unarmed aged man? Shame on you—shame!"

"He is a Jew," sullenly growled the fellow who had seized him, "and refuseth to pay in honour of St. Martin twelve silver pennies."

"And what right hast thou to force him? Release thy hold upon his garments, or, by the saint whose name thou hast profaned, I'll crack thy casque, to teach thee mercy, knave!"

This declaration was received with a murmur of discontent, not only from the ringleader, but by his companions, who were indignant that a Christian noble should interfere on behalf of an Israelite, and whose appetites were excited by the hope of plunder.

THE MURDER OF THE CURATE IN THE VAULTS.

"Drag him along!" cried one. "Bring him to the cathedral precincts; no one will dare to interfere with us there."

"As thou art a knight," said Abram, in a supplicating tone, as the ruffians were dragging him away; "for the honour of her who bore thee, leave me not in the hands of these rude men."

"Disperse the rabble!" exclaimed Ulrick to his followers. "What!" he added, as their leader, who still held his grasp upon his prisoner, drew his sword to resist him, "art bent upon thy punishment?—this,

knave, to teach thee humanity, and this to remember Ulrick of Stanfield."

The indignant speaker made but two blows at the ruffian as he spoke. The first shivered the iron helmet on his brow; the second inflicted a deep wound which seamed his head from the temple to the jaw. His companions, seeing that the knight was in earnest, took to their heels; and the wounded man sullenly released his captive, who immediately threw himself at his protector's feet, blessing him for his humanity to one of the despised and persecuted race of Israel.

No. 15.

"Follow your companions," said Ulrick, pointing with his sword to the fellow he had wounded, and who was stanching his gashed cheek with the end of his sleeve; "and thank my mercy I do not consign thee to the care of my seneschal. A rope were a fitter instrument of punishment for a robber than a noble's sword. Begone! and, as you value life, beware how you ——— my path again."

"Beware, sir knight," shouted the villain, when he had withdrawn out of the reach of the party, "how you cross mine. You have set your mark upon my face; mine shall be graven in your heart. ——— ——— never forgave an injury yet. We ——— ——— again to pay our score."

"Follow him not," said Ulrick to his followers, who, ——— at the ———'s threat, were about to ——— him. "Has head once healed, he will forget the ———, or if he remember it, ——— ———."

"And now, ——— ———," said Abram, who had arranged his ——— ———, "let your valuer state at what price you set the old Jew's ransom; and ——— ——— is, he will beg from ——— ——— of his tribe, but he will pay it."

"Ransom?" said Ulrick, in a tone of compassion; "and dost thou think, old man, I saved thee from yon ——— but to plunder thee myself? I should be then the greater robber. No! tell me but where thou livest, and two of my followers shall see thee safely to thy dwelling."

The Israelite listened to him in astonishment; so extraordinary did it appear to him that a Christian noble should render protection to one of his nation without extorting gold as the price of his service.

"Am I then free?" he demanded.

"Free as the air."

"And without ransom?"

"Without ransom."

Abram bowed to the ground before the young noble, and repeated his thanks, declining at the same time the escort that was proffered him. Perhaps he was fearful of attracting attention to his dwelling.

Ulrick, who was too enlightened to be entirely the slave of the barbarous, rude prejudice of the age, which regarded the Hebrews as a people accursed by God, and fit only to be oppressed by Christians, gazed on the venerable old man, who had resumed his way, with interest and pity.

"It cannot be," he thought to himself—for he was too careful to shock the prejudice of the age by uttering the sentiment aloud—"that Heaven intended man to be its avenger; Omnipotence needs not our finite strength to crush its enemies. See," he added aloud,

"the Jew returns; he hath thought better of our proffered escort."

Something had been cogitating in the old man's mind as he pursued his way. The being whose ruin he was commissioned to accomplish by the prior, by denouncing his journey to London to William, had preserved him from the brutal outrage of the ruffians into whose hands he had fallen. Deeply as he had been wronged by Christians, his humanity was not quite changed to gall. He resolved, therefore, on his steps, to warn him of his danger, and, if possible, provide him with a shield against it.

"Well, Israelite, what wouldst thou?"

"I would speak with thee," said the old man, bowing servilely, "speak with thee, alone, sir knight."

Ulrick motioned his followers to retire. No sooner were they out of hearing, than Abram threw off the cringing manner which he had hitherto assumed, and spoke with the dignity and firmness of a prince addressing his equal—a tone which he maintained during their interview.

"Sir knight," he began, "I little thought ever to feel interest or care for one of Christian blood. Nay, frown not," he added; "didst thou but know half the wrongs, the bitter mockeries I have endured, thy anger would be less. Enough, I would serve thee. The journey thou art about to take will be a dangerous one. The messenger of Odo of Bayeux would meet with little mercy at William's hands, were he discovered."

"Knowest thou," interrupted Ulrick, struck with surprise, "knowest thou thus much?"

"More—much more than this," continued Abram. "A messenger already is commissioned to inform the prince of thy arrival, but for thy sake he shall not depart. I have the power, as well as will, to stay him. Where wilt thou lodge, supposing thou arrivest in safety at thy journey's end?"

"At White Friars. I have letters from the bishop there."

"Then art thou lost. The prior is devoted to Prince William. He looks to be a bishop."

"With the Earl of Brittany then."

"Worse; he would sell thee for a mess of pottage."

"At some hostel, then," added Ulrick, scarcely knowing where or what to say.

"They are filled with spies. No," continued the old man; "thou hast served me for the sake of that common humanity which Christians would deny all of my race; I, in my turn, will serve thee. Take these," he added, offering him a set of tablets on which he rapidly traced something in Hebrew characters; "it will provide thee with a secure retreat, where hatred would fail to find thee, and power lack means to drag thee forth. Not an Israelite within the realm but, at the sight of them, will count down gold at thy necessity—will shelter thee within his dwelling."

"Who art thou, man of mystery?" demanded Ulrick; "and whence this power over thy peculiar people?"

"Question not that," said Abram, "but use it for thy safety. Should closer danger press thee, this ring will prove thy safeguard. Farewell! And may that Being, who is alike the God of Jew and Gentile, bless thee for thy kindness to my age."

There was something so truthful in the old man's voice, so honest in its tone, that Ulrick doubted not, even for a moment, of his sincerity or ability to serve him. He concealed the tablets, as a precious gage of safety, in his vest, and gazed upon the ring, which he still retained in his grasp.

"By every saint!" he exclaimed, "but this is more mysterious still—'tis William's signet."

With thoughtful mien he pursued his way to the palace, debating in his mind whether to lay the singular gifts, and relate the interview, before the prelates, or keep silence upon the subject.

In a vaulted chamber in the house of Abram the Jew, the entrance to which was so cunningly concealed as to defy detection, sat, or rather was bound, in an iron chair, the gaunt form of Robert of Artois. The wound which Rachel had inflicted was more dangerous in appearance than reality, and the skill of her father had quickly caused it to heal. During his progress to convalescence, the old man had treated him with the tender solicitude of a parent. He had preserved him not for love, but vengeance; for as soon as the cure was complete he had removed him, whilst in a deep sleep, by the aid of Erza, from the apartment above, and securely bound him in his seat of torture. The room in which the victim was confined was a low arched vault, built of unhewn stone, and lighted by an iron cresset suspended from the ceiling.

The first idea of Robert, on recovering from the stupor in which he had been plunged, was, that he was dead, and the gloomy cell his assigned place of punishment; for before him was an object well calculated to strike terror to a soul more firm than his. The Jewess, embalmed by her father's skill, was seated on a species of tribune before him, her dark hair, as when living, glittering with gems—her eyes, glazed by death, fixed with a stony glare upon him. Vainly he sought to shut out that fearful image; if he closed his eyes it presented itself but more vividly to his mental sight—there was a species of fascination from which he could not fly. Memory presented her as he first beheld her —young and unpolluted, innocent and happy, till, like a serpent, he had left the trail of his destroying passions on her young heart, and blighted its existence. There was something too horrible for reason in this silent commune between the living and the dead; his mind began to wander; at times he would entreat her to forgive him, then revile, and curse her. Still the impassible accuser gazed upon him, unmoved alike by imprecation or by prayer. The countenance of Robert of Artois gradually became distorted by passion and terror; Rachel's retained the cold expression of the dead. It is impossible to say how long the guilty man could have remained in this frightful solitude and lived; his ravings already began to be incoherent, when Abram, with a case of instruments under his arm, entered the chamber of death.

"Dog!" exclaimed the indignant noble, as soon as he beheld him, relieved from the worst apprehensions that he was dead. "What sorcery is this? why am I bound like a thing for sacrifice in this dark cavern, and what means this carrion here?"

"It means," exclaimed the old man, with a passionate burst of grief, "that she was my child, and thou wert her destroyer. It means that she was betrayed, and that I am her avenger."

"Beware!" shouted the captive, writhing with impotent rage; "beware how thou attemptst my life. My uncle, the prior, will soon return to claim me; his wrath will light a fire that will consume thee."

"He will return no more," calmly replied the Jew; "he hath seen thee, as he believes, dead. Brantone, thy esquire, witnessed thy interment in the neighbouring church from which I have released thee, for not e'en the grave could shield thee from a hate like mine."

"What wilt thou do?" demanded Robert, blanched with terror when he saw how completely he was in the speaker's power.

"I'll tell thee," said Abram; "I will not take thy life, for that were mercy, not revenge; but I will so change thee, that e'en thy mother could not, were she living, recognise her child. A premature old age shall replace thy manly strength—a gift thou hast so oft abused; the muscles of thy scornful brow and haughty cheek I will dissect away, till not one lineament remains of Robert of Artois. I'll change thy raven hair to grey, and pluck thy beard from off thy living face. Then, when thou art deformed in person as well as mind, when not one trace remains for men to know thee by, I'll send the in the world to beg, to rot, to starve, to be the scoff of those who lately licked the dust from off thy feet. What thinkest thou, Christian, shall I not be avenged?"

"Horrible!" shrieked his prisoner. "Mercy! Mercy!"

"Ay," continued the old man, drawing a scapel from his case of instruments; "such mercy as thou showdst to her. Writhe on, serpent," he added, "thou canst not escape me."

A groan of anguish broke from the unhappy man, as Abram plunged the instrument into his cheek, and began to remove the skin. Cries and supplications, mingled with threats and curses, were repeated, as with a firm hand and unmoved heart the avenger pursued his fearful task within the vault—the only witness the cold and passionless dead.

Day after day he returned to his victim, and relentlessly pursued his vengeance. By some corrosive preparation the beard was utterly destroyed, and the deep-brown clustering hair thinned almost to baldness; as the Jew foretold, agony and terror turned it grey. At last, when the transformation was entirely accomplished, when the once haughty features of Robert of Artois, seared by a thousand minute cicatrices, were no longer to be recognised either by the eye of love or hate, Abram resolved to release him from his seat of pain; the preparation for his own departure from England had long been secretly made. Again the powerful narcotic was administered, and the disfigured tyrant found himself, when he awoke from his deep slumber, reclining beneath a tree, not far from the castle of Ormsby, once his own domain; he was clothed in rags; an oaken staff and wallet were on the ground beside him. Slowly he dragged his enfeebled steps towards the porch, where several men-at-arms were amusing themselves with Brantone, discussing the late siege of Filby Hold; not an eye recognised in the wretched object before them their once haughty lord, and one, a fellow more surly than the rest, asked why he came prowling round the maner.

"Do you know me?" he demanded in a trembling voice.

"Know thee!" exclaimed Brantone. "No, fellow, the servitors of the prior of Dominicans keep better company. Get thee to the convent; the reverend father bestows no alms here."

"The prior! do I dream?" said Robert. "Methought this manor belonged to his once powerful nephew."

"Did belong," replied the men; "but since our young lord's death, it hath been granted to his uncle."

A low groan was the unhappy man's only reply to the announcement.

"Lost!" he murmured to himself—"lost for ever! The accursed Jew spoke truly. My own menials spurn me from my door."

At this moment an old hound, which had long been useless for the hunt, but which had once been his companion in many a gallant chase, approached, and began to whine and sniff the air uneasily around him.

"Look," observed Brantone, "if old Rollo does not seem to recognise him."

"Because," said Robert, dashing aside the indignant tear which the faithful animal's recognition had caused him to shed, "he is more faithful in his instinct than thou art in thy reason. Changed as I am, he knows his wretched master, Robert of Artois."

A shout of laughter followed the announcement.

"Master," said, one "ha, ha, ha! the noble knight returned from purgatory! Ha, ha, ha!"

"From a worse place," observed another, pointing to his scarred face. "Satan has left the mark of his claws; he must have battled stoutly to have got back again."

"Peace," cried Brantone; "don't you see the poor wretch is mad? There," he added, throwing a small copper coin; "there is a mite for thee; stoop for it, and begone."

The o'erfraught heart of his quondam master swelled bitterly at this last insult. Alms to be offered him at his own gate, by one of his own creatures, a thing whom but a few days before he could have crushed, was more than his haughty spirit could endure.

"Slave!" he exclaimed, "it was not thus thou didst promise to obey me when my mistaken pity saved thee from the gibbet to which thy life was forfeit, for plundering the abbey at Lissieux; hast thou forgot thine oath of gratitude?"

The loud laugh of the men, to whom the tale was imperfectly known, roused the anger of the esquire almost to madness, and catching up a quarterstaff which was near him, he would have felled the seeming beggar to the ground, had not the faithful hound sprang from his, by all but him, forgotten master's side, and pulled him to the ground. In an instant a dozen weapons were raised, and the brains of the faithful animal dashed out upon the spot.

"Villains! you shall dearly pay for this!" exclaimed the excited Robert. "Deeply shall my poor hound's death be revenged!"

"Begone!" cried Brantone, rising from the earth. "I am a fool to listen or be angered at a madman's ravings. Use your staves," he added sternly to the men, "and drive the beggar forth."

The men-at-arms, eager to recover the good graces of the esquire, who was known to be high in favour with their new master, eagerly o eyed his commands, and, despite his curses and imprecations, drove the wanderer from the gate.

"God!" exclaimed Robert, as soon as he was alone, "can this be real? is it not some hideous dream? Rachael," he added, as the horror of his position flashed upon him in all its bitter reality, "thou art fearfully avenged!"

Then commenced the real punishment of Robert of Artois—a punishment only to be equalled by his former crimes.

CHAPTER XXII.

Take then my hand; it is a bond between u]
Of faith and good companionship.
The miser to his hoarded treasure—love to the one
Whom it hath shrined an idol in its heart,
Will not more constant prove than I
Will prove to thee.—Hub of the Sept.

EAR the hour of sunset, just before the guard of the night was set, a traveller, dressed in the sober garb of a peaceful citizen, and mounted on a strong grey horse, which seemed more fitted for a belted knight than an humble trader, approached the barrier of Ludgate; not, as now, in the very heart of the metropolis, the busy nest of active industry, but one of the fortified entrances of the city, and connected by a low wall with the barbican. Cheapsyde, at the period of which we write, was a narrow street, far different from the Cheapside of the present day; quaintly-built houses, chiefly of timber, overshadowed the roadway with their rudely-carved projecting balconies, few of which were glazed —strong shutters of wood, raised or depressed with cords, serving the inhabitants to exclude both air and rain. As the buildings approached Cornhill they became more and more straggling, with gardens or patches of land between them. Sometimes a mansion of more goodly appearance than the rest might be seen a little removed from the wretched unpaved road, but more frequently the eye encountered only miserable huts inhabited by watermen and small traffickers, or families whose fortunes were as doubtful as their characters.

As Ulrick—for the traveller was no other than the disguised Lord of Stanfield—neared the gate, his steed attracted the attention of the men-at-arms, always ready to discuss the merits of a horse, or speculate upon the character of its rider. The warder—a grey-headed man, who still retained evidence of great personal strength, and whose keen blue eye, glancing from beneath an overhanging brow, would have prepossessed a physiognomist with anything but an opinion in his favour—stood by, listening to them in silence.

"Marry," said one, "but our citizen is well mounted; I have seen a worse piece of flesh than that sold for a hundred marks; it seems of Flemish breed; perhaps its master is some foreign trader."

"Trader indeed!" observed a second; "where are his saddle-bags? He holds his seat more like a man accustomed to crack crowns than count them. There again! How well we reined him up over the broken ground! No, no; the rider of yon goodly steed has never been a trader."

The warder, who had been scrutinising the traveller, nodded his head with the air of a man who hears an opinion which coincides with his own, but continued his observation in silence.

"Welcome, my master," said the first speaker, as Ulrick reached the gate. "Art come to witness the coronation of our young King William? It takes place in two days. That steed would fetch a goodly price to figure in the pageant. Many a noble will appear worse mounted."

"Coronation!" repeated the traveller in evident surprise; "'tis rather sudden; it is but lately that I heard of his father's death. He is in haste, methinks, to grasp his crown."

"Traitors, 'tis whispered, dispute it with him," replied his questioner; "and the holy primate is resolved to make short work of it. Hast never heard of the king's elder brother, Prince Robert?"

"Not often," said Ulrick, trying to look indifferent; "princes and kings trouble me but little; I strive to make an honest living, and leaves the great ones to settle their disputes."

"Thou art a trader, then?" demanded the warder, speaking for the first time.

The traveller merely bowed his head, so hateful to him was the subterfuge to which prudence compelled him to have recourse.

"And what dost thou deal in?"

"Steel, sir warder, steel."

"I thought so," drily observed the fellow, whose suspicions were excited, although but vaguely.

"An you lack a sword, good friend, I shall be happy to furnish you, and at a reasonable price," said Ulrick, willing to avoid further questions, which began to annoy him.

"Perhaps I may use the occasion," replied the warder. "I have long thought of cheapening one. Where shall I find you—in the city?"

"Not, at the St. Dunstan, the patron saint of all good armourers," answered Ulrick, at the same time giving his horse the rein to continue his route. "Good night, my masters. I love not the late hour, and mine host of the jovial saint will be uneasy if I tarry longer."

The traveller with these words quietly resumed his way, much to the annoyance of the warder, who gladly would have detained him till the arrival of the officer and guard who were to relieve his post. Once or twice he had thought to have arrested him on his own authority, but the lack of warrant and the idea that after all he might perhaps turn out to be some wealthy merchant, restrained him, for the city was extremely jealous of its privileges, and he was their immediate servant; still he determined not to lose sight of him, but set some one to dog his steps.

"Gilbert, Gilbert!" he exclaimed, directing the voice to the interior of the tower. "Why, how the hound sleeps! Gilbert, I say! Ho! some of you break your quarterstaff over his sleepy head!"

A shrill cry of pain from within announced that his brutal order had been complied with. A thin, pale, half-starved looking youth, of about seventeen, came from the guard room, wiping the drops of blood which trickled down his high and not unintellectual forehead. No tear, however, dimmed his bright blue eye, which shone from its caverned socket with almost unnatural lustre, indicative either of disease or insanity. Calmly the poor boy stood before his tyrant, who this time, either because he thought him sufficiently punished, or that time pressed, forebore to ill-use him further.

"Dost see yon traveller, hangdog?" he demanded, pointing to Ulrick.

"I do," replied the boy, meekly.

"Follow him—dog him to his home. Better lose thine eyes than lose the sight of him. When thou hast housed him, bring me word, fast as thy lazy limbs can carry thee."

"I will."

"Away, then," continued the ruffian, "and make good speed. If I find thou tarriest but one second I'll lash thee with my bow-string till I lay bare thy bones. Thou knowest me; do not trifle with my anger."

A slight and almost imperceptible shudder passed through the frame of Gilbert as he heard the threat. The next minute he was following the track of Ulrick, as he wound his way through the many intricacies of the crowded city.

It was not long before our hero percieved that he was watched: every time he turned his head he perceived the pale visaged boy, whose glance instinctively shunned his, as if conscious of the degradation of his employment. As he approached Temple Bar considerable confusion was caused by a party of the city guard, who were escorting the civic authorities on their return from Westminster, where they had been to pay their homage to the new king, who had solemnly confirmed their charter, to attach them to his interests. Ulrick saw that the occasion of avoiding his pursuer was too favourable to be lost; spurring his powerful horse, he dashed through the cavalcade, regardless of oaths and menaces, and quickly disappeared down one of the numerous lanes which led to the water side, by which means he avoided the Strand and the village of Charing, following the banks of the river till he arrived at Westminster, where he expected to find Anselm, abbot of Bec, in Normandy, a known partisan of Robert, to whom he was more especially addressed by Odo of Bayeux.

"Back, boy!" exclaimed one of the guard, rudely seizing Gilbert by the shoulders, as he was endeavouring to force a passage through their ranks to follow the horseman. "What will happen next, when traders take the crown of the causeway in the teeth of the city magistrates, and boys break through the city guard?"

"Pray let me pass," cried the youth, struggling to release himself from the speaker's grasp; "my errand is of speed—you know not how much depends on my fulfilling it."

A loud laugh, accompanied by blows, was the only reply of the angry official, and the poor lad was thrust back until the procession had passed; when he had threaded the barrier Ulrick had disappeared.

Anselm, the abbot of Bec, who was afterwards destined to fill so important a niche in the history of his times, lodged with the prior of Westminster, to whom he was distantly related. In his manner he was cold and stately, concealing an ambition atoned for by great benevolence under a veil of self-possession. Perhaps in early life he had met with one of those misfortunes which chill without freezing the heart; he had looked upon the world, and scorned its worthlessness. Deliberately he perused the missive of his brother prelate, glancing occasionally from the letter to the bearer, who met his gaze with that unembarrassed ease which only truth or long habits of dissimulation give; the scrutiny was apparently satisfactory.

"We meet, my lord, in strange times," he observed, "and your enterprise is one which only zeal and courage could undertake; not that I venture to pronounce it hopeless. Many of the nobles prefer Robert's claim to William's, but unfortunately the primate is against him. In two days the church will consecrate the usurper's rights; Lanfranc will place the crown upon his head in the ancient abbey of St. Peter's."

"Have the nobles, then, no voice in his election?" demanded Ulrick; "for election it clearly is if the law of primogeniture be set aside. The barons of the Angles already have proclaimed his brother king, and even now, with Robert at their head, are on their march to London."

"Robert," said the churchman, "possesses many kingly qualities; but he is rash as generous, and lacks the perseverance to assure the triumph of his cause. Who are his chief advisers?"

"His uncle, Odo of Bayeux," replied our hero.

"Better in the field than at the council board," observed the priest. "Who next?"

"Odo of Caen."

"A valiant knight. Proceed."

"Edda the Saxon, Herbert de Lozinga, the Earl of Norwich, with many chiefs and franklins of less note, and, last and least, myself."

"Good men, I doubt not," muttered Anselm, musing more to himself than addressing his visitor, "William de Warrenne, Roger of Shrewsbury, De Vere, and Neville, will, I doubt not, join him. Prince Henry, too, justly offended at his father's will, might throw his influence in the scale.—Hear me, sir knight," he added; "I will see the men I speak of. Born no subject of this land—owing it no allegiance—I can securely do so. Visit me again to-morrow at the coming hour. Where art thou lodged? with secure friends, I trust."

Ulrick briefly informed him that he was a stranger in the capital, and had as yet to seek a lodging for the night.

"Imprudent," replied the churchman; "tyranny is ever suspicious; the city swarms with spies: the very appearance of thy steed —for I noticed it from my casement—in a common hostelry would create inquiry. I will send it to the house of our order at Eltham. Leave it with me. Shouldst thou be compelled to fly, Kent must be thy hiding-place; 'tis there the battle will be lost or won, for there lies Robert's strength."

Anselm's words were prophetic: it was in that fertile county, of which Odo of Bayeux was earl, that the struggle terminated which placed William Rufus on the throne of England.

"I would guard thee here," continued the abbot, kindly, "were I other than a guest, or did I deem it a safe hiding-place. Be careful of thy safety; remember that prudence is sometimes better than courage. Farewell," he added; "peace and security go with thee."

There was something so calculating, if not cold, in the churchman's manner, that Ulrick scarcely knew what to think of him, his very caution seemed dictated more by prudence than regard; still the high character he had received of him from those who had sent him did not permit even for an instant a doubt of his good faith. "Perhaps," he thought, as he traversed the fields between the abbey and Charing, "it is but the coldness of the cloister." All men, he knew, possessed not the warm heart of his benefactor, whose nature was as genial as his own.

The unhappy Gilbert had vainly made his way along the crowded Strand, and from thence to the village of Charing, demanding of the passengers if they had encountered a citizen, whose person and steed he described. Some listened to him patiently; others answered with a surly negative. All trace of the object of his pursuit had vanished, and what to do he knew not; to return was out of the question. The brutal rage of his father-in-law—for such was the relationship between the warder and himself—increased, as it was sure to be, by disappointed avarice, was more than he dared encounter. He wandered for some time in the fields and open grounds between Charing and Westminster; and at last, overcome with fatigue, seated himself beneath a tree, and reflected bitterly on his lonely, unprotected situation.

He had not been long thus occupied, before he was aroused by the lash of a bow-string vigorously applied to his shoulders; and starting to his feet beheld, to his terror, the warder standing beside him. The disappointed ruffian, weary of waiting his return, had tracked him even there. "Cur," he exclaimed, repeating the blow, "is it for this I feed thee? is it thus my orders are obeyed? Where hast thou left the man I bid thee watch?"

Vainly Gilbert endeavoured to appease his wrath by relating the manner in which he had lost sight of him: the evil passion of the fellow was aroused; and like the tiger, whose appetite for blood is increased by the first taste of it, so the terror and cries of the youth increased his persecutor's fury. "I have lost a fortune by the heedlessness," he muttered between his clenched teeth. "I have seen Sir Walter Tyrrel, the newly appointed captain of the king's guard; he recognised the rider from my description of his steed; a price is on his head; and thus to lose it!—Ay, shriek," he added; "I'll cut the flesh from off thy lazy bones. I'll show thee as little mercy as thou hast shown obedience."

It is impossible to say how long the enraged warder would have continued his cruel usage of his victim, had not Ulrick, who was returning from his visit to the abbot, chanced to pass the spot. Attracted by the cries of the boy, and disgusted with the cowardly conduct of the ruffian, whom, in the twilight hour, he failed to recognise, his first impulse was to interfere. Seizing him by the neck, he hurled him to a considerable distance from the tree, exclaiming, as he did so, "Shame on thee, thus to abuse thy strength! The lash is fit but for the hound, not for a boy."

The first thought of the warder, on regaining his feet, was to attack the unceremonious speaker, whom he recognised at a glance; but prudence, and the hope of gain, changed his purpose: perhaps, too, the proof of strength which he had just received made him doubtful of the result, should he venture to encounter him; he pretended, however, not to know him.

"Marry, master," he growled, "but you are ready with your hands, though I bear you no ill-will for that: my temper is sometimes hotter than my reason. 'Tis the third time since Monday this disobedient boy hath given me the trouble to seek him. Let a drum but beat, or a banner wave, and, presto! there is no keeping him within the house. Come, Gilbert," he added, in a voice intended to be affectionate, "thou knowest, if I am hasty of speech, and sometimes rough of hand, that at heart I am not an unkind father-in-law. Come," he added, in a low peculiar tone, seeing that his victim hesitated, "I am not to be trifled with. Good night, sir," he continued, turning to his assailant; "I bear you no ill-blood; but for the future, be less ready with your hands."

Ulrick, who had quickly recognised both the speaker and the boy, was uneasy at the encounter; for he felt more convinced than ever that he had been dogged, and suspected that the scene he had just witnessed had merely been got up to detain him till assistance should arrive to secure his person. With a brief "good night," he turned coldly, therefore, from the mute supplicating look of Gilbert, which seemed to implore his protection, and directed his way towards Charing, turning from time to time a cautious glance, to see if he were followed.

Scarcely was he out of earshot, than the warder whispered to his son-in-law, "Follow him—trail after him like a serpent on thy belly;—lose sight of him again, and I'll rend the skin from off thy flesh. Raise thy head from time to time, that I may see the track."

The poor boy, his limbs still smarting with the chastisement he had received, threw himself, as he was bid, upon the ground, and glided after Ulrick, who, unable to distinguish the creeping form in the distance, pursued his way, in the confidence that he had escaped them.

In his way to Westminster our hero had observed by the water side a quiet solitary house, where a bundle of straw hung out, denoting that entertainment might be had for man and beast: thither he directed his steps, to secure accommodation for the night.

"'Tis rather late," replied the host, eyeing him carefully, "for a respectable citizen, such as you seem to be, to seek his lodging; but perhaps you are a stranger, a trader from distant parts, or—"

"I am," said Ulrick, "from a distant land, though not altogether a stranger in England. If the hour is too late to please you, I can seek elsewhere—a man with crowns in his pouch need never lack for shelter in a city like to London."

"Not so hasty, good master," quickly exclaimed the Boniface, in whose ear the word "crowns" tingled most musically; "you might go farther and fare worse; if we are careful whom we admit, it is that our house is honest; were your gown quilted with nobles, you might sleep in surety here. Will it please you to sit here, or shall I serve you in the inner room?"

Ulrick cast a glance upon the company, which consisted of one or two mendicant friars, several small traders, and three or four men whom it would have been impossible to place in any class, unless in that comprehensive one, cosmopolite. With a nob he signified to the host that he should prefer the inner room, where he ordered him to bring a flask of his best wine, and leave him undisturbed till supper time.

As the master of the house returned to

THE DWARF RESPONDS TO EBORARD'S TERRIBLE OATH.

the kitchen after serving his guest, a scowling figure, the cap carefully drawn over the brow, appeared at the outward door, and beckoned him out. It was the warder.

No sooner was Ulrick alone than his thoughts naturally reverted to his home and his young bride, whom he had left in the first hours of wedded happiness at the stern call of honour. Matilda, neither by tears, entreaties, nor sighs, had endeavoured to detain him; for, in her gentle nature, even the passion of love was controlled by the sentiment of duty, and the resignation with which she endured the separation increased,

if possible, her husband's admiration of her character and virtues. For some time he paced the floor of his lonely chamber, plunged in one of those delightful waking dreams in which youth cradles an unreal future; wisely, perhaps, consoling itself for the turmoils, cares, deceits, trials, and disappointments of the present, by the anticipation of happiness never to be realised. He was startled, at length, from this dreamy reflective mood, by a gentle tapping at the window; at first he deemed it accident, and continued his solitary walk; but its repetition soon became too frequent and too loud

No. 16.

to admit of his remaining under the impression. Lowering the cord which held the shutter, he thrust his head into the night air to see who it was that had disturbed him.

"Silence, sir knight," whispered the trembling voice of Gilbert; "you are beset like a tracked deer. The warder and myself have dogged you to your lair. He is gone to fetch the guard, and will be back within the hour. I am set to watch you here. For the sake of our dear Lady, fly, if you value life."

"And what, boy, makes thee take so great an interest in my favour?" coolly demanded Ulrick, who doubted whether the speaker's zeal in his service was not assumed to lure him from the protection of the house, so little did he think of the slight kindness he had shown him in saving him from his assailant.

"What makes me feel an interest?" iterated the youth. "Didst thou not defend me?"

"Granted."

"Speak for me with pity?"

"Well?"

"Well!" said the boy; "oh, 'tis plain you have always been beloved, have never missed the voice of kindness, or you would not ask that question. If you knew how crushed I had been in heart and spirit, how unused e'en to as much kindness as men would show a dog, you'd feel and understand the reason why I risk my life to serve you; though, perhaps," added the speaker, with a sigh, "it is so poor a thing that I should be a gainer by the loss."

There was a tone of sincerity, mingled with such utter hopelessness, in Gilbert's words, that, despite his resolution to be cautious, Ulrick felt convinced of the poor fellow's sincerity and purpose. Eager, like most generous natures, to atone for the pain his doubts had caused, he answered kindly—

"I believe thee, my good boy; forgive me that I wronged thy honesty by my suspicion. But tell me," he added, "whence comes the danger I must fear?"

"From the captain of the king's guard, to whom the warder described your steed and person. Perhaps, sir knight, you know him, for 'tis plain he recognises you?"

"How do you name him, boy?"

"Sir Walter Tyrrel. He hath promised gold to the warder if he succeeds in apprehending you."

The last doubt disappeared from Ulrick's mind; the name of Tyrrel was a fearful omen; for, although reared from childhood together by the good bishop, they had never loved each other. The open, warm heart of the young Lord of Stanfield had never found one affinity of feeling in his cold, calculating companion.

"Thou hast convinced me," he exclaimed, "of thy sincerity. In naming Sir Walter Tyrrel thou hast named my bitterest foe. Wait for a few minutes, and I will rejoin thee."

The speaker was about to quit the window, when the voice of Gilbert again arrested him.

"Not by the door, sir knight, not by the door. My father-in-law and the host of the hostel are friends. He hath already put him on his guard. The outward door is fastened; you would be beset and overpowered. By the window—by the window, if you value life."

The advice appeared too reasonable to be neglected. The height was not very considerable to drop. Drawing his sword, which he wore concealed beneath his dress, he held it in his teeth, so as to be ready in case of treachery. He threw his legs over the low balustrade, and let himself fall upon the ground.

"Thank Heaven, you are safe!"

"And thanks to thee, boy," replied Ulrick; "for without thy warning I had small chance of escaping them. There," he added, offering Gilbert at the same time a gold piece, "is a token for thee. Haste to thy home, and thy share in my deliverance may pass unsuspected."

The youth hesitated to take the money. The speaker thought that he perhaps deemed it insufficient; and, drawing another coin from his pouch, of equal value with the first, offered them both.

"It is not gold, sir knight," sobbed the boy; "it is not gold. You bid me return to my home; alas! I have now no home. I was set here to watch, and not to warn you. Farewell! If you knew the price at which I have paid my debt of gratitude, you would not think so little of my heart that gold could recompense its devotion to your service."

"Then come with me," said Ulrick, extending his hand, which Gilbert joyfully seized and kissed. "I am but a fugitive myself; yet it shall go hard but I will protect thee. But first to provide for our escape. Unchain the boat, and take the oars out of the others beside it, to prevent their following us."

These orders were quickly executed. The oars were removed from the two larger barks into a light skiff lying close to the water's edge: when Tyrrel, accompanied by the warder and two men-at-arms, rushed down upon them. As soon as his father-in-law perceived Gilbert, his rage knew no bounds. Once more the recompense seemed likely to escape him, through the treachery of his ill-used victim, on whom, whatever might be the result of the adventure, he determined to be revenged. Drawing an arrow to the head, he let fly the shaft; and the devoted boy sank, wounded in the chest, upon the shelving bank.

Ulrick, whose foot was upon the edge of the boat, might have escaped without risking an encounter, could he have consented to abandon his preserver—a baseness which, even for a moment, never crossed his thoughts. To rush to the side of his wounded companion, and raise him on his left arm, whilst with his right he defended their retreat, was but the work of a moment; indeed, so rapidly was the movement executed, that he had retreated several paces before his assailants had recovered from their surprise.

"Yield!" exclaimed Tyrrel, rushing upon him with his two followers; for the warder had prudently ran to the hostel to summon the assistance of his friend the host. "Ulrick of Stanfield, in the king's name I arrest you!"

A blow from the quick sword of Ulrick was his only reply, as he continued his retreat towards the bark, his face sternly turned towards his assailants, his left arm still supporting the form of the unconscious Gilbert. One of the men-at-arms had already received a deep cut across the arm, which rendered it nearly useless, and the second evinced but little zeal in approaching the keen blade of the fugitive, which flashed like lightning round his head, and occasionally whizzed most unpleasantly in the ears of his enemy. Ulrick and Tyrrel had the encounter nearly to themselves.

"Dogs!" exclaimed the latter, fearing the man he hated would escape him, "must I do your duty? Upon him! take him alive if possible, but, as you value your heads, suffer him not to escape."

Thus exhorted, the two fellows pressed yet nearer, when, by a dextrous feint, Ulrick avoided the sword of his chief opponent, and let fall his own upon his helmet; so tremendous was the blow that the straps of the head-piece gave way, and Tyrrel fell half stunned to the ground. For Ulrick to place his foot upon his chest to keep him there was the work of an instant.

"Back!" he cried, for the first time breaking silence, and holding the point of his sword within an inch of the throat of his enemy; "another step, and the blood of your leader dyes my blade."

The men hesitated between the desire of saving their captain and the fear of punishment.

"Order them to throw aside their weapons," said Ulrick, addressing his prostrate enemy.

"Never!" shouted Tyrrel, with a look of defiance.

The point of his conqueror's sword entered his throat about an inch.

"Stay, stay!" he groaned; "if I command them to give up their swords, wilt thou spare my life?"

"I will."

"By the honour of a knight?"

"By the honour of a knight," added Ulrick.

"Well then," said Tyrrel, with a look of hate, "obey him! throw down your arms, I command you."

The men, who wished no better excuse than the orders of their leader for relinquishing a contest of which they were both tired, instantly obeyed, and cast their weapons half a bow-shot from them.

"Command them to retire a hundred paces from the shore," continued Ulrick, seeing that his first order was complied with.

"That thou mayst murder me!" shrieked the prostrate man, writhing in mingled agony and shame beneath the foot of his victorious foe.

"Carrion!" said the generous youth, pressing him yet more firmly down; "the thought was worthy only thee. Decide! I speak not twice."

Again the point of the sword approached the villain's throat.

The command was given, and, like the former, as promptly executed. As soon as the men had retired the prescribed distance, Ulrick released his enemy, first taking care to secure his sword. No sooner was his foot removed than Tyrrel rose doggedly from the ground. His rage was too deep for words—his humiliation too profound ever to be forgotten.

"For the sake of this poor boy," said Ulrick, after he had placed the wounded Gilbert in the boat, and was about to push off, "I spare thy life; but remember, Tyrrel, when next we meet, our strife is mortal."

"I will remember it," shouted the baffled traitor, shaking his clenched fist after the receding boat. "By heavens!" he muttered to himself, "my promised earldom could not give me half the joy as once to feel my foot upon thy neck."

The scene we have described had passed so rapidly, that by the time the warder had called the inmates of the hostel to his assistance, the boat which contained the fugitives had reached the middle of the stream, where the tide carried it down rapidly towards London bridge.

"Follow them!" shouted the ruffian; "they have not escaped us yet."

The men rushed to the remaining boats, and found that every oar was gone; curses loud and deep accompanied the discovery: meanwhile, the skiff pursued its way.

Ulrick's position was an embarrassing one: alone upon the water with his wounded companion, whom honour and humanity alike forbad him to desert; no refuge near; no friend whom he could consult; his liberty menaced at a moment when the gravest interests depended upon his activity and freedom. The recollection of his young bride pressed painfully upon him: what would be her fate and sufferings should he fall into the hands of his relentless enemy? He was startled from his painful reverie by a deep groan from Gilbert; the sound recalled him to himself. Abandoning the boat to the direction of the current, which bore it rapidly along, he approached the youth, and, with a gentle but firm hand, he drew the arrow from his breast, and felt considerably relieved when he beheld a gush of blood follow it; for, like most knights of the age, he knew something of leechcraft, and was aware that the wounds which bled internally were the most dangerous. Opening his vest to tear a piece of linen to stanch the hurt, his finger felt something hard; mechanically he drew it forth, and beheld the tablets of the Jew. It seemed as if Providence, in the hour of his need, had brought them to his recollection; for he remembered the words which accompanied the gift, though how to find the residence, at such an hour of the night, of any of the peculiar people, he knew not.

"How dost thou feel, boy?" he demanded of his charge; "art better?"

"Much—much, sir knight," replied Gilbert, in a feeble tone, "since you have withdrawn the arrow. I shall be strong soon, and able to assist you with the oar. Thank Heaven, you are not hurt."

"Knowest thou where we are?"

"Upon the river."

"Knowest thou where reside the principal Jews of the city, merchants, or leeches?" continued Ulrick.

"In Lombard-street, sir knight. Why dost thou ask?"

"Because it is with one of them we must find refuge. My life is close beset; my enemies will never think of searching for me there. Tell me," he added, "where must we land?"

"There," said the boy, raising himself in the boat and pointing to a distant part of the bank; "from thence, at the distance of a bow-shot, stands the house of Falk, of Cologne. Men say that he is good and charitable; he is well skilled, too, in leech-craft. 'Tis said he cured the late king of the black fever, when all hope had failed him. But you will never gain shelter there."

"Why not, boy?"

"He is too rich to need your gold. Men say he hath lent large sums to the king; it may be to his interest to betray you; and Jews, I've heard, would sell their souls to spite a Christian. Pray go not there!"

"It is our only hope," said Ulrick, with a sigh; "persecution may have taught him mercy; besides, you yourself say that he is good and charitable; added to which, I have a means to secure his favour, which something whispers me cannot fail of success."

Gilbert remained silent; he was either too much exhausted, or felt too much respect and gratitude to his companion, to urge his objections further. Ulrick, as soon as they reached the shore, assisted him carefully from the boat, which, with his foot, he sent once more adrift, lest, being found near the spot where they had landed, it should set the bloodhounds on their track. The boy was so far recovered by the night breeze as to be able to walk, with the support of his protector's arm. Slowly they wound their way amid the various small craft drawn up on the shore, to be out of the reach of the tide and the empty barrels and pieces of timber scattered about, till they approached a narrow lane, inhabited chiefly by watermen, and which conducted to Lombard-street. Fortunately, from the lateness of the hour, there were few stragglers about to watch their progress; a light might be seen occasionally through the crevices of the rude shutters, intimating that all the inhabitants of the place had not retired to rest. They proceeded without interruption, till they stood before the house they sought, the habitation of Falk, the richest merchant of his tribe. The house, though the most considerable in the street, presented, externally, but a poor appearance, it being entirely denuded of those quaintly carved attempts at ornament which already began to characterise the age. It was impossible, however, not to observe that the doors and shutters were framed with a careful attention to strength; the latter, particularly, were so well joined together, that when closed not a single ray of light could find egress from within or from without. Its master, like the rest of his nation, at the fierce period of which we write, although rich, enjoyed his wealth with fear and trembling; for the populace, taught to consider the once chosen people of God but as beings fit only to be hunted and persecuted, frequently attacked the dwellings of the Jews, veiling their appetite for plunder under the convenient cloak of fanaticism and religious pretext. It is astonishing how many of the descendants of the same ruffian populace may be found even at the present day—ay, and in high places, too—their savage and persecuting propensities only a little modified by the times in which they live.

The two fugitives, after looking carefully round them to see that they were unobserved, approached the door. Just as Ulrick was about to knock with the handle of his sword, it was unexpectedly opened, and a hand extended, which, grasping his, drew him and his companion into the house, a voice at the same time whispering:

"You are late; breathe not a word, but follow me."

For a few minutes, Ulrick and his companion followed their mysterious guide in silence; a thick cloth curtain, which screened a low arch, was drawn aside, and in an instant they found themselves in the midst of a brilliantly-lighted saloon. Lovely women, richly dressed, were seated upon cushions in the oriental fashion; high-browed, dark-bearded men, conversing in groups, standing beside them. It would be difficult to say which were the most surprised—the assembled Hebrews, or the two strangers so unexpectedly introduced among them. The women hastily let fall their veils, and their fathers and brothers, drawing their long knives—for swords were forbidden them—prepared to defend themselves from some expected outrage.

The guide, a youth, whose error had brought the two parties thus in contact, stood transfixed with anger and fear.

"Who art thou? and what brings a Christian at this hour beneath my roof?" demanded a tall, venerable-looking man, in a tone which proclaimed him to be the master of the house.

Ulrick placed the tablets in his hand, which the old man retired to read by the light of a silver lamp suspended from the ceiling in an inner recess of the apartment.

"What have I done?" exclaimed the young Israelite whose heedlessness had occasioned the unexpected introduction; "by my imprudence the Nazarene hath entered in the tent of my fathers."

The men, still grasping their knives, thronged round the intruders, their black eyes flashing in fearful wrath upon them. The terrified Gilbert clung to his companion, who, in the midst of the menacing throng around them, retained his calmness and usual presence of mind. He felt, from the manner in which they were hemmed in, that the least attempt at resistance would but provoke their fate. Several arms were already raised to strike, when the voice of the old man was heard as he issued from the recess, holding the tablets of Abram in his hands.

"Harm them not," he cried. "Respect the guests of the high priest."

In an instant every hostile expression disappeared, and instead of being surrounded by ferocious faces, Ulrick and his companion found themselves amongst friends.

CHAPTER XXIII.

Heard ye the din of battle bray,
Lance to lance, and horse to horse?
Long years of havoc urge their destin'd course,
And thro' the kindred squadrons mow their way:—GRAY.

LRICK and his companion were conducted to a well furnished apartment, provided with two couches, by their host, who, like most of his nation, possessed a considerable knowledge of surgery. The wound of Gilbert was carefully dressed, and the tired fugitives, after being refreshed, were left to their repose. Early in the morning the Jew visited them again, when our hero expressed to him their thanks.

"You owe me nothing," interrupted the old man; "my house and services are freely yours; he who hath served one so honoured of our nation hath a claim upon the gratitude of every Hebrew; only point out the way in which it may be further useful to you. It seems that you are a personage of some note, for search hath been made in every hostel of the city, and severe penalties denounced against all who harbour you."

"And yet you, one of earth's persecuted race, venture to conceal me."

"I am accustomed to danger," resumed

the old man, with a mournful smile, "and therefore almost indifferent to it. In childhood, when I ventured from my home to breathe the fresh air of heaven, I was hooted, beaten, and reviled by those of my own age. I bore it patiently, for I was but a sickly boy—so patiently that at last my persecutors got tired of tormenting me. My dawning manhood was but a series of dangers and humiliations. Three days after my first marriage the home of my wedded love was burnt and plundered, and my young bride, the idol of my soul, life's richest pearl, the descendant of a princely race—for the despised sons of Abraham count names as lofty, Christian, as thine own—perished in the flames. The years which followed were a blank; but I was revenged, fearfully revenged."

"Thy wrongs indeed were terrible. But how wert thou avenged?" demanded Ulrick.

"By the captivity of the accursed city whose brutal rabble fired my peaceful home," sternly replied the Hebrew. "It was Jewish gold which armed the Conqueror's fleets—which paid his mercenary troops; the despised Jew forged the yoke destined for a nation's neck. William was but the agent of his wrath. Had I not procured him vast loans from amongst my people, his barks had never left the Norman shore: the very jewels of his ducal crown were pledged to me—his father's cup—all but his knightly sword."

"Is it possible?" demanded his hearer. "Could a being whom the world deemed so abject forge the fetters to enchain my country? Thou speakest truly, Jew: thou hast been fearfully avenged."

"And yet it has not shut out all humanity from my heart. Had Herold listened to my cry for justice, his b as had rested by the Confessor's. I pointe. cut the hands to him, red with my Sarah' blood, and asked for judgment; he refused me—why? Those hands were Christian. In his pride he proffered gold—gold!" added the old man, scornfully, "for the life of my young bride—gold to the man who could have counted treasure with him ten times o'er!"

"Thou hast suffered much!" exclaimed his guest "and I marvel that, at the request e'en of thy dearest friend, thy door should open to a Christian. Should any of thy friends who witnessed my arrival here last night prove treacherous and denounce thee?"

"Fear not," said Faulk, with a smile; "such are not the vices of our nation; persecution hath made us faithful to each other. There is not of the vilest of our race who, on the sight of Abram's tablets, would not risk his life to shelter thee; besides, even the red king's wrath would pause, ere it reached me; he hath need of gold, is negotiating a loan amongst our people, and I am not the poorest of my tribe."

"Beware," said our hero, who felt deeply interested in the old man's story, "how you hazard your wealth on so poor a surety as William's faith; know you not that many of the nobles have already acknowledged Robert as their king? that his uncle, the warlike Odo of Bayeux, is at the head of the confederacy? that, in a few days, the army of his brother will besiege him in his capital? This pageant of a coronation will but render the tyrant's fall more signal; his reign will be a brief one."

"All," said the Jew; "I know it all; and can foresee the end as truly as though an angel whispered me."

"And that will be?"

"The downfall of your hopes. Robert hath courage, but not that dogged energy of purpose which wins and guards a crown; he is too much the bacchanal of the cup and kiss; his ally, Roger of Shrewsbury, is half won over. You smile," continued the speaker, "and wonder how the poor Jew should prate of such high matter; but learn that, if we have no voice at the council board of nations, our gold finds ears there. Yours will prove the phantom king, and mine the real one. But, tell me, how can I assist your present purpose?"

"By procuring me a safe disguise. I have friends whom I must speak with."

"The Abbot of Bec?" demanded his mysterious host, with a smile. "Beware! there is danger in the visit."

Ulrick started at the query, and a suspicion of the churchman's treachery glanced across his mind: how else could he reconcile the Jew's knowledge of his intentions? Falk smiled at his suspicions, for he read them as clearly in his changing countenance as though he had given utterance to them.

"You wrong him," he said, replying to his guest's unspoken thoughts; "Anselm is incapable of treachery. He is the firm friend of Bishop Odo; and, knowing that he is so, I guessed it was to him your letters were addressed. How do you propose to visit him?"

"Dressed in the poorest garb your friendship can supply me with," was the answer of Ulrick.

"Then you are sure to be detected. Suspicion is awakened; and humble weeds are more likely to conceal a messenger than knightly armour or a courtly garb. If you go forth, do so like yourself."

"I have no armour," observed Ulrick, who saw at once the shrewdness of the advice, "and my good steed is sent to Eltham. It hath already once betrayed its master."

"I can supply you with both. When will you set forth?"

"At the sunset hour."

"Be it so," replied the Jew.

"But my poor wounded boy," said our hero, pointing to Gilbert, who lay wondering on his couch what could be the subject of conversation between his protector and the Jew; for they had both spoken in French, the common language of the higher classes at the time, and he understood only his rude mother Saxon.

"I will take care of him. As soon as he is strong enough I will provide him with the means to join you. Can I do more," demanded the Hebrew, "for the friend of the honoured Abram?"

"Nothing," answered Ulrick, "but to accept his thanks for the generous hospitality thou hast accorded. Thou hast opened to me a new page in the history of mankind: doubt not I will peruse it. For thine and Abram's sake, the Israelite shall henceforth be in deed, as well as in humanity, a brother to me. Despite the church's dicta," added Ulrick, "reason tells me that Heaven never intended man to judge his fellow dust."

"In that I am repaid," said Falk. "Farewell! Three hours before sunset the steed and armour shall be ready."

At the appointed time our hero, nobly mounted, and clad in steel a monarch might have envied, wearing his visor down, threaded his way through the city towards Westminster. Several times during his progress he encountered various portions of the royal guard, but none presumed to stop or question him. If, as he supposed, they were on the scent of the fugitive, his appearance was so different from what Tyrrel and the warder had described, that none could recognise him in the stately knight who slowly made his way through the crowded streets of the busy metropolis. He arrived without interruption at his destination, and once more stood face to face with the mitred Abbot of Bee.

"Welcome, sir knight," said the quiet, astute churchman; "there has been hot quest after you; Tyrrel is seriously wounded, and the king furious at your escape; you must have warm and true friends to shelter you, for they have done so at the peril of their lives. As you value your own," he added, "quit London instantly, for the city swarms with spies. A large reward is offered for your apprehension."

"Not with my errand unachieved."

"Leave that to me; I am unsuspected," observed the abbot; "your presence cannot advance the cause."

"But my letters, father; my letters to the nobles?"

"I will deliver them."

"I have friends, too, whom my absence—"

"May compromise," urged the priest, glancing uneasily around; "soon as you quit the abbey, depart at once for Eltham; there you will find your good steed waiting, together with letters, which I have forwarded you by a sure hand for our friends in Kent. You play a game for life, young man; throw not a chance away, for you have crafty enemies upon the watch to seize it."

The advice was too reasonable to be neglected, and Ulrick saw that the cautious speaker had taken the precaution of forwarding his letters to Eltham, not to risk compromising either himself or friends, should their bearer unfortunately be taken. Hastily, therefore, bidding the priest adieu, he mounted his horse, determined, without further hesitation, to quit a spot which menaced him with so many dangers. Unfortunately, in the hurry of his departure, he neglected the precaution which alone had prevented his arrest in his progress through the city. He wore his visor up; and the warder, whom he had so severely chastised the previous evening, and who, in the hope of encountering him, had been on the look out with a party of his men the entire day, saw, and instantly recognised him. To seize his horse by the rein, and secure his sword, was but the work of a moment. He was so securely held, that resistance would have been as foolish as vain.

"What means this outrage, knaves?" demanded Ulrick. "Do you take me for a thief, that you lay hands upon me in open day? Beware that you have sure warrant for the deed; it else may cost you dear."

"Warrant!" exclaimed the warder, with a malicious grin. "The headsman shall be my warrant, since, ere nightfall, he will have to deal upon thee. By Saint Martin, to hear thee speak, one would think that coat of mail covered a belted earl, and not a scheming traitor. Away with him, my masters."

"And whither must I go?" inquired their prisoner.

"To the Tower—his highness holds his court there. To think," added the fellow, with a laugh, "that silly head of thine should bring me fifty silver marks! They will buy plasters for the hard blows I got last night. Most of my debtors pay me one way or another—some with their coin, others with their blood; but thou shalt pay with both."

"And thou shalt have more, knave, than thou dreamest of, an' thou letst not go my rein. I tell thee, I bear a message from the king; at peril of your lives detain me."

"Ho, ho, ho! which king?" shouted the

men, to whom Ulrick's assertion appeared an excellent jest, so sure were they of his identity. "The King of the Saxons," as they contemptuously styled Robert, "or William the Red King?"

At this instant a party of the royal guard, headed by John of Montgomery, who was a secret partisan of the elder prince, whose cause he soon after openly espoused, approached the spot, and seeing a knight in rich armour surrounded by several common men-at-arms, who evidently held him prisoner, halted to inquire the cause.

"The traitor who last night nearly slew Sir Walter Tyrrel!" shouted the warder, fearful lest the new comers should interfere with his prisoner, and secure the merits of his capture to themselves.

"There is a reward of fifty marks upon his head," cried a second.

"Peace, fool!" growled the chief of Ulrick's captors, in an under-tone; "do you want to have the bone snatched from between your teeth? You see, sir knight, that we have fairly taken him; our party is quite numerous enough to conduct him to the Tower."

"You, sir knight," said Ulrick, calmly, as soon as he could obtain a hearing, "doubtless will listen to reason. I know not whether these fellows are mad or drunk, or take me for another. I told them, as I tell you, that I came here on a message from the king. Question the men: they saw me quit the abbey—you know it is the residence of the venerable primate."

John of Montgomery shook his head. He was not deceived either by Ulrick's calmness or the equivocal truth he told of coming with a message from the king. His secret inclinations prompted him to release him; but prudence whispered that such a step might prove dangerous to himself. He was one of the few nobles with whom the Abbot of Bec had tampered, and he doubted not but in the knight before him he beheld the messenger of Robert to the priest.

"In times less doubtful than the present," he replied, "the word of a knight would be sufficient; but duty compels me to ask if you have no other proof?"

"None," said Ulrick, carelessly.

"No papers?"

"No."

"To be sure he has not," replied the warder, echoing his words; "come, my masters, away with him."

"Back, churl!" exclaimed the commander of the guard, regarding him sternly; "it is not for a peasant to arrest a noble. Sir knight, I must demand your sword," he added, turning courteously to Ulrick; "you

are my prisoner. If your tale be true, your captivity will be but brief; if not, I shall not ask excuse for performing an act of duty."

As Ulrick was about to yield himself a prisoner, he suddenly recollected the signet-ring which Abram had given him. To draw his mailed glove from his hand, and hold it to Montgomery's sight, was the impulse of a moment. The officer recognised it in an instant.

"By heavens!" he cried, "it is the king's own signet-ring."

The confusion of the warder and his men may be more easily imagined than described; like tigers who had missed their spring, they were about to sneak away, fearful of the consequence of their mistake, when the voice of their late captive arrested them.

"Secure those men."

The guard obeyed him in an instant.

"How is it your pleasure we should dispose of them?" demanded their leader.

"To prison with them."

Montgomery waved his hand, and, despite their protestations, they were dragged away, amid the sneer of the crowd who had collected round the spot, and who were delighted at the sight of the warder and his men being sent to prison. They had too often suffered from their brutality to pity them, but followed their escort, shouting and triumphing in their disgrace. In a few minutes Ulrick and the captain of the guard were left alone.

"And now," said the latter, "please you to give me the ring. I ask not too curiously how you obtained possession of it; to me it is sufficient warrant for releasing you from the rude clutches of these men. Ride you to Eltham?" he added, with a peculiar smile.

Our hero started, for the words conveyed a deeper knowledge of his movements than he suspected him possessed of. For a few moments they regarded each other in silence.

"Perhaps," slowly pronounced Ulrick, at last drawing the signet from his finger and giving it.

"Then ride quickly," continued his questioner. "There you may chance to find a steed and friends; every hour you rest in London may bring those less easy to be satisfied by your story than myself. Farewell! sir knight; perhaps when next we meet we may meet as friends."

Waving their hands as a signal of adieu, the two knights separated; Ulrick to cross the neighbouring ferry on his way to the rendezvous designated by the worthy abbot, and Montgomery to relate the history of his capture, and justify his share in his release by returning William his lost signet-ring.

Our hero had journeyed several miles

ROGER OF SHREWSBURY DASHES HIS MAILED GLOVE IN TYRREL'S FACE.

before he perceived that he was followed by a young fellow dressed in the ordinary travelling costume of the times, who rode a light horse, whose active pace enabled him to keep up with his own good steed, encumbered as it was by the weight of a rider armed *cap-à-pie*. Turn which way he would, still the rider pursued the same route; once, to avoid the persevering horseman, he made a considerable detour by a wood which took him a winding distance from the main road towards Croydon; but, faithful as his shadow, his pursuer followed him—stopped when he stopped, and resumed his way as soon as he gave his steed the rein.

Although Ulrick felt little uneasiness at the idea of a single enemy, still he was annoyed at being so perseveringly tracked, and determined to ascertain at once the purpose of the traveller, whose route, by some caprice, seemed so exactly to tally with his own.

Emerging from the wood, he turned an acute angle of the road, and reined his horse to await the arrival of the fellow, who could not possibly ascertain whether he had pursued his way or not till he was close upon him. The *ruse* succeeded, for in a few minutes he heard the quick light step of the horse. Wheeling his own round, he met the rider face to face. It was a lonely, retired spot, fit for an encounter; to avoid him was impossible.

The fellow who had so closely dogged him proved to be a young man about three-and-twenty; a light pointed beard, rather inclined to red, adorned his chin, and connected it, by a few straggling silky hairs, with his moustache; his air, despite the simplicity of his dress, was martial; and he rode his horse with the air of a man accustomed alike to war or to the chase.

Ulrick was the first to speak.

"It seems, friend, that we ride the same way; whither are you bound?"

"That is a question," replied the stranger, "which a prudent man scarce cares to answer."

"Still it must be answered," said our hero with a determined air, "if we are to remain at peace. I suffer no man to dog my steps."

"Nor I any man to question mine, whether my errand be of pleasure or caprice, business or danger. Ride on, sir knight," continued the young man, with a quiet smile; "we shall soon see if our affairs or inclinations lead us the same way."

There was an easy, half mocking tone in the speaker's voice which jarred upon Ulrick's ear, not that there was anything in the words at which he could fairly take offence; still it annoyed him. Pointing to the two roads which diverged from the corner of the wood, and fixing his eyes sternly upon the intruder, who seemed more amused than frightened by the encounter, he said—

"It is my pleasure to ride alone; choose your way."

"And mine to ride in company," coolly answered his tormentor. "The society of so brave a knight is a safe guard to a poor citizen. It is your own fault that we have come in contact; I was content with the protection of your shadow."

Fully convinced that he was followed by some spy or agent of the tyrant's, the Lord of Stanfield drew his sword, determined at once to end the contest, for he doubted not but the speaker only waited their arrival in some village, or an encounter with some of the partisans of William who patrolled the country, to order his arrest. A glance of haughty surprise, more than fear, passed over his tormentor's countenance at the action, and he quietly observed that he was unarmed—an assertion which, in appearance at least, was true, since neither sword nor weapon of any kind was visible upon his person; he seemed totally unarmed.

"I cannot raise my sword," exclaimed Ulrick, petulantly, as soon as he was convinced of the fact, "upon an unarmed man, whatever may be his intentions, be he spy or enemy."

"Of course you can't," coolly answered the horseman, "so you may as well sheathe it again. It would be murder! Besides, if our roads should prove the same, why not pursue them in goodfellowship together?"

"Because it is my pleasure to be alone."

"An unsocial humour that, and savours more of the cloisters than the camp."

The fugitive started at the speech, and asked himself, could the strange horseman know him? or was it but one of those random shafts which shrewdness or hazard sometimes wing? Whichever it might be, he felt that it was more necessary than ever to separate from his obtrusive companion, whom he once more sternly bade to choose his way, as he was resolved to ride alone.

"What if it leads to Eltham? would you wish me to arrive there before you?"

Ere Ulrick could reply, another horseman, well armed and powerfully mounted, dashed round the corner of the wood, and seizing the bridle of the stranger's horse, commanded him in peremptory but respectful tones to follow him.

"To my grave as soon," replied the young man; "villain! let go my rein; quick, sir knight! your sword! lend me your sword!"

Ulrick, who deemed the pretended arrest a new pretext to detain him, set spurs to his horse, and had already gained a short distance from the scene, when the sound of his own name arrested his attention; involuntarily he wheeled round to listen—it was repeated louder than before.

"Ulrick of Stanfield! craven, false knight! is it thus you fulfil your vow of chivalry to aid the unarmed and defenceless? Thy blazon will be stained for ever!"

The language of the stranger, together with the mingled tones of entreaty and indignation in his voice, convinced our hero that, whatever might have been the young man's object in pursuing him, he was at least no spy. A few seconds brought him to the spot where the last comer was still dragging the steed and his prisoner after him.

"By what authority do you arrest this young man?" he demanded.

"By one not lightly to be disputed," replied the knight, for such his golden spurs proclaimed him—"the king's!"

"Produce it, then."

"Fool! dost think a belted knight requires other warrant than his sword? Mine shall always answer for its master's deeds to all who dare to question them. This, to teach thee a lesson of more caution."

Holding the rein of his prisoner's steed in his left hand, the speaker made a dash at Ulrick, from whose well tempered helmet the blow of his sword glanced as from a block of adamant. In the fierce encounter which ensued he had ample occasion to prove the value of the Jew's gift—the armour, weapon, and horse were admirable. Both knights were masters of their weapons, which flashed with fearful celerity, describing fiery segments round each other's heads. Their steeds seemed to take part in the struggle; so firmly were their riders seated, that one mind appeared to animate them. The blows of his opponent—and they were rained both thick and heavily on Ulrick's armour—tried its strength, but made little impression; whilst, on the contrary, the red blood followed in several places the stroke of his own good sword. Several times they retreated to short distances to draw breath, which they had no sooner recovered than, wheeling round, they returned again to the assault. Although the life-stream damasked the well-polished mail of the aggressor, his strength was by no means exhausted; and our hero, who was apprehensive of the arrival of succour, felt the necessity of finishing with him. Relying on the training of his steed, the third time they renewed the encounter, instead of meeting the shock, he dexterously avoided it by passing to the right, striking a furious blow with his long weapon as he did so on his opponent's helmet; so well was it directed, that the steel clasps which united it with the neck-piece were cut asunder, and a severe wound inflicted. The wearer's head sank upon his breast, for one of the principal arteries was severed, and in a few seconds he fell, exhausted by rapid loss of blood, upon the ground. By the time his enemy had alighted all was over—the strong man was a corse.

"A knightly blow, and well struck," exclaimed the young stranger. "I took thee from the first to be a man of courage. 'Tis well for both of us that we are not deceived. But mount thy steed, and let us hasten onward; but first reach me yon traitor's sword; perchance," he added, "I may have occasion for it yet."

There was too much reason in the advice not to be followed; the victor remounted, and for a few minutes rode silently with the stranger, whom he had rescued, by his side.

"How didst thou learn my name?" he at last demanded.

"I know the name of most men," drily

answered the horseman. "Methinks you were in no haste to claim it."

"Indeed," said Ulrick; "then perhaps you can favour me with the name of my opponent?"

"Perhaps; enough for the present that he was as brave a soldier, and as unscrupulous a villain, as ever followed banner to the field. Many a knight whose hold might else have blazed, and many a mother who else had mourned her dishonoured child, may thank thy arm. His last course on earth is run. But come," added the speaker, "let us understand each other. Ride we to Eltham?"

"We do."

"In fellowship?"

"In fellowship," said Ulrick; "but tell me what is thy name?"

"Henry," replied his companion, "for the lack of a nobler; my father gave me little else beside; so call me simply Henry, or Henry the simple—which you will; I am no stickler for ceremony—it irks me."

"So it should seem," replied our traveller, who began to be rather amused than angry with the fellow's humour; "may a man, without being thought too curious, demand how you became acquainted with his name? By our lady of the rood, it came most opportunely to thy tongue; perhaps some starling whispered it?"

"By my faith," said the young man, "it was more like a raven than a starling; there was blood upon his beak."

"And his name?"

Henry, as the stranger called himself, shrugged his shoulders, and looked at him with a peculiar smile, as much as to inform the questioner that that was his secret; but seeing a frown upon Ulrick's brow, and probably reflecting that want of confidence was but a poor return for the services he had received, he answered frankly that Sir Walter Tyrrel had first told it to him—a piece of intelligence which caused his companion to regard him once more with suspicion.

"Tyrrel!" he exclaimed; "why, he is my bitterest enemy."

"Save one," drily added the strange horseman.

"And that is 'the king,' as William of Normandy hath styled himself."

"Ay," said Henry; "and as, to-morrow, Lanfranc will crown him. The fellow whose throat you so cleverly cut brought me an invitation to the ceremony; his method of delivering it was a rough one, so I declined it."

The easy, familiar tone of the speaker puzzled our hero, who was at a loss to understand the rank of his companion, and his avowed connection with Walter Tyrrel. Had his purpose been unfriendly, nothing would have been more unlikely than his owning it; besides, he was, till Ulrick gave him the dead man's sword, unarmed, and every step their horses took lessened the distance between them and danger.

"Thou art a riddle!" he cried, speaking as much to his own thoughts as to Henry.

"And thou no sphinx to solve me. Have a little patience; and in time, like the serpent's tail in the emblem of eternity, the puzzle will unfold itself. Thou seest," he added, "I have dealt with bookcraft in my time—though more, perchance, with men; but with thy cloister-breeding thou canst understand me."

"Perhaps," replied Ulrick, secretly annoyed at the increased mystification to which he was being subjected.

"I tell thee that thou shalt, then. Let that content thee," resumed the speaker; "only, I bide my time. And now tell me, sir knight of Stanfield—how dost thou like the strange companion fortune hath sent thee?"

"So well," said the party he addressed, laughing at the oddity of the question, "that I will put no more interrogations; lest, knowing thee better, I should like thee less."

"Frankly spoken; there is something fresh in truth; I know the sound, although it is so seldom in my short life that I have heard it spoken. At Eltham the riddle shall be explained."

"At Eltham be it," answered Ulrick.

A short ride brought the travellers to the priory of White Friars, a dependency on the rich abbey of Bec, in Normandy. It was situated near the village of Eltham, in one of those secluded, quiet, sunny nooks which the monks of old so loved, and so well knew how to select, and which in no country are more frequently found than in merry England. It was one of those spots where silent sanctity might build its cell, or the broken passions of humanity, shipwrecked on the sea of life, seek and find repose. The evening hour; the stately heron, winging its solitary way to the distant wood; the glorious sunset, whose last rays, lingering like a lover's kiss, gilded the slender pinnacle of the church,—were all in harmony, forming a soft dreamy picture, which the horsemen completed.

On their arrival, they were immediately conducted to the apartment of the prior, a stately-looking personage, who received them alone, and who hastened to inform Ulrick that his steed, and the promised letters from his brother Anselm, had already arrived; at the same time informing him that a lodging was already prepared for him for the night within the walls.

"And where am I to lodge?" demanded the stranger, in a half petulant tone, displeased at being overlooked by the lordly churchman; "is there no room for me, good father, in your pious rookery?"

The priest answered haughtily that a cell should be prepared for him near his master; he was evidently offended by the irreverent tone of the speaker, whom he took for an esquire or attendant upon the person of his visitor.

"A cell?" iterated Henry; "well, a cell be it; we will do penance for our sins, since the hospitality of our host so limits our entertainment; but when last we hunted in this neighbourhood, if our memory fails not, we were better lodged; 'tis true we were not then a fugitive."

The prior started from his seat, and approaching the stranger, overwhelmed him with excuses for not having at once recognised him; adding, that he must reproach the Lord of Stanfield for neglecting to inform him that his walls were graced by the presence of such an honoured guest.

"Faith," said the young man, laughingly, "you must grant the good knight absolution there; for he dreams as little that his troublesome companion is the youngest son of the Conqueror, as you, holy father, did yourself."

"Prince Henry!" exclaimed Ulrick in astonishment, at the same time bending the knee.

"Ay," said his highness, "Henry the simple, as men call me, though perhaps, after all, I have more wit than my scoffing brother dreams, whose fraternal love was so disinterested he could not bear me from his own safe keeping. My lodging is already furnished in the Tower, but, like a wilful youth, I preferred my liberty, or Robert's guardianship to his. Tut, man," he added, "never kneel to me; I am as poor, nay poorer than thyself. Our father's love, of all his vast possessions, left us but one poor hold in Normandy, and a remembrance upon his treasurer, to be paid when we can get it."

There was something so frank and soldier-like in Henry's manner, that our hero felt instantly at his ease; for, after all, he had only taken such precautions at their first meeting as necessary prudence and his safety dictated. The young prince explained that it was by the advice of Anselm he had quitted London to join himself to Robert's fortunes, and that he had recognised Ulrick's person from having been a concealed witness of his first interview with the abbot.

"And who was the traitor," demanded our hero, "who would have forced your highness back?"

"Richard of Lissieu, our brother's pander, tool, and executioner. William will miss him sorely when there is some act which fears the light of heaven to be accomplished. Stanfield," he added, kindly taking his protector by the hand, "we owe thee a debt of gratitude for that good blow; it moved a stumbling-block from out my path—a bloodhound from my track. Few persons live to tell the tale of their captivity whom that bad man has guarded."

It was finally arranged that no notice should be taken to the community either of the arrival or of the high rank of the prior's guests, who both supped in his apartment, and soon afterwards, fatigued with the events of the day, retired to rest, each throwing himself upon his pallet ready dressed, in order to be prepared in case of danger or surprise.

The prince and Ulrick had not been long sleeping, when they were roused by their host, who, attended by Father Segsil—an aged Saxon monk, who of the community alone possessed his confidence—entered their cell.

"Rouse, sir knight!" he exclaimed; "in less than an hour the enemy will be upon us. They must not find you here; Jesu, Maria! they would burn our convent with as little ceremony as a burgher's hold."

"And whence comes this intelligence, good prior?" demanded Henry, starting from his couch. "Would it had tarried some two or three hours later; I was indulged by Mistress Fancy with a dream too glorious ever to be realised. I should like to have revelled in it some few hours longer."

"The intelligence," replied their host, paying little attention to the latter part of the prince's speech, "is from brother Segsil," pointing as he spoke to his companion, who stood regarding Henry with a look in which hate and interest were strangely mingled.

"May he not be mistaken?" demanded Ulrick.

"Father Segsil is never mistaken," replied the prior: "in an hour the satellites of William will be here."

"Hath any messenger arrived at the convent?"

"No."

"May not the good father be mistaken in his intelligence?"

"Father Segsil is never mistaken," repeated their host gravely; "his warnings are not to be neglected."

"Why, then," said Prince Henry, laughing, "we must e'en obey them, as our fathers did the oracles of old, blindly and in confidence. Forgive me, holy man," he added, turning to the aged monk, whose dark eyes were still fixed immovably upon him, "if I am somewhat more sceptic than the prior here; perchance it is the fault of unclerkly breeding."

"Shall I convince thee?" demanded the old man, in a tone which seemed to echo from a sepulchre.

"Faith! I demand no better," replied the young man, extending his left palm, which the monk thrust contemptuously aside; and seizing his right hand firmly, fixed the prince's attention by the intense expression of his gaze.

"Thy dream shall yet be realised, proud boy—the crown of England waits thee."

The prince started: that which at first he had treated as a jest became serious, for the monk had indeed interpreted his vision rightly. The flush of hope and surprise suffused his brow as he demanded of the soothsayer:—

"When?"

"When the Red King sleeps his last sleep, when the blood of the Conqueror's favourite son hath gladdened the oppressed soil of England, and bid her children hope for peaceful days. Then," added the old man, "the crown thou hast so often dreamt of shall be thine."

"But shall I keep as well as win it?" demanded Henry; who, although less influenced by the superstition of the age, could not avoid placing confidence in the man who had so singularly interpreted his dream.

"That will depend upon thy marriage," replied Father Segsil; "if thou art fortunate enough to win a bride of the royal Saxon blood, thou shalt die king of England; if not, the curse of thy race will overtake thee. Now, then, away! I speak of the future to thee no more."

"Tell me but this: shall we meet again?" demanded Henry.

"If thou art wise enough to follow my counsel, yes. At the proudest moment of thy life, if not when the last trumpet summons earth together, I'll meet thee face to face. Farewell."

"Hast thou no good fortune, father, to predict to me?" said Ulrick.

The old man gazed mournfully upon him, and shook his head, muttering to himself:

"Saxon—Saxon; I read it in his open brow and bright blue eye. Thou hast asked the old priest for a prediction—better have sought his blessing; but since the choice is made, take it and begone—a career of honour, an unstained faith, a soldier's laurel, but a broken heart. Once more I charge thee," he added, impatiently, "to begone—ride for your lives. Once past the bridge, you may slack the rein—no living thing will ever cross it afterwards."

The confident tone of the monk's voice, and the implicit faith which the prior placed n his intelligence, no matter how mysteriously obtained, decided the young men to depart. Hastening to the stables, they found their horses ready saddled, and after a benedicite from the prior and his companion, resumed their journey, Ulrick leading his grey steed by a loose rein with him.

Scarcely had they passed the bridge, a short mile from the convent, and which connected the high banks of a deep ravine, too steep for any horse to climb, too wide to leap, when the wooden fabric burst into a brilliant flame, which dark figures were seen feeding with bundles of straw and fagots. The monk's strange prediction came to their recollection—living thing never crossed it more.

"Think you they are demons?" whispered Ulrick.

"Demons or mortals, they are friends," said Henry. "Let us pursue our way."

CHAPTER XXIV.

How beautiful is death when caused
By virtue.—CATO.

ON the morning after Ulrick's departure from Norwich, Robert of Normandy, at the head of a considerable body of troops and the nobles who acknowledged his authority, marched from the city. Herbert de Lozinga, whose experience was of so much value in the council, accompanied him in quality of chancellor, that prelate having consented to retain his office at the entreaty of the new monarch. Edith and her daughter-in-law retired to Stanfield, which, removed as it was from the scene of war, a small party of vassals was sufficient to defend. The bride of Mirvan was their only guest; and there, in the antique oratory of the countess, they offered up their united prayer for the absent warriors' safety.

The prior of the Dominicans, who had accompanied the confiding monarch to the gate of St. Stephen on his march, had returned to his convent, and was walking in his stately garden, which extended from the church (now St. Andrew's Hall) to the water side, speculating in thoughtful mood upon the future, and not feeling perfectly in security touching the past. The absence of the curate of St. Julian's alarmed him, although few, he thought, could blame him for having extended the rites of Christian burial to a knight so valiant as Robert of Artois, and his own relative besides. The principal cause of his uneasiness arose from the Jew, who had so strangely possessed himself of the prince's signet-ring, and in whose

hands the papers found upon his nephew might be turned to dangerous account. Twice had he sent to the house of Abram; it was empty, not a trace of any living being remained. He had found, too, upon inquiry, that the vessel to whose captain he had given the leech the letter had sailed for Rouen, having taken several passengers with him.

"Let but William triumph—and he can scarcely fail to do so," he muttered to himself—"and I may laugh at enemies, open or concealed."

"Perhaps!" exclaimed a voice, so near him that the words were almost spoken in his ear. Eborard started, and beheld a pale, attenuated being, meanly clad, regarding him with a fixed look. His forehead was high and bald, his face marked with a thousand minute scars, which gave it a most ghastly appearance, and his limbs seemed to sink under him from sickness or want.

"And who art thou, fellow," demanded the prior, with a haughty stare of surprise, "who darest so boldly answer to our thoughts, and how gaindst thou entrance here?"

"By the old way!" replied the strange intruder, whom our readers have already, no doubt, recognised as Robert of Artois.

"The old way!" iterated the puzzled churchman: "what old way?"

"The secret door behind the statue of St. Dominic, in the cloisters," replied the stranger, for such he appeared to his uncle, "where you once heard a strange confession, father, and performed a stranger deed."

"And what was that?" demanded Eborard, still more and more perplexed.

"The marriage of a Christian with a Jewess."

"Hush!" exclaimed the astonished prior, turning pale at the words, which had been spoken loudly, for the mere whisper of such a sacrilege would have been sufficient to subject him to the censure of the church; and, if proved, to deposition from the high rank he held within its pale.

"Even as you please," said the mysterious man; "I wish not to offend you."

"How didst thou learn the fearful secret?"

"Because I witnessed it," replied his tormentor, whose object was to work upon the fears of his reverend uncle; for he knew him too well to expect much pity or generosity at his hands should he make himself known to him. "Added to which, I have the fact attested under the hand and seal of Robert of Artois."

"Where is it?" eagerly demanded the priest, who felt how necessary to his safety it was to possess himself of such an important document. "Hast it with thee?"

"It were a wise trick that," exclaimed his nephew, "to bring my gage of safety to the enemy's camp! No, no, sir priest, I am not to be caught in such a springe; the paper is in secure hands, who will transfer it to the primate, should aught like ill occur to me."

"Thinkest thou," stammered Eborard, "that I am capable of——"

"Everything," interrupted the wretched man; "nay, frown not, priest, nor raise thine eyes in pious mockery to heaven, to attest the innocence thou hast long since lost; enough for me, I know thee," he added; "know thee better than the confession ever yet revealed thee—better even than thou knowest thyself. Now let us deal together."

"What wouldst thou—gold?" demanded the terrified churchman, who inwardly cursed himself that he had ever yielded to the passionate menaces and entreaties of his nephew, and performed the sacred rites between him and Rachel—the only condition on which the haughty Jewess consented to be his; for, although she placed no faith in the ceremony herself, she thought it might bind him.

"I would," laconically answered Robert.

"What sum?"

"As much as will defray the expense of a knightly suit of armour and a good steed—say two thousand marks: thou seest I am moderate to begin with."

"Two thousand devils!" groaned the prior; "where should I find so vast a sum? Dost take our poor priory for a bishop's see? an I were to count you half the sum, the brotherhood would keep a twelvemonth's Lent."

"Take it, then, from the treasure which thy nephew confided to thy care," said his disfigured creditor; "ten thousand chances if ever he returns from purgatory to claim it at your hands."

"What treasure?" faltered Eborard.

"The twenty thousand marks in gold," sternly replied Robert; "to say nothing of the vessels of gold and silver torn from many an outraged shrine. The money, quick, at once; for I am sick of parleying with thee; and, now I think on't," he added, "make it three thousands marks,—it will save trouble for us both."

Eborard thought it best to comply with the demands of his unwelcome visitor at once, lest they should rise as he disputed them; he felt he was in his power, and had no resource left but to obey. His secret, whilst confined to his own breast, was his slave; in the possession of another, it became his master, and he submitted to its chains. Motioning to Robert to follow him to his cell, he counted down the gold to him with a heavy heart; for, like most worldly natures, he clung to the yellow dross; it was an idol which in his selfish breast had replaced the purer image of his God.

"There!" he exclaimed, as the last glittering piece fell from his reluctant fingers; "I trust thou art satisfied."

"For the present," coolly replied his nephew, pouching the coin. "Farewell. Perhaps we may one day meet again."

"The paper—the confession of Robert of Artois?" demanded Eborard, with an imploring look, which showed the importance he placed on the possession of it. "When shall it be mine?"

"Never," said his creditor, "till I am paid in full. Fear not—it is in safe hands; I am not likely to slay the goose which lays such golden eggs. Sleep in peace till thou hearest from me; that is," he added, "if a soul so black as thine can sleep. Hast any messenger to William of Normandy? for in three days I trust to join him. There is work to do in which I may be useful."

"None," sighed the prior; "at least, none which thou canst bear."

"I have other means to gain access to him," resumed his tormentor, with a smile —the first which, since his fearful punishment, had been seen upon his pale, disfigured countenance. "Adieu, most pious father," he added, with a sneer. "I do not ask thy benediction, lest it should turn to curses on my head."

"Adieu," said the priest, as he left the cell; "and may all the plagues of Egypt go along with thee! Who can this ruffian be," he murmured, "who thus holds my destiny in his rude hands? Can he be some agent of the accursed Jew? No matter who, I am in his toils; and resistance, like regret, is equally in vain."

In the manner which Robert of Artois had approached his uncle, he had shown a true appreciation of his character. If he had revealed himself, ten to one if he had been believed. Besides, in his own person, the crafty prior might have defied him; for he could not have denounced him for the sacrilege he had committed in marrying him to Rachel without implicating himself—a thing most anxiously to be avoided. He had suffered as few men have suffered, and the effect produced within his mind was as great as the change upon his person; but whether for good or evil, time alone can tell.

Concealing his gold carefully upon his person, he passed by the city gates, having first provided himself with a good steed, which he bought of a Saxon peasant, who had most probably stolen it from some straggler of Prince Robert's army, for the price at which he sold it was a vile one.

"Now, then, for London," muttered Robert of Artois, when he was fairly on his journey. "Like a shadow of the past, I will appear amongst them; like a voice from the tomb, I will croak my predictions in their ear. There is one being left in the world who still perchance may love me; let me seek him out; and then as destiny or inclination hereafter may decide."

As William, two days after his coronation, was leaving his capital to march to the encounter of his brother, who, by the advice of his counsellors, had thrown himself into Kent, he was accosted by a knight, sheathed in a plain black coat of mail, who demanded an audience in private. There was something in the tone of the speaker's voice which told the red king he was no stranger to him; and, despite the remonstrances of his attendants, whom he commanded to ride apart, the favour was accorded. Long and earnest was the conversation which ensued, the monarch frequently expressing by his gestures both interest and surprise. At last, at his request, the stranger raised his visor, and disclosed the features of his favourite, Robert of Artois; but so changed, as we have described, that but for the unanswerable proofs of his identity, which from former passages between them he had been enabled to adduce, and the strange tale of his metamorphosis which he had related to the king, his master never could have credited his assertion.

"This is indeed the poetry of vengeance,"

exclaimed the king, in a voice almost of pity for there were still, when his evil passions were not roused, some traces of humanity in him; "but fear not, Robert, thou shalt have ample means of paying back the Jew thy debt with interest. My lords," he added, beckoning his suite to approach, "henceforth this noble stranger is attached to our person; for the present, it is his pleasure that his name and rank should be concealed. Know him, then, but as William's friend, and the black knight. The time, I trust, will soon arrive when we may grace him with a nobler name, the one he hath so long and faithfully borne; till that hour arrives it is our pleasure that none question him of the past. Forward, my friends," he added, at the same time setting spurs to his impatient steed; "forward to Kent."

It is far from our intention to trace the course of the civil war which ensued, with varying success, between the two brothers: history hath more faithful chroniclers than we can presume to be. William, who, as crafty as Robert, was generous and rash, contrived to engage the affections of his Saxon subjects by liberal concessions in their favour. They were now so thoroughly subdued, that few longer aspired to the recovery of their ancient liberties, but were content with the promised mitigation of the iron rule of their Norman princes. The red king at last contrived to detach Roger Earl of Shrewsbury from his brother's interests, who, with his powerful fleet, prevented the arrival of succours which the confederates expected from Normandy; thus place after place fell into his hands, and, despite the devotion of Odo of Bayeux, Ulrick, and the few nobles who still adhered to a falling cause, Pevensey Castle alone held out for Robert.

It had for some time been besieged in vain; the great natural strength of its position rendered it almost impossible to be taken except by famine. Changing, therefore, his often foiled plan of assault into a blockade, William set down to besiege it in due form.

In the various battles which had been fought our hero had twice preserved the life of Robert, who repaid him by an attachment as sincere as he was capable of entertaining. Often would he, when walking with him on the ramparts, indulging in familiar conversation, express his regret that Heaven had not blessed him with such a son. "I feel," added the unhappy prince, "that then I should have something worth living for." It was evident that some secret sorrow prompted this regret; but Ulrick possessed too much delicacy to seek his confidence on

THE MYSTERIOUS STRANGER EXTORTING MONEY FROM EBORARD.

the only point where he seemed disposed to be reserved.

It was on a similar occasion, when the realmless monarch, who, for a considerable time, had been silently occupied in watching the night fires of the enemy, whose forces encircled the last spot of ground which owned his authority in England, turned suddenly round to his companion, and breaking silence, exclaimed:—

"I am weary of being cooped up like a wild fox in my den. What thinkest thou, Ulrick—are we not strong enough to lead a sortie from the keep? My sword is getting rusty for lack of use, and I feel the gall within my heart is rising daily to my lips, a bout might cure me of this folly, or end it, perchance, at once. 'Tis but the hour of ten ; by midnight all might be prepared."

The Lord of Stanfield, whose absence from Matilda made the monotony of his existence but more drear, eagerly caught at the proposal, and they were descending the ramparts to give the orders necessary to carry it into effect, when they encountered the venerable Edda and Herbert de Lozinga, who were both hurrying to a lone watch-tower at a distant angle of the castle. The prince informed them of the project he had just conceived, which the prelate listened to with a reproving air, for, although a man of peace, he saw at once that, even if successful, it would be attended with no ultimate advantage.

"You hear our pleasure doubtingly, my lord," said Robert, in a half offended tone.

"I may question its wisdom, sire," replied Herbert, "without presuming to censure it. Our only hope now is, that succours from France or Normandy may arrive; but for your unhappy quarrel with my lord of Shrewsbury, they had been here ere this. Wait but a little, and——"

"I'll wait no longer," replied the monarch sternly; then added, for he saw that his manner had given pain, "Yet still am thankful for your prudent counsel. Truth is, my lord, I am weary of this world of treachery and disappointment. The brightest gems in England's crown could not console me longer for the absence of green fields and a merry chase. I must do something to break my thrall, lest in very spleen I turn upon myself and devour my own heart. France—pshaw! by Rollo, but our brother the other side of the marche has had good reason, long ere this, to leave us to our fate. William has found the way to grease the Frenchman's palm; I have no hope from France."

"But I have, sire," quietly observed the bishop; "brighter than ever."

"You have received letters, then, my lord?" observed Ulrick, eagerly.

"No."

"Nor message?" added Robert.

"None. I see," said the prelate, with a smile, "the mystery displeases you. Deign to come with me, sire; if there be treason, it shall be explained. Trust me, it is no dangerous one; for the noble Edda and myself, together with a few poor monks, are the sole conspirators."

With these words the speaker resumed his way, followed by the aged Saxon and the two warriors; not a word was spoken till they arrived at the tower we have already mentioned.

"Now, then, for the conspiracy!" exclaimed Herbert, lighting a lamp, and placing it in one of the loop-holes of the battlement; "it will soon be answered."

Robert saw to his surprise that a similar light, in a few seconds, made its appearance in the window of a belfry attached to a small convent, removed about a bow-shot from the line of the enemy's camp.

"It is already answered," said Edda; "the intelligence is good."

By placing the lamps in different positions, questions were asked and responses made—a system of telegraphing which lasted about twenty-minutes; at the end of which time the prelate, turning with a smiling face to Robert, informed him that despatches had arrived from France.

"And their contents, my lord?" hastily demanded the prince.

"In ten days succour will arrive, winds and the will of Heaven permitting," answered Herbert.

"Is't sure?"

"Most certain."

"Still will I forth to-night. I feel an impulse not to be controlled. The fierce spirit of the founder of my race is on me," added the prince; "it is an omen presages me success. Within the hour, the moon will set. Let the soldiers arm themselves with flax and torches; bring flasks of oil to pour upon the tents. By Rollo's sword! Pevensey shall witness a blaze this night to light up its old towers! See to it, Stanfield."

Ulrick eagerly withdrew to prepare the men for the night's work, which he doubted not would be warm and bloody; for, whatever might be Robert's defects as a leader, want of courage was not one; though, unfortunately, it was of that reckless kind which, however invaluable in an individual soldier, is little to be desired in a chief.

The bishop remained silent; he saw no good could result from the attempt, but knew that it would be useless to oppose it further, for Robert had sworn by the oath of his race—the only pledge which the princes of his house were never known to violate. The experienced Edda also disapproved of the expedition.

"You, my good father," resumed the prince, "will summon our council, and impart the intelligence. You have no need of my weak head to aid you; whatever your wisdom may decide upon, Robert is always ready to approve."

"Always?" demanded Herbert, perhaps rather maliciously,

"Always, unless it cross my previous resolution. Farewell," he added; "wait but an hour longer on the ramparts, and you shall see a blaze, old friend, to cheer your drooping spirit: the camp of my rebel brother shall feed the flame."

The party had scarcely left the ramparts, when a figure, which had been hid by one of the huge embrasures of the battlements, stepped from its place of concealment into the bright moonlight, and throwing aside the cloak which enshrouded him, discovered the person of a man-at-arms, who had evidently been a spy upon their conversation. A deep red cicatrice, extending from the temple to the jaw, identified Peter Norbeck, the ruffian from whose brutality, our readers will recollect, Ulrick had saved Abram the Jew, and who had vowed vengeance for the chastisement his insolence and cruelty so well had merited. With a smile of mingled satisfaction and hatred he drew an arrow from his quiver, and shot it towards a low mound lying between the castle and the enemy's camp, and remained for a few minutes leaning on his bow to watch the result. A low flame from some kindled brushwood told the traitor that his intelligence had been received; and he left the ramparts to return to his abandoned guard, muttering as he went—

"I have kept my word. Norbeck's oath of vengeance hath never yet been broken."

The intended sortie from the castle was betrayed.

Robert of Normandy and his chosen band had halted about half a mile from William's camp, to give final instructions for the assault. The spot was a long avenue of aged oaks, opening on the plain, where the tents of the enemy were clearly to be seen in the pale moonlight. Some of the men were carrying dry furze and combustible matter, which they had hastily collected for the occasion; others were whispering together, calculating the plunder which would probably be found in the tents of the red king and his nobles, whilst the principal leaders of their own party were bidding adieu to Herbert de Lozinga and Edda, who had accompanied the expedition thus far on its way.

"Be not too rash!" exclaimed the warlike prelate; "your enemies are numerous, and should they rally after their first surprise, must overwhelm you. Remember, Ulrick, you have now a being whose existence hangs on yours; remember that your life is pledged deeply to her, as to your country, and that one rash act——"

A deep groan from the speaker interrupted the conclusion of his caution, as he sank mortally wounded by an arrow which some unseen hand had winged. The aged Edda caught him as he fell.

"Treason!" shouted Robert of Normandy, and the knights who witness with horror the cowardly assassination; "we are beset! To arms! to arms!"

A party of William's followers, who had been planted in ambush, rushed from their concealment in the forest; Tyrrel headed them, urged on by the double motive of hatred to Ulrick and the desire to distinguish himself in the cause upon whose success his earldom depended. Many of Robert's men-at-arms, encumbered by the brushwood and materials they had gathered, died ere they

could draw their weapons; others fled. The principal object of the enemy seemed to be to secure the person of the prince, whom Odo of Caen, and his namesake of Bayeux, and several knights, stoutly defended, reckless of their own lives, provided they preserved that of the unfortunate monarch to whom they had sworn allegiance. As brave as he was rash and inconsiderate, Robert for awhile resisted every attempt to reconduct him to the fortress; but with each moment's delay the danger which menaced him and his devoted defenders increased. Bands of dark, fierce-looking mercenaries were beginning to form in compact bodies round them; the one headed by Tyrrel had already taken the party in the flank, so as to cut off their retreat. Ulrick, who had vainly attempted to rally the fugitives, saw the danger, and, at the head of a dozen of his Saxon followers, threw himself between his friends and the enemy to defeat it. Here the battle raged most fiercely; the sword of Ulrick did fearful execution; each sweep left a gap in the compact Norman ranks, which their overwhelming numbers alone enabled them to fill up. The rival leader fought with all the desperate courage of humbled pride, ambition, and unslaked hate.

"Save the king!" shouted our hero, who saw that he and his gallant band would uselessly be sacrificed, unless immediate advantage were taken of their devotion to retreat to Pevensey, for longer resistance was impossible.

"Down with the traitors!" echoed Tyrrel, who felt like a famished tiger when it sees his prey escaping him. "Five hundred marks for this boaster's head!—a thousand for the person of Prince Robert!"

Animated by the hope of reward, again the mercenaries rushed on the faithful few; but though they were again repulsed by the calm courage with which they were encountered, another such attack must needs be fatal. Half of Ulrick's little band had bit the dust, and two were wounded. Again, therefore, he shouted with increased energy and desperation to save the king and to retreat to Pevensey.

Robert, who had resisted every persuasion of those around him to retreat, no sooner heard the voice of Tyrrel offering a thousand marks for his person, than he became a changed man. Flinging away his broken brand, he turned to those near him, saying in a husky voice:

"The sin of our youth hath found us. The day is against us. On, friends, to Pevensey! —'tis our last hope."

It is doubtful whether the devoted courage of the Lord of Stanfield could have secured them from falling into the hands of the enemy, had not a party, headed by Mirvan, sallied from the castle to assist them, for the shouts of the combatants had been heard through the stillness of the night upon the battlements, and the garrison judged their friends had been surprised.

Even thus supported, their retreat was with difficulty accomplished; they rushed pell-mell into the courtyard; and so close was the pursuit, that the drawbridge, which was raised the instant they had passed, let several of the enemy into the deep moat as it rose, for their feet were already upon it: the arrows of the men-at-arms upon the watch-tower soon dispatched them.

"Where is the bishop?" demanded William de Warrenne.

"Dead!" groaned Robert.

"And Ulrick?" said Mirvan, anxiously looking round.

"Dead or a prisoner, too."

That night there was scant revelry in the beleaguered fortress of Pevensey.

The following morning the warder brought notice that a gibbet was being erected within bow-shot of the walls, the ground around it was kept by a numerous body of archers, and that the troops of William were assembling in vast numbers in order to be present at an execution of more solemnity than usual.

Mirvan heard the intelligence with dismay, for his fears but too rightly foreboded that it was for Ulrick, for the companion of his youth, the friend of his heart, the husband of Matilda. Half frantic with grief and indignation, he imparted his suspicions to Prince Henry, who immediately conducted him to his brother's chamber, where the council was already assembled.

The chiefs were debating on the propriety of holding out to the last, or at least till the promised aid from France should arrive; their position, though wearying, was any thing but desperate. Pevensey was strongly garrisoned, well-provisioned, and, except from treachery within, might long protract its surrender. Robert sat listening to the debate more like an unconcerned spectator than a king whose crown and life were perchance at issue; his heart was crushed; from some secret cause the conduct of Tyrrel deeply affected him; and the probable fate of Ulrick, who had so generously devoted himself to ensure his safety, weighed deeply on his spirits. Mirvan's tale roused him from his apathy.

"What!" he exclaimed, starting from his chair, "the gibbet for the bravest knight that ever drew his sword in honour's cause? Perish thus ignominiously for my sake?—

never, never! Decide, my lords, upon som means to save him. My crown—my life—whatever my cruel brother will, to ransom' him; but cursed be my name, and stained my shield, if Ulrick perish, and through fault of mine!"

Odo of Bayeux, although deeply grieved at Ulrick's misfortune, contemplated no such sacrifice to save him. His ambitious projects, which aimed at nothing less than the papacy, demanded that his favourite nephew should be king; and to advance his views one step, he would have bartered a hundred lives, and thought the attainment of it cheaply paid. He proposed, therefore, that a herald should be sent to William's camp, offering ransom for the prisoner, and declaring that, in the event of any outrage being offered to his life, his friends would fearfully retaliate upon all of the opposite party who might fall into their hands.

Robert heard the proposal with undisguised contempt; he knew too well the ferocious disposition of his brother to suppose for one moment that any consideration of humanity could influence him. The rest of the council approved of the idea, Mirvan alone excepted.

Whilst the debate was going on, the realmless king took up a pen, and amused himself by writing, occasionally listening to what the various speakers urged. Without showing his letter to any one, he carefully sealed it with his private signet, and placing it in the hands of Mirvan, whispered him:

"Take it to William's camp; let a herald and a flag of truce precede you. I know the price of your brother's life, and, vast as it is, I am prepared to pay it. Away! before these selfish men suspect and seek to thwart our purpose."

Mirvan kissed the hand of the generous, but rash and feeble prince; he half suspected the sacrifice he was about to offer to the shrine of friendship and honour, and quitted the room in silence.

"Where goes my Lord of Norwich?" demanded Bishop Odo, looking anxiously after him; "I trust, fair nephew, you have no secrets from your friends—proved friends —such as we are?"

This was too direct a question to be evaded; from any other than so near a relative Robert would have answered haughtily, and perhaps even so to him, had not his soul been oppressed with the bitterness of its sorrows and disappointments. It was one of those moments when we feel the insufficiency of worldly grandeur—when pride appears as ashes, power as worthless, and the heart thirst to indulge in those sympathies which adorn and dignify humanity—sympathies which form the perfect part of an imperfect whole—the mortal signs of an immortal spirit.

"I can treat with my brother better," he answered, to his uncle, "than through my council, for we have long understood and known each other."

"This is folly, spleen!" exclaimed the prelate; "the very madness of misgoverned judgment! Wouldst fling a sceptre from thy hand as 'twere a spinster's distaff?"

"Perhaps," carelessly replied Robert; "especially if the toy in any way encumbered me.'

"Recal the messenger; this must be prevented."

Odo and several of the knights advanced towards the door, when the prince with great dignity placed himself between them, still holding in his hand the pen with which he had written to his unnatural brother. Possessed of great nobility of character, the outrage to his rank had roused him; the fierce passion of his race was upon him, and his eyes flashed with ill-suppressed indignation. In an instant the sadness of his heart had passed away.

"Is this your deference," he uttered sternly, "to your sovereign's will—this, my lords, your loyalty to the monarch you have sworn allegiance to? Remember," he added, "but one scratch of this pen"—here the speaker dashed it from him as he spoke— "and William is your lawful king; and you, instead of loyal nobles, become a herd of vile conspirators,—your lands given to confiscation, your heads the axe's forfeit prey. Advance one step to recal my messenger, and I declare my abdication, proclaim my brother king, without one stipulation for your lives and honours; and well you know the tender William's mercy. As it is, whatever our own fate, your shall be cared for; whatever our own sacrifice, your lands shall remain secure."

The members of the council gazed upon each other in surprise and consternation. The dilemma was too serious a one to be trifled with; they felt that without the prince they were but a band of conspirators, without hope of mercy. Before they could recover themselves, the fall of the portcullis announced that Mirvan had departed with the herald, when all thoughts of opposition ceased; for they would have been as useless as dangerous. Robert listened coldly to their protestations of respect and submission, and waved them haughtily from his presence.

"My poor brother," exclaimed Prince Henry, taking him kindly by the hand as soon as they were left alone, "is this sacrifice indeed worth making? Remember that a crown once lost is seldom e'er regained· Reflect, it is not yet too late."

"I have reflected," answered Robert, calmly. "My heart would burst were it longer prisoned here, shut up with mere lip loyalty, petty jealousies, and vile ambitions. Besides, I long for the green woods again; I am sick of human faces, and want to look on nature, to talk with her in her deep recesses. Her silent voice will pour no odious flatteries in my ear, waken no storm of passions in my heart. I would forget the past, and all that can remind me of it," he added; "its vain regrets, its broken hopes, its worm which never dies. Woman's love hath palled upon my lip, man's treachery left but a sepulchre within my heart. I have found but one being constant, in friendship devoted, generous, true; he hath sacrificed himself for me; he shall not perish if my crown can save him."

It was while labouring under feelings bitter as these that the unhappy prince, a few years later, sold his duchy of Normandy to the rapacious William, for the contemptible sum of ten thousand marks, and engaged but a band of adventurous followers in the crusades, which Peter the Hermit so successfully preached throughout the principal countries of Europe. But we are anticipating events; it is time that our readers returned to Ulrick, whom we left contending with his enemy, Tyrrel, to protect the retreat of his friend and sovereign, the unfortunate but generous Robert.

Opposed to overwhelming odds, it was the object of our hero to sell his life dearly rather than be taken, for he well knew the fate which would await him at the hands of William and his worthy minion; but, despite his frantic courage, and the numbers which fell beneath his weapon, he was at last surrounded and disarmed. The large reward which the leader of his enemies offered for securing him alive tempted many of the men-at-arms to risk their own lives in securing him. Tyrrel's joy knew no bounds when he beheld the being, whose superiority he had always hated, a helpless prisoner before him; every epithet which insulting cowardice could apply to vanquished heroism did he lavish on his captive, who bore it with that calm, silent contempt which often strikes deeper in the breasts of the unworthy than scorn or loud reproaches. When brought before William and the nobles in the tent of the former, his demeanour was cold and dignified; and when that tyrant, with a refinement of cruelty, condemned him to the gibbet, although his cheek might blanch, his glance was as firm and his mien as erect as ever. So favourable was the im pression, that even his enemies thought it hard that so noble a knight should be so unnecessarily degraded. Some interceded for him, but in vain: the red king affected to despise the history of his birth, and condemned him as a mere peasant to the shameful tree.

"It is the crime, and not the scaffold, which dishonours," answered Ulrick, proudly, as he he heard his doom. "All true hearts, fierce prince, will judge thy judgment, and infamy will brand thy memory with it."

Wounded and bleeding as he was, he was hurried from the tyrant's presence, and cast into a dungeon till the coming morning; then to be again led forth to meet his doom.

As we have described, the gibbet was erected within bow-shot of the castle, and most of William's troops were on the ground; the red king and his favourites arrived soon after to see our hero die. The coward heart of Tyrrel beat high with gratified revenge; he anticipated with ferocious joy each pang, and revelled in the idea of the agonies which such an ignominious death would cause his victim's proud and gallant spirit.

At the foot of the fatal tree stood a fellow clothed in a crimson shirt, which descended nearly to his ankles; his sleeves were rolled up to the shoulders, displaying his coarse, muscular arms; he was, perhaps, the least excited spectator of the scene. He was coolly occupied in selecting a coil of rope from a number near him, and twisting it in a slip-noose: the occupation proclaimed the executioner.

"Now, marshal," exclaimed William, turning to Sir Richard Whetstone, "how long are we to wait? Hath not the shaveling trussed the fellow for the gibbet yet, or must we lose the morning chase to wait the good father's pleasure?"

"Be not impatient," replied the knight, in deep disgust; "your victim, sir, is ready."

Many of the nobles beheld with equal indignation the execution of a man whom they had so often encountered in the battlefield, whose courage had been the theme of even the common soldier's tongue, and whose enmity to Tyrrel they thought justified by that unworthy favourite's insolence and presumption. Several of them had solicited William in his favour: he had sternly refused to listen to their prayer, or change the unknightly nature of his death.

"Ha, ha, ha!" shouted Tyrrel, as soon as Ulrick reached the fatal spot, "I thought his vaunted courage would abandon him at last. See how pale the traitor is."

"With loss of blood, then," coolly answered Ulrick; "but, coward, I parley not with thee. Once more I do protest, for the honour of my knighthood, against the degrading nature of my death, which only a head framed like a tyrant's could have conceived, or men lost to honour execute. Now then I am ready to meet my fate as becomes a Christian and a noble."

"As a traitor and a felon!" shouted Tyrrel. "Away with him to the gibbet! fit end for the vile peasant!"

So disgusted was Roger of Shrewsbury with Tyrrel's conduct, that he dashed his mailed glove in the villain's face, exclaiming as he did so:—

"Cur! another such a word, and I'll rend thy fawning, lying tongue from out thy mouth. For his treasons, his judges best can answer for their judgment; but peasant he is none: and I proclaim him liar, craven, and forsworn—ay," he added, fixing his eyes upon William—"e'en though he wore a crown—who dares to brand him one. His death is a murder, not an execution!"

A murmur of approbation from the nobles near, who were equally disgusted with the speaker, warned William that he was treading upon dangerous ground; still, in the bitterness of his hatred, he determined to persevere. Tyrrel, pale and subdued by the noble scorn and haughty glance of so powerful a noble as Roger of Shrewsbury, withdrew behind his master.

"Proceed with the execution," exclaimed the impatient monarch; "let us end this scene."

Ulrick, despite his courage and lofty resolution, turned pale as the minister of shame approached him; it was not death he feared, it was dishonour. Ere, however, the ruffian could lay hands upon him, Mirvan, his horse covered with foam, followed by the herald whom he had outridden, galloped on the ground; and, advancing to the red king, placed his brother's letter in his hand, who turned alternately pale and red with emotion as he perused it.

"What are your orders, sire?" demanded Whetstone, kindly hoping that something favourable to Ulrick had occurred.

"Suspend the execution," said William, with ill-concealed rage.

"Your highness!" exclaimed Tyrrel, fearful lest his victim should escape.

"Back, sir knight," cried his master, haughtily, and not unwilling to mortify him; "this is beyond your sphere. Guard your prisoner, marshal, but treat him well. Let us," he added, turning to the principal nobles near, "in to council."

Whetstone cut his prisoner's cords, and in an instant Ulrick and Mirvan were locked in each other's embrace; whilst Tyrrel, confounded and abashed at the strange termination of the scene, and the public insult and reproof which he had received from the king, stood looking on in mortification, rage, and silence.

CHAPTER XXV.

There, take the crown, whose weight will sear
Thy aching brow, for it is laden with a brother's curse.
Misery and discontent shall make their nest
Within its rim, and jealous doubts
And dark suspicions sting thee.—PEDRO THE CRUEL.

URING the following morning a spacious pavilion, destined for the meeting of the royal brothers, was erected on the plain, at an equal distance from the camp of the Red King and the beleaguered fortress. There, for the first time since the Conqueror's death, the two princes were to meet, and articles of peace be debated between them. The position of William, though thus far victorious, was anything but sure. The crown sat but loosely on his brow; to bind it there securely he was obliged to make concessions, at which his haughty soul revolted, to the nobles and clergy, many of whom, with all his condescensions, were but coldly satisfied.

Robert, although reduced to the strong castle of Pevensey, possessed a moral strength in his alliance with the French king, which the adherence of Lanfranc and the barons barely balanced in his rival's cause; added to which, the promised aid from France might still arrive, and turn the tide of fortune in his favour. The usurper was too keen a gamester not to calculate every chance; like most heartless men, he was capable of sacrificing even his resentments to his interests, and hence the order to suspend the execution of our hero; for the generous Robert, in his letter, expressly declared that all attempts at negotiation would be vain if a single hair of Ulrick's head were touched.

Many loiterers, attracted by the coming interview, were lingering round the spot; amongst others, Tyrrel and Robert of Artois, whom we shall henceforth designate by the name he bore in the camp, that of the Black Knight. The mystery which attached to his person—his intimacy with the king, as well as the cold habitual reserve of his manner, which forbad all attempts at approach—made him an object of curiosity with

many, and of a superstitious dread with others. Tyrrel, however, only saw in him a dangerous rival in his master's favour; he was jealous of his importance, and anxious to find some clue to his secret as a means of supplanting him, the first step to which he naturally thought would be to bring about a certain degree of intimacy: the present was too good an occasion to be thrown away.

"*Bon jour*, sir knight!" he exclaimed, in a careless, off-handed tone, as he advanced towards the spot where the object of his speculation was standing, gazing with a dreamy look upon the various preparations.

The Black Knight simply bowed his head without replying, but Tyrrel was not to be so put off.

"So," he continued, "our campaign is nearly over. Robert, though a foolish prince, is at least a generous master, since he resigns his crown to save his favourite's life."

"A sacrifice till now unheard of," replied the party addressed, "in the history of princes. Their memories, like water, retain no trace of the absent object once reflected there. The most devoted service, in their eyes, is but a duty scantily paid; their promises are as unstable as the winds, with which their favour changes."

"You, at least," said Tyrrel, "have no reason to complain, since your favour with the king exceeds the proudest nobles; his confidence in you is as unbounded as your merits. Many envy the Chevalier Noir—since it is his pleasure only to be known as such—his hold on William's friendship."

"Perhaps fools often take mere tinsel for pure gold," answered the Black Knight, carelessly; "but you," he added, "ought to be equally satisfied. The services you have rendered Rufus are deep and many:—first you released him from prison; conducted him to London to be crowned; detected the correspondence of his enemies; and since you recovered from the wounds received on the occasion, have done good service in the wars. These, sir knight," he added, sarcastically, "are claims a prince like William never can forget, e'en were his memory shorter than his love."

"And you might add," muttered Tyrrel, who began to fell anything but satisfiend at the delay in his promised earldom, "that through my agency the plans of the besieged have all been known and frustrated—witness last night's attack. Peter Norbeck is a useful agent in the fortress of our enemies."

The name of Peter Norbeck seemed to excite the surprise of his companion, for it was connected with certain passages of his life, to which he had long lost the clue; it was, therefore, no longer in the light bantering tone which he had assumed, but in accents of deep and undisguised interest, that he demanded if he alluded to a Norman man-at-arms who was formerly in the city guard.

"No," resumed the speaker; "but to his brother, whom the bastard of Stanfield punished for trying to squeeze a vile Jew's purse of a few silver pennies. The fellow hates, as such men only hate, with the ferocity of a bloodhound, as well as its determination. I have found him a faithful agent, perhaps because the prey we hunted was the same. The man you inquire after is his brother, now one of the warders of the city who first detected Ulrick's mission to the rebels."

"Is he with one of the companies who have followed Rufus to the wars?" demanded the Black Knight.

"There is the very man," exclaimed Tyrrel, pointing to the warder, who, with several of his companions, was lounging about to watch the proceedings; "he is my go-between with his brother."

Without a word of adieu, or thanks for the information, his questioner turned upon his heel, and proceeded directly, with his usual measured tread, towards the spot where the group were standing Laying his mailed hand upon the ruffian's shoulder, he simply pronounced the words, "Follow me," and without waiting to see if he was obeyed, directed his steps towards the neighbouring wood, conscious that his authority was such from his influence with William, that men even of a much higher rank would reflect twice ere they ventured to dispute it. The warder followed with the instinctive obedience of a hound at the call of its master. The Black Knight was held in a sort of mysterious terror by all, a feeling to which the ghastly expression of his countenance—now scarcely human—not a little contributed.

As soon as they reached an open sward,

bounded by a running brook, where the brushwood and grass were too low to give shelter to an eavesdropper, the foremost paused, and waited till the man whom he had so long been anxious to find stood before him face to face.

"Is your name Norbeck?" he demanded.

"It is, sir knight," answered the fellow, respectfully, at the same time feeling uneasy, although he knew not why, at the strange conference which he foresaw was about to take place between them.

"Formerly of the city guard?"

"And now one of its warders," added the fellow, hoping to create a favourable impression on the knight by the announcement of the responsible office with which he was entrusted.

"To whom," continued his questioner, "sixteen years since, a male child was entrusted by a noble knight, together with a large sum of money—the boy to be brought up as your wife's, by a former marriage; the gold to be employed for his support and future establishment in life?"

"The same," faltered the man, his uneasiness and astonishment increasing at every question.

"Doth that boy still live?"

"He does."

"And where?"

"Marry, that is more than I can tell," replied the warder; "'tis months since I beheld him. He was always a wayward, stubborn brat, even as a child; as he grew up, I had hard lines with him. The traitor who should have swung this day upon the gibbet can tell you, perhaps, more of his whereabouts than I can, since he it was who took him from me. I'd give the heaviest coin in my purse but to lay hands on him again."

"Why so?" demanded the Black Knight, a shade of haughty displeasure rendering his features still more repulsive than even their unnatural transformation had made them.

"Why so?" iterated the ruffian; "why, because is it not natural I should wish to find the runaway again? But may I ask, noble sir, why you feel so interested in his story? Perhaps he is known to you?"

"Ask me nothing," sternly replied his questioner; "but as thou valuest that neck of thine, answer truly; think not to deceive me, for I can detect the lie on falsehood's quivering lip—read it in the shifting glance or hesitating speech. I have dealt too long with men to be easily deceived, and despise them too much to pardon their treachery lightly. Tell me," he added, drawing his sword, "how the boy's fate become mixed up with the knight of Stanfield's; and

GILBERT ENCOUNTERS THE DISGUISED PILGRIM IN THE WOOD.

remember that thy first lie will prove thy last—I warn not twice!"

Finding that it would be dangerous to prevaricate, and ignorant whether the knight's motives to the boy were of good or evil, but trusting to the latter, the warder, without much disguise, described all that had passed between both Gilbert and himself, even to the beating and wounding of the former, and his rescue by Ulrick from his hands. Had the wretch, when he related the lashing with the bow-string, caught the flash of the fierce vindictive eyes fixed upon him, he would have read his doom as plainly as if voice had spoken it. When he had finished, he stood with a half doubtful, half confident air before his mysterious judge.

"And thou hast told me all?" demanded the Black Knight.

"All," said the ruffian, anxiously; "I trust, noble sir, that you are satisfied."

"I were difficult to please, an I were not satisfied," answered his questioner, sarcastically; "thou hast proved thyself a faithful guardian—a most kind one. Thou mightest have slain the boy, and yet thou only gavest the lash; as men correct a hound at fault, a restive steed, or base-born serf. There," he added, bitterly, taking a handful of coin from the pouch suspended at his girdle; "there is the first proof how much I am satisfied with thee; anon, thou shalt have another more lasting than the present: I am one who always pays his debts."

As the speaker poured the money into the warder's greedy palm, he dropped, apparently by accident, several of the pieces upon the ground; in stooping to pick them up, the head of the fellow was bent to the earth, leaving an opening about two inches wide between his helmet and rough coat of mail which left the back part of his neck totally defenceless. Before his fingers could grasp the first coin, the long heavy blade of the Black Knight's sword descended with the rapidity of a flash of lightning upon the mark, and the head of the ruffian rolled at the feet of his executioner.

"Carrion!" exclaimed the assassin; "if, indeed, he merited the name of such; the headsman should have dealt with thee, and not a noble's sword; thou art but too honoured to fall by hands like mine."

Spurning the gory head, whose eyeballs were still rolling in their sockets, contemptuously from him, he was about to quit the spot, when he observed a packet of papers in the belt of the being whose crimes he had so fearfully punished; to secure and read them were the work of a few minutes: surprise and indignation were visible on his countenance as he did so.

"Fratricide as well as usurper," he murmured, "this crime, at least, shall be prevented; if I cannot recall the past, at least I will endeavour to atone it."

With these words the unhappy man directed his steps towards the scene of meeting.

At a preconcerted signal, the royal brothers, each attended by six nobles totally unarmed, set out for the place of rendezvous; the men-at-arms, fifty in number, who escorted them, halted by agreement at a hundred paces on either side of the tent. In the train of William were Lanfranc, the primate; Roger of Shrewsbury, Aubrey de Vere, and three barons of less note. With Robert came the Earl of Norwich, Edda the Saxon, William de Warrenne, and three Norman vavasours, who still remained firm to his cause. The party of Robert were the first to enter the tent; the prince preceded his friends a few paces, leaning on the arm of Mirvan, with whom he was engaged in deep conversation.

"Had my son proved worthy of his name," said the unhappy prince, "my hand should have withered ere I set my seal to such a treaty; as it is, with me the secret dies, since I alone possess the proofs of his legitimacy and birth."

Had not the speakers' attention been occupied by the sudden blast of the trumpet which announced the arrival of William, they must have heard the rustling between the inner lining and outward canvas of the tent, occasioned by the retreating steps of one who had overheard the prince's confidence. It was the traitor Tyrrel.

"He comes," said Robert, advancing to the altar erected in the centre of the pavilion; "one struggle, and 'tis past."

At this moment William Rufus and his party entered. The heavy draperies of the pavilion were let down, and the two monarchs and their counsellors were shut from the gaze of the men-at-arms without. Prince Henry had declined being present at the interview; either he doubted the Red King's faith, or he disapproved of the sacrifice which his brother Robert was about to make. Cunning beyond his years, he veiled beneath an appearance of light-hearted, reckless humour, schemes of ambition, which the prophecy—for such he considered it—of the Saxon monk at Eltham had engraved too deeply on his heart ever to be effaced. Whilst the conference was taking place, he remained with the escort at a distance, laughing and chatting with the officers who commanded it.

"There they go," he exclaimed, as the parties entered the tent; "the vulture and falcon are at roost together. We shall soon have no better sport than to hunt the red deer in the forest, gentles; that is, if our kind brother of the red poll leaves us the liberty to do so."

"If your grace has a doubt upon the subject," observed the young noble to whom the observation was addressed, "I should advise the air of Normandy—there, at least, you may hunt in security."

"Perhaps!" said a deep voice near them. The speakers turned and beheld the Black Knight, whose person they had become too familiar with during the late struggle not to recognise. With his usual quiet step he had approached them almost unperceived.

"Back, sir knight!" exclaimed the prince. "Know you not it is forbidden by the terms of the truce for either party of the escort to approach the other?"

"I belong not to the escort," replied the intruder; "my errand is to place this packet in the hands of Henry of Normandy." The knight held out the papers he had taken from the belt of the warder as he spoke, and disappeared almost as suddenly as he had presented himself.

The prince perused the letters so mysteriously conveyed to him, and although they contained nothing less than matters touching his life, not a frown or gesture of surprise betrayed the deep emotion which the perusal of them occasioned. Trained early to the wiles and intrigues of courts, he was perfectly master of himself, and while he read the hearts of others, guarded the secrets of his own like a sealed book.

To those who knew the fiery, impatient character of Robert, it was a matter of surprise that he discussed the proposed articles of the treaty with his brother so calmly; by it he accepted his father's will, and gave up all claim to the crown of England, contenting himself with his hereditary duchy of Normandy. The only points on which he was inflexible were the safety of Ulrick, and the personal security both of life and lands of his adherents. On these no arguments could move him, and William, who saw that the primate and the nobles of his party not only coincided in the reasonableness of the terms, but were prepared to support his brother in insisting on them, was forced, though with an ill-grace, to yield. Lanfranc drew up the treaty, to which the rival princes and barons set their names and seals, both brothers swearing on the altar to observe it.

"Stay," said Robert, as William, with a cold sarcastic smile upon his face, was about to quit the altar, "thou hast sworn on the evangile—swear also by the oath of our race to keep good faith with me. Thou knowest the tradition of our house—thou knowest the fearful curse which hangs o'er him who breaks it."

"What I have sworn I have sworn!" exclaimed William, turning pale; for, superstitious as he was cruel, he knew that the required oath would deprive him of his cherished scheme of vengeance. "Why doubt my faith, or tax it further?"

"Why?" iterated Robert; "because I know that oaths are like water with thee. Didst thou not swear to our mother at the abbey of Caen never to prejudice the elder brother's right? The crown thou hast obtained by perjury best can answer how thou hast observed thy oath. Didst thou not swear to prove a loving brother to her youngest Henry, and hast thou not sought his life? Thy oath on the evangile!" he added; "as soon would I trust the inconstant wind or fickle waves as such an oath from thee. Speak, lords, have I not reason?"

"You have," replied the primate and peers, who began to feel regret at the part they had taken, and were anxious to make the treaty a lasting one between the princes —a step to which their interests impelled

them, for most held possessions in Normandy as well as England, possessions which, in all probability, they would lose should war again break out between the brothers.

Still the Norman hesitated, for vengeance was almost as dear to him as ambition; vainly he gazed upon those who had placed him on the throne for encouragement in his refusal; cold, stern glances met him on every face, and he felt that delay might prove dangerous even to his crown and life.

"Swear!" exclaimed the united nobles, unanimously, several of his own party advancing towards Robert.

"Be it so," muttered the tyrant, furiously; "propose the oath."

"By the bones of Rolla," said his brother, impressively, "you swear never to attempt aught against the life, liberty, and honour of Ulrick of Stanfield—to restore him instantly to freedom—in return for the unreserved surrender of my crown—and to hold all who have supported my rights scathless in honours, lives, and lands."

"I swear it," repeated William, faintly, "by the bones of Rollo."

"And may the curse of your race," added his brother—"of him men call the Devil's Son, whose couch of fire not all the prayers of holy church, or blood of heaven's best martyrs e'er can quench, be yours, if e'er you break your oath!"

All present shuddered as Rufus repeated the fearful imprecation; for not one but firmly believed that the soul of the common ancestor of the two princes was to remain, according to his compact with Satan, in hell, till one of his descendants, by breaking the oath of his race, should release it.

"Now, then," said Robert, "take the crown, and may it prove to thee of thorns. Care and suspicion haunt thy pillow—poison the wine-cup in thy hour of mirth—pall e'en the kiss of beauty on thy lip! Reign in terror—haunted by shadows—heartless, friendless, and alone!"

William, despite the natural hardihood of his nature, shrank at the well-merited malediction of a brother whom he had so treacherously supplanted in his birthright, and left the tent with his train in gloomy silence; leaving Robert to wait the arrival of the rescued prisoner, according to the terms of the treaty to be immediately given, set at liberty. As the monarch left the pavilion, Tyrrel, impatient to impart the important secret he had so basely obtained, arrested his steps, and demanded a moment's audience; his look and bearing indicated that it was for a communication too pressing to be refused.

"Prince," said Edda, addressing the now

crownless king, who still remained standing by the altar where Rufus had pronounced the fearful oath, "the joy I feel at the certitude of again embracing my grandson will hardly repay the sorrows which I experience at this most generous sacrifice, fatal alike for thee and for my country; history will chronicle the heroic deed long after the icy hand of Death hath effaced its record from the hearts of those who witnessed it."

"It has been greater, old man, than thou wotst of," said Robert, kindly; "but let it pass: all of my race are not alike ungrateful. In my path through life I have sown affections and gathered tares; love hath been blighted, honour lost, ambition crushed; e'en in that corner of my heart," he added, bitterly, "where I had garnered up a hope for age, the mildew of treachery and deceit hath found me."

All were impressed with the deep melancholy of the speaker's voice, and listened in respectful silence.

About half an hour after William's departure the curtains of the pavilion were once more raised. Edda and Mirvan advanced to meet their liberated friend; but found, to their surprise, that, instead of Ulrick, it was the primate, with Roger of Shrewsbury and Tyrrel, who entered the tent.

"Where is the Lord of Stanfield?" demanded Robert impatiently.

"A prisoner," replied Tyrrel, with an air of triumph and malicious satisfaction.

"By whose orders?"

"The king's."

"What!" exclaimed the indignant prince, "hath William already broken the oath of his race? This baseness is unworthy even of him. And you," he added, addressing Lanfranc, "priest of the Most High, primate of England, witness of this perjury. You announce it to me! Shame! oh, shame!"

"The king," said the churchman haughtily, "hath broken no oath; he took it but conditionally."

"Conditionally!" repeated all the nobles present.

"That his brother," resumed the speaker, "made an unreserved surrender of the crown. Hath he done so?—can he do so?"

"Why not?" demanded the prince, with a look of surprise.

"Because thou hast a son, to whom the rights devolve—if rights thou hast," replied Tyrrel impatiently. "Deny it not; I heard the avowal from thine own lips almost within the hour."

Robert turned deadly pale; it was clear to all that his very heart was torn with rage, with contempt, with deep and bitter emotions. Fixing his eyes upon the speaker with so singular an expression that even the bold traitor was awed by it, he murmured:—

"And thou heardst this?"

"I did."

"Where?"

"Behind the curtains of the tent. More," added Tyrrel, "that thou alone possessed the proofs of thy son's legitimacy and birth."

"Dishonoured villain!" exclaimed the prince, with a burst of passion. "First perjury to thy benefactor, who confided his prisoner to thy ward, and now dishonour to thy knighthood by meanly descending to be a spy. But I waste words," he added, using a violent effort to recover himself: "I'll speak with thee anon. First for the archbishop—what would our perjured brother?"

"That," said Lanfranc, "which alone can render the oath of William binding, and enable you to fulfil your stipulations in the treaty of the unreserved surrender of the crown—the proofs of your son's birth."

"What if I refuse?" said Robert.

"Your minion dies!" answered Tyrrel, with a look of exultation—"hangs on the gibbet, from which, by a trick, you would have rescued him—hangs like a dog, unless his master saves him."

It was sad to see the look of loathing and disgust with which the prince turned from him to address the primate.

"And what proof have I," he said, "if I consent to leave my son without a name, to sacrifice his birthright to my brother's fears by the surrender of these proofs, that your monarch will keep faith with me?"

"William's fearful oath," replied the prelate, "which then becomes a surety, and mine; for by my priestly vow I swear," and the speaker kissed his golden cross as he spoke, "if he keep not faith with thee, this voice, which proclaimed him king, shall launch the thunders of the church upon his head—this hand, which anointed him, shall sign his deposition. Robert of Normandy," he added, "may trust the faith of one who never broke his vow to God, to friend, or enemy."

"As friend or enemy I trust thee," said the prince, drawing at the same time a parchment, with the seals of his mother, the Queen Matilda, the Archbishop of Rouen, and Onfroy, Marshal of Normandy, from his breast. "Take the proofs; from this hour forth I am a childless man; the retribution is complete."

The hand of the archbishop trembled as he received the important document. Devoted as he was to the interests of the Red King, he could not behold without emotion the sacrifice—accomplished, as it were, against nature—wrung by treachery from a generous, noble heart.

"Let it console thee, prince," he said, "that this deed has secured a nation's peace and a true friend's safety. Within the instant Ulrick of Stanfield shall be free. Farewell! Would we had earlier met, or been for ever strangers!"

Hastily motioning to Tyrrel to remain, the primate quitted the pavilion to bear to Rufus the proofs he was so impatient to obtain.

No sooner had Lanfranc departed than Robert recovered his usual self-possession and serenity. Without deigning to cast a glance of reproach or hate upon the man who had so unscrupulously betrayed him, he began to give directions for his approaching departure for Normandy, where Mirvan, whose chief possessions lay there, as well as those of his young bride, proposed to accompany him.

"I cannot," he exclaimed, "bow the knee and profess lip loyalty to a sovereign I despise. My heart would wither in its own deceit. Let William," he added, "confiscate my English fief—my father's lands and father's honours shall content me."

"Which shall not be lessened by our favour," said his prince, embracing him. "Normandy hath forests as wide as any England boasts, to chase the red deer in, and hearts as true to welcome thee."

"Old as I am, I, too, would with thee, prince," added Edda, "were I not planted to the soil like some aged oak. Uproot me, and those who live beneath my shade must perish too."

Again the curtains of the tent were raised, and this time his impatient friends were not doomed to disappointment, for the Lord of Stanfield entered at liberty: his first impulse was to bend the knee to Robert, whose generous sacrifice had deeply touched his grateful nature; the prince welcomed him with a sad, but friendly smile, wishing internally, as he gazed upon him, that Heaven had blessed him with a son like Ulrick. Tyrrel looked upon the scene with an affectation of scorn and triumph.

"Robert, my sovereign," said our hero, "what hast thou done to preserve my worthless life? widowed this wretched kingdom of its happiness, bartered thy birthright, sacrificed thy son, all, all for me?"

"Bartered them freely," interrupted Robert, "since I have preserved my friend, rewarded virtue in its noblest form, and punished vice and measureless ambition. Ere I depart," he added, "from the realm no longer mine, I have a debt to pay. Leave us, my lords; leave Ulrick and myself with Walter Tyrrel alone within the tent; soon we will rejoin you on the road to Pevensey."

The command was instantly obeyed, the prince and the two young men alone remained within the tent. Tyrrel's first impulse was to lay his hand upon his sword, for although the speaker and the knight of Stanfield were both disarmed, his suspicious nature foreboded treachery.

"Touch not thy sword, young man," exclaimed Robert, mournfully. "It is not with such weapons I would punish thee. By Heaven, my sister's honour, or my father's bones, are not more sacred to me than thy life."

"Punish me?" faltered Tyrrel, lost in amazement at the prince's tone and manner.

"Ay, with words, which shall pierce deeper than my sword! fall like a coal of fire upon thy head! gnaw like a serpent's fang within thy heart! if, indeed," added the speaker, contemptuously "reptiles have hearts."

"Rail on, prince!" exclaimed Tyrrel, with an affected laugh; "I can forgive a baffled gamester's spleen; my promised earldom shall console me for a few sharp words."

"Can it console thee for a crown?" sternly demanded Robert.

The young man started from the pillar of the tent, against which he had been carelessly leaning; a light from heaven or hell broke on his astonished mind; for the first time he suspected that which, if true, would indeed, to a soul like his, be the most fearful punishment his treachery and ambition could receive; twice he essayed to speak, but the voice remained choked within his throat.

"A crown!" at last he hoarsely murmured.

"Ay, a crown!" repeated the prince; "ambition's dream; fortune's last gift to reckless daring minds.—Ulrick," he added, passionately, "I have been a man of pride and sin, but still of unstained honour. I gloried in the blazon of my house, the power of my race, the fame of my forefathers, their hundred victories by land and sea; judge, then, how deep the pang which rends this heart when I proclaim that man of infamy and shame—that thing I loathe and spit upon—my son, the legitimate heir of my proud name, the inheritor by birthright of Normandy and England."

The guilty man, crushed as by the voice of a denouncing angel, sank overwhelmed upon his knees; deeply as Ulrick despised him, he could not gaze upon his humiliation without pity.

"Fool!" continued the excited father, with yet greater vehemence, "go bend the knee to him who should have been thy subject—for whose hollow promise thou hast lost a throne; go cringe and fawn to beg the earldom bought with a crown, and beg for it in vain. Tread, a thing scorned and abhorred, upon the soil which should have called thee master; die as thou hast lived, without a name, self-disinherited!"

"Not without a name," faltered Tyrrel, rising from his knee; "thy son can never lack a name."

"And who will give it thee when I disown thee?—the kind uncle," added Robert, with a sneer, "whose abject tool thou hast become, and into whose hands, like an obedient hound, thou didst resign the only proof of thy high lineage? Never more shall the secret pass these lips. Fool! I but tell it thee to be thy punishment."

"Is thy justice so implacable?" replied the wretched man; "does no sentiment of nature speak within thee at least to acknowledge me thy son?"

"My son a landless beggar?—never—never."

"Normandy is still within thy gift," urged Tyrrel, for so we must continue to designate him.

"But never shall be thine!" interrupted his father, sternly. "Set but a foot in it, and I will place thee in a cage where thou shalt fret against the bars in vain. Reptile! thou art completely crushed. Hint but to William of thy birth, his jealousy will doom thee dead. By thine own arts is every hope defeated. The only witness of thy birth, the venerable guardian of thy youth, is dead —slain, I too justly fear, by thy unnatural hand."

"Then I am lost!" murmured the conscience-stricken culprit in a low voice to himself.

"Lost and accursed!" added his justly-incensed parent; "both here and hereafter! Instead of the fond heritage of a father's love, receive his malediction! I curse thee in the name of the long-cherished hopes and affection thou hast blighted! May no child e'er live to honour thee—no voice of love or duty smooth thy dying pillow! May the shadow of the greatness thou hast lost haunt thee like an avenging spirit—the secret of thy birth fester like a serpent's fang in thy vile, treacherous, proud, ambitious heart! May the death-hope which whispers peace to the repentant sinner's soul fail thee in thy last hour of need! May thy grave remain unhonoured by a human tear—shunned as a spot accursed by every foot! False knight and perjured friend, degenerate son and most unnatural traitor, farewell for ever!"

The wretched man, crushed by the fearful weight of a father's malediction, so terribly pronounced, rushed from the tent as if fiends pursued him—the avenging words echoing in his ears as he fled. More like a spectre than a human being, he passed the guards and officers who surrounded William's tent, and, dashing aside the silken curtains, entered the enclosure. It was fortunate, perhaps, for the monarch that he was absent. All that Tyrrel found there were the ashes and half melted seals of the fatal parchment, the proof of his high birth. The sight still further increased his fury, and, foaming like a maniac with impotent rage and shame, he hastily left the spot.

The broken-hearted Robert remained, after the departure of the son whom he had so fearfully cursed and justly disowned, a prey to terrible excitement. In the midst of a life of reckless dissipation, he had long counted on the moment when the Conqueror's death would have enabled him to acknowledge him; for, though not of royal birth, his mother had been noble. It was some time ere Ulrick could bring his chafed spirit to something like composure; but all his entreaties to induce him to recal his malediction were in vain.

"Never! never!" he impatiently replied, dashing, at the same time, as if ashamed of human weakness, a tear from his burning cheek. "Words wrung from a heart bruised like mine can never be recalled. 'Tis passed for ever; the last hope of my life is gone, and nothing now remains but a few years of madness, folly, the wine-cup, and the revel —the battle-field, or pilgrim's staff—an heirless name, and childless sepulchre."

"He may repent, and yet atone the past," urged our hero, willing to calm him further, by giving utterance to a hope he was far from entertaining: for none knew so well as he how radically bad was the nature, how engrafted the vices, of the being for whom he pleaded. His words, however, produced an effect the very opposite of his intent; the more he pleaded, the more obstinate the outraged prince became; and he finally extorted from Ulrick, before they left the tent, a solemn vow never to reveal the secret of what had passed, or the mystery of Tyrrel's birth, save at his express command. The oath was reluctantly taken, but faithfully kept. Directly afterwards they rejoined their friends, and returned to Pevensey.

As the train crossed the drawbridge Prince Henry encountered the warder's brother, Peter Norbeck, who, by an affectation of blunt humour and open speech, had gradually wormed himself into his favour; indeed, so much so, that, from a simple man-at-arms, he had promoted him to a post amongst hi.

personal attendants; little dreaming that, in so doing, he was but walking blindly into the net which his enemies had spread.

"Ah, good Peter!" exclaimed the young prince as soon as he beheld him; "I have employment for thee. Send Bras de Fer, the executioner, to my chamber; I would speak with him."

"With Bras de Fer!" echoed Norbeck, turning pale; for conscience whispered that it might be for himself the services of that hated functionary were about to be required.

"With Brass de Fer," repeated Henry with a loud laugh, slapping him at the same time familiarly on the shoulder. "Why, how the fellow stares! Go you before, and fix me a noose in the carved oaken beam in the great hall. And see that the cord be strong; for," added the speaker in a tone of confidence which might have deceived a more suspicious nature than Peter's, "within an hour a greater weight of treachery and crime than thy honest nature can suppose must swing there."

"Fear not, your grace," replied the ruffian, perfectly re-assured by the prince's manner on his own account; "the cord shall be strong enough to hang the fattest monk in merry England, where, as men say, the holy crows are fattest."

Had the speaker seen the cold, satirical smile which Henry sent after him as he departed on his errand, he would have gone less cheerfully on his way.

Within the hour the prince, attended by a dozen men-at-arms and the executioner, entered the hall, where Peter Norbeck, mounted on the summit of a ladder, had already strung the fatal cord. Bras de Fer eyed the preparations critically, and nodded approval.

"I think it will do, your grace," exclaimed Peter, admiring his own skill.

"I trust it will," replied the prince sarcastically; "but Bras de Fer had better try it."

The functionary, who had previously received his instructions, began to ascend the ladder, as if to try the strength of the cord, according to Henry's orders. Peter, to make way for him, mounted still higher, and thereby facilitated the purpose of the hangman.

"Perhaps I had better have descended?" he observed.

"Not at all necessary," replied his companion, with a smile of quiet humour; for he seemed to enjoy the joke exceedingly; "indeed, I could not very well do without you."

"You will find it firm," said Peter, catching at the rope and placing it in the hands of Bras de Fer, who assured him it would answer the purpose extremely well. "How do you make the knot?"

"That is a secret. Most men are bunglers at the knot; but, as you are not a likely man to betray confidence," continued the hangman, "I don't mind showing you. You perceive, on turning the rope twice thus, you allow the noose to run, but not to slip; once formed, you pass it round the neck of your subject thus."

Suiting the action to the words, the speaker quickly placed the fatal cord around the throat of Peter Norbeck, who sat listening with unsuspicious gravity, deeply interested in his explanations.

"What next?" he demanded.

"Why, the next thing we do," replied Bras de Fer, "is, perhaps, the most delicate touch of our craft—the most difficult point of all. Passing our arms thus, we pinion our man, and, springing with him from the ladder, launch our handiwork into eternity."

The executioner, who had gradually got his victim in the requisite position, sprang with him from the ladder as he spoke. Sliding down the convulsed body of the criminal he dropped to the ground, leaving Peter Norbeck swinging in the air, much to the amusement of the men-at-arms, who had watched the whole proceeding as an excellent jest.

"Cast the carrion into the moat," said Henry, as he quitted the hall when the death-struggle was over. "Such be the fate of every cowardly assassin—the doom of every traitor."

The letters which the Black Knight had placed within his hand proved that the wretched Norbeck had undertaken, for a bribe of two hundred marks, to poison him that very evening at the banquet.

CHAPTER XXVI.

England, farewell! Fresh shores will rise,
When thy white cliffs are lost to view,
With warmer suns and brighter skies,
With hearts as kind and friends as true.

AREWELL to England!" exclaimed Robert of Normandy, as he entered the bark at Rye destined to bear him from the land whose crown he had so singularly lost. "I leave thee with regret, for thou hast been the scene of many a gallant hope, of many a daring deed. Farewell, my friends," he added; "should England grow distasteful to you, remember that while Robert hath a home in Normandy, he hath a heart to share it with you. Give no fresh cause of umbrage to him who is now your king, and you are safe. William's fears will prove a sufficient safeguard. He may break his vow to God, his brother, and his people, but never will he dare to violate the fearful oath of his unhappy fated race."

Ulrick was the last whom the exiled prince embraced, exclaiming as he did so:—

"Adieu, thou noble heart! How different had been my fate had pitying Heaven but blest me with a son as true, as worthy of my love, as thou art! Living or dead, in exile or on a throne, Robert will rest thy debtor."

Odo of Bayeux and Prince Henry, who accompanied their nephew and brother to his duchy, embraced in turn their companions in arms, who, according to the stipulations, were immediately to separate, each at the head of the remnant of his followers, to return to his respective home. Edda, our hero, and Mirvan, were still at the head of a considerable number of vassals—the imposing appearance which they presented, together with the safe conduct of William, prevented their being attacked by any of the disbanded soldiery who roamed the country, plundering the weak, and frequently exacting ransom from the strong.

On a bier, in the centre of their march, was borne the body of the venerable Herbert de Lozinga, so foully slain by an assassin's hand, arrayed in his episcopal robes, his face calm as a prophet's sleeping. The body of the murdered prelate was preceded by twelve priests from the neighbouring monasteries, who sang at intervals the litany of the dead. Ulrick followed it bareheaded and unarmed.

The kind old man had been to him as a father, and he mourned him like a son. In his pious gratitude, he had had the corse embalmed, and intended to entomb it in the magnificent cathedral his munificence had built. There, in the centre of the choir, before the high altar, may still be seen the resting-place of the chancellor of William the Conqueror and first Bishop of Norwich, Herbert de Lozinga; all his predecessors, as well as himself up to the year 1094, having borne the title of Bishop of Thetford only.

On the arrival of the funeral train in the city, both people and clergy came forth in crowds to meet it; all united to pay the last act of homage to their pastor, whose benevolence had been unbounded, as his life had been holy and useful. Even his successor, Eborard, the worthless prior of the Dominicans, whom William, much to the discontent of the primate, had named to the vacant see, joined in the procession. Such is the homage which triumphant vice is sometimes bound to pay to virtue.

Those only who have felt the pangs of separation from the being whom they love— the agony of doubt, of hope, and fear, which imagination causes in the anxious heart— can picture the meeting between Ulrick and his bride, who now gave visible promise of becoming a mother, and forging by the holy claims of maternity a yet more indissoluble tie around her husband's heart. Edith, too, the once more happy Edith, embraced her son—her Edward's living image—and in the gladness of the present hour forgot the tears and trials of the past. Amongst the first to welcome him was Gilbert, the poor boy whom he had left wounded behind him in his flight from London, under the hospitable care of the rich Jew, Falk of Cologne. Four months' absence had so improved his appearance that his benefactor could scarcely recognise him; his anxious, terrified look had given place to one of modest confidence; his attenuated cheeks glowed with recovered health; his step had become elastic, and his spirits light. Still, in the midst of his joy —and it was almost childish, at again meeting with the first being who had ever shown pity or interest in his welfare—a cloud of

THE DEATH OF PETER NORBECK.

doubt obscured his open brow; something remained to be told which he feared might change his protector's smiles to frowns.

"Welcome, my faithful boy!" exclaimed Ulrick, raising him from his knee. "Beshrew me, but I should often have borne a lighter heart had I but known thou wert well housed at Stanfield. How didst thou find thy route hither?—did the Jew direct thee?"

"Not the Jew," faltered Gilbert, "but his daughter, Hester, who tended me, watched over my sick couch, and ministered like an angel to my sufferings. Oh! my lord, if indeed the sight of your poor Gil-

bert gives you pleasure, it is to her care alone you owe it, for my heart was all but broken when you returned no more."

"Indeed!" replied our hero, smiling at what he deemed the boy's grateful enthusiasm; "it seems the pretty infidel made good use of her time, and traced her image on thy young heart while within her power."

"Pardon me, my lord," said Gilbert, blushing, "but Hester is, or rather soon will be, a Christian."

"Indeed!" answered Ulrick, thoughtfully. "Of this we must speak further; meanwhile, welcome, dear boy, to Stanfield."

It needed all the influence both of his mother and Matilda to restrain our hero's anger when they informed him that the beautiful Jewess Hester had not only left her father's roof with Gilbert, but was actually at that very moment an inmate of the hall. His first impression was, that the wounded youth had availed himself of her father's hospitality to seduce her from the paths of innocence; still there was something so childish in his look, so frank in his nature, that his mother's words easily induced him to discard it.

"You wrong them," said Edith, calmly; "if they love, it is as angel's love—earthly passion hath not yet left its stain on their unsullied hearts. The maid is truly Christian; truth from the lips of a poor sick boy hath reached her soul, and Heaven, which smiles not always on the churchman's homily or scholar's page, hath worked its will through him. See her, Ulrick," she added; "question her ere you decide to scare the young-fledged soul upon redemption's threshold back from its place of rest; see her, and be convinced."

Matilda, seeing the impression which his mother's words had produced upon her husband, without waiting for his reply, raised the silver call to her lips—the signal agreed upon for Hester to enter. It was impossible not to be struck with the beauty and childish grace of her manners as she did so. Bending the knee, before he was aware of her intent, he raised his hand to her lips and kissed it. Such was the homage which in her father's house she had been accustomed to pay to the elders and chief men of her people.

"They tell me, Hester," said Ulrick, raising her kindly as he spoke, "that thou hast left thy father's house to become a Christian—is this thing so?"

"It is," replied the maiden, modestly; "else had I not abandoned my father in his age, or the sisters of my blood."

"And what hath wrought this change? Why wouldst thou leave the faith of thy father and thy nation?"

"Because I found it," said Hester, speaking in the phraseology of the East, which, from her childhood, she had been accustomed to, "as barren as the sea of my own distant land, whose waters never yet were ruffled by the sea-bird's wing; because I found in it observances without devotion, a body without a soul."

"And what hast thou found in Christianity?" demanded our hero, struck with the impressive earnestness of her manner and peculiar expression of thought.

"Love," replied the Jewess, with a modest blush; "love, with which creation teems; love, which at every step proclaims the work of an almighty hand; love, which makes suffering joy, and persecution peace; love, which is God, since God alone is perfect love. Not all the temple's awful pomp," she added—"the name at which nations trembled as they read, graved on the high priest's mitred brow—speaks the divinity like those plain words, 'Love one another.'"

"And Gilbert taught thee thus much of Christian faith?"

"Taught me," said Hester, "and taught me not; I felt as if I but remembered it like some forgotten air which memory had treasured in its cell. The note-key struck, and all the gushing melody returned."

"Hast thou no other love?" asked Ulrick.

"For my father and my sisters, yes," replied the maiden, her eyes suffused with tears at the recollection that her absence had clouded the joy of their once happy home.

"And none for Gilbert?"

"For Gilbert?" repeated the maiden, with a look of innocent childish surprise, so pure that our hero almost blushed to have asked the question. "Oh, yes, I love him as I love all things of God; I love him as your great father loved the dove which brought the branch of peace; love him as the faithful friend who guided my footsteps here; as a brother," she added, gravely—for the first time, perhaps, comprehending the drift of the question. "Hester will never love him less or more."

"Would that the venerable Herbert lived!" exclaimed Ulrick; "his pure soul would best direct and understand thee; mine is unequal to the task. Remain, Hester, with the kindred spirits of my wife and mother; they will instruct and love thee. Soon as thou art prepared, the church's rites shall welcome her stray dove back to its longing bosom."

Peaceful that night was the slumber of the Jewess; the last cloud, as she imagined, between her and happiness had disappeared; she dreamt not of the trials by which Heaven would test her fortitude, ere it crowned her triumph by making her its own.

Early the following morning, Ulrick encountered Gilbert on the ramparts; the poor youth, scarcely aware of the nature of his feelings towards the beautiful being whose destiny had become so strangely mixed with his, was listening beneath her window to the hymn into which her morning prayer broke forth:

"I have seen the Lord's might in the fair even-
    ing star—
In the bright worlds of light he hath scattered
    afar;

Not more wondrous are these as a proof of his
power,
Than the insect whose home is the bright
tinted flower.

I have heard the Lord's voice in the thunder's
loud sound,
When the lightning's red flash scattered terror
around ;
But His dread will is spoken as plain as in
these,
When borne on the delicate voice of the
breeze.

Oh ! there is not a thing that hath being or
life,
From the emmet's small form, to the ocean's
wild strife ;
Not a leaf on the shrub, or a sweet-scented
flower,
But are emblems alike of his goodness and
power.

I have seen the fierce waves by the tempest's
breath thrown—
Man left on the billow to struggle alone—
And felt that each creature was safe in His
hand
On the mad foaming sea, as when cradled on
land."

"Rash boy !" said our hero, pityingly ;
"thou art drinking of the draught that will
but increase thy thirst. Tell me, dreamer,"
he added, "what I can do best to show my
gratitude for thy past service."

"Gratitude !" echoed Gilbert. "Ah!
now you jest, my lord. What debt can you
owe to the wretched being whom your bounty
rescued from a slavery worse than death?
Besides, what more can I desire than to
remain near you,—to watch and tend you—
live for your use—die in your service?"

"Dreams, boy, dreams !" replied Ulrick,
who saw that Gilbert was a character which
mingling in the world alone could form, and
which, permitted to vegetate in peaceful
solitude, would lose even the little energy it
possessed. "The purposes of a life may not
be wasted for a caprice like this ; fortune
hath many roads to greatness, and the
courageous heart cannot fail to find one."

"I am without ambition," sighed the
youth.

"A cloister, then, perchance, would suit
thee better?"

Gilbert started ; for a monastic life was
the very last of which he had been dreaming.
His kind protector feared that his love for
the fair Jewess would prove hopeless. Hers
was one of those pure, visionary natures
which seldom descend to earthly love, but
exhale themselves away in the retirement of
the convent or the cell of the desert ; and he
was anxious to plunge him into the active
realities of life, in order to make him forget
its dreams—too often the most difficult and
painful task for youth.

"A cloister !" echoed Gilbert ; "never !

never ! My heart was never framed for
solitude. Do not send me from you," he
added ; "all my hopes and affections are
garnered here. It would break my heart to
part with them."

"This is madness, folly, boy," answered
Ulrick. "I must be the physician of thy
mind as well as the protector of thy fortunes.
In three days I will give thee letters to
Robert Duke of Normandy ; for my sake he
will cherish thee 'neath his wing. There thou
mayst achieve a name a soul like Hester's
may be proud to love. At the present hour
her heart is wedded to her faith alone ; it
knows no other rival."

"In three days?" sighed the youth.

"In three days," repeated our hero, turning away, unable to resist the pleading look
which Gilbert—to whom the decision seemed
like the stroke of death—directed towards
him.

"In three days," repeated the boy, as he
plunged into the neighbouring wood, "I
shall again be desolate. Fool, to think that
earth produced one flower of happiness for a
wretch like me ! Ungenerous Ulrick !" he
added, at the same time throwing himself
upon a low bank under one of those giant
oaks beneath which, perchance, the soldiers
of Cæsar had often halted, or the Druid
celebrated his mysterious rites ; "blessed
himself in all that love can yield, little he
reeks of the poor peasant youth, whose gratitude is perchance a burden to him. Why
send me from him? What need have I to
seek a name?"

"Thou hast a proud one, boy, as proud as
his whom thou namest thy protector," exclaimed a deep voice near him. "But thou
must prove thyself worthy of it ere thou
darest to claim it."

Gilbert started from his seat ; absorbed in
his sorrow, he had not marked, when he
threw himself upon the bank, that a stranger,
dressed in a pilgrim's russet garb, his cowl
drawn over his features, was already seated
beneath the shadow of the gnarled tree.

"What knowest thou of my name or me,
father?" demanded the astonished youth.

"More than thou knowest of thyself,"
replied the stranger ; "for that past, which
is to thee a volume sealed, my eyes can
read."

"The page would be a sad one," said Gilbert carelessly ; for he deemed the pilgrim
sporting with him.

"It may be a glad one soon."

"Father," said the young man, "'tis
plain thou knowest but little of me or my
fortunes : thy science hath deceived thee.
My birth is humble as thy russet gown ; my
name ignoble ; my life hath hitherto been

wretched—useless. Sport with me no more; I am too sad for jesting."

"And I too pressed for time," replied the stranger, whom our readers have no doubt already suspected to be no other than Robert of Artois. "Answer me this; dost thou not bear a red cross deeply printed on thy breast—near to thy heart?"

"I do," exclaimed Gilbert, feeling, for the first time, deeply interested in the pilgrim's question. "From infancy I have observed the mark; and once, when I asked my father how it came there, he answered me with blows, and bade me keep my peace."

"Vile slave!" muttered the stranger; "but his debt is paid. Tell me, boy, did no secret loathing of thy heart—no impulse whisper thee—the warder was not thy father?"

"I knew," said the young man, "he was but my step-father."

"Thy step-father!" repeated the pilgrim contemptuously. "He never saw thy mother; her proud heart would have spurned him like a cur, had such a being raised his eyes e'en to the dust she trod on."

"Maud, then, was not my parent?" exclaimed Gilbert. "Thank Heaven for that! Stranger, thou hast removed a weight from this bruised heart. The heavy blow, the taunting speech, the bitter gibe, were doubly bitter when I reflected 'twas a mother dealt them. But tell, in mercy tell me, who were my parents? Live they yet?"

"Thy mother sleeps the sleep of all; thy father lives, though men believe him dead. A fate as strange as cruel, and merciless as just, obliges him to walk the earth like some unburied shadow: but fear not thou; his crime leaves no dishonour on his name; thou yet mayest proudly bear it. It shall go hard but the hope lost to himself he will achieve for thee."

"His name! his name!"

"Merit it, boy, and thou shalt learn it," replied the pilgrim; "for the present hour, farewell. Let what has passed remain a secret, locked in thy breast like the first impulse of thy boyish love. Thou knowest the ruin called the Druid's Cell? Should danger threaten or misfortune reach thee, seek me there; for, poor and abject as the world may deem me, I may not lack the means to save or serve thee."

Ere Gilbert could recover his astonishment the speaker disappeared within the wood, leaving the bewildered youth to doubt whether what he had heard was real, or but the vision of some waking dream.

Bitterly did the poor monks and clergy regret the loss of their venerable superior, Herbert de Lozinga, whose rule had been of love. His successor's, the unworthy Eborard, proved of iron; for, conscious that he was regarded with dislike, if not contempt, he avenged himself by the annoyance with which petty tyranny torments the spirits it cannot subdue. Short as had been his reign, the chapter had already appealed against his vexatious, harsh encroachments on their privileges, to the primate, whose power alone could stand between them and the haughty bishop. Reckless as Eborard was, he trembled at the name of Lanfranc, whose indignation at his appointment had been openly expressed, and whose authority, for a canonical fault, could even yet depose him, despite the protection and favour of the king. He had just heard from one of his creatures of the proceedings of the monks, and was pacing his chamber in rage and vexation, when an attendant entered to inform him that a stranger, meanly clad, desired admittance to his presence.

"I have no humour to listen to strangers or intruders!" exclaimed the impatient prelate; "I am pestered enough with the stiff-necked brotherhood, whose spirit I must either bend or break. Send him to the prior or the almoner; and to teach thee, brother, discretion for the future, I forbid thee for the rest of the week to appear in the refectory during the evening meal."

"But the stranger, reverend father," urged the dismayed lay brother, "has letters of importance, as he says. I told him how difficult you were of access, but he would take no denial; he said they were from the king."

"The king! Imbecile, admit him instantly! And for thy want of sense," added Eborard, "in detaining this messenger from the king, add to thy penance a midnight vigil to our Lady; pray to her to teach thee common sense, and grant me patience to bear with thee."

"Now, fellow," said Eborard, as Falk of Cologne humbly bent before him, 'what is thy will with us? Have we misunderstood thy message? Dost thou indeed bring letters from the king? Or was it but a ruse to gain admittance to our presence?"

Bowing low, the aged Israelite, who seemed worn with grief as well as travel, presented a slip of parchment, sealed with the royal signet. In it the monarch recommended the bearer to the bishop, urging him to obtain for him, by every means, possession of his daughter, deluded from her home by the esquire of the Lord of Stanfield.

"He must be rich," thought the prelate to himself, "to have obtained such a missive from the Red King."

"How can I serve thee?" demanded the bishop, after having carefully perused the letter.

"By restoring me my child," replied the Jew. "Thou art a judge as well as high-priest of thy people. Thy laws forbid all intercourse between the children of our nation. Hester hath been deluded from me by a wounded snake, which in my pity I had sheltered. A shame hath fallen upon Israel; desolation is upon my hearth—sorrow on my grey hairs, for the child of my age hath dishonoured them."

"Thinkest thou," demanded Eborard, eager, in his hatred, to involve Ulrick in censures of the church, "that this boy—this esquire—is but the cloak for some more artful villain? That his master, the Lord of Stanfield——"

"Never saw my child," interrupted Falk; "at least not till she had abandoned the home of her fathers. In my desolation I will utter no injustice, lest the Lord of Israel confounded me in His wrath. Till this serpent Gilbert poured his venom in her ear, Nazarene never gazed upon her face. I had garnered her, like my life's pearl, in secret. My care was for her, my toil for her, my prayer for her. Perchance," he added, bitterly, "I had made an idol in my heart, and the God of my fathers hath punished me for my wickedness."

"Why seek, then, to regain her?" said the churchman, coldly.

"Because she is my child," answered the Jew; "and merciless as the Christian's law hath been to us—persecuted, reviled, outraged, and degraded, as we have been—the iron finger of oppression hath not effaced all trace of humanity from my breast. Because when the last trumpet shall sound, and the scattered race of Israel shall assemble in the valley of Jehoshaphat before the judgment-seat of the Most High, I would exclaim, 'Thanks, Lord, the children which thou gavest are all with Thee!'"

"Should she turn Christian?"

"Horror!" shrieked the Hebrew; "rather would I behold her dead than turned unto the strange God of the Christian. Pardon me!" he exclaimed, as he marked the haughty frown on the bishop's brow; "I know it is a great thing I demand—an unheard-of thing—for a Jew to exercise his natural right over his rebellious child, for an Israelite to find justice against a Christian; but if I am poor in prayers," he added, "I am rich in that the church prizes more than the empty triumph of an infant convert. I am rich in gold. Name what ransom, sum, mulct, or offering—call it what you will—you please; were it the last shekel of my house, I'd count it freely—restore me but my child."

The passionate grief with which Falk pronounced these last words made little impression upon the obdurate heart to which they were addressed; but his offers of gold were more favourably received; for Eborard was one of those in whom the yellow idol Mammon had long replaced the purer image of Deity; his dreams were of gold; his very prayers, if the ignoble aspirations of such a thing of clay merit the name, were all of gold. Belus had found in him a ready worshipper, for his statue was of gold. One rival passion, whose existence he dreamt not of, lay dormant in his heart; its sleep had been profound; its waking was destined to be fearful.

"Thou speakest truly, Jew," said the bishop, after a pause, in which he had mentally calculated how much he could wring out of him; "it is a great thing which thou demandest; still, as the church is merciful, and the king befriends thee, I may perchance stand thy stead in this; but thine alms for such a favour——"

"Shall content e'en thee," said Falk, eagerly; "I am no niggard to cheapen when 'tis my flesh and blood that I would redeem; name the sum at which I may secure the church's silence, and thy powerful aid."

"What thinkst thou of a thousand marks of gold?" demanded Eborard.

"'Tis a large sum, but yet it shall be paid," answered Falk—"paid were it the last coin I possess. Place but my child once more beneath my care, and the gold," he added, with a sigh, "is yours."

"Think not, Jew," said the churchman, "that I consent to this for mine own gain. Thy gold is for the poor. Penance and prayer must atone my share in this, if indeed the maid be truly christian."

"I know! I know!" impatiently interrupted the old man, fearful lest the prelate should demand an extra sum as a solace for his conscience; which, however, he shrewdly valued at its true price. "Fear not that the Israelite misjudges thy condescension. When wilt thou secure the wretched girl?"

"This very day our precept shall be issued forth," said Eborard; "and the gold——"

"Be counted to thee," replied Falk, "when Hester is restored unto her father. Farewell, my lord. To-morrow the poor Hebrew will once more kiss the dust before thy sacred presence."

With these words the dignitary and the despised Jew parted—the former to issue his mandate for the arrest of Hester, the latter to seek a lodging with one of his nation in the city.

That same evening Ulrick was seated in the oratory of his mother, listening to Matilda, who was instructing the young and beautiful neophite in the creed of her new faith. There was something so pure, so innocent, so free from every taint of earth, in the character and enthusiastic devotion of the maiden, that her protectress began to regard her almost with a sister's love. Added to which, the pious work in which she was occupied was, according to the spirit of the age, so meritorious in the eyes of the church, that it assured paradise to those who successfully completed it.

"But why," urged Matilda to Hester's wish of retiring to a convent as soon as she had been received into the church, "why quit the world? It hath duties as sacred as the cloister. Besides," she added with a smile, "your Gilbert's love merits some pity."

A blush suffused the cheek of the fair Jewess, and she was about to reply to her when the subject of their conversation rushed into the oratory, exclaiming:—

"Save her, my lord! They come to drag the victim forth to sacrifice; they would tear her alike from heaven and you; the soldiers of the church demand their prey."

Ere Ulrick could reply, the curtain which screened the entrance to the oratory was drawn aside, and a tall ferocious-looking monk, followed by an officer who bore the new bishop's arms embroidered on his vest, and a party of men-at-arms, unceremoniously entered the apartment. Indignant at the sight, Gilbert half drew his sword, and in his enthusiasm blood would have doubtless been shed, had not the hand of our hero restrained him. Matilda, offended at the intrusion, and alarmed for the safety of her *protegèe*, half encircled her with her arm, and regarded the men with an inquiring but disdainful glance. The priest read from the parchment which he held in his hand a citation for Hester, to appear before the bishop and the ecclesiastical court, to answer to the charge of having fled with a Christian; "a crime," added the fellow, "abhorrent both to God and man, and punished by the church with death." As soon as he had concluded, the civil officer advanced to arrest her.

"My dream—my dream!" exclaimed the Jewess, fixing her beautiful eyes on high, and every feature glowing with the most exalted enthusiasm, as if already she beheld the martyr's crown. "The wolf hath broke the fold; the tiger hath tracked the fawn. The words of my vision are realised—'If thou wouldst indeed be Christian, learn to

suffer, for to suffer is to love.' I am ready; whither must I go?"

"To prison," replied the officer, moved, despite himself, at the sight of so much beauty and courage; although, in the fulfilment of his office, he advanced to secure her person as he spoke.

"Back!" said Ulrick, sternly; "is Stanfield hold a brigand's den, that thus your master violates the laws of courtesy, and seizes on my guest? The maid is Christian."

"Let her prove it," replied the priest; "but till she does she is our prisoner."

Ulrick regarded him with a smile of cold contempt. Terrible as was the power of the church, he knew that it had its limits; but had it been ten time more despotic, he would have blushed to have resigned an innocent, unoffending being at its summons, who had no friends save himself.

"I will be warrant for the maid's appearance," answered our hero; "till then Stanfield is her home, and I am her protector."

"What if we resist?" demanded the monk.

"My vassals shall scourge ye to the boundaries of my lands. Hence!" he added; "pollute my home no longer; lest I forget your office in its errand, and crush ye like vipers 'neath my feet! Gilbert, haste to the seneschal; call out the guard, and bid them hurl these intruders into the moat, if, in three minutes, Stanfield is not clear of them."

Scarcely had the command escaped his lips than the youth had quitted the apartment.

"Beware, sir knight!" exclaimed the monk, as he retreated; "the church's arm is iron—it will crush thee."

"Better be crushed by it than live its slave," said Ulrick. "Away! and tempt not my patience further!"

"Not for me!" exclaimed Hester—"not for me this coil! What were my worthless, life to one moment's danger unto thee or thine? Besides," she added, "the fate my vision told must be fulfilled. Sir officer, I am your prisoner, and will follow you."

"Never," interrupted Matilda, "will I resign you to the charge of that ferocious man. If danger threatens, courage must meet it; if persecution comes, patience must bear it; if death waits us, innocence shall welcome it."

At this moment the seneschal and men, conducted by Gilbert, entered the oratory; and the baffled messengers of priestly tyranny, venting curses, withdrew to inform their employer of the failure of their mission.

Early on the following morning, as Eborard was considering how best to accomplish his designs, and secure not only the person of the Jewess, but involve Ulrick in the censure of the church, he was informed that a female demanded to see him. Finding, on inquiry, that she was young and beautiful, he gave orders to admit her—for, churchman though he was, he was not insensible to the charms of a red lip or flashing eye. Much to his annoyance, the prior, whose cold, stately manner towards him not all his courtesy and blandishments could change, entered his apartment at the same moment as his visitor.

"Welcome, reverend brother; benedicite, fair daughter!" he exclaimed, addressing each of them; "we will but hear the worthy prior's pleasure, and attend your will."

"Hear it now, my lord!" exclaimed the female, bending her knee, and at the same time throwing back her veil, which discovered features of such uncommon loveliness, that Eborard felt the warm blood rushing to his heart with most unpriestly violence. "I am your prisoner—the Jewess, Hester, whom you seek."

The prior devoutly crossed himself; for although a kind, he was a superstitious man. His superior remained gazing upon her with a flushed brow and trembling pulse. For the first time in his life he felt subjugated by the influence of beauty. Often as it had crossed his path before, it had never touched his heart.

"Is it possible? Art thou," he demanded, "the Jewess whom the Lord of Stanfield insolently refused to our behest? 'Tis well he hath thought better of it ere our wrath had crushed him."

"The knight of Stanfield sheltered me not as a Jewess, but as a Christian, reverend father."

"Now, praised be our Lady!" exclaimed the prior, with a benevolent smile; "the lost sheep of Zion returneth to the fold, and a soul is won. Thou art a Christian, maiden?"

"In all but name," replied Hester, modestly.

"And hath Ulrick," demanded the prior, in a tone of disappointment, "sent thee here to plead thy cause alone?"

"He knows not of my coming," said the maiden. "Visions had warned me of approaching danger. Could I behold my kind protector suffer through his zeal for me? That were indeed to prove myself unworthy of the name I bear in heart."

"Remove her," said the prelate to the attendant lay brothers, who appeared upon his summons.

"Where?" demanded the prior. "To the convent of St. Mary?"

"No," replied the bishop, sternly, "to the palace prison."

Despite the prior's intercession, the maiden was conducted to the prison; and the good man, whose interference had been haughtily rebuked by his superior, with a thoughtful mien returned to his cell within the cloister.

Gilbert remembered the advice which the recluse had given him, to seek him in the hour of danger or adversity; and on the arrest of Hester, he sought him in his retreat, and summoned him, with all the energy of despair, to fulfil his promise.

"Follow!" exclaimed the unknown, moved to compassion at the distress of the only being who still possessed a claim upon his affections; "it is not exactly the destiny I would choose for thee, but since Heaven hath willed it so, I will not vainly seek to thwart its purpose."

A few hours' walk brought them to the palace-gate of the haughty Eborard, where, despite their entreaties, threats, and despair, they were refused admittance by the prelate's guard, who advised them to apply to the almoner, or to come on the following Friday, which was dole-day. As they were returning, disheartened, fortunately they encountered the worthy prior, who listened with pity to Gilbert's tale, and felt his interest in the fate of the fair Jewess augmented by the artless story of her conversion.

"Hast thou courage, boy," he demanded, "to ride to London, and demand an audience of the primate?"

"To death," said Gilbert, eagerly, "in such a cause."

"'Tis well," resumed the churchman. "I will give thee a letter which will secure thee an audience of Lanfranc. Tell thy tale with the honest simplicity thou hast told it me, and doubt not the result."

"And I," replied the recluse, "will arm him with a weapon to depose and crush this mitred tyrant, whose sacerdoce is a blasphemy—whose religion hypocrisy."

The good prior's letter was speedily written; and that very day Gilbert, bearing a packet from his mysterious friend, as well as the priest's missive, started for London.

CHAPTER XXVII.

Then wakes the power, which in an age of iron
Arose to stay the weak and crush the strong.
Mark where she stands.   Around her form I draw
The awful circle of our solemn church. Set but a foot
Within the sacred line, and on thy head—yea,
Though it wore a crown, I launch the curse of Rome.
                                    BULWER'S RICHELIEU.

IN his anxiety to ascertain the fate of his *protegé*, Ulrick had several times presented himself at the palace of the new bishop to solicit an audiance, but without success; the haughty churchman refused to see him, and he returned on each occasion to the inquiring Matilda the bearer of fresh disappointment and disquietude. Short as had been Hester's residence at Stanfield, she had acquired not only the love of its generous owners, but the esteem and admiration of all its inmates. Her youth and beauty, no less than fervent piety and unfeigned humility, had won her friends. The poor whom she had solaced, the wounded she had tended, were all unanimous in their praise of her gentleness and patience; and many openly declared that, should the haughty prelate seek to wrong her, crowns should be broken and swords drawn in her defence. Meanwhile the recluse, as the Black Knight was now called, did not remain idle.

If the conduct of Eborard appeared inexplicable to the friends of the Jewess, it was still more so to the brethren of the convent and his own immediate household. Since he beheld his prisoner, his character seemed entirely changed; he no longer occupied himself in tormenting his clergy, or inventing fresh means of curtailing their privileges. Even his schemes of ambition for awhile were laid at rest; letters remained unanswered; decrees, long meditated, postponed; and his revenues unaudited. In the solemn offices of the church, the episcopal throne was frequently vacant, and the hours which should have been devoted to the service of his God were passed, to the astonishment of all, in visits to his prisoner, whose chamber was guarded by several of his minions whom he had brought with him from his priory, and on whose unscrupulous fidelity he could rely. The inmates of the convent were debarred all access to her.

The younger monks observed, too, with significant smiles, the attention which he paid to the adornment of his person; gems of price, contrary to the canons of the church, glittered on his fingers, and his hair and beard were perfumed. His table, to the great scandal of the prior, was served up with the choicest wines, and he indulged in the excitement of the cup more like some reckless soldier than the sober inmate of the cloister.

The truth was, Eborard loved—if indeed the impious sentiment which could make him forget his vow to God and priestly rank merits the name—madly, wildly loved.

Ardent piety alone can reconcile men to the cloisters, or the deepest sentiment of religion wed them to the priesthood. Eborard's union with the church had been of interest and ambition only. It is not, therefore, to be wondered at that the cold barriers which prudence and calculating hypocrisy had raised melted like wax before the breath of human passion.

Love in the virtuous, well-governed heart, is a pure, gentle stream, fertilising and refreshing all that it embraces; in the unholy breast it is a torrent, whose pathway is destruction and desolation.

It was on the fifth morning after the departure of Gilbert for London that Falk of Cologne, after much entreaty, succeeded in obtaining an audience of the bishop, whose intentions, although far from guessing the truth, he began vaguely to suspect. The prelate received him with his usual haughty indifference; indeed, he would have scarcely deigned to dissemble with the Jew, but for the letter which he had been the bearer of from the king. To his demand for his daughter, he replied that, great as was his inclination to serve him, he could not forget the duty he owed to his high station and the laws of the church; but that in a few days, after he had again consulted the chapter on the subject, he might perhaps be enabled to restore her to him.

"Perhaps!" iterated the Jew, eyeing him keenly, for he was no stranger to the character which Eborard bore; "there was no 'perhaps' when first we spoke; then all was clear and well defined. Have I," continued the agitated father, "but withdrawn my

THE JEWESS SEEKS SANCTUARY FROM EBORARD.

child from one peril to expose her to the worst extreme of fate? Nay, bend not, priest," he added, "thy haughty brows on me. While Rufus hath need of gold, I bear a charmed life beyond thy malice to assail. Give me my daughter, or I will appeal unto the primate. Little as he loves our persecuted race, he loves still less the priest, who holds his vows as feathers in the balance of his evil passions."

With difficulty the prelate restrained the scornful defiance which rose upon his lips, but prudence bade him dissemble; he more than half suspected that complaints suf-

ficiently serious had already been made to the stern Lanfranc against him, and he trembled at the idea of an additional charge; for as legate of the pope as well as Archbishop of Canterbury, the zealous primate was in all matters of ecclesiastical discipline his all but irresponsible judge; besides which, he knew him already to be prepossessed against him.

"I pardon thee, rash man," he answered trying to assume the tone of injured innocence, "thy vile, injurious suspicion; it proves how little thou knowest of holy church, or its much-slandered ministers. In thy headlong passion appeal unto the primate. I am prepared to meet the charge, and surrender him my prisoner. For me, perchance, it were the safest step, for my brethren already wonder at the clemency I have shown to the daughter of thy unbelieving race; but, remember, once in his power, not e'en the king's authority can tear her from it; and if his justice dooms her to the stake, blame thyself, not me."

"The stake!" shrieked Falk, his cheek blanching at the word. "No, no—impossible! Though priests, ye are men. Ye cannot have forgotten the mothers who bore you, the sisters who shared your love—all is not stone in your cold, selfish hearts. The stake! and for a child!" he added. "It is too horrible even for Christian cruelty."

"She hath fled, and with a Christian," said the prelate, coldly; "such is the church's law."

"Accursed be that law!" exclaimed the Hebrew, still more and more excited; "for 'tis for Moloch's creed. Devils alone could frame it, or men, save those who have renounced the ties of nature, he found to execute it."

"This in our presence, Jew? Thou blasphemest."

"Hear me," continued the aged Israelite: "I know the key-stone to your hearts; 'tis gold—the yellow idol at whose shrine your souls are daily sacrificed. Yield me my daughter back unstained, unharmed, and I will sate your avaricious thirst, though I count down the last shekel of my wealth, and wander forth the beggar of my tribe."

"It cannot be," answered Eborard, his impious passion struggling against his cupidity; "all I dare do I will—unseemly haste would compromise myself—in a few days perchance."

"A few days!" interrupted Falk, sternly; "and what in a few days will my daughter be to me? A degraded thing; abject as violence and brutal lust can make her. Deny it not—the lie would blister on thy lip; a father's fears can pierce the shallow veil of thy deceit. Man," he added, throwing himself upon his knees, "if our creeds be different, our natures are the same; our loves and hates, impulses, hopes, and fears, all spring from the same source. Beggar me, and I will bless thee; restore to me the child of my age, and at the judgment-seat of the Most High the Jew will not accuse thee."

"Thou hast my answer; lay it to thy reason, not thy passion. In five days thy daughter shall be free, and Heaven pardon thee thy unjust suspicions."

"Enough," said the suppliant, with an unnatural calmness; "I'll trust its justice further than thy mercy. Farewell, sir priest; thou hast yet to learn that if the Hebrew be slow to strike, his aim is but the surer."

Without further reverence or word the speaker quitted the apartment.

"There is some spell upon me," exclaimed the guilty man, as soon as he was alone—"a spell which drags me to perdition. It is no longer the cool blood which circles in my veins, but the volcano's burning lava. The image of this girl pursues me at the altar, in my dreams; my prayers are of her, my thoughts of her, my being is of her. Vainly I fly from restless vigils to a more restless couch. Fever is in my sleep, and mocking kisses sear my eager lips. I will possess her," he added, "e'en though my forfeit soul should be the purchase of a moment's bliss."

For a few moments he continued to pace the rush-strewn floor, and then, as if struck by a sudden thought, raised the silver call to his lips, and sounded twice. The signal brought Robert of Artois' former squire, Brantome, to his presence. His new master had already proved his usefulness, and hesitated not to trust him. Beckoning him to the window where he stood, he pointed out to him the retreating figure of his visitor, who was seen slowly wending his way across St. Martin's Plain. The fellow's eye followed him with the sagacious look of the bloodhound. Instinctively he guessed what was expected from him.

"Seest thou yon man?" demanded the prelate pointing to the Jew.

"I do, my lord."

"Wouldst know him again?"

"From a thousand," said Brantome; "it is not the first time I have seen him. For days he has been lingering round the palace, and twice asked an audience of the prior."

"Did he obtain it?" eagerly inquired Eborard, whom the intelligence confirmed in his fearful purpose.

"No, my lord; I took upon myself to drive him forth."

"And thou didst well," observed his master, with a smile; "but he had done better who had silenced his slanderous tongue for ever. Thou wert speaking to me lately," he added, "of the lands of Carrow—part of the fief of thy late master."

"True," eagerly interrupted Brantome.

"Come to me in two days," slowly continued Eborard, with a look of peculiar meaning: "and we will speak yet further on the subject. I am not one of those ungrateful masters who forget faithful service. Am I understood?"

"Perfectly," replied the esquire, with a look of intelligence. "As for yon infidel, rest satisfied, my lord, in this world he shall cross your path no more."

"I seek not to understand thy meaning," said the churchman; for he was a hypocrite even with the instruments of his crimes: "'tis true he hath menaced me—outraged my honour by his vile suspicions—threatened to denounce me," he added, bitterly, "to the primate; but, as a Christian, I forgive him. Do thou the same. Farewell."

"Umph!" muttered Brantome, as he retired from his master's presence; "such forgiveness is like that of the Bishop of Beauvais to the thief who stole his cup; he pardoned him the robbery, but burnt him for the sacrilege. Heaven keep me from such pardons as churchmen give!"

"The crime indeed is fearful!" exclaimed the prior, who, with an agitated step, was pacing the cloisters of the cathedral, accompanied by a venerable ecclesiastic, one of the members of the chapter, and our old acquaintance the recluse, during the Jew and the esquire's interview with his superior; "heard Christian men ever of such wickedness? It is enough to make the very saints tremble in their shrines, and his pious predecessor rise from his tomb to shame him; unholy love in an anointed bishop of the church! A sin indeed hath fallen on our house."

"Why not at once arrest him?" demanded the youngest of his companions; "the evidence is clear."

"Because," said the dignitary, "he is canonically our superior, and we are bound by oath to obey him in all lawful things. The primate only is his judge; without him we can do nothing. Would to our lady he were come!"

"Should he in his madness offer violence to the innocent object of his lust?" observed the aged monk.

"Fear not that," replied the recluse; "I am bound by no vow of obedience; should he attempt it, I would rush from the place of concealment where I so long have watched and strangle him with as little remorse as I would crush a serpent beneath my feet."

Both the prior and his companion crossed themselves in horror at the idea of such a necessity.

"Such a deed fits not a Christian man," said the former; "remember that, however unworthy, he is still a priest, and that no layman's hand may touch him. But, hush," he added, as Brantome entered the cloisters; "there goes the bloodhound whose fearful errand we have overheard. Heaven forfend that the life of the wretched Jew should fall a prey to his vile master's treachery!"

"Deep as is my cause of hatred to the accursed race, I will at least preserve the old Jew," whispered the disfigured man, "and baulk yon villain's purpose. The Lord of Stanfield owes him a debt of gratitude, for the Jew once preserved his life."

"Have you the means of communicating with him?" demanded the prior.

"I have."

"Is he still within the city?"

"In the city and on the watch," replied the recluse; "he is not one of those to sit contented by the ingle-side whilst danger threatens a hair of those he loves. We may trust the Jew's safety with confidence to him."

The letter was written and dispatched. That very night Brantome was an inmate of the deepest dungeon of Stanfield hold; his schemes of villany for awhile were baffled.

In the morning of the day previous to which Falk, according to Eborard's promise, was to receive his daughter, two Carmelite friars arrived at the convent, and demanded hospitality for the night—a request which the prior, to whom such matters were generally referred, instantly accorded. There was nothing in the manner of their reception to convey the idea that the strangers were no other than they seemed; yet all the brotherhood appeared to feel that a deeply observant eye was upon them. The stately demeanour of the elder chilled as well as awed them. The service of the day was performed with more than usual attention on the part of all; and when at night the prior, who, in the absence of the bishop, gave the usual benediction, the monks retired to their cells with a vague impression that some event of moment threatened their house. The elder ones, who were members of the chapter, were seen about an hour afterwards, when all was silent in the cloisters, to glide singly with stealthy tread and thoughtful brow into the apartment of the prior.

That very night the worthless prelate had resolved to accomplish his design. The fever of his blood, excited by the wine-cup, had mounted to his brain, and in the gratification of his unholy passion he was prepared to violate alike the laws of God and man—the sanctity of his order, and the innocence he should have guarded.

The great bell of the cathedral tolled the hour of midnight as he rose from the table where he had been carousing in solitary sin, and directed his steps towards the tower where his prisoner was confined.

The chamber of Hester was a long disused oratory, of an octagonal form, each side containing an arch quaintly carved in stone. In the one opposite to the door an altar formerly stood, but the steps which led to it, together with the crucifix, carved in the wall itself, remained; the former having, perhaps, been too cumbrous to be removed. To the left of the entrance was a strongly grated window, which by day alone gave light to the apartment. The arch facing it had formerly conducted to another recess, in which most probably a similar window had been situated, but it was now blocked by a solid screen of coarse oak panel work, on which some faint attempts at ornament had carelessly been traced. A lamp, suspended from the ceiling by an iron chain, shed a feeble light upon the kneeling person of the fair Jewess, whose pale cheek and sunken eye showed the mental torture to which she had been subjected by her impious persecutor. But if the maiden's eye was hollow, its brightness was not dimmed. In her enthusiastic nature she regarded the trials to which she was exposed as sent to test her faith, for which she would have sacrificed her innocent blood with joy, and like the Christian virgins in the first ages of the church, have hailed the martyr's crown as the proudest boon which Heaven could bestow.

Still, despite her courage, and the confidence which she felt in her delivery, even though it should prove by death, from the loathsome offers of her persecutor, the human portion of her nature trembled as the door of her prison opened, and the excited Eborard, still under the influence of wine, entered the apartment. Having first secured the door, he placed his torch upon the ground, and for a few moments surveyed his victim in silence. It was a picture angels might have wept to witness: a priest of the Most High meditating sin, and purity unarmed, except by prayer. The priest was the first to break the silence.

"Maiden," he murmured, in a voice thick with emotion, "the hour has arrived which decides the fate of both of us. Why didst thou cross my path? Till I beheld thee my dreams were but of ambition—my days of calm content. I have appealed to reason, and reason fleeth from me; religion mocks my prayer. Grant me thy love, and all that wealth can purchase, hope desire, or man achieve, are thine."

"All?" replied the Jewess scornfully; "all save Heaven."

"We will make earth our heaven," replied Eborard. "Our paradise shall rival Eden's bowers—its fierce delights fall with reviving freshness on thy heart, truer than the dull, placid dream which angels dream. Hast thou no pity in thy nature? Can a form so framed for love enshrine a heart of stone? Name but the price at which I may attain thee, I'll ransack earth to find it. This heart, so cold to all, hath now become love's glowing temple, and thou the idol of its shrine. Thou art my life—my destiny!—I live but in thy smile. Be merciful."

"Be merciful unto thyself," replied Hester, "and cast this hateful passion like a leprous garment from thee. What have I done, that thou shouldst strive to scare my unfledged soul from its salvation? Why seek to change the light of my young days to darkness so profound no after ray of hope can pierce it? Thou art a teacher of thy people, a shepherd of thy fold; lead not the steps of thy people astray; act not like the fell wolf unto thy charge. God," she added, "let not this man's wickedness shake my new-born faith! let not his triumph make me doubt e'en thee! Save me from him, and him from his weak self!"

"Thou prayest in vain," said the apostate with increasing resolution; "not Heaven itself can save thee. I tell thee, maid, thou wert created mine, ages before this world was framed—twin stars, loved in heaven, and at last were, in time's fulness, born on earth in form of frail humanity. With restless love I've sought the sacred partner of my soul. Beauty's light hath beamed athwart my path, but never touched my heart; music's voice wanted thy breath to give it melody. I cannot live but in thy presence. Thou wert not sure created to destroy me, or, if thou wert," he added with increased excitement, at the same time seizing her by the arm, and attempting to enfold her in his accursed embrace, "the same bolt shall crush us both; but ere it falls thou shalt be mine!"

"Release me!" shrieked the trembling girl, vainly attempting to free herself from his passionate hold, "I am but a child; think on thy priestly vow. Hath Heaven no aid? or are its thunders silent?"

"This is coyness," whispered Eborard; "soon wilt thou laugh at these old prejudices, and thank love's teacher for the gentle violence which woos thee to happiness. These struggles," he added, tearing aside the veil which shrouded her virgin form, "do but accelerate my triumph."

The wretched girl strove with almost superhuman strength against the attempts of the apostate priest, whose excitement increased with every convulsion of her graceful form. Placing his hand upon her waist, he endeavoured to polute her lips with his detested kiss. Horror gave additional force to her frantic efforts; and, thrusting him from her, she sprang upon the steps beneath the crucifix. Clasping the sacred emblem as her last refuge, she exclaimed, in a voice which woke the silent echoes of her dungeon :—

"Priest of God, darest thou brave thy Master ?"

For a few moments the wretched man was appalled. With the confiding confidence of an infant clinging to its parent, Hester embraced the crucifix; her eyes lit with the confidence of faith—her dishevelled tresses veiling the bosom whose modest covering the rude hand of her persecutor had torn aside.

"Ay, even there," cried Eborard, the dark passions of his evil nature doubly inflamed by the contest, and disappointed—"even there will I claim thee. If Heaven hath thunders, let it strike and save thee."

"It hath !" exclaimed a solemn voice, whose deep tones transfixed the guilty wretch with terror, as he was about to drag his victim from her last protection; "Heaven hath heard, and by its servant answers thee."

At the same instant the rude oak panelling was drawn aside—being, in fact, a concealed door, whose existence was known only to the prior—and Lanfranc the primate, attended by the members of the chapter, Ulrick, and Gilbert, all of whom had been concealed witnesses of the impious scene, entered the apartment. The stern brow of the prelate was dark with horror and indignation at the sacrilege he had heard, the profanation which had been attempted.

"Saved ! saved !" said the Jewess, in a voice of enthusiastic gratitude, as she sank, upon her knees. "In Heaven hath been my trust, and Heaven hath not deserted me."

"Lost ! lost !" murmured Eborard, slowly recovering from his surprise, and not daring to meet the primate's indignant gaze; "the arm I braved hath struck me down at last."

In an instant Ulrick and Gilbert were at the side of Hester, whom they raised from her attitude of thanksgiving. At the sight of her friends, the energy which had so well sustained her through the fearful scene gave way, and, drooping her head upon the manly breast of her protector, she wept as sisters weep upon a brother's breast. Meanwhile, four of the monks secured the person of their apostate superior.

"Wretch !" said Lanfranc, advancing to Eborard, and tearing the golden chain and cross, the emblems of his episcopal rank from his unworthy neck; "as legate of the pope, I here degrade thee; deprive the of all authority and jurisdiction in the now widowed church; suspend thee from all priestly functions. Away with him to prison."

"Thou art mine enemy," replied the wretched man, recovering some portion of his former audacity, "and leagued with these, the rebel inmates of my convent, to destroy me. I appeal from thee unto the king."

The prior and monks listened with horror and astonishment to the accusation, mixed with some uneasiness, for they well knew his influence with the monarch, whose interference might still screen his unworthy favourite and impose him on them; but they knew not the character of the primate, who listened to the culprit unmoved.

"And what canst thou urge," demanded Lanfranc, pointing to Hester, "against the maiden's accusation ?"

"That she is an infidel—her oath against a Christian prelate will not be believed."

"What to these witnesses, the members of thy chapter ?"

"That they are mine enemies, who have rebelled against me," answered the unblushing apostate.

"And to me ?" continued the primate, willing to see how far his infamy would lead him; "what canst thou urge against my oath ?"

"Thy well known opposition to my consecration—thy insolent remonstrance with the king," replied the prisoner, hope once more beginning to dawn within his subtle mind. "Fallen as thou thinkst me, William will not forget the service I have rendered him. His powerful hand will find the means, despite thy enmity, to raise me."

"Fool !" said the archbishop, calmly, "thou dost but precipitate thy doom. Nor king nor prince shall ever judge between us. As primate, already have I suspended thee from every priestly function; as legate, I excommunicate thee; I cast thee from out the living church—cancel thy share in its inheritance. Appeal," he added, "to thy unworthy master : see if his arm be strong enough to break the curse of Rome, or cancel the sentence which I here pronounce."

All present listened to the denunciations of the speaker with a sacred terror, so univeral was the dread of excommunication in that unenlightened age. Men whispered it with fear and trembling, shrinking from the unhappy wretch on whom it fell, as from a pestilence whose slightest contact was pollution—a living corpse doomed to eternal death.

The guilty Eborard, overwhelmed and crushed by the last act of stern justice of Lanfranc, felt that every hope indeed was gone, and permitted himself to be dragged unresistingly away by those who but an hour since had trembled at his frown.

"Approach, poor girl," said the primate, addressing Hester, who still clung to Ulrick, as to a brother's side; "nay, fear not, maid —all are not wolves who guard the fold. If our voice be stern in judgments on the guilty, it is rich in blessings on a soul like thine. I bless thee!" added the old man, laying his hand upon her head, as she knelt, trembling with awe and gratitude, at his feet; "I bless thee out of Zion. Angels have watched thy heart to guard its purity, and blessed martyrs smiled upon thy triumph. The church shall receive thee, stray one, to its bosom, e'en as a mother welcomes her lost child. These hands shall pour the regenerating waters of baptism upon thine innocent head; and never shall they be raised in prayer or benediction, but thou, fair child, shalt be remembered."

The heart of Hester was too full of gratitude to Heaven to permit her tongue to express her thankfulness, but the warm tear which fell upon the venerable hand which had been extended in blessings over her spoke to the prelate's heart more eloquently than e'en her lips had done.

It was morning ere the rescued convert, escorted by Ulrick and the now happy Gilbert, returned to Stanfield, where Hester was received both by Edith and Matilda with the expression of the warmest love. Again and again was the wondrous tale of her deliverance repeated, and the youth called upon to explain his share in it. It seems that on perusing the letters of which he was the bearer, both from the prior and the mysterious recluse, the primate at once proposed to accompany the messenger to Norwich, to witness with his own eyes the truth of the fearful accusation placed within his hands. The rest is easily understood. Lanfranc and Gilbert were the two Carmelite friars who had claimed hospitality at the convent, and whose arrival had so impressed the community; for the simple russet gown could not veil the prelate's stately form, or dim the lustre of his searching eye. The members of the chapter alone were entrusted with the secret of his presence; and by them the arrangements were planned which led to Eborard's detection, even in the moment when it seemed least possible to those who calculate not that the ways of Heaven are unlike the ways of man.

On applying on the following morning for an interview with Eborard, Falk was conducted to the presence of the archbishop, who explained to him that his daughter was no longer a prisoner, and that in two days he should himself receive her into the bosom of the church. The unhappy man, overwhelmed with the intelligence, to him ten thousand times more terrible than death, withdrew, like one stunned, from the primate's presence. He saw too well the stern, sincere character of the speaker to tempt him by that universal

key to the human heart, gold; for in Lanfranc's heart it was but dust, when weighed against the triumph of his church, or the redemption of a human soul.

"Christian!" muttered the Hebrew to himself, as he directed his steps across the plain of St. Martin on his way to the city. "The curse never fell upon my house till now. Our blood hath been shed like water, but it was the sacrifice of faith; our gold hath been wrung from us by torture, oppression, and the rack; but now the richest pearl is taken from us—the fairest flower is torn from Judah's stem. Our name will become a byeword on our nation's lips—a scorn, a shame to Israel. Never!" he added, bitterly. "If the degenerate girl can thus forget her duty to her kindred and her father, he will not forget his oath to Israel's God, or that he is a judge and elder of his people."

Full of stern resolution, he directed his steps towards the market-place, where, by the corner of the church, dwelt a dealer in drugs, one of his own peculiar race. Hassack was known, not only to the city, but all the country round, for his curious skill in herbs and simples. Many a greedy heir had sought his aid; and the parent whose length of days was a check upon his will career slumbered in peace; the unfaithful wife removed the jealous husband, the perjured lover the victim of his passions. Unscrupulous, and caring for nought but gold, the amassing of which formed the only pleasure of his withered heart, Hassack's skill was at the disposition of all who could gratify his ruling passion. So crude were the tests which science has since perfected, that the detection of poison was almost impossible; and the murderer pursued his guilty trade, suspected but in safety—too many great ones whom he had served being bound to interest themselves in his protection. Just as Falk reached the dingy, wretched-looking spot where the poisoner retailed his drugs and nostrums, he encountered the recluse, to whom he had formerly been known, having in his days of extravagance and pride frequently advanced him money upon his knightly bond. Fortunately the change which Abram's vengeance had wrought in him precluded the possibility of a recognition; the pale, agitated countenance of the Jew excited his attention; and crossing to the old stone pulpit, near which, in Catholic times, the priests and monks used to address their flocks, and the proclamations of the city authorities were made, he hid himself behind one of the heavy pillars, to watch his proceedings, which an instinctive feeling told him were dangerous to the life of Hester, and consequently to the happiness of Gilbert. After half an hour's converse, the old man quitted the den, the character of whose owner was well known to the observant spy, who marked the sigh of deep drawn agony which broke from the bosom of the wretched father as he passed him. As soon as he was out of sight, the recluse, in his turn, entered the house of Hassack. At first the conversation between him and its master was violent, but the Jew's tone of defiance gradually subsided to one of deference, and at last to entreaty. For once he found his master.

Lights were blazing on the high altar of Norwich Cathedral, and the font was decked with earliest flowers of spring, on the morning of the day which was to receive the fair Hester into the bosom of the church, which put forth on the occasion that imposing pomp which no ritual has ever yet equalled either in grandeur or sublimity.

Despite the silence which had been observed respecting the sacrilegious conduct of the unworthy Eborard—and the silence of the cloister is proverbial—strange rumours, connecting his name with that of the youthful Jewess, were rife amongst the people,—rumours which the absence of the suspended prelate from the service at which the primate had twice publicly officiated only tended to confirm. At an early hour the vast aisles were crowded by the curious citizens and their buxom wives and daughters. Many of the latter had heard wonderful descriptions of the neophite's beauty, and most of them came, woman-like, to criticise and to compare. A few, and but a few, came for the nobler purpose of joining in the hymn of triumph for a soul redeemed from error.

Amongst the crowd of spectators was an aged man, bent more by sorrow than by age, whose compressed lips and blanched cheek gave but faint indications of the fearful struggle passing in his breast,—a struggle which rent his very entrails with its anguish, maddened his reeling brain, and whispered him despair. Disguised in the loose gown and hood then commonly worn by the superior class of citizens, the miserable Falk —for it was no other than the father of the convert—had been one or the first to enter the church, where the discovery of his presence would probably have caused his death. He had seen with a bitter smile the decoration of the font, to him the altar of sacrifice, and remained to await the completion of the rite which was to sever him for ever, as he thought, from the child of his age, and bring shame and humiliation upon his name and race.

The procession at last approached: first came four boys clothed in long white rochets, tossing the silver censers from side to side,

filling the air with costly perfumes; then a monk bearing the primate's cross; after him the priests and brothers of the community, headed by the prior holding his staff of office. A shade of sorrow was on the good man's brow, for he thought on the dishonour which the church had received in the crimes of his late unworthy superior, Lanfranc, adorned with the insignia of his high office, closed the procession, walking under a canopy borne by four knights. As the prelate proceeded along the aisles, he scattered his benediction on the kneeling crowd, which rose and sank like an undulating wave as he approached and passed them. But the principal object of all eyes was the fair convert, who, clothed in white and veiled by drapery, was led by her sponsors, Ulrick and Matilda, towards the sacred font. Gilbert watched her approach with the same delight with which an infant might, in the early ages of creation, ere sin had drawn its curtain between men and the bright beings of another world, have watched an angel's steps. His heart was almost too full for breathing, his happiness far too great for words; yet a few moments, and Hester, his boyhood's hope, his earliest dream of love, would become a partaker of the same faith—the same hope as himself. The recluse, who felt a deeper interest in the proceedings of the day than any yet suspected, watched his excited looks, and, for reasons best known unto himself, determined not to lose sight of him.

The venerable primate had already poured the regenerating waters, and pronounced the words whose might opens the gates of the lost inheritance of Adam to his fallen race, when a loud cry startled the more distant spectators. Hester was seen to sink into the arms of Matilda and Isabel, who with her husband had graced the solemnity with their presence. At first they thought that the young Christian, overcome by her emotions, had fainted; but the increased agitation of those around her, and the astonishment of the priests, many of whom in their zeal were disposed to cry "A miracle!" soon convinced them that something far more singular had happened. The voice of Matilda at last was heard distinctly to exclaim, in accents of anguish and terror:

"Alas! she is dying—she is dying!"

"Dying!" re-echoed the crowd, impatiently, pressing nearer to obtain a view of what was passing.

"Dying!" shrieked Gilbert, thrusting those who stood between him and Hester aside; "let me once more behold her, that her image may be impressed on my young heart—its first and latest idol."

Despite the resistance of the crowd, the

agitated youth broke through the compact mass, and rushed into the circle which, overwhelmed with grief and horror, surrounded the apparently dying Hester. The wreath of flowers and veil had been removed from her fair brow, and her long dark tresses, damp with the regenerating stream, contrasted fearfully with her pale cheek; her eyes were closed, and large tears hung on their soft silken fringes. As the innocent child lay with her head pillowed upon Matilda's gentle breast, she looked like Purity expiring in the arms of Religion.

" 'Tis past!" exclaimed Lanfranc, signing the cross over the unconscious girl; "Heaven has claimed its own."

"She is not dead," murmured Gilbert, his voice choked with the deep agony which consumed him. "Cold as she was to earthly passion, she could not leave me without one look for memory to treasure in its cell—one word, to break at once the heart her gentle nature was too merciful to crush, and leave to linger in an unpitying world. Hester," he added, taking her hand, and fixing his despairing eyes upon her already rigid features, "hear the voice of my agony, the cry of my broken hope. A look, a word, a sign for the poor boy whose love was like the love which angels feel, on whose dull path no future ray of happiness may shine."

It seemed as if the sound of his voice had arrested her pure soul for a moment in its flight, or that its guardian spirit, with a human tear, permitted it one moment to return to grant the boon he asked. As if waking from a heavy sleep, Hester opened once more her veiled eyes, and cast on the speaker a glance, such as a dying sister might bestow upon an only brother—a glance where the sorrow of parting, where piety and love were unstained by human passion or regret.

As the maid sank with all the rigidity of death into the arms which supported her, the primate motioned to his attendants to remove the frantic Gilbert from the church—an office which they accomplished with firmness, but with kindness, closing the gates to prevent his return.

The unhappy youth plunged into the wood which lay between the cathedral and the river. Despair was in his heart, and madness in his eye; but there was one who read his purpose—his guardian genius hovered near him. The recluse, who had followed him from the church, was hard upon his footsteps.

Another yet more wretched being left the cathedral at the same instant as Gilbert—the unhappy Falk, whose bigotry had, as our readers have doubtless long ere this suspected,

plotted the death of his daughter at the very moment of her conversion. The claims of his nation and abandoned faith to vengeance were even to his morbid mind completely satisfied; but now a new avenger, the father, awoke within him—nature spoke with a voice which neither sophistry, anger nor superstition could silence. Hester was his only girl—had been the light of his solitude—the pupil of his leisure hours; and he loved her as all men love the thing they teach—as old men love the children of their age.

The priests had already commenced the litanies for the dead, when the calm voice of Lanfranc, who had recovered his usual composure, interrupted them.

"Not the prayer of intercession, brothers, but the hymn of triumph. Heaven hath taken the maiden to itself ere sin or human passion had time to sully with their breath the seal of redemption upon her unpolluted brow; we have seen an angel wing its flight to heaven, claiming its new-won heritage, and not a sinner trusting for pardon, part doubtful on its way. Bear her to the church, strew flowers before her, as for its virgin bride, and raise the song of joy."

In the enthusiasm of the moment, the young maidens who had come to witness the ceremony of Hester's admission into the Christian pale raised the inanimate body in their arms, and bore it to the high altar, before which a bier had been hastily arranged; others strewed flowers, as the primate directed, in their way; while the attendant clergy rose the solemn song with which the church marks its rejoicings and consecrates its triumphs:

" *Te Deum Laudamus te*,
Rejoice and raise the grateful strain,
Heaven from earth a soul shall gain,
Scatter the incense round,
Salvation's news to Israel tell,
The church's note of triumph swell,
And the pealing anthem sound.

To Deum Laudamus te,
She comes, she comes, lost Judah's child,
No more from Thee and heaven exiled,
We bear before Thy shrine,
'Tis done—life's early threshold past,
The Hebrew maid redeemed at last,
Is sealed for ever thine."

The multitude joined in the strain; and the service, which was begun in the baptismal rite, ended with the dirge for the dead. At a late hour in the evening, at the request of Hester's protector, the body was removed to Stanfield, to be placed in the ancient vault of the old chapel, were Ulrick and Matilda were in the habit of offering up their daily supplications for the repose of their murdered fathers' souls. After the service they had

THE INTERVIEW BETWEEN GILBERT AND THE JEWESS.

retired to the oratory, as usual, indulging in that deep communion which hearts devoted to each other alone can know, when Gilbert, his eyes excited by hope, his lips quivering with eager emotion, followed by the recluse, entered the apartment.

CHAPTER XXVIII.

ULRICK and Matilda were both startled at the appearance of Gilbert, the wild look of happiness, amounting almost to insanity, which glistened in his eyes; his eager words cut short and broken by the deep emotion under which he laboured while endeavouring to unfold the secret which had caused him such tumultuous joy, that reason was almost shaken on its seated throne. Finding it impossible to explain himself, he sank upon his knee, and caught the hand to the latter in his, exclaiming, as he did so: "Heaven hath not yet claimed its own! Lady, she lives! Our angel lives to gladden earth with virtues all her own—lives to give sunlight to my path, and waken music once more to my ear."

"Alas!" said Matilda, in a voice of pity, "he is mad; grief hath distraught him. Poor boy! poor boy!"

Ulrick inclined to the same opinion as his wife. He looked first at Gilbert, then at the recluse, whom he recognised, despite his disguise, as the mysterious Black Knight he had so frequently seen during his own imprisonment in the camp of Rufus, and whose influence with the King he was no stranger to; indeed, from the unearthly character of his features, the once handsome Robert of Artois was now a being whom, having encountered, it was all but impossible to forget.

"He is not mad," replied the intruder, in answer to Ulrick's inquiring look. "Heaven, to permit me to atone for my crimes, has enabled me to perform one good act. Hester, the Jewess, indeed no longer exists; but Mary, the Christian, sleepeth."

Mary was the name the fair convert had received in baptism.

"Sleepeth!" repeated Matilda, in a voice which trembled between hope and incredulity.

"Sleepeth!" repeated the recluse. "I wonder not, lady, at thy incredulity; but her fate is not more wondrous than my own. Aware, from cruel experience, how bitter is the hatred, how undying the vengeance of her race, I have permitted the seeming triumph of her father's purpose to secure her safety; he and all the world, except her friends, must deem her dead; but to them— to the true hearts that love her—I again repeat, the maiden lives."

"Explain this mystery," said Ulrick; "if thy words be sooth, more welcome sounds ne'er fell upon mine ear."

"You all," resumed the narrator, "know Hassack the Jew, who vends his nostrums in the market-place?"

"We do!" impatiently answered his excited listeners.

"Also his fearful skill in poisons and such drugs as minister to the worst of passions?"

"By reputation, well."

"And I, perchance, by evil, sad experience. The day previous to Hester's baptism," continued the recluse, "I encountered her distracted father; e'en my seared heart could pity him, for I read the storm of human passion raging in his heart; bigotry contending with paternal love—vengeance

with pity—the cry of nature with the voice of hate; 'twas the mind's agony, more lasting than the body's pain, leaving scars deeper than vulgar eyes can read—burning, although unseen. I traced him to the house of the vile mediciner—saw him, with trembling hand, count down his gold—instinctively I guessed it was the price of blood."

"His child's!" exclaimed Matilda. "Impossible! Jew though he be, thou wrongst him."

"So judge the pure in heart, lady," resumed the speaker; "but so judge not those whom crime or sad necessity hath forced to watch the hearts of others—to trace deceit lurking beneath the brow of seeming frankness—falsehood peeping through the mask of truth—the voice of cruelty with mercy's accents burning on its lips. Reason tells us what men should be; bitter experience shows us what they are. What followed proves I judged the Jew and his rash purpose rightly."

There was a tone of sarcasm and subdued passion in the voice of the recluse, which startled the ear of Matilda; she felt confident that she had heard its sound before; it woke an echo in her heart at which memory trembled; but was confused, for not one feature of the wretched man could she recal to mind. Fixing her eyes upon him almost with a look of terror, she involuntarily exclaimed:—

"Surely we have met before."

The scared brow of her ancient persecutor flushed as if he had heard an accusing angel's voice; but his repentance was too sincere to equivocate or deny the truth. Feeling that the time for revealing himself had not yet arrived, he contented himself by simply admitting that they had.

"When and where?" demanded the lady, with increased interest and curiosity.

"That, too, ere I quit this land for ever, thou shalt learn; this present hour permit me to proceed. On Falk's departure from the poisoner's den, I entered. It matters little to my story by what means I forced him to confess the purpose of the old man's visit; enough, he did confess it. It was to bribe him to prepare a liquid, which, mixed with the water in the sacred font, would cause the death of all upon whose brow 'twas sprinkled."

"Villain!" cried Gilbert; "unnatural monster! e'en at the gate of heaven to sacrifice his child!"

"Why not have denounced the fearful sacrilege?" demanded Ulrick, who, with the horror-stricken Edith and Matilda, listened with anxious heart for the conclusion of his tale.

"Denounced him?" repeated the recluse.

"Little dost thou know the fearful race. For good or ill they far surpass the dogged bloodhound in unwearying patience; the snake is not more subtle in its windings, the tiger more ferocious in its spring. I was born noble as the noblest in my land, was honoured, rich in lands and friends, possessed a form the eye of beauty had not always loathed to gaze upon. In evil hour I wronged an aged Jew—a thing," he added, fiercely, "whom, in my pride of strength, I could have crushed like a vile worm beneath my feet—whose life, to human thinking, was a reed within my iron hand; and yet he vanquished me."

"Vanquished thee!" repeated Ulrick, in a tone of incredulity.

"Vanquished and judged me. Not, indeed, with knightly arms, but more than devilish cunning; deprived me of my very name—robbed me of the rights I drew e'en from my mother's womb—tore from my seared and blistered front the seal of individuality which God had stamped upon my brow—made me the wretch I am."

"Fearful man!" shrieked Matilda, "I know thee now—know why my heart trembled at they voice—why nature shuddered at thy presence. Ulrick, it is——"

"My father, lady," interrupted Gilbert, clasping her robe, "my father!"

The agitation of the poor youth, his imploring glance, and the recollection that he had saved the life of Ulrick, sealed the secret upon her lips; though how her ancient persecutor could be the parent of the speaker was a mystery she could scarcely comprehend.

"What means this strange terror," demanded Ulrick, "and still stranger recognition? However evil," he added, addressing the recluse, "I know that thou art capable of good, for thy timely warning saved Prince Henry's life."

"Then for that one good act," said Matilda, "question him no more; if he hath deeply sinned he hath been sorely punished. Unhappy man!" she added, "Heaven forgive thee; I never will accuse thee at its bar."

"Thanks, lady, thanks, for thy most generous pardon," replied the repentant man, at the same time gracefully bending his knee before her; "it will lighten the anguish of remorse in many a bitter hour. But concealment comes too late. Ulrick of Stanfield," he added, rising as he spoke, and speaking in a firm and almost haughty tone, "thou seest a man whom friends and kindred alike deem dead—a man whose dirge holy church hath long since sung—whose heritage his greedy heirs have ta'en—a man who, pander-ing to a tyrant's lust, would have aided Rufus to deprive thee of thy fair bride. I need not say the wreck of Robert of Artois stands unarmed before thee."

"Robert of Artois!" repeated Ulrick, with an air of incredulity—"impossible!"

"Why so indeed men might deem it," replied his ancient enemy, "who judge by outward show; but I repeat it—all that the Jew's vengeance left of the once reckless knight, Robert of Artois, stands before thee."

For a few moments there was a powerful struggle in Ulrick's breast. The man who had caused him so much fearful misery stood before him. The idea of injuring an unarmed man never for an instant presented itself to his imagination; but when he reflected upon his wrongs, twice did he feel tempted to bid him arm himself, and meet him knightly in the field, but each time he encountered Gilbert's pleading look and Matilda's forgiving smile. The better principle of his nature prevailed. He could not crush a heart already torn and bruised.

"Robert," he exclaimed, "friendship there can never be; let there be peace between us, however great thy crimes. Thou hast truly spoken—they have been fearfully avenged. This boy," pointing to Gilbert, "whom thou callest thy son, shall be a bond of mutual forbearance between us. On with the tale this strange discovery broke."

"Enough!" resumed Robert, as we again must call him. "I had the means to compel the poisoner to my purpose. The nature of the drug was changed, and a mixture prepared which caused the appearance of death only. From the opening of the cathedral doors I watched the arrival of each comer. Despite his disguise, I recognised the Jew, saw him stealthily pour into the font the means, as he thought, of vengeance on his child. You know the rest."

"Let us haste," said Matilda, "to the vault; should the poor child awake amid the horrors of the charnel-house, reason might totter on its throne."

"Fear not for that," observed the preserver of Hester; "since I alone possess the power to wake her."

He drew from his vest a small box filled with a pungent aromatic as he spoke,

"Come, father," cried Gilbert, impatiently, "to the vault—the vault."

"Caution, boy," said Robert, calmly; "for we have to contend with those who know no scruple where their vengeance is concerned; the hatred of her race would reach the maiden e'en at the altar's foot, should they once suspect her life has been preserved. Can you," he added, addressing

Ulrick, "answer for the caution of all within these walls ?"

"All," replied our hero; "there is not one in Stanfield but loves the maiden for her gentleness and virtue; but as already the shades of night draw on, it were better, perchance, to wait till the household are retired to rest ere we descend into the chapel. For a few days Hester can remain concealed within my wife's apartments; none can enter unbidden there; we can afterwards consult the means of safety—now our first step must be to rescue her."

Ulrick's proposition was too reasonable to be rejected; and, despite the impatient eagerness of Gilbert and the anxiety of Matilda, the party remained within the antique oratory waiting the hour of midnight. Never did the tardy foot of time advance more slowly than to the excited watchers. At last the turret-clock struck the hour, and our hero and Robert of Artois, each taking a waxen torch from the iron sconces in the walls, prepared to descend.

The chapel of Stanfield was a low, irregular building of unhewn stone, of even greater antiquity than the hall itself, its architecture being of the earliest Saxon age. Rude stone coffins, containing the ashes of many of its ancient lords, from their ponderous size more resembling tombs than sarcophagi, were ranged in the aisles, in deep recesses cut within the walls. The one in which Hester had been enclosed was in a niche nearest to the altar. Over it frowned the image of some long-forgotten saint :

Carved in grey stone and cunning work,
The labour of some rustic sculptor's hand.

As the party entered the quaint old edifice, their torches flashed upon the salient points of the building, lighting the massive shrines with a dim, religious light, which brought them into a faint relief, and cast broad, deep shadows, such as Rembrandt would have loved, upon the roughly jointed pavement. In fact, the scene was one equally suited for the poet or the painter :

Regardless of the night's dull gloom,
They cast around a curious gaze
On low broad arch and massive tomb
Seen by the red light's flickering rays.
Saints in sculptured stone were there,
Whose spirits in the noiseless air
        Watched o'er the sacred pile.
At this perchance the world may deem
My words a visionary's dream,
        Philosophy may smile;
But if communion e'er be given
With beings less of earth than heaven,
        'Tis in some lone hour, when
The relics of long ages past,
Their shadows o'er the rapt soul cast,
        Our thoughts are spirits then.

"How still and solemn is the night!" whispered Matilda, who, despite her husband's entreaty, had insisted on accompanying them upon their expedition; "not a breath of air sighs through the vaults of the old chapel. The very echoes of our footsteps fall noiseless as the feet of Time upon eternity's dull sand. Yet here sleeps one," she added, advancing from the entrance of the chapel, where, with the rest of the party, she had paused to contemplate the scene, and pointing to the tomb of Hester, "whom, living or dead, his breath cannot corrupt, whose nobler essence his scythe cannot destroy, for her mortal covering was no more to Hester than the casket to the gem it guards and holds."

"True!" exclaimed the recluse; "and from this bed of death—this living tomb, replete with life and beauty, shall arise creation's masterpiece, pure, lovely woman. Whilst all is silent, let us hasten to hurl back the ponderous stone, and wake her back to life and its warm ties—its tears, humanities, and tendernesses—if possible, to love."

As pale as monumental marble, Gilbert was standing by the tomb; life and passion seemed to have deserted his cold cheek; his heart was too full for words—one would have broken it; a tear would have been a blessing, and yet he could not weep. Rooted he stood, like a statue, by the spot—animation and life suspended in the deep struggles of doubt and hope.

"Aid me," said Ulrick, drawing from his vest a bar of iron, which he had brought with him for the purpose, and at the same time placing his torch in the hands of Matilda; "should the poor girl awake within her tomb, it were too much for reason; aid me to lift the stone."

By the repeated efforts of the speaker and the recluse—for Gilbert remained perfectly incapable of rendering the least assistance—the ponderous lid of the coffin was at length removed, and the fair form of the inmate met their gaze. Her countenance was as calm as that of an angel sleeping. The flowers with which affection had strewed her resting-place were still unfaded. Her hand, Matilda thought, grasped the silver crucifix, which the primate himself had placed upon her breast, as if to press the image of her Saviour nearer to her heart. Stooping, she imprinted a kiss upon the sleeper's brow, and felt, as she did so, more than a dawn of hope, for a gentle moisture, different from the cold, clammy dew of death, remained upon her lips.

At the sight of the being whom he so tenderly, passionately, though hopelessly, loved, the spell which had bound the senses of Gilbert was broken. With a loud cry he flung himself at the foot of the coffin, and called upon her, with a thousand endearing expressions, to awake and gladden those who loved her by her presence.

"Wake, Hester!" he exclaimed, "that earth may once more gladden in thy smile. Wake, and save me from the living death, which existence without hope or love must bring. Wake," he continued, in a strain of yet deeper passion, "though but to enshrine thy beauty in a cloister. I still might hover round thy home, as restless spirits pine around Eden's gates. Wake," he added, with a cry of despair, seeing that his adjurations were unanswered, "e'en though it be to smile upon another, to break the heart whose idol thou hast been, and whose last words shall bless thee."

"Patience, Gilbert," said Ulrick, laying his hand kindly upon his shoulder; "prayers and tears are for the dead, and Hester, I trust, is living. See, her brow is unchanged, the rose on her lips unfaded; be firm, and wait with patience."

"She'll wake no more," groaned the excited boy; "Death is too greedy of his prey to resign so fair a victim—heaven too proud of such a conquest to yield back the brightest angel of its virgin choir. Father," he added, wildly, "thou hast deceived me—broken alike thy faith and my torn heart; for this is death—not sleep—not sleep."

The recluse, deeply moved by his son's agitation, drew from his vest a small silver box, which he carefully opened, and poured a portion of its highly aromatic contents upon a sponge. So powerful was the perfume that the chapel was filled with the sweet odour. Placing the sponge in the hand of Gilbert, he said—

"Apply it to her brow and nostrils: the subtle incense will evaporise the foul drug which holds the maiden in this lethargy. Be firm; trust to thy father's word—he will not fail thee, boy."

Eagerly did his son receive the precious gift, and kneeling by the side of the fair girl, applied it, as he was directed, to her brow and nostrils. The effect was slow but curious; no sooner did the essence come in contact with the spots where the poisoned water had fallen, than a thin vapour was seen to arise from the sleeper's skin, a profuse perspiration followed, and, to the inexpressible joy of all, a deep-drawn sigh proved that the breath of life was not extinct within her form.

"Thank Heaven!" whispered Matilda, who had watched the process with intense interest as well as hope, "she breathes." Had not a flood of tears come to her relief, she must have fainted, so violent had been her emotion.

At last, to the frantic delight of Gilbert, Hester slowly opened her eyes, but as if overcome by the light of the torches round the coffin, or oppressed by the soporific influence of the drug, heavily closed them again: her lips moved twice—nothing but inarticulate sounds, however, broke from them.

"Hush," said Ulrick, "she would speak—there again," he added, at the second effort.

"Gilbert!" faintly murmured the waking girl, again opening her eyes, and fixing them upon the youth.

"She speaks!" he shrieked, starting from his knees, and raising her in his arms. "Heaven hath heard its wretched creature's prayer—the cry of his lone agony—the voice of his bruised heart. God!" he added, "dares the impious wretched who doubted of thy mercy, dares he thank thee?"

Matilda received the scarcely awakened girl within her arms from Gilbert, who reluctantly resigned her; so greedy did he feel of the privilege of once more supporting her weak, trembling form, that he felt jealous of resigning it even to one of her own sex.

"Let us quit this gloomy place," said Matilda, in her turn resigning the precious burthen to her husband's stalwart arm. "Bear her to my chamber; she is cold—but half recovered still. I and my women are the best nurses now."

The proposal was too rational to be opposed even by Gilbert, who entreated, however, to be permitted to kiss her hand ere Ulrick bore her from the chapel. He had the happiness of again hearing her murmur his name as she was carried from him, a circumstance which neither Matilda nor her husband failed to remark.

On the following day, when Gilbert was admitted to the presence of Hester, he observed with joy the faint blush of pleasure which suffused her cheek as he entered the chamber. Our readers will remember the effort which she made at the moment of her supposed death to open her sealed eyes—the look she had cast upon him—the half murmured expression of his name. The cry of his despairing love had waked an echo in her heart never heard till then; and the same name had been the first word her lips pronounced when recalled from the living tomb to which she had been consigned. Living it might indeed be called, for, although animation had been suspended, consciousness had all the while remained. She remembered the death-dirge which had been chanted over her, had felt the warm tears of Matilda as she imprinted the parting kiss upon her brow, and endured for four-and-twenty hours all the terrors of the grave; felt, in anticipation, the earthworm preying on her beating heart. Vain had been all her efforts either to move or speak; the drug was too potent for her will to break: every faculty seemed changed to stone; she felt like a living statue imprisoned in a rock.

In the desolation of her loneliness the memory of Gilbert had returned to her—his boyish but devoted love—the agony of his parting look—and the first feeling of love engendered in her heart, as it faintly beat within its sepulchre. Many days had not elapsed before the ardent youth obtained from her the confession that she was content to live for him, that gratitude had given birth to a yet warmer passion.

How sweet, how exciting is the sensation when first the lip of woman tells us we are beloved! The soul expands, it merges into a new existence. The flowers appear more fragrant to the sense; earth seems full of music; we hear its melodies in every murmuring wind or babbling brook, catch beauty from the stars, revel in nature's harmonies, and find a shrine in every nook and dell. Pity the heart can feel the spell but once! Other and fairer lips may breathe the words again, but they will never fall so sweetly on the ear as when man hears them first.

For days Gilbert was plunged in this intoxicating bliss. When driven from the chamber by Matilda's anxious care, he wandered in the umbrageous woods of Stanfield, told to the trees his tale of happiness, or whispered it to every running stream. Hester was soon sufficiently recovered to share his walks; and often at the evening hour, deeply veiled, accompanied by Ulrick and Matilda, she would venture forth to catch fresh health from the pure breeze of heaven.

The Lord of Stanfield felt it to be his duty to inform the venerable primate, whom the proceedings which necessarily followed Eborard's deposition detained in the city, of the wonderful recovery of Mary; for it is by her Christian name that we shall henceforth designate the beautiful convert. The good man listened with astonishment to the strange tale, with indulgent kindness to the history of her love. Stern only to himself, his heart was not insensible to the happiness of others; and after a long interview with Robert of Artois, in which that unhappy man revealed to him under the seal of confession the secret of Gilbert's birth, Lanfranc not only gave his approbation to the marriage, but offered himself to visit Stanfield, and secretly to celebrate the rite. Addressing himself to Ulrick, as he bade him farewell, he said—

"Heaven, it seems, hath designed them for each other, and mine shall not be the voice to part them. Go," he added; "in five days I will meet you at your ancestral home. There shall their love be consecrated by the church's blessing; that done, let them quit England, and for ever. The unnatural fury of her father, should he discover that his child yet lives, may else prove fatal to her, despite a husband's watchful care and love."

It were needless to describe the ecstasy of Gilbert or the blushes of Mary when they heard the primate's decision; the first was wild with joy, the latter calm in the deep sentiment of her happiness—a happiness she was too pure a child of nature to conceal, too artless to deny—a happiness which their friends witnessed with a joy but second to their own.

Our readers may remember that on the retirement of Robert of Normandy from England, Mirvan, whose principal possessions, as well as those of his bride, were situated in that country, resolved to follow him, being too much disgusted with William's tyranny to accept him as his sovereign. With the consent of both princes he had succeeded in exchanging his English fiefs for estates of equal value in the land of his fathers, where it was his intention to sail, as soon as Ralph de Gael, his successor as governor of the city, should arrive. Under his protection it was decided that Gilbert and his young bride should retire to Normandy, where, with the wealth which Robert of Artois had rescued from his unworthy uncle, they could live in happiness, if not in splendour. Fain would Ulrick and Matilda have accompanied them, but they were bound to England by other ties and other claims. Edith and the venerable Edda still lived to claim their care.

The day at last arrived which was to unite the youthful lovers in those indissoluble bonds which death alone can break. Faithful to his promise, the venerable Lanfranc arrived at Stanfield; the chapel was secretly prepared, and at midnight, in the presence of Ulrick and Matilda, the nuptial benediction was pronounced. Three days afterwards the happy pair sailed under the protection of Mirvan and Isabel for Normandy, their future home of love and happiness. The letter which their kind protector furnished them with for the duke ensured them a princely welcome, and Gilbert gradually rose to offices of trust and honour. As the party were assembled on the Denes at Yarmouth, watching the arrival of the boat which was to convey them to their ship, the happy bridegroom was made aware that his separation from his father was to be eternal. To all his remonstrances the repentant Robert of Artois answered that his resolution was fixed, and that his future days, under the approbation of the primate, were devoted to his God alone.

"Go, my children," he added, "and if the blessing of a guilty man may weigh with heaven, mine shall fall like its soft dews upon your innocent heads! Whether in the cloister's shade or the far distant plains of Palestine, my last thoughts will be of you; my latest prayers be yours! Farewell! Pray that at the judgment seat of the Most High we all may meet again!"

There is nothing more painful to the heart than the bitter task of bidding adieu to those we love; linger over it as we will, the fatal word must at last be spoken. Happily the agony it occasions is seldom lasting, or o'ercharged nature would succumb beneath the pain. Still it was long, very long, ere the sundered friends forgot the anguish of that sad hour. Mary clung to Ulrick and Matilda, with all the passionate grief which an infant feels when separated from the parents who have loved it. The former was at last obliged to untwine her arms from the agitated Matilda's neck, and place her in the boat where, on the shoulder of her equally affectionate Gilbert, her sorrow gradually exhausted itself in tears and prayers for the generous beings who had so warmly sheltered and protected her.

As the vessel receded from their view the primate bestowed his benediction on the exiles; it accompanied them on their journey over the deep waters, even to the country of their future home: the good man's prayers were heard in heaven.

Three months after the scene we have endeavoured to describe Matilda became a mother, and the joy which she and Ulrick both felt as they clasped their infant daughter to their breasts blunted the edge of their regret. The aged Edda lived long enough to hold the little stranger at the font: perhaps, in the secret wishes of his heart, he would rather it had been a boy; but as its parents were both young enough to be the authors of a numerous race, he concealed his disappointment, and expired in the arms of his grandson—blessing him and the infant shoot whose graceful maturity he was not destined to witness. Seven years afterwards a second daughter completed the domestic happiness of our hero, who welcomed it with as fond a smile as though it had been a son destined to bear to distant time the noble name and manly virtues of his father.

Robert had acted wisely in exacting from his brother William the oath of his race with regard to the safety of the Lord of Stanfield. Although frequently urged by his unworthy minion Tyrrel—whose hatred of Ulrick since the dreadful interview in the tent had, if possible, increased—to exert the regal power to oppress him, the king remained faithful to his vow; the fearful penalty which he superstitiously believed attached to its violation he dared not brave. Securely seated on the throne, he even permitted the return of his younger brother, Prince Henry, to England, where he doled out to him at intervals the scanty appanage which the Conqueror had left him.

Rufus had reigned about eight years, when the death of Lanfranc rendered the primacy vacant: an occasion which the greedy monarch eagerly seized for regaining its revenues in his hands, as he had already done those of several other vacant bishoprics; but falling into a dangerous sickness, he was seized with remorse; and the clergy representing to him that he was in danger of eternal perdition if he did not make atonement, he sent for Anselm, Abbot of Bec, who, our readers will remember, had been one of his brother's most devoted partisans. The churchman, on his arrival, humbly refused the dignity—fell upon his knees, and entreated the king to change his purpose; and when he found the monarch resolved, kept his hand so closed that it required considerable violence to force him to receive the insignia of his spiritual office; but once within his grasp, he held it firmly, and William had more than once occasion to repent the choice he had made, for the new prelate was as courageous as he was incorruptible; in short, for once the tyrant had found his master. Anselm's reputation for sanctity and humility was too great for even the regal authority to venture to assail him.

In the midst of his career William had often experienced one bitter pang, the thought that on his death-bed his brother Robert, whom he detested, or Henry, who was equally the object of his aversion, would succeed him. He resolved, therefore, to marry, and secure, if possible, a direct successor to his crown. By means of spies, he discovered that his younger brother frequently visited the convent at Rumsey, where the Princess Matilda, daughter of Malcolm, the third king of Scotland, resided, under the protection of her aunt, the abbess Christina. Although, during the lifetime of her uncle and brothers, Matilda was not the heir of the Saxon line, still she was dear to the nation on account of her connection with it. Her lover—for such Prince Henry in secret was—had never forgotten the prediction of the aged monk, Father Segsil, at Croydon. Ambition had tempted him in his first visit to the convent; but the virtues and beauty of the recluse soon inspired him with a purer motive, and he loved, truly, passionately loved. Nor was it long ere he won from the fair girl's lips the confession that he was beloved again. We may imagine, therefore, his fury and despair when Tyrrel, with a malicious smile, announced to him his brother's intentions of proceeding to the convent, and to give England a queen in the person of the Saxon princess. Deeply as he felt wounded, both in love and in ambition, by the intelligence, he was too much a courtier to give his enemy the triumph of perceiving that the shaft had reached him, and he parried the thrust by demanding, in his turn, when the king was to bestow on him the so long promised earldom, which his services merited. This was a sore subject with the traitor, and he winced beneath the thrust. Despite all that he had done, and his services to William had been as varied as they were unscrupulous, the recompense was as distant as ever. The monarch still put him off with promises; nay, seemed to take a malicious pleasure in exciting his hopes only to disappoint them. Indeed, his intention in this respect was frequently so apparent, that the traitor often questioned whether the secret of his birth was not either known or guessed at by the tyrant, and the suspicion but added to his shame and disappointment.

"William will find," said Tyrrel, with a scowl, "that even my loyalty may be urged too far. He hath broken promise and oath with me; and yet the latter," he added, with a peculiar smile, "was a strange one."

"It would have been stranger," observed Prince Henry, "had he kept it. Humph!" he added, as he turned upon his heel and left the knight, "that fellow might be useful; he hath a conscience as pliant as a courtier's back."

That very night the unhappy lover sought an interview with Anselm; an achievement of no common danger, for since the recovery of his health the Red King's remorse had disappeared, and he bitterly regretted that ever he had been induced to bestow the primacy upon a character so cold and so unyielding as Anselm. Since their dispute, the episcopal palace had been continually surrounded with spies; and those nobles were sure of being visited with their monarch's displeasure who either visited or entertained relations of amity with its master. It was not, therefore, without reason that the prince took the precaution of disguising himself in a monk's gown and Capuchin to obtain access to him. Cold as Anselm was, he was not incapable of friendship. He had not forgotten the previous visits of Henry to Westminster, when he was only Abbot of Bec,

and he received him again, if not with warmth, at least with cordiality, and listened to his tale with more than common interest.

"What!" exclaimed the primate, when Henry had related his tale; "wed with a nun professed! Is William mad? or does he dream the church's thunders slumber in our land? There must be some deceit in this; he never dares attempt it."

"You mistake, venerable father," sighed the anxious lover; "Matilda is not a nun, she has only worn the veil as a protection in these lawless times, when even the altar can scarce protect its own. Her lips as yet have breathed no vow which sunders her for ever from the world."

"Then am I powerless!" exclaimed the churchman. "Had she been wedded to the altar, I would have snatched her from a hundred kings; but, as it is, Rufus may claim her person; he is the guardian of every orphan in the realm."

"But still," said Henry, and then paused.

"Still what?" demanded Anselm, fixing his eyes upon the hesitating speaker.

"The church may claim her still. Who is to know her vow is yet unspoken, if you assert it is? Pardon me, holy father," he added, sinking on his knee as he marked the frown on the prelate's brow; "but despair hath made me mad. I love the fair Matilda, not with the rash impulse of a lawless love, but truly, nobly, with a passion worthy her name and mine. Again," he added, "my tyrant brother threatens to cross my path. He hath despoiled me, and I have borne it patiently; plotted against my life, and I have forgiven him; but let him touch my love, my heart's first hope, my manhood's prize, and I will beard him in his strength. Like himself, I have the blood of the same fiend-begotten ancestor within my veins. Let him beware how he arouses it."

"This is the very frenzy of despair. Hast thou forgot he is thy king as well as brother?" demanded Anselm. "But perchance it is ambition leads thee to seek the Saxon princess's hand. Her name, in the event of William's death, would pave her husband's pathway to the throne. And I have not now to learn that Henry of Normandy aspires to the crown."

"At present he aspires only to the love of the fair Matilda," answered the young man.

"And I will aid thee!" exclaimed Anselm, after a pause, during which he had well scrutinised the features of his visitor; "when does Rufus start for Rumsey?"

"With the dawn. With him to will is to perform. He knows no procrastination in the search of interest or pleasure."

"I will place a bar between him and his hopes," resumend the primate, "which, powerful as he is, he cannot break. Farewell, and thank thy fortunes for this visit, it hath saved the maiden from the tiger's fangs. No words—I know the gratitude of princes. I will save Matilda for her own sake as well as thine."

That very night the archbishop, attended only by a slender train, left the metropolis, and directed his way towards the convent where the princess, unconscious of her danger, resided, in her holy, calm retirement.

On the second day after his departure,

William, attended by a numerous suite of nobles and retainers, entered the small town of Rumsey. With a refinement of cruelty which only a heart like his would have been capable of, Prince Henry was forced to be of the party. The only hope of the unhappy lover was in the promise which Anselm had made. Although he could not foresee the means, he doubted not of the power of the holy man to perform his word, for his influence was scarcely second to that of the Red King himself.

On arriving at the front of the convent, they found the gates closely barred; nor was it till the third summons of the herald, who demanded admittance in the name of the monarch, that the venerable and noble abbess condescended to make her appearance at the gate. Proud of her royal birth, and still more of her spiritual authority, the aged Christina demanded, in a cold, calm tone, the cause of the king's visit to her humble cell; for so, in the mock humility of the age, she designated the truly magnificent establishment over which she had so long and honourably presided.

"I come to claim my ward," impatiently exclaimed the tyrant—"the Saxon princess, Matilda, who hath too long been lost in the obscurity of the cloister—to place her in a sphere where the homage due alike unto her birth and matchless beauty shall encircle her —in a word, good mother, to place her on the throne to which she is so nearly allied in blood."

"Matilda is the bride of Heaven," answered the abbess, "and earthly love, e'en though a monarch's, were a sacrilege too fearful to be dwelt on. Retire then, prince, and leave the house of God to its poor inmates, who ask but liberty to pray for the welfare of their country and the salvation of their souls in solitude and silence. Again I do repeat it, Matilda is professed."

"'Tis false," said the infuriated Rufus; "none of your holy trickery with me, your pious mummery, and holy cant! Give entrance to the convent, or by my father's soul, I'll batter the sacred rookery down! Fit fate for such a nest of treason and rebellion!"

"The will of Heaven be done!" exclaimed the aged abbess. "Come then, and, if thou darest, rend the church's bride e'en from the nuptial altar; but beware," she added, sternly, "the curse of the saint from whose embrace you tear her. Weak as my voice is, it shall yet be heard in heaven for vengeance on the sacrilege and crime. Unbar the gates," she added to her attendants, "and let the monarch enter."

Without deigning an obeisance to the tyrant, the venerable speaker retired from the gate, and in a few minutes the ponderous doors of the church were flung wide, and Rufus and his nobles entered.

The scene which met their view was well calculated to impress the superstitious nobles with awe. As they advanced slowly down the centre aisle, in every stall of the choir was seated the immovable form of a veiled nun. The superior had resumed her seat upon her abbatial throne, close to the high altar, which blazed with a hundred lighted tapers; clouds of rich incense filled the air, and partially obscured the group of priests who officiated before the sacred shrine. In the centre of them might be perceived the kneeling form of the young princess, divested of her rich attire, and robed in the simple habit of a nun; a long tress of her golden hair, lately severed from her fair head, lay upon the altar; and as William and his train gained the centre of the church, the black veil held by the officiating priest descended like a cloud upon her head. The heart of the unhappy Henry failed him at the sight; it seemed the knell of hope.

"What trickery is this?" demanded William, his cheek and brow flushed with rage at the sight. "Where is the Saxon princess, the niece of Edgar Atheling?"

"Dead!" replied the abbess; "the princess Matilda lives no more."

"Dead!" echoed the king and nobles.

"Dead," resumed the abbess, "to the world; she is a nun professed. Raise, sisters, the hymn to invoke the blessing of the Most High upon the sacrifice."

In obedience to the command of their superior, the nuns had commenced the "Veni Creator" before the disappointed king had recovered himself sufficiently to interrupt them. His harsh discordant voice was soon, however, heard above the choral strain of the trembling cloistered maids.

"And who," he exclaimed, "without my license, hath dared to do this? Bear witness all," he added, "the rites are not yet complete; that, without my sanction, they are invalid. Matilda is destined to a throne; she is my ward, and thus I claim my right."

The speaker strode to the rails of the altar, which he burst recklessly open, and advanced to seize the trembling girl, who clung to the sanctuary for protection. Already had his rude hands grasped her veil, when the deep voice of the primate, whose presence he had not perceived amongst the crowd of priests, arrested the impious act; he started at the sound; the hiss of a serpent had been more grateful in his ear.

"'Tis well, prince," said the churchman; "is not the measure of thy iniquity yet full? Thou has widowed the church of her bishops; applied to ambition and ungodly waste the revenues of the sequestered sees, the patrimony of heaven and the poor; and now, to complete thy guilt, thou comest with armed men and sinful violence to rend the spotless bride of Christ from his insulted altar. Back," he added, "ere the justice of offended Deity levels the thunder of its wrath against thee; back, ere I place thy realm in interdict, and breathe on thee, and all that aid thy evil passions, the sentence of the church."

At the sound of Anselm's voice the most devoted followers of Rufus drew back; they knew too well his stern unbending nature and vast influence with the people, from his reputed sanctity, to brave him. The Red King alone maintained his ground, and confronted the courageous primate.

"I will at once appoint bishops to the vacant sees!" he exclaimed, trusting to bribe Anselm to acquiescence by the promise; "restore the revenues!"

"Back," repeated the archbishop, sternly. "Yield on the point of the investitures," he added.

"Back," continued the unmoved prelate. "Confirm the church's liberties."

"Back," iterated the churchman, who knew too well the character of the monarch to trust his promises, or be deceived by them into a dereliction of his duty.

Seeing that his commands were not obeyed, the archbishop advanced to the altar, and taking in his hands the legatine cross, held it up slowly before the people: every knee, except William's, was bent in the church at the sight. Then followed a breathless pause, for all guessed the fearful words about to follow.

"Let all who would not share in the excommunication," he continued, "pass the threshold of the church. If a single armed foot but cross the sacred line an inch, a breadth, a hair, on him and on his race I breathe the curse of Heaven."

"What!" exclaimed William, as he saw the nobles slowly quit the church, "will you desert me at yon shaveling's bidding? Salisbury, Mortimer, Warrenne! is this your loyalty? Traitors!" he added, when he saw that all but himself had passed the limit prescribed by the primate, "your lands shall pay the forfeit of this treason."

"We will not war against the church!" exclaimed the nobles. "Our lands were won by our good swords; our swords shall still maintain them. Thou art the king, but he is the archbishop."

"He is a traitor!" hoarsely muttered the king, at the same time laying his hand upon his sword.

"Strike!" said the prelate, "and crown my pilgrimage with the martyr's glorious crown; strike, and deluge the shrine of God with blood; strike, and set the seal of death upon thy guilty soul. Lo!" he added, snatching the veil of Matilda from his grasp, "I defy thee; king as thou art, I thrust thee forth from out the sacred precincts. Armed with the church's banner, I oppose thee—drive thee like a fierce wolf from out the scared fold."

The instant William drew his sword the horror-stricken nobles cried out, "Sacrilege!" and had rushed into the church, had not the previous command of the archbishop restrained them.

William, subdued by the firmness of his enemy, and alarmed at the spirit displayed by his hitherto obsequious barons, recoiled as the prelate advanced, and retreated backwards till he had passed the threshold, Anselm following him all the while under the protection of his cross. As soon as the royal intruder was expelled, the primate with his own hands closed the gates, and the choir burst forth spontaneously in a hymn of triumph.

In an irritated mood, the baffled tyrant returned to London, and immediately afterwards, attended only by Tyrrel and a few of his immediate followers, started for the New Forest, created by the devastation of his father, to indulge in the pleasure of the chase.

On the third morning after his arrival, at an early hour, he left Winchester, accompanied by William de Bretuil. Tyrrel, and others, for the hunt. Fortunately for the fair fame of his brother, Prince Henry on that fatal day remained in Winchester, or a share in the death of the tyrant had doubtless been attributed to him.

Rufus, like all the princes of his line, was extremely jealous of his prerogatives in hunting. Volumes might be filled with the cruelties inflicted by the Norman sovereigns upon the transgressors of the game-laws. The chase was their ruling passion, and Tyrrel shared in the instincts of his race. In a sylvan glade of the forest he had stricken a royal deer, which was so designated from the number of branches on its antlers; his foot was already upon the neck of the palpitating victim—the knife in his hand ready to give the *coup de grace*, when a horseman broke through the intervening brushwood. It was Rufus, whose evil genius had sent him to be a witness of the act.

"Villain!" he exclaimed, "it is a royal hart. What insolence is this?—e'en in our very presence to strike our prize!"

Tyrrel murmured something about not having counted the number of branches on its antlers.

"I'll teach thee how to count!" interrupted the furious monarch. "By heavens, it is a hart of grease fit for a king to chase! A prison may teach thee better manners, knave. Should the hound be served before its master?"

Stung by the insult, and alarmed at the menaces of the tyrant, who had never been known to pardon an offence against the forest laws, Tyrrel became desperate. The consciousness of high birth and merited degradation—of William's broken promises, had engendered a flood of venom in his heart, which wanted but one added drop to make it overflow. That drop the last words of Rufus gave.

"Hound!" iterated Tyrrel. "Hear! 'Tis thou who art the hound, and I thy master. Remember thy oath—'*May the keenest arrow in thy quiver pierce my perjured heart if I break faith with thee.*' The faith hath been broken, and the hour of vengeance hath at last arrived."

"Traitor!" said Rufus, half drawing his sword.

"Traitor to thy teeth!" exclaimed Tyrrel, as he fixed the fatal arrow to his bow. "Know 'tis thy injured brother Robert's son who strikes—whose avenging arrow rids England of her tyrant, and peoples hell with another of his fated race."

That very night the body of the Red King was conveyed to Winchester in a common cart by a peasant family named Purkiss, who had found it in the forest, and the guilty Tyrrel sailed in a fishing boat from the land where his birth entitled him to reign.

CHAPTER XIX.

The coronation ring of the Kyngs of England is sayed to have bene won by St. George, the champion saynt of that countrie, in Egypt, and brought fyrste into the island bye hym. It is a matchlyss rubye, with the holy crosse cunnyingly engraved thereon.

CHRONICLE OF WILLIAM OF COTTESSEY.

 N hearing the death of his brother, Prince Henry felt that the moment had arrived for the realisation of his long cherished and deeply meditated schemes of ambition. His first step was to hasten to the episcopal palace in Winchester, and secure the treasures of the late king—an act which he successfully accomplished, despite the remonstrances of their keeper, De Breteuil, who frankly told him that they were the property of his legitimate sovereign and elder brother, Robert. The impetuous prince drew his sword, and menaced him with death, in the event of his resisting him; and being backed by a considerable number of barons, whom he had gained over to his cause, that faithful officer was compelled to yield. Two days afterwards, feeling himself sufficiently strong, Henry threw off the mask, and proclaimed himself king; his elder brother's absence from the kingdom materially facilitated his obtaining possession of the crown. Thus the rights of Robert were a second time set aside by the successful usurpation of the younger princes. After a short struggle, during which that unfortunate man displayed his usual reckless courage and inconsistency, a compromise was entered into, chiefly by the influence of the primate Anselm. The elder brother resumed his duchy of Normandy, and acknowledged Henry as king, on condition that the latter paid him a considerable pension annually.

Ulrick had been amongst the first of the few nobles who joined the standard of the legitimate monarch, and the very last to counsel his abdication of his rights—a conduct which, when the struggle had terminated, did him no injury in the friendship of Henry, who, of all his brother's partisans, excepted the lord of Stanfield alone from feeling the weight of his resentment, and even invited him to be present at his nuptials with the Princess Matilda, which, as soon as the peace was concluded, he prepared to celebrate with all due pomp at Westminster.

A council of prelates had been previously held by Anselm, who declared before them that the vow taken by the Saxon maiden had only been conditional, as a means of protecting her from the tyranny of the late king. The reasons were found valid, and Matilda pronounced at liberty to marry by the unanimous judgment of the assembly.

The abbey church was crowded by nobles and their high-born dames, who vied with each other in the cumbrous magnificence of their costume. Despite the censures of the church (and the primate had fulminated them loud and frequently) against the prevailing fashion of the day—the long-toed shoes, looped with silver, and not unfrequently golden chains, to the knee—the wearers of these forbidden ornaments were numerous and bold; the occasion of displaying their preposterous finery was too tempting to be lost, only the most prudent took care to draw back from the circle which surrounded the archbishop, whose inflexibility they well knew and dreaded. This ridiculous mode lasted nearly two centuries, despite the prohibition of the church, which even in the plenitude of its power, when its thunders could crush a throne, found them impotent against a fashion. Such are the anomalies of poor, weak human nature.

The shouts of the people, who were transported at the idea of the descendant of their ancient monarch sharing the Conqueror's throne, announced the arrival of Henry and his bride, who soon afterwards entered the church, followed by the abbess of Rumsey, the aged Princess Christina, Ulrick, Matilda, and a stately train of chivalry and beauty. As the bridal procession moved towards the high altar, where Anselm, attended by his suffragan bishops, stood ready to perform the rite, Ulrick's thoughts naturally reverted to the aged monk at Eltham, who had prophesied to Henry his high fortune, and its continuance, provided he married in the royal Saxon line; nor did he fail to remember the prediction touching his own fate—"a life of unblemished honour, but a broken heart." "Let it come," he murmured to himself; "provided it spare those I love, I fear not the bolt myself."

He was soon, however, diverted from such sombre thoughts by the commencement of the ceremony.

The archbishop had scarcely pronounced the first words of the service, when a loud voice from the back of the altar commanded him to forbear. In an instant all was confusion; men gazed upon each other, and with inquiring eyes seemed to demand the cause of such unseemly interruption. The superstitious trembled, for the sound evidently came from the shrine of St. Edward the Confessor, whose canonised bones rested behind the altar. After a few moments' pause, during which Henry endeavoured to reassure his trembling bride, just as Anselm was about to recommence the ceremony, the command was repeated in a still louder tone than before, and the tall, stately form of Father Segsil, the aged monk of Eltham, was seen slowly advancing from the tomb of the sainted king, whose name was still so dear to every Saxon heart. Though clad merely in the ample, flowing, dark robe of his order, prelates and nobles were alike impressed with awe at his appearance. A long silver beard fell in waving masses upon his breast, his features, sharp with age and vigil, retained traces of former beauty as well as dignity;

bright blue eyes flashed from beneath a lofty brow, such as the divine Angelo in after years gave to the prophet Moses. Time, as loth to touch perfection, had laid his hand most gently upon him; his noble form was but slightly bent with the weight of a hundred years; and as he slowly advanced, guiding his steps with a simple staff, all involuntarily made way for him, till he stood before the altar, confronting Henry and the archbishop.

Fixing a searching glance upon the bridegroom, he demanded in a tone in which a monarch might have addressed his vassal, or the priest of Jove proclaimed his antique oracle to some expectant worshipper:

"Dost thou remember me, O king?"

Henry, who was too much impressed by the sudden apparition to reply, bowed his head in token of his recognition of the speaker, whom, from his vast age, he had long since considered as numbered with the dead.

"All I foretold thee is accomplished," resumed the old man: "the Red King sleeps within his grave, and thou art king."

"Most true, good father," replied the monarch, who had quickly recovered from his surprise.

"I told thee, prince, that we should meet again—meet at the proudest moment of thy life—and I have kept my word. But if this marriage," added the monk, "is indeed to bind the Norman and the Saxon race in the strong chain of love—to heal the wounds of mutual hate, and give a long divided country peace—no voice but mine must celebrate the rite. It is for this that I have lived. This one act accomplished, I have done with life, and all its waking dreams."

"Art mad, my brother?" exclaimed the archbishop, indignant that a simple monk should interfere with his high office. "Who art thou that, at thy bidding, England's primate should resign his functions?—speak! I love not priests who deal in mysteries."

With a faint smile, Father Segsil approached the angry prelate, and whispered a single word into his ear; the effect was electrical. Anselm started, and regarded the old man with an air of mingled awe, astonishment, and respect. Bowing his head in acquiescence, he took from one of the attendant bishops his consecrated stole, and placed it with his own hands around the neck of the aged man; saying as he did so:—

"It is most just. The will of Heaven be done."

Henry and his bride were both too much struck by the lofty bearing of Father Segsil, and the sudden act of the archbishop, to offer the least opposition. On a motion of the old man's hand they knelt before him, whilst with a firm voice, which sounded through the lofty aisles of the church like an echo from the grave, he pronounced the nuptial benediction. At the conclusion of the ceremony he laid his hand upon the head of the youthful queen, and blessed her even as a father might have blessed his child.

"Thou daughter of a hundred kings!" he cried; "yet a few moments, and the voice which blesses thee shall be heard no more on earth, but it shall rise before the throne of the Most High, to implore His mercies upon thee and on thy people. Protect thy oppressed country; be thou a refuge to the weak—a hope to the despairing; so shall men bless thy name on earth, and angels write it in the book of life in heaven. So shall thy race—no, no," he murmured, as, overcome by some sudden emotion, he sank into the arms of those around him. "Dark! dark! The spirit hath passed from me. I can see no more."

"He is dying!" exclaimed Anselm, who had placed his finger upon the pulse of the aged monk; "his race has run."

"Hast thou no blessing, no gift for me?" demanded Henry, bending his knees, and catching the hand of the expiring man, whose sudden death, after the accomplishment of the events he had so singularly foretold, struck him with religious awe and astonishment.

"I have," faintly replied Father Segsil, opening with an effort his nearly closed eyes. "Where is St. Edward's crown?"

"Upon my brow," answered the king.

"And where his sceptre?" he resumed, in a still weaker tone.

"I bear it in my hand."

"All," murmured the old man to himself; "all but the ring are there—St. Edward's ring, the matchless gem, graved with the holy cross. St. George, who won the ruby stone in Palestine, predicted it should ne'er be worn, except by England's kings. Where," he added, speaking in a still louder tone to the Norman prince, "where is the coronation ring of England's monarchs?"

"Lost!" exclaimed the abbot of Westminster, who, from his office, was guardian of the regalia; "lost on the field of Hastings. It is well known the Saxon monarch wore it in the battle; it hath never since been found, despite the recompense the Conqueror offered, the search his soldiers made."

Father Segsil, with an effort which seemed far beyond his expiring strength, raised himself from the arms of those who supported him, and gazed with an expression of mingled benevolence and dignity upon the youthful sovereign at his feet. Thrusting his hand into his bosom, he slowly drew from it the long lost gem, and placed it with a mournful smile on Henry's finger, whispering as he did so—

"Now thou indeed art king!" and, exhausted by the effort, he fell back into the arms of those who were near him—a corse. The young queen and her aunt, the aged abbess Christina, sank upon their knees and offered up their prayers for the dead.

"This is indeed a precious gift," said Henry, pointing to the ring and addressing the archbishop. "The good monk hath been its faithful guardian. He was a holy man," he added: "he foretold our succession to the crown—our marriage with Matilda. Bury him, my lord, like a prophet and a saint."

"Bury him like a king," replied the primate, "for such, in truth, he was."

"A king!" repeated Henry and the nobles who were near.

"A king," iterated Anselm. "God hath miraculously prolonged his days beyond the usual span. But I repeat, the voice which all heard pronounce upon our monarch and his queen the nuptial benediction was the voice of Harold the Saxon king, so long thought slain upon the field of Hastings. Peace to his memory—honour to the brave and the unfortunate!"

This strange discovery accounted for the interest the monk had taken in the marriage of Henry and Matilda. It was afterwards fully confirmed by documents left by the preceding abbot of Eltham, to whom the defeated monarch, immediately after the battle of Hastings, had made himself known, and by whose advice he had devoted himself to the church.

The obsequies of the aged prince were privately, but regally, celebrated by night, in the church where he had resigned his latest breath, his last resting-place being at the foot of the holy Confessor's tomb, and known but to the few who assisted at his interment, and to whom the secret was confided.

Immediately after the marriage of Henry, Ulrick returned to Stanfield. All hope of throwing off the yoke of the Norman race was abandoned on the union of the princess Matilda, whom the people loved for her charities and many virtues, as well as for her Saxon descent, and prayed that she might be the mother of a race of monarchs to succeed her—a prayer destined to disappointment, as she died without issue many years before Henry, who, soon after her death, married again, in the hope of an heir, but was equally doomed to hope in vain.

Ethra, Ulrick's eldest born, was at the age of sixteen a tall, graceful, capricious, wayward girl; in her Madonna-like beauty she more resembled her grandmother, the once beautiful Edith, than either her father or Matilda. From her earliest childhood she had betrayed a strange passion for solitude, and frequently had alarmed her anxious parents, and terrified attendants, by escaping from them to bury herself in the deepest recesses of the surrounding forests, where the distracted Ulrick had, on more than one occasion, found her seated by some babbling brook, singing to the murmuring waters, or couched, like a young fawn, within a mossy dell or flowery nook, weaving wild garlands of the simple flowers which were around her. The sight of her innocent amusement and infantine beauty would arrest the reproof upon her father's lips. How was it possible to scold the fairy being whose musical laugh at the sight of him rang through the woodland glade? Ofttimes the words of anger were checked by a shower of kisses; for, despite her wild temper and strange taste for solitude, she loved her father with all the deep affection of her thoughtful nature; her heart clung to his as the graceful ivy clings around the majestic oak. She was proud of his courage and manly strength—proud of his fame, and the devotion of the Saxon race, who looked upon him as their protector—proud of his urbanity, and proud that he was her father.

Finding it impossible to restrain this peculiar disposition in his child, Ulrick resolved, as far as possible, to provide for her safety; for which purpose he trained two young bloodhounds, who gradually became so much attached to their fairy charge that they followed her in all her wanderings, stopped when she stayed, guarded her whilst she slept, and, with the wonderful instinct of their nature, permitted no one who was a stranger on the domain to approach her person. Ethra loved her savage, wild companions; for savage they truly were to all but her. Often, in sport, would she try to baffle their peculiar powers of tracking out those they sought, by concealing herself within the cleft of a rock, or climbing into the leafy branches of some lofty tree. The faithful animals seemed to understand and enjoy the sport. Aided by their exquisite scent, they invariably found her, and bayed with joy at the discovery. Some of the aged servants of the household predicted that no good could possibly arise from this strange companionship; and the old chaplain remembered a prophecy said to have been written by a former lord of Stanfield, which ran thus:—

Woe to our house, when the maiden and hound
A home in the halls of the stranger hath found;
The raven and owl shall inhabit it then,
And the wolf and the fox make its turrets their den.

Our hero, although far from superstitious, could not avoid being struck by the singularity of the prediction, which he commanded to be carefully concealed from his wife, threatening with his severe displeasure any who should reveal it to her—a prohibition which caused the domestics but to repeat it the more frequently amongst themselves, till at last they became persuaded that their young mistress was the being whose evil fortune was to bring the long-predicted desolation upon the house of her fathers. They shook their heads ominously when the maiden and her dogs passed by them, and not unfrequently signed the cross, or dropped a bead to Heaven for her safety; for, strange and capricious as was her disposition, all who knew felt themselves impelled to love her.

It was on a fine morning in September that the young heiress, clad in her simple dress of white, crossed the drawbridge, attended by her faithful followers, Thor and Woden; for so they had been named, in honour of their pure Saxon blood. The warder shook his head as they passed him, and whispered to the seneschal his fears that the dreaded prediction was not far from its fulfilment, a confidence which the officer returned by informing him that death-lights had been seen in the chapel, a sure sign of misfortune to their master's race. The deep bay of the bloodhounds, and the joyous laugh of their charge, was soon lost in the recesses of the forest into which they plunged. Their cry startled the timid fawn from its secret lair, and roused the antlered stag to direct its flight far from the nut-brown woods of Stanfield. The thoughtless, happy girl was making her way through the intricacies of the underwood—now recalling the dogs from the scent of the flying deer, now urging them on, when the animals suddenly uttered a deep growl, and darted down a narrow path which led to a fountain known by the name of the Druid's Well. Ethra immediately followed, fearful lest her companions, so ferocious to all but her, should attack some traveller, or peasant hastening to his labours. On reaching the spot she discovered the hounds both crouching, as if to spring upon an aged woman, who had evidently climbed the low projecting rock on which she stood for safety. Although dressed in mean attire, there was an air of dignity in her manner which struck the beholder with respect. Her foot was firmly planted, and a sort of staff, with a long knife at the end, such as might be used for cutting water plants, was grasped in her right hand, ready to strike her assailants in case they should approach her.

"Down, Woden—down, Thor!" cried the maiden, rushing between the excited dogs and the object of their attack; "down, I say! Do not fear, good mother," she added; "they are obedient to my voice, and will not harm you."

"Do I look as if I feared them?" exclaimed the woman, in a harsh voice. "It is long, very long, since I feared aught of earth, and I might add of heaven; the first can take from me nothing but life, and the latter is too merciful to harm me."

The woman descended as she spoke, and fixed a curious glance upon the fair girl who had so opportunely appeared to rescue her; for, despite her weapon and the courage with which she might have used it, the two dogs, who lay whining and crouching at their mistress's feet, would doubtless have torn her in pieces but for her interference.

"You are a stranger, mother, in these parts," said the maiden, meeting her glance with a look as bold and searching as her own. "If you have lost your way, I will guide you; if you are in distress, follow me to the castle, and I will relieve you. One good, at least, results from my strange wandering propensities—they lead me frequently to the succour of my fellow-creatures."

"Thou art, then, the daughter of Ulrick of Stanfield," exclaimed the woman; "she whom the superstitious peasants call the Forest Fairy? Thy beauty well deserves the name—thy goodness even more so than thy beauty. Farewell. I have no need of human guidance—human help. I dare not longer stay, lest, as I gaze upon thee, and read thy fate, my heart should feel once more the throb of sympathy and pity."

"And what will be my fate?" demanded Ethra, whose curiosity was excited, but not her fears.

"Canst thou bear to listen to it?" said the stranger, peering curiously at her from beneath her bushy brows.

"I can bear much," answered the maiden, proudly. "Armed in my innocence, I have never yet experienced fear, though I have passed lone hours in the forest, and marked the lengthening shadows creep silently upon my path—have felt the lightning's kiss upon my cheek, yet hath it never harmed me. While innocent, I laugh at fear."

"But when innocence hath left thee?" interrupted the woman, with a bitter laugh.

"I first must cease to be," replied Ethra, with offended dignity; "thou ravest of things impossible, good mother."

"I thought so once," shrieked the hag; "but, like thee, I was deceived. Hear me proud daughter of a still prouder line. Thou hast asked to know thy fate, and I will not deny thee. Thou shalt love and be beloved, be won and scorned, be injured and avenged. Thou art in the toils: fly as thou wilt, thou canst not escape thy doom; for there is one upon thy track who never yet spared woman in his lust, or man in his revenge. Farewell. Perchance, when thy fate shall be accomplished, we may meet again."

The speaker had no sooner concluded her prediction that she plunged into the thick underwood which grew around the borders of the well, and disappeared ere the astonished Ethra could detain her. The two dogs, who had watched her with suspicion, sprang forward, and would have followed her, had not their mistress once more restrained them. The affectionate brutes looked wistfully into her face, as if to ask the reason why she forbad them to follow the instinct of their nature, which told them the object of their fury was dangerous to their mistress's happiness and peace.

"She is mad!" exclaimed the maiden, seating herself close to the well; "and I were as mad as she is to heed her strange predictions. I must keep more at home, and check this rambling disposition, fitting the daughter of some village serf, but not the heiress of the Lord of Stanfield."

Whilst thus seated, indulging in her many fancies, her eye was attracted by a water-lily which floated on the well, almost within reach of her arm from the projecting piece of rock on which she sat. Bending to secure the flower, whose beauty pleased her, the maiden overbalanced herself and fell. The pool was deep and dangerous; and despite the efforts of her faithful hounds, who leaped in and supported her, she must have perished but for the arrival of a stranger, who, seeing that the dogs were incapable of dragging their burden over the species of natural parapet formed by the rock, hastened to assist them by leaning over the water where the barrier was lowest. The sagacious animals swam with their inanimate mistress directly towards him. Catching her by the arm, he drew her forth, and, laying the insensible form upon the grass, busily occupied himself in endeavouring to restore her. Relieved from the weight which they had for a considerable time sustained, Woden and Thor soon contrived to release themselves from their watery prison by leaping over the rock. Jealous, as they generally were, of the approach of strangers near their charge, they seemed to feel that in the present crisis he was a friend, and they aided the exertions

THE KING RESCUES ULRICK FROM THE DUNGEONS OF NORWICH CA   STLI

of the young hunter—for such the preserver of Ethra, by his costume, seemed to be—by licking the hands and face of the inanimate girl, occasionally howling piteously in evidence of their distress.

After chafing her hands and forehead for a considerable time, the young man applied a small silver flask to her lips; and observed with pleasure, after swallowing a few drops of the rich cordial it contained, that the object of his care heaved a deep sigh, and half opened her eyes, which, overcome with languor, she immediately closed again.

"How beautiful!" exclaimed the stranger, gazing upon her with sudden and passionate admiration; "could I, ere life returns snatch from her lips one kiss, memory should treasure it with those golden hours which, like the oasis in the desert, cheer life's pilgrim in his dreary way."

Ardent as was the speaker's admiration of beauty, and reckless as were the means by which he gratified it, the very helplessness of Ethra protected her from further outrage than the burning kiss which he imprinted on her lips, and which many of my fair readers may feel inclined to think he had fairly earned by the service he had rendered in dragging her out of the water—only it was not quite generous to pay himself; one kiss bestowed is worth a thousand stolen ones.

The impression upon the still half-conscious girl was electrical; a tremulous agitation ran through every limb, and a faint blush instantly suffused her features.

"Where am I?" she murmured.

"In safety, lady," replied her preserver—"guarded by one who would give his worthless life a thousand times ere danger should approach you, or sorrow blight one smile upon thy brow. But tell me," he added—for he had noticed the golden girdle and bracelets, the badges of her high rank—"whom have I had the happiness of serving?"

"I am the daughter of the Lord of Stanfield," said the maiden, casting down her eyes, for she felt uneasy beneath his gaze.

Had she seen the frown upon the inquirer's brow as she announced her lineage, Ethra might have been spared the long corroding sorrow of after years—for it was a frown of bitterest, deepest hate, black as a thundercloud, but transient as the lightning's flash. Recovering himself, he demanded, in the same bland voice:—

"And you have lost your attendants in the forest?"

"These are my attendants," replied Ethra, with a blush, as, for the first time, the impropriety of her rambling disposition was forced upon her. "Thor and Woden are faithful guardians; besides," she added, "on our own domain, surrounded by the serfs and vassals of our house, what should I have to fear?"

"Fear!" exclaimed the hunter; "who that wears human form could harm thee? No, lady, thou art as safe within the forest shade as within thy father's halls; thy beauty and thy innocence protect thee."

Ethra started from the bank upon which the stranger had placed her; the word innocence had recalled to her mind the hag's prediction. She felt, she knew not why, that it would be wiser to end the scene at once. Gracefully thanking him for the service he had rendered her, she asked him his name, that her father might know whom to thank for the preservation of his child.

"My name," said the young man, with well-acted humility, "is too obscure to dwell upon the Lord of Stanfied's memory; nor is it from his hands I seek reward. One thought of the wandering hunter, lady, when you pass this spot, one kind recollection of his services, and they are overpaid."

Gracefully bending the knee, he kissed the hand which the maiden extended to him, and disappeared up the winding pathway which conducted from the dell.

Ethra remained for several minutes fixed to the spot, absorbed in her reflections; the kiss which the bold stranger had impressed upon her lips when he thought her insensible shocked her delicacy, but haunted her imagination; the deep but respectful admiration with which he regarded her, the service he had rendered her, all created in her heart an interest for the stranger dangerous to her peace.

"I wonder," she whispered to herself, as slowly she directed her way from the Druids' Well, "if ever we shall meet again. I fear that he will think me ungrateful, for I but coldly thanked him."

It was in this pensive mood that Ethra arrived at Stanfield. On her way the gambols of her faithful companions had been unheeded, or repressed with an impatient word. With a light step, she regained her chamber, and changed her still soiled, damp dress, for fresh attire. Resolving to conceal her adventure from her parents, the excuse for so doing was the fear of distressing them by an account of the danger she had run; the reason must be sought in those instincts with which love baffles the wisdom of experience. Ethra already contemplated meeting with the preserver of her life again; the relation of her adventure might prevent it, and hence her silence. I need not inform my readers that already the maiden loved.

It was not long before the meeting of Ethra and her lover—for such the stranger soon became—was an event of daily occurrence. It were needless to repeat the arguments by which he won from his destined victim the promise of concealment of their passion; persuasion is sweet from the lips of those we love, and the young heiress was, despite her high birth, but a mere child of nature. What to her were the distinctions of rank or country in the being to whom she had given her affections? His land became her land, his God became her God. Once, and once only, she had pressed him for his name—the reply struck horror to her heart.

"Ask it not, dearest; it is proscribed in the halls of Stanfield. Sooner would thy proud father see thee dead than the bride of thy Norman lover. He hates alike my name and lineage."

"You wrong him," exclaimed Ethra, weeping—"I am sure you wrong him. Ulrick hates none but the cruel and depraved. Is not my mother, too, of Norman blood? And think you he would hate the race from which she springs? Of all your countrymen, I know but one of whom he speaks with anger or disdain."

"And that one?" demanded the stranger.

"Is Ralph de Gael, the cruel constable of

the king within the Angles. Men say he hath a demon's heart shrined in a glorious form. His name is famed for cruelties. How many outraged maidens mourn the hour he ever crossed their path! how many desolated homes hath not his fierce vengeance made!"

"And yet," observed her lover, with a peculiar smile, "you do not seem to fear him."

"I," replied the maiden, "am too high a mark for his fierce, lawless passion. He fears as well as hates my father, whose influence with the people would raise a storm to overwhelm him, should he dare to lift his eyes to a daughter of his house. Besides," she added, "I have never seen him."

It were useless to follow the subtle windings by which Ralph de Gael—for the stranger was no other than the dreaded Norman—entwined himself, like a venomous snake, around the pure heart of the fair girl, whom, from the first moment he beheld her, he destined to become his victim. With a refinement of wickedness, he resolved not only that her love should lead her to abandon her home, but that it should be made the means of destruction upon those she left behind. Of all the nobles in the Angles, Ulrick alone had dared to brave his tyranny, and protect the weaker vavasours and merchants from his exactions; he had even, on more than one occasion, appealed from his decision to the king, who, anxious to conciliate the support of one so powerful with his nation as our hero, had done prompt justice to his complaint; hence the bitter hatred which the unworthy tyrant felt; and the triumph of inflicting a death-blow to the happiness of the man he feared was dearer to him than even the gratification of his selfish passion.

By degrees he led the wretched girl to contemplate the crime, at which at first she shuddered, with a lenient eye, and finally to consent to abandon her home to become his wife; trusting, as many have trusted, to the honour of a villain, and to time and natural affection to reconcile her offended parents to her choice. Could she have seen the real aim of the monster's project, she would have shrunk with horror from his words as from a demon's whisper; but the poison was veiled by flowers, and the unwary victim fell.

Stanfield, like most of the mansions of the time, was well fortified and guarded—prepared to resist every attack from open force, and only to be taken by treachery or surprise. At sunset, the drawbridge was every evening regularly raised, nor ever permitted to be lowered, except by the command of the lord of the hold himself. The most accessible part of the hall was at the back, near the chapel, where a small postern, which was never fastened till a later hour, gave ingress to the building. Persuaded by the treacherous Ralph, Ethra, whose feelings had been worked on by his tears and despair, whose enthusiastic nature had lent itself to the excitement of the life of love and happiness which in glowing colours his eloquent tongue depicted, consented to secure the keys and fly with him. The night was fixed for the event; he promised to come alone: we shall see how the false craven kept his word.

The last light had long disappeared from the towers of the hall, and every inmate save one retired to rest, when a party of men were seen to steal one by one from the neighbouring forest, and approach the moat at the back of the hall. Four of them launched a small boat, which they carried with them, upon the stream; and their leader, clad no longer in his hunting garb, but cased in knightly steel, entered the frail bark, and directed it towards the fatal postern where the unhappy Ethra had promised to await him. Finding the postern open, he beckoned to two of his followers to pass over before he penetrated into the interior in order to seek his victim. Cautiously he traversed the great hall, attended by his minions, whom he directed to lower the drawbridge and admit the rest of his destroying band.

Scarcely was the order accomplished, when Ethra, who, with a touch of her better nature, had lingered to kiss her sleeping sister, and breathe a parting prayer at the door which led to her mother's chamber, descended the great staircase and entered the apartment. The villain flew to meet her and enfold her in his serpent embrace.

"What means these men?" whispered the trembling girl, terror-struck at the sight of a numerous band in possession of her ancient home. "What do they here?—hast thou deceived me?"

"They are here to protect our flight. Come," urged the impatient tyrant, "time is too precious to be lost. Should thy father wake, blood might be shed—the blood of him thou lovest—and all our hopes destroyed."

At this moment one of the men who had been stationed at the bridge entered the hall, and addressing Ralph de Gael by his title, told him to decide quickly, for that a light had been seen in one of the turrets, and that doubtless some of the inmates were alarmed.

"Ralph de Gael!" shrieked the unhappy girl; "then I am lost! Hear me," she added, sinking on her knees: "let me be the only victim—trample on my heart—satiate thy hatred in my tears; but spare the authors of my being—spare my innocent sister. God!" she continued, convulsively, ".betrayed, and through me!"

Without a word the triumphant tyrant seized her in his arms, and giving her to his esquire, told him to remove her from the scene—an order which, despite her shrieks and struggles, he was preparing to obey, when the frantic girl burst from him, and seizing the cord which communicated with the alarm-bell, rang a peal which startled the unconscious sleepers from their rest.

"Monsters!" she cried, "they shall not be butchered in their sleep. Ho! Ulrick, to the rescue!—arm, arm!—the foe, the foe! The Norman is upon us!"

"Curses upon her fury!" exclaimed Ralph, seizing her a second time, and placing her in the hands of a party of his men, who this time succeeded in bearing her over the draw-bridge; "away with her. Now, then," he added to his men, as the sound of their horses' hoofs assured him he was obeyed, "fire the castle; fire it on every side; let not one escape to tell the tale of Ralph de Gael's vengeance."

The alarm which Ethra in her despair had sounded unfortunately came too late. As fast as the men-at-arms descended they were butchered by their cowardly assailants, who from their place of ambush shot them off at their ease. Ulrick raged like a lion from tower to tower; every step of ground his enemies gained upon him was bought with blood. His position was a fearful one. A sea of flames—for the enormous oaken rafters of the hall had taken fire—waved over his head; and the shrieks of the women, mingled with the groans of the wounded and dying, added to the horror of the scene. Our unhappy hero was fiercely contending with Ralph de Gael and two of his esquires, when the voice of Matilda fell upon his ear. With a cry of agony, which burst from the deepest recess of his heart, he cast away his sword, and rushed up the burning staircase. The father and the husband only lived within him—the warrior was extinct. As he reached the corridor, which led to his mother and Matilda's apartment, a burning mass of wood and stone fell from the ceiling, and barred his further passage. Vainly, with his naked hands, he tossed the blazing beams aside, till the seared flesh fell from his fingers. The barrier was too solid to be removed by his single strength, and the wretched man heard the last shrieks of his adored wife and mother as the crumbling roof fell with the crash of thunder upon that part of the building where they slept. Ulrick, in his despair, would have leaped into the blazing gulf, and shared in the destruction of those most dear to him,

had not a new interest in life been suddenly awakened. His youngest child, the lovely Myrra, a girl about eight years old, had, in the first terror of the alarm, hastened from the chamber where she slept, and thus escaped the fearful death of her mother and the Countess Edith. To raise her in his arms, to clasp her to his aching breast, was the impulse of an instant; he felt that, wretched as he was, life had still one tie for which he wished to live; and catching up a blazing brand, he directed his steps to the chapel, from whence a vaulted passage, could he but once obtain the entrance to it, conducted to a place of safety. As a son, a parent, and a husband, our hero had been sufficiently tried that night; and Heaven, which had permitted the crimes of that fearful hour for its own wise purposes, preserved him to avenge them. The fugitive, with his weeping burden, reached the place of concealment in silence and in safety, when the last tower of the once stately hold of Stanfield had fallen a prey to the devouring flames, and nothing remained of the abode of hospitality and virtue but a mouldering mass of ruin.

Ralph de Gael, attended by his followers, loaded with plunder, returned to Norwich. Good men cursed them on their way, and even the lawless and the vicious thanked Heaven that their souls at least were free from such a deed. The rage and indignation of the Saxon nobles was deep and loud; but, in losing Ulrick, unfortunately, they had lost the only leader upon whom they could rely. The triumphant oppressor loudly proclaimed that he had proofs of a meditated rebellion in his hands—called upon the Norman barons to join him with their vassals, provisioned his strong hold, Norwich Castle—a fortress almost impregnable before the invention of artillery—and prepared to act vigorously upon the defensive. Thus weeks and even months passed away, and Ulrick's most ardent friends, who all believed him dead, agreed to await the return of the king from Normandy, whither he had gone to invade the duchy of his gallant but unfortunate brother.

It was long, very long, ere the unhappy Ethra, whose existence her betrayer carefully guarded as a secret from all, recovered from the raging fever into which the events of that fearful night had plunged her. Youth and care ultimately prevailed, and the poor girl, the shadow of her former self, was at last pronounced from danger; it is true, that with time her health, and even the beauty for which she had been remarkable, gradually returned, but her mind remained partially obscured, nor was it till years afterwards that it recovered the full vigour and energy of its early tone. Weakened, as she was, in spirit as well as body—friendless, and in the power of an unprincipled villain, whom, despite his crimes, she still loved—those who know the human heart will wonder little that Ethra, won by his prayers and tears, his oaths of penitence and eternal love, consented to become his in the presence of a few friends in whom he could confide. The marriage rites were celebrated. It was neither to her birth nor virtues the unhappy girl was indebted for the consideration which made her his wife instead of mistress, but to his thirst for her possessions. The heiress of Stanfield was too rich a prize to be permitted to escape him, or to be obtained by other means than marriage.

The wedding feast was cold and solitary, as Ralph and his chosen friends caroused in the great hall of the castle. The golden cup was in his hands as he was about to pledge his guests. The pride of successful villany flashed in his eye, and seemed to say, "World! I may brave thee now;" when a herald, wearing the royal arms upon his vest, entered his presence unannounced, and summoned him in the name of his liege lord to appear before his court in ten days, to answer for the crimes of murder and treason.

"And who is my accuser?" he demanded, with a haughty smile.

"Ulrick of Stanfield," replied the herald in a solemn voice.

The cup fell from the villain's hand untasted, and the unhappy Ethra was borne senseless to her chamber.

CHAPTER XXX.

Divinity of hell! when devils would their blackest sins
Put on, they do suggest at first with heavenly shews,
As I do now.—SHAKSPERE.

AFTER the unhappy Lord of Stanfield, the most powerful chief of the Angles was Arad, a noble whose large possessions and high military reputation gave him a merited influence with the warlike and still but half-subdued Saxon race. To him, as to his surest friend, Ulrick fled on the destruction of his once happy home, and was, with his infant Myrra—the only living pledge, as he believed, of his Matilda's love—secretly received and sheltered until the raging fever, brought on by bodily as well as mental suffering, yielded to time and the devoted care by which he was surrounded. All but his host believed him dead. The poor wept for him, the good lamented him, and none but the wicked triumphed in his fall. The generous Arad felt the wrongs of the suffering man as keenly as though the brand of the Norman savage had desolated his own hearth; and, in the indignation of his honest nature, would have summoned his countrymen to arms to avenge them, had not the precautions of the tyrant in proclaiming the pretended conspiracy, and calling upon the great vassals of the crown for aid, deprived him of every chance of doing so with success. The rough nature of the old franklin frequently melted as he listened to the wild ravings of his guest calling with the most endearing epithets upon his murdered wife and eldest born, and reproaching them for their delay in coming to soothe him in his agony. At such moments his host would bring the little Myrra, and place her in her distracted father's arms. True to nature's instinct, even in the most violent paroxysms of his grief Ulrick recognised his child. Comparative calmness would gradually succeed to frenzy, and burning tears and passionate kisses relieve his o'er-fraught heart. Sometimes he would rave of the monk of Eltham, who had predicted his unhappy destiny, and adjure him by the double name of priest and king to revoke his fearful prophecy; demanding, with almost infantine simplicity, what crime he had committed to merit such a fate. As time, however, rolled on, these outbreaks of reason became less frequent, a calm deep melancholy succeeded to the fever of his heart and brain; and if his tears unconsciously fell upon his slumbering child, they were tears which soothed and not inflamed his sorrows. Well was it for Ralph de Gael that the existence of the unhappy Ethra was unsuspected beyond the limits of his castle; for the knowledge of her being in the hands of his enemy would have restored to the bereaved father the energy of action which slumbered but was not extinct. His horror and indignation

would have been like the volcano's wrath, or the destroying angel's breath. As it was, he decided, before he attempted to rouse his friends to arms, and plunge his beloved country in all the miseries of civil war, to appeal to Henry's justice for redress; and, not till that should fail, to draw the sword to avenge his private wrongs. As soon, therefore, as the monarch's return from his expedition in Normandy was known, Ulrick once more directed his pilgrim steps towards London. How different were his feelings from those which animated him on his first journey! He was then the happy husband of an adoring wife; full of the confidence of youth—its hopes and bright imaginings— where were they now? buried in the ashes of his once peaceful home; extinct for ever in an unhallowed grave. As the solitary wanderer passed along, bowed and changed by sorrow, friends and foes, as they gazed upon his pale cheek and emaciated form, failed to recognise the once gallant Lord of Stanfield.

The result of his appeal to the king did not belie the opinion which Ulrick had formed of Henry's gratitude to the preserver of his life; both the monarch and his queen listened with indignation and interest to the story of his sorrows. A herald was instantly dispatched to Norwich to summon Ralph de Gael to answer for his crimes before the royal presence. The citation, as our readers may remember, fell like a thunder-clap upon the assassin at the impious banquet which he gave to celebrate his nuptials with the unhappy Ethra, whose ill-requited love had been the means of bringing desolation upon the home of her youth and all who loved her, and whose crime was destined to be yet fearfully avenged.

Ralph de Gael was not a man to remain idle under the accusation which remained suspended over him; he was too much accustomed to mix in the political intrigues of the day, too well acquainted with courts and courtiers, not to know that a falling favourite has seldom friends. Many of his countrymen had envied him his influence with Henry, and the almost independent command which the monarch had entrusted to him. He felt that an instant and complete justification of the crimes he had committed could alone prevent his fall, and he resolved to recoil from no means, no matter how odious, to clear himself in the eyes of his sovereign—a point only to be accomplished by forging proofs of the pretended conspiracy of the oppressed Saxons to throw off the yoke of their Norman masters; for he well knew that to alarm Henry for the security of his crown, and the nobles for the safety of their ill-ac-

quired possessions in England, was to assure himself of oblivion for the past, and full indemnity for the future, or any act of tyranny or spoliation his avarice or licentious passion might lead him to commit.

Like most of the great religious establishments of the age, the monks of the cathedral were celebrated for the beauty of their illuminated manuscripts, and the skill of the laborious writers, who spent their lives in multiplying those precious works of art which, at the present day, form the pride of collectors and the glory of our libraries. Amongst the brothers the most renowned for their skill was a certain Father Onfroy, a man whose time was equally devoted to religion and the exercise of his pencil. Although not many years professed, none knew his name or country, or the reasons which had driven him from the world: the charitable attributed his retirement to sorrows; those who envied his renown as an illuminator darkly hinted that it was caused by crime —an opinion which his unsocial disposition and reserved manner, to say nothing of the care with which on all occasions he wore his capuchin over his features, gradually obtained credence. His labours were incessant; he seemed to fly to them as to a shelter from himself, or as a penance rather than an occupation. His hours were equally divided between prayer and the exercise of his voluntary labour; the only relaxation which he permitted himself was an occasional evening walk upon the banks of the quiet river which bounded the domain of his convent.

Two days after the arrival of the herald at the castle the solitary was missing. Great search was made by order of the prior and chapter; the stream was dragged for miles, rewards offered, but all in vain; before the unhappy man again saw the light of heaven years were fated to elapse.

As my readers have doubtless surmised, Father Onfroy had been secretly carried off, and was a prisoner in the castle, to serve the guilty purposes of Ralph de Gael, who hesitated at no means, however vile, which were likely to ensure his safety.

Amongst the many spoils of Stanfield Hall which the midnight marauders had carried off, was a chest of deeds, charters, and letters, the latter chiefly in the handwriting of Ulrick, sent by him to his anxious wife during the siege of Pevensy. These were sufficient for the tyrant's purpose. He doubted not but that by threats and promises he could so work upon the hopes and terrors of his skilful prisoner, that he should forge him proofs of a conspiracy in a writing so like to Ulrick's that even the affectionate wife to whom the models were addressed would have pronounced them genuine. In this, however, he calculated erroneously. Father Onfroy rejected the proposition with indignation; nor was it till the torture had been twice employed that he consented to lend his assistance to the fraud, which was to be the signal of our hero's further ruin.

"It will not thrive with thee, Ralph de Gael!" exclaimed the monk, as with a trembling hand he gave his gaoler a list of the materials necessary to tinge the paper, and gave an appearance of age to the forgeries; "it will not thrive with thee. Like thee, I have been a man of violence and blood; but Heaven hath smitten me, as it will smite thee in the pride of thy security, the triumph of thy guilt. Repent ere repentance comes too late."

Under the threat of the torture, which De Gael was even obliged to repeat, the monk at length completed his odious task, and the proofs damning to Ulrick's fame were at last in the hands of his bitter enemy. True, they were forgeries; but who was to detect them, whilst the only living witness was a captive, consigned, despite his employer's oath to the contrary, to the deepest dungeon of Norwich Castle?

The morning at last dawned on which Ralph de Gael was to meet his accuser face to face, in the presence of the king and council. The courtiers frowned or turned their backs upon him as he traversed the court-yard of the Tower, where Henry held his court. In the certitude of his triumph, the villain met their silent reproach with a brow as haughty as their own, for well he knew that his safety depended not upon their favour.

"Weather-cocks!" he muttered to himself; "in an hour you will fawn upon the man whom now ye affect to despise, and whose favour ye so long have envied. My safety depends upon myself, not on such weak instruments."

With a firm step he ascended the stairs conducting to the privy chamber, and found himself confronted with his outraged victim and the sovereign whose confidence he had so unworthily abused. It required all our hero's firmness to endure the presence of the man whose crimes had widowed his heart of happiness, and made his home a desert.

Reckless as the Norman nobles generally were in their schemes of oppressing the unhappy Saxons, there was a point at which even their fierce license stopped. The midnight surprise and wholesale slaughter of Stanfield filled even their stern natures with horror; added to which, Matilda was of their race, the daughter of one of the oldest of their companions in arms, related by blood to many. And it was evident, from the cold greeting with which many returned his salutation to the assembly, that most were disposed against him.

"We have summoned you, Ralph de Gael," said Henry, "to answer to a charge which, if true, will leave a stain upon the Norman name which not your worthless blood can wipe away—to answer for midnight robbery and murder; for assailing, like some midnight thief, cowardly and in disguise, the castle of a faithful subject, giving his house to flames, his heart to desolation. Ulrick of Stanfield," he added, turning to the accuser, "produce your charge."

All eyes were turned upon our hero, who, with a countenance flushed with emotion, and a heart lacerated by memory, related the destruction of his home and the loss of his wife and child. "Face to face," he added, with an expression of scorn beneath which De Gael writhed, "the villain dared not meet me. His craven heart, like some vile thief's, bold only 'neath the veil of night, shrank at the thought of manly open combat, where knightly swords, and not the assassin's steel, decide men's quarrels. He hated, too, as well as feared me; for my voice, as all here know, was ever raised against his exactions and oppressions; my home the shelter of his victims."

"Go on," said the accused, with a sarcastic sneer; "anon I'll answer thee."

"No; for my home destroyed," resumed Ulrick, with a burst of natural eloquence, "not for the plundered treasures of my house; but for those dearer treasures of the heart—those ties no wealth can purchase or after life renew,—for my murdered mother, wife, and child, I call for justice on him; I demand it in the name of the monarch whose confidence he hath abused, and the blest spirits whose voices long ere this have been raised against him at the bar of heaven. If he fails to clear himself, I demand judgment, a felon's judgment, on his accursed head; if he dispute any charge, the knightly combat in the lists against him."

All were surprised at the cool effrontery with which Ralph de Gael listened to the overwhelming accusation against him, and rose to refute it. Taking a packet of letters from his bosom, he threw them on the council-board, saying, with a haughty tone, "There lies my justification; let my accuser dispute it, if he can. For the loss of the innocents who were dear to him, I mourn; but, statesmen and soldiers, you, noble lords, can well understand the stern necessity which, when the kingdom was in peril, led me to draw the sword. Read, and be convinced."

"What means the traitor?" demanded

Ulrick, whose astonishment was only equalled by the king's.

"Are these," said the wily Norman, pointing to the letters, "your handwriting?"

"Certainly," answered our hero, slightly glancing over the well imitated superscription, "the hand is mine; but what wouldst thou infer from that?"

"You hear," exclaimed the triumphant villain, "he hath acknowledged them! Read, noble lords, the proofs of his vile treason; a plot to sacrifice each Norman noble in his hold—to drive us from the land our swords have won, not by open fight, but by assassination. The means are well contrived, the scheme is deeply laid. Now ask me why I crushed the serpent in its very den; why I gave to offended Justice's sword the plotting murderers of your wives and children. Those papers are my answer."

Ulrick, overwhelmed with horror, heard one by one the artful forgeries read. Their author had well calculated on the interests and passions of his judges, the most influential of whom were singled out by name as the first victims of the intended outbreak.

The indignation of Henry was as unbounded as his interest for the injured Saxon had been sincere.

"What answer," he demanded, "makes the Lord of Stanfield to these proofs against him?"

"That they are forgeries!" exclaimed Ulrick, recovering his self-possession, "mean, cowardly forgeries. My life disproves them; and my sword shall wring confession from my accuser's lips, let but the king grant the combat."

"It may not be," said the chancellor, rising; "the Saxon already hath avowed the writing his. What faith can be placed upon his truth who, in the same breath, owns and disowns his acts as interest and his safety prompt him? The sword only may be appealed to," he added, "where material proofs are wanting; but we have evidence which leaves no doubt upon the mind of Justice—the traitor's own confession."

"Hear me, lords," interrupted Ulrick, "not for my life—sorrows have made it worthless; but for my honour, that nobler part of man which not the tomb can hold or time destroy. I do protest my innocence. The very frankness with which I owned those letters might have convinced you they were forgeries. Compare my character with my accuser's. Would he who stoops to murder shrink from lying? Would the midnight thief hesitate at any act, however vile, to screen his worthless life? My own and my outraged country's cause," he added, "might drive me to draw the sword; but to

become an assassin, never, never. The thought was worthy only of the fiend whose soul conceived it; mine scorns and rejects the cowardly accusation."

"You hear him," said his accuser, with a cold, satisfied smile; "the traitor half avows his treason. But I have one proof more; a witness none will venture to dispute—one on whose testimony I place my life and honour. Prince," he continued, in well-affected humility, "do thou decide between us; to thee the writing of this man is known; thy clerkly knowledge cannot be deceived—do thou decide between us."

The piece of flattery was well-timed; for Henry was vain of the title which men already gave him of Beauclerc, in allusion to his skill in letters. Bending over the papers, the monarch perused them attentively, and a shade of sorrow and regret passed over his brow as the last fell from his hands.

"On my kingly word," he exclaimed with a sigh, "I do pronounce them real."

"Enough!" said the chancellor, a haughty Norman, devoted to the interests of his countrymen, and, like most hackneyed statesmen, ever ready to judge the worst of human nature. "We can no longer hesitate; the constable is fully justified in all that he hath done—the Saxon is the traitor. Sire," he added in an under tone to his still hesitating sovereign, "no weakness now; private friendship must not trifle with the safety of a crown, the honour of a nation. The culprit must to prison. Leave him to the council. The rack may wring from him the confession of his crimes, the name of his accomplices."

Henry shuddered; for it was not without a struggle that he resolved to consign the preserver of his life to the tender mercies of his nobles. Despite the apparent proofs, something whispered him that our hero might be innocent; but policy commanded alike the suppression of his feelings and the concealment of his opinion. Bowing his head in token of assent, without bestowing a parting glance upon Ulrick, he quitted the council chamber to inform the queen of the unexpected turn which the accusation had taken; for the Saxon princess, whose influence over him was unbounded, felt deeply for the wrongs of her outraged countryman, whose gallant bearing had won her good opinion, whose treachery it was difficult to persuade her to believe.

"No!" exclaimed the generous woman, when Henry related to her De Gael's charge, and the proofs by which he had supported it; "let who will pronounce him guilty, I cannot believe it. Truth dwells on the unhappy Ulrick's tongue; his life belies the

THE CONSTABLE CONDUCTS THE QUEEN TO ULRICK'S DUNGEON.

deed; I would almost pledge my own that he is innocent!"

"Matilda," said her husband gravely, "thou judgest warmly. Thou, too, art a Saxon."

"Have I loved thee less?" replied his wife, turning her blue eyes upon him reproachfully.

Not for an instant could the affectionate prince endure the look; folding his arms around her, he imprinted a kiss on her fair, open brow, and begged, with all a lover's earnestness, to be forgiven.

"I fain would think like you," he said;

"but proofs are strong against him. Were I convinced of his innocence—nay, had I but a doubt that he is guilty—despite the council and the angry peers, I'd interpose and save him."

"And you will save him, Henry," said the queen. "You owe him life for life; remember, even if guilty, he preserved yours. What would be your remorse—your future agony and shame—if time should prove him guiltless?"

"Perhaps," whispered the monarch, "there is a way to save him. We will think more of this; and trust me, love, the Saxon

Ulrick shall not fare the worst for thy sweet prayer and good opinion of him."

On the departure of Henry from the council-chamber the unfortunate Lord of Stanfield had been removed, by command of the haughty chancellor, to one of the subterranean dungeons beneath the White Tower, close to the water-passage known by the name of the Traitor's Gate. Too proud to descend to reproaches or entreaties—too hopeless to offer further vindication, our hero suffered himself to be conveyed to his damp cell in silence. To him death had no terrors, for his heart was already ashes; and, but for the stain upon his name, he could have contemplated his approaching fate, if not with joy, at least with resignation. Even in his prison his heart beat lighter than his accuser's; for, despite his momentary triumph, something whispered to De Gael that truth would yet be heard; and even while listening to the congratulations of the courtiers who once more flocked around him, and the compliments of the members of the council, his spirit sank within him. The coldness of the queen during the evening banquet, to which he was invited, was remarked by all; she shuddered visibly as his lips pressed her reluctantly extended hand; and it was clear to all, however the king and nobles might esteem his truth, that Matilda's heart was enlisted in the cause of her unhappy countryman.

At an early hour her majesty quitted the circle, and her departure was followed by an encouraging smile from her husband, who remained, however, for some time after her, in deep conversation with William de Neville, the aged constable of the Tower, a man whose fidelity to his prince was above all suspicion, and on whom Henry looked as on a second father.

"I'll do it, sire," whispered the old man, hesitatingly: "but 'tis against my judgment. Heaven grant we both repent not of it; but be it as you will."

As the knight concluded his remonstrance, he bowed and left the presence. With his departure a weight seemed to be removed from Henry's soul. Calling for a cup of wine, he drained it to the dregs in honour of his queen, and many a gallant lip and heart responded to the pledge.

Whilst the banquet in the great hall was at its height—for the Tower, at the period of our tale, was both a fortress and a palace—two persons, closely disguised, were threading the cold damp passages which conducted to the prison of our hero. One was the aged constable, to whom alone the clue was confided of the various secret entrances and means of egress from the prison, used more frequently for purposes of tyranny and death than freedom to the unfortunate and innocent. His companion was the generous queen, whose prayers and tears had won from Henry the liberty of his prisoner.

On entering the dungeon, they found our hero sleeping on the ground as calmly as an infant sleeps upon it mother's breast. The constable was surprised, for it was not often that his captives slept.

"And can this man be guilty?" whispered Matilda to her companion, as she gazed upon Ulrick's placid features. "Such, believe me, is not the sleep of those whose waking thoughts are of murder and of treason. I should like to compare the Saxon's slumbers with those of his accuser."

"'Tis hard to judge," replied the knight; "for who can read the heart of man?—it is a mystery even to the angels nearest the throne of God. He who framed, alone can comprehend it. But time presses; morning must not dawn upon our enterprise and see it unaccomplished. 'Tis strange," he added, with a smile, "that William de Neville, who bore the Conqueror's standard at Hastings, should be aiding a Saxon to escape from Norman justice!—few would believe it."

"Say, rather," replied his companion, "aiding thy king to pay his debt of gratitude. Yon sleeper saved his life, and all of Rolla's race are not alike ungrateful."

"Enough, 'tis Henry's will," observed the old man; "that hath ever been my law. What ho!" he added, in a louder tone. "Ulrick, sir knight, awake."

The sleeping man slowly opened his eyes, not with that sudden start with which unquiet guilt springs from its restless couch, but with the composure which a fearless conscience gives.

"What would you?" he exclaimed. "Hath the night passed so soon? Well, I am ready."

"Ready for what?" demanded the constable, with a look of surprise.

"For aught which pleases Heaven," replied Ulrick; "for beyond the tortures and the cruelties with which man goads his fellows, I behold the spirit's triumph and the freed soul's emancipation; plains of eternal light and waving palms; long-silent voices whisper in mine ear, 'Welcome at last to peace.'"

"To liberty as well!" exclaimed Matilda, raising her veil. "The path is free, the dungeon door unbarred. Away at once. Use fortune while thou mayst."

"The queen!" said the astonished prisoner, gracefully bending his knee; "what errand brings an angel's presence to this dreary dungeon?"

"To pay the debt thy grateful monarch owes—to set thee free," replied the generous woman; "to preserve a father for his helpless child, an avenger for the outraged Saxon honour."

Ulrick's natural hesitation to fly and leave a branded name behind him was overruled by the allusion to his infant Myrra, and the hope of one day returning to prove his innocence and avenge his murdered race. He suffered himself, therefore, to be conducted by the aged constable to the boat which by Henry's orders waited at the Tower-stairs to convey him to Normandy, where he soon afterwards joined a band of crusaders on their march to Palestine; where, in knightly action under the burning sun of Syria, he endeavoured for a while to forget the wrongs and sorrows which drove him from his native land.

With Ulrick's disappearance the last barrier to the triumph of the infamous Ralph de Gael was removed; for whatever might be Henry's secret opinion of his services, and the truth of the conspiracy which he had alleged against the Saxons, he was too politic to express it; seeing that it was firmly believed by the great Norman barons, to whom he was chiefly indebted for his crown, and whom, such was their power, it might have been dangerous to offend.

Ten years had elapsed since our hero's departure from England, during which period the oppression and tyranny of the worthless governor of the Angles had risen beyond human forbearance. The eyes of the suffering people, vavassours and franklins, were, in the absence of Ulrick, all turned towards Arad, whose watchful prudence had hitherto defeated every attempt to surprise or to subdue him. Men's minds were in this unsettled state when it became gradually whispered that midnight assemblies were being held on Monkshold Heath, and in the Druid's cave at Whitlingham, in which many of the inhabitants of the city joined. These rumours were not long in reaching the ears of the suspicious Ralph, whose spies were everywhere, and he provisioned the stronghold of Norwich Castle in expectation of the approaching outbreak.

Amongst the few national festivals which the oppressed Saxons still continued to celebrate was the anniversary of St. Edward, on which occasion the elder nobles met to exchange the courtesies of life, and the younger ones and commons to indulge in knightly sports, archery, wrestling, and quarter-staff—exercises in which few people could excel them. Arad, attended by a more numerous train than usual, was one of the last to reach the heath where the assembly was held. The spot marked out was an undulating plain broken by hills, now forming part of the enclosed lands of Thorpe, extending from the chapel of St. William in the wood down to the river's bank. The arrival of the man whom the oppressed Saxons looked upon as their leader was hailed with shouts of joy, and "Long live the valiant Arad," and "Success to the Lord of Ormsby," echoed far and near. The aged chief was attended by his only son and heir Edward, and his nephew Ethwold of the Rath, a young man to whom he had been guardian.

It was observed that the young men were unremitting in their attention to a fair girl who rode in the midst of the train, and who was received by the more aged Saxons with tokens of affection and respect. The maiden was no other than Myrra, who, from the period of her father's exile, had shared the home and paternal love of Arad, and whom rumour had long since assigned as the destined bride of either his son or nephew, for both the young men loved her, and hence the looks of jealous rivalry which occasionally passed between them; but the openhearted, generous Edward was evidently the favoured lover. A shade of sadness passed over the features of the exile's daughter as she returned the greetings of her friends, for to her the projected outbreak was no secret, and she knew not how soon the home of her adoption might be made a desert, and the friends who had protected her reduced, like her gallant father, to misery and exile.

As the day proceeded, the people noted with great satisfaction that one by one their leaders slowly retired to the depths of the wood which skirted the place of their assembly, to deliberate, they fondly trusted, on the means of redressing the wrongs beneath which they groaned, and throwing off a yoke as humiliating as it was burthensome to them. Let it not be imagined that all the nobles and franklins who were present at what might not inappropriately be called the council of the angles were unanimous in their views. Some were restrained by their doubts of success, or the more worldly consideration of personal security; others were content to live on any terms, however vile or degrading.

Considerable uneasiness existed amongst the wavering and timid at the presence of a tall, war-worn pilgrim, who stood by Arad's side, and to whom alone, of all the assembly, he seemed personally known. The red cross on his shoulder denoted he had served in Palestine; and the golden spurs upon his heels vouched for his knightly rank. Some whispered that he was a spy, a supposition instantly rejected by those who gazed upon his gallant bearing, and the evident recognition of him by their brother noble.

The business of the day was opened by Arad, who, in a speech replete with energy, drew their attention to the condition of their unhappy country, to the continued oppressions of Ralph de Gael, and the little hope of redress at the hands of the monarch, who, since the death of his Saxon queen, Matilda, had given himself entirely up to his Norman ministers and counsellors. "Are we," continued the aged chief, " once more to draw the sword for Saxon independence, or yield our necks, without one further effort, to the debasing yoke our masters place upon us? Shall we decide to live as freemen, or to die as slaves?"

There was a pause. The assembly felt the importance of the reply they were called upon to make, and remained silent. Ethwold of the Rath, the speaker's nephew, was the first to break it. Though not naturally a coward, he was selfish. Hitherto the brand of the Conqueror had not assailed his hearth —added to which, the importance which his rival cousin would obtain in Myrra's eyes, should the insurrection prove successful, at once determined him. Briefly and confidently he spoke of the hopelessness, the madness of the attempt, and called upon the meeting to disperse, ere the knowledge of their designs should give their rulers fresh pretext for further spoliation.

With a triumphant smile Ethwold remarked the effect his speech produced. Many of the vavassours and petty nobles were retiring, when the deep-toned voice of the pilgrim arrested their ignoble purpose.

"Men !" he exclaimed, dashing into the midst of them. " Can ye be men, and tamely thus resign all chance of freedom? Are ye so debased, ye cast the sword aside and kiss your chains? Prove yourselves worthy of your fathers' fame, and free your daughters from the Norman's lust. Your future sons, drawing the love of freedom from their mothers' breasts, nobly shall defend the rights their fathers bled to win, the stream of life with nobler impulse beat, and one brave deed regenerate our race."

Few as were the impassioned words of the speaker, they found an echo in the hearts even of those who wavered. Men crowded around him—the young with enthusiasm, the old in admiration. But Ethwold was not a man to be easily silenced; he was one of those who, if not eloquent, at least are plausible.

"Who is this stranger," he demanded, "who takes upon him to give lessons unto men and nobles? Beware," he added, " lest this seeming zeal should hide a traitor."

"Traitor !" repeated the pilgrim; " England, my own, my father's land, have I for thee wandered o'er Asia's burning sands, or froze amid the horrors of the north, thus to be branded with a traitor's name? Hear me, Saxons," he continued, " 'tis not the first time ye have hung upon my words, or followed my broad pennon to the fields. Exiled for freedom and my country's rights, for years I wandered 'neath a burning sun, yet felt it not—the fire was in my brain: oft o'er the pathless deserts of the east my steps have strayed—the simoom harmed me not; in storm, in danger, in the battle's heat, I courted death in vain. Once, when Despair usurped fair Reason's throne, I gained the craggy mountain's topmost height, and would have plunged in the abyss beneath, but at that moment some spirit whispered 'England might be free!' My heart, my sword, were all my country's claim, and Ulrick would not rob her of her right."

The shout of the astonished Saxons at the announcement of their banished hero's name rung far and wide. Many a gallant heart beat with admiration at the sight of him, and eager hands were stretched to welcome him. In the midst of their enthusiasm, however, a voice was heard at whose sound all gave way. The youthful Myrra had heard her father's name. Gliding like a spirit of light and beauty though the circle that surrounded him, she sank upon her knees, her voice shaking with emotion: all she could find strength to utter was :—

"Your blessing—your blessing, father— for your long orphan child."

As the stern warrior gazed upon the kneeling seraph at his feet, the thoughts of other days and other ties came over him. Placing his hand upon her head, he answered, while tears coursed each other down his manly cheek :—

" Sweet as the dew which fell on Israel's race my blessing rest upon thee, thou only blossom of my marriage bed the hand of tyranny hath spared me. Look on her, chiefs," he added, addressing the franklins, who had respectfully drawn back not to intrude upon so sacred a meeting; "say, should a form like this give birth to slaves? should beauties rare as these become the Norman's prey? Here, on the hills where free your fathers trod, I call upon you, in the sacred name of freedom—call you to burst wide your bonds—cast back to earth the fetters which enthrall you—renounce the oppressor's yoke, and rise erect and free as God and nature's chartered laws have made you."

One wild enthusiastic cry for liberty was the result of the appeal; men drew their swords, and swore no longer to hold their lives but at their master's pleasures; even Ethwold, carried away by the feelings of the moment, joined in the shout for war.

"Noble Ulrick," he exclaimed, "forgive me. I knew not the nature my suspicions wronged. Let Myrra's hand become the pledge of amity between us; my fortune and my friends will then be thine; my vassals know no other leader, my inexperienced years no other guide."

It needed not the pale cheek of Myrra, or the ill-suppressed indignation of the youthful Edward, whose imploring eyes were fixed on Ulrick, to induce his generous nature how to decide. Drawing the trembling girl yet nearer to his heart, as if to shield her even from the outrage of such a proposition, he answered with a bitterness and scorn, to which in other years his lips were strangers:

"Yield her to thee! consign her pure and spotless to thy arms! Rather would I strike her to my feet! rather behold her perish in the pile in which her sister fell, than yield her beauties to a willing slave! Go," he added, with an expression of, if possible, increased contempt,—"go, count thy gold, and view thy hords increase! Breed sons to swell thy Norman master's train, and daughters to be victims of their lust! Go, live securely, but thy nation's scorn!"

Slowly, and with a look of unutterable hate, Ethwold withdrew from the assembly, the eyes of which were turned reproachfully upon him. Curses were on his lips, yet he spake them not. Revenge, like a vulture, was gnawing at his heart; and he resolved, even at the sacrifice of those who shared his blood, it should be gratified.

That same day saw him closeted with Ralph de Gael, to whom, however, with the usual cunning of his nature, he only half confided the danger which threatened him; spoke of the meditated rising of the Saxons; but forbore to name Ulrick as their chief, promising, however, to deliver him into the hands of a party of his men, provided he might retain his daughter as his sole reward. The double traitor was in some degree forced to this; for, without the aid of the Norman soldiers, he knew it would be impossible to complete the outrage he meditated, as he well knew no Saxon could be found to lay a hand upon the Lord of Stanfield—such was the influence of his name—the love which his gallant fame and devotion to his country had inspired. The compact was accepted,

the necessary force placed at his disposal, and Ethwold retired from the castle, bound to the bidding of his master, like a worthless hound.

The name of Ulrick, and the shouts which welcomed it, spread far and near amongst the excited Saxons. The games were rapidly broken up, and the serfs and peasants burst in upon the circle hitherto reserved for their masters; all were eager to gaze upon the man whose name had been the watchword of their youth, whose arm the protection of their homes, and whose memory in their grateful hearts had survived even his services. In the enthusiasm of the moment all distinction of rank was forgotten, and it became necessary, men were so mingled together, for the leaders to retire to mature their plans ere the news of Ulrick's return should be noised abroad—a secret which, after the public recognition of his person, could not be long concealed. In the hurried council which followed, it was decided that the exile should at once proceed to Stanfield to raise the ancient vassals of his house, who, writhing under the exactions of their new master, would rise to a man, and strike for their ancient lord and freedom.

That very evening, near the old cross where the road divided from Cotessey to Wynmondham, an aged woman, leaning on an oaken staff, might have been seen watching the setting sun, whose last ray kissed the graceful spire of the cathedral, and crowned with a flood of golden light its slender pinnacles; her quick, restless eye was directed to a copse of stunted beech and brushwood near, from which a steel-clad Norman man-at-arms might occasionally be seen peeping, casting down the road impatient glances, such as the hungry wolf might cast upon its loitering prey.

"Ay," muttered the old woman, resuming her occupation of gathering herbs, "wait; he will not tarry long. The noble stag and timid fawn are both within the toils. First, the mother," she added, counting with her fingers, "then the wife and eldest born, and now the sire, and the last shoot of his doomed, blighted race. Blood will be shed. I feel—I scent it. I saw the corpse-lights flitter in the ruins of Stanfield—a sure token of death in its lordly line. He comes, the victim to the sacrifice—the eagle to the archer's aim."

At this moment Ethwold and several of his followers left their ambush to secrete themselves behind the cross, in order that they might secure their prey between two nets, and so cut off all chance of escape.

"What dost thou here, wretched hag?" exclaimed the haughty Saxon. "Away! we want no spy upon our deeds. Hence, ere my archers lash thee with their bow-strings till the flesh falls from thy accursed bones."

"There needs small wit to guess the deed," replied the beldame, sharply, "when Saxon joins with Norman to oppress his country. Hell is sure to register it, and Heaven to punish it."

A laugh from the men-at-arms stung the traitor at whom the bitter sneer was levelled. Striking the speaker with the back of his weapon brutally over the temple, he once more bade her begone.

"Ethwold," screamed the hag, in a voice rendered painfully sharp by passion, as she wiped the blood which trickled down her haggard features, "thou art a doomed man! Saxon and Norman shall alike reject thee; the gallows-tree shall end thy vile career; the pie shall chatter on thy fleshless skull, and the winds whistle through thy unburied bones. Craven and traitor, the curse of her whose words ne'er fall to earth be on thee! Thou hast struck a woman; by a woman's hand thy fate shall be accomplished."

Ere the astonished Ethwold could give orders to secure her, the hag fled into the wood, whose intricate windings forbade all hope of pursuit.

It was with bitter, sad reflections that Ulrick and his daughter, whose tears had drawn from her father a reluctant permission to accompany him to Stanfield, approached the once happy home of love and childhood. A thousand recollections rose in the mind of each as they remarked the well remembered cross which divided the two domains. Both, as by a mutual impulse, reined their steeds, to repeat an ave for the safe conclusion of their journey. The action was too favourable for the intentions of the ambushed ruffians to escape their notice. In an instant the travellers were surrounded, and the male rider disarmed.

"What would. you, masters?" he exclaimed, taking them for robbers; "gold? I have but little, and to that ye are freely welcome. What," he added, seeing that they were about to bind his arms, "would ye offer violence to a pilgrim of the cross?"

"Ethwold!" shrieked Myrra, as the eyes of the triumphant villain encountered hers, "betrayed! betrayed!"

At the name of the perjured Saxon, the fearful truth flashed at once in all its horror upon the mind of the unhappy father. Bursting with a frantic effort from the men-at-arms who held him, he sprang upon the traitor, whose life, unarmed though the indignant Ulrick was, would have fallen a just sacrifice, had not numbers overpowered him.

"It is accomplished," murmured our hero to himself; "man may not struggle with destiny."

There was a something so calm and dignified in the resignation of their captive, so touching in the tears and affectionate caresses of his fair child, that even the rude Normans felt moved, and conducted them to the city with respect and silence.

Ethwold, to avoid being seen with the party, and his treason to his countrymen thereby at once made know, lingered behind, triumphing in the anticipated possession of the high-minded girl who had rejected him, and the despair of his rival cousin, whom he hated.

"Now, then," he exclaimed, "I can meet scorn with scorn, and hate with hate. Ulrick dishonoured me before my nation; the scaffold soon will claim him. Myrra preferred the boyish love of a mere stripling to my fervent vows—ha! ha! ha! Soon shall she sue and learn to wait my smiles, come at my beck, and tremble at my frown. I'll break her haughty spirit," he added, "and find more pleasure in the task than e'en her love could yield me."

"You must be brief then," whispered a voice near him, "for your courtship will prove but short."

He started, and found the hag whom he had so brutally treated grinning maliciously at his side. The first impulse of the haughty franklin was to repeat the chastisement; but on a motion of her hand, he was disarmed by a dozen wretched looking men, who had crept through the underwood and gradually surrounded him, and who immediately hurried him from the high road into the depth of the forest.

"Dogs!" he exclaimed, as one of them drew from his vest a rope, "would you bind me?"

"Ay," replied the hag; "bind thee where Satan's hand alone shall loose thee—where thy crimes long since should have consigned thee—to the gallows-tree!"

"Thou darest not, woman," he answered. "Knowest thou who I am? Slaves! I will rack ye limb from limb for this! Hear me," he added, seriously alarmed for his safety, for one of the ruffians had already made a noose at one end of the cord, and advanced with the intention of placing it round his neck, "I am rich; I'll buy my life with gold—gold, which will purchase wine and beauty—all that men's hearts desire, all that their wish can frame."

"All but thy life!" screamed the woman; "for couldst thou coin the earth in gold, any count it down before me, I'd trample on thd offer. Do you hesitate?" continued the fury, observing that some of the outlaws were pondering on the Saxon's offer. "Fools! would the man who sold his country e'er keep faith with you? Obey me, or I break all ties between us—denounce ye to your Norman tyrants' mercies, and leave ye to your fate."

The outlaws, who were dependent on the hag for the necessary supplies of food, and whose influence over them was still further increased by her skill in wounds, not unfrequently called into requisition in the hazardous life they led, hesitated no longer. Despite his yells and frantic struggles, Ethwold was attached to the fatal tree. As soon as the men retired he caught with his unbound hands to the branch to which he was suspended, and for a few moments procrastinated his fate.

"A priest, a priest!" he shrieked. "Let me not perish body and soul! Save me, woman, and I will be thy slave, thy hound; chain me in the deep centre of the earth, feed me on carrion, use me as a foot-stool; spare my life, but for repentance."

"Ha, ha, ha! how the hang-dog howls!"
"Mercy! mercy!"
"The pie shall chatter on thy fleshless skull!" repeated the fury.
"But for one hour to pray."
"The winds shall whistle through thy fleshless bones!" she added.
"No hope—no hope!"
"None!" exclaimed the aged woman, sternly. "My word is kept; thou hast struck a woman, and a woman's hand consigns thee to thy doom."

Raising her long staff, she struck the struggling wretch upon his hands till the repeated blows forced him to let go his desperate hold, but not till bruised bones and mangled flesh had lost all power of supporting him. He fell with a heavy jerk, and, after a few convulsive struggles, Ethwold, the betrayer of his country, swung a corse; cut off in the moment of his triumph by the agency of a weak creature, whom in his strength he could have crushed, and whom in the wantonness of his power he had treated cruelly.

CHAPTER XXXI.

Thy numbers, jealousy, to naught were fixed,
Sad proof of thy distressful state;
Of differing themes thy vereing son was mixed,
And now it courted love—now raving called on hate.
COLLINS' ODE TO THE PASSIONS.

 ALPH DE GAEL paced the great hall of the castle, impatiently awaiting the arrival of his prisoners. Had he been aware who the redoubted leader was was, he would hardly have entrusted to a subordinate the task of securing his person; for despite the number of years which had elapsed since the exile of our hero, conscience—the busy monitor—at times whispered in his ear that Ulrick might return to exact fearful retribution for his murdered wife, his home destroyed, and outraged honour; and the thought would poison the wine cup, and arrest the smile upon his lip. Prudence had prevented his ever making public his marriage with the guilty, the unhappy Ethra; the greater part of the estates of Stanfield had become his by confiscation, and the knowledge of his union with the child of the man whom he had so cruelly persecuted could have answered no other purpose than to cover his name with additional infamy. The betrayer and betrayed lived still: her remarkable beauty, which even sorrow and remorse had failed to touch, held the tyrant in a bond which habitude had contributed to rivet; for, although his infidelities were frequent, they were carefully concealed from the eyes of his injured wife.

"Where stay the loiterers?" he demanded of an esquire who at a respectful distance awaited his commands. "Night hath already fallen. Can the Saxon have escaped me? Who leads the men?"

"Herbert," replied the officer. "A cool head, my lord, and a still better sword."

"I know his qualities," interrupted the impatient Norman, who loved not to hear the praise even of the instruments most faithful to his crimes. "Let the torturers be summoned. I'll wring confession from the Saxon's lips. No mercy, no weakness now. The cord and axe shall be each rebel's doom. I'll crush the traitors like a nest of vipers 'neath my iron heel."

The warders, however, cut short his threats by announcing the arrival of his prisoners, who were instantly conducted by their captors to his presence. Ulrick, although heavily chained, still supported the steps of his fair child; his paternal arm encircled her waist, half veiling her form in the folds of his dark mantle. Time and the burning sun of Syria had so changed him, that even the eye of hate, whose glance is often keener than that of love, failed to recognise him. His step was erect, in the conscious integrity of his life and the dignity of his nature; his eye, like that of an imprisoned eagle, shrank not from the gaze of his captor, which, on the contrary, gradually quailed beneath its glance.

"Who art thou?" said Ralph de Gael, in a much less haughty tone than he usually assumed towards his victims, for the bearing of the soldier of the cross had involuntarily awed him.

"A Saxon," was the reply.

"Humph! I guessed as much," interrupted the Norman, "from thy insolent bearing. What else?"

"Thy foe!" added Ulrick, sternly, "thy deadly foe. Mine is no common hate. I tell thee, Ralph de Gael, were we both struggling on the wave, but with one plank between us and eternity, my hand should dash that plank aside rather than float with thee."

"Father, father!" whispered Myrra, alarmed at the effect his words produced upon the astonished tyrant, "patience, patience for mine and for thy country's sake."

"Indeed!" exclaimed the surprised Norman, for it was not often that such words had fallen upon his ears, more used to prayers and supplications than reproaches from his victims; "and what cause?"

"What cause!" iterated our hero, approaching him; "have I not told thee that I am a Saxon; and can't thou ask the cause? Look well around thee; view the groaning earth, which once teemed plenty to her children's toil, made wild and barren 'neath the Norman sway; view well the happy homes, the antique towers, in which of old the Saxon lived and ruled, now desolate beneath the Norman brand. Dost thou still ask the cause?" and here the expression of the captive's eye, as he repeated the question, was like the forked lightning's point, or the concentrated glance of the fierce basilisk. "Again look forth, and view our offspring, children of our blood, fettered like slaves to pamper up your pride, or made the victims of their tyrant's lust. Our county lost, our homes profaned, our trampled liberties, our broken hearts—all, all proclaim the cause."

For a few moments Ralph de Gael remained pale with rage, and speechless from the mere impotence of passion. There was a tone, too, in the speaker's voice which jarred upon his soul like the return in manhood's years of childhood's half-remembered terror. He felt convinced that he and his prisoner had met before; but memory, so changed was his victim, failed to whisper where. His pride was galled at the proud glance beneath which his own had quailed.

"Fool!" he at last replied; "ours is the right of conquest; victory places the yoke upon your necks, and justifies our sway."

"Nothing can justify a tyrant's sway," answered the prisoner calmly. "Freedom is man's inalienable right, stamped by the Godhead on his form when he went forth creation's chartered lord. Nor conquest's law, nor deed on vellum sealed, nor e'en man's own assent, can ratify its loss. Though ages more than e'er the world has seen had passed since first your fetters bound us down, yet from the moment that we spurned our chain, and felt our rights, humanity's lost charter was restored. Wretch!" he added, "the measure of thy cruelties is full—a people rise in their indignant strength—despite thy guards, thy crouching slaves, their justice yet shall reach thee. When thou shalt see this bloodstained hold, the seat of thy dark tyranny and crime, a prey to flames—when frantic fear shall play upon thy heart, and wild remorse call Heaven in vain for mercy, think on the wrongs of Ulrick, and despair."

"Ulrick!" repeated Ralph aloud. His cheeks blanched as he beheld the secret terror of his life before him; then muttering to himself, he uttered, "'twas instinct, then, which made me shudder as I looked upon him."

"Wretch!" echoed his victim; "where is the home thy sword hath made a desert?—the wife thy bloodhounds hunted to the grave?—the child that perished in the blazing pile? Deep in the grave I may forget my wrongs, but whilst one spark of waking life remains, 'twill be employed in precious, dear revenge. Off, vile chains!" he added, "more terrible than death. Oh! for the lightning's arm to strike thee!"

The unhappy man became so excited by the recollection of his wrongs, that, unarmed as he was, he rushed upon the destroyer of his happiness, and raising his chains as a weapon above his head, doubtless would have inflicted a summary vengeance upon the tyrant, had not his guards restrained him

THE DEATH OF RU'US.

One more zealous than the rest held the point of his sword at the throat of the fallen Saxon, and waited but a nod or look from his unworthy chief to strike—a sign which would most probably have been given, had not Myrra, alarmed for her father's life, forget the natural timidity of her nature and the horror which the name of her enemy inspired. Kneeling at the Norman's feet, she even clasped his hand, nay, bathed it with her tears, and implored him by every sentiment of pity and humanity to spare a being whose heart his cruelties had already crushed, whose brain was maddened by the memory of his sorrows. It would have been impossible for any one, even less the slave than Ralph de Gael of beauty, to gaze unmoved upon so fair a suppliant; her ripening form, like the swelling bud of the fragrant rose, gave delicious promise of its bursting beauties; her blue eyes, like sapphires, gemmed in tears, were turned imploringly upon him; while from her prostrate position his licentious eye caught the rich contour of her heaving bosom. It was long since he had gazed on aught so fair, so fresh, so

No. 26.

beautiful; and the heart of the voluptuary throbbed with an emotion to which it had been for years a stranger.

"Rise!" exclaimed Ulrick, who beheld with a sickening sensation the looks of lawless admiration which the Norman cast upon the innocent dove trembling within his clutches. "Plead not to him for mercy, lest from the tomb thy mother's shade indignant rise and curse the child who bends to the destroyer of her race. Thinkst thou," he added, "I could value life as that man's loathsome gift?"

"Fear not," said the tyrant; "thou shalt have thy wish—the trial first, and then the headsman's office. Away with him to a dungeon! Guard him, fellows, as you would your lives; your heads are on your faith."

"To a dungeon!" replied Ulrick; "even there my spirit still can scorn thee. Come, Myrra," he added, opening his fettered arms to receive his terror-stricken child; "even in a prison a father's heart can shield thee—a father's breast pillow thy innocent head."

"Not so!" exclaimed Ralph, with a sardonic smile; "it were a stain upon our chivalry to consign so fair a prisoner to so foul a den; our castle hath a bower more suited to her beauty and her years."

"No, no!" shrieked Myrra; for as he spoke a nameless terror struck upon her heart; "my father's dungeon, the scaffold, or the grave—any where with him. I dare not—will not quit my father's side."

Despite her tears and entreaties, despite the desperate efforts of her distracted father, the unhappy girl was torn from his protecting arms, and placed by the guards in the hands of their chief, whose admiration of her beauty was, if possible, increased by the charm of its sorrows, and who listened to Ulrick's frantic curse with a triumphant laugh.

At a wave of his hand the captive was dragged by overwhelming numbers to his dungeon, and the helpless Myrra left in the power of the object of her terror.

It is impossible to say, in the excitement of the moment, to what excess his passions might have hurried him, had not the frightful convulsions into which his victim fell on beholding him approach for awhile proved her protection. Calling to some of the female attendants of Ethra, he ordered them to bear her to a chamber remote from the apartment of his wife, from whom, on peril of his wrath, they were to conceal the knowledge of her being in the castle.

Ralph de Gael knew how much he was detested, not only by the Saxon franklins and nobles whom he had oppressed, but by the inhabitants of the city generally, whom his exactions had on more than one occasion driven into unsuccessful outbreaks against his authority, the suppression of which had served as pretexts for fresh spoliation. But the present danger was of unusual gravity. Nobles and serfs, peasants and artisans, all seemed leagued against him. In his arrogance he had so offended the neighbouring Norman nobles that even from them he could count on faint support. He dispatched, therefore, that very night, a message to the king, then holding his parliament at Bury St. Edmund's, to demand prompt succour, at the same time informing him that the exiled traitor, Ulrick of Stanfield, was his prisoner. A council of war was afterwards called, and means debated to best provide against the threatened attack; for the Norman, whatever might have been his crimes, was no carpet knight, but as prompt in battle as in evil deeds.

Ethra—the neglected, the heartbroken, but still loving Ethra—had on this eventful night remained long after the vesper hymn had ceased, praying in the castle chapel, unheeded and alone; an unusual depression weighed upon her soul, a secret warning of the realisation of those undefined terrors which haunt the predestined and foredoomed. The only light within the sacred place proceeded from the ever burning lamps before our lady's shrine, and as their reflection fell upon the pale but still beautiful features of the penitent, they lit up a picture which a painter might have copied with advantage.

"Peace," whispered the suppliant. "Holy Mother, pray that my heart finds peace! Pour thou the balm of kind oblivion on its bleeding sorrows! Save me from madness! save me from myself!"

"Thy prayer will soon be heard," exclaimed a voice near to her; indeed, so near that the breath of the speaker bore the words to her very ear. "Soon will my prediction be accomplished."

Ethra started, and beheld the woman whom ten years before she had saved from the fury of her two hounds on the fatal morning when she first beheld Ralph de Gael. Although so long a period had elapsed, she had not forgotten either the adventure or the strange prediction.

"It is accomplished, mother," she answered humbly; "I am indeed outraged—scorned."

"But not avenged," sternly interrupted her strange visitor.

"What meanest thou?"

"Art thou so poor in spirit," demanded the hag, "as to ask that question? While thou art praying, wasting thy hours in solitary tears, thy husband—but no," she added, checking herself, "why should I tell the tale thou hast no wish to hear? what is't to thee with whom he wastes his hours, so thou canst weep and pray? Thou hast thy Norman mother's blood, not the proud spirit of thy Saxon race."

"What meanest thou?" replied Ethra, drawing herself up with fearful calmness. "Nay, torture me not with dark surmises or womanish conceits, to raise false jealousy within my heart; but if thou knowest aught touching my husband's faith, I charge thee tell it me!"

"He hath a mistress in these very walls—young, beautiful, and good as thou wert once," said the hag. "Soon will thy lord become the slave of her caprice, and know no law but the fair idol's pleasure."

"Thanks!" said the unhappy Ethra—"thanks! Thy words have fallen like coals of fire upon my head; but still I thank thee. Monster!" she added, with a burst of grief apostrophising her destroyer, "here, in my very home, to trample on my heart! As yet," she exclaimed, and a fearful expression passed over her excited features, "Ralph but little knows the nature he has wronged: he hath seen it only in the weakness of its love; let him beware of the strength of its revenge!"

"And thy fair rival?" demanded the woman.

"Dies," whispered Ethra, sternly; "this very night my sleeping rival dies. Then will despair rage high in my destroyer's breast—then will he feel, in agonising throes, a portion of that hell which rages here."

Drawing her veil around her, with a calm step the speaker left the chapel to return to her apartments in the castle. Her informant remained gazing after her a few moments in silence.

"Now," she exclaimed, "are my years of plotting turned to some account; mischief is high afloat, and misery rears its pale still standard o'er us. The jealous wife will not fail to recognise her sister—her sister to impart their father's danger; remorse and jealousy will find a means to save them both. Ulrick once free, these blood-stained towers must fall; and with them their destroying, heartless tyrant. Curse him!" she added, sinking on her knees; "the widow's lonely curse rest on him! Avenge me, Heaven, on the destroyer of my husband, the seducer of my child, and earth and I will then be quits."

The speaker, who had twice so strangely crossed the path of Ethra, had, indeed, no common cause of hatred to the Norman governor, for her husband had been murdered by Ralph de Gael for resisting his violence towards their only child, whom the tyrant, in a fit of caprice, had torn from her humble home; it was, therefore, with a mother's and a widow's lacerated heart that the Saxon crone had cursed him.

On reaching her apartment Ethra dismissed her attendants, from whose confusion and evasive manners, when she demanded if any strangers had arrived within the castle, she read the confirmation of her fears. As soon as she was alone she removed the jewels from her neck and arms, and changed her dress for a dark mantle and veil, such as, in the long corridors through which she had to pass, were likely to be least observed. Opening a small cabinet, she drew from it a dagger of highly-tempered steel. Despite her resolution a sickening sensation came over her as she grasped the weapon in her hand.

"What am I about to do?" she murmured. "Stain my soul with blood! Better to end my own wretched, blighted existence. 'Tis but a blow, and——No, no," she added, after a pause, "gladly as I would welcome death, mine must not be the hand. There still remains a task to be performed. The captive priest, whose dismal dungeon I discovered in my wanderings, assures me he is armed with the means to prove my father's innocence—to crush my vile betrayer. Ulrick!" she exclaimed, and a flood of tears followed the word, "thy guilty but repentant child shall vindicate thy name, and ask forgiveness only in the tomb."

In a chamber within the keep of Norwich Castle, worn with grief and terror, the innocent Myrra slept. The female attendants to whose care she had been consigned, knowing all escape to be impossible, had withdrawn to their apartments, situated in Bigod's tower, and thus the helpless girl was deprived of even the feeble protection which their presence would have afforded. The room would have been in utter darkness, but for the stream of moonlight which entered through the large grated window and fell upon the couch, lighting the heavy crimson draperies with its silver light. Myrra had always entertained a deep love, and almost superstitious veneration, for the memory of her mother, whose spirit she devoutly believed still watched over the safety of her child with all a mother's affection, with all a guardian angel's care. In all her sorrows she was accustomed to address her prayers to her loved shade; and her portrait, which she wore suspended from a pomander chain round her neck, was to her fond imagination a relic to which some mysterious influence was attached.

Perhaps there is no feeling of the human

heart so unstained by selfishness or passion, as the love which children bear their mother. How often, in after life, when the grave has closed around that tender parent's form, will a word, a look, recall to mind that guardian of our infant years—that confidant of childhood's sorrows! Again her eyes, beaming with affection, seem to dwell on ours. Again her voice breathes sweet reproof, or whispers consolation in our ears. A mother's name claims from the world respect, and from her children honour.

Myrra's was not that calm and peaceful sleep which rests upon the brow of those who slumber in the security of home and watchful friends. Her restless dreams were wild and troubled as her fortunes; dark threatening shadows weighed upon her spirit, and her deep-drawn breathings were interrupted by sighs and moanings, such as might break from an imprisoned cherub's unquiet rest. Her long chestnut hair, nature's own screen to modesty, had escaped from the embroidered veil which bound it, and fell in curling masses over her innocent bosom, which rose and sank with every exhalation of her fragrant breath. Her right hand grasped the chain and portrait, as the protecting ægis beneath whose influence she slept; and her left arm rested carelessly on her dark robe, contrasting like sculptured ivory upon an ebon ground. It was a picture an angel might have contemplated with pleasure, a fiend should have shuddered to approach.

Cautiously the arras which covered the entrance to the apartment was drawn aside, and Ethra, bearing a lamp and the poniard she had taken from the cabinet, approached. Her step was slow and stealthy as the pace of the midnight murderer; her breath escaped from her clenched teeth more like the faint hiss of a cautious snake than the free breathings of a human being. Perhaps the strong effort of self-control was more fearful in the still beautiful creature than even the wildest storm of passion would have been. Her cheek was pale with the horror of the resolution which her knit brow conveyed, and her dark, brilliant eyes flashed with the lcteric sparks of her contending passions.

"She sleeps," she murmured to herself, "thank Heaven she sleeps! Oh! when shall I know rest? Calmly she sleeps, as if watchful angers hovered o'er her couch to shield their charge from danger. 'Tis but a blow—a bubbling gush—a moment's struggle—and life's fitful dream is ended! Let me look on her fair face," she added, "gaze on the charms whose fatal beauty has robbed me of the love bought with so many crimes; the sight will steel my heart and nerve my hand."

Twice did the speaker flash the light of the small silver lamp she bore over the features of her sleeping rival. So many years had elapsed since they had met, or jealousy had so blinded her, that not one trait recalled the infant sister, whom she had abandoned, to her memory.

"Young, too," she continued; "perhaps innocent. No matter, she hath crossed my solitary path; her fatal beauty disputes with me the only heart I ever prized. Away remorse, and weak blinding pity. She dies!"

The hand of the jealous woman was raised—another instant, and the sleep of the gentle, innocent Myrra would have been eternal, when Heaven, whose wisest purposes so oft seem accident, interposed to save her soul from crime. Despite her resolution, the doubt that her rival might be the victim, and not the accomplice of her betrayer, shook her purpose. The chain and portrait which attracted her attention promised to confirm or dissipate her doubts. Gently releasing if from the sleeper's hand, she raised it to the lamp, and saw it was—her mother's! Twice did she press her hand upon her care-worn brow, deeming that memory had deceived her, or conscience conjured the accusing shadow to her blasted sight. Her burning eyeballs, incapable of tears, were rivetted on the unconscious ivory. Convinced that it was, indeed, her mother's portrait, her first impulse was to cover it with kisses, but a blush of shame, which suffused her cheek at the recollection of her crime, restrained her.

"It is no mockery of my senses," she exclaimed, "but real—my mother, such as in life she looked and smiled upon her child. Who is this sleeper, then?" she added, fixing her eyes with pitiable terror upon the couch. "Why does she wear my mother's portrait? Can it be?—no, no!" she shudderingly continued, as the fearful suspicion of who Myrra really was flashed upon her; "God is too merciful for that; madness were bliss to such adamning thought—yet doubt is worse than madness."

Rushing to the bed, she grasped the sleeper frantically, calling upon her to awaken. Myrra started at the voice from her uneasy dreams, and beholding a female, whose agitated features were more like those of the inspired pythoness than cold humanity, called in her fears for mercy.

"Call not to Heaven," exclaimed Ethra, "in idle adjurations, but answer me. Whose portrait is this?"

"My mother's," replied the astonished girl. "Oh, give it back—it is my mother's!"

Her request was alike unheard and unheeded, for at the words, "my mother's!" the unhappy woman fell to the ground with a shriek so piercing, so unearthly, that it sounded like the yell which the departing spirit gives when driven from this world hopeless of the next.

Despite her terror and astonishment, Myrra sufficiently mastered her emotions to assist the incomprehensible being who had so rudely broke upon her slumbers. Pouring water from the vase of flowers in the window of her chamber into her hands, she bathed her burning brow, and chafed her hands; but it was long ere life, with a deep-drawn sigh, recalled the insensible Ethra back to the sense of misery and guilt. Her first feeling was to end her blighted, lonely existence; shame and remorse bowed her crushed spirit to the dust, and she feared death less than she feared to meet her innocent sister's eye.

"Where," she exclaimed, wildly starting to her feet, "where is the poniard—misery's last friend, dishonour's sole resource?"

"What!" said Myrra, misconceiving her intention, "and wouldst thou take my life?"

"Thy life!" iterated Ethra, her feelings suddenly diverted from their fearful nature by the question. "Am I then quite a monster? Thy life! Oh, I would give the wretched remnant of my days to save thy heart one pang—pour the blood freely from my guilty breast, ere harm approached to thee, my guileless, innocent sister!"

"Sister!" repeated Myrra in astonishment.

"Ay, sister! thy elder born! she who taught thy infant lips to utter their first prayer! whose last kiss within her father's ruined halls was pressed upon thy cheek! Let me, ere I die," she added, "taste the last happiness my soul can know—a sister's fond embrace! Come to this heart, which throbs as it would burst to meet thee—this broken heart, which, crushed by guilt and sorrow, still can spring to thee!"

With passionate tenderness the speaker threw her arms around her long lost sister, pressed her with almost a mother's love to her agitated bosom, and printed a thousand kisses upon her unsullied brow and cheeks. Encircled in the weeping Myrra's arms, she felt as if not quite abandoned by Heaven; it was the first ray of mercy which had fallen upon her soul. Nature had struck the rock, and melted it.

"Ethra! dear Ethra!" whispered her sister, "why this mystery? Why so long concealed the secret of your escape upon that fearful night, which gave our home to flames, our hearts to desolation?"

"Ask me not; there's crime and madness in the fearful tale."

"And shame?" added Myrra, mournfully, in an inquiring voice.

Her sister started from her at the word, and gazed with a haughty but not angry look upon her.

"No," she answered slowly; "those who loved me once, may curse my memory, but never blush for it. Thinkst I had clasped thee, my pure and innocent sister, to my breast, had I been the polluted thing my cheek would burn to name? No, though it freeze thy ear to hear the damning truth, blister my lips to utter it, still it must be told that Ethra is a wife."

"Whose?" demanded her sister, with a look in which terror and pity were mingled.

"His," she exclaimed, "whose sword left a desert where he found a paradise—who made thee motherless, and me a wretch—the wife of Ralph de Gael."

"Of Ralph de Gael!" repeated Myrra, in a voice of horror, "of him who holds thy father captive, whose licentious passion threatens thy sister with far worse than death! Save me from him," she continued, "for our mother's memory, for the honour of our name—save me, or kill me here."

The agony with which the speaker urged her request proved how deeply grounded were her terrors; and despite the impulse of her better nature, her sister felt a pang of jealousy that another should be preferred by him for whom she had sacrificed her hope of heaven, the world, and self-esteem. The sentiment was but momentary. Throwing her arm around the fair girl, as if to protect her even from imaginary outrage, she reassured her that she possessed the will as well as power to release both her and her parent from their tyrant's hold, and that long ere morning's dawn they should be both at liberty.

"And thou too, Ethra?" urged the trembling pleader; "thou too wilt quit this scene of shame and crime?"

"No," replied her sister, sternly; "I know my fate, and will not shrink from its fulfilment. Fearful hath been my crime; as fearful shall be my expiation. Let me but obtain my father's pardon ere I die, and I have done with life; but see," she added, pointing to the evening star, which began to glitter faintly in the heavens, "time presses; ere the glorious sun shall gladden earth, I have much to do. Come, Myrra, come; banish all dread from thy pure, guiltless breast; indulge that hope I never more must know."

The prison in which Ulrick was confined was a deep subterranean cell, lying between the inner and outward moat, and, from the rude massive character of its architecture, as well as the absence of anything like ornament, was evidently of much older date than the castle itself, having most probably formed, with the winding passages which led to it, a part of the ancient fortress erected by Canute, who held his court in Norwich. It was one of those dungeons which tyranny alone could have conceived, or the eye of cruelty have gazed on without a shudder. The green, fœtid lichen had tapestried its unequal walls with its unwholesome vegetation; and monstrous fungi—the undisturbed growth of years, the home of the bloated toad and slimy reptile—carpeted the cold, damp floor. The thick greasy plants were crushed beneath the impatient tread of our hero as he paced the cell, and the scared inmates lazily crawled from his path, trailing their hideous forms to some undisturbed retreat.

At first his storm of passion had been fearful—perchance its violence had exhausted itself, or the cold heavy air reduced the raging fever of his blood; for, after a few hours' pacing of his cell, he gradually became calm and collected, his thoughts reverted to the past, and if hope whispered him no promise for the future, it was that a secret monitor assured him, that for him time had, indeed, no future.

On approaching one corner of his dungeon, he observed an indistinct heap thrown carelessly together, half hid by the same rank vegetation which every where encroached around him; the indistinct light of the solitary lamp suspended from the ceiling did not at first allow him to examine it distinctly; but as his eyes gradually became habituated to the place, he perceived the object of his attention to be a human skeleton; doubtless the remains of some former inmate, left to moulder in the den where its last prayer had been raised to Heaven, its last sigh echoed unheeded in its flinty walls. As he reverently raised the skull, a serpent, which had found it a convenient hiding-place, glided through his fingers, and fell upon the ground. The faint hiss of the reptile lacked that acute sound peculiar in those of its species who dwell in sun and light; it was weak and sickly, as the atmosphere of its damp, cheerless home.

"And this," he mused, "is man! The noblest temple Deity has reared becomes a reptile's hiding-place! Thought, which is Deity, ousted from its shrine, that the foul toad may dwell there! What lofty thoughts, what noble purposes may have had birth within this hollow skull! Perchance," he added, after a pause, "what fearful crimes engendered there! Its dreams, like mine, may have been those of liberty, and this the don't."e

"The end of all on earth!" exclaimed a deep-toned voice, which sounded at a distance.

Ulrick started, and looked eagerly around his prison. He was alone.

"Who spoke?" he demanded, "or have my senses mocked me?"

"One who hath counted ten long years of solitude, yet never for a moment doubted justice on earth, or Heaven's absolving mercy in a better world."

"I hear thee," said our hero, "and yet I see thee not. Where art thou, whose voice breathes hope and consolation, when hope and consolation seem to fail?"

"Art thou alone?" continued the speaker.

"Alone, with solitude and death," was the reply.

"Wait, then, a moment, till I get my tools," resumed the unknown. "I laboured years to forge them from a fragment of my broken chain—ground them with untiring patience upon my dungeon stone, less hard than my obdurate tyrant's heart. Wonder not, then, I prize them," he added, "and conceal them carefully from my suspicious gaoler's curious eye."

In a few moments Ulrick heard a noise against the wall which evidently divided the vast vault into two distinct prisons. One by one the huge stones were removed, until an aperture sufficiently large to admit the ingress of a human being was made in the solid masonry.

"Can I assist you?" he demanded.

"No," replied the stranger; "I am used to the attempt, and require no aid."

The next moment the speaker stood before him—a tall, emaciated figure, whose beard, straggling and thin, descended to his girdle; whose haggard features, from long seclusion, were of that death-like waxy hue we see upon the corpse. The tattered robe which enshrouded him, and the torn scapulary, denoted that the wearer was a member of some religious order; but the fragments were too ragged, and too much soiled and worn by time, to tell the gazer which.

"Welcome, brother in affliction!" exclaimed Ulrick, extending his hand to the strange phantom; "doubly welcome if I read aright thy priestly office in these sullied robes. Religion's minister, in such an hour, is more than welcome to the captive's heart."

"I am, indeed," replied the wretched being, "an unworthy priest of the Most High."

"And what virtue made thee the prisoner of Ralph de Gael?"

"My weakness and his crimes. Like some midnight thief, he stole upon my peaceful path, and tore me from the only shelter sin and the world had left me. Long I refused compliance with his will—refused to aid him in the vile scheme of vengeance he had formed, to crush the foe he had too deeply injured; torture was used; I yielded, and am punished."

"Torture—and a priest!" repeated his hearer, with horror.

"Ay," said Father Onfroy; for our readers have doubtless recognised in the captive, thus singularly brought in contact with our hero, the priest whose skill in caligraphy had been so successfully employed by Ralph de Gael to forge the documents which justified his attack upon Stanfield, and established a charge of conspiracy upon Ulrick; "the torture, the burning pincers, and the cruel rack. In my early days I had often gazed upon the victims bound there—counted their groans and shrieks—looked coldly on whilst every limb was stretched in mortal agony—each muscle quivering with pain too exquisite for nature to support. I have felt it since," he added, with a shudder; "felt all that I was—all that I inflicted. My punishment hath not been more fearful than my crimes."

"Who art thou?" demanded Ulrick, struck by the tone of his voice, which wakened painful recollections in his soul. "We have met before; for as I hear thee speak, the memory of many a year gone by passes in shadowy visions o'er my mind. I know not where or when, or under what circumstances, but I could swear that we have met before."

Seizing his visitor by the arm, the speaker led, or rather dragged, him to the centre of the dungeon, directly beneath the lamp, which hung suspended by an iron chain above them. They recognised each other instantly. There was no mistaking, worn and preternaturally aged as long captivity had made him, the unearthly features, disfigured by a thousand minute scars, of the unhappy monk, who equally traced, amid the ravages of grief and change of clime, the noble countenance of the Saxon.

"Robert of Artois!" "Ulrick of Stanfield!" they mutually exclaimed, and remained gazing on each other; each, from different emotions, unable to pronounce another word.

The priest was indeed no other than that most unhappy man, who, on the departure of his son Gilbert with his bride to Normandy, had, by the advice and consent of Lanfranc, concealed his crimes and reputation within the cloister, where, under the name of Brother Onfroy, he became remarkable for that fatal skill in caligraphy which had made

him the tool and victim of his unprincipled persecutor.

The monk was the first to recover from his surprise. Long suffering had extinguished in him the pride which had rendered his earlier penitence imperfect. The hand of Heaven seemed to have brought about their meeting. Sinking on his knees, he could only utter the indistinctly pronounced words, "Pardon—pardon!"

"Rise!" said our hero. "The knee devoted to the altar should not be bent to sinful man. Whatever thy crimes, long suffering has atoned them; an angel while on earth pronounced forgiveness—fear not I shall revoke it."

"Ulrick," faltered the still kneeling suppliant, "in this dark hour I feel the bitterness, the shame of vice, the holiness of virtue. As yet thou knowest not half thy injuries: my first crime failed to deprive thee of thy love; my second robbed thee of thine honour."

"What meanest thou?" his astonished hearer demanded.

"The letters which Ralph de Gael doubtless produced before the king to justify his outrage—the details of the Saxon plot to break the Norman yoke—to assassinate, cowardly assassinate each noble in his hold—which gave thy name to infamy, thy memory to scorn—were forged by this degraded hand."

"Horror!" exclaimed his victim. "Did that blow come from thee?"

"From me," continued the guilty man, "whose early crime thou hadst forgiven, whose deserted son thou hadst protected. Loathing existence, yet afraid to die, I yielded to the racks of sharp agony, and stained my knightly honour and my priestly vow by forgery—by a vile felon's weakness and a felon's act."

For a few moments there was a struggle in the generous Saxon's breast; but, fearfully as he had been wronged, he felt that Heaven had sufficiently avenged him, and that man had nought to add to its punishment. His own span of life he looked upon as counted, and trembled to appear before its bar with the sin of unforgiveness on his soul.

"Rise!" he said. "Where Heaven hath punished, man can only pardon. As freely as the creature can forgive its fellow creature, so do I pardon thee."

"Thanks," murmured Robert of Artois; "armed with thy forgiveness, I may present myself at Heaven's bar, trusting it will not prove less merciful than thou hast. Oh!" he added, passionately, "but for one moment's liberty, to wash this foul dishonour from my soul—to rend the mask from this

detested tyrant—to atone the wrong my unwilling hand hath done thee, and place thy
honour, in the minds of men, pure as the
angels who record it see it!"

"Dreams! dreams!" said our hero, mournfully shaking his head; "this dungeon is a
tomb from whence life finds no egress. Behold," he added, pointing to the skeleton,
"my history and its moral. Some future
inmate of this cell will muse o'er my remains, wondering whose nameless bones remain here."

"I'll not believe it," replied his companion; "such fate might be mine. There
would be justice in it; but Heaven hath
tried thy virtues far too deeply not to reward
at last; its purposes are ne'er so darkly
veiled from human eye as when near their
fulfilment. It speaks in parables and strikes
through clouds. Why," he added, with
increased confidence, "hath my worthless
being been preserved? Why do we both
meet here, but that the crime of years
should be atoned, and truth made clear at
last?"

"Impossible!" exclaimed Ulrick; "who
would heed thy tale?"

"Ali," answered Robert. "Were I free,
I'd find the means to place thy innocence
beyond suspicion's breath."

At this moment, through the grating of
the iron door which barred their path to
freedom, the rays of a distant light became
faintly visible. The monk was the first to
observe it. Pointing it out to his companion,
he whispered—

"Have I not prophesied?"

"'Tis but the gaoler, or my executioner."

"Say rather thy deliverer, and mine; the
hour so long dreamt and prayed for is at
hand."

Hastening to the door, he applied his eyes
to the grating, and saw at a distance, in the
long damp passage, a veiled female form
bearing a lamp—it was the same figure which
had often visited him in his dungeon, consoled his sorrows and lone captivity, and
alleviated his miseries. His heart beat high
with hope and expectation.

"She comes!" he cried; "the avenger
comes at last. Farewell, I must retire within
my cell: none must know of our communication. If I err not, soon wilt thou have
another trial to thy generous heart; but it
will bear thee through it. Say not that we
have met. Shouldst thou obtain thy liberty
without me, lead on thy friends to the
attack: living release, or dead avenge me. If
I fall," he added, "dig in the corner of my
dungeon nearest the iron ring to which for
years my body was enchained, and thou wilt
find a scrap of parchment concealed within

the skull of some lone victim who preceded
me; guard it as thou wouldst thy life and
honour, for it may serve to vindicate them
both."

Scarcely had Robert of Artois time to regain his den, and replace the means of communication between the two cells, than the
bar which fastened the iron door of Ulrick's
prison on the outside was removed, and
Ethra, the guilty and repentant Ethra, her
features concealed beneath the long sable veil
which enshrouded her trembling form, entered
the dungeon.

For awhile parent and child remained
gazing upon each other in silence—Ulrick from
surprise, and Ethra from the deep emotion
which consumed her. Years had elapsed
since she last gazed upon that stately form
—since his deep accents had fallen upon her
ear; and yet it seemed as they had met but
yesterday—so true to memory are the first
characters time traces on its tablets. She
feared to speak, lest the cry of her bruised
heart should reach her lips, and nature
vindicate her rights, in the sweet name of
father.

"Who art thou?" demanded the captive
—"some spirit of consolation haunting these
fearful cells, sent to prepare me for the parting hour, when life and grief are ended;
shrouding the ministry of heaven in veils,
that thy glad beauty break not too soon upon
us?"

"Not the bright being of another world,"
quickly answered his despairing visitant;
"but one upon whose brow misery hath set
its burning seal, hath come to weep in pity
o'er thy woes—to soothe and to relieve them
—to ope thy dungeon door, and bid thee
forth to liberty and vengeance."

"To liberty!" exclaimed her astonished
listener. "Is that word breathed in these
dungeons, which for years have heard no
sound but captives' groans and supplicating
sighs? Who, then, art thou? Thy speech
bespeaks thee Saxon, but thy words imply a
speech which none but damning crimes could
purchase thee in Ralph de Gael's halls."

Although Ethra had addressed her father
in the Norman tongue, the accent with which
she spoke it to his practised ear betrayed
her race. Ulrick's allusion to her country
touched her heart—it seemed like the first
step towards his recognition of his child; she
forgot that for ten years he had deemed her
dead—dwelt upon her memory as on a
seraph's early called from earth, not as a
guilty living thing of shame and sorrow.

"Thou hast guessed rightly," she faltered;
"I am of Saxon blood." Then hastily added,
as if fearful of the consequences of her admission—"But years have passed since I be-

THE DEATH OF ETHWOLD.

held my home—years since the sound of kindred voice hath fallen on my ear, or kindred love gladdened the desolation of my heart. Wonder not, then, that I became its victim—wedded the man stained with a parent's blood—brought foul dishonour on a noble name, unsullied save by me."

"What!" interrupted the horror-stricken Saxon, "wedded with one whose hand was red with the same blood which flows within thy veins?—perchance a father's or a brother's blood. Oh, woman, woman! affrighted furies spread thy nuptial couch, and hell and terror drew its curtains round thee."

His reproving words and lofty indignation fell like a sentence upon her self-accusing soul, and had not a burst of tears relieved her heart, its agony had broken it.

"Hear me!" she cried; "judge not my crime unheard! No common snares were spread to catch my soul. With mercy and compassion listen to my tale; weigh my long years of agony and deep remorse, my blighted youth and outraged heart, against my crime. Hear ere thou condemn me."

Moved by her passionate grief, Ulrick pointed to the rude stone in the centre of his dungeon, on which his trembling visitor sank exhausted by the strength of her emotions. With one of those violent efforts which strong minds only can exert, she, after a few moments' pause, collected her wandering thoughts, and then commenced her tale of many sorrows.

CHAPTER XXXII.

'Tis not in words to tell the power,
The despotism which from that hour
Passion held on me.—MOORE'S LOVES OF THE ANGELS.

LOVED !" said Ethra. "Knowest thou the power those words imply? They are the key to the soul's mysteries —the ciphers of its passions. I loved, not with the light feeling of a girlish heart, whose smiles and tears, like April's sun-lit showers, succeed; but with the strength of summer's ardent rage, whose smile consumes, whose burning kiss destroys. We met in secret, but not in sin," she added quickly, as she caught the expression of Ulrick's eye. "Fallen as I am, that shame at least was spared me. I am not of a race that could survive dishonour."

"So shall thy soul prove lighter by a crime," said her hearer; "but tell me, woman, why this concealment? Was thy father cold, insensible, or churlish in his love—one who ruled by fear and not affection's ministry?"

"No," answered the unhappy Ethra, "my heart hath not even that mean excuse to ease its burden. Oh! he was good, affection's self, tender, considerate, generous, loving, wise in all but his weak love for his degenerate child."

"And thou abandoned him? left him in his age, perchance to pass in childless solitude the remnant of his days in his once happy home—fitting return for all his care and fond parental love?"

"Worse," added Ethra, with a violent effort at self-command; "I brought destruction on that happy home; these guilty hands unbarred the door to the triumphant foe—gave to the fury of the Norman sword, parents, kindred, friends—brought desolation on my name and race, and misery on myself."

"Horror!" exclaimed our hero, starting from her, for her words brought to his mind the destruction of his own lordly halls, and he recoiled from her as from a loathsome thing; "I had a child—in tears of anguish oft I mourn her lost; I now thank Heaven she lives not, such a wretch as thou art. But why," he added, "why this sad tale of grief and sin to me?"

"Thou art my father's friend," replied the penitent. "Chance has revealed to me that still he lives; therefore it is I ope thy prison door, that thou, in turn, mayst plead for my forgiveness."

"Avoid that father," sternly answered Ulrick; "never meet his sight, lest, recognising thee, his heart-strings break, and, dying, he should curse thee."

At these fearful words, which seemed like a sentence to her despairing soul, Ethra wrung her hands bitterly; and the convulsive sobs and deep-drawn sighs which shook her form showed how deep was the remorse and agony of her bruised heart. Little did the returned exile deem the trembling, guilty creature before him was his own child; the once happy, smiling girl, whose arm a hundred times had been entwined around his neck—whose innocent kisses had so often sealed the words of warning on his lips.

"I have lived," she at last sobbed forth, "till life has been a curse; lived to become the scorn of all I loved—of all who ever loved me. Wouldst thou, stern judge," she added, throwing herself upon her knees suddenly before him, "thus harshly judge thy child? Would not thy iron nature melt while thus in agony she sued to be forgiven —pleaded her girlish years, her fatal passion, her long remorse, and broken heart, for mercy? Wouldst thou bid her on to her great sacrifice——"

"Sacrifice!" repeated Ulrick, "what sacrifice?"

"One," said Ethra, rising proudly from her knees, "which shall give this blood-stained hold to the avenging Saxon's sword, and hurl the tyrant to the doom he merits—

one that shall end this guilty life and the oppressor's reign together."

"Meanest thou," demanded Ulrick, gazing on her with a look of admiration as well as pity, "that——"

"I mean," interrupted Ethra, "that as this guilty hand unbarred the entrance to the Norman foe, and let the wolf upon the slumbering fold of my own kindred, it now shall ope the Norman gates to the avenger's hand. Methinks," she added, glancing wildly round, "the spirits of my slaughtered race are all assembled here, and, sternly pointing to these blood-stained towers, claim the great sacrifice to soothe their shades."

"This is, indeed, atonement," said Ulrick —"a deed to win a pardon for a crime like thine; a deed to gain a father's forfeit love, and crown thy days with penitence and peace."

"What!" exclaimed the unhappy woman; "thinkest thou so meanly of me that I seek to live, to bear upon my faded brow the brand of double treason? Oh, never—never! To avenge my country, my murdered kindred, and my outraged heart—to save thee, Ulrick, and thy innocent child from Ralph de Gael's rage, I yield him to the doom; but think not," she added mournfully—"think not I will survive him."

"Thy country's gratitude, thy kindred's love——"

"Say rather their pity, their humiliating pity," interrupted Ethra. "I know man's ingrate nature, and will not trust it. Thinkst thou I could bear to meet the world's reproving gaze, or hear it whisper, 'Behold the being who betrayed father and husband, duty and country,' forgetful that no choice was left me in my sorrow—no loop-hole to escape in my despair? No; I can welcome death, slumber in peace within the quiet grave, where passion moves not and the heart's at rest, let but a father's pardon rest upon it."

"And if he have a heart," said Ulrick, "it will."

These words fell like balm upon the listener's soul; they were the first rays of hope which pierced through the dark night of her despair. Laying her trembling hand upon his arm, she answered—

"Thou art his friend; no voice will touch his heart like thine, no reasoning reach his ear."

"His name?" demanded Ulrick, with surprise.

"That," resumed the speaker, "thou wilt know hereafter; this paper tells the rest of my sad history. Not now," she hastily added, as her father was about to unfold it; "read it not now. Leading from these dungeons, a passage conducts us to the outer moat. I have secured the skiff—a boat is ready to convey thee on."

"And my child?"

"Already awaits thee there," answered Ethra. "Thinkst thou I would leave thy innocent child within the tiger's fangs? Once free, summon thy friends, and return by the same means. Like Sin guarding the gates of Death, I will remain and give them entrance. But swear," she added, "that the great sacrifice accomplished—my country freed—my kindred blood avenged,—swear that my father's pardon shall reward the deed."

"You tax me past my power," answered the bewildered Ulrick, astonished at the vehemence of her words and the deep passion which shook her soul; "but if my prayers can win the boon, I promise it shall be yours."

"It can, it can," resumed the agitated Ethra, with a burst of tears which relieved her heart. "He will listen to thy pleading. If thou shouldst find him harsh, if the absolving words should linger on his lips, lead him," she added, "to my grave—paint to him my sorrows and remorse, my blighted years, life's withered hopes—bid him forget my sin in its atonement; then will the voice of nature speak within him, and his heart melt in precious, dear forgiveness."

There was something so desolate, so heart-broken and despairing in the speaker's voice, that the firm nature of the soldier melted at its tone. In the agitation of the moment her veil had partially fallen aside, displaying her still beautiful though care-worn features. Perhaps it may be wondered that he failed to recognise them; but ten years of womanhood and sorrow had so altered their expression from those of the wild joyous girl his heart so long had mourned as with the dead, and the pale lamp's uncertain light so shadowed them, that the suspicion never crossed his brain. Had it, oh! with what eager love his arms would have enfolded his lost treasure—with what absolving tears his yearning heart pronounced forgiveness of her crime, oblivion of the past! But it was not to be; the sacrifice to conscience was voluntary and accepted.

"Live," he exclaimed, "to hear the pardon thy repentance merits from a parent's lips; to feel once more the joy of his paternal kiss; to rest thy heart, after life's storms and shipwrecks, in the calm haven of a father's love."

"Never," said his daughter, with an impression of resolution, amounting almost to sternness, upon her brow; "my heart would wither should I see the blush of shame suffuse my father's cheek if men but named his child. Thinkst thou I could bear the world's forgiveness, or, far more hateful, its insulting pity? No," she added, "my life hath been the comet's fearful path—my death be like its end. Time presses: in my father's name, pronounce a blessing and forgiveness on me."

The speaker sank upon her knees as humbly as a child before the absolving priests; and Ulrick, with an emotion of pity and admiration, exclaimed, as he raised his hands above her head :

"In His awful name, Parent of all, and in thy earthly parent's name, I bless and pardon thee; this deed shall be, in after times, by poets sung, thy virtues only live in our remembrance. But stay," he added, as his visitor resumed the lamp, and pointed towards the door of the cell; "I have a companion, one whose life hath for ten long years been wasted in these dungeons, one whose safety is necessary to clear my honour of the foul stain the tyrant cast upon it."

"The priest," said Ethra; "I have not forgotten him; he, too, shall be the companion of thy flight; the path is open to ye both, for liberty and vengeance."

At the summons of our hero the wretched Robert of Artois issued from his den, and gazed for a few moments, with inquiring eye, upon his two companions. A sign from the female informed him that Ulrick knew not that it was to his repentant child he was about to owe his liberty; as his own knowledge of the tie between them was obtained only in the confessional, he was bound to silence. The unhappy woman, it would seem, had often sought him in his dungeon to receive consolation from his ministry, as well as to alleviate the horrors of his lone captivity with the sweet solace of sympathy and pity.

Bearing the lamp, Ethra preceded the liberated captives through the long damp passages which led to a small ruined tower beyond the second moat, and not far distant from the water's edge. From the unequal nature of the ground, they progressed slowly; in many parts the stone-work had partially fallen, and they had to climb over the obstructing masses. At length they reached a low iron door, firmly imbedded in the solid walls. A figure, wrapped in a dark warm mantle, sprang impatiently to meet them: it was Myrra, who had been long impatiently expecting them. Throwing herself into her sister's arms, she exclaimed:

"Arrived—arrived at last! How fearfully the dreary hour hath passed!"

"Silence," whispered Ethra; "remember your promise. Till safe beyond these walls our father must not know his wretched

daughter lives—wedded to him who caused his house's ruin."

The next moment the still trembling girl was folded to Ulrick's manly breast. A deep pang wrung the heart of the elder sister, as she saw the fond parental kiss—a kiss her blighted cheek was destined never more to feel—a kiss which would have been dearer to her heart than the first smile e'en of an angle's love.

Drawing from her vest the ponderous key, with a firm hand she applied it to the lock; years had most probably elapsed since last the rusty door had groaned upon it hinges. Like some surly guardian, it seemed unwilling to give egress to the captives, resisting all her efforts to force back the ponderous bolt. It required the united strength of Ulrick and his companion to turn the key within the corroded wards. At last it slowly turned upon its axle, and the first breath of morning entered freshly the narrow passage.

"Free!" exclaimed Robert of Artois, drinking with delight the pure air to which for ten long years he had been a stranger. "I have dreamt of this, prayed for this, and it hath come at last. Relenting Heaven hath heard the lonely captive's supplication, and sent him forth for vengeance and atonement!"

"We shall meet again," said Myrra, in an under tone, to her sister. "Promise me that we shall meet again."

"No tears," murmured Ethra, calmly—"no lamentation now! Yes, we shall meet again; if not on earth, at least in heaven, if penitence may win my forfeit place there. Ulrick of Stanfield," she added, in a loud, firm tone, "haste to thy friends; wait not for numbers, lest thy foe escape thee. Here will I station one to give thee ingress to the Norman's hold. Once there, thy sword must do the rest."

"The second night from this," replied our hero, "thou mayest expect me. On every hill the Saxon torch shall gleam, on every breeze the Saxon banner float. Yes, Ralph de Gael, a nation rises in its strength to crush thee. These towers, the scene of thy polluted sway, shall fall before the cry of liberty."

"Let it but sound," added his deliverer, "and fearfully my acts shall answer it. Away!" she exclaimed, impatiently; "each moment of delay is fraught with danger to thy safety."

Despite the entreaties of Ulrick and the silent pleading of her sister, Ethra remained firm in her resolution not to accompany them; her soul was fixed on the accomplishment of her fearful destiny, and she resolved to meet it calmly and alone.

"'Tis past!" she said, as after repeated efforts she succeeded in rolling back the ponderous door which shut her from liberty and those she loved for ever—"life's last weakness is past, and the few hours which remain are due to prayer, to penitence, and vengeance. My heart is lighter now that I feel a father's curse will not rest upon his poor girl's grave—armed with his forgiveness, I dare to hope for Heaven's. No weakness," she added, as with an impatient gesture she dashed aside the tears which, despite her resolution, chased each other down her burning cheek; "no vain regrets, no weak relenting pity. Here will I wait, and watch the hour whose sound shall strike for freedom and for justice, shall calm the tempests of life's stormy passions, and bring this weary, long-worn, restless spirit peace."

Seating herself upon a rough fragment of the fallen arch, Ethra passed the first hour of her lonely watch in silent, fervent prayer.

As soon as the fugitives emerged from the ruined tower in which the secret passage terminated, Robert of Artois bade adieu to his companions, and directed his steps towards the convent, where, after much difficulty, he succeeded in obtaining an interview with the prior, and making himself known to him. The indignation of the monks was boundless at the outrage offered to their order in the person of their brother. In its first burst, they threatened nothing less than death and excommunication upon the Norman governor, whose tyranny and exactions they had frequently felt in common with their oppressed and insulted Saxon neighbours.

Despite the secrecy with which the arrest of Ulrick had been conducted, the news soon reached the ears of the insurgent leaders, and spread dismay amongst them. It required all the influence of Arad and his son Edward to prevent many of the lesser franklins and chiefs from returning to their homes. Without Ulrick to conduct them, they looked upon their cause as hopeless; so well they knew, not only his skill in war, but the influence his name exercised with the serfs and people. His sudden appearance amongst them, therefore, the morning after his escape, decided their deliberations; the shout of joy which welcomed him was as sincere as the relief from their uncertainty was great. In an instant Edward was by the side of his loved Myrra, whispering those thousand tender consolations which love so well can utter.

"Welcome!" cried Arad, grasping the hand of his recovered friend; "think not we have been idle in your cause; this very day we marched to share your fate, or tear you from the tyrant's cruel power; but say," he added, "how fell you in his hands?"

"By Saxon treachery," replied Ulrick; "the cause so oft of England's weakness in the hour of trial. Ethwold, to revenge my refusal of his proffered union with my child, betrayed me to the Norman."

The name of his betrayer was received with a shout of execration by the assembled chiefs.

"And how escaped?" they demanded.

"By the remorse of one who long has lived a wretched victim to her wayward passions, but in whose heart all trace of Eden is not yet extinguished. Despite her thrall, she feels her country's wrongs—despite the tie which binds her to its tyrants, will avenge them."

"Her name—her name?" was demanded on all sides.

"That," resumed our hero, "have I still to learn; this packet tell the rest of her sad history."

Ulrick hastily broke the silken thread which bound the parchment Ethra had given to him ere he left the dungeon. It contained a ring, and a tress of her long, dark hair. For a few seconds he gazed upon the trinket with mute surprise, deeming that memory had played him false, or that he had seen the gem before.

"Surely," he murmured, "I have seen this glittering toy in happier days! It was Matilda's! given on the morning that I called her bride. Thou precious bauble, in whose magic circle recollection, with enchanter's power, recalls to mind past scenes of happiness and joys long fled! Something," he added wildly, "she told me of her home destroyed—her father, long thought dead. Could it?——No—no, I should have known my child; and yet this ring, once the fond pledge of chaste connubial love, gives token of a dreadful tale to come. Read, Myrra, read, and save me from the rack."

With a trembling hand he passed the parchment to his equally agitated child, whose eyes could scarcely decipher the few characters, so blinded were their orbs by tears. In a voice broken by sobs and sighs she read—

"Father, mourn not for Ethra; in freedom's cause she dies—happy at last if thy forgiveness rest upon her grave."

The writing fell from her hand as she concluded, and with a burst of grief she threw herself into her father's arms, who remained for several moments as if transfixed to stone—his misery so vast that at first he neither felt nor comprehended its extent. As it gradually broke upon him, the tempest of his soul became terrific, his hand wandered over his burning brow, as if to reseat reason on her tottering throne; and when at last his words broke forth, they but faintly indicated the agony of his tortured mind.

"My child," he murmured; "my lost, suffering child! left by her father in that den of crime! Nature, that now canst struggle with convulsive throes, why wert thou silent when in agony she cried to be forgiven? Earth should have shook, the heavens sent forth portentous and prodigious signs, to see a father murder his own child. Yes, chieftains," he added, gazing wildly on the assembled Saxons round him, "unknowing whom I judged, I, sternly zealous for my country's good, praised her resolve, and let her stay to die."

"Horror!" said Arad; "thy child?"

"Ay," continued the agitated parent, with a burst of passionate love; "my elder born—the first fond pledge of my connubial bliss, is by her father doomed and sacrificed. Friends, these tears I am not used to shed, flow from me like a girl's; bear with me; nature will claim her rights, despite the heart's resolve, or cold philosophy's stern reasoning. The weakness past, I am once more my country's."

Drawing his mantle over his visage, the speaker retreated to a short distance from the assembly, to commune with his heart, and seek consolation where, in life's shipwrecks and the storms of passion, weak, erring man alone can find it—in prayer. Although the blow had been terrible, it had wounded but not crushed his soul; it rose with the elasticity of faith to meet the last trial Heaven had reserved to test his fortitude and patience. In a short time he returned to his silent, sympathising friends, pale with the fearful struggle he had passed, but calm and self-possessed. Many thought, as they beheld him, they saw the stamp of death upon his face, so colourless, so worn and rigid, his agony of soul had made it. His was, indeed, the majesty of sorrow. The first burst of natural weakness past, and it became far too deep for words, too proud for tears; like death, it veiled its dignity in silence, and only spoke its presence in its impress.

Calmly he proceeded to give his orders to the different leaders: some were dispatched to raise the country round; others sent into the city to urge the discontented citizens to join them—a task more than half accomplished to their hands; as, on their arrival, they found the indignant monks preaching not only in the market-place, but in every spot where a group could be collected, detailing to their horror-stricken hearers the imprisonment and sufferings of the tortured and persecuted Father Onfroy. The vast

piles of wood collected for the purpose on St. James's Hill and the neighbouring heights, at the first stroke of midnight, were ordered to be fired, as signals for the coming onslaught, which Ulrick, in person, undertook to direct. To Edward and a party of his own retainers, who, on the first news of his return, had marched to the place of meeting, our hero confided the entrance of the secret passage, which Ethra had promised should be opened to their ingress. Had he dreamt that his child would have unbarred the door, her anxious father would himself have conducted the enterprise, and resigned to another the more dangerous post of leading the assault without the walls—but it was not to be; their last words on earth were spoken. In life the heart-broken parent and his repentant child were doomed never to meet again. When all was arranged, and not till then, Ulrick and the weeping Myrra retired to mourn together.

Our readers may well imagine the rage and terror of Ralph de Gael when informed not only of the flight of his captives, but the absence of his scorned and long-neglected wife, whose remorse and jealousy he doubted not had opened their dungeon doors. Fortunately, the men who searched the prisons proceeded no farther than the empty cells; had they done so, they would have found the patient Ethra, watching the arrival of the foe, praying for the hour to strike—the signal of her triumph and her death. The tyrant knew too well the energy of his enemy and the danger which threatened him not to prepare to meet it. The garrison were all recalled within the walls of the castle, every tower was manned, the furnaces for heating the boiling lead and oil to pour upon the assailants were got ready; but his chief reliance was on the arrival of the king, to whom our readers will remember, on the first news of the intended outbreak, he had dispatched a trusty messenger.

"Let but Henry come," he exclaimed, "within three days, and I will crush this nest of hornets—trample them like mire beneath my feet. Our walls," he added, as he cast a glance around the lofty battlements, and surveyed the various preparations for the siege, "may hold the Saxon scum at bay, and mock their idle efforts."

The boaster either forgot in his pride, or was ignorant of the passages which conducted, one to the lonely tower where outraged woman's vengeance watched; the other to the cloisters of the cathedral, by which on a previous occasion Ulrick, guided by Father Oswald, had escaped.

As the day rolled on, parties of men, variously armed, might be seen entering the city at every gate. The place of rendezvous was the vast plain which surrounded the castle—not, as now, partially built upon, and occupied by narrow dirty streets, but open and level to the river's edge. Crowds of citizens gradually joined them; and even before the arrival of the more regular forces of the Saxon chiefs, the insurgents presented a formidable array of undisciplined numbers.

The inhabitants of Norwich had long been dissatisfied with the tyranny and grinding exactions of their worthless governor, whose interest had twice defeated them in their attempts to obtain a charter for their city—a boon frequently promised and as frequently withheld by their vacillating monarch.

Ralph de Gael was far too experienced a commander to waste the energies of his men before the moment of attack. He permitted, therefore, the assembling of the insurgents without attempting to disperse them. His policy was to rest on the defensive until the arrival of the royal forces, which Henry, he doubted not, would dispatch to his assistance on the first news of the intended outbreak. Doubly did he applaud his own prudence and foresight in sending a messenger to the king, when banner after banner of the Saxon nobles appeared upon the ground. He saw that it was no petty feud he had to encounter; but the strength of the Angles arrayed against him. Once, and once only, did his cheek turn pale, as the crane-emblazoned pennon of the Lord of Stanfield was planted, amidst the enthusiastic cheers of the enemy, upon a small rising mound almost within bowshot of the walls. Conscience whispered him the contest about to commence was to be one of life and death; and secretly the tyrant prayed that Henry might arrive in time to his assistance. The day rolled on, and still he saw no symptoms of an attack from the tents and huts which the Saxons erected. It was evident that they contemplated reducing him by siege rather than assault.

" Good !" he murmured ; " the fools fall in the snare. Do they think to starve the lion in his den ? Soon shall they find that Norman swords are sharper than their wits !"

Turning upon his heel with a shrug of disdain to those about him, to indicate his contempt of the foe, he left the battlements and descended to the banquet hall, where the evening repast was spread.

At the midnight hour the assailants divided their forces into three equal parties. The first, under the conduct of Ulrick, advanced towards the drawbridge, where a strong body of archers and billmen were stationed, to protect the only approach to the elevated mound on which the castle stood. Their position was further strengthened by a numerous body of men-at-arms, who, from the summit of the lofty tower which formed the principal entrance to the fortress, were ready to pour down boiling lead, oil, stones, and missiles on all who should approach the gates. So that, in the event of the first attack upon the bridge proving successful, the retreat of the defenders into the interior would be effectually covered.

The second party, guided by the indignant monks, were conducted, under the command of Arad, to the secret passage which our readers will remember connected the cathedral with the castle chapel, and which would enable the Saxons to attack the building in the rear, where perhaps it was the most assailable.

The third, guided by Edward, proceeded to the lone round watch-tower by the water's edge. This was the most dangerous to the safety of the garrison of all; for it conducted to the very heart of the stronghold. Its existence, either forgotten or unsuspected by Ralph de Gael, baffled alike his calculation and his courage. Little did the heartless voluptuary imagine, whilst he gave the necessary orders for the defence, and smiled in the fancied security of his position, that the hand of a weak woman would render his precautions unavailing. In his pride and wantonness, he had sown the seed of desolation; the hour had struck when he must reap the harvest of the whirlwind and the storm.

At the first signal of the Saxons, the ponderous iron door rolled slowly upon its hinges, and Ethra, pale as her destiny, appeared before them. The first glance assured her that Ulrick was not the leader of the host, and her heart beat lighter. In the long lonely hours of her silent watch her fear had been to meet her father's eye—to listen to his voice again—to expose her stern resolve to perish in the ruins she had caused—to the entreaties of paternal love, or the weak pleadings of her woman's nature.

"Ascend the passage branching to the left !" she exclaimed to the foremost of the band; " it will conduct ye to your victims. I need not tell you let your hearts be firm and your good weapons strong."

A shout from the eager Saxons proved that she was understood. Despite her worn appearance—for she had neither quitted her post nor tasted food since Ulrick's departure —and the simplicity of her dark robe and veil, there was a commanding dignity in her manner which enabled Edward to recognise the unhappy wife of Ralph de Gael. Eager for her safety, he entreated her to allow him to send her, under escort, to the camp, urging that the terrors of so fearful a night were ill suited to a woman's presence.

"I will not keep one soldier," she impatiently interrupted, "from the work of vengeance. Is this an hour to think of women's safety, when knightly blows are to be struck, and freedom to be won? Away, and leave me here." Turning to the men, she added, with a voice and gesture such as Boadicea might have used when urging her subjects against the Romans. "As ye rush on triumphant through the halls, think on the homes your foes have made a desert! the blood they shed in mockery and scorn! Let the remembrance of your country's wrongs nerve well each arm to strike the oppressor dead!"

With an eager shout, the Saxons, excited by her words, sprang forward, and Edward, despite his reluctance to leave her unprotected, was compelled to follow in the stream.

"'Tis well," she exclaimed, as the last flash of their torches disappeared in the windings of the low subterranean passage; "once more I am alone, and mistress of myself. Triumph, my soul—exult, and taste of joy. My genius rises o'er my foe victorious; and this great deed satiates at once my hate and my revenge. 'Tis worth long years o suffering to live for such an hour as this. Yes, Ralph de Gael," she added, bitterly, "I pay thee now for heartless scorn, neglect, insulted love. The Saxon wife hath set the Saxon bloodhound on thy track—the outraged child avenges her murdered mother."

In the excitement of the moment, which partook more of madness than of passion, Ethra continued to pace, with hurried step, the entrance of the vault, muttering alternately words of reproach, or giving vent to the insane expression of her triumph. Soon the shouts of the Saxons, as they burst upon their astonished foe, reached her, and her pale lips quivered, her dark eyes flashed with redoubled brilliancy at the signal which told her fearful vengeance was accomplished. Catching up a torch which one of the followers of Edward had dropped in his haste, she began to trace her way to the scene of blood and slaughter.

"The conflict is begun," she cried; "I go to perish in the storm my breath hath raised."

Despite the impetuosity with which Ulrick commenced his attack upon the bridge, it would have proved unsuccessful against the compact body of archers stationed there, had not the party of Saxons under Arad, whom the monks had guided, burst from the chapel and attacked them in the rear. The Normans, thus doubly assailed, seeing all hope of retreat into the interior of the castle cut off, fought with desperate courage, but in vain; the conflict became too close to permit them to use their bows, and the missiles which the men-at-arms stationed on the tower continued to hurl down were not more destructive to their enemies than to themselves. Their light steel barrets proved but an inefficient protection against the heavy clubs with which the Saxon serfs were armed; heads and helmets were alike crushed beneath their blows, and many chose death by plunging into the deep moat beneath, which soon ran purple with their blood, rather than meet it from the desperate Saxons' hands.

After an hour's hard fighting the bridge was cleared, and the assailants remained masters of the position, which, however, advanced them but little in their general attack, for the iron studded gates resisted all their efforts, while from the lofty battlements directly over them the besieged kept raining down showers of boiling oil and melted lead, and ponderous beams of wood, which crushed by dozens the unhappy mutilated wretches upon whom they fell.

Ralph de Gael, who directed the defence, beheld with pleasure the foe recoil before the destructive missiles. In the insolence of his triumph he addressed their leader with every taunt and insult his malice could suggest.

"What!" he exclaimed, ironically, "retreat so soon! strike one blow more! or is Saxon courage cooled with its first check? For the future, women and girls shall guard our walls, and hold them too 'gainst such assailants. Ulrick," he added, "had Stanfield towers been kept like mine, my sword had found its task less easy. I almost blush to have crushed so poor an enemy."

"Coward!—cool, insulting coward!" replied our hero, his eyes flashing fire at the allusion to his once happy home, "descend from thy stronghold, and let the sword decide between us. I'll stake my country's wrongs and rights upon the issue."

"Thinkst thou I am so poor a gamester," shouted the tyrant, with an insulting laugh, "to risk that which is mine already? The gibbet, knave, and not a noble's sword, is the fit doom thy rash presumption merits. Slaves," he continued, addressing the Saxons, who had retreated beyond the reach of the burning shower, "Henry will soon be here; long ere this the royal banner floats upon the breeze. To your homes—your homes; wait not the lion's wrath, lest it consume ye."

The assertion of the expected arrival of

ULRICK'S ATTACK UPON RALPH DE GAEL.

the king, who was known to be at a day's march from the city, struck a damp on the hearts of many, and might have produced the effect the speaker artfully intended, had not the shouts and cries within the walls informed them that one part at least of their attack had been successful—that Edward and his troop had obtained an entrance in the castle. The tyrant's flushed cheek turned pale as the war-cry of the victorious Saxons fell upon his ear.

The next moment Richard de Montmar, the seneschal, his sword broken, and his gashed brow streaming with blood, appeared upon the walls before his terror-stricked master.

"What meant that cry?" he faltered.

"The foe are in our walls; like Cadmus' sons, they rise from earth. Our men, discouraged, murmur treason, and demand their leader. To the hall, or all is lost."

For a few moments his chief stood as if struck by the destroying angel's sword, so wild, so improbable did the intelligence appear: nor was it till the renewed cries of the combatants burst upon the air that he started from his mental palsy. Calling to his men, he rushed from the walls, to stem the tide which Heaven had so mysteriously turned against him. In a few minutes the battlements were deserted, except by the wounded and the dying who had fallen beneath the arrows of the Saxons.

Ulrick, who judged the cause of the confusion, suffered not the advantage to be lost; but redoubled his efforts against the no longer well-defended gates, which, from their massive strength for a time continued to defy his utmost efforts. While the assailants, with renewed vigour, are continuing the attack, let us followed the dismayed Norman to the scene which met his gaze within his hitherto deemed impregnable stronghold.

A large portion of the garrison were assembled in the great hall of the castle, fighting desperately with the Saxons, who, under the conduct of Edward, occupied the low arched galleries which ran round the apartment, and from which their arrows did fearful execution upon their enemies; the floor was strewed with the dead and dying, whose mingled groans, yells of agony, and execrations added to the horrors of the scene. In the centre of the hall stood the excited Ethra; her right hand holding a torch; her long dark hair, freed from the veil which she had lost in the tumult, streaming like a meteor in the wind. Regardless of her own safety, she urged on her countrymen to the attack, her shrill voice rising above the din of arms as she reminded them of the wrongs and shames their Norman tyrants had inflicted on their hearths and homes.

"Traitoress!" exclaimed Ralph, as he confronted her, "it is to thee I owe this desolation, this ruin of my hopes. Thine was the accursed hand to release my deadly foes, and bring the Saxon hound upon my track."

Ethra surveyed him with a look of withering scorn, and an unblanched cheek; the haughty spirit of her race was on her, and though a secret instinct told her that the dark thread of her existence in a few moments would be severed, her heart trembled not, neither did her voice falter as she answered him—

"Monster! thinkst thou I would leave my gallant father in thy grasp, and have the power to save him? Is't not enough thou hast lured me to foul perdition's brink, but thou wouldst plunge my guileless sister in the dread abyss? Hark to that shout!" she added, as the triumphant voices of the assailants, who had just broken in the outward gates, burst upon her ear; "'tis the

victorious cry of Liberty rejoicing to behold her children free. The Saxon, the despised Saxon, hunts thee now; the spirits of my slaughtered kindred ride upon the storm; the furies claim thee as their destined prey. Soon shall they be avenged."

The passion of her tyrant was too intense for words; surprise, too, held him chained. His hitherto submissive victim, whose heart he had trampled on, whose feelings wantonly sported with, had turned like a lioness to rend him. With a look of concentrated hatred, he twice passed his sword through her defenceless body, and the betrayed, unhappy Ethra fell, without one groan or sigh, a corse at her destroyer's feet. She had met the fate she sought. Love, honour, happiness were lost; and as freely as the sea-bird dashes the spray from its soiled wing, she cast her life away, a cold smile of triumph lighting her features even in death.

The murderer had not long to exult over his revenge, for the voice of Ulrick urging on his followers, or calling with passionate vehemence upon his child, alarmed him for his own worthless safety. Calling on his esquire and a party of the most determined of his men to follow him, he made his way over the mangled and the dying to a corner of the hall, where a narrow staircase led to a solitary turret, the flat roof of which was large enough, perhaps, to hold fifty men, and which one determined sword might defend against a host of enemies.

"Turn, craven hound!" shouted our hero to him, as he ascended the steps. The defiance which would have followed was cut short by a pang such as a father's heart alone could feel. His child—his deeply loved, long mourned, repentant child—lay weltering in her life's blood, e'en at his very feet. With a cry like that a breaking heart sends forth, he sank upon his knee beside her. The warrior was extinct—the parent only lived within his breast.

"Wake!" he sobbed, as he pressed his lips with passionate tenderness to her cold brow; "wake to hear the pardon thou hast so dearly won. Ethra—child of my love, first-born of my hope—one look, one little pressure of thy hand! Dead—dead!" he murmured. "God, my brain is on fire—my heart is broken!"

So majestic was the grief of the bereaved parent, that even his enemies respected it. These, however, were soon driven from the hall by the arrival of Arad and the party under his command. The slaughter on both sides had been fearful, for Norman and Saxon fought with all the bitterness of long-garnered hate. The castle, with the exception of the solitary tower into which Ralph and his party had retreated, was in possession of the assailants, when an unexpected event entirely changed the fortunes of the night.

Henry, who had been holding his parliament at Bury St. Edmund's, was in council when the mission of the governor of the East Angles was presented to him. His indignation, as well as that of his nobles, was extreme. That the man whom he had snatched from justice should so ungratefully repay his mercy, stung him to the quick; and he swore, by the oath of his race, to proceed at once to Norwich, and execute strict justice on the offenders. Despite the haste of his march, the battle was fought ere he arrived. But the overwhelming force which accompanied him rendered all resistance on the part of the victorious Saxons unavailing; and they saw the fruits of victory snatched from them even in the moment of success. The larger body of them retired to their homes; and Ulrick, Arad, Edward, and most of the chiefs, remained prisoners in the hands of the Normans.

At an early hour on the following morning a council was held in the chapter-house of the cathedral, at which the king presided in person. Ralph de Gael, Salisbury, De Warrenne, De Vere of Oxford, and many barons of less note, were seated at the board. When the chancellor, our hero's old enemy, took his seat, the forgeries, upon which on a previous occasion the lord of Stanfield had been condemned, lay open on the table. At a signal from Henry, Ulrick and his companions in misfortune were introduced. His cheek was pale from loss of blood and the fierce emotions which had so lately wrung his soul. But if his step faltered from weakness, his eye was bright and proud as ever; it shrank not from the stern gaze of his judges, nor quailed beneath the triumphant sneer of his oppressor. Henry was the first to speak.

"My lords," he exclaimed, "we are here to judge an ingrate and a traitor, whom I confess that, with a weakness unworthy of a king, yielding to an angel's prayer, I saved from your resentment. Of Ralph de Gael's administration, and the oppressions of which he is accused, we will decide hereafter. But however they may palliate," he added, pointing to the other Saxon chiefs, "the outbreak of these misguided men, they excuse not the ungrateful lord of Stanfield—the plotter, the assassin."

"The wronged—the slandered!" exclaimed a deep-toned voice, at whose sound all present started.

The doors of the chapter-house were thrown open, and Robert of Artois, dressed in his priestly rags, just as Ethra had released him from his dungeon, stood before them.

"Wretch!" he cried, fixing a glance of scorn upon the man who had so long held him captive; "here, within these holy walls—here, in the presence of Heaven and of man, avow your treachery and Ulrick's wrongs, detested, grovelling, most unknightly villain!"

"Who art thou?" demanded the chancellor.

"Ask of yon monster," resumed the speaker, pointing to the astonished Ralph de Gael—"of him who for ten years hath held me captive in a loathsome cell, till of humanity its memory only rests—of him who, to conceal his murders, outrages, and crimes, forced me, an unworthy priest of the Most High—by tortures forced me to forge the proofs on which you would condemn the preserver of your monarch's life, and crush the noblest heart that tyranny e'er reached."

"Liar!" faltered the detected but unabashed miscreant—"what proof?"

"What proof!" iterated his accuser, with a cold smile, whose serpent-like expression was far more terrible than even his impassioned scorn. "Fear not, thou shalt hear proof enough to satisfy the doubt of incredulity itself—to brand the festering lie upon thy brow—to show thee to the world the monster that thou art, and strip thee of the last defence falsehood and infamy have left thee."

"Assertion is not evidence," interrupted the chancellor, rising uneasily from his seat.

"True," said the repentant man; "and an angel's oath would lack conviction to a heart like thine—seared in the subtle trickeries of office, dead to every generous, natural impulse. Behold the proof!"

Hastily taking up the forged letters one by one, he laid them before the king. Passing over them, at the same time, a sponge dipped in some aromatic essence which he drew from his breast to the surprise of the monarch and his counsellors, and the confusion of Ralph, a second inscription appeared beneath the first.

Henry seized the paper and eagerly read as follows—

"I, Onfroy, caligrapher, and priest of the cathedral church of Norwich, trusting that Heaven will one day bring my weakness and the cruelty of Ralph de Gael to light, declare that having been twice put to the torture, I have reluctantly consented to forge these letters, being prisoner the while to the aforesaid Ralph de Gael."

Our readers need scarcely be reminded that the composition of the sympathetic ink was, in the age of which we write, a secret confined chiefly to the cloister.

"Monster! unknightly felon!" exclaimed the king, as the last letter fell from his indignant hand, "what answer for thy worthless life—what subterfuge or subtle turn can serve thee now?"

"Sorcery," replied Ralph, desperately resolved to brave it to the last. "Relying on my innocence and Heaven's assistance, I demand the knightly combat."

Henry, surnamed "Beauclerk," was not to be deceived by an excuse which the more superstitious of his council took into their serious consideration. Whilst they clustered round the council-table to consult on the demand, the king approached the prisoner, whose cheek had proudly flushed on hearing the proofs of his innocence, but in a few seconds became paler than before.

"Lord of Stanfield," demanded the agitated monarch, "canst thou forgive the involuntary wrong I most unwittingly have done thee?"

"Protect my child—redress my country's wrongs," sighed our hero, "and all is well."

"God!" exclaimed the king, "he is dying!"

His fears were but too true. Worn by loss of blood, and the many bitter trials he had undergone, the tired spirit of our hero was rapidly passing away to rejoin those he had loved, but failed to avenge on earth. His eyelids were half-closed in death when the voice of the chancellor for a few moments recalled him to the world.

"The battle is accorded," he coldly pronounced; "let the sword decide between the accused and the accuser."

The usages of chivalry with the Normans were sacred. Monarchs and nobles alike were bound by them; and the chancellor and his party thought by their decision to avoid the odium of so foul an accusation being proved against a member of their own order. Henry heard their decision with indignation, anger, and contempt.

"The combat!" he repeated; "and with a dying man!"

"I am ready!" faintly exclaimed Ulrick, like some wounded lion rearing his form erect to meet the hunter's last attack; "where is my sword?" and weakened by the effort, he fell back into the arms of Arad.

Henry pointed to his feeble state in silence.

"Let him appear by champion!" exclaimed the council, in answer to his mute appeal.

"Be it so!" said Henry, with a burst of wrath, which told the presuming barons they had gone too far. "I'll be his champion.

Ulrick of Stanfield," he continued, taking the dying hero's hand, "I here proclaim thee innocent—the soul of honour and the light of truth. Most foully hath thy vile accuser lied. There lies my glove—a monarch's glove shall be thy gage of battle."

Suiting the action to the word, the excited king threw his embroidered glove upon the ground. None presumed to raise it. The Norman nobles would have gone far to save one of their order, but not one felt disposed to brave a wrath which, once roused, might consume them. Even the chancellor was silenced, for he knew that Henry, when really excited, was capable of daring everything. There was a solemn silence in the hall, which the monarch was the first to break.

"No answer!" he exclaimed. "Away with him, then! De Vere, you act as marshal. In ten minutes let the trumpet's breath proclaim that he hath met a felon's doom."

Despite his protestations, Ralph de Gael was dragged from the assembly, and in a less space of time than even the king had announced, the fearful signal was heard, and his last sigh passed from him on the gibbet.

"Ulrick," said his champion, "preserver of my life, I have avenged thee."

"More," answered our hero, with a last effort; "thou hast preserved my honour. All is over, and the prediction of the prophet priest of Eltham is accomplished."

"I remember," added Henry; "a life of honour, a soldier's triumph, but a broken heart."

A smile of gratitude passed over the features of the dying man, as he fixed his last look upon the speaker. That smile remained after the spirit of Ulrick had passed away.

Most of the Saxons were pardoned. Henry kept his Christmas at Norwich, and granted the citizens their first charter, in compensation for the exactions which they had suffered from their unprincipled governor, who was found to have amassed enormous wealth by his oppression. Before the monarch left the city, the marriage of Myrra and Edward was solemnised in the presence of the court by Robert of Artois, who did not long survive his restoration to liberty, but was found dead at the tomb of Ulrick, whither he went daily to offer up his prayers.

END OF THE CHRONICLE OF ULRICK THE SAXON, AND BOOK I. OF STANFIELD HALL.

BOOK II.

THE CHRONICLE OF THE HEIRESS.

In 1515 Henry VIII. reigned, and Wolsey swayed the destinies of the English nation. The moral portraiture of the monarch and his minister presents the same peculiarities which their likeness, painted on canvas by the united pencils of Titian and Rembrandt, might have done: masses of glorious colouring—brilliant, dazzling, and life-like—starting from deep and gloomy shadows—the contrast of the sunbeam and the thundercloud, midnight and the glare of noon. Europe, in the beginning of the sixteenth century, presented a gallery of living portraits such as few ages have seen. The magnificent Leo X., the astute Charles V., the gallant Francis I., Henry, Wolsey, Luther, Erasmus, and Melancthon, all left the impress of their minds upon the destiny of the world.

Henry at this period began to manifest, although but slightly, that distaste towards his wife which ultimately led to the downfall of his favourite, and the separation of the kingdom from the church of Rome. In estimating the character of this prince, it ought to be remembered that the marriage with his brother's widow was a political one, and that he was a mere boy when it was consummated. Henry VII., touched by remorse, it is said, on his death-bed, had strongly advised him not to fulfil the contract, which Warham, Archbishop of Canterbury, despite the dispensation of the Pope, never could be brought to approve. Unfortunately, the interests and opinions of his father's ministers and council prevailed; and six weeks after he became king he gave his hand to the unfortunate Catharine of Arragon—a princess who had actually been married to his elder, and afterwards affianced to his younger brother, the Duke of York.

This inauspicious union, from the very first, was distasteful to the clergy and a great portion of his subjects, who justly considered that the bull of Julius II., which dispensed with the canon of the church, was granted by that pontiff more from the desire of embarrassing his enemy, Louis XII. of France, by thus cementing the alliance between England and Spain, than a due consideration of those higher motives which ought to have guided the head of the Catholic world.

We have touched thus lightly upon the subject at the commencement of our tale, to avoid those dry historical details which might interfere with its progress and action, and to enable our readers to understand that Henry was not altogether swayed by caprice in seeking to dissolve a marriage so opposed to the prejudice of the age and the faith of his subjects, many of whom regarded the death of his sons by Catharine as a punishment for his incestuous union.

At the period at which our tale commences, Wolsey had attained as a subject all but the climax of his ambition; the great seal of England, held by the primate, Warham, alone was wanting to complete his authority. Rome had decorated him with the purple, and his confiding master had bestowed on him not only the archbishopric of York, but the rich see of Durham, the abbey of St. Alban's, which he held in commendum, and the revenues of the bishoprics of Bath, Worcester, and Hereford, the incumbents of which being foreigners, residing in Italy, were glad to compound with the haughty cardinal for a pension in lieu of the income of their preferments. From these resources the magnificent churchman displayed a state which rivalled the crown in pomp. He had lords and knights in the number of his household servants; when he said mass in the royal chapel, two dukes presented him the water; indeed, so tenacious was he of this service, that it is said the cause of his enmity to Buckingham arose from that haughty nobleman insultingly emptying the basin at his feet after he had unwillingly performed it.

The usual crowd of idlers were assembled on the rude embankment near the Tower of London, to watch the unloading of a foreign ship which had cast anchor on the preceding night. Amongst them might be counted city 'prentices, with their short clubs and saucy looks, idling away their masters' time; old sailors, who were past service; merchants, eager to receive their long-expected merchandize; bowmen, on their way to the archery grounds—large unenclosed fields, lying between Shoreditch and Rotherhithe; besides the usual proportion of citizens' wives and daughters, who, with the curiosity natural to their sex, were gathered in little neighbourly cotteries, commenting on the appearance of the crew of jolly fresh-looking Flemings who commanded the vessel.

"More broadcloth from Ghent!" exclaimed Master Sleeveboard, a rich draper in Cheapside, as he eyed the carefully-packed bales which were being landed on the wharf. "Surely the produce of our English looms might content the gallants of the court; but no, forsooth! nothing but foreign braveries will go down with them. I have not sold an ell of honest linsey wolsey these three days; and the taxes, we all know, my masters," he added, lowering his voice, "must be paid the same; trade or no trade, money must be had."

"Shame!" cried several who stood round; for the complaint was a popular one, the city being extremely dissatisfied at the preference given to foreign traders and their goods by the court; a dissatisfaction which, a few years later, broke out into serious disturbances, and cost the lives of many of the citizens.

"At the last tourney at Greenwich," observed a member of the company of the passamentiers, or embroiderers, "his grace of Buckingham was the only noble who wore English braidings on his trappings."

"A cheer for the Duke of Buckingham!" exclaimed the crowd who had gathered round; "he is a true Englishman."

"And a friend to the commons," observed one.

"Of the blood of John of Gaunt," added another.

"If you love him," observed a grave, elderly personage, dressed in a mulberry-coloured gown and hood, "the less you remind his enemies of his descent the better. Henry loves not those who stand too near the throne. The hart is a gallant beast, but it is no match for the lion."

This allusion to the armorial bearings of the king and duke was perfectly understood by the people, who at that time, from the frequency of pageants, tilts, masques, and processions, were better acquainted with the devices of the nobility than even are the better classes of the present day, so hath the noble science of heraldry unfortunately fallen into disuse.

"How are the imposts to be paid," demanded a burly little citizen, "if we are to be inundated with foreign goods? The last war sweated the city sorely, and there are whispers of another benevolence."

"Not a word against the war," cried a young fellow, an armourer by trade, whose jaunty cap, rapier, and love-locks gave him a rakish appearance; "I'll not hear a word against the late war. I am an armourer. Live and let live. I sold more blades and corslets in that one year than my father did in all the late king's reign. Besides, did not the emperor himself take soldier's service under our noble Henry?"

"Ay, and a general's pay," interrupted several.

"Ask Martin, of St. Paul's, if the tent of cloth of gold in which the recruit was lodged was ever paid for," added Sleeveboard.

"The war cost half a million."

"And what advantage did we gain by that?" shouted the crowd.

"Advantage!" iterated the armourer with indignation; "why we beat the French, and Henry won the city of Tournay."

"And the cardinal," quietly added the stranger in the mulberry-coloured gown and hood, the same who had just before rebuked them for their imprudent zeal for the Duke of Buckingham, "obtained the bishopric—the usual division between intelligence and strength, or church and state—the king the shell, the subtle priest the oyster. What, in the name of fortune, will he aim at next?"

"The great seal, perhaps," suggested Sleeveboard timidly, for he liked not speaking of his eminence of York; "he hath long had an eye to it, and will not withhold his hand."

"Or the papal chair?" observed the armourer, with whom Wolsey was no favourite; "sure that might content him."

"Would anything content him?" continued the stranger; "once pope, he would quarrel with St. Peter for his keys; he hath an appetite more greedy than his fortunes; besides, who ever yet beheld that *rara avis*, a contented priest?"

At this last speech there was an instant pause in the conversation—if that may be called such, where every speaker vociferated at his pleasure. So great was the terror which Wolsey's name inspired, from his arrogance and well-known vindictiveness of character, that few men cared to mention him: in fact, Henry himself was scarcely more feared than his all-powerful minister. The old substantial citizens, therefore, walked quietly away, leaving the indiscreet stranger and a knot of the lower classes, such as the 'prentices and sailors, standing by themselves upon the quay. Of the better order, the armourer alone remained, and he continued for some time to eye the speaker with a look of droll surprise; the former met his gaze as if perfectly unaware of the effect his words had produced.

"Thou hadst more care for the duke's safety than for thine own," quietly observed the young man at last.

"Perhaps not," said the stranger; "at least, my purpose is answered."

"And that was?"

"To get rid of the meddling citizens—fellows who attend to every man's business except their own—who grumble at cent. per cent. upon their dealings, calling it scant profit."

"You expect merchandise, then," observed the armourer, "by yonder vessel?"

"I do."

"Contraband?" continued his questioner.

"Ay," answered the stranger bluntly. "Wilt thou assist me? There is a broad noble to be won."

At this moment a boat put off from the shore. Instead of bales of goods, it was charged with three passengers—a lady and child, together with a male attendant. The latter was a burly, honest-looking Englishman, of about forty, whose bronzed face told that he had been exposed to the wars; whilst his round, half bald head, short neck, and broad shoulders, gave a sort of bulldog character to his appearance. The female, who was dressed in deep mourning, was evidently in the last stage of consumption. The hectic colour on her thin cheek contrasted painfully with its unearthly whiteness; her attenuated hand shook as she held the dark veil which partially shaded her features, and which her feeble strength could scarcely retain in its place against the gusts of wind, which was blowing freshly. A beautiful child, with long curling hair, and blue, thoughtful eyes, was seated next her, endeavouring, with infantine grace and watchfulness, to prevent the breeze from incommoding her mother, by assisting to hold, with her little hands, the rebellious veil in its proper place.

"Behold the merchandise I expect," coolly observed the elder, fixing his eyes intently on the boat. "Mother, child, and servitor, all three are there;" and he counted them deliberately upon his fingers as he named them.

"And are they your wife, child, and servitor?" observed the young man, curiously; for he began to suspect, although but vaguely, that the intentions of the speaker were anything but friendly towards the travellers; besides, there was something unnatural to him in designating human beings as merchandise.

A momentary contraction of the muscles, as if a spasm had suddenly seized him, passed over the countenance of the stranger, as he answered with the monosyllable, "No," in a voice so cold and iron-like, it sounded as an ice-drop as it fell.

"Occupy not thyself with me or with my motives, young man," he said, in his usual tone, in answer to the look of mute inquiry with which the armourer regarded him, "since both are past thy scrutiny. Enough;

I am of those who pay for service rendered. The task I ask of thee is easy to perform."

"And honest?" demanded the young man, doubtfully.

"And honest," continued the speaker. "It is but to follow yon strangers through the city, and bring me word where they reside. There," he added, "is a piece of gold for thy present service; its fellow shall be thine on thy return. Are we agreed in this?"

"We are—where shall we meet?"

"At St. Paul's Cross—before the vesper hymn."

With this understanding the two strangely assorted companions parted; the elder, evidently wishing to avoid recognition, drew his velvet hood over his face; the younger observed, as he did so, that his fingers were encircled by gems of price, such as by the sumptuary laws none but a noble might presume to wear.

The young man, Cuthbert the armourer, whom we have thus introduced to our readers, like most of the city roysterers of the day, possessed more heart than head—more courage than prudence. Accustomed from the very nature of his trade to the profession of arms, there were few skirmishes with the city watch in which he failed to bear a part; but as he was ever ready to stand up for his ward, and bore a good character, these little outbreaks had hitherto been winked at by the alderman, whose niece, it was whispered, more than shared her uncle's partiality for the handsome craftsman. Although, from the wars, feuds, and quarrels—to say nothing of the tournaments of the age—he was seldom without work, it was quite as seldom, from his reckless, generous habits, that he had anything beyond a few silver pennies in his purse; and the lightly won golden noble, together with the promise of a second, elated his spirits accordingly.

"Faith, friend Cuthbert, thou art in luck's way," he muttered to himself; "thou mightst have hammered long enough at the forge ere thou hadst put a rose noble in thy pouch. I don't half like the duty I have undertaken, though," he added, musingly; "it is but the lurcher's part to dog these strangers. If I thought the stranger meant them falsely, I'd cast his gold into the Thames, and warn them of their danger."

The words had scarcely passed his lips when the boat reached the landing-place, and the pale, sickly lady, leaning on the arm of her attendant, and holding the child by the hand, made her appearance on the quay.

"Thank Heaven," she exclaimed, "good

Steadman, we are once more in England. 'Tis sweet to tread my native shores again, though I return to lay my bones there."

"Psha!" said the blunt yeoman; "the air of England will bring back the rose of health into your cheek. I begin to feel the benefit already," he added; "I am as hungry as though I had not tasted food since we sailed from the Low Countries, where, God willing, would we had never been."

The sigh of his lady, and her tearful glances at the garments of her widowhood, told him his wish was understood.

Cuthbert, who had been eyeing the party for some time, as if to assure himself that he was right in his surmise, hastily approached, and slapping the stout servitor on the back, saluted him by the name of "uncle."

"Uncle!" repeated Steadman, suspiciously; "well, perhaps I am, for I have a springal of a nephew much about thy age; but since I am thine uncle, tell me my name. I have been so long absent in foreign parts that I have almost forgot the sound of it."

"Why, Steadman, to be sure — Uncle Steadman," replied the young man, with a smile whose frankness might have disarmed suspicion's self; "the same who followed my mother's noble foster-brother, the knight of Stanfield, to the wars, now ten years since; and who promised, the evening before his departure, to take me with him, but, like most uncles when they promise, broke his word."

"Cuthbert, boy, give me your hand!" exclaimed the old soldier, now fully convinced of the identity of the speaker. "Blame thy mother's tears at the dread of parting with thee for my broken word, and bear me no ill-will. Is my sister living yet, or have thy scapegrace follies broke her heart?"

"Living; and, praise to my namesake, holy St. Cuthbert, well."

"Alone?" demanded her brother.

"Alone!" said the young man, with a look of surprise; "yes, quite alone, unless you choose to reckon me something in her household. But why these questions, uncle? Surely you cannot doubt a welcome from your sister's son?"

Steadman and his suffering mistress exchanged a few whispered words together; he was evidently urging something to which she yielded a reluctant assent.

"But may we trust him?" she demanded. "Remember what fearful perils still surround us."

"To be sure we may; he is the son of your late noble husband's foster-sister and my nephew. He knows me well, though the stripling is so grown that I had well nigh forgotten him. He knows, too, that I would brain him with as little remorse as I would set my heel upon a viper, should he prove treacherous."

"You may trust me, lady," said Cuthbert, taking off his cap and standing respectfully before her, for his young heart was touched by the sorrowful expression of her countenance, and the hand of death so evident upon it. "I am a thoughtless, gay fellow, too much addicted perhaps to shooting at the butts, wrestling, and quarter-staff; and when the cry of 'clubs and 'prentices' is heard, am generally first upon the causeway; but I never yet broke confidence, or betrayed a fellow-creature in my life."

"Yes, mama, you may trust him," said the child, quietly; "his eyes do not shift and fall, and blink, as Robert's used to do; besides, he is Father Steadman's nephew, and must be faithful."

"Be it so!" sighed the lady. "Lead us, young man, to your mother's dwelling. Thought poor in seeming, and hunted by my foes, I am not without the means of rewarding fidelity."

The speaker, exhausted with the effort to speak, immediately resumed the arm of her companion, and Cuthbert passed before to guide them on their way, revolving, as he did so, what extraordinary scenes a child so young must have passed through to have been so precocious an observer of her fellow-creatures.

After winding their way through several of the narrow streets, the party emerged into Cheapside, and stopped at a small but substantial house, known by the sign of the Golden Sword, the lodge of Cuthbert's handicraft; such ensigns in the reign of Henry VIII. not being, as now, confined to hostels and wine-houses, but common to all trades. Having assured himself, by careful observation, that they had not been followed, the young man led his guests through the well-furnished shop into a neat low room at the back of the house, where his mother, Dame Maud, sat plying her needle, and waiting the return of her truant son. The greeting between Steadman and his sister was affectionate and sincere; he was many years her senior, and she looked upon him almost in the light of a parent as well as brother. No jar of worldly interests had ever passed between them, to lessen the bond of love. They had both been poor—sorrow had been their sole inheritance, and they had divided it ungrudgingly together. Nor was the widow of the good Sir Richard Stanfield and his orphan child made less welcome. Maud felt a grateful pride in being useful to

RALPH DE GAEL BEFORE KING HENRY.

her high-born guests, and as soon as the first words of welcome, surprise, and salutation were past, conducted the lady to her own quiet chamber, and entreated her to repose.

Whilst the hostess is thus hospitably engaged, it may be as well to enlighten our readers as to the circumstances under which the widow and infant heiress of a race for which, we flatter ourselves, they have long since felt a degree of interest, returned as fugitives to the land of their birth.

Calais still formed a portion of the English possessions in France; it was the key to the country—the door by which our armies could always enter, during the long and desperate wars which raged between us and our Gallic neighbours. The defence of the city and territory round it, known by the name of the March, was generally entrusted to a soldier of high repute; it being considered the most honourable as well as dangerous post the crown could confer. The pride of the English nation, from the highest to the lowest, was gratified by the barren honour of this possession; and nothing, perhaps, tended to alienate the affections of her subjects from Mary so much as the ultimate loss of it. They could have pardoned her marriage with the Spaniard, the judicial murder of Lady Jane Grey, and the burning of the bishops; but the loss of Calais was a death-blow to her popularity. The people never forgave it; and the unhappy queen, when dying, frequently was heard to exclaim that Calais would be found engraven on her heart.

Sir Richard Stanfield, the last of his ancient race, nine years before the commencement of our tale, had espoused the only daughter of Walter de Mauny, deputy-governor of this so long-disputed city; and being of an adventurous disposition, easily yielded to the entreaties of his wife to remain in France, that she might not be separated from her father. A year after their marriage, their only child, Mary, was born. When Henry, in his war with Louis XII., yielded to the persuasion of the emperor, and attacked Tournay, both Sir Richard and his father-in-law accompanied the chivalrous monarch in his expedition. The latter fell, full of age and honour, during the siege, in fighting by the side of his king, whose life he saved by the sacrifice of his own; for a party of Walloon Lanskenettiers having recognised the royal person and surrounded it, the brave old knight kept them at bay till a party of English cavalry, in their turn, came up and rescued them — the monarch living and unharmed, his defender a corse.

This act of devotion induced Henry, who was not then ungrateful, on the taking of the city a few days afterwards to name Sir Richard Stanfield governor, much to the jealousy and anger of many who thought they had a better claim to such an honour; so true it is that kings seldom can reward one friend without creating a dozen enemies. Such always has been, and such, I suppose, always will be the character of courtiers. During the knight's absence from England his estates were administered by his kinsman Sir John de Corbey, a proud, ambitious, disappointed man, whose fortune had been squandered in the wars in Italy, where he had been a partisan of the house of Medici in their aggressions upon the liberty of their country.

Sir Richard's conduct in his government secured him during five years not only the commendation of Henry, but what at that time was of far more consequence—the approbation of Wolsey. Still it was certain that he had some secret enemy. Several times, when out on a reconnoitring party, he had been shot at in a way which proved that the ball could only have come from one of his own men. Despite the entreaties of his wife, and the warning of his friends, all of whom attributed the attempts to the vengeance of some unsuccessful rival, he refused to resign his office, urging that it was one of honour as well as danger, and that, come what would, his enemies should never say they frightened him from the post his sovereign had confided to him.

This resolution, as chivalrous as rash, proved fatal. His body was one morning found upon the ramparts, where he had incautiously made his rounds without the attendance of his faithful esquire Steadman, pierced through the back by the blow of one of those long spears or partisans which sentinels use, evidently foully murdered by one of his own garrison. Strange as it may appear, the hatred of his enemies did not end here: scarcely were the funeral rites performed, than various suits were suscitated against his widow in the courts of equity and common law in the city, who found herself unexpectedly called upon to answer for bonds for moneys lent, of whose existence she had never dreamt, and whose validity she, anxious for the honour of her husband, as well as the inheritance of her child, unwisely contested. We say unwisely, because it was the contest of the lamb against the wolf—subtilty against unsuspicious frankness, fraud against honour. Had she at once proceeded to England, the machinations of her enemies could not have pursued her so boldly there. Twice an attempt was made to destroy the house in which, with a few faithful domestics, she resided; and more than one plot frustrated for the abduction of her child. Worn out at last by the unequal and iniquitous contest, the widowed lady at last resolved to fly secretly to England, and to trust to Henry's recollection of her father's services and death as a protection against the schemes which were evidently laid for her ruin. Gathering together her jewels and the remains of former wealth, she embarked at night in the small trading vessel whose arrival we have already noticed at the Tower quay, attended only by the faithful Steadman, whose love for his late master was now devoted to his helpless widow and her child.

"Humph!" exclaimed Cuthbert, as soon as his uncle had explained to him the melancholy story we have so briefly sketched. "And this kinsman—this Sir John de Corbey—did you never suspect?"

"Frequently," whispered the old man; "I know him well. He is a man whose windings are more difficult to trace than those of the venomed snake; so secret are his movements, that not a trace remains to tell the serpent has been there. Besides, he is high in favour with the king; and as we have no proof that he ever received my lady's letters, it would be dangerous as well as impolitic to accuse him."

"Perhaps not," said his nephew. "Tell me, what sort of a person is this Sir John?"

"Tall—dark hair—a face cold as a marble statue, and, if I err not, a heart still colder; he hath a scar on his left cheek, from the thrust of a lance, received at the siege of Pisa, in the Italian wars."

"It can't be he, then," muttered Cuthbert, musingly.

"He! Whom?"

"The man who gave me this golden noble to dog you on your arrival to your lodging," said the armourer, opening his hand and displaying the glittering coin; "and who promised me the fellow if I brought him word of your whereabouts to St. Paul's Cross."

"This must be seen to," exclaimed the old man, thoughtfully. "Wouldst know the man again?"

"From a hundred, with his deep-toned earnest voice. The devil, when he tempted our grandmother Eve, was never half so persuasive; he would have wiled a bird from the tree," added the speaker, "or an abbot from his dinner."

Steadman rose impatiently from off his stool, and paced the narrow chamber with an agitated step; not that he doubted in the least his nephew's fidelity; he would have answered with his life for that. Indeed, it seemed as if Providence had sent him especially to their assistance; but he felt that an humble uneducated being like himself was ill-calculated to act in such important matters. He was like a child in a labyrinth, and saw no means of escape. Cuthbert eyed him for some time in silence.

"Uncle," he at last observed, "for an old soldier who has battled in the Low Countries, you seem sadly puzzled with this tangled skein. Shall I unravel it?"

"How, boy—how? Tell that, for it is past my wits," replied the old man.

"Was not our lady one of the maids of honour to Queen Catherine?"

"True."

"And this Sir John de Corbey, if I mistake not, is a favourite with the chancellor Warham?"

"I have heard as much."

"Go to, then," resumed the armourer; "the game's not lost, play but the last cards boldly. The cardinal, whose stomach is of a singular capacity, e'en for a churchman's, longs for the great seal, and piously would miss his prayers to spite his brother prelate. The queen, whose goodness is as proverbial

as Wolsey's appetite, will lend a helping hand. Why not claim her highness's protection?"

"I have thought of that before," answered Steadman; "but how to accomplish it?"

"Leave that to me. My godfather is her cofferer. I have free access to the palace; I'll place myself in the white gallery as she returns from vespers and give it her myself; that is," added the young man, with a half frown, for he liked not the doubtful expression of his uncle's countenance, "if you like to trust me."

"It is not that, boy—it is not that," said his uncle, replying more to the thought of his nephew than his words. "I would trust thee with my own life freely, without a word, a thought; but I must consult my lady ere I take upon myself to act in this."

The old man passed up the narrow staircase to his sister's chamber, and in about an hour returned with the petition of his mistress to the queen, which the unhappy widow saw no other means of conveying to her hand than by the agency of Cuthbert.

"I bid thee be careful, boy, not faithful," he said, as he placed the packet in his hand; "the last I am sure thou'lt be. Double like a fox on thy return, lest any watch thee. Thou hast to deal with subtle foes; be thou as subtle."

"Fear not for me," interrupted the armourer, at the same time secreting the packet in his bosom; "I know the city well; they must have a keen scent and a quick eye who chase me through its windings. I'd cross their trail, and throw the best bloodhound of them out, ere they suspected that the game had doubled."

"'Tis well," said his uncle, pleased with his confidence and zeal; "but beware of force."

"Force!" exclaimed his nephew, laughingly; "those who weld the sword can wield it, uncle. I have not been in the Low Countries, but I can turn a point and give a thrust, with here and there a slasher. Ask my friends, else, of the city watch," he added, with a knowing smile; "most of them bear my mark."

Without waiting for any further reply, Cuthbert buckled on a light rapier, set his bonnet jauntily on his head, and started on his errand.

That very evening, as Catherine passed from the chapel-royal with her train from vespers, Cuthbert, true to his promise, bent the knee before her.

This unhappy princess, then in the very bloom of womanhood, possessed much of the gravity as well as pride for which the Spanish nation were distinguished; but, although haughty and reserved towards the nobles of her court, who too often enticed her husband into follies which she disapproved, she was easy of access and affable to the poor. "They are God's children," she used to say, when any wondered at her charities which were distributed with a lavish hand, "he blesseth those who aid them."

As was the custom in all cases of petitions, when the presenter was not noble, one of her highness's attendants—a tall, stately nobleman, dressed in black, and wearing a Spanish order of knighthood—on a motion of Catherine's hand advanced to take it; but the armourer knew well the necessity, if possible, of interesting the queen herself—petitions so received being referred to the almoner to decide.

"Not to the almoner, gracious lady!" he exclaimed, fixing his eyes upon her with an imploring look; "though my jerkin be of fustian, I am the messenger of one who is entitled to velvet and miniver in your grace's court. There is a tale of sorrow to be told, of injury to be redressed, and none may come between your heart and you. As you hope," he added, "that our Lady will smile upon the prayer you uttered at her shrine this night, let your own eyes be judge of that I bring."

Catherine seemed struck by the earnestness as well as the simple eloquence of his words; perhaps her own prayer had been that Henry's heart might be turned from its estrangement; or, perhaps, with all a mother's love, she had asked for the health of her young child, the infant Mary, who alone survived of all the issue of her marriage-bed. Whatever was her secret motive, she determined to grant his prayer.

"Thou art a bold knave," she cried, extending her gloved hand to receive the packet, "to dictate in our very court; and we," she added, with a melancholy smile, probably at her own little superstition, "are as weak as thou art bold, to yield to thy request. Let's see what mighty interests are at stake, that a queen's eye alone may read them."

Catherine retired to one of the lofty windows of the hall, and broke the seal of the packet. At first she seemed surprised, then interested. Her eye glanced by turns from the missive to the bearer. Hastily tearing off the lower part of the letter, which probably contained the unfortunate lady of Stanfield's address, she placed the fragment in her bosom. She had lived so long in courts that she mistrusted all.

"Forgive our chiding," she said, advancing a step towards the still kneeling Cuthbert;

"thou hast shown both zeal and prudence. Let them guide thee still."

These last word were accompanied by a look which plainly said, "There is danger—be upon your guard!"

The young man felt it as such; and he answered it by one of respectful determination and intelligence.

Most of her attendants were intrigued and curious at the nature of the communication her majesty had received; but respect and etiquette kept them silent.

"Has my lord of York yet gone from court?" demanded Catherine, after a pause.

Ere those around her could reply, the great doors of the hall were thrown open, and Wolsey, who had been celebrating vespers in the chapel-royal, entered, proceded by the officers of his household, pages, and the usual procession of cross-bearers and priests. At any other moment, perhaps, Catherine would have resented his intrusion unannounced, for she was tenacious of her rank; but at the present instant she required his services. The cardinal, who deemed that she had long since reached her private apartments, excused himself with the courtly ease of a favourite. Placing her letter she had so lately received within his hands, Catherine watched his countenance with a searching glance whilst he perused it.

"What think you, my good lord?" she demanded, as the churchman raised his eyes from the paper.

"Does your highness feel interested in this?" was the reply.

"Deeply. She was one of my earliest friends in my adopted country," she answered. "I would set my life upon her truth."

"'Tis a vast pledge," exclaimed Wolsey with a bitter smile; "and you are happy, lady, that your heart can so trust, though it should be to be deceived. Was that youth," he added, pointing to Cuthbert, "the messenger?"

Catherine gravely bowed her head in affirmation, when the cardinal immediately beckoned him towards the window, where he was still standing with the queen.

In an instant the young man stood modestly before them.

"Thou has performed thy message," said Wolsey, "faithfully; return to those who sent thee, and bid them wait with patience; justice, though slow of step, is sure. In thy way home," he added, "if but a shadow cross thy path, start from it as from an enemy. See that none follow thee. Give every man the crown of the causeway; and cross thyself, and tell thy beads to Heaven when thou reachest thy house in safety."

"Are her enemies so powerful, then?" whispered the queen, as the young man disappeared at the lower end of the hall.

"The chancellor and his minion, Sir John de Corbey," replied his eminence; "a man whose path 'tis dangerous to cross. Did I not see him when I entered?"

"He hath left the presence," replied Catherine, glancing round the circle.

"Poor boy!" muttered the churchman with an imperceptible shrug, as he took leave of her highness; "his wit must be keen and his arm strong if he reach home in safety."

On his way to York House the prelate meditated how best to turn the occasion to his advantage; for, despite his great influence with Henry, the latter still retained a great esteem for Warham, who had been his father's chancellor as well as his own, and never could be persuaded to demand the great seal from him. The guilt of Sir John de Corbey, who was his kinsman as well as favourite, seemed admirably fitted for Wolsey's views; since, could he involve the one in the discredit of the other, he might be either forced or driven into a resignation. Under any circumstances, he determined to protect with his powerful interest the widow of the knight of Stanfield; if it served no other purpose, it would gratify the queen, and mortify his brother prelate and less ambitious rival.

Cuthbert had reached the banks of the Thames, intending to take boat to the city, when an arm was laid upon his shoulder, just as he was about to embark. He started beneath the pressure, mortified at his want of precaution. The fact is, his interview with Catherine and Wolsey had bewildered him. Turning, he saw by his side the nobleman who had so lately offered to take his petition to the queen.

"You pay little heed to the caution of his eminence," observed the stranger, with a quiet smile.

"Faith, my lord," answered Cuthbert, completely thrown off his guard by the encounter and apparent knowledge of Wolsey's whispered words, "I believe I have been dreaming; but what is your good pleasure?"

"Her highness has bethought her of your lady's suit, and thinks it better the widow of the knight of Stanfield should be under her protection than in her present retreat."

"And where may that be?" demanded Cuthbert, eyeing him suspiciously.

"Where, I neither guess nor seek to know," replied the stranger, haughtily, but at the same time with an open frankness, which might have disarmed suspicion's self; "but doubtless the messenger will be provided with a clue. I have but to conduct you to the house of her highness's master of the horse, and there my mission ends."

There was something so plausible in the manner as well as words of the speaker, that the unfortunate armourer fell into the snare. He had seen the envoy in close attendance upon Catherine, and it seemed the very madness of credulity to doubt him. Unhesitatingly, therefore, he entered into a barge to which the stranger pointed. It was rowed by four stout fellows, in rich liveries, who pushed off the moment they had received their freight, and directed their oars towards a lofty turreted mansion on the opposite side of the river.

So unsuspicious was the young man of the intentions of his companion, that he followed him into the house; nor did the closing of the iron gates behind them, as soon as they had entered, in the slightest degree shake his confidence. Taking a torch from the hands of one of the numerous attendants in the hall, the noble host mounted a stone staircase, which led to the principal tower of the building, his victim following him. Nor was it till they had entered a low-arched, desolate-looking room, unfurnished, hung with tattered, antique arras, which floated with the night breeze from the walls, that the chill of suspicion struck upon his heart. Glancing uneasily round, he ventured to observed that it was a strange place to await the arrival of the queen's messenger in.

"It will suit our purpose," drily answered his conductor, at the same time removing his jewelled cap and casting it upon the dusty oaken table. "Few who enter here ever complain of the accommodation or reception."

The act of throwing off his cap at once revealed to Cuthbert the danger in which he stood, for the long dark plume which had hitherto shaded the left side of the wearer's face being removed, left distinctly visible a scar, such as a wound from a lance-head might have made. The young man remembered the words of his uncle, and felt that he was betrayed.

"Sir John de Corbey!" he exclaimed; "then I am lost."

"Thou knowest me, knave," said his captor. "'Tis well; it will save words between us, for I am of those who do not love to waste them. Where is the wanton who calls herself the widow of my kinsman?—where the bastard she would palm upon the world as Stanfield's heiress?"

"By what right do you interrogate me?" demanded the young man.

"The right which rules the world—force," replied Sir John.

He struck his hands together as he spoke, when three men immediately appeared from behind the arras; two were common-looking ruffians, who evidently had long been at war with humanity as well as fortune—Mercy would have turned from them with a hopeless eye, so strongly marked were the lines of avarice and cruelty upon their features. They were fellows who would have strangled the priest at the altar, or the smiling infant at its mother's breast — strangled them for sport, had the incentive of gold been wanting. The third was our old acquaintance in the mulberry coloured gown and hood. Cuthbert had scarcely time to lay his hand upon his sword, when the two former sprang upon him, and he was disarmed.

"Thou art a faithful messenger!" observed the last-mentioned personage, in his usual, low, musical voice, whose tones fell fearfully upon the armourer's ear from the very absence of anger or of passion in it.

"Silence, good Adam," said Sir John; "we complain not of the treason, though we punish the traitor. Behold, young man," he continued, pointing to the lower end of the room; "tell me, what seest thou there?"

"A dark recess," answered Cuthbert, "left in the solid wall."

"What else?"

"A pile of brick and stone."

"Enough to fill the entrance to that recess, is't not?" demanded his questioner, with a cold smile.

"Enough to fill the entrance to that recess!" repeated the youth, with a faltering voice. "Mean you—no—no! God! 'tis too horrible for human malice to conceive, or nature to endure—you do not mean——"

"To what?" demanded his tormentor, with the same unmoved expression.

"Nothing," said Cuthbert, "nothing: one of those monstrous dreams such as scare children in their sleep, and old men cross their brows when they relate—a thought too wild for madness, too horrible for truth—a thought," he added, with increased excitement, "which hell would pause to listen to, if uttered in its centre, and laughing fiends approve."

"At last," exclaimed Sir John, "we understand each other. Mark well my words: name to me the retreat of those I seek, or, living, I'll immure thee in yon tomb. Thou shalt woo Death, and coyly he shall hear thee; hunger shall gnaw thee; burning thirst consume thee; the screech, owl only echo back thy shrieks, and hell and darkness mock at thy despair. Decide; time waits for both, eternity for one of us."

"Then Heaven have mercy on me!" replied the armourer, firmly; "for I will not betray the trust reposed in me, or sell the blood of innocence."

At a sign from their employer, the two ruffians sprang upon their prisoner, whom, after a desperate struggle, they dragged to the recess, and, despite his shrieks and frantic cry for aid, bound him by a chain fixed in the solid wall.

"Monsters!" said the youth, exhausted with the fearful efforts he had made; "Heaven will avenge me!"

"It had better save thee," observed Adam, with a sneer.

The men immediately commenced their labour; and in a few minutes the enclosures reached as high as the breast of the youthful and unhappy victim.

"Stay!" he gasped, overcome with the terror and horror of his doom: "if I accede to your demand, what pledge have I that you will keep faith with me?"

"My word, slave," uttered the knight, in the same calm voice.

"Or his oath, if thou canst trust it better," added his cynical companion in villany.

"I can trust neither!" shrieked the youth; "oaths are for men, not monsters. You would mock my simple faith—profit by my credulity. I must die," he added; "but oh! God, such a death! If you are human show me some mercy—the sword, the cord, or axe, but not a doom like this."

"Proceed!" cried the villain, who saw that his crimes had left him no guarantee to offer on which the armourer could depend, and whose death now became necessary to his safety.

The men rapidly resumed their fearful work, impatient to end a scene which was appalling even to their ferocious natures.

"Monsters!" said Cuthbert, as the wall rose rapidly before him; "the heaven whose laws you outrage will yet avenge me; my restless spirit shall haunt ye to the scaffold; my murdered form shall ever be beside you; remorse shall palsy the unspoken prayer upon your lips. God," he added, "be deaf to them as they are deaf to me; harden their hearts; deprive them of the power of penitence. Avenge me, if thou wilt not save me. Mercy — darkness — darkness — darkness!"

The last brick was inserted in the wall, and the words of the still living tenant of the tomb sounded faintly from behind the arras, which the trembling executioners of their master's will let fall over their fiend-like butchery.

"You are pale," said Adam, going to an old cupboard and filling a goblet of wine, which he presented to the ruffians; "this will refresh you."

"After you," said one of the men suspiciously, for the gentle Adam was held in dread and doubt by all who knew him.

"Fools!" replied the leech—for such was his profession—with a quiet smile, at the same time draining half the contents of the cup. "What is't ye fear? Such instruments are too useful to be parted with; our mutual guilt is a bond between us, as sure as death could make it."

Replenishing the cup, he presented it to the men, who drained it without suspicion. The next morning they were both found dead within their beds.

On descending after the scene we have described into the great hall, Adam and his master found a messenger with a summons from the council, commanding the attendance of Sir John De Corbey on the following morning before the king.

"I have lost the game!" exclaimed the assassin, pale with rage, to his worthy assistant, as soon as they had retired to the chamber of the former; "the estates for which I stained my hand in kindred blood are lost."

"But life is saved," replied the leech; "dead men can bear no evidence against us."

"And honour?"

"Pshaw!" added the cynic; "hast lived these years to grieve for a shadow? Honour! thou wilt grow moral next. Honour! it was thy inheritance; fools only grieve when they have spent it."

With this sneer the confederates parted.

On the following morning, Sir John de Corbey, attended by his minister and accomplice Adam, made his appearance in the presence-chamber, where a scene presented itself which might have shaken even his iron nerves, had he not been prepared to meet it. The widow whom his machinations had deprived of a husband and driven to the verge of madness, and the orphan whom he so long had plotted to rob of her inheritance, were kneeling before the throne where Henry and his queen, surrounded by their court, both sat. Wolsey was standing near the person of the monarch, listening to the story of her wrongs, and commenting upon it, as she proceeded, to his master.

"So, sir knight," exclaimed the impatient king, "you are come at last to answer for yourself. God wot, but we had nearly sent in other guise to fetch you. Knowest thou this lady?" he added sternly, pointing to the still kneeling suppliant before him.

"My noble kinsman, Richard of Stanfield's widow!" said the traitor, with well-acted affection and surprise; "this is indeed a joyful meeting. Why, noble lady, have my letters and my prayers for your return so long remained unanswered?"

"Letters!" faltered the widow; "I received none."

"Received none!" repeated the false guardian; "and the large sums of money sent to your orders?"

"Never reached me," said the lady. "I have been forced to sell plate, jewels, and all I possessed, for bread."

"There hath been treachery here!" cried the knight, with so natural an appearance of indignation that all but Wolsey was deceived by it. He, with his usual astuteness, saw that the speaker was acting the only part prudence and safety left him.

"You admit, then," said Henry, in an under tone, "this lady to be the widow of your kinsman."

"Who dares to doubt it?" answered the artful villain, "or brand the unblemished honour of your old servant, Walter Manny's daughter?"

The allusion to Henry's preserver was well timed, and confirmed the good impression his previous words created.

"And this his child?" added Wolsey, pointing to the infant, whose deep, thoughtful eyes were fixed upon the party questioned, with an expression of intelligence beyond her years.

"His child and undoubted heiress," was the reply.

"You are prepared, then, to resign your trust?" continued his eminence.

"This very hour," said Sir John, sinking on his knee; "and I entreat my royal master to relieve me from it. I am poor—but hitherto my honour is unquestioned. Appoint what arbiters your grace shall please, and if they find a silver penny unaccounted for, a rood of land wrung from my kinsman's trust, I pledge my life to make the forfeit good."

"God's writ! but we have wronged the man," exclaimed Henry, starting from his seat; "thy speech is far more honest than thy look. My lord of York, see to it. Knavery must be skilled indeed if it blind thee. Lady," he added, kindly, "old Manny's daughter shall not lack a friend whilst Henry lives. Embrace thy kinsman. It seems to our discernment both have been victims of the same deceit. Look to her safety, my lord cardinal, and follow to our closet."

With these words the impatient Henry, who hated business, and was anxious to depart for Greenwich, where his sister, Margaret of Scotland, was hourly expected to arrive, broke up the presence, and, followed by all but Wolsey, Sir John de Corbey, Adam, and the helpless widow and her child, withdrew from the apartment.

The murderer approached, and would have saluted the widow of his kinsman, but with an instinctive shudder she drew back. A serpent's kiss would have been more welcome to her.

Wolsey, not oversatisfied with the turn the affair had taken—for he trusted to involve the patron of Sir John, Warham the chancellor, in the knight's disgrace—seeing the agony and repugnance of the lady, interfered, observing, that when the accounts of his trust were audited and acquitted it would be full time to claim the kiss of peace.

Turning to one of his officers, he gave orders for the departure of the widow and her child.

"Where to, your grace?" demanded the unabashed knight; "to Stanfield?"

"No," answered Wolsey, coldly; "to the convent of St. John."

Three days afterwards the suffering, broken-hearted victim slept the last sleep, and the orphan heiress of Stanfield was left the only bar between the assassin and the prize he sued for. But an eye was upon him, and, despite his daring, and unscrupulousness, he quailed beneath its glare: that eye was Wolsey's.

CHAPTER II.

A tale of wonder, and of terror too,
Such as old men by chimney-nook relate,
When winter draws around some gossip's hearth
The listening awe-struck group.

HE Lady Mary, as the orphan heiress of Stanfield was generally named, remained for several years in the same retreat to which Wolsey had consigned her. So fair did the investigation of Sir John de Corbey's guardianship, which took place upon the death of her widowed mother, appear, that no reasonable motive could be assigned for depriving him of his trust, and he still remained in the management of her vast possessions. He was no vulgar gamester—the stake he played for was character as well as life; and every species of forgery and artifice were resorted to by himself and his agent, Adam, to account for the large sums appropriated to the furtherance of his schemes of ambition. Even in the blackest natures one trait will still be found, one link between humanity and Eden's forfeit heritage. Cold, subtle, and remorseless, as was the heart of her false guardian, it was not for himself that he had sinned, but for his son, the impoverished heir of his proud name; doomed by his father's extravagance, crime, and folly, to that worst of fates—a noble beggar's. Henry de Corbey was two years younger than our heroine, a gallant, noble boy, whose mind, nurtured by feeling and high thought, was free from every worldly stain, from every selfish passion; with him the beautiful in nature or in sentiment found a ready worshipper; his soul was framed for the ideal, and like the sensitive plant, recoiled at all contact with the base and worldly. He was a youth such as the noble Surrey might have modelled, or the fair Geraldine have loved.

It was in vain that Adam, to whom his education was entrusted, sought to fashion him to his own dark purpose; no matter how artful the veil which hid the poison of his lessons, how specious the sophistry, his pupil rejected them, and, by a species of mental analysis, separated the good from evil. So sudden and startling were at times the intuitive perceptions of the scholar, that the atheist and cynic were tempted to exclaim, "Hath this thing a soul?" Opposite as were their characters, the guilty father proudly and passionately loved his son: in him every ambitious thought was centred, every future hope and wish; for him alone had he sinned, and the motive of his crime was made at last his punishment.

Sir John's communications with his ward during her residence in the convent were chiefly made through the medium of his secretary, a young man of decayed but noble family, named Walter Lucas. His father had been the knight's companion in the war in Italy, had fallen fighting by his side, and

THE ESCAPE OF ULRICK AND THE CALIGROPHER.

he deemed his promise of providing for his orphan son amply fulfilled by appointing him to a station in his household. Young, ardent, and chivalrous, it is not to be wondered that the ripening beauty of the Lady Mary, now merging into womanhood, made an impression on his heart; and that, although his lips were silent, his eyes were eloquent with thoughts of passion. Repeated interviews confirmed the dangerous feelings, and, despite the disparity of their fortunes, the madness of his hopes, the poor dependant loved. Mary became the star of his existence, the

dreams of his young life: if he sighed for honours, it was to raise him nearer to her sphere; if he wished for wealth, it was to render him more worthy to her. Like some miser, he garnered the precious secret in his breast; lived with it, prayed with it. She was the idol of his heart's shrine; his very soul offered its incense to her.

The heiress possessed that peculiar style of beauty which Raffaelle might have loved to paint, or Petrarch to immortalise; the intellectual blended with the corporeal, the aerial with the earthly; feeling and sentiment beamed from her dark blue eyes, which were so deep and clear in their expression, that love and purity seemed to have made their homes there. Add to the portrait a nostril delicately chiselled; a mouth formed like Cupid's bow, from which a breath exhaled sweet as the last fragrant air which Adam drew from Eden's half-closed gates; and auburn hair falling in wavy masses, like a cloud of gold, over her neck and bosom. Imagine this, and you complete the picture.

> Her step was grace; her bosom's swell
> Seemed like love's own gentle pillow—
> A nest for young desire to dwell—
> A sea of sweets—a snowy billow.

On the secretary's first visits, the orphan received him with a diffidence, which soon gave way to smiles at the warm interest he expressed in all that could contribute to her happiness. How mistaken have those poets been who describe love as timid! Those who really read the human heart will find that it makes weakness strong, and hath a courage peculiarly its own. On one occasion, while on his way to the convent, Walter rescued a dove from the beak of a falcon; the bird was slightly wounded, and in the instinct of its terror flew into his very arms for protection; its disappointed pursuer wheeled slowly round his head, and sailed at last majestically away. Not daring to present it as a gift, he ventured to implore her campassion for his *protege*—a prayer at once accorded. A pang of jealous envy struck his heart as he beheld the gentle girl place the trembling flutterer on her breast, and cover it with kisses. That bird was the first tie between them.

From welcoming him with smiles the maiden soon began to receive him with blushes—to count the time which would elapse before he should return; and more than once her virgin dreams were of him. The presence of the abbess, or some member of the sisterhood, on the occasions of his visits, prevented more than the interchange of looks; but these, to lovers, have ever been more eloquent than words; and at last the enthusiastic, happy Walter felt convinced he was beloved, as though her lips confirmed the blest assurance.

Despite the vague feeling of childish terror which the Lady Mary retained of her guardian, it was almost with satisfaction she was informed that Wolsey had consented to her being withdrawn from the convent, and placed under his protection. Henry himself had recommended it. The crafty knight had secured the friendship of the brother of the rising favourite, Anne Boleyne; and the cardinal, all powerful as he was, deemed it imprudent to oppose it; added to which, he had nothing but surmise and vague objection to offer—so artfully had Sir John contrived to keep down all suspicion.

It was not till the heiress reached her own halls of Stanfield that the secretary found occasion to breathe the tale his glances had so often told, or that he received in words the blest assurance that he was beloved. Trained in the simplicity of conventual life Mary was ignorant of the coquetting of her sex—the thousand little arts by which they enhance the value of their smiles. In the frankness and truthfulness of her heart, she confessed their passion to be mutual; and although her cheek burnt at the confession, it was with a blush as pure as infant's joy or virgin's modesty.

Amongst the first to welcome our heroine on her arrival at Stanfield was our old friend Steadman, who, on the death of her mother, had settled at Norwich, where he introduced the Flemish manner of wool-combing, which he had acquired in the Low Countries, and drove a profitable trade. Our readers may imagine the delight with which this faithful servitor beheld the child of his loved master, from whom he had so long been separated. With almost a father's fondness he admired her graceful form and ripening beauties, and prayed that her fate might be happier than her parents'. Indeed, nothing but this species of devotion to the memory of the past, so common in the servitors of the olden time, could have induced the blunt old soldier to have remained a single instant under the asme roof with Sir John de Corbey, whom he looked upon, with reason, as the cause of the mysterious disappearance of his nephew, the unfortunate Cuthbert, the armourer; whose murder, he used to say, Heaven would in its own good time both discover and avenge. Maud, his widowed sister, whose wits had been unsettled ever since the loss of her only son, resided with him. Like her brother, she too was impressed with the fixed idea that Sir John was the assassin of her boy; and although gentle as a child at all other times, the sight of the man she hated, or the mere mention of his name, excited her to fury; and she would fall upon her knees, and curse him as only a mother's broken heart could curse.

For a month after the return of Lady Mary to her paternal hall there was nothing but a succession of feasts and mirth. The only drawback to her happiness was the persevering boyish passion of her cousin, Henry de Corbey. Young as he was, his heart had long pined for something to cling to. The graceful girl appeared to him like a sunbeam in his path. She was the realization of his dreams—a thing to love, to serve and worship. Did she wander on the terrace, he was by her side—in the silent nook of the forest, he was at her feet, pleading his suit with an eloquence and grace which nearly drove poor Walter mad with jealousy, but which, with woman's tact, the orphan playfully turned aside as the light language of chivalry and romance—meeting his burning vows with smiles and jests. As a brother, she could have loved him for his generous qualities, his daring spirit, and his open heart—his scorn of all things mean and earthly. Perhaps, had not her heart been won—boy though he was—he might have gained an interest in time: some boys are dangerous.

But soon a more serious cause of apprehension clouded her clear brow. Despite the disparity of years between them, Sir John de Corbey became a candidate for the maiden's hand; not from love—for his heart had long been dead to every passion but ambition—but as the means of securing those possessions for which already he had so deeply sinned. Although his ward tremblingly declined his offer, it was evident to all that he still retained his pretensions; and, like the patient bloodhound which never quits its track, persevered in attentions which, he trusted, would in time weary the unprotected girl into consent.

The intentions of her guardian at last became so apparent that it was commented upon in the household—several of the old retainers of which, as well as the chaplain, were indignant at the attempt to profit by the friendless condition of their young mistress to weary her with a match so unsuited to her years and inclinations.

"Were our young lord," observed the steward, "about five years older, the lady might do worse than to choose him. He hath a noble spirit and a generous heart."

Had the speaker known how keen a pang his words inflicted upon the unhappy Walter, who sat listening on thorns to the discussion, he would have pitied him. Despite the secretary's efforts at self-control, he could not forbid his cheek to flush or lip to quiver; and his confusion was still further increased by the observation of Adam, who was seated in a nook of the old hall, apparently poring over the quaintly illuminated page of a rich manuscript, but in reality watching him with furtive glances. The leech suspected him.

"For my part," observed the seneschal, "I never thought Sir John possessed a heart to love aught but himself. What can be his motive for persevering in a suit distasteful to his ward, dishonouring to his years?"

"Necessity!" exclaimed Bertha, the attached female attendant of the heiress; "a rich wife to mend a poor fortune."

"Necessity!" repeated the chaplain, impatiently; "a mean excuse for a still meaner action. Let him amend his ruinous style of living—he else must leave his brave son a lean inheritance."

"Right, right," chimed in Adam, with his usual quiet tone; "retrenchment, by all means. Half his retinue he might well dismiss, part with his steward and servitors; a chaplain, too," he added, with a peculiar smile, "in such a household, were superfluous."

The merry laugh which followed the last observation roused the temper of the priest, between whom and the speaker a species of silent warfare had long waged. The churchman, with the instinct of his profession and natural piety of his heart, hated the sceptic and the mediciner; the leech despised the unlettered chaplain. Strange that between science and religion the seeds of enmity ever should be springing.

"Out on thee, heretic!" retorted the worthy man. "Wouldst have a knight o worship like Sir John dine with his meat unblessed?"

"The expense, father," continued the leech, unmoved by the opprobrious epithet the former had bestowed upon him, "consider the expense; four score marks a year and dainty living—something too much, methinks, for mumbling homilies and doggrel Latin."

The question of latinity was a sore subject between them; the man of science treating the churchman's monkish learning with most superb disdain: indeed, the latter had been so frequently wounded in the contest, that he prudently avoided the subject, and took refuge in the religious side of the question, where the cynic was compelled, in words at least, to be respectful; for the persecution against the Lollards was raging at its height.

"Out, heretic!" exclaimed the chaplain, with a look of horror. "Rail at the holy mass! Beware! the church's arm can punish."

Several of his hearers, to prove their orthodoxy, piously crossed themselves; and even Adam feared that he had gone too far.

"You wrong me, father, with a forced construction," he replied. "I spoke not of thy doctrines, but latinity; in which, as holy church claims no infallibility, I, or any other man, may call thy skill in question. Heaven forfend I should attack thy faith," added the speaker, with an affectation of humility; "it is a thing toosublimated r human reason to analyse—at east, a rea weak as mine."

"Thy words," said the ecclesiastic, gravely, and not altogether displeased at withdrawing his antagonist from a position where he was master, "deceive not me; no, nor thy feigned humility: thou hast deeply studied."

"Not much—not much," said the leech, musingly. "Sometimes before my eyes dreams of far distant lands will rise—of marble palaces—of gilded domes, which in my youth I saw, or fancied so—of shrines where science was the goddess worshipped— of silent temples, whose eternal walls breathe the deep spirit of the painter's art."

"You speak of Italy," exclaimed Walter, deeply interested in his words; for it was not often that the cold and reserved Adam could be brought to dwell upon the subject of his country, or the events of his early years.

"Ay, of Italia," continued the old man mournfully; "of that land where art and nature, like two rivals, strive in generous emulation. I have stood within her temples— breathed her balmy air—gazed enrapt upon her sculptured treasures, till the soul hath e'en been drunk with beauty; but still found her choicest statues in her living forms."

As if ashamed of the weakness and gar-rulity he had displayed, the leech closed the illuminated page over which he had been poring, and slowly quitted the hall. His departure was the signal for breaking up the conversation. The worthy chaplain retired to his devotions—or his bottle; for he was not of those who despise the creature com-forts of existence; Bertha, to attend her lady in her usual walk; and the amorous secretary, as the poet quaintly expresses it, "to chew the cud of sweet and bitter fancies," or to watch patiently but for one glance from the blue eyes he loved. Despite his confidence in Mary's faith, and the hopeful-ness so natural to youth, his heart was ill at ease. The persevering suit of the knight aroused his fears, and the boyish love of the son his jealousy; for he could not avoid feeling there was something in the gallant bearing of the noble, generous boy to touch a woman's heart. He had not been long ensconced within his favourite bower upon the old terrace-walk of Stanfield, before his mistress and her attendant, followed by the passionate, loving Henry, approached; and he was compelled to remain the concealed spectator of a scene which wrung his heart and awoke his admiration.

"But one poor kiss, sweet coz," exclaimed the youth; "grant it as you would alms to

a beggar's importunity; if not from charity, from weariness. They deal in fable," he added, "who assert that Heaven is won by prayers; I find it deaf to me."

"For shame, rude boy!" answered his cousin, half playfully, half petulantly, de-termined not to treat his suit as serious. "A kiss! your beard would frighten me."

"Manhood lies not always in the beard," replied the youth quickly. "In hawking for a husband, Mary, cast not your bird that way, lest you should find the quarry struck more precious in the plumage than the sub-stance. You call me boy; methinks 'tis time you treat me like a man, since you deny me the boy's privilege—a cousin's kiss."

"Why, Henry," said the unhappy girl, "why follow my sad steps to pour a tale whose mirth is sadness to me?"

"Why do I follow thee?" repeated the amorous boy, fixing on her a look, and blush-ing at his own boldness. "Because I love thee! Thou hast a pearly skin, and a red lip, whose pouting blush invites a thousand kisses; a figure whose light grace haunts me in my dreams. But 'tis not these," he added; "'tis thy mind, seen through the glorious veil of these its outward graces. Let me be sworn thy knight."

"What!" exclaimed Bertha, who in her own heart would have preferred the hand-some boy to twenty secretaries; "wouldst rival thine own father?"

Henry de Corbey started, and, perhaps for the first time in his life, his cheek turned pale. An idea so preposterous as a marriage between his cousin and his father never once struck him. From delicacy, Mary had con-cealed her guardian's tyranny from his son, whom, despite his importunities, she loved with a sister's love. The proud and generous boy spurned at the thought of such a sacrifice.

"Rival my father!" he repeated gravely. "Maiden, this is some ill-timed jest."

"My lady finds it none," answered the attendant petulantly; "for the knight woos not with smiles, but threats."

"Threats!" said Henry, his eyes flashing with indignation; "who dares accuse my father of dishonour? This is some loose talk—the gossip of the hall, bred from in-vention and mere idleness. Mary," he added, throwing himself upon his knees, and seizing her hand, "thy words are truth; thou hast a soul too pure to lend to falsehood even the sanction of a look: is this thing so?"

"It is," faltered the lovely girl, her neck and brow suffused with a thousand blushes. "Would I had been born a beggar!"

"What!" continued the youth, starting to

his feet; "marry my father! couple age with you! bid the dull stream of sluggish winter and of genial spring in the same current flow! Oh! never, never! Nature revolts at such a prostitution. No, Mary, no! thou shalt not change thy girlhood's smile into a stepdame's frown; the opening bud of love's first flower shall not wither on the icy breast of heartless age. Love whom thou wilt," he added passionately, "my arm shall aid thy choice; wed whom thou wilt, my breaking heart shall bless it."

Despite his resolution, and the manly tone in which he spoke, the effort was too much for him, and tears of mingled rage and grief chased each other down his burning cheeks. Vainly he endeavoured to dash them aside—vainly endeavoured to conceal them; he was Nature's child, and had not yet acquired the art of smiling on the pangs which turned his heart to ashes, or bearing a calm front with the iron hand of shame upon his soul.

"You were right, Mary," he exclaimed, "quite right, to mock my childish suit. I prove myself a boy by these unmanly tears. Do not despise me for them; I am not yet accustomed to dishonour."

"Thou art my own dear noble-hearted cousin!" replied Mary; "and these tears honour thy manhood, not disprove it, Henry. Come, thou shalt be my friend—Heaven knows I need one—my knight, my brother."

"Brother!" repeated the youth with a sigh; "well, be it so. I'll prove a brother to thee, watch over thy happiness like a miser over his most precious treasure, seeking contentment in the task, since I have lost my own."

The speaker sadly turned away to leave her.

"Whither goest thou?" replied the Lady Mary.

"To my father!" replied the boy, with a degree of resolution beyond his years.

"What to do?"

"To plead thy cause—to purge this foul dishonour from his heart," said her cousin; "to bid him choose between this madness and his son; to show him in a mirror the monster he hath engendered in his brain, till he shall loathe and scorn it. Farewell, dear Mary! soon shall I see thee smile again, glad in the light of thine own heart, thine innocence and virtue. Doubt not my eloquence when 'tis for thee I plead."

The sad-hearted boy left her on his generous errand as he spoke. Scarcely had he left the terrace, than Walter, who had been an agitated spectator of the scene between the cousins, emerged from his concealment. He was too just not to appreciate the maiden's confidence and his young rival's worth. The agitated girl advanced to meet him; placing her hand in his, she sobbed, as he knelt to press it to his lips.

"Walter, our dream of happiness is over. The evil fortune of my house prevails, and we must part."

"Part!" said her lover. "Dost thou, then, repent the love which blessed the humble secretary?"

"Are these sad tears," replied the unhappy heiress, "the proofs of love estratged or faith decayed? But I am beset with snares, with terrors for thy safety; my guardian——"

"Loves thee," added Walter, finishing the words her lips refused to speak.

"Call it not love!" exclaimed his mistress; "profane not the pure flame. Base avarice is the shrine at which he worships—to restore the fallen greatness of his house his fixed ambition, and I the sacrifice. By lingering here thou wilt but pull destruction on thy head, yet fail to rescue me. Too well thou knowest," she continued, "his stern, unbending nature. Alone I have the heart to brave the storm, yet not to share it with thee. Fly, then, at once; for oh! I see no haven for our fears—no power to save me from the last despair."

"Yes; Wolsey," replied her lover; "he whose all-powerful arm shielded thy infant years from thy false guardian's tyranny."

"Wolsey's!" repeated the maiden; "he hath abandoned me. What chance—what hope to interest him in my fortunes?"

"Listen," said Walter; "when boys, my father and the cardinal were friends—sworn confidents in study, pleasure, mischief. Some childish words divided them. One morn, when walking on the banks of the swift Orwell, which skirts their native city, my father's ears were struck by the faint cry of a spent swimmer. His jerkin doffed, he plunged into the stream, and bore the half-drowned soul to shore. 'Twas his quondam friend."

"Did he not, in his greatness, remember the preserver of his life?" demanded Mary.

"The great have treacherous memories," resumed the youth. "Ere my father died, he left a letter for his grace, begging protection for his orphan son; I have it still."

"Why didst thou not present it?"

"Dost thou ask why?" said the secretary, gazing upon her with earnest tenderness. "What was to me the chance of earthly favour—of buzzing, like some hapless moth, around the lamp of greatness, to perish at last, perchance, within its blaze—if it removed me from thy presence, lady?"

Mary would never have known the sacrifice

of which her lover spoke so slightingly, but for the hope he entertained that it might not yet be too late to use the letter as a means of saving her. Generous herself, she had never considered the inequalities of their fortune; and if for a moment she remembered her high lineage and broad lands, it was to wish them ten times greater, to bestow them on the man she loved. Hers was a heart which, in the fulness of its love, could all bestow, without vaunting, like a churl, the value of the gift; and yet she felt the sacrifice of Walter, so apt is sensibility to weigh the merit in another it sees not in itself.

"Didst thou for me resign the hope of life—the step which leads to greatness?" she exclaimed; "my weakness must not shame thy noble nature. Let the storm rage, it still shall find me firm. My heart shall draw fresh courage from thy pure devotion. Death may divide our hands, but not our loves; but never shall the faith once pledged to thee be given to another."

The maiden raised the cross which hung from her rosary as she spoke, and pressed it to her lips; and Walter—for the moment, the happy Walter—bent the knee before the idol of his soul, and pressed with impassioned lips the hand dearer to him than the richest treasure earth possessed, or heaven itself could bestow. His dream of happiness—like most dreams of happiness in this world—was doomed to be brief; for Adam—who, like Satan watching the first pair in Paradise, concealed behind the balustrades of the terrace, had observed their interview—advanced with his usual stealthy step from his lurking place. He took no notice either of the secretary's position or the Lady Mary's confusion, but seemed to regard them both as the most natural circumstances in the world. The fabled basilisk, it is said, is never more dangerous than in repose. Such, at least, was the case with the cold, subtle agent of Sir John de Corbey's unnumbered villanies.

"Our lady," stammered the secretary, endeavouring to hide his confusion, "had conferred a favour on her servant, when you stepped in, and——"

"Broke the current of your gratitude," added the old man, with a sarcastic smile. "She is a liberal mistress."

"What mean you?" demanded the young man, impatiently, for he liked not the look or manner.

"What should I mean?" replied the intruder, in the same sneering tone. "The blush upon her cheek doth but betoken kindness to a menial, and in thy shifting eye I read thy heart's true character. Thou wouldst not deceive me," he added, ironically, "wouldst not lie to screen thy lady, e'en though she loved her servant."

Turning from the young man as if he deemed it waste of time to continue the discussion, he addressed himself to the heiress, informing her with an air of mocking respect that her guardian wished to speak with her.

"Fly!" whispered Mary to the secretary, as she passed him on her way to the hall. "Wolsey is now our only hope." The close attendance of Adam prevented any adieu beyond the look which accompanied the words; but that was eloquent as love could make it.

"I must away," exclaimed Walter, as soon as he was alone upon the terrace. "Soon as Sir John hears of my daring passion my life will be beset. Those who have crossed his path had better live, cameleon-like, on air: though yon cursed leech has skill enough to poison the very atmosphere I breathe, so even that were dangerous."

As the speaker descended the steps which led from the raised walk to the open grounds, two of the knight's foreign retainers sprang upon him; and, despite his resistance, he was borne to a strong room at the top of the loftiest tower of the hold; the window of which, it is true, was unbarred, but at such a distance from the ground that nought could fall from it and live. A cloak had been thrown over his head to stifle his cries; for the young man was so beloved, that many of the household would have drawn their swords in his defence, despite the terror which the knight and his minister, Adam, universally inspired. Here the captive was left to meditate alone; a thousand times did he curse the imprudence which had betrayed his secret, and indulge in gloomy anticipations of the future.

The Lady Mary found her guardian seated in the library of Stanfield, a low-arched room, which received its distinctive appellation from a few books and manuscripts kept in an ancient oaken press, where many of the deeds and charters concerning the estates were likewise preserved. A village schoolmaster of the present age would have smiled at such a library; but, in the reign of Henry VIII., it was thought sufficiently considerable to merit an especial notice in the chronicles of the Monk of Cotessey—a writer whom, in the course of our work, we have before referred to.

"You summoned me, Sir John," said the trembling girl; for years had not diminished the terror which in childhood he had inspired her with.

"I did," replied the knight, leading her

to a seat : "for converse which concerns your happiness and mine. Why," he added, taking her hand, "are you thus obstinately blind to your own good? Rank, observance, and respect await my bride—a noble state my widow."

"Such," said his ward, "are to me superfluous; nobly born, I need not their advantage. Besides," she added, "ask your own heart, do they give happiness?"

"A philosopher!" exclaimed her tormentor, with a sneer.

"No, sir," replied Mary, spiritedly, "a Christian. I have no wish to wed; the difference of our years renders this suit impossible. Be generous, then, and urge the theme no more; be just to your own honour, lest men should say Sir John de Corbey broke his kinsman's trust, and gained by fraud the lands he failed to win by blood."

Hitherto the conduct of his ward had been so submissive and respectful, that the knight was both astonished at her firmness and stung by the knowledge of the fact her words conveyed. The scenes of terror and distress which in her infancy she had experienced had never been effaced from the memory of the thoughtful child, but had been pondered over from year to year, almost from day to day. The relations of Steadman, too, and the wild, melancholy ravings of his mad sister, had impressed her mind with fearful doubts of her dark guardian's character.

The thrust had been a home one, and for a few minutes he regarded her with a glance of cold and stony hatred, which, while it made her young heart beat with terror, served but to confirm her resolution.

"And yet," he said, regarding her with an insulting look, "this cold, coy, and contented maid can love in secret, and, forgetful of her blood, receive the homage of a menial's heart. Mary of Stanfield, thou art disgraced!"

The blush which suffused the cheek of the fair girl at the brutal words was in itself sufficient refutation: morning might have envied it for its purity — innocence have offered it to cruelty for its justification; it was a witness fresh from the heart—pure as the life-stream which coloured it. She felt that the moment had arrived when further concealment would not only be unwise, but useless; and trusting that her lover was already on his way to implore the powerful protection of the cardinal, she answered with the courage of insulted virtue:

"'Tis false, sir knight! Nay, frown not at my boldness," she added; "the pride of innocence and womanhood compels me now to speak. Walter's love is pure and generous, and cannot disgrace me. He does not seek to raise his fortunes by my wreck of happiness; he would not force me to the arms of wrinkled age—extorting vows love only should bestow——"

"Insulted, rejected!" interrupted De Corbey, pale with passion, "and for a peasant!"

"Peasant!" repeated Lady Mary, scornfully. "He hath a prouder title, sir, than king ere gave or herald's pen inscribed—Nature's nobility, a generous heart; besides, I have often heard you yourself declare that Walter's birth was gentle."

"Let him prove it, then, before his judges."

"His judges! of what crime can you accuse him?" demanded the astonished maiden.

"Of an attempt to steal an heiress from her guardian's trust," replied the villain. "Wisely our laws protect the high born maid from the weak promptings of her yielding heart, guarding the honour of a noble line left in such frail keeping. In wooing thee Walter hath sinned against the law. He is my prisoner, and his doom——"

"Mercy!" exclaimed the agitated girl, all her assumed firmness giving way at the thought of her lover's danger, which, from the law cited by her guardian, she knew to be no imaginary one; "kinsman, mercy!"

Like pleading angel, she sank upon her knees before her persecutor, who surveyed her with a dark smile of triumph, for he fancied that he had found the means to bend her resolution and mould her to his purpose—the means of Walter's danger.

"Mary," he answered, calmly, "I will be just."

At this moment Henry de Corbey, eager to have an explanation with his father, entered the apartment. From one of his attendants he had just heard of the secretary's arrest, but he wisely kept that knowledge, and the resolution he had framed in consequence, to himself. When he beheld his cousin kneeling at the feet of his stern parent, his agitation for a moment deprived him of his firmness; recovering himself, he passed between her and the knight, and raising her, said in a tone of gravity beyond his boyish years:

"Rise, Mary, rise—nor shame my father's manhood by your knee."

"Retire, Henry," cried her persecutor, ashamed of being detected in an unworthy position by the son for whom he had so deeply sinned, and of whom he was so justly proud. "Leave me to guard the honour of our house."

"Your pardon, sir," replied the youth, respectfully, "but we are both its guardians. Mary," he added, leading her to the door of the apartment, "leave me to reason with my father. Fear not for Walter," he whispered; "I possess the means to save him."

The kind look of sympathy and affection which accompanied the words of her cousin gave hope to the despairing victim's heart. She knew the truthfulness and devotion of the being in whom she trusted. "Be cautious," she replied, in the same low tone, as she left the room; "he is your father—urge not his wrath too far."

As soon as they were alone, father and son, for a few moments, regarded each other in silence. The high-minded youth had hitherto treated his parent with almost childish obedience and respect; and this sudden opposition to his will was as astounding, therefore, as it was unexpected.

"Art thou, indeed, my son?" demanded the knight, with a look beneath which Henry would once have quailed.

"Thy wretched son," replied the youth, mournfully; "for my happiness was built upon my father's love—my pride upon my father's honour—now dust and ashes both. Father, is this the way to fill thy kinsman's trust? Knaves betray the living—cowards the dead: retrace thy steps, lest men should call thee both."

The guilty man was struck, but not moved from his fixed purpose by the sorrowful appeal. The very admiration which he felt for the courage, generous impulse, and lofty bearing of the speaker, determined him more strongly than ever, no matter by what means, to atone the wrong he had done him by squandering his inheritance. The thought that the gifted being, the heir of his proud name, must struggle through the world with life's bare competence—a mere adventurer, with no fortune but honour and his sword—was madness to him. He had sworn to rebuild the greatness of his house, even if he perilled his soul in the attempt. Unable to reason the youth, he thought to overawe him.

"Boy," he exclaimed, trying to assume a look of outraged dignity, "retire to your studies!"

"Such scenes," replied Henry, firmly, "change boys to men, throw age upon the heart, turn youthful smiles to manhood's line of thought. What means this persecution? I will not shame thy ears to call it love. Would that I wronged thy honour to suspect it avarice."

Finding that evasion or concealment with his son was no longer possible, the knight of Corbey motioned him to a seat beside him.

"Henry," he began, "though of strong passions in my youth, once, like yourself, I had a generous heart; the time has been when death had not one terror like dishonour—when I believed the world all truth, and trusted its delusive smiles—when friendship was not, as now, a sound without a sense to my dull ear, or love a stranger to my heart. I trusted all—by all to be deceived. In Italy, that land which hell hath decked to look like paradise—where serpents lurk 'neath flowers—whose very air, fanning the ashes of unhonoured age, revives the dormant passions they should hide —I entered as a soldier into life. I will not tire thy patience with my career. Enough, I mixed in the intrigues of courts, drained pleasure's cup e'en to its bitter dregs, revelled in beauty till its sweetness palled me! What was my fate? The prince I bled for sold me to the foe; my triumphs hurt the ingrate's vanity; the love I sinned for sought a richer dupe; fortune, which smiled upon my early youth, was quits with me in manhood. I was left a beggar."

"And if left with honour, left with every thing," interrupted Henry.

"I will not die one," sternly resumed the speaker. "I will, at least, redeem thy heritage. Justice, and nature, as her nearest kinsman, gave me the disposal of the Lady Mary. I offer her no unhonoured name, no undistinguished hand. Not a word," he added, seeing that his son was about to speak —"thou mayest as well try to arrest the meteor in its course as turn me from my will. If the path be crooked, I alone shall trace it. How couldst thou bear a life of poverty? the jest of bloated wealth? the pity of thy equals? the sneers of thy inferiors? Never—never! The honours of our house shall not end in a beggar's dish and wallet!"

Deeming that he had sufficiently impressed his son with the necessity of the sacrifice of his cousin at the shrine of interest, he left the apartment, his haughty soul stung to the quick at the explanation he had been compelled to offer, and unable longer to endure the alternate glances of astonishment and shame the unhappy youth cast on him.

"God!" he exclaimed, "and is this man my father? the being I have held in honour —fancied the model of all chivalry! Surely some demon hath possessed his mind, poisoning his better nature. For me—for me he sins. What were the wealth of worlds bought with a tear from Mary's eye—one stain upon the honour of my name? I swore to be her knight—boy as I am, I'll keep my oath. Perchance," he added, "she may love me in my grave. Yes, Mary, yes; I'll save thee from my father's selfish passion— my father from himself."

With this resolve the youth retired to his apartment, there to plan the means of putting into execution the noble purpose he had formed of freeing Walter from his prison, and watching over Mary's safety.

A stormy night had closed the eventful day we have endeavoured to describe. The wind whistled mournfully round the lofty tower in which the prisoner sat; his food untasted—Adam had brought it to him; and although tormented with thirst, he feared to touch the draught within his reach. The old man's skill in poison was no secret

to him. One after another the various instruments employed by Sir John had disappeared or suddenly died; till, at length, the members of the household began to look upon their master's confidence as a dangerous favour, and shrank from it with terror. Still so artfully the murders, if murders they were, had been committed, that no tangible evidence had been found to fix the crime. One fellow, who had been heard to mutter threats, died in the servants' hall on opening a letter which some stranger, it was said, had left for him at the gates. The leech pronounced it apoplexy. Another expired after being bled for a fall from his horse. The old members of the household shook their heads, but prudently remained silent.

"Thus ends my dream of life," murmured the prisoner to himself; "hope bids farewell at the door to those who enter here. Fool! I was amply warned, but, like the giddy moth, have lingered round the flame whose fire at last consumes me. I burn with thirst," he added, "but fear to drink."

Fearful lest the thirst which tormented him should overcome his resolution, with a blow of his foot he shivered the earthen vessel containing the water, which he justly feared to be poisoned.

"I'll not die like a drugged cat in this old tower!" he exclaimed; "they shall not make me accessory to my own murder. Oh!" he added, impatiently, "but for one hour of liberty! I'd use the gift so well, they should have swift steeds who caught me."

At this moment a tapping at the window was heard. At first the captive, deeming it the fluttering of an owl attracted by the light within his chamber, paid slight attention to the signal; but, on its being repeated, he hastened to the casement, and to his admiration as well as terror, found Henry de Corbey hanging by a rope which he had fastened on to the battlements above. The wind was so high, and the weight of the youth so light, that his form vibrated fearfully in the air at the dizzy height at which it was suspended, alternately appearing or disappearing, like some spectre floating on the winds, before the eyes of the prisoner. His features were pale, not from the danger of his position, but from the recent agitation he had undergone.

"Are you unfettered?" he demanded; and again a gust of wind blew him from the casement.

"I am," replied the prisoner, when the wind brough the youth within the sound of his voice again.

"Follow me, then," said the boy; "the cord is strong enough for both of us. Stay, I will slide down a few feet lower to leave you space—'tis well."

Suiting the action to the word, the adventurous boy permitted the rope to glide through his hands till he had descended some ten or fifteen feet lower; when, twining it over his arm, he paused in his descent, till he beheld the prisoner emerge from the casement of his chamber and follow his perilous example. It required both a firm eye and a strong hand; the cord vibrated fearfully against the side of the lofty tower, like the pendule of some giant clock. Fortunately the young men both reached the ground in safety. Walter would have expressed his gratitude for his deliverance, but Henry stopped him.

"You owe me nothing—away! you will find my horse saddled and ready by the Druid's well. Waste not the moments precious to safety by words of thriftless gratitude."

"But Mary?" interrupted the secretary.

"Is safe while I have life. The angel which watches over innocence will not prove more faithful to his trust than I shall."

With a silent pressure of the hand the young men parted—though rivals, they esteemed each other—Walter to the Druid's well, where, according to his deliverer's direction, he found a gallant steed awaiting him; and Henry to the tower, to remove the rope by which he had effected the escape of the prisoner.

Great was the anger and confusion of Sir John de Corbey on the following morning when informed of his secretary's escape. Adam and two trusty domestics were immediately dispatched in pursuit, while he himself, with the unhappy Lady Mary, now little less than a prisoner, removed from Stanfield to a mansion which he possessed in Norwich. There the household were entirely devoted to his purposes, and the heiress would be effectually removed from those who might protect her.

CHAPTER III.

Though human cunning hide each sinful deed
In its recess, dark as the womb of time,
Justice at last shall break each barrier through,
Holding the guilty and the proof to light.

ELL did the gallant steed on which the fugitive was mounted answer to the rider. In less than an hour the distance between Stanfield and Norwich was passed in safety; and there did the breathless Walter first draw rein. Like a Will-o'-the-wisp he had dashed over bog and fern, forded the stream, skirted the wood, and galloped down the rough broken road, till he reached St. Giles's Gate, a massive, lofty tower, built with flint and stone, long since consigned by the cupidity and brutal ignorance of the corporation to destruction.

Few cities have more suffered from the Vandalism of its rulers than the capital of the Angles. How many monuments of the religious, civil, and domestic architecture of our fathers have they not destroyed! The fine old keep of the castle erected by Roger Bigod in the reign of William the Conqueror remained almost uninjured till 1824: 'tis true the elaborated Norman carving was much time-worn, grey, mouldering, and weather-stained, giving it that tone of antiquity which painters love; but it was determined to restore Norwich Castle, or rather "smarten" it, as the authorities profanely called it; and the plan chosen was the very worst which could possibly have been adopted —that of entirely recasing it. In the new stone facing which the old keep now carries, the arcades and tracery have been copied, but the effect produced is just as if a noble antique statue had been restored by chipping away the entire surface, and replacing it by an imitation of vulgar workmanship. All that rendered it valuable is gone for ever, and it is atoned for by a copy, to make which it was necessary to destroy the original. Fit instrument for such a sacrilege, Wilkins, of National Gallery fame, was the architect selected, most probably because he was a native of Norwich. What other city could have produced him?

It is not often that we indulge in digressions foreign to our tale; such of our readers as have mourned over the destruction or degradation of the monuments of their birth-place will sympathise with and pardon us.

Much as Walter wished to consult his old friend Steadman in the emergency in which he found himself placed, he dared not venture to enter the city: but, turning to his right, skirted the moat and walls till he arrived at St. Stephen's Gates—since destroyed by the same barbarians—and broke into the high road leading direct to London. Although the night was dark, Walter had not passed the post unobserved. The citizens kept careful watch, for disputes were running high between them and the prior and monks of the cathedral respecting their jurisdictions: to such a length had they been carried, that blood had been shed on both sides, and it was rumoured that Wolsey himself was about to visit the city in order to decide between them. It was therefore to the interest of the authorities to prevent their priestly opponents from sending any *ex-parte* statement of their cause to the all-powerful minister. Several messengers had already been intercepted and detained; they had subtle enemies to contend with, and they took their precautions accordingly.

The horseman had not proceeded more than eight miles in his present direction than he encountered a party which attracted his attention. Two soldiers of the city guard, mounted on serviceable steeds, were leading a sleek mule between them, on which a rider in the dress of a priest lay, bound by cords. His captors had thrown him, like a sack of corn, over the pillion, and despite his cries, groans, threats of excommunication, and prayers, were jogging along with him over the rough, uneven road at a pitiless rate. The unfortunate man was one of the prior's messengers, a brother of the convent, who, with more zeal than prudence, had undertaken to convey his superior's appeal and denunciations against the citizens to Wolsey. Like the secretary, he had been seen from the city gates, and his captors sent in pursuit of him. Despite the fleetness of his mule, they had succeeded.

"We have bagged the holy fox," shouted one of the men, laughingly, as Walter approached him, doubtless, in the obscurity of the night, mistaking him for a comrade sent to assist in the chase. "If the shaveling only prays as heartily as he curses, by our Lady, but he will win heaven by storm."

"Holy fox! and shaveling!" ejaculated the captive, in a voice of terror and indignation; "who ever heard Christian men speak in such ungodly terms? Know you not," he added, "that you will both be damned for this? For what says the canon of the church? Accursed are they who touch—"

Here a terrible jolting on the road and scantiness of breath interrupted the priest's quotation.

"You ride fast, young sir," said the man who had first spoken, as Walter's nearer approached showed him the error into which he had fallen; "'tis a late hour, and your journey seems suspicious. Stand to the city guard, and answer for your errand, name, and quality."

"I am beyond the city bounds," replied the young man, "and you have no right to question me. Stand back," he added, as he saw the fellow draw his horse into the centre of the road to dispute his passage; "I am armed; your blood be upon your own head if you assail me. Therefore beware."

"Strike!" roared the monk, who, on nearing the dispute, began to entertain hopes of a rescue. "They are accursed, and thou mayst lawfully slay them. They have laid hands upon a priest; de facto, they are excommunicate; they have seized me and my mule upon the king's highway—ergo, they are robbers. I do deliver their souls to Satan, and their bodies to the sword. Smite them with good conscience."

A sharp blow which the second soldier—who still continued to hold the rein of the priest's mule—administered with the butt-end of his lance, admonished the churchman to be silent.

"Holy Mother!" he muttered to himself, "I shall be made a martyr of at last. It is not exactly the honour in the church I should have preferred," he added; "but I suppose the saints know best what is fit for me."

Walter, seeing that his assailant was about to level his heavy partisan, the mere weight of which, had it fallen upon his head, must have stunned him, drew his sword, and, putting spurs to his gallant, though jaded steed, pressed upon him. The encounter—if it deserved the name of such—was over in an instant; for, avoiding the ponderous weapon of his adversary by wheeling his horse round, he succeeded in inflicting so severe a wound upon his right arm, that it fell useless by his side.

"By heaven, Gilbert," shouted the fellow, "but the springal hath wounded me; my arm is powerless. Upon him cautiously, for the knave fights well."

"Would he had slain thee outright!" thought the monk to himself; for he had been too severely admonished to give utterance to his thoughts aloud.

Now it was that the struggle commenced in earnest. The second soldier, warned by the fate of his comrade, stood not less carefully than manfully upon his guard; it was in vain that Walter wheeled round and round him, describing a circle of which his opponent remained the centre; the fellow, turn which way he would, confronted him—his ponderous partisan raised above his head, ready to crush him. So lightly armed was our hero, having nothing but his sword, that, unless he had seen a fair opening, it would have been madness to have closed with him—a single blow from that rude weapon being sufficient to slay both man and horse. Finding that their evolutions were in vain, as if by mutual accord, they drew up, and remained for several seconds regarding each other in silence.

"You use your partisan well, friend," said Walter; "pity that you do not employ it in a better cause than plundering lawful travellers upon their journey. Your name will prove a credit to the city-guard, which, sooth to say, boasts not too good a one already, if men speak truth of it."

"Plunder!" repeated the fellow; "he must have a doublet thinly lined who would stop thee, or yon prating monk, for gain. By my patron saint! I question if ye are not both richer in blows and curses than marvedes! I'd not give a silver mark for the quiltings of both your jackets."

"Why do you bar my path, then? Do you take me for a robber?" demanded the young man.

"No," resumed the speaker, in a dogged tone, like one determined not to be thrown off his guard.

"For what, then?"

"For a messenger of the wily prior, charged with more lies than virtues—more frauds than truth. If we must put our city's rights under the cowl of mother church, at least it shall be the cardinal's—we will not yield to a crow of our own nest; so either give up your letters, or return with me."

"What if I assure thee that I am a stranger to your city broils, and bear no letters?" said the secretary, who began to feel impatient at the delay occasioned by the encounter.

"Thy assurance will exceed the measure of my credulity," replied the fellow, with a laugh.

"Thou art determined, then, to bar my passage?"

"Indisputably."

"Why, then," exclaimed Walter, "St. George decide between us! Have at thee for as obstinate a knave as ever gained a broken crown in a fool's cause! Since we must play at loggats, let the sides be equal!"

Clapping spurs to his highly trained but almost exhausted steed, the speaker turned suddenly round, and galloped to the spot where the monk still lay bound upon his mule. With a single stroke of his sword he cut the cords, and set the captive at liberty; calling out to him at the same time, "If ever mother church struck a sure blow, strike it now; up, priest, and be doing."

The worthy brother needed no second invitation. No sooner did he feel his limbs at liberty than he slid from his mule, and, after giving himself a hearty shake, secured the long partisan which the wounded man had dropped in the previous encounter with Walter. With a prudence peculiar to his profession, before he advanced to the assistance of our hero, now furiously assailed by his opponent, whose rage at the liberation of the monk knew no bounds, he quietly dealt the fellow, who was stanching his wound, a blow on the head with the butt-end of his weapon—so scientifically applied, that it effectually prevented him, for some time at least, from either witnessing or taking any part in the affray. We beg our readers most particularly to remember that it was with the butt-end of the partisan the blow was given; for brother Hugo, even in his wrath, remembered the canon of the church, which forbids a priest to smite with steel, lest it lead to the shedding of blood; added to which, knocking him down answered his purpose quite as well. After this exploit, had the liberated captive followed the dictates of prudence only, he would have remounted his mule, and continued his route; but anger, and a sense of something like gratitude, restrained him; he remembered the hard blows he had received, and, like an honest man, was anxious to acquit himself of the debt. With a bold front he advanced to Walter's assistance, who, sooth to say, was hard pressed by his assailant, whose superiority of weapon gave him an advantange over him. In his early days the monk had evidently been used to arms; for he not only handled the partisan skilfully, but took up a position at the foot of a tree, round which the combatants were repeatedly wheeling, which evinced considerable tact in strategy. With the long tough ash pole raised above his head—for he still remembered the canon—he stood, as it were, the

arbiter of the fight, ready to throw down his warder, and bid the contest cease. At least he did throw it down, and so effectually, that it fell on the young soldier's head-piece, with a force which, had it not been well-tempered, must have shivered it to splinters; as it was, the wearer fell, from his horse as suddenly as if he had been shot. The frightened animal, freed from its rider, galloped off, and was soon out of hearing.

"Fairly aimed and fairly struck, holy brother," exclaimed Walter, who, had he not been so unequally opposed in point of weapons in the encounter, would have blushed at such assistance.

"Pretty well," modestly replied the priest; "the spirit was willing, although the flesh was weak. But what are we to do with our prisoners?—heathens as they are, we cannot leave them thus."

The speaker, who, after all, possessed more of the milk of human kindness than its gall, took from the huge pocket of his gown a well-filled flask, and applied it to the lips of the senseless man, first bathing his brow with a portion of its contents. The fellow, who had been stunned more than seriously hurt by the blow, gradually recovered his senses, although at first they were naturally disposed to wander after the severe concussion which they had received.

"Holy mother, how my brain dances!" he exclaimed. "What a flash of lightning was that which blinded me! Where am I? I dreamt I had been in purgatory!"

"A very natural dream, too, my son," replied the monk; "take care how you realise it."

"You here! and at liberty!" said the man; "why, where is Martin, then?" This was the name of his comrade.

"Much in the same state as yourself," meekly answered the priest; "the Lord hath smitten ye both: your companion sorely."

"I suspect," said the fellow, "the Lord has had very little to do with it. It was more like felling an ox than chastising a Christian."

After binding up the wounds of the two fellows, and cutting the saddle-girth of their remaining steed, so to delay their arrival in the city that all further pursuit would prove in vain, Walter and the monk pursued their way.

Upon more familiar acquaintance, it seemed that they were both bound to the same destination, London, and each to implore the protection of Wolsey; the churchman for the rights of his convent in their disputes with the citizens, the secretary for himself and the Lady Mary.

Making good speed, they arrived in the metropolis, and learnt that the minister was at his newly-erected manor-house of Hampton, the magnificence of which, it was whispered, excited the jealousy of his master and induced the favourite, at last, to surrender it to him, receiving Richmond in exchange. Here the two travellers parted—the priest to lodge with those of his order in the city, the young man to the house of Sir John de Corbey on the banks of the Thames; the only inhabitant of which was an old chaplain, who had protected him in his infancy, and finally introduced him to the family of his patron : the mansion for several years had been abandoned by its owner—too many fearful associations were connected with it to permit him to dwell in peace there.

Independent of the affection which he bore to his venerable friend, it was necessary that he should see him, in order to obtain the letter which his father had written to the cardinal, and which, for many years, had been left in the old man's care. Otherwise, perhaps, he had not ventured near the fatal spot, even though deserted by its designing master. So unused was Father Celestine to receive visitors, that Walter had to ring at the closely-barred gates several times before the worthy man could be roused from his studies. He was a man learned beyond the spirit of his times; a ripe good scholar, but unbeneficed churchman. Although removed from all active interconse with the world, even he had heard of the effect produced by Luther's preaching, and obtained from a brother in Germany, who was one of that fiery apostle's earliest disciples, copies of his writings, in perusing which he was so intently absorbed, that it was not till the fifth or sixth peal of the great bell that the idea struck him of some one desiring admittance at the gate.

Wondering who, at such an hour, for it was already nightfall, had arrived to break in upon his solitude, the recluse closed the volume, and, taking the lamp from the table, proceeded to the great entrance whence the ringing came. At the sound of his favourite's voice he quickly let fall the massive bars, and bade him a thousand welcomes. There was one green spot in the old man's heart—one oasis in his life's desert, and Walter was the being who inhabited it. He had watched over him in his infancy, and he loved him in his manhood; the very anxieties he had occasioned him increased his affection. His feelings had found but one trunk round which to twine themselves, and gratefully expended all their foliage on it.

"What unexpected fortune," he demanded, brings you at such an hour ?"

"Are you alone ?" replied the young man.

"Alone with solitude," answered the priest, eyeing him uneasily at the question.

"Then bar the gates."

"Bar the gates !"

"I am a fugitive—pursued, I doubt not; and my life in danger."

Without a second word Father Celestine did as he was requested. The thought that his *protegé* was in danger, armed him with unusual presence of mind. As soon as the fastenings were secure, he quietly resumed the lamp, and led the way to his own cell, from which he had so lately been disturbed.

"In times like the present, Walter," he began, "when virtues are too often punished as crimes—when vice lords it openly, and truth finds no security but in concealment or the grave, I will not ask thee what fault, but rather what merit, hath drawn this danger on thee, and driven thee a fugitive from Stanfield."

Charmed with the old man's simple confidence in his integrity, the secretary related the story of the Lady Mary's persecution, his own ill-starred passion, his danger and escape, and the hopes he built upon the letter of his father to the cardinal. His friend heard him with patience, occasionally shaking his head at the history of his love; for, recluse as he was, he knew sufficient of the world to appreciate the distance between his orphan favourite and the wealthy object of his wishes. His first words, therefore, were to discourage him in a pursuit which he feared was hopeless; added to which, although he knew much of books, he had not the least idea of the tender passion.

"This comes of love and women," he exclaimed, "the source of evil since the commencement of the world; the last lost Paradise—the first perilled the empire of the world. Perhaps, after all," he continued, a ray of kindlier feeling crossing his heart as he saw the mortified looks of his listener, "there may be something delightful in having a being to confide in—to share our pleasures—to relieve our cares—in having children to resemble us. Yes, yes," he added, ater a pause, as if reasoning with himself, "'tis just that man should love; the heart alone must not be barren. So thou art right, boy, to obey its instincts; would I could say wise in the object of thy choice !"

Ere Walter could reply a loud ringing at the bell startled them both from their seats.

"I am tracked !" whispered the fugitive; "the bloodhounds are upon me."

"Perhaps not," replied the priest; "but should it prove so, here are nooks enough to shelter thee in this old mansion."

The summons was again impatiently repeated. Walter quietly drew his sword, determined to sell his life dearly, if, as he doubted not, pursuers from Stanfield were upon his steps. Father Celestine laid his hand upon his arm to restrain him, for he loved not bloodshed, and violence, he saw, would be useless, should his suspicions prove correct.

"The fox must be met with cunning, Walter," he said, "and the lion with strength; when thou art assailed it will be time enough to use thy sword. Here is the key of the great tower—fly to the upper chamber; neither Sir John de Corbey nor his minion, Adam, will venture to pursue thee there; couch behind the arras; anon I'll seek thee. But to prevent surprise, make fast the oaken door at the foot of the staircase."

"How wilt thou gain admittance," demanded the young man, "if I make fast the door?"

"Leave that to me—away—draw bolt and bar behind thee. I know a way to reach thee."

The bell once more sounded violently. With a silent pressure of the hand the priest and secretary parted—the former to open the gates to his unwelcome visitors, the latter to his hiding-place within the tower.

"What seek ye at such an hour?" demanded the former, as soon as he reached the grated door.

"Messengers from Stanfield," was the answer.

"I must have surer token than your words," replied the old man, "ere I open to you."

"Good, master chaplain," said Adam for it was the leech, who, with his two companions, were dispatched in pursuit of Walter, that demanded admittance. "Surely you know my voice: that is sufficient token."

With an appearance of alacrity which ill accorded with the secret terror of his heart, the priest withdrew the heavy bolts, and admitted the party into the mansion; and instantly, as a matter of course, replaced the several fastenings.

"You arrive late," he quietly observed. "Had not an idle book detained me, I should long ere this have retired to rest."

"'Tis well you came at last," replied the leech, eyeing him suspiciously, for he was no stranger to the friendship existing between the chaplain and the object of his pursuit; "but, perhaps, you have had visitors?"

This was uttered with an half-inquiring voice, as if the question were the most indifferent one in the world; the old man, who knew his character, perfectly understood him, and answered in a similar tone—

"Visitors indeed! Few of the neighbours like to pass the house even when the sun is shining brightly. I know not one who would set a foot in it after nightfall: it bears an evil name. The boatmen speak of shrieks and cries of murder heard from the old tower at midnight; and many have assured me they have seen lights flitting in the upper chamber, when no human hands could have carried them; but that I am a priest, I should bear an ill name, simply as its tenant."

Adam was silent: like most infidels, he was superstitious, and he liked not any allusion to the old tower or its chamber.

"Come," resumed the speaker; "you seemed well drenched with the storm; 'tis fortunate I have a fire to dry you."

With these words he conducted his unwelcome guests to the little chamber where he had lately listened to the tale of Walter, and with an appearance of hospitable zeal began to make preparations for their entertainment. Whilst thus occupied, the leech took up the book the good man had been reading. It was Luther's reply to Henry's defence of the seven sacraments; the same work which procured for the kings of England, from Leo X., the title of defenders of the faith, inconsistently retained to the present day. In it the royal disputant was most unceremoniously treated; the fiery monk had been unsparing of the qualities in which he most excelled— sarcasm and abuse. The work was strictly prohibited by the furious tyrant; the mere reading of it was looked upon as little short of treason, and cruelly punished. While the unfortunate chaplain's back was turned, Adam glanced his eye upon the title-page, and instantly secured it; it added to his strength, for it placed the reader's life within his power.

"Good!" he muttered within himself; "we shall understand each other soon."

The frugal meal was quickly dispatched, and the two assistants in his crimes were conducted by Adam to their chamber in a remote corner of the mansion, in which, with his usual precaution, he locked them. On his return, he found Father Celestine hunting over the closets, corners, and nooks of his room, with an air of nervous anxiety. The poor man missed his book, and well knew the importance of his loss.

"You miss something?" observed the leech, with a cold smile.

"Yes—yes," hurriedly answered the old man, continuing his search.

"What?"

"Nothing—a trifle—a book that—have you seen it?" he added.

"I!" replied the Italian, with an air of surprise; "I am little likely to waste my time with homilies, or lives of saints, or legends, for such I doubt not are the nature of your pious studies."

"I shall find it, doubtless, in the morning," said the chaplain, trying to look indifferent on the subject; but he was not deceived—he knew that Adam was the master of his secret; his sneer convinced him.

Despite the danger which threatened, Father Celestine determined to secure the escape of his guest, ere he cast a thought upon his own personal safety. With a composed countenance, therefore, he bade the leech good-night, and retired to the solitude of his cell—there to reflect on the best means of releasing Walter, and disappointing the malice and cunning of his enemy.

On reaching the upper chamber of the tower, to which his friend had directed him, a sickening sense of loneliness and desolation fell upon the young secretary's heart. The half-rotten tapestry, torn by its own weight, hung in huge fragments from the walls, or floated lazily like funeral banners on the stagnant air. The night was wild, as the fortunes of the fugitive; gusts of heavy wind swept at intervals, howling like fiends broke loose, around the tower, dashing the rain against the rattling casement, and then gradually subsiding with a low and sullen moan to dismal silence. Anon the thunder-cloud would burst above his head, shaking the massive pile e'en to its dark foundations, and lighting, by the red flash which accompanied it, each nook and corner of the unhallowed chamber where he sat. As the hours rolled on, despite his courage, Walter became nervous and excited; a hundred times he fancied he heard the slow and stealthy tread of some one on the stairs—indeed, so positive was he upon one occasion, that he rose from the crumbling chair on which he had been seated, and opened the door; but, no! imagination had deceived him, there was no one there. Darkness itself would have been less terrible than the obscure light his simple lamp afforded; its sickly flame rose and fell with the various currents of air to which it was exposed—dancing like some *ignis fatuus* in its socket, and casting life-like, mysterious shadows on the walls and ceiling.

"There is some spell upon me!" he exclaimed. "This old tower might give mirth itself the horrors, freezing the smile upon his rosy lip; but what have I to fear? the door is well secured below—against earthly visitants, I possess my sword. As for unearthly beings, I believe not in them. Why should the dead revisit earth?"

Scarcely had the words escaped his lips,

when, as if to test their sincerity, an owl, attracted doubtless by the lamp, dashed with its harsh, shrill cry against the casement. Walter started from his seat, and, despite his vaunted incredulity, felt that his heart beat quicker. Nor was it till the creature had repeated its lonely cry that he recovered his self-possession, or could smile at his boyish terror.

"Poor philosophy!" he muttered to himself; "how strong in theory, how weak in practice—a giant in repose, a child in action! We learn rules but to disregard them, demonstrate truths but to disbelieve them. I'll be no more," he added, "the slave of my imagination or the fool of fancy; better darkness than uncertain light; besides, my lamp may attract the attention of others than yon obscene bird to my window."

Scarcely had he extinguished the light than the storm burst with increased violence around the towers; and the monotonous patter of the rain was broken by the whistle of the wind, at times sharp and piercing, then low and moaning. Walter was approaching the window to watch the battle of the elements, when his attention was struck by a streak of light along the wall of the room, as if some person were standing with a lamp behind a closet door. At first he thought that fancy had deceived him; but no, there was the light, more brilliant than it perhaps would otherwise have been, from the darkness through which it penetrated.

Not knowing what cause to attribute it to, and naturally dreading the approach of some secret enemy, the young man cautiously retreated from the window to a distant part of the room, where a fragment of arras larger than the rest promised him at least a temporary concealment. Hiding behind the damp tapestry, which flapped like a pall against his face, he watched through a hole which he made with his sword the mysterious light, which gradually became to his imagination stronger and stronger, till at last its brilliancy almost dazzled him. Just as expectation was wrought to its greatest power of endurance, a door, curiously concealed within the wall, which it was made to resemble, opened, and Father Celestine, bearing a lamp and a basket of provisions, entered the apartment. In an instant all our hero's terrors, superstitions, and wayward fancies—the mental phantasmagoria which had so long tormented him—vanished, and he saw the room, with its torn arras and distant shadows, as it really was, and not as his imagination had peopled it.

"Welcome, father!" he exclaimed, step-

STEADMAN'S INTERVIEW WITH THE MENDICANT FRIAR.

ping from his concealment; "your presence breaks more than my solitude; it puts to flight the idle thoughts which disturbed it. Did I not fear that you would laugh at me for the confession, I would relate the terrors which this deserted room and midnight have inspired me with."

"It is, indeed," replied the priest, glancing uneasily round, "a cheerless place—fit for the deeds which have been perpetrated in it. Heaven, which witnessed, will doubtless, in its own good time, avenge them."

"Deeds! what deeds?" demanded Walter.

"Those of the olden time, as well as those of our own day," replied the old man. "How often has the stealthy murderer's footstep mounted the secret stairs by which I came! Chance, whilst roaming over the old house, discovered to me their existence—unknown, I feel assured, to all beside. Here, in this very room, whilst the unconscious victim slept, death by the cord or steel has done its work; these walls have echoed to the last cry of nature. I never enter here," he added, "but I repeat a *De Profundis* for the dead."

No. 32.

"You speak of the past," said the secretary, replacing on the table the flask of wine which the chaplain had brought him. "Know you anything of the crimes committed here by those of our own day?"

"Nothing," replied the priest; "whatever I may suspect, I know absolutely nothing. There is one below, perhaps, who would relate a tale of terror suited to the night and the occasion."

"Adam?" said the secretary, inquiringly. His visitor nodded assent.

"He it was, then, who arrived to dog me. The bloodhound little dreams his victim hides 'neath the same roof with him. Strange he should devote the energies of such a mind to serve the purpose of so foul a master. He must love him well, to damn his soul for his advancement."

"Love," replied the chaplain, "is not the bond between them."

"What then? interest?"

"No—hate."

"Hate!" repeated the youth; "father, you surely jest. No spaniel ever followed in his master's steps more faithfully than Adam in Sir John's. His intellect, his energies, are but the servants of his will; his conscience know no voice beyond his pleasure; his heart feels no remorse. Such, old friend, are not the services of hate."

"Nor yet of love," added the priest. "I tell thee, boy, he hates his subtle master. I have seen his proud lip curl at his command, his dark eye glance, when unobserved, upon him, as Satan's might on the Archangel's brow. Doubt not but he will one day turn and rend him. Then, perhaps, and not till then, will the dark secrets of this chamber be revealed."

"Tell me, father," said Walter, fixing his eyes upon him, "what is it you know?"

"Nothing."

"What suspect, then?"

"Much. It occurred years before you entered in the service of the knight of Corbey, that a young man, having the appearance of a citizen, accompanied Sir John to the house; he seemed under no restraint, for he followed his conductor freely to this chamber. He was never seen to quit it," he added, slowly.

"That was strange," said the secretary, deeply interested in the narrative; "pray proceed."

"Stranger still," resumed the narrator, "Jarrold and Carl, two of the household supposed to be deepest in their master's confidence, the next morning were found dead within their beds. From that period—almost from that day—the house has been abandoned. Strange noises have been heard and lights, 'tis said, seen from this chamber window."

"Superstition!" exclaimed Walter—"mere superstition! Think you that Heaven suspends the laws of nature e'en to unveil a murder? Improbable! impossible!"

The words had scarcely passed his lips than the large piece of tapestry, behind which the speaker had lately concealed himself, suddenly fell from the carved cornice to which it had been suspended: the rustling noise which it made in its descent startled both the inmates of the room. The priest regarded the young philosopher with a smile, which seemed to ask the value of his philosophy, when so simple an accident could cause his heart to beat and his cheek to lose its hue of manly resolution.

"'Tis strange," said the secretary, after a pause. "Why should it fall?"

"It must have fallen at some time or another," answered the chaplain; "why not now?"

"You must confess it is at least a curious commentary on my words."

"Experience," replied the elder, "is full of such matters. Imagination might draw from it a thousand inferences, which sober reason would reject. Had the rotten arras revealed in its descent a cabinet, a treasure, a secret door, or any proof of crime, we might suppose that there was something more than accident in it."

"By heaven! but there is!" exclaimed Walter, who had been anxiously scanning the wall. "See, father, here is a recess rudely built up; observe how unevenly the stones are placed, as though terror urged the hands of guilt to its completion. My soul upon the issue, but it contains some mystery."

"I think so too," replied the priest, carefully examining the wall. "What are we about to learn?"

"Shall we proceed?" demanded the young man; "I can easily wrench one of the loose bars of iron from the window, and break open the recess."

"Proceed," said the priest: "man is but the instrument in the hand of Heaven to work its ends. Who, in tracing the action of Providence, shall venture to declare how much is accident, how much design?"

Walter, encouraged by the words of the chaplain, easily wrenched an iron bar from the window, where the corroding tooth of time had already loosened it in its socket, and commenced his attack upon the stonework which filled up the recess. The first stroke of the instrument fell with a hollow sound, like a blow struck upon a tomb. An unwonted energy nerved his arm; he felt as if supernaturally called upon to bring some long hidden crime to light—to proclaim and to avenge it.

Slowly, and with difficulty, as if reluctant to yield up the secret they so long had guarded, the rough, unhewn stones gave way beneath the repeated blows of the secretary, and fell, one by one, with a dull, heavy sound upon the floor, disclosing a ghastly skeleton, bound by chains to iron staples in the wall. There was little doubt but the wretched victim had been confined there living, the arms and shoulders being dislocated by the frantic struggles it had made; fragments of cloth and linen still adhered to the mouldering bones, and innumerable beetles were seen hurrying in every direction along the walls, alarmed at the flood of light so suddenly let in on their disgusting banquet.

"Father," exclaimed the young man, turning with an expression of pity and terror from the revolting sight, "God hath not permitted this mystery to be revealed, that we should seal our tongues. Heaven, which heard the victim's cries, counted his groans, measured his tears, wills that we should avenge them."

A flash of lightning more intense than any which had preceded it, followed by a tremendous thunderclap which shook the old tower, lit up the apartment, throwing with its intense sulphurous light the feeble flame of the dying lamp into the shade. Whether attracted or not by the iron belt which encircled the waist of the skeleton, it is impossible to say; but certain the electric fluid seemed to linger longer there than on any other object upon which it rested. Finally, it disappeared, leaving the recess in greater darkness than before.

On looking closer into the unhallowed tomb, Walter perceived a steel sword-chain and scabbard, still hanging round the marrowless bones. The lightning had attracted his attention to them first. With a trembling hand he removed them, and bringing them to the light—despite the rust and mildew which covered them—distinctly traced upon the clasp of the belt the name of Cuthbert.

"Cuthbert!" repeated the old man, crossing himself in terror. "How wondrous are the ways of Providence! Such was the name of the young stranger who so mysteriously disappeared several years back in this very chamber."

"The nephew of Steadman?" demanded the young man; "the son of the maniac Maud?"

"The same."

"The hour of retribution, then, hath arrived at last. The dead seems to have chosen me as his avenger. I accept the task. I here devote my soul to its fulfilment, and Heaven smile upon me as I keep the oath! Morning soon will dawn. Tell me, father," he added, "have you brought me my dead father's letter, the only legacy his broken fortunes had to leave me?"

"Take it, my son," replied Father Celestine, placing it in his hand; "and may the writer's spirit watch over and protect thee! 'Tis time for thy departure."

"But should Adam enter here," exclaimed the young man, glancing uneasily round, "he would at once remove the proofs of his and his master's crimes, or contrive some tale to explain them."

"Slight fear of that," replied the priest; "the door is barred below, and, save myself, no living being knows the secret access to the tower. Follow me, Walter," he added, "I will conduct thee first to liberty. Lose not a moment; with the earliest dawn make thy best way to Hampton. Wolsey hath a proud heart, but not an ungenerous nature. If I rightly judge him, he will protect the Lady Mary, and avenge her wrongs for her own sake—something perchance for thine."

"And thou?" demanded Walter.

"Will wait thy coming here," continued the old man; "my duty accomplished to the living, I have not one less sacred to perform towards the dead."

Taking the scabbard and sword-belt with him, the secretary followed the speaker down the secret stairs, and, after a long descent through vaults and passages cut in the thickness of the massive walls, found himself in one of the offices of the mansion, detached from the principal building.

"The light of morning breaks," whispered the old man; "away! God and a good conscience speed thee on thine errand!"

He remained for a few minutes listening to the retreating footsteps of his favourite, and then returned to the chamber where so fearful a discovery had been made. The first rays of the sun, as it gleamed through the time-stained windows, found him at his duty.

The priest was praying for the dead.

CHAPTER IV.

"My buildings sumptuous, the roofs with gold and byse,
Shone like the sun in mid-day sphere;
Craftily entailed as cunning could devise,
With images embossed most lively did appear."
From an old poem on Hampton Court, written
by Cavendish, Wolsey's secretary.

N the beginning of the sixteenth century the Knights Hospitallers of St. John of Jerusalem were a rich and powerful community; the gates of their magnificent preceptory of Clerkenwell attests even to the present day the stateliness of their habitations, and the style in which they lived. Amongst the numerous possessions of this order of military monks was a district of some thousand acres, through which the Thames flowed from Ditton to Walton on the Surrey side, and from Teddington to Hanworth on the Middlesex bank. This manor, known by the name of Hampton, was a low sandy level, producing but little corn, and inhabited chiefly by a few priests and lay brothers, till Wolsey purchased it of the prior in 1515; when, employing the vast resources at his command, he quickly changed the character of the place. The ancient hostel and chapel were swept away, and a splendid palace arose, as if by enchantment, at the bidding of the wealthy cardinal; and here, within two years of his purchase of the place, did he surround himself with the pomp of kings, and maintained a state superior to his master's.

In the presence-chamber, waiting his coming from his private apartments, were assembled the chief noblemen and gentlemen of his eminence's household; the two cross-bearers, with their silver crosses; the Earl of Derby, to bear the hat to the chapel, and lay it on the altar; Cavendish, his secretary; and a crowd of suitors, both laymen and ecclesiastics; the fortunes of most of whom depended on the smile or frown of the favourite.

Amongst the various groups assembled in the hall—and they were both remarkable and splendid—were three personages who claimed particular attention. The first was Sir John Hervey, vice-chamberlain to his grace—a stiff, tall, formal courtier, whose face was a faithful mirror of his master's—smiling where he smiled, frowning where he frowned. The pages nick-named him the "Weathercock," as they could generally tell what kind of humour the cardinal was it by gazing on the countenance of the worthy knight—that is, after he had had his first audience of his uncertain master; previous to that it was as impassible as a statue's—meaningless as the pliant wax waiting for the impress of the seal. In his right hand he held his wand of office, with which he marshalled visitors according to their due degrees. The second was Fisher, Bishop of Rochester; the prelate whom Henry VIII. afterwards beheaded for his opposition to the reformation, and to show his hatred of the Holy See, which had just conferred upon its unfortunate defender the dignity of cardinal. The third was Wolsey's fool, Patch—the inimitable, faithful, shrewd, sarcastic Patch—the only person who, perhaps, ever ventured to speak his mind freely to the all-powerful minister, and who, upon his fall, presented him as a valuable present to the king. Such, however, was the poor creature's fidelity to his master, that he was obliged to be dragged from his presence, and conveyed by force to Greenwich, from whence he twice endeavoured to escape.

"Does his grace ride to day?" demanded the prelate, addressing the functionary with the white wand.

The officer looked embarrassed. He had not yet seen his capricious lord, and he never committed himself by giving an opinion; he contented himself, therefore, by merely elevating his eyebrows and looking more stolid than usual.

Patch, who heard the question, answered it in his own whimsical way. Plucking one of the feathers from the crest at the end of his bauble, he threw it into the air, and blew it with his breath, exclaiming, as he did so, till it reached the ground, "Ride—not ride—ride—not ride—ride—not ride. You are answered, my lord, with as much certainty as the knight's perspicuity and my wisdom can divine."

The churchman smiled. He understood both the satire and wit of the speaker.

"Perhaps," he added, "he goes to Greenwich; I saw the barge getting ready on the river as I arrived."

"Perhaps," replied Sir Henry, solemnly, fearing even by that equivocal expression of committing himself.

At this moment the Earl of Derby approached, and invited the bishop to inspect the new tapestry—a present from Francis the First to his friend and counsellor, as he invariably styled Wolsey in his letters—for the first time displayed at the lower end of the hall. No sooner had they withdrawn than the jester drew the arm of the vice-chamberlain through his, and took him, as if for the purpose of some important communication he had to deliver to him, a little on one side.

"How prudent should they be," he whispered, with a gravity to which the laughing expression of his eyes gave the lie, "who are entrusted with a great man's confidence! You have seriously compromised his reverend grace."

"How so?" demanded the astonished courtier.

"How so!" repeated Patch, with a look of comical contempt. "Sir knight, thou art more obtuse than an angle: a chamberlain should see further into a mile-stone than most men. I had some thoughts of retiring from my office, but I see I must look further for a successor. 'How so!' Hast thou not given authority to all present to suppose, nay, positively assert, that his eminence may or may not go to Greenwich? The fact is patented; thou wilt be cited as its author—men will quote thee for thy master's whereabouts—spies will be set to dog thee—statesmen to pump thee; knowing," he added, with an indescribable leer, "how deep thou art in Wolsey's confidence."

The loud laugh of the noblemen and gentlemen ushers in waiting at the jester's hit proved that his wit had told. The eye of the angry officer glanced round the hall, but encountered only the glance of those whom he was far too prudent to quarrel with. At last it fell upon a young man whose travel-stained dress and haggard features indicated both bodily fatigue and mental suffering. It was our old friend Walter, who, by dint of perseverance, had made his way to the great hall of Hampton, in the hope of presenting his letter to the cardinal.

"Now," exclaimed the knight, in a haughty tone, for he could be haughty with his inferiors, "what brings you into the presence-chamber?—methinks the Almonry might better serve your errand."

"Your pardon," replied the fugitive, colouring with ill suppressed indignation at being thus addressed, "I am here to deliver a letter to his grace."

"A letter to his grace!" repeated Patch. "Oh, the simplicity, the beautiful simplicity of youth! Were it known that his eminence had received a letter from a mysterious messenger in a soiled doublet, though of goodly presence, the couriers of half the cabinets in Europe would be set in motion; France and Spain would send special ambassadors to demand explanations of the vice chamberlain or of me, and probably the peace of Europe would only be preserved but on condition of our joint dismissal."

A second hearty laugh still further predisposed the pompous functionary against our hero. Before, however, he took upon himself the decided step of dismissing him from the hall, he prudently inquired the name of the writer of the letter, lest unwittingly he should compromise himself by such an act.

"It was written," replied Walter, a tear involuntarily dimming his eye, "by my late father—his grace's earliest friend."

The words had no sooner passed his lips, than the jester immediately put out both his hands, as though he had something in the hollow of each, and was balancing them to ascertain which was the heaviest. One of the secretaries, Master Cavendish, observed the action, and asked what he was doing.

"Trying which weighs the most," quietly answered Patch, "a dead man's influence, or a great man's memory."

"And you find——" said the questioner.

"That I have no just weight by which to try them," continued the fool. "It must be heavier than thought," he added, "and lighter than a thistledown. When you find me such, I will solve the question, sir."

There was a tone of feeling and sadness in the speaker's voice which jarred strangely with his motley office.

"You must deliver your letter at the Almonry, young man, and attend in three days for a reply. None but those who have been presented to his grace have the *entrée* to the presence-chamber. Retire! No words!" added the chamberlain; "oblige me not to give orders to remove you from the hall."

There was no disputing a command so peremptorily given, and the disheartened fugitive reluctantly quitted the brilliant assembly, where in sooth his soiled garments were somewhat displaced. The jester followed him.

The above incident had scarcely passed, when a gentleman usher cried out—

"Place, my lords and gentlemen—place for my Lord Cardinal of York!"

In an instant the various conversations and whisperings which had taken place were broken off, and the assembled officers and courtiers assumed that air of respectful attention which cringing humility so well knows how to pay to greatness. The large doors were thrown open by the yeomen of the hall, and the almost royal churchman entered from his private apartments. Wolsey was at this period in the prime of intellect and manhood, his features marked by that slight animal expression which indicates energy of character, gives action to mind, and denotes determination in all who possess it. In person he was above the usual height, extremely dignified in his carriage, an advantage to which his rich flowing robes of engrained crimson satin more than slightly contributed. He spoke with the confidence of one long accustomed to be listened to with attention and respect. It is recorded of him that he was kind and indulgent in his household, and took a pleasure in showing his haughtiness only to such as were of great estate, or had offended him; in the latter case he was implacable. With all his defects, and they were great and many, let it not be forgot that he was the munificent patron both of letters and of art. Hampton Court attests the latter, whilst Oxford bears witness to the first.

"Good day, my lords and gentlemen!" he exclaimed, slightly bending in acknowledgment of the profound salutation of the circle—"Good day, Hervey," he demanded, without deigning a second glance on men of the highest rank, who were suitors, or dancing attendance on him, "what letters have arrived?"

According to the usual etiquette Cavendish advanced to the bag, and gave them, one by one, to the vice-chamberlain, who handed them to his eminence. The first was from the king, and dated Greenwich. The minister kissed it with an affectation of respect as he broke the seal; it announced the expected arrival of Campeggio, whom the reigning pontiff, Clement VII., had joined with himself in the legatine commission for deciding the divorce between Henry and his queen. A slight shade passed over the lofty brow of the statesman as he perused the epistle; perhaps he already foresaw the difficulties to which the question ultimately gave rise, not only between his sovereign and himself, but England and the see of Rome.

"So this is his answer to a memorial of the state of Europe and the emperor's intrigues," he murmured, as he placed the letter in the belt of his soutan. "I must decide without him. A childish toy, an hour's caprice, and a kingdom's interest are cast aside. Earth! earth! such are thy rulers!"

The succeeding letters, after being slightly glanced over, were handed to an officer, whose duty it was to receive them and deliver them to the secretaries to be answered. The contents of the bag which Cavendish held were nearly exhausted, when Patch, who had followed Walter from the hall, returned. Holding the letter in his hand which the youth had vainly attempted to deliver, the jester had good-naturedly undertaken to do so for him. Quietly coming between Sir Henry and the secretary, just as the former held out his hand mechanically for another letter to give to Wolsey, he placed Walter's in his palm, and the unsuspicious courtier instantly handed it to his master, who had watched the jester's manœuvre, and smiled at its success; for the shrewd-witted fool was a favourite with him.

A strange change came over the countenance of the cardinal when the signature of the letter met his gaze; he was like a man who found a reproach where he expected a smile—a thorn where he looked for a flower. The writer had been the companion of his youth—the first, perhaps the only friend he ever loved or trusted, and yet he had neglected him with a kingdom's wealth and patronage at his disposal, had never once inquired if he were living or dead, poor or in prosperity. Such is the value of a great man's memory.

"Who brought this letter?" he demanded, after a pause, during which he had been revolving in his mind how to atone for his past neglect, and remove from his heart the reproach of ingratitude.

The question was addressed to the astonished chamberlain, but the speaking glance to Patch intimated that it was from him the answer was expected.

"A youth sore spent with travel," replied the jester, more seriously than he was wont to speak, "but his soiled doublet offended the chamberlain's knighthood. His want of quarterings ruined his humility, so he dismissed him to the Almonry, your grace—to flirt with Patience, whilst waiting on her lean sister, Charity."

"Almonry! charity!" repeated Wolsey, in a tone which boded a tempest to the unfortunate object of his wrath. "It is the curse of greatness to be aped by the fools that cringe and circle round it. Seek out the youth," he added to the terrified officer of his household, who stood, or rather tottered, before him. "Lead him to our presence, and beware how you obtrude yourself again till he be found."

Sir Henry Hervey, curving his back to

the very ground, sneaked out of the presence-chamber.

"I owe this young man's father a deep debt of gratitude," continued Wolsey, half aloud and half talking to himself, "which, though unclaimed till now, shall now be paid."

"It must be to the youth himself, then, master," replied the jester, "for his father is long since dead."

"Dead!" repeated the churchman, dropping the letter, "Oh, power! how empty is thy greatness! My word can clothe the naked wretch with ermine; deal war or peace, as to my will seems meet; say to my foe, thou shalt not live an hour, yet cannot bid my friend exist one minute! The crozier, like the sceptre, smells of earth. I am sick of greatness. The boy I loved, the first friend of my youth, the saviour of my life," he added, bitterly, "gone to his grave — weighed down, perhaps, by my ingratitude! — cold, heartless, selfish Wolsey!"

The self-accusing tone in which the words were uttered made a deep impression on all who heard them, for his eminence was not a man to "wear his heart upon his sleeve;" if he felt deeply, he rarely expressed his feelings; and many argued favourably of the young man's fortunes from the terms in which Wolsey reproached himself for his neglect of his father.

In a few moments the abashed chamberlain reappeared, ushering in our hero with as much respect as he would have paid to a crowned head, so suddenly had he risen in importance since his master had reproved him in his favour.

"Approach, young man," said the cardinal, fixing his keen grey eye upon his countenance, as if to read his very soul, "and let me gaze upon thee. Thou hast thy father's features," he added, after a pause, during which he scanned him well; "nature stamped their impress on thy face as witness of his blood. We will not forget our former friendship for him: to give thee standing in the world and mark our favour, we name thee of our chamber."

"Gentlemen of the chamber!" whispered Cavendish to one of the ushers; "who is this stripling?"

"One of whom 'twere well to court," replied the latter personage. "Hennage solicited the post for his son these two months past."

Instead of kissing the hand which the churchman extended to him as usual on receiving such an appointment, Walter knelt and offered a paper to his eminence, containing the history of Lady Mary's wrongs, and Sir John's oppression.

"How!" exclaimed Wolsey, his brow suddenly flushed with anger and surprise. "What wouldst thou more?—the office is indifferent good, and for a young beginner——"

"More — much more than I deserve," replied the young man, still offering him the writing; "I did not come, as many do, to push vile interest, or to sue for favour. I came to add another laurel to your wreath of fame; to guide your guardian Ægis o'er the head of innocence devoted to destruction. Oh, my dread lord, in after times, when Wolsey's name shall stand recorded on his country's page, one act like this shall shed a greater lustre than all his bounties on the mean and worthless."

"His favour's gone!" whispered the usher; "fool to play with fortune while within his reach!"

"Not so," said Cavendish; "whate'er the suit, 'tis granted—his grace hath ta'en the paper."

The latter was right in his surmise; for, after eyeing him a few moments searchingly, the minister took the document from the suppliant's trembling hand, and read it attentively.

"What pledge," he demanded, "have I for the truth of this?"

"My life—my faith!" exclaimed Walter, radiant with hope and expectation.

The cardinal advanced a step towards the speaker, and gazed upon his open, candid brow; and then, as if satisfied with the scrutiny, muttered to himself—

"His eye shrinks not from my gaze; there is a blush upon his cheek, yet it appears like youth's and warm ingenuous nature's. Enough, young man," he added, addressing himself more directly to the still-kneeling youth; "I'll trust thee."

"My thanks—my gratitude!" faltered the lover.

"Hold!" resumed his eminence; "thou hast some dearer interest in this matter. Speak freely, if I am not to doubt thee."

"I love Mary of Stanfield," whispered Walter; "her guardian would have imprisoned me for an attempt upon an heiress."

"Thy suit shall fare the better that it is avowed," replied the churchman in the same under tone. "Follow me to my closet; for here are ears I trust not—lip service, but no hearts. Order my barge," he added, in a loud voice; "within an hour we start for Greenwich. And for the future know this gentleman as one of our household and especial favour."

All bowed, and many a look of envy was cast upon the fortunate object of their master's commendation. Without casting a second look upon the nobles who were waiting to press their various suits with him, the cardinal left the amazed circle of courtiers, and was followed by our hero to his closet, where, with the simplicity of truth, he related, not only the story of his love, but the oppressive cruelty of Sir John de Corbey; and finished by the discovery of the skeleton of the unfortunate armourer, producing, at the same time, the belt and scabbard of the murdered man in proof of his assertion.

"Good!" exclaimed the cardinal with a smile of quiet satisfation; for he remembered the intrigue by which her guardian had removed the Lady Mary from his protection. "The knight has played a desperate game; but we shall balk him yet."

The same evening, after a long conference with Henry at Greenwich, the favourite gave orders to his house to depart for Norwich, ostensibly to settle the dispute between the prior and the citizens, to which we have previously alluded, but which, fortunately for our lovers, was not the only motive for his journey. Walter travelled in his suite.

Despite the decided step which he had taken in removing the heiress from her own domain of Stanfield to his manor-house within the city, Sir John de Corbey was ill at ease. The escape of his secretary alarmed him; and the prolonged absence of his counsellor and minister Adam was another source of vexation to his unquiet spirit.

He was pacing the great hall of the mansion about a week after the interview we have just endeavoured to describe, when the leech, with his usual stealthy tread, entered the apartment. There was no hurry, no anxiety upon his features. He saluted his employer as slightly as though he had been absent from him but a few minutes, instead of twelve or fourteen days. After carefully closing the doors, the knight advanced towards him, and, in a voice broken by excitement and passion, eagerly demanded if he had succeeded in finding the fugitive.

Adam simply nodded his head in answer to his questions.

"And where?"

"Where least you would expect or wish," replied the Italian, for the first time breaking silence; "safe under Wolsey's shelter and protection."

"Confusion!" exclaimed the guilty man; "the butcher's son hath crossed my path once more! Out of thy store of subtle wit invent some scheme to counteract this mischief, or I am lost."

A close observer might have seen a smile of mingled satisfaction and contempt flit, like a passing shadow, over the countenance of the leech as he noted the agony and rage of the speaker. The expression was but momentary; his features instantly resumed their usual cold and statue-like character, as he demanded, in a tone of affected humility, how his poor skill could serve when his own had failed. This time the mask was too transparent—the sneer was seen through the humility.

"Italian," said his master, bending his brow, for he keenly felt the contempt of the being whom he dared not quarrel with, "from thy derision I can gather hope. Lost to the ties of country, kindred, friends, the pride of knowledge lives within thee yet. Thou hast a secret joy to play man's passions against himself, and from opposing natures work out thy hidden purpose. Tell me, what is thy project—bribery?"

"Bribery will do much," slowly answered the old man, as if weighing some important project in his brain.

"I have heard thee say that all men have their price," interrupted the knight, with a gesture of impatience.

"True," resumed the leech; "the difficulty is to get, not to name it. Monarchs, by flattery and beauty's smiles, sometimes by gold, are moulded out at will. Gross sensual appetite is some men's god. Priests mostly feed them: and they are yours. I have bribed chiefs and rulers in my time," he added; "played as I list with ministers and princes; but Wolsey is no common man. Yet he, too, hath his price."

"Where shall I seek it?" eagerly demanded Sir John, deceived by the leech's manner, and deeming that he had found the key to every difficulty — so much was he accustomed to rely upon his contrivances.

Adam raised his eyes and gazed for a few moments upon the speaker with an expression of mingled pride and shrewdness, as if he felt a triumph in solving a problem which had puzzled his unscrupulous employer.

"On that seven-crowned hill," he answered slowly, "where, decked in harlot pride, the mockery of imperial Rome is found—the shadow only of departed greatness. Pluck the tiara from the pontiff's brow, bear it to Wolsey's footstool. Were thy soul blackened with his father's blood, his blessing would be on thee, his hand be knit to thine."

"You mock me!" exclaimed the knight, in a tone of irritation; "is there no other way?"

"I know of none," carelessly answered the Italian, as if to him it were the least important matter in the world.

"Why, then I know the worst," said his master. "Never shall Wolsey's mandate

THE INTERRUPTION TO THE MEETING BETWEEN WALTER AND LADY MARY.

tear her from me, beggar my son, the heir of my proud name, to enrich a base-born peasant. She must be mine," he added, "or——"

"Hush!" whispered his companion, laying his hand upon his arm, and glancing cautiously round the room, "speak not so loudly. Her death might serve you better than her love. Wives are expensive; and 'tis her wealth alone that you require."

The wretched man, but half resolved on crime, started, as the tempter placed the deed before him, and the vile motives which incited him to perpetrate it.

"No—no," he faltered, "'tis not her wealth alone—the honour of our house——"

Something between a chuckle and a hiss issued from the thin lips of the leech at the attempt of the speaker to palliate to himself the incentive to the deed. Throwing the arm which he still held contemptuously from him, he answered, "Psha! we understand each other."

The accomplices in crime remained gazing upon each other for some time in silence; there was something unearthly in their stare. The expression of the Italian's countenance was like that of the demon, waiting to be solicited. Sir John's resembled the doubting votary's, fearful to name the impious deadly gift. The man of science was resolved not to speak; the man of crime for some time hesitated, but was forced at last to give way in the contest of resolution, were they were so unequally matched.

"It must be by poison," he faltered; "other means were dangerous."

Still the leech was silent.

"A poison," he resumed, "which leaves no trace for justice's curious eye to dwell upon. Thou must supply me with it."

The leech bowed his head in token of assent, as though it were the simplest thing in the world he had been requested to do. Indeed, it was ... for their plottings and villanies ... passed between them. Could ... right in his conjecture ... the tie which bound them indeed ...

"Thou ... in my laboratory," said Adam, "the draught shall be prepared. Fear not ... assured that men of skill the ... the cause of death; they will ... apoplexy."

"Farewell," ... John; "I will once more ... I must to my ward."

"And I," added Adam, drawing the heavy key of the ... from his vest, "must to my ..."

With these words the worthless plotters against the life of the youthful heiress of Stanfield parted on their different errands. Scarcely had they left the chamber, than the door of a carved oaken press, which stood in a recess near the window, was slowly opened, and Henry de Corbey, who had been a concealed witness of the interview between the Italian and his father, staggered from his hiding-place. His cheek was pale with horror, and the heavy cold perspiration which stood upon his brow showed like drops of dew trickling down a marble statue. His very blood felt stagnant in his veins, yet he distinctly felt the strong and slow pulsation of his heart. Nay, he could almost hear it. He felt as if he had been suddenly transformed from youth to age, so utter was the desolation that had fallen upon him; for it was not a passing tempest which had dimmed the sunshine of his soul, but an eclipse which had obscured it.

"What have I heard?" he murmured to himself. "Words that hiss like serpents' whisperings in my ear. My father an assassin! Mary his victim! God! it cannot be! This is some horrible dream! Thou art too just, too merciful," he added, bursting into tears, and burying his face in his hands, "to try a boy, a child, with terrors such as these.

Wake me from it," he sobbed, "ere reason quits its throne, and I go mad, doubting of heaven and Thee!"

For some time the wretched youth gave way to the natural weakness of his age, and relieved his burdened heart.

Courage in the young is generally accompanied by sensibility, because it is an impulse: it is only where it is the result of calculation that we remark the absence of its best companion. The boyish lover, who had devoted himself to the protection of his outraged cousin, was not the less firm in his resolution because he shed a few natural tears over his voluntary task. Had the intended assassin been any other than his father, he would immediately have denounced him; but not only his parent's life, but the honour of his name was at stake; and pride, duty, as well as the dread of ... fettered his tongue in silence. For a while he paced the oaken floor of the apartment in deep and painful meditation, revolving in his mind how best to spare his parent's name and secure the Lady Mary's safety. A melancholy smile, like a dying sunbeam, flitted over his pale countenance as the means of succeeding in ... presented itself to his imagination ... the sacrifice was a costly one, but he ... that it would be effectual.

"...," he cried, after he had well meditated and resolved his purpose, "the son for whom thou wouldst have sinned shall yet preserve thy honour."

That same day, whilst his cousin was taking her guarded walk upon the terrace, Henry de Corbey concealed himself within her chamber.

About ten o'clock in the evening of the same day the streets of Norwich were almost clear. Here and there a solitary figure might be seen hurrying towards home, his step quickened by the double anticipation of a scolding tongue and an encounter with a straggling 'prentice, who, since they had been called upon by the citizens to keep watch and ward with the guard, in consequence of the dispute between the city and clergy, were more than usually insolent. Several such parties had passed by the Palace Plain, where formerly stood the residence of the dukes of Norfolk, chanting their noisy songs, and hustling into the middle of the street such quiet passengers as business or pleasure called from their homes at that late hour. Under one of the old-fashioned porticos of a mansion at the end of a street stood, or rather leant upon his staff, a tall mendicant friar, his hood drawn over his face, in all probability more for warmth than concealment, for the wind was blowing keenly. As the sound of footsteps approached his lurking-place, he several times quitted his retreat, but instantly shrank back to it on perceiving the riotous character of the parties who approached and passed him. At last a solitary passenger, a man of staid demeanour, such as became a substantial citizen, who had a voice and was well respected in his ward, was seen walking towards the palace. After eyeing him for some moments, as if to assure himself of the character or identity of the party, the friar emerged freely in the street to address him.

"Benedicite, my son!" he exclaimed; "the night promises to be a rough one."

The citizen whom he addressed respectfully raised his cap from his head, and uncovered an open lofty brow, frosted with age, yet marked with health and resolution. It was our old friend Steadman, the now opulent wool-comber, who was retracing his steps to his quiet domicile. The old man had served, and had seen the brethren of St. Francis, as the mendicant friars were called, in the battle field, whispering consolation to the dying and hope to the wounded. He had watched their labours in the hospital and in the camp, in the prison and on the scaffold; wherever, in the course of his long life, he had encountered misery, danger, distress, or sorrow, there had he also met the humble brothers of the order; and the bluff veteran raised his bonnet to the russet gown and cord of the mendicant priest with deeper reverence than he had paid to a mitred prelate or a belted earl.

"Knowest thou, my son," demanded the friar, "where in this city stands the mansion of Sir John de Corbey?"

The citizen eyed the speaker narrowly. Between himself and the knight existed a sense of unmerited injury and slumbering hate. He had just heard too that the Lady Mary was little better than a prisoner in her home, that Walter was a fugitive, and he naturally regarded with suspicion all who seemed in any way allied or connected with the oppressor.

"I know both it and its owner," he answered, in a tone which contrasted strangely with the courtesy of his previous action. "Would I had less reason to boast of his acquaintance, for I hold it but slight honour."

"He seems, my son," replied the friar, calmly, "to hold scant place in your favour; yet report speaks of him as a valiant knight, and of unblemished honour."

"Not the first lie report has trumpeted foolishly," exclaimed the old man, who deemed it imprudent, however, to enter into further conversation with one who might be a spy or agent of the subtle knight: so

hastily turning on his heel, he drily bade his interrogator good night, and prepared to resume his walk towards home, when the voice of the mendicant again arrested him.

"You forget you have not yet shown me the house in question."

"Follow me," replied Steadman, in a tone which plainly indicated his dissatisfaction at the task imposed; and, without waiting to see if the friar obeyed his injunction, he turned upon his steps, and marched sturdily along till he reached the church of the Dominican friars, now St. Andrew's Hall. Passing over the bridge, he pointed to a large house, isolated in its own grounds, on the opposite side of the river, which watered the lawn in front.

"That's it, friend," said the old soldier; "God and our Lady speed your errand, if it be good; if evil, may they pardon thee. Farewell! the hour is late for honest men to be abroad in; I must to my home."

The monk drew from his pouch a piece of gold, and proffered it to the speaker for his acceptance in recompense for the service he had rendered him. Much to his astonishment, his guide rejected it, almost with contempt.

"I want not your gold!" he exclaimed. "You must be rich to pay so large for so slight a service. Humph!" he added, eyeing him both leisurely and suspiciously, "gold and a friar! I question if the cardinal himself, whose revenue, they say, would buy a county, had been more liberal."

"Why do you refuse the gold?" demanded the mendicant.

"Because I have not earned it," replied the wool-comber, "and wish to keep my conscience cleaner than my hands. A foolish whim, you'll say, as the world goes; but still it is my whim; and, thanks to industry and care, I am rich enough to indulge it."

"All men are not so scrupulous," observed the stranger, replacing the broad piece within his pouch.

"No: only the honest ones," said Steadman.

"Art thou honest?"

The question seemed to arouse the anger of the old soldier—more, perhaps, from the half-sneering, half-doubtful tone in which it was uttered, than from the words themselves. Grasping the stout staff with which he guided his steps through the city, as though he longed to break it over the inquirer's back, he answered him—

"Too honest to accept of gold from the friend of Sir John de Corbey."

"I am not his friend," coolly replied the stranger.

"Well, then, from his enemy."

"Nor am I his enemy."

"In the devil's name," exclaimed the old soldier, "what art thou then?"

"His judge."

"His judge!" repeated our old soldier, yet more and more surprised; "who and what art thou?"

"As thou seest; an unworthy priest of the Most High," said the mendicant, bowing with profound humility.

"Priests are not judges," observed the citizen; angry, as he conceived, at being trifled with by an unworthy jest.

"And are there none who judge," demanded the friar, "save those who interpret the law's stern letter; or, clothed in ermine and in purple, speak its life-condemning word? He who shall rend the veil from Justice's bandaged brow, point out the den where crime hath hid its terrors and its proofs, guide the keen blade in its descent, and mark the hour to strike, He is the Judge —earth's judges are His agents."

The tone of dignity with which the friar spoke convinced Steadman that he was in contact with no common mind. In a moment his mistrust had vanished. The old soldier had seen sufficient of the world to know that such a man would never be the agent of a criminal like Sir John de Corbey; his confidence was complete.

"How can I serve thee?" he inquired, in a tone of cordiality, different from his former one of suspicion; "you seem wandering here," he added; "if not without a purpose, at least without a shelter. Come with me; a mattress and supper shall be yours. It is not much I have to offer—but it is given freely."

"No," answered the friar; "and yet I thank thee. But duty detains me here. Tell me, what is thy name?"

"Steadman, the wool-stapler," said the old man; more than a little mortified that his proffered hospitality had been so unceremoniously rejected; for he was anxious to see more of the wandering priest.

"Formerly in the service of the Lord of Stanfield?" demanded the friar; "he who was foully murdered at Tournay?"

"The same."

"And afterwards of his lady, during her widowhood?"

"True."

"And uncle to a young man named Cuthbert, the armourer, who eight years since suddenly disappeared, after delivering a letter to her majesty, the queen, from your former mistress?"

"The very same," replied Steadman, greatly agitated, for he had never ceased to reproach himself as having been indirectly the cause of his nephew's destruction, by sending him upon the fatal expedition. "If you possess any clue to the poor boy's fate, in mercy make it plain; his widowed mother's blessing, an old soldier's thanks, and Heaven's approving smile, will recompense you."

"His fate," replied the friar, "has been a sad one; the time hath not arrived to speak more plainly."

"But shall it be avenged?" demanded the uncle of the unfortunate armourer.

"It shall."

"And soon?"

"And soon," repeated the mendicant; "Heaven is always just. Guilt for awhile may flourish, innocence sink 'neath the shade of calumny and ill; justice at last, like the bright sun, shall break majestic forth—the shield of innocence, the guard of truth. We can but watch the hand upon the dial of old time," he added; "our vain regrets, impatient murmurings, will not accelerate its pace one hour."

"Let me but live to hear it strike," said the old man, passionately, "and I have lived long enough; my noble master will then be avenged, my murdered nephew sleep in peace."

The friar fixed his keen eyes upon the speaker, like one accustomed to read men at a glance. The scrutiny was apparently satisfactory, for the bluff old soldier met his gaze with the unshrinking confidence of an honest nature and a guileless heart; indeed, he had nothing to conceal—his life from boyhood upwards had ever been as open as his speech.

"Hast thou confidence in me?" he demanded of the wool-comber.

"I have."

"And wilt thou follow my directions?" continued the speaker.

"I will, to the very letter."

"And ask no questions?"

"And ask no questions," repeated Steadman, who would have been puzzled to have accounted even to himself for the extraordinary influence which, in so short a time, the friar had acquired over him.

"'Tis well; so shall thy wishes be accomplished and thy nephew's memory be avenged. Remain here," continued the mendicant, "till morning; watch well the windows of yon gloomy mansion. If you perceive a signal from them, haste for the officers of justice; the life of the Lady Mary will be then in danger."

"The life of the Lady Mary!" repeated his hearer, in a tone of horror. "Oh! do not trifle with me. She is my master's child; I love her like my own. I have held her a prattling, smiling infant on my knees.

God!" he added, with an expression of energy and resolution beyond his years, "if any harm befal her, noble though he is, these hands shall rend her false guardian limb from limb, though I die upon a gibbet for the act. But how—how should you know this?"

"Remember thy promise—no question!" replied the mysterious stranger,

"Tell me at least," said Steadman, "who is to give the signal which I must watch for?"

"I am."

"How will you gain admittance to the house?" demanded the puzzled citizen.

"Leave that to me."

"You are not deceiving me?"

"Rely upon my faith."

With these words the mendicant approached the house. Avoiding the principal porch, he passed to a side entrance used chiefly by the servants of the household, and knocked gently with his staff three times. It was evident that he was expected, as the door was immediately opened, and the stranger entered; first turning round and laying his finger upon his lip, as a signal to Steadman for silence and discretion as he did so.

For more than an hour the old soldier continued to pace up and down in front of the house, listening for every sound, and pondering over in his mind the character, words, and bearing of the mysterious being whose commands he found himself so strangely fulfilling. At times he thought it was some friend or servant of the knight's who had been amusing himself with his credulity—a suspicion which his knowledge of the past events of his life tended to confirm; and then again he doubted; there was a dignity and truthfulness in his manner, which, despite appearances, inspired confidence.

"Be he in earnest or in jest," murmured the old man, "I'll do his bidding; if the latter, 'tis but one night passed as I have passed many in my youth, beside the watch-fire's blaze; if the former, if danger really threatens my master's child, her enemies shall find that I am not too old to strike in her defence."

With this resolution he resumed his walk before the house, and night still found him at his post.

CHAPTER V.

"Night's iron tongue hath told the birth of morn;
Now is the hour when pale-faced murder walks:
And impious deeds, which shun men's gaze,
By guilty hands are wrought."—*Old Play.*

N a large oaken panelled chamber, whose projecting bay windows faced the river, the Lady Mary was kept almost a prisoner by her false guardian, whose fearful courage rose with the crisis which his villany had provoked. The farther he advanced in his dark purposes, the more intense became his resolution, for his heart had long been a stranger to the compunctious visitings of conscience. Mercy might have turned with a hopeless sigh from his stern visage, and meek-eyed pity appealed to his humanity or sympathy in vain. Of all the domestics of Stanfield, Bertha alone had been permitted to attend the unhappy heiress to her new abode. Had Sir John known the devotion of the faithful girl to her persecuted mistress, even that poor indulgence would have been denied. The apartment was as desolate in its appearance as the fortunes of its youthful inmate; it had originally been the reception or state-room of the mansion, and the faded splendour of its gilt furniture and purple hangings showed like mildewed tinsel on a funeral pall. At one end a pair of richly-carved folding-doors led to a long-deserted oratory, and from thence, by a winding staircase, to the cell of the chaplain beneath; these doors were invariably kept locked. Directly facing them was the general entrance to the chamber. The heavy curtains were drawn before the windows, and fell in massive sombre folds upon the floor. Nothing, in fact, could be more gloomy, more calculated to crush the spirit of a captive—the stern reality of a dungeon would have been cheerfulness compared to it

" 'Tis past the hour of midnight!" sighed the orphan, as she turned the hour-glass, and replaced it on the table beside her; "no chance, no hope that Walter will arrive to-night! Should he have fallen into my guardian's power, or Wolsey's ear can prove deaf to my sad tale, how drear a fate will then be mine! Oh! there is madness in that thought!" she cried, emphatically, starting from her chair and pacing her lone prison. "Each way I turn is doubt and misery. I am alone, friendless and un-protected—all have deserted me; no friend, no aid—lost, lost!"

In the passionate excitement of her sorrow the unhappy girl approached the oratory, and was startled by a deep-drawn sigh. Advancing to the door, she listened attentively—hope and fear alternately causing her heart to beat with fearful expectation; the sound, however, whatever the cause, was not repeated, and she resumed her agitated walk, satisfied that it was nothing more than the moaning of the night wind as it swept through the halls and passages of the old mansion.

It is strange, when labouring under the influence of fear, how quick the eye and ear become; the falling of a leaf, the rustling of a veil, the waving of a plume, fixes the latter, while the sight measures the depth and out-line of a shadow.

The sound which next attracted the Lady Mary's attention was her own name, breathed in a voice so low it scarce broke silence. She paused; it was repeated; the second time she felt assured that she was not deceived: it was the faithful Bertha at the door of her chamber, demanding if she were alone.

"Alone with terror and despair," whispered her mistress, in the same low and melancholy tone.

The door was gently unbarred from with-out: as it slowly moved upon its rusty, time-worn hinges, it gave a loud creak, something like the shrill scream of a screech-owl dis-appointed of its prey. Had an arrow been driven through the trembling captive's heart she could not have felt a keener pang. It seemed impossible the noise should not alarm the house. There was a pause; a minute seemed an age; her breath became suspended; her arteries ceased to beat; nor did the life-impelling stream resume its course till, with-out further noise, the portal was opened sufficiently wide to admit her faithful atten-dant to her presence. She was cautiously followed by a friar—the same who had set our old friend, Steadman, on the outside of the ouse to watch.

" ady, dear lady," whispered Bertha, sinki g upon her knee, and kissin her

mistress's hand; "thank Heaven, we meet again!"

"Who is yon stranger?" demanded the orphan, pointing to the mendicant, whose features were hidden in his cowl.

"A wandering friar."

"Who gave him admittance to the house?"

"I did," replied the courageous girl. "I was on the watch, determined to ask assis-tance of the first stranger who might ap-proach: Heaven has sent this good man to our aid. Courage," she added; "courage, and you are saved."

The words of the speaker will explain the readiness with which the stranger obtained entrance to the mansion. Perhaps he had expected to find some other on the watch, for he had twice inquired after the chaplain of his conductress, who explained to him that the worthy man had that very evening been sent by Sir John to Stanfield, in order most probably that he might not be a witness to the scene of cruelty and oppres-sion he was about to enact. The friar had evinced both surprise and disappointment at his absence; for he had counted on him to baffle the plotters in their dark scheme of blood.

"A friar!" exclaimed the captive; "then hope remains; and with hope, life and love. Father," she added, approaching the holy man, and fixing her tearful, trusting eyes upon him, "you will remain till morn or Walter comes; you will protect me? Hea-ven knows I need protection. Will you not save me, father?"

"Save thee from what or whom?" de-manded the mendicant, in a tone of assumed surprise.

"From my base kinsman's tyranny—from death," whispered the suppliant, "or worse than death. He seeks my hand, not from love or base desire—from a still darker passion, avarice. Walter hath fled to Wol-sey; this my stern guardian knows, and on my head will wreak a mean revenge. Would," she added, "would I had been born a beggar!"

"Doubt not Wolsey's justice," replied the stranger, kindly; "he will protect thy lover and redress thy wrongs. But you spoke of death," he continued, lowering his voice; "think you he would dare——"

"Dare!" whispered the Lady Mary, with a shudder; "what would not Sir John de Corbey dare? This very night he hath sworn to make me his. Earth hath no respect, Heaven no law, he hath not broken. You, even you—a priest of the Most High—he would hold your blood as water, if the shedding of it advanced his interest or his purpose."

"Indeed!" said the priest, drily, and much with the air of a man who finds himself called upon suddenly and, unarmed to encounter a ferocious savage; "is he so desperate a villain? Then we must use the best defence time and circumstances permit. Girl," he added, turning to Bertha, "dost thou love thy mistress?"

"With my life," answered the devoted maiden.

"Go to the gate," resumed the mendicant—"the same at which I entered. Aid will soon arrive; friends whom I possess the means to summon. You must admit them. If they or you should fail," he added, solemnly, at the same time taking the orphan by the hand, "why, Heaven have mercy on us both!"

"And you?" said Bertha, half doubtingly, for she liked not the thought of separation from her mistress.

"Remain here with your lady," continued the friar.

There was a pause. The speaker, with the keen, quick perception of a man accustomed to read the human heart, saw that he was doubted. Without a moment's hesitation he advanced towards the window, and drawing the heavy drapery aside, beckoned the two trembling females to approach the spot where he stood.

"See you no one?" he demanded, pointing to the burly figure of Steadman, who, with his eyes fixed upon the mansion, still kept watch.

"We do," they answered both together.

Carefully opening the huge casement, he leant forward and waved his handkerchief in the air. The old soldier understood the signal, and instantly set off in quest of the city guard.

"'Tis Steadman!" exclaimed the Lady Mary, who had recognised him in the moonlight.

"Are you convinced?" demanded the friar.

"I am," said Bertha, kneeling and kissing the hem of his robe. "Assign me, father, what penance you think fit; were it to walk barefoot to St. Edmund's shrine, I merit it for having doubted thy faith one moment."

On a sign from the mendicant the speaker took a mute farewell of her mistress, and cautiously descended the great staircase, barring the door on the outside to prevent suspicion. No sooner were the Lady Mary and the priest alone, than the latter advanced to the curtains, and drawing a long sharp weapon from beneath his robe, began cutting the silken cords which confined them; these he knotted together till he formed one of sufficient length to reach from the window to the ground. In a few minutes it was fixed.

"Dare you venture?" he demanded, as soon as he had accomplished his task.

Before the prisoner could reply, a deep, firm tread was heard upon the staircase. The orphan trembled, for she recognised her guardian's step: nor did the friar seem quite at ease on hearing it.

"Too late, too late!" he whispered; "but fear not—succour will soon arrive; or, at the worst, I am armed and near thee. Should the necessity arise, priest though I am, thine enemy shall find I have the nerve to strike."

With these words the speaker retreated behind the curtains of the window where he had affixed the rope, and where he could watch the arrival of the aid which Steadman could not fail to bring.

Scarcely had he ensconced himself than Sir John de Corbey entered the apartment, bearing in his hand a small silver cup. The features of the knight were cold and stern —pale as a statue on a tomb, and marked by the fixed lines which speak a mind resolved on its purpose, be it for good or ill. As he slowly crossed the room to place his burthen upon a table, the friar could almost have imagined him the ministering priest of some infernal shrine; nor would he have been far wrong, for the evil heart is indeed a demon's shrine, and the offerings humanity's worst passions.

It was painful to witness the expression of agony and terror in the eye of the poor orphan as she watched the action of her guardian. Like the bird fascinated by the rattlesnake, she could not withdraw her gaze. For several moments the murderer and his victim regarded each other in silence. So violently beat the heart of the trembling girl, that you might almost have heard its deep pulsations. She was the first to speak, and despite the terrors which appalled her, her voice was calm, even as the horror of the scene.

"Guardian," she exclaimed, "in that hollow eye, that frowning brow, and fixed compression of thy lip, I read a soul resolved upon its purpose. Murder," she added, almost in a whisper, "foul, unmanly, midnight murder."

"Mary," replied Sir John, in a tone whose coldness rendered his words more terrible; "thou seest thy kinsman and judge."

"My judge! what crime have I committed?"

"Thou hast disgraced thy lineage," resumed the knight, "by listening to a base-born peasant's love; but never shall the proud escutcheon of our house be dishonoured by thy marriage with the unworthy object of thy headstrong passion."

"Dishonoured!" repeated the girl, with a look of withering scorn and contempt, which even the sense of the peril in which she stood could not restrain. "The murderer talks of dishonour! Oh, specious sophistry! oh, vile pretence to cloak a deed thy cheek would blush to name! I am thy kinsman's orphan child—no friend save thee. Break not the reed which hath no other stay. Thou hast a son—what wouldst thou feel to see him thus opprest? Guardian," she added, sinking on one knee before him, "stain not thy soul with blood—mercy, mercy!"

"Wilt thou be mine?" he whispered, and the words hissed with fearful passion through his clenched teeth.

"For my dead father's sake," she continued, still fixing her imploring eyes upon him, "whose blood will rise against thee at the bar of Heaven—by my mother's broken heart, whose spirit now is watching over us, reflect, have pity!"

"Wilt thou be mine?" he repeated with increased but still suppressed passion.

"Never," said the orphan, rising from her knees, and fixing her eyes with the mingled resignation and firmness of a martyr upon him; "death were less fearful than thy loathed embrace; think not of it, dream not of it; life thou mayest destroy, but never crush my soul. Wed with thee," she continued with energy, "a man of blood and mystery! my father's murderer! never—demons would dance around our nuptial couch, and yelling furies draw the curtain round us. Thy bride! even in madness such horror would be spared me."

The accusation of murder so suddenly brought against him startled even her guardian's equanimity. The suspicions which had connected his name with the death of the knight of Stanfield he had deemed long since buried in the grave of his victim; but now they rose again in stern reality before him. There was something in the energy with which the unprotected girl accused him of the murder of her father, terrible as well as dangerous; should she live, the accusation might be repeated and believed. Instead of relenting from his purpose, her words confirmed it. Pointing to the cup upon the table, he exclaimed, while passion struggled with hate and mortification—

"Then you behold your doom!"

"I will not die!" shrieked the heiress, with a struggle; "help—murder—help!"

The tyrant sprang upon her; with one hand he stifled her despairing cries, and with the other drew a short stiletto from his bosom, and held it over her, as, overcome with terror, she sank half fainting across a chair between them. The friar, who all the while had been upon the watch, was about to dart forward, when, to his surprise, the doors of the deserted oratory were thrown open, and a new actor appeared upon the scene. Henry de Corbey, his hair bristling with horror, like an avenging angel darted between his father and his victim; with one hand he held the murderer's wrist, who, like a spirit spellbound, gazed upon him, and with the other raised the fatal chalice to his own innocent lips, and slowly drained it off.

"Father," he exclaimed as he let fall the cup, "I drink forgiveness of the crime; thou art a childless man."

A yell of hopeless, dark despair, frantic as that which the archangel gave when hurled from heaven, burst from the breast of the guilty, wretched father, who stood tranfixed like Cain when the brand first seared his aching brow; an idiotic laugh succeeded, so loud and vacant that echo trembled to repeat the sound. The assassin was already punished. The friar, who, with his hood half drawn over his features, had emerged from his concealment, seeing the danger to the orphan past, quickly regained his covert place behind the curtain.

"Heaven help thee, gallant youth!" exclaimed the agitated Mary, as her preserver sank upon the floor beside her; "he is dying—Henry, dear Henry—alas! for me he dies! Is there no help—no aid?"

"None," sighed her cousin, on whom the draught had already commenced its deadly work. "I am past the leech's skill; but thou art safe, dear Mary—safe, quite safe. Give me one kiss, sweet coz," he added with a faint smile; "Walter need not be jealous now! Do not forget the boy who loved you like a man—the kiss, the kiss!"

With passionate grief the object of his early and devoted love bent over him, and kissed the dying youth. At that moment, in the impulse of her grateful and affectionate nature, gladly would she have given her own life to have saved her deliverer. Had he lived, the secretary might have found in him a dangerous rival; for such pure devotion was well calculated to win a woman's heart.

At this moment a loud knocking and the sound of many voices were heard at the great gate of the mansion. Steadman and the expected assistance had arrived.

"Think of me sometimes in your hours of mirth," sighed the victim, whose faculties began gradually to be obscured; for it was the peculiar quality of the Italian's poison

EVERIL IN THE LOLLARDS' TOWER.

to destroy the principle of life by acting on the brain. "Where is my father? How dark the room grows!—dark—dark—dark!"

"He is sinking—going!" shrieked Mary, kneeling on the floor beside him, and trying to raise the sufferer's head, which fell heavily upon her breast. "His eyes are glazed; God! is there no aid—no help?"

The agony of her voice roused the expiring youth, who, with a last effort, raised his head from its throbbing pillow, and fixed his bloodshot eyes with mournful tenderness upon her, and imprinted the last kiss of love and devotion on her lips, his soul exhaling in the act. The smiling angel which welcomed his pure soul to paradise repaid it back as seraph hands threw wide the gates to give him entrance.

Scarcely was the last sigh breathed, and the sacrifice of the devoted boy accomplished, than Adam, followed by Steadman and a portion of the city guard, rushed up the staircase and entered the apartment. The sound aroused the knight from his deathlike torpor. For a moment consciousness returned, and his eyes rolled wildly round the room, till they rested on the body of his son, when, with a deep groan, he sank beside it. The leech comprehended in a moment all that had passed, and a cold smile played for an instant over his features. There must have been something unusual in the tie which bound the Italian to his employer; whether of love or hate, he at least was faithful to him—for, with the fact of the deed and the plausibility of a witness, he instantly accused the Lady Mary of the murder.

"No, no!" cried the orphan, wildly, as soon as she perfectly comprehended the fearful accusation, "his father did the deed into the fatal—the poisoned cup. Henry, Henry——"

[several lines obscured by ink blot] ... the recollection of the ... under ... with in ... and accused ... death ... addressing the officer who ... the watch.

"... do ... the man, reluctantly; "but I also remember that she accused his father."

"His father!" exclaimed the Italian, in a tone of well-affected indignation "—impious belief ... where that father lies," he ... upon the insensible Sir John, who had ... himself upon the body of his son. "Who ever saw the murderer pillowed on the victim's breast? You must perform your duty."

Stayed were Steadman, whose brow reeled with the confusion of the scene, so different from the one he expected to witness, but whose confidence in his master's child was never for one moment shaken. "Some fiend hath been at work here; wait but a moment—she will explain it all—she is innocent. My soul—life—honour, on the forfeit, if my words prove false. Mary," he added, in a tone of almost childish affection and remonstrance, "Lady Mary, rouse—rouse, for the honour of your father's name; speak—confound this lying villain with a word."

"Where am I?" sighed the heiress, with a look which indicated the return of reason. "Steadman! oh, I am safe with you—safe—quite safe. You," she continued, bursting into a passionate flood of tears, and throwing her arms, like a frightened infant, round the old man's neck, "you will not desert me?"

"Not while this tongue can wag," replied the old man, endeavouring to speak firmly, "or this arm strike in thy defence. But thou art accused of this night's fearful crime; speak, and clear thy fame of this suspicion."

"I!" said the girl, with a look of surprise and incredulity, "I accused of my dear cousin's death? No, no; malice itself could never forge a charge so base. I have a witness."

"A witness!" repeated Adam, with a start of surprise.

"A witness!" repeated the officer.

"Behold!" she continued.

Rushing up to the curtain behind which the friar had been concealed, she hastily tore it aside. He was gone. The cord which remained fastened to the window explained the means of his flight.

"Gone!" she exclaimed, her mind again beginning to wander with the shock. "Then I am right; it is a dream, a fearful dream, and not reality. Wake me—wake me! or I shall go mad."

To all interrogations the orphan persisted in asserting that it was but a dream that had passed, and that her cousin lived; nor could the entreaties of Steadman, or the questions of the officer, elicit further explanation from her. Despite his wish to believe her innocent, his suspicions were confirmed, and he felt it his duty to guard her till morning in her chamber. To add to the confusion of the scene, Bertha was nowhere to be found; all seemed to conspire against her.

The next day the magistrates arrived, and a more lengthened investigation took place, at the end of which, despite the evidence of Steadman, the plausible reasoning of Adam prevailed, and the orphan heiress of Stanfield was committed, on the charge of murdering her cousin, to the city prison. The absence of her attendant, who was deemed an accomplice, told against her; and the old soldier's story of having been informed of her danger, and set on to watch by a wandering friar, was treated as a fable invented to save her.

After the arrest of the Lady Mary, Sir John de Corbey, who was still insensible, was borne from the chamber to his couch, where, for four-and-twenty hours, he lay raving and struggling between life and death. The leech was his only attendant—the only witness of the fearful accusations uttered by the sick man in his frenzy. The skill of his physician at last, however, prevailed, and he sank into a slumber so deep and still that the slightest pulsation of his wrist, to which the Italian repeatedly applied his finger, alone indicated a difference between it and death.

On the second morning after the murder—for the sacrifice of the gallant youth was at least a moral assassination—the wretched man awoke. At first he imagined that he had been labouring under a fearful dream, and gazed with a degree of satisfaction on the well-remembered objects in the apartment, which the sun already lighted with its sickly rays as they penetrated through the time-stained windows, rich with the armorial bearings of his ancient house.

"Thank Heaven," he murmured, "it was but a dream; but, oh! a dream of terror; it hath quelled the raging fever of my blood, broken my heart's stern purpose. Perhaps Heaven," he added, after a pause, "hath sent it, in its mercy, to warn me from perdition. Memory! memory! would I could recall the past!—would I could repent!"

The wretched man, still labouring under the impression that the fearful scene he had witnessed was but a vision, raised his hands as if to pray, when a low, hissing laugh startled him. Springing from the couch, he beheld the minister of his crimes, the cold and serpent-like Adam, regarding him with a mocking and scornful lip; the expression of his countenance resembled Satan's watching the unavailing regret of a falling spirit. In an instant the reality, the dreadful reality, that he was a childless man — that the scene of blood, the recollection of which shook his iron frame with agony, had really passed, and was no creation of his distempered fancy, flashed upon him. With a shriek he exclaimed, as he started to his feet—

"Tormentor—fiend—avoid me! thy presence scares the pitying angel from my side. My boy—my boy——"

"Fiend!" repeated the Italian, in a tone of derision—"you mistake, I am an angel."

"An angel!"

"Ay. Lucifer was one. Am I worse than he? But this is weak and imbecile," he added; "did not friendship plead, I would desert thee—leave thee a wreck upon misfortune's tide—the sport of Wolsey and his minion, Walter—the scoff of fools—the landmark of dishonour!"

"Dishonour! Hath it not fallen?" said the wretched man, writhing; but, at the same time, listening to the subtle tempter with a kind of latent hope. "Is not my name pronounced with execration?"

"No."

"Do not all curse the murderer?"

"Yes."

"Shall I not be dragged," resumed Sir John, "'mid hootings, forth, to shameful trial, and a more shameful death?"

"Not unless you seek it," replied Adam, in the same quiet, passionless tone with which one answers an impatient woman or a fretful child; "that fate at least may be avoided."

"How?" demanded the knight; "how to be avoided?"

"The Lady Mary is accused as the assassin."

"By whom?"

"By me."

There was something so monstrous, so fiend-like in the accusation, that even Sir John de Corbey, tutored and hardened as he was in villany, shrank with horror and shame at the thought of sacrificing the innocent girl even to secure his own vile safety: sorrow had touched his heart till it felt almost human.

"Mary accused as the assassin!" he exclaimed. "My kinsman's orphan child—she who loved him with a sister's love—perish on a scaffold for my crime! I never will consent."

"Oh, yes, you will," said the Italian, with his usual cool sneer; "for the doom you dread must be her fate or yours—or yours," he repeated in a low, impressive tone, which gave a fearful meaning to his words.

"What chance, what likelihood, to give a colour to the charge?" faltered his dupe.

"Your son removed, does she not become your heiress?"

"Heiress! to a beggar!"

The leech quietly drew a sealed packet from his bosom, and silently gave it to the knight, who hastily broke the seal; cold drops of agony fell from his forehead as his eye glanced rapidly over its contents. It informed him that his cousin, Richard de Corbey, with whom for years he had been at variance, was dead, and had left him heir of all his broad possessions. He was rich, rich enough to glut the desire of avarice; but wealth arrived too late—he was a childless man. From the date of the letter, it ought to have arrived at least two days sooner. The murderer's punishment even in this world had commenced.

"Too late, too late!" he groaned, as he crushed the letter which Adam, for some reason of his own, had purposely kept from him; "had it arrived but two days sooner, hell had been spared its triumph, heaven its saint. Henry, my boy!" he added, frantically; "in whom alone I lived—for whom I sinned—my own heart's pride—the tie which made it human—wake from thy grave, e'en though it be to curse me! Henry! Henry!"

Mad with despair and remorse, the guilty father dashed himself upon the couch where he had so lately lain, and continued to call upon his murdered son till exhausted nature took refuge in insensibility.

"Not yet, not yet," muttered the leech, as, like an exulting fiend, he glared upon him; "each pang, each groan and tear are mine, and I will not abate one jot of the account. My debt is lessened, but not paid. Death, with repentance on his lip, might win him heaven; and he would meet her there," he added. "Memory, I thank thee for that thought; it steels my heart again; 'tis iron, iron!"

With these fearful words, which expressed the speaker's long-smothered hate, and gave some clue to the cause, the Italian poured into a small cup the remaining portion of the draught which he had previously administered, and poured it down the throat of the unhappy victim of artifice and passion. The effect was speedy, for the wretched man recovered again to life and consciousness.

Probably the drug possessed some peculiar power of deadening all violent emotion, for he was calm, and spoke like one reviving from a stupor, or perhaps his better angel had deserted him.

"So," he muttered, more in the tone of a man conversing with himself than one who addresses his conversation to another, "Mary is accused as the assassin?"

The tempter smiled, for he felt certain of his victim.

"Yes—yes," he continued, "I am resolved; my name shall yet descend unspotted to the tomb. This great act passed, within the cloister's shade I'll hide my misery and despair for ever."

"A cloister!" repeated Adam in a tone of contempt; "psha! pray by proxy! Besides," he added, in a low, bland voice, "you are not yet so old but that a son may bear to time unborn the proud name of De Corbey."

This time the probe had gone too far, and the sufferer winced beneath the pang; he felt the bitter sneer the words conveyed, the biting mockery; but was too much exhausted, too spiritless, to resent them.

"Sleep—give me sleep!" he murmured; "heart and brain can bear no more."

The leech arose from his seat, and drew the heavy curtains round the couch; further drugs he knew to be unnecessary, for exhausted humanity was sure to seek relief in nature's best medicine, sleep.

He was not deceived; in a few minutes the deep breathings of the knight assured him that his prayer was granted; and he reseated himself at the foot of his couch to watch patiently by his side.

While thus occupied, the thoughts of many an early year and blighted hope passed through his burning brain; perhaps his recollections were of that sunny land in which he first drew breath—of home, of friends, of youthful love, or passion's broken vow. Whatever were the subjects of his thoughts or workings of his mind, they produced a strange effect upon the old man's countenance. The rigid lines which the long habitude of self-command had marked upon his features gradually softened; his thin lip slightly quivered, and a tear, a large round tear, fell like a drop of liquid lava on his cheek—the first he had shed for years, and doomed to be the last.

"Why this weakness?" he sighed, as he dashed the stranger aside; "why this relenting, when life and its sole purpose are so near accomplished? Do I regret the oath I swore—to be revenged, though I lost Heaven in the attempt? It is fulfilled," he added, gazing on the speaker; "for I have steeped his soul so deep in crime, that mercy's tears, gushing through endless time would fail to cleanse it. He is lost, body and soul—here and hereafter lost. My years of misery soon will be atoned."

Why the Italian took the fearful oath our readers will not long wait to learn; how he had kept it they know already.

The day at last arrived which was to consign the remains of the young and gallant Henry de Corbey to their final resting-place. His father, whose short-lived fit of remorse had passed, had given orders that the funeral should be conducted with a magnificence proportionate to his newly acquired wealth and sorrow, as if the escutcheoned banner and emblazoned pall could render death less terrible, mocking the pomp of woe. The grave had been dug in the chapel of our Lady, in the cathedral of the city, the burying-place of all the house of Corbey.

In honour of the family of the deceased, whose ancestors had been amongst the earliest benefactors of the church, every altar of the majestic edifice was illuminated and adorned with funeral pomp. At the high altar the prior himself officiated, whilst low masses for the dead were celebrated at all the others. As usual, the body was placed under a catafalque in the centre of the choir; the childless father, the now wealthy Sir John, was seated at the head as chief mourner; whilst many who shared his blood, or had been the companions of his son, were gathered round the bier. The solemn right had reached that part where the priest pronounces the introit:

Requiem æternum dona eis, Domine,
Et lux perpetua luceat eis;

when a laugh—a maniac laugh—of unearthly triumph rang through the vaulted aisles, and startled the officiating ministers. Most who heard it crossed themselves, and even the heart of the hardened murderer beat wildly as at the anticipation of some fresh horror. There was a pause in the service, and it was some time before the prior, with a faltering voice, could proceed with the words—

To dicet hymnus, Deus, in Sion,
Et tibi redditur votum in Jerusalem—

when a second yell, more fearful than the first—a yell which spoke the very madness of mirth—again startled the assistants' ears. This time the confusion was complete; the affrighted priests replaced the half-raised chalice on the altar, and men gazed upon each other in superstitious terror.

The prior took the crucifix in his hand, and, turning towards the crowd at the lower end of the church, demanded who it was who had dared to interrupt, by such unchristian levity, the holy sacrifice.

The people divided, and a female figure advanced from among them; her long white hair, bleached more by sorrow than by age, had escaped from the linen coif which should have confined it; her grey eyes flashed with all the fearful brightness of insanity; and her withered arm, which she kept waving wildly above her head, as if in triumph, gave her more the appearance of a pagan priestess than a Christian widow. It was the mother of the unfortunate Cuthbert, the armourer, the maniac sister of our old acquaintance Steadman. She was well known in the church, where she was a constant attendant; for unless she came in contact with Sir John de Corbey, or his name was mentioned before her, her demeanour was quiet and inoffensive, but at such times the fever of her brain returned with double violence, and her imprecations on the supposed murderer of her son were wild and terrible to listen to.

The knight gazed on her, as she advanced towards him, with ill-suppressed terror; to his superstitious imagination—for, like most infidels, he was superstitious—there was something ominous in the encounter at such a time and occasion.

"Ha!" exclaimed the unhappy Maud, "the vulture hath lost its young—the tiger mourns its cub—ha! ha! ha!—I knew that Heaven would avenge me in its own good time. Please," she added, in an almost imploring voice, "where is my son? We will bury them together. My brain—my hot brain would be cooler could I but pray beside my poor boy's grave!"

"Retire, Maud," said one of the priests, mildly, at the same time so placing himself between her and the catafalque as to prevent her approaching further.

"I'll not retire," shrieked the maniac, "till he has given me back my son. I've been a patient wretch too long. When God hath smitten him," she added, pointing to the coffin, "why should I hesitate to curse? He hath blighted my widowed years—plucked the only flower in my life's path; and when I ask his bones—my poor boy's bones—that I may lay them by his father's side, and sleep myself there, you bid me peace! Peace to a mother's heart! peace to a childless widow! Ha! ha! ha! There is no peace whilst yet the murderer lives!"

"Maud—Maud!" exclaimed the priest, mildly—"this is madness; think on the time, and on the sacred place."

"And you defend him," continued the unhappy mother, in the same excited strain; "but priests and all—all are set against me. Oh! would, like thee, I had the power as well as the will to curse him!"

"Woman," faltered the knight, and the expression of his countenance was ghastly as he spoke, "I know nought of thy son; leave me in my sorrow to mourn for mine."

"Remove her from the church," said the prior, in a voice of authority, "and let the rites proceed."

In obedience to the command of their superior several monks left their stalls, and surrounded the desolate creature, who violently resisted their firm but humane efforts to lead her from the church. Several of her friends and neighbours assisted them.

"We shall meet again!" she screamed, shaking her meagre arm at Sir John; "twice shall we meet again! I see it now—the trial and the scaffold—ha! the scaffold! ha, ha, ha! Cuthbert shall be avenged—bravely avenged; and his mother's broken heart repose at last in peace."

Exhausted by the force of her struggles, poor Maud ceased to resist their efforts, and was at last conducted from the cathedral by her friends and the priests. As soon as she was gone the mass for the dead was resumed; but a chill had fallen upon the spirits of all who assisted. The calm spirit of devotion had been scared from their breasts, and a vague sentiment of terror supplied its place; so that, although the rites proceeded, they proceeded coldly.

As soon as the service was accomplished the body was removed to the chapel of our Lady—there to remain till night, when the workmen would arrive to place it in the final resting-place of its race. One by one the mourners, with a cold salutation to the knight, departed, leaving the bereaved father alone with the dead. In quitting him no friendly hand had grasped his, no soothing voice had whispered consolation in his ear; it was evident that even those who shared his blood, or who had loved his son, regarded him with distrust; even his bereavement occasioned little sympathy. Men regretted the gallant Henry de Corbey for his own sake; but pronounced his death—they knew not wherefore yet—a judgment upon his dark, unsocial parent.

It was a melancholy picture—the fierce victim of his own evil passions standing alone in that solitary chapel, before the last of his children. Where were now the hopes for which he had steeped his soul in crime, and bartered his heart's repose?—ashes, ashes. Whilst standing before the coffin of the being he had loved with all the strong energy of his nature, how many a faded dream recalled itself—how many a broken promise! And bitterly did his self-accusing heart regret that he had been deaf to his high-spirited boy's entreaties. The tempter Adam was no longer near him. For an instant his long inculcated lessons of infidelity were forgot; the shadow of holy thoughts fell on him, and for the first time for years he felt disposed to pray.

Just as he was about to bend the knee, the same wild laugh which had startled him in the church fell on his ear. He looked up, and beheld the maniac Maud threatening him through the window of the chapel; despair fell on his soul, and he rushed from the spot.

For him the hour of mercy was for ever past. The infidel and assassin could not pray.

CHAPTER VI.

O N the morning after the interment of Henry de Corbey, crowds of citizens, in their holiday costume, accompanied by their sight-loving wives and daughters, might be seen wending their way towards St. Stephen's Gate, then, as now, the principal entrance to the city from the London road. Here and there an alderman, in his furred gown and wand of office, who had been too late at the Guildhall for the procession, fended the crowd, impatient to join his brethren at the above-named gate. The more substantial citizens ventured a familiar jest with these tardy dignitaries as they hurried by, which was repaid by a smile or passed with indifference, according to the relative importance of each man in his ward. The jokes of the weavers and handicraftsmen only reached their ears after they had passed them; for the speakers were far too politic to annoy—unless upon the sly—those who might one day have it in their power to repay them tenfold for their want of prudence. The centre of the street was occupied by a procession of the clergy, who, with banner and cross in air, marched in stately pomp to the place of rendezvous. First came the Dominicans, who were much disliked by the lower order of people, on account of a toll which they exacted from all who passed the bridge adjoining their monastery. Then the secular clergy of the city, the only ecclesiastics who were well received; for their faces were familiar to the people as household friends—comforters whom they applied to in affliction for consolation or advice. After these came the prior and monks of the cathedral, escorted by a strong body of their tenants and dependents, who, well armed, marched on each side of them.

We have before alluded to the disputes between the city and the church, touching their respective jurisdiction, and the privileges of their offices. Matters had risen to such a crisis, that Wolsey himself was expected to arbitrate between them: and it was to await the arrival of the all-powerful minister that the citizens and dignitaries of Norwich were thus hurrying to the city gates.

The armed force by which the prior and monks were accompanied was an unnecessary display. The inhabitants, who had right upon their side, were far too prudent to prejudice their cause by any act of violence at such a moment, especially as it was known that the Duke of Suffolk, the brother-in-law of the king, with a body of eight hundred of the militia of the adjoining counties, accompanied the Cardinal of York in his almost regal progress.

The slow pomp of Wolsey's journey was torture to the impatient, fiery Walter, who rode in his splendid train. They had journeyed rapidly enough till they reached Bury St. Edmund's, where his eminence thought fit to make a retreat at the shrine of the martyred king and saint. By the term retreat, in the Catholic church, is meant the absolute seclusion during two, three, or more days from all worldly occupation, and devoting the time to penitence and prayer. The spot selected is generally some religious house, where the harassed soul, yielding to the influence of solitude and prayer, retempers its weakened energies in blest religious, holy, calm repose.

During the three days which Wolsey devoted to this pious purpose, he remained close shut up in his cell; the abbot of the monastery alone had access to him. All earthly pomp and distinction of rank were cast aside; nor could the officers of his household distinguish their imperious master from the numerous penitents who knelt before the shrine. The same robe enveloped all,—noble and burgher, layman and priest.

On the fourth day orders were given to resume their march to Thetford, where the procession was joined by the Duke of Suffolk and his men, under whose escort it advanced to Norwich.

"Here come the loiterers!" exclaimed a thin, sallow-looking personage, whose robe and chain denoted that he filled the important office of mayor of the ancient and then flourishing city. "Holy St. George! to be behind at such a moment, when the magistracy should put their best face forward! See," he continued, pointing out the procession of the clergy to the two aldermen who joined him under the noble archway of the gate, "how well our enemies are arrayed—no loiterers, no absentees there. A wise man should take a lesson even from his foes."

"Why, ay," said the elder of the party to whom the reproof had been addressed, "St. Peter has used his crook to some purpose—not a sheep of the holy flock seems wanting. How the pious wethers bleat!" he added, as the hymn of the monks rose above the murmurs of the crowd, thickly ranged on each side of the street.

"For shame!" said the town-clerk, who, being a priest—no unusual circumstance at that period—did not relish the jest upon his order; "is it thus you speak of the church? Out upon thee for a Lollard, and no true Christian!"

"Not of the church, father," replied the burly alderman, "but of the shepherds, who think more of the fleece than the flock, more of Peter's peace than Peter; and as for being a Lollard, I pay my Easter dues as regular as e'er a citizen in my ward."

By this time the rival parties faced each other, the corporation and their officers occupying one side of the gate—the clergy, with their banner-bearers and retainers, the other. In their respective positions they very much resembled a cat and dog, restrained from biting or scratching by the presence of their master with the whip—Wolsey was that master.

Scarcely had the parties arranged themselves, than a horseman was seen approaching from the high road. He dashed along at a rapid rate, nor drew rein till the nostrils of his reeking charger were in a line with the mayor's face, which absolutely became purple with indignation at the want of respect paid to his scarlet robe and chain of office. The rider wore the livery of the Duke of Suffolk, who had married the Queen Dowager of France—the rapacious Henry's sister. It was in allusion to this unequal alliance that his grace assumed the well-known device—

Cloth of frieze, be not too bold,
Though thou art match'd with cloth of gold;
Cloth of gold, do not despise,
Though thou art match'd with cloth of frieze.

The conduct of the fortunate noble was as prudent as his device, since he retained through life the favour of his capricious and tyrannical brother-in-law, whose friendship, generally speaking, was as uncertain as his love.

"Advance, my masters!" exclaimed the horseman; "his eminence the cardinal, and my lord of Suffolk, are within bow-shot of your walls. Advance, and quickly, unless you churlishly wish such honourable guests to knock at your very gates before you bid them welcome."

The speaker being in the service of so great a man as the duke, deemed it unnecessary to use more courteous phrase in addressing the authorities of the city, whom, as a military man, he looked down upon with disdain, as a parcel of weavers, traders, and spinners.

"Humph!" whispered the mayor to the senior alderman; "if the jackal barks so loudly, what will the lion's roar be? Would we were well out of the quarrel with our neighbours! See how confidently the prior smiles! I suppose we must move on."

Before his worship could give the necessary order to advance, the question was decided for him by the town-clerk, who quietly told the fellow to return to his master, and say that the magistrates and citizens, in conformity with ancient usage, would receive both himself and his eminence of York at the city gate. Astonished at the order, the messenger was about to reply, but was cut short by the speaker, who, eyeing him with an expression of contempt, demanded how long he had been promoted from the guard-room to the council-chamber of his grace; and bade him at once, without further parley, retire with his message—a piece of advice which the discomfited horseman obeyed.

"Treachery!" exclaimed the mayor, appealing to the aldermen; "clear treachery! The priest has sold us to the prior! Wolsey will never pardon such a message! Let all who love the city follow me," he added;

"it may not yet be too late to retrieve the evil impression of his words."

Several of the less clear-sighted dignitaries who shared his worship's opinion were about to follow him; the officer with the mace had already shouldered the ensign to precede them, when the voice of the town-clerk arrested the man.

"Whither go you?" he demanded.

"To precede his worship and the aldermen," replied the functionary.

"Remain where you are," said the priest; "if Caleb Brown, the cloth-weaver, chooses to pay his respects to the Duke of Suffolk and the Cardinal of York, Heaven forbid that I should prevent him. Doubtless he will be honourably received," he added, sarcastically; "but, as mayor of Norwich, his dignity and office leave him the moment he passes the city gates."

"Ha—ha!" chuckled the alderman whom the peppery chief magistrate had reproved for being late; "broad-cloth within, linsey wolsey without! Who would have thought that standing on the right side of a stone wall could so have improved the quality of a man? Ha—ha—ha! Pity it can't do as much for our merchandise; it would raise the value of the city tolls."

The jovial laugh of the speaker was echoed by most of the corporation, who, sooth to say, were becoming somewhat tired of the pompous, dictatorial manner of his worship, and enjoyed his confusion.

"You have hit me hard, Master Bolton," said the little man—for that was the town clerk's name—trying to swallow his mortification; "but I forgive you, inasmuch as my own zeal outran discretion. You are right—quite right," he continued, in a patronising tone; "it is not for the dignity of the city that the chief magistrate should quit the walls."

"Nor his own," added the previous speaker, who seemed mightily to enjoy the joke.

Eager to secure the favourable opinion of the judge, upon whose opinion so much depended, the prior and monks took advantage of the dispute amongst their rival's party to advance, that they might be the first to bid his eminence welcome to the ancient city, and by contrasting their zeal with the citizens' supineness, offer a delicate flattery, of which no man of his age was perhaps more susceptible than Wolsey. They reached the spot where the cardinal and duke had halted just as the returned messenger repeated, with certain additions, the town-clerk's reply. Suffolk, who was anything but a proud man, listened to it with indifference; but there was an angry spot on the churchman's brow, which presaged the reception of the city authorities when they should meet; the prior, on the contrary, was most graciously received.

"We are pleased to believe so!" exclaimed Wolsey, with a flushed brow, at the conclusion of the address which the town-clerk read, and which expressed the joy of the magistrates and citizens at receiving him within their ancient walls; "although, God's truth, you gave scant earnest of it, in waiting, like unwilling hosts, till we approached your gates before you bade us welcome."

"So please your eminence, it was to testify our deep respect."

"Respect!" repeated the cardinal in a doubtful tone; "the mode was somewhat novel."

"Respect," repeated the town-clerk, modestly but firmly; "here for ages the city has been accustomed to receive its sovereigns and rulers; the usage, my good lord, is older even than our earliest charter."

Wolsey's brow cleared up—the storm was passing.

"Here we are magistrates and authorities, our voices have a respect and mirage value; beyond this gate we are nothing more than simple citizens, unfit to thrust ourselves into your gracious presence, where reverend respect alone should greet, and bold, presuming confidence be dumb."

This time the churchman smiled, for the flattery, though apparent, was neither uncalled for nor indelicate.

"Enough, master clerk," he said, "enough; we knew not that the charter of your goodly city was so limited. Ere our departure we will speak further on the matter, and see if it cannot be amended; meanwhile, let the mayor and aldermen precede us to our lodging. We are my Lord of Norfolk's guests," he added, bowing to the duke, who rode upon his right hand, "and trust to spend some days within your walls."

The windows in St. Stephen's Street and the Market Place, through which the procession passed, were filled with the wives and daughters of the gentry and citizens, all eager to catch a glimpse of the magnificent minister, whose state was said to rival his master's. Anxiously did Walter, who rode in the cavalcade, scrutinise each fair face as he slowly moved along, in the hope of recognising the heiress of Stanfield. Little did he deem that the object of his search was a prisoner in the ancient keep of Norwich Castle, upon a charge of murdering her kinsman. Lovely were the forms, red the lips, and bright the eyes which met his gaze; but unfortunately they were neither the forms, the lips, nor eyes he sought, and the chill of dis-

WALTER DISCOVERING THE SKELETON OF CUTHBERT.

appointment fell upon his heart as he reined his steed in the court-yard of the Duke of Norfolk's stately palace, without having met with one familiar face amongst the crowd, or heard a single voice to bid him welcome. As soon as his eminence and the two dukes had entered the house, he threw the reins of his horse to one of the numerous grooms, and rushed into the street to make his way to Steadman's, where he felt assured of obtaining some tidings of his mistress. He found the old man disconsolately seated in the chamber at the end of his warehouse, his

pale, anxious face reclined upon his hand, and his eyes red with weeping. Walter was much shocked, deeming at first that it was illness which had changed him. His sister Maud was tranquilly seated by the diamond latticed window, which looked upon the river, reading her missal. The excitement of the previous day had passed away, and the maniac was comparatively calm.

As the spurs upon the heels of the young man rang upon the stone floor, the honest wool-comber raised his eyes and recognised him. Their meeting, though cordial, was a

No. 35.

sad one. Nothing could equal the astonishment and indignation of Walter Lucas on hearing the death of Henry de Corbey, and the accusation which it had brought upon the Lady Mary. The old man's tale of the mendicant friar who held and him on the watch, and his inexplicable .... alarmed and confused him. The future appeared like a mist, through which appalling shadows alone were dimly visible.

"Oh! 'tis a deep-laid scheme," he said, "to ....

.... pale—oh! so .... my ...... gaze on it. Shall I tell you what he ... posed me?—that I should be revenged ... had revenged at last—and as I ...... patient. Yes yes," she added, ... as if replying to her own .... thoughts, "it will be cleared up soon."

"It will indeed," said Walter; "forgotten deeds are hourly brought to light; no book so sealed but time unfolds the page, and keen-eyed justice reads the damning record of our crimes at last."

"What mean you?" demanded Steadman, struck by the solemnity of his words and manner.

"Nothing," replied the young man; for the strict command of Wolsey to keep silence respecting the discovery of the unfortunate armourer's bones fettered his tongue, "or at least nothing more than to inculcate faith and patience." Fearing to be questioned upon the subject, their visitor hastily took his leave, promising to return the following day. The first spot to which he directed his steps was the castle, where he vainly prayed for an interview with the prisoner; for the governor was in the interests of her accuser, whose newly acquired wealth gave him the means of paying largely for the services of

all who sell their souls for gain. Disappointed in his intention, with a heavy heart he turned from the ancient keep, and retraced his way to the palace of the Duke of Norfolk, where our readers may remember the cardinal was .... His purpose was, if possible, to obtain an audience of Wolsey, the last anchor on which he could rely in this sudden shipwreck of his hopes.

It was not till after the evening banquet that our hero found the opportunity he ....

.... of the king, ... the inflexi-................ who demanded the .... firmness .... and the .... equally .... honour it must .... the final sentence which Campeggio .... pronounced, the .... Katherine was treated by him with all .... Wolsey was too clear-sighted not to perceive the rocks and quicksands by which he was surrounded, and even his firm spirit trembled at the danger. It was, therefore, with something like pleasure that he beheld the tapestried entrance to his chamber drawn aside, and Walter present himself. The presence of the youth was a relief to his weary, overtaxed mind. The great man almost smiled as the youth bent the knee before him.

"We have heard it all!" he exclaimed; "Henry de Corbey's death and the knight's accusation. I fear me our retreat at Bury has had an evil influence on the poor maid's fortunes."

"It has indeed!" sighed Walter, who felt that, if his master had but arrived in Norwich those three days sooner, all would have been well.

"But not irreparable," said the cardinal.

"That is," he added, gravely, "if she be innocent."

"If she be innocent!" repeated her lover. "My life that she is innocent! Mary—the good, the gentle Mary—guilty of murder! Should an angel's tongue, my lord, proclaim her guilty, I never could believe it."

"You vouch it boldly," observed Wolsey.

"Because I know her heart—her soul—her mind; and all are sinless as a young seraph's thought. I have watched their opening dawn—weighed in love's balance each rising impulse, action, word — and found, like angels' smiles, each purer than the last."

"Such," said the churchman, "is the blind confidence of youth, which believeth all things where it loves. The heart's bitter task from the cradle to the grave is but to forget its trust in man's integrity and woman's faith. As we advance," he continued, "in life's dull road, mask after mask is rent aside, till we behold the idol of our dreams stripped of the grace imagination lent it. In all humanity's sad, stern reality, we wake from dreaming only with our footsteps in the grave."

"If this be true, my lord," answered his hearer, "let me descend there with unbroken dreams. Better to live the world's blind fool, than its far-seeing cynic. I could not bear to feel within my heart no other tenant than dark mistrust, or thrust forth friendship and confiding love, to make the seat of life a charnel-house."

A cold, bitter smile passed over the features of his eminence as he listened to the impassioned words of the speaker. Perhaps he remembered the time when he believed like him; perhaps he doubted his sincerity, and demanded of himself if the young man was not acting a part to win his confidence. He resolved to try him further.

"Think you," he demanded, "that Sir John de Corbey could have been accessory to his son's death?"

"Heaven forbid that I should wrong mine enemy," said Walter; "not willingly, my lord. He loved the boy too well; he was his hope, his life's ambition — a being of generous impulse and high thought — a heart so pure, a spirit so ingenuous, they made men wonder at capricious nature that such a son should spring from such a father."

Wolsey's brow relaxed, for he *knew* that the youth had measured justice both to his rival and his enemy.

"There is some mystery," continued his visitor, "which time or chance may give the key to. Oh, my dread lord," he added, "one word, one little word from you will save her. We have a witness, a wandering friar, who, concealed within the chamber, witnessed young Henry's death."

"A wandering friar!" repeated his hearer.

"Put off the trial till that man be found," continued Walter; "upon my knees I ask it —for life, fame, love, all hang upon his breath. Can you hesitate, my lord, when you already have such fearful proof of what her enemies are capable?"

"I cannot stay the course of justice," said Wolsey. "There are respects where even power must pause."

"But you can guide her steps, my lord," interrupted the pleader. "Remember, she is blindfold, and her sword, without your arm to stay it, may strike the innocent and spare the guilty."

"What I dare do, I will," resumed his master; "orders shall be given to find the man you speak of. Have you," he demanded, fixing his eyes keenly upon him, "revealed to any one the mystery of the murderer's death?"

"No," replied Walter; "and yet the secret burns upon my tongue! I long to brand the villain to the public scorn, strip him of the cloak hypocrisy has cast around him, and show the world the foul deformity it hides. But I have been silent."

"Be silent still," said the churchman. "Why I demand this you are not the judge; how I shall use it you have yet to learn. Of what order," he added, carelessly, "was this friar you spoke of?"

"Of the Mendicants?"

"Good; and now retire; in the morning my chancellor will give you an order to admit you to the Lady Mary; hear her version of this fearful story; it may perchance present a clue to guide us through the labyrinth. Go," continued his grace, "and remember Heaven is not the less prepared to strike, because its arm is veiled in clouds. Go, and if the maid be really innocent, go in confidence and hope."

"I could almost trust that boy," he murmured to himself, after Walter had withdrawn; "the world hath not spoiled him yet —ambition's fire not quite corrupted his young heart. As he spoke how the memories of my youth returned! Methought I listened to his dead father's voice—to the companion of my boyhood's years—to him whose merry laugh mocked the aspiring hopes of greatness, which childish confidence oft pictured forth in friendship's trusting hour. They are realised," he added, proudly; "dreams have become realities; but am I happier? I must not ask myself that question, lest I should find the hill I mounted with such toilsome steps is ashes—ashes—ashes!"

With an effort the speaker dismissed from his mind the train of thought into which he had fallen, and resumed the perusal of his papers. In a few moments he was again the statesman.

Early on the following morning, as Walter left the palace, he was accosted by Patch, who, for once, had doffed his motley suit of office, and was attired in a dress of black, more befitting a reverend divine than a jester.

"Whither goest thou?" he demanded, as our hero passed the gate. "Thou hast a face as long as the chamberlain's wand, and as woe-begone as a rejected suitor's."

"It reflects my heart," replied the young man, "for my errand is a sad one."

"Take folly with thee, then," said Patch; "it is the salt which seasons life—the antidote to melancholy and the spleen. They are your fools, who rail at mirth and cannot see a sermon in a jest."

"Not now," exclaimed the impatient lover; "I am too sad for jesting."

"I will be dull then, too," continued the intruder; "why, man, it is my nature. I am like Janus, double-faced—a moral death's head with a painted mask, folly on one side, wisdom on the other. There," he added, screwing his features into an expression of solemnity, to which his laughing, mischief-loving eye gave the silent lie—"a mourning heir at a miser's funeral could not better act his part. What, not one smile! Then thou art sad indeed."

"I go," said Walter, "to visit innocence in a dungeon."

"Ah! then I must go with thee," resumed the persevering jester; "in such a case a fool will be, in the world's opinion, thy fit companion; for sober wisdom, boy, will scout thee for it. Visit innocence in a palace," he continued, "an thou wilt. Nay, even in a cottage, without great imprudence, it may be sometimes risked—upon the sly; but in a prison? Psha! Had I not been too long at court to blush, my cheek would crimson for thee."

"Thou hast a kind heart," exclaimed the young man, who perfectly understood the speaker's bitter humour.

"Have I?" said Patch. "Keep the discovery a secret, then, I pray you."

"Why so?"

"The world would only find it out to wound it. Hearts are like flying fish—the shark and albatros both prey upon them."

"Have with thee," said the young man, with a melancholy smile; "since thou art resolved on such dull company, take it not amiss if I entreat thy presence no further than——"

"Fear not, I have a character to lose," interrupted his companion, resuming at once his former sarcastic tone, "and know the world too well to let it catch me in an act so foolish as visiting the unfortunate—a crime were nothing to it. I shall intrude no further than the gate."

Walter was struck with the natural delicacy of the speaker, and the tact with which he understood his wishes. On their way to the castle he related to him the story of his love—its trials, hopes, and fears; painted with a lover's eloquence the grace and virtue of the Lady Mary, and the knight's heartless, cold oppression. On hearing the relation of the murder of Henry de Corbet, and the sudden disappearance of the mendicant friar, the jester became deeply interested, and weighed his words attentively.

"You still believe her innocent?" he demanded.

"I could swear it," replied our hero.

"So could I."

"You!"

"I?" repeated Patch; "look not so surprised, for folly hath a logic of its own, which, after all, is nearer allied to wisdom than men think. As thus: sober reason slowly proceeds from the premise into the consequence, while folly jumps it—a process far more expeditious," he added, with a cheerful smile, "and quite as satisfactory."

"Wolsey hath promised to seek out this man," continued Walter, "upon whose evidence so much depends."

"He'll keep his word," drily observed the jester, "be it for good or ill."

By this time they had reached the castle, which, for many years, had been converted into a county and city prison. This time the governor, who seemed disconcerted at their arrival, was all civility and smiles; the sight of the cardinal's seal to the order of admission had wrought a wondrous change in him.

How shall we describe the interview of the long separated lovers—its tears and confidence, its hopes and fears? The prisoner, who, since the death of her cousin, had listened to no friendly voice, had met no sympathising look, sobbed on the breast of the scarcely less agitated Walter, as with broken words and sighs she related all the terrors of that fearful night—his father's cruelty—Henry's devoted death, and the mysterious conduct of the mendicant friar, in whose integrity, despite his unaccountable disappearance, she placed firm faith, declaring her firm conviction that his absence was owing to the machinations of her enemies, and not to any participation in their crimes. Her suitor, in his turn, described his reception by Wolsey, and the interest which the still powerful minister expressed in her sad fate. Bitterly did he lament the delay occasioned by the retreat at St. Edmund's shrine, a delay which had given the ruthless knight time to spread the net in which his victim was so fearfully entangled.

Whilst the youthful pair are thus occupied in sweet intercourse of mutual consolation, let us return to the jester, who remained in the court-yard of the castle, gravely occupied in examining the curious architecture of the ancient pile, in the contemplation of which he seemed absorbed, but whose restless, prying eyes, in reality, noticed every trifling incident that occurred.

Nearly an hour had thus passed, when the door of the turret, which led to the governor's apartment, opened, and the functionary, whose confusion on their arrival Patch had noticed, appeared, accompanied by a tall, thin, grey-haired man, whose aquiline nose, piercing black eyes, and sharp intellectual features, denoted an Italian, rather than Saxon origin. There was a degree of affectation in the indifference with which they crossed the court, and the careless adieu of the functionary to his companion at the gate, which the shrewd observer failed not to note. The likeness to the physician of Sir John de Corbey, a personage whom Walter, during their walk, had minutely described, instantly struck him. The fool was not far wrong in his guess.

"You seem interested, sir, in these old walls," said the governor, with a cringing civility; "many a curious deed has passed within them."

"Doubtless," said Patch, drily.

"Many have died here by the axe and cord," continued the man, not altogether pleased with the tone of the reply.

"Any by poisoning?" demanded the jester, fixing his eyes upon the speaker.

"Poi—poisoning?" repeated the fellow, the blood, despite his habitude of self-control, rushing into his cheek; "not—that—I know of; how should I?"

"Ah! I thought you might."

There was a pause; the governor mentally cursing his folly for having provoked a conversation upon a subject which circumstances rendered dangerous and unpleasant. He felt that it was necessary to say something, for each moment's silence added to his embarrassment.

"You belong to his good grace of York?" he at last faltered out.

"No."

"No!"

"His good grace of York belongs to me," said the jester, with a gravity which might have deceived keener wits than the dull gaoler's. "I have dined and supped upon him for these twelve years past."

"I understand you," replied the fellow, with a broad grin. "Doubtless he is a profitable master; you turn the penny by him."

The jester relaxed the gravity of his expression, and screwed up his features with so knowing a look, that the gaoler's grin gradually expanded itself into a hearty laugh, in which his visitor joined. From a protuberance about the chest of the rascal's doublet, he judged that a bag of coin, or a parcel of some kind, had been hastily thrust there, and he determined in his own peculiar way to ascertain the fact. Continuing, therefore, to laugh and twist his face into every possible variety of expression, he gradually approached the governor, and in the paroxysm of their mirth gave him a friendly poke, such as one man might familiarly offer to another in good fellowship, upon the chest, just where the appearance excited his suspicion. A faint chink followed the blow. The gaoler's laugh instantly ceased, and he eyed him suspiciously.

"Par Dieu!" said Patch, wiping his eyes, which overflowed, "but you keep your keys in a curious pocket."

"I can't be too careful," replied the man.

"Of course not," answered his companion, gravely, fully convinced in his own mind that the sound proceeded from coin of some kind.

"Would you like to see the dungeons?" demanded the governor; "some of them are curious in their architecture. I can show you places," he added, "which common eyes have seldom gazed upon."

The proposal was assented to, and calling for a torch, the governor preceded his guest down a low arched passage, leading to the subterranean dungeons which had existed from the Saxon times, and where Canute had doubtless kept his prisoners. They were excavated in the mound on which the keep stood.

In less than an hour Patch returned whistling, alone; and on the following morning a new governor, who had been appointed by Wolsey, took possession of his office in the castle.

It was a dangerous thing to play at cross purposes with the jester.

The morning at last arrived on which the anxiously-expected trial was to take place, and the county hall was crowded with the rank and beauty of the neighbourhood. The youth of the prisoner, the historic name she bore, and the many dark rumours which attached themselves to the fame of her guardian, had contributed to excite interest and curiosity to the highest pitch. At one end of the court the three judges were seated; the presiding one was the father of the celebrated Sir Thomas More, who succeeded Wolsey as chancellor of England. At a table beneath their elevated seat were the advocates and prosecutors in the cause. The Lady Mary, attended only by her lover and the faithful Steadman, was, in consideration of her station, accommodated with a chair, and spared the humiliation of the felon's dock. Her features were pale, but dignified. The friar, upon whose evidence so much depended, despite the exertions and promise of the cardinal, had not been found; and her only hope was that her judges might be induced to postpone the trial in order to give further time to find him.

It was remarked that, during the proceedings, Sir John de Corbey never once raised his eyes towards his injured kinswoman; whilst Adam, on the contrary, was frequently seen to regard her with an expression of pity and interest.

As soon as the jury had been sworn, the advocate for the prosecution rose to address the court. He began by painting the virtues of the deceased — his noble character and ancient lineage — and the love it was well known he bore to the accused; "a love," he added, "which has severed the last branch of a noble tree — a love which, instead of awakening sympathy, engendered hate — a love whose bridal couch hath been the grave. This honourable court," continued the speaker, "can well imagine that Sir John de Corbey received with pleasure the prospect of a union which promised to cement the happiness of his son and the honour of his family. Unfortunately, the wishes, the passions of the prisoner were opposed to such arrangements; her affections, I regret to say, having been artfully seduced by one whom her guardian, from a mistaken charity, had reared in his household, warmed the half-frozen viper till it stung him, and who does not hesitate to appear in this solemn presence — affronting justice by his hardiness, insulting the childless parent, of whose bereavement he has indirectly been the cause."

Walter bit his lips till the blood started to hear himself so characterised, but for the prisoner's sake was silent.

The advocate, after concluding his vituperative charge, was about to call his witnesses, when the counsel for the Lady Mary arose, and demanded a postponement of the trial, on the ground of the absence of a necessary witness — a mendicant friar, who, concealed within the chamber, witnessed the whole transaction, and whose evidence he contended would not only prove the innocence of the presumed culprit, but turn the accusation most fearfully on her accusers.

The judges whispered together, and, after some minutes' consultation, demanded of the speaker if he had any corroborative proofs to offer of the existence of such a person and friar.

Steadman was sworn before the court.

"I object to that man's evidence!" exclaimed the opposing advocate; "I can call witnesses before this honourable court to prove that for years he has been known to entertain a deadly rancour towards Sir John de Corbey; that he has frequently threatened him with vengeance — predicted dishonour, ruin to his house — nay, often boasted that he would bring him to a scaffold yet."

Witnesses were called, who, unfortunately, were but too well able to prove the intemperate threats of the bluff old soldier. It was decided by the judges that his evidence should not be taken, and as no other person had seen the friar, the objection was overruled, and the trial ordered to proceed.

"Lost!" sighed the unhappy girl, as she sank with her head upon her lover's shoulder; "my last hope gone!"

Steadman, half mad with passion and indignation, rushed from the court, where perjury and corruption for a time carried everything before them. Flying anywhere to avoid the crowd, the broken-hearted man directed his steps towards the church of the Domincians, in which Wolsey held his legitimate court, where, however, he seldom presided in person, leaving that office to his chancellor and two doctors of divinity retained for that especial purpose. As the wool-comber crossed the cloister he beheld to his astonishment the stately figure of the mendicant hurrying before him; for a moment he could scarcely believe his senses, but deemed it was some vision; once convinced of the reality, however, he sprang upon the friar, and seizing him by his robe, exclaimed—

"Friar or devil, I've found you, then, at last."

"What means the slave?" demanded the astonished man.

"Slave! I am an Englishman—no slave," replied Steadman; "more, I am a constable, and I seize on you as a witness in the cause of the heiress of Stanfield, accused of murder. Will you go with me?"

"No."

"Then," said his captor, most inconveniently tightening his grasp, "I'll make you."

"I'm a priest," exclaimed the friar.

"If you were a bishop you should go," coolly answeerd Steadman, "though I did penance for a month for laying hands upon your rochet. So come," he added, dragging the friar, with a grasp of iron, towards the gate. "You may as well come quietly; for, by our bluff king Harry's oath, dead or alive, you follow me."

"Madman!" exclaimed the prisoner; "loose your hold. What, ho, guard! treason! treason!"

In an instant the officers and soldiers who were in attendance on the vice-legates rushed from the church, for the voice was not unknown to them. The struggling men were surrounded and separated.

"An attack upon the cardinal!" exclaimed one of the officers, who recognised the friar's face—"cut the villain to pieces!"

A slight wave of the hand restrained them.

"The cardinal!" repeated Steadman, sinking on his knee.

For a few moments Wolsey regarded the old man with a flushed brow and angry eye; which gradually, however, gave place to a kindlier look, when he remembered how he had been mystified.

"Knowest thou the penalty incurred," he demanded, "for laying hands upon a prelate?"

"No," replied the prisoner, bluntly; "but I daresay death. You are great and powerful—I poor and honest. I care not for myself, but for one I love like my own child. They drove me from the court," he added, "because, forsooth, my tongue had been sometimes faster than my wits—refused my evidence, as if I could bring my soul to lie even against my enemy. Mary says one word from you will save her. Ah! I see a gracious smile upon your lip, which tells or imports she is——"

"Innocent!" interrupted Wolsey, kindly. "Away to the court-house! I shall be there as soon as you—to do a deed that shall strike earth's guilty great ones with dismay. Captain," added the speaker, "I

do discharge you of your prisoner. Summon my escort and my household; we will but doff this guise, and then set forth at once."

Steadman was no sooner released than he flew with the rapidity of a far younger man towards the court-house, from which he had so lately rushed. How different were his feelings on his return! He felt that he was the bearer of hope, life, love; his heart was full of its intelligence, and every instant seemed an age till he discharged the burthen. During his absence the work of perjury and crime had advanced towards its completion; despite the prisoner's simple tale, the defence of her advocate, and the indignant, impassioned appeal of Walter, the jury had pronounced her guilty, and the presiding judge was about to pronounce sentence.

"Death!" exclaimed the old man, bursting into the court, and repeating that word of the judge; "who talks of death, when I bring life and honour? He's found—the witness found!"

Adam laid his hand upon Sir John's arm, who had involuntarily started from his seat at the intelligence.

"A mere subterfuge, my lord," said the advocate, rising, "they have no witness."

"No witness!" repeated Steadman; "you lie. No witness! Ha! ha! ha! he will soon be here."

At this moment the clash of arms without announced the arrival of the cardinal.

"No witness!" he continued, with an hysterical laugh. "Behold!"

The great entrance to the court was thrown open, and Wolsey, in his robes of state, attended by his officers, entered the court. All rose to receive him. Walter's heart beat wildly—he remembered his master's promise.

"Be seated, my good lords," exclaimed his eminence to the judges; "we are here to perform an act of justice."

The heiress of Stanfield sank upon her knees in gratitude; she knew that she was saved; she recognised in the deep-toned voice of the speaker the witness she had sought—that the mendicant friar and Wolsey were the same.

CHAPTER VII.

But Truth shall yet be heard—no human power
Can stifle or corrupt her purposes.
Through Superstition's gloom her voice is heard—
It pierces through the veil of barbarous ages,
And injured Virtue walks triumphant forth,
Freed from the taint of calumny and crime.—CREON.

ITH a precision, every word of which sounded in the ears of the astounded Sir John de Corbey and his accomplice like a death-knell, Wolsey related all that had passed in the chamber of the prisoner on the evening of her cousin's death. Many a bright eye was gemmed with tears as their fair hearers listened to the story of a boy's devotion and a father's crime. The persecutions to which the orphan heiress had been subjected were detailed at length, and the heartless villany of her false guardian made clear as day. Not content, it seems, with the accusation to which she had so nearly fallen a sacrifice, the knight had, through the ministry of his agent, Adam, attempted to poison his victim even in the last fearful sanctuary of the laws—her prison. The late governor of the castle—whom Patch, the jester, had cleverly made a prisoner, at the very moment when that functionary, under the pretence of showing him the dungeons, had intended him the same kind office, was produced in court, and acknowledged that he had received a certain sum of money to mix a powder, which the Italian had provided him with, in the Lady Mary's food. From the promptitude with which he had been secured, both the poison and the bribe were found upon him. The wretch confessed to everything, for he knew into whose iron grasp he had fallen, and that his only hope of mercy was in truth. A yell of execration, which even the majesty of justice failed to repress, rose from the auditory, as one by one the crimes of the prosecutor were laid bare. Warm, sympathising friends thronged round the agitated and still weeping prisoner, eager to atone by present kindness the injustice of their past suspicion. But the interest and excitement of the scene were still further increased, when, on a signal from the cardinal, four officers appeared in court bearing a black chest, which they deposited on the table before the judges, who commanded it to be opened. Expectation was raised to its utmost pitch, as the usher of the court raised the lid and disclosed a human skeleton; the girdle of iron and the collar round the neck, together with the staples which had riveted them to the wall, still remaining on the mouldering bones. At the same instant several of the halberdiers secured the persons of the knight and Adam. The brow of Sir John became suddenly flushed, and he was observed to stagger at the sight. Even the usually pale face of the leech became paler as he gazed on the fearful evidence of a crime which he deemed long since buried in oblivion.

On perceiving that his eminence was about to speak, there was a breathless silence in the court. Men felt that a strange revelation was taking place, one of those extraordinary developments in which unerring Providence vindicates the justice of its ways to man—hunts guilt from out the cunning labyrinth where it hides, demolishes its subtle guard, its covered trenches, its well planned citadel, and from the fragments of its vain defences constructs the proofs which send it to the scaffold.

"Knowest thou," he demanded, fixing his cold glance upon the murderer, "knowest thou these bones?"

Shame and desperation gave to the guilty man a courage to which the terror of his glance and quivering lip gave the silent lie. With an effort worthy of a better cause he firmly answered in the negative.

"Nor these fetters?" continued his interrogator, pointing to the manacles remaining on the skeleton.

"No."

"This may, perhaps, refresh your memory, sir knight," said Wolsey, at the same time throwing upon the table the scabbard which Walter had found in the recess. "It bears a name should wake an echo in thy conscience, unless, like them, it is of iron—Cuthbert, the armourer's."

"My dream, my dream comes true at last!" shrieked the maniac mother of the victim, who, with the cunning peculiar to insanity, remembering her former forcible expulsion from the church, had remained a quiet spectator of the trial. "Heaven hath

HENRY DRAINS THE POISONED CHALICE TO SAVE THE LADY MARY.

heard the widow's prayer, and will avenge her wrong!"

There is a majesty in sorrow which even the vulgar must respect. The people made way for the wretched Maud, who advanced from the crowd of spectators into the body of the court. Approaching the table where the ghastly remains of her son were placed, she raised the crumbling skeleton in her arms, and imprinted a maternal kiss upon the fleshless brow. The skull of the murdered youth reclined upon her bosom, upon the pillow where in smiling infancy it so oft had lain, and whence its innocent lips had drawn the first pure stream of life. It was an appalling picture to behold the living and the dead locked in that close embrace. Even the judges, accustomed from their painful office to scenes of misery, were moved to pity, and all but the assassins wept.

"Curse him!" she exclaimed, in a voice broken by convulsive sobs, and raising at the same time her withered hand to heaven, "curse him, thou righteous Judge! Bare thy red arm in justice forth, and launch the eternal bolt within his heart! Dry the springs of penitence within him, that no absolving tears gush forth to cleanse it of its foulness! Strike him with unbelief! harden him to his perdition! Living, let fiends possess his impious soul, and mocking devils jibber at his prayers! Withhold the boon of madness from him! Sleep fly his burning eye-lids as from a couch accursed! Let him loathe life, yet shrink with childhood's terror at death's coming shadow. Despair and infamy go with him to his dungeon, and mock him on the scaffold! I am heard!" she added, with a laugh, whose frantic mirth made the stoutest present shudder. "John de Corbey, the widow and the mother's curse is writ against thee in the Book of Life—ha! ha! ha! My boy and I will sit in heaven together and laugh at thy eternal agony; laugh as thy black soul writhes in its lake of fire!"

"Peace, woman!" said the presiding judge, after a silence which lasted several minutes, and which even he almost feared to break, so intense was the horror and excitement created by her passionate imprecations. "Even the guilty have feelings to be respected; the majesty of justice must not be outraged by a scene like this. Remove her from the court," he added, turning to the ushers who were standing behind the sheriff; "but do it with all gentleness."

Two of the officers approached to obey the order, but Maud, clasping the remains of her son still closer to her heart as for protection, fixed on them a look so wild that even they hesitated to approach her.

"Withered be the hand that touches me!" she cried; "accursed of God and man! Would you separate the mother from her child—from her long-hidden treasure? I'll be calm," she added; "silent as the voice which made life's only music to my widowed heart; but I must remain: I shall go mad else—mad with man's injustice—mad with my grief and wrongs. There—the dead and I will wait in silence and in patience—wait for earth's justice on our woes together."

With as much tenderness as a young mother could have shown her first-born child, the maniac placed her frightful burden upon the ground, and seated herself beside it. Removing the long black wimple from her head, she covered the remains with it as with a funeral pall. The action permitted her long white hair to fall dishevelled, like a silver veil, upon her shoulders. Judges and spectators alike were deeply moved; the former motioned to the officers to permit her to remain. Indeed it would have been difficult, in all that vast assembly to have found a heart sufficiently hard, or an arm strong enough to remove her.

As the verdict against the heiress of Stanfield had not been recorded, no further process was necessary than that the jury, on the recommendation of the judges, should reconsider their judgment, which for form's sake they did, and unanimously and instantly pronounced her not guilty. The joy of the assembly would have been far more boisterously expressed, had not the strange emotions they had been subjected to damped their ardour. They respected also the presence of the dead, and the desolate mother who watched beside it. The fervent pressure of her lover's hand was more grateful to the rescued victim than a hundred congratulations.

"Come," said Wolsey, in a kind and serious voice, taking her by the hand, "this scene fits not a woman's presence; for the present, the convent's walls will be your best retreat—at least till you depart for London."

"For London!" answered the Lady Mary, with surprise; "and why not, my lord, for Stanfield?"

"For London," he repeated, gravely; "our gracious master remembers the debt of gratitude due to your ancient house, and the good queen intends to guard you near her person till a fitting marriage relieve her of your care."

The heiress sighed. The words "a fitting marriage" seemed a fresh barrier to her happiness. The churchman smiled, for he read the maiden's thought, and whispered a word, as he glanced at Walter, which brought the warm blood once more to her pale cheek, and reassured her heart. Both were deceived; trials which neither the cardinal nor the heiress dreamt of were in store for both.

"Farewell, my lords," said Wolsey, addressing the judges, who, with all present, rose on his departure. "I have performed my duty; you," he added, pointing to Sir John de Corbey and his accomplice, "doubtless will do yours. Let the trial commence at once, lest justice should accuse us of delay."

"Save me," whispered the knight to the leech, who watched the departure of the cardinal as coolly as if he were a mere spectator in the court, and not a criminal arraigned upon a charge touching his life; "is there no way to snatch me from dishonour and the grave?"

"None," laconically answered Adam, in the same undertone; "the butcher's cur hath got firm hold."

"I would live," continued the wretched man—"live for repentance, for atonement."

"Psha!"

"Live," he iterated, "even in a cloister or a dungeon."

"What difference," demanded the Italian, "between them and the grave? I blush to call thee pupil. Dismiss these idle terrors from thy mind—feeble humanity's first and last weakness—and welcome, like me, thy long, eternal sleep."

About an hour after the departure of the cardinal the trial of Sir John de Corbey and his accomplice commenced. The first witness who appeared against them was Father Celestine, whom Walter, to his surprise, afterwards found had all the while travelled in Wolsey's train from London; but so secretly had his eminence taken his precautions, and such were the means at his command, that to all but himself his presence had been unsuspected.

The good priest's deposition proved the arrival of the armourer in company with the prisoner on the night of his disappearance at the old mansion on the bank of the Thames; also, the sudden death of two of the servants the ensuing morning—men who were known to have been deep in the confidence of their master, and who had been present during the fatal interview in the chamber of the tower; which chamber, by Sir John's order, had been afterwards closed, and the household for years carefully kept from all admission to it. He afterwards related the arrival of the fugitive, and the circumstances which led to the discovery of the fatal recess during his concealment from Adam and his pursuers.

As soon as his evidence was completed, the leech, who all the while had eyed him with the glance of a basilisk, wrote a few hasty words upon a slip of paper, and gave it to one of the servants who had attended him and the knight to court. The fellow instantly disappeared with it. The colour of the witness slightly changed; he guessed the purport of the writing; he knew the thunderbolt was launched, but was prepared to meet it.

If the spectators had been appalled at the simple relation of the priest, their indignation was roused to the highest pitch by the eloquent description of Walter, who described with the energetic eloquence of youth the horrors of the victim's death—his distorted limbs, dislocated by his fearful despairing struggles in the living tomb to which his merciless destroyers had consigned him. A thrill of pity and terror ran through the veins of all; men listened with a silent fascination to the tale which charmed their senses and caused their blood to creep like the spell of the nightmare. The only sounds to be heard were the stifled convulsive sobs of the heart-broken widow of the victim.

"Merciless—merciless villains!" she exclaimed, "was it for this I bore him?—did Heaven permit me to become a parent only to lose him thus? Cuthbert, my boy, my martyred child!" she added, apostrophising the sad remains beside her, "would that the life blood of thy mother could have saved thee from these butchers!"

Thrice did Sir John, when called on by the judges for his defence, rise and essay to speak. On every face he read his condemnation; every eye turned from his gaze with loathing and abhorrence. Confusion, and not remorse, overwhelmed him. The last time he sank upon his seat in sullen, hopeless despair. What could he urge against a tale so clear?—what plea advance to touch the heart of Justice?—what subtle lie, what plausible excuse avail him against the mute pleading of that lonely woman? Mourning like Eve over her murdered child, her very presence was his condemnation. The Heaven he so long had braved with impunity confounded him at last.

At this moment the domestic whom Adam had dispatched returned, and placed a sealed packet in the leech's hand, who hastily breaking the envelope, drew from it the book Luther had written in reply to Henry's defence of the seven sacraments of the church, and which our readers may remember he had found in the chamber of Father Celestine on the night of his visit to the house in London.

The jury, directly after the summing of the judges, returned a verdict of guilty against both.

When asked why sentence of death should not be pronounced, Adam alone replied; his voice was as low and musical as ever, and it was only from the bitter sarcasm which occasionally broke forth that men could perceive his heart of stone was moved.

"Were the question you have asked, my lords," he began, "other than one of those bitter mockeries in which humanity delights, I might, perhaps, dispute the right to punish one murder by another—the right for dust to judge its fellow dust—to wrest the high prerogative of Deity, by annihilating life, as if its hands had grown too feeble to uphold the balance. Such a plea, however, would serve me little here—it would be urged ages too soon. But a time will come when it must be heard; when mankind, starting like sleepers from a dream, will ask of earth's pale rulers and their laws questions which kings and priests will find it hard to answer. Not yet," he added, "not yet—not yet."

"Heretic!" exclaimed the presiding judge, in a tone of indignation.

"Your children's cuildren," said Adam, with a smile, "perchance may call me by another name."

"And that is——"

"Philosopher."

"Philosopher!" iterated the legist, with a look of scorn—"what school?"

"Of one which yet hath known few pupils and still less admirers," replied the leech, unmoved by the expression of contempt—"of one whose lessons, like the lines traced by the eternal wave upon the rock, imprinted once, become indelible; men even now begin to mark its letters, and soon will learn to read them."

"Perish such doctrines," said another of the judges; "they pervert mankind."

"Thought cannot perish," mildly answered the Italian. "You may destroy the temple in your blind madness," he added, at the same time slightly touching his brow; "but the God defies your feeble malice; a truth once uttered is immortal, and cannot be destroyed; like an event, it slumbers cradled on the wing of time, sure to arrive at last."

"Cursed follower of Luther!"

"Of Luther!" interrupted Adam; "of him who broke one chain to forge mankind another—of the beer-swilling German, whose dull eyes mistook truth's shadow for its substance? No; he dreams as little of my school as thou dost. Of Luther!" he repeated. "To prove that our affinities approach no nearer than our common dust, I'll yield another victim to the list of those who suffer through his errors."

The book, the mere possession of which was looked upon by the vindictive Henry and his ministers as a species of treason and sacrilege, was handed by the prisoner to one of the ushers, who gave it to the judge. The man of law piously crossed himself as he read the title. Unfortunately, it contained within its leaves the letter which the brother of the unfortunate Celestine had written to him from Germany when he forwarded the fatal volume, and the poor priest was instantly arrested. He submitted with a sigh of resignation, for he knew that his doom was fixed, and sought not by useless struggles to avert it.

"Monster!" said Walter to the Italian; "hast thou not crimes enough upon my soul already? Is this thy vain philosophy?"

"Why not?" replied the leech; "did he spare me? Besides, the hecatomb of dust is numbered! Why should I save one victim from the list? When earth is drunk with the blood of superstitious martyrs—when, like a sponge, it hath sucked up the appointed sacrifice of life, then will the reign of reason be at hand. I but advance the dial," he added, with a sarcastic smile; "why should I retard it?"

After a short consultation amongst the judges, the presiding one pronounced the sentence on the prisoners.

Sir John de Corbey, in consideration of his rank, was doomed to perish by the axe; but for the heretic, as well as murderer, Adam, a more fearful punishment was assigned—the stake; his body to be consumed to ashes, and those ashes given to the winds, in order, as the speaker concluded, that no remnant of so vile a wretch might find a resting place upon the earth his career of crime had so long polluted.

The old man heard the sentence with a bitter smile, for he felt that it made him and his judges equal; his guilt was not more atrocious, in his judgment, than his punishment.

Father Celestine was to be removed to London, to answer in the court established by Archbishop Warham for the punishment of heresy for his imputed crime.

Despite his entreaties and the influence of Wolsey's name, which Walter scrupled not to use, he was refused permission even to shake his old friend by the hand, or whisper one word of consolation. In the impetuous indignation of his heart he would yet further have committed himself, had not his friend the jester, who had been an interested spectator of the trial, succeeded in dragging him away.

"By my faith," said Patch, as soon as they had cleared the court-house, and were alone upon the plain which surrounds the castle, "but my search is ended. I have for a long time been looking for a successor to my office, and at last have found one. Come with me," he continued, "that with all due ceremony and celerity I may resign the ensigns of my authority in your favour."

"Spare me!" said the young man, painfully agitated; "I pray you, spare me! The good priest was the friend of my otherwise unfriended youth — my tutor — guide — my second father—and for me he dies! Had I not sought shelter of his quiet home, had not his fears for me disarmed all prudence, yon fiend's relentless malice had been baulked."

By this time the speakers had reached the second moat, some traces of which, twenty years since, were plainly visible, but they have since been filled up and built over; at the period of which we write it was a deep dry ditch, with steep banks on either side. They both naturally paused upon the brink.

"I think," said the jester, "that, as the world wags, thou hast some liking for me— a sort of kind caprice—something like the love born half of pity, half endurance."

"Have I not proved thy worth?" demanded his companion, grasping him warmly by the hand. "Be more just to thyself, and call the feeling by its true name—friendship."

"Friendship be it then," said Patch; "the name will serve as well as any other. Supposing, now, that I should fall in this same moat before us, what would this friendship prompt thee to do?"

"Why help thee out again," answered Walter, with a faint smile.

"How?" demanded the querist; "by jumping in thyself, or remaining on the bank, whence thou could reach a helping hand to drag me safe again?"

"Certes, by remaining on the bank," replied the young man, who did not yet perceive the drift of the jester's questions, which our readers, doubtless, have already devised.

"Good," said Patch; "time will bring something more than a beard upon thy chin. Celestine is in the ditch, where but for me thou wouldst have jumped beside him, instead of standing on the bank to aid him. There's nothing," he added, "so useful as an illustration to a truth; 'tis like a picture in a primer—it shows the child its lesson."

"Kindly and wisely hast thou shown me mine," exclaimed his hearer, who saw at once, not only the necessity, but the wisdom of his friend's advice, so characteristically conveyed. "In my folly, I would neglect the only means to save him. I must to Wolsey; one word from him——"

"That word will never be spoken," interrupted the jester. "Alas! poor dreamer, how little dost thou know the world! To hear thee speak, one would imagine it a simple path,—straight as integrity, and not a winding maze, which none may traverse without its subtle clue. Had the good priest," he added, "but simply broke his vows, our master might have cast the shadow of the Roman purple o'er him—winked at treason—shut his eyes at murder—turned a deaf ear to any accusation, save that which touches Henry's vanity. Celestine hath wounded that, and Mercy's voice is dumb."

"Surely his grace's influence with the king—" urged Walter, unwilling to abandon his last hope.

"Whew!" whistled Patch. "I thought the child could read, and find it only knows its letters. Didst ever ask thyself this simple question: Why the child loves its paper kite—the air-buoyed toy, whose flight resembles so well ambition's short career?"

"Even for its buoyant qualities," replied his companion.

"Because *he holds the string*," continued the speaker, with a glance of deep meaning, "and knows he can recall it at his pleasure."

"What if the string should break?"

"The kite falls still the same," drily answered the jester.

This familiar illustration at once revealed to the young man the relative positions of the minister and his master; the former was all-powerful alone, so long as his views crossed not Henry's inclinations, whose pride was flattered by the homage paid his servant, and who saw in him, as in a glass, his own reflected greatness. When he considered the character of the monarch, and the crime of Celestine, he felt hopeless alike of Wolsey's mediation or the sovereign's mercy.

It must be remembered that, during the lifetime of Arthur Prince of Wales, Henry VII., according to some historians, designed his second son for the archbishopric of Canterbury, and educated him accordingly. His preceptor Skelton sought to make him rather a scholar than an enlightened statesman. He tutored him in the dry philosophy of the schools, especially the Aristotlean, then most in credit with the learned. To theological studies the royal pupil, in early life, devoted himself with ardour and success; but their good effect on the character of the future king may be questioned. Divinity, as it was at that period taught in the schools, tended little to enlarge the views or give soundness to the opinions of its students; and hence, probably, the violent prejudices of Henry—his conceit and intemperance in polemical discussions—his vacillations on important points, and his obstinacy in those of less moment. He was never known to forgive any man who either differed in opinion or had once offended him; and when, at a more advanced period of the reformation, Luther sought, by the most abject flattery, to conciliate the royal reformer, he found his advances treated by the king with disdain.

It was hopeless, therefore, to expect that any who knew the monarch, or valued his favour, would venture to intercede for one who had so deeply offended him where he was most sensitive.

"My hope ends here!" exclaimed Walter, sadly, as he pondered these things in his mind. "Where shall I look for aid—where trust?"

"Trust much to thyself," said Patch, "and something, perhaps, to me. Folly succeeds where wit will often fail."

"Folly!" repeated the young man, earnestly. "By my faith, thou hast mistaken thine office; thou wert born to be a statesman, not a jester."

"Are they, then, so much unlike?" demanded his companion. "For my poor part, I see only this difference in them—the jester's office is a merry, whilst the statesman's is a sad one; and when I think on't, I prefer my own—kings smile at mine, while nations weep at his."

There was a touch of sadness in the motley wearer's tone, which showed that Walter was in the right. The jester had, indeed, mistaken his calling, or perchance the world had done so for him.

It was finally arranged that our hero should take no step in the matter without the counsel of his friend, whose shrewdness equalled his devotion. There were but few men in the world before whom Patch condescended to unmask, and when he did so, his confidence was complete. Ardently did the youth desire his return to London, where alone his efforts could be of use. Gratitude, to his uncorrupted heart, was a sacred debt; and, like an honest mind, he felt impatient till he had discharged it.

On parting with Patch, the impatient secretary hastened to the convent to which the heiress of Stanfield had been conveyed, on her liberation from prison, by order of the cardinal. We trust that but few of our readers are too old or too hackneyed in the mysteries of the heart not to feel the joy of such a meeting—its smiles and tears—its hopes renewed—its quiet, deep content, more eloquent in silence than in words. Those who have seen the being in whom their heart hath centred, restored to them at life's last gasp—the shipwrecked mariner who with but one plank between him and destruction, when the dark waters roared around him, and his reeling brain was drunk with terror, caught the rope cast by some friendly hand to save him—can well imagine the change the lovers felt from dark despair to hope's returning dawn. Even the veiled sister who, in accordance with conventual rule, was present at the interview, let fall a tear in witness of her sympathy. Though divorced from earth, and dead to human passion, the poor nun was not insensible to human joy. Perhaps she remembered, too, the time when such feelings and such hopes were not quite a stranger to her breast—when she herself had loved and been loved.

"Farewell!" exclaimed Walter reluctantly, after the repeated intimation of the recluse had warned him it was time he should separate from his mistress. "You will soon change this calm retreat for the allurements of a court. Greatness will beam upon you —young hearts proffer the incense of their homage, and flatterers woo you. Do not forget me then; do not forget the humble youth whose only sunshine is your smile— whose faith is centred in your vow as an angel's promise. Why," he added, fixing his eyes with melting tenderness upon her, "why was I not born a prince, or you a

beggar? Why hath fate placed this cruel distance 'twixt us?"

"Unkind one," said the orphan, with a smile, "why see a distance which my eyes regard not? Why envy me the happiness to o'erleap it? Art thou so churlish in thy love to grudge so poor a vantage o'er thee? Dismiss the torment of such vain suspicions —the love death's terror could not shake, greatness or flattery would strive in vain to win. Thou art like a child," she continued, "who, having found a pebble on the beach more pleasing than its fellows to his fancy, deems it a treasure every one would steal, though few save he would prize it."

With this gentle reproof, so calculated to make the youth forget the disparity between their fortunes, and to display the speaker's modest appreciation of her merits, the lovers separated, with an understanding that they should daily meet again. The Lady Mary went to the retirement of her cell, there to give thanks to Heaven for her preservation from her guardian's tyranny, and offer prayers for the repose of the generous, gallant Henry de Corbey's soul; Walter to his attendance upon his patron, Wolsey.

Our hero's first act, on his arrival at the palace of the Duke of Norfolk, was to throw himself at the feet of the cardinal, and thank him for his generous protection of the orphan heiress—a protection which our readers may remember was not extended without some danger to himself; as, had his presence in the chamber been detected on the night of the attempted murder, his priestly character would have been slight protection against the desperate resolution of the two assassins.

During the stay at Bury St. Edmund's and his eminence's supposed retreat at the martyr's shrine, Patch alone suspected his absence: he knew his master's humour— knew that he sometimes loved to throw aside his cumbrous state, and mingle, unknown and unsuspected, in the world. Hence the jester's positive assurance that the mendicant friar would be found upon the trial, when Walter informed him of Wolsey's promise. 'Tis strange how well he knew the churchman.

"Rise," said his eminence, graciously extending his hand to the kneeling youth; "I have but performed my duty; although, perchance," he added, with a complacent smile, at the recollection of the coolness and courage he had shown, "it was somewhat boldly done."

"Say nobly, my good lord!" exclaimed the young man; "let not the tongue whose praise is fame to all beside, be unjust to yourself alone."

"Hast learned to flatter?" demanded Wolsey in a tone which showed that, secretly, he was far from displeased at the compliment, which, sooth to say, gratitude, if not truth, excused.

"Thou wilt thrive at court, where a smooth tongue maketh way better than a sharp wit. Tell me," he added, "what followed after I left the court?"

"The assassins were condemned."

"Of course," said Wolsey, coolly; "did they think Justice was lame as well as blind, and that her silent step would never overtake them? Fools! her blow is not less sure because delayed. That widowed mother's curse," he added, "must haunt them to the scaffold—ring in their ears even at the death stroke; mine echo with it still. Proceed."

Encouraged by the familiar tone of the speaker, Walter related the last triumphant act of the Italian's malice, and Father Celestine's arrest. His hearer's brow darkened as he proceeded. The astute churchman perhaps already foresaw the solicitations to which he should be exposed, and felt the impossibility of lending an ear to them; for none knew so well as he how implacable was the king's resentment.

"Madman!" muttered his eminence to himself, "to mix with matters of such fearful moment! Better to have sat on the volcano's brow, or hung suspended o'er the burning gulf but by a single thread, than brave the wrath of Henry! But speak of him no more; his fate is sealed beyond all human aid—all human hope."

"Alas, my lord!" said Walter, mournfully, "he is my friend—the protector of my youth. Can I be silent, and his dear life in danger? My heart would sicken with the burning curse of its ingratitude. Grant me the means to save him."

"Impossible!" said Wolsey, coldly; "I can do all but step between the lion and his prey. Walter," he added, kindly, seeing that the young man turned from him with a sad, despairing look, "I would do much for thee. Men call me heartless where I am only powerless. Meddle not thou in this high matter; it would but bring destruction on thy head—not save thy friend one pang. For thy dead father's sake, I fain would guide thy sea-tossed bark to shore—not see it wrecked upon a rock like this."

With these words the speaker retired to his private chamber, where, without special invitation, none might presume to follow him. His visitor observed a shade of sadness in his tone—indeed, all who have studied the character of Wolsey can conceive how severe a struggle it must have cost his haughty nature to avow that, where his master's pas-

sions were concealed, his boasted influence was powerless. Such is but too often the condition of poor reflected greatness.

"Patch was right," thought the young man to himself: "the fool hath judged the world more wisely than the scholar. I must rely upon myself to save him."

The three days allotted between the sentence and the execution of Sir John de Corbey had at last expired. The scaffold for the knight was erected close to the keep of Norwich Castle—the stake for his accomplice between the inner and the outward moats. Attracted by the fearful spectacle, the city at an early hour poured forth its population. Strange that such a magnetic power should exist in terror; despite philosophy, its influence is felt even by the strongest mind; and those whose humanity or sensibility shrink from the sight of human suffering listen with excited interest to its tale. Gentry and citizens alike were there, the unwashed artisan, the hooded friar, the prowling mendicant, and lively soldier, all drawn together by the excitement of the scene. To the honour of the sex, but few of the wives and daughters of the spectators were present, and those of the lowest grade. The morbid passion of marking the last struggle of the victim to offended justice, counting its agonies and tears, is, at least amongst females of the higher class, to the dishonour of the age, a passion of pure modern growth.

Whilst the mob are congregating round the scaffold, impatient for the commencement of its horrors—as for the opening of some masque or pageant—let us enter the precincts of the gloomy prison, and visit the condemned murderers in their cell.

In consideration of the rank of the principal culprit, both he and his minister were confined in a strong chamber in Bigod's Tower, less dreary than the gloomy cells where prisoners were generally kept. The rudely sculptured crucifix and massive chain sealed in the wall marked the past and present use to which it had been and was applied—first a chapel, now a prison. The physiognomy of the captives presented a singular picture of the two extremes of human passion—its tempest and its calm. Sir John, agonised with shame at the approach of an ignominious death, his heart seared by disappointed ambition, raged in his wild despair like some fierce tiger caught in the hunter's snare; whilst the philosophic Adam, on the contrary, was as unmoved at the prospect of his fearful death, as the Indian sage whose own hand lights the pile which wafts him to the stars. The knight, faithful to the infidelity which he doubted, but professed, had obstinately refused all religion's did, and driven its horror-stricken minister from his dungeon by his imprecations and his blasphemies. Adam, on the contrary, had contented himself by quietly declining it.

"I will not die!" exclaimed the frantic noble, pacing the narrow limits of his cell; "I will not meet the gaze of the vile mob, or hear their insulting yell. If the fable which galls mankind be true—if there be a devil—I call on him to save me. I dare not die," he added, with increased terror—"life in a dungeon, where the foul toad or spotted snake meanders—anything rather than annihilation."

His companion listened to him with a composed smile.

"...." continued the priest, "...reason ... ? What ... there be ... the avenger of blood, the ... stern and implacable, the ... of ... Call him again—'tis not too late for penitence; for, oh! ... there is a ... worse than annihilation."

"There is," said Adam coldly.

"You tell me so! You, who so oft have mocked at——"

"Priestcraft," interrupted the Italian, "not at Deity. Fool! the flower, the tender blade of grass, thy impious foot so oft hath crushed proclaim the holy truth. There is a God—the judge and the avenger. Passion's clouds may veil Him from our gaze, the mists of sophistry obscure the eye of reason, but His all-glorious presence is not less reflected back from nature as a mirror.

"Call back the priest!" shrieked his astonished master to the leech, in a voice of frenzy; "'tis not too late to pray, to make atonement. Oh! for a year, a month, a week—one little week of life—for penitence and prayer!"

"Too late!" exclaimed Adam, pointing to the door of the cell; "when next it opens, the executioner will withdraw the bolt, the hour for prayer or penitence is past."

"Then I am lost."

"Here and hereafter lost," solemnly repeated his fellow-prisoner.

"You tell me so," said the unhappy man, glaring on him with the mingled rage of insanity and despair; "you, who have been my minister in crime!—you, who played with human life as with a childish toy!—you, who more than once have steeled my heart and urged me to perdition!"

"Ay," said Adam, "I have lured thee to destruction's brink, and joyed to see thee damning thyself with crime."

"For what?" demanded the knight, in a voice of surprise.

"For vengeance."

"What cause?"

"What cause!" iterated the wily Italian, drawing up his figure to its full height, and regarding his master with a look of withering hate, "what cause? Hast thou forgot the maid whose home was by old Arno's palaced shores—my affianced bride? Pure as the first thought of a young angel's heart, I left her to prepare our future home of love; returning, found her all thy degrading lust and brutal violence could make her. From that hour I cast off human ties and bound myself to vengeance. I have achieved it," he added, slowly, "and I are quits."

"My sin—my sin hath found me!" murmured ... in a hopeless tone; the leech's ... words recalling to his memory the ... of blood and violence with which ...

"Ho ... the frantic ... despair. "The avenging judge holds forth the balance in his red right hand; it ... the measure of thy crime is ... Rejoicing fiends already circle round ... waiting the headsman's stroke to seize their prey!"

"Mercy!" ... , falling on knee, overcome with terror; "mercy!"

"Mercy!" ... the ... "think on thy crimes."

"I do repent them."

"Thy kinsman's blood," he continued, "may be forgiven."

"The armourer's living death—his widowed mother's curse."

"Heaven is merciful."

"Thy son—thy murdered son," added his tormentor, in the tone of an exulting fiend.

"Shall be avenged!" shrieked the frantic knight, starting to his feet, and seizing the leech by the neck with a grasp of iron. "Thou croaking raven, I will stop thy cry! triumphant devil, I'll disappoint thee yet! Thou shalt not drive hope's pitying angel from my side! Be this," he added, as he dashed his victim with a giant's strength against the wall of the prison, "my first atonement! Ah," he continued, as the convulsed features, bursting eye-balls, and blood-stained foam which bubbled from the Italian's lips, proclaimed the struggle nearly over, "thou art human! Ha! ha! ha! I shall escape thee yet! Writhe on, serpent, writhe on! thy sting is powerless now!"

With these words he gradually relaxed his grasp, and the corpse of the once-gifted

THE TWO COURTIERS WATCHING THE BARGE OF THE CARDINAL.

Adam fell at his feet. In the triumph of his mad revenge, the wretched man little thought that he had but fulfilled the intentions of the dead man, who had provoked him to the deed, in order to escape the stake and executioner. His prediction to the knight proved true. The first who unbarred the cell, was the executioner.

CHAPTER VIII.

Death is indeed most terrible; e'en when it comes
Unto the sinless couch, and weeping friends
Whisper religion's last consoling prayer.
But on the scaffold, amid the rabble's curse,
When conscience echoes back the accusing cry,
It comes with tenfold terror.—CREON.

IN the foremost rank of spectators nearest the fatal scaffold were our friend, Stead- man, and his maniac sister, Maud. Vainly had the honest wool-comber, together with

Walter and many of her friends, tried
to persuade her from the fearful spectacle.
To all entreaties she opposed but one reply,
"That justice would be defeated, and the
murderer of her boy, on account of his vast
wealth and ancient name, be permitted to
escape the punishment due to his crimes."

"I will be present!" she exclaimed; "I
will behold the death-pangs of the tiger who
hath robbed me of my child, and curse him
as he dies. I know—I know," she muttered
sullenly, "you would break the snare, and
set the monster free—free him for gold—for
his accursed gold—as if this earth coined in
one yellow heap should buy my poor son's
blood—no—no!"

So fixed had this idea become, that the
leech who attended her saw it was impossible
to remove it. He, therefore, advised her
brother to comply with her request, suggesting that the shock would in all probability restore her reason, or snap asunder
the frail thread of her lonely, blighted existence. To such an argument, and from
such a source, there was nothing to reply;
and the unhappy woman, despite the wishes
of Steadman, whose soul revolted at the
anticipation of the sight, was permitted to
gratify her undying hatred of the murderer
by being present at their execution. All
made way for her—some with pity, others
with terror—for the mad ravings of her
triumph were terrible to hear. Ere we blame,
let it be remembered that her brain was
turned, and how fearful was the crime which
made her childless.

"One—two—three!" she cried with
frantic delight, as she counted the strokes of
the great bell of the cathedral, which announced the hour appointed for the consummation of the last solemn act of justice
—"he comes!—ha! ha! ha!—he comes!
You will not let them disappoint me," she
added, turning to the people; "you will not
let them save him. If they attempt it,
pluck him from the scaffold; tear him limb
from limb; show him the poor man's blood
is not to be purchased by the rich man's
coin."

"Shame," exclaimed her brother, angrily;
"as thou art a Christian woman, peace.
Heed her not, friends," he continued, turning to the mob—"she is mad; she is the
mother of the murdered boy, whom Sir
John——"

"Buried alive!" shrieked Maud—"consigned in the full bloom of health, while the
young blood ran freely in his veins, giving
fresh impulse to his generous heart, to a
living tomb, to gnaw his flesh with hunger
—tear his poor veins to quench his burning
thirst—to madness—frenzy—to such dark

despair that death became a mercy. Who
that hath a mother," she continued, looking
wildly round, "will dare dispute my right
to curse him?"

There is generally a natural sense of justice
in the mob—alas! when will education
entitle them to be called the people? It
was so in the present instance. Although
they shuddered at the maniac's maledictions,
they felt her wrongs excused, even if they
failed to justify her curse. The great gates
of the castle were thrown open, and the procession appeared at last before the impatient
multitude. First came the sheriffs in their
robes, with their wands of office; they were
followed by some half dozen soldiers of the
city guard, who carried their long partisans
upon their shoulders. The next was the
executioner, a tall, brawny, muscular man,
whose features were rigid with the hard lines
of iron resolution—coldly rigid, as if the repeated horrors he had witnessed had had the
same effect upon him as on others—had
transformed them into stone. In his right
hand he bore the axe, with its broad
sharpened glittering edge turned towards the
prisoner. The fellow, for the greater ease
in the performance of his disgusting office,
was naked to the waist; there was nothing
to impede the action of his strong arm, the
corded sinews of which were as visible to the
spectators as the stems of the withered
leafless ivy are when clinging round the
branches of some blasted oak.

A thrill of horror ran through the crowd
at the sight of the law's last terrible avenger,
and a stifled murmur of execration followed
his appearance. Is it not strange that the
man whose office is more awful than either
king's or priest's; that the being in whose
hands society places the prerogative it has im-
piously wrenched from Deity—the privilege
of taking life—should be held in such
universal detestation by the people?—a sentiment which, par parenthesis, is not the
least powerful protest against it.

On the appearance of Sir John de Corbey,
who was led, or rather half-dragged, between
two of the headsman's assistants, the indignant populace broke out into a loud
triumphant yell, for the haughty knight had
never been a favourite amongst them, and
the nature of his crime was such as steeled
all hearts against him. From his torn doublet
and flushed features, it was evident his conductors had had a desperate struggle before
they had pinioned him; nor will it be wondered at when it is remembered that when
they entered his cell, they found him almost
mad, gloating over the dead body of his
victim and accomplice, Adam.

The sheriffs, who were responsible for the

conducting of the execution, trembled at the effect which the expression of popular opinion might have upon the prisoner. To their astonishment, however, instead of increasing his excitement, it rendered him quite calm—the noble survived the man in him. With a violent effort at self-control, he repressed his agitation, and walked quietly to the block, where the principal executioner was already occupied in arranging cords to drag him down in the event of his resisting.

"Spare thy trouble, fellow," he said; "the madness of the hour is past. I might contend with death, but not with thee. Are there any," he added, "who for the love of the ancient house of Corbey will do a dying man a last poor favour?"

One of the soldiers who followed the sheriffs advanced towards him: he had served him in the wars.

"Thanks, good fellow," said the knight. "Remove my doublet, and place the bandage so around my eyes as to confine my hair; then lead me to the block. I can endure yon wretch's axe, but not his hand."

The two functionaries motioned to the soldier to comply with the prisoner's request, for they were anxious to end the scene. Once, and once only, the unhappy man was observed to tremble and his cheek turn pale. It was when the voice of the maniac Maud fell upon his ear, as they were blindfolding him, before leading him to the block.

"There is a God," she cried; "monster! thou feel'st him now. His hand hath struck thee—die, like the ban wolf, howling, unpitied—scorned and despised of earth—hopeless of heaven!—die," she shrieked, with frantic exultation, as the executioner swung the glittering axe in a semi-circle round his head to give greater impetus to the blow, "accursed of God and man—despairing die!"

The axe fell, and the soul of Sir John de Corbey, ere the echo of the blow had faded on the ears of the terror-stricken spectators, stood before the tribunal of the Most High. Man's judgment may not pursue it further.

"It is accomplished," said the widow, all passion and excitement suddenly leaving her; "my boy's blood hath not fallen to earth unavenged. Lead me home," she added, turning to her brother, and half-sinking into his arms—"lead me home, for every minute of my life is numbered."

The leech proved right in both his predictions—her senses were restored, and she was dying.

"Maud!" exclaimed her brother, the tears streaming down his weather-beaten cheeks, "thou art dying. Go not to the grave with curses on thy lips. Remember His words, who preaches pardon, that we may be pardoned. As thou dost hope to meet thy boy in heaven, recall thy maledictions on the dead."

The expiring woman opened her half-closed eyes, and cast a look of hatred towards the scaffold and its still palpitating victim—a look such as the wounded pantheress might regard the destroyer of her young with. It was the last she ever gave on earth; the sorrows and triumph of the heart-broken mother of the armourer in this world were over. The sympathising crowd slowly divided for Steadman and his friends, as they bore the body of his sister from the scene.

Walter was joined by Wolsey in the commission to the sheriffs, authorising them to take possession of the property of Sir John de Corbey, now confiscated to the king and seized on for his use. Patch, whose keen restless disposition rendered him unhappy unless when occupied, thought proper to accompany him; for, as he judiciously remarked, there were occasions on which two heads had the advantage over one, and this promised to be one of them. While the officials were occupied in taking an inventory of the plate and furniture, the jester demanded to be shown to the apartment of Adam.

"What think'st to find there?" demanded his companion.

"The key to a riddle which hath puzzled me," replied Patch, "the leech's character. For a fool, I act on philosophic principles. Naturalists tell us, if we would gain a knowledge of an animal, its habits, manners, and propensities, to examine well its den. Adam's the animal I would study; I'd gain a knowledge of his habits, manners, and propensities; his room the den I would examine."

The door of the apartment was locked; it had been fastened by its occupant on the morning of the trial; they were compelled, therefore, to break it open, for the key was nowhere to be found. It was one of those large old-fashioned rooms, full of quaint nooks and convenient corners, such as are still occasionally to be found in country mansions. The furniture resembled more the odds and ends of an artist's studio than the garniture of a well-ordered chamber. Cabinets, no two of which were alike, were stuck in the different recesses. On one side of the walls was a collection of arms of various dates and countries, together with several strangely contrived instruments, which the visitors took for implements of torture or divination; they knew not which. Most probably the modern man of science would have smiled at their error; for the late owner of the objects of their curiosity was in advance of his time. One cabinet of ebony, inlaid with silver, particularly attracted their attention. Walter had often heard speak of it; for the inmates of Stanfield, as well as those of the knight's house in the city, regarded it with a feeling of superstitious terror. No eye save its master's had ever been known to gaze on its contents. The others had frequently been seen open; they contained books, manuscripts, chiefly on medicine and the sciences, drugs, minerals, and a small collection of medals, several of them from the hand of Adam's countryman and contemporary, the unrivalled Benvenuto Cellini.

Perhaps the peculiar appearance of the cabinet in question had given birth to the species of awe with which the household spoke of it. The workmanship, which was even more costly than the materials, was of Florentine marquetterie, adorned in the panels with sculpture, a style much older than the renaissance which belonged to the reigns of Francis I. and Henry, both of whom patronised it at their respective courts.

After vainly trying the various keys which they found upon the table, Walter proposed to force it open, which Patch prudently declined. The jester judged wisely, for the cunning Italian had so contrived the lock of the cabinet, that on the first attempt to pick or break it the tube of a small pistol would discharge itself full in the face of the imprudent intruder on his secret—a piece of ingenuity which was only discovered on the production of the real key, which was obtained from the governor of the castle, who had found it suspended by a silver chain round the neck of Adam, after his death, by the hands of Sir John de Corbey.

On opening the door of the cabinet they found that it contained a small altar, over which was suspended the portrait of a young girl of almost celestial beauty, one of those glorious faces of sun-lit joy and innocence which Guido loved to paint; golden hair, bright as the pure ray which falls from morning's wing when first it flashes o'er the awakening world; violet eyes—eyes of that indescribable deep thoughtful blue which poets love, as Petrarch felt too well; and a lip—Damascus's budding rose were pale beside it.

> Her face was of Italia's mould,
> Such as her daughters bore of old;
> A classic head, whose golden hair
> Fell o'er a brow like marble fair;
> A chisell'd nostril: a rich lip,
> Sweet as the dew the wild bees sip.

"Beautiful!" exclaimed the young man, gazing on the portrait with enthusiastic admiration; "who ever saw a form more fair—a brow more intellectual? Who can it be?"

"Stay," said Patch, approaching nearer, "here is an inscription." He advanced, and read, engraved as if with the point of a dagger, beneath the frame—

"Betrayed—June 1st, 1500. Avenged—June 1st, 1529."

The latter, it must be remembered, was the date of Henry de Corbey's death and his father's desolation.

"What art thou dreaming of?" demanded Walter of his companion, who had remained a considerable time silently musing before the shrine; "upon the woman?"

"No," replied Patch, "on the Italian. The world has lost an epic by his death. What food for conjecture," he added, pointing to the inscription, "do those words convey! Betrayed! avenged! who would believe a few scratches could be so eloquent? Scholar, burn thy books, since two brief words can better tell the history of the heart and its fierce passions than all thy musty treatises!"

"Adam must have calculated shrewdly," said Walter, "since month for month, perchance hour for hour, the crime and the atonement were the same. Fearful, doubtless, were the wrongs which demanded such relentless retribution. Father Celestine was right in his conjecture—the bond between the destroyer and the avenger must have been of hate."

"This, at least," said the jester, removing the picture, "shall not fall into the hands of those who would indulge in ribald jests, perhaps, over its owner's fate. I'll keep his treasure as a memento, not of his crimes, but sorrows. It will serve my spirit to converse with, when 'tis sad."

"Where wilt thou hang it?" inquired the young man.

"In an old museum," replied the melancholy jester, "where I have treasured up stray waifs like these; books which have no meaning but to memory—relics which the heart's devotion alone can venerate. I shall live to glean more treasures for it yet; Rome's sullied purple, a queenly crown, and, perhaps," he added, fixing his eyes sadly upon his companion, "the vow of broken friendship. No matter; the collection will only be the more curious from the contrast."

"Cynic!" exclaimed Walter; "with thoughts like these, wronging thyself no less than friendship, thou art more suited to a cloister than a court. Thou wouldst preach well in a cowl."

"Right," said Patch; "it should have been a cloister."

"And what wouldst thou have done there?"

Debauched the monks with merry jests? cheated old Time with quaint philosophy, and made his hours pass lightly?"

"Neither."

"What then?"

"Why," said the jester, with an effort to cast off the melancholy which oppressed him, "in gulling others I should at least have learned to forget myself; but," he added, "leave spleen to statesmen—'tis their heritage —morals to priest, who best should understand them, and let us to our duty. What wilt thou claim for thy museum?"

"I do not understand thee. My museum! I have not yet begun to form one."

"Then the collecting it will last the longer. Poor boy—poor boy! Those," he added, "who begin in early life to count the shipwrecks of their happiness—to store up the relics of the hearts they prized—the hopes which dazzled only to mislead—have half gone through their task."

Walter understood at last what the speaker meant by his museum.

It was curious to observe the rapidity and knowing look with which the jester examined the contents of the remaining cabinets. Articles apparently of no inconsiderable value were thrown by him carelessly aside, whilst certain oddly shaped phials and packets of drugs were crammed in his capacious pockets; neither was a small manuscript which related to their use forgotten.

"More subjects for your museum," observed the young man, who for some time had been silently watching the proceedings of his companion. Patch raised his head and answered him—

"No, these are for the world—arms for its miseries and its treacheries. Folly is the legitimate executor of wisdom, and in nine cases out of ten its heir. Thou and I may live to bless the day which made us the leech's heritors. Here," he added, "is a trinket the Egyptian queen would have purchased with her crown, after she had failed to move the love or pity of Octavius."

He held up a ring of massive gold, which he had found in a small drawer in the cabinet.

As he spoke Walter examined it, but could perceive nothing either remarkable or valuable in it, beyond the workmanship and the metal.

"A vast treasure, truly!" he exclaimed, returning it to the jester, who carefully put it in his pocket. "The bells upon thy cap, friend Patch, were worth a dozen such."

The speaker knew not it was one of those rings, invented first in the east, made hollow and charged with a subtle poison, so mild, yet so sure in its effects, that the curious eye of science might vainly try to trace the cause. When Walter saw it next it glittered on the hand of Wolsey.

Finding that the dispute between the prior and the citizens was not to be settled so easily as he at first imagined, the cardinal broke up his legatine court, and adjourned the cause to London, where he was anxiously expected by the impatient Henry—eager to prosecute the favourite project of his divorce. The heiress of Stanfield travelled in his eminence's train, the good Queen Katherine having determined to receive the helpless orphan under her own immediate protection, an arrangement which gave the anxious lover of the maiden more uneasiness than he ventured to express.

On the arrival of the travellers at York House, the magnificent residence of Wolsey, better known to our readers perhaps by its modern appellation of Whitehall, the churchman was informed that her majesty was at Greenwich; and thither, without even being permitted to alight, the Lady Mary and the lay sister from the convent who attended her were compelled to continue their journey, her protector being anxious, not only to oblige the queen, who expected her, but to avoid a pretext for scandal; for, as a prelate, he was a strict observer of all the outward proprieties of life.

"Whither goest thou?" demanded Patch of the disappointed Walter, as he turned from the river, after watching the barge which conveyed his mistress to her royal protectress out of sight.

"To seek out the prison of Father Celestine," replied our hero.

"I thought as much; but spare thyself the pains. I have found it out for thee."

"You?" said the young man, with an expression of incredulity upon his countenance. "Why, we have but just arrived, and thou hast spoken with no one save thyself."

"And the messenger who yesterday brought letters from the primate," observed his friend. "The poor old man is a prisoner in the Lollards' Tower; that priestly den," he added, "where men with mercy and religion on their lips enact the part of fiends. If things continue so thus, it will soon become a question where the Thames flows reddest—at Lambeth or the Tower. Strange rivalry, between the church and state!"

Walter shuddered, for he had heard of the horrors which even Warham, Archbishop of Canterbury, had caused to be exercised towards his prisoners; not that the primate was particularly distinguished for his severity. Cruelty, unfortunately, was the peculiar characteristic of the age. Even the virtuous and enlightened Sir Thomas More is not exempt from the charge. During his chancellorship he caused one James Barnham, a gentleman of the Middle Temple, to be arrested on a charge of heresy, and brought to his house at Chelsea. As one means of converting him, the philosophic judge caused him to be tied to a tree in his garden, called the "Tree of Life," and flogged him severely with his own hands. The unhappy victim of the enlightened chancellor was afterwards burned at Smithfield as a relapsed heretic. So much for More's philosophy.

"I'll save him from their grasp," exclaimed the excited youth, "though I fire Lambeth to achieve it!"

"Psha!" interrupted Patch; "that were about as wise a thing to do as to burn the nut to reach the kernel. Thou hadst better crack it."

"But how?"

"Hast faith in me?"

A silent pressure of the jester's hand from his companion was the reply.

"And canst thou act a part to save thy friend," continued the speaker, "smile where thou wouldst frown, grasp the hands of men, and feel that thou wouldst rather have thy fingers on their throats,—teach thy young lips to praise the deeds thy very soul abhors, forget the honest impulse of thy nature, and make thyself a necessary lie?"

"I can descend to dissembling," replied the anxious friend of Celestine, "to save the good priest's life."

"Follow me, then," said his companion, "and like two serpents, let us cast our skins. Consider it but as a Christmas masque, in which thou dost enact the devil's part. The mummery o'er, thou'lt be again thyself."

At a distance of about three hundred yards from the principal gateway leading to Lambeth Palace, stood a substantial-looking hostel, close to the water's edge, and known by the name of the Golden Rose. From its proximity to the river, it was frequented chiefly by watermen, and the lower officials and domestics of the archbishop. Occasionally, however, some poor gentleman or priest, who were either suitors, or had business to transact in the ecclesiastical court of the primate, mingled with the motley group who assembled every night within its walls. The appearance of such guests, although not of ordinary occurrence, was not sufficiently rare to occasion observation or surprise.

On the night which followed the return of Wolsey and his train to town, the vast kitchen, which also served as a general room for the guests at the Golden Rose, was occupied by three different parties, each party having a table to themselves. At the one

nearest the fire were seated two citizens—an old man and a young one—the quiet richness of whose dress proclaimed that they belonged to a superior class. A stoup of wine, scarcely touched, stood before them. From their abstracted air and occasional whisperings, it was evident that they were not there for drinking, or for the pleasure of society, for they conversed with none. The elder of the two had all the appearance of a man who had served. His air was erect and soldier-like, his eyes clear and open, and his beard cut in the peculiar fashion which distinguished the Walloon mercenaries of the period. His companion, on the contrary, possessed the shy, reserved manner of a student.

At the long table, which extended the entire length of the apartment, were the general company, or ordinary frequenters of the house—traders, watermen, and three or four fellows wearing the prelate's livery. They were not more noisy than such persons generally are. Perhaps the presence of their neighbours somewhat restrained them. The third party consisted of four men, whose table was drawn as far out of sight as possible in a recess formed by the large bay window, the only one which gave light to the apartment. These men were, perhaps, the most remarkable personages in the hostel. They were the two gaolers and torturers of the archbishop's prison—ruffians, who made a pleasure of tormenting their fellow-creatures—of exciting agony to the limits of endurance—who watched with the apathy of science the fluttering pulse, the glazed eye, and quivering muscles of their victims, and descanted on each fresh discovery in their hellish art with the gusto of professors.

Conversation was going on with considerable animation at the principal table. The subject in dispute was whether Lollards were Christians or Pagans. The retainers of the church swore they were the latter; else, they philosophically argued, they would not be so frequently sentenced to the stake. One obstinate old man, the orator of the neighbourhood, refused to be convinced even by this authority; perhaps, like many others who were silent on the subject, he already doubted its infallibility. The dispute and uproar were at the highest, when the door of the hostel opened, and two friars entered the room.

"Benedicite!" exclaimed the elder, a portly tun-bellied fellow, whose flushed face and pimpled nose gave evidence of what kind of fasting and mortification he indulged in. His companion, who was evidently many years younger than himself, remained modestly silent.

"Now, then, you shall be satisfied," cried one of the disputants; "this holy father shall decide between us. You will not doubt the church's judgment, though you do mine."

"He that doth," said the red-nose brother, "let him be anathema. Doubt the judgment of the church—the corner stone on which the fabric rests! the very sublimation of impiety. Tapster," he added, "bring me a flask of sack; my heart sickens at the infidelity of the age—an old man too—fie! fie!"

"But you have not yet heard the point in question," boldly interrupted the advocate of the Lollards' Christianity. "Listen, at least, ere you decide between us."

"It needs not, my son," meekly answered the friar; "since by that infinitesimal particle of infallibility which pertaineth to me as an unworthy unit of the church, I see already that thou art in error. But propound," he added, with an air of contemptuous pity such as is so frequently met with in churchmen; "propound—our ears are open to the cause between ye."

"Are Lollards, father," demanded the archbishop's servitor, "Christians or Pagans?"

"Mistaken Christians," meekly interrupted the little man. "State the question fairly; do me no wrong in the good father's judgment."

"Pagans!" exclaimed the reverend judge; "worse than Pagans! wretches on whom the tender mercies of holy church, its pious faggots and celestial stripes, are thrown away—deaf adders, whom its fervid arguments cannot convince; although," he added, with a twinkle of the eye, observed only by his companion, "latterly they have been warm enough to melt a heart of lead."

"If neither Pagans nor Christians, father," demanded the persevering little champion of toleration, subdued, but not convinced, by the speaker's vehemence, "what are they, then?"

The speaker eyed the friar slily as he spoke. He flattered himself that he had puzzled him.

"Anthropophagi!" solemnly answered the religious man; "the most horrible of that species of heresy which the church terms carnivorous, and in atonement for which Christians are taught to fast on Fridays."

There was a pause. Many of the listeners piously crossed themselves, convinced from the high-sounding words which the friar had used that Lollardism must be something more dreadful than any other ism they had ever heard of. Its little advocate sneaked quietly away; and the speaker and his young companion seated themselves at the same table where the two strangers whom we have before described were discussing their flask of wine. The elder regarded the new comers, as they took their places opposite to them at table, with a mingled expression of amusement and disgust. The friar's hard words had not confounded him.

"Are you for the archbishop's court tomorrow?" demanded the host, as he placed the stoup of wine before them. The good man always attended upon gentlemen of their cloth himself—it looked respectful, and prevented any dispute about the reckoning, which invariably occurred whenever the tapster served them.

"No, son, no," replied the elder, after tasting the wine, which he replaced upon the table with disgust. "Host of the Golden Rose, hast thou no conscience? Wouldst poison thy guests? Is a strong woody wine like this fit for a delicate stomach?"

"It's the best I have," answered the man, in a surly tone, who thought that the abuse of the wine was merely intended to excuse the payment of the reckoning.

"Have I mistaken the hostel, then? Is this the Golden Rose?"

"It is."

"Hath my old friend and compeer, Gilbert of York, deceived me," continued the friar, "who boasted that I should find here wine fit for an abbot's table, and a reasonable host? Wine!" he repeated, with a look of disdain. "I drank better when I was a novice. 'Tis as sour as the grape of Picardie."

On hearing the name of Gilbert of York, the manner of the host was completely changed. He immediately offered to exchange the wine, observing that although it was of excellent quality, he certainly had a few flasks of a superior kind, reserved only for such customers as knew how to appreciate it, or were personal friends; and concluded his harangue by demanding if his reverence intended to remain long.

"But two or three days, good host," replied the friar, in a patronising tone. "I had hoped to have witnessed the burning of a Lollard or two ere my departure, but am doomed to disappointment. There is no zeal left in the world," he added; "we are no longer a Christian people. I would have given a rose noble for the sight of one."

The old soldier frowned, and his young companion gazed upon the speaker with an expression of disgust too plain to be mistaken. On hearing the liberal proffer of the speaker, the principal gaoler started from the table where he was sitting with his companions in the recess, and advanced into the middle of the room.

"I will show you three," exclaimed the fellow with a grin, "and charge you only for the price of one. I have them all ready cooped up in my cage there—three as bitter specimens of heresy—ay, and as tough, too —as Smithfield ever boasted. What say you, master, to a peep at my raree-show?"

"Who art thou, friend?" coolly demanded the party to whom he made the proffer.

"The gaoler of Lambeth," was the reply.

"My offer," said the monk, with the air of a man who wishes to withdraw from a rash bargain, "extended to the burning of the heretics, not the mere sight of them; but perhaps," he added, "you would not make that a difficulty between us?"

"No, father," said the fellow, with a broad grin, "I cannot promise that; but Michael here shall put the thumbscrews on them to amuse you. There's one young fellow from the north, a Master Everil, who had them on to-day—bold as a lion—who would show rare sport!"

The old soldier's companion half started from his seat at the words, and turned so pale that the speaker must have observed him, had not the younger of the friars at the same moment leant before him, as if to reach the wine which the host had just placed upon the table. As he did so, he whispered the word "Caution!" in an under tone. A quiet pressure of the hand beneath the table, when he resumed his seat, thanked him, and conveyed the intelligence that he was understood.

"Not to-night, friend," said the man of the ruby nose; "not to-night. Besides, I have another novice of my convent whom I should like to witness the lesson—perhaps to-morrow."

"Remember, it must be at night," said the fellow, in a disappointed tone; for his avarice had been excited by the proffer of the rose noble; "what say you; is it agreed?"

"Why, really, I——"

"And you shall apply the screws yourself, holy father," whispered the ruffian, thinking that would clench the bargain.

"Shall I?" said the friar, his eyes flashing with a very different expression than that of satisfaction at the offer; "agreed: *I will apply them!* Here," he added, pouring out a stoup of wine and offering it to the gaoler; "drink! this is to seal the bond."

The fellow drained the cup with gusto—it was not often such liquor passed his lips— and extended his hand to the donor, exclaiming, "It is a bargain; you will not fail?"

"When did mother Church ever fail to keep her word, especially if an act of charity was to be performed, such as roasting an heretic or torturing an unbeliever? I and my brethren will be with you. It will be a

lesson for them," he added, "and an edification for me."

It was finally arranged that on the following night the friars were to be admitted to the Lollards' Tower, there to amuse themselves by the sight of the tortures inflicted by demons, in the name of religion, upon the prisoners. More wine was called for, and at a late hour the two monks left the house, on their way, as they said, to a convent of their order in the city, where they meant to pass the night. The other travellers who had been seated at the same table with them, after a whispered consultation, hastily paid for their scarcely tasted flask, and followed them.

"Thank Heaven!" exclaimed the talkative brother to his companion, whom our readers have ere this doubtless recognised as Walter, and the speaker as Patch. "Thank Heaven that we are out of that den. If hypocrisy would make men sick, I have had a dose of it. But I suppose," he added in his usual sarcastic vein, "we get accustomed to it."

"Success—success is certain," said Walter, warmly pressing the jester by the hand; "we shall tear the victim from his merciless tormentors yet. We shall require a boat."

"And friends," added a deep musical voice so near them that they caught the speaker's breath upon their cheeks. They turned round in consternation at the sound. Their two companions at the table in the hostel were beside them. Walter laid his hand upon a weapon which he wore beneath his disguise, ready to defend both Patch and himself if attacked. For a few seconds the parties regarded each other in silence; the old soldier was the first to speak.

"You are no friars!" he exclaimed.

"Perhaps not," said the jester; "but whatever we are can matter little to Sir Richard Everil."

"You know me!"

"At least I name you," replied the disguised friar; "and that, too, without ever having given you shrift. Put up your sword," he whispered to his friend, "there is no danger. I know the man; his purpose at the wine house, if I mistake not, was kindred to our own. His son is a prisoner in the Lollards' Tower."

"Can you name me, too?" demanded the young man who accompanied Sir Richard.

"As readily as your godfather," said Patch; "you are a scholar at Oxford, who, on hearing of his cousin's danger, fled from the university to London to work out his deliverance; an act which, in the eyes of the world, proves you have more heart than head, gratitude than prudence."

THE ESCAPE OF FATHER CELESTINE FROM THE LOLLARD'S TOWER.

"Who are you?" exclaimed the knight, more surprised at the recognition of his nephew than of himself.

"We live in times," said the jester, "when names are dangerous; pardon me that I have uttered yours. Me you will never know but by my deeds; and to balance the advantage which my knowledge gives me over you, I promise to restore your nephew to his college—his absence overlooked; that is," he added, "if he have the wit to keep good counsel on his expedition."

When the speaker's favour with Wolsey, who was founding a college at the university, is remembered, his promise will not be deemed a rash one.

"How canst thou do this thing?" demanded the young man, curiously.

"As miracles are worked—by faith," replied the friar. "I am one of those whose promises become realities only by being trusted. And now, sir knight, without further confidence, shall we understand each other?"

"How is that possible?" demanded Sir Richard.

No. 38.

"Nothing more easy," said Patch, "to men who judge the thing implied, and not the thought expressed. You will have a boat to-morrow at midnight on the Thames?—say for your caprice or pleasure."

"I will."

"With four stout rowers on whom you can depend?"

"As on myself."

"And if I, or two or three of my brethren, on returning from the Lollards' Tower, should wish to drop down the river, your boat will be at our disposal?" slowly demanded the speaker.

"Provided," said the knight, hesitatingly, "that you bring——"

"A certain layman with us? Right—'tis just the party should be equal. We understand each other?"

"Perfectly."

"Your nephew," continued Patch, "is about the height of my young novice here. Perhaps he would like to try how he would look in such a frock and cowl? I'll bring them with me, for I have heard there will be masking on the river."

"Agreed."

"To-morrow, then, we meet again," said the jester.

"To-morrow," repeated the knight and his companion; and with this brief understanding they parted to their respective homes.

The jester and our hero reached York House without further adventures, entering by a private door, of which the former had the key.

"Thou art a suspicious being," said Walter to his friend, as he was removing the paint and false nose from his face; "why not have trusted to Sir Richard Everil?"

"I trust to few men," replied Patch, seriously; "whilst I keep my secret I am its master; when I reveal it, I become its slave. Besides," he added, "my name might compromise my master's, even as from the leaf men guess the tree."

"Can it be possible," exclaimed Walter, "that Wolsey knows of——"

"Hush!" said the jester, "that is a subject on which I have no half confidence to give; with me, 'tis all or none."

CHAPTER IX.

When headstrong cruelty o'erbeareth right;
Wresting the sword of justice unto malice,
Straining authority to evil ends:
The fox's cunning, and the serpent's wiles;
Virtue permitteth them.—*Heir of the Sept.*

N the following night Patch and his companion resumed their disguise, and left York House by the private postern for the place of rendezvous, keeping a sharp lookout, as they crept along the bank of the Thames, for Sir Richard Everil and his nephew. Every boat was carefully scrutinised as it passed up or down the river; one or two were even hailed, the rowers of which either answered by abuse or passed on in silence. By this time they had reached Westminster, where they crossed the stream to Lambeth.

"Surely they cannot intend to play us false," whispered Walter, "or to fail us?"

"Neither," said the jester, in an under tone. "The knight is an artful fox, who hath served under the emperor Maximilian in the Low Countries; he was mixed up, too, with Perkin Warbeck's troubles in the late king's reign, when Lord Stanley lost his head and the poor youth his crown. The old soldier hath but taken his precautions against our treachery; he is more suspicious of us than thou canst be of him."

A loud shout from a long rakish-looking cutter which was moored close to the palace wharf prevented our hero's reply. By the light of the moon, which was at its full, every object was distinctly visible upon the stream; and he counted ten or twelve men seated on the benches. Judging from their laughter, and the frequent snatches of songs, he took them for foreign sailors who had been drinking.

"Let us avoid them," he said, laying his hand upon the jester's sleeve, who, after a few moments' hesitation, had quickened his pace towards the boat; "doubtless they have frightened our friends from the place of meeting."

"My priesthood against my cap and bells," replied Patch, "but they are our friends."

"For once, I tell thee, that thou art in error; they are Germans—listen to their song."

A second shout of laughter interrupted the speaker; it was followed by the last verse of the song—

" Du Heilige ! hor Deiner Kinder Flehen
  Es dringe machteg auf zu Deinem Licht.
  Kannst wieder freundlich auf uns niedersehen
  Verklarter Engel ! Langer weine nicht !

"Are you convinced?" demanded Walter, as the echo of their voices died away.

"As much," answered his companion, "as by a rogue's profession of his honesty, or a courtier's vow of disinterestedness. But we shall soon see," he added; "for, if I mistake not, here comes two of the crew to reconnoitre us."

An old sailor and a young one, both in the Flemish costume, advanced towards them as he spoke. It was impossible to recognise them from their features, for they wore their shaggy caps pulled closely over their brows; while their beards, worn long, after the fashion of their country, equally hid the lower part of their faces. Without the slightest salutation, or sign of acquaintance-ship, they passed the two pretended friars, apparently disputing warmly between them-selves, in their own language, on their way. Walter cast a smile of good-natured triumph on his friend, whom he was delighted to find, as he thought, for once in his life, at fault.

"What say you now?" he demanded.

"As I did before," coolly replied the jester; "they are our friends. As soon as they have reached the end of the walk, and ascertained that we are unaccompanied—for I told you the knight was an old soldier, and as suspicious as a fox—they will return and accost us."

The speaker was right, for at the very point he indicated, the two sailors paused, looked sharply round them, and, as if satisfied with the survey, began to retrace their steps towards the spot where he and his companion were standing. It was now the former's turn to smile, which he did so comically that Walter scarcely winced at the retaliation.

"Goot naicht, mine holy faders!" cried the elder of the mariners, in a strong German accent, as he overtook them. "You come to make some prayers to de vish to-night, or say your penance to de moon?"

"Really, Sir Richard," answered the elder of the party to whom the question was ad-dressed, "considering your age, and long ab-sence from court, you have a pretty talent for intrigue; your accent deceived my young companion here."

"Outflanked !" exclaimed the knight, frankly extending his hand; "you will ad-mit my strategy at least was fair—mask for mask, battery for battery. Old soldier as I am," he added, "you have beaten me; in masquerading I am no match for you."

"Probably not," said Patch, with a sigh; "for my whole life hath been one. Yon boat," he continued, pointing to the one where the singers were seated, "is yours?"

"It is."

"And the rowers?"

"Are my friends."

"And she belongs?" added the jester.

"To a vessel at Gravesend, which is ready to lift anchor and make sail for Antwerp the moment I and my son set foot on board."

"You must take a companion in your flight."

"Willingly," said Sir Richard.

"A good old man," interrupted Walter, "whose only crime hath been the reading of Luther's book against King Henry's treatise—a schoolman's curiosity, and not a sceptic's thirst. The gaoler boasted," he added, "that there was a third within the tower."

"There will be room for all," said the knight, eagerly; "persecution teacheth its victims mercy. Heaven forbid that we, from any selfish motives, should leave the just work half accomplished; but time presses."

Patch and his comrade produced from under their disguise a frock and capuchin similar to their own, in which the nephew of the speaker, with a little assistance, quickly arrayed himself—retaining, however, by way of precaution, his arms beneath his dress. As soon as the metamorphosis was complete, the three friends directed their steps towards the palace; where, by this time, its ruffianly guardians were expecting them. Before bidding adieu to their companion, it was arranged that the gaoler and his satel-lites, in the event of their leaving their post, should be secured, and conveyed in safety on board the boat, with which understanding they parted.

"You are late," said the gaoler, as the three pretended friars arrived at the foot of the Lollards' Tower; "I have been on the look-out for you for the last two hours, and began to think your zeal had cooled."

"It is more than my thirst has," replied Patch, as, with an affectation of fatigue, he waddled up the narrow stone staircase leading to the warder's room, which served also as a question chamber for the judges and examiners of the primate's court. "Holy St. John," he added, "but these steps are hard to mount; they take away the little breath fasting and prayer have left me."

"Hard to mount!" repeated his conductor, with a broad grin upon his face; "many complain that they are harder to descend. The screams of the heretics will sometimes startle even the screech owls from the hiding-places."

The young men shuddered; for they understood the allusion to the mangled limbs and sufferings of the prisoners. The short dry cough of their companion warned them to be silent.

The apartment into which they were shown was, with the exception of the one in which the captives were confined, the loftiest in the tower. The entrance to it was directly opposite the narrow iron-barred windows, which grudgingly admitted but scanty portions both of air and light. On the wall facing the open chimney, in which a cheerful fire was burning, were ranged a collection of instruments, whose use would puzzle an antiquary of the present day; but which was perfectly understood by the brutal inmates of the place, whose business it was to employ them. Thumb-screws, gyves, iron boots, maiden's collars and belts, whose jagged spikes at every turn of the wretched wearer's body lacerated the flesh, were amongst the most simple of the contrivances. There were other inventions, of so complicated a nature, so scientifically devilish, so capable of stimulating the palsied nerves to the endurance of fresh agony, that even the guardians who had the care of them looked upon them with a species of terror and respect. Had Satan, as is the case on the visit of one potentate to another, passed in review the artillery of mother Church, he might have carried back several useful hints, and complained sadly, on his return to his dominions, *that his mechanists were in arrear.*

"A goodly collection," said the jester, after he and his two companions had for some time silently examined them; "they must be obstinate heretics whom such arguments will not convince. What do you call this, friend gaoler?" he added, pointing to a frame which contained a most suspicious looking arrangement of pulleys, knives, and cords.

"That," said the ruffian, "is called the bishop's cradle; it was invented by a German prelate in the time of the crusades, and proved the means of converting thou-

sands of infidels: he was afterwards canonised"

"Was he," said Patch, "the blessed man? *But, doubtless, he has his reward.* It must have been far more officacious than argument, which the benighted heathen would not have understood. Do you ever use it now?" he added.

The gaoler shook his head mournfully as he replied—

"No, holy father; it is unfortunately out of order. We tried it twice, but somehow it killed the prisoner each time; so his grace, who is of a sweet pitiful nature, has given orders that it should be used no more. We keep it now merely as a sort of——"

"Pious relic," continued the friar, seeing that he was at a loss for a word; "I understand."

"But what are these?" He pointed to a row of small instruments as he spoke.

"Those," said the gaoler, taking three or four of them down, and throwing them upon the table, "are thumb-screws. We shall want them by-and-by," he added, with a leer at the friar as he did so.

"*I trust we shall,*" replied the jester, with a look equally expressive; "but first, friend, for the love of our Lady, give me a cup of wine. I have not moistened my lips since vespers, as I'm a Christian priest."

The fellow walked to a corner of the room, and poured out a cup of wine from a large stone bottle, which he carefully placed upon the table, after handing the cup to the speaker, who prudently smelt it before applying it to his lips.

"Excellent liquor, no doubt, friend," he said drily, "for thy prisoners, but somewhat too thin for thy guests; hast thou no better wine than this?"

"None," answered the gaoler; "but I know where it may be procured."

"Where?"

"At the Rose," replied the ruffian, smacking his lips, for he remembered the flavour of the draught the friar had given him to seal their bargain with on the previous evening.

"Out on thee for a rogue," said Patch, poking him playfully in the ribs; "dost think that holy church is as rich in carnal wealth as spiritual treasure? Well, well," he continued, as if melted by the recollection of the good quality of the liquor of mine host of the Golden Rose, "it is not often that we indulge in creature-comforts; there is a testoon, send for the wine, and then to our goodly work."

He threw the piece upon the table as he spoke.

"You, Bernard, go for the wine," said the

fellow, who exercised a sort of authority over the rest; "and you, Gills, to see that he does not drink it on the way; remember fair play is a jewel."

"Regarded even amongst thieves," added the donor of the coin, who saw the two fellows depart with ill-concealed satisfaction, for the parties were now three to two.

"When shall we begin?" demanded Walter of the gaoler, for he began to be impatient of the delay.

"As soon as the captain has been his round."

"And that," said the jester, carelessly, as if he were asking the most innocent question in the world, "will be——"

"Exactly at midnight," replied the unsuspecting functionary.

It wanted rather more than a quarter to the time.

"Does he visit your prisoners?" said Patch, taking up one of the thumb-screws and examining it very attentively, as if to make himself quite master of the mechanism of the instrument.

"A mere form," said the fellow; "he knocks with his halberd at the door of the tower, and calls, 'Safe ward?' I reply, 'All's well,' unless," added the fellow, "I happen to be drunk, in which case I answer——"

"In the devil's keeping," said the assistant gaoler, with a laugh, imitating at the same time the gruff voice of his superior.

A glance of intelligence passed between the three friars; they probably thought the information worth noting, and not the less so that it was gratuitous.

"And what is this, friend?" demanded the eldest of them, taking up a short bar of wood, covered in the centre with cork, and having strong leathern thongs at each end.

"Oh! that," said the gaoler, "is a gag; his grace the primate is a humane man, and cannot bear to hear the cries of the prisoners, as they are undergoing the question in the tower; it disturbs his meditations."

"So I should think," observed Patch, drily.

"A childish contrivance," continued the fellow, with an air of contempt, "since thrust it into their mouths as far as you will, it cannot hurt them, provided they bite deeply enough into the cork—otherwise it might, perhaps, dislocate their jaws, nothing more."

"Really," said his questioner, "the weakness of the reverend lord almost makes me blush; "but holy church is so merciful."

"Very," chimed in the two novices.

The speaker took up one of the thumb-screws, and began opening the machine,

turning the vices awkwardly, as if to see how they acted. The gaoler looked upon him with a smile of pity at his ignorance.

"Not that way, holy father—not that way!" he exclaimed. "Bless me, how ignorant men become by living in the cloister! See," he added, taking the instrument from his hand, "this is the way they are applied."

The speaker offered to fix them upon the hands of the friar, who drew back with an air of childish timidity. It was no part of his intention that they should be tried upon himself.

"What!" continued the fellow with a laugh, "are you afraid that I should give your pious fingers a squeeze? Here," he said, turning to his companion, "hold out your dainty thumbs, and let his reverence see how they should be used."

His companion did as he was directed, and in an instant the instrument was closed upon him, and the screw turned, not sufficiently to hurt him, but only to hold him tight. Again the three friars exchanged looks, which seemed to say that the decisive moment had arrived.

"By our Lady," cried the jester, with the most candid air imaginable, taking up a second instrument from the table, "but it does seem very easy. I almost think I could manage it myself. Hold out thy thumbs, friend, and let me try."

The unsuspecting gaoler, with a laugh, did as he was requested; in fact, he lent himself to the caprice of his guest much with the air of an old soldier who lends his weapon to a child to play with, giving the bungler directions all the while to use it. He found Patch an apt scholar.

"Now," he said, as soon as he had placed his digits in the hollow, "close the lid—quite right; don't be afraid of hurting me."

"I won't," muttered the learner to himself.

"That's it," he continued, "turn the screw—bravo!—excellent!—you'll do it as well as I can in time. Gently—the other way—the other way, I tell you—curse it, the fool has crushed my fingers."

The gaoler and his companion being thus cleverly secured, the three friars immediately proceeded to action. The young men drew their concealed weapons from beneath their gowns, whilst their comrade hastily barred the doors of the apartment.

"Betrayed!" roared the astonished ruffian, who saw too late that he had been made a fool of. "What, ho! captain of the guard—treason; the prisoners will es——"

His further exclamations, as well as his attempt to reach the window, were cut short by Patch, who thrust one of the gags, the use of which he had so elaborately explained, into his mouth, and tied it with the leathern thongs tightly at the back of his head. Walter and his brother novice did the same kind office for his assistant—a stolid, stupid-looking fellow, who appeared too much surprised at the whole proceedings to offer the least resistance.

"Not badly arranged," said the jester, with a smile of satisfaction, to his friend, as soon as the operation was complete. "I question if our old acquaintance Adam could have managed it much better. We must, however, secure them to the staples in the wall."

Despite the mute resistance of the wretches, they were compelled at last to yield. An extra turn or two of the thumbscrews made them as tractable as lambs. It was truly astonishing how very clever their pupil had become; certes, he was an apt scholar.

"Where are the keys of the upper chamber?" he demanded of the chief gaoler.

The fellow remained with his eyes obstinately fixed upon the ceiling; it required more than an extra twinge before he pointed with his manacled hands to the hook where they were hanging; for, of course, he could not speak.

"Good!" said Patch, with a patronising air; "we shall understand each other in time."

The ruffian's eyes flashed with fearful fury; for the first time in his life he had been made to feel a slight portion of the pangs he had so frequently inflicted; and, like most brutal natures, he was cowardly sensitive of pain. At this moment thee distinct knocks were given with the but-end of a halberd upon the door below, and the voice of the captain of the guard was heard demanding, "Safe ward?"

This was the most critical moment of the whole. The captives naturally imagined that the captain of the watch, not hearing the usual reply, would mount the stairs to ascertain the cause, and already they indulged in the anticipation of a ferocious vengeance. They were doomed, however, to disappointment; for the jester advanced coolly to the window, and imitating the gaoler's voice, for he was an excellent mimic, roared out in a drunken tone, "In the devil's keeping."

A low inarticulate growl announced the fellow's hopeless rage at the success of the trick. In a few minutes the tramp of the guard died away, and the three adventurers mounted to the upper chamber to release their friends, whom they found barbarously chained against the wall, in such a position that it was impossible for them to lie or sit.

Walter and his young companion hastily released Father Celestine and the son of Sir Richard Everil from their chains. The third prisoner was a youth of not more than sixteen, whose emaciated frame and terror-stricken gaze announced that his sufferings, both mentally and physically, must have been great.

"God!" muttered Patch to himself, as he unlocked the poor boy's fetters, "can such cruelties exist?"

No sooner was the captive released than he sank upon his knees to the supposed friar, imploring his pity. The sight of a churchman's robe had lately been to him a sign of persecution. No wonder that it inspired him with fear. It was not without some difficulty that its wearer reassured him.

"How came you within their toils?" he demanded. "Thou art too young for heresy. Tell me thy name."

"Louis," replied the youth, hesitatingly.

"Louis! what else?"

"D'Auverne," he faltered.

"D'Auverne!" almost shrieked his liberator, dreadfully agitated at the name. "It cannot be; devils would pause at such a deed. Poor boy! thou shalt be avenged—terribly, fearfully avenged! This present hour I must devote to thy security. That once assured, thine enemies may tremble. Give me a token," he added, "that thou hast not deceived me."

The rescued youth whispered something in his ear which perfectly assured the speaker of the truth; for, with a burst of almost parental fondness, he pressed him to his heart. It was not often the jester was thus moved.

The late captives could scarcely believe in their good fortune when told that they were free. Their situation was still one, however, of too much danger to permit any time to be wasted in idle congratulations. Holding his young charge, in whose safety he had so suddenly become interested, by the hand, Patch conducted the fugitives from their prison; nor did the party once pause to draw breath till they reached the boat, where they found the knight and his friends most anxiously expecting them. The two warders, who had been sent to the Golden Rose for wine, were lying gagged and fast bound at the bottom of the vessel.

"We have performed our promise," said the leader of the expedition to Sir Richard, pointing to his companions; "now, then, keep yours."

"And must we never meet again?" demanded the grateful father, who could scarcely keep his eyes from the contemplation of his rescued son, or sufficiently thank his mysterious deliverer.

"Never," said the friar, sadly; "our paths in life are different. Those who see me masked must never know me, should we meet face to face."

"Is there no proof of my gratitude——"

"Yes," interrupted the jester, "take this boy; protect his flight to Antwerp; guard him as you would the token on which depends your safety. Save him for my sake, love him for his own."

"He will deserve it, father," exclaimed his fellow-prisoner; "he hath cheered my heart in many a lonely hour."

"By heaven!" said the knight solemnly, taking the boy by the hand, "I will; he shall be unto me even as a son."

The youth silently kissed his hand, and fixed his eyes inquiringly on Patch, on whom he suddenly seemed to place unbounded confidence.

"What are we to do with these ruffians?" demanded one of the rowers, pointing to the prisoners at the bottom of the boat. "To release them were madness—to slay them unnecessary cruelty."

"Take them with you," said the jester; "they are more fortunate than their comrades in the tower yonder, whose lives must pay the penalty of this night's work. Now, then, away at once," he added—"pull for your lives. If assailed, defend yourselves like men for whom mercy is no more; remember that the axe and cord are suspended over the neck of every one till he sets foot in Antwerp."

Walter hastily embraced his venerable friend, and placed him in the vessel, where the other fugitives were already seated. Waving his hand in silent adieu, he and his companion remained standing on the bank watching them as they disappeared. The tide, most fortunately, was running down, and the bark shot like an arrow towards London Bridge.

At this moment the beacon, which was always kept ready, was lit on the summit of the Lollards' Tower, to warn the water-guard that some prisoners had escaped. The palace-watch, on their return, finding the door of the prison open, and obtaining no answer to their summons, had mounted to the chamber of the gaoler, and all was consequently discovered.

"We may still give them time," said Patch, rushing to the only boat near the bank, and tossing the oars into the middle of the stream. "Now, then," he added, "off with your frock and cowl."

Walter did as he was directed.

"Can you swim?"

A plunge in the water was the reply. It was followed by a second; and ere the pursuers could reach even the bank the two friends had gained the current, and were making way rapidly towards York House, on the opposite side of the river. A discharge of fire-arms which took place indicated that they were seen, and the splashing of the balls in the water near them warned the swimmers that they were not yet entirely out of danger.

The tide being in their favour, a very short time brought them to the landing-place, up which they carefully crept, for the moon was shining so brightly that they were fearful of being seen making their way to the postern, which the jester carefully opened. Once inside, the fugitives were safe.

"Our friends," whispered Walter, anxiously, "think you they will escape?"

"If they show a bold front they will," replied his companion, shaking himself like a great water dog. "Young man," he added, "there is a strange sort of confidence between us—something like that which, in my boyhood's days, I once called friendship, till the world taught me another name."

"Call it so still," said our hero; "old names are most familiar to the heart, certain to the ear."

"I mean to try it," continued Patch.

"How so?" demanded the youth, anxious to prove the strength of his attachment to his capricious friend.

"You saw my meeting with yon poor boy to-night?"

"I did, with wonder—what of it?"

"What wouldst thou do if I should bid thee by this friendship, then—this school-boy dream which thou believest in—to forget it?"

"Forget it!" answered Walter, with a simplicity which was at once a pledge of his sincerity and truth.

"I think thou art right, after all—old names are best," said the jester. "Therefore we'll call it friendship." With these words the speakers separated, each one to press a sleepless, anxious pillow.

On the following morning, Wolsey, with his usual attendants, took water to visit the court at Greenwich. During the voyage, Patch, who had once more donned his official costume, remained close behind his master's seat, occasionally leaning over it in earnest conversation. Once or twice, from the expression of his countenance, Walter imagined that he was relating to his eminence the history of their last night's adventure. While thus engaged, none of the household, not even Cromwell or Cavendish, ventured to approach the churchman; it being an understood thing that when thus occupied with the fool, the cardinal desired no listeners to what passed between them. The gilded barge at last drew up close to the landing-place, where the college now stands. A group of courtiers and lacqueys, in the royal liveries, were watching its arrival.

"Welcome, my Lord of York," said Sir Thomas Wyat, more favourably known as a poet than a courtier, and whose after connection, real or supposed, with Anne Boleyn nearly cost him his life. "His majesty is walking in the park. I am honoured with his commands to conduct your grace to his presence. He is impatient for your company."

The haughty prelate merely bowed, and taking a packet which the Earl of Derby presented to him, motioned to the speaker to precede him. The jester fell back into his usual place in the train, near to his favourite Walter. They had not proceeded far across the park before they encountered Henry, who, with his attendants, was amusing himself by shooting with a cross bow at the butts. As soon as he beheld his minister, he cast the instrument aside, and advanced to meet him. The monarch was, at this time, in the prime of life, of that goodly presence which the portraits of him by Holbein have rendered familiar to the English people. Although stout, his person presented no indication of that frightful obesity which in the latter years of his life rendered him incapable of all active sports, and so soured his temper that he became an object of terror to all who ventured to approach him.

"You have returned in right good time, my lord," he exclaimed, graciously extending his hand, which Wolsey kissed. "By my halidom, but we began to grudge the Norfolk boors so much of your fair presence. But you have heard the news?—Clement hath found his reason."

"I have," replied the churchman.

"Ha! this looks like business," continued the king, rubbing his hands with an air of satisfaction. "The holy father tires, it seems, of the double part the emperor imposes, and sends his legates with full powers to decide 'twixt me and Kate. Campeggio has arrived at Calais."

A close observer might have remarked a troubled expression in the eye of Wolsey at the intelligence.

"Never hath Rome sent so beggarly an ambassador," continued the speaker. "No matter, we must honour him, if not for his master's sake, for the cause he comes to judge. See to it, Wolsey—see to it; the honour of thy purple is concerned."

The minister gravely bowed in token of obedience.

"And now," said Henry, "come with me to the terrace. Thou must see Kate and prepare her for the coming trial. Heaven knows," he added, hypocritically, "it is not for the vain pleasures of concupiscence that we have raised the question, but for the satisfaction of our conscience. Conscience, cardinal," he repeated, throwing his arm at the same time familiarly over his favourite's shoulder, "the only monitor of kings."

"And the one," whispered Patch to his companion Walter, "which they least attend to."

Katherine of Arragon, the unhappy wife of Henry VIII., was seated on the terrace of Greenwich Palace, attended by her maids of honour, enjoying the morning breeze. Amongst the bevy of fair girls and noble dames who, divided into various groups, were indulging in the usual gossip of a court, was the beautiful but thoughtless Anne Bullen, or Boleyn—for the name is spelt indifferently by contemporary writers—the queen's still more unfortunate successor. At this period, although the attentions of Henry were sufficiently marked, the lively object of them was far from indulging in the hope that his capricious love would one day raise her to the crown. Still less did she dream that it would precipitate her from it to the scaffold. Educated in the gallant court of France, whither she accompanied the king's sister on her marriage with Louis XII., admiration was familiar to her; perhaps it also afforded her an opportunity of tormenting a young nobleman, to whom at this time she was engaged, Lord Percy, eldest son of the Earl of Northumberland, which engagement, at the secret instigation of Henry, Wolsey contrived to break, and hence the future queen's bitter animosity towards the cardinal.

"And you really think her pretty?" said Anne to the Countess of Derby, glancing at the same time towards the heiress of Stanfield, who, seated at Katherine's feet, was for the second time relating to her royal benefactress the trials and dangers to which she had been exposed.

The countess nodded assent; and added, "Wyat thinks her so."

"Oh!" resumed the fair questioner poutingly; "like his friend Surrey, he admires every fair woman. Poets are seldom judges of beauty. Has the king seen her yet?"

This was asked with an air of indifference, as if it were the most unimportant question in the world. Her companion smiled; she was too long accustomed to the amosphere of a court to be deceived.

THE QUARREL BETWEEN THE MERCHANTS AND CITIZENS.

"Not yet," she replied. "The lady, it seems, was too much fatigued with her journey to be present at last night's masque; but here comes his majesty; now, then, we shall judge."

Katherine rose at the approach of her unkind husband, who saluted her with the ceremonious politeness due to her rank—a respect which, to his credit it may be observed, he never forgot. Casting his eyes round the circle, perhaps to avoid the mute imploring look of the queen, they fell upon the Lady Mary. With his usual brusque manner, he demanded—

"Hey, May-bird! who have we here?"

Wolsey named his protegée to the monarch, who was still leaning on his shoulder.

"What!" he exclaimed, "my old friend Manny's grandchild? Hast any semblance of his honest face?"

The queen whispered her to approach, which the orphan did with graceful modesty, and bent the knee before the speaker, whose evident admiration was commented on by all present.

Anne Boleyn looked furious, and Walter unhappy.

Patch, who loved a game of cross purposes, was, perhaps, the only party present who was amused.

"By my faith!" continued the king, half-playfully and half-wantonly touching her burning cheek with his finger, "thou hast thy grandsire's clear bright eye—though, not to wrong the good knight's memory, a some-what fairer visage. Welcome, sweetheart, to our court. 'Tis the fairest maiden," he added, turning to Wolsey, "I have set eyes upon since Lammastide."

Covered with blushes, the trembling orphan withdrew to her place beside the queen. The eyes of Anne Boleyn were fixed upon her with an angry expression as she did so. Half the court already set them down as rivals.

"Kate," said Henry, turning to his wife, who still retained her seat upon the terrace, "before vespers my lord of York will visit you in your closet; his errand is of special import—touching our future peace."

The unhappy Katherine meekly bowed her head in token of acquiescence—or perhaps it was to hide a tear. She dreaded Wolsey's visits: they had of late been fatal to her happiness. Nor was the cardinal himself much less embarrassed.

"Who is that youth?" demanded the king, glancing at Walter, whose agitated countenance during the interview between the heiress and himself had not escaped his observation.

"Walter Lucas, the youth I named to your majesty," answered his eminence, at the same time making a sign to the young man to approach, who immediately bent the knee before the monarch, who eyed him with an expression of countenance which those who knew him judged to be anything but favourable.

"By St. George! a stalwart youngster, well knit, and stout of limb," he exclaimed, "whose services have merited our favour. Let him," he added, turning to the minister, "be the bearer of your letters to Campeggio; we owe him so much grace."

Radiant with smiles, the unsuspecting youth would have expressed his gratitude, for he deemed the unexpected command of the monarch the first step in the ladder which was to elevate him nearer to the object of his wishes. But a peculiar look from his protector restrained him; he contented him-self, therefore, by bowing and retreating to his old position by the side of Patch.

"I am fortunate," he whispered to his companion.

"Very," said the jester, drily; "as fortu-nate as the starving traveller in the desert who found a pearl."

"What mean you?" demanded the youth.

"Simply that a loaf would have been better," replied his friend; "nothing more —but silence," he continued, "the game is but beginning; we shall have more sport yet."

At this moment, to the terror of Walter, Archbishop Warham, attended by the cap-tain of his guard and a party of yeomen, leading the gaoler and his companion prisoner, appeared upon the terrace.

The aged primate's voice trembled with agitation as he addressed the king, and in-formed him of the escape of Father Celes-tine, whose crime was in Henry's eyes second only to treason.

"What," said the tyrant, his eyes flashing with ill-suppressed rage, "have we traitors so near us? 'Tis time we took the reins in our own hands, since delegated rule grows weak, and rank offence aims at our very person. Knew you of this, my lord?" he added, turning fiercely upon Wolsey.

"No such report," said his eminence, calmly, "hath been made to me. The prisoner was not in my keeping. The mo-ment I heard of his monstrous crime I for-warded him under a sure escort to the Tower. It was by your majesty's own order, as I hear," concluded the speaker, "that he was transferred to Lambeth."

"Right!" exclaimed Henry, in a milder tone. "I was a fool to trust the villain to the guard of doting age. Thou art always right, good Wolsey; we are as a child when counselled by another."

"Sire," said the venerable Warham, deeply moved by the brutal passion of his master, "my age indeed is heavy, since you reproach me with it."

"Tut, tut, tut—let that pass," muttered the king; "when our blood is chafed we measure not the letter of our words. What hang-dogs," he added, glaring ferociously upon the prisoners, "bring you with you?"

"So please your majesty, the gaolers," said the primate, "by whose treachery or carelessness the prisoners have escaped."

The terrified wretches sank upon their knees before their inexorable judge, exclaim-ing, "Mercy!"

Walter was about to start forward and avow the whole transaction. Hardened as their office had rendered them, he could not endure the thought of their suffering death through any act of his. Patch saw his intention, and laying his hand upon his arm, quietly whispered him:

"There is a better way: follow me."

The youth obeyed him like a child, and retreated after him from the circle. In a few minutes they were seated in a chamber in one of the smaller turrets of the palace, the jester's usual lodging when at Greenwich with his master. First carefully locking the door, he pointed to a seat, and took one opposite to him : Walter's back was to the window.

"Thou hast one peculiar talent for a courtier," said Patch, as soon as they were seated.

"Indeed! What is that?"

"The art of compromising thy friends."

"No matter," exclaimed the young man; "I cannot bear the thought that yon poor wretches should suffer for my crime; their dying groans would haunt me in my dreams. I grant them heartless, cruel, hardened in their fearful office, till it hath brutalised their nature; bad as they are, they are but what society hath made them."

"A philosopher," interrupted his companion.

"No," resumed the speaker, "but a man who would risk something to keep a quiet conscience. Henry lately spoke to me with favour, commended my zeal and service. I will confess all, and——"

"Die," added the jester; "I have no wish to hang even in thy company."

"Thinkest thou I could betray thee?"

"No," answered Patch; "but I might betray myself. Poor boy, thou art surrounded with dangers enough already; from this, at least, I have preserved thee. Whither wouldst thou go?" he demanded, observing that Walter was advancing towards the door.

"To the king."

"Too late," said his friend, pointing to the window. "Behold!"

The gaoler and his companion were swinging from the branches of a lofty oak in front of the tower where they sat.

CHAPTER X.

The cunning net which fraud and treachery weave
Shall oft by Providence o'erruling hand
Be spread to their confusion, and the mesh
In which they sought to snare their victim's steps
Prove their own pitfall.—CREON

IMMEDIATELY after the execution of the gaoler and his assistant, Henry took the arm of his favourite, Sir John Perrot, a courtier, who continued longer, perhaps, than any other to retain the friendship of the capricious monarch, and drew him aside towards the park, a signal to those in attendance to keep out of ear shot. Such confidence was not uncommon between the king and knight, who exercised a sort of secret ministry under his suspicious master; and who was frequently employed by him in certain delicate transactions, the nature of which even Wolsey was supposed to be a stranger to.

The divorce between Henry VIII. and Katherine of Arragon is one of the many questions of history which have never been fairly judged. As one of the leading causes of the Reformation in England, it has been regarded by Protestants with favour, and on the other side as severely censured by Catholics. Two points, at least, may be urged in its justification—first, that the principal universities of Europe, when consulted upon the subject, unanimously pronounced against the validity of the marriage; secondly, that when a treaty of union was proposed between the Princess Mary and the Duke of Orleans, Francis I. expressed considerable doubts as to her legitimacy.

Knowing how completely the reigning pope, Clement, was in the interests of the emperor, the nephew of Katherine, Henry was naturally suspicious of the impartiality of the judges before whom the question was to be tried, even though one of those judges was his own subject and favourite, Wolsey. As legates, they were completely under the control of the pontiff, whose insincerity throughout the entire proceedings was unworthy the head of the church.

"So, Perrot," said the monarch, as soon as they were alone, "this beggarly Italian hath arrived at Calais, where our governor writes me word he is detained for lack of means. Methinks," he added, bitterly, "the holy father, when he sends a legate to our court, might at least furnish him with the necessary *viaticum*. By St. Paul! but he takes tithe enough to do so."

"St. Peter's net," replied the courtier, with a smile, "is like a mouse-trap."

"How so?" demanded his master.

"It lets all in, but nothing out," answered the knight.

"Right, Perrot, right!" exclaimed Henry, with a hearty laugh; for the simile, coarse as it was, pleased him. "Rome swallows up in agnats enough to support an army. Perhaps we may one day take some measure with it touching the subject; but of this no word at present; the time is far from ripe. Didst mark that stripling lately—Lucas I think my Lord of York named him in our presence."

"I did, your grace," said the courtier; "also the impatient look which followed the mark of favour your highness bestowed upon the maid of Stanfield!"

"I noted him," replied the monarch, with a look which was anything but a favourable augury for the subject of their conversation.

"In sooth, the maid is fair," continued the courtier, "and merits a sovereign's favour."

"Dost thou think so?" demanded the prince, with an affectation of indifference, which did not deceive his companion, who knew how seldom the speaker gave expression, even to him, of his real sentiments. "Of her, perhaps, hereafter; for the present," he added, "of this Lucas. He is to be the bearer of Wolsey's letters to his brother legate—to this Italian priest Campeggio."

"True, your grace."

"I must have those letters," continued Henry, in a whisper, as if fearful that the trees should echo back his words. "I am consumed with doubts which burn like an overflowing gall within me. I will be satisfied. Priest to priest, they will be confidential. I'd know the writer's mind; I'd have his heart, Perrot, here in my hand, like an open book before me—read each thought, trace every subtle turning. Then, if I find the mitred puppet plays me false, I'll trample him, despite Rome's purple, like mire beneath my feet."

The courtier trembled at the dangerous confidence of his imperious master; he felt like a man who was walking blindfold upon the edge of a precipice—to advance or to retreat alike were dangerous.

"Hast heard my will, man?" continued the speaker, harshly. "We are not used to speak our pleasure twice."

"Your highness's favour," replied Sir John, "must be my shield, should my Lord of York suspect my agency in this said matter."

The request was not an unwise precaution, for Perrot well knew that the king had on more than one occasion sacrificed his private agents to the vengeance of his minister. This time, however, there was less danger; for Henry was in love, and suspected his powerful favourite.

"What!" he exclaimed, "hath the shadow become more powerful than the substance—the servant more dreaded than his master? 'Tis time I look about me, since a churchman's hat bears down a kingly crown."

"Your grace has misconceived me," faltered the courtier; "Heaven forbid a thought like this should wrong my master's honour. The letters shall be obtained—if possible, without violence," he added, fixing his eyes meaningly upon the king; "but should the bearer resist, and be slain——"

"Bury him," said Henry, carelessly; "what is a peasant's life against a monarch's pleasure? How now, my lords!" he continued, turning to his train, who, during the conversation, had kept at a respectful distance; "it seems that we must wait your service. It is not often princes complain they are alone."

The nobles, who understood the reproof as an ungracious intimation that they might approach the speaker, immediately thronged round their capricious master, who entered into conversation with them on the merits of a cast of hawks, which his brother-in-law, the Duke of Suffolk, had that very morning presented him with, and which he intended to fly on the morrow.

As the party proceeded through the royal chase of Greenwich, Sir John Perrot contrived gradually to fall into the rear of the courtiers; and soon afterwards, taking advantage of a turn in the wood, the knight detached himself from the royal train altogether, and retraced his way to the palace. As he mounted the steps of the terrace he encountered Patch, who, as usual, was loitering in the sun—a jest upon his lips for most men, and a sneer for some.

The courtier and the fool entered the courtyard together.

That very night a Benedictine monk and an esquire of the king's guard left the royal residence for Calais, each unsuspicious of the other's errand. The game had commenced; neither the cardinal nor the monarch trusted each other.

Early on the following morning Walter was prepared for his departure. He encountered his protector on his way to mass, attended by the noblemen and officers of the household; for even in the residence of the king, Wolsey maintained his state. The poor youth's heart was heavy, for he was about to undertake a journey without one farewell to the object of his love—one opportunity of entreating for her the watchful care of one whom, in his ignorance of courts, he believed to be all-powerful.

"'Tis well, young man," said his eminence, as the messenger knelt before him; "here are your credentials; spare not for spur or rein till you arrive at Dover, where the captain of the port, on the production of your despatches, will place a boat at your disposal. It is a high trust," he continued, "for one so young; execute it wisely, that our royal master may not find his favour thrown away upon the heedless or the worthless."

Cromwell, Wolsey's secretary, placed in the young man's hand a packet bound with a silken thread, and sealed with the cardinal's legantine seal. It was addressed to Campeggio. Walter placed it carefully in the breast of his doublet, exclaiming as he did so—

"They must reach my heart, my lord, who would deprive me of it. Fast as man can do your errand I will do it. Deign but to add your benediction on my way."

A close observer might have seen an uneasy expression in the churchman's eye, as he traced the air-drawn cross over the speaker's head, and bade God speed him.

The traveller had not proceeded far upon his journey before he heard the clatter of a heavy horse upon the lone stony road behind him. Turning his head, he was surprised to see the rider, whose features from the distance it was impossible to recognise, making signs to him to stop. Concluding that some portion, perhaps, of his instructions had been forgotten, he drew rein, and was shortly afterwards joined by his old friend Patch, who had ridden hard to join him.

"What errand brings thee here?" demanded the young man, holding out his hand.

"A fool's!" added the jester; "at least, the world would deem it so. I come to serve a friend. A pest upon thee, boy," he added, with a melancholy smile; "I shall get human soon, and all thy fault. Already I begin to dream, e'en as I dreamt in childhood's thoughtless days, when trust and friendship were not mockeries to me. But let that pass; we must speak touching thy journey and thy safety. The packet with the letters from our master to Campeggio——"

"Are safe in my possession," interrupted Walter, with surprise. "But what of them?"

"Thou wilt guard them well?" said the jester, in a tone of inquiry.

"Dost doubt my courage or my honesty?" exclaimed the young man, deeply wounded by the suspicion which he thought the words of the speaker were intended to convey. "Guard them well!" he repeated; "I'll guard them even with my life, should any try to deprive me of them."

"The trial will be made," coolly interrupted his companion. "'Tis to forewarn thee that I am here."

"Indeed! by whom?"

"A kingly robber, though not a kingly hand," continued Patch. "Canst thou, even when the knife is at thy throat, appear to sleep, and let no quivering lip, no blinking of the eye, or start of fear, betray thy trembling consciousness?"

"I can. But what of this?" demanded his hearer, still more and more confounded at his words.

"Simply," resumed the speaker, "that the letters which thou bearest, though addressed to the Italian priest Campeggio, are written for the king. Henry suspects his minister, and descends not to act the robber to satisfy his doubts. Now dost thou understand?"

"I do."

"And at the hostel on the road, where the attempt will be first made, wilt lend thyself to this apparent theft?"

"I will."

"Without one doubt of me or thought of treachery?" added the jester.

"Without one doubt of thee or thought of treachery," said Walter, firmly, and at the same time extending his hand to his companion; "for what is friendship if a doubt can shake it?"

"And I will prove a friend," exclaimed Patch, returning the pressure warmly. "Thy hand shall not be truer to thy purpose than I will be to thee. Clouds thou canst not see are gathering round thee; thy bark will soon be tossed upon a sea where sunken rocks and shifting sands threaten the inexperienced mariner. But fear not thou; the fool," he added, bitterly, "whose wit is only sharp enough to barb a jest, or win a courtier's smile, shall pilot thee in safety through the storm."

"Thanks," replied the young man, alarmed at the warning tone of the speaker, even while he gathered confidence from his promise of safety. He had already tried his faithfulness, and he knew he could rely on him.

"When the masque is played," resumed the jester, "and thou art fairly robbed, write as in deep despair to Wolsey; say thou hast retired to France until his indignation shall be passed; implore his pardon, curse thy luckless stars, act all the madness of the ambitious boy whose dream of greatness accident hath blighted."

"Retire to France!" faltered his bewildered hearer, to whom the idea of a separation from the object of his affections was insupportable. "Is there no other way?"

"Tut!" interrupted his friend, "I did not mean to put thy patience to so hard a trial. Old as I am, I still remember what love is — its self-tormenting doubts and jealousies, its sighs and April tears. The seeming robbery accomplished and thy letter to the cardinal dispatched, return at once to London."

"To London!" repeated Walter, in a tone of joy, which showed how great a burden was removed.

"Knowest thou one Marriet, a rich Lombard merchant and money-lender in the city?" demanded Patch, without paying any seeming attention to his emotion.

The reassured lover inclined his head to intimate that he did.

"Show him this token," continued the speaker, plucking one of the innumerable silver bells from his cap, and placing it in his companion's hand, "and he will shelter thee. Shouldst thou need gold, the miser's hand will count it down unsparingly before thee upon no better pledge than this same worthless bauble. Remain with him till I come or send for thee. Fear not," he added, seeing that the young man was about to speak—"fear not for the Lady Mary. She shall not lack protection in thy absence. I will watch over her with more than a lover's care—with all a father's love. She will be safe until we meet again."

Patch kept his promise; for, as our readers have doubtless long ere this discovered, he was no ordinary man, but one who pinned his faith upon his word. There were more mysteries about the jester than his cap and bells, as time will most probably unfold; but we must not anticipate our story.

An object is not more truly reflected in a mirror than are the frowns and smiles of greatness in a court. The old nobility, at the head of whom was the Duke of Norfolk, had never forgiven Wolsey his extraordinary rise in Henry's favour, or his magnificence, which eclipsed their own feudal state; still less could they understand his character, for they were as far removed from his genius as his greatness. The Catholic party, who were chiefly led by Warham, the primate, and Fisher, Bishop of Rochester, beheld with mistrust the suppression of the smaller mon-

asteries, which the cardinal had commenced, having obtained bulls to authorise the measure both from Clement and the preceding popes, intending to devote their revenues to the foundation of colleges and schools of learning.

Both of these parties beheld with pleasure the first appearance of coldness in the monarch towards his minister. Many who had been constant attendants on his levées now neglected them, and the chapel of the palace, which was formerly thronged when his eminence officiated, was, unless the king was present, comparatively deserted. Wolsey, though secretly galled, bore the insults of the court with proud indifference or cold contempt. Although, in all probability, he foresaw his downfall, he knew that the hour was not yet at hand; fate had reserved the favourite one triumph more.

On the Sunday after the departure of Walter the sacred edifice was thronged; Henry, as usual, was present. But little attention was paid by the crowd of nobles and courtiers to the mass; all were in expectation of a scene; it having been whispered that, as soon as the ceremony was over, the captain of the guard had received orders to arrest the cardinal, and the dukes of Norfolk and Suffolk to demand from him, in the king's name, the great seal.

Anne Boleyn, too, was there, in all the pride of her beauty, and ambitious whisperings of her heart, doubtless anticipating the downfall of her enemy, for such she regarded Wolsey to be, since in council he had recommended her removal from court until the question of the divorce should be decided. The only drawback to her contentment was the sight of the fair girl who knelt by the seat of the unhappy Katherine, and on whom Henry, from time to time, cast glances which ill accorded with the sacred precincts.

Just as the solemn service had commenced, Sir John Perrot, whose absence for several days had been noticed, made his appearance with a large missal under his arm. Advancing to the *prie Dieu* before the king, he reverentially placed the book upon it, and withdrew to his seat amongst the courtiers, as unconcerned as though he had but performed his customary service.

There were two hearts which beat the lighter as they beheld the act of the knight —the cardinal's and our old friend Patch's, who from a gallery above was intently watching the scene.

The impatient tyrant, who imagined that he alone understood what was meant, opened the jewelled-clasped volume, and found, as he expected, a letter between its illuminated leaves; it was bound, after the fashion of the times, with a silken thread, and sealed. We need not inform our readers that it was Wolsey's letter to Campeggio.

As the ceremony proceeded, the monarch broke the seal, and, whilst his courtiers imagined him absorbed in prayer, eagerly occupied himself in perusing its contents. After the usual salutations to his brother legate, the letter continued thus—

"Knowing that his grace hath a most subtle judgment, and, by his learning and skill in confuting heresy, hath deserved well, not only of the holy father, but the whole church,—I trust that the commission directed to us will extend to the satisfying of this matter, which proceedeth from no vain lusts, but an unquiet conscience. He hath ever been to me a princely master, and my greatness is but the shadow of his favour, exalting my unworthiness; wherefore I will bear with no injustice towards him. I have recommended the withdrawal of Mistress Anne Boleyn, of whom you speak, from court, to silence all unnecessary scandal; albeit she is of unblemished name touching her woman's prudence. Should the emperor, who taketh bitterly the cause of his aunt, albeit he once made question of the legitimacy of the Princess Mary when proposed that he should marry her, tamper on this matter, either with thee or with Rome, set both thy words and countenance, as I shall do, against it. Remember that justice is due to all, but how much more so to the illustrious prince who demands it from the church at our unworthy hands! Trust not too implicitly to the bearer of this; he is one in whom I have slight confidence. His grace's commands, which to me are laws, made him my messenger in this, which else had been trusted to another."

The concluding part of the letter treated of the manner of Campeggio's travelling, and the ceremonial of his entry into London, where their joint court was to be held. It is easy to understand now why Walter was directed to permit himself to be robbed so easily.

"So," muttered Henry, after had perused the missive, so different from what he expected, "this is the servant they would deprive me of! Faithful as when first I trusted him; cautious only for my advantage; prudent, even to his own danger, when 'tis to serve his master. Knaves!" he added, glancing on the principal enemies of his re-established favourite a look which, could they have interpreted, would have made many tremble. "I'll punish them as reptiles should be punished. I'll make them lick the very dust beneath their victim's feet."

Like all men of violent passion, Henry proceeded to extremes. The circumstance which had most weakened his minister in his favour was the recommending the retirement of Anne Boleyn; but it was now, if not satisfactorily, at least sufficiently explained. Perhaps the passion which the licentious monarch began to feel for the orphan heiress of Stanfield rendered him less susceptible in the matter, and he determined that the reparation to his favourite should be as signal as his former coldness had been unmerited.

At that part of the mass where the officiating priest pronounces—

"Lavabo inter innocentes manus meas—"
I will wash my hands among the innocent—

it is customary to present him with water, into which he dips his fingers—figuratively to purify himself for the approaching sacrifice. On all previous occasions when Wolsey had celebrated the sacred mystery in the royal chapel, there had been a struggle amongst the nobles for the honour of serving him, but on the present no one offered to stir. It was too tempting an opportunity to realise the fable of the ass kicking at the dying lion for the courtiers to neglect it. There was naturally a pause from the circumstance in the solemn rite. His enemies smiled at the cardinal's embarrassment, and wondered how he would extricate himself from it. Their wonder, however, was but of short duration; for, to their astonishment and terror, the king, leaving his elevated seat, advanced towards the altar, and, taking the golden ewer and basin from the attendant deacon, offered it himself to Wolsey,—an honour never, perhaps, conferred before or since by a crowned head upon any but the sovereign pontiff.

"Not to the unworthy servant!" exclaimed the cardinal in a voice of deep emotion, "but to the heavenly Master whose livery he wears, be all the honour of the king's humility."

Bowing his head to conceal the grateful tears which fell upon Henry's hand, the speaker dipped his fingers in the water, and as soon as the monarch had returned to his seat, resumed the celebration of the mass.

"I thought," whispered the Duke of Norfolk to the Earl of Oxford, "we should fail. Henry will not suffer a hair of his favourite's head to fall—despite his fits of anger, he loves the butcher's cur too well."

"His pride," replied the last named noble, "will rise with the unlooked-for honour. I had rather than a thousand marks I had been absent at the insult offered him. Though, after all," he added, "it was your grace's place to serve his eminence rather than mine."

"So, my lords," exclaimed the king, as he left the chapel, leaning on the arm of the triumphant churchman, "it seems that we must do your duty for you. Perhaps," he added, "the blood of Howard, Warrenne, and De Vere is too proud to serve where Henry Tudor leads, as if our favour could not raise the vilest scullion to be your equals."

"In rank," said De Vere firmly, the proud stream of his Norman ancestors rushing to his temples, "but not in blood."

This was a sore point with the fiery monarch, who frequently imagined that his Norman nobles looked down upon him as the descendant of Owen Tudor, a simple Welsh gentleman, forgetful that by his mother's side he was equally a Plantagenet.

"'Tis well, my lords," he exclaimed; "we may find the means, perchance, to tame this pride of blood. The hand which struck the traitor Buckingham is not palsied yet."

This was strong language, even from Henry VIII., to the son of a man who had so materially contributed to place his father upon the throne; but gratitude was never the failing of his race.

Wolsey, who foresaw how necessary the assistance of the nobility would be to the accomplishment of his master's designs, interposed, and skilfully played the mediator.

Oxford apologised for his warmth, for the allusion to the unfortunate Duke of Buckingham showed him that he was treading near a precipice. His excuses were not too gracefully received, and the prince, muttering something about fools and fantastic knaves, withdrew to his cabinet, still leaning on the arm of his minister.

"You have done an unwise thing, De Vere," whispered the Duke of Norfolk, as their sovereign and his favourite left them; "you have made a relentless enemy, and disposed the king against you."

"Be it so," replied the haughty peer, turning upon his heel; "I can yield to the lion, but disdain to crouch before the jackal. Your grace's humour is more pliant, perhaps."

A dark scowl from the duke followed the retreating form of the speaker. His grace was one of the most servile courtiers of the day; indeed, so much so that he afterwards pronounced sentence of death upon his own niece, the unfortunate Anne Boleyn, after repeatedly interrupting her defence. A few minutes afterwards, and he was seated in the cabinet with Henry and Wolsey.

That same day two orders were given which occasioned much surprise and gossiping at court. The Earl of Oxford was commanded to retire to his estates, and Sir Thomas Boleyn quietly ordered to withdraw his daughter to Hever Castle, his family residence in Kent, until the question of the queen's divorce should be decided.

On the 8th of November, 1528, Campeggio, after a tedious journey from Dover, arrived near London; but refused, contrary to custom, to make a triumphal entry into the city, wishing, most probably, to give a mournful rather than a joyful air to his mission. He took up his abode at Bath House, a mansion belonging to Wolsey, close to Temple Bar, some remains of which are still to be seen bearing the cardinal's arms.

At the first public interview between the legate and the king, everything passed in the usual smooth and complimentary style. He addressed Henry as the defender of the faith and deliverer of the pope, who had recently been a prisoner to the emperor, with other flattering remarks, particularly gratifying at such a period from a papal legate, although at the present day they would be thought dearly purchased by the gift of two hundred and forty thousand pounds, which sum Henry had lately presented to the pope to assist him in his difficulties.

In their private interview, however, the tone of Campeggio was altered. He used many arguments to persuade the king from the steps he wished to pursue—an interference which the impatient prince resented, declaring that he feared the pope had broken his word with him, since it seemed that his eminence had rather come to annul than confirm his marriage. To these reproaches the legate replied by showing the decretal bull, but refused to let it out of his hands, even for a moment. With all this conduct the anxious monarch was greatly dissatisfied, but received some consolation from the assurance of Campeggio that he was deputed to address the queen in the name of the pope, and exhort her to enter a religious house; ending the question by her voluntary retirement from the world. But this advice, coming even from so venerable a quarter, had no weight with Katherine, who modestly but firmly replied, that she could not break the sacrament of her marriage, for that, if others were disposed to do so, she felt it binding on her conscience still. While the subject was thus agitated, Henry's deportment towards his unfortunate queen was such as to maintain the appearance of regard and respect which he professed to feel towards her.

Finding all hopes of persuading the queen to a compromise, by entering a cloister, useless, preparations were made for holding the legatine court in the great hall of Blackfriars, which had been selected from its close proximity to the old palace of Bridewell,

WALTER AND PATCH, DISGUISED, ACCOSTED BY THE EVERILS.

where both Henry and Katherine were re- siding.

On the day appointed, the two legates entered the court in state, and seated them- selves as judges on chairs covered with cloths of gold. On the right and left were rich canopies and seats for the king and queen. Wolsey, as Hall in his Chronicles takes care to specify, assumed precedence over his brother cardinal. The scribes, who were doctors in divinity, sat below the judges, while the counsel for their majesties were ranged at each end within the court.

Henry was seated upon his throne. To his impatient spirit the slow procedure of legates was like oil poured upon his passions; he felt humiliated in appearing as a plaintiff before his own subject, whose zeal to serve his master was curbed by the delays which the pope purposely occasioned to the proceed- ings. With that revengeful policy which frequently characterises churchmen, Clement VII. bitterly resented the attempts which Wolsey had lately made during his illness to engage the votes of the Sacred College in his favour : this, and his obligations and fears

No. 40.

of the emperor, are the true reasons of that vacillating policy which finally lost to Rome the richest gem of its triple crown. History proves that revenge is sometimes a costly luxury even to priests.

Anne Boleyn, according to the authority above quoted, was in the hall amongst the other spectators, and surveyed, no doubt, with feelings which could not easily be described, the strange scene acted before her; although, since the order for her removal from court, the ambitious dreams in which she had indulged had gradually faded away.

But the personage in the court on whom all eyes were fixed was the injured queen, who was seated upon the chair of state nearly opposite to her relentless husband. Katherine, on this occasion, sustained her part with all the spirit and dignity which her previous conduct had led the public mind to expect, and with passionate indignation manifested her last ineffectual resistance to the power of those who were appointed to hear and decide her cause.

After silence had been proclaimed, and the commission of the judges read, a herald advanced into the centre of the court, and, bowing before the king's throne, exclaimed in a loud voice, "Henry, King of England!"

"Here," said the prince, not giving him time to complete the citation so galling to his pride.

Wolsey marked the tone of his master's voice and trembled.

The herald then proceeded to the spot where the queen was seated. This time he was permitted to complete his duty without interruption.

"Katherine, Queen of England," he pronounced, "come into court."

All eyes were fixed upon the party summoned, who rose with quiet majesty from her seat, and, looking round the court twice, essayed to speak. It was a bitter moment with the unhappy princess, called upon, after so many years, to defend the validity of her marriage and the legitimacy of her child. The proud blood of her imperial race flushed her generally pale features as she at last broke silence—

"Alas! my lords, and is it now a question whether I be a king's wife or no, when I have been wedded to him almost twenty years, and in this fashion doubt never been made before, when I have borne unto him divers children? Alas! sir," she added, turning to the king, "in what have I offended you? Have I not been to you a true and humble wife, ever conformable to your will and pleasure? If there be any just cause ye can allege against me, either of dishonesty or other matter, I am content to depart, to my

shame and rebuke; but if there be none, pray you let me have justice at your hands. I am a poor, weak woman, uncounselled and unfriended."

"Counsel hath been named," replied Wolsey, "and your majesty——"

"My lords," continued the queen, casting on both the cardinals a withering glance, "I do reject ye as my judges. My lord of York, whose pestilent breath hath blown the coal of discord 'twixt the king and me, is mine enemy—my husband's subject—his greatness the creation of his favour;—how then shall I expect justice at such hands? Therefore I do appeal to Rome—there only can my cause be truly judged. And humbly do entreat your majesty, even in the way of charity, to spare me until I know what counsel and advice my friends in Spain may give me; and if you will not, then must your pleasure be fulfilled."

Having thus spoken, Katherine of Arragon made a low curtsey to the king, and leaning on the arm of Griffith, her receiver-general, was about to leave the court, when Henry commanded the herald to summon her again.

The heiress of Stanfield, who had been amongst the few attendants who adhered to the falling fortunes of the unhappy queen, whispered her as she reached the door that she was summoned.

"On," said Katherine, in a loud tone, so as to be heard by all the assembly; "it is no matter; that is no court for me; therefore I will not tarry."

Nor could she be prevailed on to return or appear again before the legates.

Even the lustful Henry, moved by the noble bearing of his afflicted wife, declared that she had been as true and obedient to him as he could desire.

"She hath," he continued,—melted, perhaps, to some portion of his former tenderness by the pitiable condition of one who little merited to be thus degraded,—"all the virtuous qualities that ought to be in a woman of her dignity. My first doubts," he continued, "were suggested by the demurs of the Bishop of Tarbe, concerning the legitimacy of the Princess Mary, question being at that time entertained of her marriage. These doubts, once suggested, were nurtured by despair of issue from the queen, and not by any disinclination for her person or her age; with which I could be as well content," he hypocritically added, "as with any woman's living."

The falsehood of this assertion could only be equalled by the unblushing coolness with which it was made.

"This declining of our authority and appeal to Rome," observed Campeggio, who had his private instructions from the pope, "controls our will, and must prolong your highness's doubt in this same matter."

"Indeed!" replied the king, casting a ferocious glance upon the legates: "methinks you trifle with me; beware, lest I contrive to solve the knot without Rome's further aid."

The Italian priest, who trembled for his bishopric which he held in England, hastened to assure the angry prince that he would immediately write to the holy father, stating to him the opinions of the English prelates, and the obstinacy of the queen in refusing to listen to the advice which in his name he had tendered to her, of retiring to a convent.

"Add," said Henry, rising from his seat, "that there are other churches than the church of Rome—other barks on which men seek salvation than the bark of Peter. Hitherto I have been an obedient son—let him beware how his injustice forces me to pry into his title. Justice refused when sued for may be at last demanded. By Saint George!" he added, striking with his clenched fist upon the table, "rather than live this puppet slave—this toy of Rome—I'll try my sceptre's strength against his crozier. Mince not my words. The wrath of kings may raise as fierce a storm as Luther's preaching, or as Bourbon's sword. Clement's deceit and Charles's treachery have not yet subdued me."

Without deigning further look or salutation to the two cardinals, the enraged and disappointed suitor left the court, followed by most of the nobles and several of the bishops, who were already disposed towards, or foresaw the reformation. Cold drops of perspiration stood upon the brow of Wolsey, who saw the pit beneath his feet, into which he could not choose but fall. As a priest and cardinal he doubly bowed to Rome, but as the subject of the ferocious Henry he was every way in his power. The nobility and courtiers, whom his pride had offended, he knew to be disposed against him; in the bitterness of anticipation his punishment already had commenced.

On the retirement of the legates the spectators slowly dispersed, scarcely daring to whisper even to themselves the purport of their monarch's threats; they were like men who had assisted at the first act of a fearful spectacle, whose conclusion might be yet more terrible.

As soon as the unhappy queen reached her privy chamber, the pride which had sustained her when before the legates at once gave way, and casting her arms about the neck of her only child, the Princess Mary—who was quite old enough to feel her mother's wrongs and the peril of her own position—the high-souled woman wept bitterly. The orphan of Stanfield, who felt grateful to her royal mistress for the protection she had extended both to her mother and herself, hastily poured a small quantity of Cyprus wine into a golden cup which stood upon the manchet table; and, with the tears of sympathy yet warm upon her cheek, presented it to the crushed and humbled Katherine. To her surprise and terror the young princess dashed it from her hand, and fixing upon her an indignant, sullen look, demanded if she wished to poison her sovereign.

"Poison!" repeated the astonished maiden.

"Poison, minion, was the word," repeated the gloomy child; for even at that early age the princess gave indications of the jealous, suspicious, cruel character which rendered her after-reign so unpopular in England; and which, perhaps, after all, her mother's sorrows and the many bitter mortifications of her childhood contributed to form, for women are seldom naturally cruel.

For a few moments our heroine was thunder struck. For several days she had observed that the wayward speaker had treated her with marked dislike, but had attributed it to her temper, which displayed itself in passionate ebullitions to all, rather than to any personal distaste. The innocent girl was far from suspecting that the openly expressed admiration of the king, and the licentious glances which he so lavishly bestowed upon her, but which, in the natural purity of her heart, she had passd unnoticed, had caused a suspicion both in the mind of the queen and princess unfavourable to her devotion to their service.

"Katherine—royal mistress!" she exclaimed, throwing herself at the footstool of the unhappy wife of Henry—"you do not think me false—you do not believe the orphan girl you have befriended capable of treachery? One smile—one look—nay, but a word," she added, "to dispel this horrid doubt, or my heart will break!"

"So young," murmured the still agitated queen, recoiling from her touch, "and so deceitful! Heaven forgive thee, girl; for thou hast much to answer."

"You hear!" said the princess sternly, at the same time pointing to the door.

"What mystery is this? Indeed you wrong me!"

"Begone!" continued the scowling child.

"Who are my accusers?"

"The queen would be alone," exclaimed Katherine of Arragon, rising from her chair, and drawing up her stately person to its full height. "We are not yet uncrowned; the seat you dream of is not empty yet."

"Heaven forgive my gracious mistress her unjust suspicions," sobbed the orphan heiress of Stanfield as she retired from the chamber, "and protect her servant, who now indeed is friendless."

Scarcely knowing which way to direct her steps, overwhelmed by the sudden and degrading suspicion, the bewildered girl tottered through several of the apartments which formed the suite of her deceived benefactress, nor paused till she reached a large saloon hung with arras and furnished with rich cushions. Here her little remaining strength gave way, and she would have fallen to the ground had not a strong arm sustained her.

She started at the touch. That arm was Henry's.

CHAPTER XI.

Love seeks not happiness obtained through tears;
Knoweth no pleasure in a selfish joy,
Blights not the flower beyond its eager reach,
Or planteth thorns lest other hands should pluck;
Its abnegation is it seal of truth.—THE PURITAN.

N tears, sweetheart!" exclaimed the amorous king, gazing upon her with an expression which brought the warm blood into the maiden's cheek. "Marry, beshrew their hearts whose lack of kindness could dim such eyes as thine! What is thy cause of sorrow? Let those who have angered thee take heed of me."

"A whim, a girl's caprice, a thought, the oppression of a wayward heart; nothing, your highness, that should raise a serious thought within a monarch's mind," answered the generous girl, determined, under any circumstances, not to allude to Katherine's unkindness, or the Princess Mary's unjust suspicions.

"Tut, May-bird! it is fixed on thee oftner than thy modesty supposes. We feel no common interest in thee, and will mark that interest by no common favour. The arrows of thine eyes have hit a loftier mark than thou has dreamt of yet. Tell me," he added, in a softer tone, "why do I find thee weeping?"

"Sire," said the orphan, trembling with apprehension of an avowal which, even from a king, her soul would have repelled with scorn, "my heart acknowledges your bounty to your old servant's grandchild, but the protection of my royal mistress more than repays the service of his life. 'Tis past," she added, struggling to regain her composure; "woman's tears are but as April showers, falling 'twixt sunshine. Permit me to retire."

Henry fixed his keen blue eyes upon her, and regarded her for a few moments in silence. The desire to avoid rather than attract his attentions, as others did, served to augment his passion, for he was too clear-sighted not to perceive that the speaker both saw and feared his love, which, indeed, was already suspected by the whole court; nor was he far from guessing the real cause of the sorrow in which he had discovered her.

"So," he muttered, in a lower tone of voice, still retaining her hand, "Kate hath rated thee, sweet wench?"

"Your highness!"

"Tut! I see it all; I know a jealous woman's tongue lacketh discretion, breaketh all bounds, and runs a tilt with prudence."

"Alas! your grace, but she hath many griefs," interrupted his prisoner, for she had not yet been able to withdraw her hand from his grasp, "threatened by the loss of your most princely favour and affection."

"Is such a loss a grief?" demanded Henry, with a meaning smile.

"As queen and mother doubly so to her."

"And have not I my sorrows?" interrupted the monarch, "and few to feel for me? Bound by a chain which conscience tells me Heaven approves not, tormented by a love," he added, fixing on her a glance which spoke the passionate admiration of his heart, "which even I must pause ere I avow, for I would be loved as kings are seldom loved—not for my crown, but for myself alone—I would possess a love such——"

"Such," added the heiress, determined, if possible, to prevent the avowal of his passion by not appearing to understand him, "such as the royal Katherine feels, whose birth, though less than her virtues, renders her the mate of an imperial throne. Besides," she continued, "whose love, my liege, can ever equal hers, who is the mother of your gracious child?"

"Yours!" exclaimed Henry, attempting to retain her hand. "Yours, for which I sigh. I gaze upon you, and forget my sceptre. I listen to the music of your voice, and earth seems dull without you. I tire," he continued, "of woman's flattery and man's deceit. I pine to find a heart which can forget I am a king, a tongue to speak with me in simple truth. The song of the untaught bird will oft entrance the ear, more than the practised warbler in its gilded cage. Say, sweet one, canst thou love me?"

"As my king," replied the maiden, turning as pale as the marble pedestal against which she leant for support. "Yes—truly, and humbly, as a subject ought."

"Forget I am your king," impatiently interrupted the royal libertine; "I have enough already of such lip homage. Canst love me as a man? as your own knight? as Henry would be loved?"

The speaker's voice had gradually changed from the tender and almost respectful tone in which he at first had spoken, to its habitual one of authority and almost of irritation, and, perhaps, his manner was never more imperious than when he commanded her to forget his rank and state. 'Tis strange how frequently the courage, both physical and moral, will sometimes rise with danger and temptation; both are frequently confronted by the weakest natures, when unexpectedly called to brave them. It was so in the present instance; for the timid girl no sooner saw that all hope of avoiding the avowal she so much dreaded was at an end, than her terror instantly left her, and she answered with a firmness and calmness which appeared stranger even to herself than to the licentious monarch.

"No such evil thought hath ever tempted me. Frown not, sire, if I prefer the smile of heaven even to yours; remember that, humble as I am, the love which failed to raise might still debase me."

"But it can raise thee, girl," he whispered, thinking that her objections to become his mistress might give way before the temptation of even the distant hope of becoming his wife. "This hand can lead thee to so vast a height, the world shall lie like some rich garden riant at thy feet—place thee where men shall pin their fortunes on thy smile—where sorrow's chills and the sad storms of life shall never reach thee."

"I should turn giddy, my dread lord, and fall from such a pinnacle. I was not born for gazing on the sun—the valley suits my humble footsteps best; the path you name leads not to happiness."

"What," said Henry, "if it lead you to a throne?"

"It would not tempt me; conscience would haunt me with unholy dreams, memory remind me of her wrongs who sat there, terror and guilt overshadow it with evil. I see your grace," she added, "sports with my inexperience, or wished, perchance, to try me; but believe me, prince, I am too grateful to my royal mistress—too long the witness of her many virtues—to suffer such weak dreams to mock my reason."

"By heavens, girl," said Henry—for even his coarse brutal nature could appreciate the purity of her motives—"but I am serious! The thrall which binds me in unholy fetters, despite Rome's subtle policy and wire-drawn pleadings, soon shall be dissolved. Then, when the chair is empty, and my hand is free——"

"My answer will be still unchanged," said the orphan, mildly. "Were your grace's state in life fitting to mine as now, tis far above it, such wishes would be equally vain."

"Dost tell me so?" exclaimed Henry, in a tone so harsh that the girl sank almost fainting on the pile of cushions near which she had been standing. "'Tis well; the whisperings I have heard, it seems, are true. Sir John de Corbey's accusation was not all a falsehood—the heiress of Stanfield loves a menial."

"Your highness, he you name is gently born, though little graced with fortune's misused gifts."

"A peasant knave who broke his trust to Wolsey, and lost or sold his letters to Campeggio."

"My life, your highness, upon Walter's faith."

"Dost brave me, minion!" continued the incensed and mortified monarch, his still handsome features flushed with anger. "Heed, lest I take thee at thy word. For thy springal, let him beware; the hour he sets his foot on English ground, by my unbroken faith, shall be his last! For thee," he added, "forget our passing jest—ha! ha! ha! But, by St. George, it was not badly played! Henry refused, and by a simple girl—ha! ha! As if a king would condescend to sue hen with a word he might command—ha! ha!"

Turning on his heel, without deigning further notice of the maiden, the burly speaker quitted the apartment, still forcing the hoarse laugh beneath which he endeavoured to hide the shame of his disappointment: his flashing eyes and compressed lips showed how little he had been in jest.

No sooner had the tyrant disappeared than the unhappy heiress felt the full misery of her position. Alone, without one friend to whom to apply for counsel or protection—persecuted by Henry, rejected by the queen—suspected, menaced, and trembling for her lover's safety more than for her own—many and bitter were the thoughts which crowded on her mind. She was startled from her painful revery by the rustling of the arras near her, which, as the echo of the angry monarch's footsteps died away, was hastily drawn aside, and Katherine of Arragon, accompanied by the Princess Mary, entered the chamber. There was a noble sorrow on the countenance of the royal matron, for her own ears had convinced her how unfounded were her suspicions of the orphan girl; and with the impulse of a generous heart she hastened to make atonement. Even the features of the scowling child were softened from their usual harsh expression.

"Thou wilt forgive me my injustice," exclaimed the queen, "and Mary's petulance; alas! poor child, her mother's griefs, and not her nature spoke. I have witnessed all," she added—"thy unavailing generous defence of the rights of those who had so lately scorned thee."

"My gracious mistress," sobbed the heiress, sinking upon her knees and kissing her extended hand, for her heart felt relieved of more than half its burden since she found her innocence acknowledged by Katherine,—"how can the object of your care atone for the sorrow of which she is the involuntary cause?"

"Not thou—not thou the cause," sighed the queen, "but Henry; his passions are as untamed as the relentless tiger's will. Heaven grant hereafter they prove not as destructive!"

"Madam," said the heiress, her former terrors of the king returning, "remove me from the court, restore me to my peaceful convent's shade; I have known few happy moments since I quitted it. Alas!" she added, "how beautiful were earth, how rich in joys, did not man's evil nature mar the bounteous gifts! The serpent which tempted him in Eden dwells no longer in the garden, but in his heart."

"True, girl," said Katherine; "and where

the reptile's venom fails to poison, its fangs will strive to wound. To-morrow," continued the speaker, trying to restrain her emotion, "I quit the palace of my husband for my manor of Kimbolton. I know the separation is doomed to be eternal. They would divorce me from my crown, from Henry's heart; separate me from my child, and brand upon my matron brow the seal of shame; but never," she added, "shall act of mine give sanction to a deed which robs my Mary of her birthright. My child may yet avenge me."

The eyes of the young princess, generally so dull and inexpressive, were suddenly lit up with a fire which made them terrible to look upon, as she fixed them upon the countenance of her mother; the rest of her features, strange to say, were as impassible and cold as usual.

"I will avenge thee, mother," she slowly pronounced, as if, at the same time, she mentally registered some fearful vow—"if Mary lives the wrongs of Katherine of Arragon shall be atoned."

History proves, when, after her brother's death, she mounted the throne, how fearfully the speaker kept her word.

"Fallen as I am," continued the queen, without apparently noticing her daughter's promise, but addressing herself to the orphan, "I can still offer an humble shelter to the child of my faithful servant, unless," she added with a bitter smile, "the exile from the court affrights you."

"The mariner quits not the sea-tossed wreck to tread on land again, with half the joy which I shall fly with you from its treacherous precincts."

"'Tis well," said Katherine; "follow me to my closet. I will arrange with Griffiths for thy departure. Thou clingest to a broken fortune, girl, but a firm heart; and Heaven may one day recompense thee."

With these words the speaker once more raised the arras and retreated through the private door by which she had entered; the heiress caught the curtain as it fell, and drew back to make way for the princess, who was about to follow; when suddenly the young girl seemed to recollect something she wished to say, and motioned her to let fall the hangings. There was generally an unamiability of manner in all she did; but at the present moment she was positively gracious. Fixing her eyes upon her namesake, she said in her usually quiet voice—

"I have been unjust; but Lady Bouchier was to blame. I am but a child, and naturally feel my mother's injuries as keenly as my own. Do you forgive me?"

The only reply of the late object of her

anger and suspicion was to kneel and kiss her hand.

"Perhaps," said the speaker, "I may one day be able to atone it; and here is a token that I will do so, I make few gifts; for to each gift there is a promise. Return this reliquary to me should fortune ever place it in my power to redeem my word. Whatever you ask," she added solemnly, "shall be granted; *be it a life, an honour, or a vengeance*, Mary will not fail to keep her word."

The child kissed the small jewelled shrine, which had been presented to her by her cousin the emperor on her birthday, as she spoke; and removing the chain to which it was suspended from her neck, she passed it over the head of the heiress of Stanfield, who once more bent the knee to receive it. Little did she dream how precious would the gift in after years become.

"Hide it," said the donor, resuming her apathetic manner, "and attend me to the closet of the queen: and guard it well; for I make not such gifts often."

The curtained entrance to the apartments of Katherine was once more drawn aside, and the haughty daughter of Henry VIII. proceeded with her usual quiet step to the chamber of her unhappy mother.

When Walter parted with Patch on his way to Calais with Wolsey's letters to Campeggio his mind was agitated by a thousand doubts and fears. Not that he suspected the jester of treachery; on that point he felt at least secure. But his words pointed to some portending danger—something fatal to his love—perhaps to the happiness of Mary; and that future, which had lately seemed so bright and fair, so full of hope and promise, was once more clouded by the gathering tempest and approaching storm.

At Feversham, where he halted on the second night of his journey, he encountered, in the little inn at which he had been directed to stop, a party of travellers—merchants seemingly, whose conduct, without the clue given to him by his friend, would have excited his suspicions. They conversed freely upon the subject of the divorce, then the engrossing topic of the day, and appeared, despite their peaceful occupation, ready to pick a quarrel and cut the throat of any man who argued that Henry was not justified in his demand. The host of the golden crown was equally loyal.

"Of course our bluff King Hal is right," he exclaimed, as he ladled the soup into the wooden bowls which were ranged for the guests upon a clumsy oaken table, strewed with herbs by way of garniture. "What is the use of being king, if he is not to have his own way? Marry!" he added, "if things progress as they have done of late, I should not wonder if men dispute, at last, his grace's right to govern his kingdom as he pleases, since disloyal knaves begin to cavil at his pleasure."

What would the speaker have said had he lived to witness the altered state of royalty at the present day? He but spoke, however, in the spirit of the times in which he lived.

By this time the soup was served, and the benedicite pronounced by a friar, who chanced to be amongst the company, and not an unobservant spectator of what was passing. Each traveller being served, they produced from their pockets, or from the small satchels which the better orders wore at their sides, spoons of boxwood or metal, and set lustily to their repast, for few houses of entertainment at the period of which we write furnished their guests with such conveniences, each one being obliged to find his knife; as for forks, they were generally unknown.

"Is it far you travel, sir?" demanded the elder of the merchants, addressing Walter, who was seated next him.

"To Calais," replied our hero, who fancied that he was not entirely a stranger to the voice of the speaker, whose person, however, was too well disguised, if his conjectures were right, for him to recognise.

"I, too, am bound for France, to purchase merchandise; which, sooth to say, finds a ready sale at courts where foreign braveries are all the favour, and turn the honest penny to the trader's hand."

This was touching upon one of the most delicate topics of the day, for there had lately been fierce disputes between the citizens of London and the foreign merchants, who engrossed the trade of the metropolis in their hands. Henry VII., with a view to benefit his dominions, had laid down stipulations in most of the treaties which he formed with foreign powers for establishing a commercial intercourse between them and Great Britain. He encouraged Italians and Germans to visit his kingdom to dispose of foreign goods, and to take in exchange woollen cloths, tin, and lead. At first these foreigners were compelled to pay double duty on the goods which they imported; but this being found detrimental to commerce, the customs were abated, and the trade rapidly increased. Thus we see that even in the fifteenth century the principle of free trade was beginning to be understood. In the reign of his son, the display and amusements, the dress and extravagance of the court, the emulation to excel in every species of splendour amongst the nobility, and the intercourse with the French, who have always excelled us in all that is gay and costly, naturally occasioned an enormous demand for silks, damasks, jewels, wines, and luxuries of every description. These articles were chiefly supplied by Florentine or Venetian merchants, to whom great protection was given, and who acquired by their monopoly of the trade vast wealth in this country. Hence jealousies had arisen; and these insolent foreigners, boasting of the favour of the king, inflicted all those petty insults upon the English mechanics and traders, which persons accustomed themselves to obnoxious deportment to their superiors delight to offer whenever they have an opportunity. The conflict broke out between the two parties upon the following occasion.

Williamson, a carpenter, having purchased two pigeons, was rudely deprived of them by a Frenchman, who insolently declared that they were not fit meat for a fellow like him. The poor man urged in vain that, having paid for them he had a right to regale himself with them. The thief ran off, declaring that he would carry them to the French ambassador. He did so, and found shelter in his house. The poor Englishman, disappointed of his birds, naturally gave vent to his indignation in no very measured language, for which he was committed by the mayor of the minster, to prison. The ambassador not being satisfied, wards made to the mayor himself for the delivery of the prisoner, and a demand that by the law of the land the English knave should lose his life, and that no Englishman should venture such language a Frenchman required; nor could he get any other reply to the friends of the poor carpenter.

This, and similar acts of tyranny, so incensed the citizens that they requested Dr. Edee to preach against the privileges which the foreigners enjoyed. Encounters between them and the 'prentices became of frequent, nay, almost hourly occurrence; till at last the mob attacked Newgate, and released not only the carpenter, but several other prisoners, who had been committed for insulting these pampered, insolent strangers.

The riot at last reached such a pitch that the Earls of Surrey and Shrewsbury were sent with a body of troops to subdue them. The ringleaders being secured, commissioners were appointed to decide on the fate of the offenders. The court, over which the Duke of Norfolk presided, sat in Guildhall, and the prisoners, to the number of 270, were introduced, tied together with ropes. Thirteen of the citizens were executed upon gibbets erected in those parts of the city where the principal disturbances had occurred, to the disgust as well as terror of the inhabitants.

Henry, perceiving that the commissioners were pushing the affair with too much severity, pretended to yield to the entreaties of the three queens—Katherine of Arragon and his sisters Mary of France and Margaret of Scotland, who fell upon their knees and demanded pardon for the citizens—a petition which the king, as Stowe informs us in his Chronicles, reluctantly accorded. Only imagine thirteen citizens being executed in the present age for a simple riot caused by the overbearing insolence of a Frenchman! This little episode is, however, but a faithful picture of what took place in the good old times, which the blind idolaters of the past sometimes tell us we shall never see again, to which I doubt not but that the majority of my readers will exclaim, "Heaven forbid they should!"

No sooner had the supposed trader, therefore declared his intention of proceeding to France to purchase merchandise than a volley of abuse from several of the guests broke out, and words at last rose to such a pitch that swords were drawn. Walter, whose disposition naturally inclined him to side with the weaker party, had already drawn his and ranged himself by the person assailed, when the friar, who had remained an unconcerned spectator of the scene, approached him and whispered in his ear a caution to remain quiet. His trusted word the stranger who had remained near him.

"Whilst you remain tranquil," said the speaker, "there will be no danger there is against you their swords are drawn, and not against each other."

The observation, which accorded so well with the information which his friend Patch had given him, decided him to his silence, and he quietly resumed his seat when, as the friar had predicted, the disturbance generally subsided, and the quarrellers became once more friends.

"Leave the packet!" whispered the churchman, as he withdrew for the night, "upon the stool beside the bed, and take no heed of what passes; there is danger even in the blinking of an eye; act as you have been recommended, and you are safe."

Whatever might have been our hero's previous determination, he now resolved to follow implicitly the advice of the speaker, whom he judged at once to be an agent of Wolsey's. Bidding him, therefore, a goodnight, he proceeded to his chamber, which contained two beds, one of them occupied by the trader whose avowal had occasioned the pretended dispute amongst the guests. Following the directions of his unknown friend, he placed the packet by the side of

WALTER'S VISIT TO STEADMAN AMD MAUD.

his pallet, and cast himself, half-dressed, upon the straw-covered couch. Few inns in the reign of Henry VIII. afforded better accommodation than that simple, but not very luxurious material. Despite the repeated assurance of safety which he had received, he took the precaution of taking his sword to bed with him; for, as he wisely argued to himself, it was at least one guarantee the more.

In the extraordinary position in which he was placed, our hero found it, despite the fatigue he had undergone, impossible to sleep.

With his half-closed eyes he lay for some time watching the pallet opposite to him: the hard, regular breathings of its occupant announced that he slept, or pretended to do so. Gradually these breathings became less and less distinct, till at last they entirely ceased, and Walter saw the pretended trader rise from the bed, upon which he had thrown himself half-dressed, and cautiously creep towards the stool upon which he had placed the important packet, quietly possess himself of it, and hasten from the apartment. In less than ten minutes afterwards the sound of horses' feet upon the stony road informed him that the successful robber had departed with his prize.

"But for the word of one I am bound to trust," muttered the dissatisfied youth, "I had not lain here to be plundered like a sleeping cur. 'Sdeath! how I longed to spring upon the thief and try the metal of his courage! though, perhaps," he added with a sigh, "'tis better as it is."

"Much better," murmured a voice, which must have been near him for the speaker to have caught his words.

Walter with one bound started from his couch, and stood upon the floor of the chamber, sword in hand.

"Who is there?" he demanded, glancing round the room, which was imperfectly lighted by the small lamp hanging from a rafter in the ceiling, the ponderous timbers of which, rudely put together, supported the roof of the house.

"Look up," was the reply, "and you will see."

He did so, and beheld the friar, who had given him the warning below, crouching like a squatting Indian behind one of the massive pieces of wood-work directly over the bed on which he had been resting. From the gloom of the chamber it required a strong sight, as well as a minute examination, to trace the outline of a human figure amongst the beams and timbers of the roof. When, however, he could sufficiently distinguish, he saw, not without a vague feeling of terror, that the speaker held an arbalette in his hand; so that, in fact, all the while he had been reclining on the couch, his life had been entirely at his mysterious friend's disposal.

"Help me down," said the speaker.

The young man did as he was directed; and as soon as the stranger reached the floor, he seated himself upon the bed, and motioned to Walter to take a seat on the stool beside him.

"If Sir John had remained much longer, I must have called out," said the pretended friar; "I have had the cramp this half hour."

"Sir John! You know the robber then?" demanded the messenger.

"I should think I do," replied the fellow, with a comical expression of countenance.

"And his name?"

"Sir John Perrot, the favourite of the king."

"And what was thy errand here?" demanded Walter.

"To watch over thy safety," replied the fellow; "and no unnecessary one, judging from thy want of prudence whilst below."

"And thine arbalette——"

"Would have sent a bullet to the false knight's heart, had he broken faith with us and played thee false. You may sleep securely now," continued the speaker; "in the morning write the letter as directed—I will be the bearer. Then wend your way to where you are directed."

"And that," said Walter, willing to ascertain how far the friar was entrusted by his friend, "is to——"

"Where concerns not me," interrupted his companion; "Patch is a cunning gamester, and never shows his hand; he may at times let fall a card or two, but holds the leading trumps. Good-night," he added, at the same time throwing himself upon the pallet where Sir John Perrot had so lately lain; "my task is ended, thine perchance begins."

The young man followed his example, but it was a long time before he could compose himself to sleep. The events of the last few days appeared a mystery to him. One thing, at least, was clear to his understanding, that Henry's favourite servant and confidant was in the interests either of the cardinal or the jester; how else could the intended robbery have been made to answer the purpose of the former, by substituting such a letter as the ambitious statesman knew would serve him with his master, whilst the one really intended for Campeggio was forwarded by a second messenger? But whether his eminence was a party to the warning he had received, or that he owed it, as well as the precautions taken to ensure his safety, to the friendship of Patch, he was at a loss to decide. His tired thoughts gradually gave way to nature's sweet restorative, and he closed his eyes at last, to dream of love and its delusive hopes.

In the reign of Henry VIII. the chief bankers and money-lenders were the Jews and foreign merchants, who advanced their treasures oftentimes upon the security of plate and lands, or the charter-deeds of religious houses, which often required such advances to enable them to complete the sumptuous edifices whose ruins even now excite astonishment and admiration at their vast design and magnificent proportions. Not unfrequently a relic of well-known sanctity was pledged for some large amount. This was considered one of the safest securities the merchants could obtain, as it was a point of honour as well as religion with the convent or church to which it belonged to redeem such treasures.

At the time of the reformation and suppression of the monasteries many of the usurers were ruined by the comparatively valueless pledges thus left upon their hands. A Lombard Jew, who had lent a considerable sum to the monks at Canterbury upon the mitre and arm-bones of St. Thomas à Becket, carried them to France, where they may still be seen in the rich chapel erected in honour of the saint in the cathedral of Sens; indeed, little more than a year has elapsed since the writer of these chronicles beheld them there.

Marrietti, one of the most considerable of these money-lenders, was seated in his shop, in Lombard-street, expatiating upon the beauty of a Venetian chain which a gallant of the court was cheapening, when a young man, apparently much fatigued with travel, crossed the threshold of his house.

"Ha! nephew," said the Italian, extending his hand to him, "welcome home again! You found the merchandise, I trust, all right at Calais?"

"Merchandise!" repeated the young man, who in fact was no other than our old friend Walter.

"Ay, merchandise," repeated the little old man, sharply. "Marry, this comes of giving boys a holiday, as if thou couldst not have combined pleasure and profit at the same time. I warrant me thou hast not forgot to spend the five crowns I gave thee. But get thee in," he added; "it was an evil hour when I consented at my sister's bidding to take such a scapegrace 'prentice."

Without giving the astonished youth time to speak a word, the irascible little usurer pushed him into a small inner room at the back of his shop, and closed the door upon him.

"Ah! my lord," he said to the nobleman, who had been too much occupied in admiring his purchase to pay much attention to the features of the young man, "you are fortunate; you are not plagued with the care of such a nephew. Two hundred ducats," he continued, returning to the previous subject of their conversation, "is the lowest price; the carbuncles and rare pearls, as I am an honest man, are worth the money."

The bargain was speedily concluded, and the lover of the fair Geraldine—for it was no other than the gallant Surrey—left the merchant's house on his way to London Bridge, there to take water for Hampton, where the object of his poetic love was residing with her father, the Earl of Kildare, whose family, according to the learned Dr. Knott, trace their descent from the Geraldi of Florence, and is not, as is generally supposed, of Irish origin; hence the fair girl's romantic name of Geraldine.

No sooner had the young nobleman departed than the merchant let fall the heavy wooden shutters which hung suspended, as it were, by strong cords over the unglazed windows of his shop, and drew the ponderous bolts. Before closing the outward door he methodically lit his lamp, and then proceeded to make it fast. Satisfied at last that all was secure, he opened the door of communication, and entered the little dark chamber where Walter was sitting.

"Well, nephew," exclaimed the old man, with a shrewd smile, "how feel you after your voyage?"

"Somewhat fatigued, uncle," replied the young traveller, in the same bantering tone, "since I find that such is the relationship between us; though I question if our fathers would not have been more surprised at it than we are."

"Perhaps so," said the merchant, eyeing him keenly, and muttering something to himself about the impossibility of his being mistaken. "But doubtless you have a token to convince those who are sceptical," he added.

His guest thrust his hand into his bosom, and produced the little silver bell which Patch had given him. The usurer's doubts were satisfied. Cordially holding out his hand, he bade him welcome to his humble roof, and informed him that he had been prepared for his reception by the jester, who had so minutely described his person that he had recognised him the instant he entered the shop, and treated him as he had, fearful lest the Earl of Surrey, who was so much about the court, should recognise him, as he had done.

The speaker seemed astonished when his guest assured him that the danger had been purely an imaginary one; for that, with the exception of a late occasion, he had never placed his foot within a royal residence.

"No matter, my lord," replied the old man with a smile of incredulity; "I seek not your name or quality. The token you have brought answers for all."

"But I am no lord," said Walter, not wishing to assume a rank to which he possessed no claim.

"I have no right to pry into your secrets," replied the old man with an incredulous smile, as he led the way into the interior of the house. "Were you the poorest horse-boy that ever rode in a noble's train, and brought that token with you, you were equally welcome to my roof."

In the course of the evening the fugitive was joined by his old friend Patch, who conducted himself in the house of the usurer as if he were at home, ordering him to bring up the wines he named, and prepare supper for himself and guest.

"One word," exclaimed our hero, "to relieve my anxious heart; the Lady Mary—"

"Is well and safe as yet."

"As yet," repeated Walter; "tell me?"

"Patience — patience!" interrupted the jester; "I know 'tis difficult for young blood to curb the restless whisperings of the heart, its doubts and jealous fears; but thou hast seen more than most men of thy gossip's prudence; with thee I have almost laid aside my mask; thou knowest that thou canst trust me. Give thanks and eat," he added, as the repast was placed upon the table, "for we must ride to-night."

"Where?" demanded his companion.

"To chase the moonbeams or the wild fire's light," said Patch, with a laugh; "those who ride with me must ride with confidence as blind as faith, leap at destruction, and without a doubt. Dost question me, roysterer?" he continued; "knowest thou not old Mammon here and I are of earth's kings the kings, since gold and folly rule the gore-stained earth?"

"I'll question thee no more!" exclaimed the young man; "thou art a sphinx, which Œdipus himself had never guessed — a thing to be admired, not understood."

"What, boy!" replied the jester, "wouldst batter me with thy humanities? compare me to Thebes' monster? And yet," he added, "the simile is just, for both were never rightly understood."

"How dost thou understand it?"

"As the Greeks of old," answered the humourist; "the sphinx is nothing more than poor humanity, as tyranny and superstition have disfigured it: when once its rights are known, its wrongs redressed, the monster is destroyed, but all the god remains. Come," he continued, rising from the table, "a cup of Cyprus wine ere we depart, as yellow as thy gold, old Plutus, and a thousand times more precious. Are our horses ready?"

"They are," answered the obsequious merchant, at the same time pouring the costly wine into two small silver cups which he handed Patch and his guest.

"Success to our enterprise," exclaimed the former as he drained the cup, "and now then to horse. Keep careful watch," he added, "that we wait not an instant on our return."

After seeing that his companion as well as himself were well armed, they quitted the mansion of their host by the back part of the house, and mounted two horses, which they found waiting for them. The jester led a third one by the rein. It was a gloomy night; the rain fell in torrents as they set out, but gradually subsided ere they reached their journey's end, which Walter found, to his surprise, to be the palace of the king at Greenwich. Following the example of his guide, he fastened his steed to a tree at the outskirt of the park, and followed him cautiously to a small pavilion, situated at the end of the terrace, where but a few days since he had been presented to the king, and where he last beheld the object of his passion. It was evident that the isolated chamber was inhabited, or than an inmate was expected, for lights streamed through the richly stained window in the chamber above, and cast party-coloured rays upon the sward where they were standing.

"Thank Heaven, we are in time!" exclaimed the jester.

"In time for what?"

"Thou wilt see. Follow me to the terrace, but above all be silent."

Walter did as he was directed. They had not ensconced themselves more than an hour behind a clump of shrubs, when they beheld a man muffled in an ample mantle, and preceded by a page bearing a torch, quit the palace, and direct his steps towards the pavilion. From his burly port, they knew it was the king. As soon as he entered, Patch quitted the concealment, and hastening to the door, securely fastened it by a contrivance which he had brought with him for the purpose.

"Now, then, to the front of the pavilion," he whispered; "not a moment is to be lost."

"What mean you?"

"The heiress of Stanfield is in that temple of iniquity with the king."

Walter needed no further inducement; his very heart seemed to be on fire; the earth scarcely bent beneath the elastic pressure of his tread. As soon as they were beneath the windows, Patch drew a ladder from the bushes, which our hero hastily ascended. As he reached the topmost stave, a shriek fell upon his ear. With a giant's strength he dashed open the casement, and leaped into the chamber, and found the orphan struggling with the king.

"Saved!" she exclaimed, as she cast herself upon his neck; "oh! Walter, you have indeed preserved me from perdition."

The baffled Henry absolutely foamed with rage and disappointment, for he was unarmed. Yet, relying on his great personal strength, he seemed at one moment inclined to brave the contest, which Walter perceiving, drew his sword.

"Back, tyrant!" said the young man, sternly, at the same time bring the point of his weapon to a level with his breast; "one step nearer, and I forget thou art my sovereign, as thou hast long since forgotten the ties of honour, knighthood, and humanity."

"Slave!" muttered Henry, "down at my feet—crouch for thy beggar's life! Let me but raise my voice——"

"And thy last cry shall follow it!" interrupted the young man. "Thy hot blood stains my sword. Why should I hesitate?" he added, "why spare the wolf who knows no touch of mercy?"

"He is thy king," whispered the orphan. "Stain not thy soul with treason; leave him to Heaven and his conscience."

At this moment Patch appeared upon the summit of the ladder, and motioned to them that it was time to depart. Hastily passing the rescued maiden towards the window, Walter stood upon his guard, between her and the king, whilst she descended. Several times Henry essayed to speak, but passion held him silent. In his mind he resolved, the instant the intruder should follow the example of his intended victim, to raise an alarm and cause them to be pursued. The young man he destined for the rack and cord, the orphan for his infamous embrace.

Scarcely had these thoughts revolved within his head, than Patch once more mounted to the window-sill, and whispered to his companion to descend.

"What, ho! treason!" exclaimed the monarch, as our hero placed his foot on the window-sill.

His further words were silenced by Patch, who hastily cast a small ball into the window, which burst as it fell, and filled the chamber with a dense vapour;—in a moment the excited monarch sank senseless upon the floor.

"You have killed him," whispered Walter, as they reached the ground.

"Small fear of that," replied the jester, "and even if I had, monarch as he is, he would have been lawfully judged and executed. I told you," he added, "we should one day bless the chance which made us the leech's heritors. You see my words come true."

As quickly as possible the three fugitives gained their horses, and never drew rein until they were safely housed with the friendly merchant in Lombard-street.

CHAPTER XII.

'Tis sweet to roam with those we love,
When the pretty stars are peeping,
Like angels watching from above,
But at distance kindly keeping.—*Serenade from "The Venetian."*

THE next morning even those most accustomed to the capricious temper of the king were astonished at the brutal ferocity which he displayed towards all who approached him. The adventure and disappointment of the preceding night rankled deeply in his revengeful soul, and in his fury he mentally threatened destruction not only to the hero of it, but to the innocent object of his licentious passion. Private orders, sealed with his own signet, were dispatched to the governors of the principal sea-ports, giving a minute description of the person both of Walter and the heiress of Stanfield, and commanding their arrest should they attempt to quit the kingdom. As for Patch, he had been so carefully disguised and kept so far in the background, that his share in the transaction was not likely to be suspected.

"Leo seems in an amiable mood this morning," whispered the last-named personage to the poet, Sir Thomas Wyat, who stood conversing with him in one of the deep bay windows of the presence-chamber at Greenwich, where the jester had attended Wolsey in his usual visit to the king. "At least," added the speaker, "if we may judge from the scared looks of the jackal. See how he sneaks from the royal den; perhaps he has encountered the fangs of the regal brute as well as his growl."

This observation was occasioned by the crest-fallen appearance of Sir John Perrot, who issued from the king's closet with the air of a man not quite assured whether or no his head still sat upon his shoulders. The fact is, the terrified knight had passed a fearful hour with his incensed master, who had bitterly threatened him, declaring that through his stupidity or treachery alone could the abduction of his intended victim have been known to her friends and deliverer. The humbled courtier cast a reproachful glance at Patch as he passed the window where he and his companion stood. To the latter it seemed to deprecate the jester's usually sarcastic humour, who, however, perfectly understood it, and returned it by a triumphant smile, for he feared not the minion's treachery—he was completely in his power.

"Why, Sir John," he exclaimed, advancing from the window to meet him, "from thy woe-begone countenance one would imagine there was an end to all intrigue at court—that honesty was to be henceforth the language of the day, or that, like a whipped scholar, thou wert pouting over a new lesson. Courage, man," he added, bitterly; "let courts become as honest as they may, there will still be found use for such as thee."

"Thou art a hard taskmaster, Patch," replied the knight, in an under-tone; "a man may as well give hand to Satan as take service with thee; the king," he added, "is furious."

"More so than you expected?" coolly demanded the jester.

"Hath threatened to disgrace me," continued the knight.

"Impossible," said his tormentor, in a tone of undisguised contempt, which made the courtier writhe, for he perfectly understood the speaker's meaning, "not even Henry's power can accomplish that; despot as he is, you may defy him there. Kings, like other men," he added, "fail at impossibilities."

"At least," faltered Sir John, blushing with shame and anger as he spoke, "it can affect my life. This very hour his highness swore to trample me as mire beneath his feet, should he but prove my treachery."

"Indeed!" replied the jester, with a quiet laugh, at the same time turning on his heel and leaving him, "fortune favours thee in thy disgrace, for, like the worthless fish cast back into the lake, thou'lt find thy element."

The knight, unable to conceal his mortification at the sarcasm, which conscience told him he merited, hastened from the presence-chamber, revolving in his mind whether it were not wisest to confess all, and trust to Henry's mercy, than to continue the slave of such an ungracious task-master as the jester. Reflection, however, soon convinced him that the bark of his tormentor was worse than his bite, and he resolved to let things take their usual course.

The fact is, Sir John Perrot was a needy man. In his office of keeper of the privy purse he had been detected in sundry peculations by Wolsey, who not only overlooked them, but continued to feed his extravagance and necessities, on condition that he consented to act as his spy upon the king, whose secret movements were thus made known to the wily minister, even by the very agent chosen by Henry to conceal them from him. No wonder that the enemies of the churchman were so frequently defeated. It is needless, perhaps, to add that Patch was the usual channel of communication between the cardinal and the dishonest courtier, and that his friendship for Walter had induced him to exercise his power further than his master would have approved, since it had raised the anger of the monarch to such a furious pitch.

At this moment Henry issued from the royal closet. He was wrapped in a long loose gown of cloth of gold, lined with sables; and instead of the barret or hat which Holbein has rendered familiar to most English readers, his head was covered with a purple velvet hood, which gave a ghastly expression to his unusually pale features. In short, it was evident from his whole appearance that he still felt the effects of the jester's parting gift, which left him for a long time senseless on the floor of the pavilion.

"Where be these legates?" he exclaimed, "the sloths of Rome—these Fabian politicians, who trust to tire our patience by delay? Knows my Lord of York," he added, in a loud harsh tone, "that we have twice demanded his fair presence?"

"His eminence is in the chapel with Campeggio, sire," faltered Sir Henry Denny, who, more perhaps than any courtier present, trembled at the ungovernable temper of the king.

"'Sdeath! go tell the red-caps we attend them here, and by their own appointing. The sun is bright, the air of heaven blows keenly. We would not lose our match for twenty times their bidding. Go, Suffolk," he added in a kinder tone, turning to his brother-in-law, "order our train to mount; and tell Le March we'll fly the Norway falcon our sister Margaret sent me."

The duke bowed, and left the presence-chamber to execute the orders he had received.

No one knew better than the infuriated monarch that both Wolsey and Campeggio had been above three hours waiting to obtain an interview; for, in fact, it was by his own private orders that they were thus discourteously received, for virtually their mission was at an end, since an inhibition had been received to stop their proceedings as legates. The pope, who was devoted to Katherine's nephew, the Emperor Charles, had, however, with his usual duplicity, exempted the king from the penalties which the inhibition imposed on all such as should abet the process of the divorce. The politics of Clement VII. were most disastrous to the Holy See; they lost eventually three kingdoms to its triple crown.

"'Tis well, my lord!" exclaimed Henry,

at the same time contemptuously crushing in his hand the papal indulgence which Campeggio, in the hope of soothing his wrath, had presented him with. "Since Rome denies us justice, we must seek a remedy within ourselves. Your mission ended as it began, in bitter mockery and deceit, albeit in that we blame not you. We will not longer detain you at our court. Your brother of York," he added, for the first time during the interview, casting a cold glance on Wolsey, "will order your departure with all honour. Farewell! St. George and our Lady speed you!"

Without waiting for a reply, or deigning further salutation to either of the legates, the king turned upon his heel and entered the royal closet to prepare for his morning ride, calling lustily to Sir Henry Norris to see the falconers were in readiness. The mortified churchmen, humbled and confused by their reception, retired to the lodging of Wolsey amid the sneers of the courtiers, who already anticipated the haughty favourite's downfal.

"The period of your master's favour has arrived, friend Patch," whispered Sir Thomas Wyat, as they crossed the court-yard of the palace; "the bark of Peter is in peril."

"It has weathered," replied the jester carelessly, "a rougher storm than this; the tempest is never so near exhausted as when it rages loudest."

"Thou art poetical in thy description, man: fortune hath misplaced thee; she should have made a minstrel, not a jester, of thee; thou hast a poet's soul, if not his verse."

His companion fixed his eyes upon him with an expression half-mocking, half-serious, as he replied to him in his own quaint style.

"Are there no poets, then, but such as deal in rhyme? Tut, man! they are but the scholars of their art. Those who can play with human passion—oppose the fox's cunning to the lion's strength—trace even through crime the fine connecting link, the golden thread which holds humanity in one vast whole—or touch the secret key-notes of the heart, making deep melodies or fearful discords,—such are your poets; those who write are rhymesters."

"A lesson! and in mine own art!" exclaimed the knight, astonished at the new phase in his strange companion's character. "Thou art a very protean personage. I find as many changes in thee——"

"As in thy mistress's humour or dame Fortune's smiles," said the jester, finishing the sentence for him; "but fare thee well. I must to my master—you, doubtless, to the hawking with the king. Beware," he added, with a significant look, "how you cross the royal falconer in his sport. Should you ride towards Hever, loose not the jesses of your bird—cast not your hawk that way."

Hever Castle was the residence of Anne Boleyn, for whom the poet's passion was more than suspected by the court.

Sir Thomas understood the hint, and, nodding adieu to the friendly giver, walked musingly away.

On entering the cardinal's chamber, Patch found his eminence pacing up and down the apartment alone; the courtiers who generally thronged his ante-chamber had already deserted it in anticipation of his disgrace. The usually flushed features of the churchman were pale, and it was evident, from the compressed lips, that he was struggling to subdue an emotion which, once given way to, would, like a torrent, bear everything before it.

"Alone, my lord!" said the jester, with a well-affected expression of surprise.

"Doth that astonish thee?" exclaimed Wolsey, bitterly; "the sun hath set, and friends are, like shadows, seen only when it shines. This worse than folly, this madness of the court of Rome, joined with the king's hot passion for Anne Boleyn, hath ruined me. I have touched the climax of my greatness, and must, perforce, descend. My enemies prevail at last."

"One way," observed the person whom the speaker had so singularly chosen for his confidant, "remains to crush them, and knit thyself yet closer to the capricious Henry's heart."

"Name it," said the astonished churchman, surprised that the speaker should have found a clue to escape the danger at which even his experience felt appalled.

"Your eminence is still legate?" demanded Patch.

"Thou knowest I am."

"And can convoke the prelates and the clergy?"

"Assuredly."

"Convoke them, then; and despite Rome's threats, pronounce for the divorce. Leave Henry's sword and Clement's crosier to decide the rest."

It would be singular to calculate the effect which the carrying out of the advice so boldly given might have produced upon the religious destinies of England. Rome, most probably, would have yielded, or been reconciled in time, and Wolsey have remained till death Henry's all-powerful minister. It was by a similar line of conduct that Cranmer secured the favour of the king, who maintained him in his proceedings against all his enemies merely because he could not suffer the authority to be assailed which had given judgment in his favour in his divorce both from Katherine of Arragon and her more unfortunate successor, Anne Boleyn.

"It were, indeed, one way," slowly repeated Wolsey, more like a man replying to himself than answering another; "but it would cast a brand whose conflagration ages would not extinguish. Heresy even now is rife within the land."

"What matter," observed the jester, "so you escaped the flames? As for the brand you speak of, it is cast already—Henry and Rome are twain at this moment."

"It would stain my purple," added the cardinal.

"Cast the shadow of the imperial rag aside; men are beginning to hold it at its value."

"Destroy all hopes of the tiara which Clement's age and failing years hold out?"

"Dreams," interrupted the counsellor, "dreams, which France and Spain alike have fostered only to deceive. France fears; Charles hates as well as fears thee. As a subject already hast thou menaced the world—as a sovereign thou wouldst command it. Rivals as they are, they would unite on this one point against thee. The tiara," he continued, scornfully, "it is the *ignis fatuus* which leads thy steps astray, and blinds thy sight where thou shouldst see most clearly. Why, like a wayward child, pine for a bauble placed beyond thy reach?"

"Dream though it be," exclaimed the churchman, rising from his cushioned seat and pacing the chamber, "it is a glorious one, and crowned my sleep from boyhood. It cheered the obscure student in his patient toil—urged the aspiring statesman on to greatness—armed him against the nation's murmurs and the noble's scorn. I will not turn my footsteps from the path," he added, with a determination which showed how deeply the ambitious hope was wedded to his soul, "though Death, clad in his grisly terrors, bar my passage, pointing with mocking finger to a timeless grave."

"Heaven grant," said his hearer, disappointed perhaps that his counsel was not followed, "that Henry's wrath leaves it a bloodless one."

Wolsey started as the thought which had dimly haunted him of late was thus forced palpably, as it were, upon his sight. He well knew how he was hated both by the nobility and people, chiefly on account of the death of the Duke of Buckingham; although, when his master's jealousy of all who stood in any way related to the throne is considered, it is doubtful if he was anything more than

a passive instrument in the matter; added to which, even in disguise, exile, or poverty, from his position in the church, the vast influence of his name and talents, he would be a dangerous enemy—too dangerous for those who had overthrown to suffer him to live.

"Think'st thou," he demanded, in a voice so low that it sounded like a whisper, "he would dare to violate Rome's purple and lay a sacrilegious hand upon our life?"

"Henry is fond of innovation," replied Patch, in his usual quiet tone; "the novelty might tempt him."

It might almost have been thought the speaker prophesied, when it is remembered the tyrant decided at once upon beheading Fisher, the venerable Bishop of Rochester, who was afterwards condemned, together with the illustrious Sir Thomas More, for denying his supremacy, upon hearing that the pontiff had raised him to the dignity of cardinal, brutally declaring that Rome might send the hat, but he would make sure it found no head to fit it. Like all the Tudors, he had a thirst for blood.

"There at least," said the tottering favourite, "I may defy him. Thanks to thy friendship, I am armed against that last extreme of fate; even at the scaffold's foot the jester's gift should baulk his malice."

He raised his jewelled hand as he spoke, and displayed the poisoned ring which Patch and Walter had found in the cabinet of the Italian, Adam, after the execution of Sir John de Corbey. The faithful donor smiled mournfully as he beheld it. Perhaps he already saw that the hour was nearer than the speaker imagined.

"Away," continued the speaker; "join thou this hawking party. Have ears for every word which falls from Henry's lips—eyes for each glance; a straw, the thistle's floating down, will show which way the wind blows; above all, take heed if he rides towards Hever — there lies our chiefest danger."

With a nod of intelligence, which intimated that his intentions and wishes were perfectly understood, the strangely selected confidant quitted the apartment, which Wolsey continued to pace in thoughtful silence long after his departure, pondering over the storm which menaced him and the bold advice he had received.

"It cannot be," he murmured to himself, "that the fabric I have reared, the hopes for which I toiled and sinned, should fade in air like childhood's fairy dream; yet why should I regret it? for what is rank and state?—a tinsel robe which fools and knaves alone are dazzled by. The wise man knows its worth-

PATCH COMMITS LOUIS TO THE PROTECTION OF SIR RICHARD EVERIL.

lessness and scorns it. But power," he slowly added, " is earth's real substantial good; life's only purpose and reality; as drowning wretches clutch at straws, I'll hold it to the last."

With these words, which illustrate, perhaps, alike the strength and weakness of the great man's character, he reseated himself, and began to compile from the papers on the table a list of his vast wealth, with which he vainly hoped to bribe the king when the impending crisis should arrive. Whilst the falling favourite is thus occupied, let us fol-

low our old friend Patch, who had joined th royal party.

Hawking or falconry in the reign of Henry VIII., and even to a much later period, had this distinctive character from the other pastimes of the age—it could only be practised by persons of rank. The possession of a hawk was considered as one of the ensigns of nobility, and those who were entitled to be the owners of this bird generally travelled with them, took them into the field of battle, and refused to part with them even when taken prisoner. No action was deemed so disgraceful to a nobleman as the surrendering of his hawk or dog. The laws of etiquette, which prohibited the use of the hawk to the vulgar, regulated in the same aristocratic spirit the species of the bird which, according to the degree of an individual, he was permitted to possess. An emperor might have an eagle, a vulture, or a melawn ; a king must descend to a gerfalcon; whilst a falcon gentle and a tercel gentle were permitted to a prince, a falcon of the rock to a duke, a falcon peregrin to an earl, a merlyn to a lady, and a sparrow hawk for a priest.

The ladies and clergy both joined in this amusement, in which the fair sex frequently equalled and sometimes excelled the sportsmen. To a lady we are indebted for one of the most elaborate treatises on hawking which time has handed down to us. Dame Julian Berners, sister of Richard, Lord Berners, and prioress of the nunnery of Sopewell, wrote a work both on hawking and heraldry, which was printed in the neighbouring abbey of St. Albans, in 1481. The style in which this work is written is an instance of the want of refinement in the females of the fifteenth century.

The mode in which hawking was practised varied according to circumstances; for it was pursued either on foot or on horseback, or by the side of the lakes or smooth water. Henry seems to have preferred the land amusement, and to have entered into it with so much ardour as sometimes to have encountered inconvenient and dangerous accidents. On foot, the sportsmen were provided with a long pole to assist them in leaping over hedges, ditches, or fences, which might obstruct their progress. The party who pursued water-hawking were, on the contrary, obliged to wait by the side of a river or pool until the game arose, or if that did not take place soon they employed their attendant falconers to beat long the banks to alarm the birds, which arose aloft only to encounter their destruction.

The falcon, which was brought to the scene of action hoodwinked and seated on the hand, was now uncovered and allowed to fly at the prey, but was not left to its own discretion, being retained by straps of leather called jesses, which were fastened round the legs of the bird, and to these jesses were attached lines which the sportsman would loosely wind round his little finger. The legs of the hawk were adorned with bells, to which was fastened a creance, or long thread, by which the bird was drawn back after she had begun to fly; this, in technical language, was called reclaiming the falcon. Milan bells, from their sweet musical sound, were generally preferred.

It may easily be supposed how important a personage the falconer in those days must have been, and how valuable the well-tutored birds must have been considered, when this sport was thought so important to the happiness both of the king and his nobles, that stringent laws were made for the protection of the young falcons. Henry VII. made a law, in the eleventh year of his reign, enacting that if any one were convicted of destroying the eggs of a falcon, a goshawk, or a lance, he should suffer imprisonment for a year and a day, and be fined at the king's pleasure.

The loud shouts of the party, as they dashed along the banks of the Thames, following the falconers who rode before to rouse the birds, directed Patch where to follow them. He was no timid horseman, and half an hour's hard riding brought him up with the royal sportsman. Just as he reached the ground a stately bird had been started from the low sedgy banks where it had been feeding, and with repeated gyrations rose till it appeared like a speck in the clear blue sky above it. This was the critical moment for the sportsman to display his skill by assuring himself that his falcon had seen its victim before he loosed the jesses and launched it from his hand.

"Whoo! lie til ho!" cried Henry, as he cast his bird—a magnificent Norway falcon, the gift of his sister, the Queen of Scotland, and which he had named after the donor. "Now, Margaret, do thy best; by St. Hubert, but 'tis a royal bird," he continued, as the liberated falcon rose majestically in pursuit of its prey; "how steadily it rises on the wing! Now, heron, wing thy way!"

The hunted bird had evidently caught sight of its pursuer, for instead of attempting to rise higher, it wheeled round and made way towards a grove of lofty pines, in which most probably its nest was situated, and whose tall tops were visible to the sportsmen, even from the flat marshy ground where they were riding. Dashing his spurs deep into his horse's sides, Henry started off to follow the aerial chase. Many a gay halloo was given, and many a merry laugh rang on the banks of silver Thames, as the nobles and courtiers followed in the wake of their excited master.

"Fly, Margaret!" shouted the king; "a cast of golden balls if thou strikest down the heron before he reaches wood. Hip, ho, whoo!" he continued, his excitement every moment increasing; "he gains upon him—now the long-shanks sees he cannot reach the wood, and rises on his wing again."

To have watched the chase one might really have thought that the gallant falcon had both heard and understood the encouraging cry of his royal master, for it had redoubled its efforts and so far gained upon its flying victim, that perceiving the combat inevitable, the persecuted heron had once more changed its lateral course and risen on its wing. Its pursuer followed it.

"Rise, falcon! rise heron!" shouted the Duke of Suffolk, who was an enthusiastic admirer of the sport, and who, together with the king and principal personages of the party, drew their horses into a circle, as the contest once more became confined to that portion of the heavens directly over their heads.

"Fly, cardinal! rise, king!" shouted a voice from a distant group of falconers and courtiers who were gathered at a distance. There was an instant pause in the laugh and vociferation of those nearest the monarch, not knowing how Henry would approve the daring jest. For a moment his brow was clouded, but a quiet smile gradually, and apparently without his wishing it, appeared upon his lip. Those who watched it and knew him intimately, saw that the fate of his favourite was sealed, and many a heart beat the lighter.

"Well, my lords," he exclaimed, bursting into a good-humoured laugh, as if unable longer to control himself, "dare you refuse the challenge? Shrewsbury, a hundred pieces on my gallant falcon, and a glove for thy lady—is it a wager?"

"A royal one, sire," replied the politic noble, bowing at the offer, "and I accept it."

"Dost thou?" cried Henry; "why, then, fly, cardinal! rise, king!"

No sooner had the words passed the lips of the speaker than they were joyously echoed by nearly every noble present, for there were few who did not secretly desire the downfal of the churchman. The faithful Patch listened to them in silence, for which he was roughly reproved by the obsequious Earl of Shrewsbury.

"Why, thou disloyal knave," exclaimed the earl, "refuse to repeat the war-cry of the king?"

"I am no courtier," replied the jester, scornfully.

"Thou art an insolent traitor," retorted the haughty noble, who felt the bitter satire of the speaker more than he cared to show; for during his prosperity he had been one of Wolsey's most obsequious worshippers, which no one knew better than the faithful fool.

"And thou a noble weathercock," answered Patch, in his usual unmoved tone, "a thing to show which way the wind of royal favour sits."

"What dispute is this?" demanded Henry, riding up to the group, followed by Suffolk, Surrey, and his immediate attendants. "Wrangling in our presence, knave?"

"A slight dispute between my brother of Shrewsbury and myself," said the jester, coolly. "He wears your majesty's bells, I the cardinal's. We could not agree as to the sound; each fool preferred his own."

A general laugh followed the explanation; for, strange as such license would now appear, the jester in those days was a privileged person, who might address even to a crowned head with impunity reproof or advice, which the gravest statesman or counsellor in the kingdon would hesitate to offer.

"Thou art a merry knave," observed the king, joining in the mirth, "and I believe a faithful one. Wilt thou take service with me?"

"No, gossip, no," replied the jester, gravely shaking his head. "Why, to make room for one, displace so many? Besides," he added, "I am in my humour something like Minerva's bird, as fits our state and wisdom."

"How so?" demanded Henry.

"I quit not a ruined house."

There was a tone of melancholy reproof in the voice of the speaker, which awoke a kindlier sentiment towards his master in the breast of the king, and alarmed the courtiers for the success of their schemes to displace him. Suffolk saw the impression, and hastened to remove it.

"Look, sire!" he exclaimed; "see how royally your falcon merits its name—a pair of spurs to a dozen nobles that he gears his bird."

"Not without feeling his heron's beak," replied the jester, fixing his keen grey eyes upon the contest; "see how nobly he watches for the swoop—it will be fatal to them both."

The eyes of the speaker and the monarch encountered as he spoke. They understood each other.

"Be it so," said Henry; "it is too late to stay it."

The falcon, as usual, had soared and soared till it had gained a height considerably above that of its victim, whose long neck was turned back, watching for the pounce which the pursuer was sure to make, and which, if once avoided, generally gave the heron an opportunity to escape, as it was made with such violence that the descending bird could neither stop midway nor recover its wing till some minutes after. Every eye was fixed upon the royal bird as it made its fatal swoop, and the cry of "Fly, cardinal!" was again mockingly repeated; but, to the disappointment of all, save Patch, the cardinal or heron disdained to fly, but extending its long sharp beak like a lance, it received its enemy upon the point, literally impaling it by the force of its descent. The falcon, however, although wounded, was not subdued; but, fixing its talons in the breast of its adversary it clung with tenacity to its conqueror, which it struck with its powerful beak repeatedly upon the head. Both fell together. Henry was the first to dismount to relieve his favourite from its position, in the hope that it might be only slightly wounded. The hope, however, was vain—both heron and falcon were dead.

"I would sooner," exclaimed Henry, "have given a thousand marks than this should have happened. Poor Margaret! thy flight has been a short one."

"But a victorious one," observed the Duke of Suffolk; "its enemy has fallen with it."

"To your pleasure, gentlemen," said the king, gloomily—"to your pleasure. I'll hawk no more to-day. Suffolk and Surrey will ride with me, the rest dispose themselves as their caprice and humour lead them, till the banquet hour."

This was the general intimation given when the speaker wished to be alone, or to start on one of those amatory expeditions in which he so frequently indulged, and in which his brother-in-law and another favoured noble were generally his companions.

"How far is it, Sir Thomas, to Hever Castle?" demanded Patch of the poet knight, who, like most of the courtiers, had drawn rein, not to follow even by inadvertence the same route as the king; "thinkst thou a good horseman might be there by dusk?"

"Undoubtedly," replied the party addressed, trying to look unconcerned.

"I will bet thee a rose noble to a flask of sack that Henry sups there," continued the jester.

"If he does," replied Sir Thomas, turning pale, but trying to appear unconcerned, "what is that to me?"

"To thee?" repeated the querist; "why, what indeed! If the king loved fify Mistress Boleyns, what would it be to thee, since thou hast no inkling of affection there—no idle dreams such as boys muse on, when spring's sweet breath wooes them to wander by the rippling stream, or 'neath the hawthorn's budding shade? To thee, indeed! Who could suspect thee of such folly?"

The unhappy poet, who felt all the sarcasm of the jester's words, winced like a man stung by a hornet; indeed, at times the jester's tongue was not less venomous, though this time he thought the caution was perhaps kindly meant.

"Thanks, friend Patch," said Sir Thomas "I understand thee—the warning is well-timed and well-meant. I know the danger of crossing the lion's path, and shall not ride to Hever."

With these words he turned his horse aside, and plunged in the woods which skirted the river. His companion remained for a few moments gazing in silence after him. He knew the human heart too well to trust its weakness or its promise.

"And I," he exclaimed, as the white plume of the knight disappeared amid the trees, "prophesy that I must ride hard to reach Hever before thee. What so deceitful as a lover's resolution, or a woman's promise?"

With these reflections, the jester gave rein, and pursued his way to the residence of the beautiful Anne Boleyn. Hever Castle was erected by William de Hever, a Norman baron, who under Edward III. obtained the king's license to embattle his manor house, as well as to have free warren within his demesne. It is situated on the western border of the county of Kent, hard by Penshurst. His two daughters and so-heiresses conveyed it by marriage to the families of Cobham and Brocas. The former, who had acquired the whole estate by purchase, resold it to Sir Geoffrey Boleyn, a wealthy mercer of London, and lord mayor of the city in the thirty-seventh year of the reign of Henry VI. The wealthy merchant was the great grandfather of the beautiful Anne whom Wyat and Henry both passionately loved.

The castle itself was an interesting specimen of the domestic fortress,—a large massive building, with buttresses, square towers, embrasures, and a deep moat supplied by water from the neighbouring river Eden. The entrance gateway was further flanked by two towers, embattled, strongly machicolated, and defended by a portcullis. Considerable remains of the once stately structure still exist.

The moon was shining brightly down the broad avenue which led to the principal entrance, when a horseman, whose foaming steed and soiled dress showed how hard he had ridden, drew rein at the foot of an enormous chestnut tree, whose branches shaded a vase and statue which in the Italian style graced the bottom of the walk.

"So," he exclaimed, at the same time removing the bit from the mouth of his good steed, "I am here the first; more than are invited will meet at the place of rendezvous. Should Henry encounter Wyat at the place of tryst, it may cool his hot impetuous love; if not," he added, "I must trust to the chapter of accidents. Human folly or hum passion will not fail to supply me with some clue."

We need not tell our readers that the speaker was their old acquaintance Patch.

Twisting the rein round the neck of the animal, he released it, and the well-trained steed made its way into the underwood to feed upon the tender herbage; its master knew that with a whistle he could at any moment recall him. After looking cautiously round as if to assure himself that he was unobserved, or had not mistaken the place, the jester climbed the chestnut tree we have before alluded to, and cradled himself at his ease in the enormous branches, still watching with an eager eye and an attentive ear for any sight or sound which might indicate the approach of any of those whom he expected. He had patiently maintained his position for more than an hour, when a light rustling step roused his attention. At first, he deemed the sound proceeded from some stray fawn, so lightly did the footfall break upon his ear. He was, however, quickly undeceived; for a graceful figure emerged from the shade of the narrow footpath into the full moon's light; her veil floating in the evening breeze, displayed the animated, beautiful features of the wearer, as, with a timid step, she advanced towards the vase beneath the tree to deposit a letter under the marble pedestal, starting at every rustling leaf or nameless sound the forest shades sighed forth.

"Good!" murmured the watchful jester to himself, "the game begins. Anne Boleyn has well commenced her part; Wyat and Henry next."

No sooner had the maiden deposited her letter than she retired towards the castle by the narrow footpath, fearful of being observed if she ventured in the open avenue, which the full moon rendered almost as clear as the light of day. The moment she was gone Patch nimbly descended from his hiding place and secured the precious document, which he hid within his breast, for something whispered to him that it would one day be useful. He was seldom wrong.

Scarcely had he regained his former secure position than a second horseman approached, who, however, took the precaution of dismounting at a considerable distance, and fastened his steed to a tree—it was the poet and once favoured lover of Anne Boleyn, Sir Thomas Wyat, whose muse, although scarcely worthy of that honour, has been coupled with the gallant Surrey's in his impassioned lays to Geraldine.

Taking his rebeck from his shoulder, he hastily touched a few chords by way of prelude, and then accompanied himself as in a deep manly voice he sang the following serenade:—

> The stars from heaven are peeping
>   Less beautiful than thee;
> Come while the world is sleeping,
>   To change love's vows with me.
>
> Come with thy bright eyes beaming,
>   Brightly in beauty's spell;
> Come while the earth is dreaming,
>   Our tale of love to tell.
>
> Night's holiest guards are keeping
>   Their vigil round thy tower;
> Then while the world is sleeping,
>   Sweet lady, quit thy bower.
>
> The stars from heaven are beaming
>   Less beautiful than thee;
> Come while the earth is dreaming
>   To change love's vows with me.

"An this piping win her not," murmured Patch, "I would advise the knight never to pinch rebeck more: for, to do him justice, he does it daintily."

The skill of the songster was not thrown away: the step of the maiden again rustled through the wood, and in a few moments Anne Boleyn stood in the avenue, and the enamoured Wyat at her feet.

"Good!" said the jester; "an Henry comes, all may yet be well."

CHAPTER XIII.

" Cromwell, I charge thee fling away ambition ;
By that sin angels fell ; how then shall man,
Although the image of his Maker, hope to win by it ?"
"Had I but served my God
With half the zeal I served my king ; He would not in my age
Have left me naked to mine enemies."—Shakspeare, Henry VIII.

 NCE more I behold thee !" exclaimed Sir Thomas Wyat, passionately kissing the yielding hand of Anne Boleyn ; " once more I hear the music of that voice whose melting tone haunts e'en my sleeping hours, making rich melodies in dreams. Anne," he continued, fixing his eyes with eager fondness upon the blushing girl, " mine is not a love to dazzle or destroy thee ; the throne to which I would raise thee is a faithful heart which only beats for thee. The homage I would surround thee with, its every thought and wish. Were I a king, by heaven I should only prize my crown but as it rendered me more worth thee."

"Nay, now you mock me," replied the inconstant maiden, whose love towards the knight, since her retirement to Hever Castle, had suddenly returned, for she deemed the capricious Henry's passion extinct. " 'Tis true I have been dazzled, but not misled ; my head may have turned giddy with the honeyed flatteries of Henry's tongue, but not my heart—that has been constant to thee."

"Say'st thou, sweet one ?" whispered the enamoured poet, gently circling her waist with his trembling arm. "Oh ! repeat the blest assurance ; let me gaze in thy bright eyes as thy dear lips pronounce it. Nay, thou shalt not deny me," he added, pressing her closer to his manly breast, "for every word will fall like precious balm upon my wounded heart, healing the pangs of jealousy and love."

"Must I repeat it ?" demanded Anne, coquettishly raising her eyes to his, but quickly dropping them beneath the burning ardour of his gaze, which brought the blush into her conscious cheek.

"An thou really lovest me," replied Sir Thomas, intoxicated with the brilliant glance. "Love is exacting in its privileges, and I have been too long debarred from mine."

"Well, then," said the future queen, with a sincerity which at that time, perhaps, she really felt, "I repeat it : the king might win

my ear, for women seldom frown when told that they are fair ; but never, Wyat, by our early vows, breathed in the deep confidence of mutual love, never hath he touched my heart."

"I knew it was ambition," muttered Patch, who from his position in the chestnut tree overheard the conversation. "Oh, woman ! how like an angel to those who know ye not !"

"And that heart ?" exclaimed her lover, sinking upon his knee and gazing upon her as if life and death hung on the words which followed from her lips.

"Is, as it ever hath been," she continued, "thine, and thine only. But why this cruel doubt ?—have you not read my letter ?"

"What letter ?" demanded her enraptured lover.

"What letter, ingrate !" repeated Anne ; "why the one I placed but an hour since for thee beneath the pedestal of yonder vase, our usual hiding-place : hast thou not found it ?"

The knight rushed to the well-known spot, and searched impatiently, and, as our readers are aware, in vain, for Patch had already secured it.

"Alas !" he exclaimed, " 'tis gone !"

"Gone !" said his mistress ; and a cold shudder ran through her frame as she echoed the words, as if already she anticipated the fearful retribution it would one day cause to fall upon her. "Impossible ! I placed it there but now. Surely you jest."

"The wind, perhaps, hath caught it," observed her lover ; "but fear not, sweet ; I will remain till daylight, and search each bush to find it. Tell me," he added, tenderly, "what did it contain ?"

"The assurance of my love," replied the troubled maiden, with a sigh, "and my indifference to the king. Should it fall into evil hands it might work my ruin."

"How so ?"

"Henry might forgive an injury, but ne'er an insult to his vanity. Oh ! 'tis a cruel nature ! Selfish in all things, doubly so in love."

"She is warned," muttered the jester to

himself; "if she falls, her blood be on her head."

"Fear not, love," whispered Sir Thomas; "he must come armed in more than mortal terrors that would injure thee. Once mine, king though the tyrant be, I would protect thee against his malice. Besides," he added, "there are other climes fairer than England's soil, where faithful hearts might make this earth a paradise of love; e'en there where thy young days were passed—the sunny land of France."

"True," sighed Anne, not without a pang, as her ambitious dream of greatness vanished at the thought.

At this moment the gleam of distant torches was seen flitting through the woods, and voices heard calling on the fair fugitive by name.

"Good," muttered the concealed spy; "it is the king. Now, then, to test her promises."

"Fly!" exclaimed Anne Boleyn, "I am called; let them not find thee here."

The speaker's sister-in-law, afterwards the infamous Lady Rochfort, rushed from the wood, and casting her arms round her fair relative, whispered a word which flushed her cheek, but whether with hope or fear it were difficult to tell.

"It is the king," whispered Wyat, fixing his eyes expressively upon her.

"True," said his mistress; "he must not find thee here—my hitherto unsullied name were compromised."

There was a candour in the avowal which would have disarmed any suspicions except a jealous lover's. Sir Thomas trembled at the word, but hesitated not to obey her.

"Farewell," he cried, imprinting a kiss upon her burning cheek; "remember that my life is in thy keeping. Heed not the tyrant's promises or threats; love watches over thee."

The agitated knight hastily plunged into the underwood and disappeared, but not, as his mistress thought, out of hearing; for, creeping cautiously round to the back of the tree where Patch had ensconced himself, he cautiously began climbing the giant trunk.

"Good," muttered the jester; "the plot thickens, the scene grows interesting."

"Art mad, to cast thy fortune from thee?" demanded the artful confidant. "Quick, and seat thyself; 'tis well, Anne, thou hast wiser heads to screen thy folly from the jealous king."

Although surprised and confused, the maiden, with all a woman's tact, did as she was directed, and cast herself upon the seat close to the friendly tree, where her lover by this time had hid himself. Her sister, more versed in intrigue than herself, hastily caught up the rebeck which Wyat had left upon the sward, and, reclining at her feet, began to touch the chords. The sound soon drew the party to the spot.

"Who art thou, villain?" demanded the astonished poet, as he felt the form of Patch reclining on one of the massive branches where he intruded himself—"a spy or thief?"

"Whichever thou wilt," coolly whispered the party thus apostrophised; "but be patient, now—calm thy hot temper, lest it cost thy head. Henry loves not those who poach upon his rights; besides, thou now canst test thy mistress's faith, if it be worth the trial. Kings seldom woo in vain."

"Patch!" said the astonished knight, recognising his voice, for he was too much shaded to permit him to distinguish his features.

"Silence," said the jester, drily; "do as thou wilt with thy own life, but risk not mine. 'Tis a strange whim, perhaps, but I prefer nestling mid the leaves to hanging from the branches."

A cordial pressure of the hand was the only reply to the speaker's well-meant caution. In an instant other thoughts and other feelings wrung his heart, for Henry was at the feet of his fickle mistress, who started with well-affected surprise as her royal lover knelt before her.

The convenient sister-in-law, seeing that her task was ended, discreetly withdrew to a suitable distance, taking, however, the poet's rebeck with her: it might have told a tale.

"Henry!" exclaimed Anne; "that is," she added, pretending to recover from her confusion, "the king."

"Henry," said the monarch; "call me Henry, your own true, devoted Henry, who casts aside the splendour of his state, the world's stale homage, and his flatterers' praise, to taste an hour of pure delight with thee."

"Rise, your grace; I have listened to these honoured words before, and once, like a weak child, because my heart wished them true, believed them. My folly has been punished—in my banishment I have in part atoned it."

"Banishment!" repeated the monarch.

"How else am I to consider my forced retirement to Hever Castle?" continued the fair speaker, whose ambitious hopes returned with the presence of her suitor.

"But as love's guise, to hide its secret purpose," replied the amorous king. "Perchance, too, as a trial of thy faith; for I would be loved not for my crown, but for myself."

"As the fair maid of Stanfield doubtless loves thee!" exclaimed his listener in a tone of well-acted reproach; "oh! Henry! Henry! was't not enough to win a hopeless love; shadow my girlhood's years; but thou must cast it like a worthless flower aside, crushing my heart with jealousy and shame?"

"Tut, tut!" whispered the delighted wooer, whose vanity was gratified at the well-acted passion of his aspiring mistress; "thou has been bred too long at courts not to see through a flimsy veil like this. The maid of Stanfield," he repeated, "a pale-faced chit, whom we selected purposely to blind observant eyes, and not to wound thy trusting nature. Thou wilt scarce persuade me now that thou wert really jealous of a child like her; it were too flattering to my love."

Anne Boleyn smiled upon him; she was too politic not to be convinced.

"Heavens!" whispered Wyat; "can such treachery dwell in woman's form?"

"Where else should it dwell?" replied his companion in the same under tone; "the devil, when he tempts mankind, is sure to wear an angel's face."

"Come," said the enamoured Henry; "the dews of night are falling fast, and the keen air may chill thee; let us to the castle—the morning, fair one, sees thee again the light and joy of England's court."

"Alas!" sighed Anne Boleyn coquettishly; "the court, your grace, is not the place for me."

"Thy place there," exclaimed the king, "soon shall be the highest; we have found the way to cut this Gordian knot without the aid of Rome. Patience a little, sweet one, and thine enemies shall fall like reeds before thee."

"There is one, sire," replied the maiden, "no storm can shake; one who has thriven so lordly in your favour, that his pride and state shadow the throne, and to vulgar eyes makes e'en your glories dim. Why recal me when a word from Wolsey will at any time banish me from your presence and your heart? Henry rules England, as men say, but Wolsey rules the king."

"Thou think'st so!" said the monarch, knitting his brow, for he was becoming impatient at being schooled even by so fair a speaker.

"I repeat, your grace, but what all who love their king affirm."

"To-morrow witnesses his downfall, Maybird," whispered the amorous monarch, fearful lest even the passing wind should catch the important secret; "wilt thou now refuse to be present at thine enemy's disgrace?

Suffolk and Norfolk, this very night, received the mission to demand from him the seal of England in our royal name. Art thou content?"

"Content," repeated his mistress, looking into his eyes with a glance such as she had so lately cast on Wyat; "I am most happy. Teach me, Henry," she added in her syren voice, "to bear this most unlooked-for bliss; my heart will break else with its conscious joy."

A kiss, whose echo nearly drove the distracted knight from his ambush, sealed the monarch's promise and Anne Boleyn's fate. On a signal from the king, the torch-bearers, who, together with Suffolk and Sir Thomas Boleyn, had remained at a convenient distance, surrounded the happy pair, and escorted Henry and his inconstant mistress to Hever Castle.

No sooner had the cortège disappeared than Patch and his companion descended from their place of concealment. The countenance of the knight was pale with conflicting passion. Scorn, love, and jealousy, by turns, assumed their fearful empire over him. He was like a man suddenly awakened from a fearful dream, doubtful of the reality of the scene of perjury and deceit he had witnessed.

"Henceforth," he cried, "let woman's promises be writ in sand—or, better still, in water—for they are fools who trust them. Who would believe that such deceit dwelt in so fair a form?"

"All," said the jester, "who have studied them. They little know the world who deem the gaudiest casket hides the richest gem. Psha! man," he added, "let not thy heart dissolve in bitterness; thou art not the first who hast mistaken tinsel for pure gold—the counterfeit for the pure gem; choose again, but choose with more discretion."

"Never," replied Sir Thomas; "she was my love's first dream—my manhood's hope. Banish me to a desert, and, despite her falsehood, memory would find some verdant spot, and there enshrine her image."

"Is the wound so deep?" said his companion, musingly; "time only can effect a cure."

"Time!" repeated the poet; "will it restore a broken heart?"

"It will bind it, boy," resumed Patch. "What! pine like a love-sick girl, and waste the energies of thy existence for one who coldly sells herself for idle state—barters the vow fresh spoken on her lips for a polluted greatness—perjures herself to gain a crown, whose weight at last will crush her! Weakness, folly!"

"You name it truly, yet I love her still."

"Respect thyself," said the jester, at the

THE DEATH OF SIR JOHN DE CORBEY.

same time giving the customary signal to his faithful steed, which in a few moments came bounding towards him from the neighbouring wood, "and fate will then respect thee. Stained as earth's flowers are by the trail of Eden's serpent, buds may yet be found untainted by the venom of its falsehood; but seek them not in courts," he added, "or in the busy haunts of man. The deeper the solitude, the fresher will the plant be found. Farewell!"

With these words the men who had been so strangely thrown together separated—the

lover to brood over the loss of his fickle mistress, and Patch on his return to London, where our old friend Walter and the heiress of Stanfield impatiently expected his arrival.

On the rescue of Lady Mary from the licentious violence of the king, she was rapidly conveyed by her two protectors to the house of Marietti, the wealthy merchant in Lombard-street, where, for the first time, Walter was made acquainted with all the mysteries of the mansion, which was connected by a low stone passage with the large storehouses at the back, where the owner

No. 43.

kept the bales of foreign goods, in which he dealt. In the centre of these storehouses, three rooms were strongly built, and so carefully protected from observation by the surrounding edifice that it was only upon a minute survey their existence could be suspected. A second passage, still more artfully concealed, led to a subterranean chamber, well provisioned, so as to enable the fugitives to withstand a siege in case of necessity. To the existence of this second place of refuge even Marco, the old and confidential servant of the merchant, was a stranger to the knowledge of its existence. It was shared only by the jester and his friend, who instructed Walter how to reach it, should their retreat, by any unfortunate accident, become suspected. The precaution was a wise one.

As the jester approached the house early on the morning after his adventure in the forest, he found, to his terror and surprise, a party of the city guard, headed by his old acquaintance, Sir John Perrot, had taken possession of each end of the street, and carefully examined the passengers before allowing them egress from it. Patch being well known, no difficulty of course was made to his passing freely. The name of his master, Wolsey, was still a talisman few would venture to brave.

"How now, Sir John?" he exclaimed, carelessly, as if the answer to the question he was about to put was the most indifferent thing in the world to him. "Out birding so early? What kind of game are you beating for, that you ride with so many huntsmen in your train?"

"Traitors," replied the knight, with more than his usual gravity.

"What, have the Lombard merchants turned politicians? Hath the Emperor Charles sent an army from his Milan duchy, packed up in a bale of silks?"

"Worse," said Sir John; "two fugitives, for whose apprehension our royal master has offered a vast reward, are concealed within the house of Marietti, the rich money lender."

"How know you that?"

"We are sure," replied the courtier.

"What, has he taken them in pledge?" demanded Patch, anxious by every means in his power to gain time, in order that the heiress and Walter might reach their place of concealment.

"Information was given to the marshal by a fellow named Marco," said the knight, "a servant of the house. I was ordered on this expedition—an office," he added, in an under tone, for he well knew the jester's connection with the merchant, from whom he had frequently received money on his account, "which I dared not refuse."

"It could not have fallen better; they must be saved," whispered the fool.

"Impossible! my life would pay the penalty."

"Did it cost fifty, still it must be done," interrupted the jester, in the same low tone; "search where thou art shown, and leave the rest to me. Nay, stare not, man, thou shalt have thy price—a hundred nobles of as pure gold as ever bought a courtier's conscience or a soldier's weapon. Are we agreed?"

The leader of the expedition merely bowed his head. He had, in the course of his career at court, had many dealings with the jester, and knew that his simple word was as a noble's bond.

By this time Marietti, who had been reconnoitring from one of the loopholes practised in the door, let down one of the huge wooden shutters which served to admit light into his shop instead of windows, and with the air of a man startled by some unexpected alarm from his sleep, demanded:

"Who is there?"

"Friends," replied Sir John Perrot; "so open at once, good Lombard, and fear not for thy merchandise."

"Open in the king's name!" exclaimed Sir Edward Darrel, a young knight who had been joined with him in the command of the party, and who, like most young courtiers, was anxious to distinguish his zeal, especially before Patch, whom he knew to be the confidant of Wolsey, and whose good report he thought might serve him; "dost take us for robbers, man?"

"I scarcely know what I took you for," answered the merchant, at the same time opening the door: for he felt re-assured by the appearance of the jester, whose ready wit he doubted not would find some means to extricate them from the dilemma, but whom he was too prudent to be the first to recognise. "If this is not some drunken jest," he continued—"if you really come in the king's name, before I permit you to enter my house, tell me, at least, what is his grace's pleasure."

"A most reasonable request, truly!" exclaimed Patch; "as if two valiant knights, with the city guard to back them, were to give a reason, on compulsion, for their proceedings! Perhaps, old Mammon, we come to ransack thy money-bags, set free thy hoarded gems, toy with thy wife, or kiss thy daughter; that is," he added, "if such a piece of dried humanity can father any thing except an ingot."

"You have given shelter to two fugitives," said Sir John Perrot.

"Traitors," added Darrel, "upon whose heads the king hath set a princely recompense."

"Alack!" replied the merchant, apparently relieved from his fears, "but some one has sadly sported with your credulity; but trust not to my words, trust your own eyes—search well the house; and if you find any living thing except my faithful servant and myself, deal with us after his good grace's pleasure. I am a merchant, sirs," he added, "and meddle not with politics."

The two knights, accompanied by four of the halberdiers, followed the speaker into the little room at the back of the shop. Once there, much to the old man's astonishment, they proceeded to the secret door which opened into the passage leading to the rooms constructed in his warehouses. Despite his usual self-possession, he trembled, for he felt convinced that some domestic treachery must have been at work; and he doubted whether the mystery of the subterranean chamber had been betrayed or not.

"Go," he said sternly to Marco, whose guilty conscience spoke in his shifting eye and burning cheek, "dost thou not see that there are strangers in the shop? Holy Mary!" he added, "but I left the Duke of Suffolk's diamond George and the bracelets for Mistress Boleyn in the inner cabinet. Go and secure the key."

The aged wretch, who had eaten the speaker's bread for years, but whose thirst for gold had tempted him to betray a generous master, slunk from the chamber at his bidding, and while the rest continued their search, returned to our old friend Patch, who was expecting him in the outward room or shop.

"What brings thee back, faithful Marco?" whispered the jester, in a tone so full of confidence that the father of deceit himself could scarcely have suspected any sinister design to lurk beneath it. "They are a long while searching."

"Because," replied the fellow, "they have discovered the passage leading to the rooms within the warehouse."

"That's strange," said Patch, eyeing him closely.

"Of course it is; but it does not follow, because the secret is discovered, that I have betrayed it."

"Thou betrayed it!" repeated the fool, in a tone in which a close observer might have detected a slight vein of irony, "preposterous! No, bad as humanity becomes, it has reached that pitch of degradation. We took hee a starving man, of broken fortunes, to our service, in which thou hast grown grey;

thou hast amassed, for one of thy state, gold beyond thy dream or wish, for thou art a childless man, so near, too, to thy grave, that the bare thought of such a deed would damn thee. Thou sell, like a thankless cur, thy master's blood for a few pieces more to grease an itching palm!—improbable, impossible!"

"I trust—I—I am sure so," faltered the man, writhing beneath the sarcasm of the speaker, which he received for unmerited but well-meant praise.

"But thou hast not yet answered my question: what brought thee here?"

"Jewels of price are in the inner cabinet; my master sent me for the key."

"The inner cabinet," said the jester, with a peculiar emphasis; "you are sure?"

"Quite," replied Marco, advancing towards the ponderous iron-bound piece of furniture in which Marietti was supposed to keep the most precious of his merchandise, and which stood in a recess cut in the solid wall at the back of the shop. As he did so, Patch took a long key of a peculiar construction from the merchant's desk, and applied it to an opening in the counter beneath. The outward cabinet, which was level with the stone floor when opened, presented an appearance something like a sentry-box; but with this difference, that instead of a back or shelves as one would naturally expect to find in such a place, a second door, strongly studded with nails, presented itself. This was the entrance to the real treasure chamber; the exterior one was merely a blind. As the merchant had stated, a large key had been left in the massive lock. The moment the false servant laid his hand upon it to withdraw it, the floor of the outward cabinet, upon which he was standing, gave way, and before he had time to utter one prayer for mercy, one shriek for aid, the wretched man sank into an abyss beneath, whose stagnant waters soon ended his sufferings and his crimes.

When the party, after their ineffectual search, returned, the cabinet was closed, and the jester busily employed in examining a curious suit of inlaid Milan armour exposed for sale in the Lombard's shop.

"Well, have you limed the birds?" he demanded of the two knights.

"We have been placed upon a false scent," replied Darrel, "and have discovered nothing but two chambers daintily furnished, and tasted a flask of Greek wine fit for an emperor."

"Henceforth," said Perrot, who was something of an epicure, "thou shalt be my vintner. Why, man," he added, clapping the Lombard on the shoulders, "thy wine is melted rubies. Jove never drank sweeter nectar."

"I have but a few flasks," replied the merchant, drily, "and they were a present from my Greek correspondent, Mavoryeni, who is more chary of it than his gold. 'Tis the Chian vintage."

"Write to him again," exclaimed the jester, "and let me peruse thy correspondence. I am a judge of letters."

The two knights, fully persuaded that they had been sent upon a fool's errand, and that all further search would be useless, dismissed the city guard, and, remounting their horses, rode, accompanied by Patch, to York House, from whence the latter personage, after a brief interview with his master, once more returned to the city.

On the first alarm given at the house of Marietti, the old man rose, and, hastily waking Walter, conducted him and the heiress to the subterranean chamber whose existence we have previously described, but which was happily unknown to the treacherous Marco; nor was it till he had seen his guests safe within their hiding place, and removed every vestige of their presence, that he entered the little chamber at the back of the shop, where his domestic slept. The scene which followed our readers have already read.

The orphan heiress, whose fate we have for some time lost sight of, was praying within the low vaulted chamber, the close air of which had already caused her cheek to pale. Walter, his sword freed from its scabbard ready for use, was watching beside her, when a distant step in the long passage which conducted to their retreat fell upon the listener's ear.

"They come," faltered the maiden. "Walter, by the love you bear me, and the faith which I have sworn, let me not fall alive into the tyrant's hand. Death hath no terror compared to such a fate. Remember your promise."

"I will remember," replied the young man, his lip quivering with emotion as he spoke, for he had sworn to offer her a pure, unsullied sacrifice at the shrine of honour, rather than permit her to be polluted by the licentious passions of the vindictive Henry. With one arm he encircled her waist, and remained on guard, ready at the first signal to defend the trembling creature, who clung to him with all a woman's confidence for protection, or, if defence were vain, to die together.

The footsteps approached nearer and nearer; and although only a few instants had elapsed since first they heard them, yet every one was so fraught with agony and expectation, that it seemed an age; the very beatings of their hearts became suspended; nor was it till their eccentric protector, Walter's old friend, the jester, had been some time in the chamber, and all fear of a surprise had ceased, that their lifestream flowed again in its calm, usual current.

"What news dost thou bring?" exclaimed the young man, extending his hand to him; "let me know the worst, for danger is less appalling than suspense."

"The worst," repeated his visitor, with a faint smile, for his heart was heavy with the anticipation of his master's fate. "For thee, thank Heaven, the worst is past. For once," he added, "relentless cruelty has been defeated by honest cunning; but you must away, England is no longer an asylum for you. The barque is ready, and the wind sets fair for Antwerp."

"For Antwerp!" repeated the Lady Mary, blushing, for an intuitive sense of delicacy showed her the impropriety of her being the companion of Walter in his flight in any other character than his wife.

"All is arranged," continued the speaker, kindly, "this very night a chaplain of the queen, who still feels warmly for your welfare, will unite your fates. Here is a token from her grace."

He handed to the agitated and astonished girl a small slip of parchment, recommending, or rather commanding her marriage and temporary exile. It was signed "Katherine."

It fell from her hand the moment she had perused it. In an instant Walter was at her feet, entreating her by a thousand persuasive words, such as have weight in maidens' ears, to confirm his happiness. The transition was so sudden, so unexpected, that the orphan could not sufficiently recover her agitation to reply to his passionate asseverations of eternal constancy and faith.

"I will be his bondsman," said the jester, observing her hesitation—"if a true heart can merit such a sacrifice—that thou wilt not repent the generous confidence; besides," he added, "better a hasty marriage than an eternal separation."

These words at once decided her.

"Walter," she replied, at the same time extending her hand to him, "it is not thus a daughter of my house should wed, but I know thou wilt not think less kindly of me if in the hour of danger I cast aside the scruples of my rank and womanhood, and yield to this most hasty marriage. My heart hath long been given to thy keeping. I here entrust my person to thy honour—my happiness to thy protection. Let the priest come, the bride will not say nay."

We may pass over the passionate gratitude of the lover and the approving words of Patch, who had already begun to take as deep an interest in the persecuted orphan as in the welfare of his friend. As he and the queen had secretly arranged, a chaplain that very night visited the house of the Lombard merchant, and with no other witnesses than Marietti and the jester, the heiress pronounced the vow which bound her destiny irrevocably with Walter's, the vow which set the seal upon his boyish dreams by crowning them with a reality of bliss. No sooner had the trembling priest departed, for he knew the risk he ran, than disguises were brought, and the fugitives, dressed as two sailor boys, were smuggled on board a small vessel lying below the Tower. Patch accompanied them till they were safe on deck.

"Farewell!" he whispered; "noble lady, in Antwerp you will meet Sir Richard Everil and his son, also a gentle youth, whom your husband rescued from that den of cruelty, the Lollard's Tower. Be kind to the poor boy for my sake—you will soon, I doubt not, learn to love him for his own."

Our readers may suppose how readily and gratefully the promise was given.

"You will find, on your arrival," continued the speaker, "a letter from the queen. Keep a good heart; for while I live you have at least one friend to watch over and protect you."

"And that one a kind one," exclaimed Walter, warmly pressing his hand. "This heart must be cold indeed ere it forgets thy matchless friendship and thy generous service."

The last adieu was spoken, and the lugger, which had been specially engaged and manned for the purpose, spread her canvas to the wind, and rapidly made sail down the river. As it passed Gravesend, a boat, well armed, put off from the fort, evidently with the intention of boarding it : but the jester had taken his precaution; for no sooner did it approach alongside, than a carronade, which had been brought to a level with the watermark, was discharged at it, and the shot sent clean through its slender planks. Fortunately for the rowers, they were sufficiently near shore to regain it without loss of life. Long ere further preparations for pursuit were made, the craft which bore the fugitives was out of sight; nor did they encounter further accident till they arrived at Antwerp.

On the following day Henry returned to Greenwich, accompanied by Anne Boleyn and her father, to whom the monarch had clearly explained his intention towards the object of his passion, whom, as an earnest of her future greatness, he created Marshioness

of Pembroke, giving her a thousand a year to support her dignity; but while Wolsey still remained in power, the aspiring woman trembled at the realisation of her ambitious dreams, and every wile which her sex so well know how to employ when they would subjugate the master mind of man to their caprice, was tried to keep up Henry's indignation against his favourite, whose pride was exaggerated, whose wealth dwelt upon to excite the monarch's cupidity, and whose services only were overlooked.

"Thou wilt keep thy promise, Henry?" she exclaimed, leaning softly upon his arm and looking up into his eyes with that expression of thoughtful tenderness so difficult to resist in women, even when we know it to be assumed, "Thou wilt not listen to the glozing speech of this priestly traitor—this enemy of our happiness? Wilt thou?"

"Thou shalt see, May-bird," replied the amorous monarch: "thine own eyes shall witness his disgrace. See," he added, leading her to the window, "he comes. Behind the arras, in the presence-chamber, we may observe what passes; Suffolk and Norfolk have their charge."

Leading the fair temptress from the royal closet, where the above brief dialogue had taken place, Henry and Anne Boleyn proceeded to the withdrawing-room, which was separated from the throne-room only by a heavy curtain of Utrecht velvet, the massive folds of which were easily drawn aside.

Wolsey, on his arrival, had been purposely received without those customary marks of respect which on all previous occasions had been shown him by the officers of the household on his visits to his sovereign; but he came prepared to meet the worst, for the faithful Patch had informed him of the mortification prepared for him by his ungrateful master; and he resolved, if he must fall, to fall at least with dignity.

Regardless, to all appearance, of the studied neglect, he slowly advanced up the great staircase, and entered the crowded presence-chamber with as proud a step as in the days of his favour and undisputed power. The courtiers, most of whom had received their cue, remained covered in his presence; several even went so far as to turn their backs upon him; these were chiefly the younger ones, for the old and prudent could not but remember how frequently his downfall had been predicted, and how often his enemies had been disappointed.

As a cardinal, Wolsey was the only subject admitted to sit in the presence of the king—a privilege claimed at that period by all the members of the Sacred College at the courts of European sovereigns

Without deigning to cast a look upon the pack by whom he was surrounded, the stately churchman seated himself for the last time upon the gilded chair reserved for his especial use, and motioning to one of his ushers, directed him to place a species of desk or prie-dieu before him, upon which was a book containing the minutes of the council, which he began to read. While thus occupied, the curtain was drawn slowly aside, and Norfolk and Suffolk approached the spot where the still dreaded minister was seated. Henry and Anne remained behind the hangings, watching the proceedings.

"My lord," said Norfolk, "we are the bearers of unpleasant tidings."

"The messenger is most fit, then," coolly answered Wolsey, gazing upon the embarrassed courtier with a glance of keen contempt. "But to your news, my lord."

"We are commissioned, cardinal," exclaimed the impatient Suffolk, "to demand from you in the king's name the seal of England."

"And your authority?" demanded Wolsey.

"Our master's royal word," replied the nobleman; "is not that sufficient?"

"No!" replied the fallen favourite, haughtily.

"You refuse to resign it, then?"

"To you, and such as you. When Henry gave it to my charge, he bound it by patent to me for life; and such gifts," continued the churchman, with a haughty smile, "are not resumed upon a courtier's word or an intriguer's faith."

"Intriguers!" echoed the two peers.

"Vex me not, lords," exclaimed Wolsey, "with idle words. I know my doom is sealed, that Henry's ears and Henry's heart are closed against his servant; but I have been his friend, and he hath still a nature too princely to insult me. Go to your master and to mine," he added; "tell him that to his pleasure I submit myself in all things; but to himself alone, or to his warrant, will I resign the trust of former confidence, the gift of other years. Not on the faith of creatures who have cringed like reptiles in my path, sworn that their fortunes flourished in my smile, and offered flattery's incense as to a god before me. Minions of fortune, sycophants, or knaves, I know and scorn ye."

"Arrest the traitor!" whispered Anne Boleyn to her royal lover.

"He hath reason, sweetheart," gravely resumed the king, taking up a pen and signing his name at the bottom of a blank sheet of paper; "it is not thus the seal should be demanded."

CHAPTER XIV.

With thee every passion is still,
Each tempest of feeling is o'er,
Hearts falsehood hath broken are still,
The eye weeps with anguish no more,
What is fortune? what honour? what fame's fleeting breath,
Compared to thy slumbers, oh! beautiful death?—*Old Ballad.*

N presenting the warrant, attested by the sign manual of the king, Wolsey immediately resigned the great seal; and about an hour afterwards, amid the sneers of the courtiers and the triumphant jeers of his enemies, left Greenwich for his mansion of York House, the scene of his past splendour, pride, and munificence. It was the last time he was ever permitted to visit it, the dukes of Suffolk and Norfolk having intimated to him that within four-and-twenty hours he was to retire to Esher, a palace which belonged to him as bishop of Win-chester, which see had been added to his other preferments in 1521, by his then indulgent master. Henry and Anne Boleyn stood at the oriel window of the great chamber, to watch the departure of the fallen favourite. The countenance of the monarch was marked by an unusual expression of gravity; indeed, a close observer might have noted something like regret or peevishness. That of the beautiful being by his side, upon the contrary, was radiant with smiles and joy. She had humbled her enemy: the only influence which stood between her and the gratification of her ambitious hopes was at last overthrown; and as the disgraced minister, leaning upon the arm of his chap-

lain, followed his attendants to the sumptuous barge which lay moored upon the banks of the river, she felt herself in all but name a queen. The pertinacity with which she had pursued the downfall of the cardinal was not amongst the least acts of imprudence which Anne Boleyn committed; for although the man yielded to her influence, the monarch was insensibly offended, since he knew the secret cause of her resentment. Wolsey, at his private command, had broken the contract of marriage which existed between her and Lord Percy, which contract was afterwards made the ground of the divorce which the convenient Cranmer pronounced between her and the king, when satiety had palled the cruel husband's love, and the scaffold and the axe were waiting to receive her.

"You are sad, Henry," she exclaimed, as she caught the moody expression of her companion's countenance. "Alas! I see that Wolsey's influence lies nearer to your heart than Anne's love."

"Not so," replied the king, turning from the window, and gazing upon her animated features; "but men uproot not readily the tree they planted, e'en though its growth be somewhat rank; were it not wiser, sweetheart, to lop the branches, trim the foliage deftly, but let the trunk remain?"

These words, which showed, even at the decisive moment, the regret with which Henry parted from his former favourite, alarmed his capricious mistress, who felt that if Wolsey were restored to favour, her dream of grandeur would be short—she feared his cold observant eye upon her.

"No," she exclaimed, passionately, "his downfall is necessary to my peace of mind; for who would see their bitterest foe lodged in the heart they love? He hath a tongue might wile a song-bird from the forest bough —deceive even thy princely wisdom by its speciousness. How, then, could Anne, with nothing but her simple love to guide her, contend with him in cunning? Besides," she added, throwing her graceful arm round the shoulder of the amorous king, "thy promise, Henry?—thy knightly promise!"

"Shall be kept," he replied, yielding to the fascination of her beauty and the influence of the moment; for few men can resist a caress, or the influence of the eyes of those they love.

"And thou wilt not retract it?" she continued.

"No, by this kiss! Nay, thou shalt not deny me," said the monarch, as Anne Boleyn coyly turned her head aside; for, to do her justice, however light and suspicious her conduct in other respects towards her royal suitor, it was up to the period of her marriage marked by extreme prudence—a circumstance which doubtless tended to increase his passion. "Be it," he added, "the seal of Wolsey's downfall and of Henry's faith."

His mistress resisted no longer, but blushingly received the pledge. It was not the first time that a statesman's downfall or a courtier's favour had been bartered for a kiss. Such is the weakness of earth's rulers—such the frail tenure of a favourite's power!

At this moment a low shout from the lawn before the palace attracted the speaker's attention, who, with his arm encircling the slender waist of his mistress, led her back to their former position by the window. Wolsey was already seated in his gilded barge, which the rowers were pushing into the middle of the river. The cry which attracted the king's attention was from an insolent knot of courtiers, who, in the days of the cardinal's prosperity, had been ready to lick the dust before him. True worshippers of the sun—butterflies of fortune—they had adored him in prosperity, and now, like yelping curs, turned on him in adversity.

As Henry reached the window the cry was repeated. Wolsey was unmoved by it; his long experience of men had taught him most probably what to expect, or how to value them. But Henry felt indignant at the insult, not for his former favourite's sake, perhaps, so much as for his own. Fallen as he was, the man who had been his confidant for years—his friend, his *alter ego*, or other self, as he had familiarly called him —was still too important a personage for a courtier's sneer. Dashing open the casement near him, he called to the captain of the guard, Sir Hugh Neville, a brave old knight who was standing in the court below, reflecting, most probably, upon the moral of the scene.

"Neville, clear the court!" exclaimed his fierce master, in that harsh deep tone which he invariably spoke in when angry or excited. "Is our palace-yard a bear-garden, that every hound should bark in it? Clear the court, and let none pass but such as have the entrance to our privy chamber."

With these words the speaker closed the casement, and in a few seconds the troop of courtiers, like an affrighted herd of deer, had left the forbidden precincts—many of them speculating on the probable return of Wolsey to power, and cursing the precipitation with which they had so incautiously developed the genuine qualities of their time-serving nature —a fear which was not without foundation, when the vacillation which Henry showed throughout the affair of his favourite's downfall is considered—his repeated messages of kindness to him—the ring which he sent him, and the restoration of a part, although a small one, of his wealth.

On Wolsey's arrival at York House he summoned the officers of his household, and proceeded to make inventories of all that his noble palace contained. He caused several tables to be placed in his gallery, and these were covered with pieces of rich velvet, damask, grograine, tufted taffeta, satin, and holland, in such immense quantities that when he afterwards complained of a robbery having been committed, he stated that no less than five hundred pieces had been conveyed away.

He ordered the most sumptuous preparation to be made for the inspection and arrival of the king. The walls of the apartments were hung with cloth of gold and silver, and with rich copes, which had been fabricated at his own expense for his colleges at Oxford and Ipswich. His plate was arranged upon two long broad tables in his counsel and gilt chamber; and being not only costly but in great profusion, it astonished the eyes of all beholders, for until the reign of Henry VIII. pewter was used daily, even at the table of the monarch.

As soon as these various preparations were finished the cardinal retired to his closet, attended only by his faithful Patch. For some time they busied themselves in destroying various papers and correspondence in silence. The churchman was the first to break it.

"The hour my enemies have so long waited for has arrived; my robe and cross," here the speaker touched the pectoral gem upon his breast, the ensign of his episcopal rank, "are all that fate hath left me. The once wealthy Wolsey is a beggar now."

"Not so," replied the jester, carefully dropping the velvet arras over the door, to prevent the possibility of eavesdropping. "Thou art rich even in that the yellow worshippers of Mammon reverence — in gold, rich enough to glut the thirst of avarice, or create on earth a paradise—if," he added, "thou couldst find one from which ambition was excluded."

"What mean you?" demanded the fallen churchman.

"It means," resumed the speaker, "that for many long years I have traded with a portion of thy wealth, hoarded thy gifts to be lent out on interest, watched for gain as for a crown in heaven, trafficked in men, in promises and favours, sold and bought human passions, feelings like things of vilest merchandise, when great returns were promised."

"And the result?"

"That you are rich; the wealth you leave to the rapacious king exceeds not the jester's store."

"Sayst thou so?" whispered the cardinal, breathless with astonishment at the unexpected good fortune, for he knew the speaker's truthfulness too well to doubt his words. "Why, then, the game of life's not yet played out; my foes have not disarmed me."

"True," said Patch, "in Italy thou mayst pass the remnant of thy days in honourable calm repose, and show that, great as was thy nature in prosperity, that it became still greater in ill-fortune. In our retreat," he added, gaily, "like the earth's oracles of old, we will pronounce the truths which shake or move the world."

At this moment Sir William Gascoigne knocked at the door of the closet to inform his eminence that everything was in readiness for his departure. To this officer, who had long been the treasurer of his household, Wolsey gave in charge his vast wealth for delivery to the king.

"We will speak further of this," whispered the cardinal to Patch, as they left the chamber; "at present eyes are upon us, which watch our every turn—ears pricked to catch our lightest breath. We hold it as a proof that Heaven inclines towards us that we have still a friend so true as thou art."

"Friend!" repeated the jester, fixing his eyes upon the pale countenance of the speaker with an expression which showed how the word had elevated him in his own esteem; "that name repays a harder bondage, a longer servitude than mine."

When the preparations for the journey were completed, the fallen favourite entered his barge at the private stairs of York House, and was rowed over to Putney, where his horses awaited him.

His embarkation was eagerly watched by crowds of citizens and courtiers, both in boats and on land; but when they perceived that he was not, as they had anticipated, conveyed to the Tower, their disappointment was visible. On arriving at Putney, the cardinal took his mule, and his train their horses, to proceed on their way. They had not advanced far from the town before they encountered Sir Henry Norris, who, saluting Wolsey with great respect, bade him be of good cheer, for that he knew by certain knowledge that he should speedily be restored again to his sovereign's favour and his former power. The exile smiled incredulously.

"Thy wish deceives thee," he replied: "men who fall like me seldom rise again."

"Yours hath been a stumble, my good lord," continued the messenger of Henry,

WOLSEY PERFORMS HIGH MASS FOR THE LAST TIME BEFORE THE KING.

for such indeed he was, "and not a fall. Indeed, I can give token I am right."

"I would gladly see one," exclaimed his eminence.

"Would this, my lord, content you?"

Sir Henry Norris ungloved his hand and drew from his finger a small ruby ring, graved with a rose and portcullis, one of the badges of the royal house of Tudor, and which Wolsey had seen a hundred times worn by his capricious master; indeed, it had on more than one occasion served as a token of his will between them.

"Take it, lord cardinal," said the messenger; "the words of prophecy I utter were the giver's; you in your wisdom best can judge whether or no he hath the power to make them truths."

Immediately on receiving the gem followed one of those scenes which show of what brass and clay the strongest minds are framed. The man whose genius had wielded the destinies of a mighty nation, made war or peace at his caprice, been courted by kings, aspired to the proudest throne on earth, wept like a child for joy on receiving the well-known token from the king. Alighting from his mule, and bare-headed, the once haughty Wolsey returned thanks to God at the first sign of returning favour from a man whom in his heart he knew to be treacherous, remorseless, cruel — his only virtue courage, and his least vice deceit.

The jester gazed upon the scene with a mingled expression of pity and contempt.

Taking a chain and reliquary containing fragments of the holy cross from his person, the cardinal presented it to Norris in requital of the yet more precious gift of which he was the messenger.

"And has your grace no token for the king?" demanded the knight, after kissing the churchman's hand, who had condescended to pass the chain round his neck himself.

"Methinks," said Patch, "the goodly plate and furniture of York House were sufficient token, or is Henry's affection so intense that he would have his eminence's skin as well as robe?"

The knight smiled as he replied—

"His grace desires not these, but there is a gift I know would please him well, and do thy master service."

"Name it."

"Thyself," said Sir John; "the king remembers well thy merry humour and thy biting jests, thy quips and bitter fancies. 'Twas but this very day I heard his grace declare he would not grudge a thousand nobles to purchase such a fool. He swears thou art unrivalled."

"Indeed!" exclaimed the jester, his eyes flashing fire at the degrading proposition of transferring him, like a sumpter mule or beast of burden, from one master to another. "His highness wrongs himself, as well as those around him. He must be difficult of choice, where all are to be sold—thought, soul, word, conscience, faith, and honour— e'en at a more vile price, than their vile thews and bones."

"Impossible!" added Wolsey, who saw that in losing Patch he should part with his right hand, his intelligence, his minister. "He is the only solace of my broken fortunes, — all that reminds me I once had friends. I cannot, will not, send him from me."

A look of gratitude, which Wolsey alone understood, thanked him for the generous resolution.

"Farewell, my lord," said Sir John Norris; "I have pointed out the means of pleasuring his grace; 'tis yours to accept or to reject it. Your friends must wish you had decided otherwise."

With these words he put spurs to his horse, and set forward on his return to Greenwich.

For some minutes the cavalcade renewed their journey in silence. The hopes which the favourable message and gift of Henry to their master had at first inspired in the minds of the attendants were considerably damped by the refusal of Wolsey to part with his jester, who continued to ride by the mule of his eminence, but without exchanging a word with him. The fallen favourite was the first to speak.

"This refusal will incense Henry more than the report of enemies, the sneers of courtiers, or e'en Anne Boleyn's malice. I fear me, Patch, that Italy, after all, must be my place of exile—my last dreams vanish here."

"Are they the last?" demanded his companion, fixing upon him an inquiring look, which showed how little faith the speaker put in the extinction of that ambition which had been the ruling passion of his life, or merely the lull which precedes the renewal of the storm.

The fallen man shook his head with a mournful smile, and they continued their progress towards Esher again in silence. Patch was evidently cogitating some important point within himself — the cardinal chewing the cud of vain regret and bitter fancies. Just as they reached a point where the roads separated, the jester drew rein with the air of a man who had decided on a distasteful task.

"After all, my lord," he whispered, "I think I had better humour this strange fancy of the king, and return to Greenwich: it will at least secure one friend at court to arm or to forewarn you."

Wolsey's countenance cleared; for despite the loss which his absence would occasion to himself, as far as his personal feelings were concerned, he could not but perceive the advantage which might accrue by having so devoted a friend continually near the person of the capricious Henry.

"And wilt thou make this sacrifice for thy master?" he demanded.

"No," replied the jester, sternly.

"For thy friend then?" said Wolsey, who perfectly understood his humour.

"For my friend willingly," replied Patch, his features lit with an expression such as men seldom read there; "that word hath bound me to thee faster than gold or interest. The voluntary service outweighs a thousand bought ones. Farewell," he added; "dream on thy dream of greatness: if human wit or courage can avail, it shall become a truth; if not, one faithful heart at least shall share thy fall—one faithful arm avenge thee."

An hour's hard riding enabled the speaker to overtake the messenger of the king, to whom he announced that the cardinal, returning on his first hasty resolution, had transferred his service to the king.

That same night the jester resumed his old quarters in the palace at Greenwich.

On the following morning Patch was warmly welcomed by Henry, who had long wished to attach him to his service. By Anne Boleyn he was viewed with distaste; something whispered her that the confidant of Wolsey was a dangerous person near her future husband, and all the enemies of the cardinal shared the feeling.

"So," she exclaimed, and a slight sneer curled her beautiful lip as she uttered the disobliging words, "fidelity hath taken a lesson from prudence, and changed sides at last!"

"Why not," replied the jester, bowing before her with mock respect, "when love hath done the same? Are fools less easy to be wooed than women? Kings seldom sue for any thing in vain."

The future queen blushed slightly and was silent.

"Thou art a slanderer on the sex," said Henry, "and hast never loved."

"Your grace's pardon," interrupted Patch, "but, like other great men, I have had my weaknesses; and she I loved was faithful too for three whole days, till I betrayed myself and proved I was a fool."

"How so?"

"By believing her," he added sarcastically. "Show me the man could give a greater proof of folly, and I'll change liveries with him—ay, caps and bells to boot."

At this moment the Duke of Norfolk, who had witnessed the discomfiture of his kinswoman, whose union with the king he was anxious to secure, as a stepping-stone to his own aggrandisement, drew near the royal circle, and eyeing the speaker with a look of superb disdain, observed—

"So, knave, thou hast returned to court?"

"Don't be alarmed, my lord," replied Patch, mimicking his look and tone of voice so admirably that Henry and all who heard him were convulsed with laughter at the retort, "*there is room for two of us.*"

"This fellow must be disposed of," muttered the mortified noble to himself, as he turned angrily away.

Anne Boleyn shared the feeling, for the jester's words had stung if not alarmed her.

"Come," exclaimed Henry, whose coarse nature cared little for the feelings of others, provided his own were unscathed; "the fool defends himself with his wit, the noble with his sword—each one to his weapon. The

challenge hath been fairly given, and as fairly answered. As judge of the lists, I throw down my warder and bid the combat cease."

With these words Henry, attended by his courtiers, left the great hall for the terrace, to amuse himself with shooting at the butts which were erected on the sward before it—an amusement of which he was passionately fond, and indulged in with his favourites, whilst the ladies of the court overlooked the sport.

"Thou art a child, Anne," exclaimed the newly created Lady Rochfort to her sister-in-law, Anne Boleyn, who, with an affectation of state, walked apart from the rest of the ladies; "thy countenance is as a book, where every child may read. The jester's random hit hath quite discomfited thee."

"It was no random blow," whispered Anne, "but levelled with design. That fatal letter, in the weakness of returning fondness, I wrote to Wyat, something assures me hath fallen into Wolsey's hands."

"Impossible! it is thy terror speaks, and not thy sober reason."

"Armed with such a weapon, what have I not to fear?" added the future queen, with increased agitation.

"Crush him," said Lady Rochfort, with a fiend-like look—"crush him ere he can use it; set thy heel upon the serpent's head ere it can use its fangs to sting thee. Didst thou know the power," she continued, contemptuously, "women can exercise o'er those who love them, Henry would only hold the sceptre, thine the hand to sway it. Creation's lords are puppets in our hands; we pull the strings and move them at our pleasure; nature hath armed our weakness with a power to mould the masters of the world at will."

"But should my fears be right?" urged Anne; "should Henry see that fatal letter, farewell the thought of marriage."

"Better before than after," replied her shrewd confidant, with a terrible emphasis, which proved how thoroughly she understood the character of the king; "better to temporise with fate than brave it. As for this speechmonger, the jester, this fellow whose weapons are his words, leave him to me; if he possess the secret, I know a way to wring the knowledge from him."

"And the agent?"

"Is a shrewd one," said the unprincipled woman, whose beauty was only equalled by her licentiousness.

"Enough; he is one of those soft fools who set their lives upon a woman's smile—things to be used, but laughed at. Trust to my friendship, and leave all to me."

"To thy ambition rather," murmured her

sister-in-law, as her counsellor quitted the terrace to meet Sir John Norris, who had been wistfully eyeing her for some time from the sward beneath. "How eagerly the love-stricken minion spurns the dull earth as he advances! Look to thy honour, Rochfort," she added, with a frown; "for by my womanhood, yon galliard's face might win a woman's heart more guarded than thy wife's."

The fair speaker was not wrong in her observation, for the features of the knight partook of that Antinous-like beauty in which the animal and intellectual are so exquisitely blended that none but women of strong minds can resist. Such admire it more in the statue than in the life, where its melancholy voluptuous expression alarms ere it can fascinate them. As she continued to gaze, Sir John Norris raised his dark lustrous eyes till they encountered hers; their glances met but for a moment; that moment, however, was decisive of their fate; she trembled, blushed, and turned away. It was well that Lady Rochfort did not see that glance, or it would have filled her soul with suspicions similar to those which crossed the mind of our old acquaintance Patch, who unperceived had approached the spot where Anne Boleyn stood, and watched the whole proceeding: she started as from a serpent in her path when she beheld him.

"How!" she exclaimed, assuming a haughtiness of manner to hide her confusion, at which the jester smiled; "our privacy broken in upon! Have we spies upon our steps?"

"Lady," he replied, and his voice was low and musical, as suited the earnestness of his purpose, "why should we be foes? Smile not; 'tis in my strength, not in my weakness that I speak. The contest is unequal: thou art fair and young, with all youth's glorious dreams fresh in thy soul—with all its ties around thee; I have passed alike the age of hope and promise. If it is sometimes hard to feel that earth hath not one link, there is at least this advantage—that death presents no terror. Why should we continue it?"

"At what price?" demanded Anne, who imagined she saw in the submission of the speaker a proof that neither he nor Wolsey dreamt of the existence of the fatal letter. "At what sacrifice are we to secure the friendship of so great a man as Patch the jester? Think'st thou," she added, with a sneer, "a quip will efface our image from the heart of Henry, or break a purpose kings have failed to shake?"

"No sacrifice," answered the singular being, his eye slightly kindling at the sarcastic manner in which she addressed him. "Since it will bring thee honour, be generous to a fallen foe."

"To Wolsey!" interrupted Anne Boleyn; "never! There is a hate between us which all thy cunning sophistry would fail to cure."

"Be content with his disgrace—his absence from the court," urged the suitor in his still humble manner. "If he hath wronged thee," he continued, "his downfall hath atoned it. Why extort from Henry's lips a pledge for his destruction?"

"He is mine enemy," said the future queen.

"At least a noble on," said the jester, proudly; "for he will leave a trace upon the earth for men to ponder and to wonder at. The memories of such men fade not, like idle dreams."

"His dreams will soon end!" exclaimed the now reassured Anne triumphantly. "This very night Henry hath promised to sign the order for his impeachment and committal to the Tower."

"Were it already signed," said Patch, coolly, "I should not fear; he hath a powerful friend to plead for him; one whose favour with the king is paramount against all other influence."

"Whose?" demanded the astonished listener.

"Yours," whispered the jester; "judge if I overrate it; the king will not resist your sighs and tears; for, if needs must, you shall both lie and kneel, and feign and pray to shake him. It will make Satan laugh," he added in the same under tone, "to see the perjured hypocrite fawn on the man she loathes, to win the safety of one she hates; to undo the mesh her cunning heart devised; bribing her royal dupe with a kiss, false as the one which sealed her faith to Wyat, or transferred it, a short hour after, to the amorous king."

As these fearful words fell upon the ear of Anne Boleyn, all her pride gave way, and she sank humbled in the dust before the man whom she had treated with scorn and contumely. Patch, fortunately, was not of a revengeful nature; although he despised, he pitied her distress and terror.

"I would have spared thy woman's shame," he continued; "but thou hast forced this from me. Hadst thou been true to nature, to thy sex—had one generous impulse, one spark of Eden, lingered in thy soul, I would have spared this last humiliation. Remember the blow aimed by thy malice must be stayed, or it will crush thee with thine enemy."

"I am lost," sighed the overwhelmed

woman, who so lately deemed herself a queen.

"Not lost, but warned. One step further against thy fallen foe, and thy letter to Wyat—the one which paints thy loathing of the king and thy warm love to his more youthful rival, is placed in Henry's hand. Knit thy fair brow," he added, " and act the puppet-queen ; mock at me ; scorn me in public as thou wilt ; but mark my will in this. I am one of those who warn not twice."

Bowing low, in mock humility, before her, that those who from a distance had marked their interview might not suspect the singular tone in which it had been conducted, the jester took his leave, and continued his walk upon the terrace, satisfied that the danger which threatened the man he so faithfully served and loved, at least for the present hour, had been avoided.

When Lady Rochfort returned to her sister-in-law, after her interview with Sir John Norris, she found her pale as marble, seated upon a bench which fortunately happened to be near, and into which she sank as soon as the horrible interview between her and Patch was ended.

"Anne !" exclaimed the alarmed confidant, " in the name of every saint, tell me what has happened."

"Mine enemy hath found me," sobbed her relative, sinking upon her shoulder. " The jester has my letter, and threatened to lay it before the king. I am lost !" she added, passionately. " Why did I ever listen to the whisperings of ambition, or break the only vow my heart e'er sanctioned ?"

"Threatened !" repeated Lady Rochfort ; " if he hath only threatened we may defy him. Rouse thyself," she continued, loosening, at the same time, a golden flacon of perfumes which hung suspended by a chain from her jewelled girdle, and applying the contents to the brow and nostrils of her kinswoman. " Be but as true to thyself as I will prove to thee, and, despite the jester and his proofs, all will yet go well."

The speaker, as our readers doubtless already have perceived, was a woman of resolution. She kept her word. During the month which followed the interview between Anne Boleyn and the jester, the oldest courtiers were mystified by the proceedings of the king towards his former favourite. It is true that Hales, the attorney-general, filed an information against Wolsey for having procured and published bulls from Rome securing the office of legate contrary to a law passed in the reign of Richard II., to which indictment the cardinal pleaded guilty, but professed ignorance of the statute,

and submitted himself to the king's mercy, who not only granted him protection and pardon, but restored to him a portion of his forfeited wealth, amounting to six thousand three hundred and seventy-four pounds—a large sum in those days, and finally restored him to the sees of York and Winchester, from which he had been suspended.

All this was gall and wormwood to the future queen, who found herself compelled to use her interest and blandishments to secure the safety of the man she hated, and whom, whether justly or not, she considered her bitterest enemy. Patch, when he pleased, was an inexorable task-master, and amply avenged her broken faith to Wyat, who at her express instigation had been sent into a kind of honourable exile, under pretence of a mission to the court of France.

This gleam of sunshine was the last doomed to fall upon the fortunes of the illustrious man, whose name, with all his failings, pride, ambition, and despotism, must ever fill a brilliant page in English annals. The tutelary genius and protector of the fallen minister suddenly disappeared from court; vain were all the inquiries which Henry set on foot to trace him—Patch was nowhere to be found, and the enemies of his master once more raised their heads. Anne Boleyn and her infamous sister-in-law exchanged triumphant smiles as blow after blow was rapidly levelled at the object of her hate, whose conduct in his retirement at York, where he occupied himself in the duties of his high office, was beyond all praise. He even refused to join in the diversion of hunting, which he had formerly passionately enjoyed, and devoted himself to works of charity, learning, and piety. But while Wolsey was receiving proofs of respect and popularity from the people, which he had never obtained in the days of his too brilliant greatness, his foes were more than ever impressed with the necessity of destroying a man who could render himself thus powerful even in adversity. Reports were conveyed to Henry's ears of the state and hospitality which his degraded favourite still maintained, and these accounts were exaggerated in order to impress the mind of the jealous king with the danger of suffering so ambitious and unsubdued a character to exercise so great an influence in society.

Unfortunately there were circumstances which seemed to favour these representations. The cardinal had never been installed into his archbishopric, and prepared to celebrate that ceremony soon after Allhallows. The king was informed of this innocent project, with all the additions that envy could suggest ; and the warrant commanding his arrest upon a charge of high treason was directed to the Earl of Northumberland, the former lover of Anne Boleyn, who wished to make her victim feel, by the choice of the noble charged to execute her will, that the hands which levelled and struck the blow were those of the lovers whose contract he had broken. There is always a refinement of cruelty in a woman's vengeance.

Wolsey was at his residence of Cawood Castle when the arrival of the earl was announced to him. He foresaw his fate, and prepared to meet it with dignity. He received his unwelcome guest with courtly hospitality, and conducted him to his own chamber, that he might change his apparel. There it was, according to Cavendish, who, as gentleman usher, alone was present, that the arrest was made. The captor laid his hand upon the cardinal's arm, and in a voice broken by emotion faltered out:

"My lord, I arrest you of high treason!"

The keys of the castle were given up, and consternation spread throughout the household.

On the following morning the commissioner, after arranging everything according to his instructions, dispatched Dr. Augustine, Wolsey's chaplain, bound like a common felon, to London, and prepared to set forward himself with his illustrious prisoner; but, as the cardinal had chosen to celebrate mass for the last time before his household, it was late before the procession set out. At the gates of the castle it was joined by a number of country gentlemen, whom Northumberland had summoned to attend on the occasion, and more than three thousand persons were assembled, who expressed their good-will and commiseration to the unfortunate captive, by crying out:

"God save your grace! evil take them who have taken you!"

These and similar cries followed the train of the earl through the town of Cawood, where Wolsey had endeared himself to the poor and the rich by his hospitality and charity.

As the prisoner progressed towards London, his strength was observed visibly to decline; and, by the time he reached Leicester, he was so exhausted that his attendants were obliged to lift him from his mule at the gate of the great monastery where they halted for the night.

"Father abbot," exclaimed the dying man to the superior, who, at the head of his monks, had advanced to the gates to receive him, "I am come to lay my bones amongst you."

The speaker was too exhausted to utter more, but on being supported to his chamber, retired to his couch, whence he never rose again.

The first care of his eminence was to confess himself to an aged monk, whose reputation for sanctity was deservedly spread over the country round. What passed at that awful interview can never be disclosed till priest and penitent both stand before the judgment seat of the Most High, and the secrets of all hearts are known. Certain it is that the absolving words were at last pronounced by the aged minister, whose power, according to the faith of the Catholic world, unseals the gates of Paradise to man.

It was midnight. Northumberland and Kingston, the keeper of the tower, stood conversing by the watch-fire which burnt cheerfully in the centre of the cloisters, and lit the dim arcades with its red light, when the sleeping guard, who lay scattered in groups around, were startled by a violent knocking at the great gate. The earl, who, since his arrival at the monastery, had retained the keys in his own possession, gave them to his companion to unlock the door, not doubting but that the summons proceeded from a messenger, charged with orders from the king, as he had been continually receiving such during his journey with his important prisoner. No sooner was the gate unbarred than a man, wrapped in a horseman's cloak, dashed through it. He looked like a being resuscitated from the grave; so haggard, pale, and worn, were his features, that those who gazed upon him would have taken him for a corpse, had not the unearthly energy of his eye assured them that it was a living thing which stood before them.

"Am I too late, my lord?" exclaimed the intruder, addressing the earl, to whom he was well known, the former having held, when Lord Henry Percy, an office in the household of the cardinal — "have treason and cruelty accomplished their work? Is the proudest heart, the noblest mind in England, yet extinct?"

"Patch," said the young noble, recognising him, "whence come you?"

"From the grave," continued the jester; "from the living tomb to which my enemies consigned me. But tell me," he added, "does our master, friend, still live?"

"The hand of death is on him."

"Too late — too late," murmured the faithful confidant; "but he must not die and dream that I betrayed him. His great heart must not descend into the tomb ere it hath done me justice. My lord," he added, "by our hours of old companionship—by a poor man's honour and a true man's faith— by your own generous nature, grant me one boon—let me behold my master ere he dies."

There was something so energetic in the jester's tone and face that Northumberland could not resist it; he knew his captive's dissolution was hourly, if not momentarily, expected; and he considered that he should run small risk in granting so poor a boon. Motioning to the speaker to follow him, he led the way to the interior of the monastery to the abbot's chamber, where the once powerful Wolsey lay in the agonies of his last hour.

On a low covered couch was stretched the emaciated form of the once powerful man; his full features so fallen and emaciated that even Patch recognised him with difficulty. The priests, who had just administered the last office of the church, were slowly quitting the cell when the jester entered it. Kneeling on a cushion at the foot of the pallet, he gazed for a few moments in silence upon the melancholy wreck of so much intelligence and ambition.

The dying cardinal was the first to speak. Fixing his hollow eyes upon his former favourite, he faintly smiled, and pronounced the name of "Patch."

The tone and look all spoke unbroken confidence and trust; the kneeling man required no further assurance that Wolsey, even to the last, had rightly judged him.

"We have escaped them," murmured the sufferer; "Rome's purple hath not been sullied in our person; the curs who yelp to lap our blood are disappointed, Patch; but, oh! at what a price!"

Here some internal spasm so fearfully wrung the dying man that he was incapable of uttering more.

"I, too, have suffered," whispered the ester; "prison, torture, all that cruelty could devise; but I am free again—if not to save, at least to avenge thee."

"I deemed thee dead," faltered Wolsey. "but never faithless. Who was thine enemy?"

"Anne Boleyn."

The name seemed to rouse the wrath and latent energies of the expiring man. "Anne Boleyn!" he exclaimed, "the destroyer! Ere long her beauty shall be quenched in blood. The crown she seeks shall crush her. See!" he added, pointing with his emaciated hand to some imaginary scene before him, "the scaffold rears its hideous front. Another and another still succeeds. Blood! Henry will slake his thirst in the hot stream. Does he think our thunders sleep, or that Rome's arm is nerveless? Summon a council of the church—unveil the dread artillery of heaven. Heresy descends like Egypt's plague upon the land—England is lost—the rock of faith split with dissention—the rein escapes me, Martyrs and saints, *ora, ora, pro nobis!*"

With this invocation on his lips, the haughty spirit passed away from earth, and Wolsey lay beyond the reach of human malice or of human sympathy.

No sooner was the last struggle over than Patch approached the side of the couch, and kissed the dead man's hand—a burning tear fell upon it as he did so. Amongst the jewelled rings which glittered on the nerveless fingers was the poisoned one, which had been his own gift. He slowly drew it off, and touched the secret spring.

As he suspected, it was empty.

"Pale corse," he murmured, extending his hand towards the body, "thou shalt be avenged—I swear it by our compact and our sufferings!"

Could Anne Boleyn, Rochfort, and Norris have heard his words, they might have trembled at the jester's oath.

CHAPTER XV.

Ambition first sprang from your blest abodes,
The glorious fault of angels and of gods;
Thence to their images on earth it flows,
And in the breasts of kings and heroes glows,
Most souls, 'tis true, peep forth but once an age,
Dull, sullen prisoners in the body's cage;
Like eastern kings a lazy state they keep,
And undisturbed in their own palace sleep.—POPE.

 HE night after Wolsey's death, all that remained of the once powerful favourite was consigned to its final resting-place, in the chapel of Leicester Abbey, by torch-light, with all the ceremonies due to his ecclesiastical dignities; but previous to this solemnity it was thought proper that the mayor and aldermen of the town should see the body, in order to prevent any false rumour respecting his death. On inspection, it was found that Wolsey had constantly worn a hair shirt

next his skin—a mark of penitence which none of his attendants suspected his having adopted. It is not specified by Cavendish, his gentleman usher, who was faithful to him to the last, that any appearances of poison were observed upon the body; and although several contemporary writers repeat the assertion that the cardinal poisoned himself, the fact of his having done so must always remain an historical doubt.

We trust that during the course of our narrative our readers have felt sufficiently interested in the fate of this great man, whose portrait, like one of those gorgeously illuminated figures in our ancient missals, stands in such rich relief, to render a brief summary of his character acceptable.

The qualities of Wolsey may be better collected from a review of his history than from the observations of his numerous biographers. His faults are, indeed, sufficiently apparent, but they will be found to be more than balanced by those great and useful qualities which he has been allowed by various historians to have possessed, and of which his enemies could not withhold from him the credit. In his office of chancellor, he is admitted by all to have been regular and diligent in the execution of business, and usually equitable in his decrees. Yet, as a legislator, unqualified praise cannot be accorded him; the means by which he forced subsidies from the reluctant commons and nobles for the king were unconstitutional and severe.

As a churchman, if we deny that Wolsey had the true spirit of religion at heart, we must at least admit that he was zealous in his devotion to the interests of the hierarchy under which he served, and that his exertions in its behalf were of an enlightened nature. In the regulation and the suppression of monasteries, and in his efforts to oppose learning in the church to the learning of the reformers, he evinced a just conception of the disease which preyed upon the vitals of pontifical supremacy, and of the means by which the seeds of its corruptions alone could have been eradicated. As a patron of learning and art, Wolsey shines without a speck upon his character. His philosophical attainments were obscured by the subtleties of the Thomists; and although not eminent in literary acquirements, he was aware of their importance to religion, and of the superiority which they gave to a nation in general. His endowment of the colleges, and his patronage of the fine arts in general, are not the only testimonies which he gave of his regard for intellectual attainments. It was by his intervention Erasmus was invited by Henry VIII. to reside in England; and

although the offer of a permanent provision in this country was afterwards declined by that great scholar, who plainly perceived that the king and his favourite were no masters for him, yet he ever accorded the meed o praise to Wolsey in promoting the interests of learning. This commendation is the more valuable, as bestowed upon the cardinal by one who loved him not, however he may have eulogised his public virtues. "The household of Wolsey," says the impartial historian Strype, "was composed of no slight and trivial literature, since they were dear to their master and Erasmus."

With regard to the private character of this great churchman, if we look for that correctness of deportment which distinguishes the prelates of the present day, our expectations will be disappointed. It is well known that he left a son named Winter, who received a liberal education in Paris, and who was amply provided for by his putative father.

Accusations upon the score of moral conduct were not refuted, or even denied, by Wolsey. Hypocrisy was not the vice of his lofty mind; he had too much penetration not to see that in private life it is seldom successful in deluding any but the weak and credulous, while in the exercise of his public functions he will knew that it was far easier to retain power by open, daring measures, than by dastardly pusillanimous intrigues. This line of conduct affords in some degree a clue for the long duration of those high and dazzling honours by which his eminence was distinguished, for he had to deal with a prince who could endure his arrogance and usurpation of power, but who could not forgive deception when practised by another than himself. The real cause of Wolsey's downfall was the hatred of Anne Boleyn and the vacillating policy of Clement VII. on the subject of the divorce.

A hundred torches lit the chapel in which the remains of the once haughty cardinal were being lowered to the grave. Twelve knights held the ropes upon which the coffin, adorned with the mitre, crozier, and hat, was supported; and as it slowly descended, the flashing of the tapers upon their bright steel armour contrasted finely with the sombre vestments of the abbots and monks, grouped around, and chanting a *de profundis* for the dead. Bareheaded at the foot of the grave, stood the Earl of Northumberland, and Sir William Kingston, the Keeper of the Tower, opposite him; both most probably reflecting on the instability of human grandeur and human wisdom. The former, while Lord Henry Percy, had been an officer of the dead man's household, and could judge

THE LOVERS AFTER LADY MARY'S RESCUE FROM THE KING'S BRUTALITY.

better than most of the virtues and weaknesses of his late prisoner, whose conduct in dissolving his hasty contract with Anne Boleyn he had long ceased to resent, nay, even felt grateful for.

But where was Patch all the while,—the inimitable Patch—the melancholy jester— the kind cynic—the man whose gall was in his tongue alone, for the rich milk of human love left it no room within his generous heart? Far from the pomp of death, from the official grief of those around him, the last true friend of fallen greatness knelt in a retired corner of the chapel, anxious to vile his tears from every eye. Vainly the jester tried to pray; his attention at every word was broken by old memories, and passages of former kindness, confidence, and faith, between him and the master who had called him friend, and by that word restored him to his own respect, and which he had repaid by services such as no gold could purchase.

Just as the service was concluded, a violent ringing at the great gate startled the assistants. The earl gravely whispered something to one of his attendants, who left the chapel, and returned with a packet, which he delivered into his master's hand, who, thinking probably that it contained some fresh instructions from Henry, hastily broke the seal and perused its contents.

"Marchmont," he said, to an esquire who stood near him, as soon as he had finished it, "go to the gate, give the bearer of this missive four crowns, and direct him to the town. On your life, neither draw bolt nor bar; and, above all," he added, in a low whisper, "not a word of the jester being here."

The young man bowed, and withdrew upon his errand.

The ceremony was completed, and one by one the knights and attendant priests withdrew from the chapel, leaving only the massive lamp which hung before the altar of Our Lady to give light to the interior. Of the many lately assembled there, Patch and the earl alone remained; the latter advanced to the remote corner where the jester was kneeling, and laying a friendly hand upon his shoulder, commanded him to rise: the mourner obeyed him without a word.

"I have received orders, which I dare not openly disobey, to arrest you."

"From Anne Boleyn," said Patch, quietly; "I guessed as much when I heard of the arrival of a messenger; she plays a bold game, but will lose at last."

"You think so?"

"I am sure so."

"Patch," said the earl, "thou hast a kind heart, and that head of thine, which is stuffed with something more than whims and crotchets, has guided me from many a boyish folly. Twelve hours' grace is all I dare venture for thee; take the best horse in my stable, and my purse if thou hast need of it —put what space you can between us, and for thy safety and my honour, until better times, cross my path no more."

"You shall not tamper, my dear lord, with honour or with safety for my sake; perform your duty," replied the jester.

"What, arrest you?"

"Even so."

"Art mad, or tired of life—that, like an idle thing, you cast it from you?"

"My life, my lord, is as safe as your own. I have a powerful protectress in Anne Boleyn."

"Why, man," exclaimed the earl, "this is the excess of wilfulness; blindness that will not see. I tell thee that it is by the request of her thou namest I am commanded to arrest thee."

"And I reply," answered Patch, in the same earnest tone, "that I possess the means to work my safety; nay, make mine enemy the step to reach it. Therefore, my lord, send me with Marchmont and the messenger."

"One moment," said the friendly noble, "and I have done. Approach, for the words I am about to utter bear death, even in their echo, to the unguarded speaker, and may prove scarcely less fatal to him that listens to them: Henry and Anne are married."

The jester received the intelligence with a gleam of satisfaction. It assured him that vengeance was within his power. He cast a look upon the unclosed grave, and his heart felt strengthened. "Still, my lord, I repeat my words; perform your duty."

"Be it so," replied Northumberland, reluctanly advancing to the door of the chapel, and calling for his esquire Marchmont, to whom he pointed out the person of Patch, and pronounced the simple words "Arrest him. Blame not me, should Fortune have deceived thee."

With these words the speaker quitted the spot, in order to give directions for the departure of the prisoner, who resumed his former attitude of prayer or meditation for the dead.

The exact date of Anne Boleyn's marriage with Henry VIII. is uncertain. Hall, whose accuracy in dates is remarkable, fixes it on the 14th of November, 1532; Stowe, on the feast of St. Paul, 25th of January, 1533. The truth appears that the ceremony was performed with so much privacy that it was only from conjecture that any specific date was subsequently assigned. The most decisive evidence upon the point is given by Cranmer, who in a letter to Hawkins, ambassador at the imperial court, mentions that the ceremony was performed somewhere about St. Paul's day. The divine selected to perform the marriage was Roland Lee, who was soon after promoted to the bishopric of Chester as a reward for his complaisance. At an early hour, according to an old manuscript account of the divorce presented to Queen Mary, Lee was commanded to repair to a garret at the western extremity of Whitehall Palace, and in that apartment the bond which afterwards proved so fatal to two of the parties present, namely, Anne and Sir Henry Norris, was secured; the latter, with Ann Savage, afterwards Lady Berkeley, were the only witnesses of the ill-fated union, which was not publicly announced till the ensuing Easter.

The unacknowledged queen was seated in a luxurious apartment in Hampton Court. The tables were piled with silver and gilt plate, many of the pieces from the exquisite chisel of the unrivalled Florentine, Benvenuto Cellini. One of them, known as the dragon cup, had been the gift of Francis I. to

Wolsey, on the meeting of the two sovereigns at Andres, in the field of the cloth of gold. On the downfall of the favourite, it had fallen with the rest of his confiscated wealth into Henry's hands, who had presented it to his new wife as a portion of his marriage gift. Anne was seated in a species of chair of state, for although not openly acknowledged as queen, it was generally whispered at court that the marriage had really taken place, and the rumour was confirmed not only by the respect and tenderness with which the king treated her, but by the state which in private she hesitated not to assume. Lady Rochfort and Lady Rivers were standing behind her chair, half familiarly and half respectfully, conversing with her, while a sober, acute-looking man displayed a portrait, which he had just completed, for her approbation. The painter was the Fleming Holbein; the portrait was her own.

"It is like, very like," exclaimed the thoughtless woman; "and yet methinks, Master Holbein, you might have done more justice to our poor merits. Painting should be something more than a dry copy of nature, a dry detail of beauties and defects: it should cast its broad lights upon perfections only, and veil defect beneath its friendly shades. Was it necessary to be so very truthful?"

Anne alluded to the slight deformity in one of her hands, which the truthful artist had given in the portrait. Some chroniclers describe this to have been an additional thumb, others represent it as being a bony excrescence merely, which protruded from the second joint.

The Fleming bowed, and observed, as he removed the picture from the easel, that the error should be remedied; gallantly adding, that the defect, like the spots upon the sun, was the only thing which enabled men to contemplate the splendour of her beauty.

"He has mistaken his vocation," whispered Lady Rochfort, as the artist withdrew; "he should have been a courtier, not a painter."

The portrait was the celebrated one, known, doubtless, by the engraving, to most of our readers, in which the second wife of Henry is represented with her hands somewhat demurely folded over her jewelled stomacher.

At this moment Sir Henry Norris entered the apartment. Anne blushed at the look of open admiration with which he regarded her, and which caused her sister-in-law and Lady Rivers to exchange significant glances.

"Speak!" she exclaimed starting from her seat; "are our orders obeyed—is the traitor found?"

"He is, most gracious madam," replied the knight, with an affectation of respect.

"And a prisoner?"

"Safe in the strong chamber of Wolsey's tower," he replied.

A smile of triumph lit the countenance of the questioner, to whom the imprisonment or death of Patch was an object of the utmost moment, as touching her future safety. The expression gradually changed to one which destroyed its beauty, for it denoted cruelty.

With an impatient wave of the hand she motioned Lady Rivers from the apartment, and remained alone with the confidants of her danger and her weakness. For several minutes she paced up and down, her resolution struggling with her better nature; then suddenly stopped, and with her tiny foot beat impatiently the inlaid floor.

"This is folly, Anne," whispered her sister-in-law; "what you decide must be decided quickly."

"Better a thousand lives be sacrificed," added Sir Henry Norris, "than one unquiet thought should e'er disturb the serenity of your repose."

"I know," answered Anne Boleyn, hurriedly, "I know that he must die, for not till he is in the grave can I believe myself a queen; my own safety and the fortunes of all who love me depend upon his silence."

"Be resolute," said Lady Rochfort; "you will sleep securely when you know that your enemy sleeps his last sleep on earth. Had the fool resigned the letter he might have lived in dull obscurity; his obstinacy falls on his own head."

"Were every means employed," demanded Anne, whose naturally timid nature shrank at the thought of bloodshed, "to wring it from him?"

"Ay," said the knight, "and some sharp ones, too; if senseless stones had memory or tongue, Hever Castle could tell a tale of groans and sufferings might blanch the cheek to hear. But he was firm; threats passed him like the wind; his resolution, like his chains, was iron; how he found strength to escape after he had bribed his gaolers baffles my wisdom."

"Is there no other way?" exclaimed the hesitating queen.

"Perhaps," said Sir Henry, "for he hath demanded to see you; indeed, I am partly bound that you shall grant him audience, for Marmont, who delivered him into my hands, refused to do so till I had pledged my knightly word he should have speech with you. Such, he said, were Northumberland's commands."

"Northumberland!" repeated Anne, still

further unnerved by the mention of her former lover; "this must be met at once. I'll visit him."

The speaker and Lady Rochfort quickly disguised themselves in long mantles and masks, which so completely concealed their persons and figures, that but for the presence of the knight, whose intrigues with the latter were generally whispered, they might have passed in that age of gallantry and romance unknown and unsuspected. As it was, the respect with which all made way for the party in their progress to Wolsey's gate-house, the place where the prisoner was confined, proved that they were recognised.

On mounting the narrow staircase which led to the strong chamber over the archway, the queen and her attendants found the outward room guarded by six ruffian-looking fellows, who had, from their reckless appearance, evidently long been at odds with fortune. Not wishing to be seen by these men, she whispered to Norris and his companion to remain whilst she tried her eloquence upon the prisoner, whom she vainly thought to bend or influence to confess where he had hid the fatal letter, the possession of which was so necessary to her peace.

On entering the room which served as his temporary prison, she found him calmly seated at the grated window, watching the various constellations, which, like gems upon night's mantle, sparkled in the heavens. So absorbed was the jester in his occupation, that either he heard not the fairy footfall in the chamber, or did not choose to notice it. Patch's conduct was a puzzle sometimes to himself.

"So, jester, we meet again," she exclaimed, removing her mask, and fixing her piercing eyes upon him. "Thou hast forgotten me?"

The captive rose, and stripping up the sleeve of his doublet, slowly bared his arm, displaying the shrivelled muscles and half-healed scars, which proved how fearfully the torturers had accomplished their task. His visitor shuddered as she gazed upon the mute accusation of her cruelty and vengeance.

"Forget you, lady?" he replied, in a calm passionless voice, "The miser forgets not his debtor; and though I bide my time, the hour for payment is but deferred—not past."

"Payment?" faltered Anne, attempting to hide beneath a smile the secret terror which his words had occasioned. "A look, a sign from me, and every debt is cancelled. There are those without will strike a balance 'twixt us."

"Doubtless," said the jester—"those who deal in perjury seldom hesitate at murder."

"Be advised," continued the fair speaker,

regardless of the interruption, "and resign this proof of my girlhood's folly. Do this, and not only will I forget the past, but recompense, by future bounties, the ills thou hast suffered from thy misplaced firmness—load thee with wealth and honours. For know," she added, "we have reached a height which sets all foes at nought."

"True," said Patch, eyeing her sarcastically—"thou art married."

Anne Boleyn bowed her head in token of assent.

"And that same act," continued the speaker, "which gave a sceptre to thy hand placed an axe in mine."

"An axe!" iterated the new made queen, gazing upon him in surprise, not unmixed with terror.

"Thou hast a dainty foot to tread the blood-stained scaffold's creaking planks—a slender neck to meet the headsman's office. For know," he added, "that ere to-morrow's sun reaches the mid arch of Heaven, a sure hand will place thy letter before thy jealous husband's eyes. Henry will read thy vows of love to the deceived and exiled Wyat—the written proofs of thy distaste of him, scorn of his person, loathing of his passion."

"Mercy!" exclaimed the terrified queen, clasping her hands in agony; "Henry will divorce me."

"Divorce!" repeated Patch, with a laugh which might have thrilled a stouter heart than Anne's; "no, lady—no; Henry will not divorce you. With Katherine of Arragon—the daughter of a king, the niece of an emperor, the unspotted mother of his child—such tedious process might be necessary; but with the woman who has sold herself for the mockery of a crown—the woman who has deceived him—wounded his pride, self-vanity, and love—his subject born—there is a shorter way,—the axe—the axe!"

Although outwardly unexcited, the last words escaped from between the speaker's clenched teeth with the vehemence of a serpent's hiss. His late triumphant foe was completely crushed.

At this moment Sir Henry Norris and Lady Rochfort, who had overheard every word of the conversation, entered the chamber to the terrified queen's relief.

"Fear him not, Anne!" exclaimed the latter, whose courage was of the same masculine character as her mind; "fear him not! 'tis but a tale invented by the braggart to purchase his vile safety."

Patch listened to her bold assertion with his usual quiet smile, and calmly advancing to one of the corners of the room, touched a spring concealed within the richly carved mouldings of the wainscot, which opening discovered a secret staircase artfully formed in one of the angular turrets of the gateway, which communicated with a passage leading far beyond the palace; it had been originally contrived by Wolsey when he built Hampton Court, for what purpose it is not now necessary to inquire. Like all his master's secrets, the jester was well acquainted with it.

"You see," he said, "how much I value life, when, for three hours past, escape has been within my reach,—nay, wooing me to tread the path of safety. Judge now how much I fear you."

He withdrew his hands as he spoke; the panel fell into it proper place. Incredulity itself could no longer resist so convincing a proof of his sincerity. Anne and her companions gazed upon each other in hopeless dark despair. To contend with such a being seemed like a struggle against destiny itself; even the haughty spirit of Lady Rochfort quailed before him.

"Be merciful!" exclaimed the agitated queen, clasping her hands, and fixing a terrified, imploring glance upon him.

"Merciful!" iterated the jester with a laugh; "the woman whose mind even now was bent on murder can prate of mercy! No," he added, sternly, "not for my own wrongs and sufferings, but for your victim's fate, whose heart you broke, whose great soul crushed, o'er whose untimely grave I breathed an oath of vengeance. I leave thee to thy fate — to Henry's mercy — to thy deceived husband's justice."

"For the sake of my unborn child!" gasped the suppliant.

The jester started. At first he deemed it but a stratagem to awaken his pity and forbearance, but a searching glance at the form of the speaker, on whose person the tokens of maternity had already developed themselves, convinced him of the truthfulness of her assertion.

"For thy child's sake be it so," he answered; "that is a plea might stay the avenging angel's sword For one year from this day thou art safe—count every minute of thy greatness—sate thy soul with the false glare of pomp; but when the year is passed," he added, "expect me here again!"

"An it prove a boy," whispered Lady Rochfort to her sister-in-law, "thou mayst defy him. The passion of Henry's life has been to have a son. Remorseless as he has proved himself, he will never sacrifice the mother of his heir."

A slight pressure of the hand was the only answer the reassured queen had strength to give.

"And now," resumed the jester, "I must away, if I am to keep the promise pity for thy child extorted from me. I already fear," he added, once more regarding the heavens, "that it may prove too late."

"Fly!" exclaimed Anne, rousing herself from the stupor into which the agitation of the interview had thrown her; "away at once! Trifle not with my life as well as thine!"

The jester once more opened the secret panel, and pointing to one of the torches fixed in an iron sconce against the wall, bade the queen remove it.

"For what?" demanded Sir Henry Norris, with a look of astonishment.

"To light me through the passages," answered the singular being, with a laugh which echoed through the chamber; "ha! ha! the Queen of England performs a menial's office for the jester!"

"Never," exclaimed the indignant Lady Rochfort, "never shall her majesty stoop to such humiliation."

"She has stooped to vice," coolly answered Patch, once more seating himself upon the oaken settle by the window; "can she descend much lower? But be it at her pleasure; *I am in no hurry to depart.*"

"It is useless," muttered the terrified Anne, conquering with a violent effort her pride and shame, "to struggle with my fate; I am ready to attend him."

Grasping the torch in her delicate hand, she advanced towards the opening, ready to descend as soon as he should give the signal. The jester gazed upon her agitated features and heaving heart for a few moments in silence. Despite his sufferings, and scorn of her duplicity, the better feelings of his nature prevailed, and he resolved to spare her this last humiliation.

"Lady," he said, removing at the same time the torch from her trembling hand, "the lesson is complete. I will not tax thy feeble strength. Thou now must feel there is a dignity which crowns cannot bestow, or tyranny destroy — the dignity of virtue. Farewell! Use the time wisely: the year will soon be past; when, true as the gnomon to the hour, we meet again."

With these last fearful words, which showed that his purpose was unchanged, the speaker disappeared, closing the secret entrance after him, and leaving the inmates of the chamber in consternation too deep to be described, too terrible for words. The knight was the first to break the painful silence.

"This is no man," he exclaimed; "a thing of heart, of thews and sinews, of warm flesh and blood; but a cold, sneering devil. We have been tricked," he added, "by a braggart's boast. Curses on the weakness which has spared him! Would I had riven his body with my sword!"

The only reply of Anne Boleyn was to point to the secret entrance, the proof that the jester needed not their aid to have secured his safety by flight, had he felt so disposed.

Norris was silent.

"A year," said Lady Rochfort, who was the first to recover her self-possession, "is still before us. Wisely employed, it shall bring us safety. Courage, Anne, courage," she continued; "could we but find into whose hands the letter hath been trusted, all would still be well."

"Right," added Norris, starting from his reverie: "the jester will doubtless direct his steps to find his confidant. He must be watched."

"By whom?" demanded the queen.

"By me," replied the knight, casting upon her a look which the worthless sister-in-law of Anne Boleyn observed with secret displeasure; "to whom else would I trust the happiness of proving useful to my queen? This fatal letter once in your grace's hand, leave me to deal with these same boasters."

"Accomplish that, and count upon my lasting gratitude."

At this moment the sound of trumpets in the great court announced the return of Henry, who had not been expected from London, where he had been to hold a council with the new primate, Cranmer, till the morrow, but whose unabated passion for his wife had induced him to return even at that late hour.

"Hasten to your apartment," whispered Norris; "and deign to excuse my absence for awhile. I ask it the more boldly as the heavy hours will be employed in your best service, madam."

With a few hasty words of adieu, Anne once more resumed her mask, and passing through the guard-chamber, contrived to reach her lodgings in the palace a few minutes before Henry entered them.

The morning after the interview between the queen and the jester in Wolsey's gateway proved to be a bitter cold one; the sleet, driven by a piercing wind, fell thickly and pitilessly upon the few straggling beings whom business or necessity compelled to tread the streets of London. The hour was still early when a foot-passenger, wrapped in a horseman's warm cloak, was seen to direct his steps towards the monastery of White-friars, the residence of the celebrated Fisher, Bishop of Rochester, whom Katherine of Ar-ragon had selected as one of her advocates in the question of her divorce. The traveller,

who was no other than our old friend Patch, glanced keenly round the street to ascertain if he was observed, and seeing no one but a porter, who, with a ballot of goods upon his head, doubtless intended for some merchant in the city, had followed his footsteps from Charing Cross, he rapidly plunged down one of those narrow lanes in which the principal entrance to the abbatial mansion stood. Before ringing at the gate he cast a second glance around, and saw no one but the same eternal porter, who had placed his burthen at the corner of the street and was resting himself upon it.

He rang and was admitted.

The porter no sooner saw where he entered than he quietly resumed his burden, and continued to carry it for a short distance down Fleet Street, till he was overtaken by a city 'prentice, to whom he resigned it, and, placing a silver crown in his hand, walked hastily away.

"I am in luck," muttered the 'prentice; "it is not every day I meet with a fool to carry my load and pay me for allowing him to do my work. Some madman, doubtless, with more money than wit."

The speaker was in error; Sir Henry Norris, on the contrary, had a great deal more wit than money.

That same night a party of pilgrims, who had remained to perform penance in the church, broke into Fisher's lodgings, and ransacked his private cabinet. They were no common robbers, for gold and many jewelled relics were left untouched, and but a single paper removed. Once possessed of that, they retreated in various directions before the community could assemble to interrupt them. That paper was the letter of Anne Boleyn to her lover Wyat—the robber, Norris, who trusted to make it the interest of his amorous designs. It was some time before the jester was made acquainted with his loss, as immediately after his interview with Fisher he had set sail for Antwerp.

Cranmer, whose convenient policy made him a favourite with the king, by the authority of the latter held a court at Dunstable, which place was chosen from its vicinity to Ampt-hill, the residence of Katherine, who refused, however, to acknowledge its jurisdiction, and never condescended to take the slightest notice of the citation addressed to her. The divorce was notwithstanding duly pronounced, and Anne Boleyn openly acknowledged as queen.

This complaisance on the part of Cranmer was the price which he paid for the primacy, which, on the death of Warham, Henry had conferred on him.

The coronation of Anne was now determined on, and by the splendour of its arrangements the king no doubt intended at once to evince his contempt of Clement and the vacillating line of conduct which that unworthy pontiff had pursued.

Early in May the king caused proclamation to be made, commanding all those persons who possessed the right of hereditary service to put in their claim before the Duke of Suffolk, High Steward of England, for the occasion. The Duke of Norfolk claimed to bear the staff of gold, and to exercise the office of Earl Marshal. This title had been conferred on his father and his heirs by Henry VIII. It had been previously held by the house of Howard, although first conferred by Richard II. on Mowbrow, Earl of Nottingham, whose female descendant conveyed the right into the Norfolk family.

A few days previous to the ceremony the queen was brought in great state from Greenwich to the Tower by water, the mayor and aldermen of London having the charge of conveying her thither in their barges. The boat in which the queen was seated was preceded by a wafter full of ordnance, in which was a dragoon casting different coloured fires about him. Then followed the barges of the different companies, with their coverings of cloth of gold, and in some instances hung with innumerable little bells, which danced in the wind. On one side of the mayor's barge was another wafter, on which was a mount, on the summit whereof stood a white falcon crowned, upon a pedestal of gold, encircled with white and red roses. Round the mount were virgins singing and playing. This was the device of Anne, who appeared in her own barge, attended by her father, by the Marquis of Dorset, the Earl of Arundel, and many nobles and bishops, each one in his barge.

On landing at the Tower, Henry received her with a loving kiss. Little did the thoughtless queen, in the intoxicating triumph of the hour, suspect how different would be her next reception there.

The next morning the queen was carried through the city in a litter open at the top, in order that the people might behold the object of their sovereign's affections. The carriage was drawn with two white palfreys covered with cloth of gold, whilst over the head of Anne was borne a canopy adorned by silver bells, supported alternately by sixteen knights. The beautiful queen was attired in a circote of white tissue, furred with ermine; her hair hung down in tresses, and her head was bound with a circlet set with precious stones. The litter was followed by the queen's chamberlain, master of the horse, and most of the nobility and clergy.

On Whit-Sunday Anne went in still greater state from Westminster Hall, where the procession assembled, to the high altar of the Abbey; the monks and clergy in rich copes, and most of the nobility of the kingdom in their coronets and robes, preceded her.

Then followed the Marquis of Dorset, bearing the sceptre; the Earl of Arundel, the rod of ivory and the dove; and the Earl of Oxford, St. Edward's crown; last appeared the young and lovely queen, attired in a circote of purple velvet, under a canopy which was held over her head by the five barons of the Cinque Ports; the bishops of London and Winchester held the lappets of her robe, and the old Duchess of Norfolk bore up her train.

During the ceremonies of her coronation the youthful queen was attended, according to custom, throughout the day by one of the monks of Westminster, whose duty it was to dictate the responses she should make, and instruct her in the ceremonial as it proceeded. Just as the primate placed the crown upon the brow of the fair creature who knelt before him, and the shouts of all present hailed her with the cry of "Long live the queen! may the queen live for ever!" a single drop of blood fell apparently from the ceiling of the church upon her neck.

"What is that?" demanded Anne of the attendant monk, who trembled as he beheld it.

Before he could reply, Cranmer motioned him to keep silence.

The newly-crowned queen returned to her chair of state, but was no sooner seated than she repeated the question.

"Nothing, your majesty," replied Lady Rochfort, who, as her lady of the bed-chamber, stood near the throne; "a drop of moisture has fallen from the roof of the church upon your highness's neck—nothing more."

With these words the speaker applied the kerchief to remove the stain, and pretended to be satisfied; but whilst the anthem was pealing in her ears, her altered look proclaimed to those who knew her that her mind was ill at ease.

The feast was spread, according to ancient usage, in Westminster Hall. Wyat, who had been permitted to return from exile, served his former mistress at dinner, on the occasion, as sewer. Henry and the ambassadors beheld the banquet from a sort of closet erected on the north side of the hall.

During the removes, before the wafer, cup, and comfits passed round, Anne, attended by her ladies, retired to her private chamber—there, as the old chronicler observes, to disport herself with dainty recreations. Many a musical laugh rang midst the fair group, nor was the voice of the queen silent on the occasion.

When the mirth was at the highest, she turned suddenly to Lady Rochfort, and asked her for her handkerchief. The artful woman, taken off her guard, without a thought presented it. Anne slowly unfolded it, and saw that it was stained with blood.

The next moment all was consternation—the queen had fainted.

CHAPTER XVI.

A city, sir, of palaces and towers,
Where busy trade once held its golden mart,
And the rich east poured gems and perfumes rare
Into the merchant's lap.—*Merchant of Antwerp.*

N reaching Antwerp, the once proud city of palaces and trade, Walter and his youthful bride found Sir Richard Everil and his son anxiously expecting their arrival, of which they had been forewarned by the vigilant care of Patch, whose friendship, like the influence of their tutelary angel, still seemed to watch over and protect them. The hospitable old knight insisted on their taking up their abode with him in a mansion he had purchased close to the cathedral—that wondrous pile, where religion has enshrined itself in art. Here Walter had the happiness of once more embracing his old friend, tutor, and guardian, Father Celestine, whose escape from the Lollards' tower had been attended with such fearful risks. The venerable priest wept as he blest him and his new-made bride. Debarred from the holy pleasures of paternity by his religious vows, his heart yearned over the son of his adoption with all a father's love; and as he listened to the story of Henry's cruelty and the orphan's almost miraculous escape, he gave thanks to Heaven and the generous hand which had befriended them.

The other inmates of their host's house were his son Edward and the youth Louis d'Auverne, whom the jester, as our readers will not fail to remember, had so peculiarly recommended to Sir Richard's care. The first was a religious enthusiast, deeply imbued with those gloomy doctrines which paint the God of love as the inexorable judge—the stern avenger; which reject the innocent flowers scattered by His hand to cheer man's path through life, and find a morbid pleasure in seeking out the thorns. The second, although fast verging into manhood, was in thought and feeling still a child; persecution had made him timid, but failed to chill his confidence in human nature. Mutual suffering had made him and Edward Everil friends; he looked up to him as to a superior being, and his early faith was already gradually being shaken by the stern tenets of his companion.

As in the gradual development of our story these young men are destined to act a conspicuous part, this slight key to their respective characters will not be found useless to our readers.

Absorbed in their mutual happiness, here Walter and the heiress passed the first days of their wedded life; earth was to them a paradise, into which no serpent as yet had crept. The trials and the sorrows of the past served but to increase the deep content of the present—to render more brilliant the prospects of the future. Like children who had launched their tiny bark on the calm surface of a sun-lit lake, they dreamt not that the murmuring breeze might deepen to a storm, or the dancing ripple on the waters be lashed to foaming waves.

About two months after their arrival they were visited by the governor of Antwerp, Don Juan de Castro, a noble of high birth and military reputation, whose services on the field of Pavia had won for him the confidence, nay almost the friendship of his ambitious sovereign, the Emperor Charles V., to whose favour he owed his present post: he had but just returned from Madrid, where he had been summoned but three days previous to the exiles' departure from England.

Like most of his nation, a rigid Catholic, he had never condescended to visit the Lollard Everil or his son, deeming that he amply fulfilled his politic master's instructions in protecting them against the influence of the clergy, who already began to whisper strange tales respecting them. Charles's toleration must be attributed to his position as Emperor of Germany, in

which country his power was limited, and where the reformation had already taken root too deeply to be eradicated. But Walter and his bride, in the eyes of the governor, were very different personages; they were of his own faith, exiles in the cause of Katherine of Arragon, whose honour, with all the chivalrous devotion of a Spaniard, he was ready at the sword's point to maintain; added to which, he had received orders from the monarch's own lips not only to treat them with all courtesy, but as his special guests.

The hidalgo in person was far below the average height; he possessed the head of a sage, placed by some caprice of nature upon the shoulders of a dwarf. The grave melancholy of his handsome countenance contrasted strangely with his almost child-like form, which, although well knit and of faultless symmetry, scarcely reached to the shoulder of the one who had honoured him with her hand. The Lady Inez had long been the reigning beauty of Madrid, and when, at the command of the emperor, she became the wife of his favourite general, there was no lack of epigrams to celebrate the event. These did not entirely cease till the bridegroom had killed three of the most distinguished wits of Spain in single combat, after which men became careful how they spoke of Don Juan de Castro and his beautiful wife, who, if not happy, at least appeared reconciled to her fate.

"Welcome, lady and cavalier," said their visitor, raising his plumed hat gracefully as Mary and Walter entered the apartment; "welcome to Antwerp. Although the voice is that of its unworthy governor, his words are those of a powerful prince—his gracious master Charles the Fifth, who honours in your person the cause of his wronged aunt, Katherine the queen."

There was something so grave and stately in the address that Walter could not forbear a smile, which fortunately the speaker did not see, for with the courtly gallantry of the time his head was bent over the extended hand of the lady, to whom the compliment was addressed, in order to salute it.

"In obedience to my instructions," continued the don, "I have given orders that apartments should be prepared for you at the palace, where the senora anxiously awaits the pleasure of being presented to you."

These and similar obliging offers were gratefully declined, to the surprise and secret dissatisfaction of the governor, whose orthodox notions of propriety were offended at the idea of guests of his Catholic majesty residing under the same roof with a Lollard; an objection which the presence of Father Celestine scarcely served to remove.

After presenting the Lady Mary with a letter from the grateful Katherine, the visitor took a ceremonious leave, but not till he had forced upon them an invitation to a grand *fete*, to be given in five days' time, in honour of the birthday of the emperor,—a courtesy which it would have appeared ungrateful and impolitic to have refused.

The day of the emperor's fete at last arrived, when Walter and his bride, arrayed with a simplicity suited to their present fortunes, set forth to join the gay throng already assembled in the palace of the governor. Mary's dress consisted of a robe of white silk,. seamed with silver, worn under a circote of black velvet, which, fitting tightly to her figure, displayed to advantage her graceful bust; a few pearls were twisted in her luxuriant hair, which, tied with knots of riband, fell in clustering curls over her fair shoulders. The golden chain and reliquary, the princess Mary's parting gift, hung round her lovely neck. Nor was the appearance of the gallant bridegroom less distinguished: his bright orange-coloured hose, of the finest

Flanders cloth, fitted his well-knit limbs, showing the play and movement of his muscles at every turn; his doublet, of pale green damask, fastened closely to his waist by an enamelled belt, from which hung a dagger and rapier, of Milan steel, the jester's parting gift; his barret, shaded by a white plume, which waved jauntily in the air, added to the grace of his simple costume. As they mounted the great staircase, adorned with orange-trees and flowers, and lined by the Spanish guard, a murmur of admiration was distinctly audible; in sooth, a nobler pair had seldom pressed the marble steps. Like the first inhabitants of Eden, they moved

In nature's simple grace, unstudied beauty.

In a rich saloon hung with the precious tapestries of Flanders, under a canopy adorned with the arms of Spain and Germany, stood the governor and his lady to receive the assembled guests. The person of the former we have already described, but to the beauty of the latter it would require the pen of a poet or the skill of a Titian to do full justice. It was of that voluptuous goddess-like style which kindled admiration in some hearts more frequently than love. Her hair, black as the raven's wing, was gathered in a net of silver fillagree, adorned with gems, whose lustre was eclipsed by the brilliant expression of her soul-subduing eyes,—whose glances, when shaded by the passionate dreams of her young heart, rivalled the combustion of the diamond, or the melting tenderness of the dove. Her countenance was as changeable in its expression as the surface of a lake, which reflects alike the gathering tempest and sleeping sunbeam. Her form, as stately as the antelope's, was draperied in a ruby-coloured velvet robe, which displayed to perfection its statue-like proportions: the rich jewels which hung upon her arms and neck veiled rather than added to their dazzling beauty. In brief, she was a mortal whom Juno, even after she had obtained the cestus of Venus, might have envied, or Circe borrowed a still deeper spell form. She had been listening with a stately coldness to the compliments addressed to her by the heavy Flemish nobles and dignified Spaniards who formed a circle round her. When the English exiles were presented to her, both Walter and his bride thought they had never gazed upon a form more faultless, or a brow more fair. As with an animated air she returned their salutation, the listlessness of expression gradually gave place to one of interest and pleasure, and her face became radiant with smiles and pleasure.

"You are welcome—most welcome," she

exclaimed, "to our poor festival; but it is not thus I would have met you, surrounded by a crowd and idle ceremony, in which the heart is chilled and the lips bound by cold observance. Here," she added in a half reproachful tone, "you should have been my guests, not formal visitors."

After this and several similar amiable compliments, Walter and the Lady Mary retired to make way for fresh guests, who were continually arriving. The eyes of the fair speaker followed them with a lingering look, till they were lost amid the throng, which was continually changing place in the vast and gorgeous saloon.

The little governor cast a surprised and puzzled look of inquiry upon his wife, who had expressed bitter disappointment when he had made known to her the wish of his sovereign that the English strangers should be lodged in his own palace and treated as his guests—he did not as yet fully comprehend her.

Many of the visitors who had previously been presented came masked, and the variety of costume, the glittering armour of the commanders, the stately robes of the clergy, the waving plumes of the knights, and gorgeous dresses of the ladies, rendered the scene at once brilliant and amusing. After wandering some time through the room, Walter led his companion to a seat formed in an alcove, shaded by citron trees and rare exotics, where the guests, like moving pictures, passed in review before them.

"How beautiful!" exclaimed Mary, who was delighted with the novelty of the scene; "and yet," she added, "it is sad to think that in a few brief years all who are here assembled—the brave, the young, the fair and happy—will have passed away like summer's flowers, and only leave a memory and a name."

"No more !" exclaimed a deep voice near them.

They started, for they had not perceived the approach of the speaker, a slim figure, in a plain Spanish dress, whose features were closely masked. There was something in the tone of the voice which impressed them with the idea that they had heard it before, but it was slightly altered by the mask.

"A countryman?" said Walter, for the stranger had spoken in English.

The mask bowed, and quietly took a seat beside them.

"Have you lately arrived from England?" demanded the Lady Mary, hesitatingly.

"But six hours since."

"Then," said Walter, "you can, perhaps, inform me of the fate of those in whom we are most interested. Does Henry still pursue his former favourite to destruction, or hath his heart relented?"

"The cardinal of York is now where Henry's friendship or Henry's hate are alike indifferent. Wolsey's sleeps his last sleep in Leicester's holy pile."

"Dead !" exclaimed the exiles, in a voice of deep emotion, for theirs were not the hearts to forget the favours they had received at his once powerful hands.

The tears of the young bride fell fast as she remembered the interest which the cardinal had taken in her fate—his presence at the scene of her brave cousin's death—his sudden appearance on her trial, and subsequent protection.

"Lady," said the stranger, "these tears are Wolsey's noblest epitaph. Wealth may command the marble's stately lie, the herald's blazon, and the poet's verse, giving to infamy the reward of honour; but one simple tear on grateful virtue's cheek is praise which speaks the judgment of the heart. I should prefer it to a hundred tombs."

"Henry," said Walter, "has lost the glory of his reign, learning its patron, England its statesman, and I," added he, in a melancholy tone, "a generous benefactor—a liberal friend."

"And Anne Boleyn?" inquired the heiress; "her ambitious dream——"

"At last is gratified," answered the stranger; "she is queen. But the crown," he continued, bitterly, "will prove a burden to her aching brow, the sceptre tire her hand. Her path lies by the precipice—death lies in ambush 'neath her very steps."

"I envy not her greatness," observed the fair questioner.

"Nor I her husband," drily added their singular companion; "but tell me, are there no other friends, no nearer ties whose fate may interest you?"

"Yes," exclaimed Mary, "there is one who——"

Here the speaker suddenly paused as her eye met Walter's. The name of the jester was in the thought of both, but prudence whispered to name him not.

"Who—what?" demanded the mask.

"Must not be named," said Walter, in a decided tone, for he began to entertain suspicion that his countryman might prove to be a spy.

"Perhaps," observed the stranger, with a bitterness of tone which contrasted harshly with his previous voice, "he you would name may be of lowly birth—one poor in the world's gifts, of mean estate, despised of those who judge by glare and tinsel; so, you are wise — most wise to forget him."

* "He I would name," replied Walter, haughtily, for he was now confirmed in his suspicion, "was Wolsey's friend, who trusted few men lightly; his birth I reck not; but his mind is noble, stored with such generous qualities as dwell in good men's hearts."

"Ah! you mean Cromwell?"

"No."

"Or Cavendish, the usher of his grace?"

"Nor he."

"You cannot mean his worthless jester, Patch?"

"Worthless!" exclaimed the indignant Walter, now thoroughly thrown off his guard by the slander of the man who had proved himself so true a friend. "To some minds virtue is ever worthless; there are men who judge mankind after their own vile standard, and you, sir, seem of these."

The speaker had started from his seat, and with flushed brow stood gazing upon the intruder, who, with provoking calmness, remained quietly by the side of the Lady Mary, who for some time had been regarding him. To her husband's astonishment, she gradually passed one arm round the shoulder of the stranger, and with her disengaged hand removed his mask. In an instant the young man's anger was changed to joy—he beheld his old friend Patch.

"I am a fool," said Walter, as he pressed him warmly by the hand; "I ought to have known the tree from its bitter fruit; but prithee, friend, blaspheme no more 'gainst friendship and thyself."

"Lady," said the jester, with a smile, "you have saved me from a false position. After such commendation, modesty had glued my mask so tightly to my face, I should have risked my skin ere I removed it."

"Had I but known, I would have caught thee," continued his friend, "like a woodcock in thine own springe—have probed that moral ulcer of thy mind, which makes thee doubt of all but vice, mistrusting thyself e'en more than thou mistrustest virtue."

"One thing is certain," replied the cynical being, shaking his head mournfully at the accusation, "that I mistrust not thee. But tell me," he added, willing to change the subject, which was evidently a painful one, "how likest thou this gay mart of commerce and beauty? Look to him, lady; here are flashing eyes and stately forms, lips that persuade feeble hearts to play the truant."

The young bride raised her eyes to the features of her husband, and saw a look so full of tenderness and love, that she smiled at the half-playful, half-mischievous caution of the speaker.

"I fear them not," answered the Lady Mary; "they must have hearts as well as eyes to win him."

"And even then," said Walter, "they would fail. Mine is so full of thee, it hath scant room for any second guest. But how knew you we were here?"

"From Sir Richard Everil," said Patch: "and so the governor and I being old friends, I took a gossip's leave, and came in search for you. Have you seen his wife?"

"I have."

"And what think you of her?" demanded his questioner, who had been an observer of the interview, and watched the expression of the lady's countenance.

"That she is beautiful," replied his friend, in an unembarrassed manner, which showed that for the present he at least was heart-whole, "perhaps too beautiful; more of humanity would please me better—to me there is always something heartless in a faultless face."

The jester smiled, for the opinion was his own.

Anxious to converse without restraint, the three friends returned to the grand saloon to make their excuses and adieus to their hospitable host. The governor bowed gravely as he listened to them; and the fair brow of his wife, before all radiant with smiles, became suddenly clouded.

"So soon!" she exclaimed; "not at least till you have partaken of our worthless banquet."

The courtesy was again gratefully declined; but Walter and his bride were not permitted to depart till they had promised their fair hostess speedily to renew their visit at her villa beyond the Mechlin gate,—"where," she observed, "she could receive her guest without the form which surrounded her in the city, where, as wife of the governor, she was compelled to hold a kind of petty court."

"Farewell," she softly murmured, as Walter, according to Spanish etiquette, bent to kiss her hand. The word was accompanied by a look which, but for his love for the heiress, would have dwelt long upon his memory. Fortunately Patch was the only person who noticed it; but, indeed, few things escaped the jester's vigilance.

"She certainly is very beautiful," said the young man, as they descended the marble stairs.

"And seems as good as she is lovely," added the Lady Mary.

Their companion heard both the observations, but continued silent.

It soon became evident that the Lady Inez had conceived a violent friendship for the gentle English girl, whose quiet nature contrasted so strongly with her own; not but the fair Spaniard could be quiet, too, when it answered her purpose to appear so. To Walter she displayed an easy, polite indifference, leaving the little don to dispose of his time either in hawking, or in hunting the wild boar—a species of game still occasionally found in the woods lying between Antwerp and Malines. To please his wife, whose will on most points was law, the governor had even consented that the Lollards, as he disdainfully termed them, should be sometimes invited to the villa; and Edward Everil and Louis d'Auverne became in time frequent guests there. The latter, since the arrival of Patch, had shaken off, though but in a slight degree, the influence which his companion exercised over him. The heart of the poor boy was naturally affectionate and trusting; the jester's counsel and Walter's example bade him look upon the world as something brighter than a vale of tears. They impressed him with the conviction that there was sunshine too. As time rolled on, the philosophy of Patch, and the affectionate reasonings of the Lady Mary, who already regarded him as a brother, produced a still more beneficial effect, and cleansed his brain of the gloomy dreams which shaded it.

It was at the close of a sultry day that the strangers were assembled at the villa, for in the summer Inez seldom visited the city. The governor, during his noon repast, had received a summons of so important a nature that he left his meal unfinished, and, despite the burning heat, started on horseback for Antwerp,—not, however, without offering his usual punctilious excuses to his visitors. There had been a pause in the amusements, conversation had become languid, when some one proposed that they should sally forth to meet Don Juan de Castro on his return; an idea which seemed to hit the taste of all, for it was instantly adopted, and the party sallied forth, the lady of the mansion leaning on the arm of Walter, and the Lady Mary accompanied by Louis, Edward, and others of the guests.

As they proceeded, the party gradually got dispersed, and Walter and Inex found themselves alone in one of the most retired parts of the wood, into which they had strayed, unintentionally no doubt. It was a night such as love revels in; the air was thick with balm as beauty's voice struggling against passion, and the gentle breeze which fanned the wanderers' cheeks was faint as the checked breath of an approaching kiss. The light was of that mellow tone which golden sunset and the rising moon cast on the twilight east. At such an hour and in such a place the lovely Spaniard was a dangerous companion. Even the constant heart of Walter beat with unusual quickness as he felt her arm tremble within his, and her glorious eyes fixed like twin stars upon him, pouring a flood of light into his very soul.

"How often have I wished at such an hour," sighed the fair syren, "that destiny had cast my lot far from the world's vain grandeurs, and that with one loved object I had lived in peace, listening to no deeper music than the song-bird's note, breathing no richer perfume than the wild flower's breath. Alas! why was not such a fate reserved for me?"

"For you, lady," replied her companion, "you who are born to rule a court, whose queen-like step mocks the dull earth it treads on!—a cottage and a rustic life for you! You jest."

"The heart never jests—and 'twas from the heart I spake."

"This is a thought of sadness, lady," continued the young man, moved by the melancholy tones in which she answered him; "one of those spots upon the sun's bright disc, which aid to bear its lustre, or jealous cloud marring a summer sky. With your lord's return, I shall again behold thy beauty decked in smiles and gladness."

"In smiles," repeated Inez, "possibly; but never more in gladness; that hath been long an exile from my breast. Mine," she added, "is a wayward nature—my smiles are for those I love not; my tears for those I love. Fools who think that gems upon the brow can heal the wound which rankles in the heart, deem that I am happy, and envy me. God!" she continued, pressing her hand on Walter's arm, "they little know the wretchedness they envy."

"Wretchedness!" exclaimed Walter, deeply moved, "impossible! Thou hast station, wealth, thy husband's love, the world's respect. What wouldst thou more?"

"A heart to feel with mine," replied Inez, passionately—"a soul to comprehend me—a temple where I could enshrine myself, and know no world beyond. Canst thou not," she continued, moving her ivory arm from his, and passing it gradually round his neck, "imagine to a nature framed like mine the strength of such a love?"

"Lady," said Walter, faintly, struggling with his resolution, for it was scarcely in human virtue to resist the glance, the intoxicating dream of such a passion, "tempt not humanity beyond its strength. Let us return; our absence will be made the theme of comment."

"Ingrate," softly sighed the temptress, at the same time letting her head sink upon his shoulder, and raising her eyes, no longer brilliant, but subdued by languor, to his, "thousands have sighed to gain the heart which only beats for thee."

How the struggle between virtue and temptation would have ended it is impossible to decide, for at this moment the voice of Patch was heard calling on Walter from a thicket near them. Pressing a burning kiss upon his lips, the guilty woman—guilty in heart, at least—started from his embrace, and fled by a narrow footpath towards the villa.

"Thank Heaven !" sighed Walter, "she is gone, and I can still respect myself and meet my Mary's smile. We must not meet alone again. The cup of Circe is less dangerous than her beauty."

"Hilloa, Walter !" continued the jester, advancing still nearer towards the spot where the speaker stood. "So," said Patch, "thou art found at last. Prithee, man, what has detained thee? a sonnet to the moon? or hath some wood nymph crossed thy path while gazing on the stars?"

"Neither," replied his friend, holding out his hand to him : "but for once a truce to jesting. Never came friend more welcome to his friend than thou to me this hour."

"Truly?" replied the jester, fixing an inquiring glance upon him.

"Truly," repeated Walter; "dost thou doubt me?"

"Then all is well," said Patch, "and now let's in together. Don Juan de Castro has arrived and twice demanded you; it seems his sudden departure for Antwerp had some relation unto us. We must return to-night."

On entering the saloon where the party were once more assembled, Walter found his fair hostess seated by the side of his unsuspecting wife, whose quiet smile of welcome spoke the unbroken confidence of her young trusting heart. All trace of passion or excitement had disappeared from the features of the Lady Inez, which were once more radiant in smiles. The young man shuddered as he remembered the words she had so lately uttered in his hearing, that her smiles were for those she loved not.

And there she sat, like some demon clothed in light, smiling on his wife.

As the two friends entered the room the governor advanced to meet them, and drawing them into one of the recesses formed by the projecting windows, conversed with them for a considerable time, but in so low a tone that even the watchful ear of the lady of the villa failed to catch a word. From his calm manner she judged, however, and truly, that her husband had no suspicion of her inter-

view with Walter in the wood ; and that conviction reassured her.

"I have ordered the escort to remain," said Don Juan de Castro, as he advanced with his guests into the centre of the apartment to take leave of his wife. "They will ride with you through the wood."

"What !" exclaimed Inez ; "do you depart to-night?"

"Intelligence has arrived which compels me," replied Walter; "my lord will be my voucher."

The governor bowed in confirmation of his words.

"I cannot part with all my guests at once," said their hostess; "at least, let my fair friend remain."

Walter felt, he knew not why, a sudden disinclination to be separated, even for an hour, from his young bride, especially under the roof of the governor's lady. Throwing his arm round her waist, he answered, playfully, that she was used to travel, and that a night ride of a few miles was soon achieved. A look from the Lady Mary thanked her husband for deciding for her. Inez beheld that look ; and the pang it caused her jealous heart atoned, if suffering could atone, her folly.

The great bell of the cathedral struck the hour of twelve as the travellers drew rein before the mansion of Sir Richard Everil. Walter and Patch, however, did not enter ; but after seeing their companion safely housed, they made their way, according to the governor's instruction, to the church of the Dominicans, so well known in Antwerp.

"Who can this stranger be, or what his errand?" demanded Walter of his companion, as they walked along.

The jester suggested that it was probably a messenger from the emperor.

Their curiosity was soon gratified, for on reaching the church in question they found a brother waiting for them, who, after ascertaining that they were the right parties, conducted them to the house of the superior, where they were presented to a short, shrewd-looking man, dressed in black velvet, but without any ensign to mark his rank beyond those nameless characteristics which denote the gentleman. He bowed as his visitors approached, but without quitting his chair or removing the plumed hat which partially shaded his countenance. The superior of the Dominicans, with folded hands, stood beside him.

"Welcome, gentlemen," he exclaimed, in a low, musical voice. "Don Juan has doubtless informed you that I am commissioned by the emperor to inquire from your own lips what more is in his power to offer to prove his gratitude for your service in the cause of his unhappy aunt."

"For myself," said Walter, "the friend-ship of the governor, and the generous pro-tection of his majesty, leaves me nothing more to ask."

"And I," said the jester, "have done little to merit either your master's interest or his favour."

"I fear me, then," said the stranger, "my mission will be vain, for Charles has a ser-vice to solicit at your hands of too much danger to be lightly undertaken, or meanly paid when done."

"Does your monarch think," demanded Patch, "that services are only to be bought? that men sell deeds of honour as vile truck-sters barter merchandise, for the ignoble gain? 'Tis a common error, this mistrust of human nature—monarchs should be above it. Name the service," he added, "and if honour sanctions it, or courage can achieve it, tell your imperial master to conclude it done."

The Spaniard fixed his eyes upon the speaker with a searching glance, as if he would read his very thoughts; but the jester met his regard with a look as haughty as his own. The former was the first to break the silence.

"Katherine of Arragon," he said, "crushed by her wrongs and her false husband's tyranny, draws near her end. The injured queen hath not perchance another month to live."

"Her throne hath proved to her a seat of thorns," observed the jester; "earth hath few ties to bind her."

"You forget one," interrupted the stranger; "she is a mother."

"True," said Patch; "I imagined you thought only of the queen."

"Henry," continued the envoy, his pale face flushed with anger as he spoke, "refuses her the last consolation left a dying mother's heart—her child's embrace—unless she ad-mits the dishonour of her blood, and ac-knowledges the divorce which placed Anne Boleyn on the throne."

"And Charles," observed the jester with a sneer, "feels for the honour of his aunt more than the yearnings of her love."

"The friends of the unhappy queen," added the speaker, without heeding the in-terruption, "who reside in England are strictly watched. The Lady Salisbury, under whose ward the Princess Mary lies, hath, after much prayer, consented to conceal her highness's absence for three days to visit her dying mother, receive her blessing, and her last embrace."

"And the service you demand?" said Walter.

"Is to proceed to England, conduct the princess to her mother, guide her in safety back, and then return."

"When must we depart?"

"To-morrow."

"As soon as the bark is ready we set sail; but how," continued our hero, "am I to obtain the confidence of Lady Salisbury, to whom I am a stranger?"

"That," replied the envoy, "is provided for:" here the speaker drew a gemnal ring from his finger, and placed it in Walter's hand; "this token will prove a pledge between you."

"Farewell!" said Walter. "Should I fall in the attempt, I trust to Charles's honour to protect my helpless wife."

"Doubt not his gratitude," replied the stranger, "or my promise."

"What think you of our expedition, Patch?" demanded his companion, as they left the church of the Dominicans. "Why, man, thou art as silent as the graves we tread upon. Dost thou suspect treachery?" he whispered, for the idea struck him that the envoy might be an agent sent by the vindictive Henry to entrap him into his power.

"The world is full of treachery," answered the jester, "and he thrives best who is best prepared to meet it."

"Ha! this is no envoy from the em-peror?"

"No."

"I guessed as much."

"Unless," continued Patch, with a smile, "a man can be an envoy from himself."

"What mean you?"

"That we have spoken face to face with Charles the Fifth. The envoy is the emperor himself."

The following morning a vessel, well armed, under the Spanish flag, sailed from Antwerp—Walter and Patch were both on board.

Immediately after the birth of the Princess Elizabeth, a second attempt was made to overcome the resistance of Katherine of Arragon to the divorce which Cranmer had pronounced; her daughter Mary was inhu-manly taken from her, and every indignity offered which it was thought could subdue her lofty spirit. But the repudiated queen, whose maternal tenderness, far more even than her pride, instigated her to resistance, refused, to her last moments, to accede to a sentence, a compliance with which would have degraded her in the eyes of the country, and injured the prospects of her daughter with regard to the succession, by casting the stain of illegitimacy upon her birth. Katherine was still, therefore, treated as queen by her attendants; nor would she suffer any person to enter her presence who had presumed to address her by an inferior title.

The constitution of the unhappy wife and mother at last gave way. As the hour of her death drew near she entreated to be permitted once more to embrace her child, a request which Henry brutally refused, unless she first subscribed to the divorce, a copy of which was sent her for that purpose.

Upon a couch in one of the large rooms in the old manor of Kimbolton reclined the wasted form of Katherine of Arragon. Her disease was a broken heart. In the midst of her sufferings no word of anger towards the king had ever been permitted to escape her, and the last letter which she addressed to him previous to her death is a model of touching simplicity and tenderness. Lady Willoughby, the attached friend of the queen, hung over her couch. On the first intelligence of her danger, she had flown on the wings of friendship to console her, and her arrival was quickly followed by Eustachio Chapuys, the ambassador of Charles V., whom Henry dispatched to visit her—not from any lingering tenderness towards the woman whose affection he had so cruelly requited, but that his presence might give the lie to any rumours of unfair practices, which were sure to be circulated by the enemies of Anne Boleyn in the event of her death.

Sir John Perrot, who had been the bearer of the condition upon the acceding to which she was to be permitted to behold the Princess Mary, was in the room. Courtier as he was, even his callous nature was moved at the sufferings of the mother and the woman, and he quitted the apartment till she should come to a decision.

"This is agony," sighed the queen, gazing with an irresolute eye upon the paper, her signature to which would secure the last happiness which she was capable on earth of tasting. "None but a heart of iron could make a mother's love for her poor child the means to torture her."

"Henry," said Eustachio, "is well skilled in the art of finding out the means of cruelty."

"Not Henry," interrupted Katherine, "but Anne Boleyn. Oh, may she one day reap the harvest she has sown! May he prove as obdurate to her prayer as she has tutored him to prove to mine! It is not much," she added, bursting into tears, "for a dying mother to solicit at their hands—a last kiss from her child ere her lips become cold and insensible to nature's sweet caress, her ears dull to affection's voice."

"Heaven at last," cried the sorrowing Lady Willoughby, "will requite her."

"I am becoming weak," said the dying woman, knitting her brow with sudden resolution; "feeling's at war with judgment. Strange that the heart should be the last to die. I must not suffer the strong cry of nature to shake my steadfast purpose. Raise me," she added, "raise me for one moment."

Her weeping attendants did as she desired.

"Now, then, call in the messenger."

Sir John Perrot re-entered the apartment.

"Witness all," she continued, tearing, with a strong effort, the paper which she held in her hand, and by that act rendering all compromise between honour and nature impossible, for her very hours were numbered, "that I deny the sentence which has robbed me of a crown, my daughter of her birthright; and that I die as I have lived, the queen, the lawful wife of Henry."

Exhausted by the effort, she sank fainting into the arms of her supporters.

"Decided like the daughter of a King of Spain," exclaimed the ambassador, whose great aim was to prevent a compromise, which would have so deeply wounded the pride and honour of his master.

"Decided like a mother," added Lady Willoughby, whose tears half choked her utterance.

"Here my mission ends," said Sir John Perrot, kneeling at the foot of the couch, and kissing the cold hand of Katherine; "would that, consistently with honour, it could have met a different termination!"

In a few moments the clatter of a horse's hoofs announced that he had left the manor-house.

No sooner had Henry's messenger departed, than Eustachio proceeded to one of the windows, and blew with a silver whistle three distinct notes. The signal caught the attention of the queen, who faintly demanded what new trials awaited her.

Ere the ambassador could answer, a horseman, stained with travel, and wrapped in a huge cloak, entered the apartment: a young girl accompanied him. The horseman was our old friend Walter, the maiden the Princess Mary, whom he had succeeded in conveying from Lady Salisbury's protection to the couch of her dying mother.

"Mary!" exclaimed Katherine, throwing her arms with passionate tenderness around her, and clasping her to her breast with all the energy of maternal love; "the last wish of my broken heart is granted, the last desire of my dim eyes fulfilled! I once more bless my child—feel her soft skin upon my lips—her warm tears on my cheek—gaze

upon her without one blush of shame; for not even for the bliss of thus beholding and of blessing her have I forgot I was a queen, or tampered with her birthright. I bless thee," she continued, "with a dying mother's blessing! The orphan's God become a parent to thee—sustain and strengthen thee with signal mercies! Should He reserve thee for a crown, remember all but thy mother's enemies—leave them to His judgment whose strong arm hath sustained thee! Nearer!" she added, "nearer to my heart. My eyes grow dim. Bury me like a queen. Henry—pray for him, Mary. My heart, my heart is broken!"

With these words the suffering spirit of Katherine of Arragon passed from earth for ever.

No. 47.

CHAPTER XVII.

In a rude hut, fast by a stagnant pool,
Dwells the weird woman; good men shun her door,
Or mutter prayers as with a hasty step
They pass her dwelling by: for she hath skill
To blight the cattle, and dry up the springs
Which make the green earth fruitful.—*The Witch-Finder.*

AMONGST the many waiters upon fortune in the court of Henry VIII. was the Viscount Lisle, the eldest son of that Edmund Dudley whom Henry VII. made, conjointly with Richard Empson, surveyor of his Commission of Forfeitures—perhaps the most iniquitous means ever yet employed by an English monarch to extort wealth from an oppressed and impoverished people. The mode of proceeding was by means of spies and informers, to find out all those persons of good estate who had in any way offended against the penal statutes, and to exact large fines as the price of their pardon from the king. Although the mere tools of Henry in the gratification of the ruling passion of his existence, avarice, on his death the popular indignation against them became so strong that it was felt necessary to sacrifice them. They were accordingly committed to the Tower, and shortly after tried and executed. Thus while the royal robber slept in his gorgeous tomb at Westminster, the instruments of his cupidity paid the penalty of his crimes.

Henry VIII. was so sensible of the iniquity of the sentence, that in 1511 he raised John Dudley, the son of the legally-murdered man, to the dignity of viscount; restoring to him at the same time a portion of his father's confiscated estates. The Dudleys, it must be remembered, were of ancient descent. Edmund, during his imprisonment in the Tower, wrote a singular book, entitled "The Tree of the Commonwealth," with the intention of conciliating the favour of the young king; but it is questioned whether he ever saw it. It was afterwards discovered by Stowe, who transcribed and presented the copy to the Earl of Warwick, the author's descendant; the Earl of Oxford purchased the original.

But for the family of the unfortunate Empson nothing was done; perhaps, as their father was only the son of a sievemaker, Henry felt but little interest in their fate.

The young viscount, destined to act so conspicuous a part in the following reign, was possessed of all the requisites for a successful courtier: he was brave, subtle, pliant, and unscrupulous—patient in counting his chances in the game of life, eager in embracing them. In his boyhood he had been indebted to Katherine of Arragon for protection and advancement; but no sooner did the star of Anne Boleyn appear in the ascendant, than he became one of its enthusiastic and most assiduous worshippers; and the new queen rewarded his devotion by frequently employing him on occasions of confidence and secrecy.

On the evening of the day on which Sir John Perrot had been dispatched to Kimbolton with Henry's cruel decision to the dying Katherine, that she must either admit the validity of the divorce or forego the happiness of embracing her child, a grand masque was held at York House, once the seat of Wolsey, but now the property of the rapacious king.

On the 15th of September, scarcely five months after her coronation, the queen had been delivered of a girl, to the great disappointment of Henry, who passionately desired a son. The discontented father little thought, when lamenting the sex of the new-born infant, that the princess who caused him this vexation would afterwards, in the person of Queen Elizabeth, raise the glory of this country to a greater height than that which it had attained under his own government—would prosecute his own designs with respect to the reformation with far greater zeal and judgment than he had ever done, and would evince in her personal character so much of his own temper and spirit, that no one could doubt her affinity to her royal father. The little princess had been christened soon after her birth, with great ceremony, the old Duchess of Norfolk and the Marchioness of Dorset acting as godmothers, and Cranmer, Archbishop of Canterbury, as godfather. The royal infant was nursed in the palace of the Bishop of Winchester, at Chelsea, and her household arranged as that of the presumptive heir to the crown as soon as she had attained the age of three months.

About this time it began to be whispered amongst the ladies of the bedchamber that Anne Boleyn was again likely to become a mother.

The masque was one of those stately unmeaning pageants in which Henry so much delighted, but which at the present day would be considered as a dull amusement, even by the most slavish of the worshippers of the past. The king, who, from his increasing obesity, seldom joined in the dances, played at shovel-board with his brother-in-law, the Duke of Suffolk, and a knot of favourite courtiers, who vied with each other for the honour of emptying their purses with the royal gamester, and amongst whom Viscount Lisle, or Dudley, as we shall, for the future, call him, was always conspicuous; he had for some time been intriguing for the post of lord-admiral, and neglected no means that might ingratiate himself with his capricious monarch and the queen, however vile and unworthy. Anne had just finished dancing with the Duke of Richmond, Henry's natural son, who had been educated by Wolsey, and who, had he lived, would doubtless have been placed in succession to the crown before either of his daughters by his father, who evinced much love towards him, and deeply mourned his untimely end. The joyous, thoughtless woman was about to resume her chair of state, when her evil genius, Lady Rochfort, approached, and whispered to her that Smeton had returned.

"Admit him," said the queen, carelessly.

"Impossible, your majesty; he has ridden hard, and is in no fitting habit for such a presence."

"Tell him," said Anne, after a few moments' reflection, and in the same under tone, "to make his way to the terrace; from the window of my closet I can speak with him; and you," she added, "rejoin me here."

In a few minutes the speaker, complaining of the heat of the apartment, which was no other than Wolsey's banqueting-hall, made her excuses to the king, and retired. Henry regarded her with a complacent smile, which the mirror-like features of the courtiers instantly reflected.

"Her majesty seems slightly indisposed," observed Brandon.

"Qualms, women's qualms," said Henry. "Anne hath promised me there shall be no disappointment this time. An she makes me father of a boy, we'll have a christening, lords, shall cause pale cheeks in Rome. Strange," he added, musingly, "that hungry knaves, the very serfs of the earth, should have strong sons born daily, hourly, to them; whilst I, who have a kingdom to bequeath, have only puling girls to heir me."

The crowd of courtiers could only express their conviction that the next would be a prince.

"I trust so," muttered Henry moodily; "if not—well—we shall see—we shall see."

The king returned to his game; and the friends of Anne Boleyn, who marked his manner, secretly prayed that her next child might prove a boy: their fortunes depended on it.

"Now, Smeton," exclaimed the impatient Anne to a tall dark-looking personage, who, wrapped in a horseman's cloak, stood conversing with her at the window of her closet, "what intelligence? Are my suspicions true? or was the assertion of Eustachio—that the Princess Dowager of Wales and the Lady Mary yet should meet—an empty boast?"

"Most true, your majesty," replied the messenger. "Last night we watched the house of the Lady Salisbury, and saw her ward, the Lady Mary, leave the manor, attended by two horsemen."

"Art sure?"

"Most certain. Despite her disguise, I knew her person well; fear was in every look. Fast as their panting steeds could carry them they crossed the chase, and took the road to Kimbolton."

A triumphant smile lit the beautiful features of Anne Boleyn, as she listened to the intelligence, which so deeply compromised, not only the Countess of Salisbury, whom she disliked, but the Princess Mary, whom she feared as well as hated. Henry she knew would never forgive so daring a defiance of his will; for, like most despots, he was as relentless as he was cruel.

"And who," she demanded, "were the companions of her flight?—surely not the ambassador of Spain?"

"No, gracious lady," answered Smeton; "one was a stranger to me, but I am sure that it was not Eustachio. The other was as well known to me as to your grace—Wolsey's late jester, Patch."

"Patch!" cried, or rather almost shrieked the conscience-stricken queen; "hath he returned to cross my path once more?"

"Madam!" exclaimed the astonished messenger, wondering at her sudden terror.

"Fear not," whispered Lady Rochfort, drawing near to her trembling sister-in-law; "the serpent's fangs are drawn. Without the letter he is as powerless as the dust thou treadst on."

"Perhaps," said Anne, "perhaps. I know not why, but I fear that man; his image haunts me sometimes in my dreams. I see him," she added, "with his cold sarcastic smile, pointing to the axe. He is my destiny, and I cannot avoid him."

"But you can silence him," replied her companion. "Take courage—I tell you he is powerless. Shall I send for Norris?"

"No — at least not for the present. Smeton," said the queen, advancing once more to the window, "we are again your debtor; fear not but we will find a time to well requite your service; meanwhile, be this the gage of our intention and good favour."

The imprudent queen placed in his hand a ring of price which Henry had lately given her, and motioning that their conference was ended, closed the window.

"Why not entrust Norris with this affair?" demanded Lady Rochfort, who was anxious by every means in her power to advance the interests of her paramour, to whom she was as passionately as criminally attached.

"Because he hath taken an ungenerous advantage of my secret, and refuses the fatal letter to my prayers. Were that destroyed, I should breathe freely, scoff at the frowns of fate, and hold capricious fortune as my slave; but as it is, I am racked by doubts which sometimes freeze the smile upon my lips."

"He holds it as the pledge of payment of his services," answered the confidante, coolly; "sovereigns have fickle memories."

"And knowest thou, Rochfort," inquired Anne, "the kind of payment he expects?"

"Doubtless the promised earldom," replied his infatuated mistress, fixing a keen look of suspicion upon the speaker, whom she had more than once seen regarded by Norris with passionate admiration.

"Perhaps," said the queen, with a laugh, which even at that moment, from the natural levity of her disposition, she could not resist—"perhaps. I thought he had higher views."

"He must forget them, then," exclaimed Lady Rochfort, in a voice so harsh and deep, that the thoughtless Anne was startled. "Death lies crouching in the path you glance at; let him advance one step, and——"

"Tut—tut! Art jealous, sister?" said the queen.

"Not jealous," replied the excited woman; "not jealous, but forewarned."

The complaisant Dudley was finally summoned to the presence of Anne Boleyn, and trusted with the secret of the Princess Mary's visit to Kimbolton, where he was directed instantly to follow her, and on her return to bring both her and her companions to London.

By this stroke of policy the queen trusted to secure the downfall of the three persons whom she most feared—the Princess Mary, the jester, and the aged Countess of Salisbury—who would all three be caught in breaking the commands of the king, without the possibility of denial or excuse.

"Accomplish this with your usual skill," said Anne, "and the post of lord admiral shall be yours; that is," she added, with a smile, "if our weak means may help you to it."

Before the speaker returned to the masque, the expeditious Dudley, attended by a party of men on whom he could rely, was on his road to Kimbolton.

Our readers must remember that the scene and events above narrated took place previous to the death of the high-minded Katherine of Arragon, described in our last chapter.

Although not of an affectionate disposition, for through life she had few attachments, the Princess Mary deeply mourned the loss of her mother. Mutual misfortune had endeared them to each other; and the spirited resistance which the deceased queen to the last moment of her existence opposed to the divorce, and her perseverance in defending the rights of her child, created a strong claim both upon memory and gratitude, and to which in after life her daughter showed that she was not insensible.

When all was over, Mary rose from the side of the couch where she had knelt, and imprinted a last kiss upon the lips of her parent, whose eyes she closed with her own hand. This pious duty done, she retired, leaning on the arm of Lady Willoughby, to the chapel, there to prostrate herself before the altar, to compose her soul by prayer. Although outwardly calm, it was evident to her companion, who had known her from infancy, that she was deeply moved. Not a tear glistened in her small grey eyes, which sparkled with the concentrated expression of sorrow, pride, and hate. A tear would have relieved her; but she was one of those who seldom wept, either for others' miseries or her own. No sooner did she reach the marble steps leading to the altar, than she released the arm of her companion, and, with a firm step, advanced to the uppermost. Placing her hand upon the crucifix, she exclaimed, in a voice so deep, yet low, that it scarcely broke the stillness of the sacred place—

"Mother, I will avenge thee, in a prison, in exile, or on the throne; that one thought shall ever be present to my memory—be graven on my heart. Upon thy persecutors' heads, upon their children, and upon their children's children, will I, if possible, visit thy broken heart, thy tears and wrongs, thy outraged honour, and thy patient suffering. I'll give thee blood for tears, groans for thy sighs, and death for thy disgrace. Thy daughter's heart shall prove as deaf to their prayers of mercy as they have proved to thee. *Agnus Dei qui tollis peccata mundi,*" she added, bowing before the sacred symbol; "may thy smile welcome me to paradise, or thy wrath consume me, as I keep or break my oath!"

There was something fearful in the cold pitiless resolution and determined hate of one so young. Her aged companion shuddered as she listened to it, and almost fancied that the image of the crucified Redeemer—whose words, even on the cross, were of forgiveness—frowned on the impious vow, to sanction which he was invoked. How Mary kept her oath history explains too well.

A few minutes after the above incident, whilst the princess was engaged in reciting a *de profundis* for the dead, the Spanish ambassador, Eustachio, entered the chapel. Approaching the object of his search, he silently stood beside her, holding in his hand a letter sealed with the broad seal of her cousin, the Emperor Charles V.

"For me?" said Mary, as soon as she had finished her devotions.

The diplomatist half bent the knee as he presented it.

The princess broke the seal, and rapidly glanced over its contents; as she did so her pale cheek became flushed, partly with anger and partly with surprise. Fixing her eyes upon the messenger, she exclaimed—

"Have I read rightly? Without consulting our dead mother's pleasure, or our own will, the emperor decides on our escape to Spain?"

Eustachio bowed his head in confirmation of her words.

"What if we refuse?"

"Your highness cannot refuse," replied the ambassador; "my imperial master now holds himself as your guardian, and has decided for you. A vessel waits, and there are those at Kimbolton who have instructions to escort you."

"Unless by her own pleasure," said Lady Willoughby firmly, "the princess shall not be removed. Consider," she added, turning to Mary, whose features had recovered their usual calm expression; "consider the consequences, both to Lady Salisbury and yourself; for her the axe, for you the lost chance of a throne."

"I have considered," said Mary quietly; "here I have few friends and many enemies, in Spain are those who love me. When," she added, turning to Eustachio, "must we depart?"

"With the dawn," replied the triumphant minister, who was fully sensible of the importance of the resolution, apparently so decided; for Mary in the hands of Charles might prove a source of terrible uneasiness to Henry. "Your highness has decided wisely."

"Fatally," interrupted Lady Willoughby, "both to herself and friends."

"Press all things for our departure," continued Mary, without heeding the exclamation of her companion, who, as well as the statesman, was deceived by her cool decided manner. "Time tards till we leave Kimbolton behind us."

"With the dawn," said Eustachio, as he quitted the chapel, "all shall be prepared."

"And with the dawn, traitor," exclaimed the princess, as soon as he was out of hearing, "will I be far away. Willoughby," she added, with a faint smile, "thou, too, deceived!—misfortune teaches dissimulation rarely, then. Thinkest thou I am so heartless as to risk the blood of those who love me—so weak as to be made a tool in the hands of my ambitious cousin—so mad as to throw away the chance of England's crown by consenting to this exile?"

"What means your promise, then?"

"To gain time, no more. Charles is bent upon his scheme; his minister is well attended, and has the means to execute it. So where resistance cannot avail, cunning must work the road to safety. Fetch hither, and quickly," she continued, "my two conductors—they are sworn to restore me in safety to the countess."

"Can you trust them?"

"I can," said the royal maiden, thoughtfully, for even at that early age misfortune had made her a judge of character. "They are Englishmen, and will not betray me."

The youthful speaker was not deceived in the opinion she had formed; for both Patch and Walter, on hearing of the project of Eustachio, not only approved her resolution, but declared their readiness, at the risk of life, to second it. By their advice the horses were quietly led round to the outskirts of the chase or forest which surrounded the old manor of Kimbolton; and while the ambassador, who was completely thrown off his guard by the manner of the princess, was arranging for her departure, Mary, on foot, attended only by Lady Willoughby, made her way to the place of rendezvous, where her guides and protectors awaited her. Here she parted with the friend of her mother, who, to avoid suspicion, returned to the house, and after recommending herself to the protection of Heaven and the saints, plunged into the depths of the forest as the surest way of avoiding alike detection and pursuit. About an hour after her departure, a party of eight or ten horsemen, well armed, drew near the house, which they cautiously reconnoitred at a distance. Their leader, who was no other than Dudley, after a few moments' consideration, placed his men within the shelter of the chase—not that there was much chance of their being observed, for the night was dark and lowering; whilst he himself, muffled in his riding cloak, crept towards the mansion, directly opposite to the principal entrance of which was an aged oak, known even as late as the time of Charles II. by the name of Queen Katherine's tree, so called from that unhappy princess having been in the habit, during her last illness, of frequently reclining under its shade.

"This will answer my purpose," muttered Dudley, as he climbed into its venerable branches; "here I can observe all that passes, and, like a skilful general, direct my operations securely and unseen."

The speaker had not remained more than an hour in his uncomfortable position when, from the sudden glancing of lights from room to room, he guessed that some extraordinary event had taken place. At first he imagined that Katherine had just expired; and, hardened even as his nature had become, his heart smote him when he reflected on her former kindness and his present purpose. Short as proverbially are the reckonings of a courtier's conscience, his were cut still shorter by Eustachio issuing from the house, and calling on his train to horse.

"Good," said the spy to himself; "the Lady Mary is about to depart."

"She cannot have fled far," observed the envoy to his secretary, a Spanish priest, as they passed beneath the tree; "who would have thought her capable of such decision and reflection?"

"Think you," demanded his companion, "she hath returned to the Lady Salisbury?"

"Where else," replied Eustachio, "should she fly?"

"'Twill be a bold stroke," continued the priest, "if it succeeds. Mary, once in Spain, will prove a hostage for her father's submission to the church. Backed by her friends in England, who mourn the destruction of the ancient faith, and by the armies of our sovereign Charles, Henry must yield."

"All which, reverend father," interrupted his superior, "depends upon overtaking this wayward girl."

Here the speakers advanced towards the offices, where their attendants were already mounted for the pursuit, far out of the listener's hearing. In a few minutes the sound of their horses' hoofs along the road announced they had departed.

"So," said Dudley, as he descended from his hiding-place, "a pretty knot of treason I have discovered;—how best to turn it to my own advantage must be an after thought: for the present, to secure the runaway. She hath not taken to the road," he muttered, after a few moments' reflection; "I should have met them else. No. Where then? Ha!—the wood—the wood!"

Hastily making his way towards the place where his men were concealed, he ordered them to dismount, and search for the traces of any travellers who might have lately entered it.

"A useless trouble, my lord," replied a fellow named Black Will, who had served with his master in the Low Countries, and who was supposed to possess his confidence; "I have detected them already. There are three riders, and two of them are men, the third a woman."

"How know you that?" demanded his leader, not wishing to be deceived on so important a point, although generally speaking he had the fullest confidence in his sagacity.

"By the prints," answered the ruffian; "feel them yourself, my lord; two are deep and well cut in the turf, which prove the steeds to have been heavily mounted; the third is faint but half impressed, save at the rise of yonder bank, where, as I guess, the rider stumbled."

"You are right," said Dudley, who, like an Indian following a trail through the prairie, had crept on his hands and knees to feel the imprint of the horses' hoofs upon the grass; "they have passed this way. As you value your lives, whatever may be your danger, harm not a hair of the female rider's head; for her companions, deal with them as you may. A hundred nobles," he added, "if you o'ertake them before dawn, and double the sum if you show me the traitors lying with their faces upwards on the sward."

A low murmur of assent was heard amongst the men; and the speaker, remounting his steed, placed himself once more at their head, and led on the pursuit.

The fugitives had ridden about two hours over the uneven ground without interruption or encountering a human being; occasionally the night-owl, disturbed in its nocturnal rambles, uttered its shrill and melancholy cry as it flitted across their path; and once the howl of the savage wolf caused their terrified horses to prick their ears, start, and tremble at the unwelcome sound, nor could they be induced to proceed but by the application of the whip and spur. The night, which all along had been dark and gloomy, now threatened a storm; the masses of black clouds which here and there floated in the heavens gradually extended, till they formed a sombre veil, enveloping the earth in its gloomy folds, and shutting out the stars, which seemed, like guardian angels, fixed to watch it while it slept. At intervals, the jagged lightning whizzed through the murky air, and was followed by the lazy thunder-peal, rolling heavily after it. Huge drops of rain began to fall—splash, splash—through the autumnal foliage, which was too thin to resist the heavy shower, or afford much shelter to the lonely travellers who were silently pursuing their way beneath it. To increase the discomfort of their journey, the sharp easterly wind whistled mockingly in the branches of the trees which lined their road, and blew directly in their faces, adding its cold, watery blast to the miseries of the night. Still the princess, wrapped in the additional cloak which Walter insisted upon depriving himself of to give her, pursued with unflinching courage her desolate way. Once, and once only, did a murmur escape her lips, when her terrified steed fell back upon its haunches, scared by a flash of light-ning so wild and vivid that it illuminated the deepest recesses of the chase, and showed for a moment the horrors and perils of her path with frightful distinctness, and then left her plunged in a darkness made more palpable by the sudden contrast.

"This is fearful," exclaimed Patch. "Old traveller as I am, I should prefer a quiet nook by the chimney-side on such a night as this. Is there no shelter?" he continued, turning to his companion, who was already drenched to the skin. "The storm seems to increase rather than dimish; one would imagine the forest fiend let loose. It is impossible her highness much longer should endure it."

"Ride on," said Mary, sternly; "there are worse dangers than the tempest—man is more pitiless than heaven. I can proceed."

Again the party set spurs to their flagging horses, and rode till they came to a stream, which the heavy rain, now falling in torrents, had swelled into a cataract. There it was directly in their path, foaming and dancing like a mad fiend or living thing instinct with malice to impede their future progress. For the first time the heart of the royal maiden sunk as she drew rein upon the bank.

This unexpected barrier brought the party to a stand-still, for, ignorant as they were of the depth and current of the water, to permit their precious charge to attempt the fording it would have been folly. Patch with his usual sagacity, at once opposed it.

"I can but venture," said the courageous girl, regarding the dashing waters with an invountary look of terror; "there will be few left in the world to mourn, though many will rejoice, at my untimely fate. I question," she added, bitterly, "if, through all my father's realm, there wanders this night an outcast so lonely and helpless as his wretched child."

Despite her tender years, her recent loss, and sufferings from the pitiless rain and piercing wind, not a tear was seen in Mary's eye: as we before observed, the princess sel-dom wept.

"Lady," said Walter, who was touched at the desolate state of the speaker, once the heiress of a throne, but now a fugitive, help-less, and by all, save his companion and himself, unfriended, "this is, indeed, a sorry trial for your grace; but, perhaps it is but the probation with which Heaven tests your virtues ere it rewards them. Trust to my words, that many a joyous hour in England's regal halls shall well repay you for the present hour."

Their young charge shook her head mourn-fully, but did not trust herself to answer. While they were thus deliberating, the storm continued to descend, if possible, with re-doubled violence; and it became necessary, if they wished to preserve life, to find some shelter, not only for themselves, but for their steeds, which, scared by the lightning, be-came almost mad and ungovernable through terror. Placing the princess for a few mo-ments under the shelter of a tree, whose giant branches stretched half over the road, the two horsemen galloped in contrary direc-tions along the banks of the foaming stream, not without considerable danger to them-selves, for the ground was so slippery that several times they were nearly precipitated, horse and all, into the current.

A peculiar whistle from Patch, resembling the cry of a plover, a signal which his com-panion well understood, announced to Walter that he had been successful in his search.

"Courage," said the jester, "but for a few moments," taking, at the same time, the rein from the cold benumbed hand of the princess—"but a few paces; shelter and fire are at hand."

Overcome with fatigue, and incapable of further exertion, Mary yielded to his guidance. In a low marshy swamp, close to the river which barred their progress, stood a wretched hovel, built of mud and stones, and thatched with weeds; indeed, so slight and fragile were the materials of which it was constructed, that but for a low projecting rock against which it had been reared, the storm would ere this have levelled it with the ground, so frail was the lonely tenement. Stunted elder bushes and other dank shrubs concealed it on either side, so that it was only on a close examination that anything in the shape of a habitation was to be found. To this solitary hut did the three drenched travellers direct their way; Patch, who had made the discovery, taking the lead. No sooner had they reached the hut than he knocked lustily against the rough planks which formed the door, and through the interstices of which the light from either a fire or lamp was streaming. This it was which first attracted the jester's notice to the spot. On their repeated summons the door was at last opened by a weird-looking woman, whose tall figure and commanding features gave to her person a dignity which her squalid, though clean, attire could not conceal. Courageous as the Princess Mary naturally was, she could not avoid betraying something like fear on her appearance. In her left hand she held a lamp, made of coarse baked clay, whilst her right one grasped a long narrow sword, whose bright blade glittered in the flickering beams of the uncertain light. The knit brows and stern expression about the mouth showed that in case of danger she had the resolution to use it.

"Dost take us for robbers, good mother," exclaimed Patch, eyeing her curiously, for he was fond of studying character, either in courts or hovels, "that you welcome us glove in hand?"

"We seek but shelter till the storm is past," added Walter; "and this, dame, is not a night to turn a dog from your door, should it howl for pity, much more one of your own sex."

The female glanced her eye rapidly over the party, and apparently satisfied with the scrutiny, gave way for them to enter, observing, as she did so, that the presence of their companion answered better for their purpose than their smooth speech or Flemish broadcloth.

The hut, though desolate and cheerless on the outside, proved comparatively warm and comfortable within. A cheerful fire was blazing in a rude chimney, formed by the supporting rock at the back, and a couple of rough wooden benches enabled the drenched fugitives to seat and dry themselves.

The jester glanced quietly round the walls. A few wooden platters and bowls, such as in the reign of Henry VIII. were the common furniture of every cottage, and even of some hostels in England, were ranged on a shelf against the wall; over them hung bundles of various herbs and berries, more or less dried for use, together with other fanciful odds and ends, more curious than useful. The only attempt at ornament was a simple cross, fashioned, most probably, by the lazy hand of some shepherd or woodman from a piece of holly wood, plenty of which was found within the forest. A large raven, whose whitened bill denoted its vast age, was basking in the warmth before the fire; with a low, sullen croak, he hopped to a distant corner of the hut as they approached, as if angry at being disturbed.

"You have chosen a singular companion," observed Walter, pointing to the bird; for at the time we speak of all its species were regarded with superstitious dislike, especially by the ignorant.

"It is almost the only one," said the woman, "which the persecution of the world hath left me. He at least will neither flatter nor betray me—not so with man," observed their hostess.

"You are bitter against the world, good mother."

"I am as it hath made me," continued the woman. "But heed not my speech; take the shelter accident affords, dry your garments, and, soon as it lists you, pass on your way."

"You at least," said the Princess Mary, proffering at the same time a purse of gold nobles, "shall have no cause to regret our visit. Take it," she added, seeing that the female hesitated; "it will at least add something to your comforts, which are, alas! but scanty."

"Gold!" exclaimed the woman, "what should I do with gold, and sleep in peace? I knew I should be tempted," she muttered, "for I dreamt last night of the bright yellow devil. Put it back, girl—put it back; with such a treasure beneath my roof I could not rest at nights. The fear my son might murder me would haunt me in my sleep; there's evil in the sight of it—put it back."

"You have a son, then?" demanded Patch, at the same time exchanging a glance with his companion, which the keen-eyed hag saw and interpreted rightly.

"A son," she repeated; "why else do I live? Could any but a mother endure the load of an existence wretched and lone as mine? Yes, I have a son, wild as the forest fiend—almost as lawless, too; for he hunts the deer despite man's edicts and his cruelty, as if God," she added with a scornful laugh, "had made the creatures of the earth for lords and princes only."

At this moment the door, which had been left unbarred, was pushed hastily open, and the person spoken of entered with a fawn, which he had just slain, upon his shoulders. His parent had not unfitly described him as a forest fiend. He was apparently about twenty; his strong, shapely limbs were cast

in a youthful giant's mould; his features, like his mother's, were strongly marked— their haggard, wild appearance considerably heightened by the long dark hair which fell down his neck and shoulders. No sooner had he thrown the slaughtered game upon the floor than the old raven hopped from its corner towards it, and begun smearing its bill in the still flowing blood, in its endeavours to tear and enlarge the wound.

"Croak—croak!" went the bird, delighted with its unusual banquet.

No. 48.

"Silence, Harro," screamed the hag "thy note seldom bodes good."

"Strangers here?" said the young man, regarding the party attentively; "but I guessed as much, when I saw your steeds tied to the chestnut tree beside the cottage. You have lost your companions in the forest?"

"No."

"I have no wish to be curious," said the fellow, doggedly, for he fancied the speaker was deceiving him, "but I saw them abou a mile hence. More, I listened to their conversation while I lay crouched on the damp grass as they rode by me, and heard their leader, whom one called Dudley, refusing to draw rein till he overtook you."

"Dudley!" exclaimed Princess Mary, starting from her seat.

"Dudley!" shrieked the hag; "the oppressor, the assassin! Hath the scaffold given up the dead? Did men deceive me when I heard that justice had been done, and that the axe had fallen on his accursed neck?"

"He speaks of the son of the man you name."

"Father or son, vengeance is still the same," continued the woman. "Degenerate dog!" she added, turning to her son, "hadst thou not an arrow in thy belt to avenge thy widowed mother's tears — thy father's blood?"

"'Tis not too late," muttered the young giant, seizing the brand, which his mother had laid aside as soon as she was satisfied of the character of her guests.

In an instant Walter and Patch drew their swords, and placed themselves before the princess, whom it was evident the young ruffian took to be connected with the enemy.

"Avoid this broil," said Mary, speaking in Norman-French, so as not to be understood, "if it be possible. Dudley is an enemy more fearful than e'en my father's frown, or Eustachio's ill-timed zeal. We must cross the stream before them."

"Trust to our prudence," replied Patch, in the same language; "but our first duty is to secure your highness's safety. Fear not; the sainted queen, your mother, watches over you."

The fury of the mistress of the hut suddenly was calmed; and, on a sign, her son threw down his weapon. All were surprised at the change, and thought at first that she had understood them.

"You would fly?" demanded the woman.

"We would," said Mary, "but, alas! our horses are exhausted."

"I will give them a drug," said their hostess, "which for twelve hours shall restore their strength—nay, give them tenfold vigour."

"And the torrent?"

"May be passed by one who knows the track, even though it raged with ten times greater fury. Trust to my guidance and you shall cross in safety."

The speaker was at least in earnest in her boast, for taking down three of the wooden bowls, with the assistance of her son she half filled them with water, into which she poured the contents of a stone jar. As soon as it was opened a strong and not unpleasant perfume filled the place.

As soon as the young forester had left the hut to administer the drugs to the horses, the manner of the female entirely changed. Approaching the princess, she bent the knee and would have kissed her hand.

"What mean you?" said Mary.

"Fear not," whispered the woman; "they should tear me limb from limb ere I betrayed you. Prop of the ancient faith, daughter of kings, go forth in safety. Think not that I am mad; my words are strange, but my deeds may prove yet stranger. Years since it was foretold," she added, "that this withered hand should place the daughter of Katherine of Arragon upon the throne: it will one day be accomplished."

"Thou art mad."

"Hark!" she continued, as the lively neighing of the steeds announced that the drug had taken effect, "the first boast is at least accomplished. Fear not the rest; you will have small need for whip or spur; they must bestride the wind who follow you. Once past the torrent, you may defy pursuit."

To the astonishment of the fugitives, they found their horses, lately half dead with fatigue, pawing impatiently the ground, full of life and animation, as if anxious to proceed.

"Heaven is on our side," said Mary, as, preceded by their conductress, they set forward.

"And the weird woman of the chase," added their mysterious guide.

The young hunter, left alone in the hut, began to prepare the fawn for supper, to do which he was obliged several times to chase the obstinate raven from the carcase, where for some time it had been gorging unobserved at its ease.

"Croak! croak!" cried the bird, as its master impatiently kicked it away for the third time. The sullen creature, offended at the chastisement, retreated to a corner, which the various morsels of offal the operator threw to it could not tempt it to quit.

"It's a bad sign, Harro," he observed, "when we cease to be friends."

Just as he had finished his task, Dudley and his companions, who had been baffled in their search, entered the cottage.

"What art thou doing, knave?" demanded the leader of the party, who was a stout upholder of the forest laws.

"Canst thou not see?" replied the young man, doggedly; "skinning a deer."

"Insolent! knowest thou not many a better man has been hanged for this?"

"I know it. My father hung for it."

"Yet thou art not forewarned," said Dudley.

"No more than thou art; for thine lost his head soon after."

This was an allusion which the fierce soldier was never known to forgive; his cheek became ashy pale, and his eyes flashed with the fury of an excited rattlesnake. Without a word, he drew his sword, and before his victim could stand upon his guard, passed it twice through his heart.

"Creak!" shrieked the raven, as it hopped from its hiding-place and perched upon the body of the dying man; "croak—croak!"

In a few moments its beak was again stained with blood.

"This passes patience," said Dudley; "but the fool is rightly served."

At this moment the mother, who had just returned from guiding the fugitives, who had safely crossed the torrent, entered the hut; at a glance she comprehended the full extent of her misery, and all that had passed.

"Monster!" she cried, "a widowed mother's curse rest on thy head. As was the father, so is the son—cruel, remorseless, bloody, pitiless; and so the fate of both—the scaffold—the scaffold—the scaffold!"

The excited woman approached close to the assassin, and shrieked the last words in his ear.

"What means the hag?"

"That I shall see thy head higher than e'en thy pride would place it. Dudley," she continued, "when thy step is nearest to the throne—when ambition holds the prize almost within thy reach—then will thy doom be near, then shall we meet again. As I foretold thy father's fate, so do I tell thee thine!"

Dudley, as if stung by a serpent—for there was a memory in her words which caused even his heart to quail—cast a furious look upon the speaker, and darted from the hut.

"Croak—croak!" cried the raven, hopping after him.

For a long time the wretched mother remained insensible upon the body of her murdered son.

CHAPTER XVIII.

"Proud of her lofty birth, but gracing it
By acts of charity and holy deeds,
Such as approving angels smile and write
In the eternal register of heaven."—*Mabel.*

 N a lofty chamber in Montague Manor was seated a venerable lady, whose unbroken form and stately person showed that time had dealt most gently with her. Her dress was sober, as became her years, yet distinguished by the ensigns of high rank, such as miniver and sable, with which her circote of deep purple velvet was lined—a distinction almost peculiar to royalty. Her long grey hair was carefully rolled under a linen coif, displaying to advantage her lofty forehead. Blue eyes, whose lustre time had tempered but not dimmed, gave animation to her still handsome countenance, when not, as now, clouded by anxiety and care.

This remarkable personage was no other than the celebrated Countess of Salisbury, the grand-daughter of Richard Neville, Earl of Warwick and Salisbury, and the daughter of George Duke of Clarence, brother of Edward IV., who was drowned in a butt of malmsey in the Tower. She was Countess of Salisbury and Baroness Montague in her own right. Descended from the line of Plantagenet—a name which Fuller quaintly remarks outsyllabled Tudor, both in the affections and mouths of the English nation —she possessed the high and courageous spirit of her race, and was a fit representative of that proud ancestry whose lowest descendant regarded with contempt the inferior family of the Tudors. Induced, perhaps, by the calamities of her earlier days, she had condescended to bestow her hand upon Sir Richard Pole, whose blood, although it had flowed through many honourable veins, was scarcely worthy to mingle with the pure stream by which the existence of the noble Margaret was cherished. Misfortune had at an early age given her lessons of wisdom and humility, by which, if we may judge of the character of her children, they seem to have profited more than their mother. Her son, the celebrated Cardinal Pope, was through life humble and unaffected. Her brother, Edward Plantagenet, Earl of Warwick, had been conveyed at an early age from the house where he was born to the Tower, and immured there on account of the jealousy of his uncles, Edward IV. and Richard III., who both dreaded his pretensions to the crown. It was reserved for the dastardly spirit of Henry VII. to sacrifice this youth, grown almost imbecile by long confinement, to the mean policy of Ferdinand of Spain. The royal victim was led forth and beheaded on Tower Hill, in order to secure the marriage between Prince Arthur and Katherine of Arragon. No wonder that an union so concluded was unhappy.

Henry VIII., conscious of the injustice with which her brother had been treated, for many years showed her great distinction, and committed the Princess Mary to her keeping after his divorce from her mother.

The anxiety which we noticed in her countenance arose from the absence of her ward, whom she had permitted, contrary to the strict injunctions of the king, to visit her dying parent at Kimbolton, and whose escape from the political machinations of Eustachio, the Spanish ambassador, and the pursuit of Dudley, we described in our last chapter. The absence of the princess had been carefully concealed from the household, under the pretence of an indisposition, which compelled her to keep her chamber, where the countess and her physician alone were supposed to enter. The form of serving her grace had been regularly kept up, as a blind, during her absence, the venerable lady herself carrying the dishes into the apartment of the presumed invalid.

"Five days," she murmured, rising and pacing the rush-strewn floor uneasily; "five whole days, and not a sign of their return! It will be impossible much longer to conceal her absence from the household, many of whom are little better than spies upon us. Our lady aid her!" she added; "it is for the desolate child I feel, more than for myself. My days cannot be many; and whether in a dungeon, on a scaffold, or her ancestral halls, Margaret Plantagenet will know how to die!"

Little did the venerable matron dream how near she was to being called on to fulfill her boast.

Dr. Mansel, her physician, entered from the inner chamber, where it was supposed he had passed the night watching by the sick ward, as she finished her soliloquy.

"See you any signs of their approach?" she demanded.

"None, madam, none; but that is not the worst—a party of horsemen are directing their way towards the house."

"Horsemen!" repeated the countess, her pale features slightly flushed. "Horsemen! then I guess the rest. The absence of the princess has been discovered. I am betrayed; and these are the messengers of Henry's vengeance."

"Hope for the best," said the physician; "he may be merciful."

"Merciful!" she repeated, with a look of scorn; "oh! well I know the Tudor's mercy—it is written in the blood of my murdered brother, my persecuted kindred. The Welsh Wolf fears the English hart too much to spare its aged dam."

"They are but few," observed the old man; "should their errand in truth prove hostile, we are strong enough to resist them, and at least gain time for flight."

"Flight!" repeated the lady, mournfully; "and whither should I fly?"

"To your son Reginald, in Italy."

"Hopeless—hopeless! You may transplant the tender sapling, but not the gnarled tree. I will cause no man destruction in my cause; the fate we can't avoid, true courage shows itself in yielding to."

At this instant an usher entered the apartment to announce that Viscount Lisle, who was on his way from court, and was charged with a message to the Lady Mary from her father, demanded admission at the gates.

"Admit him," said the countess, firmly; "we will descend to meet him; let not the pliant courtier say that Margaret Plantagenet sent him hungry from her dates."

"What, noble lady, do you intend to do?"

"Confess all," was the calm reply. "Think you," she added, proudly, "I would descend to falsehood?"

"I am not so scrupulous," interrupted the physician; "let me descend to meet this Dudley—keep him in play until the latest moment. In the game of life, we should never throw one chance away."

"At my time it is scarcely worth a struggle to preserve it," observed the countess; "but be it as you advise. I will retire to the Lady Mary's room, and wait as you advise."

Taking up her missal from the prie-dieu, near which she had been sitting during the long watching of the night, Margaret Plantagenet left the apartment with as unconcerned an air as if she had been unconscious of the danger near her.

On descending to the great hall, Dr. Mansel found Dudley and his companions, who, although not invested with any official character, had already begun examining the domestics.

"And so," he said, "the Lady Mary has been sick for five days?"

"Even so, my lord," replied the physician, who came just in time to catch the question.

"And who has seen her?" he demanded, rudely.

"I and the countess," was the reply.

A smile of incredulity lit the features of the artful Dudley, who was puzzled how to proceed; for, as we before observed, he was invested with no official character, and he knew that the stern old countess was not a person whom he could either bully or terrify; still it was absolutely necessary that he should obtain proofs of the absence of the princess.

"This is folly, doctor," he exclaimed; "I well know the Lady Mary is not at Montague Manor."

The household exchanged looks amongst themselves, for such for three days past had been the general opinion.

"More," resumed the speaker; "that she hath been to Kimbolton."

"Indeed!" said Mansel, who was a shrewd man, and began to suspect the true state of the case; "your lordship is pleased to jest at the expense of our credulity. If you will favour me with your credentials to the princess, I will request an immediate audience of her grace, that you may be satisfied."

"I tell you she is absent," repeated Dudley, who was almost as much embarrassed as the doctor how to extricate himself from his false position.

"And I repeat, show your letters—give some token that this intrusion is authorised by the king, or I advise the countess to give orders to have you tossed into the moat," replied the physician.

It is impossible to decide how the dispute might have terminated, for it continued to wax warm on either side. The domestics, who were both numerous and attached to their venerable mistress, naturally took courage, and sided with the speaker when they found that Dudley came unarmed by the authority of the king. Swords were already drawn on both sides, when the stern

voice of Margaret Plantagenet was heard to exclaim from the inner room—

"Peace, knaves! Place for her grace, the Princess Mary!"

The next moment the countess entered, preceded by her ward, whose pale face and haggard eyes gave proof that she was ill, and that the doctor's story was not all a fiction.

It would have been difficult to decide as she entered the apartment which was the most surprised, Mansel or Dudley; the latter, who was an accomplished courtier, bowed to hide his chagrin.

"I understand, my lord," said the princess, "you are the bearer of letters from my father?"

"Not—not exactly letters," stammered the discomfited intriguer.

"Have we misunderstood the Lady Salisbury?" demanded Mary, turning to her companion.

"Such, I understood, was the pretence which gained him admission here," replied the countess, haughtily.

"His lordship said so at the gate," observed the warder.

"And since then," added the secretary, "he hath been questioning all the household, asserting that your grace was absent—fled to Kimbolton—not ill; and that for two night's past he had chased you through the country."

"And is it so, my lord?" said Mary, sternly; "was it to gratify an idle curiosity, or still more idle spleen, we have been dragged from our sick couch under the thought of doing honour to our father's messenger? We congratulate you, my lord, upon your honourable conduct, and trust an hour will come to prove our gratitude."

Bold as Dudley constitutionally was, he quailed beneath the speaker's cold grey eye. Could he have seen into futurity, her glance would have given him an uncomfortable sensation about the neck.

"Gods! what!" cried the aged countess, "have I lived to be braved in my own halls by the son of the extortioner, Dudley, whom the rope would have requited better than the axe? Arm, knaves!" she continued, turning to the domestics, whom the sight of the princess had given fresh courage to—"arm, and drive the intruders from my house."

"Madam," said the baffled man, pale with passion at the fierce taunt respecting his father, "the residence of the Lady Mary must not be made the scene of strife. I can respect my master's daughter, though by descending to artifice she has lost the respect due to herself. For you, proud woman, I shall find another way to thank you."

Without waiting for a reply, the speaker left the house. He was a man of his word, and kept his threat as far as the Countess of Salisbury was concerned, against whom Henry was already sufficiently predisposed on account of the intrigues of her son, Reginald de la Pole, at the papal court, against him.

A few days after Dudley's return to London, orders were issued for the arrest of the aged countess, and her committal to the Tower.

On her trial the illustrious lady defended herself with great spirit and presence of mind, indignantly denying the charge of treason, which, in the legal phrase of the day, was merely constructive, and supported by no better proof than the assertion that she had entertained certain Italian domestics in her service, who might possibly be spies of Rome. The subservient peers, with Henry's tool, the Duke of Norfolk, at their head, who would doubtless have devoted his own mother to the block rather than offend the royal brute he called his master, found the aged daughter of the Plantagenets guilty, and sentence of death was accordingly pronounced. Vainly Mary interceded for her mother's friend. Henry was inexorable; and the queen, to whom the princess in her grief wrote to urge her influence with the king, never condescended to reply.

On the scaffold, the high courage for which her illustrious race had been celebrated did not belie itself in Margaret Plantagenet. When told to lay her head upon the block, she stoutly refused, saying that she had committed no treason, and that if the tyrant Tudor wanted her head, he might get it as he could. It was a fearful sight to see an aged woman running round the scaffold, her white hair streaming in the wind, followed by the executioner, striking at her with the axe. It was not till after repeated blows that she fell, and the bloody tragedy was accomplished.

This scene occurred in England, while such men as Cranmer and Cromwell lived; and not one voice was heard in execration of the deed. No wonder kings are tyrants when men are curs.

Anne Boleyn was shortly after punished for her heartlessness by the premature birth of a son. Had the child lived, her fate might have been different. Her last hold on Henry was all but broken.

The intelligence of Katherine's death inspired Anne Boleyn with triumphant joy, and she indicated her satisfaction by wearing yellow for mourning—an instance of bad taste, which her admirers have vainly attempted to palliate by urging that yellow was the colour usually worn in France as mourning for queens; but this interpretation is too far-fetched, especially as she exultingly exclaimed, when the Duke of Suffolk brought the news to her, "That now indeed she was a queen!" Her satisfaction, however, was of short duration; for the season of her adversity was shortly to arise—her husband's love was already on the wane.

"Could I but persuade Norris," she thought, "to resign that fatal letter, I might defy the malice of my stars."

She did persuade him, but the result was fatal to both.

A few nights after the events we have described there was a masque at court, during which Henry's attention to Jane Seymour became a subject of general remark.

The young lady whom Anne had so imprudently retained about her person as maid of honour was of great beauty, and of a mind and disposition suitable in gentleness and delicacy to her external loveliness. She was one of the four daughters of Sir John Seymour, of Wolf Hall, in Wiltshire; her father was descended from the Lords Beauchamp, and had married into the honourable family of the Wentworths, from whom descended the present Fitzwilliam family. He had maintained a reputation for valour in the wars, both in the present and late reigns, and at the time we speak of held the office of governor of Bristol Castle.

The birth of Jane Seymour was therefore respectable, and nature seemed to have destined her for an elevated station. Possessing, perhaps, less attractive loveliness than Anne, her person was characterised by more perfect symmetry, and her features by greater regularity than those of her royal mistress, whilst her deportment displayed the dignity without the reserve of Katherine. To these advantages Jane possessed that of an easy temper, which neither the late nor present queen were blest with; and her conversation, while it was free from the austerity and national gravity which had cast a gloom upon the social character of Katherine, had yet a more correct and elevated tone than the discourse in which Anne too frequently indulged—the result, perhaps, of a careless, playful disposition and exuberant spirits.

Intoxicated with her beauty and position, the young queen thought merely of her pleasure; like a giddy child, she basked in the sunshine of fortune, and dreamed not it had also shadows. With an imprudence which not even innocence could excuse, she danced, not only with her old lover Wyat, but with Sir Henry Norris, whose favour with his royal mistress was already too freely talked about, and had excited the jealousy of his mistress, Lady Rochfort. Anne forgot in her thoughtlessness that there is no enemy so dangerous as a jealous woman. After having made her appearance with the king in state, she seized the moment of his absence to withdraw, but soon returned, masked, and in a domino, like any other lady of the court; a disguise which, although not sufficient to conceal her, permitted those around her to address her with a familiarity which would have shocked the ears of her virtuous predecessor.

Henry, who witnessed her conduct with displeasure, withdrew into a closet communicating by folding doors with the saloon. Jane Seymour was already seated there, half-pensively, half-coquettishly perhaps, and, strange to say, alone; for since it was observed that the king viewed her with admiration, the younger courtiers were afraid to flirt with her: the jackals knew their place.

"Alone, May-bird!" exclaimed Henry, gallantly taking her hand; "I thought I had been the only one deserted here."

Jane noted not only the words, but the tone in which they were uttered.

"The sun, sire, shineth where it listeth," replied Jane; "and we should not complain of solitude, since its rays give light and animation to the world: it is a desert only where it shines not."

"Say'st thou, sweetheart?" said the enamoured monarch, gazing upon her with the same looks of admiration with which, but a few months before, he had gazed upon his queen. "Why, then, art thou insensible?"

The maid of honour raised her eyes and gazed upon him with a look of reproachful tenderness, which she was far from feeling for a man of Henry's years, person, and character; but he was a king, whom recent example had proved would divorce one wife to elevate another; and women, even the most virtuous, after a certain age, are generally coquettes or else ambitious. Jane Seymour most probably was the latter only, and employed the arts of the former but as a battery to advance her design. In love affairs women are born generals.

"You are silent," whispered her admirer.

"What can I say, your highness?" timidly replied his companion. "Honour is dearer to me even than life or love. Woman's heart is weak, but Heaven hath wisely placed virtue as its guardian. Why force the blush into my conscious cheek—why seek for an avowal whose very shame consumes me?"

Despite his general self-possession, Henry could not repress a smile, the reply so reminded him of his courtship with Anne Boleyn. He must have had a curious knowledge of the sex from his intercourse with his six wives. Pity the royal Bluebeard, who was so fond of scribbling, never left us the fruit of his discoveries and experience; it would have been quite as instructive as his "Assertio Septem Sacramentorum," and a great deal more amusing.

"All ties," said the king, meaningly, "are not indissoluble."

"But marriage is, sire."

"Unless upon just grounds," added Henry, moodily, his virtuous resentment at Anne's levities increased by Jane's opposition to his wishes.

At this moment a courtier, dressed in a long gown of crimson taffeta, ornamented with Venetian passementerie, who, like the speakers, was masked, approached the spot where they were sitting, and pretending not to know them, exclaimed—

"Lovers! lovers, on my life?"

"Do you read the stars, friend?" demanded Henry, disguising his voice, willing to humour the supposed mistake.

"The heavens, like the earth, to me," replied the intruder, oracularly, "are as an open page; to me the present is as was the past, the future as the present. I can read the very inward thoughts of those who trust in me."

"Indeed," said Jane, either believing in his assertion, or feigning to do so. "What, then, are my fortunes?"

"Show me your hand. I see—I see," he murmured, after surveying it carefully; "a lofty fortune, a noble state—a life of honour, lady, and of love."

"Wedded?" she inquired, timidly.

"Wedded," repeated the stranger—for such he appeared both to the monarch and his companion.

"And mine?" said the king, at the same time extending his palm.

"The lion's path—the lordly eagle's flight—a career for men to wonder at and fear. There are ears," he added, bowing respectfully, "to which I dare not utter more."

"But my thought—my thought, man?"

"He were a bold man would presume to speak it," replied the pretended soothsayer.

"But thou shalt speak it," replied the monarch; "or I will find a way to wring it from thee. If, as you say, mine is the lion's path, remember it is dangerous to cross it. If my career is, indeed, the eagle's flight, beware its swoop."

"Should it offend you?" faltered the stranger.

"I can laugh at it," answered the king, carelessly.

"Should it prove true?"

"I can pardon it."

"And let me pass unquestioned?" demanded the intruder.

"Even so."

"Upon your knightly honour?"

"Upon my knightly honour," repeated the king.

He was daring, whoever the intruder might be; for he leant toward the speaker, and whispered in his ear—"A wife's fidelity—a woman's love;" and ere Henry could recover from his surprise, walked hastily away, and was seen no more. The monarch, who was naturally suspicious, eyed his companion doubtfully: at first he deemed it a plot of hers to shake his faith in Anne's fidelity; a moment's reflection, however, showed him that he was mistaken. Hastily rising from his seat, he cast his glance around the chamber, by this time filled with courtiers and noble dames. The queen was nowhere to be seen. The brow of Henry grew fearfully dark, as he turned from the crowded presence-chamber towards the private apartments of the palace. Sir John Perrot was about to follow him, when the stern voice of his master warned him back. "I need no attendance," he whispered. "Remain here, and tell Suffolk to let a guard be ready at my call. Where is the queen?"

"She retired a few moments since to her private chamber, your grace."

"We shall see," muttered Henry, as he walked away—"we shall see. If I prove her the thing I dread to name, this night she sleeps within the Tower."

On reaching the terrace the impatient speaker saw or fancied that the same mysterious personage who had excited his suspicions flitted in the darkness before him. As a precaution he drew his sword; for, like most tyrants, he had an instinctive conviction that he was not beloved, and prepared himself accordingly.

Despite his jealousy and indignation, he had sufficient control over his passion not to let it defeat his purpose by its ebullitions; he, therefore, slackened his pace as he reached the windows of the private apartment of the queen. A light was streaming from one of them, casting the reflection of the coloured glass upon the stone balustrade. Carefully approaching, he beheld Norris in earnest conversation with Anne Boleyn.

"Traitress!" he muttered to himself; "was it for this I risked a crown?"

"Even so," whispered some one near him.

He turned, and beheld his masked acquaintance in the gown of taffeta with Venetian passementerie. Seizing him by the arm, he muttered—

"Silence, on your life!"

"I have no wish to speak—my tale is told—my task all but ended."

The evening had been sultry, and the window, which opened into a species of balcony projecting from the apartment, was but partially closed. Henry carefully drew the casement towards him, in order that he might hear all that passed: the inmates of the chamber were too much occupied with their conversation to note him.

"This is ungenerous, Norris," were the first words Anne was heard to utter. "Why seek a love fatal alike to both of us? Hast thou forgot my honour is fenced round by death and sin, or that a yawning grave lies between thee and thy presumptuous hopes?"

"Were it the eternal gulf that bigots preach of, or where churchmen say the noblest spirits writhe in immortal agony," replied the amorous knight, "and such a bliss in view, still would I tempt it. Anne," he continued, passionately, "thou art the day-star of my life—the aim of my existence! The thought that thou art another's is distraction to me! Like the bold Greek who braved Olympian Jove, I, too, bear the vulture preying on my heart; but what were his feebled pangs compared to mine—the pangs of unrequited love?"

Henry's companion observed that the monarch's teeth absolutely grinned with rage, and he smiled beneath his mask.

"Love!" repeated Anne; "do not pollute the word; for true love sues for that it seeks; it is love's semblance only that extorts it. That letter, Norris," she added—"that fatal letter!"

"Is safe within my cabinet."

"Yield it to my tears—my prayers! Should it be found, I tremble as I think on Henry's wrath."

"I cannot part with it," interrupted the knight; "it is my talisman—the key which opens to me a bower of bliss—the ladder by whose aid I one day trust to mount to joy. The brightest jewel in King Henry's crown would not tempt me to resign it."

"Not e'en my love?" demanded Anne, coquettishly; for she felt that she was playing for a fearful stake, and trusted to delude him by hopes she never meant to realise.

"Thy love," iterated Norris; "what would it not purchase?—my soul, my life, an eternity of chains. Give me that hope," he added, sinking on his knees and catching her scarcely resisting hand, "and I will be thy slave—wait on thy smile with all a lover's fondness—repay the boon with all a lover's truth."

The indignant monarch had seen enough; his furious nature could endure no more.

Motioning to his companion to remain, he hastily left the terrace and returned to the great hall, where Suffolk, in obedience to his orders, had already assembled a party of the guard.

"Go to the chamber of the queen," he hoarsely whispered; "arrest the adultress."

"Sire!" exclaimed the duke, speechless with surprise.

"Dost understand me?" demanded his master, ferociously: "or art thou, too, leagued against me? Arrest Anne Boleyn, the wanton whom my folly raised to a crown,

and for whom justice reserves the axe. Secure the person of Sir Henry Norris, and bring them both unto the council-chamber. Not a moment's delay, or thy head, Suffolk.— ay, even thine——"

The obsequious brother-in-law knew too well the furious disposition he had to deal with. Without another word, he quitted the hall.

"Parrot!" roared the king.

In an instant the courtier stood beside him.

"Go to the lodging of Sir John Norris,

and bring to the council-chamber his cabinet. Let no one touch it, man, on thy life—on thy life. Stay," he added, as the terrified favourite was about to depart, "send to the terrace; there is a mummer there—a masking devil, who—no matter; man or devil, he hath spoken truth; see that he escapes not. Away!"

The messenger needed no second command, but disappeared upon the instant. The excited speaker continued, like a chafed lion, to pace up and down the hall, amid the profound silence of the guards, and the astonishment of the courtiers, who neither ventured to raise their eyes, or whisper in his presence—so much was the relentless tyrant feared by all who knew him.

"Dupe!" he kept muttering to himself—"dupe! dupe! I shall be the laughing-stock of Europe! How Rome will triumph in my shame! Let them," he added; "it shall be washed out with blood—the axe for the sceptre; the scaffold for a throne. Ha! ha! ha! It will be brave sport to Spain and Katherine's friends."

Norris was still at the feet of Anne, when the guard sent by Henry to arrest his companion on the terrace approached. The heavy tread of the soldiers startled the imprudent, but not guilty Anne; and turning to the window, she beheld, to her astonishment, that it was wide open, and a figure wrapped in a cloak sternly regarding her.

"Fly!" she whispered, "we are betrayed!"

Norris sprang through the window just in time to be arrested with the stranger who had caused his alarm, and who he doubted not had betrayed him. As the torches flashed upon his features he recognised his former victim, and the reader's old acquaintance—Patch.

"The jester!" he exclaimed.

"I told you we should meet once more," said Patch, in an under tone, "and I have kept my word."

"Mercy for her!" cried the knight, in a tone of agony, "whom my imprudence has destroyed."

There was a generosity in the request which almost touched the pity of the jester, for it in part redeemed the speaker's error; but he caught sight of the ring which he had taken from the dead hand of Wolsey; and his heart was once more hard as iron.

Anne Boleyn was not kept long in suspense as to the full extent of her misery, for in a few moments the Duke of Suffolk, attended by a party of the yeomen of the guard, entered the chamber where her interview with Norris had taken place, and found her overwhelmed with despair and terror, half fainting in her seat.

"What means this intrusion, my lord?" she demanded, trying to assume a firmness she did not possess. "Armed men in the closet of the queen? Doubtless some jest! ha, ha, ha, a jest! Say it is a jest, and I forgive you."

"Would that it were no other!" replied the duke; "but my orders respecting you are most imperative."

"Respecting me?" repeated the queen.

"You are a prisoner."

"Prisoner!" shrieked Anne, completely overwhelmed by the realisaton of her worst fears; "then I am lost, for who can name the prisoner that ever Henry spared? Suffolk, brother," she added, clinging to his arm, "go to my husband; tell him I can explain all—all. Mark! all," she added, laughing hysterically, "if he will let me speak with him one moment."

"Your highness can do that before the council," observed the duke, "who will be delighted to prove their duty to the king by justice to his wife."

"Justice!" repeated Anne, with an impatient gesture; "justice from them! You mock me, duke. None know so well as you they are but puppets to my husband's will—things that move, breathe, speak, swear, and lie as he directs. Justice from them!" she added, bursting into a flood of tears; "the vulture's justice on the fluttering dove. Oh! Suffolk, I have been imprudent, but not guilty—not guilty to my lord."

"It is my duty, madam, to hope that you may prove it."

"I assure you I have not," she iterated, wringing her hands in agony; "if you have any pity left, conduct me to my husband."

"Guards, form her highness's escort," said the duke, turning coldly away.

"Where do you lead me?" she demanded; "to Henry?"

"To the council, madam."

"Then I am lost."

Preceded by the Duke of Suffolk, who walked bare-headed before her, and surrounded by the yeomen of the guard, Anne Boleyn was conducted from her apartment to the council chamber.

On reaching the ante-room Sir John Perrot informed his grace that he must remain there with his prisoner till summoned to appear, and whispered that Sir Henry Norris was already under examination.

The council chamber in the old palace at Greenwich, where the discovery and arrest had taken place, that night presented a curious picture of passion, crime, weakness, and subserviency. Henry, who either really was, or pretended to be, convinced of Anne's inconstancy, kept pacing up and down the room much in the same way as he had done in the great hall. Besides Cromwell, the king's vicegerent for ecclesiastical affairs—the same who had been Wolsey's secretary—there were present Cranmer, who wore a troubled look; Norfolk, cold and supple, ready to pronounce a sentence, even upon his own blood, if it would please his capricious master; the Earl of Oxford, and one or two councillors of less note.

In the centre of the room was a cabinet of Florence marqueterie; the same which Leo X. had sent to Wolsey at the commencement of his prosperous career, and which may still be seen in Windsor Castle. Drawer after drawer had been ransacked, every recess thrown open, but still no paper or letter compromising the queen could be found. Norris, who, together with Patch, was strictly guarded at the lower end of the council table, began to breathe freely, but he counted without his host.

"The rack," said Henry, "may force it from him; make out his committal to the Tower; Kingston will find the means to make him speak."

Sir William Kingston was governor at the time.

"Perhaps," said Cranmer, timidly—for, although a friend of Anne Boleyn, like most priests he was a cautious man—"this villain hath belied her majesty—there may be no letter."

"Perhaps you are a fool," said the king. "Am I a dolt—an idiot? Have I nor eyes nor ears? Did I not see the traitor on his knee to the adultress—hear her implore him to give her back the letter? I, by my crown and honour, believe it treason, priest, to doubt the existence of that letter."

After such a declaration, Cranmer was perfectly convinced. Henry had a most persuasive way of bringing his councillors to think with him.

"Your highness is deceived," exclaimed Norris, who, to do him justice, was more anxious for the safety of the queen than for himself; "there is no letter. It was an idle boast—an empty threat. I alone am culpable. Her majesty is innocent."

"Liar!" muttered the king.

Patch only smiled.

"I think, sire," observed the Duke of Norfolk, "that the jester here could throw some light upon the matter."

"Why, ay," said the king, "he hath rendered us a good, though painful service; and now I recollect, the cabinet was Wolsey's. Hast seen it, knave, before?"

The jester nodded.

"Have all the drawers been opened?"

"All, save one," replied Patch.

Norris fixed an imploring glance upon him; but it was useless—his own torture and imprisonment he might have forgiven; but his master's wrongs, and Anne Boleyn's persecution of him after he had fallen from his once dazzling greatness, were graved too deeply on his memory for pity to efface. Approaching the cabinet, he pressed his finger on a spring concealed beneath a shield blazoned with the arms of the cardinal, when a species of flap fell from what appeared the solid front of the lid, and disclosed the letter of Anne Boleyn to her former lover, Wyat. Fortunately for the poet, and unfortunately for the writer, it was without address or date, and Henry naturally believed that it had been written since his marriage, and addressed by the queen to Norris; nor could all the knight's protestations to the contrary dissuade him. He had advanced too far to recede—his mind was already made up to sacrifice his wife at the shrine of his new passion. Henry perused the letter for some time in silence; scarcely a counsellor present ventured to draw his breath; for he knew not which way the storm of passion might be swayed, or on whom his wrath would fall. All, however, augured unfavourably for the queen, for his face became livid with passion as he perused the lines so mortifying to his vanity; we would add love, did we believe that such a being ever felt it. Turning towards Cranmer, who trembled as he approached, he thrust the letter into his hand, exclaiming—

"Read, read the wanton's condemnation, and then defend her if you can."

In proportion to his former zeal on her behalf, the primate now expressed himself shocked at the levity of her highness in writing such a letter.

"Levity!" repeated Henry, in a dissatisfied tone; "levity! call it treason, lord, when next you speak."

"It is treason," faltered the archbishop.

Turning to the captain of the guard, the king commanded that Sir Henry Norris should, that very night, be carried under strong escort to the Tower, and discharged the jester from custody, reserving, as he said, to hear his story, and question him upon the cause of his long absence, in private.

"And now, my lords," he continued, as soon as the knight was removed, "for our most painful duty as a king, a husband, and a father. The queen must to the Tower after him."

There was a deep silence on hearing the determination, but not one voice was raised against it. Even Dudley, for whom she had succeeded in procuring the office of lord admiral, was silent.

The fallen have seldom friends.

"I dare not trust the weakness of my nature were I to see her again," said the tyrant, whose hypocrisy deceived no one but himself; "you must inform her of my determination."

The Duke of Norfolk bowed, and Cranmer ventured to demand upon what authority they should commit her highness, as such a proceeding was without precedent.

"Upon our royal warrant," exclaimed Henry, seizing a pen, and writing his name at the head of a roll of parchment, plenty of which, prepared for such purposes, was lying on the council table.

"And touching her treatment?"

"Let it be queenly to the last—at least till the peers pronounce her guilty. Farewell, my lords," he added; "I have done my duty; look well that you shrink not from yours!"

Dashing aside the velvet curtain which led from the council chamber to his closet, the king, with this indistinct menace, passed from the room. Most of those present breathed more freely after his departure.

On a signal from the chancellor, the doors at the lower end of the apartment were thrown open, and Anne Boleyn, preceded as before by the Duke of Suffolk, and surrounded by her guard, made her appearance before them. All rose on her approach; and one of the attendants drew to the foot of the table a chair of state.

"Where is my husband?" she faintly demanded.

"In pity to his feelings," replied the Duke of Norfolk, "we have advised his highness to withdraw."

"His feelings!" repeated Anne. "Have you no thought of mine? What mean these strange proceedings—this midnight council, and these guards? Of what am I accused?"

"It is our duty to inform your highness—of being faithless to the king."

"He cannot believe it; you cannot believe it. Show me the when or where, the probability of such an act of black ingratitude. Cranmer—father—friend—my Lord of Norfolk—uncle—go for me to the king—fall on your knees—entreat that he will hear me—tell him I can explain all—that my love is still unchanged—that I am true as the hour when first he knew me.

"It must be proved, niece," said the Duke of Norfolk, coldly; "it must be proved. Meanwhile, his highness, with the full advice and consent of his council, hath decided that for the present you take up your abode at the royal lodging in the Tower."

"The Tower!" faltered Anne, who felt that all was over; "when must I depart?"

"With the dawn," said the duke, rising, and all the councillors followed his example.

"No hope, no aid," she murmured; "all are false; Cranmer, Norfolk, Dudley, all alike desert me. Oh! may they one day feel at their great need the sting of such ingratitude!"

The malediction of the speaker was prophetic, as history seems to have recorded it; for all these were condemned to death in after years, but one; and he, perhaps the worst, escaped the doom.

As she was about to retire to her apartment she encountered the eye of Patch, who whispered in her ear the name of Wolsey, and the aged Countess of Salisbury, Margaret Plantagenet.

"The hand of Heaven hath reached me!" she cried, "and I am crushed beneath the blow."

By daybreak the following day the unhappy queen was conveyed in her own barge to the Tower.

In this world she and the jester never met again.

CHAPTER XIX.

For man, the lawless libertine, may rove
Free and unlicensed through the wiles of love;
But woman, sense, and nature's easy fool—
If poor weak woman swerve from virtue's rule—
If strongly tempt, she quits the thorny way,
And in the softer paths of pleasure stray,
Ruin ensues, reproach, and endless shame,
And one false step entirely damns her fame.—Rows.

N the following morning, Henry, after an interview with the infamous Lady Rochfort, commanded that her husband — who, as our readers will recollect, was Anne Boleyn's brother—Weston and Brereton, gentlemen of her privy chamber, and Smeton, a musician, should be arrested and submitted to the torture, in order to wring from them an accusation against the unfortunate queen, whose chief crime, in her husband's eye, was that she had outlived his liking. None of them, however, could be induced to confess anything against her; but Smeton, who, in the vain hope of saving his life, or unable to support the agonies of which he was most mercilessly subjected, acknowledged that he had dishonoured his royal master's bed—an admission which at once silenced the pleadings of Cranmer and the leaders of the reformers, to whom she was deservedly dear, as it gave a legal colouring to the charge against her. Henry either was, or affected to be, furious at the intelligence, and gave orders to expedite the trial with all possible celerity; he was impatient to vindicate the honour of his crown, and dissolve the knot it had cost him so many years of violence and perseverance to tie. One charge against the unhappy queen has been treated lightly by historians of all parties—namely, that she had been culpable with her own brother—an accusation so monstrous and incredible, that it could only have found place in a mind as depraved as Lady Rochfort's, who was anxious by the same stroke to get rid of her husband and sister-in-law, the latter having rivalled her in the affections of her minion Norris.

There is no pang like love to hatred turned;
Hell hath no fury like a woman scorned.

On the trial of Lord Rochfort, the only proof advanced against him was that he had on one occasion been seen to lean upon his sister's bed. On this he was condemned and executed.

When left in the Tower with Kingston and her female attendants, Anne fell upon her knees, exclaiming, "Jesus, have mercy upon me!" She derived, however, some consolation from repeated communion; but even this relief to her distracted mind was frequently interrupted by bursts of hysterical laughter. She repeatedly declared her innocence to the governor, calling herself the king's true wedded wife. These asseverations were mingled with pathetic inquiries after her parents and her "sweet brother," of whose arrest she was for some days kept in ignorance. In this harassed and feverish state, rendered almost childish by misery and terror, which were aggravated by contrast with the dazzling splendour of her former state—trembling with the apprehension of a cruel death, and induced to believe that those accused with her had confessed their guilt, when, in fact, all that could be extracted from them, with the exception of Smeton, amounted only to a confession of her levity —her days were passed in misery and tears.

Anne appears to have encouraged a species of gossiping flirtation with the gentlemen of her privy chamber, who, it must be observed, were of respectable descent, and could not be considered in the light of menials. Her former condition, too, as maid of honour, must be taken into account. While in that position she had doubtless become accustomed to that flippant discourse, which, whilst it proves that she was deficient in delicacy and prudence, does not justify those rigorous measures by which her faults and foibles were so severely expiated.

On her first examination she confessed that on one occasion, while the king was at Winchester, Smeton came to her chamber to play upon the virginals; that when she saw him, she asked him why he was so sad, and that he replied, with a sigh, "It was no matter." She owned that Weston had said to her that Norris came to her chamber more on her account than for Madge (one of her women), whom he pretended to be in love with, and that Weston himself had declared to her his love, which she had repelled with scorn and displeasure.

These confessions from the vain and thoughtless queen, trivial as they were, had the effect of increasing the irritation of the king, who was offended by the liberties taken with his dignity; and his indignation was aggravated by the enemies of the queen, who hated her for her religious opinions, and influenced Henry against her.

On the 12th of May, 1536, the trials of Norris, Smeton, Brereton, and Weston took place in Westminster Hall. They were found guilty, and condemned, although each protested his innocence, except Smeton, who, from his birth and character, was the least likely to have found favour in the sight of Anne. It is remarkable that Smeton should never have been confronted with the queen. He shared, however, the sentence with the rest: they were all beheaded and afterwards quartered, as guilty of high treason.

Previous to her trial, Anne addressed the following letter to the king. A copy of it is preserved in the Cottonian MSS. with many others of the same period, as a model of eloquence and simplicity, and the only letter which is extant of so celebrated a personage: we give it for the pleasure of our readers:—

"SIR,—Your grace's displeasure and my imprisonment are things so strange to me, that what to write, or what to excuse, I am altogether ignorant. Whereas you send unto me, willing me to confess a truth, and so obtain your favour, by one whom you know to be mine ancient and professed enemy. I no sooner received your message from him than I rightly conceived your meaning; and if, as you say, willing to confess a truth indeed may procure my safety, I shall with all willingness and duty perform your command. But let not your grace ever imagine that your poor wife will ever be brought to acknowledge a fault where not so much as a thought ever preceded. And to speak a truth, never prince had a wife more loyal in all duty and in all true affection than you have ever found in Anne Boleyn, with which name and place, I could willingly have contented myself, if God and your grace's pleasure had been so pleased. Neither did I at any time so far forget myself in my exaltation and received queenship, but that I always looked for such an alteration as I now find; for the ground of my preferment being on no surer foundation than your grace's fancy, the least alteration I know was fit and sufficient to draw that fancy to another object. You

have chosen me from a low estate to be your queen and companion, far beyond my desert and desire. If, then, you found me worthy of such honour, good your grace, let not any light fancy, or bad counsel of my enemies, withdraw your princely favour from me; neither let that stain—that unworthy stain, of a disloyal heart towards your grace—ever cast so foul a blot on your most dutiful wife, and the infant princess your daughter. Try me, good king; but let me have a lawful trial, and let not my sworn enemies and judges sit as my accusers; yea, let me have an open trial, for my truth shall fear no open shame. Then shall you see either mine innocency cleared, your suspicions and conscience satisfied, the ignominy and slander of the world stopped, or my guilt openly declared. So that, whatever God or you may determine of me, your grace may be freed of an open censure; and, my offence being lawfully proved, your grace is at liberty, both before God and man, not only to execute punishment on me as an unfaithful wife, but to follow your affection, already settled on that party for whose sake I am now as I am, whose name I could, some good while since, have pointed unto, your grace not being ignorant of my suspicions therein. But if you have already determined of me, and that not only my death, but an infamous slander, must bring you the enjoying of your desired happiness, then I desire of God that He will pardon your great sin therein; and likewise mine enemies, the instruments thereof; and that He will not call you to a strict account, for your unprincely and cruel usage of me, at His great judgment seat, where both you and myself must shortly appear, and in whose judgment, I doubt not—whatever the world may think of me—mine innocence shall be openly known and sufficiently declared.

"My last and only request shall be, that myself may only bear the burthen of your grace's displeasure, and that it may not touch the innocent souls of those poor gentlewomen who, as I understand, are in strict confinement for my sake. If ever I found favour in your sight—if ever the name of Anne Boleyn has been pleasing in your ears— then let me obtain this request, and I will so leave to trouble your grace any further.

"With my earnest prayers to the Trinity to have your grace in His good keeping, and to direct your grace in all his actions,

"From my doleful prison in the Tower, your most loyal and ever-faithful wife,
                              "ANNE BOLEYN."

Upon the mind of Henry, this letter, which was most probably written by Cranmer, produced little effect. His love for Jane Seymour, who, to avoid scandal, had

.etired, during the process of the queen, to her father's seat of Wolf's Castle, rendered him deaf to pity; and, unfortunately, the levity, to use the mildest term, of the prisoner's conduct, gave but too colourable a character to the heavy charge against her.

It was a lovely morning, on the 15th of May, when a crowd of citizens and idlers were assembled in the great yard of the Tower. It was evidently not for a joyous occasion, for there were few smiling faces to be seen amongst them; all eyes were turned towards the chapel, where prayers were being read before the Dukes of Norfolk, Suffolk, and twenty-five peers, appointed to try the queen. The spectators were waiting impatiently for the procession to issue forth on its way to the great hall of the Tower, where the ceremony was to take place. Amongst the persons assembled were many whose severe countenances and sober costume denoted their adherence to the reformed faith, and who naturally considered the downfall of the queen—who was looked upon as its head—as a blow to its stability. The Catholics, who were far more numerous, on the contrary, were openly rejoicing in the prospect of Anne Boleyn's death. They hated her, as the chief cause of the separation of Henry from the see of Rome, and considered her as the only bar to a reconciliation; but they were mistaken.

"So Hal has found her out at last!" exclaimed a fellow in a buff jerkin and barret, whose appearance denoted that he had been formerly an ecclesiastic, though now thrown upon the world by the suppression of the monasteries. "What better could he expect, when he took to his bed a heretic, and discarded his lawful queen? whose soul God assoil."

"Lawful queen!" repeated a young man near him, who evidently belonged to the opposite party; "your zeal, friend, outruns your discretion. Have you forgot that by a late statute it is declared penal to deny the validity of the king's divorce?"

The fellow looked wondrously embarrassed; and many who had been annoyed at his speeches enjoyed his discomfiture.

"Here comes the lieutenant of the Tower," continued the young man; "we shall hear his opinion of your loyalty. The queen, after all," he added, "may keep her head longer than her enemies their liberty."

The unfrocked monk did not wait the arrival of Sir William Kingston, but slunk into the crowd, which opened for him on either side, for they were chiefly of his way of thinking. The first impulse of the young man who had reproved his brutal speech was to follow and secure him; but a tall, grave-looking personage, who was standing near, laid his hand upon his arm and whispered, "Let him depart—we have a holier, higher aim in view; it would be folly to turn from the path even to punish a reviler, when the ark itself is in danger. Be patient, Louis; let us bide our time."

The young man yielded, and the incident passed without further notice.

By this time the religious service was ended, and the great doors of the chapel were thrown open. First came a party of the yeomen of the king's guard, their partisans reversed in sign of mourning; these were followed by a herald, bearing the writ which authorised the trial; then came the peers, two by two, dressed in their robes, but without their coronets. There was a serious gravity upon the countenance of each, for it was the first time that any one bearing the title of queen had been put upon a trial for life or death; and although they had been chiefly selected from their supposed enmity to her person as judges on the occasion, they most probably felt that in its turn posterity would judge them. The Chancellor Audley and the Duke of Norfolk, uncle to Anne, but her bitterest enemy, who had been created high steward on the occasion, closed the procession.

Curses or benedictions were muttered, according to the sentiments of the crowd, as the judges passed to the great hall in the White Tower, which had been fitted up as a court on the occasion, and where a chair of state had been placed for Anne Boleyn. No sooner had the peers taken their seats than the doors were closed and guarded by a party of the city guard. Then, and not till then, was Anne Boleyn conducted from her prison in the royal lodgings and brought before the court—an arrangement which occasioned great dissatisfaction amongst the people, who had hoped to have gratified either their sympathy or curiosity by a glimpse of her.

On being brought to the bar, the unhappy queen was accused by the chancellor of adultery with her brother and the four other prisoners already convicted, and also with having conspired against the life of the king.

"Answer," said her uncle, in a cold, harsh voice, as soon as the indictment was finished. "Anne, queen-consort of England, are you guilty or not guilty?"

"Not guilty!" she replied, rising from her seat with dignity; "in word, in thought, or deed, or aught that can be construed by malice self to treason against my husband, to whom I am bound by honour, gratitude, and unchanged love."

"Gratitude!" repeated Norfolk, with a sneer; "tut—tut!"

"Gratitude," repeated Anne; "for my lord first from a mean woman raised me to be a marchioness, next to be his queen; and now," she added, bitterly, "seeing that he has no further honour to bestow on earth, he seeks by martyrdom to make of me a saint in heaven. Wonder you, then, that I am grateful—oh, most grateful!"

Amongst other charges alleged against her, she was accused of having said to each of her supposed paramours, that the king never had her heart, and that she loved him better than any person whatsoever, which was to the slander of the issue begotten between the king and her.

This, according to the law which was made for the succession of Anne's children, was treason; so that, with a degree of ingenious perversion quite congenial with the temper of Henry, the act which had been passed on account of his unhappy wife was made the instrument to destroy her. Few witnesses were called. Smeton was never confronted with her; all that was alleged was merely hearsay; she was nevertheless found guilty, and sentenced to be beheaded or burned, according to the king's pleasure. No sooner did the wretched woman hear the sentence than she fell upon her knees, exclaiming—

"Oh, Father—oh, Creator! Thou that art the Way, the Truth, and the Life, thou knowest that I have not deserved this death?"

An awful adjuration, if she were really culpable; but sublime, if she were innocent.

"Sir William Kingston," said Norfolk, "re-conduct her majesty to her apartments."

"Uncle," said Anne, turning proudly to him, "my blood rest upon your soul. You have stamped infamy upon your name, immortality upon mine. You, my kinsman, have been both judge and accuser; you have interrupted my defence, mocked at my reasonings, turned a deaf ear to my plea. An hour, perhaps, will come when others will prove as deaf to you as you have been to me."

With these words the speaker left the great hall of the Tower, and, preceded by the governor and her guards, retired to her prison in the royal lodgings.

Lord Rochfort was next arraigned, and replied to the charge in the same way his sister had done, declaring his innocence. The only grounds of accusation against him were, that he had been seen leaning against the bed of the queen; yet he was condemned to be beheaded and quartered—a sentence which was executed on the 17th of May, without any confession either from him or his com-

panions, all of whom, with the exception of Smeton, declared their innocence to the last. Great obscurity must ever rest upon the guilt or innocence of the queen. The minutes of her trial were carefully destroyed, but whether by the orders of her infuriated husband, or by those of her daughter Elizabeth, has never been ascertained.

While Henry meditated the destruction of his queen, he also resolved, with an inconsistency peculiar to himself, to dissolve the marriage for which he had risked so much, and which had once been the object of his dearest wishes. Cranmer—the convenient Cranmer—called an ecclesiastical court; and on the plea of Anne's previous contract with the young Lord Percy, dissolved the union which he had formerly pronounced valid, and thereby pronouncing his own goddaughter, the Princess Elizabeth, illegitimate.

No sooner did Anne reach her private apartments than she gave way to all the violence of her grief, and indulged in passionate exclamations of anguish and terror.

"For this," she exclaimed, "I broke my faith to Wyat; for this urged Henry to dethrone his queen. God! the lesson I have taught falls on my head with fearful judgment—my throne has become a scaffold—my sceptre is turned into an axe—the omen of my coronation is complete."

"Courage, madam," said the compassionate Lady Kingston, who pitied her distress, "the king may yet relent, and mercy——"

"Mercy!" shrieked Anne, hysterically—"Henry's mercy—ha—ha—ha! Preach of the tiger's mildness or the vulture's pity. These prison stones are not more deaf to mercy than his selfish heart. I must die," she added. "From her regal tomb Katherine of Arragon rises to beckon me—coldly she smiles, and, with her bony fingers, points to a yawning grave. Save me from her, Kingston!—shield me!—cover me from her destroying gaze!"

The terrified creature veiled her burning eyelids with her trembling hand, as if to shut out from her sight the fearful spectre which her excited imagination had conjured up. Lady Kingston, who really felt for her charge, for she was of the reformed faith herself, hastily advanced to the manchet table, and pouring some wine into a small silver cup, offered it to the unhappy woman, who mechanically raised it to her lips, and was about to drink it, when her eye caught the colour; shudderingly she cast it from her, exclaiming that it was blood—Salisbury's blood—and that she dared not drink it.

"Not so, madam—it is wine I proffer you."

THE STOLEN INTERVIEW BETWEEN WALTER AND LADY INEZ.

"I tell you it is blood!" repeated Anne, passionately, for her excitement now approached delirium; "I ought to know—'tis not the first time I have tasted it. See how my victims stalk before me: — the royal Katherine, her uncrowned brow furrowed by grief, her pale cheek wet with tears; Wolsey, with his proud look and broken heart—the fierce Plantagenet, who mocked my state, and called me Henry's minion—ha! did I not well requite her? and Mary—no, not Mary; thank Heaven, she never will accuse me at its bar."

Here a flood of tears fortunately came to her relief, and she sunk, sobbing like an exhausted child, upon the shoulder of Lady Kingston, whose heart was torn between her duty and her sympathy; for, as we said before, she was of the reformed faith, and had already been practised on by the friends of the unhappy queen.

"All is not lost," she whispered soothingly, "you have friends who love you still."

"Friends!" petulantly repeated Anne, "ay, in my summer hours; but they all vanished when misfortune came; Death is the only friend which now remains to me."

"Yes, one more—Hope."

"Hope!" said the queen.

"Can you be cautious — hide from the prying eye of those around, who are but spies upon us," demanded Lady Kingston, "the secret joy—the hidden confidence—the promises of safety?"

"I can," eagerly answered Anne, in whose heart the love of life began to prevail over her terrors.

Her companion, after first carefully securing the door which led to the ante-chamber, where the queen's women were seated, approached a panel in the wainscot, directly opposite to the chimney, and gave three distinct knocks. To the prisoner's astonishment they were returned.

"What—who is that?" she whispered in breathless agitation.

"Hope," replied the lady in the same under tone.

Taking a peculiarly formed key from her bosom, she applied it to an aperture in one of the interstices of the elaborately-carved mouldings, and the panel revolved upon a sort of axis, displaying to the astonished queen an opening, at the back of which appeared a flight of stairs. Two young men— the same who had reproved the fellow for his insolence in the court-yard of the Tower— entered from the recess. They were no other than the son of Sir Richard Everil and Louis d'Auverne, who had been chosen by the reformers to execute the plan which, with the assistance of Lady Kingston, they had formed for Anne Boleyn's escape. They had both, unknown to Patch or to Sir Richard, quitted Antwerp for that purpose. With a respect to which the captive had long been a stranger, they bent the knee, and kissed the hand she extended to them.

"Not the knee," she murmured—"not the knee. I am no longer Henry's queen, whose smile gave life and honour; but a poor captive, defenceless wretch, whom cruel men have doomed to die; then do not mock me with a state no longer mine."

"Thine, lady," said Louis, gazing on her with a look of intense admiration, for his young heart was touched by her distress and danger—"thine is the royalty of soul which no adversity can shake. Thou art an Esther to thy people. He whose cause thou hast served on earth will still uphold thee, and warring angels combat on thy side."

At any other time Anne would have smiled at an enthusiasm so flattering to her vanity, but the sense of her present danger was too imminent to permit her yielding to the levity of her nature. Eagerly she glanced from Lady Kingston to the strangers, as if to demand an explanation of their purpose, and the mysterious means by which they had entered her apartment.

"I told you," whispered the former, "there was hope."

"They are but boys," mournfully observed Anne, who could not conceive how her safety could possibly be achieved by such instruments.

"Philistia's host," observed Everil, who overheard the observation, "was scattered by a boy. A rush is a better weapon than a sword, when His will gives courage to the arm which wields it. The path which brought us to thy prison, queen, may serve thee to escape."

"True," said Anne eagerly, at the same time starting from the seat into which from mere exhaustion she had thrown herself; "lose not a moment. Death lurks within these walls; in every shadow I see his grisly presence. Let us away at once."

"Impossible! our vessel is not yet prepared, and night must veil our footsteps, for we have the inner as well as the outward ward to cross. For two days be patient, lady."

"Two days!" repeated the captive; "still two days of doubt, suspense, and terror? But whither," she added, "whither can I fly? In all my husband's wide domains, where is the nook to shelter me?"

"You have friends at Antwerp, lady," observed Louis—"friends who would die to serve you. There, till happier days shall dawn, you can repose in confidence and peace."

"Antwerp!" repeated Anne, after a moment's reflection. "Good! place seas between me and Henry's wrath."

"You will trust us, then?" eagerly demanded the younger of her two mysterious visitors.

"Trust thee! I never thought of that," she murmured. "Trust thee! who can the wretched Anne Boleyn trust, when all conspire her ruin? But thou," she added, fixing her tearful eyes upon the youth, "hast never dwelt in courts, art young in years, hast all the freshness of the heart upon thee. Yes, I will trust thee, for I have no other trust, no other hope."

"Save God," added Everil, solemnly.

"Save God," repeated Anne, for her pride and levity were gone.

It was finally agreed that two nights hence they were to return with a disguise for the captive queen, and conduct her by the secret passage to a boat moored near the Traitor's Gate, where sure friends would wait them. Once more kissing the hand of the prisoner, they disappeared down the mysterious staircase, and Lady Kingston closed the panel after them.

"Will they keep faith with me?" demanded the prisoner of her companion, "or is it but one of those delusive rays which malignant Fortune sends to mock the wretch's hope?"

"Fear not they will keep faith with you," said Lady Kingston. "You will meet again."

The two Lollards—for, under the influence of his friend Everil, d'Auverne had become one—left the chamber of the captive queen, and descended the stairs, artfully concealed in the walls of the White Tower, where the royal lodgings were situated. The secret passage terminated in a low, arched room, upon the basement story, inhabited by the widow of an ancient warder, who, in consideration of her husband's services, was allowed to drag out the remnant of her miserable existence there. Quiet and unassuming in her manner, she had frequently been the unsuspected means of intercourse between the captives of tyranny and superstition with their friends. She was deeply attached to the reformed tenets, and looked upon the queen as a martyr in the cause of the reformed faith.

"Bless ye!" she exclaimed emphatically, as the two young men left her lowly shelter. "The Lord shall send ye a blessing out of Zion, and strengthen ye with signal mercies! How fares the sainted captive? Are the waters of affliction bitter to her taste?"

"The bitterness hath passed away, good mother," replied Everil. "She hath Heaven and her good conscience to support her, and both have whispered hope."

The two conspirators made their way, on quitting the Tower, to a small house of entertainment frequented chiefly by watermen, soldiers, and warders of the Tower, and known by the name of the King's Staff. The host, Joe Hoskins, or, as he was more familiarly called, Tun-bellied Joe, was a model of a landlord; provided a guest paid his reckoning, he asked no questions, made no speculations as to his whereabouts, or idle comments upon his means. In the upper part of his tenement were five or six small chambers, rather better furnished than was usual in houses of a similar class. These were let to such travellers as could afford to pay for the accommodation; the rest slept, as was the habit at the period, upon the rush-strewn floor.

As Everil and his companion crossed the hill, they did not observe that they were followed by a man, dressed in the garb of a sailor, who dodged them to their lodging,

and, entering the lower room, chose a position so near the window that he could watch all who either entered or left the house. As may be supposed, the trial and condemnation were the topics of conversation of Joe's customers.

"So," exclaimed a fellow, the same who had so freely expressed his opinion in the Tower yard, "the eyes of our good king have been opened at last, and the harlotries of the young queen made clear."

"Harlotries!" repeated several in a dissatisfied tone; for Anne Boleyn was becoming popular since her misfortunes.

"Proved!" continued the speaker, in a voice of triumph; "proved! else would her own uncle have condemned her, so near a relative and friend?"

"Here comes her last friend," observed one of the warders; "few complain of the world's cares who have passed by his hands."

The party assembled at the King's Staff rose and looked through the window. A man with a venerable long white beard was passing; his dress proclaimed him an ecclesiastic. It was the chaplain of the Tower.

He was a singular character, was Father Anselm; grave, as became his office, shy of conversation and vain gossiping. It was to the unfortunate, the hopeless, the condemned, that he devoted his sympathies; in the prison cell, or by the scaffold, he spoke with an unction which earnestness rendered eloquent, and faith sublime. In the course of his long career, what strange confidences had he not received—what fearful mysteries had been made known to him! Were it possible to call the old man from his grave in the Tower chapel, and place the page of history before him, what curious errors would he not be able to correct! Clarence—he of the malmsey draught—Rivers, Stanley, Dudley, the aged Countess of Salisbury, and her sons, all had passed the solemn hour which precedes death with him—hung on his words of promise, or breathed their last maddening curse into his aged ear, as they either met their fate with hope, or died despairing.

The sailor who had followed the two young men into the house had risen like the rest to notice him, but an expression of pain and sickness came over his countenance as he fixed his eyes upon him, and he resumed his seat.

A few moments afterwards young Everil left the house. The spy, for such he appeared, noticed his departure, and paying for the mead he had been drinking, left the room, but not the house, for instead of turning to the door, he leisurely mounted the narrow wooden stair which conducted to the chambers above, in one of which Louis d'Auverne was seated, waiting the return of his companion. The book he had been reading fell from his hand as the door opened and the sailor entered the apartment.

"Patch!" he exclaimed, rising and throwing his arms around the jester's neck; "I thought you in Antwerp."

"Where you should have been, rash boy," interrupted his visitor. "why have you left the secure asylum where I placed you with Sir Richard Everil?"

"My motive was a virtuous one."

"Say rather a foolish one. Canst thou struggle, boy, with fate? tear from the book of time the page which destiny hath writ? As easy may thou think to accomplish this, as save Anne Boleyn."

"How know you my project?" demanded Louis in a tone of surprise.

"I am an interpreter of dreams," replied Patch, "and thine is one."

"Which shall be realised, if wit or courage can achieve it. Friend, father, guardian!" he added, "hadst thou but seen her in her wondrous beauty—in the lone desolation of her heart—e'en thy cold nature would have pitied her."

"I do pity her," quietly observed his visitor.

"And wilt join with us to save her?"

"No!" exclaimed the jester sternly; "not for the tortures and the wrongs I have myself endured, but for her unrelenting hate of one whose mind, with all its faults, was great and noble, whose heart, despite its weakness, generous, whose high career she thwarted, whose fallen state she mocked. Hadst thou, as I did, seen him on the death-bed where Anne Boleyn brought him, torturing him by insult, hopes deferred, and bitter mockeries, thy heart would be as cold and fixed as mine."

"You speak of Wolsey?" observed Louis.

"Ay—of her victim."

"The victim of his measureless ambition, of pride and——"

"Hold!" said the jester, in a voice so stern and harsh that the speaker started from his seat; "whatever his faults, presume not thou to judge him."

"Was he more than man?" demanded the youth with a smile.

"Yes, to thee. One word of censure from thy lips were to blaspheme 'gainst nature—to reverse creation's laws. Let ignorance mock the pang it cannot feel, or malice brand where mercy fain would hide; ants judge the stars, and pigmies war with fate; but let not the son presume to judge his father."

"Father!" shrieked Louis. "Is this the mystery which, like a shadow, hath followed me through life—the cloud o'er my young path, the gloom upon my heart? Was that great, bold man indeed my father?"

Overcome by the excitement of the discovery, the speaker sank upon his seat, and, for awhile, wept bitterly. For a few minutes the jester suffered the natural sorrow to have way, nor attempted to check it by ill-timed consolation. When, by its violence, his emotion had exhausted itself, he drew his chair beside him, and commenced the narrative of his father's fall, his own sufferings and tortures, and Anne Boleyn's treachery. The commencement was breathed into the ear of one who would have died to serve her; its last words were listened to by her bitterest enemy.

It was near midnight when the jester took his leave.

The night previous to the day fixed upon for her execution Anne Boleyn had obtained permission of Sir William Kingston should be passed with her confessor alone; for the species of Protestantism which the queen professed retained much of Catholicity both in its forms and dogmas: it was reserved for Edward VI. and Elizabeth to render the separation complete. At midnight she was told the folding doors at the back of her chamber would be opened, and the priest be seated in his oratory, ready to receive her; from his ministry she would pass to the executioner.

"Courage!" whispered Lady Kingston to the captive, as she followed her husband from the chamber; "all is arranged; before the hour of midnight friends will be here."

She glanced at the panel leading to the secret passage; the next minute the prisoner was alone. For awhile she continued to pace her prison-floor, meditating on the past, or laying plans for the future—a future she was never doomed to see—and her eye alternately brightened or was dimmed by tears, as hope or fear prevailed. That very day she had been privately conveyed to Lambeth to listen to the sentence of divorce which Cranmer had not hesitated, at the will of her capricious husband, to pronounce. Her soul was bitter, and her regret at the prospect of quitting England, even though she had worn a crown there, was considerably lessened.

"Fool!" she sighed, "I have been a fool, dazzled by a bauble, whose reality has mocked my hope; for Henry and his detested love I sacrificed the heart of Wyat, my own joy, my girlhood's preference, and my happiness. Thank Heaven that I am free from the gilded chain at last; and once in France—dear France—my harassed soul may taste again of peace. Peace," she added, gloomily; "no, Henry's hate will pursue me even there.

I must seek out some desolate nook, if I would live secure from his resentment."

At this moment a creaking noise was heard, the panel opened, and Louis entered the chamber.

"They come," she whispered to herself in a triumphant voice. "The scaffold and the headsman are in vain. Oh! how the tyrant's heart will flow with gall when he shall hear I have escaped him!"

By this time the young man stood in the centre of the room, regarding her with an expression at once so stern and melancholy, that, despite her confidence and hope, the speaker trembled.

"Let us not lose an instant!" she exclaimed, at the same time throwing a large mantle which Lady Kingstone had purposely left in her apartment over her usual dress. "At twelve the priest will await me; after him the axe. We have no time to lose."

"Lady," said Louis, coldly, "you say truly—*you have no time to lose.*"

"What mean you?"

"That at twelve the priest will wait you, and after him the axe."

"How!" shrieked Anne, "have my hopes played me false, or treachery deceived them? Are friends untrue, or their vile agent faithless?"

"Thy friends are true to thee," replied Louis; "the boat is manned—the secret path is clear—the road to freedom unsuspected. I only bar the passage."

"Thou," repeated Anne, in a tone of surprise. "What cause?"

"What cause? Lady, I will tell thee for what cause. I had a father—a noble-gifted man; humble in birth, but lofty in his pride; he had a mind to grasp an empire, or to rule the world: and yet a woman's will—a wanton's smile—could hurl this master-spirit from its height, and take a pigmy's pleasure in a giant's pangs. Art thou answered?"

"Wolsey!" murmured Anne.

"I had a friend," continued the excited speaker, "who, to save my father, obtained a written proof that Anne Boleyn sold herself, like vilest merchandise, to the man she loathed—breaking her plighted faith to wear a crown. This faithful friend—faithful upon the rack—was captured, tortured by Anne Boleyn's will. Art thou answered?"

"Patch!" exclaimed the conscience-stricken queen.

"The Lady Salisbury—Pole—" added Louis.

"Are fearfully avenged," interrupted Anne. "Save me! for I am not fit to die. My soul is charged with such a black account, I fear to sum it o'er. Save me!" she almost shrieked, clinging to him in wild alarm, for the light began to gleam through the crevices of the oratory door, showing that the priest was at his post. "Another minute it will be too late. Oh! by your soul's young hope, have mercy!"

"Wolsey!" sternly interrupted Louis.

"As, at your last hour, you trust for mercy!"

"Patch!" continued the young man.

"Lost!" said Anne Boleyn, "lost."

At the same instant the doors of the oratory slowly unfolded, displaying the altar ready lit, and the priest of the Tower waiting to receive her. As she tottered towards him Louis disappeared through the secret passage. Anne Boleyn and the minister of consolation remained alone.

CHAPTER XX.

It is the crime, and not the scaffold, makes
The headsman's death a shame.—*Catiline.*

AT an early hour the following morning, on entering the apartment of the royal captive, Lady Kingston was astonished to find Anne Boleyn kneeling before the altar in the oratory, absorbed in prayer. The last storm of human passion had passed over, and the lull of peace, the calm forerunner of the grave, succeeded. She was about to die—to quit the joyous scenes of this fair earth, which never seems so beautiful as at the hour we leave it—to pass from a brilliant idolised existence to the dark shadows of the tomb. The approach of death made her, with all her frailties, almost sublime. She had searched into her heart, and found its bitterness; she had washed the plague-spot of her soul with the tears of penitence, whose regenerating drops had made her a new being. The noblest portion of Anne Boleyn's life were the few hours which preceded its final close.

"Alas, madam!" exclaimed the astonished wife of the governor, "why do I find you here? have your friends proved treacherous or weak? Long ere this I deemed the waters of the deep rose between you and this sad unhappy day. Know you not—that—— Spare my tongue the rest."

Here the speaker, who was deeply attached to the condemned queen, burst into tears, and wrung her hands in the impotence of her sorrow.

"I know what you would say," replied Anne, with a faint smile, "the day that I must die. If God has willed it so, it were impious to repine. I am glad," she added, "the morning is o'ercast and gloomy; I shall feel less reluctance to meet my doom than if the sun shone brightly and the heavens were rife with balm and music."

"Such as the day," observed Lady Kingston, "you landed at the Tower previous to your coronation."

"The day of the month?" exclaimed the captive, turning deadly pale.

"The nineteenth of May."

Three years previously, day for day, in all the flush of beauty and the pomp of royalty, she had been conveyed by her then loving husband from Greenwich to the Tower, previous to her coronation. The coincidence of date was striking, and its contrasts appalled her. Now she was a captive, about to die. The gathering crowd, whose murmurs, like the hum of clustering bees, penetrated even the walls of her prison, were assembling to line her passage to the scaffold—not, as before, to cheer her progress to a throne. For a few moments her fortitude gave way, and pressing her hands to her throbbing temples, she wept the bitter tears of terror and despair.

"To feel the life-blood beating at my heart," she cried, "life in each vein—life in all around—yet know that I must die! Cursed," she continued, "be the hour in which my fatal beauty caught the tyrant's lust, and doubly cursed the folly which believed him, which sold my young heart for an empty pageant! Had I been bleared, deformed, ill-favoured, I might at least have lived securely, though unloved. Oh, Katherine — Katherine! dearly art thou avenged!"

"Madam," said Lady Kingston, "remember you have been a queen."

"And am," continued Anne, proudly. "Let the convenient Cranmer—doubly per-

jured—dissolve the knot he tied; let venal councils confirm the trickster's sentence; despite them all, I am a queen—queen of a mightier king than Tudor's blood-stained line can boast: the queen of Death."

"Daughter," said the aged priest, rising from the steps of the altar, where he had passed the night with her in prayer, "let not the veils of earth obscure thy view of heaven; let not the regrets, the weak affections, or the heart's strong passions, cause thee to cast one lingering look upon the shore thou art about to quit for ever; direct it rather to that better land where the worn soul, like to some desperate bark tossed on misfortune's sea, may find a haven of repose at last."

At the calm, passionless voice of the chaplain, the bitterness and excitement which had so strongly shaken her became subdued, and Anne Boleyn once more regained a degree of self-possession, which, to the last moment, did not again desert her.

"What is the hour?" she demanded of her compassionate friend.

"Nine," replied Lady Kingston.

"And the one appointed for my execution?" added the queen calmly.

"Twelve," sobbed the generous lady. "The Duke of Norfolk and of Richmond, together with the chancellor and Cromwell, already have arrived. Still there must be hope; the king may yet relent; he cannot shed the blood once so dear to him, rendering his child motherless, and himself a murderer."

The victim faintly smiled. She knew too well the heart of Henry to entertain the least hope of mercy; indeed, for some time she had been haunted with terror, lest he should have executed, in all its horrors, the sentence of the court, which condemned her to be burnt alive; the dread of which alone, it is supposed, induced her to comply with the tyrant's will, and confess a previous contract with Lord Percy, when examined before the primate and several of the peers at Lambeth, and which confession was afterwards made the ground of the divorce between Henry and herself. The king, with an inconsistency peculiar to his character, beheaded Anne Boleyn for being faithless to a marriage which Cranmer had just declared to have been no marriage at all.

"Lady Kingston," said the queen, "I have a request,—I will not say which you must grant; but which, if dying words have weight, or gentle thoughts of pity dwell in woman's heart, you will not sure refuse me."

The party thus adjured could only answer by her tears. The speaker understood them.

and, taking her by the hand, led her to the canopied chair of state, which still remained in the apartment—for to the last the prisoner was treated as a queen—and, after some resistance, forced her to seat herself in it.

Lady Kingston was surprised; and the priest looked on her with an inquiring eye.

"When you shall see the Lady Mary, Katherine's injured child," exclaimed Anne, "do in my name as I do now." Here she cast herself upon her knees before the chair. "And as you shall answer to God for the fidelity of your promise, repeat my very words:—In His name who suffered for us all, I ask her pardon for the wrongs she has received. I sue for it in her sainted mother's name. Paint to her my tears and my remorse, my woman's agony and shame, my fall and fearful death; nor rise till she relents."

"The bitterness of death indeed is past," exclaimed the chaplain of the Tower, "when thou hast gained this victory o'er thy heart; that once subdued, all that remains is easy."

At this moment there were three distict knocks at the door of the apartment. Lady Kingston started from the chair of state and turned deadly pale. A noise at the same moment was heard, as if from the weeping of women in the ante-chamber. Anne calmly seated herself in the vacated seat, and motioned to the priest to unbar the door.

The dukes of Norfolk and Richmond, together with the nobles deputed by Henry to witness her last moments, were announced by Sir William Kingston, whose countenance was unusually grave.

"Admit them," said the captive, calmly.

"Will not your majesty first be served?" demanded the governor.

"I have supped," said Anne, "on angels' food, and will not break my fast again on earth. I hear," she added, "that I am not to die till noon. I regret it; by this time I had thought to have been past all pain."

"Fear not for the pain, madam," said Sir William, respectfully; "it will be no pain —it is so sottle" (quick).

"Fear!" repeated Anne: "I have no fear. I have heard that the executioner is very quick. Besides," she added, "I have a little neck—it will soon be over."

And clasping her hands about it, she laughed heartily.

The above trait of levity, at such an awful moment, would scarcely have been believed, had not the governor of the Tower recorded it in a letter to Cromwell, which is still extant.

The lords commissioners now entered the chamber. Despite his effrontery, the Duke of Norfolk, Anne's unworthy uncle, who had condemned her, could not meet the eye of his injured kinswoman. He felt the degraded part he had acted towards her, but more so towards her brother, the unfortunate Rochfort, whom he had sent to the scaffold upon a charge as monstrous as the proofs by which it was supported were weak and frivolous. The Duke of Richmond, Henry's illegitimate son, appeared overwhelmed with grief. He was young; and the unhappy queen, in the days of her influence and prosperity, had ever treated him with kindness. The chancellor and Cromwell were cold and impassible as usual.

Anne motioned to them that she was prepared to hear them.

"Marchioness of Pembroke," began the chancellor.

"Marchioness of Pembroke!" repeated Anne, her countenance suddenly flushed with virtuous indignation.

"Such," continued the chancellor, "is your fitting title, since the ecclesiastical courts have declared your marriage with his majesty the king null and void."

"Marchioness, then," said Anne, with a bitter smile. "Pray proceed."

The great law officers of the crown proceeded to read the parchment, which bore the great seal of England. By it the king pardoned her death by the stake, to which she had been originally condemned, and changed the sentence into beheading.

"If Marchioness of Pembroke," said Anne, when he had concluded, "the sentence affects not me; it is as Henry's wife alone that I can be condemned. Knaves!" she added, "sorry knaves! do you not see your malice but defeats its vile intent, and justifies mine innocence in this?"

The addressing of the speaker as marchioness had been a gratuitous piece of insolence on the part of Lord Audley, the chancellor, who was strongly attached to the party of Katherine, and who had laboured hard to induce the king to pass the act which subsequently declared the Princess Elizabeth illegitimate, thereby placing both of Henry's daughters on an equal footing. The calm reply of the queen was too forcible to be overlooked. From that moment to the last of her existence the commissioners never omitted to address her as queen.

"You have heard the merciful intentions of the king," said Norfolk, harshly, "and we are here to see them carried into execution."

"Your fitting office, my kind uncle, would have been the executioner's; but pray proceed."

"In an hour," added Richmond, "we shall attend your grace."

"You will find me ready, my good lord; my spirit longs to cast earth's garments off. Mine enemies this night may envy me my sleep. I presume my women may attend me?"

The commissioners bowed assent, and demanded if she had any further request to make which their duty to the king or the strict letter of their instructions would enable them to grant.

"Nothing."

"In an hour, then, we will attend your grace."

"An hour."

And the commissioners, struck by her dignity of manner and firm bearing, bowed, as they left the chamber, with a respect deeper, perhaps, than they had shown in her days of pride and power, when her smile with Henry was law, and her breath could make or mar the fortunes of a courtier.

The precincts of the White Tower were crowded by persons of all ranks and ages to behold the fearful tragedy about to be consummated. Amongst the common people an idea prevailed that the sentence would never be carried into execution. The death of a crowned head by the axe was something new in England; even under the haughty Plantagenets such an event had never occurred, and the lower classes are generally slow to believe in innovation. Amongst the Catholics, we regret to say that many were present to glut their hatred by witnessing the execution of a woman whose elevation had been not only fatal to their interests, but destructive to their faith. Many thought that with Anne Boleyn's death the days of the reformed faith were counted; but Henry and his parliament too keenly appreciated the sweets of plunder to forego the spoliation. Many of the reformers were also gathered there, gazing with anxious faces on the gloomy scaffold hung with black, and its dread paraphernalia, the block, the axe, and the masked executioner, that being whom human laws have invested with the attributes which Deity seems to have reserved unto itself, till Vengeance, disguised in the robe of Justice, entered Heaven and stole it—the awful power of taking human life.

"How old Kate," observed a fellow, who, by dint of squeezing, had obtained a place directly opposite to the scaffold, "must chuckle in her grave at Peterborough at this morning's work! The fall of the axe will be enough to startle even her earth-plugged ear. Her rival has not long enjoyed her crown."

"Longer than she will enjoy one in Heaven," muttered an old woman near him.

She had been a sister of the convent at Eltham, and, like many others of her order, on the suppression of the house, cast inhumanly upon the world, to beg or starve, by Henry's vicegerent, Cromwell, whose rapacity was only equalled by the infamy of the means by which he gratified it. As we have before stated, he was one of the commissioners appointed to witness the death of the unhappy queen. He little thought, as he walked proudly through the court-yard of the Tower, that the next procession he would figure in there would be to his own execution. Although he had been Wolsey's secretary, he had not learnt this truth, that the further you advance in royal favour, the more slippery the path becomes.

By the ramparts, close to the archway leading to the royal lodgings, where the prisoner had been kept, were several courtiers and gentlemen, who were either in attendance on the commissioners, or had made interest with the authorities to witness the procession, which they were as eager to behold as their descendants, our modern aristocracy, possibly can be to witness a hanging match at Newgate.

The bell of the chapel of the Tower announced that they were about to be gratified.

First walked a strong body of the trainbands, headed by their respective officers; for rumours of an attempt at rescue had been rife in the city for several days, and Sir William Kingston had taken his precautions. He little knew how nearly the sympathy or weakness of his lady had succeeded in defeating them.

Next came the commissioners in their robes of state, followed by the Lord Mayor of London—the same who had so boldly declared upon her trial that the only thing he could understand from the proceedings was, that everybody wanted to get rid of her—king, witnesses, and judges. He walked with a discontented air, as ill satisfied with the part he was compelled to take in the doleful pageant, for the young queen had been a favourite with the city.

The civic functionary was succeeded by a party of the yeomen of the guard, dressed in the same quaint costume in which we behold them at the present day, with the arms and cypher of Henry VIII. embroidered on their backs and breasts; as usual, they bore their long gilt partizans.

Sir William Kingston, governor of the Tower, bareheaded, and bearing his staff of office, followed next; but all eyes were fixed upon the queen, who, dressed in black velvet, her features partially veiled by the sombre drapery which fell from her lovely head,

THE BRAWL AT THE ROAD-SIDE HOSTELRY.

walked firmly after him. In her right hand she held a book of prayers, the same which she afterwards gave to a sister of Sir Thomas Wyat, who attended to disrobe her on the scaffold, which was for many years guarded as a relic by the poet's descendants.

There was neither fever nor excitement in the victim's face; she appeared neither awed by the thronging multitude, nor weakly cast down by the approach of death; an air of holy resignation showed that, as the aged priest had predicted, the sting of death was really passed: a martyr going to the stake could not have looked more beautiful or more resigned.

As the mournful procession passed along, many an eye was dimmed with tears; men remembered her charity, and contrasted the splendour of her past existence with the terror of the present hour. Even the more Catholic portion of the spectators, who looked upon her as the primeval cause of the downfall of the ancient faith in England, changed the half-muttered curse and smile of triumph to a look of commiseration and a parting prayer.

Arrived at the foot of the scaffold, the halberdiers divided, and the victim mounted with a firm step the fatal stairs. A chair, covered with black cloth, had been placed for her reception, in which she seated herself, whilst her weeping female attendants ranged themselves at the back. Every tower and parapet of the old fortress, that regal den of blood and crime, was lined with spectators, entranced by the interest and horror of the scene. A queen was about to die—a criminal or a martyr, according as men judged her, about to appear before the throne of Him to whom the heart and its deep mysteries are as an open page. Faithful to his mission, the aged priest, bearing the crucifix, stood beside her, whispering the last consolation—the parting prayer—in her sad ears; whilst Sir William Kingston read, in a deep voice, the warrant for her execution, and concluded with the usual formula of "God save the king!" Not one voice in that breathless, vast assemblage echoed him; and of the commissioners, the obsequious Duke of Norfolk alone bowed his head; Richmond was drowned in tears, and the chancellor occupied in whispering the orders to the executioner.

"See that your axe is sharp and your arm steady," he muttered to the gaunt figure, who, clothed in scarlet, watched, with professional indifference, the scene in which he was to perform so dreadful a part, and at which so many were drowned in tears.

"Fear not, my lord," replied the headsman; "Hugo of Calais never yet struck twice."

The assurance was not altogether an idle boast. The speaker, who was the public executioner of Calais, at that time an English possession, had been sent for expressly to perform his disgusting office on account of his dexterity. He was as unmoved at the beauty and rank of his victims as the senseless block against which his axe was placed; their innocence or guilt was to him a matter of indifference; he was a mere machine, who struck as his masters or the law directed, and left them to settle the justice or the crime of their proceedings.

As soon as the reading of the fatal document was finished, Anne rose from her chair, and briefly addressed the noblemen around her. Her voice was silvery and clear; and so hushed were the spectators, that it was heard by nearly all the numerous assembly.

"I am come," she said, "to die as I am judged by law. I accuse none, or say anything of the grounds upon which I am judged." Falling on her knees, she added: "Father of all, be gracious to that most merciful and pious prince my husband. He hath been to me a good and gentle lord, full of kindness and forbearing." Rising, she expressed a wish that if any one would meddle in her cause they would judge it for the best, and concluded by entreating all present to pray for her, and her friends to pardon her if she had not always showed them as much kindness as her means enabled her to do.

Was this an implied acknowledgment of her guilt, or a penance imposed on her proud heart by the consciousness of her treachery to Katherine and Wyat, as an atonement for her broken vows to her husband or her lover, is a question now almost impossible to decide, every minute of her trial having been carefully destroyed by her enraged husband, or her crafty daughter Elizabeth.

These words, which are historical, leave her advocates in one of two dilemmas—that she was either a wanton or a hypocrite. Who shall decide?

One of her women, the sister of the poet Wyat—the only man whom perhaps she had ever sincerely loved—half drowned in tears, approached to render her the last sad offices; Anne had herself selected her for the occasion.

"Courage," she whispered, with a placid smile, at the same time placing her manuscript prayer-book, which was set in gold and enamelled black, in her hands.

The attendant knew for whom it was intended.

Her women now removed the long black veil which, like a sombre cloud, shaded her pale face; at which moment a sickly gleam of sunshine broke forth and fell upon her countenance, never more beautiful, perhaps, than at that hour; her long fair locks fell on her neck—that hair, so lately hung with gems, amid whose silken curls the wanton fingers of her cruel husband so oft had strayed. A groan of anguish burst from the crowd as Mary Wyat gathered those curls in her fingers, and twisted them tightly round the victim's head.

The executioner quietly removed the axe, on which he had hitherto been leaning, from the block, and coolly passed his practised fingers along the edge as if to reassure himself of its sharpness. A shudder ran through the crowd: they felt that the last fearful scene of a dismal tragedy was approaching.

One of her women offered her an embroidered handkerchief to bind her eyes, which Anne rejected with a motion of her hand, and advanced firmly towards the block, declining all support. As she passed that portion of the scaffold where her uncle the Duke of Norfolk was standing, she paused for an instant, and her brow became suddenly flushed; it was but a momentary weakness; a glance from the aged priest, who walked beside her, holding the crucifix to her view, recalled her to herself. The hour for all human resentment was past; and she continued her way, uttering, as she moved along: "Pray for me! Pray for me!"

Kneeling upon the cushion placed for her at the foot of the block, she prayed long and fervently. Her last words were: "To Christ I commend my spirit!" In this hope she died, for her soul accompanied her parting prayer to the judgment seat of heaven. The words had scarcely passed her lips than she bowed her head; an arm was raised, and the swift flashing of steel seen in the air. A dull heavy sound followed, and all was over.

The executioner kept his boast: there was no occasion to strike twice.

Thus was ended a life of much celebrity and of great importance in the annals of this country. A few hours afterwards the body of this once idolised woman, whom Henry had risked his kingdom to obtain, was thrown into a common chest made of elm tree, used for the purpose of keeping arrows, and buried in the chapel of the Tower.

Tradition still points out the mound at Richmond where Henry went alone to watch for the signal which announced that he was once more free to wed.

When we compare the position of the unfortunate Anne Boleyn, intoxicated with the dazzling splendour of her rank as queen, the admiration which she excited as a woman, with the degradation which attended the close of her career, her frailties and levities, it must be admitted, were sufficiently punished. One strong ground for believing in her guilt is, that her daughter Elizabeth, through a long and prosperous reign, forbore to vindicate her mother's character by any written defence or legal investigation of the charge against her. The best defence ever offered for her conduct was the immediate marriage of her husband with Jane Seymour, in the course of the very week in which her predecessor suffered decapitation, Henry having first testified his indifference to the horrible event which had occurred by wearing white as mourning for *one day*. The simple lines of the poet Churchyard appear singularly applicable to this unhappy queen:

"They frowned on me that fawned on me before,
 They hated me by whom I set much store;
 They knew full well my fortune dyd not last,
 In every place I was condemned and caste;
 I plead my cause at barre; it was no boote,
 For every man dyd tread me under foote."

The remains of the once gay Anne were scarcely conveyed to their resting place, than a bark, which had for several days been lying near the Tower stairs, left its moorings, and glided slowly down the river. Patch, Walter, and Louis d'Auverne, who had witnessed the execution, were on deck. The former, whose agency had been so fatal to the queen, was pacing it in moody silence. Vainly he argued with himself that he had but avenged his friend and master by an act of justice. He felt, perhaps for the first time in his life, dissatisfied with his conduct, and wished that he had left the task of vengeance unto Him who has so solemnly declared that it is His.

Walter, who read what was passing in the mind of his friend, forbore to interrupt him; he felt that there were moments when the heart is fitted only for its own communings, when even the voice of friendship falls distastefully on the ear, and consolation appears like mockery. Louis d'Auverne, on the contrary, needed consolation; the momentary excitement which had induced him, at the last hour, to defeat the projects of the reformers with respect to the escape of Anne had passed away, and he trembled like a child at the idea of encountering his friend Everil, whose strong mind had subjugated his.

"Yet it was to avenge my father," he murmured; "and if a weakness, Heaven will surely pardon it."

The voyage to Antwerp, from which they had now been absent several months, occupied them nearly five days, for the wind was against them. Oh, with what eagerness did Walter contemplate once more folding Mary in his arms! time had seemed an age since he beheld her; and as the stately towers of the queen-like city rose in sight, his heart beat wilder and wilder with anticipated happiness: he dreamt not that, during his absence, a serpent had entered the abode of happiness and peace, and that the infection of its venom had already corrupted the source of his bliss—the life of his young bride.

The jester and Louis could scarcely keep pace with him as he threaded the crowded quays, at most hours thronged with merchants, sailors, and traders of all nations, but more particularly on the arrival of a ship signalled from the fort below. A few minutes brought the impatient rover to the house in the grand place, where he had left his treasure under the trusty care of Sir Richard Everil. The heart of the young husband sank within him as the servant—a faithful Fleming whom he had engaged—opened the gate of the old-fashioned mansion on his approach. There was not a smile upon the honest creature's countenance, nor even a look of satisfaction at his return.

"What has happened?" faltered Walter.

A tear fell from the eye of the domestic; his heart was too full to speak; he could only point to the marble staircase which led to the apartments. Our hero staggered rather than walked up the steps, followed by Louis and the jester, and made his way to the chamber of his wife.

Reduced almost to a shadow by suffering and sickness, upon a low couch reclined the once graceful form of the heiress of Stanfield. Shortly after the departure of her husband, her appetite had gradually failed her, and burning pains consumed her in the chest; every breath of air she drew seemed like a flame, or a stream of burning oil poured on her exhausted lungs. The only nourishment she could be prevailed upon to taste was fruit, which the *affectionate care* of the Lady Inez constantly supplied her with. Indeed, during the absence of Walter, the beautiful Spaniard had scarcely ever been absent from her side; and so attached had the grateful invalid become, that she would take the orange or raisin from her hands when she rejected them from all beside.

"Could I but once more behold him," murmured the confiding girl, speaking of her husband to the lovely fiend who was seated by her side. "I could die happy then. Methinks," she added, "my brow would not ache reclined upon his breast. I could brave death, if it found me in his arms."

The exhausted sufferer fixed her glassy eyes with so mournful an expression of confidence and love on her supposed friend, that even she, hardened as she was in a career of crime, felt a passing pang. Mary observed the changing colour of her cheek, and deeming it the unspoken pledge of sympathy for her sad fate, repaid her for it with a sister's kiss, which the fiend returned. Strange to say, it left no blister on her victim's cheek.

"Try, dearest," she whispered, soothingly, at the same time pressing upon the invalid the half of a pomegranate—the native, like herself, of sunny Spain, where treachery is veiled beneath smiles, and poison with a kiss—"it will moisten your parched lips, and cool the burning pain you speak of."

Just as Mary was about to place the treacherous gift to her lips, the sound of a hasty step was heard upon the stairs. With a strength which surprised herself, she started from her recumbent position. She knew the tread — the instinct of affection told her whose was the impatient foot. With a scream of joy, she rushed across the room as Walter entered it, and sank in his arms. For a long time she remained insensible to the tears which fell upon her brow, or the warm kisses on her burning cheek.

Patch, who had followed his friend, observed that on their entrance the governor's wife turned deadly pale, and dropped the pomegranate in her agitation and surprise. He made no remark, but quietly stooped for it and conveyed it to his doublet before she recovered from the state of confusion into which their arrival had thrown her, or, indeed, before any one had observed the action.

It is impossible to describe the grief and despair of Walter, as he hung over the emaciated form of his idolised wife. His agony was too deep for words; he could only look upon her, press her to his heart, and reproach himself that even for a moment he had wandered from her side. At each fresh burst of passionate sorrow the now comparatively happy Mary would reply to him, "that all was well, that death had lost its terrors, since she encountered it in his embrace."

"Angel!" sobbed the husband, with a burst of love and agony; "death shall not divide us: the same blow kills us both."

The sensitive feelings of the governor's lady were so excited by the sorrows of the youthful pair, that she was compelled to return to her palace. She made her adieu with her hypocritical face bathed in tears, and uttering vows for the speedy restoration of her sweet friend. The jester followed her with a cold, observant eye, and shortly afterwards left the house. The illness of the Lady Mary was too sudden and too rapid in its fearful progress to be the result of natural causes. Of that Patch felt convinced, and he determined to consult an old friar of the Dominican convent, renowned for his skill in chemistry, a Father Rimeriez, a native of Spain, but whose life had been passed in exploring the antiquities and learning of the East. The cell of the learned monk was at the north end of the cloister, and had been assigned to him, as the largest in the convent, in consequence of the nature of his pursuits, which required room for his alembics, retorts, and furnaces. Books, sigillums, minerals, earths, plants, bones, and all the odds and ends of science, were scattered round the chamber, or piled upon the massive oaken shelves which extended from the ceiling to the floor. Fortunately, the possessor of this treasure was at home, and he received the jester with the courtesy of an old friend.

Patch related the object of his visit, described the altered appearance of the Lady Mary, her glassy eyes, attenuated form, and pale transparent complexion; but without, at the same time, uttering a word of his suspicions.

"How long," demanded Rimeriez, "is it since her husband left her in health?"

"About four months," replied his visitor.

"*Poisoned!*" said the priest.

Such was the jester's own opinion; he could scarcely trust himself as yet to speak his doubts, but they pointed to the Lady Inez; he remembered her interview with Walter in the wood the last night they had passed in Antwerp, and his suspicions became strengthened. Without a word, he drew from his pocket the piece of pomegranate, and place it in the chemist's hand.

The man of science perfectly understood its meaning. Placing it on a marble slab, he carefully divided it into four pieces, one of which he dropped into a glass filled with spirits of wine, and kept adding portions of various acids and alkalics; but still no visible change was produced, the contents retained their colour.

"It is by no vegetable poison," he exclaimed, "or I should have discovered it. Umph! we have to do with no common bungler in the trade of death."

A different course of operation was tried, but without success. The contents of the crucible remained unchanged.

"Nor by mineral poison either," murmured the operator, slightly vexed at the skill which defied even his experienced eye to detect it. Suddenly recollecting himself, he placed the apparatus on the table, and opening a cabinet, drew from it a manuscript written in Eastern characters upon vellum, and for nearly an hour remained poring over the contents, Patch watching him all the while with curious eye; for the old man's countenance was a study, now flashing with intelligence when he had obtained, as he thought, some clue; now puzzled and embarrassed when the thread escaped him. With a quiet smile of satisfaction he closed the page at last, and returned it to its resting place.

"Have you succeeded?" demanded his visitor.

The old man nodded, as much as to say, Be patient—we shall see. Taking up one of the remaining pieces of the pomegranate, he placed it upon a plate of hardened metal, and brought a couple of wires which hung from a coil in the ceiling in contact with it.

Going into a closet adjoining his cell, the worthy monk set some machine in motion, for Patch could distinctly hear the evolutions of a wheel. With the interest and almost the affection of a father hanging over a sick child, the man of science watched the result. Suddenly a succession of brilliant flashes, so intense that the eye could scarcely support them, parted from the pomegranate, and the metal plate was melted into a shapeless mass.

"Ah! I thought so!" exclaimed the monk, in a voice of triumph—"poisoned by the powder of diamonds."

"Art sure?" demanded the jester.

"Sure!" repeated the monk, with a scornful smile. "Had man sworn it, thou mightest have doubted it. Hadst thou administered it thyself, it would not have been wisdom to have been too certain. But when science prove it, incredulity is dumb; there is no disputing the truths she vouches, for she is the only witness who never lies. Science and truth are one."

"And is there no hope—no remedy to arrest the fatal poison in its career—to recall the light to the exhausted eye—the blush of health to the wan cheek and wasted form?"

The old man shook his head doubtfully.

"The poison," he observed, "was used chiefly in the East; its tests were known but to few;" indeed, it was not till ages afterwards that the combustion of the diamond, the one he had applied, became known, or *discovered*, as they call it, in Europe. In the East, that land of learning and of mystery, the aged monk had made himself acquainted with secrets which modern science as yet has scarcely dreamt of; but even he, so virulent was the poison, was not sure that he possessed an antidote; but he would try—he would try.

Independent of the feelings of humanity which naturally prompted him to use his best endeavours, the pride of the chemist was excited; the case was an unusual one, and he would rather have the triumph of success than the honours of the church to which he was devoted. To the latter he was more than indifferent; like many others, he had taken orders as a means of dignified retirement and ease.

After various manipulations, he placed a small phial, filled with a dark green liquid, in his bosom, and drawing his cowl over his thin, parchment-like features, started to accompany his visitor to the house of Sir Richard Everil, first carefully locking the door of the chamber, which was at once his cell and laboratory. They soon arrived there.

The Lady Mary was still upon the couch, her head resting on her husband's breast, and her hand clasped in his, when Patch and his companion entered the apartment. She could only welcome her old friend with a smile. Upon the monk she gazed with an air of resignation; she thought he had been sent for to administer the last offices of religion. A life pure as hers had been had not much preparation to require, or many sins to confess; her heaviest crimes were but the weaknesses of a virtuous heart—such sins as make angels smile when they record them.

"You need not leave me," she murmured; "I have no thought, no action of my life, I would conceal from you."

This was whispered in Walter's ear, who turned with an inquiring, piteous look towards his friend.

"It is not a confessor I have brought with me," said Patch, struggling to maintain his firmness, "but a physician, lady—one whose skill gives hope."

"Hope!" said the sufferer, faintly; "too late, too late—my last hope has passed, and almost my last regret," she added, turning her eyes with a look of undying love towards Walter, "since I expire in my husband's arms."

Without uttering a word, the monk advanced and felt her pulse. Through his long life women had been to him but as the zoophytes, minerals, polypi, or any other production of nature which came within his way—things to be examined, classed, and forgotten; but the sweetness and patience of Mary amidst the fearful agonies which he knew she must endure interested him; and he resolved, if human skill could avail, that the grave should be disappointed of its prey.

Motioning to Patch to reach him a silver goblet from the manchet table, he filled it with the mixture he had so carefully compounded, and offered it to his patient to drink; she would have refused, but the imploring look of Walter, who clung to it as his last hope, and the tearful eye of the jester, restrained her. For their sakes she determined to endure the agony of another draught, for it must be observed that the only moisture which for weeks had passed her burning lips had been the fruit which the perfidious Inez presented her; liquid was, in any shape, like a draught of molten lead.

No sooner had she swallowed the contents of the goblet than the change in her appearance became terrific; her hair bristled with the agony, which caused the cold damp

perspiration to stream at every pore, and her chest heaved as though the swelling heart would burst its marble prison. So intense were the pains and throbbings, that Walter at one time thought her strained eyeballs would have burst from her burning sockets. Unable to endure their horrible expression, he covered them with his hand, and sobbed like a child as he wiped the blood-tinged froth from her quivering lips.

The monk, who witnessed the effect of his potion, regardless of her sufferings, rubbed his hands in quiet satisfaction. He knew that there was hope.

"God!" said Walter, "she is dying!"

"Nonsense," said the man of science; "she is too strong to die yet. See how bravely she bears up against the spasm. I knew it would succeed; I knew it must succeed."

At this instant, with a shriek of pain which no resolution could suppress, the object of his solicitude sank upon the couch, to all appearance senseless; her husband thought that she was dead, but the friendly monk once more reassured him.

"In a few moments you will perceive her returning breath," exclaimed the man of science, "but faint, as if exhaling from the lungs of a new-born child. Watch her as men watch the thing they love, the hope they live for. If in three hours the spasm does not return she is saved."

"Saved!" iterated Walter, scarcely daring to trust his ears with the blest assurance.

"Saved," repeated the monk, gravely; "the agonies you have witnessed were occasioned by the solution of the poison, which, like a thousand serpents' fangs, were preying upon her frame."

"Poison!" shrieked the astonished husband; "breathes there a wretch whose malice could engender such a monstrous crime? Name the fiend, that I may avenge humanity's insulted form, and tread the monster's heart out! Poison!" he added, wildly; "who could have envied bliss like ours, or sought to change it to such dark despair as reason shrinks to contemplate?"

"Leave that to me," said the jester, sternly. "*I am the Lady Mary's best avenger!*"

He kept his word.

CHAPTER XXI.

He was a monarch fit to judge the world,
A warrior who knew how to conquer it;
Justice he loved with equal hand to deal,
Still tempering it with mercy.—*Charles V.*

AT the time predicted by the Dominican, the heiress awoke from her deep slumber. The burning fever which for so many weeks had wasted her young life was extinct within her veins, and the keen pangs of the heaving lungs, so long irritated by the particles of the diamond poison, subdued. But she was feeble as the new-born child, when its first faint cry intimates that it has received the breath of life. At the decisive moment, nature, like a gallant soldier who disdains to desert his post, had gathered all its energies for the struggle, and found itself victorious, although exhausted by the fearful effort. No kneeling votary, breathless with awe, trembling with hope, ever awaited the reply of the Delphic oracle of old with deeper faith, or more intense agony, than Walter did the decision of the priest, who, with his finger upon the fluttering pulse of his newly-awakened patient, was seated by the couch. The sufferer's eyes were fixed upon her husband; in their expressive tenderness she found a balm more precious than even the leech's healing draught. Patch stood gazing on the scene in silence. The anxious expression of the old monk's face gradually relaxed into a smile as he became more and more assured that his skill had triumphed. That smile was to the young husband's heart like the first beam of paradise. Mary caught its radiant reflection from his care-worn countenance, and answered by one

——as pure as e'er was given
By a soul redeemed just winged for heaven.

"Speak, father," exclaimed the young man, eagerly; "have I aright interpreted thy smile?—do I awake from my dark hopeless dream of sad despair to hail the promise of a glorious dawn, or is it but a hope which cheats me with a moment's bliss to plunge me deeper in my misery?"

"It is no dream," replied the benevolent Dominican, "but a reality as truthful as thy love. The hour I feared has passed, and left the victim of the foulest treachery which ever dwelt in human form weak and exhausted with the struggle, but saved—the poison is extinct."

Walter's first impulse was to cast himself by the couch and imprint a thousand kisses on the fair thin hand extended to him. He tried to speak, but the full heart denied him the power of language; and bending his face in the coverlid, as if ashamed of his weakness, the strong man wept, but they were tears of joy.

There was a slight convulsive twitching about the features of Patch, who stood a not uninterested spectator of the scene. Something must have been the matter with his eyes too, for they were dimmed with tears. Following the example of the priest, he left the young exiles by themselves, and hastened from the chamber.

Crossing the Grand Platz, the jester overtook his old acquaintance, who was returning to his monastery and his books, speculating, perhaps, upon the scene he had witnessed, and asking his heart whether all the wisdom, all the science he possessed, were worthy of the sacrifice at which he had attained them. A silent pressure of his friend's hand, as he overtook him, was, to him, sufficient recompense for the service he had rendered, and changed at once the current of his thoughts.

"You think," demanded Patch, willing to be re-assured, "that the life of your charge is out of danger?"

"For the present," replied the monk; "but should the attempt be made again, not even my art could save her. It is not in nature to endure two such trials. She has bitter and subtle enemies," he added, "to employ such desperate means of vengeance; they must be wealthy too, for the preparation is most costly."

"She is rich," observed his companion, with a bitter smile.

"She! who?"

"Her enemy."

"Do you know her then?" demanded the Dominican.

Patch nodded in the affirmative, and related to the monk the scene he had witnessed between the Lady Inez and Walter in the wood previous to their leaving Antwerp—her burning words of passion, her looks of love; added to which, the morsel of pomegranate which fell from her guilty hand on the unexpected arrival of Walter and himself, which the monk's own experiments had proved to have been the vehicle of the poison, left her guilt no longer a matter of doubt.

"I know the lady of old," exclaimed the priest; "it is not the first time she has crossed my path, but it shall be the last. Mercy with some degenerates to weakness, and even pity may become a crime. She must be punished."

"She shall," quietly observed his companion.

"By whom?"

"By me."

"Better reserve her fate to one whose justice is as terrible as his power is undisputed—the emperor."

"He loves the husband too well to shame the wife," replied Patch.

"You do not know him," replied the Dominican. "Charles prides himself more upon the strict execution of justice in his dominions, than even their wide extent or boundless wealth. He has ever entertained a pious horror of the poisoner's craft, for it is well known that his unhappy mother was first deprived of reason, then of life, by means of drugs and philters. Fear not he will do you justice on the murderess."

"And spare the husband's honour?" demanded the jester.

"I can venture to answer even for that, if you are ruled by me; but the first step must be to discover her accomplice."

"That is already done. You know the German, Hermes, the chemist, who lives in the corner of the Alt Mart?"

His companion nodded that he did so.

"He is also a dealer in gold and gems, philters and charms. I have discovered, by sure means, that a lady, deeply veiled, has several nights visited him, leaving her servants at the door—that, after long conference, they have parted—nay, more, that he hath obtained of her a ruby ring, a jewel of inestimable value, which I had noticed on her hand."

"'Tis well," said the monk; "come with me."

"Where—to the German's?"

"No—to the emperor."

Charles V. had as much of the monk as the monarch in his character; his very morality was ascetic. In his own dominions he upheld the extravagant pretensions of the church; and even while he held the Pope a prisoner in his own capital, he hypocritically caused prayers to be offered up in all the churches of Spain for the pontiff's deliverance. The Inquisition, the most tremendous weapon which despotism ever wrenched from

superstition, found especial favour in his sight; although, with his usual sagacity, he retained, for political purposes, the power of directing and restraining it in his own hands. He prided himself on the strict administration of justice, and felt a secret delight in directing its blows as from a cloud unseen. The tincture of insanity which he inherited from his mother could only be repressed by the restless energy of his character. When he, in after life, resigned his crown to his son, the unworthy Philip, it broke forth the stronger, perhaps, for having been so long subjected to the discipline of his body as well as mind. Of this no greater proof can be given than the celebration of his own obsequies in the monastery to which he had retired, which he did with terrible pomp, repeating the responses to the officiating priest himself as he lay prostrate on the pall-covered bier in the church of his convent.

On reaching the cloister of the Dominicans, Patch and his companion found the emperor seated in the same cell where he and Walter had been introduced to him previous to their expedition to Kimbolton.

"So," exclaimed Charles, in a hoarse voice, as soon as he beheld him, "you have returned at last to claim the recompense no doubt due for your *faithful* service?"

"Senhor," replied the jester, "such actions find their best reward in the hearts of those who achieve them."

There was a pause. Charles knew perfectly well that he was recognised, although, with his usual tact, the speaker had addressed him as he would have done any hidalgo of the Spanish court.

"It was but half performed," at last muttered the monarch, with a dissatisfied air, for to him the possession of Mary's person had been of far greater moment than the mere gratification of the maternal feelings of his dying relative. "You have braved the emperor's anger in baffling his minister."

"There is something yet more terrible than even the imperial Charles's anger."

"And what may that be?" demanded the questioner haughtily.

"His contempt," coolly answered Patch.

The frown upon the brow of Charles relaxed.

"We are English," added the speaker, "both Walter and myself. Our first duties are to God and our country; let the emperor ask his own princely heart how we should have performed them had we consented to steal the Princess Mary from her father; his answer will acquit me."

"Thou art right," replied the monarch kindly, for he felt secretly gratified with the compliment, "and I will so represent your

condnct to his majesty that you shall not suffer in his judgment. To-morrow he makes his public entrance into Antwerp. See that you and your countryman present yourselves. You will there find if princes have faithless memories or no."

The jester bowed low at the command.

The usually placid brow of Charles became threatening as a thunder-cloud while his visitors related to him the attempt made upon the life of the exiled heiress of Stanfield, her fearful agonies, and the fiend-like artifice by which they had been caused; he felt that

he was doubly called upon to vindicate the majesty of justice—first as a monarch, whose protection had been violated in the injury offered to his guest, and, secondly, as a knight sworn to protect the helpless and defenceless.

"And who," he demanded, when his visitors had concluded their narration, "composed the hellish poison ?"

"Hermes, the chemist of Prague," replied the Dominican, "whose practices caused him to fly from Paris."

"The same who aided Louise of Savoy in

her attempt upon the life of the constable Bourbon?"

"The same," replied the monk.

"The motive," continued Charles, "of the fair devil who employed him?"

"Jealousy; a wanton's love for Walter."

"Which he no doubt returned," observed the emperor, drily; "for such women as the Lady Inez seldom sue in vain. Oh, woman, woman!" he added, "will the serpent's lessons never be rooted from thy heart?"

The jester's vindication of his friend was too complete to leave a doubt upon the royal mind.

Charles sounded a small silver bell upon the table beside him, and the captain of his guard, a tall, stern, soldier-like personage, whose jet black plumes brushed against the doorway of the humble cell as he crossed its threshold, stood before him, and seemed like an automaton waiting his commands.

"Bring hither the chemist Hermes within the hour, quietly and without observation. You understand?"

The officer slightly inclined his head in token of obedience.

The Dominican approached the speaker, and whispered something respectful into his ear.

"And see," added the prince, "that he removes nothing from his person, not even a kerchief from his pouch, or a ring from his hand. Away!"

The captain of the guard made a military salute, and disappeared without offering a word. He was, in fact, as remarkable for his taciturnity as his courage. It was the former quality which rendered him a favourite with his imperial master, to whom he never opened his lips unless when strictly necessary, and whose secret commands were executed with a fidelity too long tried ever to be doubted.

Hermes, the chemist, was a man of no ordinary skill in the science which he disgraced by prostituting it to the vilest purposes. Although he had long passed the hot summer of licentious manhood, his passions were untamed, and he scrupled at no means to ensure their gratification. The voluptuous beauty of the governor's wife had long excited his desire; and when she applied to him for a subtle poison, as a means of removing the innocent object of her hatred—the only bar, as she imagined, between her and Walter's love—the subtle German had exacted a ruby of matchless beauty, one which the emperor himself had presented to her upon her wedding-day, as the price of his services. Vainly she proffered gold enough to glut even his avarice; he was inexorable. The evil passions of her heart at last pre-

vailed, and the gem was given as the price of life.

At the very moment the jester and the Dominican were relating the history of her crimes to the emperor, she was closeted with her confederate.

"Is this thy boasted science?" she scornfully exclaimed, as soon as the chemist, who had been summoned to attend her at the government palace, appeared before her; "are these thy promises? My rival has recovered."

"Impossible!" replied her visitor, fixing a bold glance of admiration upon her person; "there is no medicament in nature, no secret in art, to counteract the slow but certain action of the poison. 'Tis but the pause which precedes the last sigh of exhausted life."

"Would I could think so!" murmured the fair fiend; "but I am well assured from good report that the Dominican priest, Father Xavier, who attended her, pronounced her cured."

"Father Xavier!" repeated Hermes in a voice of terror; "what devil brings him to Antwerp?"

"You know him?" demanded Inez.

The German bowed his head in token that he did so.

"Is he very skilful?"

"Very," muttered the chemist in a tone of spite, which showed that his confidence, although he did not choose to avow it, was somewhat shaken; "he hath many curious secrets obtained in Araby, that land of perfume and of wisdom; but even his skill must fail him here. Impossible, lady," he added, "I tell you it is impossible."

The confident tone in which the speaker declared his conviction of the efficacy of his poison in some degree reassured his depraved employer, who now adverted to the real object of her interview with him—the obtaining back the fatal ring which in the headlong passion of jealousy and hate she had so imprudently parted with. Going to a cabinet which stood in a recess of the chamber, she took from it a curious casket of inlaid Milan steel, and, touching a secret spring, poured its rich contents upon a table before the astonished German. Diamonds, which might have formed the zone of Venus, were mixed with sapphires, whose deep blue rivalled the colour of her eyes, or ruby gems, less brilliant only than the Paphian goddess's lips, were scattered in glorious confusion before him. Raising his eyes, he fixed them upon the beautiful being who thus tempted him, as if to inquire her meaning.

"Take thy choice of these," she whispered; "nay take them all, but give me back my ring."

Hermes was rarely tempted. The struggle was between avarice and his daring love; his avarice was strong, but love at last prevailed. He knew that the emperor was expected, that his intended victim, at *any price*, must repossess her ring—and he refused.

"And what canst thou hope for from its possession?" demanded Inez, glaring on him like a baffled tigress; "wealth?—I have proffered it."

"Love," answered the poisoner boldly, casting upon her at the same time a look which fully explained his meaning.

The stately creature drew herself up at the word, like some startled doe when first she hears the baying of the distant hound; and the expression of her dark eyes, in which scorn and astonishment were mingled, became so intensely brilliant, that the speaker, unable to endure their gaze, bent his orbs to earth. A laugh, not loud, but deep—one which had no note of mirth—broke from her quivering lips, as she repeated, in an accent of cold contempt, his declaration:

"Love! and thee!"

"Dost thou scorn me, lady?"

"Scorn!" repeated Inez; "scorn is too weak to express my loathing of thine insolence. Love, and thee! Sooner would I meet the embrace of the fierce tiger or the rattlesnake—make Death my bridegroom and the grave my couch—ere sink to such pollution as a thought of thee!"

"Charles will expect to see his gift," coolly answered her visitor.

"And he shall see it," as coolly retorted the beautiful fiend, rapidly revolving in her mind the means to accomplish her purpose. "Thou hast baffled many, but thou escapest not me. Hide thee in the deepest recess of the caverned earth, my vengeance shall find the means to reach thee. Fool, without judgment or remorse, thou hast studied much, art skilled in many lores; but there is still one page closed to thy wondrous knowledge—the page of woman's heart. Begone!"

"Yet thou canst love," observed the man of science, awed by her manner, but too much fascinated to tear himself away.

A blush suffused the face and neck of Inez as she replied to him:

"That I can love, let my degradation witness—my crime, which hath reduced me to so vile a level, a slave dares lift his eyes to me. Begone," she added, passionately, "lest I call those whose wrath will wash out this insult in thy blood, give thy craven heart to feed the carrion kite, thy limbs to blister in the sun."

She laid her hand upon the golden cord which communicated with a bell in the antechamber, and rung so violent a peal, that in an instant the apartment was filled with pages and waiting-women. The countenance of the German became still paler as they entered.

"You have my answer," continued the speaker, haughtily. "I have no time to waste further words with thee."

"Should your resolution change," said the prisoner, bowing in mock humility, "you have but to send to me. For three days, lady, the gem shall remain at your disposal."

"*I will send to thee*," replied Inez, with a glance of concentrated hate. "Fear not," she added, suppressing with difficulty a low hissing laugh, "but thou shalt hear from me soon—very soon."

Hermes, inclining once more to the ground, quitted the apartment of the governor's lady, who, after commanding one of her attendants to gather up the scattered jewels, and restore them to their casket, quitted the apartment, leaving the wondering pages and waiting women to speculate upon the scene they had witnessed.

"She must be mine," murmured the chemist, as he retraced his steps towards his gloomy mansion in the Alt Mart; "she is in the toils, and struggle as she will, cannot escape me. How wrath becomes her!—how her wondrous beauties rise and fall, like the wind-beaten sea from whose white foam Venus, they tell us, sprang. 'Tis worth a life of study and privation," he added, "the proud world's scorn, and superstition's rage, to clasp so fair a prize at last. Part with thee!" he continued, drawing the ruby signet from his breast, where he had concealed it during his interview with Inez, and placing it upon his finger, "part with thee, loadstone of my happiness—the pilot to my wishes—not for Peru's richest mine!"

Excited by the anticipation of a triumph he was never destined to achieve, Hermes entered his house, left in the care of a dumb boy, whom he had purchased from the Moors, and whose intelligence could only be equalled by his fidelity. As soon as he beheld his master, he fixed upon him a glance, which at once conveyed to him an intimation that there was danger.

"Where?" demanded the German.

A similar look directed his attention to a distant corner of the shop; as he turned he felt an iron hand upon his shoulder—it was the captain of the guard.

"Follow me!" exclaimed the taciturn messenger.

"Follow you!" repeated the chemist, who began to feel alarmed; "where?"

"You will see."

"I will not follow you," replied Hermes, gathering courage; "I am in Antwerp, protected by the laws of our good emperor, I pay the city dues, and, as a burgher, cannot be arrested without an order from the governor."

"Yes, you can."

"By whose?"

"His master's."

The speaker drew the mailed glove from his hand, and displayed upon his finger a broad signet of gold, graved with the imperial arms. It was the badge of his authority. At sight of it every officer, civil and military, either in Spain, Germany, or the Netherlands, was bound to render him obedience and assistance. Its production would open the long-barred prison-door, or close it upon the culprit for ever.

The prisoner turned deadly pale as he beheld it; he knew into whose hand he had fallen.

"Permit me," he faltered, "at least to change my garments."

"No."

"To replenish my purse with gold?" continued the wretch, significantly, trusting by this hint to bribe the messenger, but whose fidelity had long been proved to be beyond temptation.

"You will need no gold where you are going."

"At least," he added, "to leave this ring, which is not mine, for the noble dame who, in an hour, will send for it. Hafez knows to whom, and on what condition, to deliver it."

He fixed his eyes with a peculiar expression upon his dumb confidant, who answered it with a look of intelligence which showed that his real meaning, which was to conceal it, was perfectly understood, but his visitor remembered too well the commands of his imperial master to be so duped.

"Not a hair from thy head," he whispered, "nor a word from thy lips, shalt thou leave behind thee. Attempt to speak again, and I dash my gauntlet in thy face; resist, I call those who will drag thee like a captured wolf through the streets of Antwerp. Accompany me to the Dominican convent," he added, "there my task is ended, and thine, perchance, begins. Remember, eyes thou dreamest not of will follow us. Escape is hopeless—resistance madness. Submit," he added, "and, if thou art wise, submit in silence."

This was perhaps the longest speech the speaker had ever been known to utter. Hermes,

who read in the resolute eye of the fierce soldier that force and expostulation would be alike useless, sullenly submitted to his destiny, and accompanied his conductor, who, on their way, walked gravely by his side. Many who encountered them imagined that the skilful mediciner had been called upon to exert his art in some case of emergency by his companion; none dreamt that he was under an arrest. On his road to the convent he pondered over and over in his mind the cause of his misfortune, and came to the conclusion that the Lady Inez was the secret mover in the affair; and bitterly he cursed the folly which had led him to brave her indignation. Twenty times he was on the point of demanding of his silent conductor the cause of his arrest, but the sullen glance of the officer, who carried his mailed glove in his hand, and the recollection of his threat, restrained him. He felt that the charge must be serious, from the peculiar manner in which he had been taken, and the precautions used to prevent his escape, for he saw that several persons dressed in the usual burgher costume followed him, without appearing to do so. In fact, every avenue of escape was beset.

"At all events," he murmured, "the traitress shall not triumph. If I perish, she shall perish too!"

On entering the cell with the captain of the guard, Hermes saw the emperor, whose person he instantly recognised, Patch, and his old enemy the Dominican monk—we say enemy, for in science they had long been rivals, long followed the same pursuit, but with this difference, that the priest, as became his sacred calling, devoted his knowledge to the benefit of humanity, while the prisoner prostituted his by pandering to its vilest passions.

As soon as he saw in whose presence he stood the confounded criminal sank upon his knees.

Charles rang his silver bell, and four soldiers, accompanied by an executioner, armed with a long German beheading sword, entered the cell. The latter placed himself directly behind the prisoner, whose blood ran cold as he approached him.

"Hermes," said the monarch, in a voice as calm as if he were giving directions to his minister, "it is our will to question thee touching matters which concern a lady's honour and thy forfeit life. We have the means," he added, "to detect the lie on falsehood's trembling lip—the power as well as the will to punish it. Now, then, to thy shrift, and remember that the first attempt to deceive us will be the signal of thy death. We question not again those who once deceive us, or threaten twice. Knowst thou the lady of the governor?"

"I do," murmured the captive, in a voice broken by terror and emotion; "she has been my bane—my——"

"To my questions!" interrupted Charles, in a stern voice; "keep well to them! Where got you that ruby ring upon your finger?"

"From the Lady Inez," answered the chemist, after a pause.

"For what service? for what reason?" repeated the monarch.

Still the culprit hesitated.

The speaker removed his glance from the kneeling man, and fixed it upon the executioner.

"For preparing a subtle poison," gasped Hermes, the cold perspiration trickling down his features, for he felt that he was pronouncing his own condemnation.

"Of powdered diamonds, was it not?"

"It was," groaned the unhappy man; "but, oh! dread sire, remember my temptation. The victim, I hear, has escaped the fatal draught. No life has yet been sacrificed. Be merciful, as you are great."

"No victim has yet been sacrificed," said Charles, coolly; "the sacrifice is yet to come. Secure the ring," he added, nodding to the captain of the guard, who drew it from the prisoner's finger, and kneeling, offered it to his imperial master, who motioned to the Dominican to receive it.

"Take it, holy father; it would pollute our hands to receive it from a criminal. It must be cleansed by holy church ere we again can touch it."

The priest crossed himself as he received it from the captain's hand.

"Remove your prisoner," added Charles.

"Mercy!" shrieked the despairing wretch; "mercy, mighty emperor! Banish me from Europe—confine me in a dungeon—let me drag out in darkness and in chains a wretched, lone existence—toil in the mines; but let me live, if only to repent."

A wave of the hand was the only reply vouchsafed, and the criminal, like to some crushed reptile, writhing in agony and terror, was dragged from his relentless judge's presence.

Charles, Patch, and the Dominican alone remained within the cell. For awhile the monarch remained silently revolving in his mind how to spare the honour of his servant and friend Don Juan de Castro, and yet execute the terrible judgment he had resolved upon. In a few moments his resolution was taken.

"Let what has passed remain as a secret breathed in the confessional—a thing whispered to God and your own hearts alone. Englishman, thou shalt have justice as fearful as the wrong to thy fair countrywoman has been great. Seek not to know how or when. My word is pledged; it shall be kept as sacredly as the honour of my crown—the responsibility of my high office. Priest," he added, "cleanse me yon gem from the pollution of the felon's touch; we have a use for it."

The monk advanced to the table, upon which he first placed a basin of water, and then cast salt, which he took from the bouffet where the monarch's simple repast had been served, into it, muttering the usual exorcism. As soon as the water was consecrated, he dropped the ring into it, and pronounced it purified.

"'Tis well," said the emperor, placing the sparkling ruby on his finger; "to-morrow, at the palace of the governor, we shall meet again. Summon a chapter of the holy office, father; let them assemble at midnight; there we will make known our purpose, and the means for its fulfilment."

This was understood to be the signal for them to withdraw, and the jester and his friend left the gloomy prince once more to his reflections.

Loudly pealed the bells from the hundred towers of Antwerp, when, on the following morning, Charles V., attended by a brilliant retinue, made his public entry within its ancient walls. Four knights of the Roman empire held the canopy over his august head; and his valiant nobles, who had so stoutly fought by him on the field of Pavia, or accompanied the constable Bourbon to the siege of Rome, followed in his train. Every balcony in the city of palaces was filled with noble dames or the fair wives and daughters of the merchant princes, who rivalled them in magnificence as well as beauty. The monarch gravely bowed his head to the plaudits of the people, which, in the present instance, were unbought and sincere. The honest Flemings loved their prince, who had passed many of his earliest years amongst them, protected their commerce, and governed them with an equity and mildness practised by few crowned heads at the period. Charles was a keen reckoner, and estimated his flock according to the value of his fleece. In his expensive, though glorious wars, his faithful subjects in the Low Countries stood by him to the last. It was reserved for the succeeding reign, by cruel persecution and unwise exaction, to shake their strong fidelity.

On reaching the government house, where Don Juan de Castro was standing bareheaded to receive his sovereign, a shower of bouquets fell from the balcony as the cortege stopped.

The emperor looked up; but no smile passed over his saturnine countenance as he recognised the fair hand which threw them. The heart of the Lady Inez, who, surrounded by a bevy of dames, was seated there, radiant in smiles and beauty, sank within her; and the jester, who, from an opposite window, was an observer of the scene, whispered to himself—

"Charles will keep his promise; she is already judged."

"It cannot be in nobler hands," exclaimed the emperor, in a tone of unusual kindness, as the governor offered on his knee the golden baton of his high office to his august master. "Keep it, Don Juan de Castro; I cannot trust it better than to your loyalty and faith."

Descending from his richly-caparisoned steed, the speaker, preceded by his governor, and followed by the nobles who had figured in the procession, mounted the marble stairs which led to the tapestried hall, where Inez and the ladies of Antwerp were waiting to be presented to him, and whom the stately etiquette of the age allowed to remain standing, whilst he seated himself at the banquet, where he was served by the magistrates in their robes of office, and the governor, in solitary state, alone.

The feast, which was a mere matter of ceremony, was soon concluded, and the solitary guest at the groaning board, rising from his chair of state, bowed to the assembled circle, and withdrew to his private apartments, leaving the repast to the magistrates and nobles, who, with the governor at the head, immediately occupied the table. Then, and not till then, did the banquet really commence. This, in the parlance of the day, was termed by the emperor dining with the city of Antwerp.

The Duchess de Medina held the golden basin in which the monarch dipped his fingers, whilst Inez, in virtue of her husband's office, presented him with the embroidered napkin to dry his hands.

"Service from such fair dames must not pass unrequited," exclaimed Charles, and drawing a sapphire and the fatal ruby from his fingers, he presented the former to the duchess with a smile; the latter, with a cold stern air, to the guilty Inez, whose agitation was so excessive that, despite her strong nerve and more than woman's courage, she nearly fainted. Her confusion became at last so remarkable, that the attendants thronged around her, fearing she was ill.

"Give her air," said the sovereign, coolly; "the ceremony has fatigued her."

In an instant she stood alone, trembling and confused, before her judge.

"Silence!" whispered Charles, "for the honour of the name you have disgraced—the child which calls you mother. Retire to your chateau; *you shall hear from me anon.*"

These last words struck upon her ear with fearful import. She knew well what the speaker meant by hearing from him anon; with the same fearful words he had dismissed Calvano, his secretary, to the block. With a deep murmur she retired from the circle, and, under pretence of indisposition, gave orders for her departure to the chateau, as the emperor had commanded.

The sudden illness of his wife was subsequently announced to the governor, who, despite his anxiety, was chained for the rest of the day, by the duties of his office, to the side of his master, who never perhaps displayed more kindness to his favourite than on that fatal morning.

Just as the evening closed, an officer arrived with the intelligence that the boat in which the guilty Inez was crossing the river, on her way to the chateau, had been upset, and the lady of the governor unfortunately drowned. Distracted with the intelligence, Don Juan de Castro rushed from the assembly, and paced like a madman the banks of the river, offering immense rewards for the recovery of the body; but all was useless. *It was never found.*

A few days after this mournful event, his sympathising master, in order to remove him from the scene of his past happiness, sent him on an embassy to Paris, where Francis I. then held his court.

About a fortnight after the departure of the governor, all Antwerp was assembled in the great square to witness the execution of two criminals, condemned, it was whispered, by the holy office to die for sorcery and other crimes. There was evidently a degree of mystery in the transaction; no one knew their names, or when they had been judged, their station in the world, or who had been their victims. At an early hour a body of Spanish troops were marched into the open space, where the pile already was erected, and a still larger number lined the streets from and leading to the Dominican convent, and through which the procession was to pass. All was expectation, mystery, and terror.

"Who can they be?" whispered one of the Flemish burghers to his neighbour; "not Flemings, we are certain. Methinks the emperor might execute his criminals at home, and spare our honest city the shame of such a spectacle."

"Hush!" replied the party to whom the observation was addressed, in the same cautious tone; "Charles is as jealous of his right of justice as of his imperial crown. See how yon stranger eyes us."

The stranger was no other than Patch, who, with a presentiment as to who the culprits really were, had been led to the spot.

The great bell of the cathedral now tolled out the signal for the execution. First came the monks of St. Dominick, bearing the banner of the saint, with its long-abused motto of " Justice and mercy ;" then a body of soldiers marching in double file, between whom the prisoners were led, each attended by a confessor, whispering in their despairing ears the last prayers of the church.

To the horror of the people, it was observed that one was a woman. The features of both of the culprits were concealed beneath an iron mask, and they were gagged as well as bound.

It was the remark of all that the female marched with a resolute air, while her companion in misfortune, on the contrary, was overwhelmed with terror, and could scarcely support his fear-stricken limbs. As soon as they were attached to the fatal pile, a herald advanced into the centre of the square, and proclaimed their crimes :

" Hermes, a convicted poisoner and assassin, and an *unknown female* his accomplice, both of whom had confessed their crimes, were about to die. By the mercy of the emperor the woman was to be strangled first and burnt afterwards; the ashes to be scattered to the winds."

" Pray for them," added the office, as he finished his mournful office; " all good Christian people pray for the culprits whom the justice of man is compelled to punish, but whom God may pardon; pray for the culprits and the Emperor Charles."

At the close of the above singular exordium, which was the form invariably used, the executioner advanced to the pile, and casting a silken noose round the neck of the female, gave one end of it to his assistant, and both began to pull in an opposite direction. A few convulsive movements followed—a drop or two of blood trickled from beneath the mask, and all was over. The jester sickened at the sight, and turned hastily away.

" Fire the pile !" exclaimed the officer, as soon as the first part of the tragedy was finished.

In a few moments the wood, which had been piled to an unusual height, caught the flame, which rose and fell like a living thing around the dying and the dead. Pitch, oil, and other inflammable materials were profusely cast upon the pile, which burnt so fiercely, and emitted so much smoke, that even if the masks by accident had fallen, it would have been impossible to have recognised the features of the victims. Long even after the flames were extinct, and nothing remained but a heap of smouldering ashes, the guard with jealous vigilance forbade all approach. The remains were carefully gathered up, and cast into the river.

That very day the souls of Inez and her accomplice stood before a tribunal more terrible even than the emperor's—the judgment seat of God.

CHAPTER XXII.

The herald's pomp, the crown and pall,
Emblem that Death is lord of all,
And his rude grasp relentless flings
On crouching slaves and sceptred kings.—*Creon.*

FTER the fatal events described in the last chapter, Antwerp became no residence for the exiles; too many painful associations were connected with it. The cry of blood was in the streets—poison seemed to linger in the very air; even the iron nerves of our old friend Patch were shaken by the terrible justice of Charles V.; and he never passed the Grand Platz, where the execution of the guilty Inez had taken place, without a shudder. Her husband and the world firmly believed that the unfortunate lady had been drowned by the upsetting of the boat on her way to the chateau. The emperor, the Dominican, and the jester were perhaps the only three persons who really knew her fate. As soon as the Lady Mary was sufficiently recovered, a voyage to a more genial climate was proposed, and Italy selected as the future place of their abode. Patch, who had twice visited that classic

land on secret missions for his master Wolsey, became their guide, and a few weeks saw them quietly settled on the banks of the golden Arno, waiting, but not impatiently, for the hour when the death of Henry would restore them to their native land.

It would be trenching too much on the province of the historian to trace the progress of the blood-stained king, step by step, in his career of crime; still a slight synopsis may not be uninteresting to our readers.

As we before stated, the same week witnessed the execution of Anne Boleyn and the marriage of Jane Seymour, which was doomed, although in a different manner, to prove as unfortunate as the preceding ones. Indeed, there seems to have been a fatality about all of Henry's wives, as if at each succeeding union the angry spirits of his outraged queens flitted by the altar and pronounced a curse.

On the eighth of June, not a month after the death of Anne, a new parliament was summoned. The chancellor, Lord Audley, in addressing the house, stated that the king had two reasons for commanding their attendance: first, to settle an heir to the crown, in case he died without children lawfully begotten; secondly, to repeal the act by which the succession was settled on the issue of his late marriage. The compliant tools—for under Henry the houses of legislature were little more—passed without the least opposition the acts he required. Both the divorces were confirmed, and Elizabeth declared a bastard, as her sister Mary previously had been. Nay, the parliament even went so far as to give the king, in the event of failure of legitimate issue, full power to appoint a successor, either by letters patent or by will—a servility which proves how little understood were the true principles of constitutional government in those days; the form, however, shadowed forth the substance.

The act, which proves the extraordinary power that Henry possessed over his parliaments, was the means of pacifying the mind of the emperor, since it was not impossible that under it his niece, Mary, might still succeed to the crown by an act of her father's will; and it probably induced that princess to conform more readily to his pleasure than hitherto she had done, since about this time she consented to sign an acknowledgment of the illegitimacy of her mother's marriage.

Her sister, too, who was now placed upon a level with herself, was no longer an object of envy; indeed, a certain degree of affection seems to have been displayed, if not actually felt, by Mary towards the infant daughter of Anne Boleyn, whom she called in one of her letters a "toward darling."

Elizabeth appears in her infancy to have been possessed of many engaging qualities, which procured her friends even amongst the interested panders upon royalty; whilst the new queen treated her with kindness and affection. Educated under the charge of Lady Margaret Brian, the future queen remained at Hudson, where she had been removed previous to the execution of her mother. Upon that event, a difficulty arose with regard to the management of the household regulations of the young princess, and to the state which it was suitable to keep about her. In a letter to Cromwell from Lady Brian, she alludes to the alteration in the degree of her young charge, of which she states he was informed only by report, and complains that *no mourning had been provided for Elizabeth on her mother's account*—a neglect which proves that Henry was as coarsely-minded as he was heartless. The death of Anne was not the only sacrifice to the tyrant's jealousy during the year; for Lord Thomas Howard, brother to the Duke of Norfolk, for having married the Lady Margaret Douglas, daughter of the Queen of Scotland, and niece to Henry, was committed to the Tower, where he died—poisoned, some say—others, of a broken heart. The Lady Margaret afterwards became the mother of the celebrated Darnley, husband of Mary, Queen of Scots.

Whilst cares and vicissitudes disturbed the domestic concerns of Henry, the reformation advanced with rapid strides throughout the kingdom. Cromwell, who had obtained an ascendancy over the mind of his master scarcely inferior to that which Wolsey once possessed, proved a powerful supporter of the new doctrines. The regal supremacy having already been acknowledged by the bishops, who were seconded by the king, although some opposition had been offered by the people, Henry at once determined to exercise that authority with which his submissive parliaments had invested him. For this purpose he appointed Cromwell his vicegerent, or vicar-general, an office little inferior in honour and power to that which Wolsey, as legate, had formerly exercised. In this capacity his representative was invested with entire authority in religious affairs, and he was entitled not only to correct and visit all abuses, but to superintend the conduct of bishops and archbishops, of whom he took precedence in convocation.

The important charge was placed in energetic but not in careful hands. In the suppression of the monasteries, the only object of the vicegerent and his commissioners seems to have been the plunder of the establish-

FATHER XAVIER IN HIS CELL.

ments. They visited the churches, abatial houses, the cloisters; the monuments precious to art, the pages in which were writ the chronicles of the Saxon, Norman, and mediæval ages, were ruthlessly destroyed. This Vandalism has and ever must remain a reproach to the memory of Cromwell. Abuses might have been corrected, false miracles exposed, without perverting the charitable intentions of the founders of these establishments, by giving the wealth destined for the poor, education, and religion, to a rapacious set of courtiers, who, like a pack of hungry curs in full cry, yelled after the spoil. The reformation created, by the wealth it gave, the most powerful aristocracy in Europe; but then, by way of drawback, it necessitated the poor laws for the starving and unfortunate, formerly entertained at the convents and religious houses. On more than one occasion they were rendered so desperate by the misery which the change occasioned, that they broke into open rebellion.

There is little doubt but that great abuses had crept into the religious orders, and that the ease and luxury enjoyed in the great convents was frequently a stronger inducement to a monastic life than religious motives. The repasts of the monks were generally prepared with a lavish hand, and resembled a modern banquet much more than the meals of humble and self-denying devotees. At the monastery of St. Alban's fifty-three farms, every one of which was estimated at forty-six shillings per annum, were devoted to the kitchen. Provisions were brought from London, and nine carriers appointed to convey them to the abbey, which also possessed a house in Yarmouth for the purpose of storing up salt fish for Lent. The dinner was served upon plate, which was carried up an ascent of fifteen steps to the abbot's table —the monks, it is true, enduring a tantalising penance of making a pause and singing a hymn at every fifth step. At Canterbury and Peterborough the priors had usually repasts consisting of sixteen dishes; various kinds of strong liquors were used; and claret, piment, and mead, regaled the jovial churchmen.

But in none of these establishments did greater luxury and enjoyment prevail than in the great monastery of Furness, in Lancashire, where the monks were of the order of St. Savigny, under the rule of St. Benedict. They lived like nobles round the court of their abbot, who was a prince in his territory —a ness or nese of land, as the Saxons termed it, which nature had singularly protected on the north and south by dangerous quicksands, on the west by St. George's Channel, and on the east by the fells of Furness, which, until the thirteenth century, were entirely covered with wood. No sheriffs were permitted to enter this privileged spot—no tolls were collected within these hallowed precincts; nor was any one permitted to molest the abbot or any of his tenants under a penalty of ten pounds. Secured from all interference, and emancipated from the censure and inspection of the public eye, the monks of Furness had every means of indolence and ease. Their forests abounded with the buck, the doe, the wild boar—once common in England—and the legh, or large deer; the convent was also supplied with wheat from its own fields, which were celebrated for their produce; and the abbot was enabled to purchase such luxuries as the domains did not produce, by the large revenue arising from the iron mines in the county of which he had the sole direction and profit. Besides the possession of a breed of hawks, these princely churchmen had free chase through Furness; and that border territory as frequently rang with the echoes of the abbot's hounds as with those of the lay nobles. Besides this privilege, the abbey possessed large paddocks, and an enclosure called the "deer-park," which may still be traced near to the ruins of the monastery. The building, situated in a deep, narrow vale, of which it occupied the entire breadth, was surrounded by a stone wall, which enclosed the abbey mills, its stews for receiving fish, its kilns and ovens; while the luxurious vale, stretching down towards the south, was watered by rivulets, which spread beauty and fertility around.

Although nothing more serious could be proved against the monks than their luxury, the abbot was terrified into the surrender of his lands to the king. Most of them were annexed to the crown. Charles II. afterwards bestowed them upon the Duke of Albemarle, through whom they finally reverted to the duchesses of Montague and Manchester, coheiresses of the Duke of Montague.

It is not the reformation which we feel disposed to quarrel with; but the use which was made of the wealth wrung from the indolent but charitable priests, to be bestowed upon the rapacious, exacting nobles. Many of the monasteries were so well governed, and the lives of their inmates proved to be so blameless, that even the infamous commissioners, Layton and Dr. Lee, were compelled to give unwilling testimony in their favour. At Westrope, the abbot is described as a right honest man, having about him only religious persons. The nunnery of Catesby, in Northamptonshire, was proved to be in excellent order and rule, as was the priory of Great Malvern, in Worcestershire, the superior of which, says Latimer in a letter to Cromwell, "is old, feedeth many, and that daily." As may naturally be supposed, the breaking up of so many establishments caused much confusion as well as distress. At court it was a scramble for the plunder—in the cities, weeping and distress. Lord Audley obtained Christ Church, in Aldgate, whose prior was always an alderman of London, and rode in the city processions as such; but when he offered the magnificent church to any person who chose to be at the expense of demolishing it, and clearing away the stone, not an inhabitant could be found to join in the act, and he was obliged to employ workmen at an expense, when he demolished the steeple and priory, which far exceeded the value of the materials.

We have dwelt a little too long, perhaps, upon the theme; but it was impossible, in a work pretending to an historical character, to pass over so important a subject as the progress of the reformation; and the picture of the life, government, and manners of so celebrated a monastery as Furness can scarcely prove unacceptable—it shows what such establishments were,

"When rosy monks and mitred priests
Ruled o'er the ferti e vale."

This severe measure against the church caused a serious rebellion in the northern counties, where the Pilgrims of Grace, under the leadership of one Robert Aske, took possession of Pomfret, York, and Hull, obliging the Archbishop of York and Lord Dacey, who commanded the castle in the former place, to surrender that fortress and take the oath to the association. If at this time a competent leader had appeared, Henry's reign, and the progress of the reformation, would have terminated together. The terms on which the rebels finally laid down their arms were somewhat exorbitant. They required that a parliament should be held in the north, and a court of justice established; that no person north of the Trent might be forced to attend the courts at Westminster; that the Princess Mary should be declared legitimate, the pope restored to his authority, the monks to their houses; that Cromwell and Audley should not be allowed to sit in the next parliament; and that the commissioners, Layton and Lee, should be imprisoned for bribery and extortion.

These articles induced Henry to keep his army still in the field, and circumstances proved that the provision was a wise one, for a second insurrection broke out the February after, in which eight thousand insurgents were driven from Carlisle by the Duke of Norfolk, who, after their defeat, executed seventy-four of their leaders. Thus we see that the reformation was not universally received by Englishmen as a boon.

The day, or rather the morning, for it had but just struck one, which was to make Henry VIII. the father of a son, at last arrived. The queen was in labour; and Cranmer, together with the chief officers of state, were summoned, according to ancient usage, to be present at the birth. The king, who impatiently expected the event, was pacing, with hasty strides, the floor of the royal closet at Hampton Court. The Duke of Norfolk, Sir John Russell, the founder of the Bedford family, and the Marquis of Exeter, were with him.

"An Jane brings me a boy, my lords," exclaimed the anxious monarch, at the same time rubbing his hands in pleasing anticipation, "we will have a christening shall make the roof of Hampton ring again. What day will this be?"

"The vigil of St. Edward," replied the duke.

"If I am to have a son, I would not wish him born upon a better day, or to bear a nobler name. What was the last report?"

"That her majesty was still in labour," said the marquis.

"Would she were quick about it!" observed the king, yawning, for he had been up all night, and, like most stout persons, suffered if deprived of his usual rest.

At this moment a low knock was heard at the door of the royal closet.

"Come in," said Henry, sharply, for he was naturally excited between fear and hope.

The queen's physician entered. Sir Anthony Browne was with him. There was a serious expression upon the countenance of both of them which augured evil news.

"What mean these hang-dog looks?" demanded the king in a harsh grating voice. "Umph!" he added, "I can read them; another girl, I suppose. Was ever father doomed to be cursed as I am?"

"Not so," replied the physician; "but——"

"But what? speak out!"

The man of science, as well as his companion, glanced towards the persons who were with the king, in a manner which seemed to say that it would be impossible to explain themselves in their presence. Henry understood the hint, and motioned them to withdraw. As soon as they were alone, he drew the bolt upon the door, and hastily approaching the physician, laid his hand upon his arm, and gazing upon him with a peculiar expression of countenance, whispered—

"I understand you; the difficulty you anticipated has arrived?"

"It has."

"And the child?" he demanded, with an agitation which rendered him almost breathless.

"Is a boy," gasped the physician, turning as pale as a maiden's shroud as he pronounced the words.

Henry paced the chamber for a few minutes; more than once he essayed to speak, but the words trembled upon his cruel lips, and a cold perspiration trickled down his already furrowed forehead; his mind was at last made up.

"It is impossible, you say, that her majesty should prove the living mother of a *living child?*"

"In the present instance, sire, impossible."

"When you return, let it be to announce the birth of the Prince of Wales."

Whatever he might have felt, the cold tyrant pronounced the order in a voice as clear and free as though the mother had never been the object of his love. An hour after, it was announced to him that his dearest wish was at last gratified—that he was the father of a boy, but that the queen was dying.

It is singular that the precise day of the death of Jane Seymour should have been so variously stated. Herbert fixes it on two days after the birth of her son; Burnet on the day after. The ceremonial of her funeral in the Heralds' Office affirms that she died twelve days after the prince was born. It appears from the register of the "Garter," page 410, that the queen was in childbed two days, and suffered exceedingly. It is certain, however, that she lived long enough to receive extreme unction, and hear that the young prince had undergone the rite of baptism; for on the day of his entrance into the world, in which he was destined to act so conspicuous, although so brief a part, the infant was solemnly constituted a member of that church which at this period it is impossible to know whether to designate as Catholic or Protestant. The baptismal service was performed in the chapel of Hampton Palace, Cranmer and the Duke of Norfolk acting as godfathers, and the princess, or Lady Mary, as she was now called, standing as godmother. The font, which was of silver, was guarded by Sir John Russell, Sir Francis Brian, Sir Nicholas Carewe, and Sir Anthony Browne, in aprons, and with towels about their shoulders. The Earl of Wiltshire, *father of the late queen,* bore the taper of virgin wax. Then came the Princess Elizabeth, holding the chrism, and supported, on account of her tender age, in the arms of Lords Morly and Beauchamp. The Marchioness of Exeter, assisted by her husband and the Duke of Suffolk, carried the child.

As soon as the ceremony was performed, and the usual gifts offered at the font, the unconscious infant was borne in state to the apartment of the dying queen, to receive her last blessing ere she expired.

Unlike Anne Boleyn, who had been carelessly buried to an obscure grave, the body of Jane Seymour was conveyed with great solemnity to Windsor, and there buried in the middle of the choir of the castle church. At St. Paul's, and at every parish church in London, masses were said, and dirges sung, after the manner of the Catholic ritual. The king kept his Christmas at Greenwich, in his mourning apparel, which neither he nor the court changed till after Candlemas Day.

The birth of a male heir to the throne was an event deeply interesting both to prince and people. The estimation in which the former was held by foreign courts was greatly enhanced by the security which this event gave to the continuance of his line; and the latter rejoiced that the evil of a disputed succession was avoided: for there is little doubt but, had Henry died before the birth of a son, the utmost perplexity with regard to the crown must have been the consequence of his inconsistent proceed-

ings. To him, therefore, the birth of Edward was an event of such vast importance that it justified, in his selfish nature, the death of his amiable queen, Jane Seymour.

Henry's fourth marriage was with Anne of Cleves, to whose person he took a disgust on the very first interview. On the 11th of December, 1539, she was received at Calais by the Earl of Southampton, lord high admiral of England, and several members of the royal household. The Flemish beauty at last reached the shores of England, and was met by the Duke and Duchess of Suffolk. The primate conducted her to Rochester, where the Duke of Norfolk, together with the barons of the exchequer, and a great train of nobility and knights, were waiting to receive her. Henry, who was at Greenwich, could no longer restrain his curiosity; he left the palace without pomp. The first interview with his bride must have been highly diverting to those who had no anticipation of the serious consequences which resulted to his minister Cromwell from the disappointment. Sir Anthony Browne, the husband of the Lady Elizabeth Fitzgerald, Surrey's "Geraldine," describes the king as overwhelmed at the sight of the unwieldy consort they had chosen him. In the retirement of his chamber he gave vent to bitter disappointment, declaring that they had haltered him to a Flemish mare, and not a Christian princess.

From that hour the fate of Cromwell, who had concluded the marriage, was sealed.

He overcame his repugnance, according to the above quoted authority, sufficiently on the following morning to send her, according to ancient custom, a marriage gift, which consisted of a partlet furred with sables, and richly garnished with sable skins; a muffley furred, and a cap. The bearer was Sir Anthony Browne, and the message was as cold and civil as possible.

The disgust of the king increasing, he determined to break his marriage at all hazards; and as he could not decently behead the queen, he thought fit to divorce her. A parliament was summoned, Cromwell arrested, and committed to the Tower, upon a charge of high treason, on which he was afterwards beheaded, and the dissolution of the union pronounced by the obsequious legislature, upon the ground that the king's *internal consent* had been wanting. To do the fickle monarch justice, however, he behaved liberally upon the occasion; sufficient revenues were assigned for the honourable maintenance of the princess, who received by letters patent the title of Henry's adopted sister ; a poor compensation for the loss of a crown.

Catherine Howard, the beautiful, the frail, the culpable Catherine Howard, niece to the Duke of Norfolk, was next elevated to the blood-stained throne. The lady, as cousin-german to Anne Boleyn, was within the degrees of affinity to the king forbidden by the canon law; it was therefore found necessary to frame a bill, in which it was specified that no pretence of pre-contract or degree of affinity, except those mentioned in the laws of God, should be made use of to annul a marriage. This act involved the proceedings of the king in the greatest absurdity, since it condemned his proceedings both towards Katherine of Arragon and her successor. The only lasting result of this law was the precedent it gave for cousins-german to marry—a thing unheard of before, unless by dispensation from the pope.

The life of incontinence which the new-made queen had led, both before and after her marriage, coming to the knowledge of Cranmer, he revealed it to the king; her paramours were arrested, and she herself, together with her confidant, the infamous Lady Rochfort, committed to close ward at Sion House, where, however, she continued to be served with all the dignity of a queen. They were both executed on the 20th of February, on Tower Hill.

Henry's last marriage was with Catherine Parr, who survived him.

Influenced most probably by the disgust which the conduct of Catherine Howard had excited, the king conceived a hatred towards the family, and gave private orders for the arrest of the Duke of Norfolk and his son, the gallant, incomparable Surrey, who was condemned for having quartered the arms of Edward the Confessor in his shield. What availed his eloquent defence, his high renown, his poetic genius, and his knightly services? An obsequious jury found him guilty, and he was immediately executed.

About this period the primate lost his most powerful friend, Charles Brandon, Duke of Suffolk, whose wife, the queen dowager of France, had long since disappeared from the scene of life. Henry, who was sitting in council when the intelligence was brought him, declared that, during the whole course of their friendship, his brother-in-law had never once whispered a word to the disparagement of any person, and added, looking round the circle of abashed nobles, " Which of you can say as much?"

All were silent, and the king quitted them with a strong expression of contempt.

Cranmer, deprived of this support, became the more exposed to the cabals of the court, who, with the chancellor at their head, endeavoured to undermine his favour with the king, who, seeing the point at which they aimed, feigned compliance, and desired them to make inquiry into the prelate's conduct. Even his best friends looked upon Cranmer as lost. He was obliged to stand several hours at the door of the council chamber in the manner so graphically described by Shakspeare, before he was called in; and when at last admitted, his enemies told him they had decided on his committal to the Tower. The primate appealed to the king, and, finding his remonstrance disregarded, to the terror and confusion of the council, produced the royal signet, by virtue of which he removed his cause from their unjust decision. The members, who were compelled to convey the token to their master, were severely reproved by him for their perfidy and jealousy.

But if Henry shielded his friends, he proved relentless to all beside. Anne Ascue, a young and beautiful creature, who had great interest with the ladies of the court, and who was an especial favourite with Catherine Parr, was committed to th- Tower. The morning before her examination upon a charge of denial of the king's supremacy and heresy, Lord Seymour, the maternal uncle of the Prince of Wales, who had long been calculating the approaching death of the monarch, paid a visit to that regal den of infamy and cruelty. He had learned from Gardner that the queen had incautiously given the enthusiast a ring—a gift from her crpricious husband. His object was to possess himself of it, and by that means obtain an influence over the fate of his sister-in-law useful for his future purposes. Sir William Kingston, who was his friend, assisted him in the object of his pursuit; for, like his wife, the governor of the Tower was attached to the reformed religion, whose perfect development the still Catholic dogmas of Henry were opposed to.

The prisoner, a fair, delicate-looking girl in the first blush of womanhood, entered the chamber where the intriguing noble awaited her. There was an air of patient courage in her pale countenance which martyrs might have envied, and her blue eyes were lit with the pure light of faith. Modestly she inclined her head before the chair where Seymour had thrown himself, awaiting his commands.

" This is a sorry place," he observed, " for one so young and fair."

" It is the place," replied the maid, " to

which Heaven hath called me. A palace or a grave, while I perform my Master's service, are to me alike."

"Know you," continued the courtier, "the fearful nature of the charge against you? that it affects your life?"

"My life is in His hands who holds the breath of kings; if it be His will that I bear witness to His truth, His servant will be ready."

"You court death, then?"

"No; but I do not fear it."

"Hast thou been questioned," demanded Seymour, in a whisper, "touching thy knowledge of the queen?"

Anne Ascue remained silent.

"Thou art a courageous girl," he continued, "worthy of Catherine's confidence."

Still no answer.

"Hear me," said the speaker, who saw that he must obtain her confidence, "for every moment is fraught with danger to her whom in these walls I dare not name. Two of her predecessors have left their names written in blood upon their fatal threshold: it depends on thee whether a third be added to the list."

"On me!" repeated the prisoner with surprise.

"Ay. It is known she we speak of gave thee a token of her favour—a ballas ruby; and unless the fatal gift be produced to-morrow, when Henry shall demand it, the executioner of Calais will have another journey and another victim."

"Supposing," said Anne, "that what you assert were true, how could a simple gift affect her?"

"How?" repeated the ambitious Seymour; "men call thee wise as fair! Ask thy own heart whom in his anger or his lust did Henry ever spare? His favourite Wolsey, his consort Katherine, the joyous Boleyn, or my gentle sister, sacrificed—brutally sacrificed—to his ambition or caprice; but perhaps," he added, "thou wilt find a joy on falling not alone."

The prisoner, without deigning a word in reply to the accusation, advanced nearer to the seat, and fixed her penetrating glance upon him.

"Art thou," she demanded, "the brother of the pious queen, Jane Seymour?"

"Dost doubt it?"

"No, no," she muttered to herself, after a pause; "thou hast spoken truth; and yet I fear me for no godly purpose, for I can read ambition in thine eye, pride in thy heart. Strange," she added, "that two such natures should be so near akin!"

Seymour had heard of the peculiar powers of reading the thoughts of all who came in contact with her, as well as the supposed gift of prophecy which, according to popular belief, the prisoner possessed, and he asked her smilingly if she still hesitated to trust him.

Anne fell upon her knees, and remained for a few minutes absorbed in prayer. So fervent were her devotions, that while they lasted she seemed insensible to all around. Her visitor became at last impatient.

"Thou hast sought a pledge," she answered, "and it shall not be denied thee, since I feel assured that it will work the safety of the royal hand which gave it; but woe! woe!" she added, "to the messenger!"

"What mean you?"

"If," continued the maid, "thou dost, without one second purpose, one unworthy dream of future profit, seek to restore the token to my mistress, take it freely."

Seymour extended his eager hand.

"But if," added the speaker, "one earthly thought, one base desire, doth linger in thy heart, it leads thee to the scaffold."

The courtier smiled at the prediction, for he was no believer in her supposed gift of prophecy, although in the present instance it was singularly fulfilled; for the return of the fatal pledge so wrought upon the gratitude of the soon-widowed queen that she bestowed on him her hand almost immediately after her husband's death; the ambitious hopes nourished by which alliance ultimately led him to the block. He thought of Anne Ascue as he mounted the fatal steps.

"Take it," said Anne, drawing the sparkling jewel from her bosom, and placing it in his extended hand; "thou hast received thy warning—and thy doom."

"Doubt not my fidelity."

"I doubt it not," said the enthusiast, "for it is thy interest. Farewell," she added; "on earth my task and sufferings will soon be over; thine," she continued, with a cold smile, "are yet to come."

Catherine Parr, in her zeal for the reformation, frequently ventured to converse, and even to dispute, with Henry upon points of faith. At such times, her natural talents and strong sense would often embarrass and irritate the fretful temper of her capricious husband, who had on several occasions complained to the Chancellor Wriothesley and Gardner, both of whom were her mortal enemies. These so inflamed his anger and his pride, by representing how glorious it would be to show to the world that no rank or station was independent of the law, that Henry consented to articles of impeachment being drawn up against her, the circumstance which finally decided him being the assurance which the chancellor gave that his queen was one of the secret supporters of Anne Ascue, and had even given her a ruby ring in token of her favour.

"If this be true, my lord, she dies," muttered the incensed monarch between his teeth, "were she ten times closer knit to our weak heart."

"It is easily ascertained," observed the crafty Gardner, who knew the danger of delay; "send for her majesty; question her. If she produce the ring——"

"Not to-night," interrupted the king, "not to-night; I am weary, and my tired spirit needs repose. You will find me in the palace garden, my good lords, to-morrow. Let a party of the guard attend. I should like to see the terror in her face," he added, with a malignant smile, "when ordered to the Tower."

The procrastination of Henry saved the life of Catherine Parr.

The following morning the heroic Anne Ascue was placed upon the rack—yes, in that age miscalled the age of chivalry, monsters could be found to consign a woman, a fair young creature, to torments which demons only could behold without a shudder, and yet her murderers were born of women, and had sisters! mothers! Wriothesley demanded twice of the virgin the nature of her relations with the queen, and what she had done with the costly token of her favour. The sufferer was silent.

"Stretch the rack!" he exclaimed to the governor of the Tower; "we will wring an answer from her yet."

Sir William Kingston, to the honour of his memory and his manhood, positively refused.

The infuriated chancellor placed his own hand upon the wheel, and turned it till the delicate limbs of the sufferer were nearly torn asunder. Even the executioner turned aside, disgusted at the sight. The maiden's constancy was still unmoved.

Baffled in their attempts, the still palpitating victim was removed from her bed of torture, and condemned by the pitiless Wriothesley to be burnt alive—a sentence which was afterwards executed in all its barbarity, the noble-hearted girl, whose courage had preserved her friend, being carried in a chair to the stake.

The above is no exaggerated picture; on the contrary, but a faint sketch of what the martyred Anne endured; for she was a martyr alike to honour, conscience, friendship, and her God; and yet posterity, which has erected a stately monument to the time-serving Cranmer, who never once lifted his priestly voice against such barbarity, has not inscribed the maiden's name upon a simple stone. Such is the vaunted justice of time!

On the afternoon of the same day Henry and his queen were seated in the gardens of the palace, for the ulcers in the monarch's legs debarred him from all but the simplest exercise. The countenance of Catherine was placid, as usual, and yet her heart beat terribly, for she had been forewarned of her danger, but was partially armed against it.

"And so, Kate," said her husband, with a malicious leer, "thou art grown a theologian—a very doctor in dispute. We must be cautious how we encounter thee."

"You jest, my lord," replied the queen, secretly rejoiced at the favourable opportunity. "Women are unfit for argument, unless," she added, "in the hour of sickness to beguile their husbands of its tediousness, and make them smile, as I have done your highness."

"Umph!—say'st thou?" demanded the king, suspiciously.

"Man," answered Catherine, "is the stronger vessel, moulded in God's own image;—woman's was ta'en from man's: so should she draw her judgments from his wisdom, as he draws his from a still higher source."

The bloated countenance of the tyrant relaxed almost to a smile.

"Your grace, I see," she added, "is laughing at my want of skill; but if I failed to amuse your mind by my weak arguments, the attempt was not without its use."

"How so?"

"In the rich lessons it elicited."

Henry, who, like most sensualists, was susceptible to flattery, would have been perfectly convinced by the unembarrassed ease of the speaker's manner, had not the doubt respecting the ring still rankled in his mind.

"May be, Kate," he replied—"may be."

"Nay, it is, your grace," she unhesitatingly replied.

"Where is the ring?" he suddenly demanded, "which I gave thee on thy birthday?"

"Which, my lord?" demanded Catherine, with coolness.

"The ruby, wench—the ruby."

With an air of well acted astonishment, Catherine ungloved her hand, and drew the ring from her finger—Seymour that very morning had returned it to her.

"Gad's death!" exclaimed Henry, furiously; for he imagined that both the chancellor and Gardner had deceived him; "have we been trifled with—duped by a prating priest and lying courtier? There is work for the headsman here."

"Your majesty!" said the terrified queen

"We are chafed, Kate—but not with thee, wench—not with thee."

At this moment Wriothesley, attended by a party of the guard, ready to arrest the queen, entered the garden. Henry, despite his infirmity, hastened to meet him, for he felt a touch of shame at the idea of Catherine knowing how nearly he had been led into giving his consent for her destruction.

"Beast!" he roared, as soon as he reached the astonished functionary. "Fool! without wit or sense; one word of thy knave's errand here, and thy resting-place shall be the Tower!"

"Sire!" faltered the chancellor.

"Another moment, and, by St. George, I'll hang thee, like a cur, from the highest tower of my palace. Brave not my wrath. Be wise, and quit my sight directly."

In an instant the garden was cleared, and the still indignant monarch returned to where he had left the apparently astonished, but secretly delighted, Catherine.

"Be not angry, my dear lord," she ventured timidly to exclaim; "I'm afraid it wears your health too much."

"The idiot!" growled Henry.

"Perhaps he has sinned in ignorance," she observed, "for I have ever thought that he was honest. Let me plead for him."

"Kate," said the king, in a voice which was softened by an unusual expression of kindness, "thou art too good to suspect worthlessness in others. He does not deserve much mercy at thy hands. Speak of him no more."

It must be admitted that the queen managed her husband cleverly on this occasion; but then *she was a widow when he married her.*

CHAPTER XXIII.

"Henry of haughty mind and sturdy mien,
With fury reigned, and often changed his queen;
Disowned the Pope, yet kept us Papists still,
And burned both sides which dared contest his will."

THE death of Anne Ascue, and of other distinguished sufferers, during the reign of Henry, inspires the mind with sympathy; but, perhaps, the most lamentable, if not the most affecting, instance of his injustice is still to be related. During the small portion of his remaining life, the Seymours, with the Earl of Hertford at their head, acquired a complete influence over the king; and thus suddenly raised to power, of which they ultimately proved themselves both incapable and unworthy, they endeavoured to secure their greatness more firmly by the death of others. It is melancholy to view the consequences of faction on the reign of those princes whose passions have rendered them the prey of designing men. The brothers of Jane Seymour were supposed to be warmly attached to the Protestant faith, whose establishment had so enriched them. Between them and the Howards the most inveterate jealousy existed. This fatal passion proved the ruin of the noblest scion of the worthless stem of the house of Norfolk, a house which, in its long existence, like the aloe, has produced but one glorious flower.

Henry, Earl of Surrey, son of the Duke of Norfolk, had set the bright example, not of deriving his lustre merely from the splendour of his descent, but of adding to it from his personal merit. One of the most chivalrous of warriors, and esteemed of the poets of his day, the virtues and accomplishments of this gallant nobleman gave more glory to his race than all the honours which flattery or apostacy have since secured them. In one respect only Surrey was deficient—he wanted prudence to give security to his pre-eminence in rank, in fortune, and in genius. Jealous of honour, and fearless of personal danger, he could neither brook the slightest appearance of insult, nor the shadow of reproach upon his military reputation. During the last war in France, he had distinguished himself in various reckless enterprises, and at the close of the campaign had received the important office of governor of Boulogne, where he sought incessantly to add to the renown of the English chivalry by sallies and skirmishes with the French, and even by personally engaging with the enemy, to which he also

incited his followers in imitation of the days of old,

"When Christian chiefs, by good Godfredo led,
Planted the holy cross in Palestine."

After an imprudent but glorious adventure, in which many knights and officers were slain, Surrey was recalled, and Lord Hertford appointed captain-general over the English pale in France, whilst Lord Gray, his bitterest enemy, succeeded him in his command of governor of Boulogne.

The warrior-poet was not of a temper to bear this unjust and insulting measure with patience. Like the rest of his family, he re-

garded the Seymours as upstarts, and attributed his disgrace to their influence. His expressions of indignation were uttered in that unguarded and forcible manner which showed a soul incapable of treachery, by proving that he was above fearing it.

Unhappily, some secret foe conveyed this transport of indignation to Hertford and the king, and the noblest ornament of the court was committed to the Tower.

Hertford naturally dreaded the power of the Howards, should they ever be restored to favour; and the Duke of Norfolk, politic and experienced in courts, feared the ascendancy of the Seymour interest; he even sought to avert the impending storm by an alliance between that family and his own. His daughter, the Duchess of Richmond, was solicited to marry Sir Thomas Seymour, brother to the earl; but that lady, although beautiful in person, was a fiend in mind, hating her father and her illustrious brother. She refused, *because the union would have saved them.* It has also been stated by historians that Surrey, on his part, rejected the daughter of the earl; but this is disproved by the fact that his wife was at this time living in the bonds of affection with him. The duke, who had long been separated from his duchess, lived with a Mrs. Holland, a lady of an ancient Norfolk family; and on the trial of that unhappy, but worthless man, both his wife, daughter, and mistress appeared against him.

That the outraged wife should have forgotten the vow pronounced at the altar—the mistress the man who had sacrificed so much for her—might not have surprised the judges of the father; but what experience, what calculation of human depravity could have taught them to behold with patience, a *sister,* young, beautiful, and accomplished, appearing at the bar of justice *an unsought witness to criminate her brother?* The chief point of her evidence, and that which most influenced the judges of the noble Surrey in their condemnation, was, that he had borne on his arms what *seemed* to her judgment a kingly crown, together with a cypher, which she *took* to be H. R. Oh, woman! woman!

"Angels when good—devils when virtue leaves ye."

The defence of Surrey was worthy of his high fame as a soldier and a man. In his replies to the allegations of the witnesses, he showed that his acuteness and wit were equal to that fine imagination which had made him the ornament of the age. In his indignation at the perjury of his accusers, he evinced the spirit of a knight who held his honour dearer than his life. But this display of a great and upright mind availed not; the base jury found him guilty; and Wriothesley, to his eternal disgrace, pronounced sentence of death upon the gallant Howard—the model of chivalry, the mirror of true love—whose genius alone would have rescued the age in which he lived from oblivion or contempt. He was remanded to the Tower, where, about a week after his trial, he was privately beheaded.

The closing scene of the life of this celebrated man is enveloped in oblivion, and we are denied the gratification of beholding one of the noblest pictures which human nature has ever presented to the contemplation of mankind—the death of the poet, warrior, and Christian. The execution was carefully concealed from public view, the contrivers of the iniquitous transaction well knowing how the opinions of the populace would be expressed on the occasion.

With the lover of Geraldine expired the chivalry of England. The last *preux chevalier,* and one of the sweetest of her poets, died upon the scaffold, with the bitter feeling upon his gallant mind that a traitor sent him there.

Henry VIII. had a peculiar taste for extinguishing the glories of his reign. But Providence at last seemed tired of the iniquity of the crime-stained tyrant in shedding the blood of the poet Surrey, the mirror of chivalry and knightly virtue. The cup of his infamy was filled, and the forbearance of Heaven exhausted. Yet even in this world the monster endured a portion of the punishment reserved for cruelty and vice. His obesity became extreme; he was incapable of moving without assistance, and frightful ulcers broke out upon his limbs, eating to his very flesh; in this state he became so furious that all trembled to approach him. The queen, with her own hands—for, according to the fashion of the times, she was skilled in surgery—dressed his wounds, and endeavoured by the most devoted attentions to beguile him of his pains. We have already seen how narrowly she escaped death as her reward. All saw his end approaching, but no one durst inform him of his condition, for several persons had suffered death merely for predicting such an event, and each one was afraid lest in the transport of his fury he might punish capitally the author of such unwelcome intelligence.

Cranmer, the queen, and members of the privy council, were assembled in the antechamber of the royal closet, on the morning which released England from its tyrant. They had been summoned to see the stamp affixed to the warrant for the execution of the Duke of Norfolk, lying under sentence in the Tower; for the sufferings of the English Nero had become so intense that he was no longer capable of affixing the sign manual to the instruments of his will, and an act had been passed declaring the affixing of such stamp or seal in the presence of the council, by order of the king, equivalent to the regal signature. But although thus specially summoned, all feared to enter the chamber where the monster slept; each felt that his dissolution would be the guarantee of his individual safety—each secretly prayed for it, expected it; yet such was the force of terror, that no one ventured to give utterance to his secret hope, but continued to speak of the dying king's recovery as a thing of course. Cran-

...ner, the primate, never showed his want of moral courage more than at the dissolution of his master.

Seated in a chair, in the royal closet, from which he was unable to move without assistance, Henry sat, awaiting, with fretful impatience, the arrival of his council. Although so near the grave, his thirst for blood remained undiminished. The dread that Norfolk, whom, since the fall of Catherine Howard, he hated, should escape him, was wormwood to his revengeful heart; added to which, in exciting the terrors of all who approached him by the brutal ferocity of his manner, he found the only solace to his sufferings; on the rack himself, it was a consolation to see others writhe in agony as well.

For three days and nights sleep had not visited his weary eyes, whose bloodshot, restless expression denoted the ill-suppressed rage and impatience which consumed him. His once comely form was bloated with excess, and his cheeks hung like bags of water on his neck, adding, by their wax-like, sickly hue, to the horror of his appearance. His voice, once so clear and manly, was now broken to a low hoarse growl, and interrupted, when he endeavoured to speak, by a cough which filled his mouth with foam and blood. Of all the royal attendants, Sir Anthony Denny was the only one who fearlessly approached him; he had served him faithfully for many years, and, despite his cruelties and vices, felt, from long habit, attached to his troubled master.

"Denny! ugh! Denny!" murmured the king.

"Sire!" whispered the attendant, who was in an instant at his side.

"Have the council yet arrived?"

"They wait your highness's pleasure."

"It seems I must wait them. Ugh! But we shall live to thank them for their duty, shall we not, Denny, eh?"

The faithful servant was silent.

"Shall we not live?" hoarsely roared Henry, impatient that his question had not been answered as he wished; for, like most dying men, the flattery of hope was dear to him.

"I trust so, sire."

"*We will live,*" continued the tyrant, furiously; "our will is stronger than our body; ulcers may eat our flesh, but they can't destroy that—they can't destroy that!"

"The soul, indeed, is immortal," observed Sir Anthony.

"Who spoke of soul?" demanded the king gloomily; "I spoke of will—the unconquerable mind's resolve can subdue agony; it may defeat death, or at least postpone the fatal blow. I am better, Denny, am I not?" he added, fixing at the same time a painfully inquiring glance upon the knight; "do I not look better?"

"In sooth, your majesty speaks with more cheerfulness than you have been wont of late."

"I have my answer," growled Henry; "when the human curs who fawn on kings avoid their questions, the answer must be fatal. Dog," he added, "couldst thou not have lied and cheated me with the charlatan's last consolation—hope? or dost thou think the lion's breath so nearly spent that flattery were thrown away?"

Here a violent fit of coughing interrupted the speaker's furious reproaches, at the end of which he sank back exhausted in his cushioned seat. The knight took a sponge steeped in aromatics from a golden cup, and bathed his face and temples.

"Ah, Denny!" sighed the king, who felt relieved by the attention, "heed not my impatience; Henry knows thy faithful service; but would it not chafe an angel's patience to lie like a crippled hound a prisoner here, living to feel the grave's corruption in my corroding flesh—to taste its sickening taint in every breath I draw—to know that I, the king, the master of fair England's soil, lord of the lives of crouching millions, must die—be borne, like common carrion, to the grave—the grave?"

"It is the lot of all, sire."

"Perchance men dream there," continued the sufferer; "that's the terror, to lie fettered in bonds of ice upon the narrow bier, whilst the racked brain is seared by burning visions, yet not possess the strength, e'en by a groan or yell, to ease the o'erfraught heart. God! it is terrible." Then, after a pause, he added, "No, no, thy justice never imagined punishment like that."

"Shall I inform the council that your highness waits?" demanded the knight, who feared from the sudden change which came over the countenance of his master that his end was not far distant.

"No—no! I have scarce strength to make known my will. My pains have suddenly grown easier. I feel as I could sleep. I shall recover, Denny. I am sure I shall recover," he continued, in a voice of exultation, "if I could only sleep."

As is usual when mortification has once taken place, the more violent agonies were calmed; and that which was the forerunner of immediate death the speaker took for symptoms of amelioration. Sir Anthony Denny carefully raised the cushions at the back of the royal patient's chair, and stood watchfully beside him, ready to execute his first command.

"Stay," said Henry, "I shall sleep the better when it is done. Dost see you parchment?"

His glance pointed to a deed lying on the table at a short distance from him; it was the death-warrant of his former favourite, the Duke of Norfolk.

"I do," replied the knight.

With difficulty the king drew from his bosom the golden stamp on which his name had been engraved, and which with jealous vigilance he kept on his person.

"Fix it," he muttered, in a low tone.

The attendant hesitated.

"Must I speak twice?" added Henry. "Dost thou forget that I am still a king—still thy master; and that there are chains and the block for traitors who dispute their sovereign's will?"

Sir Anthony applied the fatal signet, and returned it upon his knee to his master.

"Well, 'tis well," continued the speaker, with a horrible smile of satisfaction. "Take it to the council; bid them dispatch it to the Tower; the rest concerns Kingston and the executioner. That done, return, place thyself at my closet-door, and watch me while I sleep."

Henry's command was obeyed by the obsequious council, who were kept, like lacqueys, trembling at the door, whilst the modern Nero slept the sleep which preceded his dissolution.

Henry, in his sleep, experienced one of those remarkable dreams which puzzle philosophy to explain, and give the lie to the materialist. Time, for once, inverted his glass, his nearly exhausted sands ran back, and the Moloch king beheld his victims, like Banquo's vision, pass before him. First Wolsey—he of the eagle's pride and lofty flight, whose magnificence and love of art cast a veil over his weaknesses. With a cold glance the stately shade swept before the sleeper's sight, and pointed with his finger to an open grave. Death seemed to have purified him; he wore his purple gracefully, not proudly, and his expressive features had more of pity in them than of scorn.

Katherine, the lofty Katherine of Arragon, followed next, her crownless brow pale in the majesty of death. With a forgiving, melancholy smile, she seemed to gaze upon the father of her child, then melted, like the morning mist, into thin air.

Anne Boleyn, the fair, the false, the beautiful Anne Boleyn, succeeded her stately predecessor. The smile upon her ruby lip was of unearthly beauty, and her eyes, like sunbeams resting on twin gems, flashed with supernatural brightness. The sleeper's heart beat as wildly as when he first wooed and won his fickle prize from the embraces of her poet lover. In his dream once more he would have clasped her, when a hissing sound, like that of a falling axe, fell on his ear, and streams of blood gushed round and round him. Then commenced the long agony of Henry's dream, the foretaste of his punishment. The thunder-peal rolled heavily, and the forked lightning seemed to blind him with its sulphurous flashes. The heavens rained blood; the groaning earth heaved with thick bubbles of the clotted gore which it had drunk; till, as if a second deluge were unloosed, the tyrant floated in one crimson sea. Vainly he attempted in his slumber to escape. He seemed to know that he was dreaming, but at the same time felt that it was no natural dream. Conscience whispered that he saw his final doom. Madly he seemed to dash and splash through the billowy gore. The heads, the fresh bleeding heads of his victims met him at every turn —the venerable More, who died for conscience sake—the aged Fisher—the last of the female Plantagenets and her two sons—the gallant Surrey, and the guilty Catherine Howard. The trunkless heads glared on him with their death-fixed eyes, and the tyrant groaned and yelled in the agony of remorse and terror. Cold drops of perspiration fell from his throbbing temples, and trickled down his livid cheeks.

Sir Anthony Denny was alarmed at the noise; and deeming that it was the death struggle which choked the sleeper's utterance, rushed into the ante-chamber, where the council were still waiting to be summoned. His appearance startled the whispering nobles.

"Now!" exclaimed the primate, who was conversing with the queen.

"The king——"

"Go on," added the impatient Seymour, uncle to the young prince, who was present.

"Is in his last agony," added the knight.

The queen instantly retired to her apartment, and the council in a body proceeded to the chamber of the dying monarch.

The knight who preceded them threw open the folding doors at their approach, for he knew that in a few moments the sovereign power would pass from Henry's hand into those of his council, and, like most courtiers, he bent to the rising power.

The king was still struggling in his dream.

"God!" he murmured, "terrible are Thy judgments—not for ever—oh! not for ever!"

The groan of anguish which followed was so intense that it seemed to have been wrung from the agony of a despairing soul. All who heard it trembled, and Cranmer, although little given to superstition, turned pale.

"It was the last," observed the Earl of Southampton; "Henry VIII. is dust."

"God save King Edward the Sixth of England!" cried the council, with wonderful unanimity, and with voices which showed that they spoke like men released from an oppressive fear.

Their acclamations, however, had been premature. Henry was exhausted by the terrors he had undergone, not dead. A second groan, as fearful as the first, assured them of the important fact. Like most men who have committed themselves by an excessive zeal, they looked foolish and confused.

Cranmer approached the chair and placed his finger on the sufferer's wrist.

"It still beats," he observed in a whisper to Denny, who was near him.

The touch dissolved the hideous spell, or species of nightmare, under which Henry laboured. Opening his eyes, he stared wildly upon the intruders, and, still under the influence of his dream, muttered to himself—

"These too! why are they here? I have not ta'en the lives of these yet—not yet!"

A peculiar glance was exchanged between the councillors.

"Sire!"

"Cranmer," exclaimed the monarch, recognising him, "I am dying!"

The primate was silent; it was no moment for flattery; and yet he felt that it would be scarcely prudent to confirm the speaker's assertion.

"Art silent? Hast thou no prayer," faintly demanded the nearly exhausted prince, "to bribe the ear of Mercy?—no atoning work to wash my crimes away—to cheat hell of its victim?"

"Sire," said Cranmer, in a low voice, "give some sign that you die at last in the faith of Christ, our Redeemer!"

Henry pressed the hand of the prelate; but before he could reply, the last string gave way, and he sank back a corse!

The death-rattle had not ceased to be heard in his throat, when the cry of "God save King Edward!" was repeated more cheerfully even than before, for this time it was uttered by men who had been trembling a moment before for their lives, as Henry, had he survived, would never have forgiven their zeal, even in favour of his son.

Like all the Tudors, his natural thirst was for blood.

The body of the king, who had died at his palace at Westminster, was conveyed to Leadenhall, there to lie in state until the funeral. By his will Henry desired that his remains might be interred in the choir of the church at Windsor, between the stalls and the altar, and that the bones of Jane Seymour, already entombed within the chapel, might be interred under the same monument. Before the death of Wolsey, a splendid fabric had been begun for a mausoleum. Although erroneously stated by late historians as having been intended by the cardinal for his own tomb, the inscription upon it of "Henry, Lord of Ireland," proved, as Fuller judiciously remarked, that at first it must have been designed for the king. The monarch enjoined also that the sepulchre of Henry VI., whom he *facetiously* designated as his uncle, and that of Edward IV., his progenitor of the house of York, should be beautified and repaired. The *Protestant* prince, as the reformers delight to call him, commanded that *masses* should be sung for the good of his soul, and that four solemn obits should be kept yearly; at each obit ten pounds were to be distributed amongst thirteen poor knights of Windsor, of whom he was the first patron; and that twelvepence, a long gown of cloth, with a garter embroidered thereon, and a mantle of the same material, should be distributed to each knight.

With regard to the succession in case of Edward, Mary, or Elizabeth dying without issue, it was to devolve upon the descendants of Mary, Queen of France, who had married his favourite, the Duke of Suffolk; the children of Margaret, the Scottish queen, being unjustly omitted in this arrangement of Henry's.

It is remarkable that all the arrangements of Henry's will were passed over or annulled by uncontrollable events. The throne was ultimately occupied by the descendants of Margaret, whom he had excluded, and the tombs of Henry VI. and Edward IV. suffered to fall into decay, and the very monument of the king himself was never completed, his coffin, and that of Jane Seymour, being discovered by chance, when the vault underneath the choir was opened for the purpose of entombing Charles I. Mary, from horror of the dubious sentiment attributed to her father, and Elizabeth from penuriousness, left the half-finished work untouched, and the monument was finally taken down and sold in the civil wars, when many of the noblest works of art and antiquity were sacrificed to the levelling, rapacious hands of the infuriated soldiery. It is, however, not a little singular that not a single stone should mark the spot where rest the remains of a monarch whose actions and character are more familiar perhaps to the minds of

Englishmen than any other British king who either followed or preceded him.

The character of Henry VIII. has been so frequently and so fully described, that any elaborate description of his character would now appear like plagiarism. By contemporary writers the sum of his virtues and his vices was either aggravated or diminished as party views or religious opinions influenced them.

Henry, with all his vices, possessed a cultivated taste, and while under the influence of Wolsey did much for the advancement of literature and art. In his reign it has been observed that no dunce ever wore a mitre; and history proves the observation to be correct. His appreciation of men of letters and artists is undisputed. Skelton the poet educated him. Although a priest, he was a licentious writer, and something of a satirist. This would not have prevented his preferment in the church had he not offended Wolsey by his famous lines, "Why come ye not to Court," a poem which excited great sensation at the period, and so roused the indignation of the haughty cardinal, that the writer was obliged to fly from his resentment. He took sanctuary in Westminster, where the abbot Islip protected him until the year 1529, when he expired shortly before his renowned persecutor, and was buried in the churchyard at Westminster.

Wyat and Surrey at one period stood high in Henry's favour.

The Chronicles of Froissart, at his command, were first translated by Lord Berners in 1513, and Pinson printed them. The celebrated Leland, whose works are dear to every lover of the antiquities of England, was keeper of his libraries, and employed at Henry's expense upon his vast and interesting records. Borde, the earliest medical writer, flourished in his reign; nor must the names of Parker, Lord Morley, Thomas Vaux, Rochford, Bryan, and Sir Thomas Sternhold, who translated the Psalms in imitation of the French poet, Marot, be forgotten. More and Erasmus have been already named. It was at the house of the former that the king first became acquainted with the painter Holbein, and being delighted with the productions of his pencil, took him home and employed him for the rest of his reign. He was decidedly the first English monarch who seriously encouraged the art of painting. He had several artists in his pay besides Holbein, such as Quintin Matsys, Johannus Corvus, Gerard Luke, Anthony Joto, Jerome de Trevisi, Homeband, Bartti, and others. He also invited the immortal Rafaelle and Titian to shed the lustre of their genius upon his kingdom and

his reign. It was the misfortune of England that those glorious men declined to comply with his request, supposing, it is said, that amongst a people where portrait painting was so much encouraged, their peculiar talents would not be called forth into play, yet it was the frequent practice of the king to cause his battles and other memorable events to be commemorated by the pencil of the painter as well as in the page of the chronicler.

There is no doubt but that the reformation checked, for a time, the progress of literature and the arts, and frustrated Henry's exertions in their behalf. The wealth and taste of the monastic bodies, which had hitherto proved the great supporters of painters, sculptors, and architects, were now destroyed, and no patrons for many years arose to supply their place.

It is in judging Henry *as a man* that the conscientious writer turns with disgust and loathing from the task. In friendship he was insincere, in love capricious, in revenge a Nero, in deceit a Judas. Where he once hated, no sentiment of justice or religion withheld his arm. His sceptre became an axe; and the offence, however trivial, and the punishment, were alike written in blood. In short, in one comprehensive phrase, he had every vice which renders humanity terrible and despicable, without one solitary virtue— unless courage may be termed so—to redeem it. And yet such was the state of public morals at the time, that the bloated savage was regretted by the people, whose liberties he trampled under foot, whose intelligence he submitted to the standard of his own uncertain, capricious, changing faith. No monarch ever mounted the throne under more favourable auspices, or possessed greater opportunities of good, than Henry VIII. Truth reluctantly compels us to add, that no sovereign ever more abused them.

No sooner had the breath left the body of their late dreaded master, than the council proceeded to the chamber of his son—now Edward VI., then in his tenth year. The royal child was busily occupied in reading his book of prayers—the same which Holbein had illuminated for his father previous to his marriage with Anne Boleyn. The young prince was, from his earliest infancy, of a melancholy temperament, which gave an appearance of dignity unusual in one so young. As the nobles, with his uncle Hertford at their head, thronged eagerly round him, his cheek became suddenly pale; he guessed the melancholy truth, and burst into tears. He was too young not to have loved his father.

"The king," he sobbed, "the king!"

Cranmer bent the knee, and kissed his little hand, conveying to him by that act of homage the intelligence that the crown had descended to his brow, and that he was doubly an orphan.

The desolate child wept long and bitterly. Never was crown less joyously received.

Taking him by the hand, his uncle, the Earl of Hertford, led the boy-king from his private apartment towards the council chamber, the lords preceding them bareheaded, and the youth still sobbing with ill-suppressed grief. The primate placed him in the chair of state, amid a unanimous cry of "God save King Edward."

On breaking the seals of Henry's will, it was discovered that he had fixed the majority of his son at the completion of his eighteenth year, and that the executors, sixteen in number, were to be entrusted with the administration of the kingdom during his minority. Their names were: Cranmer, archbishop of Canterbury; Wriothesley, the chancellor; St. John, great master; Lord Russell, privy seal; the Earl of Hertford, chamberlain; Viscount Lisle, admiral; Tonstal, bishop of Durham; Sir Anthony Browne, master of the horse; Sir William Paget, secretary of state; Sir Edward North; Sir Edward Montague, chief justice of the Common Pleas; Judge Bromley; Sir Anthony Denny; Sir William Herbert, chief gentleman of the privy chamber; Sir Edward Wotton, the treasurer of Calais; and Dr. Wotton, dean of Canterbury.

In the hands of these persons was invested the regal power. They were to be assisted by a council, whose office was limited to offering advice. Amongst the latter were the Earl of Arundel and Sir Thomas Seymour, the king's uncle—the same who, in a few weeks after the death of his brother-in-law, espoused the queen dowger, Catherine Parr.

This will gave satisfaction neither to one party nor the other. The chancellor was, perhaps, the only person contented with it, as, from his office, he felt assured that a great portion of the authority of the state must fall into his hands. No sooner had the document been read than Hertford quickly observed that the government would lose its dignity without an ostensible head, who might represent the royal majesty, and receive addresses from the foreign ambassadors.

"The president of the council might suffice, I think," observed the chancellor, bitterly.

"Meaning yourself, no doubt, my lord?" said Hertford.

Wriothesley bowed.

"The king's blood," replied Hertford, tauntingly, "may best represent his crown."

"Alas, my lord, where are we to look for it?" demanded the lawyer, with a sneer; "our late sovereign took good care to leave few descendants of York or of Plantagenet to embarrass his successor. The nearest relative, in such a case, is the Cardinal de la Pole, and I presume you would not vote for him."

Lisle, whose ambitious projects had long been maturing, smiled at the seeds of division thus early sown. He saw that he should reap a good harvest in the end. He did so.

Sir Thomas Seymour, although he hated his brother, felt that it would be but politic to join his interest with his in this; and their united interest prevailed. Hertford was elected Lord Protector, and soon after created Duke of Somerset; by which name he is, perhaps, better known in history: the cunning Lisle, who was secretly plotting his ruin, receiving as the price of his consent the earldom of Warwick. But our old acquaintance had yet higher views, which touched the crown itself.

Just as the council was about to disperse, some one suddenly recollected the Duke of Norfolk.

"Behead him!" exclaimed Hertford.

"Impossible," replied the chancellor, coolly, for he was secretly inclined towards the duke, and sought to mortify the protector for the triumph he had obtained over him.

"Impossible!" repeated the haughty peer; "know, my lord, that when speaking in our royal nephew's name, we speak our will—that nothing is impossible."

"By we, does your lordship mean the regency?" demanded the subtle lawyer.

Hertford was silent. The chancellor continued:

"It is fit we understand, my lords, the meaning of the noble earl—the royal WE."

The nobles turned an inquiring glance towards the uncle of the king, who, fearing that he had too soon unmasked his game, replied, in some confusion—

"Of course I meant the council, and that the regal power, full and entire, is centred in its hands."

"I thank your lordship," exclaimed Wriothesley, bowing mockingly, "and call upon our colleagues here to remember the admission. *The regal power, full and entire*," he solemnly repeated, "*is vested in our hands*; consequently, to conspire against it would be treason."

The admission afterwards proved fatal to him who made it.

"My lords, the warrant is already signed," exclaimed Hertford, who was most anxious to secure the destruction of his wily enemy; "the duke, therefore, is——"

"Improperly so," interrupted the chancellor; "the royal stamp should have been affixed in our presence—without which it is invalid."

"Certainly," replied the council, who began to fear that they had been too precipitate in yielding to the pretensions of the uncle of the king, and were willing to prove to him that they knew how to defend their rights; "the warrant is illegal."

The chancellor drew the parchment from his bosom and deliberately tore the royal monogram from the margin. From that moment it was worthless.

Hertford, although furious, was from prudence silent.

For three days the death of Henry was kept secret from the people, and on the fourth, the lord mayor being summoned, and the city filled with troops, his infant successor was proclaimed king.

About six months after the accession of Edward VI., at the close of a sultry evening in July, a ship, evidently of a foreign build, was seen lazily making its way through the pool towards old London Bridge; the sluggish wind scarcely removed a crease from the folds of her heavy sails, and she moved with as much deliberation and state as a city alderman, or a pimple-nosed abbot after a solemn feast. Amongst the spectators who watched her progress was a fine old white-haired man, whose unbroken height and erect carriage showed that time had dealt most kindly with him; his attire, without being rich, showed that he belonged to the wealthy class; a stranger gazing on him would most probably judging from the eager look with which he watched the ship, have taken him for the owner, or, at least, a merchant who had a rich freight on board. In both surmises he would have been mistaken; the only treasures which the gallant bark contained for him were the orphan child and grandchildren of his old master, whom he served and loved in his youth—Sir Richard Stanfield.

We scarcely need inform our readers that the old man was no other than the faithful Steadman. Like a statue of ancient fidelity, he remained upon the bank of the river waiting the arrival of the ship. At times, the thought of the evening when he and his widowed mistress last landed there—his gallant nephew's fate — his sister's wrongs—and Sir John de Corbey's crimes, would dim his eyes; but the hope of once more embracing the child of his adoption—

the heiress of the race he loved—perhaps of dancing her children on his knee, cleared them again, as April's sun disperses the descending showers.

As the boat neared the shore, the old man's heart beat quickly. It touched the quay at last, and a lady, whose matron form and graceful person were still redolent of beauty, leaning upon the arm of a foreign looking cavalier, set foot upon the soil of England, the first time for fourteen years.

It was Walter and his devoted wife. The two children — a boy and a girl — who followed, each holding the hand of a quiet, shrewd looking personage, were the only issue of their marriage. The youth, who was about twelve years of age, already fancied himself a man; he was a brave, gallant little fellow, who feared nothing but the reproof of his mother, or a tear in the blue eyes of his sister. After her parents, the girl would have been puzzled to say which she loved most, her brother or her conductor, our old friend Patch.

"Lady," exclaimed the old soldier, as the heiress of Stanfield set foot upon land, "Mary——"

He was too much overcome by emotion to be able to utter more, but would have knelt to kiss the hand which she extended towards him. With true woman's tact and feeling she prevented his design, and drawing him towards her, kissed him affectionately upon the cheek.

"My kind—my second father!" she exclaimed.

Walter's hand was in an instant grasped in his.

"Welcome—a thousand times welcome to your country!" murmured the faithful, humble friend. "Time has seemed long—very long, since I beheld you. I often thought," he added, "that a stranger would close the old man's eyes, and not his master's child."

"We shall have many a year of happiness and love to pass together yet, old soldier," observed Walter, for he saw that Mary's heart was too full of former recollections to permit her to speak.

"And are these your children?" demanded Steadman, pointing to the boy and girl, who stood with their guardian, Patch, gazing on with an inquiring eye, and wondering who the white-haired man could be.

"They are," said Walter.

"It is Steadman!" added the jester, who at once had recognised him.

"Steadman!" they both repeated, throwing their arms round the old man's neck; "what dear old Steadman, who followed grandfather to the wars, and protected

mamma from her cruel guardian when a child? Oh! how we shall love him!"

The yeoman's honest heart was full; his fidelity in exile and absence had been remembered; the child he had so truly loved had taught her children to repeat his name. The service of a life was well repaid.

"What a pity," exclaimed the boy, "that you are too old to go with me to the wars!" He dreamed of nothing else. "But never mind," he added; "when I return from each campaign we will sit cosily by the fireside, and I will relate to you my adventures,

and listen by turns to yours. Oh! we shall be such friends!"

"Your name?" sobbed the old man to the youth.

"Richard."

It was the same as his old lord's, whom he had loved and followed when a boy. He could almost have imagined that Time had inverted his glass, and suffered the sands to run back for more than half a century. Catching the sturdy little fellow in his arms, he pressed him to his heart; then confused at the freedom he had taken with the heir of

No. 55.

his master's house, he would have kissed his hands.

The scene was becoming too painful for the feelings of the Lady Mary. Fortunately the house of the aged faithful Mariette was not far distant; a few moments sufficed to bring them there, where the most hospitable preparations had been made for their arrival. As they crossed the threshold two persons muffled in cloaks passed them, seemingly anxious to avoid recognition: but the quick eye of Patch was not to be deceived. He recognised them in an instant—the first was the fanatical son of Sir Richard Everil, the other Louis d'Auverne, Wolsey's son.

"This is indeed a joyful meeting," exclaimed the jester, who willingly would have embraced him.

"Louis!" sternly uttered his grave companion.

"Why," resumed the speaker, "have we so long remained estranged? Why have you not written?"

"Louis!" repeated the Lollard, in a tone more impatient than before.

"A moment," replied the youth. "It can scarcely be a sin to express our gratitude to those who love us; 'tis the last weakness," he added, "Heaven will pardon it. Father—friend, our paths are different; but my heart to you is still unchanged. Pray for me—pray for me; and farewell."

With these words Louis d'Auverne sprang from the doorway, and in an instant was out of sight. The jester stood gazing mournfully after him.

CHAPTER XXIV.

Vaulting ambition, which o'erleaps itself,
And falls on the other side.—*Shakspeare.*

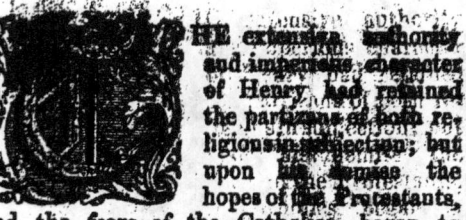

THE extensive authority and imperious character of Henry had retained the partizans of both religions in subjection; but upon his demise the hopes of the Protestants, and the fears of the Catholics, began to revive, and the zeal of these parties produced everywhere disputes and animosities,—the usual prelude to more fatal divisions. The protector, the Duke of Somerset, had long been regarded as a secret partizan of the reformers; and being now invested with the regal authority, he threw aside all restraint, and at once discovered his intention of correcting the abuses of the ancient religion, and of adopting still more Protestant innovations. He took care that every person entrusted with the education of the young king should be imbued with the same principles as himself; and as the youthful Edward discovered a taste for every kind of literature—especially theological—far beyond his tender years, all men foresaw, in the course of his reign, the total abolition of the Catholic faith; and many, in the usual time-serving spirit of courtiers, declared themselves in favour of those tenets which were likely to prevail. The wealth which most of the nobles had acquired from the spoils of the clergy induced them to widen the breach between England and Rome; and, by establishing a contrariety of speculative doctrines—as well of discipline as of faith—to render a coalition with the mother church impracticable. Their rapacity also was still further excited by the prospect of pillaging the secular, as they had already done the regular clergy; and they knew that while any share of the old doctrines prevailed, or any respect to ecclesiastical authority remained, that they could never hope to succeed in their enterprise.

This condition of things induced Sir Richard Everil and his son to leave their retreat at Antwerp, and once more venture into the arena of polemical adventure. The state of toleration was favourable even to their extreme opinions; and Louis d'Auverne, whose naturally gentle spirit had been gradually subjected by the stern enthusiasm of his friend, accompanied them. The Lollards, so bitterly persecuted in the preceding reign, now began to show their heads; although, with considerable prudence, they veiled many of their peculiar views, and confounded themselves under the general name of reformers. Of the most fanatical portion of this sect young Everil soon became the leader, and the new-made Earl of Warwick, who aspired in secret to the protectorship and the downfall of the Seymours, leagued himself with him : he saw that he was one of those men who in times like the present were powerful either in favour or against any cause to which they allied or opposed themselves.

The protector, in his schemes for advancing the reformation, had always recourse to the counsels of Cranmer, who, being a man of moderation and prudence, was averse to all violent changes, and desired to bring over the people by insensible innovations to that system of doctrine and discipline which he deemed most perfect. He also, probably, foresaw that a reformation which carefully avoided extremes was likely to be most lasting; and that a devotion merely spiritual was fitted only to the fervour of a new sect. He seems, therefore, to have contemplated the establishment of a hierarchy which might stand as a perpetual barrier against Rome, and retain the reverence of the people, even after their enthusiastic zeal had diminished or entirely evaporated. The person who opposed with greatest authority any further advances towards the reformation was Gardner, Bishop of Winchester, who was secretly supported by Warwick in the council as a means of embarrassing the protector, whose younger brother, Lord Seymour, had so wrought on the affections of the queen dowager, that she married him within a few months of Henry's death—a union which so increased his wealth and credit, that he aimed at nothing less than the overthrow of the regent, and seizing the reins of power himself. To increase his popularity, he affected the opinions of the most fanatical of the reformers—spoke of reducing the number of bishops—lessening the power of the convocation of the clergy—and, indeed, gave it to be secretly understood that he was opposed to the establishment of any hierarchy, as savouring too much of the doctrines of Rome.

The great aim of Somerset's policy was to carry out the plan of the late king, and secure the union between England and Scotland, by the marriage of Edward with the infant queen; but as the Catholic party in the latter country was still dominant, all overtures for the alliance were courteously refused, and a war was the consequence, in which the Scots, as usual, were worsted; but the advantages not being pushed to the last extremity, it only inspired that impetuous people with a still greater aversion to a union so violently courted.

The queen dowager of Scotland, finding that such was the general feeling of the nation, called a parliament at Haddington, and it was there proposed that the youthful Mary should, for still further security, be sent to France, and committed to the guardianship of that ancient ally; which, after a stormy debate, was agreed to—the clergy, who dreaded the consequence of the English alliance, seconding the measure with all their influence.

It was while the protector was engaged in the war to which these circumstances gave rise, that Lord Seymour sought the occasion of his overthrow, and made an attempt which ultimately recoiled upon himself.

He represented to his friends that formerly, during a minority, the office of protector of the kingdom had ever been kept distinct from that of governor of the king's person, and that the union of these important offices in one person conferred an authority dangerous to the well-being of the kingdom. He even procured a letter from the young king, addressed to the parliament, in which Edward desired that Seymour might be appointed his governor. The design, however, was discovered, and a party of nobles sent to remonstrate with him. He received them haughtily, and threatened, if his just claims were rejected, to make the parliament the blackest which ever sat in England. Alarmed at his proceedings, the council summoned him before them to answer for his conduct. He refused to attend; upon which they threatened to order him to the Tower; at the same time stating that, so far from the young king's letter being a protection, it would be considered as an aggravation of his offence. This firmness, added to the loss of influence which he experienced on the death of his wife, the queen dowager, who expired in childbed, induced him to submit to his brother, and a hollow reconciliation was patched up between them.

Once more a widower, Seymour now turned his ambitious views towards the throne itself. He saw that Edward's constitution was weak, that in all probability he would not live long; he therefore secretly made his addresses to the Princess Elizabeth, then in the sixteenth year of her age; and that lady, whom even the pursuit of ambition and the hurry of political intrigue could not, in her more advanced years, entirely disengage from the influence of the tender passion, seems to have listened to his overtures with considerable complacency. But as Henry, by his will, had excluded his daughters from all share in the succession, unless they married with the consent of his executors, and that consent it was certain Seymour never could obtain, it was concluded that he meant to effect his purpose by expedients even more rash and criminal. Secretly as these proceedings had been carried on, they reached the ears of the council, and several secret meetings had been held to consider whether the moment had not arrived to arrest the daring conspirator. Warwick, to the astonishment of all, was against such a proceeding, his secret aim being to involve the Lady Elizabeth in Seymour's downfall, and so remove one barrier to him and the long-cherished object of his ambition.

It is not to be supposed that on his return to England our old acquaintance Walter suffered much time to elapse before he petitioned for the raising of the sequestration which Henry in his wrath had laid upon the lands of Stanfield. Day after day he attended the council, and was as frequently put off with promises never intended to be kept, for the spoil was too rich to be lightly disgorged. It was on one of these occasions, while waiting in the ante-chamber with his friend and adviser Patch, that he heard voices in loud and stormy debate within. This was the more unusual, as Edward himself presided at the council board.

"One would imagine," said the jester, in his usual sarcastic tone, "that the king amused himself at shovel-board, instead of presiding at a council-board. Didst hear that voice?"

"'Twas Warwick's," observed his companion; "his fortune swells him."

"And will," added Patch, "until the bubble bursts. When the oak hath fallen, the reed imagines itself an oak. There are shades which haunt these walls must smile in bitter mockery at the fantastic tricks of their successors—pigmies playing at the Titans' games.

"The dispute grows warmer."

"Wouldst like to see the interior of the ant-hill?" demanded Patch.

"What mean you?"

"Follow me," continued his friend; "the Syracusan tyrant was not the only one who framed an error to test his courtiers' truth. There are secrets in this palace would make Satan smile with admiration, were he planning one for his own home."

"Mean you——"

"Follow me, and see."

Hastily passing from the ante-chamber, they entered the armoury, where goodly suits were piled in niches, some inlaid with gold, others curiously damascened in Milan steel; and at the east end of the room, in a recess, was the magnificent one, both for man and horse, worn by the late king, and presented to him by his sometime ally and friend, and sometime enemy, the Emperor Charles the Fifth. The species of arch under which it stood was panelled in oak, to correspond with the rest of the apartment. After carefully looking round to see that they were not

observed, the jester pushed back an acorn in the centre of one of the mouldings, when a portion of the wainscot, large enough to admit of a stout person passing, rolled back, and discovered a passage dimly lit by loop-holes, irregularly left in the deeply moulded cornice, which ran round the alcove. Obeying a motion of his hand, Walter followed his conductor, who, despite the obscurity, walked like one certain of his whereabouts, till they reached a small closet, in which were two chairs covered with rich brocade, but enveloped in dust from long disuse. They were both placed close to the wall, in which apertures were pierced, extending to the back of the throne, and through which the voices of the speakers at the council board were conveyed as by so many speaking trumpets to the inmates of the room.

"An ingenious contrivance," observed Walter, as he gazed curiously around.

"What is more ingenious than tyranny?" demanded his companion.

"Was this the late king's contrivance?"

"No, his father's," replied the jester, "the man with a kingly crown and a scrivener's heart; whose wisdom was to suspect all and trust to no man—who loved gold better than heaven, and who only left his hoards behind because he could hit on no means of taking them with him—whose life was one incarnate lie—who murdered the heir he pretended to avenge, and blackened Richard's memory to justify his own."

"You speak of the impostor Perkin Warbeck?" said Walter.

"Impostor!" repeated Patch, his lip quivering with suppressed emotion as he echoed the word.

"At least I have been taught to consider him as such."

"Then think so still," exclaimed his friend; "'tis not the first lie honest men have trusted. It were a curious speculation, Walter," he added kindly, "to calculate how many truths and errors time will one day set in their true light—how many fames purge of the damning spots which miscalled history has splashed them o'er with—how many earthly glories will it dim."

"True."

"To time, then, leave Perkin Warbeck and his cause," said the jester; "the old destroyer will prove his best avenger. Hark!" he added, as the sound of voices rose high within the council chamber, "that is Warwick speaking."

"Warwick!" repeated Walter, puzzled at the new title, although he recognised the voice.

"Or Dudley," added Patch, "an thou likest the popinjay by his old plumage better.

Hast thou forgot the chase he led thee the night we fled from Kimbolton with the Princess Mary? He plays a daring game; but, if I read the royal orphan's star aright, a losing one. Both Somerset and Seymour are his tools. He plays the brothers each against the other, striving to ruin both."

"He is a traitor!" muttered Walter.

"You mistake," said his friend; "he is a politician."

On applying their ears to the apertures, they heard Warwick propose that a warrant should be made out for Seymour's committal to the Tower, to be used only in the event of his completing his projected marriage with the Princess Elizabeth, whose want of duty and respect to her brother and sovereign, Edward, in listening to such clandestine proposals, he painted in language but too well calculated to excite the young prince's resentment.

"Why not proceed at once?" demanded the Duke of Somerset, who was seated upon a stool placed on the throne itself, beside his nephew; "I cannot see the motive for this delay."

"Nor I," modestly added the youthful prince.

"These are the things the world calls statesmen," muttered the jester; "the motive is as clear as any sunbeam; aught save a bat or barn owl might see through it."

"Were it not wiser," continued Warwick, he prudently put the question interrogatively, in order to feel his ground as he went along, "to let the princess still further commit herself, even to the consenting to a private marriage with this ambitious man? and by that act forfeit all chance of succession to the crown?"

"And then?" said Cranmer, fixing an inquiring glance upon the speaker.

"Arrest them both together: Seymour will be ta'en in the overt act of treason, Elizabeth in rebellion to her brother's will."

All the members of the council present, except Cranmer, whose affection for his goddaughter induced him to oppose it, voted in favour of the proposition of the earl, to whom the warrant, signed by the king and Somerset's own hands, was accordingly entrusted, to be put in force the moment he should find the act of treason accomplished; indeed, so excited were both the protector and the youthful Edward, that it required all the primate's eloquence to prevent the name of the imprudent princess from being included in the order of arrest; as it was, he only postponed it.

"We have witnessed a strange scene," observed Walter, in a whisper to his companion; "what can be Warwick's motive?"

"Ambition," replied Patch; "he plays one brother off against the other."

"But his hostility to the Lady Elizabeth?"

"She stands between him and the crown."

"The crown!" repeated Walter, with a look of astonishment.

"Not for himself," added the jester,—"that were a flight too lofty e'en for his ambition,—but for another, under whose name he trusts to reign, and through whose marriage he will place his own blood on England's throne. I have watched his game with interest; he plays it boldly, but will fall at last."

"You think so?"

"I am sure so," replied Patch; "the devil, whom he serves, will place his foot upon the throne, then change it to a scaffold. It is not often I predict in vain."

"The princess must be warned in time," exclaimed Walter, after a few moments' pause.

"The daughter of Anne Boleyn," said the jester, fixing his eye upon the speaker.

"Is not answerable for her mother's cruelty," replied our hero; "besides, she is an orphan and a woman, beset by enemies, waylaid with cruel snares. Trust me, old friend, we shall sleep better for the rescuing her."

His companion pressed his hand with the air of a man who felt that he had wronged him by a doubt, which he never ought to have entertained, of his generosity and justice.

"The serpent's trail," he whispered, "despite man's fall, hath not left its venom in every heart—earth were indeed a desert else."

The discussion before the council on the fate of Seymour was followed by one of still greater importance to our hero—the consideration of his petition for the restoration of his wife's estates. Patch, through the agency of his partner Mariette, had solicited the influence of several of the members of the board, who being under great pecuniary obligations to the wealthy merchant, had faithfully promised their best services when the question came before them. It was amusing to witness how they kept their faith; not one who had pledged himself but spoke and argued against the impolicy of restoring the rich domain of Stanfield to its owner; the great plea urged was, that if the business of restoration were once commenced, there was no knowing where the claims might stop, and that the crown would become impoverished by such acts of justice. Warwick, who had an eye to the possession for himself, was particularly opposed to it; it was not the only project in which he was doomed to disappointment.

"Farewell to Stanfield!" exclaimed Walter, bitterly, as he listened to the discussion. "Justice, Justice, how is thy name perverted!"

"Fear not," said Patch; "the heir shall win it yet."

His friend shook his head incredulously.

"I tell thee so," continued the speaker; "nay, more, I promise thee—and experience hath by this time convinced thee that the jester's promise is more to be relied on than a prince's oath. But come," he added, "let us retrace our steps; we have heard all that concerns us, more than we came to hear. Home—home—and there consider the best means to baffle Warwick and preserve Elizabeth."

"And Seymour," added his companion, with earnestness.

"Is past hope," added the jester; "one of those stubborn men who think fate may be vanquished by braving it—who try to stare danger out of countenance, nor find their error till they fall o'er the precipice."

That very night two horsemen, dressed as Italian merchants, each carrying a small bale of merchandise upon his saddle-bow, set out for Hatfield, the residence of the Princess Elizabeth, who, although regarded with more favour by her Protestant brother than the Catholic Princess Mary, was still, from her proximity to the crown, an object of suspicion; and from the attachment which the great body of reformers bore her person — almost of rivalry — Seymour was not far wrong in his calculation when he thought that the possession of her hand would prove a stepping-stone to the realisation of his dreams of ambition.

It is impossible to ascertain at this remote period how far the courtship was really carried between Seymour and the youthful princess, but there is every reason to believe that she was fascinated with the elegant manners and eloquent tongue of her suitor, and but for the interference of the council, would have married him, despite the clause in her father's will, which, as Edward was then in health, and Mary stood between her and the succession, affected her but little. It would have been a singular marriage that of the brother of Jane Seymour and the daughter of Anne Boleyn.

Elizabeth was walking in the grounds of Hatfield, attended by the ladies of her little court, who, in point of fact, were no other than spies upon her conduct, placed there by the jealous Somerset and intriguing Warwick to watch her conduct, when two traders, having all the appearance of Italian merchants, were seen making their way towards the house.

The heart of the princess was ill at ease. With her usual penetration—for she was remarkable for that quality even at that early age—she saw that she was surrounded by those who, under the mask of respect, were little better than enemies, ready to catch at each unguarded word. She had promised that very evening to meet her lover—to listen to his vows, if not to yield to his importunate entreaties for a secret marriage, which something whispered her would be the signal of his ruin, if not her own. Time hung, as it always does in moments of anxiety, with leaden pinions; and despite her habit of self-command, a close observer might have seen by her restless eye that her heart was ill at ease.

No sooner did the horsemen perceive the princess than they dismounted from their steeds, which they consigned to two stout serving men who followed them. They approached the group of ladies.

"Back, fellows!" said Lady Mortimer, who acted as mistress of the little household at Hatfield, where, at this period, Elizabeth was only a temporary visitor; "no strangers are permitted to approach her grace."

The intruders instantly paused, not to alarm the party, and respectfully uncovered to the future queen, who gently inclined her head, at the same time demanding of the speaker who the strangers were.

"Traders, I believe," replied her ladyship.

"From Milan, your grace," added the elder of the strangers, who was, in fact, no other than Patch. "I have passementeries might serve an empress for her coronation robes, and taffety fit to line them, jewel work from Florence, a ring from Cellini's own hand, and a pearl which her highness Louise of Savoy sent to the constable Bourbon when she offered him her hand in marriage, as a means of settling their disputes; laces of Venice," he added, "and cunning work from Flanders—merchandise worthy of beauty's eyes to dwell upon."

Walter, whose experience in the nature of the baubles they carried was less than his companion's, was occupied during this speech in unbuckling the straps of the packs, and displaying their contents to view. Elizabeth, not suspecting that the traders were other than what they seemed, was turning coldly away, when the entreaties of her attendants arrested her step, and she suffered herself to be persuaded to examine the strangers' merchandise, much of which was really curious and valuable.

Never had the fair dames found so reasonable a trader. The Venitial laces and passementeries changed owners at a price far short of the value of the precious metals in which they were worked. A small mirror of smoked crystal attracted the attention of Lady Mortimer, whom female curiosity had thrown off her guard.

"And what is this, Sir Italian?" she demanded.

"An Egyptian mirror," replied the jester, "in which the past may be recalled and the future predicted. It was a similar one in which Cleopatra foresaw the choice between death and the dishonour of a Roman triumph, and chose the latter. The wise Cornelius, in this very one, showed the late Earl of Surrey his lady love; and in this—provided," he added, "that your ladyship is still unmarried—you may see the features of your future husband."

"Thou knowest I am a widow, cunning knave," replied the dame, laughingly; "to me thy glass is useless."

"In that case others may read your fortunes for you," observed Patch.

Lady Mortimer, like most of the females of the age, was superstitious, and although she professed the while her utter disbelief in the virtues of the glass, she suffered herself to be persuaded to step aside with the merchant to consult it. As soon as they were out of hearing of the circle, the jester asked her upon what point she wished to consult his skill.

"A promise hath been made me," said the lady, in a low tone, fearful lest even the trees should hear her; "canst tell by whom?"

Patch looked for several moments in the glass.

"A tall dark man," he replied, "who has a scar on his right temple; a soldier, I should judge from his martial air; a noble certain, for he wears the chain and badge of some knightly order, and a bear's head upon the pommel of his sword. Have I described him rightly, lady?"

"As faithfully as I could myself," replied the awe-stricken woman.

It was no great wonder that he did so, for he had long been acquainted with the Earl of Warwick, and knew that Lady Mortimer was in his interests.

"Will he keep faith with me?" she demanded.

Again the mirror was consulted, with the same apparent confidence, by the stranger.

"No," he boldly answered.

"No!" repeated the lady.

"He himself will not possess the power. I see him crushed by a pile he has been endeavouring to rear; a scaffold—an axe—and woe," he added, "woe to those who trust him."

From his knowledge of mankind and pecu-

liar means of information, it required no very profound knowledge in the black art for the speaker to predict the downfall of the ambitious Warwick. His listener was both surprised and intimidated at his skill, and received his predictions with superstitious reverence.

"What," said the princess, advancing towards them, for she had observed the changing countenance of Lady Mortimer, "hath the cunning man told thee of a second husband, or predicted that thy first one should return?"

"Neither," replied the lady, drawing a little on one side, that Elizabeth might consult the oracle, if such were her pleasure.

The princess eyed our old acquaintance for some time with a cool, steady glance, as if she were mentally reading him.

"Thou art a clever knave," she at last exclaimed, "to have wrought this on the Lady Mortimer! But come," she added, good humouredly, "let me try thy skill. Tell me, what has fate in reserve for me?"

"A crown," replied Patch, without a moment's hesitation.

"Speak lower," said the princess, who began to feel alarmed at her imprudence, well knowing that such a predicton might materially injure her both with Edward and her sister Mary, should any of the spies around her overhear it. "When?" she added.

"After trials which will wear your patience, and dangers which it will require all your prudence to avoid," whispered the jester.

"From whence arises my chief danger?" anxiously inquired the princess.

"Love."

The questioner started—it seemed as if a warning was thus singularly conveyed to her of the precipice upon the brink of which she so incautiously was treading.

"Keep not your rendezvous to-night," continued the speaker, "nor write the promise which ambition, and not love, demands. Evil eyes are upon you, lady—evil hands ready to work you ill. The warrant is already signed for Seymour's arrest."

"His arrest?" faltered Elizabeth.

"You cannot save him, but may share his ruin. Farewell, lady," added the speaker; "my task is ended. Be faithful to yourself, and let not a moment's weakness mar your fortunes."

The rest of the ladies were so astonished at the effect produced both upon the princess and Lady Mortimer, that they feared to make a trial of the merchant's skill, but suffered both him and his companion to depart without further question. As soon as they were gone, Elizabeth, under plea of indisposition, retired to Hatfield House, where she immediately secluded herself from the observation of her household to reflect upon the warning she had received.

In the delightful grounds which surrounded the mansion stood a species of labyrinth or grotto, adorned with shells and minerals wrought into quaint devices. At the further end a fountain gave an artificial coolness during the heat of summer to the recess, in which Seymour and the thoughtless object of his passion were accustomed to meet. In this grotto a pursuivant-at-arms and a dozen halberdiers had been for several hours concealed, when a horseman gallantly mounted drew rein near the mouth of their retreat. They had received their orders, and it seems their instructions were not to secure the intruder alone. Warwick's plan was to arrest the lovers at the very moment of their meeting. The night, fortunately for their intentions, was a dark one, and suited to their purpose.

"Curse on this delay!" exclaimed the impatient Seymour, after he had paced for upwards of an hour the moss-covered floor of the place of rendezvous. "What can have detained her? Were she once mine," he thought, "I would throw off the mask, and brave my serpent brother. Wedded to Elizabeth, the reformers would unhesitatingly throw themselves into my hands; and so supported, what might I not achieve? The protectorship—the crown itself," he slowly added; "for there are those who think with me that Edward's life is worth but little purchase, and Mary's title bad by her mother's most unholy marriage. Would she were here!"

Scarcely had the aspiring lover—if lover he might be called, whose love was but a stepping-stone to his ambition—finished his reflections, than a figure, dressed in white, and covered with a thickly embroidered veil, was seen cautiously to approach the grotto. Seymour no sooner beheld her than he exclaimed "Elizabeth!" and instantly enfolded her in his embrace. Before one word of warning or reproof could be uttered, the concealed halberdiers, headed by the pursuivant, burst from their concealment, and the latter, laying his hand upon the shoulder of the noble, in the king's name arrested him. Knowing the fiery temper of the man they had to deal with, the captors prudently disarmed him before he recovered from his surprise; and throwing a cloak over his head, to drown his cries, should he attempt to call assistance, they hurried him to a litter which they had left concealed within the grove,

and quietly left the domain of Hatfield for the high-road, where a troop of horse was waiting to escort them back to London.

"Princess," said the pursuivant bending the knee before the veiled figure, "pardon me the office it is my duty to perform. You are a prisoner."

"I am no princess," replied the lady, haughtily, attempting at the same time to pass him.

"My orders," resumed the officer, intercepting her passage, "are to arrest any lady whom I may find in company with the Lord Seymour. Will it please you follow me?"

"This is some error!" exclaimed the female in a supplicating voice; "indeed it is an error! let me return to the house and I will reward you amply. You will repent this," she added.

"Lady," said the officer, more than ever convinced of the high rank of the speaker, "I am faithful. The order for your arrest is sealed with the king's own seal, signed by his hand. Think you without due warrant I had ventured to this extremity? Force me not, I beseech your grace, to use measures unworthy of your dignity."

On a signal given by the speaker, a second litter was brought from the wood, into which the reluctant lady was compelled to enter, and the whole party started on their return, the pursuivant fully satisfied that he had succeeded in the object of his mission and captured both the lovers, an achievement for which he well knew both the protector and Warwick would liberally reward him.

The following day he arrived with his prisoners at the Tower. Seymour was instantly conveyed to the prison in the governor's keep, and the second litter, with a great mystery and respect, to the royal lodgings.

It was whispered, as it passed, that it contained the Princess Elizabeth.

"Poor thing!" exclaimed an old warder, when he heard it; "I can well remember the arrival of her mother."

About noon on the following day, Cheapside was thrown into confusion by the arrival of the king, who, attended by the Duke of Somerset, Warwick, Cranmer, and the rest of the lords of the council, was on his way to the Tower. Edward at this time was in his fifteenth year, tall, and remarkably graceful for his years, and highly popular with the citizens both on account of his youth and the comparative mildness of his government, so different from the iron rule of his father. The young king bitterly regretted the step into which he had been betrayed in ordering the arrest of his sister, and he evinced a determination to investigate

the charges against her himself,—so unusual, that both Warwick and the protector had cause for reflection. The lion's cub began to show that in time it would be a lion too.

The monarch bowed gracefully to the acclamations of his subjects as he passed along, and with a gallantry worthy of the descendant of Edward the Fourth, doffed his plumed cap to the fair ladies in the balconies, whence loving eyes darted their light upon him, and gentle lips spoke blessings as he went.

On his arrival at the Tower, Sir William

Kingston presented the keys of the fortress on a golden salver; the prince merely touched them, in token of his sovereignty, then smilingly returned them, observing as he did so, that they could not be in more faithful hands.

The proud Duke of Somerset was so thrown into the shade by the royal bearing of his nephew, that he experienced a pang of jealousy at the change, and instead of yielding to the assumption of the monarch gracefully, he vented his spleen during the day by endeavouring at every step to thwart him; a proceeding as impolitic as it was useless.

"Our uncle seems in no very gracious humour," whispered the king to Cranmer, as, leaning on his arm, he entered the council chamber, where Seymour had been already brought.

Edward had come with the express intention of acting favourably towards the unhappy man, whose violence, unfortunately for himself, and fortunately for his enemies, broke forth at the very first question put to him by the primate. On this his nephew at once ordered him to be conveyed to his prison, and from henceforth took little, if any, interest in his fate.

"We have another prisoner to question here," observed Warwick, as soon as Seymour had been removed; "the Princess Elizabeth."

"Say rather an explanation to hear," interrupted Edward, gravely; for Elizabeth had ever been the favourite of his sisters.

"Here is the warrant for her apprehension," said Somerset, pointing at the same time to the parchment bearing his own and nephew's signatures lying on the council table. The monarch motioned to the primate to pass it to him. He read it carefully as soon as he received it, and retained it in his hand.

"A chair of state," he exclaimed to the governor of the Tower, "for our sister."

The supposed princess was introduced, still wearing her veil. The council rose upon her entrance, and the king himself motioned her to the seat which had been placed for her.

"This is not the Princess Elizabeth," exclaimed the Earl of Warwick, who had been scanning her figure narrowly; "there is some mistake here."

"I told them so," said the lady; "but no one would believe me."

She threw aside her veil as she spoke, and discovered the features of Lady Mortimer.

"What means this mummery?" coarsely demanded Somerset. "Answer to me, or——"

"Answer to me," mildly interrupted Edward. "Rise, Lady Mortimer. Our uncle is a soldier, and his manners savour somewhat too rudely of the camp. Explain this mystery."

"I was sent with this letter by my royal mistress."

"Where?"

"To the grotto at Hatfield, sire."

"Whom to give it to?"

"The Lord Seymour."

"I see it all, sire," blandly exclaimed Warwick; "this lady has been mistaken for her grace. There still is time to execute the warrant."

"Had we not better read the letter first?"

The letter, which was in the hand-writing of Elizabeth, was handed by Edward to the primate, who, hastily breaking the seal, read aloud to the astonished conclave as follows:—

"My lord.—I thank you in all honesty for your good opinion of me, which is doubtless flattering to one of my inexperience and years. I neither accept nor decline it, referring myself in all things touching the disposition of my unworthy hand to the pleasure of my dear brother and sovereign lord your master, as well as mine. Unless you come armed with his authority, my lord, to Hatfield come no more.

"ELIZABETH."

"A prudent and a wise reply," added Cranmer, as he passed the letter to the members of the council.

"A juggling one," exclaimed Somerset, impatient that the princess had eluded the snare; "but it is not too late. Let a troop of horsemen, with Sir William Kingston, start this very hour for Hatfield. We have other evidence, and——"

"Let them not stir," said Edward, rising and tearing the warrant into several pieces; "our sister is absolved in our judgment."

"But not in mine," interrupted the imprudent duke.

Edward eyed him for a few moments with an air of cold surprise; and, for the first time perhaps, the idea struck him that he should like to throw off the tutelage of *both his uncles*. Warwick watched the glance, and was not slow to profit by it.

"We have heard the expression of his highness's pleasure," he exclaimed; "my lords, the council, I presume, is ended."

Then did the first doubt of Warwick enter the mind of the protector.

CHAPTER XXV.

This is no natural sleep; some cruel hand
Hath nipp'd the bud ere it became a flower;
Stifled the goodly promises of youth
E'en in their sweet unfoldings.

HE protector having called a session of parliament, it was resolved to proceed against Lord Seymour by bill of attainder; and the young king, whom his uncle's violence and imprudence had disgusted, was, without much difficulty, induced to give his assent to the proceeding, an approbation upon which the peers laid much weight. The matter was first brought before the upper house, and several nobles rose in their places, and gave an account of what they knew concerning the intentions of the accused; his criminal projects, words, and actions. These narratives, framed, for the most part, of violated confidences or vague suspicions, were, through the influence of Warwick, received as so much legal evidence; and although the prisoner had formerly many partizans and friends in that august assembly, not one of them had the courage or honesty to move that he should be heard in his defence, or that he should be confronted with the witnesses. A little more scruple was made in the House of Commons, where all our battles for the civil rights of England were ultimately fought. There were even some members who objected against the whole method of proceeding by bill of attainder, and insisted that a formal trial should be given to every man before his condemnation. Soon after, on the 20th of March, the following month, a message was sent by the king, commanding the house to proceed upon the same evidence as the House of Peers. The commons were induced to acquiesce. The bill passed in a full house, with not more than ten dissentient voices.

The sentence was afterwards executed upon Tower Hill, and the warrant signed by the criminal's own brother, Somerset, who was universally execrated for the unnatural proceeding. The attempts of the admiral had been levelled chiefly against his brother's usurped authority; and, although his ambitious enterprising character, encouraged by a marriage with Elizabeth, might have endangered the public tranquillity had he succeeded in his design, the danger was remote and the remedy illegal.

While we have occasionally given sketches of the state of society amongst the noble and great at this period of England's transition from catholicity to the reformed religion, let it not be supposed that we are unmindful of the condition of the people. History proves to us that there is scarcely any abuse in civil society so great as not to be attended with some beneficial consequence, and that, on the attempt to reform them, the loss of these advantages is very sensibly felt; whilst the benefit resulting from the change is the slow effect of time, and seldom perceived by the bulk of the nation. Scarcely any institution can be imagined at first sight less favourable to the interests of mankind than that of monks and friars; yet it was followed with many good effects which, having ceased with the suppression of the monasteries, were regretted by the people of England. The monks always, residing in their convents in the centre of their estates, spent their money in the provinces amongst their tenants, and were a sure resource for the poor and indigent; though there is little doubt but their indiscriminate charity gave but too much encouragement to the idle and vicious. Restricted, also, to a certain mode of living, they had not equal motives of extortion with other men, and they are acknowledged to have been the most indulgent landlords. The abbots and priors were permitted to give leases at an under-value on the payment of a fine, which practice has been continued by their successors, the Protestant bishops, to this day: hence the impossibility of ascertaining their incomes. But when the church lands were distributed amongst the nobles and courtiers, they fell under a different management. Rents were raised, while the unfortunate tenants no longer found the same market for their produce. The rents were spent in the capital; and the farmers, living at a distance from their lords, were exposed to oppression from the rapacity of stewards and underlings. The grievances in the reign of Edward VI. were heightened by other causes. The manufacturing arts were much more advanced in foreign countries than in England. A great demand arose abroad for English wool, and pasturage was consequently found more profitable by the new lords of the soil that tillage. Whole estates were laid waste; the tenants, regarded as a useless burden, were expelled their habitations; even the cottagers, deprived of the commons on which they fed their cattle, were reduced to misery. Sir Thomas More alluded to this grievance in his "Utopia," when he observed that a sheep had become a more ravenous animal than a lion or a wolf; for that it devoured whole villages, cities, and provinces; alluding, of course, to the distress caused by the introducing of sheep-farming, which had deprived so many thousands both of work and bread.

The general increase also of gold and silver in Europe, after the discoveries of Columbus and his companions, had a tendency to influence these complaints. The growing demand in more commercial countries had heightened everywhere the price of commodities which could rarely be transported thither. But in England the labour of men who could not do easily change their markets remained at the ancient rates, and the poor complained bitterly that they could no longer obtain a subsistence by their industry. The protector, who loved popularity and pitied the condition of the people, encouraged these complaints by the very steps he took to redress them. He appointed a commission for making an inquiry concerning enclosures, and issued a proclamation ordering all the late ones to be laid open by a certain day. The populace meeting such countenance from the government, rose in several places, and committed great excesses; and, under pretence that the commission would be eluded, sought for a remedy for their complaints by force of arms.

The rising began in several parts of England, as if a universal conspiracy had been formed by the commonalty. The rebels in Wiltshire were dispersed by Sir William Herbert; those in the neighbouring counties of Oxford and Gloucester by Lord Grey of Wilton. Many of the rioters were killed in the field, others executed by martial law. The commotions in Hampshire, Sussex, and Kent were quelled by gentler expedients; but the disorders in Devonshire and Norfolk threatened more dangerous consequences. At the head of the insurrection in the latter county was one Ket, a tanner, a man of strong passions and some natural talent, who had excited the people by his eloquence.

A few days before the insurrection broke out, Walter and Mary had, after an absence of many years, returned to Norwich, and taken possession of the humble but comfortable abode of their old friend Steadman, who felt prouder on the day which enabled him to offer a home to his master's child, than if a kingly sword had dubbed him a knight upon the field of battle. One chief object of the visit to Norfolk was to abstract, if possible, from the muniment room at Stanfield certain papers, the possession of which, in happier times, might restore the children of the heiress of their mother's lost inheritance.

It was market-day, and vast quantities of wool were exposed to the buyers or agents, who regularly attended to purchase it for the foreign manufacturer. The wives of the poorer classes wandered through the then unpaved square, with discontented looks, but little food was exposed for sale. Turn where they would, they found nothing but wool—wool; while the poor creatures required bread—bread.

"Pass on, gossips! pass on!" exclaimed Mike Maze, the burly tax-collector, who, escorted by a couple of halberdiers, was receiving the corporation dues; "this is not the flesh-market!"

"We know that as well as you do," murmured several of the women.

"Oh! do you?" replied the functionary; "then clear the way, and don't interrupt me in the execution of my duty; the corn-market lies at the other end of the church; off with you!"

"And where are we to get the money to buy bread with?" demanded several; "and at such a price?"

"Or bread to buy, even if we had the money?" added another; "England is turned into a sheep-walk!"

"Would I had been born a sheep!" cried a hump-backed little tailor, whose lean appearance showed that he had long been a stranger to good food, or else that it had been thrown away upon him; "I should be well fed then, and taken care of."

"That's a seditious wish," observed the collector with disgust, for his stomach absolutely recoiled at the idea of Bumpy Jem, the cognomen by which the half-starved tailor was generally known, being converted into a sheep, an animal for certain portions of which he had great respect; "but you were always an ambitious rascal, and ought to be punished."

"What! for wishing to be a sheep?" demanded the offender, who was the wit of the mob.

"Certainly."

"What, then, do you deserve," added the tailor with a grin, "whose offence so much exceeds mine?"

"How so?" said the functionary; "how so?"

"In wishing all your life to be a calf, and having been one without knowing it."

The burst of applause which followed this retort of poor Bumpy Jem told that the jest was relished, and excited the ire of the collector to a furious pitch. Snatching the partisan from the hand of one of his attendants, he struck the poor fellow a violent blow over the head with it; the stroke was followed by blood; and the poor little hunchback measured his length upon the ground.

"Shame! shame!" exclaimed the women, raising him; "that's a foul blow."

Mike Maze was about to repeat the outrage, when a burly, thick-set man, in the dress of a respectable tradesman, sprang through the mob and wrenched the weapon from his hand.

"Bravo, Ket—bravo! down with him! the tunbelly—down with!"

The remaining officer was about to use his halberd, when a stone thrown by some unseen hand struck him on the temple. The blow was fatal: with a groan the instrument of tyranny fell a corse in the market place. The collector and the disarmed companion of the dead man fled. For the space of a minute there was a breathless pause amongst the crowd of idlers whom the dispute had attracted to the spot. Ket looked pale but determined; he knew that he had long made himself obnoxious to the authorities by his advocacy of the people, and that the whole weight of their resentment would fall on him. It was a relief, therefore, when one loud hearty cheer from the populace told him that the action was approved.

The news spread like wildfire through the market-place. Bumpy Jem had hitherto been the people's fool, their wit, and sometimes their counsellor. Wounded and bleeding, he now appeared to them as their martyr. Some of the men began quietly to break up the stalls for weapons; many of the women ran screaming through the streets, so that in an inconceivable short space of time a report was spread that an insurrection, headed by Ket the tanner, had broken out before he had even thought of defence.

"Friends," he exclaimed, "patience has its limits. Are we to be trampled like dust beneath our proud masters' feet, or show ourselves like men?"

"We will—we will!" chorussed the mob.

"A crisis has arrived—nothing like meeting danger boldly."

"Nothing—nothing!" echoed his admirers.

"Always take the bull by the horns, Ro-

bert," quietly observed his brother, who was a butcher, a fellow of the most stolid temperament, and strongly attached to his more sanguine relative.

"Strike, then," exclaimed the bold, adventurous man, "for your birthright—your fair share in the soil of England. The poor man's farm—the common—is enclosed. Why should the noble's chase be more respected? Your honest labour—the means which God had given you to repair the injustice of your fellow man—is rendered valueless; the fields remain untilled, the land unsown. 'Wool, wool!' is the noble's cry. Let him not complain if the people answer, 'Bread!'"

"Hurrah!" cried the now excited mob, "our cry is bread—bread for our wives and children."

"Meet me, then, at Wymondham. There let us throw down the enclosures and encamp; it will give the starving peasant and the labourer an opportunity to rally round us. Shut up within the walls of Norwich, we are powerless."

"But we can return," exclaimed Bumpy Jem, who had recovered from the blow which was the original cause of the tumult, "and crack the walls of the city like a hazel nut."

"And roast the kernel," added a voice in the crowd.

"We will return," resumed the orator, "clad in the people's strength and the justice of their cause. Away at once: here we may be crushed. In the city we are within the grasp of a pigmy's glove; in the country a giant's hand were powerless. Remember our cry—'God and the commons!'"

"God and the commons!" repeated the people; and in a few minutes the market-place was cleared. During the day the unemployed workmen and the discontented of every class poured in one continuous stream through St. Stephen's Gate on their way to Wymondham. The authorities were paralysed, and the city was morally lost before the enemy returned to attack it.

The rebels—for such, we presume, they must be called—occupied themselves for several days in throwing open the enclosed lands, and burning, wherever they found them, the farmers' and the nobles' stocks of wool, which, as the rents were not unfrequently paid in kind, were often considerable.

Their numbers at last became so vast, that they decided on something further than the throwing open of the commons—restoring the old religious establishments, the loss of which, before the establishment of poor laws, was so severely felt by the poorer classes. As the first step to their design, it was agreed the following morning to attack the city. Wymondham, where the insurgents were encamped, our readers will recollect, is close to the old domain of Stanfield.

The moon was shining clearly, darting its silver rays through the green foliage, and lighting at broken intervals the mossy glade, along which three horsemen were quietly wending their way. The foremost was our old acquaintance Patch, his companions Walter and Steadman.

"How beautifully," observed the younger of the three, "the moon holds forth her lamp to light us on our way!"

"Say, rather, like a coquette dealing out her smiles and frowns; for several times a black cloud, like the veil of a Spanish beauty, has obscured her visage, and caused my steed to stumble."

"Give me a dark night, especially when I know my ground," observed the old soldier; "the moon, like the lovely dames you speak of, has betrayed many a gallant fellow to death. I ask for no better light than the glowworm's lamp to-night."

"Why so, old honesty?" demanded the jester.

"We are too near the rebels," replied the veteran, "to render it either desirable or safe; and the less we converse the better. We shall soon reach the hall; let us ride on in silence."

It was seen that the caution was not a vain one, for the little party had not proceeded many paces further before they were challenged by the rough voice of a sentinel, demanding with an affectation of military discipline—

"Who goes there?"

"Minions of the moon," was the jester's quick reply.

"That's not the word," replied the insurgent; "shall I shoot him, Jem?"

"No," replied the sharp voice of the hunchback; "let's take them prisoners."

"But there are three," urged his companion.

"The greater the honour," said the tailor, at the same time emerging from the underwood, where, with his comrade, he had been concealed, and confronting the party as they advanced down the glade. "Stand!"

"In whose name?" inquired Walter.

"The people's."

A momentary halt took place, and the three travellers, inwardly cursing the interruption, hastily consulted what would be the best course to pursue, when a shrill whistle rang through the wood. It was answered, although at considerable distances, on every side, and in a few minutes various bodies of men, armed with scythes, bows, and roughly-

formed pikes, were seen emerging in every direction from the underwood. Resistance would have been useless; it was plain they were surrounded by the insurgents, and completely in their power.

"Three of the enemy," exclaimed Ket the butcher, who was one of the leaders.

"Spies," echoed the band. "String them up to the loftiest oak."

"The lowest of these might answer," interrupted Patch; pointing, at the same time, to the superb forest of trees on either side. "But before you proceed to extremities, ask yourselves one question, my good fellows."

"What is that?" exclaimed their captors.

"What good will it do you? Our purses are not very heavy; but, such as they are, you are welcome to them. Our steeds may serve to mount your cavalry," he added, with an imperceptible sneer; "and as for our skins, although your leader is a tanner, he would hardly wish you to hang us for the sake of them."

"That's more than I'll answer for," replied the butcher.

"At least," observed Walter, "let him decide for himself."

After a few moments' consultation, it was arranged that the prisoners should be conducted to the hall, where Robert Ket had taken up his quarters; for, like most popular leaders, as soon as he became formidable, he aped the state he had previously denounced. It is astonishing how very seldom patriotism can stand the test of success.

"And where are you taking us to?" demanded Steadman, as they urged the horses of the captives onward.

"To Stanfield," was the reply.

"To Stanfield," said the old soldier, his countenance suddenly brightening up—"with all my heart; there are worse places to pass the night in than Stanfield, at least to my thinking."

By his companions in misfortune this was understood as a secret encouragement to them not to despair, and the event proved that they were not wrong in their supposition.

In the great hall of the old mansion was a fire composed of fragments of carved benches and broken furniture, which had hastily been piled together, to spare the insurgents the trouble of cutting fuel; as in most cases of popular commotion, the men who were in arms for their own rights respected very little those of others. Sheep and deer, half-skinned and mangled in an uncraftsmanlike manner, were lying piled together in different parts of the hall; some of the carcases serving as pillows for the drunken, sleeping patriots; others were busy in furbishing up partizans and weapons from the armory, which neglect and long disuse had rendered unfit for service.

Robert Ket, the leader of the motley band, was pacing with moody strides before the blazing fire when his prisoners were introduced. He had heard from sure intelligence that the Marquis of Northampton, with a considerable body of troops, had been dispatched against him. This nobleman had just returned from the relief of Exeter, which had been besieged by the rebels. There, in conjunction with Lord Grey and Batista Spinola, leader of the German horse in the English pay, he had defeated the insurgents, and hanged one of their leaders, the Catholic vicar of St. Thomas, from the steeple of his own church, arrayed in his vestments. He threatened to do the same with Robert Ket. The threat was fulfilled, although the marquis did not live to witness it. These and other circumstances had induced the chief of the rebels to march at once to Norwich.

"Who are these?" he demanded of Bumpy Jem and his companions, as they marshalled the captives before him.

"Prisoners," replied the hunchback, at the same time making a ludicrous effort to salute the tanner in a military style.

"Where taken?"

"In the chase of Stanfield."

"Where, I presume," interrupted Walter, "none will dispute my right to ride, when it is remembered that I am the husband of the heiress of its ancient lords."

"We'll have no lords," said one of the men. "The land is for those who till it."

"We'll be our own lords," exclaimed the hunchback, with a gravity which produced a smile upon the features of the jester, despite the critical position in which he and his companions stood.

"Are you Walter Lucas?" demanded Ket, walking close to our hero, and scanning him narrowly.

"I am."

"What proof can you give?"

"Proof!" exclaimed the old soldier; "I'll vouch for him. You know me, Master Ket, and no man who does that ever could accuse John Steadman of a lie. This is Walter Lucas, our lady's husband."

"And where is your lady?" continued their interrogator.

"In London with her family," replied the jester, whose conscience was not quite so susceptible as the veteran's.

"That's bad," said the tanner; "her presence here would have had great influence with the people. Still you may, perchance, serve the cause as well. We require men of experience," he added; "practical men. We have thows and limbs enough, but lack the skill to train them. You and the old soldier both have served, and——"

"Hear me," replied Walter; "much as I feel for the wrongs of the commons, violence and bloodshed are not the means to redress them. Let not the flush of a first and last success deceive you."

"And what are the means?" exclaimed the tanner, sternly. "To crouch like slaves and lick the armed heel which treads the life-blood from a land—crushes the cottage while it respects the palace; to wait with hound-like patience till the insatiate maw of our oppressors is so gorged with victims that repletion leaves the worn helot a moment's time to breathe. You are not the first from whom I've heard such doctrines. Wilt thou join us?"

"Never!" exclaimed the captive firmly.

A low murmur rose amongst the men. It is astonishing, when once unchained, how soon our passions lead us to cruelty. The taste of blood and plunder which the rebels had enjoyed increased their appetite for more; they were like young tigers, who just began to feel that they had claws and fangs, and longed to use them.

"At least," said Patch, with a look of caution, "you will consider of the offer. Remember you, too, have suffered by the tyranny of Edward and his father. You have wrongs to avenge, rights to assert, and a triumphant people are, as history proves, *sure to be grateful.*"

The sneer which the last words conveyed —if even the look had been wanting—convinced our hero that the speaker's real object was to procrastinate and obtain time or opportunity for escape. He determined to follow it, but did not think it prudent to appear to yield too soon.

"Give me a few hours to reflect," he cried.

"To escape, you mean," replied the tanner, with a frown.

"If you think that," interrupted Steadman, "place us in the chamber of the warder's tower; there is not a loophole in it that a well-fed cat could creep through, and the door of solid iron. Doubt not but by the morning you will find him reasonable."

"Be it so," said the leader; "the people give you till to-morrow."

"Good," observed Patch; "the people are always generous."

"Hear!" cried several of the rustics near him; "give him a flask of wine," added another, "from the cellar, are plunder at Cotessy. He is an excellent patriot."

"You mistake, friend," said the jester, taking the proffered gift from the hand of the speaker; "*I am only a philosopher.*"

"I suppose you don't mean to starve us?" exclaimed Steadman.

The appeal was met by hugh pieces of meat being stuffed into the hands of the speaker; the donors kindly assuring him that if they hanged him in the morning they would at least feed him to-night.

So important did the insurgents deem the safe keeping of his prisoners, that he accompanied them himself to the warder's tower, the upper chamber of which was without even a window to admit the light of day, and the inhabitants were only enabled to breathe from the air supplied by the narrow loopholes in the walls. After satisfying himself of the security of his captives, Ket turned the key in the massive lock of the iron door, thrust it into his bosom, and left them to their reflections.

"You have selected an agreeable lodging, old friend," exclaimed Walter, after he had paced for a few minutes up and down the chamber.

"At any rate, a secure one," quietly replied Steadman.

The jester, in his turn, was somewhat puzzled; he had carefully examined the walls, and convinced himself that there was no secret passage, or hidden means of egress, as he at first suspected; still there was a cheerful look about the old soldier in which he trusted.

"Secure enough," repeated our hero; "the butchers will find us in the pen to-morrow when they seek us."

"Doubtless, master," said the aged follower; "but the difficulty will be to get into the pen to-morrow."

"What mean you?"

"My life on it," said Ketch, "but Steadman winds them still."

The faithful servitor of the former lord of Stanfield led his companions towards the door, which, as we before stated, was of iron, and locked in a frame of the same material, the whole of which was apparently a fixture in the masonry. We say apparently, for on pressing certain knobs in the lock, the door, frame and all, sank in the grooves cut in the solid wall beneath, and a second door and frame descended from the corresponding grooves cut in the wall above: the only difference was this, that the massive lock and bars which fastened them on the first door were on the outside, but on the second they were placed within.

"A contrivance worthy of the Medici," said the jester, struck by the ingenuity of the arrangement.

"At least, it has well served our turn," added Walter.

The coarse jests and loud mirth of the rebels, as they became gorged with the strong ale, wine, and mead, plundered from the neighbouring nobles, had been for some time lulled to rest before the three captives ventured to release themselves from their prison, and, guided by Steadman, descend to the muniment-room, where they found, amid the fragments of papers, books, and parchments, the precious charters which conferred the lands originally upon the ancestors of the Lady Mary, William the Conqueror's confirmation of them, as well as those of the succeeding Norman kings.

The great purport of their visit being accomplished, fearful of detection, they left the house as secretly as possible, and finding horses in the chase, returned to Norwich, from whence they started again at an early hour to London, long before the rebels thought of advancing towards the city.

On the following day Ket and his followers took possession of Monkshold Heath, near the city, and there held a species of tribunal under an oak, which for many ages after was known as the Oak of Reformation; from which place he summoned the gentry to appear before him, and issued decrees as despotic as they were ridiculous and cruel. On the heath was a noble mansion, called Mount Surrey, which the Earl of Surrey had built on the priory of St. Leonard's. This was seized, and plundered of its contents, and converted into a prison; the priory chapel, which the earl had previously changed into a dovecote, was burnt, and its ruins still go by the popular name of Ket's Castle.

During the time which the chief and his followers remained in their camp, seemingly without any definite purpose, a constant intercourse was kept up between the insurgents and the city, the mayor of which had been several times summoned before the oak of reformation, where, as Fuller quaintly remarks, justice was so religiously administered, that one of the city vicars was compelled to read morning and evening prayers to men whose hands were red with blood. All the deer in the neighbouring parks were brought to the camp, and so plentiful was the supply of other meat, that a fat sheep sold for fourpence; twenty thousand, it is said, were consumed in a few days. While they were thus spending their time in feasting and rioting, the authorities were equally neglectful. The council at first only sent a herald with an offer of pardon if they would disperse; nor was it till the Marquis of Northampton, at the head of an army of fifteen hundred men, had been defeated, and Lord Sheffield slain by the rebels, that serious measures were adopted, and the Earl of War-

wick, who was about departing with an army to renew the war with Scotland, sent to Norwich instead, whither he arrived, and encamped in the market-place. For a while the good fortune which had hitherto attended the insurgents followed them; the whole of the ammunition belonging to the royal army fell into their hands, and shortly after they succeeded in capturing the artillery also. The earl was now obliged to shut himself up in the city, and defend himself by fortifying the gates, streets, lanes, and dykes, in the best manner he was able. Some of his officers were urgent that he should quit the city as untenable, but Warwick replied that he would do so only with his life, and compelled his captains, in accordance with an ancient custom observed in times of great danger, to kiss each other's swords and vow to defend the place and each other to the last extremity. The next day a reinforcement of fourteen hundred men, consisting of a Swiss regiment and veterans, arrived, and the general resolved upon attacking the rebels in their camp.

But Ket did not wait for the attack. An

ancient prophecy, said to be of ancient date, was circulated amongst his followers to animate their courage. To this day it is repeated by village gossips and aged crones. It ran thus:

> "The country gnoffes, Hob, Dick, and Hick,
>   With clubs and clouted shoon,
>   Shall fill the vale
>   Of Dussin's dale
>   With slaughter'd bodies soon."

Either trusting the prediction, which was first delivered to him by an old woman renowned for her skill in herbs and spells, or desirous of availing himself of the enthusiasm it had excited amongst his followers, Ket resolved to quit his vantage-ground and attack the enemy. It was on the 27th of August that the rebels marched from Monkshold Heath into the adjacent dale, where they made hasty preparations for battle, by cutting a ditch and planting stakes in front of their position.

The Swiss troops commenced the attack by a furious charge, in which several of the most important citizens, who had been detained as hostages by Ket, and inhumanly placed, bound, in the van, were killed. The insurgents were beaten after the first charge of the cavalry, and the battle became a mere scene of flight and slaughter. About three thousand were slain in the pursuit. Ket fled so swiftly that his horse broke down at the end of a few miles; he was recognised by the servants of a house where he took refuge, and, together with his brother, delivered into the hands of the triumphant Warwick. Many of the prisoners were hung upon the oak of reformation, and forty-nine hung and quartered in the market-place: altogether three hundred were hung, to strike terror to the hearts of others.

In the council-chamber, which had been hastily fitted up in Norwich Castle, were assembled, besides the victorious Warwick, the principal leaders of his army, the captains of the foreign mercenaries, the mayor and gentry of the city, and a mixed crowd of citizens and civilians. Strongly guarded and heavily chained were two captives—the butcher and the tanner. Dick, the former, retained his usual impassibility of feature; the latter, on the contrary, like most men of sanguine temperament who experience violent reverses, was completely crushed by his misfortune; vainly his companion tried to cheer him.

"Do what they will to us, brother," he whispered, "it can't last long: we have only so much life to be expended—so much blood to shed; and even if they take it drop by drop, it must come to an end at last."

"True," sighed Robert.

"I never knew," continued the comforter, "an ox linger more than ten minutes; and I don't think I am half as strong as an ox."

The speaker's well-meant consolations were interrupted by the Earl of Warwick, who proceeded at once to the purpose for which the prisoners had been brought before him—namely, to sentence them to death—a death so fearful, that its horror almost redeems the madness of their crime.

"Rebels and traitors," he began, "the hand of outraged authority at last is raised to avenge society, religion, and all that is estimable in the great social compact which binds mankind together. Yours have been no common crimes, and you shall meet no common doom. *Alive* you shall both be hanged in an iron frame—one from the keep of Norwich Castle, the other from the spire of Wymondham church—a warning to all traitors."

"An example," added Ket, whose energy the indignation which he felt at the barbarity of his sentence had revived—"an example to all future martyrs for the people's rights. The chattering crow may perch upon my swinging bones, and, as the night wind whistles through them, contented tyranny rejoice my spirit's fled: it will but cheat itself. In every groan of my creaking fetters that spirit shall revive, and children through future ages mark the spot, where, like an avenging beacon placed on high, the poor man's martyr died."

"Silence him!" exclaimed Warwick.

"You cannot silence time," replied the prisoner. "Think of me, earl, when thine own hour shall come."

On a signal from the earl, the two brothers were secured by a party of the Swiss soldiery, and dragged from the council-chamber to the courtyard of the castle, where the elder Ket, who was to suffer at Wymondham, was bound hand and foot with cords, and cast, like a sack of wheat, over the back of a trooper's horse; in which fashion, amidst the derision of the soldiery, and the jeers of the multitude, he was conveyed to the place of execution.

"Good-by, Robert!" he exclaimed; "I have a rough ride before me; but the longest journey has an end, and we shall meet again at last."

His brother would have kissed him, but the foreign mercenaries would not allow him even that consolation. In this world they never met again.

By Warwick's orders a strong iron frame had been prepared, large enough to hold the body of a man in an upright position, but not sufficiently roomy to permit him to turn. A chain was attached to the cross-bar at the top by means of a swivel, so that the infernal contrivance could be hung from the walls of the castle, and turn as it swung in the night air.

Ket gazed upon his living tomb with an unmoved countenance, and submitted, with a look of resignation, to be stripped by the executioners to his hose, which was no sooner done than they thrust him into the iron frame, and riveted the bars in front so firmly, that it would have required the blow of a sledge-hammer to break them. No sooner was the victim enclosed, than Warwick and the members of the council descended into the courtyard. The preparations were complete.

"Now, traitor," exclaimed the cruel earl, "dost thou repent thy treason?"

"I repent my sins," replied the unhappy Ket, "but I go to a Judge more merciful than thou art."

"Up with the villain!"

"We shall meet again," shrieked the victim; "be it thy terror here to know that we shall meet again. When the headsman's stroke shall sunder the thread of thy polluted life, and thy scared soul shall yell before the judgment-seat for mercy, thy victim's voice shall drown the cry, deafening the ear of Pity. Monster! the curse of blood is on thy soul—coward as cruel—fiend!"

The fearful denunciations of the speaker ceased to be heard, as the frightful machine in which he was confined rose to the level of the lofty battlements, to which it was drawn by a party of men who were stationed on the walls. Here the end of the chain was passed over a thick iron bar, which bar was again cemented into the solid stone-work. For many hours not a cry escaped the victim, but as the day wore on the pangs of thirst became dreadful, and his groans were distinctly heard. Horror chained many of the spectators, who were assembled within the enclosed space between the moats, like statues to the spot. The shrieks of the sufferer at last became so terrific that the people fled, and even the obscene night bird who had been fluttering near, impatient of its prey, lazily flapped its heavy wings and retired, scared from its living banquet.

By this time it was midnight, and the earl, wrapped in a horseman's cloak, issued quietly and stealthily from a small postern opposite the drawbridge. No sentinel challenged him as he passed, for it was an order given to the guard that all who either left or arrived by that postern should pass unquestioned. When on the bridge, Warwick paused, and cast a cold, ferocious glance upon his victim, who swung in the night air, and

whose occasional shrieks startled the soldier on his lonely rounds.

"The headsman?—no—no," he muttered, alluding to Ket's prediction, which had made a deeper impression on him than he chose to acknowledge. "I will at least provide against that. I play a bold, and consequently a dangerous game, but it shall never lead me to the scaffold."

So thought the speaker's father, Dudley the extortioner, as he was called, and both were alike deceived.

The earl made his way cautiously to a small stone cottage, built out of the ruins of the monastery of Grey Friars, which were scattered about at random over the piece of land formerly the convent close. This was a locality carefully avoided by the superstitious citizens, especially at night; for the inmate, an aged woman, known by the name of Mother Alice, was supposed to hold communication with the beings of another world. In her intercourse with those who sought her—and they were neither few nor poor who did so—she conducted herself more like a priestess of some long-forgotten superstition, than a simple vendor of poisons, drugs, and medicines; for it was generally believed that all the three might be bought of Alice by those who could pay down the sum she asked for her doubtful ministry. The only inmate beside herself of the lonely hut was a raven, superstitiously believed to be a familiar spirit; although, to judge from its appearance it was nothing more than an ordinary bird.

"Enter!" exclaimed a deep voice, as Warwick knocked with the handle of his dagger on the oaken door. "Enter, if you come in the name of sin and despair."

"What if I come in the name of Heaven, dame?" replied the earl.

"Then you have mistaken your road. Pass no—pass on; for sin and sorrow only visit here."

There was something so peculiarly sad in the speaker's tone, that the visitor resolved at once to speak with her, and, raising the rude latch, entered the house.

"Croak—croak," went the voice of the raven, and the bird, generally so bold to all visitors, retreated at once to its usual resting-place. Dame Alice started hurriedly to her feet.

The cottage was so dark that the visitor could scarcely distinguish the person of its mistress; she seemed like an ill-defined shadow, flitting between him and the rude species of stone hearth on which a fire of wood was, or rather had been, burning; for the red embers only remained, and cast a sickly, uncertain light around.

"What would the Earl of Warwick with me?" demanded the mistress of the house.

"You know me, mother?"

"Yes," said the woman, "as you do me —by fame?"

"Fame!"

"Ay, we have both our reputations," added the hag, with a sneer, "and both alike are evil."

"'Tis well," said her visitor. "I would have a draught which at a soldier's need might defeat the malice of his enemies— place death between him and the headsman's office. Dost understand me, mother?"

"Ay," groaned the woman.

"Wilt serve my will in this?"

He heard the mistress of the cottage moving about the floor, and occasionally a dark shadow passed between him and the faint light which the red embers gave. At last, an arm from the mass of thick drapery which screened her figure was extended towards him: in the hand was a small phial.

"Take it," said the woman; "but do not touch me, as you value your life."

He took the phial, and cast a purse of money upon the table.

"Keep thy gold," said the woman. "In serving thee I serve myself."

"Hast thou no other poison?" demanded the earl; "one of a nature so subtle that, dropped upon a flower or kerchief, it would war with life, nor quit the contest till victorious?"

"Ay," said the sorceress, "one *fit for a king to fall by.*"

"Give it me," said the speaker, eagerly, "and I will pay thee for it ten times more than for the first."

"Take it," again exclaimed the woman, "and now begone. We shall meet again— once again—and then, my lord, both our careers will be near their close."

"What mean you, hag?"

The woman cast a handful of some perfumed wood upon the fire, and in an instant the cottage of the mediciner was filled not only with a sweet perfume, but illuminated by a light so intense that every nook and corner became distinctly visible; and, to Warwick's terror and surprise, he discovered in the woman the mother of the boy whom he had so brutally slain on the night of the Princess Mary's escape from Kimbolton.

"Murderer!" she shrieked, "thy career will soon be ended—my boy will be avenged."

The earl rushed upon her with his sword, which he had hastily drawn, when she darted on one side, and, seizing a species of staff, struck a violent blow upon an earthen globe suspended over the fire. The vessel was shivered into a thousand fragments, and the contents fell upon the blazing embers. In an instant the hut was filled with a vapour so intense, that Warwick was blinded by its effects, and wildly struck at random. When the mist dispersed, he was alone within the cottage—the hag was gone.

CHAPTER XXVI.

Should man the open palm extend,
Woo thee with smiles, and call thee friend,
Praise thee for merits not thine own,
Condemn thy foes, their fault unknown—
Shrink from that man—avoid him—fly!—
Friendship, like love, can masque and lie.

ARWICK'S success against the rebels considerably increased his interest with the court party, whom the pride and arrogance of Somerset had gradually disgusted; for no sooner had he obtained the patent which invested him with the exercise of the regal authority, than he ceased to pay attention to the other executors and councillors of the king's will. All who were not devoted to him were certain to be neglected, and whoever opposed his views were sure to be treated with neglect and contempt. Unfortunately, while he thus manifested a resolution to govern everything his own way, his capacity did not appear proportioned to his ambition. Warwick, more subtle and artful, concealed his dangerous views under fairer appearances. He still professed himself the friend of the man whose downfall he was secretly plotting; and having associated himself with the Earl of Southampton, he formed a strong party, who were determined to free themselves from the yoke of the protector.

Although Somerset courted the people,

the interest which he had formed with them was in no degree answerable to his expectations. The Catholic party, who retained influence with the lower classes, were his declared enemies, and took advantage of every opportunity to decry his conduct. The attainder and execution of his brother bore an odious aspect. The introduction of foreign troops into the kingdom was represented in invidious colours; and the great estate which he had suddenly acquired, at the expense of the church and crown, rendered him obnoxious. But the final blow to his popularity was given by the magnificent palace which he was imprudently building. Three bishops' houses and the parish church of St. Mary were pulled down to furnish materials for the structure. Not content with his first sacrilege, he ordered St. Margaret's, Westminster, to be demolished, in order to employ the stones for the same purpose; but the parishioners rose in tumult, and drove away the workmen. He next laid his hands upon a chapel in St. Paul's Churchyard, with a cloister and charnel-house annexed to it; and these edifices, together with the singular old church of St. John of Jerusalem, were made use of to raise his palace. What rendered the matter more odious to the people was, that the tombs and other monuments of the dead were defaced, and the bones carried away to be buried in unconsecrated ground. These proceedings gave such disaffection in the city, that remonstrances were made; and the council, emboldened by assurances of support from the principal nobility, proceeded at once to assert their authority, without any regard to Somerset. They laid the same injunction on the lieutenant of the Tower, who expressed his resolution to obey them.

No sooner did the protector hear of the disaffection of the council and the city than he removed the young king from Hampton Court to Windsor Castle, and arming his friends and retainers, resolved to defend himself against all his enemies. But finding that no man of rank, except Cranmer and Paget, adhered to him, he lost all hopes of success, and began to apply to his foes for pardon and forgiveness.

No sooner was this despondency known, than Lord Russell and the speaker of the House of Commons abandoned him. The latter was bound to him by many obligations; and the former meanly sold him for the earldom of Bedford and a grant of abbey lands, which he degraded himself by receiving at the hands of his enemies. Such is the unworthy origin of the vast fortunes of the house of Bedford. Warwick had thrown off the mask, and gone too far to recede.

The council, under his direction, sent dutiful letters to the king, complaining that his uncle, whom they had created protector on condition that he consented to be guided by their advice, had usurped the whole authority of the realm; that he had, in levying forces against them, and placing them round the person of the king, been guilty of treason. These letters made a considerable impression on the youthful mind of Edward, whose cold manner to his uncle indicated to all about him that the hour of his disgrace had arrived.

Seeing that in the disaffection of his nephew his last stay was gone, Somerset resigned the protectorship, and was immediately committed to the Tower. Articles of impeachment were drawn up and exhibited against him; and while that haughty, weak, ambitious man was a lonely prisoner in the very cell which had held his brother captive, his daring rival Warwick was raised to the dignity of Duke of Northumberland; the last earl of that name, and first lover of Anne Boleyn, having died without issue, and his brother, Sir Thomas Percy, being attainted for his share in the Yorkshire rebellion in the late reign.

Somerset was brought to trial before the Marquis of Winchester—created high steward—and a jury of twenty-seven peers. He was acquitted on the charge of treason, but condemned to death for felony, in having conspired against the lives of the council, and executed on the 22nd of January, 1552.

No sooner had Northumberland, as we must now style him, obtained the supreme direction of affairs, than it was observed by the attendants of the young king that his health began gradually to decline. This might have proceeded from innate weakness of constitution; but men began to whisper and assert strange things, not openly, indeed, but under the seal of confidence, which rendered them more terrible.

It was not till the strength of the monarch, both mental and physical, was undermined that the new-made duke ventured to broach the grand scheme which had been the object of so many years of treachery and scheming. He gradually represented to the prince that his two sisters, Mary and Elizabeth, had both of them been declared illegitimate by parliament; and that, although Henry had restored them to their place in the succession by his will, the nation would never consent to see a bastard seated on the throne. That the inevitable consequence of Mary's succession would be the return of the nation to the church of Rome; that of the young Queen of Scots to make England a province of France, in consequence of her betrothment to the dauphin; in fact, that these princesses were both legally and morally excluded, and that the legitimate heir was the Marchioness of Dorset, eldest daughter of the French Queen Mary, by her second husband, the Duke of Suffolk; and that, in the event of her death or resignation, her eldest daughter, Lady Jane Grey, would become her successor. Finding that his arguments made a great impression on the mind of Edward, he next persuaded him to create the Marquis of Dorset Duke of Suffolk, who, as the price of his elevation to that dignity, bestowed the hand of his daughter, Lady Jane Grey, upon Lord Guilford Dudley, Northumberland's fourth son.

It was shortly after the above marriage that a council was summoned by the young king. Cranmer and the judges were invited to assist. Everything denoted that the subject to be debated was one of those on which the lives and fortunes of its mooters, as well as the destiny of a people, sometimes depend.

Edward was seated upon the throne, at the head of a long table, by the sides of which the members of the council had taken their places. Cranmer, as primate, was next the king; Northumberland faced him; Sir Edward Montague, chief justice of the Common Pleas, Sir John Baker, Sir Thomas Bromley, and Sir James Hale, were seated near the chancellor, the Bishop of Ely, who had reluctantly consented to give directions to draw the letters patent which transferred the crown from Mary and Elizabeth to Lady Jane Grey; but that wily prelate absolutely refused to sign it, or affix the great seal to it, till the judges had previously affixed their signatures; and it required the personal entreaties of the king ere Cranmer could be prevailed upon to follow the chancellor's example. An expedient was at last hit upon. A special commission was issued by the king and council to the judges, requiring them to draw a patent for the new settlement of the crown; and a pardon under the great seal was immediately granted them for any offence they might have been guilty of by their compliance. Of all the members, Sir James Hale, although a zealous Protestant, alone refused compliance. Cecil, who afterwards became so distinguished in the reign of Elizabeth, pretended that he only signed as witness to the subscription of the prince.

"You have signed your ruin, my lord," whispered the sturdy Hale, as he followed Cranmer down the staircase of York House, where the council had been held.

"What mean you?" demanded Cranmer.

"That the letters patent, in the event of our young monarch's death, would become so much waste paper. The emperor will assert the rights of the Princess Mary; the people, who resent the spoliation of the church, and still more the corrupt uses to which its wealth has been applied, will rise in her defence. Methought I saw, as I sat at the council-board, a skeleton, with an axe, behind the chair of every one who signed—save one," he added, sorrowfully — "save one."

"And whose was that?" demanded the primate, with a smile, for he was too enlightened to yield easily to superstition.

"Your grace's," answered the speaker, sorrowfully.

"And what saw you in its place?" demanded the archbishop.

"A brand," replied the judge, shudderingly — "a blazing torch, such as the executioner uses when he lights the pile to which some despairing guilty wretch is bound. In vain I tried to persuade myself that my imagination deceived me. The glare of the red flame was not to be mistaken; like a living thing, instinct with malice, it seemed to leap towards you, eager to reach your robes."

"The effect of an excited imagination," observed the prelate, who, despite his philosophy, could not avoid being struck by the singularity of the speaker's dream, for such he termed it. "You must have slept during the council."

"Your pardon, my lord; nothing slept at that eventful meeting except the prudence of the members; and I could well wish, for the love I bear your grace, you had been absent."

"Why so?" demanded Cranmer, in an uneasy tone of voice; "the pardon of the king secures us against charges, even should our enemies prevail."

"Would it secure you against the wrath of Mary? Think you, my lord, the daughter of Katherine of Arragon will ever forgive the man who pronounced her mother's marriage illegal, branded the stain of bastardy upon her proud brow, and lent no nerveless hand to uproot the ancient faith? Do not deceive yourself. Prudence could not so guard your steps that she would not find a false one; for power seldom lacks means to make occasions which justify its ends."

"True—alas! too true. But Edward, our young prince, is young, and may recover."

"Never!"

"What mean you?" demanded the churchman.

"Simply that the king has not a year to live," replied Sir James.

"A strange prediction,"

"Your grace will find it a true one."

"But on what grounds," exclaimed the unsuspecting prelate, "do you draw such an inference? He is young, and quite recovered from the maladies which last year threatened him, the measles and small-pox."

"That was the time, I think, Lord Robert Dudley was named gentleman of the bed-chamber?"

"It was. What then?"

"Nothing, only that his highness's health hath been declining ever since."

"Mean you?" exclaimed the horror-stricken Cranmer.

"I mean nothing, my good lord, more than my words express, that from the time the Duke of Northumberland placed his son, Lord Robert Dudley, near the person of the king, his highness's health declined. It would puzzle a lawyer's wit to make treason out of that. Youth dies as well as age. The bud which promises the sweetest flower is oft the earliest plucked."

"Woe—woe to England, and her suffering church!" sighed Cranmer.

"Fear not for the church!" exclaimed the sturdy knight; "it's life is not like human life, and cannot be destroyed. Fare-well, your grace! I shall to my country seat, and wait for better times. Remember my advice: when Edward dies look to your-self, and wisely place the sea betwixt you and the soil of England."

With these words the speakers separated, and entered their respective barges — Sir James to his house in the city, the primate to his palace at Lambeth; the latter with a heavy heart. The conversation with the knight had given him food for reflection; for, as his friend had hinted, his position was a dangerous one.

After the settlement of the crown was made, with so many suspicious circum-stances, Edward visibly declined every day, and small hopes were entertained of his recovery. To make matters worse, his physicians were dismissed by Northumber-land's advice, who prudently, however, obtained an order in council previously; and the dying youth was put into the hands of an ignorant old woman, who undertook in a little time to restore him to health. After the use of her medicines the bad symptoms increased in a violent degree; he felt a difficulty both of speech and breathing; his pulse failed, his legs swelled, his colour became livid, and all saw that his end was approaching. Now came Northumberland's last stroke of policy. He caused letters to be written in the name of the council both to the Princess Mary and Elizabeth, desiring

their attendance on their brother, whose infirm state of health required the assistance of their counsel and the consolation of their company. His real object was to get them into his power, in order that no opposition might be made to the succession of his daughter-in-law, the unfortunate but inno-cent Lady Jane Grey.

It was the night before their expected arrival that the guard, by Northumberland's orders, had been doubled round the old palace of Greenwich, where the young king lay. There was an air of gloom in the features of the servitors as they hurried to and fro with noiseless step, fearful to wake an echo which might disturb their dying master. All but the great gates were closed, and there a guard of Swiss were placed with orders to admit all such nobles or members of the council as might arrive, but to suffer none to depart. Many had already fallen into the snare; others were continually arriving.

"You are riding a dangerous road, my lord," exclaimed a sturdy yeoman, who was mounted on a powerful nag; "an earldom has been lost by a foolish ride ere this."

"What mean you, knave?" demanded the horseman to whom the above remark had been addressed. "Is it thus you venture to sport with the Earl of Arundel?"

"Earls are but men, my lord," replied the stranger; "hoodwink them, they see no better than the vilest clown, and fall into the snare the same."

The noble rider was too experienced a courtier not to understand that there was some allusion to the present state of affairs, and the summons which he had received to attend the king at Greenwich; for, as one of the old nobility who still adhered to the ancient faith, Northumberland felt anxious to secure his person. Sir John Bates, an officer of the duke's household, rode near him; so that in effect, although not in appearance, the earl was a prisoner.

"Thou art an impudent knave," said Arundel, in an altered tone, which showed that he fully understood the speaker's intention was to get speech with him. "Another time I'll speak with thee; at present, maugre the night, wind, and the rain, I must pursue my journey."

The scene of the above rencontre was Blackheath, about three miles from the ancient palace, and the night, as the speaker alluded, was a wet and rough one.

"No time like the present, sir earl." said the stranger.

Here Sir John Bates rode between the speakers, and in a peremptory manner ordered the stranger to ride on, observing that he could not permit the earl to be annoyed by a beggar's insolence.

"The beggar's importunity," replied the yeoman, "is better than the gaoler's care. One would think the valiant knight conducted a prisoner or a hostage to Greenwich, rather than a belted earl and an honoured guest, that he is so churlish in his speech to those who accost him."

"Villain!" exclaimed the knight, raising the handle of his heavy riding-whip, and levelling a blow at the speaker, which, had it taken effect, must have proved fatal. Then the intruder, as if terrified at the impending danger, put spurs to his steed, and started off, pursued by the infuriated knight. No sooner had they disappeared in the darkness, than the real object of the pretended flight became apparent; for a second horseman, who had hitherto remained at a distance, rode up to the side of the earl, and entered into a hurried conversation with him.

"Are you the friend of the Princess Mary?" he demanded.

"I am."

"And in communication with her?"

The earl of Arundel hesitated

"My lord, moments are precious, for there is not one upon which there does not hang a life. If the Earl of Arundel has belied a long and noble line of ancestry, the faith of his fathers, and forgotten the friends of his youth, let him pass on; his degradation be his punishment; but if his heart be honourable, still let him trust to one whose word was never yet broken to friend or enemy."

"And who is that one?"

The stranger approached so near to the peer, that he felt his hot breath upon his cheek; and fearing that his intention might be hostile, would have started back; but before he could wheel his horse round, the pretended yeoman raised the slouched barret which concealed his visage, and discovered to him the well-known features of Wolsey's former favourite—the jester, Patch.

"Enough," said the earl; "I know that I may trust thee; but be brief."

"Edward is dying."

"I guessed as much; his illness hath assumed a strange character of late."

"Poison," whispered the jester; "nay, start not, but hear me. Northumberland plays a daring game, and one which might prove successful, had not the Princess Mary firm friends to watch over and protect her. I baffled the villain once, and mean to do so again, Heaven willing. He has caused letters to be written to her and Elizabeth, in the council's name, commanding their attendance at court. They will arrive and find the king a corpse."

"Insolent traitor!" muttered the noble between his teeth.

"You, and the Catholic peers, as well as the princesses, have been summoned by the same hellish policy. Like a wary fowler he has spread the net; bid hope farewell, my lord, should he have time to draw it close."

"What mean you? What can the aspiring villain aim at?"

"A prison for the royal maidens; the block and axe for those who espouse their escape."

"What can I do?—my escort," observed the earl, "is composed of Northumberland's followers. I have scarcely half-a-dozen fellows of my own in all the train. Fool, fool!" he added, "to be thus caught!"

"While the princesses are at liberty, my lord, your life is safe. You must accompany your gaolers to the palace."

"What then?"

"The moment Edward has drawn the last breath of his young life, cast this ball from the window of the palace upon the marble pavement of the court beneath. It will convey a signal which I shall understand."

Patch placed a small ball, apparently of glass, in the hands of the nobleman, who contrived to thrust it, unseen by his attendants, into the bosom of his doublet. It felt cold as an icicle against his skin.

"What next am I to do?" demanded the earl.

"Take no part of the traitorous proceedings which will follow, as you value your head and your broad lands. But tell me," he added, "have you the token about you which was to serve as a sure pledge between you and the Princess Mary in the hour of danger?"

"I have."

"Give it to me."

Arundel slowly drew from his finger a sapphire ring, graved with the cognisance of his ancient house, and placed it, with a confidence almost amounting to simplicity, in the jester's hand, who, cynic as he was, felt gratified with the reliance upon his honour which the act conveyed.

"It shall not be abused, my lord; and now, farewell! For see," he added, "the chase has ended—for once the sparrowhawk has chased the falcon, but the noble bird disdains to turn and slay him."

As he spoke, the first yeoman who had addressed the Earl of Arundel in his progress, galloped up to the speakers, still pursued by the infuriated Sir John, whose steed was almost blown.

"Have you finished?" he demanded of the jester.

"I have."

"And the token?"

"Is in my possession. Farewell, sir earl," said Patch, as the knight approached; "forget not my instructions. When next we meet, Mary will be queen of England, or—"

"Or what?" demanded the peer.

"We shall meet no more."

With these words the horsemen rode away just as Sir John Bates rejoined his prisoner; for such in reality the earl considered himself, and was, however courteously the affair was disguised.

"You have had a conference, my lord," exclaimed the knight, who saw that he had been duped.

"Possible," said the noble, coolly.

"There is treason in this, my lord."

"That treason exists somewhere I have long suspected," said Arundel, impatiently; "but where, time must show; meanwhile, good fellow, as the peers of England are not yet sunk so low as to be accountable for their conduct to every saucy squire or knight invested with a little brief authority, let's drop the subject, and resume our ride towards the palace. The air is almost as unmannerly as thy tongue—the one has ruffled my temper, and the other all but blown the cloak from off my shoulders. Forward, man," he added; "I thirst for a cup of ———— to warm me."

Thus admonished, Sir John ———— thought it best to take no further notice, but proceed at once with his charge towards the palace. On his way he decided upon not relating to his master the circumstance which had occurred, and the earl, he felt assured, for his own sake, would be silent. It was near midnight when they reached their destination.

In the ———— chamber of the palace, known by the name of the King's Lodging, were assembled the various members of the council round a heavily carved and ———— upon which lay the person of the ———— monarch. Cranmer was praying ———— of the royal sufferer, whose thin ———— but faintly articulated the responses to the prayers. North———— like the ———— genius of the ———— hovering ———— him, ———— ————

———— succession ———— piece ———— and the honours of his race in jeopardy. The danger which they had braved ———— at a distance seemed terrible when near at hand; and but for the fear of Northumberland — whose foreign troops and northern dependants guarded the palace—they would gladly, ——— and ———— have left him to settle the question of succession with the nation and the Princess Mary ————

"A———— ————," whispered the Bishop of Ely, who ———— to Sir Thomas Browne, as the Earl of Arundel entered the royal chamber; "he plays his game with skill."

"But it does not always ensure success," was the reply.

The new-comer advanced to the foot of the couch, and bent the knee before the suffering mass which, while it moved and breathed, was king of England. It would have pained a sterner heart than his to behold the fearful alteration which had taken place in the youthful form of the dying Edward. His graceful limbs were swollen from all proportion; and while his body had become unnaturally large, his features were sunk and shrivelled till the expression of the countenance was really ghastly. Such was the influence which Northumberland retained over

the mind of the prince, that, even so near his end, his chief anxiety was to secure the fulfilment of the settlement which he had made of the crown and kingdom. To this he was still further urged by his fears for the stability of the reformation, to which ———— every reason to conclude he was ———— not bigotedly attached.

"———— Arundel," he muttered with difficulty, ———— the ———— time extending his hand; "you are ———— time to see the last of Edward."

"Not so. I trust to Heaven that your grace has many years ———— in store. You are young, and ———— ————. Your highness's physicians are the best ————."

There was a peculiar look which passed between the members of the ———— and the duke, by whose orders the physicians had been removed.

"I have no physicians," said the king; "perhaps it might have been better ———— I ———— them."

"It might, indeed," said the earl.

"I sent for you," added the royal sufferer, who had been well instructed in his lesson, "first, that you were the friend of our father; secondly, that you might sign the deed by which, with the advice and consent of our council, we have regulated the succession to the crown."

"Your grace," said the earl, seriously—"your father's will has already settled that. Your royal sisters——"

"Are bastards," fiercely interrupted Northumberland, "and incapable of ————."

"Yes—yes," added the king, "Dudley" —he always called him by his family name —"is right. Besides," he added, "the holy faith might suffer should Mary succeed me. Elizabeth—yes, I am sure for Elizabeth."

As this last observation fell upon the ear of Cranmer, he regretted that he had not availed himself of this partiality of the dying prince for the daughter of Anne Boleyn to facilitate her accession to the throne. Her Protestantism was undoubted, and she was his goddaughter—a tie in that age almost superstitiously respected.

"You will sign it?" demanded Edward, anxious to have the assent of so influential a person as the Earl of Arundel, whose acquiescence would entrain that of a great number of Catholic families in the same arrangement."

"I must have time to consider, my dear lord," replied the peer, anxious not to irritate the suffer. "If they be legal, the letters patent can receive no additional authority from my approval or otherwise. I have a duty to my country and myself——"

"Which you shall have time well to consider of at the Tower," said Northumberland. "Think not, my lord, we fear your name or influence. Accusations of disaffection had been brought against you, and his highness wished to convince himself if they were true or groundless. He is convinced. What, ho!" he added, "let a boat be manned and a party of the yeomen of the guard convey my lord of Arundel close prisoner to the Tower."

"No," said Edward, faintly attempting to raise himself from his couch of suffering.

"It must be so, my dear lord," whispered Northumberland, with but little affectation, even of reverence, for he felt that the speaker in a few minutes would be past asserting or expressing his wishes.

"It shall not be so!" exclaimed Edward, with an effort to make himself heard. "My lord, I charge you on your allegiance that no harm befal our cousin of Arundel; he must not be pressed in this. Perhaps it might have been wiser if others had considered it as well."

"He is a traitor!" exclaimed the exasperated duke.

"Robert Dudley, thou liest to thy teeth. Thou art the traitor, and this dying prince thy victim. Who dismissed his attendants," he continued, "to try the drugs of poisoners and quacks?"

"Poisoners!" repeated Cranmer aghast; "no—no! it is too horrible!"

"Poisoners," said Edward, the word for the first time waking a strange suspicion in his soul. "Listen to me, Dudley. From the hour I smelt the flowers you gave me on my birth-day, I have had a sickness in my heart; their perfume has never been absent from my sense; but poison—impossible—no, no—the boy who trusted you, raised you to honour, loved you like a father, has never fallen a victim to so black a treachery. You did not, could not do it."

"Rather a thousand deaths myself," exclaimed the duke, throwing himself at the side of the couch. "Oh, my dear master, could my heart's blood, poured drop by drop, assuage one pang, or lengthen your life one day, I'd give it freely."

"I am sure of Dudley," replied Edward, trying to smile, and at the same time extending his hand in sign of renewed confidence. "I am sure of it. Stay by me, and let me have no more brawls. Peace—peace should dwell in the chamber of a dying king. I am going; pray for me, father; pray for me."

The excitement of the dispute between Northumberland and Arundel had been too much for the exhausted sufferer, and his spirit gradually sank, like the wick of an unfed lamp expiring for want of oil. He expired in the seventeenth year of his age, grasping with touching confidence his murderer's hand.

No sooner was he assured that the final breath had parted than Northumberland sprang upon his feet, and, advancing to the centre of the room, exclaimed—

"God save Queen Jane!"

"Amen!" added Cranmer, solemnly, at the same time with gentle hands closing the eyes of the inanimate Edward.

Arundel advanced towards the window, and, following the instructions he had received, cast the ball he had so mysteriously obtained upon the pavement of the court-yard. It broke without any detonating explosion, and a lofty column of violet-coloured flame illuminated the old towers of the palace, shooting up into the air considerably above them. Fortunately the action had been unobserved.

"Treachery!" exclaimed the duke, who, with several members of the council, had advanced towards the window. "Have we traitors here?"

Each regarded his companion with mistrust; like men who had committed some crime, they feared that one would denounce the other.

"Perdition!" added Northumberland, as he perceived that the signal-fire was answered by a similar column on the opposite side of the Thames—"there seems a preconcerted code of signals. This must be looked to. In the meanwhile, my lords, until we have proclaimed the Lady Jane, and taken such measures as the safety of the kingdom may require, I hold it prudent that the council do not dissolve, but remain in permanency, attached to the executive, to advise and to control it."

The proposal was agreed to, and the Earl of Arundel was, by the consent of all, consigned a prisoner to the keep of the old palace, were several strong rooms to serve as dungeons, in case of emergency, had been preserved.

Cranmer remained praying by the royal corse, absorbed in bitter, deep reflections, for he felt that a crisis was at hand, not only for the church, but for himself, and he almost felt inclined to follow the advice which Sir James Hale had hinted at, and seek safety in Holland. Had he fortunately done so, how foul a page had been spared in England's annals!

"Let Everil, and the mad enthusiast he calls his friend, but follow my instructions," muttered Northumberland to himself, as he retired from the chamber of death to hold consultation with the council, "and fortune, I defy thee. My blood, mine!" he added, "shall fill the throne of England."

Like many other dreamers, he was born to be deceived.

On the morning after the death of Edward VI., a gallant train of nobles and knights was passing over the heath at Hoddesden; they were both preceded and followed by a clump of spears, consisting of the followers of Sir Henry Beddingfield and Sir Henry Jerningham, two of the most ancient families of Norfolk, and devoted to the old religion. On receiving the summons of her dying brother, Mary had hastened to set out upon her journey, but, with her usual forethought, she sent word to several of the Catholic nobility of her journey and intended route; so that by the time she advanced towards the metropolis, the followers of those who came under pretence of doing her honour so completely outnumbered the attendants of young Everil and his companions, whom Northumberland had sent to escort his victim, that she found herself in a position, if necessary, to defy them.

"Mark you how the papists throng her passage?" whispered Everil to his companion, a tall, thin young man, who rode beside him. "Should she succeed to the crown, woe to this now Protestant land."

"She never shall succeed," was the cool reply.

Everil fixed his eye upon the speaker as if to read his very thought, but the expression of his countenance was calm as usual. A close observer might, perhaps, have imagined that there was a degree of insanity, of that peculiar kind which results from religious enthusiasm, in the sullen expression of his deep blue eye and attenuated features, which were sharp and almost painfully intellectual. Every line in their expressive lineaments was thought — deep, morbid, soul-consuming thought.

While advancing in the freshness of the morning, two cavaliers were observed directing their foaming steeds towards them. They were Patch and his old friend Walter. Everil at once recognised them, and a frown upon his gloomy brow marked how little pleasure the rencontre gave him. His companion pulled his beaver yet closer over his brow, as if he wished to avoid being recognised. The two horsemen wheeled round to avoid the spearmen who preceded the cavalcade of the princess, and directed their steeds towards the centre. When they arrived within bowshot of the principal personages, Sir Henry Beddingfield left the side of the Lady Mary, with whom he had been conversing, and spurred his horse to meet them.

"Whence come you?" he demanded.

"From Greenwich," was the reply.

"And whither go you?"

"I suspect," said Patch, "our journey ends here. We would have speech of the Princess Mary."

"Impossible."

"Very likely," was the cool rejoinder; "but we must see her highness, for all that. Know, Sir Henry, you have to do with a man who has long dealt in impossibilities, and who knows how to appreciate them. Give her highness this token."

He pulled from his finger the sapphire ring given him by the Earl of Arundel, and presented it to Sir Henry Beddinfield, who regarded it, for a moment, in silence.

"What thinkst thou, sir knight, of the doctrine of impossibilities now?" demanded Patch.

"Follow," said the noble. "I know this ring, and the name of him who sent it."

Riding hastily before, Sir Henry whispered a few words to the princess, who instantly checked her steed and dismounted on the heath. Walter thought she looked unusually pale as they approached; for the rest, her demeanour was calm and self-possessed as ever.

"Now, your intelligence?" she demanded, in a low harsh tone; "our brother?"

"Sleeps with his royal sire," replied Patch, bending the knee; "God save Queen Mary!"

In the enthusiasm of the moment, the two noblemen who were standing near repeated the cry; the spearmen who followed them caught up the shout, and in a few moments the heath resounded with the cry of "God save Queen Mary!"

"We thank you, gentlemen," she exclaimed, without appearing in the least excited by the unexpected intelligence; "but reserve your shouts till we are seated on the throne, which treason would hold from us. Is't not so, old friend?" she added, turning to the jester.

"Letters patent have passed the great seal, setting aside your majesty's and the Lady Elizabeth's claim in favour of the Lady Jane Grey. London is in the hands of Northumberland's troops, and the Tower is garrisoned by his creatures."

"So then it would seem I am a queen without a kingdom. Heaven bear me witness, this crown hath fallen at an untimely hour; but since it hath fallen," she added, proudly, "upon our unworthy brows, Heaven will doubtless give me strength to bear it. Our council has been brief, friends, but 'tis ended. Sir Henry Beddingfield——"

"Madam!" said the gallant nobleman, bending his knee to the ground before her.

"To you we entrust the care of our royal person. Conduct us back to Framlingham. You, my faithful Jerningham, write letters to our nobles and the mayors of our cities and towns, commanding them to assemble their followers and the citizens in arms to defend our rights. Pardon to those who submit."

"Pardon to all?" demanded the party to whom the order had been given.

"No," she replied, passionately; "not even for the crown of which they would deprive me. Will Mary stain her lips with falsehood? There are amongst them those whom, if I reign, shall pay their treasons and their crimes with life—men whom Mary can never pardon. Now then, once more, to horse, and on to Framlingham!"

The speaker's hand was on the saddle to remount the palfrey standing near her, when the young companion of Everil, who had been Northumberland's messenger with the letter to Mary, rushed between the gentlemen who surrounded her. Madness was in his eye: the shouts which proclaimed her accession had unhinged his mind. Deeming himself called upon by God to save his church—proud in the holiness of his mission, he drew a long Venetian knife from his belt, and rushed to his sacrifice of fanaticism and murder, exclaiming—

"Die, Jezebel, in the pride of thy sin, ere yet the land is drunk with the blood of saints!"

The blow must have proved fatal, but for the presence of mind of Patch, who darted between the princess and the fanatic, and received the long blade of the weapon through the flesh part of his arm. The assassin was instantly secured.

"Art hurt, old friend?" demanded Walter.

"Not much," was the reply; "but who is the mad fool who sought his sovereign's life?"

"Behold him," cried the youth.

The jester turned, and a sudden sickness came over him as he recognised in the speaker the son of his old master, Wolsey, Louis D'Auverne.

CHAPTER XXVII.

"In which strange tales are ended, scenes wound up,
And gloomy evils brought to sunny close."

 N hearing of the flight of the Princess Mary to Framlingham, Northumberland found that further dissimulation was fruitless; he went therefore at once to Sion House, accompanied by the Duke of Suffolk, the Earl of Pembroke, and the members of the council. Approaching his daughter-in-law, Lady Jane, who resided there, the messengers sank upon their knees, and offered their homage to her as queen of England. Jane, who was ignorant of the young king's death, and the letters patent which had been executed in her favour, received them with equal surprise and grief. It was long, very long, before the entreaties of her parents, whom she tenderly loved, or the remonstrances of Northumberland, could induce her to accept the crown. Indeed, it was the influence of her husband which ultimately wrung a reluctant assent from her quivering lips.

"Evil will come of this, my lords," she exclaimed—"evil to all of us. God permitteth not the inheritance of the orphan to be wrongfully taken. Speedily, speedily will He avenge it."

The words of the youthful speaker were but too prophetic.

The unfortunate Lady Jane was of the same age, and had been educated with the late king. Young as she was, she had attained to a familiar knowledge both of the Latin and Greek languages, as well as several modern tongues. The learned Roger Ascham, tutor to the Princess Elizabeth, relates that one day, having paid her a visit, he found her reading Plato, whilst the rest of the family were engaged in a party of hunting in the park; and on admiring the singularity of her choice, she told him that she derived more pleasure from the perusal of that author than the others could reap from all their sport and gaiety. Her heart, full of this passion for literature and tenderness for her husband, who well deserved her affection, had never opened itself to the flattering allurements of ambition, and there is every reason to believe that her first rejection of the crown was a sincere one.

It was then usual for the sovereigns of England, on their accession, to pass the first few days at the Tower, and thither Northumberland immediately conveyed the phantom sovereign. All the members of the council were obliged to attend her to that fortress, and by this means became in reality the prisoners of her father-in-law, whose will they were forced to obey. Orders were given by them to proclaim Jane throughout the kingdom, but these orders were executed only in London and the immediate neighbourhood. No applause ensued; the people heard the proclamation with silence and concern; some even expressed their scorn, and one Pot, a vintner's apprentice, was cruelly punished by having his ears cut off for this offence. The Protestant teachers themselves, who were employed to convince the people of the lawfulness of Jane's usurpation, found their eloquence unavailing. Even Ridley, Bishop of London, who preached a sermon for that purpose, wrought no effect upon his audience.

Mary, meanwhile, remained at Framlingham, the nobility daily flocking to her standard, till she soon saw herself surrounded by a considerable army ready to take the field. The partisans of her rival daily deserted to her; and even the fleet which Northumberland had ordered to the coast of Suffolk declared for the Princess Mary, who commenced her triumphant march towards London.

In this critical position the ambitious duke resolved to take the field himself to oppose her progress, but on reaching Bury St. Edmonds he found that his army, which amounted to only six thousand men, was too feeble to encounter the queen's; he therefore wrote to the council for reinforcements, who instantly seized the occasion to free themselves from confinement. They left the Tower as if they meant to execute Northumberland's commands, but being assembled in Baynard's Castle, a house well fortified, belonging to the Earl of Pembroke, they deliberated on the means of sliding out of the dangerous position in which they found themselves. Arundel commenced the conference by representing the injustice and cruelty of the duke, the exorbitancy of his ambition, the criminal enterprise which he had projected, and the guilt in which he had

succeeded in involving the council, and concluded by offering that the only means of making atonement for their past offences was by a speedy return to the duty which they owed their lawful sovereign.

This motion was seconded by Pembroke, who, clapping his hand to his sword, swore he was ready to fight any man who expressed a contrary opinion. Not a voice amongst all those who had so lately bent the knee to Lady Jane, was raised in defence of her claim. The lord mayor and aldermen were immediately sent for, and orders given to proclaim Mary. The citizens expressed their approbation by shouts of applause; and even Suffolk, the father of Lady Jane, who commanded in the Tower, finding resistance useless, opened the gates and declared for the queen. His innocent daughter, after wearing the crown ten days, joyfully resigned it, and retired to private life. Northumberland, deserted by his troops, proclaimed Mary queen, throwing up his jewelled cap and exhibiting every exterior mark of joy.

Mary's approach to London was one continued triumph. Elizabeth met her at the head of a thousand horse, which she had levied to support their joint title; and in a few days the queen took possession of the metropolis of her kingdom amidst the rejoicings of all her faithful subjects. Her first orders on entering the Tower were for the arrest of Lady Jane, her husband, father-in-law, and the Duke of Suffolk, whose incapacity caused his life to be ultimately spared. But the guilt of Northumberland was too great, and his courage and ambition too dangerous to permit him to entertain any reasonable hope of life; and he was ordered to be brought immediately before the council, at which the queen, together with Gardner, Tonstal, and Bonner, who had been confined during the late reign, assisted. They found favour in the eyes of Mary from their adherence to the Catholic cause.

The royal lodgings in the Tower once more presented a scene of courtly splendour and confusion. The long panelled antechamber leading to the council was crowded with noblemen and dignitaries eager to pay their homage to the now firmly established queen, by whom it was generally observed that the Catholic was received with peculiar favour. As yet, no overt act had been committed which announced her secret resolution of restoring the ancient faith, an intention which those who knew her more than guessed at. Among the assembly, Patch, who still wore his arm in a sling, and who appeared pale with mental as well as bodily suffering, together with Walter and his wife, were not the least conspicuous personages. Short as had been the sojourn of the heiress of Stanfield at the court of Henry VIII., her person was well remembered, as well as that monarch's open admiration of her; and those who knew how bitterly the Princess Mary resented the injuries of her mother, augured unfavourably of her reception. They knew not that none was more firmly convinced of her innocence than the new queen, or of the pledge which, in atonement of her unjust suspicion, she had so solemnly given her, and which, amidst all the changes, trials, and vicissitudes of her eventful life, the exile had carefully preserved. The members of the new council passed through the crowd to the chamber where they were, for the first time, to assemble, with an air of importance and dignity, at which the jester would have smiled, had not his heart been occupied with fears for his old master's son; for the baffled assassin, Louis d'Auverne, was that very morning to be brought up to receive judgment.

"How proudly," whispered one of the spectators, "the old fox Norfolk struts along! Ill-fortune befal the council where his voice is heard!"

"Pshaw!" said another, who was a time-serving trimmer; "he is only using the freedom of limbs which he has just recovered. Lock you up eight years in a cage like the Tower, and you would walk stiffly too."

At this moment the Duke of Northumberland, dressed in deep mourning, pale and dejected with anxiety and the mental sufferings he had undergone, was led in a prisoner; the lieutenant of the Tower and a party of the yeomen of the guard had him in charge. As he passed, all shrank from him—some with real feelings of disgust, for his crimes were flagrant and many; others, with an affected horror, in order to show their zeal for the new order of things. Humbled as he was, he cast a look of scorn around him when he saw the coldness of those who but a few days before had sworn by his fortunes, and built their own upon his favour.

On a slightly elevated chair of state, Mary, as pale and collected as usual, presided at the head of the council-table. Bonner was seated on her left hand; Gardner, Norfolk, Tonstal, and Courtenay, who was soon after created Duke of Devonshire, on her right. By some historians she is supposed to have entertained an affection for that accomplished nobleman, who was the son of the Marquis of Exeter, and had been detained a prisoner merely on suspicion during the late reign. His attachment to the Princess Elizabeth, it is said, prevented their union, and was one of the causes of the queen's hatred and jealousy of her sister.

As soon as the oaths of allegiance and supremacy were administered—for Mary still retained the title of "Head of the Church" —Northumberland was introduced; the lieutenant with his drawn sword standing behind him, and the yeomen at the lower end of the room guarding the door.

"So, my lord," said the queen, sarcastically, "we meet at last, somewhat later than you calculated, had your traitorous design succeeded in obtaining possession of our person after our dear brother's death."

"Of what, then, am I accused?" demanded the duke.

"Treason," replied the Earl of Pembroke, who had been one of the first of Edward's council to desert him.

"Treason!" repeated Northumberland "treason! Show me the law, how a man can be guilty of treason who obeys orders given him under the great seal, or the justice of those who are involved in the same crime, if crime it be, sitting as his judges."

"Fear not," said Mary, quietly, "but you shall have both law and justice."

"If," said the Earl of Arundel, "this great knave hath so fenced his villanies that he escapes upon the present charge, I have another, still more hideous, to bring against him."

There was an expression of mingled surprise and contentment upon the countenances of many present, for they felt that the defence would have involved them in the prisoner's guilt.

"Name it!" exclaimed the accused.

"Murder as well as treason; not against our gracious mistress, whom God preserve, but her late royal brother Edward, the victim of his crimes and mad ambition."

There was a general expression of horror at the speaker's words, and Northumberland turned deadly pale.

"Proceed," said the queen, calmly; "my Lord of Arundel, we trust, has too much discretion to accuse without due proof."

"Not only proof, my royal mistress," replied the peer, "but witness."

On a signal given by the speaker, a side door opened, and a female figure, deeply veiled, advanced to the lower end of the council table. The prisoner seemed as much surprised at her appearance as the members of the board.

"What mummery is this?" he exclaimed. "Who is the woman?"

"A mother whom thy sword has rendered childless," exclaimed the female, throwing back her long veil, and discovering the features of Dame Alice. "I told thee we should meet again. Mary Tudor," she added, "the prophecy is fulfilled; this withered hand has placed the child of Katherine of Arragon upon the throne, and avenged the blood shed on the night you fled from Kimbolton."

Mary recognised in the speaker the hag in whose cottage she had found shelter.

"What means the woman?" she demanded.

"It means," said the wretched being, "that these hands prepared the poison which sent your brother to his long account; a poison so subtle, that dropped upon a flower, a handkerchief, or glove, would dry the wearer's blood, dissolve the marrow in the crumbling bones, and waste the sickening brain."

"'Tis false," faltered the duke.

"Swear it," said the woman; "call God to witness it; do it, and damn thyself! My vengeance would be but half complete if thy crimes left thee but one faint glimmering hope of Heaven's pardon."

Several of the members of the council who had been present at the death of the young king remembered his words—that he had never been free from a sensation of sickness from the hour he smelt of a nosegay which Northumberland had presented to him on his birthday.

"And what," said Mary, sternly, addressing herself to her former hostess, "hast thou to hope from this fearful confession? Our justice—"

"Justice!" hoarsely shrieked the hag. "I expect nothing from human justice; no fear from that of Heaven; my hell has been on earth—my punishment anticipated here. I have been hunted from the hearth-stone of my fellow creatures like the dam of the red wolf. I and my cub, even in the desert hut which gave us miserable shelter, the hunters—the human vultures—found us—slew my boy—but left his aged mother to avenge him. And now, Mary Tudor, shall I tell thee what I would do were I the queen of England, and thou the wretched guilty thing before thee?"

"What?" demanded the queen.

"I'd bid the ministers of my wrath heap in the court-yard of the Tower the holly-bush and oak. Alive I'd chain you trembling cur, whose selfish heart ne'er beat but for ambition or revenge, and his vile accomplice to the pile, and from the balcony of yonder window watch them burn, burn, till their flesh was ashes. Such is the law of England," she added, casting a glance of intense hatred on the prisoner; "and such, if I were queen, should be the prisoner's doom."

All shuddered as they listened to her, for there was something terribly unnatural in a criminal of her age and sex suggesting the details of such a fearful death. Mary alone gazed upon her unmoved.

"Thou hearest," she said, addressing Northumberland; "the woman hath spoken truly. Such is the law of England, and such, if convicted, by my crown and faith, shall be the poisoner's punishment."

The quiet tone in which the queen uttered her determination sent a chill through the veins of all who heard her. Northumberland, overcome with terror, threw himself upon his knees, and solicited in the most abject terms permission to retract his plea of having acted under order of the great seal, and confessed his guilt; his confession was taken down by the clerk of the council, and read over to him.

"Sign it," said Mary, sternly.

He did so, and was immediately removed.

After a brief consultation, it was decided that he should be brought to trial upon his confession; it was not thought prudent to allude to the death of Edward, who was extremely beloved by the Protestant party. The fact of the poison having been prepared by one who had foretold the accession of the queen, and a devoted Catholic, might have engendered strange suspicions in the minds of the people, ever apt to believe in the crimes of their rulers.

That very night Dame Alice was privately strangled in her prison.

It was upon this confession that the Duke of Northumberland was condemned and executed upon Tower Hill. Previous to his death he turned Catholic, and exhorted the people, when upon the scaffold, to return to the religion of their fathers, as the only means of healing the wounds of the nation. There is every reason to believe his conversion was sincere.

"And now, my lords," exclaimed the new sovereign, "we have another act of justice to perform. The wretched fanatic whose impious hand was raised against our life is to be punished, and our preserver recompensed. Admit them to our presence."

The doors of the council chamber were thrown open, and Louis d'Auverne, Patch, Walter, and the heiress admitted to the royal presence. Immediately after the attempt, the enthusiast had been deserted by his tutor and companion, Everil, who wisely fled the kingdom, nor did he venture to return till the following reign. Louis was pale, but calm and collected; the being abandoned by his friend caused his heart a keener pang than the anticipations of the cruel death which he knew awaited him. Mary was struck by his calm, collected demeanour, and whispered to Gardner, who stood beside her chair of state:

"See, my lord, the courage which fanaticism inspires."

"It may not accompany him to the scaffold," replied the prelate; "the devil generally abandons his instruments at the supreme moment."

"So," said the queen, addressing herself to the prisoner, "I see by thy unbroken spirit and unblushing front that penitence is still a stranger to thy hardened nature. What had I done, what injury inflicted, that thou shouldst raise thy hand against thy sovereign and a woman?"

No. 59.

"I deemed thee the enemy of my country and my faith," answered Louis, firmly.

"Coward and traitor!" replied Mary, contemptuously.

"Heretic!" added the bishop.

The Protestant members of the council exchanged uneasy glances, for the queen smiled graciously upon the speaker.

"Madam," said the prisoner, "your faith teaches you to persecute the light of truth—mine to die for it. Heaven, that nerved my arm, will sustain my courage in the hour of trial."

"Heaven?" interrupted Patch. "Deluded boy! Are the eternal thunders still? Wait life and death no longer on the Godhead's will? Canst so deceive thyself to think that Deity would break its own first law to arm the regicide, when but to will is to perform? Madam," he added, sinking on his knee, "shed not the blood of this deluded youth. He is misled—not naturally wicked. The fanatic preaching of the Lollard hath blinded both faith and reason. Commence thy reign by imitating Him whose words, e'en on the cross, were of forgiveness. Pardon—pardon!"

"The attempt against our life, as a Christian, we might forgive," said Mary, coldly; "but as a queen, we feel bound to punish it. Were such great offence o'erlooked, riot would soon usurp the place of reverend authority, unbridled license and nerveless justice from her judgment seat, and wild confusion desolate the land. Thou art mad to ask it."

"By thy mother's memory," exclaimed the jester, sinking on his knees; "by the service I have paid—by the sacrifice of my own life, in saving thine! Mercy, sovereign, mercy!"

"The sacrifice of thy life!" repeated the queen, in a tone of surprise.

"The knife with which he struck was poisoned," continued Patch. "Had it but touched thy blood, yea, grazed thy skin the tythe part of a hair, not all the drugs which nature yields had saved thy life. Yet twelve days, and the voice of thy murderer will be silent as the destroying angel's wing sent on death's sudden mission."

There was a mournful silence for some moments after the jester had announced his approaching end. The heiress of Stanfield, who loved the jester as she would a father had fortune permitted him to live, sank weeping on her husband's breast, even the iron features of Mary were slightly moved; but what words can paint the agony and remorse of the prisoner, whose affection for his victim was, perhaps, the last human weakness which lingered round his heart. He had been the guardian, the friend, the instructor of his childhood; and although years had separated them, the feelings and memories of old times returned. He knew not that the knife was poisoned; Everil, who had supplied him with the weapon, had kept that fearful knowledge to himself.

"Queen," said Louis d'Auverne, "the mask has fallen. Heaven could never have inspired me to commit an act at which e'en fiends would shudder—the destruction of my childhood's earliest friend. I have been deceived," he added; "hell saw my spiritual

pride, and sent its agent clothed in religious garb to tempt me. Friend—father," he added, throwing himself upon his knees and embracing the feet of Patch, "trample—spit upon me—spurn and scorn me, but ere I die say that you forgive me!"

The tears rolled fast down the speaker's countenance as he fixed an imploring glance upon his victim, who raised him with a smile of quiet deep contentment, and folded him in his embrace. He had done so a thousand times when the criminal was a child.

"The bitterness of death is past," he whispered in his ear, "when I shall meet thy father face to face, I will tell his son is worthy of him. Madam," he cried aloud, "an act of clemency befits your gracious self—mercy for this poor youth!"

"Impossible," said the queen. "Ask any other boon, and it is thine."

"God!" said the jester, "are the hearts of all earth's rulers cast in the same iron mould? I have served thee truly—given my life for her—saved her from many dangers—from false friends, and yet the only recompense I ask is heartlessly denied! I have lived," he added, "to thank thee for thy memory that I am not a king——"

"It was thy duty," interrupted Mary, in an angry tone.

"I remember it, madam," replied Patch, proudly; "though you had forgotten yours. No matter now," he added, passing his arm over the shoulder of Louis d'Auverne; "our separation will be a brief one."

"True," said the queen; "so by my crown, there is one whose prayer can move me."

"Thy oath, great queen—the oath I exclaimed the jester of Stanfield, taking from her neck the golden chain and reliquary which Mary had worn. "Remember thy royal words: 'Whate'er the boon—be it a vengeance, an honour, or a life—I swear to grant it.'"

She sank upon her knees before the chair of state where Mary was sitting, and held the long-forgotten reliquary to her astonished sight.

"The Lady of Stanfield!" she exclaimed in a harsh, dissatisfied voice. "We do remember some such promise, but this is not the hour or place to claim it."

"Pardon, gracious princess, but no hour so fit as when the voice of gratitude demands it; it is the heart's memory, and mine must be cold indeed when it is deaf to its strong claim."

"What would you?" demanded Mary.

"The life of Louis d'Auverne," firmly and respectfully answered the heiress.

The queen half started from her chair in indignant astonishment; but the sight of the talisman, which was supposed to contain a particle of the true cross, restrained her. She remembered her oath, and was too superstitious, if not too religious, to break it.

"Lady of Stanfield," she said, mastering her anger, and extending her hand to receive back her gift, "the promise is sacred, and, whate'er it be, shall religiously be kept. Heaven forbid Mary should commence her reign with a broken vow upon her conscience; but reflect well on what you ask."

"Madam," whispered Gardner, "the church has a dispensing power, which——"

"Would be useless here, my lord," interrupted the queen; "deeply as we reverence it. Lady of Stanfield," she continued, "forget not that your lands are confiscated, that you have children, and a husband; that my signature at the foot of this sheet of parchment restores both you and them to lordships, wealth, and honour. Speak!"

She advanced to the council-table, took up a pen as if she set to write, and paused for a reply. The suppliant hesitated not an instant, but still repeated:

"The life of Louis d'Auverne!"

"An earldom to redeem my inconsiderate oath," added Mary.

"The life of Louis d'Auverne," said the heiress, without a moment's hesitation.

"Consult thy husband."

"Madam, I should offend him by the insult. Could you divide your sceptre, coin the wealth of England's realm, and pour it down before me, it would not tempt me. My cry would still be, 'The life of Louis d'Auverne.'"

Her husband, with a burst of love and admiration, which not even the presence of royalty could restrain, raised her from her suppliant position, and pressed her to his manly heart; and a tear stole unheeded down the jester's cheek at the proof that their love for him was superior to all that wealth or state could offer.

"Take it," said the queen, coldly, at the same time affixing her signature to the parchment; "but blame not me if it has left your children beggars."

"They will be happy," replied the heiress, receiving it upon her knee, "since it has paid the debt of gratitude and honour which their mother owes."

"Louis d'Auverne!" exclaimed Mary, "to redeem an inconsiderate vow we spare thy forfeit life, but we banish thee from England's soil for ever. Four and twenty hours we give thee to depart the land; that once expired, if found within our realm, thou diest a traitor's death. Look to it,

lords," she added, striking her hand upon the table in a way which reminded the council of her father. "We shall hold those as traitors to our crown who plead for him again, if found within our kingdom."

Without deigning to cast a look upon the heiress, the queen, preceded by Gardner and Bonner, left the council-chamber, followed by all the members of the board. The clerk only remained, to give orders to the captain of the guard, to let a party of the yeomen follow their late prisoner, and keep a close watch upon him till he was embarked, or, the four-and-twenty hours once expired, to arrest him if he had not quitted England.

"For me," said Patch, raising the hand of the heiress to his lips, "you have bartered the halls of your fathers—the heritage of your children."

"They love their kind friend too well to reproach me," replied the high-minded woman, with a faint smile. "I have news for them worse than the loss of home and lands, exile and poverty."

"And that?" said the jester, in a tone of surprise.

Walter finding that the heart of his wife was too full to speak, took the speaker by the hand, and sorrowfully answered for her.

"Thy fearful danger, Richard," he added, naming his son, "will grieve for his instructor, and Mary break her tender heart for her kind playmate."

"Yes," said Patch; "yes, children are always grateful, they will regret me. But no more of this. I need the present hour for action, not lamenting. Perhaps," he added, "I have a balm in store you little dream of."

Walter was not deceived by the expression; he knew too well the truthfulness of his friend's nature; but Mary, with a trusting hope, permitted herself to be deceived. We are easily persuaded to believe the thing we wish.

Patch, accompanied by his rescued pupil, returned to the house of Marietti, his partner; the party of the guard appointed to watch over Louis till the moment of his embarkation attending him. The strong coffers of the partners were opened, and the exile supplied with funds to ensure an honourable existence in the land of his retreat.

"Too much, too much!" exclaimed the deeply repentant man; "let me owe my existence rather to my daily toil than to the bounty of the man whose love I have so cruelly requited."

"Take it," said the jester; "thy father's son must not live a beggar."

"But it will leave thee poor," urged Louis.

"Enough will remain for the only task I have left in life," said Patch, with a smile; "I have paid my debt of gratitude. Friendship's" he added, "is all that now remains."

A ship bound to France was easily found, and the captain, urged by the golden arguments of Marietti, set sail before the twenty-four hours had expired. Louis d'Auverne repeatedly embraced his victim and preserver, before he set his reluctant foot on board, demanding pardon and forgiveness, which were as repeatedly accorded. The exile arrived in France in safety; there he passed under the name of Winter a secluded life. From the chalice and stole upon his tomb, it would seem that he returned to the faith in which he had been educated, and died a priest of the Romish church.

"I have saved him," exclaimed Patch, as he watched the lessening sails of the vessel, "saved my master's son. Wolsey," he added, "glorious spirit! soon shall we be reunited; thy gracious smile will be the first to welcome thy old friend, when his tired soul reaches that peaceful land where earth's delusions fade and mind holds converse in the pure light of truth."

On the return of the jester to the house, Marietti met him at the threshold. The Italian's countenance was clouded, not at the attack which had been made upon his coffers —for all he had was at his friend's disposal —but at the approaching separation; for Patch's danger was no secret to him.

"The Earl of Arundel hath been here," he whispered.

"What sought he?"

"What seek the nobles generally when they visit the roof of those whose honest industry they affect to despise, prizing their blazon and their feudal rights above the arts of industry and peace? He wanted gold, not for himself, but for a greater one."

"For whom?" demanded the jester.

"The queen."

"Good!" said his partner; "she shall have enough to glut the thirst of avarice. Oh, gold!" he added, "'tis thou that art earth's god; the sceptre which rules it may be of iron, but the hand which sways it is of gold. Farewell! I must to the Tower to see the queen."

"You are pale and worn," exclaimed Marietti, whom long years of intercourse and friendship had unite to the speaker as to a brother: "rest, rest until to-morrow."

"I shall soon have an eternity of rest," replied the jester, and will not forestall it. To render my sleep a calm one, I must not lay my head upon my pillow leaving my greatest debt unpaid."

"What debt is that?" demanded the Italian.

"A long and just one—the debt of friendship and of human love."

Despite his friend's remonstrance, the speaker, without a moment's rest, turned upon his steps, and made his way to the Tower, where the queen still held her court. Like all sovereigns at the commencement of a new reign, she wanted money. The Protestant portion of the kingdom, jealous of her intentions, were certain to oppose the granting of a subsidy, unless accompanied by conditions which Mary was determined not to accept; and Marietti had been applied to as one of the wealthiest, to advance an immense sum to enable the government to act at first independently of the commons, who began to show themselves far more jealous of their money than of their liberties or religion. Patch was too well known by all about the court to find much difficulty in obtaining an audience of Gardner, now the queen's chief adviser. The prelate, remembering the scene which had lately passed before the council, received him haughtily and coldly.

"Now," said the churchman, "your pleasure, master jester; time with those who have a nation's welfare on their hands, the burden of the state upon their minds, is precious.'

"And yet I have seen it borne with no less grace than strength," observed his visitor; "but we have outlived the age of fable. There were giants in the olden time."

Gardner winced at the sarcastic tone in which the comparison between himself and Wolsey had been drawn, and again demanded his pleasure.

"You have sent the Earl of Arundel to Marietti, the merchant, to negotiate for certain moneys."

"How know you that?" demanded the prelate.

"Is there anything astonishing," quietly demanded Patch, "in the junior partner, in a transaction of such magnitude, referring to the head of his house?"

"Partner!" repeated the now astonished bishop; "you jest."

"No so," said his visitor. "Since modern statesmen have taken up the trade, I have laid it down. Besides," he added, "our masters now would rival us."

"You, then, really are the person to whom Marietti said he must refer?"

"No other," said the jester.

"You know the terms proposed?" demanded Gardner.

"I came not to listen to terms in such a matter, but to dictate them."

"Dictate them?"

"Ay, for not one stiver shall be counted down unless they are agreed to. The hand which holds the sceptre may be another's, but the sinews that give it strength are mine."

"I trust the conditions will be reasonable."

"More; like myself, I will be generous; nay, princely in my terms. First, I double the sum your royal mistress named."

"Doubled!" exclaimed the prelate, his eyes sparkling with satisfaction. "Good, good! And the terms?"

Patch approached the speaker, and whispered something in his ear; at which the expression of satisfaction on Gardner's countenance suddenly changed to disappointment.

"Impossible!" he replied; "she hath sworn never to restore them."

"It was a rash oath, my lord, and therefore sinful."

"She will keep it."

"And I my gold. Farewell."

"Stay," said the bishop, thoughtfully; "money must be had, despite a thousand oaths."

"True," said the jester, "the church's power can well dispense with them."

"Wait for me," said the prelate; "in a few minutes I will return."

Gardner was as good as his promise. In less time than Patch could have expected he entered the room, his countenance flushed, for he had endured a rough scene with the queen, who yielded at last to his reasons on the necessity of her position. In his hand he held a document signed by the royal hand, and sealed with the great seal.

That same night the secret vault in the house of Marietti was emptied of a great part of its long-hoarded treasures, which were conveyed by water to the Tower. The jester paid with no niggard hand for the favour he had asked.

The transaction once concluded, he disappeared, and returned to the dwelling of his partner no more.

Walter and his wife were speculating upon the absence of their old friend, whom young Richard and little Mary were hourly inquiring for, when a messenger from the town arrived, and placed in the hands of our hero an order, signed by Gardner, commanding him and his family, in the queen's name, to depart from London and take up their residence at Stanfield Hall. Conjecture and opposition alike were useless; and in three hours after the receipt of the royal rescript, the party, including old Steadman and Marietti, set out upon their journey.

It was at the close of a lovely evening that the long exiled heiress approached the home of her fathers; whether to remain there as a prisoner, or rule there as a mistress, seemed equally uncertain. Tears and smiles were on her cheek, like alternate showers and rays of sunshine, as the towers of the hall, rising in stately pride above the wood, first met her view. Her life had indeed been an eventful one since last she trod its floors. The recollections of her youth returned; and gentle sorrow, which the conflicting nature of her feelings excited, refreshed her heart, till she felt young again. As the horses of the party rounded the point of the chase which admitted the full front of the building to their view, a loud enthusiastic shout burst from the assembled tenantry and peasants assembled on the green sward before the principal entrance, and a hundred voices cried—

"Welcome to our rightful lady — welcome to the child of the old lords of Stanfield!"

Mary could only weep and bow her gratitude.

"Is that our future home?" demanded young Richard, proudly. "We must fight, father, ere we lose such a heritage; the very bones of our ancestors would rise to reprove us else."

"What beautiful woods and flowers!" exclaimed his little sister. "Would Patch were here to walk with me and tell me tales of fairies, and speak of the merry birds and busy insects as we walked beneath their shade!"

The rejoicing tenants escorted the wanderers till they entered the great hall, where a fresh surprise awaited them. All the old retainers of the house whom time and the late commotions had spared, attired in the livery of her house, were drawn up to meet the heiress, who, like one bewildered, passed on, still pursued by the blessings and acclamations of the crowd, till she reached the chamber where she passed so many solitary hours. There the party found the enchanter who had contrived the scene. Poor Patch, propped upon his couch, pleasure and death struggling for mastery in his expressive countenance, was waiting to receiving them. In an instant the grateful Mary was at his side, her warm tears falling on his attenuated hand, while Walter's grief almost unmanned him. His little favourites, too—Richard and his sister, who slowly understood the loss they were about to experience—hung sobbing round his couch.

"You are come at last," said the jester, with a faint smile; "come to take possession of your home—the future abode of innocence and virtue. Take it, Walter," he added; "'tis my last gift. The wealthy merchants for the future are dependants on your bounty. But I," he added, "shall not be a burden to you long."

He placed in the hand of his friend the deed which restored the domain of Stanfield to him and his heirs for ever.

"Matchless friend!" exclaimed our hero; "why hath Heaven denied the only boon that could complete our happiness—thy life?"

"Better as it is. Walter, my heart yearned to thee when thou wert a boy as I first saw thee a suppliant in the halls of Hampton. Thou art the only man, save one, who never yet deceived me. Thou needst not blush to be the jester's heir; for 'twas on the turn of fortune whether I became your king or friend."

"My king!" exclaimed Walter and Mary, with surprise.

"Ay. Bury this with me; I would not common eyes should gaze upon it, or vulgar hands rend it from the senseless clay."

He took a chain and miniature from his neck as he spoke, and placed it in the hands of his friend. The portrait was that of a young man dressed in the regal robes. There was a name in small letters round the setting. Walter held it to the light and read it aloud:

"Perkin Warbeck!"

"My father," said the jester.

Whether Perkin really was, as he asserted, the son of Edward the Fourth, supposed to have been murdered by the order of Richard, in the Tower, or an impostor, has never been decided. Historians disagree. One thing alone is certain, that Patch was his son. Wolsey have saved him when a boy from the jealous cruelty of Henry the Seventh; hence the attachment which, through life, the jester evinced towards him —his fidelity and love.

"Farewell, Richard," said the dying man, extending his hand to the kneeling boy beside him. "Don't forget your old friend, nor the lessons he has given you; they will

sustain your heart in many an hour o trial."

"True," replied the boy, "for they have been of honour."

"Mary," continued the sufferer, "kiss your old playmate and companion. When spring comes and you gather wild flowers in the woods of Stanfield, spare one for the grave of your merry jester, and he will ask no other monument."

The weeping child clung with a passionate sorrow round his neck, and imprinted a hundred kisses on his lips. It was extraordinary how her caresses moved him.

"Take her away," he murmured; "or I shall wish to live. I am going," he whispered to Walter, "but do not grieve. I leave my name as a household thing amongst you. With my wealth I might have bought honours, titles, pleasures, or revenge. I have purchased in its stead the love of two young hearts, whose smiles have cheered me living, whose tears will embalm my memory when dead. Strew flowers upon my grave —I need no marble; and, Walter, when you are a grey-haired man, bring your grandchildren to the jester's resting-place, and bid them play there. Seek it sometimes at evening hour, alone, or with Mary by your side. If in the world of shadows we retain a knowledge of what passes here on earth, 'twill sooth my restless spirit."

"Patch—friend—my only friend!" exclaimed Walter, sinking on his knee, and kissing the hand of the dying man, "thy memory is graved too deeply on my heart ever to be erased. When it is mouldered in the turf beside thee—then, and then only, wilt thou be forgotten."

"And then our spirits will have renewed the amity of earth in heaven. Faint, and fainter still, life's pulse is ebbing. Like the jester's wit, life's vocation's past. Master, I come! Walter—Wolsey—Wol——"

With one long-drawn sigh the model of friendship, fidelity, and honour resigned his breath, amidst the tears and prayers of those who loved and mourned him.

LONDON: PRINTED BY E. LLOYD, SALISBURY-SQUARE, FLEET-STREET.